Tania Blanchard writes historical fiction inspired by the true stories and the rich cultural heritage of her family's history. Her bestselling, acclaimed stories of love, loss and hope and the challenges facing women in defining moments in modern history span world wars and pivotal moments in time during great social and political upheaval, and are beloved by readers everywhere. Her books *A Woman of Courage*, *The Girl from Munich*, *Suitcase of Dreams*, *Letters from Berlin* and *Daughter of Calabria* are bestsellers. She lives in Sydney with her husband and three children.

Visit www.taniablanchard.com.au

TANIA BLANCHARD

AN UNDENIABLE VOICE

HarperCollinsPublishers

HarperCollins*Publishers*
Australia • Brazil • Canada • France • Germany • Holland • India
Italy • Japan • Mexico • New Zealand • Poland • Spain • Sweden
Switzerland • United Kingdom • United States of America

HarperCollins acknowledges the Traditional Custodians of the lands upon which we live and work, and pays respect to Elders past and present.

First published on Gadigal Country in Australia in 2024
by HarperCollins*Publishers* Australia Pty Limited
ABN 36 009 913 517
harpercollins.com.au

A catalogue record for this book is available from the National Library of Australia

ISBN 978 1 4607 6411 4 (paperback)
ISBN 978 1 4607 1625 0 (ebook)
ISBN 978 1 4607 3796 5 (audiobook)

Cover design by Louisa Maggio, HarperCollins Design Studio
Cover images: Woman © Abigail Miles/Arcangel; Zeppelins by PA Images/Alamy Stock Photo; Gotha G.V bomber by De Luan/Alamy Stock Photo; all other images by shutterstock.com
Author photograph by Kate Buechner
Typeset in Sabon LT Std by Kelli Lonergan
Printed and bound in Australia by McPherson's Printing Group

FSC
www.fsc.org
MIX
Paper | Supporting responsible forestry
FSC® C001695

To all the women who change the world and make it a better place, one small step at a time.

To Hollie, Trish and Jane, descendants of Eleanor Blanchard, who light up the lives around them and make a difference, each in their own way. The world is better because of you.

Remember the dignity of your womanhood.
Do not appeal, do not beg, do not grovel. Take courage,
join hands, stand beside us, fight with us.

– Christabel Pankhurst

PROLOGUE

Photographs are memories on paper that show the truth of the moment. They have the capacity to evoke all the thoughts and feelings of those who experienced the event, a window into that moment. It is history frozen in time. Photographs are much more accurate than the drawings I taught my students to do in the naturalist club before Annie was born.

From the journal of Hannah Todd Rainforth

EBBERFIELD, NORTHERN ENGLAND

DECEMBER 1906

Peals of laughter broke the silence of the ancient forest, and as I reached a break in the trees I saw flashes of the children running up ahead. The sound of dogs barking drifted up the dene. Roger walked beside me, dried leaves crunching underfoot. It was my thirty-sixth birthday and my wish was to spend the day with my family. We'd taken advantage of the clear winter sky to be outdoors, and I'd packed a delicious picnic and Roger and the children had made me a cake.

'Let's stop here and have lunch,' I said.

'Duke, Shandy!' called Roger. There was a lull in the noise, as though everything had paused; nature taking a breath as it inched closer to its hibernation. Then dogs and children were racing towards us.

'Stop!' I cried. But it was too late, the dogs launched themselves at Tommy, muddy paws and wet fur plastered against his clothes.

'Yuck! Get off,' he yelled while William and Annie giggled uncontrollably.

'Down,' said Roger sternly.

Duke and Shandy looked at Roger, panting heavily after the run, pink tongues lolling, but they did as they were told. They shook themselves vigorously, droplets of water flying, making Annie and William shriek and collapse into fits of laughter. The dogs ran excitedly around the small clearing, rolling in the grass and leaf litter, attempting to dry themselves. I couldn't help but laugh myself. I glanced at Roger, who grinned from ear to ear and gestured to the path.

'All right,' I said to the children. 'Why don't you go down to Minerva's Pool and wash your hands and faces? Take the dogs with you.'

'Can we go for a swim too?' asked Tommy, looking at me hopefully. At ten, he already loved pushing the boundaries.

'It will be too cold, son,' said Roger, ruffling Tommy's dark hair, which was just like mine. 'The dogs have a nice coat to keep them warm.'

'I'll bring you some tadpoles,' said William, brandishing the net and jar he'd brought.

I smiled. My baby, still blond, like Roger had been as a child, but already eight years old. He was such a sweet boy. 'When you come back we'll eat, and after we'll see if we can find some deer, badgers or spotted woodpeckers.'

'And Dadda can show me how to take photographs of the birds and butterflies,' said Annie, taking the camera case from Roger and hanging it around her neck, pulling her long, honey-coloured hair free.

Roger encircled my waist with one arm and kissed me. He was just as exuberant as the children and the dogs. 'We'll be back soon. And maybe then we can lie in the sunshine while the children play with the dogs.'

I arched an eyebrow in scepticism. Although we'd walked a good part of the morning, the children, like the dogs, had boundless energy and wouldn't rest until bedtime, when the day's activities would finally catch up with them – I hoped, anyway. 'We can try but perhaps we have to come on our own next time.' I thought back to the time we'd picnicked here when I was pregnant with Annie, and the glint in Roger's eyes told me he remembered too. 'Go on with you,' I said, batting him away, grinning in response to his wide smile.

'Come on,' he said to the children. 'Let's give your mother a few minutes' peace.'

I spread the picnic rug out and unpacked the sandwiches and lemonade. I left the vanilla cake with lemon icing sitting in the basket on top of the folded newspaper. I pushed wayward strands of hair back into my bun, and breathed in the fresh air, cool against my face. Gazing at the bare trees around me, surrounded by small bushes and undergrowth, I was grateful for the time to myself. It was peaceful, even with the distant sounds of Roger and the children and the two dogs, and I decided to take advantage of the quiet to read until they returned. I removed the newspaper from the basket.

An advertisement for Kodak Brownie cameras reminded me that Christmas wasn't far away, and I wondered if we might buy one for Annie, now she was eleven. My thoughts turned to the community projects I was involved in with the Ebberfield Suffrage Society, including our visits to families with Christmas hampers and clothing drives for schoolchildren. It was always a difficult time of year for those desperate not to enter the workhouse, especially the many tenant farmers who had been unable to find allotments when the coal company had bought up the farms on the edge of the village recently for the colliery. Perhaps we could include small toys in our hampers for families who couldn't afford gifts. I made a mental note to talk to Mrs Burrows and the church aid society committee about it too.

I shook my head in amazement, remembering back to the first time I'd met Mrs Burrows, about fifteen years ago. I was still fairly new to Ebberfield, arriving after teachers' college to help my parents with their pub, The Ox and Plough. I was a suffragist – I'd wanted to change the world and that began with first helping the local community. I'd never expected to fall in love, much less marry. But here I was with the love of my life and three beautiful children, running the pub and contributing to our village becoming a better place for everyone, especially women and children.

'Have a listen to this,' I exclaimed after Roger and the children returned and the children had taken their sandwiches to sit on the nearby rocks, passing crusts of bread to Duke and Shandy. 'Did you know that hot air balloons have travelled from Paris to the Yorkshire coast now? It's the furthest distance any flying machine has gone before. And now an all-women French crew has launched and flown balloons too.' I showed Roger the article and photos in the newspaper. 'They're pioneers in their own right.' I looked at my daughter, laughing at something one of the boys had said. 'I wonder what the world will be like when Annie is a woman. What daring things might she do?'

My children and the pub had taken up much of my time and, for some years, I'd stepped back from the national suffrage fight, focusing on local community projects, like literacy for women and providing care packages for the poor. Private Members' bills were still failing in Parliament, but for the first time, a demonstration inviting women from all over Britain to come together in support of women's suffrage was planned for the new year. It was an exciting development for the movement, and now that the children were older and I was able to breathe, I was beginning to think it might be time to join the national fight once again.

Roger smiled. 'She'll be just like you. Fiercely determined to take on the world, facing injustice and all of life's challenges.'

'Is that how you see me?' A rush of tenderness and gratitude filled me as I touched his face, the dark afternoon stubble rough under my hand, and looked into his startlingly blue eyes. Roger was a couple of years older than me and still just as beautiful as the day we'd met: tall, athletic; silver beginning to thread through his dark, curly hair in a way that made him look distinguished. The creases that lined his face showed his character to the world. He was just as strong, steadfast, generous and loving, and as passionate about our family as I was, and my greatest supporter in life.

'You know I do. But maybe I don't tell you enough.' He leant in to kiss me. 'You're strong and resilient, caring and kind. How can Annie or any of our children want to do anything but take on life with passion and try to make the world a better place?'

I gazed at the children playing hide and seek with the dogs and smiled. 'Well, we've done something right then, you and I.'

1

My dearest Clementine is a 'Suffragette'! Once it was an insult invented by the press, but now the Women's Social and Political Union use it with pride as a badge of honour. I always knew it would be a matter of time before she joined the WSPU. She was thrilled to be part of their very first march through London to the House of Commons, led by their leader, Mrs Emmeline Pankhurst, and her daughters Christabel and Sylvia.

'Hannah!'

Walking down the main street of Ebberfield, I turned to the sound of my name. 'Mrs Scruton,' I said, as she rushed out from the council chambers. Despite her age, she was still just as energetic as when she'd joined our suffrage society fourteen years earlier. She had been one of the first members and was a stalwart supporter of women's rights and the many community projects we were involved in.

'Oh, Hannah, dear,' she said. 'You heard Charlie, Mr Franks' boy, is runnin' for parish council? He's hardly out of short trousers!' Mrs Scruton made it her business to know everything there was to know in the village. Running the local tea room came in handy for that.

I chuckled. 'Charlie's in his twenties now.'

She flicked a hand in dismissal. 'It's ridiculous. No one'll respect him. He don't have the life experience or wisdom to be a parish councillor. We all know why he's runnin' – to do his father's biddin' – and that won't end well.' She shook her head in disgust. 'If he gets in, it'll be three years of trouble.'

I smiled and nodded as villagers walked past us. I understood Mrs Scruton's point. Mr Franks was the publican and owner of The Rose and Crown. Sixteen years ago, he had tried to force my father out not long after he'd bought The Ox and Plough, and then my mother and me when Papa had become too ill to continue working. There had been many disagreements with him over the years but we had prevailed and The Ox and Plough had grown to become a favourite with locals. Our pub was thriving, but it was more than just a pub, it was the heart of the community, the lighthouse that sought to protect and champion women, children and the vulnerable.

'When Mr Franks and Esther were on the parish council,' I said, shifting the ledgers I was carrying to the other arm, 'she stood up to him and stopped him from causing all manner of trouble. Perhaps we just need someone on the council to keep Charlie and his father in check.' Esther Burrows was one of the women who'd helped me start the suffrage society, along with Clementine Foster, who I'd taught with at the local elementary school, and they were my closest friends. Esther had been one of the first women elected as a parish councillor ten years ago and was in office for five years before joining Clementine in London, to follow her passion for engineering.

Mrs Scruton chuckled. 'Oh, yes, I remember.' Her eyes narrowed. 'Why not put your name forward? Give young Charlie a run for his money?'

I shook my head. 'I'm not eligible.'

'But surely now that your dear mother has passed, you'll inherit the pub?'

'No, the pub has been left to my sisters and me, and it's still under probate.' I gestured to the ledgers, which I was taking to the brewery to discuss the possibility of a loan extension to buy my sisters out. 'Besides, Roger's name is registered on the electoral register at our address.' Even if I became the owner of the pub, as his wife, I couldn't vote or run for council registering under the same address. The only way I could qualify was to own a property that Roger didn't own or occupy.

She frowned. 'You've been publican of The Ox and Plough and president of the suffrage society for years. If anyone's eligible, it's you. The law's gotta change.'

'Women need the vote,' I said simply. 'It's the only way we can change the law.'

'Mrs Fawcett will get it done,' said Mrs Scruton sagely. 'Then you should think about parish council. Keep those stuffy codgers on their toes.'

Millicent Fawcett, who I was pleased to call a friend and an inspiration, and the National Union of Women's Suffrage Societies continued the fight in Parliament. But discontent was growing with each failed Private Members' bill and a new group had split from the national body three years ago: the Women's Social and Political Union.

'What about you, Mrs Scruton? You could run against Charlie.'

'Me?' She laughed. 'Oh, no, dear. I'm too old and crotchety. I'd be a cat among the pigeons.' I tried to keep a straight face. The image her words conjured in my mind was amusing and accurate. She would shake things up, that was for sure. 'You, on the other hand,' she said, 'have youth, patience and wisdom.'

I smiled at the compliment. 'One day, perhaps.'

I found Annie in my room one day after school, rummaging through my drawers. 'I have to take my costume to school soon. Can you help me find something? It has to be just right,' she said, looking up at me with worry in her big blue eyes.

Christmas was around the corner, traditionally the pub's busiest time. Christmas Eve was our biggest night of the year, when families came to watch the magic show, sing carols and play games. The children were very excited. All three were in the elementary school nativity play; Annie, now in one of the older classes, believed it was her right to play the Virgin Mary after years of minor roles and was a little annoyed that Tommy, the year below her, had been picked as one of the wise men. He had always been impatient in his attempts to keep up with his sister, racing ahead and insistent on proving that he was ready for whatever Annie was doing. William had been relegated to playing one of the stable animals and didn't seem to care that he had no lines.

I glanced out the window. It was dark already but I had a few minutes before I had to check on the new girl, Bella, who I'd employed in the scullery and kitchen next door at the pub. She had recently replaced a maid who had found work as a secretary with my encouragement. I still missed my niece Jenny, who had left seven years ago after marrying Robert Brown. They only lived over the road above the butcher shop of Jenny's father-in-law, Tom, and I saw her most days, but she was more like a sister than a niece to me and it had been a balm to have her here with me. These days, Jenny had her hands full with Oliver, soon turning seven, five-year-old Lily and a newborn daughter, Rose.

'Now, let's see what we can find. You'll need a veil and a gown for Mary,' I said, opening the cupboard. 'What about this?' I asked, pulling out a length of blue velveteen fabric that I'd had for longer than I cared to admit. I'd intended to make something for Annie when she was little but I never seemed to have the time, but a simple gown wouldn't take long now with the Singer sewing machine Roger had bought me.

Annie's face fell. 'But it's just a piece of material.'

'Ah, that's what you say now, but you have to have a little imagination.' I draped the fabric around her and hoped there was enough. She was getting tall, with long, thin legs like a colt. 'We'll make a gown with wide sleeves,' I said, looping the fabric to show her what I meant.

'What about the veil?'

'Well, let's see.' I turned back to the cupboard where I kept old clothes that could be repurposed, my hand hovering over folded skirts and blouses, the sharp smell of camphor making my nostrils flare.

'How about this?' Annie lifted out a piece of champagne silk satin.

I stared at it a moment, a small smile playing on my lips. 'Do you know what this is from?' I asked softly.

She shook her head. 'But it's pretty.'

I let the smooth material glide over my hand. 'This was part of my wedding dress, when I married Dadda. I used some of it to make the christening dress for you and your brothers. This is one of the pieces that was left over.' I'd packed the christening dress away after I'd lost my last baby partway through my pregnancy, when William was three. I'd decided then that I didn't want to feel that kind of pain and loss again. Roger and I felt blessed with the children we had and agreed to not have any more, as much as was within our power. The pessaries and sponges had done their job so far.

'Will you make me a wedding dress when I marry one day?' Annie asked, putting the fabric against her cheek.

The breath caught in my throat. The innocence of childhood was a precious thing and I'd begun to feel it slip away as Annie approached her twelfth birthday. It wouldn't be long before she'd have to face the injustices of the world and fight for her rights as a woman.

'My sweet girl, of course.' I draped the silk satin over her hair, letting it cascade down her back. With a little ribboned border, it would be perfect.

As loving and affectionate as she was, Annie also had a wise head on her shoulders and never ceased to amaze me with her inquiring mind, much like my own mother had said about me. Annie's wisdom and intelligence often challenged me about how best to answer her questions and guide her on her path to knowledge and discovery. Tommy, on the other hand, was my live wire, a more physical child; he lived in the moment and was instinctive in his reactions to the world around him. As for eight-year-old William, he was the sensitive one, but outgoing and always kind. He was able to talk to anyone and was loved by everyone, so much like my father, his namesake.

I kissed Annie's forehead. 'Now, what are we going to find for Tommy's wise man and William's cow?'

'There you are,' said Roger.

I noticed the tight lines around his eyes and said to Annie, 'Off you go. We'll finish this later.'

Roger smoothed Annie's hair as she left the room. 'We received the reply from the brewery,' he said once she'd gone. The valuation of the pub had been accepted by the probate court, but Roger and I couldn't afford to give my sisters their share of the inheritance unless we sold the pub or took out a loan to buy them out.

I took the envelope from him, pulled out the letter and read the tight handwriting with Roger reading over my shoulder.

Dear Mrs Rainforth,

Thank you for your application regarding the extension of your current loan.

I believe this loan was first taken out by your father, Mr William Todd, on the purchase of The Ox and Plough, in 1890. On reviewing this loan's history since then, I am aware that you and your mother, Mrs Todd, continued the payments after Mr Todd's death in 1895. It is to your credit that all payments have been on time with no arrears.

I understand that, with your mother's passing, you intend to purchase your sisters' shares of their inheritance and continue to run the pub as you have done. However, although your current figures are showing good profits, it is not in my power to grant you an extension of this loan solely in your name. If you require the assistance of the brewery in this matter, I suggest you advise your husband that his signature will be required to secure the loan extension and on the liquor licence as equal owner to yourself.

Yours sincerely,

Harold Hargraves

I glanced at Roger in disbelief. Part of me was relieved to find the same look of shock and outrage on his face that I was sure was on mine. 'After all these years of dealing with the brewery, I'm still not trustworthy, just because I'm a woman.' The paper quivered in my shaking hand.

'It's ridiculous,' he said. 'Hargraves must have it wrong.'

'Mr Worthington would have given it to me in a heartbeat, but this new brewery manager doesn't know me.'

I'd thought women had more standing in the community after everything we'd done to prove that we were as capable as men, especially in matters of business, but nothing had really changed. I would have to speak with my sisters to see if they were willing to keep their shares in the pub until I could sort out this business with the brewery.

*

December 1906
Dear Mrs Rainforth,
I'm still in London, working on the new typhoid vaccine with Dr Almroth Wright and won't be back until Christmas. I'm worried about the rise of influenza, which has reached epidemic proportions here, and the growing rates of mortality. You know how rapidly these epidemics spread, but because of the short incubation period and the difficulty of diagnosing the early stages of the disease – with its indistinct symptoms – too many are falling ill fast. I think it prudent to remind the town about disease prevention and management.

You know what to tell them. What we have learnt is that the predominant cause of death from influenza is pneumonia. Anyone with underlying respiratory conditions is at higher risk of the secondary infection.

I always appreciated letters from Dr Jenkins, one of our local doctors. He was a member of the suffrage society, and I'd worked closely with him on projects such as the new isolation hospital, building the reservoir to hold fresh water for the town, the pumping station and installing street taps, and the smallpox vaccination program.

With Christmas so close, I only hoped we could rouse the small agricultural village of Ebberfield from its apathy after more than a decade free from waves of infectious disease and encourage them to take the safety measures required to halt influenza in its tracks.

2

The vast coal fields of the north have been mined for decades, and it was inevitable that progress would come to our sleepy village. We are one of the last untapped areas, access to the coal deposits under the limestone and the North Sea made possible by the technology of freezing the shafts to prevent water from filling them. But it's been fraught with problems. Work on sinking the shafts has stopped and nobody knows when the coal mine will be operational.

It was Christmas Eve. We'd closed the doors of The Ox and Plough after a busy and successful evening of music, magicians and games aimed at bringing the community together.

'I still have to put the children's presents under the tree,' I said to Roger with a yawn as I brought the clean glasses from the scullery to the bar. 'Tomorrow will be too busy to do it.' My sisters and I had decided that we should all be together on Christmas Day. It was the first time we'd be without Mama and I was glad to host Christmas lunch and have all my family in one place.

'Have you wrapped them all?' he asked.

I nodded and then noticed his sheepish expression. I raised an eyebrow.

'I have a couple of things to wrap.'

I sighed. 'We'd better do it now then.'

He shook his head, lips pressed in a determined line. 'I'll do it.'

'Why, Roger?' I grinned. 'Do you have something to hide?'

He frowned. 'I don't know what you're talking about.'

I draped my arms around him from behind. 'Have you got me something?'

'No.'

I nibbled the tender lobe of his ear. 'Are you sure?'

'Hannah, you know I can't think when you do that.'

'That's the point,' I whispered.

'Is it now?' He turned quickly, surprising me, and tickled me in the ribs.

I collapsed into his arms, my giggles becoming helpless fits of laughter. 'Stop, Roger,' I wheezed.

'Have you had enough then?'

I nodded vigorously.

He pulled me to him and I slid into the hard, inviting planes of his body. It was quiet and we were alone. Opportunities didn't come along like this too often.

'I don't care about wrapping presents,' I said throatily, leaning in to kiss him. 'I want you to unwrap *me*.'

My sisters, Sarah, Mary and Jane, and their families joined us for Christmas Day. As did Roger's brothers David, Matthew and Anthony, and sisters, Alice and Maude, and their families.

After lunch, the Christmas cake was cut and served and tea was poured. Silence descended as children and adults alike relaxed in the parlour. I took a moment to survey the room, our entire family together. Roger worked long hours managing the pub, while I was often in the office, looking after the business side of things, or on the floor, making sure everything flowed smoothly. It made socialising very difficult. Thankfully, we had Reg, once our potman, now Roger's right-hand man behind the bar, and Bobby Duggan who stepped up from his role of cellarman to help Reg during the busy times, whenever Roger was absent.

After the cake was devoured, Mary, Sarah and Jane joined me in the kitchen to help clean up. I'd waited all day to find the right time to broach the subject of the pub. If I didn't do it now, I might not find another opportunity.

'Have any of you thought more about The Ox and Plough?' I asked.

All three of my sisters bristled uncomfortably as they scraped plates and put food into the larder.

'We know how hard you and Roger have worked to maintain the pub,' said Mary. Her eyes slid away. 'But ...'

'Why don't you leave your shares in the business?' I suggested hopefully. 'You'll receive your share of the profits.'

'You don't make enough to support more than one family,' replied Mary gently. There was real regret in her face.

Sarah turned to me. 'We all need the money. I'm sorry about the fact that you and Roger have been running the place for years but it's all Mama and Papa had to leave us.' She could be blunt, on the verge of being brutal, but she was never malicious. Nevertheless, I felt my hackles rise.

Jane nodded and rested her hand on my arm. 'Money like this doesn't come along every day. It will allow Bert and me to make some much-needed repairs to the cottage. And I know it will be life-changing for Mary and Sarah too.'

'We can't afford to buy you out unless we get a significant loan,' I said bleakly, feeling hollow inside.

'I don't know what you're worried about,' said Sarah shortly. 'You'll be able to pay it off when the mine opens. Business will boom, like it did for us in Trimdon. It will be worth it to you and Roger in the end.'

'Then keep your shares in and reap the rewards with me,' I urged.

'If it was just us girls, maybe we could manage something, but we have to answer to our husbands and they want us to take the money,' said Mary, squeezing my hand.

My anger flared and I pulled my hand away. 'What? Don't any of you have a voice? This is your inheritance, not your husbands'. What about your say? Isn't this your decision to make?'

Sarah's eyes flashed as she banged a pot down hard on the table. 'We've never had the opportunities you've had. This money is *our* opportunity to make our lives better.'

'I've had to work for every opportunity I've had!' I was livid. 'I've been managing The Ox and Plough for twelve years, ever since Papa become too unwell to remain as publican. My name went above the door then and on the liquor licence as the new publican. I was the one who struggled to keep it afloat when Mama became the new owner.'

'We know what you went through,' said Jane, trying to appease me.

'No, you don't. What you don't understand is that *you* gave me no choice. You all had a choice to live the lives you wanted and insisted I was the only one who could help Mama and Papa when they bought the pub. I was the only one unmarried, with no other responsibilities, you said. It was me who had to give up my dreams of teaching in the city. I'm the one who's been invested in the pub since the beginning, I'm the one who worked hard and sacrificed so much to continue our father's legacy. Doesn't that count for something now?'

I thought of the day I'd arrived straight from teachers' college. I was young, idealistic, and could never imagine a future in a place like Ebberfield. Here I was, sixteen years later, married with three children and desperate to find a way to stay. The Ox and Plough was my life, my future and the future of my family.

'If the pub is a burden to you, why not sell it?' asked Sarah, spreading her hands wide.

'It's fine for you to say,' I said, raising my voice. 'Roger and I have put our hearts and souls into this place and all you can say is that we should sell?' I shook my head. 'You know I'd never do that! I've done everything to ensure that Papa's legacy would live on and look what we've built. This place is the centre of the community, a place for everyone. They don't call it "The Lighthouse" for nothing.' I glared at each of them. 'I won't sell. I'll find a way to buy you all out.'

I yanked open the back door and stormed into the yard, headed for the field beyond. I needed to let off steam before I said anything I regretted. I loved each of them but at times they infuriated me.

Later that night, I told Roger about the conversation.

'It's not your fault, my love.' He brought my hand to his lips. 'Probate is a bloody business and you can't blame your sisters and their husbands for accepting what's been offered to them. In matters of money, compassion and fair-mindedness fly out the door.'

He cupped my face. His hands were cool and soothing against my flushed cheeks. 'I'm as invested in the pub as you are, but don't hold this against your sisters. Perhaps you have to go in and see Mr Hargraves and explain your family's history with the brewery, so he understands how capable you are?'

I took a deep breath, the familiar feel of Roger's skin on mine, the faint smell of beer on his shirt, making me feel safe and anchored.

'You've been my partner in the pub for years and I'm happy for us to do this together as we always have. I don't have a problem with you cosigning but I *do* have a problem with the fact that I'm seen only as a wife, unequal to her husband in matters of business.'

Roger nodded. 'I know.'

'It's a matter of principle,' I said, my spine growing straight. 'I have to convince the brewery men that I should be able to get this loan on my own. If I can set a precedent, then change will follow more easily. I have to try for Annie's sake, and for all women.'

'Talk to the brewery, but the decision is yours.' In his eyes, I saw only love and support.

'I don't understand why you're concerned that your husband has to cosign the loan,' Mr Hargraves said after I'd explained my position. 'You work with each other and you're in this together, after all.'

I clenched my fists to stop my hands from shaking. Any man in the same situation would never have faced this opposition – financial institutions would be lining up to loan him the money he needed to buy his siblings out. And women weren't asked to cosign their husband's loans when they worked together.

'But I suggest you speak with Mr Phelps, our financial officer,' he continued hurriedly, seeing me frown deeply. 'To get a full understanding of the brewery's policy with loans and to discuss your situation. I have only acted on his advice.'

I was ushered down the hall to Mr Phelps's office.

'I'm sorry, Mrs Rainforth,' Mr Phelps said. 'Your visit is most irregular. Mr Hargraves conducts the business with our tied-house customers and unfortunately, I can't approve the extra funds without the security of joint ownership and your husband's signature on the loan document. We're only following standard banking conventions.' It was ridiculous that the banks didn't permit a woman to hold bank accounts in her own name – they required a signatory from a husband, father, male relative or friend.

'What about my mother? She owned the pub after my father's death. She didn't need joint ownership with a male relative.'

'Your mother was no longer a married woman. A married woman is considered half of a marital unit and therefore her husband must be included.' He shrugged. 'Mr Worthington may have given you hope if he were still here, but unfortunately, I do not have the long-standing relationship with you and your family that he had. The proper process must be followed and it is this brewery's policy that, in the case of a married woman, a tied-house must be in the names of husband and wife to execute loan documents.'

'If my husband had come to you for a loan extension and The Ox and Plough was his inheritance, would you have given it to him without requiring my signature or joint ownership with me?'

Mr Phelps stood suddenly. 'I'm sorry, Mrs Rainforth. If you and your husband make an appointment to see Mr Hargraves with the correct paperwork in order, I assure you, as valued clients, the brewery will be only too happy to help you in this matter.' He gestured towards the door.

I felt my cheeks flood with heat. I was being dismissed just like a child.

'Thank you, Mr Phelps,' I said tightly.

My first stop after I left the brewery was Mr Sanderson's office. He was the local solicitor and clerk of the Ebberfield Rural District Council, and a great supporter of our suffrage society. I was very grateful that he had a few moments between clients to see me.

'Mr Phelps is right,' he said, once I'd finished explaining my situation. 'The brewery can execute loans in the same manner as banks and financial institutions.'

'I understand that,' I said. 'But how can he insist that Roger and I both sign the loan contract? Under the *Married Women's Property Act*, I can own property in my own right. Surely, I can also take out a loan?' The last amendment to the law had been over twenty years ago, giving married women an independent financial and legal identity.

Mr Sanderson leant forward, steepling his fingers. 'The law does allow married women to own property in their own right but it also allows for certain interpretations in practice.'

'What do you mean?'

'It comes down to coverture and common law. These laws have been around for hundreds of years and the new married women's acts haven't completely displaced their influence. There is still an overriding attitude, especially in men in positions of power, that married women are better off being guided by their husbands in matters of property and finance. The husband is generally the breadwinner, with greater earning capacity and experience with money, whereas the wife often works solely within the home, in an unpaid capacity.'

'But that's just opinion, not the law,' I replied impatiently.

'Hannah, you know better than most how long it takes for attitudes to change to influence legislation. Tradition and public opinion still establish interpretations of those laws.'

I did know. Fighting for women's rights and the vote for women, I'd seen resistance to change demonstrated overtly, violently and also subversively.

'But what possible reason could the brewery have to need Roger's signature? I'm the one who has paid the loan repayments ever since Papa left the pub. I have extensive experience in business and in dealing with money.'

'You will find that all banks and reputable lending establishments insist on a husband's signature. This ensures that the loan is guaranteed by the marital unit, should you default or the loan be recalled.'

I sighed. 'There's nothing I can do?'

He shook his head. 'I'm sorry. You could take them to court and fight the interpretation of the law but there are no guarantees the judge will rule in your favour. If you want the loan soon, I can't see any other option but to accept their terms. The banks are no different and will only offer you a higher interest rate.'

I couldn't go home after; I was too angry. I called on Emily Duffield at the farm instead. She had married Roger's best friend, John, around the same time as Roger and I had married and their children were similar ages to Tommy and William.

'I haven't put a foot wrong with the brewery in all these years,' I said, seated in her parlour. 'Don't get me wrong, Roger and I have been doing this together for so long and cosigning a loan document makes no difference to how we work, but it's about the principle.'

She passed me a cup of strong tea. 'There's no way around it?'

I shook my head. 'We're a long way from independence when we can't even exercise our financial freedom.'

'What are you going to do?'

I put my cup down. 'We could sell. I could take my share of the proceeds and Roger and I could start another business.'

'Would you really do that? After everything you've done? I know how much the pub means to you – means to us all. It wouldn't be the same if you weren't there.'

I dropped my head in my hands. 'You know I can't leave. The Ox and Plough is part of who I am. I want to fight this.

I keep thinking about Annie and how I so want the world to be different for her, but I don't have the money to fight the brewery's decision. Anywhere else I go will be the same. At least the brewery is offering a decent interest rate. But it's about something bigger and if I sign this, I'll have lost my independence as a property-owning woman before I've even had it.'

3

I miss Mama and her wisdom. Her reassurances that whatever the children were going through at each stage of their development was normal and that I would manage each of the trials of parenthood with my own mother's intuition gave me confidence. Trusting this sense now, I feel ready for the next stage of parenthood. It's time for a little separation, for the children to explore some independence from me and for me to return to my lifelong passion – fighting for the vote for women.

A few days later I woke feeling unrefreshed after I'd been up and down with William all night. He'd been fretful, complaining of a sore tummy, and his skin was hot to the touch. Only when he'd vomited into the bucket by his bed and I'd straightened his bedding did he finally fall asleep. I always hated when the children got sick like this, but I remembered my mother telling me how childhood illnesses were an inevitable part of having children the first time Annie was ill as a baby. The worry associated with it was common to all mothers and the best we could do was to follow commonsense measures, make them comfortable and watch for troubling signs and symptoms. But high temperature and fever always concerned me.

'Stay in bed. Get a little more sleep. You've been up half the night,' said Roger, rolling over to kiss me lightly on the lips.

I shook my head and then stopped, feeling slightly nauseous. 'I can't,' I said. 'There's too much to do. I have the brewery orders to send in today and I still don't know what we're going to do about my sisters' shares.'

'I've been making inquiries as well. The brewery is still our best option, with the lowest interest rate. Perhaps if we go to see Mr Hargraves together, we can persuade him to waive the requirement of my name on the deed after we buy your sisters out.'

'You shouldn't have to get involved, Roger.' I felt the irritation rising from the base of my spine and shivered, suddenly cold.

'I know, my darling, but if there's no other way to keep the pub ...'

'I just want this resolved. Let's go and see him today. I'll take the orders myself and we can talk to him then.' I swung out of bed and grasped the side table as my vision swam.

'Are you all right?'

'I'll manage,' I said, as the wave of dizziness passed. 'Just a little tired.' I wondered for a moment whether I was pregnant but then I heard Tommy's feet on the floor of the hallway, the bathroom door slamming and the unmistakable sound of retching. 'Oh, no, not Tommy as well.' I threw a look to Roger before I went to Tommy's side.

'Feeling sick, my boy?' I asked, holding his forehead as he heaved over the toilet. He was hot, but not as bad as William had been.

'I don't feel good, Mama,' he said in a small and pitiful voice once the vomiting had stopped. He sat on the floor and put his hands to his head, looking so wretched that it made my heart break. 'And my head hurts.' A flash of worry sliced through me.

'Come on, let's get you back to bed.'

'But what if I'm going to be sick again?'

'I'll bring you a bucket, just like I did for William.'

He nodded, allowing me to lead him back to bed. He had his own room since Mama had gone and I was thankful he did, as he wouldn't wake William.

I settled him back into bed with a bucket by his side. 'Are you cold?' I asked.

He nodded and then grimaced.

'I'll get a bed warmer from the kitchen.'

I met Roger outside William's door, where I could hear him whimpering.

'Will's awake and hot as hell,' he whispered in concern.

'Tommy's sick too. Can you ask Bella to bring up a foot warmer for him? I want to see how much worse William is. We might have to call Dr Jenkins.'

Roger nodded. 'Shall I ask Bella to stay with you and the children this morning?'

I glanced at Annie's door. 'If Annie's not sick too, I might need Bella to make sure she's ready for school while I'm dealing with the boys.'

He squeezed my hand. 'I'll manage in the pub.'

I went in to William's room. His cheeks were ruddy, eyes red and glassy and bedclothes kicked to the bottom of the bed. I touched his forehead and drew my breath in. He was burning up.

'Mama!' He began to cry.

'Where does it hurt, my darling boy?'

'Mama, why are Big Bear and Little Bear talking to me?' he asked weakly.

I turned to look at the stuffed toys he'd had since he was small where they sat on his chest of drawers. 'Are they still talking to you?'

'Yes, Mama.'

I took his little hand in mine. It was limp and that troubled me even more. 'It's just because you're sick. We're going to fetch Dr Jenkins and it won't be long before you're feeling better.'

Bella looked in on us. 'I've given Tommy the bed warmer, Mrs Rainforth, and he's tucked up in bed. How's Willie?'

I shook my head. 'Could you fetch me a flannel and cold water and then walk down to Dr Jenkins' surgery and ask him to call on both the boys as soon as he can?'

'Of course, ma'am.'

Dr Jenkins finished examining Tommy and William before Annie had left for school. Thankfully, she was healthy.

'It's influenza,' he said, closing his bag. 'I've been run off my feet the last few days with growing cases. Keep the boys in bed and make sure Annie stays away from them.'

'Is it serious?' I whispered, following him into the hallway.

'Tommy should recover in a few days but it's young William we have to watch. I'll leave you a tonic and some medicine to help make them more comfortable. The sooner we can get the fever down, the better.'

I felt the blood drain from my face. 'I should have called you sooner.'

'My dear Mrs Rainforth, you couldn't have foreseen it. Influenza hits suddenly and hard. But children seem to bounce back quickly and usually recover in a few days.'

'Even William?' It took all my willpower not to allow my face to crumple then and there.

'There's no reason to worry just yet. You know what to do. Keep doing what you're doing with him and I'll be back tomorrow to see how he is. And make sure you take a few minutes to yourself while the boys are sleeping. You look exhausted.'

'I will,' I said, finding some relief in his words. 'Thank you for coming so quickly.'

But I couldn't let go of the images of seeing my boys so sick. Memories of my sister Mary and her boys, Christopher and Nicholas, ill with diphtheria eleven years ago came rushing back to me. Mary had been like a wraith after losing ten-year-old Nicholas, the disease ravaging his little body when the antitoxin had arrived too late for him.

Both the boys were sleeping by the time Bella brought the mail in to me. I noticed a letter from Mary in Hartlepool. Funny that I'd just been thinking of her.

> My dear Hannah,
>
> Just a quick note to tell you that I have influenza but Christopher and George are well. I've been feeling a little out of sorts all week but not bad enough to see the doctor. I assumed I had a cold until I took poorly yesterday with a fever and the doctor came to see me. He seems to think that I've had it all week with very few symptoms but because I haven't rested, I've become worse. I thought I'd better let you know because he says I may have been infectious at Christmas. Keep a watch for any symptoms in the children, even if they seem a little off-colour. As a mother, you'll know. And can you let Jenny know as well?
>
> I'm going back to bed now, on doctor's orders. Jane is cooking for us and will bring around food each day until I'm on my feet again.
>
> I'll write again when I'm feeling better.
>
> Your loving sister,
>
> Mary

I sighed, feeling bad about the conversation at Christmas when she was already ill. Poor Mary. But I was glad she had Jane around the corner to keep an eye on her. A few days in bed was probably just what she needed.

'Mary has influenza,' I told Roger when he came in to check on the boys. 'The boys could have picked it up from her but it's just as likely that they caught it from anyone in the village.'

'Should Annie be at school then?' he asked, pouring tea into my cup before filling his own.

'Hopefully anyone who is already feeling sick will have the good sense to stay home until they're well. Dr Jenkins has held talks at the school and across the village on what to look out for and what to do for influenza and our suffrage ladies have distributed leaflets as well. Annie was probably exposed at the same time as the boys, but I'll keep her home if she feels unwell.'

Roger nodded. 'With any luck, the boys will be on the mend in a few days. Do you want me to take the order to the brewery later today and see Mr Hargraves about the loan?'

'You might have to. I don't know when the boys will be well enough for me to leave them with Bella and we have to finalise this business with my sisters and the inheritance.' I shut my eyes as another wave of dizziness rolled over me.

'Are you feeling unwell?'

'Nothing a few hours' sleep won't fix,' I said, smiling weakly.

He grasped my hand. 'Go and have a lie down. I can watch the boys.'

'No, my darling. I'll have some breakfast in a minute and I'm sure I'll feel better.'

He swallowed the last of his tea. 'I'd better get back then if I'm going to see Hargraves later. I just hope I can persuade him to change his mind about the joint ownership.' He bent down to kiss me. 'Let me know if the boys' condition changes.'

By lunchtime, Tommy's fever had come down thanks to Dr Jenkins' tonic and he was beginning to feel better.

William's fever, however, was still very high and the cold compresses were doing little to bring it down. I was fuzzy headed with fatigue by that afternoon and was confused when Dr Jenkins arrived after surgery.

'I didn't think you were coming until tomorrow,' I said when I let him in.

'I've been thinking about William all day and wanted to check on him before I go home this evening. How is he?'

I shook my head. 'Not much better.'

I took him downstairs after he'd seen both the boys.

'Tommy's through the worst of it and will be back to normal in a couple of days,' he said. 'But I will admit that I'm a little worried about William. I've increased the dose of his medicine and the tonic and I hope to see an improvement when I stop by in the morning. If he gets any worse through the night, don't hesitate to send for me.'

'If he's not any better?' I could barely say the words. I felt heavy, as if treacle was flowing through my veins and I couldn't think straight.

'Then I'll admit him to the hospital where we can keep a close eye on him. Prolonged high fever in a child this young can be dangerous.'

The breath caught in my throat. I knew what he was saying. Infectious diseases like this could turn deadly in the blink of an eye and a patient could spiral downwards in a matter of hours, out of the control of even the most experienced medical practitioner. I couldn't lose William. He was my baby. I felt the world spin around me, my head pulsating to the beating of my heart. I thought it was going to split in two.

'Hannah?' Dr Jenkins grasped my arm. 'Come and sit in the parlour before you fall down.'

I found myself lying on the lounge, feeling the most unwell I had ever felt. I vaguely remembered Roger carrying me upstairs to my bed and, with infinite care, tucking the blankets around me as my teeth chattered hard with my shivering. I was ice cold and burning with heat all at once it seemed. I'd been plunged into a hellish nightmare.

I slipped into a restless sleep full of terrors, dreaming of William and me sinking below a river of pulsating red, me trying to reach for his little hand as we were pushed and pulled, tumbling through the rapids of the raging and boiling river. I couldn't even cry out when William slipped from my grasp and disappeared from my reach. Both our screams were silent until I was alone in my torment, my grief, anguish and pain. I was burning from the inside out; I was beginning to disappear, and I knew it would continue until there was nothing left of me, completely dissolved into the blood-red river. Until I was one with it.

When I woke, my head ached and I squeezed my eyes tight against the light that threatened to pierce my brain, but even my eyeballs ached. I heard moaning and soft hands on my arms and coolness against the burning skin of my forehead.

'How long has it been?' I heard a voice whisper.

'Two days.'

'It's too long for her temperature to be so high. If we can't find a way to bring it down soon …'

I drifted back into nothingness but the red colour of hell slowly dwindled until I drifted in a sea of black. Mama and Papa came to me in my dreams, their soothing words telling me that I was safe, that William and Mary were safe too.

An oil lamp burned on my bedside table. As my eyes adjusted to the dim light, I realised that Roger was slumped in the chair by my bed.

'Roger,' I croaked from between parched lips.

He woke immediately and sprang to my side. 'You're awake,' he whispered, clasping my hand. His felt strong and solid, anchoring me to the here and now.

'Why aren't you in bed?' I forced out, grimacing at the dryness of my throat.

'Here, have something to drink,' he said, lifting my head gently as he put the cup to my lips. It was chamomile tea, spiced with one of Dr Jenkins' tonics. I swallowed gratefully. 'I didn't want to disturb your rest,' he said, answering my question.

'I've been sick.' It was more of a statement than a question. 'How sick?'

'We were worried about you and William—'

'William, how is he?' I struggled to sit up. Last I remembered, Dr Jenkins was concerned about William's fever. I couldn't bear to think that I hadn't been there for him when he was so ill.

Roger rested his hand on my shoulder. 'No, don't get up.'

I felt a rush of panic overwhelm me as my dreams returned to me. What if we'd lost him? 'Tell me, what happened to him?'

The look of sorrow on Roger's face was almost too much. I felt my body brace for the blow that I knew was coming but I had so little energy.

'His fever came down the night you fell sick and after a couple of days of aches and pains, he's almost back to normal.'

I sighed slowly. William was safe and on the mend. 'What about Tommy?'

He kissed my forehead, cool against his comforting touch. 'Tommy's fully recovered and Annie didn't get sick at all.'

I closed my eyes, relief flooding through me, and nodded. They were all safe and well. Then I frowned. 'How long have I been ill?'

'Four days, my darling. Four days of living hell. For some reason, you and William suffered terribly with the fever. Dr Jenkins did everything he could think of to bring down your temperature. He was worried you'd develop pneumonia like Mary.'

'Four days,' I repeated in a daze. 'And Mary has pneumonia? Do you know how she is now?'

He didn't meet my eyes. 'We'll talk about it tomorrow. Now it's time for you to rest and I could do with some sleep myself.'

I had to admit that I was exhausted just with that little conversation and Roger's face looked ravaged. I brought his hand to my lips. 'I'm so sorry to have put you through this, my darling. Come to bed and sleep. I feel much better now and I want you next to me.'

'Are you sure?'

'I'll be able to sleep again with you beside me. You look like you haven't slept for days.'

He nodded, turned off the lamp and slid into bed, wrapping his body around me as though he was protecting me and willing me to get better. His nearness was all I needed and I drifted back into sleep, feeling safe and loved.

After examining me the following day, Dr Jenkins declared I was on the road to recovery. 'But you are not to get out of bed until I think you're ready,' he said sternly.

'Don't worry. I don't feel like I could manage much at the moment,' I replied. I felt incredibly weak and fatigued after the fever and still had a scratchy throat, but compared to the body aches and pains and the bursting headache, it was nothing.

'I know what you're like, Hannah. You never stop and push through your own exhaustion to get things done. You have an iron will but it will not serve you well here.' He looked at Roger, who stood on the other side of my bed. 'I must insist that you convalesce slowly.'

'You have to listen to him, Hannah,' said Roger. 'We don't want to lose you.'

I pushed myself up into a more upright position, feeling cross. I wasn't a child who needed to be told what to do. 'What are you talking about? The danger period has passed, hasn't it, Dr Jenkins?'

'I'm afraid not. You've been hit hard, but even those who haven't had a serious case have fallen victim to pneumonia because they haven't rested enough during their convalescence, and have done too much too soon.'

'But I remember you telling me it's a risk for older people and I'm young and healthy.'

'Yes, and so was Mary, and it didn't prevent her from getting pneumonia,' said Roger. The sorrow that I'd seen in his eyes the night before was back.

'How is Mary?' I asked, feeling suddenly afraid.

'Tell her, Roger,' said Dr Jenkins. 'She has to know and it may make her cautious with her own recovery.'

Roger sat on the edge of the bed and took my hand. 'Mary didn't recover from the pneumonia.'

'What do you mean? She's still unwell?'

'No, my love,' Roger said, softly. 'Mary passed away the day before yesterday.'

I felt my body pierced with pain more intense than I'd experienced over the last days, like shards of ice stabbing my heart and head.

'It can't be. I only just got a letter from her. She wasn't even unwell with influenza at first.' They were wrong, they had to be.

'Mary was vulnerable because diphtheria left her with damage to her heart and her body couldn't cope with the onslaught. I'm so sorry,' said Dr Jenkins.

'We won't take any chances with you,' said Roger in anguish. 'I can't lose you, so please listen to Dr Jenkins' advice.'

'Mary's really gone?' My eyes welled.

Roger nodded.

'No, not Mary.' Grief flooded through me, hot tears running down my cheeks as my body was racked with sobs. Roger wrapped his arms around me but all I saw in my mind's eye was Mary as a young woman, her face radiant and proud: the day she took my hand and whispered in my ear that she'd got the job she wanted at the draper's emporium and that I was the first one she'd told. I was only a child, but the honour was not lost on me. She was all excitement, jumping up and down and hugging me. Mary and I always had a special bond. It was impossible to believe she was gone.

Then my parents' words in my dream came to me. William and Mary and I were safe. Perhaps all three of us had teetered on the edge of life and death. William and I had lived but Mary had not. She truly was safe in the arms of Mama and Papa and her beautiful boy Nicholas.

I now understood the concern of Roger and Dr Jenkins. Mary would want me to do as I was bid and live. I had to get better to help Mary's family any way I could, now that she was gone.

4

> The WSPU motto 'Deeds not Words' is often interpreted as disruptive and inflammatory, but is valuable in making our cause known. If Mrs Fawcett can stand side by side with them, then why can't others? If we all unite, Parliament must hear us.

It was gloomy and raining when I arrived at King's Cross Station. Clementine and Esther were there to greet me when I stepped off the train clutching Mrs Fawcett's letter, the document I felt symbolised that all was not lost, that there was still a fight to win.

'I can't believe you're here,' said Esther, hugging me tightly. 'We've been so worried about you.'

'I can't believe I'm here either but I'm all the better for seeing you both.'

I'd had to push my feelings of grief to one side and gather my strength. Leaving my family at a time like this and after the boys had been unwell was no small thing. All I had wanted was to keep my family close, make sure they were safe and well, but Roger's mother, Elizabeth, was there to help. Now, I was eager to be going back to the engine room of the suffrage movement. I had to continue fighting the fight: for Mary, for Mama, for Annie.

'Let's have a look at you,' said Clementine, her eagle eye taking in my appearance. 'You're skin and bone, but we'll get some good London meals into you and make sure you enjoy your time away from the pub and the children.'

Clementine looked much the same as she always had: tall, slender, the same intensity to her expression but her auburn hair now shot with silver. Esther's sharp angles had softened to generous curves and her frizzy, ginger hair still defied control but didn't show the grey as clearly as Clementine's.

'We're so glad you've come,' said Esther warmly, squeezing my hand. 'Let's get you home and have a nice cup of tea.'

We caught the underground to Notting Hill, where Esther and Clementine lived.

'Welcome home,' said Esther, ushering me inside their three-storey terrace. It had been part of her mother's inheritance and she had gifted it to Esther when she'd decided to move to London. Esther's parents had both accepted that she had chosen to remain single. Mrs Burrows had tried to make what she called 'a suitable match' for her daughter but after Esther was raped by Edward Partridge, she couldn't let her prospective suitor come near her.

Edward had been a pillar of the Ebberfield community; a Justice of the Peace, district magistrate and had inherited his uncle's estate, Dalleymoor. Ten years ago, after testimony from his wife, Marjorie Partridge, as well as from Esther and me, he was convicted of manslaughter for killing Fred Duggan. Fred had violently beaten and violated his wife, Dorothy, for years and also attacked Marjorie, causing her to lose her unborn baby. It was only once Marjorie had fled Dalleymoor and Fred's body had been found that we learnt that Edward was abusive, using violence and threats, including what he'd done to Esther, to prevent the truth from being discovered.

I felt my stomach knot at the thought of inheritances. I couldn't put off resolving ours, and I couldn't push my sisters any further. I didn't want to lose another sister after losing

Mary. I had to sign the brewery loan when I returned home, as much as I resented it.

'I'm excited about Saturday,' I said, surprised at how grateful I was to receive a strong cup of sugared tea and the opportunity to put my feet up.

'It should be a good turnout,' said Clementine, pouring milk into her own cup.

'Mrs Fawcett mentioned in her letter that she's expecting about forty different women's organisations and about three thousand people. Enough for the government to sit up and take notice.'

Roger's sister Alice and our friend Emily were joining me on the day as suffrage society representatives. Mrs Fawcett had also asked to meet with me, along with Clementine and Esther, to discuss the new Private Members' bill and how best to include women's enfranchisement.

'I think the tide has turned,' said Esther. 'Since the general election last year, there are so many more men supportive of women's suffrage. Maybe this time, the bill will pass.'

It was an exciting prospect. Times had changed and, since women had been voting in local government elections for more than ten years, I hoped that Parliament was ready for women to vote in national elections.

'We've noticed the same thing at home. Men have been writing letters to the editors of the northern newspapers. And respected men too. It's certainly raised the profile of the movement.'

'I doubt it will be enough,' said Clementine, shaking her head. 'I agree that attitudes have changed, but men don't want to give up their power to women. It's going to take much more to convince them to take our cause seriously.'

'But the WSPU has already taken action that provided shock value,' said Esther. 'You've definitely raised public awareness.

But I'm sorry to say, it's not all positive. Why do you think that certain organisations don't want to be associated with anything the WSPU is involved in?'

'I know how you feel, Esther,' said Clementine hotly. 'But it doesn't change the fact that it's going to take shocking action to wake the government. A bit of poor publicity in the newspapers is nothing – the news changes day to day. But in the end, I firmly believe it will be our actions that force Parliament to recognise our legitimate claim and they're the only ones with the ability to give us what we want. If they won't listen, then we must force their hand.'

'So, you don't believe this new Private Members' bill will be successful?' I asked.

'I really hope that it is. All the WSPU hopes for that. But if it's not, then we need to do something more.'

Esther opened her mouth to retort. Clearly, they'd had this conversation before. But instead, she reached out and squeezed Clementine's hand. 'You know I worry about you getting involved in anything dangerous and unlawful. I don't want to see you in prison.'

Clementine covered Esther's hand with her own. 'Don't worry. I can look after myself.'

'Enough about us,' said Esther, standing suddenly. 'You must be peckish after your trip. Come to the kitchen. We have sandwiches and cake and I'll put on another pot of tea.'

The next day we went to the Portobello Markets, a short stroll from the house.

'Everything's at your fingertips here,' I said, gazing at the shop facades with terraces above them. There were drapers, fruiterers and greengrocers, florists, fishmongers, sweetshops, coffee houses, butchers, bakers, milliners, tobacconists, and the workshops of joiners, coopers, saddlers and even an upholsterer and decorator. 'Hard to imagine this was farmland fifty years ago.' I thought about Ebberfield and how much it might change in fifty years with the new coal mines.

'You can see why Clem and I have never become good at cooking when we can buy whatever we want here,' said Esther as we wandered among the stalls, threading our way through the crowds.

Men, women and children were hawking their wares on the street: ice cream, nuts, oysters, sandwiches, cakes and pies. Barrows of apples, oranges and potatoes were parked next to stalls selling gourds and marrows and fish displayed on tables. It was a sensory overload of sound, vibrant colours and smells – strong, offensive and exotic.

'The sandwiches last night were very nice,' I said, eyeing a large fish whose scales looked dull and listless, and which gave off a very fishy odour.

'My cooking repertoire hasn't changed,' said Clementine with a grin, steering us away from the stall. Evidently, they knew which vendors sold fresh produce and which did not.

'I thought the sandwiches were better than boiled eggs and fried sausages,' replied Esther, suppressing her own grin.

I lifted a sceptical eyebrow. 'I think it's time you both learnt how to cook properly. You can't manage on sandwiches, eggs and sausages for the rest of your lives.' Esther's family had a large estate outside Ebberfield with servants and a cook. Clementine had lived in the teacher's lodgings when she was in Ebberfield but she had never really taken to cooking either. But they'd both been in London for some years now. 'I think I'll have to teach you some simple recipes.'

I settled on a roasted chicken and vegetables, which I showed Esther how to make when we got home, while Clementine walked to the shop to buy wine to accompany our meal. The leftovers would make a good base for a chicken soup and could also be used in their favoured chicken sandwiches.

Our dear friend Marjorie Partridge joined us for dinner. We'd all become closer with the ordeal of Edward's arrest and trial. She'd been living in London since the trial, about the same amount of time as Clementine.

'How's your new job, Clem?' asked Marjorie over dinner.

'Wonderful,' said Clementine with a smile. 'Notting Hill High School is so much closer than Hackney. It's only a twenty-minute walk to school.' Esther's friend Hertha Ayrton, the well-known electrical engineer and suffragist, had taught at the school and helped Clementine get the job.

'It's a shame the school in Hackney closed,' I said, knowing that educating working-class children was close to her heart. I had been surprised when she'd written to tell me that she'd accepted the job in a more affluent area.

Clementine nodded. 'It is, but the new school has a long history of producing suffragists and I'm proud to be influencing the next generation.'

'You'd think the WSPU would pay you for the privilege,' said Marjorie with a laugh. She worked at the NUWSS as a clerk; Mrs Fawcett had given her a job when she'd left Ebberfield with nothing after Edward's trial.

'It's all for the cause,' said Clementine, smiling ruefully. She caught Esther's eye and grinned. 'And I'm learning a lot myself, thanks to this one' – she gripped Esther's hand – 'she forces me to go with her to the public Friday evening lectures on all manner of scientific topics.'

Esther smiled sweetly back at Clementine. 'You can pretend it's a chore, Clem, but I know you find it interesting – even though you pretend to be asleep sometimes.'

'All right. You have me there,' conceded Clementine.

'At least I don't drag you along to lectures at the Physical Society.'

'Thank God! But you still want me to become a member of the Advancement of Science association and join your sub-committee.'

'What's this about?' I was doing my best to contain the grin that wanted to break open on my face. They were just like an old married couple. The move to London had been good for Esther. She had spread her wings and was learning to fly. And she was pushing Clementine, who had always been one for action, out of her comfort zone.

'The sub-committee investigates the teaching of science in schools and universities. Clem's been helping me understand how science is taught in the classroom, but her contribution on the committee would be invaluable.'

'Heavens, Esther! How do you fit it all in?' asked Marjorie.

Esther shrugged. 'I have to feel useful. After eight years on the parish council in Ebberfield, I couldn't twiddle my thumbs.' Any hopes of Esther running for local council when she arrived in London had been dashed when it was ruled that women were ineligible to become councillors on town borough and county councils.

We moved to the parlour after dinner, taking our wine glasses with us.

'I just received another letter from Becky,' said Marjorie. 'Edward is still intent on finding me. He won't let up. He wants to meet with me but I don't want to see him. I never want to see him again.' Her hand trembled as she gulped the last of her wine.

'He's been out of prison for five years and he's still harassing your sister,' said Clementine. 'Can't the police stop him?'

'What's the point of making a big fuss?' asked Marjorie. 'Why do you think I don't go back to Ebberfield? It's enough that I'm still married to him. I'd divorce him if I could but then he'd find out where I was and he'd make sure we'd meet and that wouldn't end well.'

'Does he know you're in London?' asked Clementine.

'Probably. He knows I'm not at Dalleymoor any longer, as the estate was transferred to his mother while he was in prison. My aunt had a house here, but when Becky and I inherited it, we sold it so Edward would have no way of finding me. I've taken every precaution to remain safe and anonymous, even wearing wide-brimmed hats and not walking anywhere on my own.'

I could see a faraway look in Esther's eyes and knew she was remembering the events of ten years ago. She had been with Marjorie the night of Fred Duggan's murder. 'I felt safe at home on the estate but when I first moved to London, I sometimes wondered if he was following me,' Esther said softly. 'But whenever I turned, there was never anybody there.'

'Does anybody know where he is now?' I asked.

'Actually, I made some inquiries about his whereabouts,' said Marjorie, sitting tall once more. 'I enlisted the services of a private detective, a Mr Stevens. Edward is here in London, in Bethnal Green, working in a factory.' She put her hand on Esther's arm, her eyes shiny with what might have been unshed tears. 'I watched him leave the factory one day. I didn't recognise him at first, he was so hunched and defeated looking, and then he stumbled away. But when he reached into his bag and put a bottle to his lips, I knew it was him.'

'He didn't see you?' Esther whispered in horror.

'No, but now I don't fear him and you don't need to either. He's a pitiful shell of a man, broken and harmless. I'd feel sorry for any other man, but not for him, after what he's done.'

5

Esther is a true trailblazer. She has just accepted a position at the Royal Institution, while still finishing her engineering degree, as an assistant in the laboratory. She will be helping eminent researchers like professors Thomson and Dewar, Joseph Swan and James Swinburne with their work on electricity.

'I can't believe it's still raining,' I said, hunching further into my coat as we walked along The Strand. 'There was no hint of it yesterday.' It was the day of the Great Demonstration and it was cold and wet, but not unusual for February. Women had been gathering since earlier that morning in Hyde Park and congregating under the banners of their individual organisations near the statue of Achilles. It was the first time women from all over Britain had united to march on the streets to further the suffrage cause. It was a new direction for us and I was excited by what change this could bring.

'It hasn't stopped everyone from coming,' said Clementine, over the sounds of the brass band and the voices of many women as they followed the slow procession. Mrs Fawcett, Lady Balfour and Lady Strachey were at the head of the column with the banner of the NUWSS and the words *Franchise: the keystone of our liberty*. Umbrellas and banners were dotted throughout the procession as it snaked through the streets, and a number of carriages and motor cars followed the marching women, bearing red and white flags with the initials WS and red and white flowers. And we all carried red and white rosettes, to signify women's suffrage.

'I've never seen a crowd as big as this before,' said Emily, exhilarated. 'All these women together, in solidarity. It's an inspiring sight.' She and Alice had arrived from Ebberfield the night before.

'Except for the mud,' said Alice, as she slipped in her boots. I laughed. Some women had sensibly worn galoshes but the hems of long skirts were caked in mud. Although it would have been lovely to be snug and dry inside one of those cars, I was thrilled to be among it all. We were all there for the same reason, to be seen supporting the bill for women's suffrage.

'And so far, everything has gone smoothly,' said Esther.

'The picture of respectability,' replied Clementine. Esther only smiled slowly.

'I was expecting jeering from the bystanders but everyone's supporting us,' I said. I'd seen many things in our fight for women's suffrage. I knew that Clementine had been present at some of the more volatile demonstrations and been subject to vulgar taunts and jostling by men and women opposing women's enfranchisement and the WSPU tactics.

'Maybe ten years ago, but none of us is as young as we used to be,' said Marjorie. 'I've heard some of the younger women have comments thrown their way, but none of them rude or insulting, just saying how many pretty women are here to look at.'

'Why should they comment on what women look like at all?' asked Clementine.

Soon we had reached Exeter Hall for the meeting and it was a blessed relief to be inside, although all the wet, woollen coats and skirts pressed together in a confined space gave the air a particular smell. Yet the atmosphere was joyful and optimistic and everyone was anticipating the speeches. We listened to a ladies' orchestra while we waited for everyone to get settled.

The meeting finally began at four o'clock, with a round of rousing speeches by well-respected members of organisations such as the Women's Trades' Council, the Women's Liberal Federation and the Women Textile Workers' Committee. MPs Walter McLaren for the Liberals in government and Keir Hardie, leader of the Labour Party, spoke as keen supporters of women's suffrage. But chief speaker was the Jewish writer and husband of Hertha Ayrton's stepdaughter Edith, Israel Zangwill. Mr Zangwill was an excellent choice as he was engaging, witty and passionate about his thoughts on how half the population had no political rights.

Finally, the meeting's main resolution – that women receive the vote on the same basis as men – was carried.

'I'm not convinced it's the right course of action,' said Clementine as we walked back to the train station later that evening. 'If women accept the vote on the same basis as men, then only some women will be able to vote. Wouldn't it be better to fight for universal suffrage for all?'

'I think the idea is to create change slowly, so we can get some concessions in Parliament rather than throwing the whole lot at them at once and risking the government refusing to give us anything,' I argued.

'I admire Mrs Fawcett, but I don't see that making small concessions will make any difference at all, only alter the opinion of women and the suffrage movement. Give men an inch and they'll take a mile. They'll think that this is all we want, but it's not.'

'Of course not,' replied Esther rather grumpily. 'But it will take patience and persistence until all women are given the vote. First all men will have to be seen to have the vote before all women will be accepted as eligible.'

'Well, it's been a long day,' I said. 'Let's see what the committee on the suffrage bills have to say. With any luck, it will be good news and this franchise bill will be debated in the House of Commons.'

It was with the space to think and reflect in the quiet of the Notting Hill terrace that I decided to write to my sisters. Time to contemplate more than the children's needs, the pub and the day-to-day minutiae made me consider what was most important. I had to let go of my resentment.

> Dearest Sarah,
> It's still hard to believe that Mary is gone. It reminds me that life can be fleeting and that the things we say and do can be irrevocable. We only have each other, you, me and Jane. The three of us is all that is left.
>
> I'm sorry we argued about the pub at Christmas. I know we can both get fired up. The last words I spoke to Mary were in anger that day. I regret them now. I can never take them back or apologise to her but I can make things right between us. I don't want this business of the inheritance to hang over us like a shadow. Mama and Papa would never have wanted it to split us apart. Family is most important to me and I will make sure you and Jane have your share of the pub's worth. We have to keep our family together.

Four days later, Esther and I returned from the committee meeting in the parliamentary district, brimming with optimism. I had woken that morning thinking of all the women who we were fighting for. I had to channel my grief over Mary's death and fatigue from my own illness into positive action and push away thoughts of how much I missed Roger and the children.

'It feels so different this time,' I told Esther, as we stood in the kitchen making a pot of tea. 'The new enfranchisement bill is being supported by so many politicians and other men who believe this is the right thing to do that I feel there's greater hope than ever that such a bill will be voted through Parliament.' A number of Private Members' bills had attempted to pass the House of Commons since the Begg Bill had failed ten years ago, despite a petition featuring 250,000 signatures, but none had been successful.

We were interrupted by the door slamming and Clementine popped her head into the kitchen, hair dishevelled but her cheeks pink with excitement.

'What's happened, Clem?' asked Esther, frowning in worry.

'You've been at the House of Commons, haven't you?' I asked. 'The committee heard about the commotion and arrests at Parliament today.'

Clementine nodded, pulling out a cigarette. I noticed her hand was shaking as she took it to her lips. 'The WSPU held our first Women's Parliament at Caxton Hall. The King didn't mention the women's suffrage bill in his speech yesterday and we couldn't let that pass without making a noise, so we marched on the House of Commons.'

King Edward VII had been on the throne six years, following the death of his mother, Queen Victoria, who had reigned for almost sixty-four years.

Clementine drew out a lighter and made several attempts to light the cigarette. 'Politicians and powerful men think they can get what they want by omission but we won't take it.' Her eyes flashed with conviction as she puffed on her cigarette. It was the first time I'd seen her smoke. 'I told you, nothing will happen to that bill, like every other time. Not unless we hold them to account.'

Esther merely directed her steely gaze at Clementine and said nothing.

'I didn't get arrested, did I?' Clementine asked, taking her coat off. 'There were four hundred of us and sixty were arrested. Most chose prison rather than the fine.'

Esther rushed to Clementine and cupped her face with her hands. 'Thank you for not ending up in prison. I'd be worried sick about you.'

'I know.' Clementine kissed Esther's hand. 'But someone has to speak up against the underhanded tactics of politicians, so that people like Mrs Fawcett have the chance to get a fair hearing for the new bill.'

6

What is financial freedom? The right for a woman to own property? No, it's more than that. It's the right for any woman to open and control a banking account in her own name. It's the right to own her own business, to run it as any man would do, and to take out a loan on her own merits.

Roger, the children and I were at the final football game for the season. We were all fanatical about it; it was in the Rainforth blood. Roger used to play for Ebberfield but hadn't for some years now. His brother David played for Newcastle United in the Football League First Division and had been part of the FA Cup side for a few years. And I had pushed for the game to be played in the local school, all those years ago. Roger and I had coached them together until we got married, and Roger still coached the school teams that both Tommy and William played in.

'Go!' bellowed Tommy, as one of his favourite players raced down the sideline to intercept the ball.

We cheered as the player kicked an incredible pass to his teammate, who slid across the pitch as he reached the ball and skilfully kicked it into goal. The children's faces were pink with excitement as they raised their arms to celebrate the successful goal, ensuring Ebberfield won the game and proceeded to the semifinal.

Afterwards, riding the high of Ebberfield's win, Roger joined Annie, Tommy and William out on the green, kicking our football around. Since I'd returned home, I was incredibly relieved to see that all three children were healthy and well, with no lingering trace of the illness the boys had experienced.

'Pass it to me,' said William as Annie dribbled the ball and kept it out of reach of her brothers, just as Roger had shown her.

'Well done,' said Roger with pride. He was rewarded with Annie's glowing face and her pass to him. 'Now you, William.' He kicked the ball and William stopped it neatly with his foot, before kicking it to Tommy, the two passing it to each other while Annie and Roger tried to intercept.

All three children had skill and I thought it a terrible shame that Annie couldn't play in a competition the same way the boys could. But things would change. They had to. One day, all manner of things would be possible for girls and women.

I opened Mrs Fawcett's letter, hoping we'd made some progress with the women's franchise bill. I sank into a chair across from where Annie was reading *Black Beauty* again. I loved that she felt strongly about animal welfare. I'd tried to instil the value of social justice in the children and now that Annie was twelve, I had a sense that she'd really begun to understand what that meant.

> My dear Hannah,
> I write to you with a heavy heart. We had such high hopes for the enfranchisement bill. Mr Dickinson presented it to the House of Commons for a second reading but there was already a dissatisfaction with the bill not going far enough to help working women. But if we'd lobbied for any more, there was no chance the bill would have been considered at all. The ladies' gallery was closed, the MPs fearing protests by the WSPU. Mr Dickinson pleaded that

the members not be swayed by militant action during the debate, but it made no difference. The bill was talked out, without any conclusion nor any vote.

We've worked so hard for this bill and all of us had pinned our hopes on it. We step back, defeated for now, to regroup and rethink our strategy for next time.

We were right back to where we started. What a waste of time and effort. Nothing had changed.

'Why are you so sad, Mama?' asked Annie.

I looked up at her, struggling to hide my disappointment, all the frustration and futility of the last months hitting me. In that moment I realised that rather than hide my feelings, it was time to introduce her to the suffrage fight.

I explained to her about the bill and how the parliamentary process was the only way to get the vote for women, why it was important to give girls of her generation the opportunities that women of my generation were denied. 'We need the vote to be able to change the laws, to push for greater equality and ways to improve the lives of women and children and the vulnerable in society – those whose voices struggle to be heard.'

Annie nodded when I was finished, her little face solemn. 'What can we do now?'

I smiled. She wanted to understand and be involved. 'We continue to do what we can here in Ebberfield to help the community and we support the actions we feel will make a difference for the cause, here and in London.'

Everyone was worried about the radical strategies of the WSPU but perhaps we needed both: words and actions, working together and in balance.

*

It was time to settle the issue of the inheritance and as I promised my sisters in my letters, pay them for their share in the pub. I was determined to keep the family together and if that required me to sacrifice my principles, then I would do it for them. I knew the brewery loan was the best option for us, so Roger and I went to the brewery to sign the loan documents. The satisfied expression on Mr Hargraves' face made me livid and, for a second, I considered ripping up the document right in front of him instead. But it was the only way to keep the pub. He might have won this battle but one day women would be treated the same way as men in all matters, legal and financial. I'd continue the fight to ensure that happened.

With our signatures on the loan, Roger became co-owner of the pub.

When we returned home, I sagged in a chair. 'We've done it. I can give my sisters and George their money now, even though I'm sure they don't understand what it's cost.'

'I'm sorry, Hannah. I never wanted it to be this way.' Roger held my hand, his face anguished.

I brought his hand to my lips. 'We've secured our future and that of our children and the legacy we've built with my parents. That's what's most important.'

'We'll make The Ox and Plough the toast of the district. It will continue as the beacon and beating heart of this village but bigger and better than before.'

'That we will.'

I kissed him then, the unshed tears in my eyes making the world around me glisten and shine.

7

When Annie was young, I'd hoped that women would have the vote when she came of age but it seems we are no closer than we were ten years ago. Sometimes I despair that at the rate we're making progress, women's enfranchisement won't become a reality before she turns twenty-one. But I believe the suffrage marches that bring women together are the way forward. Is it time to introduce her to this new positive action? Our young women are the future of our cause.

It was the day before the Ebberfield Agricultural Show and after setting up and organising The Ox and Plough's refreshment stall at the showground, we turned our attention to our dogs. When Roger had talked about entering Duke and Shandy into the show, the children had been excited by the idea and wanted to be involved. There was no backing out after that and Roger had entered both in the two-year-old retriever category.

'Dukie!' squealed Annie, up to her elbows in soap suds, as the dog shook, spraying her with water.

'It's just a little water,' said Tommy with a grin as he kept hold of Shandy and continued to wash her, scrubbing behind her ears and under her chin.

'Here, let me help you finish washing him,' said Roger. Duke was a big dog for Annie to manage – he came up to above her knee.

Suddenly, Shandy slipped through Tommy's fingers and made a run for it.

'Get her!' yelled Roger.

William and I ran after her, Tommy in hot pursuit. Soap suds and water trailed in Shandy's wake.

'Got her!' shouted William triumphantly, trapping the dog in a corner and holding her tight. I smothered a laugh as Shandy wiggled and squirmed in his embrace, until William was as wet as she was.

I popped the lead around her neck. 'Come on, Shandy, let's get you clean,' I said, glad that she followed obediently back to the tub. We now had two wet dogs and soap suds all over the children. It was a balmy evening in August, so it didn't matter.

'Tommy, you help Annie rinse Duke while I help William rinse Shandy,' said Roger.

'Maybe we should toss the children in the tubs as well,' I said.

'We're not dogs,' said Annie indignantly, pouring water over Duke's smooth black coat.

I did laugh then. 'No, you are not,' I agreed.

'I think it would be fun,' said Tommy, splashing Annie with water.

Annie squealed again and Duke took his opportunity to escape, but I was ready for him with a large towel.

'Come on, Tommy,' said Roger. 'Leave your sister alone. I need your help to dry Shandy while I empty the tubs.

Soon both dogs were damp rather than wringing wet and chasing each other around the room, barking with excitement, as though they revelled in their new cleanliness. We all laughed at the spectacle and then Annie, Tommy and William began tossing a ball to the dogs, who attempted to catch it, dogs and children as boisterous as each other.

Roger put his arm around my waist as we watched the joyful chaos. 'Good to see them having fun,' he said.

'It is, but who'd have thought we'd have a pack of geese for children?' I shook my head and we both began to laugh.

The following day, after everything was set up, pies and sandwiches out on trays and Reg and Bobby manning the refreshment stall, Jenny and her children joined us for the walk to the show ring where the dog competition would soon begin.

'It's certainly busier this year,' said Jenny, wheeling little Rose in her pram. Lily held my hand and Annie, Tommy, William and Oliver raced ahead.

'It's because the mine people are back, now that the sinking of the shafts has begun again,' I said.

'I'm glad you kept the pub,' Jenny said softly. 'I know it was difficult for you to find the money to buy everyone out, but I can safely say that I'm not the only one who's relieved you did. The Ox and Plough was Grandda's legacy, but it's your legacy now.'

I squeezed her hand. 'Thank you, Jenny. It means the world to have your support.'

We stopped by the dog pens where the children now gathered around Roger, getting the dogs ready for showing.

'Roger is so good with the children and the dogs,' said Jenny. 'I wish Robert had a hobby.'

I nodded. 'He loves the pub as much as I do but it's always busy. He's somehow lighter since we got the dogs.'

Roger and I were fortunate. The pub was our passion, but our children and the dogs were our joy. If all people were able to follow the things they loved, were passionate about and enjoyed, what a different world it would be.

*

April 1908

Dearest Hannah,

I've done it! I've been elected as a councillor on the local borough. After the by-election because of Councillor Straun's death, I was able to run because of the recent *Qualification of Women Act*. Women can now be voted on any local council in the land, hurrah!

'Councillor Esther!' I shouted with joy into the silence of the room. I only wished I had been there to celebrate with her. I pressed the letter against my chest, her words resonating with my own hopes for the future. Esther was a pioneer. One of the first women on a parish council, a well-respected female engineer and now this. Anything seemed possible, it was almost within reach.

I had just finished tidying up after Annie's thirteenth birthday gathering. It had been wonderful to have all our families together, Roger's and mine. Even Mary's husband and son, George and Christopher, had come. Only now did I have time to read Esther's letter that had arrived with the birthday card from her and Clementine.

I'm so very pleased the bill was passed just as the work on the education committee was coming to an end. I would be tearing my hair out otherwise. The Local Education Authority is run by council, and I feel like I can step into some useful capacity right from the start. It's a big organisation with lots of moving parts but Clem assures me that if anyone can find their way through the bureaucracy, it will be me. She joked that I'd soon feel right at home and one day I might even be mayor! Who knows? I feel that soon, anything that's possible for men will be possible for women.

> We're looking forward to seeing you in June. Will you come to the NUWSS march organised by Mrs Fawcett or WSPU's Women's Sunday? I think I shall go to both and support Clem, despite my concerns about attending a WSPU event. I find the lack of democracy and the WSPU's increasing level of secrecy and militancy unsettling. Not only have they increased their disruption of public meetings and heckling of MPs, they've established regular Women's Parliaments and led demonstrations to Parliament, where many members are inciting confrontation with politicians and police and, when arrested more and more of them choose imprisonment.

Decisive action had to go hand in hand with the genteel petitions lobbying Parliament. But not everyone agreed, especially about what constituted reasonable decisive action. There was much to discuss with our suffrage society before deciding what to do.

'The decision we have to make is whether to send representatives of our suffrage society to only the NUWSS march and not the WSPU's Women's Sunday or whether we should attend both,' I said at the next suffrage meeting in the upstairs room of The Ox and Plough.

'What about loyalty to the NUWSS?' asked Mrs Burrows, her lips pressed into a thin line. I hadn't expected her to agree to support WSPU action. She was Esther's mother and the long-standing president of the church aid society and was still very conservative. She'd come around slowly to change like supporting women's suffrage.

'What's wrong with doing both?' asked Mrs Scruton. 'Ain't the idea to show those toffs in Parliament that women want the vote? The more women at each march, the better, I say.'

'But ain't that sayin' we align ourselves with the WSPU?' asked Dorothy Duggan. 'Because I ain't goin' to end up in prison like some of their folk.'

'No, Dorothy, it's not like that,' said Jenny's mother-in-law, Amelia. 'We'll only be listening to speeches about the cause.' She glanced at me. 'That's right, isn't it?'

I nodded. 'Both groups still support each other. Think of it as each doing their part to help women's suffrage.'

After a vote, we decided that representatives of the Ebberfield Suffrage Society would attend the NUWSS march and anyone who wanted to support Women's Sunday could do so individually.

'Now, let's talk about what we can do to help the Jacksons.' The coal company had recently bought more farming land on the edge of the village to build cottages and the colliery town. The Jacksons had been tenants and had been so far unable to find other land to farm. 'Can we put regular care packages together for them?' I asked. 'Food, clothing for the whole family.'

'I've already begun with that,' said Mrs Burrows. 'We should do a clothing appeal through the school since two of the children already attend.'

'Can we find a way to get them assistance with their rent? At least until they both have work.' They'd moved to a tiny place in the next hamlet but it was hardly adequate for two adults and five children. 'And what about work for Mr Jackson, perhaps as a temporary worker on the local farms?'

'I'll look into that,' said Emily. 'Maybe John can give him work, or will know who might have need of a worker. I'll ask if anyone has a vacant cottage on their farm too.'

I nodded. 'That's a great help, thanks Emily.' They owned one of the largest farms in the area. 'What about Mrs Jackson? Maybe we can find her something to supplement their income, perhaps from home, since she still has three children not at school yet.'

'Maybe Mama can help with that,' said Alice. 'She's swamped with alterations and repairs these days, and she prefers to make new garments.' Alice and Roger's mother, Elizabeth, had returned to dressmaking when Roger's father had died. She knew the tough times some families went through.

'Wonderful. That will keep them afloat until they can get back on their feet. The last thing we want is for them to end up in the workhouse.'

Mrs Scruton nodded. 'That's a fate nobody wants.'

On a cold Saturday in June, after Clementine's assurances that the procession would be peaceful, Annie and I returned to London to join her and Esther at the WSPU-organised Women's Sunday. We congregated in Hyde Park, part of one of seven processions that travelled from different directions. There were at least five times the number of those at Albert Hall the previous weekend, when Annie and I had joined tens of thousands of women, including Emily, Jenny, Alice, Marjorie, Esther and Clementine.

The NUWSS-organised rally had been Annie's first march. Although a little overwhelming for a girl from a small northern village, it had been the perfect first experience for her, filled with grandeur, dignity and the colour of a medieval festival, and she'd taken so many photographs with her new camera. Part of me wished I'd brought the boys too, but there was plenty of time to introduce them to the cause. Women had marched behind seventy beautifully designed and embroidered silk banners emblazoned with great women throughout history that rippled majestically in the wind. It had been a far cry from the demonstration of the previous year, which had been dubbed the 'Mud March'.

'Mama, there was nothing to worry about,' said Annie, looking around her in awe, the music of the brass bands loud in our ears. 'We're all here to support the vote for women.' The aim of both marches was to pressure the new Prime Minister into supporting the passage of the current women's suffrage bill through Parliament.

I smiled. The atmosphere was relaxed and genteel, much as it had been the weekend before, and there was not a trace of agitation or confrontation. I was glad I'd decided to bring her to another march. 'We are,' I replied. As far as the eye could see there were bonnets and hats and many women wore white, the colour of the WSPU. And not just women but men too. I felt a real sense of optimism with so many voices lending themselves to our cause.

'And there will be many speeches again,' said Esther, pointing in the direction of some of the twenty platforms erected in a circle to stage the various speakers.

'That's right,' said Clementine with a nod. 'Some speakers will be young women describing why they need the vote and older campaigners and men too. I believe even a well-known playwright will make a speech.'

'Now Prime Minister Asquith and Parliament will have to see that the people want this,' said Annie, her eyes widening in understanding. 'Actions can speak louder than words.'

'You've got it,' I said, exuberant. I wrapped my arms around my clever daughter and kissed her on the cheek. I was proud to be part of this moment and it gladdened my heart that Annie was here to witness it too.

We were in high spirits when it was time to leave. The crowds surged towards the exits, laughing and chatting exuberantly, and the police who had stood patiently on the periphery of the crowds all afternoon, now stepped forward to ease the crush.

'What was your favourite part of the day?' Clementine asked Annie, as we slowly made our way to the exit.

'When everyone shouted "Votes for Women" at the end and raised their arms in the air. I felt the voices of all those people in my body like a wave. It was incredible.' Her eyes shone.

'It's something we'll all remember for a long time,' agreed Esther.

'What about the speakers?' I asked, curious. We moved forward again in a cluster, like a large ponderous beast.

'The Kenney sisters who worked in a cotton factory when they were younger than me. It really opened my eyes to how vulnerable children are treated. But very inspiring that they now fight for working-class rights as well as the vote.' Annie's face was very thoughtful and I wanted to hear more of her insights but the crowd shifted again and suddenly we were at the exit. Annie went ahead and was let through, pushed along by the press of bodies, but I was stopped. I noticed that we were separated from Clem and Esther, somewhere behind us.

'Excuse me,' I said to the policeman, instructing me to wait. He had a shock of white hair, unusual in a man his age. 'Can you please let me through to join my daughter?' I pointed to Annie who was disappearing in the swarm of people converging outside the exits.

'You'll have to wait like everyone else,' he said with a scowl on his face.

I understood that it must be a trying day for him but all he had to do was allow me to pass. 'But she's only thirteen and I'm afraid I'll lose her. She doesn't know where to go.'

He stared at me for a moment, his pale eyes dispassionate, reminding me of a predatory hawk, and then turned his attention to another policeman nearby. 'You'd think these women would have learnt patience,' he said. His partner laughed.

I strained to see Annie in the crowd but she was gone. 'Annie? Annie!' I called. My heart thumped and I looked around wildly. 'I've lost my daughter,' I shouted, then tried to slip past the policeman. But he held me back by the shoulders.

'I told you to wait,' he said close to my face, his teeth gritted. 'Without order there is chaos. If everybody did whatever they wanted, like you, we'd have a panic on our hands.'

'But I've lost my daughter. She's out there,' I cried, pointing to the road outside the park.

'Let her go through,' said a gentleman, coming to my aid. 'Can't you see she's distraught?'

'Where's your common decency?' demanded a woman, joining him.

'Get your hands off her,' said a second woman in a loud voice.

I looked to the angry faces that surrounded us now, waiting for the policeman's response.

'Let her go,' said the second policeman, looking uncomfortable. 'I didn't know she'd lost her child.'

The policeman let go of me, his face flaming with embarrassment and I quailed at the fury in his eyes. He stepped aside and let me through and I breathed a sigh of relief. I ran, looking for Annie, feeling his gaze burning a hole in my back.

'Annie,' I shouted repeatedly, searching for her through the crowd.

'I'm here, Mama,' I heard her finally reply. Then I saw her, waiting by a lamp post with Dr Jenkins. My chest flooded with relief. I didn't know Richard would be here at the march, but I was so grateful to see him reassuring Annie, who was looking for me in the crowd.

I rushed up and hugged her tight. 'I thought I'd lost you,' I said, looking into her happy face.

'I saw Annie on her own and we decided to wait for you here,' said Dr Jenkins. 'I knew you wouldn't be far behind.'

'Thank you.' I gave him a smile of gratitude and relief. 'I didn't know you were coming today.'

'I was called to London and the laboratory unexpectedly and I thought I'd come.'

'Can we go for tea and cake when Aunt Clem and Esther get here?' asked Annie. 'I'm starving.'

I smiled. Oh, to be young and free of the cares of the world. If only I could shield her from them forever. 'Of course. Perhaps you'd like to join us, Dr Jenkins?'

'I'd be delighted.'

8

It's a wonder the anti-typhoid vaccine still hasn't been made available to our own military. Dr Jenkins has told me about an American Army doctor interested in taking the vaccine he and Dr Wright have been working on back to the United States to introduce to the army. But he's worried that once again it will be voluntary. During the Boer War, many more might have been saved had the vaccine been made compulsory.

I woke to the sound of tinkling crockery and opened my eyes.

'Happy birthday, my darling,' said Roger, placing the tray of tea and biscuits on the small side table. 'There's a letter arrived for you too, from Clem.' He kissed me on the lips.

'Stay,' I whispered, stretching luxuriously.

Roger smiled, a shadow of regret touching his face. 'Enjoy a few minutes to yourself before the children wake. I'll be back once I've opened the pub.'

I smiled as he left the room, marvelling at how the six months since Women's Sunday had passed by in what felt like a moment.

I sat up and took a sip of my tea, admiring how Clementine had perfectly timed the arrival of her letter.

December 1908

Dear Hannah,

Esther and I send you birthday wishes. We're celebrating with a bottle of wine after cooking your famous roast chicken, which, although not as good as yours, is still a success for our cooking prowess. So, I suppose we are celebrating this as much as your special day.

Did you hear that Mrs Fawcett has withdrawn her support for the WSPU? As if our cause isn't her cause! She wrote a letter to the Members of Parliament, condemning any violent action that destroys property. It was only a few smashed windows – surely a small inconvenience for the awareness these actions have raised to our joined cause?

But I don't believe her mind will be changed and perhaps this is better, us doing things our way while the NUWSS does things theirs.

The fire was crackling, making the room cheery and dispelling the winter chill, when I joined Roger in the pub. I'd enjoyed my tea and biscuits while reading my birthday cards and letters.

'We have to renovate the pub before the colliery opens and there are more customers,' I said as I gazed at the tired carpet in the lounge bar. 'We need an outdoor area and new male and female restrooms, as well as a family-friendly lounge. And a games room, with a billiards table and dart board.'

The law had recently prohibited children under the age of fourteen from the bars of a public house. I agreed with stricter laws around alcohol and children and was a firm believer of the temperance movement, which was ironic considering I was a publican, but The Ox and Plough was more than a drinking establishment – it was the beating heart of our village, a place where people from our district could come to enjoy a sense of community. And for us to remain relevant to the needs of the public, it required some changes to the original footprint and the uses of our available spaces.

Roger nodded. 'We've held off for as long as we can but with the refurbishment The Rose and Crown has done, I don't think we can leave it any longer. If only we could install electricity. I heard that new lines are being laid, including one between Ebberfield and the Ebberfield colliery pit. Pubs in Hartlepool have electric lighting and everyone's talking about how modern and up to date it is. Perhaps it won't be long before we have it. And after the closure of The Black Bull, we can't give the licensing board any excuse not to renew our licence.'

I sank into a chair with a sigh. 'Fancy being told that your business is no longer necessary or required to provide for the community. I know The Black Bull needed repairs, but it's been around for more than fifty years, as long as The Ox and Plough, and it had its loyal customers.'

'It was only a matter of time after the Royal Commission determined that there were too many public houses. We're lucky we didn't have to consider this sooner.'

'We'll need another loan.' The idea of borrowing more money didn't excite me.

'There's no way around it. We've proved to the brewery that we can pay our loan but we'll have to work out how much we'll need to do what we want.'

I nodded. We were managing the repayments we already had. With the extra customers a renovation would attract, we could possibly pay more. 'It might come down to what we can afford, and we might have to consider just doing the essentials,' I said, feeling suddenly tired. 'I'll put some figures together and we can look at what our priority is before we ask the brewery for more money.'

*

A letter came a few days later from Jane's husband, Bert, asking me to come to Hartlepool.

> Jane is unwell and refuses to stop and rest. She won't listen to Eliza or me. You and Sarah are the only ones who can make her see reason.

My stomach dropped and fear rushed through me. After what had happened to Mary – and so quickly – I made arrangements, leaving the children in the capable hands of Roger's mother, Elizabeth, and took the train to Hartlepool to help Jane.

'You shouldn't have come,' said Jane, shaking her head when I arrived. 'I'm perfectly fine.'

I hugged her tight and realised how thin she'd become. 'I'm here now,' I said, drawing away and searching her face for clues to how ill she was.

Jane took my hand. 'Well, since you're here, we'd better celebrate your thirty-eighth birthday.'

I shook my head. 'I don't want to create more work. I'm here to help you. How long have you been feeling unwell?'

'It will pass.' She kissed my hand, glancing at the sceptical expression on my face. 'I promise, it's not serious. But I don't see enough of you. We're always busy and since Mary …' She blinked away the tears that sprang to her eyes. 'So let me enjoy your company while you're here.'

I squeezed her hand, my own vision blurring. 'Let's enjoy each other's company,' I agreed, 'while you rest.' Despite her assurances, I could tell that she wasn't herself and with Bert's concern, I was worried about her.

I sent Roger a note, letting him know that although Jane was up and about, I would stay a week or so to make sure she recovered. He replied a few days later.

My darling Hannah,

We're all well here. I hope that Jane is feeling better under your care.

I took the figures you put together to Mr Hargraves so we can get the loan extension arranged before the new year. I wanted to ease the burden on you with your worry about Jane. At first, I wasn't sure we'd get the extra money but it's all organised now. Everything is signed off and ready to go. We can begin work soon.

The children and I miss you.

My heart is yours. Today, tomorrow and always.

All my love

I returned home in time to prepare for the Christmas Eve celebrations at the pub, one of the biggest evenings of the year, and had barely stepped in the door when I heard shrieks from the children as they rushed to greet me.

'You're home, Mama,' yelled William, almost knocking me over in his excitement. I held him tight, kissing the top of his head. I had missed his affectionate nature – his hugs, the way he took my hand in his when we walked and he sometimes still snuggled on my lap.

'How's Aunt Jane?' asked Annie, walking into my embrace.

'Much better,' I said with a smile. I smoothed Tommy's hair as he pecked me on the cheek.

'The biscuits are out of the oven,' said Roger, coming into the hallway. All three children raced to the kitchen and Roger lifted his eyebrows in amusement. 'They want to make you afternoon tea.'

I sniffed the air in appreciation. 'That's beautiful. Did you make the biscuits with them?'

He nodded. 'That was a bigger task than I expected. I think I spent more time cleaning up than making them.'

I laughed. 'Thank you for organising it, my darling.' I leant into him, his solid warmth. 'It's good to be home.' Roger often surprised me with little thoughtful gestures.

'It's good to have you home.' He wrapped his arms around me and kissed me. 'I missed you.' His hands slid lower.

I smiled. 'I need to go away more often.'

Roger took my hand and led me to the parlour. 'I'll have to help them with the tea in a minute but Annie insisted you wait here. She has the boys helping her pick some flowers out the back.'

I put my hand on my heart. 'How did we raise such beautiful children?'

Roger's eyes were dancing. 'Beats me.'

He sat beside me and I took his hand. 'Thank you for organising the loan extension. It was very thoughtful of you.' I took a breath, choosing my words carefully. 'You mentioned in your note that there was a problem with getting the extra money. We do still owe a lot with what's left of Papa's original loan and then buying my sisters out. Are you sure we can make the extra repayments?'

He nodded. 'Mr Hargraves was concerned at first about the brewery's ability to loan us the funds we need but he agreed that the pub should have the work done. He and Mr Phelps organised it all in the end, for a reasonable rate too, and I signed the loan papers. It might be a little tight at first with the extra payments but we'll manage, and when the colliery opens, we'll have more money coming in.'

My body stilled. 'I wish you'd waited until I got home,' I said quietly.

Roger frowned. 'I thought you'd be happy. One less thing to worry about.'

'I know and I appreciate that. But when you knew there might be a problem ...' I shook my head in frustration, trying to get him to see. 'Why didn't you wait so we could talk about it? You signed the loan documents without me.'

'I thought I was doing the right thing,' he said indignant, pulling his hand from mine.

We were interrupted by the sounds of the front door opening and footsteps in the hallway.

Alice burst into the parlour. She was trembling and her face was the colour of milk. I'd never seen her so discomposed. 'It's Mama, she's had an apoplexy.' My heart dropped. Elizabeth was the soul of the tight-knit family, the one who kept the Rainforth clan together. The death of Roger's father, nearly twenty years ago, had bound them together.

Roger stood. 'But I only just saw her this morning. She was here with the children.' His brow was furrowed in confusion.

Alice touched his arm. 'Dr Jenkins said you should come and see her. She won't last long.'

'You go,' I said, hugging Roger briefly. 'I'll see if Jenny can look after the children and I'll join you.' I kissed Alice's cheek, cold against my lips and squeezed her hand in sympathy and support. Then they were gone.

The days that followed were difficult. Elizabeth lingered between life and death, unable to speak or move. Christmas came and went in a blur. I managed as best I could, juggling looking after the children and running the pub while Roger was the rock that his siblings leant on. It seemed to me that Elizabeth was waiting for all her children to arrive home; David from Newcastle, Maude from Scotland, Anthony and Matthew from Yorkshire. It was when we were all by her bedside, each of us having said our goodbyes to her, that she finally slipped away.

I held Roger's hand in mine, his eyes bright with grief. As I wept softly, I thought again of my father who had also suffered an apoplexy and was taken from us suddenly, without any of us seeing him. At least Roger and his siblings had the chance to be with her when she passed. I was grateful Roger and the children had spent her last days with her, happy and oblivious of what was ahead, and I was glad that I was here for Roger and to say my own goodbyes to a woman who had given me her love and support over the years. And as the year came to a close, Elizabeth was laid to rest beside her beloved husband, the first snow of winter dusting the ground like a benediction from above. She would be sorely missed.

9

Many highly respected suffragists, like Elizabeth Clarke Wolstenholme-Elmy, have joined the WSPU. Over the last thirty years she has fought against coverture and promoted higher education for girls and women standing for election in their local councils. But even she believes greater action is needed to get us the vote.

EBBERFIELD, NORTHERN ENGLAND

APRIL 1909

'How are the renovations at the pub coming along?' asked Dr Jenkins one afternoon. We were walking along the open ground where the new terraced houses would be built for the miners. The same land where the Jacksons had farmed. I was happy that we'd been able to help them find their feet with Mr Jackson finding work on a local farm.

'It's chaos,' I said with a shrug. 'We're run off our feet but some days I can almost see what it will be like when it's all finished.'

'I can imagine how hectic it's been, especially after the loss of Elizabeth.'

'It's been difficult, but in some ways, the renovations have been good for Roger. His attention and focus to the project have been a good channel for his grief.'

Dr Jenkins nodded solemnly. After a pause, he gestured to

the land in front of us. 'The tendency is to build the houses tightly packed. The yards are generally small but if we can insist on room for families to breathe fresh air ...'

'Children can play in the garden,' I said, following his train of thought. 'In Trimdon, where Sarah lives, they have allotments, open spaces at the end of each row for community gardens, where they grow flowers, fruit and vegetables, but what if we had an area for the children to play too.' My eyes traced across the green undulating land to the colliery and then to the sparkling blue sea beyond. It was hard to imagine a whole new village springing up here.

'You mean like a park with a playground and vegetable patch,' said Dr Jenkins.

'Exactly. For the health and wellbeing of all the miners and their families.'

'Council will have to make sure reservoir water is connected to these streets too, with water pumps,' said Dr Jenkins. 'I'll make my report to the district council and hopefully we can avoid the overcrowding we see in some other colliery villages.'

I smiled. 'I hope council take on your recommendations. It's the responsibility of the parish council to provide allotments for residents as well as parks and playgrounds, so they should support our ideas.'

Dr Jenkins lifted his eyebrows. 'You never can tell with Charlie Franks on the council. Such a shame you couldn't run with those property qualifications preventing you.' Although I was busy with my commitments, including the national suffrage fight, if I'd been given the opportunity to run and work as a parish councillor, I would have taken it.

I nodded. 'Charlie Franks has certainly been a thorn in our side. Between obstructing the proposed women's shelter, refusing to allow a public library, and making sure The Rose and Crown was chosen by the festivals committee to provide refreshments at the last four events …' I shook my head. 'We just ask for fair and reasonable distribution between all the pubs in the village and for him to support projects that benefit the village, no matter that they're proposed by the suffrage society.' I checked my watch and gasped in dismay. 'I have to help with the school lunches. They're short-staffed today.'

'I'll drive you back,' said Dr Jenkins, pointing to his new motor car, a Thornycroft tourer.

I shook my head. 'I still have time if I walk quickly. You finish looking at the site and let me know if you have any more thoughts.' I waved in farewell and hiked my skirts up as I strode across the field. I wore shorter skirts above the ankle to bicycle and go walking but when I was about the village, longer skirts that skimmed the ground were more respectable.

I arrived just in time to receive the orders of groceries and fruit and vegetables from our new suppliers. The suffrage society, along with the church aid committee, organised everything we needed for school lunches from the funding supplied by the local education authority. When the law to provide food to children in elementary school had been passed three years ago, we'd celebrated it as a milestone. We'd been providing vulnerable children hot meals, often breakfast and lunch, for more than ten years.

'Let's finish cooking the mutton stew and the dumplings,' I said to the poor teacher who was frantically trying to do everything. 'I'll send Annie to fetch Jenny and Amelia to bring the meat from their butchery and help pack away the groceries and, after we've served the children, we can begin preparing for tomorrow's lunch.'

Soon the benches were filled with hungry children. Annie put on one of the aprons. 'I'll help serve,' she said.

I kissed the top of her head. 'I'm going to miss you when you go to Hartlepool in the autumn,' I said. Annie was in her last year and often helped me with the school meals when there weren't enough teachers to cook and supervise.

'You'll have to get Tommy to help then,' she said with a grin. 'You know he'll jump at the chance to skip class.'

I sighed. 'Don't I know it. But it might be good for him. I can show him what we're cooking and he can explain to the other children where the food has come from and how it's grown.'

'He'd like that, Mama,' said Annie. 'Anything to do with farming.' I handed her the first bowl of stew, which she sniffed appreciatively. 'Smells good. I think I'll miss this when I'm in high school.'

My belly clutched. It was nearly time to let her begin her own journey into life. She'd miss us as much as we'd miss her. But she was growing up, and days like today reminded me how much I relied on her. And as much as I knew going to high school was a wonderful opportunity for her and would prepare her for her future, I wasn't sure I was ready to let her go.

By summer, Roger and I had finished the refurbishment of the pub. In the end, we'd borrowed as much as we'd been able to complete all the changes we believed were necessary to bring The Ox and Plough up to date. It was exciting to open our outdoor area with the fine weather. I was surprised to see how the atmosphere was different. Not everyone was drinking beer, some were drinking only soft drink, but all had come to meet friends and family, congregating around tables, some in the sun, some in the shade. With the outdoor area open, we'd decided to offer different food options. Besides Mama's famous pork pies, roast meat or ham sandwiches, we added beef or clam stew, soups and roast joints. The timing couldn't be more perfect, as miners had begun to trickle into the village. It wouldn't be long before the mine would be producing coal.

But my joy about the success of the pub was deflated when I was called to school to see the headmaster.

'What's this about, Mr Gregg?' I asked, as I was ushered into his office and he gestured for me to sit opposite him.

'It's about Tommy,' he said gravely.

I felt the cold tendrils of unease stir within my belly.

'He's been involved in a fight with another boy and when he was told to stop by the teacher on the playground, he ignored her, and punched the other boy in the face, leaving him with a black eye. He's a smart lad and I expect him to set a good example to the younger children.'

My mouth was dry. Tommy was becoming more of a handful the older he got. I swallowed hard. 'I'm sorry. He's not normally like this.'

'I know, but he refused to tell us what the fight was about. Perhaps with an explanation we could understand what was behind it.' Mr Gregg shrugged. 'Regardless, I've given him a warning. If this behaviour continues, there will be consequences.'

'Of course,' I said. 'We don't tolerate such behaviour at home either. Roger and I will get to the bottom of this and make Tommy understand he can't hit other people.'

Later that evening, Tommy sat in front of Roger and me at the kitchen table.

'Why won't you tell me why you did it?' I asked him again, frustration rising within me.

Tommy shook his head, a defiant look on his face.

'I understand that sometimes people push you too far,' said Roger. 'It happens to all of us. As men, we see others react by hitting back all the time and think it's the answer, the manly thing to do.'

I saw Tommy straighten a little at his father's mention of him as a man.

'But, son, lashing out by hitting others isn't the thing to do. You're smart. Use your head, not your fist. You'll be the bigger man and others will respect you more.'

Tommy looked at his father with understanding and nodded slowly. 'It was one of the new miner's boys. He was making fun of Will,' he said in a low voice.

My own anger flared, hot and bright. Someone had hurt William and Tommy was punished for defending him.

Roger rested his hand over mine, to still me. 'What did he do?'

'He taunted Will, calling him dumb and slow, and when Will said nothing, he pushed him until he had him up against a wall, with his cronies laughing around him.' Tommy shook his head. 'I didn't know what else to do, Dadda. I pulled him away from Will and he threw the first punch but I ducked and he missed. I had to hit him back, to protect Will and make him see he couldn't do that to him again.'

'I understand why you did it,' said Roger. 'Bullies have to be stopped. But you should have stepped away when your teacher asked. You had proved your point and you should have respected her.'

'But she didn't see what happened.'

'No, but you could have explained and allowed the teachers to deal with this boy.'

Tommy hung his head. 'I'm sorry, Dadda,' he mumbled.

'Just think twice before you act. You're nearly thirteen years old.'

Tommy nodded.

'Now apologise to your mother and make sure this doesn't happen again.'

Roger caught my eye and I nodded imperceptibly. He knew how to deal with Tommy now that he'd hit the turbulent years of change. Our son was tall and thin as a bean pole and

I noticed a faint shadow above his upper lip. It wouldn't be long before he was a man.

The summer break eased so quickly into September that it was with trepidation and anticipation that Annie and I prepared everything she'd require for high school. Roger, the boys and I had taken her down to Hartlepool and settled her in with Jane. Now that it was time for us to leave, I could hardly believe that I was about to farewell my darling daughter.

'Do you have everything you need?' I asked, looking around the small bedroom that Jane had made welcoming with a posy of colourful flowers on the desk in the corner and a pretty coverlet on her bed.

Annie nodded. 'I'll be fine, Mama.' But I could see her eyes well and her bottom lip begin to quiver.

I wrapped my arms around her, holding her tight, willing myself not to break down. It wouldn't help her. 'You'll get used to it,' I said softly. 'Aunt Jane will look after you and Eliza will be at school with you. I'll come and visit when I can.' I kissed the top of her head, like my father used to with me. She was almost as tall as me now, with long, lanky legs. I wondered how much she would have grown when I next saw her. I blinked rapidly. That thought was nearly the undoing of me. 'You're going to love high school, learning history, literature and science, and using your mind, really challenging it. You'll have so many opportunities.'

'I know how lucky I am, Mama.' She was so earnest, it made me smile. 'I'm excited, really I am.'

We'd talked about how gaining an education gave her the ability to make choices in her life. It was less of an abstract idea after she'd heard about the girls at the cotton factories, but she wouldn't truly understand the importance of it until she was older. All the same, I wished she could stay in Ebberfield.

We needed more high schools in the rural towns, especially for girls. Everyone deserved a higher education, not just the ones who could afford to live away. But the issue of schools and education belonged to the county council. And married women, women with children who knew intimately what was needed, couldn't even get elected to the parish.

'I love you, Annie, and I'm so proud of you,' I whispered, brushing the hair from her face.

Watching her wave bravely from the front porch as we pulled away, all I could do was hold myself together as I waved back. When we turned the corner and I could no longer see her, I let the tears fall.

10

> I admire the ideas Chancellor David Lloyd George proposed in April's People's Budget. Raising the taxes of the well-off as a way of paying for welfare reforms that will address the problem of poverty seems a logical step. But forcing taxes on women who aren't involved in any of the decision making of this bill is another example of the disempowerment of women.

I was reading the newspaper out the back one afternoon in early July, looking for any news about the release of the Royal Commission on the Poor Laws report, when an article about suffragettes caught my eye.

'One of the suffragettes has gone on a hunger strike,' I exclaimed.

'What are you talking about?' asked Roger, who had come to join me in the sunshine.

'She was imprisoned after writing a passage from the Bill of Rights on the walls of the House of Commons. She refused to eat for ninety-one hours, before she was released in poor health.'

'Why would she do that?'

'I remember Clem telling me that suffragettes are imprisoned as common criminals, not political prisoners, which they believe they should be. Their offences are minor and they end up in prison only when they refuse to pay the penalty on principle. But they're not criminals and should be able to wear their own clothes and have decent food.'

'Well, I understand their frustration, but surely starving yourself is a bit extreme,' said Roger. 'Even to prove a point.'

'Perhaps, but she has certainly raised the profile of women's suffrage.' I couldn't help but marvel at women like her who were willing to put their bodies on the line for the cause.

'No!' Smoke was billowing from the oven. I opened the oven door and stared in dismay at the burned dinner. It was our fifteenth wedding anniversary. I had prepared the table with candles and flowers, had made appetisers and dessert but with the main course burned beyond salvation, the meal was ruined.

Roger came in to investigate the smoke and smell of burning as I put the tray down on the stovetop. 'What happened here?' he asked.

'I only stepped away for a short time,' I said. 'It's never happened to me before and today of all days.' I put my head in my hands, disappointment washing over me.

'It's all right,' he said, enfolding me in his arms. 'I know how busy you've been.'

'It's too late to cook anything else now.'

'I know you've gone to a lot of trouble to make this evening special. Why don't we have a picnic somewhere?'

I gazed at him dubiously, thinking about what we had.

'Come on, it will be fun. The weather is good. I'll finish up now and we can go while it's still light.' We were experiencing the last breath of summer, even though it was September.

I nodded slowly. 'I suppose the boys are at Jenny's tonight.' The boys had settled back into the routine of a new school year but my thoughts often wandered to how Annie was faring in her first week of school.

Roger grinned. 'Then we have all night.'

I packed everything in a basket, including bread and ham and cheese. Thankfully the appetisers and chocolate mousses I'd made wouldn't spoil and were easily transported. And I included a bottle of Champagne to celebrate with.

'It reminds me of when we were young,' I said when we were settled on the front of the cart. My belly was filled with butterflies and I was giddy with excitement. 'Where are we going?'

'You'll have to see,' he said mysteriously.

A short time later we were sitting on the picnic rugs and cushions on the back of the cart at a protected inlet, the calm blue sea lapping the shore in front of us.

'A perfect spot to watch the sunset,' said Roger, grasping my hand and kissing it. 'I'm sorry about the dinner. But I hope this makes up for it.'

I glanced around us at the spread of food, the flowers I'd brought straight out of the vase, the Champagne we'd opened. 'Food tastes better in the open air.' I bit into one of the little savoury tarts and gave the rest to Roger, feeling his lips brush my fingers as they closed around the tasty morsel. 'And you've picked a very romantic place.'

'Happy anniversary,' he said, clinking his cup with mine. 'Here's to the last fifteen years.'

'And here's to fifteen more,' I replied as we toasted.

'I thought I was the happiest I could ever be the day I watched you come down the aisle on your father's arm. I thought I knew what was ahead of us; the pub, family, children, hard work, difficult times and joy. But it's been so much more than that. And I could never have imagined then how much happier I'd be today because of all that – the life we've lived. But I am.'

I kissed him. 'I love you, Roger, more than ever, and I feel the same. Our love gets better, deeper, with each year we're together. And we have many more years ahead of us.'

'Just like a good wine – or Champagne,' he agreed, raising his cup then draining it. 'But I didn't bring you here just for the view and sunset.'

I raised my eyebrows. 'What then?' I asked, feigning innocence.

He took the cup from my hand. 'Do you remember the day you met me at the beach before we were married? Before you went to London to visit Millicent Fawcett?'

'I remember it very well,' I whispered. I'd waited for him in the sea. It was the night we'd conceived Annie.

'Come, swim with me.'

I gazed into his eyes, soft with promise and yet intense, just as in our early days. Away from the constant needs of children and the stresses of everyday life, nothing had changed between us.

I took my husband's hand as he helped me down from the cart and we made our way down to the water's edge, kissing and stripping off as we went, leaving a trail of clothing behind us. 'Come on,' I said, grinning, as I ran into the sea, bracing myself against the shock of cold, but gasping anyway as I submerged myself. I swam hard away from shore to dispel the violent shivering, until my body tingled and I felt a sense of exhilaration. I flipped onto my back. I'd forgotten how liberating it was, the water against my naked skin, floating free in the sea. This was living.

Roger was right behind me. 'Let me warm you up.' He wrapped his arms around me, the heat of his body, pleasant against the cool water. We floated there together, rocking with the gentle motion of the sea.

'This is the best anniversary,' I said. 'What I'd planned would never have been as good as this.'

'There's a lot to be said for spontaneity.' Roger kissed me, his touch searing my skin.

'Indeed, there is,' I said, wrapping my legs around him and surrendering myself to the moment.

A month later, Jane and I were at the new skating rink in Hartlepool. I'd taken the opportunity to come across to see Annie and find out how she was adjusting. And because I missed her. Roller-skating was the latest craze across the nation and Jane's daughter, Eliza, had invited Annie to join her and some of her school friends. Although Eliza was in the year above, I was touched by her thoughtfulness. I decided to take a photograph of the girls skating and lifted Annie's camera to my eye. They were all wearing blouses with high collars, some ruddy-faced and having discarded their short-waisted jackets already, and flared short skirts that fluttered as they glided, hemlines pressed along their shins. Strands of hair had escaped from under the small bonnets, and smiles were on every girl's face, bursts of laughter as they swayed unsteady on their skates or flew past with speed. It was wonderful to see them having so much fun. I could never have imagined roller-skating would become so popular when I was their age, living in Hartlepool.

Before long we began to talk about the reports of the forcible feeding of women hunger striking in prison that were in all the newspapers.

'One of John's buyers told him he went to a fancy-dress party in Hartlepool dressed as a suffragette on hunger strike, complete with a feeding tube,' said Jane, scandalised. John was her eldest son and a fisherman. Lady Lytton and eleven other members of the WSPU had been imprisoned for throwing stones and breaking windows while protesting at the Newcastle rally, where the Chancellor was drumming up support for the People's Budget, which was having trouble being passed through Parliament. They all commenced hunger striking but many were forcibly fed. Some supported the practice but others abhorred the idea.

I frowned. 'There's no accounting for taste then.'

'No, I agree, but do you know that there have even been comic sketches at the theatre about the suffragettes being forcibly fed in prison? I was quite shocked when I heard.'

'I can't believe people are making fun, not just of our cause, but of women's suffering. They're continuing our protest with their bodies – that's all they have,' I said. 'I think they're brave. Clem wrote to tell me that many suffragettes go on hunger strikes in prison, even knowing that they'll be made to undergo forcible feeding. When they're released, they receive a silver medal for their courage and loyalty to the cause.'

'I've heard terrible things about this forcible feeding,' said Jane.

'Yes, I can only imagine the brutality when you're already weakened by lack of food,' I said. 'I've read in the newspaper that Keir Hardie, the former Labour leader, questioned the government about how they can allow women to be subjected to this treatment. It's inhumane.'

Jane nodded. 'I agree they're brave, and loyal, but when all you see is their plight being ridiculed, it's clear public opinion is against them.'

'What other choice do they have?' I asked, shaking my head with frustration, the anger surging through me in a burst of heat. 'These women are dedicated to raising the profile of our cause and they know what's at stake. But I don't think the public understands what they go through. In any other setting it would be a form of abuse and torture. Even in prison, a woman's rights are denied. If ever there was a situation that so clearly proves that women need the vote to control their own destinies, this is it.'

*

The NUWSS was busy in the lead-up to the general election in January 1910, securing male signatures for our petition for the vote for women, which was presented to the House of Commons by the leader of the Labour Party and member for Barnard Castle, a neighbouring constituency to us in Southeast Durham, Arthur Henderson. Mrs Fawcett reported that more than 280,000 men signed the petition supporting the vote for women.

It seemed that our refurbishment of The Ox and Plough had been the right decision. Everything was running smoothly and we were managing the repayments on the new loan. Now we could accommodate families, locals, farmers coming in to the monthly livestock sales and their wives, who came with their children to meet friends and wait for their husbands. We had a games room, an outside area, our meeting rooms and new toilets.

At the colliery, the shafts had been completed and miners were arriving in the village, ready to begin mining the very first coal seam. Terrace houses had been erected near the mine but no other facilities were ready yet, so business in the village thrived. I was busier than ever with new projects aimed at welcoming the mining community and inviting new members to our suffrage society, and Roger had been elected on the parish council, wanting to do his bit to help the smooth transition of the village into a mining town. It was good to have his ear but unfortunately, Charlie Franks had been re-elected. At least Roger would be able to keep the lad under a watchful eye.

It was a cool spring morning in early May when I opened the newspaper to see the news that King Edward VII had died. It wasn't long before I noticed locals congregating on the streets to share their shock and grief. I stepped outside to find Amelia Brown crying and being consoled by a shaken Mrs Scruton.

'He was a peacemaker,' said Mrs Scruton. 'With men in power, tryin' to outdo each other, manoeuvrin' and posturin' across Europe and the colonies, claimin' their country's superior, he's the one who settled 'em down. What's gonna happen now he's gone?'

From what I'd read in the newspapers, Edward VII had been a good liaison between the European nations, a diplomat of sorts, easing the tensions caused by the colonial interests in Africa and the Russo-Japanese war. The powerful nations of Europe had split into two alliances, with the newly formed Triple Entente between Britain, Russia and France and the older Triple Alliance between Germany, Austria-Hungary and Italy. The articles and cartoons in the newspapers highlighted the trouble in the Balkans region, where states wanted independence from the failing Ottoman Empire, and European countries like Russia and Austria-Hungary wanted to expand their interests and fill the vacuum. It seemed to me to be a tug-of-war which King Edward had been able to adjudicate.

'Perhaps the new King will take over where his father left off,' I suggested.

Mrs Scruton flicked her hand dismissively. 'He's just a youngster compared to his father when he took the throne from Queen Victoria. Ain't nobody left to stop them doin' somethin' stupid and causin' us all to be drawn into a war we don't want.'

'I doubt it's that serious,' said Amelia, dabbing her eyes with her handkerchief. 'I'm sure King George will do a good job but King Edward will be missed.'

I hoped she was right, but with so many players involved, it only took one domino to cause all the rest to fall.

Later that day, William and Tommy arrived home from school and as usual devoured the lemon slice that had been my favourite as a child. It was Annie's favourite too. I wondered what she thought about the shocking news. Most likely I'd learn her thoughts in her next letter. I was grateful that she wrote home every week, even when she didn't have much to tell. I read her letters to Roger and the boys over dinner, and replied to her before bed. She'd seemed to adjust to her new life better than I had. I missed her quick, light footsteps on the stairs, the feel of her hair between my fingers when I braided it and the sense of communion we shared in those moments of quiet togetherness. But I was grateful she had Eliza to keep her company, like the sister she never had, and Jane to watch over her.

'Did you hear about the King?' asked William, crumbs clinging to his mouth.

I nodded. 'Nobody's talking about anything else,' I said, filling his cup with milky tea.

'At least it got us out of our normal lessons,' said Tommy with a grin. It was his last year of elementary school and although he was a clever child, he still didn't enjoy school. He loved football and was curious about the world around him, learning by practical application. Sometimes I wondered about our decision to send him to high school in Hartlepool. I didn't want the boys to become miners, working long shifts below ground where the risk of terrible accidents and death was still commonplace. I only hoped he'd seize the opportunity of furthering his learning, so he had the choice of a skilled occupation and the chance of a good life.

'What did you do instead?' I asked, filling his cup with black tea and adding three teaspoons of sugar.

'We had to write a story about the King, either as a newspaper article or imagining if we had met him. I wrote about meeting him out on the farm and him stepping in a cow pat.' Tommy laughed before cramming another piece of slice in his mouth. I had been surprised by my eldest son's interest in farming but it had not waned. He spent so much time on John and Emily Duffield's farm with their son Harry, who was a similar age.

'We could do the same,' said William, smiling at Tommy's irreverent antics. 'Or draw a picture of the King and what he might have looked like if we'd ever met him.'

'I bet you drew a picture,' I said, refusing to comment on Tommy's story.

William nodded and fished the drawing from his bag, smoothing it out on the table in front of him. He had drawn a very good likeness of King Edward, down to the detail around his eyes and face, and with great animation. Not only that, he'd drawn the King standing next to a motor car.

Tommy whistled. 'Not bad! Not bad at all.'

'What kind of car is that?' I asked.

'A racing motor car,' William said with a smile.

'The King would never race motor cars,' said Tommy.

William's smile broadened. 'But what if I could and the King gave me first prize?'

'Well,' said Tommy, shaking his head, 'I don't know, but it's just as likely as the King coming to the farm and stepping in a cow pat.'

We all looked at each other and burst out laughing.

'It's good to have dreams,' I said, wiping my eyes. 'And it looks like you both have imaginations that are alive and well.'

11

I was surprised to learn that King Edward, respected diplomat, had disapproved the appointment of Lady Frances Balfour and Mrs Tennant to the Royal Commission on Divorce and Matrimonial Causes, two women among a dozen influential men, even though women are the ones who suffer the most from the current laws. How can a man, even a king, really understand what women go through?

EBBERFIELD, NORTHERN ENGLAND

JULY 1910

It was finally the end of the school year and summer holidays. I was elated that Annie was coming home from high school in Hartlepool. She had spent nearly a year away, home only at Christmas and the school breaks, and I had found it so difficult without her. Tommy would be joining her at a boys' high school in the autumn. For now, I wanted to make the most of the summer months with all my children under one roof before I had to accept and endure the separation from two of my children.

'I'm just going down to check on the barrels,' said Roger. 'I want to have everything done before Annie arrives on the train, so we can spend the evening together with her.'

'Why don't you let Bobby do it?' I asked.

Roger shook his head. 'He doesn't come in until later and I

think tonight will be busy behind the bar – I doubt he'll have time to check everything.'

The miners would be out to celebrate the first coal being drawn from the northern pit. Finally, the Ebberfield colliery was operational. It was something for all of us to celebrate. With the success of the colliery, the village would flourish, and our pub would only go from strength to strength.

I kissed him briefly on the lips. 'Don't be too long. She'll be expecting you and I have to finish the dinner. I'm cooking her favourites.'

'I'll be there ready and waiting for her when she comes in,' said Roger with a grin.

Dinner was in the oven before I thought to wonder whether Roger had left yet. 'Did you hear Roger leave to get Annie?' I asked Bella.

She shook her head. 'The horse and cart are still here,' she replied, looking out the window.

I checked my watch. 'He should have left already,' I said with a frown. 'Can you finish up here while I see what's keeping him?'

'Of course,' said Bella.

I made my way to the main bar, where I found Reg.

'Have you seen Roger?' I asked.

'No. I thought he was going to get Annie.'

'Don't tell me he's forgotten the time and he's conditioning the casks.'

Annoyed, I returned to the scullery to call down the stairs, 'Roger, Annie will be here soon. You have to go now.' I didn't wait for a response but descended the stairs. 'Roger!' I yelled, impatiently. But there was no answer. Clearly, he wasn't in the cellar.

I was about to climb up the stairs again, racking my brain for where to look for him next and deciding whether to take the horse and cart myself to the station, when something caught my eye. I squinted in the gloom then made my way slowly down the stairs, the hairs on my neck raised. Something was wrong.

As I came closer to the floor of the cellar, it was then that I saw my husband, lying on the floor.

'Roger!' I screamed, rushing to his side. He didn't move, even when I shook him. 'Roger, please wake up.'

I found the oil lantern and turned on the flame with a trembling hand. He looked like he was sleeping. There was no blood, no limbs bent at odd angles. I shone the light on his face. It was grey and his eyes were wide open in surprise.

'Roger,' I sobbed, touching his face, his beloved face. And then I knew. My husband was no longer there. Roger was gone.

I felt arms pulling me away, faint voices and words in the distance.

'No,' I sobbed, wrestling free. 'Don't make me leave him.'

It was mercifully quiet again. I was alone with Roger. I held his hand, willed him to wake up, to come back to me. Maybe we could stay like this: alone, together.

But soon there were more voices, more intrusions.

'Hannah.' Someone was shaking my arm.

I slowly swivelled my head to look at the unwelcome arrival in confusion.

'Hannah, I have to examine him,' the person said gently. 'I have to see what's happened to him.'

I stared at the man. A small pinpoint of recognition. Dr Jenkins. 'Roger ...' I whispered. The horror rushed through me and I began to shake. 'Am I dreaming?'

He shook his head. 'Come away now.'

I clutched the doctor's hand. 'He's dead, isn't he?' I'd allowed the gate to open with my words and the tears flowed down my face.

Dr Jenkins nodded. 'I'm so sorry, Hannah. There's nothing I can do. He's gone.'

I covered my face with my hands. I couldn't look at his sorrowful and apologetic expression. 'No, no, no. It can't be. He's too young. He was fine after lunch. He wouldn't leave us like this.'

Arms gathered me in. Held me as I sobbed. Nothing felt real.

I was guided out of the cellar by firm hands. I didn't want to go. Soft arms gathered me up, taking me home.

I was in the parlour when Annie fell into my arms sobbing as if her heart would break. Tommy and William followed close behind.

'Mama,' sobbed William. 'Is it true? Is Papa really dead?'

His little voice penetrated my numbness as I looked into his anguished face, wishing more than anything in the world that I could tell him it wasn't true. Tommy stood silently beside me, tears rolling down his cheeks while Annie clutched my arm like she'd never let go.

'Yes, Papa is dead. Dr Jenkins said so.'

My own heart shattered with my words. I enfolded our children in my arms. I had to protect them from this pain that threatened to suffocate me.

Roger's funeral was the most difficult day of my life. The last thing I wanted was to speak to anyone, but everyone came. Roger was well loved in the district, he had been born and raised here, had just begun his term as parish councillor and had been part of The Ox and Plough for over fifteen years.

All I could do was nod and try not to weep continually. Try to put one foot in front of the other. My only clear thought was to keep my children close, make sure they were protected as much as was possible.

But as we left the church, following Roger's coffin on his final journey into the graveyard, the very first time I'd laid eyes on Roger came back to me like it was yesterday, even though it was twenty years ago, on my first day in Ebberfield. From the front of the pub, I'd seen Roger support his stricken mother and hold a weeping boy to him, his brother Anthony. They were following Roger's father to the graveyard, a man taken too soon, leaving his young family behind. Now his mother was gone too, resting these last eighteen months beside her husband.

I swayed on my feet and Tommy and William held me upright. Roger's father had died of a heart attack, suddenly and unexpectedly, just as Roger had. He'd been haunted for years by his father's loss but had had no control over this. None of us did. History had repeated itself.

Roger's coffin was lowered into the ground and my legs buckled. All I wanted to do was to fling myself on top of it, stop him from disappearing from me forever – but I had to be strong for the children. I swallowed the bile that rose to my throat and stared ahead, feeling the bones in Tommy's and William's hands rub together as I held them tighter. They were too young to lose their father, the boys only thirteen and twelve. Annie stood in front of me and I could feel her shaking as she sobbed silently. At fifteen, on the cusp of womanhood, she still needed her father. With each shovel of earth that covered my beloved, I felt myself become more distanced from the world. My children wept. I couldn't weep. I didn't have that luxury; if I started, I'd never stop.

My heart had shrivelled to a small, hard ball by the time Roger was covered, gone from sight.

*

The days after Roger's death blurred into one. I was numb. The constant ache deep in my chest was the only reminder that it was better not to feel, because every time I allowed myself to, the pain and desolation was more intense than I'd ever known. Everyone rallied around me and the children. Clementine and Esther came up from London, and Jenny, Jane, Sarah, Emily Duffield and Roger's sister Alice took it in turns to stay with us. Some days I found myself unable to get out of bed and others I couldn't settle on any one task, moving aimlessly from one to another. The dogs missed Roger too and even with the extra attention from the children and our friends, they were listless.

'Hannah, someone has to do the orders for the brewery,' said Jenny a couple of months later. Everyone had returned home, returned to their lives, but Jenny still came to see me every day.

'Tomorrow,' I said, staring at the photograph of Roger and the children on the parlour table. I kept delaying the decision to send Annie and Tommy to Hartlepool, for the beginning of the new school year. They didn't want to leave and I wanted them to stay, to have them close to me, safe and together. The idea of us being separated was too much to bear, although I believed their education was important. Ebberfield was safe and comfortable but jobs here were limited, and I knew that one day they would most likely have to look further afield to find jobs that were fulfilling and that paid well.

'You said that yesterday. And you have to pay the staff. Reg, Bobby and Bella understand, but the two new miners you put on, they won't.'

I sighed. 'Yes, I know.' It all seemed too much. Each morning, I woke after a few hours of oblivion, expecting Roger by my side. Only when I opened my eyes and turned to his side or felt the cold sheets next to me did reality hit once again, like a body blow. The loss had grown so great, I thought I'd be better off dead than live suspended between life and death. Time meant nothing, stretching, compressing. I'd lost the other half of me: my best friend, my confidant, my lover. My life.

'Come on, up you get. I'll help you.' Jenny pulled at my arm, making me get to my feet. 'You have to deal with the business. There's a letter from Mr Hargraves from the brewery, requesting you to make an appointment to see him. This month's loan payment is late. Of course, they understand your loss, but business must continue.'

I nodded and kissed her cheek. 'What would I do without you, Jenny?'

After doing the books, paying the staff and the loan, and catching up on the orders, I was exhausted. But on reading the letter from Mr Hargraves, I realised the loan required a meeting in person. It was a matter of urgency and I made the effort to visit Mr Hargraves the following day.

'My condolences, Mrs Rainforth,' said Mr Hargraves, as I took a seat opposite him at the desk. 'I apologise for asking you to come in at this time but there seems to be an issue with your loan.'

'Yes, I'm sorry the loan payment was late this month, but it's all up to date now and there won't be any problems in the future,' I said, a flush of embarrassment rising on my cheeks.

'No, no,' he replied, shaking his head and spreading his fingers wide. 'You have never missed a single payment, and in fact have never been late with any of your payments. We understand the delay for this month completely.'

I frowned. 'Then what is this about?'

He swallowed visibly. 'I'm not sure how to tell you this.'

Any tiredness I was feeling dropped away in an instant. 'Tell me what?'

'There's a problem with the loan. The last extension you and Mr Rainforth requested to refurbish The Ox and Plough raised the amount beyond our loan limit. But you and Mr Rainforth have been long-time, reliable customers and we wanted to ensure that your business continued to thrive. So we arranged for a third party to underwrite the loan.'

I stared at him a moment. 'Why didn't I know about this?'

'Mr Rainforth was the only required signatory for the loan.'

Roger, what were you thinking? I clenched my fists in my skirt, suppressing the impulse to rip shreds off this man. 'Even though I've been your customer for fifteen years and we both had to sign the loan to buy out the pub.' I was glad I sounded icy and contained.

But then I remembered the trouble we'd had to get the loan approved and how it had finally come through while I'd been away in Hartlepool when Jane was unwell. Then Elizabeth had died before we had a chance to discuss Roger accepting the loan the brewery had offered and afterwards, there was a rush to get the work done in time for our busiest season. And it would have all been well except that now he was gone.

I leant forward in my chair. 'What's the problem with this loan, Mr Hargraves?'

'Well, we received a letter from a private financial establishment asking us to remind you to meet the new repayments and fulfil the conditions of your loan.' He had the good grace to look sheepish.

'What do you mean?'

'The interest rate you've been paying was only offered for the first eighteen months. Then the rate increased ... quite a lot.'

I felt suddenly cold, all the way through to my bones. 'By how much?'

'It tripled.'

I stared at him, not sure I'd heard him correctly. 'Did you say tripled?'

'Yes, tripled.'

I gasped, comprehension slowly dripping through to my consciousness. 'But that's much more than standard rates, even among private lenders or … or even banks … '

He nodded, his face pale, a sheen across his forehead. 'It is.'

'Isn't there anything we can do about it? It's clearly irregular and exploitative.'

'I'm afraid not, Mrs Rainforth. Your husband signed the contract, which is legally binding.'

'But surely, he didn't agree to that rate? He wouldn't have.' I did the sums quickly in my head. 'He would have known we couldn't afford it.'

'I couldn't say—'

'What do you mean?' I interrupted him, raising my voice. 'You organised this loan for him. Why didn't you tell him?' I looked at Mr Hargraves sharply and my heart dropped to the pit of my stomach. 'Unless you didn't know either.'

'We only learnt about it recently with the letter.'

'Did you tell my husband about this?' Was it the reason Roger had had his heart attack? I held my breath, waiting for the answer.

'No, Mrs Rainforth. We've only just discovered it ourselves.'

I sagged. At least this news wasn't what had killed him.

'Where does this leave us, then?'

'You have to meet the new repayments. If you default, you may lose the pub.'

'But this isn't my fault,' I protested.

'I'm sorry. My hands are tied. There's nothing I can do.'

I stood abruptly. 'I want to see the loan documents and the letter you were sent.'

Mr Hargraves nodded. 'Of course. But this matter must be rectified urgently. I would hate to see any drastic action taken against you.'

I drew myself to my full height. 'Are you threatening me?'

He looked tormented. 'No. You are a valuable customer I'd hate to lose. What I suggest is that you read the documents carefully, to fully understand your obligations under the contract.'

'Thank you, Mr Hargraves, for your advice, but I have managed a successful business for many years and I would never have signed that contract, because I always read my documents carefully.' My stomach sank as soon as the words were out of my mouth. Did I blame Roger too? With that, I turned away to hide my trembling hands as I strode from his office.

It was only when I was alone in my bedroom where nobody would hear that I allowed myself to shake and sob. I had thought my life couldn't get any worse following Roger's death but the thought of losing The Ox and Plough was horrifying and chilled me to the bone. We were only just managing the repayments as it was, without this new rate rise. I couldn't accept what Mr Hargraves had told me. I'd find a way to fight this injustice. It was wrong.

I met with my lawyer, Mr Sanderson, after he'd reviewed the documents, praying for an answer to my problem.

'The brewery outsourced the loan to a reputable company who, for some unknown reason, changed the standard terms and conditions,' he said. He went on to explain the underhanded loopholes that had led to the exorbitant payments that were now expected. 'In short, Roger was tricked. He wouldn't have known signing this would lead to any greater repayments than what you were already committed to. But you see, hidden under all the legal language, there was a floating interest rate, the option they reserved, to reduce the term of the loan and with it, increase the interest rate, to cover the amount borrowed. And unfortunately, this option has been exercised.'

'We haven't had the loan long. Why now?'

He shook his head. 'I couldn't say. The pub isn't a high-risk venture.'

'Isn't there anything we can do, Robert?'

'We can fight this but it won't be easy. The contract is signed by Roger, making it a legally binding document. But I believe the brewery is culpable by introducing the financial firm to the contract when Roger believed he was only doing business with the brewery. However, as I said, the firm is legitimate and reputable.'

I frowned, not sure any of it made sense. 'Why would they change the standard conditions?'

'It certainly is strange. Something smells off to me. I don't like a contract like this at any time, but the only time such an option might be used is when the client is high risk and there are high stakes involved. If the client defaults by not repaying the loan, the money is usually secured by seizing the assets.'

'I don't understand. Why would they have made Roger sign a document like this?'

'I don't know, Hannah. It's quite a convoluted trail and it will take time to investigate what's happened here. But until then, you have little protection. If you can't pay the loan, which clearly you won't be able to, you have to rely on the goodwill of the brewery. If they can be made to feel a skerrick of remorse or guilt for their part in bringing in the underwriter and for not checking the terms of the loan, then they might hold the financial company at bay long enough for us to find our own legal loopholes or discover a reason to declare the contract null and void.'

I stared at him in horror. 'What am I going to do? If I lose the pub, I'll have nothing. And I won't be able to pay you to continue the investigation.'

'Don't worry about that now. Think about what you want to do. If it's sell the pub, it will get you out of this mess with some money left over. But if you want to fight this, know you have the village behind you. Besides, my wife and Amy would never forgive me if I let The Ox and Plough go. It means so much to all of us.'

I stood, blinking away the tears, grateful for the support of good friends. I wasn't alone.

'Thank you, Robert. I'll let you know what I decide.'

12

My darling Roger is gone. Every time I wake, all I want to do is drift back into nothingness, find some respite from reality. And the nightmare of my life is worse than the worse imaginings of sleep. How is it possible I might lose the pub as well? How can I endure this cruel twist of fate? But somehow, I must. I've gone from incredible happiness to the depths of despair.

With the mining operation underway and coal being pulled up to the surface in larger quantities every day, we were experiencing our busiest time at the pub. Miners had nothing else to do when they weren't on their shift and they congregated in the pubs, talking and playing games. They were big drinkers. I wondered if I could somehow pay the extra money on the loan with the income flowing in. But I knew I'd manage to only hold on for a little while.

I was so proud of the business we'd grown at The Ox and Plough and the knowledge that, one day, it would set the children up with a secure future. I wanted Annie to have the options that allowed her to live as an independent, liberated woman, just as the boys would have their freedom. And now, I felt sick at the thought that, after losing Roger, I might lose it all.

But it was getting more difficult to stop the drunkenness, even though we refused to serve anyone who was drunk and we always called on the constable before tensions became explosive and fights broke out in the pub between miners and locals.

One evening, I was dead on my feet serving a wedding party. A fight broke out in the main bar and I went in to beg for calm.

'Come on, Mick, you have to go now,' I said to one of the miners. His wife and children had recently left him, so I understood his pain, but he'd been like this, drunk and disruptive every night, for over a week now and enough was enough.

'No,' he yelled, agitated. He shoved me and I fell, hitting my head on the bar. I saw stars. Reg rushed from behind the bar to restrain Mick, ready to push him out the door. But Mick, in his drunken rage, was too strong for him and swung a punch, hitting Reg across the jaw but falling backwards himself and crashing into the window. The men around the bar pulled Mick away from the broken glass, and the sound of crashing brought the constable running. He escorted Mick to the police station to sober up overnight.

Reg had a deep gash on his cheek.

'Reg, go to the kitchen and wait for Dr Jenkins to come. You're going to need stitches.'

'No, Hannah, I'm all right.'

I shook my head. 'Please, get it seen to before it gets too late.' I turned to Bobby. 'Can you go to Dr Jenkins, then board up the window until we can get it fixed? The mining boys will manage behind the bar for a while.' I shut my eyes. *Of course, it's all turned to custard now that Roger's gone.* But I had to be strong.

The broken window was the last thing I needed but I began to clean up, picking up the pieces of glass from the ground. It was then that I realised that I didn't have my wedding rings and watch on. I'd taken them off earlier when I was kneading bread for the wedding party. I disposed of the glass and went to the kitchen, my heart pounding.

'Have you seen my watch and rings?' I asked Bella, who was cleaning the wound on Reg's cheek. 'I think I left them on the table when I was making the bread.'

'Yes, they're there, next to another card.' Letters and cards of sympathy and support had been coming in ever since Roger's death. I nodded and put on my watch and rings. They were treasured keepsakes from Roger and their loss would be too much to bear. I took the envelope and fled to the office. My head was aching from the fall and I was struggling to remain calm.

I slashed open the envelope and opened the card.

> My condolences, Hannah. When you lose everything, you understand the true meaning of loss.

I dropped into my chair and began to weep.

I couldn't see a way forward. I was truly on the verge of losing it all.

I stood in front of Mr Hargraves, feeling like a child in front of the school headmaster.

'I'm sorry, Mrs Rainforth. If you can't make the repayments, then the matter is out of my hands.'

'This is my livelihood. The Ox and Plough has been my life for twenty years. None of this is my fault. Please, Mr Hargraves, have some compassion.' I wasn't above pleading.

His expression softened. 'You are a good client, Mrs Rainforth. We don't want this any more than you do. It was never our intention to cripple you with this loan and it's in our best interest for you to continue our mutually successful relationship. As such, we've contacted the underwriter, but they won't budge.'

'It's impossible for me to pay. I can't lose the pub.' I clutched my hands to stop them from shaking. 'I'll fight this.'

He nodded. 'All we can do is take administration of The Ox and Plough and place one of our managers in while we look into this matter further.'

'But once I'm out, you won't want me back in.'

'That's not true. We're offering you an olive branch, a solution. Your only other option is to sell up, which means you'll lose any chance of ever getting the pub back.'

I stared at him, quivering with rage and fear. 'You give me no choice then,' I rasped, my throat thick with emotion. 'I refuse to sell, but I'll do everything in my power to prove I should never have been evicted.'

'I wouldn't expect anything less, Mrs Rainforth,' he said, standing and showing me the door. 'Good day.'

Receiving my letter of eviction, the last days and nights at the pub, the indignation of all my customers, friends and neighbours – it was all a blur.

I stood in my kitchen, Jenny, Emily and Alice helping me with the final packing. I gazed across what was still mine. For all the years Roger and I'd worked, a few boxes of crockery and household items was all I had left.

'I've lost everything. Every fibre in my body wants to scream out with the injustice of this. Women have no control over their security, their finances. I have to get the pub back, it's our home and our legacy. I can't give up, after everything my parents and Roger and I have done to build it up. I just can't.' I dropped my head in my hands and began to sob.

'I'm homeless and I have no income or savings. Everything we had, we put into the pub. I can't support myself or my children,' I continued, feeling more wretched than I could have ever imagined. 'I have to go to London. Esther has offered to take us in and won't hear of me paying rent, and Clem has found me a job as an elementary teacher.'

'Surely you can find work here?' replied Emily. 'You're a teacher and have more skills than most of us. And you've been a local in this town longer than most.'

I smiled weakly. 'There's no opening at the school. It will only be until Mr Sanderson can unravel the business with this loan.'

'You can stay with us until you get the pub back,' said Alice, squeezing my hand. 'It's a bit crowded, but we'll manage.'

Tears glistened in my eyes. 'Thank you. I mean it. But four mouths to feed is no small thing. I don't want to outstay my welcome.'

'You know we'd never see you destitute,' said Jenny, gently. 'You have always lifted us and many of the people of this town. We'll find a way to support you.'

I shook my head, shame flooding my cheeks. Now that I'd made the decision, I knew it was my only real choice.

'What about the children?' asked Alice. 'Their lives are here.'

I pushed the sob that rose to my throat down. It was too much, but I had to face the practicalities. 'They've only just lost Roger and I don't want to disrupt them any more than they have been but I can't afford to keep Annie and Tommy in school in Hartlepool. I struggle to keep Tommy in school at all and William wants to be just like him. If the children are with me in London, Esther and Clem will help me ensure they all have a good education.'

I'd never felt more alone. There were still moments when I expected Roger to be in the next room and I'd think of how we'd talk through our problems and find a solution together. But he was gone and the responsibility of the pub, my family's future and our very survival rested like a heavy burden on my shoulders.

I sat the children down in the kitchen and explained why we were moving to London.

'No,' said Tommy outright. 'I won't go.' His eyes flashed with anger and his hands were curled into tight fists. I knew they wouldn't like it but I didn't expect this resistance, especially when I listed the reasons why we had to go. I glanced at Annie and William, their faces pinched and pale, their eyes darting uneasily between Tommy and me.

'I know you miss Dadda,' I said gently. I was sure he felt alone and misunderstood. I wondered how Roger would have framed this discussion differently, in a way that Tommy would grasp the importance of my decision.

He shook his head. 'I can't believe you want to leave everything we've ever known, everything that connects us to Dadda, like he doesn't exist.' He was shouting now. 'But I won't leave! I'll get a job, do an apprenticeship.' He brushed the tears away furiously.

I looked at Annie, her face on the verge of crumpling. 'Is it the only way?' she whispered.

'I wouldn't do this to you all if there was a way we could stay.'

'If it's what we have to do, then I'll come to London, Mama,' Annie replied while William nodded his head.

I reached out for Tommy's hand. 'Please, say you'll reconsider.' I watched my son's face darken as he moved away from my outstretched hand. He was fourteen and I knew I couldn't force him to come.

He folded his arms. 'You know I don't like school. I'm better off here, getting a job on a farm. Dadda would understand.'

I jerked, like I'd been slapped. 'I don't want us to be apart.'

Will gently rested his hand over mine. 'What if I finish elementary school here, closer to Tommy? That way, he won't be alone.' The expression in his eyes belonged to someone much older.

Will's words took my breath away. My beautiful boy looking out for his brother, and for me. That one considerate gesture was my undoing. 'Come here, all of you,' I hiccoughed, pulling the three children to me and hugging them tight. 'I love you all so much. No matter what happens, never forget that.'

A week later, after long nights desperately spent planning into the small hours, everything was organised.

I couldn't believe I'd decided to let Tommy stay. After discussing it with Emily and John, they agreed to take him on as a farm labourer to learn the ropes of farming. He was settled out at the Duffields' farm, sharing a room with their eldest boy, Harry, who was home for the holidays from boarding school. They took Duke and Shandy too, as some comfort to the boys, and I knew they'd be just as happy on the farm as Tommy. He preferred to be outdoors and doing things – a life in London would confine and trample him. I was thankful for Emily's and John's kindness and the fact that Tommy and Harry were firm friends. But as much as Tommy was determined to leave school, I was secretly as determined to get him educated somehow, even if it was when I got the pub back.

But harder still was my decision to allow William to finish his last two years of school in Ebberfield. He was only twelve and I felt torn leaving him behind, even though he was going to stay at Jenny's. She'd insisted, and I knew she'd treat him like her own son. He was to share a room with Oliver and would help Robert around the butcher shop. I was relieved that Jenny had assured me that she'd have Tommy visit regularly and I was determined to come back to see them as much as possible.

Annie had a spot at the Notting Hill High School, where Clementine was teaching, so she and I would live with Esther and Clementine. Although I'd never imagined splitting my family up like this, all three of my children had a safe place to go and I had an income and a roof over my head until the matter of the pub was resolved, for however long that would take.

'Now that I know the children will be all right, promise me that you'll keep our groups at The Ox and Plough running – the literacy groups, the community projects and suffrage society,' I said to my friends as we stood on the platform, ready to board the train.

'We promise,' said Emily, grasping my hand.

'We'll make sure everything continues, even if we have to find a new home for our meetings until you return,' said Alice.

Jenny nodded, blinking tears from her eyes. 'You're the heart and soul of this town, Hannah. And I'll miss you terribly. I've never been further than across the road from you, ever since I was fifteen.'

I smiled, the tears welling once again. 'I'll be back before you know it, home with my family.' I didn't know what the future held but I had to believe I was doing the right thing.

Annie and I boarded the train to London after tearful farewells with Tommy and William. I memorised the imprint of their young bodies as I hugged them with all my might. But feeling Tommy contained and tall and William quivering was almost too much for me to take. My heart shattered as I stepped away. I couldn't believe I was leaving my two precious boys behind when their father was not long in the cold ground.

At least they were in loving hands that I trusted. All I could do was pray that it wouldn't be long until we'd be reunited with The Ox and Plough.

I couldn't stop thinking about what I'd done to my family as the train took me further away from the boys and closer to London.

Tommy had been so angry with me when I told him I'd organised him a place to stay and that I was still going to London.

'How can you leave us with strangers?' he'd yelled, his face blotchy with fury.

'They're not strangers,' I said. 'I thought you'd be happy with the Duffields. And I know how much you love the farm.'

'You think that makes up for everything?'

'No, of course not. Nothing can change what's happened. I'm doing my best to make things easier for you. You know that Emily and John love you as a son.'

'But I'm not. I'm their worker.'

I shook my head. 'You're learning a trade. One you told me you wanted to do.'

He stared at me, seething with resentment.

'If you'd rather come to London and go to high school or find some other trade—'

'I don't want to go to London! I suppose this will have to do.'

I'd watched him storm from the kitchen and heard the slam of the front door behind him, making me jump.

'Mama, I understand you have to go to London to work,' said William. He'd been sitting quietly with his cup of milky tea while I'd argued with Tommy.

'I'm sorry, love,' I said, kissing the top of his head. 'I don't want to leave you. You could always change your mind and come with us.'

'I know. I'll be all right. It will be like a long holiday with Ollie, even though we'll be going to school, and it will be fun helping in the butcher shop.'

I hugged him tight. 'I'll miss you, William.'

'I'll miss you too, Mama.'

Sitting on the train, I wondered if I'd gone crazy, but the idea of going to London seemed the only sensible choice I could make. I watched Annie sleep, the dark lashes against her fair skin, and thought through the options again.

If I ever had any chance of getting my family back together and under one roof, this was it.

I was exhausted when Clementine finally ushered Annie and me into the Notting Hill terrace.

'We have more room than we know what to do with,' said Esther, hugging me tight. 'I've made up a room for Annie and one for you. We want you to stay as long as you need without a second thought.'

I looked into Esther's face, full of love and concern, and burst into tears, the distress of the last weeks coming to a head. I was finally in the safe and loving cocoon of my oldest and dearest friends.

13

In theory, married women as property owners can be on the electoral register but they do not qualify to vote. Men abuse the words of the law and hide behind those words when it suits them. It's imperative that women be involved in creating a more equitable future. We simply must have the vote to create change.

After Annie was asleep, I talked until late with Clementine and Esther.

'When I was evicted, it was the most mortifying moment of my life,' I told them, pulling my legs up under me on the sofa. 'I could barely look my friends in the eye, let alone my neighbours, the locals and the new manager of the pub. And then to leave my children ... I'm so deeply ashamed of it all.'

'None of it is your fault,' said Esther, putting her arm around me.

'I know Roger wanted to organise the loan to take the pressure off me when Jane was ill, but if I'm honest, I'm angry he didn't read the contract thoroughly. Perhaps we'd have picked up the inconsistency sooner if I'd checked it when I got home from Hartlepool ... but with Elizabeth's death and the rush to get the renovations started, I trusted the brewery and Roger to make sure it was all in order.'

'Hannah, you can't blame yourself,' repeated Esther.

'You need to keep busy,' said Clementine with a concerned frown. 'Teaching will be good for you.'

I shook my head. 'I'm worried about going back. I haven't taught in sixteen years. What if I've forgotten everything?'

Clementine shook her head. 'It's like riding a bicycle. It will come back to you.'

'Besides, you've kept your hand in with after-school lessons for children who are struggling and you've been through the curriculum three times with your own children,' said Esther.

I nodded, more for their sake than my own. I knew how worried they were about me but I wasn't sure about anything anymore.

'Nothing much has changed,' said Clementine. 'And once you have your confidence back, you'll feel stronger, clearer, more steady on your feet.'

'I don't know ...' I said, putting my head in my hands. 'I feel rudderless.'

'Teaching will give you purpose,' said Esther, squeezing my shoulder.

'And that's exactly what you need,' said Clementine. 'You've had purpose and a strong conviction ever since I've known you. What about the pub? What can you do from here?'

I lifted my head. Clementine was always the practical one. 'Robert Sanderson is helping me with the legal side of matters. He's offered his services for free but I've always paid him for his advice and I don't know how to feel about it.'

'Take his gift in the spirit it was given,' said Esther quietly. 'You've helped many over the years with no thought of payment.'

I nodded, reflecting on the truth of her words. But it was more than that. Receiving was more difficult than giving, especially for myself. It felt like I had less control of the situation, of what I was receiving and the obligation that might go with it. As a woman in business and in leadership,

I had to prove I was in control, to keep the wolves at bay. Robert Sanderson wasn't out to ruin me, he only wanted to help right a terrible wrong. But after everything that had happened, I found it difficult to trust.

'Robert's daughter, Amy, will help with the investigations here in London. She's a fully trained solicitor working as an assistant in a legal office and is an expert at researching the background of difficult legal cases. I'll help her however I can.' Being a woman, Amy wasn't able to practise as a solicitor, even though she'd gained her law degree through the London University.

'Surely it's an open-and-shut case?' replied Esther. 'As you say, the contract is irregular.'

'I don't know. It's complex, all tied up with legal processes.'

'Well, you and the children are part of our family,' said Esther, grasping Clementine's hand. 'You can stay here as long as you need.'

I smiled for the first time in weeks. 'Thank you. It means the world to me.'

I stood in front of a class of boys beginning the new school year. I was working at the local elementary school on Portobello Road. Glowing references from Esther, Clementine and Benjamin Burnett, who was now headmaster at a large boy's school in Sussex, had secured me a permanent position here.

Some faces showed anticipation, others held looks of boredom and there were even a few displaying resentment. I wondered in passing how Annie was faring at her new school.

'Let's start with you writing about what you did over the summer,' I said cheerfully. 'Then each of you can read it in front of the class and tell me a little about yourselves.'

'I've got nothin' to write about,' said one boy.

'Did you spend time with friends or help your parents?' I asked.

He shook his head.

'What about playing football or marbles?' I asked to a blank stare. I had to find the spark, something that interested him. 'What about collecting things, like stones or tadpoles?' I asked, thinking of William. This boy was eight or nine – he should surely have a hobby.

The boy's face lit up and he nodded. 'Thank you, miss,' he said, picking up his pencil and beginning to write, tongue between his teeth. A pleasant sensation flooded my chest and came to rest in my belly: part relief, part fulfilment. Clementine was right. It *was* like riding a bicycle.

I was back to where I'd started my teaching career twenty years earlier, with similarly aged children. But I was grateful to have a job. My dream had once been to teach in a high school for girls like Clementine and perhaps even become a headmistress. However, with the new rules imposed by the Board of Education, it was difficult to find a position in high schools these days without a university degree or further training. I had gone to teachers' college in Durham but Durham University didn't allow women to obtain degrees until 1895, when I had left teaching and was already married.

Some of the boys might be a little challenging but I knew how good it would feel to get my teeth into finding ways to foster a love of learning in these children, help them discover what inspired them. Teaching boys had a different purpose for me now. Many of them were just like Tommy and William had been at that age. These boys would one day become men and if I could play my part to help them learn respect for girls and women, to broaden their perspectives and question things they were told to just accept, then perhaps the world would be a better place.

*

I met with Amy Sanderson not long after my arrival in London.

'I'm so sorry about what's happened to you,' said Amy. We were sitting in Esther and Clementine's parlour at Notting Hill. 'You inspired me to study law, watching you fight for the vote for women and the community projects you ran. I've always wanted to use my knowledge to improve the inequities that women suffer under the law.' She took my hand, almost shyly. 'And I'm incredibly grateful that I'm in a position to do that now, with you. It is my great honour to do everything I can to get you out of this contract.'

'Thank you,' I said. I wondered if Amy realised how her words and compliments had not only touched me, but lifted me too. I had made a difference. 'Where do we start?'

She pulled her notebook from her bag. 'Papa has written to me with instructions. The brewery is attempting to get to the bottom of why those clauses were added to your contract, just as we are, but they aren't willing to accept you defaulting on your loan had anything to do with them. So, first of all, I'll research the financial company and its dealings. See if anything like this has happened before and, if so, what happened and whether it was resolved.'

'And then?'

'If we can find any whiff of a problem like this, even from a reputable firm, we can pressure the brewery into accepting full responsibility. We want to prove that they were negligent for not checking the contract Mr Rainforth signed but if we can also prove that they were negligent in using this financial institution to outsource the loan without first checking its history, then it opens the door for us. They may have no choice but to deal with the financial company themselves and give you back the pub.'

I shook my head in amazement. 'It sounds so simple.'

Amy smiled wryly. 'Unfortunately, it rarely is, but we'll use every avenue to resolve this.'

A rush of gratitude swept through me. 'How can I ever repay you and your father?'

'We have to get you back into The Ox and Plough. That will be payment enough.'

14

I'd forgotten how much I enjoy stretching the minds of my students and finding what makes them passionate about the world. Clem was right, after a few weeks, it feels like I'd never left teaching. My desire to make the world a better place began when I became a teacher. I may have lost everything I've built but I can make a difference to the boys I teach. And that is enough for now.

Annie and I had been in London just over a month when the first letter arrived from the boys, accompanying one of Jenny's letters. Annie was settling in well and we'd written to them twice already, sending little packages with photographs to brighten their day, telling them about our schools and life in London.

I climbed the stairs up to my room and sank into my reading chair, putting Jenny's letter to one side and fumbling as I unfolded the letter from the boys.

Dear Mama,
School is going well. I'm in the advanced class this year. I walk with Oliver and Lily every morning and afternoon and sometimes help them with their homework. Jenny made your lemon slice the other day. She knows it's my favourite.

Football season has started and Oliver and I have been to every home game so far. We both still play in the school games. I'm striker and Ollie is goalie. Tommy has started playing for Ebberfield in left field defence and he's so good. Even Uncle David says he's playing well and might play for Newcastle United one day, just like him. We see Tommy every Sunday when he comes to Jenny's for lunch.

I'm glad that you are enjoying teaching and that you are settled with Aunt Esther and Aunt Clem. But I hope you are not too long in London.

Your loving son,
William

Tears spilled down my cheeks. William was managing. Jenny was clearly doing everything possible to help him settle in and keep contact between the boys. But I was missing all the little things that happened from day to day, the conversations that William and I would have of an afternoon or evening.

I read the short note from Tommy, written underneath William's letter.

Dear Mama,
The last of the harvest is done. Harry has gone back to boarding school, so now I have his room to myself. It means I have to take more responsibility for the work but I don't mind. I am learning lots with Uncle John and it's so much better than school. I'm up early to milk the cows and help him feed the animals and then we're ploughing, preparing the fields for seeding. Soon we will have to wean the calves.

Your son,
Tommy

I was grateful to John for keeping Tommy busy. David was Roger's brother and I was glad he was back in Ebberfield. He would look out for the boys in Roger's place, along with Alice and Jenny.

I picked up Jenny's letter, wondering if she had any extra insight into how the boys were going. I'd begun sending money to her and Emily, to help with their upkeep.

> The boys are adjusting to their new circumstances. William is doing well at school and Tommy clearly loves the farm. He talks about it every Sunday when we see him, and Emily always sends eggs with him as a gift to us, which is kindly appreciated. He won't talk about London, The Ox and Plough, Roger or you, even when William does. Perhaps it's the age and a stage boys go through. John and Emily say that Harry doesn't do much more than grunt these days either. (Heaven help us!) William talks to Ollie more than he does to me but I think he's happy enough, although I know how much he misses you. He's sleeping better than he was. Ollie tells me he has fewer nightmares and is less restless.
>
> We all miss you a great deal. The Ox and Plough isn't the same without you. The new manager is a mild-mannered man but has no idea how to make the place feel warm and welcoming. Alice, Emily and I take it in turns to help with the school meals and with Dr Jenkins' vaccination programs and plans for the colliery town. The suffrage society has welcome packs ready for the new miners' families. You should feel so proud of all the good things you have done for Ebberfield.

I dropped the letter on the little table, feeling overwhelmed. I was thankful that everything continued in Ebberfield with the help of my friends but the suffrage society, the community projects, The Ox and Plough – they were my labours of love, the results of my passion and vocation. It was like leaving my babies behind, just as I had my two boys, when what I wanted with all my heart was to return to them, nurture them, watch them grow and flourish in the world.

I rubbed at my chest where the pain had lodged like a deep ache. It rose and fell in intensity but was ever present. I didn't know how long I could endure this separation, but it was out of my hands. I just had to carry on.

It was an unusually mild Sunday afternoon in late October and I sweltered in my coat as we walked to the new Electric Cinema Theatre on Portobello Road.

'Annie is suited to London,' said Clementine.

Annie was walking up ahead with Esther, arm in arm, and I could hear her talking about the actress Mary Pickford, who starred in the movie we were going to see.

'The cinema today, and trips to the museums, galleries and the department stores to look in the display windows definitely make her happy,' I said with a smile. Clementine and Esther made sure Annie and I were both kept busy when we weren't at school. At this rate, we'd soon be cultured Londoners.

'I've been keeping an eye on her in school and she's applying herself well in class and is beginning to make friends.'

'I always thought Annie would thrive in London. She's so much like me. But I did find her crying after she read the letter William sent to her. She misses her brothers and she misses her father.'

'It's going to take time. It's hard on all of you.'

My worries faded as we entered the cinema. It was a grand building built specifically to show motion pictures using electricity, and had ornate baroque decorations on the walls and the domed ceiling, plush seating and a closed curtain over the stage.

The four of us settled into our seats. The lights dimmed and the curtains opened, revealing a big screen where the stage would normally be. Then the room went dark and the screen flickered to life. The music began to play, the pianist adding to the silent film.

Annie squeezed my hand in excitement and I smiled at her anticipation.

I glanced at Annie as the story of a young woman and her father played out on the screen. Tears filled her eyes at the high drama of *As It Is in Life* and I wondered if the story was a little close to home.

We all laughed at the moments of comedy. Annie was lost in the story, as was I, and for a while, our difficulties disappeared as we were swept up in someone else's story.

Before we knew it, the movie was over and with the return of the light, we returned to reality.

'That was incredible,' said Annie. 'I've heard girls at school talking about films but I never expected to feel like this.'

'Like what?' asked Clementine.

'Like I was in the middle of it, feeling real feelings,' Annie said in wonder.

'Have you ever been to see a play?'

Annie nodded. 'I saw one when I was at school in Hartlepool, but this was different. And Mary Pickford really is marvellous. She played the daughter perfectly.'

'Who's for afternoon tea?' asked Esther. 'There's a wonderful tea room around the corner. My treat.'

'I'm starving,' said Clementine. 'Sandwiches, scones, Victoria Sponge, all washed down with a well-brewed pot of tea or perhaps hot chocolate. You'll love it, Annie,' she said, taking Annie's arm.

Annie looked towards me, eyebrows raised hopefully.

'What a good idea,' I said, beaming.

'Definitely hot chocolate,' said Annie. 'What should we eat first, Aunt Clem?'

'Thank you, Esther,' I whispered, squeezing her hand, delighted to see my daughter happy, without the shadow of sorrow cast over her. 'This outing was a great idea.'

I picked up a handbill from the WSPU on the sideboard in Clementine and Esther's parlour.

'Are you joining the deputation to Parliament on Friday?' I asked. It was a cool November day and Annie and I had been in London nearly three months.

Clementine nodded. 'The government has made it clear that no more time will be made for the Conciliation Bill during parliamentary time this year.' This was a new bill that proposed to give wealthy, property-owning women the vote.

'After all the work that's been done by the parliamentary committee,' said Esther, shaking her head.

'But I don't think it goes far enough,' said Clementine with a frown. 'Only giving women who own property the vote dismisses the vast majority of women who don't.'

'You know it's the only way MPs in the Houses of Commons and Lords will accept a proposal of women's suffrage,' replied Esther.

'It's another Private Members' bill,' I said slowly. 'But I remember Mrs Fawcett writing to me to tell me it was passed on its second reading ... We need the vote. It's the only way we can change the law. If women had financial independence, if they could have bank accounts without their husbands' permission, if they could take up business loans, just as a man can, and sign contracts on their own merits, they could have greater control over their financial security and their future. If I'd been able to take out the loan on my own, I would have demanded to see that contract and would have checked it thoroughly. Perhaps I'd have noticed something amiss and maybe everything that happened with the pub could have been avoided.' I dropped my head. Every time I felt anger flare at Roger for not being more careful, the guilt reared its ugly head. How could I be angry at my dead husband, the man I loved?

'You can't think like that,' said Clementine. 'Do you hear me, Hannah? You'll drive yourself mad.'

'Think about Annie, Tommy and William,' said Esther.

'Channel your frustration, grief and anger into doing something about it,' said Clementine. 'We'll help you all we can with the legal process.'

I nodded and took my friends' hands, holding them tight. 'What would I do without you both?'

Suddenly everything made sense. My path was clear. I was at the lowest point in my life, everything against me, and I had to fight to claw my way back up. I couldn't physically do much else to fight for the pub, I could only wait for Mr Sanderson to mount the legal battle, but fighting for the vote would give me back my fire and help me regain my voice and my agency.

'I'm coming. I'll join the deputation and together we'll raise our voices so the government has no doubt that women want the vote.'

15

William has developed a passion for woodwork inspired by a school project. He says he's going to make Jenny a shoe rack for inside the back door. It's very kind of Robert to create a space for William and Oliver to build things with the leftover wood from John and Emily's old shed.

I joined Clementine and a big crowd of WSPU supporters at Claxton Hall for the midday rally, only to learn that Prime Minister Asquith had called a general election and any remaining time before Parliament was dissolved would be taken with government business.

Clementine and I stared at each other, our anger mirrored in the other's face.

'Good God! I can't believe the government has shut us down again. We were so close this time,' I said. I had allowed myself to believe that the bill would be passed and that soon women would be able to vote in government elections and make a difference to the laws that affected their own lives. I felt the disappointment drop like a stone to my belly, where it lodged, heavy and immovable.

'The government doesn't want the bill to see the light of day,' Clementine said bitterly.

I swallowed, but my throat remained tight. A little bit of my heart hardened. 'Just like every other Private Members' bill.' I could feel the anger and hard-edged fury swirl around the room. For the last twenty years, we'd been following parliamentary process to get a women's suffrage bill legislated. 'What do we have to do to make the government see sense?' I asked.

Clementine met my eye. 'You know what we have to do.'

I knew very well what Clementine meant – she believed it was time for action, not words. Wealthy and powerful men in Parliament had no understanding of what it was like for women; speaking for us with no idea about our struggles and dreams, and deciding our fate. After the months of disappointment and heartache, it was such a blow. But I couldn't condone violence and the destruction of property.

The lead delegation of the WSPU left in a flurry of activity, determined still to speak to the Prime Minister and persuade him to change his mind. This was our last-ditch attempt, otherwise it was back to the drawing board, to lobby new MPs to join the suffrage cause and begin the long and laborious process of drafting a new proposal and presenting it to Parliament.

A crowd of about three hundred of us, each a group of twelve delegates, followed the deputation to Parliament, led by Emmeline Pankhurst and well-known and respected community leaders, including Hertha Ayrton. Surely Asquith would see reason, speaking to such logical, practical and genteel women?

'I didn't know that Elizabeth Garrett Anderson was a member of the WSPU,' I said to Clementine, as we walked through the cold, mid-November streets, barely feeling the bite in the air, fuelled as we were by anger and desperation. Dr Garrett Anderson was Britain's first qualified female doctor and the first woman mayor in Britain, and the sister of Millicent Fawcett.

'She isn't. She doesn't support our more militant activities, even though Mrs Pankhurst has put a hold on such things until this bill is passed. But she believes in this bill, as we all do, and has come to join her daughter, Louisa, who's in the lead delegation.'

We reached Parliament and I realised the walk had done me good, given me a way to disperse my ire. I watched as the lead delegation was admitted to the St Stephen's entrance as the square filled with women holding placards that said such things as *ASQUITH HAS VETOED OUR BILL*, and purple banners advocating the bill and the vote for women. Ever the optimist, I was filled with hope. This *had* to work. My livelihood and future depended on it.

But it didn't take long before the delegation returned, some of the women shaking their heads.

'The Prime Minister turned them away!' a woman shouted across the square.

'He what? He can't even face a group of women to discuss their concerns? That's disgraceful.' I screwed my face up in disgust. Maybe we needed to do more than talk.

'He's a coward, as I knew he would be,' said Clementine scathingly.

Word spread, rippling through the crowd, as shock, anger and despair rose like plumes of smoke, thick and suffocating. Groups of women moved towards the doors to the House of Commons, seeking entry to Parliament. If the government wouldn't see respected leaders of the suffrage movement, then they'd have to hear the voices of the women in the square.

Divisions of police moved in, blocking our way. I glanced nervously at the men in uniform, their faces carefully guarded – and felt a sudden bolt of recognition. One of them was the man I'd argued with at the Women's Sunday demonstration in Hyde Park. His predatory gaze searched the crowd until it fixed on me. I shivered and clutched Clementine's arm, but she simply watched, grim-faced. She'd explained that delegations like ours could not be arrested for peaceful protest but had warned me that she'd seen this sort of behaviour before from the police. It was why Esther had decided not to come and why I'd decided Annie should remain at home with her.

Scuffles broke out as police snatched banners and flags, breaking the sticks and tearing them to pieces, forcing the women back and pushing them into the onlookers nearby. I stood transfixed, horrified by such blatant violence.

The crowd surged forward and we were swept towards the Houses of Parliament and the lines of policemen, unable to break away.

'Clementine,' I screamed, as she was grabbed by a huge policeman.

He lifted her skirts and thrust his knee between her legs then laughed at the shock on her face. 'You women think you can do whatever you like but today isn't your day. Today we can do what *we* like and nobody's going to stop us,' he snarled, pushing her into the gathering crowd of bystanders – mostly men, I now realised.

I lost sight of Clementine as I was gripped by strong hands, my arm twisted viciously behind my back until I screamed with pain, sure it would break. Before I knew what was happening, fingers were on my breast, pinching and twisting savagely, before I was shaken violently by the collar of my coat and thrown into the crowd.

My head cracked against something hard, leaving me dazed on the ground, surrounded by men reaching for me. I raised my arm to them, sure they would help me up, but my hand was kicked away by a man's boot.

'Suffragette scum,' he shouted in my face. It was the policeman with white hair, his eyes burning with hatred. 'We'll teach you a lesson you'll never forget.' Every sense in my body told me he was dangerous. I had to get away from him.

Somehow, I scrambled to my feet, only to be jostled from man to man, pulled close and grasped on my behind, my upper thighs and breasts. I realised what danger I was in, even surrounded by three hundred women, and I fought back, screaming and lashing out at my attackers, connecting with chests, faces and, for one man, the soft place between his legs, before I was punched in the face. I saw stars.

Women banded around me, escorting me to safety as the men turned to their next victim. The experience took me back to how we women had come together in the face of such hatred and violence from men: I could see Dorothy Duggan, Kitty, Marjorie and Esther. It was happening again. I shuddered.

I found myself back at Caxton Hall, where women limped, dishevelled and injured, into the safety of its walls and others left, patched up, to return to the fray.

'Those policemen are not the normal police we deal with,' said one woman, wiping the blood from my face, after I told her what had happened. 'A-Division knows us and understands our cause. They've always treated us with respect.' She shook her head. 'And there have been whispers that men in the crowd aren't just roughs, but plain-clothes policemen, some taking photographs of women up close.'

'Roughs?'

'Gangs of men the police call in to roughen women up. But we've never experienced anything like this before, and photographing women to identify them is new.' I thought about the man who had yelled in my face. He was a policeman, but his type of brutality and violence blurred the lines of traditional policing. How did he fit into all this?

I looked around the hall for Clementine but didn't find her, seeing instead women being treated by nurses for black eyes, bloody faces, bruises over their bodies and dislocated fingers and thumbs, wincing when I touched my fingers to my own throbbing eye and cheekbone. I could tell my ribs would be painful in the morning. My blood boiled at the effects of violence evident for all to see and I hoped those men had photographed the injuries the women bore with courage, evidence of police brutality. Beneath our clothes were the deeper indignities: the pain, embarrassment, fear and trauma of our attacks. But we were tough women, committed to our cause, and ready to put our bodies on the line.

After the disgusting treatment and behaviour I'd seen against women who had protested peaceably, I knew it was time for me to commit to the cause, mind, body and soul. The parliamentary process had failed and the authoritarian patriarchy had tried to quash the last hopes of rational, logical and peaceful protest in a most degrading manner. This was war and it was time to force the government to sit up and take notice. We had to make enough noise so they'd never be able to ignore us again.

I went back to Parliamentary Square to find Clementine.

'Be careful,' said one of the women as I was leaving Caxton Hall. 'They're dragging women down the side streets and you know what that means.'

I nodded and made sure I stayed well clear of the police when I could, ducking and weaving from the uniformed men and the attention of those in the crowd. My primary focus was Clementine. I was afraid for her and I wanted to get her home safely to Esther. Annie was in the back of my mind too. All around me, women were being abused – hit with sticks and helmets; grabbed around the throat; thrown to the ground and kicked. This violence was protracted and beyond any drunken bar fight I'd ever seen. But I was glad not to come face to face with the policeman again. The fact that he recognised me and was ready to continue his assault scared me most of all.

I returned to Notting Hill without Clementine. Esther's cry of shock at the sight of my face did nothing to dispel my worries for our friend.

'Clem – is she here?'

Esther shook her head, her frown growing deeper.

I glanced towards the kitchen and the stairs. 'Where's Annie?'

'She's upstairs, doing her homework.'

I nodded. 'Good. I don't want her to see me like this.'

Esther grasped my hands. 'What happened?'

'I looked for her everywhere. I'm so sorry, Esther. We were separated and I couldn't find her.' I slumped onto a chair, suddenly exhausted. 'The last thing I saw was her being pushed into the crowd.' I told her all of it, even the violence we had experienced.

Esther stared at me in astonishment when I was done. 'But the protest began over six hours ago. You mean to tell me that this abuse continued the whole time?'

I nodded. 'I've never seen anything like it. Bleeding and battered women going back into the fray. Such strength and bravery, and support for each other.'

Esther sent a note to Hertha Ayrton who replied that many women had been arrested that night; Clementine could very well have been one of them. I went back out and checked the local hospitals but didn't find her. With Annie in bed and oblivious to what had happened, Esther and I paced throughout the night, praying Clementine was safe and well.

The following morning, I heard Esther call: 'Hannah, she's here!'

I rushed to the front door to find Clementine dishevelled but in one piece. She had a cut lip and grazes across her cheek and was holding her arm, the sleeve of her jacket torn. We ushered her into the parlour, where she collapsed on the lounge.

'Are you hurt?' I asked.

Clementine shrugged. 'Just bruises and a few cuts.'

'Where were you?' asked Esther, holding her tight. 'We were worried sick.'

'I was arrested along with over one hundred other women and we were locked up overnight and brought in front of the Bow Street Police Court this morning.' She brought a shaking hand up to her face. 'We were all released without charge.'

'How could they charge you with anything?' I asked, incredulous. 'The police should be held to account for the abominable treatment of peaceful, law-abiding women.'

She shook her head, looking dazed. 'I don't know. We were told that the Home Secretary decided that there was no public advantage to prosecuting us.'

'Well, that's a good thing, isn't it?' asked Esther. Winston Churchill was the new Home Secretary and I remembered Millicent Fawcett mentioning that he was a supporter of women's suffrage. 'Surely, he'll order an inquiry into what happened at Parliament Square?'

'It's all a distraction,' Clementine said, gritting her teeth. 'It doesn't change the fact that Asquith has postponed any discussion of the bill and it's highly unlikely to get mentioned in Parliament again.'

'Come on, my love,' said Esther gently. 'You've had enough excitement for one day. Let me look at your injuries and put a salve on those cuts and grazes.'

Clementine looked at me. 'I'm so sorry, Hannah, to involve you in something like this. We had no idea the police would become so brutal.' She reached out to my swollen face and my black eye, which was still partially shut. 'Are you all right?'

'Same as you.' I grinned unexpectedly, but my grin faded at the worry in Esther's eyes. 'I'll go and fetch the salve and make us a pot of tea.'

When I returned, I found Esther weeping, kissing Clementine's face and hands fervently.

'I didn't know what happened to you. I thought I'd never see you again.'

Clementine raised a hand to stroke Esther's cheek tenderly. 'I'm fine, my love, and I'm sorry I worried you.'

I stood transfixed, almost dropping the tray. I long suspected that Clementine and Esther had become more than friends since they'd moved into Notting Hill, but I'd never seen them express their love in front of anyone before. It was confronting, two women together, but then the look on their faces reminded me of how Roger and I were together. Clementine and Esther had found that same love with each other.

'I have tea and ointment,' I said, bringing in the tray.

Clementine and Esther remained in their embrace, smiling at me, a silent acknowledgement of their relationship. They seemed completely natural, like any other loving couple. And after losing Roger, I realised that love was a treasure that lit up our lives wherever we found it.

I was worried about trying to explain what had happened to Annie. But in the end, I didn't need to say too much to her. The clash between police and the suffragettes was reported in all the main newspapers and splashed across the front page of the *Daily Mirror* was a photo of a suffragette on the ground, police and other men surrounding her.

'You know that the papers haven't reported what happened truthfully,' I said to her when she examined my face and then gazed at Clementine. But that photograph captured the truth of that afternoon.

Annie nodded. 'I know what the suffragettes do, Mama,' she said. 'The girls talk at school. But if the police can push women around like this for nothing more than wanting the same rights as men, then I understand why we have to fight back.'

I looked into her blue eyes, so much like her father's, and brushed a lock of hair from her brow. What we'd suffered was public humiliation, indecency and torture, something I'd never want my daughter to experience, yet, how could more violence be the answer? 'You know that violence should never be condoned. What happened last night was terrible, unconscionable.' I shivered at the memory. 'But more violence doesn't make it right.'

'But what's going to make the difference, Mama? If the government won't even allow discussion about a women's enfranchisement bill, then how will it even become legislated?'

I stared at her in shock. She was far more informed and aware than I'd realised. But she was fifteen years old and had grown up so much since Roger's death. I wondered how many other girls around the country cared about women's suffrage or believed the same as Annie. I hoped they were numerous – we were going to need them.

16

I used to get so frustrated with my older sisters meddling in my life. But now as a mother, I understand. I want only the best for my children and I worry about them endlessly. Tommy's lack of curiosity in his letters to me is a little concerning, though I am glad he's passionate about the farm and football. I know he's angry about losing Roger so suddenly. We all are. Annie and I will visit at Christmas, I only hope it's soon enough.

It was a Sunday and I'd persuaded Annie to join me for a trip to the British Museum.

'The most famous collections from around the world are housed here,' I said, as we climbed the stairs to the next floor.

'You're the one who loves collecting,' said Annie with a grin.

I nodded. 'Mine are nothing compared with what you'll see here.' I'd always loved gathering unusual things from nature and the outdoors. My favourite was an ancient fossilised acorn I'd found on the beach with Papa, in West Hartlepool, when I was a child. When I'd led the naturalist club at school, the girls had pinned wonderful selections of butterflies to boards that were on display even when my children were students there. But I'd also found old amber and glass beads in a field on top of the hill outside Ebberfield and an ancient stone with a refined edge and depressions that fit my fingers.

The museum wasn't big enough to house all its treasures and an additional wing was being built but the sounds of construction faded as we walked through another room.

'*The Ancient Egypt exhibit*,' read Annie.

'This looks interesting,' I said. We stopped in front of a large statue. 'Who do you think it is?'

'*Sandstone osiride statue of Amenhotep First, around 1525 to 1504 BC*,' Annie read off the sign.

'He must be an Egyptian pharaoh,' I said. I craned my head up to look at him. The statue was nearly double my own height.

'He is,' said Annie, continuing to read. '*He wears the double crown of Upper and Lower Egypt*. Do you think his beard was really that long?'

'Maybe,' I said with a smile. I wondered how a man like that had lived so long ago and how much humankind had changed and evolved over the millennia. How different were we to people back then? What kind of adaptations had we developed to help us survive as a species?

'I wonder what the writing on the back says.'

I peered at the unfamiliar etchings on the slab behind the pharaoh. '*I* wonder what insights into the past have been left to us here in the present.'

Annie nodded. She shared my fascination with the lessons history could teach us. 'Hieroglyphs. Somebody wrote those thousands of years ago. Wouldn't it be fascinating to understand what it says?' Her eyes were wide with wonder.

My heart squeezed with joy. Despite everything that had happened, part of me was happy that Annie was here in London, absorbing the culture and learning things that school didn't teach. Experiences like this were precious.

*

Later that week, I noticed an envelope addressed to me on my desk at school. I opened it absently and pulled out the note.

> We know you were at the demonstration at Parliament Square. We have evidence of your participation in the events of that day. We are watching you.

I dropped the paper as if it had burned me and scanned the room, my heart pounding in my chest, but there was nobody behaving suspiciously, just teachers going about their day.

'Do you know who left this envelope?' I asked one of my colleagues. Nobody from school knew I'd been to the demonstration. I'd taken some time off after, to give the bruises on my face the chance to fade enough for me to hide them with powder. The purple marks that bloomed on my breasts, ribs and thighs were well hidden by clothing.

She shook her head and shrugged. 'Probably came in with the rest of the mail.'

I nodded. Whoever it was knew where I worked and they were watching me. I shuddered.

I showed the note to Clementine and Esther later that evening and told them about the policeman who had assaulted me and shouted in my face.

'He might have remembered you from Hyde Park, but he's a uniformed officer. How would he know who you are or where you work?' asked Clementine. 'I think it's more likely to be one of the plain-clothes police who were taking photographs of women that day.' I nodded. Clementine's reasoning made sense but the note was still concerning, regardless of who had sent it.

'Why would a policeman photograph you?' asked Esther with a frown.

'They were photographing women throughout the demonstration and during the attacks,' said Clementine.

'But why?'

'I think as a way to identify women who regularly demonstrate and the ones they might consider to be behind the protests and deputations, whose banners were most inflammatory or whose voices were raised the loudest or who provoked other women into protest too,' I said. 'It's their evidence against us.' Photographs used as proof, but it was all relative, depending on the intention of the photographer, I now realised. I'd been thinking a lot about it and why they'd allowed the atrocities against peaceful women to continue.

'What evidence?' Esther picked up the note and read it again. 'What do they think you did? You weren't breaking any laws and you were attacked without provocation.'

I shook my head. 'I don't know.'

'I wouldn't be surprised if all the women they've photographed and identified had notes sent to them too, just to intimidate them. To scare them into staying away from demonstrations and any public activity supporting women's suffrage,' said Clementine, taking the note from Esther.

'Then where's your note, Clem?' asked Esther. 'If anyone should have one, it's you. You were arrested, after all, and they know who you are.'

Clementine's frown intensified. 'I could be next, I suppose. But Hannah, it's much more likely to be an empty threat, to just scare you off.'

I nodded slowly. I'd done nothing wrong, so there was no reason for anyone to threaten me or be watching me.

I went upstairs and took off my jacket, hanging it in the wardrobe. I still felt uneasy, as I sat on my bed and changed out of my boots, even after talking it through with Esther and Clementine.

I sighed and rubbed my stockinged feet. The light from the small reading lamp spilled across my writing desk and I noticed the letter Alice had sent me probably a week earlier. I was never tardy in my replies but I'd forgotten how much time it took at the end of my day to write out lesson plans for the boys and think of ways to make the learning experience fun and interesting.

I pulled the shawl from the end of my bed, draped it across my shoulders and settled at my desk. Writing would give me some distance from the unsettling note.

Dear Alice,

The fallout from 'Black Friday', as it's become known, has continued. We heard that the police were ordered not to arrest the demonstrators but rather teach them a lesson. You can imagine how this has inflamed many women but especially the WSPU and the women who were attacked.

Clementine tells me that many members have left, fearful of what might happen to them in the future. The deputations to Parliament have been stopped and more direct action has been approved by the WSPU, such as window breaking and rock throwing, rather than clashing with police, so that women have a chance to get away before police arrest them. I never thought I'd agree to such tactics but the memories of that day remain burned behind my eyes and on my skin. I never thought I'd see such brutal behaviour by men who are meant to protect the citizens of this country.

And now, I've agreed to join the WSPU. What other choice do I have? We have to get the vote. How can women have control over their lives without it? How can the laws that keep women disempowered, without financial security of their own, ever be possible without it? I have become a desperate woman, willing to do desperate things for the sake of my family, my home and my livelihood.

Threats, real or imagined, weren't going to stop me. I had to raise my voice and play my part in the fight for women's suffrage. It was personal for me now. A matter of survival.

I woke to the sound of a door banging closed. I'd been dreaming of Roger and half asleep, reached out, expecting him to be beside me. Sleep slipped away and in the harsh reality of morning, I remembered I was in Notting Hill and it was my fortieth birthday. My heart sank. My first birthday without Roger and the boys. I sighed, not sure I could get through the day at school while hiding my deep sadness. It was significant days like this that made my loss feel raw and immediate all over again. Cards and letters from my sisters, Jenny and friends in Ebberfield had arrived in the post but nothing had come from the boys.

The day passed in a haze and in the afternoon, Clementine, Esther and Annie made a fuss of me with thoughtful gifts, insisting we go out for an early steak dinner. Marjorie Partridge joined us.

'I've made you a cake, Mama,' said Annie when we returned from dinner. 'A chocolate cake.'

I laughed, kissing her cheek and enfolding her in a hug. 'My favourite!' We'd rarely had chocolate cake at home in Ebberfield because William disliked it so much. 'Thank you, my darling girl.'

A knock at the door disturbed us.

'We're not expecting anyone are we?'

'We do have a surprise visitor for your birthday,' said Esther smiling, as I heard Clementine open the door.

I turned to the footfall in the hallway and a tall, lean figure in the doorway. 'Dr Jenkins! How lovely of you to come.'

'Happy birthday, Mrs Rainforth,' he said with a grin. 'I was in London and thought I'd hand deliver these.' He held out a bunch of flowers.

'Thank you,' I said, smelling the flowers, touched by his thoughtfulness. 'They're beautiful.' Their riot of colours made me smile.

'Hello, Annie,' said Dr Jenkins. 'How's London?'

'Good,' said Annie with a nod. 'I'll tell you all about it later but I have something I have to do first.'

I frowned, wondering what she'd planned, as she raced off upstairs with Clementine and Marjorie following close behind.

'Come and sit down,' said Esther, gesturing to the parlour. 'We're just about to bring out the cake and a pot of tea.'

We made ourselves comfortable as Esther bustled off, then Dr Jenkins pulled out a number of packages and envelopes from his bag. 'From Jenny and the boys.'

The breath caught in my throat. 'They didn't forget,' I whispered.

'Jenny and I knew how hard this day would be for you and we wanted to make sure you received these today.'

I squeezed his hand. 'Thank you. It means the world that you did this for me.'

'It's the least I could do.'

'Now, tell me all about Ebberfield,' I said, straightening up and wiping my eyes hastily.

'The boys are well, as I'm sure their letters will tell you,' he said with a smile. 'The Ox and Plough is as busy as when you left it, thanks to everyone who wants to continue to support you. We're all still in shock that something like this could happen to you, and we're determined to keep the pub focused on the community until you return to it.'

I stared at him, trying to accept his words. His kind eyes were green in this light; his usually immaculate sandy blond hair and elegant appearance a little dishevelled. He'd clearly been in a rush to get here on time.

His eyebrows knitted together in a frown. 'I'm sorry, Mrs Rainforth. Have I upset you?'

I shook my head, swallowing the lump in my throat. 'Please, call me Hannah. And, no, Dr Jenkins. I'd expect nothing less from you than honesty. The truth is that you're the first person who has been direct with me and I'm touched by that and the fact that everyone is still behind me and continuing what I started. You're a true friend.'

'Richard,' he said with a smile. 'I've known you for far too long to be anything else.'

'How's the colliery village coming along?' I had to change the subject or I'd cry. Today, everything was close to the surface and my nerves were on edge.

'Council has sent our proposals to the district council committees, not without some objections from Mr Franks and his son.'

I groaned. 'That's right, Mr Franks won the by-election after Roger ...'

'You and Roger were a force to be reckoned with in the town and we all miss you both.'

I nodded, looking down at the carpet. 'Well, not everyone,' I said after a minute. 'I'm sure Mr Franks isn't too upset that we're gone.'

Richard gave a small laugh. 'At least we have John Duffield on the district council and Robert Sanderson as clerk and in our corner. I feel sure we can get the improvements to living conditions and sanitation passed.'

I nodded. 'And how long are you in London?'

'A week or so. I'll drive back to Ebberfield for Christmas.'

I nodded. 'Are you here to help the Americans with the typhoid vaccine?'

He shook his head. 'No, Dr Russell has taken our research to the United States to conduct clinical trials. They've inoculated volunteers in the army with a new single dose that seems to be most effective.'

'How was it, working with them?'

'I know many consider the Americans brash, but I actually found them refreshing. There was no pussyfooting around. The people I dealt with were straightforward and just got things done.'

'We could use a bit of that here,' I said with a smile.

He snorted. 'Indeed, we could. It's embarrassing, really, that our own British Army doesn't have the foresight to see how our vaccine could save so many lives.'

I remembered when he'd told me that a trial of the vaccine on British troops in India had been successful. But to safeguard all the men, the vaccination had to be mandatory, not voluntary.

'But enough about me. How are you?'

'I'm managing,' I said. 'I'm better now that I have letters from the boys.' I turned my face away to hide my grief. 'I sometimes wonder if I've done the right thing, coming to London and leaving the boys behind. I feel like I'm a terrible mother. I miss them so much. I can't wait until Annie and I see them at Christmas. We'll go on the train. I thought it best to wait until then, to give them a chance to settle, without the upheaval of goodbyes each time.'

'You're a wonderful mother,' he said. 'Don't ever doubt that. It took great courage for you to come here, and great sacrifice. But you've done it for your family, anyone can see that.'

I turned to look at him and only saw sincerity and concern in his face.

'I'll look out for them however I can. I'll bring anything from them when I next come to London and I can take back anything for Christmas. Save you carrying it on the train when you come.' He paused. 'Unless you and Annie come back with me? I can delay going back until school is finished.'

I smiled with gratitude. 'Would you do that, Richard?' I had already bought small gifts for them, wrapped and ready to take but the ease of travelling back by motor car was a godsend.

'Of course. It's no inconvenience to me. Almroth will be happy if I stay to help him in the laboratory another few days.'

'Happy birthday, Mama,' said Annie, coming in with candles lit on the cake, Esther and Marjorie behind her with the tea trays.

'And we come bearing gifts,' said Clementine, placing a couple of beautifully wrapped presents on the table.

'Oh, thank you, my friends,' I said, my heart filling with joy. 'I'm so lucky to have you.'

17

I can't believe that, despite letters written to the newspapers and testimonials collected from over one hundred women, Mr Churchill denies that there was police brutality at the Black Friday demonstration. It's appalling and I sense a recurring theme: powerful men hiding behind words. Let's see how they combat action.

Spending Christmas and then William's birthday in March in Ebberfield was wonderful but also strange. To be a family again, with Annie and the boys, was like ambrosia, and to be surrounded with the well wishes of friends and neighbours fortified me and warmed my heart. I'd felt part of me begin to come back to life, unfurling slowly like the petals of a closed flower. Seeing the boys, holding them close to me and watching them with others reassured me that they were well. Tommy couldn't stop talking about the farm and William, now thirteen, was the same as always, cheerful and loving, although he rarely left my side and his eyes followed me whenever I left the room. It was just as difficult to leave them as the first time, although now, I knew they were managing their new situations well enough, and the heavy weight on my heart lightened a little with each visit.

It had been disconcerting and at times distressing, though, to watch customers coming and going from The Ox and Plough. Something had shifted. I didn't feel I quite belonged anymore, because life in the village had gone on without me – and I had begun to adjust to life in London.

Although I missed everyone desperately, I loved the energy of London, the hustle and bustle; how accessible everything was. I was living the life I'd dreamed of, before I fell in love with Roger. You could find anything you could imagine, much of it brought into port on ships from far-flung parts of the British Empire and the world. The city was a melting pot of cultures, a centre for new ideas, but best of all, a place where those ideas were explored and practical applications discovered. When I was a young teacher, I'd wanted to change the world, make it a better place for women, children and the vulnerable and London was the perfect place to do it. That fire still burned brightly within me and London was still the place to fight for change, beginning with the vote for women.

'There are a lot of women already here,' said Annie in awe as she walked with me, Clementine and Esther towards Trafalgar Square.

I nodded. 'And there will be many more yet.'

It was census night, Sunday, 2 April 1911, and we'd enjoyed a picnic in Norland Square gardens with local supporters of women's suffrage, mostly women and their daughters, many of them Clementine's students and Annie's classmates. All around there was chattering and laughter, the air of a festival, and a strong sense of unity as we protested the census. There were some serious conversations about what action different women were prepared to follow after the picnic. Some were going home to fill in their census forms with comments like 'No votes, no census' or 'I don't count so I won't be counted'. But for those who refused to fill in the form correctly there was the risk of a five-pound penalty or a month imprisonment. Instead, many women decided they'd stay away from their homes all night and join census parties across the city, at objectors' homes or in big public venues. The census protest was supported by the WSPU and the Women's Freedom League, and thousands of women were expected to participate across the country.

'Do you feel better about coming now, Aunt Esther?' asked Annie.

Esther squeezed Annie's hand as we walked. 'I'm glad I'm doing this with you, your mother and Aunt Clem.'

I thought about the conversation Esther and I had had earlier that day. Esther had decided she would stay at home.

'What will you do?' I'd asked.

'I'll fill in the census form without your names and write my own protest on it.'

'Why not come with us? A bit of civil disobedience at Trafalgar Square after the picnic surrounded by friends and acquaintances sounds like much more fun. We're going to the Aldwych Skating Rink afterwards too – there'll be entertainment and refreshments at the Gardenia restaurant.'

'It's vegetarian!' Esther had pulled a face and I'd laughed. Vegetarianism was gaining popularity due to the anti-vivisection movement. Many activists who fought for women's rights also protested the use of live animals in scientific experiments. And with Annie's strong feelings about animal welfare, I wondered how long it would be until she'd consider becoming vegetarian.

'It will be part of the fun and we'll be together all night.' I had come a long way since pork pies at the pub.

'You know we have to do something,' Annie said to Esther now, her face earnest under the street lights. 'With this many people protesting, the government will have to listen.'

'It *is* a peaceful protest, which I quite agree with,' said Esther with a smile.

'It feels good to make a stand, doesn't it?' asked Clementine, a wicked grin on her face.

'Oh, all right,' said Esther, batting her arm playfully. 'It does feel good. Especially when so many different kinds of women support this protest.'

When we arrived at Trafalgar Square, the mood was high, with groups of mainly women talking enthusiastically and laughing as they gathered in their coats and hats. It was infectious too. We felt like we were doing something important.

'It feels good to find a way to thwart the government,' I said. 'Let's hope this puts a spanner in the works and they finally recognise how many people support women's suffrage and the lengths we'll go to for getting it.'

'Well said, Hannah.' Clementine linked arms with us. 'Come on, let's make our way to the skating rink before the singing and performances begin. Let's see who can stay awake until morning!'

But on our way to the Gardenia in the early hours of the morning, I hung back a little from Esther, Annie and the group we were with, arm in arm with Clementine. 'Do you see the men hiding in the shadows?' I asked in a low voice.

Clementine nodded, just as a flash of light caught the corner of my eye. 'The police surveillance unit. They'll be out here all night in the cold. But we'll be safe in the restaurant until morning, with good food and good company.'

'Serves them right,' I replied, walking briskly to catch up with the others.

I walked into the kitchen a few days later to begin dinner and found Clementine and Esther hunched over the table, dark and light heads almost touching. Annie and a friend from school would be home soon from skating.

'What are you two plotting?' I asked jokingly.

They looked up, their faces pale and pinched.

'Everything fine?'

'We received a note, slipped under the door,' said Esther. 'It was addressed to all three of us.'

'Like my note?'

Clementine nodded and handed me the paper. 'I don't think it's a prank.'

> We know who you are. You and your household were absent from your place of residence on census night. You may take your actions lightly but tread carefully. One misstep and we will have you. We are watching.

I stared at the note, disconcerted. 'It must be the police we saw at the Gardenia.'

Clementine nodded. 'Mrs Millar said she saw them outside the skating rink as well.'

'Why didn't you say anything?' asked Esther.

'What was the point? I didn't want to worry you, and if we'd turned around and come home, they would have noticed us,' said Clementine, lighting a cigarette.

'But they *did* notice us,' said Esther, her face strained. 'They know where we live and work and what we're doing. The threat is hard to miss.'

'We haven't done anything the police can arrest us for.' I looked at the note again. 'It can't be just us. Surely other women who were out on census night received notes too?'

Clementine blew out a long trail of smoke. 'I'll ask around. We're being bullied and threatened. The police and the government want us to back down and submit to them.'

'They're afraid of us,' I said. 'But they hide behind their laws.' I grasped their hands and looked each of them in the eye. 'We can't give in to their terror, we can't live in fear. We've done nothing wrong.'

I was delighted when I received a letter from Robert Sanderson. He only wrote when there was something to tell me about the pub loan and after my visit with him at Christmas, I hoped it was good news.

> Dear Hannah,
>
> I'm writing to you after my correspondence with Amy. When I last met with you, we were still waiting for information on the financial institution. Amy now has the list of directors, and we have uncovered some interesting information. On that list I found a name I recognised, the name of a director also on the board of Philip Usher's financial company, which was sold when Edward Partridge went to prison. I don't know if the connection means anything – both companies have good reputations. Amy will continue to search for any past impropriety by the company or any of its directors in regard to loans and dealings with clients. I will delve further into the legal situation. Unfortunately, it can be slow and tedious work, but my hope is that we can sue the brewery. We only need to collect enough evidence to construct a watertight case against them.
>
> My best regards,
>
> Robert Sanderson

I put down the letter, exhaling slowly. Lists, names and words – again, this was about men hiding behind them. But while Amy and Robert were fighting them with action, I remained hopeful. With each step they took, we were closer to a solution.

*

We were walking along Kensington Church Street one Saturday on our way home from the station at Notting Hill Gate, when I noticed one of the WSPU stores. I stopped to admire the scarves, ties, badges, posters and tea sets in the window, all in the colours of the WSPU – purple for loyalty, green for hope and white for purity.

'It belongs to our Kensington branch,' said Clementine proudly, as I wandered inside and gazed at the pamphlets, brochures and a beautiful hatpin.

'I'll take these,' I said to the volunteer, placing a hatpin and two badges on the counter.

'You'll be counting yourself as one of us if you wear them,' said Clementine, as I fished out the right money from my bag.

I nodded. 'I know. It's time for me to become a member and follow your motto, "Deeds not Words".' I'd explained my thoughts in a letter to Mrs Fawcett, but how could she really understand when her livelihood and home hadn't been pulled out from under her? Her future was secure.

Clementine grinned and hugged me tight. 'I never thought I'd see the day,' she exclaimed.

'I'm doing this for my family and for all women like me, who only want the same business opportunities as men. Women shouldn't have to struggle to maintain their livelihood and a secure future for their family.'

'You're doing the right thing,' said Clementine. 'It's the only way anything will change.'

18

I can't forget the scenes at Parliament Square on Black Friday. Women manhandled and beaten. Never have I imagined the police would behave this way. We gathered in peace, only wanting to talk about our concerns. But they were threatened by us. And we were treated like enemies of the state, with our photographs taken to identify troublemakers. How can this be right? How can this be British justice at work? Will women be silenced at any cost?

I had been deeply anxious to hear what Mrs Fawcett thought about my move to the WSPU – would she feel abandoned? Would she end our correspondence? I was happy and relieved when her reply to my letter arrived while she was on her speaking tour. She had been a good friend and mentor to me for many years and I valued her advice.

May 1911
My dear Hannah,
I understand your feelings about our fight for women's suffrage. Our progress is slow as a glacier. Some days I feel hopeless that we will ever reach our goal. But we have to stay the course – perseverance is key. I appreciate you sharing your thoughts about joining the WSPU but I still believe that violence cannot be the answer.

But perhaps the rift between the NUWSS and WSPU can be still healed. We've been invited by Mrs Pankhurst to the Coronation Procession next month. Delegations from many different suffrage groups will be attending. There will be tens of thousands of women present, including from the colonies. It will be the biggest demonstration the suffrage movement has ever seen and as women are half the population, we will be sending a message to the government that, with the Parliament's return in September, we hope the Conciliation Bill will finally be given the time it needs to progress to legislation.

I put the letter down and stared at the trees in the back garden, the tender green of the new leaves budding on the branches. I had always believed that Mrs Fawcett's method was the only way to reach our goal, but despite my admiration for her, I didn't believe in her path any longer. Roger's death, the loss of the pub and the disruption to my family had made it clear that we needed action to achieve the vote for women. Part of me felt like I was betraying her, a woman I had known most of my adult life, who had mentored me and who I called a friend, but I had to stay true to what I now believed, my new conviction. She would respect that, as much I would always respect her. It was my hope that the differences between the two organisations could be resolved or at least understood and accepted. But I had to choose action now.

There was much excitement in the build-up to the Women's Coronation Procession. The best part was that Jenny, Alice and Emily came from Ebberfield to participate.

'The colliery is producing coal now,' said Alice, as we drank tea with Esther and Clementine in their parlour. 'And a village has begun to grow around it, separate from ours. So many terraced houses have sprung up and a council school is being built.'

'It's amazing how quickly it's happened, now that coal has finally been extracted.' I shook my head in wonder and took a sip of the strong black brew I favoured now. Once, I'd loved sweet, milky tea but so much had changed after Roger's death, and everything that had followed. 'How's the pub doing with the colliery up and running?' I ventured.

I noticed the glances between my friends.

'The manager from the brewery is still there,' said Jenny softly. 'He does well enough, especially with the extra customers. Reg and Bobby and Bella have stayed. He's trying to keep things as you had it, with all the community meetings, the literacy classes and society meetings, but—'

I cut in, my heart aching. 'I'm glad the brewery has kept its word.' I was pleased the pub was doing well in my absence, but it hurt to hear it. I wasn't needed ... and if I wasn't needed, there was no place for me in Ebberfield. My shoulders slumped in dejection.

'No, wait,' said Alice, frowning. 'You didn't let Jenny finish. The manager can't do everything you did. He doesn't have the same commitment or personal touch that you do. People don't warm to him. Some of the programs aren't running as regularly and I won't be surprised if he drops them altogether.'

Emily reached out and grasped my hand. 'Don't you see? Everything has changed. *You're* not there. You were the heart and soul of The Ox and Plough. You were the light of our lighthouse. It's your passion and drive that kept everything going.'

I stared at her as her words hit me like cold water. I took a ragged breath and hid my face in my hands, awash with emotions I didn't know how to begin to explain. My time in Ebberfield seemed a lifetime ago. Could I go back to that life now? It would never be the same as it was. Would I be forever chasing ghosts of the past? Was London my future and the fight to get the vote my new focus? Without it, what happened to me with the pub would continue to happen to other women. And yet, I desperately missed the congenial community of Ebberfield and the life I'd built there.

'You'll be back there one day,' said Jenny, encouragingly.

I shook my head. 'Sorting out the loan contract is taking longer than I expected. It could take years to unravel and we still have to prove the brewery was negligent when they offered the loan to Roger.' A little voice of doubt had begun to whisper to me. *What if I never get the pub back? What will I do?*

'But you have somewhere to start,' said Alice. 'Anything we can do to help, we will.'

I sighed. 'I know. And knowing I have you all gives me strength.' I thought about my children, who gave me reason to continue every day without succumbing to despair. 'How's Tommy?'

'He seems better,' said Emily. 'John has given him more responsibility and he's stepped up. He's a natural, he doesn't need to be told twice, and he instinctively knows what to do, whether it's with livestock or the sowing and harvesting. And I try to get him to read a little every day to continue to stretch his mind, but he never does, although he'll happily sit down with magazines on agriculture.'

'I should give you some of the articles I've kept from my collection of agricultural journals,' said Esther, excitement shining in her eyes. 'I knew I kept them for a reason. I think Tommy will find them interesting and if he wants to discuss them further, I'd love to correspond with him or even put him in touch with other experts in the field.'

Deep affection bloomed in me. 'Thank you, Emily and Esther, for taking an interest in Tommy's education. You know how important it is to me.'

'There's more than one way to get an education,' Esther reminded me.

I nodded. 'And since farming is his passion, it's the natural place to start.'

'Well, that and football,' said Alice, laughing. 'Since David has been coaching Tommy and William, both the boys have been training most days and talk about little else. He thinks they have talent, real potential, and could make one of the big sides when they're older.'

Emily and Jenny nodded. 'It's made a big difference for Tommy,' said Jenny softly. 'He doesn't seem so angry anymore.'

'Maybe he can release his emotion into training and the game,' said Alice. 'I remember David was the same after our father died. That's when he started devoting all his energy to playing football. He realised he was good at it, it gave him purpose.'

'Purpose,' I repeated. It was something we all needed.

'Come on,' said Clementine, waving a cigarette in the air, 'let's go over the plans for the procession. We have to make sure we have everything for our costumes and banners. I hope you're all staying for a few days, because we'll meet women from all over the Empire, including Australia and India!'

Saturday, 17 June 1911, was a beautiful and sunny afternoon, perfect to be outdoors. Women dressed in national and historical costume assembled in Westminster and stretched along the Embankment as far as the eye could see, and crowds gathered to watch. Every detail had been planned, so that an orderly procession began to move towards the Royal Albert Hall, four miles away.

'Is that Joan of Arc on a horse?' asked Annie as we began to walk five women abreast. We were both wearing our WSPU badges and I, my hatpin. After sending money to Jenny and Emily for the boys regularly and helping with the Notting Hill bills and food shopping at my insistence, it had taken weeks to save for the membership. But now that it was paid, it felt good to be part of a group who were dedicated to action, to doing something to change the future for women.

Clementine nodded. 'She leads the Crusader section. Can you see the women dressed as knights of the crusade?'

Annie nodded, taking a photograph.

The march was a spectacle of theatre and colour, with many different pageants joining the procession, marching between the delegations from the various suffrage societies, such as the Artists' Suffrage League, which designed banners and pamphlets for the WSPU, the Actresses' Franchise League and the Woman Writers' Franchise League, carrying colourful pendants, flags and banners. The most noticeable was the sea of white – seven hundred respectable and dignified women dressed in all white to signify their terms of imprisonment and their femininity, moral virtue and purity to the cause of women's suffrage. Their banner was clear, held high above their heads – *From Prison to Citizenship.*

The Imperial Pageant contained Indian women dressed in jewel-coloured saris. The Australian and New Zealand contingents were there too, New Zealand having the honour to be the first country in the world to grant national suffrage for women and Australia, the honour of bestowing the right to hold parliamentary office on women nine years later, when Tommy was in his first year of school. Their contingent was led by the wives of the Australian Prime Minister and

Premiers of New South Wales and South Australia, who had been pointed out to us earlier.

In another section, there were nurses and midwives dressed in their uniforms. Many women had chosen to dress as significant British women of the past – queens, scientists, writers – all carrying their names mounted on sticks. These were women of power and influence, many who had wielded political power and proved that women were capable of involvement in political life and of using the vote wisely. Others dressed in their national costumes – Welsh, Irish, Scottish. The WSPU were bedecked in purple, white and green, and the NUWSS contingent, led by Mrs Fawcett, was over a thousand strong. It made me happy to see estranged organisations come together like this and my respect for Mrs Fawcett only grew.

There were many floats decked in flower garlands but the most visually stunning was the Car of Empire. It was drawn by white horses and carried figures representing women of the Empire, both east and west, and was followed by more women carrying garlands of roses, the symbol of England.

'Why didn't we do this procession as part of the King's coronation celebrations?' asked Annie.

'Because for centuries, women have never taken part in the official proceedings – only men,' said Clementine.

'Even when Queen Victoria was crowned?' asked Annie, shocked. I beamed. Annie was thinking like a woman who believed in equality. She was a suffragist.

Clementine nodded. 'But because there are so many visitors here in London for the Imperial Conference and the King's coronation in a week, it's the perfect time to showcase the women of the British Empire.'

'And women are half of King George's loyal subjects, after all,' I added with a smile, thinking of Mrs Fawcett's letter.

Annie was getting more than the education I'd wanted for her. Being with Clementine and Esther and coming to suffrage events like this was the perfect pairing with her schooling. There was nothing like learning from experience and real life. A textbook could never tell her how being part of a procession like this felt, or what impressions would remain with her as she grew into a woman and formed her own thoughts and beliefs. Excitement, hope and pride bristled through the procession like a spark of electricity. We were riding high on our shared camaraderie, united in our cause.

'Look,' said Clementine, leaning in to me and pointing towards women being pushed in wheelchairs or bathchairs. 'They were injured on Black Friday and are still unable to walk, seven months later.'

I stared, horrified. 'It could have been us,' I replied quietly.

Clementine nodded. 'But these women are the most powerful symbol here. The police and government think they can break us. They can certainly break our bodies but we're stronger than that. They'll never break our spirits.'

I took my friends shopping before they went back to Ebberfield.

The noise of traffic hit us as we reached the busy road and I had to raise my voice to be heard. 'I'm glad you were all here for the procession. Imagine, if the bill is passed, women will soon have the vote.'

'It would be better if property qualifications were removed,' said Alice. 'There are too many women ineligible to vote. But I understand that it has to be done in stages, otherwise it scares the MPs away and we won't get anything at all.'

'It's a fine line between the idealism and pragmatism,' I agreed. We turned down Oxford Street. 'There are a few big department stores in London, but Esther says Selfridges has everything you could possibly want to buy. It's only been open a couple of years but we should be able to find something special.' I wanted to find a unique gift for Tommy's birthday and a surprise for William too.

'You haven't been?' asked Emily, as we stood outside the huge neo-classical building on Oxford Street. It was bedecked in flags, bunting and garlands ahead of King George's coronation.

'I thought I'd wait, to share the experience with all of you.' Besides, I didn't have money to waste. I thought of the paperweight of the Houses of Parliament that Clementine had bought for me, from Harrods, on her very first trip to London to visit Mrs Fawcett in my place, seventeen years ago.

'Look at the windows,' said Alice in awe. It was a beautiful display of eighteenth-century French paintings; by Watteau and Fragonard, so the sign read. The rich hues of the garden and park settings and ladies in their exquisite gowns spoke of luxury and recreation, drawing customers into the store.

'Do you know that it's called "window shopping"?' I asked with a grin. 'People come just to look at the window displays, especially at Christmas.'

Next to the entrance was a display of the British Empire in all its glory, inspired by the Festival of Empire exhibiting at the Crystal Palace.

'Look at these strange animals,' said Jenny.

'They're from Australia,' said Alice, reading the display card. 'Kangaroo, koala and wombat. I've never seen anything like them.'

'I've heard that kangaroos jump down the streets of the cities,' said Jenny.

'No wonder the animals are so unusual,' said Emily. 'Australia's at the bottom of the world.'

'Very exotic,' I said, fascinated by the stuffed animals.

'This Bengal tiger is beautiful,' said Jenny, shifting her gaze to the Indian part of the display.

'Just like Shere Khan in *The Jungle Book*,' I said with a smile. 'I used to read those stories to the boys. Maybe I'll buy them a copy of the book. Selfridges has the largest bookstore in the world, you know.'

'We'll never get you out of there,' said Jenny with a laugh. 'Come on, let's see what the fuss is all about.'

Inside, we were welcomed by the dazzling scents of the perfume department. We slowly navigated our way through the various floors and departments, each with their own telephone, marvelling at the array of products on offer.

'Anything you could wish to buy and more,' said Jenny. 'And cheaper than I was expecting.' We were loaded with parcels, mostly small trinkets and toys for the children. I was glad I'd found a unique gift for Tommy's fifteenth birthday, a Swiss sports knife, which included a second smaller blade for cutting, a corkscrew and wood fibre grips.

'Let's go to the tea garden for refreshments.'

Emily groaned. 'I don't know if I can carry my parcels up any more stairs.'

'We don't have to,' I said. 'We'll take the electric lifts.'

Alice frowned, looking dubious, but both Emily and Jenny breathed a sigh of relief.

'They're reliable,' I said. 'In two years, there haven't been any reported accidents.' In truth, I was a bit nervous about trusting an electric machine to take me up and down between floors, but the contraption was progress and the way of the future, and Esther had assured me it was safe.

'Oh, stop, Hannah,' said Alice, batting me on the shoulder. 'If you're doing it, then so will I.'

'Did I mention that there's also a library here?' I asked, smiling mischievously.

'No!' said all three in mock horror. They had already been impressed with the first women's toilets in any department store. And I'd heard that Mr Selfridge was a strong supporter of women's suffrage.

'We'll starve before we get to the tea garden if we go there,' said Jenny.

'All right then,' I conceded, just as the doors of the lift opened. 'The tea garden it is.'

19

We've become a little family here in the Notting Hill terrace. Clem and Esther have given Annie and me a home and a refuge. They understand the importance of family and have had to build their own. Finding love in each other has not been easy. The law doesn't recognise such relationships and they must hide theirs from the world. But who can truly judge what form love comes in?

EBBERFIELD, NORTHERN ENGLAND
AUGUST 1911

'Happy birthday, Tommy,' I said, pulling him to me. He was fifteen now. All the time on the farm had made him broad across the shoulders and I could feel the muscles in his arms and back ripple. Annie and I were in Ebberfield for a short visit and I couldn't wait for him to open his gift.

'Time to open presents,' said William excitedly. We were in Emily and John's parlour at the farm for a small party. Duke and Shandy had flopped on the floor beside us after an exuberant reunion with William, Annie and me.

'Hold your horses,' said Tommy with a smile, but indulged his brother anyway. It was good to see them getting on so well.

'A book on football and the FA Cup,' he said, opening the cover, his brows raised in surprise. 'Interesting!'

Annie snapped another photo, and Tommy stuck his tongue out at her. She was recording the afternoon, photographs we could pore over when we were back in London.

'Show me,' said William, craning his neck as Tommy turned the pages before handing it to him.

'There's one more present,' said Annie, pointing to the wrapping paper.

Tommy unwrapped his final gift. I held my breath, waiting to see his reaction. His face lit up as he turned it over in his hands.

'Is that a Swiss knife?' asked John, leaning in to look. I nodded and he whistled. 'This will be handy on the farm.'

Tommy's eyes glistened. 'Thank you, Mama. It's brilliant. I'll take it with me, wherever I go.'

'Time for cake!' said Emily with a smile. 'And candles and birthday wishes for the year ahead.'

The day flew past quickly and I wanted some time with the children before Annie and I had to leave the next morning. After the party was over, I persuaded them to walk with me in the cool of the afternoon.

I gazed wistfully at The Ox and Plough as we walked past. My name as publican had been removed from above the door, as my liquor licence hadn't been renewed. With the manager unmotivated to continue the pub as a village hub, Jenny, Alice and Emily had taken on the responsibility of many of the community projects and had the added pressure of finding new places to hold meetings and a central place from which to run them. Without me, it was no longer the town's lighthouse and I felt a pang of sadness and deep regret. Until the mess was sorted out, I was still the legal owner of the pub, and I was grateful that the brewery hadn't forced the sale of the pub and property. I still had hope.

The boys wanted to show me the new colliery settlement.

We passed the old village and walked down the new Seaside Lane, where shops had sprung up and construction was everywhere. I had seen this area first as the Jackson's farmland and then as open fields when I had discussed the housing development with Richard. Everything was changing.

'This will be the Colliery Miners' Welfare Institute,' Tommy told me. 'Can you see where the football field and cricket pitch will be? It'll have all the modern sports facilities. And the new pub The Black Diamond will open soon. There will even be a new railway station right here in Ebberfield next year.' He and William kicked a football as we walked.

'How exciting,' I said. 'It will be much more convenient to have the station closer. No more trekking back and forth through the snow and winter rain with the horse and cart.'

'Kick it to me!' cried Annie, wanting to be involved in the ball game. It was times like this, when she was with the boys, that I realised how much she missed them.

'Shame I won't get to go to the new school when it opens,' said William, kicking the ball to her and gesturing to the massive building. It would hold many times the number of our local church school.

I nodded. 'You only have one year left.'

'You kick it like this,' said Tommy, showing Annie the finer points of football as he kicked it back to her.

'Am I still coming to London when I'm finished?' William asked, a tentative expression on his face.

'Yes, the local high school is good.' I noticed him flinch. 'Don't you want to?'

'I don't want to leave my friends behind, especially Oliver, and Tommy will be here by himself.'

'Don't worry about me,' said Tommy, kicking the ball to me before grabbing William in a headlock. 'It's better you go anyway.'

'Why, so I won't be able to show you up on the football field?'

'In your dreams,' said Tommy, finally letting go. 'Because if you want to play professional football, you can't stay here all your life.'

'That's all well and good,' said Annie, stopping the ball I'd kicked to her. If she'd had half a chance, she would have been good at football too. 'But you can't play football forever. What will you do if you don't make the professional league?'

William stopped in the middle of the street with the ball at his feet. 'I don't know!' he exclaimed, exasperated.

'What about you, Tommy? Do you still want to play professional football?' I asked.

'Uncle David says that when the season begins in a few months, he'll talk to the scouts at Newcastle to come and watch me play. Maybe I can join a squad and next year when I'm sixteen, I can be selected to a team and play with Newcastle, like Uncle David.'

'So, you might not be here anyway?' William was incredulous.

Tommy shrugged. 'I'm not sure what I'll do.'

'All right,' I said, taking the boys' arms in mine as we continued to walk. 'You can't stay here when it's time for you to go to high school,' I said to William. 'Perhaps Uncle David can suggest one of the clubs in London to try out for.'

I turned to Tommy. 'If you want to come to London with William, Esther has plenty of rooms for all of us. You can study' – Tommy's face hardened – 'or find a job,' I said quickly. 'I want us all together, but you're fifteen and almost a man, Tommy. If you want to play football, I'll talk to Uncle David about how we can ensure you're looked after.'

William had a thoughtful expression on his face but Tommy's face darkened further.

'Why can't you find a job at the colliery school when it opens? Or even at one of the new shops, until you can get one at the school?' asked Tommy. 'That way we could be all together.'

'But Tommy, you know that won't work. There's no high school here for Annie or William, and Aunt Esther has been so generous to give us a place to live. We can all be together in London and I have a job already and—'

'Don't lie,' Tommy spat. 'You're there for the suffragettes.'

I froze at his tone. I took a deep breath. 'Yes, I feel like I can also do important work with the vote for women, right at the heart of it all.'

Tommy glared at me. I pushed on. 'You know it's a cause close to my heart. And the suffragettes have been successful raising the awareness of the vote and equality for women.' I didn't like the expression on Tommy's face, the faint disdain and scorn.

'You'd rather stay in London because of the suffragettes than be with us here in Ebberfield?'

'No, of course not, Tommy!'

'You know it's not like that, Tommy,' said William, frowning with indignation.

'Her cause is more important than us,' retorted Tommy.

'Don't be ridiculous,' said Annie.

'Everyone, calm down,' I said, not feeling calm at all. 'Let's not say things we don't mean.' I needed to avoid a pile-on at any cost.

Annie and William both stared at Tommy.

Tommy dropped his head.

I huffed. 'Let's not spoil a nice day. Let's go back and get some ice cream at Mrs Scruton's.' It was his birthday, after all. I only hoped it could restore the mood. I clenched my hands to stop them from shaking.

*

Clementine and I were at one of the WSPU meetings of the Kensington branch. We'd seen men loitering outside the building, some with cameras, and when Clementine mentioned them to various members, many of them were already aware of them.

'It's the police surveillance unit, Special Branch,' said one woman. 'They follow us and photograph us and I dare say they target us at marches and protests. Why do you think the same women get arrested, time and again, even when they haven't broken the law?'

'They're trying to break us down,' said another woman. 'But if they think intimidation and bullying will work, then they have no idea who they're dealing with.'

'We're stronger than they know,' I said.

Once the meeting was underway, the conversation turned to discussing ways of protesting King George's anti-suffrage sentiments. One that seemed popular was erecting WSPU flags at each hole of the private golf course the King played at.

'I can't believe that, after all the effort we went to for the Coronation Procession, the King doesn't support women's suffrage,' whispered a woman in front of us.

'What I can't believe,' whispered Clementine next to me, 'is that we're supporting this Conciliation Bill when it goes back to Parliament next month.'

'What do you mean?'

'Sylvia and Adela Pankhurst don't agree with Christabel's and their mother's support of the bill – it only promotes the vote for women who own property. What about working women?'

'I agree.' It seemed ridiculous that Clementine would be excluded from voting simply because she didn't own property.

But Emmeline Pankhurst and her daughter Christabel led the WSPU with what many believed was an iron fist.

'Did you see any women who work in sweatshops at the Coronation Procession?'

I frowned, trying to think. 'No,' I said finally. Women who worked in sweated trades were low paid and worked long hours in poor conditions, often in their homes or small workshops, sewing, stitching shoes, making boxes and chains. I remembered the conditions at the workhouse when I'd first arrived in Ebberfield. The workhouse had since grown in size to accommodate the needy. But nothing much had changed. Women with few choices were still being exploited. 'Come to think of it, there were very few working women's groups present at all.'

'That's because most of them work Saturday mornings and would have had trouble getting to the procession in time. Working women can't afford to take time off work to demonstrate for an intangible idea like the vote.'

'What's most important to them is looking after their family – putting food in their bellies and keeping a roof over their heads,' I said with feeling, remembering the horror of being evicted from the pub without a livelihood. Although Clementine and I were working women, our education gave us opportunities, choice and better pay. But if I didn't solve the problem of Roger's loan, I would lose my property and any right I'd have to vote under this bill. So far, Amy Sanderson hadn't found any other cases of loans like ours with the financial institution.

'That's exactly right,' said Clementine. 'And it's why I support the vote for all women.'

I nodded. Clementine had always felt this way and I'd agreed with her in principle when I was younger. But now I was a working woman, widowed, essentially without property, scraping to support my family. We needed to walk a delicate balance, being at the mercy of powerful men. I agreed with universal suffrage but believed that, in practical terms, gradual enfranchisement for women was more achievable. There were hundreds of thousands of women like me, unable to secure a loan or mortgage. If the Conciliation Bill was passed, we would be one step closer to having control over our own financial freedom and security.

It was a hot Sunday afternoon in August when Richard arrived with letters from Ebberfield. I'd decided to stay in London at the end of the school year and had picked up some extra work over the summer, tutoring children from the well-to-do families in the area, so I could put some savings away. Esther and Clementine were in the parlour – Esther was writing a paper on the research she was conducting on electricity at the Royal Institution where she worked, while Clementine was reading and smoking in the cross breeze of the open windows downstairs – so I took Richard out to the back garden with a pitcher of lemonade. Annie had gone with school friends to cool off on a quiet part of the Thames.

'It's very pleasant out here,' he said, looking around.

'It's a surprising little oasis,' I agreed, putting the pitcher on the small table in the shade of an apple tree. 'Esther loves to garden and spends time out here, tending to the flowers and plants.' The garden was lush and green with colourful borders, which were a little limp with the heat. 'I've begun a small vegetable and herb patch,' I said, gesturing to one corner.

'I'd love to see it.'

I smiled, leading the way. 'We've got mint and thyme growing and we've enjoyed some carrots, cabbage and tomatoes, as well as a few blueberries.'

'Is there anything you can't turn your hand to?'

I stopped and turned to him. 'Oh, I don't know. I've been working with the school lunch programs for so long, even here at Portobello Road, that it felt like the next step to take. There's nothing like fresh home produce and I'd like to teach the boys at school how to grow them as well, if I can convince the headmaster in the autumn.'

'You're a marvel, Hannah. After everything you've been through, you're flourishing.'

I was suddenly aware that we were standing very close to each other and felt the blush bloom in my chest and throat to burn in my cheeks.

I looked into his face, the familiar green eyes filled with appreciation and ... something more – a heat between us. Suddenly his arms were around me, holding me lightly, and the blood in my veins fizzed. I gazed at his lips, and reached up to kiss him before I could think about it. He kissed me back, sure but restrained, his lips soft.

I broke away, stepping out of his embrace, my heart pounding. 'I'm so sorry, Richard. I don't know what I was thinking.' Embarrassment flooded my body and my cheeks flushed once more. What had I done?

'There's nothing to be sorry for,' Richard said, gazing at me evenly. He took my hand as if it was the most natural thing in the world. It was then that I realised the depth of his feeling. 'Let's drink our lemonade. There are things I want to say to you.' He tucked my hand into the crook of his arm and we walked back to the table under the tree.

'Richard ... I don't want to ruin our friendship because of a momentary weakness,' I said trying not to tremble as I poured the lemonade.

'I've known you for nearly twenty years, Hannah, and I've admired you from afar for many of them,' he said softly.

'But over the last year, watching your incredible strength and determination in the face of what's happened, I have to admit, my admiration has grown into something more.'

I put the pitcher down, and raised my eyes to his. 'What are you saying?' His words warmed my heart but in a few short minutes we'd gone from firm friendship to shaky ground.

He rested his ha0nd on mine and my skin tingled at his touch. 'Do you think we can ever be anything more than friends?' he asked softly.

I pulled my hand away, panic surging in my chest, making it difficult to breathe. Roger's face swam into my mind. 'I can't—'

'Please, Hannah, hear me out, for the sake of our friendship.'

I looked into his green eyes for any hint of momentary madness, but found only the steady calm I had always seen. I nodded slowly, my mouth dry.

'The kiss was unexpected ... but it gives me the strength to tell you how I feel. I've wondered if you might ever reciprocate the feelings I have and now ... there is some hope. I want to be here for you and the children, to provide an anchor and a safe harbour for you. But I've decided to join Almroth when he leaves for South Africa. I could be gone for six months or more.'

'What?'

'We're studying the outbreak of pneumonia in gold mine workers to see if we can provide a vaccination to reduce the death rate, or prevent further infections.' He swallowed hard. 'The truth is, I was going to wait until I came back to tell you of my feelings. It hasn't been long since you lost Roger and I don't want to rush you. But perhaps it's better this way. It gives you time to consider how you feel and whether there might be a future for us. We can write to each other, and if you decide there is nothing more between us, then I hope the time apart will allow us to remain friends.'

I stared at him, my mouth slightly agape. My world was spinning so fast. 'I'm sorry, Richard. I ... I don't know what to say.'

'You don't need to say anything.' He smiled, then stood. 'Please just tell me you'll think about what I've said and that you'll continue to write to me.'

I nodded, slowly. 'I will.'

'Then I'll see myself out. Give my regards to Esther and Clementine.'

He kissed my hand before he disappeared back into the house and I stared at the garden for some time after.

Finally, I glanced at the letters on the table. One from Jenny, one from Emily. I clapped my hand across my mouth to stifle the sob that burst up from my chest. I couldn't believe what had just happened.

'Hannah?' said Clementine, wandering outside. She strode to my side. 'What on earth is wrong? Is it one of the children?'

I shook my head.

'Then what is it?' She sat beside me. 'You're shaking.'

'It's Richard,' I whispered in a strangled breath.

'Dr Jenkins? What's happened?'

'I kissed him ... He has feelings for me but ...' I shrugged helplessly.

She grasped my hand, her eyes dancing with excitement. 'Esther!' she called. 'Can you come outside?'

'What is it?' asked Esther, popping her head out the door.

'It's Richard. Hannah kissed him and he said he loves her,' Clementine exclaimed across the yard.

'Why don't you tell all the neighbours,' I said testily, heat rising to my cheeks.

'We should shout it from the rooftops!' said Clementine with a wicked grin.

'Your first kiss!' Esther and Clementine exchanged a knowing glance. 'How wonderful!' gushed Esther as she joined us at the table. She took my other hand. 'Now tell us. What happened?'

I took a shuddering breath and told them all of it.

'You and Richard have always made a good team,' said Esther when I'd finished. 'We've suspected that he's been in love with you for a while now.'

If only I'd known. 'I should never have kissed him. And he didn't say he loves me.'

'Of course he loves you, just because he didn't say the word,' said Esther, waving her hand dismissively. 'The poor man was out on a limb telling you his feelings when he knew you had no idea.'

'But … it's impossible. I can't let this happen.' I stared at them, expecting them to understand.

'And why not?' asked Clem. 'You kissed him. You must be attracted to him. Don't you have feelings for him?'

I frowned, staring as the beads of water on the outside of my glass began to slide. 'I don't really know. It's not anything I've ever thought about. I've always been in love with Roger. After losing him it feels too soon to fall in love again. How can I possibly think about anyone else when he was my one true love?' I paused. This was the hardest part to admit. 'And kissing Richard feels like I've betrayed Roger's memory,' I whispered.

'But Roger's gone, Hannah,' said Clementine gently.

I shook my head violently. 'Don't you see? I'm a terrible mother. I've abandoned my boys, split my family. I've lost the pub. I don't know who I am anymore. I don't deserve to love anyone else.' I pressed my hand to my mouth.

'Everyone deserves love, Hannah,' said Esther softly. 'Look at Clem and me.' She reached out and squeezed Clementine's hand. 'Stop beating yourself up. What happened to you was not your doing. You made the best decisions you could under the circumstances.'

I knew that Clementine and Esther had fought against the odds to be together. They were as deserving of love as anyone, if not more. If not for them, I didn't know where I'd be. But my failings were too great. 'No, I have to focus on getting my family back together. If I concentrate on fighting for the vote and for the pub, then maybe I can redeem myself in the eyes of my children.'

Clementine and Esther shared a glance. 'Maybe it's for the best that Richard goes away for a while,' said Clementine. 'It gives us time to make you see that you deserve love and happiness.'

Esther kissed the top of my head. 'Richard is a good man who has always respected your decisions. Maybe he can bring you happiness again.'

It seemed that the Prime Minister's promises could be broken when we learnt of his statement in Parliament early in the November session.

Clementine and I were at Clement's Inn, the headquarters of the WSPU, visiting the editorial department of *The Suffragette* newspaper to have an article revised for the Kensington branch, when we heard the news telephoned through from Westminster.

'He's introducing a new bill for Manhood Suffrage in next year's session,' said the woman behind the desk. 'It will abolish all property qualifications and give all legitimate male citizens the vote.'

I felt my chest constrict and pulled the air into my lungs with ragged breaths. I couldn't bear it if we were back to the beginning again. 'What about the Conciliation Bill?' I asked.

The woman shook her head. 'He's invited women to persuade MPs in the House of Commons to add an amendment for women's suffrage. But it won't do us any good.'

We were no closer to the vote – perhaps even further away, given the new focus on men's suffrage. All our hopes and efforts for nothing. I felt as though my future and that of my family hung in the balance.

'That's right,' said another voice, booming across the floor.

I turned to see Christabel Pankhurst stride towards the stairs in her hat and coat.

She paused. 'Mr Asquith knows that any amendment will be easily defeated in Commons. He has the numbers for his bill and although he promises that it won't affect any further Conciliation Bill, I guarantee this one is dead in the water.'

'He's a dirty liar,' said the woman behind the desk.

'What do we do now?' asked Clementine.

'We don't trust anything the government tells us in the future. The WSPU resumes its war with greater vigour and renewed ferocity,' said Christabel, before sweeping through the doors.

I met Clementine's eye, my eyebrows raised. 'What does she mean?' I asked, anger pulsing through my veins.

'It means we fight with the only thing we have – our rage at such injustice and betrayal. And it's time to pull out all the weapons in our arsenal.'

20

The rift between the NUWSS and WSPU is deepening by the day. If we don't show how committed we are to our aims, the government will never be held to account and continue to do nothing. Militancy seems to be a language men speak, so let's use it to our advantage.

A couple of weeks later I stared in disbelief at the letter I received from Mrs Pankhurst. I had never met her and I was amazed that she'd written to me. As I read the letter, my astonishment grew, because she'd asked me to keep its contents secret.

I showed it to Clementine. 'I have one too,' she said in hushed tones. 'I think anyone at the last WSPU meeting who agreed to the next stage of action would have received one.'

'What are we whispering about?' asked Esther, walking into the room.

I thrust the pamphlet at her. 'Emmeline Pethick-Lawrence, the treasurer of the WSPU, has organised a demonstration on Tuesday evening at eight o'clock in Parliament Square to protest against the Manhood Suffrage Bill, and Clem and I have been invited.'

'Mrs Pankhurst was part of a deputation to Mr Asquith and Mr Lloyd George to demand that the Manhood Suffrage Bill be changed to include equal universal suffrage, but they refused,' said Clementine. 'This protest is a reasonable response to their refusal.'

'I'm not sure you should go,' Esther said, reading the paper. 'If male supporters are encouraged to go to keep women safe and prevent what happened on Black Friday from happening again, then they must be expecting trouble.' She frowned as the implication hit her. 'Why have you been specifically invited to take part in a public demonstration?'

'I'm sorry, Esther, we can't tell you.' Clementine spread her hands in regret.

'What are you talking about, Clem?' Esther asked in exasperation. 'And what do you mean "we"?' She looked at me, raising her eyebrows in question.

'We both received letters from Mrs Pankhurst, asking us not to tell anyone about the protest,' I said simply. I wasn't going to lie to her.

Esther glared at each of us like we were wayward schoolgirls. 'You do know that if Mrs Pankhurst tells you to keep anything secret, it involves illegal activity.'

'I can't stand by and do nothing. I can't watch while men in power make declarations about women's lives,' I said, Mrs Pankhurst's letter crumpled in my hand. 'I love teaching but part of me feels useless when the legal process to get the pub back is so slow and laborious. I have to do something productive now. I'm going to the protest.'

'Are you sure you're willing to risk it after the notes we've received?' asked Esther. 'You know we're being watched. What if you're arrested?'

'I won't be bullied any longer. I'll just have to be fast and on my guard.'

'Neither of us can afford to be arrested, Esther,' said Clementine. 'Not with the fine nor prison time if we're charged and convicted.'

'Then it's simple,' Esther said, arms folded across her chest. 'Don't go.'

'It's *not* that simple,' I said.

'It's too dangerous. You don't know where the police will be or what they'll do.'

'You know we can't let threats stop us,' said Clementine. 'If we don't do this, the police and the government will think they have us.'

'What about the children if you end up in prison, Hannah?' persisted Esther, her face pinched in concern.

I stared at her a moment. 'I'm doing it for them,' I said quietly. Tommy's words came back to me. Maybe I had sacrificed being with him and William, being together as a family. But being here and doing this work was important and I felt compelled to do it. 'This is a fight for a better future for everyone. I have to take a stand, Esther. I'll never be able to live with myself if I don't try everything I can. If I lose my job, I'll get another, even if I have to take in sewing or clean houses.'

The night before the protest, I dreamed about Roger. We were in The Ox and Plough; Roger was behind the bar and I was holding a broom.

'You don't need to do that,' he said, pouring beer.

'I have to clean up.' The floor was covered in broken bottles and glasses. 'There's too much rubbish,' I said frantically. 'I'll never get to the bottom of it.'

'Yes, you will,' said Roger, still pouring. 'Use what you have.'

I glanced desperately around the room as the mound continued to grow. Soon I would be buried in it. 'Roger,' I cried out, but he didn't seem to hear me. *Use what you have.* I pushed the shattered glass out of the way with my broom and I realised that I could fight the rubbish. I continued to sweep a path until enough space opened around me and I could make my way to Roger and the bar.

But when I turned, the bar was empty. All I heard was his voice, encouraging me: 'Keep going!'

I woke with his words resounding in my mind.

Clementine and I presented our WSPU membership cards at the Gardenia restaurant on The Strand at seven o'clock sharp – the only way to gain admission. The hostess led us to the stairs and we went up to the long room, where women sat in groups. It seemed like any gathering of respectable women in their coats and hats, perhaps a charity meeting or even waiting to go in to a school concert, but we were all here for another more serious purpose. A woman smiled and came over to us. Her face was familiar as an organiser for the London area.

'Are you prepared for a long or short sentence?' she asked us.

I looked at Clementine briefly, who nodded. My dream of Roger gave me confidence to continue. This was it then.

'Short,' I said. 'My friend too.' Esther would never forgive us if Clementine opted for a long sentence.

The woman nodded. 'The National Liberal Club. Smash one window only and do it before nine o'clock.' She handed us each a sheet of paper.

I glanced at it quickly – instructions on what to do if we were arrested.

'Now, do you have your own implements?'

We shook our heads. 'Go and see the woman at the top of the stairs. She'll give you what you need.'

The woman we'd been directed to, gave us small toffee hammers. Mine felt weighty in my hand, a small object yet ready to pack a big punch. 'I suggest you put them up your sleeves,' she said. 'And make sure you smash your windows once the demonstration starts, while there's a diversion.'

Clementine and I joined the growing crowds at Parliament Square, suffragettes as well as suffragists. Many were from the NUWSS, and there were placards and banners from all different societies, and male supporters too. The crowd was bigger than any I'd seen at a demonstration at Parliament Square. Rows of uniformed police cordoned off the St Stephens entrance. Some of the men were allowed into Central Hall and even St Stephen's Hall, where word reached us that their attempts to send for Members of Parliament had failed.

A chant broke out across the crowd – 'Votes for women!' – until the crowd was chanting as one. Mounted police tried to push back the swelling crowd but we wouldn't have it. Women reached out and took hold of horses' bridles wherever they could and others raced through the break in the lines and chained themselves to railings and lamp posts closer to the entrance of Parliament. That's when we saw stones hurled towards the windows of Parliament and heard the crash of a broken lamp on the square. Police surged towards where the stones had been thrown from as a howl went up from the crowd.

'Come on,' said Clementine, pulling me away. 'It's time.'

We left the square with other small groups of women, all moving in different directions. We nodded to a few walking with us, emboldened by the unity in our cause, until they began to disappear into the night. Clementine and I stole through the quiet streets, my heart thumping in my chest as I looked constantly behind us, worried about being under surveillance and fearful of being stopped before we'd completed our mission at the National Liberal Club. I understood why it was a target: the liberal government was deaf to women's suffrage and it was a men-only club.

'Ready?' asked Clementine after we'd picked a place shrouded in shadows. There was nobody around and the men inside the building were oblivious to our presence.

'Ready,' I whispered, wielding my little hammer. This was the first time I had ever contemplated breaking the law and my heart was pounding. But what other weapon did I have at my disposal to bring about change?

We smashed our chosen windows, the sound of breaking glass brittle against the normal sounds of the night. For just a moment, I froze in shock at what I'd done, holding my breath and listening for any sound that said we'd been heard. There was nothing. Then the thrill and danger coursed through my veins. Every sound and sight became sharper, every impression had greater clarity. I grinned at Clementine, exuberant at our success.

But my fingers brushed against the wedding ring on my hand and my children came instantly to mind. I could *not* get caught.

'Let's go,' I whispered.

We crept away, each step taking us further from the scene of our crime. I stared into the dark shadows around us for any sign of movement.

A shout and the sound of running footsteps behind us broke the stillness of the streets and turned my satisfaction into fear and cold hard determination.

'Run!' I urged Clementine, as I took off.

I pushed my senses out in front of me, turning down streets away from danger, until I realised I no longer heard Clementine's footsteps behind me. I turned to look and squinted into the inky blackness, but there was nothing. I stopped short, my breathing ragged, the roaring in my ears almost too loud to hear anything else. *Where was she?*

I slowly crept back the way I'd come until I heard voices on the street ahead. In the light of a lamp, I saw Clementine, cornered by two policemen. One was holding her hammer and inspecting it closely. I was about to run to them, explain that she hadn't done anything, when our eyes met and she shook her head imperceptibly. Still, I couldn't walk away, even as her eyes pleaded with me to go.

Only when the police escorted Clementine back towards Parliament did I turn away and slink into the darkness, pushing my guilt down as images of Annie, Tommy and William played in my mind.

Esther and I paced the floor of the terrace.

'I'm so sorry,' I kept repeating. 'One minute she was behind me and the next she wasn't. What if we were followed after all?'

'But why would Clem be arrested and not you? Show me the instructions you got if you were caught,' said Esther.

I pulled the page from my skirt pocket and together we read the sheet.

'She'll be taken to a police station and, after a time, bailed out and she can come home.'

I breathed a sigh of relief. At least Clementine wouldn't have to stay in custody until her appearance in court the following day.

'Clem knew what she was getting into,' said Esther, squeezing my hand. 'She knew there was a chance of arrest. But the fact that she only broke a single window means she won't have a long sentence.'

I nodded. 'We both knew the risks. You understand why we had to do it, don't you?'

'Clem is headstrong and sees the world in black and white. It's one of the things I love about her. She follows through on what she believes with total conviction and passion.' Esther smiled ruefully. 'I would never want to change that about her.' She gazed at a portrait photograph of Clementine she'd insisted on being taken last Christmas. 'I remember some years ago you called her a "warrior angel". That's exactly what she is.'

Clementine returned home not long after, in high spirits and grinning from ear to ear. 'Over two hundred of us were arrested,' she bragged. 'I'm in good company. Lady Lytton, Mrs Pethick-Lawrence and May Billinghurst were also arrested.' Lady Lytton was daughter of an earl and sister-in-law to Arthur Balfour, the Prime Minister in office five years ago. Emmeline Pethick-Lawrence was the WSPU treasurer and May Billinghurst was well known for fighting for the cause from her tricycle, having been crippled by polio as a child. They were all highly respected senior members of the organisation.

Esther gave me a pointed look and I had to smile back at her, in relief and embarrassment. Clementine was safe and well, and even proud of what had happened tonight. I should be proud of my involvement too.

The following day, Esther accompanied Clementine to the police court. I had to go to work and was determined to teach the boys about the value of equality between men and women.

When I returned home that afternoon, I found Esther pale-faced and staring into space, her engineering notes scattered across the table.

'What is it?'

Esther shook her head. 'I can't concentrate,' she said in a monotone.

My belly clenched in fear. 'What happened with Clem this morning? Did she receive a prison sentence?'

'Of course. There was a long line of women with their suitcases waiting outside the police court when we arrived. I would never have imagined such a sight, if I hadn't seen it with my own eyes. They all received sentences.' She shook her head. 'It was what she wanted, but it didn't go to plan. She was sentenced to a month.'

'A *month*?' I sank to a chair, stunned. 'We were told only seven days for a single window.'

'But she was charged with breaking more than one window.'

I clapped my hands over my mouth. 'This is my fault,' I whispered. 'She's been charged with my crime as well. I have to tell them it was me, not Clem.' I stood, ready to go to the police station. 'I can't let her suffer for my actions.'

Esther caught my arm. '*Don't*. Clem made me promise to keep you out of it. We can't do this to Annie and the boys. If you're in prison, it will worry them no end. Clem has already been moved to Holloway Prison, along with the others. Nothing you can do or say will change that now. The police have their pound of flesh and will make sure they're all punished.'

'But it's not right. I've let you and Clem down.' Anything could happen in prison in a month. And Clementine could lose her job.

'You have *not* let us down.' She grasped me by the shoulders. 'You being imprisoned won't help the children, and what about the battle you're fighting for the pub? You have to be free to continue and you need a clean record to renew your liquor licence and remain as publican.'

I took a deep breath and took her hands in mine. 'Then we give her all the support we can.'

21

Italy is at war with Turkey and the crumbling Ottoman Empire over Libya in North Africa. With Morocco now a French territory under the protection of its Triple Entente partners, and Egypt under British control, it's no wonder Italy thinks it can claim territory too. But do the people who live in these disputed territories want to be under the yoke of yet another power? I can sense a fight coming. There comes a time when any oppressed person, man or woman, will rise up.

As it turned out, Clementine decided to push the boundaries, even in prison.

My dearest Esther and Hannah,
I am well enough here in prison. I am with many women in the second division, each of us in isolation. We're allowed visitors and correspondence with the outside world, but only once a month, so I've had this letter smuggled out to you. When I first arrived, the prison officers tried to take a photograph of me but I'd been warned by others and distorted my face so that it was unrecognisable. I've heard whispers that they try to take photographs of us in our cells or the exercise yard without our knowledge or consent, but we are already familiar with this kind of surveillance.

We're allowed exercise in the yard every day but cannot talk to each other. May Billinghurst rides around the yard on her tricycle, which is painted in the suffragette colours and has a placard on the back: *Votes for Women*. My respect and admiration for her have increased as she wears irons on both legs and walks around on crutches inside the prison.

Our cells are basic but adequate and the meagre meals sustain us but it's not called prison for nothing. However, Lady Lytton and those ladies who are high born or from good connections are treated like political prisoners, with all the comforts afforded to them. They are housed in the first division cells, where they have all the luxuries of home: their own clothes; writing desk; fireplace; comfortable chairs and a bed with soft furnishings; and the hot meals they're used to. Suffragettes are not considered political prisoners, just common offenders, even though our crimes are minor. It's not justice, only another form of persecution, to punish us further. Lady Lytton proved the hypocrisy of this division when she used a false name when she was arrested and imprisoned in London last year, pretending to be a London seamstress.

Along with some of my fellow suffragette prisoners, I decided to make a statement. We have begun a hunger strike to draw further attention to the cause of women's suffrage and our treatment in prison. I have so far refused food for three days. It won't be long before I too will face forcible feeding. I am decidedly weak but remain mentally strong.

I think of you both more than I can say and of coming home to you at the end of my time here. But knowing how important our cause is and the difference the vote will make in all our lives keeps me strong.

All my love,

Clementine

The fact that women were being imprisoned as criminals for acts of civil disobedience was outrageous. Like Clementine, some had received long sentences. But to read about the further indignities to suffragettes in prison was mortifying and unjust. Men were exerting their power over women, trying to subjugate them into submission. Where were their basic human rights?

There was nothing Esther and I could do except send our own letters of objection to the newspapers, the Home Office and to MPs, including Keir Hardie, who was fighting against forcible feeding in the press and in Parliament. We had to find our advocates wherever we could. I found myself wishing I could talk to Richard about it but he was still in South Africa.

'Mama, do you think you could make a vegetarian dish tonight?' asked Annie, one afternoon not long after. 'I've decided I want to stop eating meat. Killing animals is cruel.'

I nodded. 'I admire your commitment my darling. Do you have something in mind?' A knock at the door interrupted our conversation. 'Preferably a dish I can make quickly and that Aunt Esther and I will like too,' I continued as I went to answer it.

I opened the door and stared in shock, speechless.

'Good afternoon, Mrs Rainforth. I'm Detective Sergeant Sykes.'

It was the white-haired policeman. I moved to slam the door but he was quicker, jamming his boot in the crack.

'Not so fast, Hannah.' He pushed the door open.

'What do you think you're doing?' Fear coursed through me like lightning. 'What do you want?' My ears strained for any sound of Annie, praying she wouldn't come out.

'I bring you a warning. Your friend has made some disturbing admissions while in prison about what you've been up to. If you don't desist, you'll land in prison too.'

'Are you following me?' My voice came out as a strangled whisper.

He smirked. 'I never said that.' He leant in, his eyes focused on his cornered quarry, cold and hard like ice, and I recoiled. 'Just remember what I've said. You don't want to see me back here.'

A wave of outrage rose, battling against my fear. 'Please leave, sir.' I stared him down.

He grinned. 'Don't forget, I'll know,' he growled as he backed away. As soon as he was off the threshold, I slammed the door shut and turned the lock.

I stood there for a moment, breathing deeply as I tried to stop my trembling. I knew he was bluffing about Clementine's admissions, even without her letter. The police were monitoring all the leaders of the WSPU, so they already knew I wasn't involved in any great clandestine activities. All I'd done was smash a window, but they couldn't prove it, otherwise I'd already have been arrested.

But I was sure of one other thing. I'd made an enemy of this man. I'd embarrassed him in front of his colleague and the public that day at Hyde Park and he'd held a grudge ever since. What was it going to take to stop him?

To make my worries worse, on my birthday, I received a letter from Alice.

Hannah, I'm worried about Tommy. David tells me he's been fighting with some of the fellows at football training, who goaded him about not making the squad for Newcastle. David said he's too young to go to Newcastle yet and has to wait until next year, when he's quite sure he will make the squad and, if he's dedicated, probably the team next season. But Tommy won't listen

> and he's easily provoked by his teammates. Emily told me he came home the other day with a black eye.

'Oh, Roger!' I whispered. He'd know what to do. Somehow, I'd have to find a way to bridge the distance with Tommy. We had left without resolving things after his birthday or speaking about the anger that coiled tightly within him. I had wanted the boys with me in London for Christmas, but Annie and I would have to go to Ebberfield instead. I had to go home.

At long last, Clementine's sentence was served. Esther, Annie and I were there at Holloway with WSPU officials on the morning of her release. Annie insisted on coming, telling me she was old enough to see what was happening. Her request pulled me up short when I realised she was right. She was sixteen years old and I couldn't shield her from the world forever – and nor should I. It was time to let her in to the realities of the battle we were fighting.

Women ran from the gates towards the waiting crowd, many crying with relief. Clementine lit up when she saw us but I had to mask the horror I felt as she walked stiffly towards us, the elegant ease with which she usually moved, gone. She looked drawn, her clothes hanging off her, and there were bruises around her neck and on her hands and wrists, in varying shades of mottled green and purple against her pale skin, her hair was lacklustre and her hands red and chapped from manual work. The women who were released with her looked no different. It was a shock I felt viscerally, like a blow to the stomach. Anger boiled in me at how she'd been treated.

Esther sobbed as she hugged Clementine. 'What have they done to you?' she hiccoughed.

'Don't fuss ...' Clementine had begun to cry.

Annie glanced at me, her face pinched in concern, and I smiled reassuringly, before she wrapped her arms around Clementine. 'It's good to see you, Aunt Clem,' she said.

Clementine brushed a lock of hair from Annie's face and tried to smile. 'Well, you're a sight for sore eyes.'

'Come on, let's get you home,' I said, taking Clementine's arm in mine.

'Those words have never sounded sweeter,' rasped Clementine, wiping her eyes.

We returned home, where Esther assisted Clementine to bathe then helped her to bed, though she refused to sleep.

'Come, sit by me,' she said to us. 'I've been on my own for a month. I promise to rest but I have to tell you what happened in there – all of it. You have to bear witness to the shame and degradation that women like us are exposed to every day.' There were dark circles under her eyes and her cheeks were hollowed, with new lines etched across her beautiful face. I wanted to cry for all she'd been through. I didn't need to hear the words from her mouth because her body told with great eloquence the story of what had transpired over the past month.

'By all means,' agreed Esther. 'As long as you let the nurse examine you when she comes and you do whatever she says.' The WSPU had offered the services of a nurse for the women who were ill when they came out of prison. Clementine nodded and Esther sat beside her. Annie sat on the end of the bed and I dragged a chair across.

'We had to undress and change into prison uniform,' began Clementine. 'The prison guards had no sympathy for us. Some women called out, insisting we were political prisoners, but the guards just turned their backs.'

'That's why you joined the others in a hunger strike?' asked Annie.

Clementine nodded. 'We broke windows. We didn't hurt anyone. It's an offence punishable with a fine, not a prison sentence. And for that, we were isolated in cells that had the bare minimum. We were given none of the comforts that would lift our spirits. The aim was to break us. I heard the cries of my fellow hunger strikers, who were forcibly fed, supposedly to prevent them from becoming unwell. It's a most inhumane process. Women cried out in defiance, then in fear when it began. The sounds became more frightening, with gagging and pitiful moaning. Twenty minutes of torture and abuse to a woman's body, twice a day. And soon I knew it would be my turn.'

Esther grasped her hand, her knuckles turning white with the strength of her emotion.

'Was it as bad as they say?' I asked, eyeing the yellow bruising that began on one side of her throat and disappeared under the neckline of her nightdress. Her nose and lips were red and covered with thick, dark scabs. I sat tall, steeling myself for what was to come.

'It was worse. Nothing prepared me for the physical and mental torture. I thought I could be brave, but I wasn't brave at all. I screamed as long and as loud as anyone, fighting against the invasion of my body with every instinct I had. I never imagined being brutalised like that.'

I glanced at Esther, whose face had turned the colour of milk. When our eyes met, I knew she was thinking about the night in the Ebberfield graveyard when she and Marjorie Partridge had been assaulted by Fred Duggan, and the rape she'd endured at the hands of Edward, and suddenly I was back in the alley next to The Ox and Plough when Edward had held a knife against my throat and over my pregnant belly, determined to stop me from speaking out about what we knew about him. I remembered the raw fear and terror and my body's instinctive response to save my life and that of my baby, William.

'Go on,' said Esther, her voice wavering.

'Twice a day four guards came in and held me down in a chair and my head was forced back so they could insert a metal clamp to pry my jaw open so far that I feared that it would dislocate. Then the doctor pushed a rubber tube into my nose and another into my throat. I thought I was going to die from suffocation. I gagged and choked, the pain like fire.' Her hand drifted to her throat as she relived the experience.

'I felt the nasal tube go all the way down to my stomach then the other tube was pulled out and before I could cry out, a mixture of milk and eggs was poured into the tube. It was too fast and, because I hadn't eaten for days, it curdled when it hit my stomach and I vomited it up while I was still being held down.' Clementine looked around at us, her eyes wide open as she remembered the horror. 'I truly believed I would die then, choking on my own vomit, but the doctor didn't relent, just waited for me to be done, then poured more mixture into my tube. I don't know how many times I gagged and vomited, but he persisted until he proclaimed I'd had enough. The tube was removed and I was escorted to my bed, barely able to walk. They left me there each time ... I was a mess.'

Esther's face was filled with anguish and Clementine paused, raising Esther's hand to her damaged lips.

'I'm all right, my love. It's over now. I will only burden you once with the telling of what happened, but I have to finish.'

Esther nodded, clasping Clementine's hand in her own.

'I heard the same screams and sounds of choking in the cell next to mine and all I could do was shudder and shake and cry, for myself as much as for them. I could barely speak, my throat was so sore, but when I knew the doctor had left,

I called out, "Never surrender." And after a moment, they called back, "Never surrender," one by one. It became our catchcry as we endured the same process again that evening and every day after that.'

'Oh, my love,' whispered Esther, the tears rolling down her cheeks.

I pulled Annie to me. My daughter was rigid with shock and repulsion.

'I'm so sorry, Clem. I should have taken my part of the blame.' It was my fault she had been in prison as long as she was and that she'd endured that dreadful suffering for so long.

'No, Hannah,' Clementine said fiercely. 'I chose to do this. I knew the risk of forcible feeding but a hunger strike is a powerful way to send the message to Parliament, the government and the public that we will continue to put our bodies on the line for the cause. The struggle for the vote for women has to remain high in the nation's awareness. And now we have to let others know how women are treated for simple acts of civil disobedience and for refusing to do what they're told.' Her eyes flashed with defiance, even now. 'I will use this experience as a weapon.'

A week later, the WSPU had a carriage take us to Queen Hall, where a breakfast reception was being held to honour the released prisoners.

'I don't know that you're well enough yet,' said Esther as Clementine prepared to leave. It was her first trip outside the house and she was still weak. She had cuts in her mouth that were yet to heal and pain in her nose, throat and stomach, making it difficult for her to eat. The nurse had told her to rest and had given her medicine and a tonic.

'I'll manage, Esther,' she said with an impatient flick of her hand. 'Some women have been through what I have dozens of times.'

I understood them both. It was difficult to see the one you love in such a state but Clementine had chosen this path for the good of all women.

'Why are there so many men here?' whispered Annie when we arrived at the breakfast reception. I scanned the room and noticed a few men at each table.

'They would be husbands, fathers, brothers and men who support the WSPU and the suffrage movement,' I said. 'Men have been imprisoned along with our women for taking part in window breaking and some have endured their own hunger strikes.' We found our seats at the long tables. 'Your father was a great supporter.'

'I don't know if he would have gone as far as going to prison or on a hunger strike,' she replied.

'No, perhaps not,' I said softly, 'but he was just as passionate a supporter for equality for men and women as I am.' I thought about Tommy for a moment and wondered if Roger had lived, whether he'd understand his father's support and why I had to do this.

Many members of the WSPU were already present, seated at the long tables in the hall with their white, green and purple sashes with *Votes for Women* written across them. Members of the committee sat at the front. We were all the same, there to show respect for the women's time in prison and their self-sacrifice.

Mrs Pankhurst presided over the breakfast, thanking the women for their courage, duty and loyalty to the cause that was so dear to all our hearts, and presenting each woman with a medal for valour in action.

When Clementine's name was called, Annie, Esther and I cheered and clapped the loudest. Her face was flushed with pleasure when Mrs Pankhurst pinned the medal to her chest and shook her hand. Annie took a photograph to commemorate the occasion.

'I never thought I'd meet her,' she whispered when she returned to the table. I'd never seen her star-struck like this but she'd acted on the directions of this woman, who was highly respected in many circles and who could galvanise action.

'The medal is beautiful, Aunt Clem,' said Annie. It was styled like a military medal, the ribbon in the suffragette colours and engraved with *For Valour* on the top silver bar and *Hunger Strike* on the silver medal below. Clementine hugged Annie and I could see tears slip from the corners of her eyes.

She only managed to eat a little after the formalities had been observed. 'My throat hurts when I try to swallow,' she murmured.

'Try some of the egg,' whispered Esther. 'It's quite soft.'

Clementine shook her head and grimaced. Then I remembered that eggs had been forced down her feeding tube. Instead, she sipped her freshly brewed coffee, buoyed by her conversation with other women who had been through forcible feeding themselves. She was part of a new sisterhood who understood her suffering. It was going to take time for her to heal.

When we returned home, there was another note slipped under our door. I waited, my dread mounting, until Clementine had gone up to her room for a rest with Annie's help before I showed it to Esther.

> Your defiance has consequences as you have seen.
> We arrest who we choose and decide the term of
> imprisonment they receive. Let this be a lesson to you.

The events of the night Clementine was arrested suddenly fell into place.

'It's Special Branch, it has to be. They targeted Clem. Made an example of her,' I said, anger and fear rising within me like two snakes intertwined, ready to strike. I clasped my hands together to stop them from shaking. Deep in my gut I knew the police were playing games with us. Why else had Clem been stopped and not me?

'There's more.' I told Esther about the visit from the policeman. 'I'm sorry I didn't tell you sooner. He must be Special Branch too. I thought it was just me he was after, but now I'm sure he's the one behind all the notes. He wants to harass and frighten us, but he's dangerous.'

Esther glanced upstairs. 'Then none of us are safe here.' I followed her gaze and realised that he knew Annie lived here too.

I took a deep breath. I had to be calm and rational. 'I think it's time we put a bit of distance between them and us. We need a chance to think about what to do.' I grasped her hand. 'Why don't you and Clem come with us to Ebberfield for Christmas?'

Esther thought for a moment and then nodded. 'We can stay with my parents. The fresh air, a change of scenery and my mother's determination and nursing skills will be good for Clem's recovery.'

'Good. They might think we're running scared but we'll never back down,' I said. 'We'll find a way to beat the bastards.'

22

I've been thinking about Richard. I miss him coming to visit, his excitement in relaying his medical research to me and how much he wants to help others with new discoveries and inventions. We're so alike in that way, wanting to make the world a better place for everyone. He's just as passionate as me. His fight is medical science and health, where mine is for equal rights for women and education.

Every time I came back to Ebberfield I felt more displaced. In some ways it felt like home but in others, I felt like an outsider. But none of that mattered when I was reunited with my boys.

'William, you've grown since August,' I said as I hugged him to me. At nearly fourteen, he was as tall as me. 'I've missed you so much.' I kissed him and was pleased when he reciprocated and hugged me tighter. He had always been an affectionate boy and it was wonderful to know that hadn't changed.

'It's good to have you home, Mama,' he said.

'You know, Tommy's here too,' said Annie, ruffling William's light hair.

'Tommy's here?' I replied, delighted. He hadn't written to me since I'd seen him for his birthday, though I continued to send him letters.

'Right here, Mama.'

I turned and pressed my hand across my mouth, overcome

with emotion. His face had changed; it was longer, with more angles and the shadow of facial hair on his cheeks. He was shaving then. He was becoming a man.

Then I was in his arms, crying. I was home, with all of my children.

Christmas was wonderful. We stayed with Jenny and Robert, who had gone to so much trouble. Sarah and Jane were there with their families, along with George and Christopher, who was now working in the Ebberfield mine.

'How is George managing on his own?' I asked as we cleaned up the kitchen after lunch. We'd insisted that Jenny go out with Annie and the children to look for Santa Claus while we placed the presents under the Christmas tree and tidied up.

'I think it was hard on him, leaving the butcher shop after so many years,' said Jane. 'But he's adjusting to his new life, working in a butchery in the colliery town. He refuses to remarry.'

I shook my head. It had been nearly five years since Mary's death. Like George, I couldn't imagine ever marrying again. After losing the pub, it was something I could have considered for the sake of the children, but Roger had been the other half of me and I still grieved for him every day. I often saw men who couldn't cope after the death of their wife, at the pub and within the village, and many married quickly and began new families. Women, on the other hand, often remained widows rather than remarry, unless they had children they couldn't support on their own.

'As much as today means the world to me, it's hard being without Mary and Roger,' I said. Coming home always ripped open the wounds of my loss, no matter how I tried to prepare for it. Every time was a visceral shock.

'How are you going in London?' asked Sarah.

'I love it, actually,' I said, washing up the platters. 'And Esther and Clementine have been incredibly good to me and Annie. I'm really enjoying teaching again and Annie only has one more year after this at Notting Hill High School.'

'Are you any closer to getting the pub back?' asked Jane.

I paused, my hands in the soap suds. 'It's taking a while to untangle, but Robert and Amy Sanderson are working on it.'

'When are you coming home?' asked Sarah. 'Your boys need you.'

I stared at her, paralysed by the truth of her words. 'I can't come back until I have my home and livelihood returned to me,' I said finally.

'But surely you can get work at the local school and rent a cottage for you and the children while you wait for the problem with the pub to resolve,' said Jane. I shook my head. *Not you too!*

Sarah huffed in exasperation. 'It's been over a year. Have you thought that you'd have some answer by now if you were going to get one? Maybe you have to let this fight go?'

I pressed my hands on the edge of the sink. 'I can't. The pub is Papa's legacy and mine too, which I worked so hard to build and hang on to. Roger and I put everything we had into it, our hearts and souls.'

'But what about your children? They're all separated. Do you think this is what Roger would have wanted? Do you think Papa would want you to hold on to this dream at the expense of your *family*? I can't imagine either of them would want you to sacrifice so much for a livelihood.' Sarah wrapped her arms around me. 'It's time to face reality, Hannah. You've always wanted to change the world, but the children need you to hold the family together.'

I stiffened in her embrace and clenched my jaw, on the verge of angry tears. 'I'm *doing* this for my family,' I ground out. 'You all received a generous sum when I bought your shares of the pub. But the increased valuation was on the back of Roger's and my hard work. Now you want me to just give up my share of the inheritance and start again with nothing?' I clasped my hands together, shaking with indignation. I looked each of my sisters in the eyes. 'You may not understand or agree with what I'm doing, but I need your support, not your condemnation. I'm alone in this situation. The weight I have to bear is so heavy some days, I feel like I'm going to break, and yet I can't, for my *family*. So please, be the love and support I need.'

My sisters stood there dumbfounded and, I hoped, chastened. But I did have to face the possibility I might not get the pub back and formulate a plan if that ever happened. Would I want to come back to Ebberfield? It was what Tommy wanted, but the idea was unsettling. I strode away, determined to enjoy the time I had with my children.

I took them to see Roger's grave, our family all together for a few minutes on Christmas Day.

'Aunt Alice brings us every Sunday after church,' said William as Annie placed the flowers we'd brought at the base of the headstone.

'I can't believe he's here, under all this dirt,' whispered Annie.

I pulled her to me. 'It still feels like yesterday.'

Tommy shifted from foot to foot. 'Dadda's not here. He's gone.' The bleak look in his eyes made me want to gather him up and protect him from his pain. I had written to Tommy after I'd heard about the fights he was getting in, but he'd never responded. At least, I noticed with some relief, that he didn't have any fresh bruises.

'He's not gone,' said William, shaking his head. 'I talk to Dadda all the time.'

'What, in your imagination?' asked Tommy. His face held curiosity, not spite.

'No,' said William, 'mainly in my dreams, but sometimes I know he's with me when I walk to school or home and we talk.'

'I dream about your father too,' I said, pulling both boys to me. 'I still miss him so much.'

I wanted to keep the feeling that Roger was with us, even if it was only because we'd spoken about him. But although it hadn't snowed yet, it was cold, the wind off the North Sea cutting right through to the bone.

'Let's go and have hot chocolate,' I said instead.

I went to visit Robert Sanderson a few days later.

'Good morning, Hannah.' Robert was sitting with a file in front of him. 'How's London?'

'I've finally settled and enjoy teaching again. And it's been lovely to see more of Amy. She's been such a help and support.' I fiddled with the edge of my sleeve. I was anxious, the conversation with my sisters going around and around in my head. 'Have you found out any more? How long until we have a case to get the pub back?' The brewery was a business and the longer I was gone, the more the current running of the pub became normal and, I worried, the less likely the brewery would be inclined to give the pub back to me.

'I have some good news,' said Robert, with a smile. 'The brewery has finally agreed to work with us to prove the liability sits with the financial institution.'

Hope surged through me. This was the best Christmas present I could ask for; this and the fact that Tommy seemed to be in better spirits. I'd spoken to Emily and David at length and Tommy had dealt with his problems by focusing on his training, to be the best he could be before the Newcastle coach watched him play again in the new year. Maybe he was finding his way. I decided to let it be. The last thing I wanted was another argument at Christmas and Tommy closing himself off to me again.

'How? Why?'

Robert steepled his fingers. 'Well, simply, the brewery doesn't want to be sued for their negligence in not checking the loan before they gave it to Roger. And with the brewery on our side, we'll have more clout and resources at our fingertips. All we need now is that one piece of irrefutable evidence to break the case open. But don't worry. I have confidence that we'll find it. Keep strong.'

I stood, elated. 'That is wonderful news. Thank you, Robert, for your efforts. I'm eternally grateful.'

'It's my pleasure. We'll have you back before too long,' he said, shaking my hand.

I met Esther outside the tea room.

'Where's Clementine?' I asked.

'In with Mrs Scruton. They're talking about her imprisonment and the forcible feeding.'

I understood why Esther had come out to wait for me in the cold. It would be hard for her to hear it again. 'How is she?'

'She's improving. Mama has taken her on as her personal nursing project.' She grinned. 'Poor Clem. You know Mama once she's decided on something. She checks the daily menu, making sure Clem has good, nutritious food she can manage to eat and insists on a schedule of massages and exercises to help strengthen her.'

I couldn't help but grin in return. 'Clem has no other choice than to get well.'

'But it's the nightmares. I can see it in the mornings when she comes down for breakfast. Her eyes are dark and heavy and I know she's had a restless night.'

'I imagine it will take time. You're the best one to know how to help her.'

Esther nodded, her face dark with memory.

We went in and joined Clementine and Mrs Scruton.

'Disgraceful business,' said Mrs Scruton, shaking her head.

'We think the police targeted her,' I said. I explained about the notes we'd been receiving and Detective Sergeant Sykes.

'That's persecution,' she said, outraged. 'Know what you're gonna do?'

We shook our heads.

'You ain't gonna live in fear – you hold 'em to account.' She leant towards us. 'Those weasels hide in the shadows. But you tell everyone you know, 'specially the women. Bet there's many more of you and they'll tell their stories too. Alone you're powerless, together you're strong again.' She gestured to the three of us. 'But you know this.'

I nodded and gave a sigh of relief. 'Sometimes it's hard to see when you're in it.'

'When this disgustin' behaviour comes to light and is public knowledge, they can't hide. They lose their power.'

The power of fear, I thought.

'Thank you, Mrs Scruton,' said Esther, squeezing the old woman's gnarled hand.

'Even better – write it all down. Everythin' you notice, everythin' that happens. You can always take your story to the newspapers in London.'

She was right, of course. Mrs Scruton had a knack of telling it how it was, stripping back the layers to what was beneath.

'Don't mess with us northerners,' I said grimly.

23

I've been thinking about the spiritualist movement and theosophy lately. Marie Curie has attended seances with her husband in Paris, visiting a famous Italian medium supposedly communicating with the dead and the spirit world. According to Esther, she remains sceptical. There are charlatans and frauds who prey on the vulnerabilities of others, and although I desperately wish I could speak to Roger again, I know it's a fantasy.

When it was time to step into the train carriage and say goodbye to the boys, I cried, hugging them to me, like I had when they were small, even though William would soon be taller than me and Tommy towered over me now. I didn't want to let go. Leaving them felt more difficult each time, even with the knowledge that William would join us in the summer and Tommy would think seriously about his future over the coming months.

All of the emotion hit me once we returned to London. It had been such a lovely visit and Tommy seemed happy. I missed the boys, being able to talk to them, hug them and know the everyday details of their lives. I'd lost so much that I could never have back. I'd lost sight of what their dreams and passions were, how they viewed their future. I knew that the best I could do to keep the family together was to be in London while Annie and William attended high school, and continue teaching and fighting for the vote for women. I could only pray that Tommy would decide to join us.

In February, a new Conciliation Bill was presented to Parliament in addition to the Manhood Suffrage Bill, which lifted my spirits.

'The new qualifications mean that women householders would be included in the vote,' I told Clementine and Esther, scanning the newspaper report. 'That's about two million women.'

'We can't agree to this,' said Clementine.

'Why ever not?' asked Esther.

'It still gives some women the vote,' I said, 'and means that women's suffrage is still in the forefront of Parliament's mind. Surely further votes will follow.'

Esther nodded. But Clementine shook her head.

'It's a drop from the previous two versions of the bill. The WSPU holds firm on its demand for the vote for women, equal to that of men. If we give in now after all the broken promises, then we'll never get what we want.'

'I have to hope, Clem. We've been fighting for the vote for about twenty years and we know it's a process that will take time.' I crushed the fabric of my skirt in my clenched hands. I agreed with Clementine in theory but it wasn't realistic. 'The sooner women get the vote, even if it's not all of them to start with, we can agitate for changes to laws affecting the financial position of women. I don't want other women to go through what I have.'

'I know how difficult this time has been for you.' Clementine's face softened. 'We all want the same thing: for women to have the same power as men.'

'Don't give up hope, Hannah,' said Esther. 'Soon you'll have William here. And Amy and Mr Sanderson continue working on the pub loan. It's just going to take time.'

But when Clementine and I received invitations from Mrs Pankhurst to become involved in a new campaign of window smashing beginning in early March in protest of this new Conciliation Bill, I agreed to go, despite the visit from the policeman and the note we received before Christmas. I'd had enough of being bullied and told what I could and couldn't do, of being expected to roll over and take any treatment dished out to me. We'd told our experiences to members of the WSPU, describing the intimidation and maltreatment by Detective Sergeant Sykes, and they in turn told us how they'd been under surveillance, followed and photographed not just at rallies but also during their private lives. We heard how Special Branch had been conducting surveillance on prominent suffragettes for some time but now they were following ordinary members.

Esther, Clementine and I wrote detailed reports about the harassment we'd received, ready to make our experiences public, but no more threatening notes came our way.

'Rather broken windows than broken promises,' said Clementine, repeating the WSPU slogan that was written on hammers and around stones.

'But we have to be careful. Watch out for anyone following,' I said. 'Especially Sykes.'

'Neither of us can get caught. It will mean prison and forcible feeding if we hunger strike. Besides, you can't afford to lose any wages or have a criminal conviction if you want the pub back and I'll lose my job if I go to prison again. The school headmistress is obviously in support of what we're doing but she can only take it so far. I still feel bad leaving her without a teacher for a month last time and even though my pay was docked until I went back in January, I know she won't tolerate me being absent again.'

'Agreed.' Although Clementine returned to school in the New Year, I was also worried she wasn't back to her full health. She still wasn't able to eat much, or keep some things down and the pain in her throat and stomach hadn't gone completely. Another stint in prison would weaken her further.

The attacks began in a coordinated approach on the first day of March 1912. Women spread across the West End of London, targeting important public buildings. Clementine and I took part in smashing windows before melting away into the busy crowds at the end of the working day. We later heard that Mrs Pankhurst was arrested for smashing windows at the Prime Minister's office and home on Downing Street. Windows had been smashed along Piccadilly and Regent and Oxford streets. The windows of Selfridges had been spared, since many a suffrage meeting had been held in its tea room and it sported window displays in the WSPU colours. Afterwards, over a hundred suffragettes had been arrested.

Later in the week everyone assembled in Parliament Square and listened to speeches delivered by prominent suffragettes. During the speeches, over one hundred and fifty women left the Gardenia restaurant armed with their weapons and instructions to continue the attacks that had begun a few nights earlier, but this time on shop and office windows. With Mrs Pankhurst in Holloway for two months, we had to rally the cause.

Excitement was high when we began to leave the Gardenia restaurant in small groups at different intervals, so as not to arouse suspicion.

Clementine and I were almost at our target on The Strand when I heard a soft voice call our names. I peered into the shadows. It was Esther.

'What are you doing here?' asked Clementine.

'Don't do it tonight,' Esther said in a low voice. 'Special Branch have been watching the Gardenia for hours. No doubt everyone has been followed.'

My heart began to race as I looked around me, but I couldn't see anyone behaving suspiciously.

Esther pulled us further into the shadows. 'I've been watching out for you. When you left the Gardenia, I saw the men following. I had an idea of where you might be going and waited here, hoping I wouldn't miss you.'

'But they'll arrest us anyway,' said Clementine. 'Especially when they find hammers on us.'

'Not if we leave separately.'

'No,' I replied vehemently. 'We are not separating. That's how we got into trouble last time.'

Esther stared into the distance for a moment. 'They're remaining out of sight behind that fountain. What if we jump into one of the taxi cabs up ahead before they know what we're doing?'

We nodded and raced along the pavement to the row of taxi cabs. The three of us climbed into the first and, as it pulled away from the kerb, I looked out the window to see two men in plain clothes emerge from behind the fountain and rush towards us. One of them was Sykes.

'Go,' I yelled to the driver, my head pounding in time to my heart. The motor car picked up speed and only once the men disappeared from view, did I release the breath I'd been holding. I grasped Clementine's and Esther's hands and found that they were shaking as much as me. Then I burst out laughing, in relief and disbelief.

'We beat them,' I exclaimed. 'Thanks to you, Esther.'

'I couldn't let the two of you get yourselves into trouble,' she said with a grin. 'But I have to admit it was a rush, getting away from them. I'm only glad I got there in time.'

'Do you remember when we came to London all together and stood on the Tower Bridge and were chased away by the authorities?' I asked.

'How can I forget?' replied Clementine softly. 'That trip to London made me realise that I wanted to live here someday.'

'And here you are,' said Esther, clasping her hand.

'When we were at the theatre that night, I remember thinking how progressive London was and dreaming about the three of us living and working here,' I said.

'We're back together after all these years,' said Clementine. 'And still running amok.'

'But this time, things are more serious.' Esther's face was shadowed with worry.

I nodded. 'It could have turned bad if you weren't there tonight, Esther. Thank you.'

'She's our guardian angel,' said Clementine, kissing Esther's hand.

'I have an idea,' I said. 'Let's put the WSPU colours up on the Tower Bridge in memory of that day.' I looked into their faces under the light of the street lamps as we passed them. Both were open with excitement after our close call. 'Let's relive the sense of freedom we had. If we can hang on to that hope and optimism, we can overcome any challenges we face.'

'Let's defy the patriarchy and the bureaucracy, you mean,' said Clementine with a harsh laugh.

'Yes, let's tell the world that we'll never submit. We'll beat them, no matter what,' I said, feeling emboldened. 'Driver, to the Tower Bridge, please.'

A few days later, Esther came home distraught.

'I've received a note at work,' she said, thrusting a sheet of paper out in her shaking hand for us to see.

> You might think that you have evaded us. We are watching you and we know about your unnatural behaviour. Make no mistake, you will be prosecuted under the full extent of the

law for criminal activities that you support. Your life and that of your co-conspirators will be ruined.

'Why you?' I asked. 'You haven't done anything wrong.'

'I helped you and Clem get away,' Esther said, her voice hoarse. Tears filled her eyes. 'But I'm worried it's more than that. What if they know about Clem and me?'

Clementine shook her head. 'How could they? We've both been so careful in public and our relationship isn't illegal anyway.'

Esther raised her hands in despair. 'But what else can it mean? The only reason our relationship isn't illegal is because male lawmakers want to pretend women like us don't exist. Heaven forbid respectable women should even wonder about that possibility and turn away from their men,' she said bitterly. 'But if it became public knowledge, there would be consequences.' She took Clementine's hands. 'You'd likely lose your job and we'd lose our respectable standing in society.'

'And we've worked hard to earn respect as women in our work and our community,' said Clementine.

'But people aren't ready for a relationship like ours,' said Esther softly.

I shook my head. 'I don't understand why this policeman and Special Branch would use your relationship to threaten you?'

'Maybe to stop us. If we continue to speak about their harassment, especially by him, perhaps they'll use that against us,' said Esther.

'You know how they are. They stick together and close ranks. But we won't remain silent,' growled Clementine.

'I know you're not worried about yourself. But what if this hurts Esther?' I asked.

Clementine glared at me, distress and anger in her eyes, then strode from the room.

Not long after, we learnt that one hundred and twenty-six women were to stand trial along with Emmeline Pethick-Lawrence and her husband, who had been arrested after a raid on Clement's Inn, even though they hadn't been involved in the campaign. Christabel Pankhurst had managed to flee.

But when the Conciliation Bill failed later that month, I felt the hope I'd harboured begin to fade.

'Thirteen Labour ministers didn't make the session in Commons because of the unrest caused by the coal strike. We lost by fourteen votes,' said Esther, returning from Parliament.

I exhaled sharply. It had been so close. We'd proven we had courage, determination and resilience, but it still wasn't enough.

I received a letter from Millicent Fawcett a few weeks later, enclosed with her birthday card to Annie.

> April 1912
>
> My dear Hannah,
>
> I remembered that Annie's birthday is soon and I write to send my birthday wishes to her. She'll be seventeen, if I recall correctly. I don't know where the years have gone. But I suppose it makes me an old lady! Please give her my love and all my best for the year ahead.

I smiled. Mrs Fawcett and I had known each other for nearly twenty years now and she never forgot any of the children's birthdays, despite the ridiculously busy schedule I knew she kept. I stayed abreast of the activities of the NUWSS, which had grown in size and complexity since its early days. Although the number of organisers was increasing, Mrs Fawcett was still its leader and president.

> It's a terrible disappointment to see the defeat of the Conciliation Bill. After all the years we've been involved in this parliamentary process, I'm still utterly appalled by the lengths politicians will go to, to pervert any matter that will not benefit their own aims. Rumours and insinuations once made public always take on a malevolent life of their own. In the end, our friends in Parliament abandoned us because of fear about their own agendas.
>
> All we can do now is turn our attention to the Manhood Suffrage Bill with the fervent hope that one of the women's suffrage amendments will be added. But I pray that the militant actions of the suffragettes don't sway public opinion against our cause and give politicians an excuse not to honour their promises. Prime Minister Asquith is not a friend of women's suffrage.

Power plays had always involved fear: find what was most important to a person and make it their weakness. The note to Esther was proof of that. Bullying, thuggery and stand-over tactics, disguised in words and layers of meaning; these were games played by men who were in positions of power and should know better. What hope did any of us have if we refused to play their game?

I admired Mrs Fawcett for her tenacity but the time of hoping that talking and petitions would be enough had passed. I believed that the government would only consider our cause seriously if we made them uncomfortable enough to be forced to do something about it. Deeds not words, indeed.

A few days later, everyone was breakfasting around the table when I opened the *Daily Mail*.

'Something's happened to the *Titanic*,' I said.

'What?' Esther was by my side in an instant. She had been following the launch and maiden voyage of the largest passenger vessel in the world, because it used the steam turbine invented by Charles and Katharine Parsons. Esther and her father had corresponded with them twenty years earlier while working on making the steam engines in farm machinery more efficient.

I clapped my hand over my mouth in horror, unable to believe what I was reading. 'It collided with an iceberg on Sunday night, somewhere in the Atlantic Ocean,' I said finally, scanning the story for more details.

'That's more than a day ago,' said Clementine from across the table.

'What's happened to the people on board?' asked Annie, her eyes huge with the thought of all those people stranded in the middle of the ocean.

'It says that the *Titanic* is still afloat and no lives have been lost. But other ships in the area are steaming towards the location to help it and save the passengers.'

'The ship sent a call for help from its wireless installation,' said Esther, reading over my shoulder. 'The paper is calling this the first reporting of an international news story with wireless messages sent to London and New York.'

'Thank goodness. The story could have been so much worse,' I said, thinking about Richard and his trip home to London soon.

But the following morning, the newspaper reported the unimaginable. I stared in disbelief at the headlines shouting that the *Titanic* had sunk.

'But it was supposed to be unsinkable,' said Esther, aghast.

'More than fifteen hundred people are missing.'

'There were two thousand, three hundred and fifty-eight on board,' said Clementine, reading alongside me. 'And only twenty lifeboats were picked up.'

I blinked as I continued to read, unable to believe what I was seeing. The magnitude of such a disaster was hard to comprehend. 'Apparently it didn't carry enough lifeboats for all the passengers. Twenty was all they had.'

'That's unconscionable,' said Clementine, shaking her head. 'Somebody will have to be held accountable.'

'Nobody could survive in those icy waters. Those poor people never had a chance.' Esther's voice was shaky.

'I wonder if everyone would have been rescued if they'd had enough boats,' I said, looking through the lists of the missing. They were mainly men: wealthy businessmen from New York; young newlyweds; passengers in first and second class and steerage as well as the crew.

Then my eye caught another story, reporting the escalation in the naval race between Germany and Britain and how the good relationship between cousin-kings had begun to fracture. My skin prickled with disquiet. Was the world rushing headlong into its future with little heed to the consequences of its actions? Men in power led the dance of diplomacy, and with Europe so divided between its alliances, ordinary people like me could only watch the rise in tension between nations with dread, and each of the signs that pointed to disaster. I shivered. It felt that we were on a precipice: one wrong move could send us all into chaos.

24

May 1912

Dear Mama,

Football has finished for the season. Our team played well but we came third on the table. It's a shame the high school doesn't have a football team, but Uncle David said he'll help me write to football clubs in London before I come. I still have a few months before I have to talk to them. Tommy will probably play in Newcastle next season. So, all of us will be gone from Ebberfield. I will miss Oliver and Jenny and Tommy too but I'm looking forward to London and all the exciting opportunities. Aunt Esther has even promised to show me her work with machines at the Royal Institute.

Your loving son,

William

I clutched the letter to my chest and smiled. I couldn't wait for William to join us in London. My family was slowly coming back together. All I needed was for Tommy to be with us. But I doubted that would ever happen unless I got the pub back.

Richard had returned from South Africa. I reread the last letter he had sent me.

The pneumonia outbreak has now been contained. I'm coming home to relieve Dr Williams, of whom I've asked enough, so he can retire. I'll return to the practice and continue the research at St Mary's into bacteria and

> pathogens. I have so much to tell you about Africa. It's a fascinating country and the different tribespeople have ancient traditions and wisdom that I'd love to explore further.

Richard had written to me regularly while he'd been away, with stories about the African people. He had never mentioned our last visit and his courtesy allowed me to consider how I felt about him from a distance. We were good friends, we had much in common with how we viewed the world and it was in that way that I came to realise I was attracted to him. Clementine and Esther kept reminding me that I deserved happiness, pulling me up every time I thought of the pub, of the boys and my sisters' words, until I began to wonder what being happy might look like for me now.

But now Richard was home and coming to visit and I was anxious and nervous as well as excited to see him. Clementine and Esther had made sure they were out, taking Annie with them, despite my pleas for them to stay.

Nearly a year had passed since his last visit and it took some adjustment to get used to each other again. I made us tea and served Mama's lemon slice to get us through the pleasantries. But soon we were settled in the parlour and I was engrossed in his stories of Africa, the wild countryside, the harsh terrain of the Rand gold mines and the extraordinary history and culture of the African people.

'What about the pneumonia? Did you find what caused it?' I asked.

Richard nodded. 'The miners who tended to contract it were often novices and migrant workers from the tropical north. They're more susceptible to the high altitude and cold winters around Johannesburg, especially after leaving the hot humid mines in damp or wet or just inadequate clothing.'

'It's the same as anywhere then? Commonsense measures that we tell parents to use with their children.'

Richard laughed shortly. 'You're exactly right.'

'It's nearly dark,' I said in surprise, as I looked out the window at the fading light. 'We've been talking all afternoon.'

'Time flies when you're having fun,' Richard said, his face alight with pleasure. 'I've so enjoyed our conversation. I can't talk like this with anyone else.'

I nodded, returning his smile. 'Me too.'

'I should go,' he said.

My stomach dropped. I didn't want him to leave. 'How long are you staying in London?'

'I'll go to Ebberfield tomorrow,' he said, fiddling with his cuff.

We were interrupted by the front door opening and Annie calling out, 'We're home and we've brought dinner.' She rushed into the hallway. 'How can you see in here?' she exclaimed, turning on the electric lights.

Richard and I blinked in the light and smiled at each other.

'Will you stay?' I asked.

He stood. 'Not this time. I've had a long day. But I'll call in before I leave for Ebberfield, if you have any letters for the boys.'

'Thank you, Richard. That will be wonderful.' I joined him at the door. 'It looks like I'm spending the evening writing then.'

He took my hand and brought it to his lips. 'Until then.'

That night I dreamed of Roger again. He was sitting on the edge of my bed, caressing my cheek, smoothing the hair from my face as he often had. I tried to open my eyes but I couldn't.

'Rest now,' he murmured. 'You have a lot of work ahead of you.'

'I don't want to fight anymore … I'm so tired,' I mumbled as sleep drew me back towards oblivion.

'Remember what you're fighting for …' My eyes flew open at his words, but a dark shadow loomed behind him and I shrank back in fear. 'Don't be afraid. You can find what you're looking for …' The shadow coalesced into an image of myself, laughing with joy, before it dissipated. 'Most of all, be happy …' He kissed me gently on the lips and was gone.

I woke and reached out but the bed beside me was empty. The memory of Roger's kiss still lingered on my lips. I squeezed my eyes shut and wished myself back to sleep, so I could return to my dream and have Roger with me just a little longer.

But sleep refused to come. Instead, tears fell, hot and salty against my skin and lips. I felt at once comforted by his presence and bereft all over again.

'Oh, Roger,' I whispered. 'I miss you so much.'

Ever since my visit to Ebberfield for Christmas, William's belief that Roger was with him had stayed with me. I'd felt Roger's presence after he died but as the days turned to weeks and months, the feeling faded. Maybe my dreams were the only way I could reach him now. Or perhaps it was my own self reminding me what I already knew.

But the message of my dream was clear as day. I had to keep fighting for what was important to me. My family, the pub, and the vote for women: but I also had to find myself again and find happiness in my life.

I wiped the dampness from my face with a shuddering breath. I was doing the best that I could. I'd punished myself enough for what had happened. Clementine and Esther were right. I deserved to be happy. And the only way I could do that was to leave the life I'd had with Roger behind. It was time to shed my skin.

*

I found reading the WSPU newspaper, *The Suffragette*, was a good way to keep up to date with all the WSPU activity. Mrs Pankhurst was released from Holloway in June after she became unwell from her hunger strike. She had not been forcibly fed but the newspaper reported that many had been with a new level of aggression. The second reading of the Government Reform Bill went ahead in July, around the time the secret arson campaign had been launched, orchestrated by Christabel Pankhurst from Paris, where her mother was visiting her, and organised and carried out by Annie Kenney. I read with consternation how homes of anti-suffrage ministers had been attacked and there had been assaults on pillar boxes. Incendiary devices had been used at the GPO, while a bomb had been planted in the Home Secretary's office, which had thankfully been discovered. Most distressing of all, the Theatre Royal in Dublin had been bombed during a performance that the Prime Minister had been attending. Thank God he escaped without harm.

Finally, the time had arrived to bring William to live with us in London. I'd taken the train to Ebberfield and was now helping him pack his things.

'We'll have to go shopping for some new clothes in London,' I said holding up a pair of his trousers. 'You've grown since Christmas.' He was taller than me now and I was glad I had savings put away for things like this.

William grinned. 'Who knows Mama? I might end up being taller than Tommy.'

I smiled. 'Yes, you might.' I packed his folded clothes into a suitcase. 'Is Tommy coming back with us to London for a few days? I have great plans to celebrate his birthday and show you both around.' He was turning sixteen, a big milestone.

He frowned, a dubious expression on his face. 'I don't know Mama. Every time I ask him, he changes the subject.' He dropped onto the bed. 'He's not happy about me leaving. But he's going to Newcastle soon with Uncle David to talk to the football club about starting with them. He knows I can't stay here.'

I kissed the top of William's head. 'Don't worry about Tommy. He's just going to miss you.' I sat beside him and put my arm around him. 'Maybe with all of us in London, he might join us after the football season.'

After dinner that evening, I pulled Tommy aside in Oliver and William's room. Jenny had kindly invited friends and family to farewell William, but Tommy had been quiet, almost to the point of being morose.

'Will you come back to London with us tomorrow?' I asked him. 'So we can celebrate your birthday?'

'You know I can't,' he snapped. 'We have to prepare for the agricultural show. But I suppose you don't think about things like that now you're in London.'

'Tommy!' I chided gently, although his words cut me. 'I know you're going to miss William but that's unfair.' I was glad we were alone.

'Unfair?' He stared at me incredulous. 'What you're doing is unfair. Taking William to London, away from his friends and everything he's ever known.'

I felt the anger begin to rise in me like a rolling wave of heat. *Not this again.* I took a deep breath, determined not to lose my patience with him. 'You know why he has to come to London. I wanted you all together to begin with. But William wanted to stay until he'd finished elementary school so he could be near you.'

'I don't know why you had to go to London in the first place. You could have stayed here if you wanted us to be together. But you chose to go, to leave us behind, for the life of a suffragette.' He shook his head. 'I've never been more embarrassed, my mother protesting on the streets. Next, I'll hear that you're in prison. Dadda would roll over in his grave.'

White-hot fury rose within me and I slapped him across the face. 'Don't you dare! Don't *ever* talk like that to me again. I've worked all my life to improve the lives of women and children, for you and your brother and for Annie. I wanted you to grow up in a better world where there is equality for all. Your father always supported me in that work, and I sure as hell brought you up with those same values.' I didn't raise him to be like this. *Where did I go wrong?*

Tommy touched his face, red from the imprint of my hand. 'And look where it's got you. Nothing to show for it, no vote for women. All you've done is made life worse for us. If that's what the suffrage cause has done, then I'm against it. Sacrificing your family for an unachievable dream.'

He may as well have hit me back. I drew in a long shaky breath, shocked by his vitriol and his hurtful words. I stared into his beautiful face, but his expression was defiant and held not one ounce of regret. He was hurting, that much I knew, but I'd given him every opportunity to join us in London. If I kept badgering him, I'd push him away altogether. Staying was his choice, one I thought would make him happy, but maybe he had to work out for himself what he wanted.

'I'm glad I know how you feel now, Tommy,' I said quietly. 'But remember that I love you and want nothing more than for you to join us. You know where I am if you want to talk.' I forced myself to turn and walk from the room, when all I wanted to do was hold him tight, until he let his tears flow.

I was grateful that Richard made conversation with William as we drove back to London the following day. I was a little quiet but William barely noticed, he was that excited. But Richard had noticed, frowning in my direction periodically, at my silence when I would normally add to the discussion. Tommy had barely spoken to me before we left, pecking me briefly on the cheek, without a hug. But as we pulled up to the Notting Hill terrace, my own joy that William was finally with us, overtook my sadness.

'We've made up a room,' I said, enthusiastically. 'A room all to yourself, with a desk to study at. The window looks over the back garden. Annie stayed behind to finish off the matching curtains and bedcover we made you.'

But he was already out of the car and before he could knock on the front door, Annie, Clementine and Esther were on the porch hugging and kissing him.

'Welcome home, my beautiful boy,' I said, as we walked inside.

'Come in here,' said Annie, taking his arm.

William stopped at the parlour door. 'For me?' he asked. On the wall was the banner we'd all made: *WELCOME HOME WILLIAM* with streamers and a vase of flowers on the table.

'Hope you're hungry,' said Clem. 'We have sandwiches, cake and Cadbury chocolate bars!'

William's eyes widened. 'I'm starving.' We all burst out laughing.

I hugged him tight. 'I'm so happy you're here,' I whispered. 'I hope you'll be happy too.' I'd been waiting for this day for so long. Our family was almost back together.

In October the WSPU offices moved to Lincoln Inn's House from Clement's Inn, where the Pethick-Lawrences had lived for some years. I was shocked to hear that Emmeline Pethick-Lawrence and her husband had been expelled from the WSPU after returning from recuperating abroad after their prison sentence, but the official line for the move of the WSPU's office was that we needed more room.

'Do you know what happened, Clem?' I asked as I cut into the lemon slice I'd made for afternoon tea. William was still adjusting to school and life in London, missing Tommy, Oliver and his friends in Ebberfield and the slice was my way of easing his difficulty.

'The talk at the meeting of the East London Federation was that the Pethick-Lawrences don't agree with the escalation of our militancy.'

I nodded. 'It's one thing to attack property, which the government seems to value above all, but another to threaten lives. What if people had been maimed or killed by those attacks?' I paused. 'But window smashing doesn't seem to have galvanised Parliament to action. There's been no further progress with the Manhood Suffrage Bill nor our amendments during this last session.'

'It's a difficult balance, I know,' Clementine said, 'but no wonder so many are pulling away from the WSPU, especially when those who disagree are expelled, despite having done so much for the organisation. Sylvia Pankhurst and her sister Adela disagree with these new methods too. The WSPU is putting working women like the ones in the East London Federation at terrible risk. They can't afford to go to prison and if they're convicted of crimes of assault or bodily harm, their sentences will be even longer. Rather than recruit them to the WSPU, Sylvia believes that we should do more to help solve poverty, low pay and harsh working conditions in the sweated industries. These problems are more immediate to the working women than the parliamentary vote for women. And I think she's right. During the first week of the recruitment campaign, we were ridiculed and laughed at by locals, and even had fish heads thrown at us.'

I shook my head. 'Any division in the organisation isn't a good sign. We need unity. Millicent Fawcett has always maintained that unity gives us strength against the opposition we face. As it is, the NUWSS and WSPU have already broken ties and I'm worried that dissension within the ranks will weaken the effect of what we're trying to do.'

'We'll persevere. But time will tell,' she said.

Richard visited London and took me to dinner at one of the grill rooms, where we enjoyed steak and chops. Afterwards we went to a dance hall, where I learnt that Richard was a good dancer. He guided me around the floor with ease, making me feel comfortable with my lack of skill, until I was breathless with the whirls and turns of the variations of the waltz.

'I had a wonderful time,' I said, as we arrived back at Notting Hill.

'So did I.' Richard's smile lit up his face. 'There's so much to do in London and I enjoyed spoiling you.' He took my hand and brought it to his lips. 'I should go.'

'Don't go,' I said in a rush, butterflies fluttering in my belly. 'It's so late. Esther has made a room up for you and tomorrow you can join us for breakfast.'

I would let this night take its own course. But it was a big step for me and I was nervous. I had never been with any man other than Roger. I wasn't young anymore and my body had changed since having the children. I wasn't sure how experienced Richard was as a lover or how attractive he would find me. But I wanted this again, this intimacy – I needed it.

I was a grown woman, a widow, and I trusted Richard to be gentle with my feelings and discreet. The guilt and shame I carried about not being a good mother were only making me miserable. I deserved love.

'If you're sure,' he whispered. I saw in his eyes a yearning that matched my own.

I nodded and took his hand, leading him into the sleeping house and up the stairs to the top-floor guest bedroom. Then, before he could say anything, I kissed him. His arms were around me in an instant. I threaded my fingers through his hair, surprisingly soft, as the kiss deepened. I yielded to him as we slowly undressed each other, our exploration of each other's body punctuated by kisses.

'I love you, Hannah,' whispered Richard as he lay above me.

He wasn't Roger, he never would be, but I knew that what I had with Richard was something different and just as enduring.

I gave myself to him.

25

Victory at last! Tommy visited the Notting Hill terrace for Christmas, and I thought my heart would explode to see my family reunited in London. Tommy couldn't stop talking about football and Newcastle, and he seemed lighter. How it had torn at me to put him on the train home.

It was a cold and miserable night in January 1913 when Clementine, Esther, Marjorie and I arrived at a packed Holborn Hall for a special WSPU meeting. I'd left William at home with Annie. He was settling into life in London, enjoying high school and training with Chelsea FC, although he was still too young to play with them. But he missed Tommy.

Mrs Pankhurst had called the meeting to discuss the withdrawal of the Manhood Suffrage Bill on a technicality by the Speaker of the House before it even made it to the floor of Commons. It was Marjorie's first meeting as a fee-paying member. She'd finally come to the realisation that we weren't getting anywhere with a women's suffrage bill and had little faith in parliamentary process.

'A new era of militancy begins today,' Mrs Pankhurst announced over the murmurs of the crowd. 'Unless Mr Lloyd George and the other ministers who made promises resign tomorrow, we will resume our fight. We have stern business to attend to and will continue to target property. But we are not men who give no thought to human life in times of war.

We must always remember that human life is sacred and shall remain close to our hearts.'

'Guerilla warfare,' said Clementine, nodding in satisfaction. 'Just like Garibaldi did to bring freedom to all of Italy.'

'How do you mean?' asked Esther. Clementine had been overjoyed when Esther had joined the meeting but I think her attendance was to better understand Clementine's position and possibly to protect her. Forewarned was to be forearmed.

'We're facing an enemy with all the power and resources at their disposal while we have little. We'll use wit rather than force, maximum chaos with minimum effort, and take our enemies by surprise,' explained Clementine.

'But damaging innocent people's property?'

'When people have had enough of our tactics and the monetary cost to them, they'll have no choice but to force the government to make it stop. And the only way to make it stop will be to give women the vote. Because we will never stop until we get it.'

'They've betrayed everything they promised,' I said. 'We have to do all we can to make them see the injustices that all women suffer. If our petitions and words don't work, we have to put our bodies on the line, because we have nothing else. War it is.'

In the following months, after a deputation of women were refused entrance to Parliament to see Mr Lloyd George, the smashing of windows began at the Home Office, Treasury and other government buildings, as well as nearby shops. Mrs Drummond and Sylvia Pankhurst were arrested immediately, along with twenty-eight other women. The campaign of arson and bombings escalated and there was no doubt who had carried out such attacks when, each week, pages were devoted to coverage in *The Suffragette*.

Clementine, Marjorie and I met with the WSPU at Selfridges

tea rooms one afternoon in April. It would be more difficult to be under surveillance here, hiding in plain sight. We were especially vigilant, after the threats we'd received in the notes.

'We have codes,' said one of the organisers, handing sheets to each of us. 'This is the only way we will communicate about any of our campaign details.'

I looked at the page. 'Mixture' meant 'Letter follows, do nothing until you hear again'; 'Fox' was 'Are you prepared for arrest?'; 'Thistle' was 'Asquith'; 'F' was 'Mrs Pankhurst'; 'Almonds' was 'Public meeting'; and 'Gatwick' was 'Caxton Hall'.

The organiser leant forward. 'Make sure nobody gets a hold of this list. Hide it in a safe place.'

'It's very clandestine,' I whispered to Clementine.

'Hopefully we're one step ahead of Special Branch,' she replied.

'What do you think we'll be asked to do?' asked Marjorie.

'It will be arson,' said Clementine.

Marjorie looked shocked. 'What if we hurt someone?'

'We won't,' I said. 'We won't put anyone at risk.'

'That's right,' said Clementine. 'We only target buildings that are empty.'

'Not that it helped Mrs Pankhurst,' I said.

But outrage followed Mrs Pankhurst's conviction and sentencing with a series of more high-profile bombings in public places.

'A bomb was discovered outside the Bank of England last night,' said Esther, reading the newspaper in the parlour, only days later. She shook her head. 'Thankfully it was defused by a police officer.'

'It didn't go off,' said Clementine in annoyance, stubbing out her cigarette. 'It was supposed to go off at midnight when nobody was there.'

'You knew about this?' asked Esther.

Clementine nodded. 'I know the women who made it using a milk tin and the mechanism from a watch. Very clever, really.' I frowned at Clem's flippant attitude and stopped the letter I was writing to Jane.

'Bombs. Is this how low the WSPU have stooped?' Esther shook with anger.

'Men use bombs in their wars and call their acts heroic,' said Clementine hotly. 'Why shouldn't women?'

But not all attacks went to plan. The bombs became increasingly dangerous due to the use of nitroglycerin, and were responsible for unexpected or unintended deaths, especially among postal workers.

'I thought we agreed we wouldn't hurt anyone,' I said softly. 'Bombs are unpredictable. They can go off unexpectedly and maim innocent people.' I knew that I couldn't step over that line. 'Please don't get involved in bombs, Clem. Neither of us wants to be responsible for hurting or killing someone. We want to make people's lives better, not worse.'

Clementine's lips were pressed together in determination or obstinacy, I wasn't sure which. She turned away, tears in her eyes. I worried about her. Her health hadn't been the same since her time in prison. She was still troubled with periodic pain in her stomach and throat, unable to eat much when it was bad and she was smoking more.

'Hannah's right,' said Esther. 'It's a line none of us wants to cross. It's terrorism, and you could be charged with murder if someone is killed. Not to mention that planting a bomb is a hangable offence.'

'We can continue our fight by hitting the men in power where it hurts them but not like this,' I said. 'We have to draw the line at what's acceptable.'

Clementine and I received instructions while we were at the home of one of the WSPU members. Our new target was a local golf club.

'We'll meet at two o'clock in the morning,' said the organiser as we left in groups of two or three, careful to evade those who might be watching us.

On the chosen night, Clem and I were picked up from a nearby park in the motor car of one of the members.

'Do we have everything?' asked the driver as we stopped outside the golf course. The clubhouse was dark.

'Garden trowels and acid,' said a woman, handing supplies to us.

'You each know what to do,' said the driver.

We left in pairs. Clementine and I made our way towards the greens, the light from a small torch showing us the way. I squinted into the inky blackness, imagining police behind every bush or tree but nobody was there. We couldn't afford to be arrested and sent to prison. We'd both lose our jobs and I could say goodbye to ever running the pub. I'd shame the children if I was caught and Tommy would never speak to me again.

'Here?' whispered Clementine, shining the light on a patch of neat lawn.

I checked the map and nodded, dropping to my knees. 'For women everywhere,' I whispered back as I plunged my trowel into the dirt, slicing a section of the grass.

We worked hurriedly, digging up the lawn, my ears straining as we listened for every sound in the darkness that surrounded us, our ragged breath amplified in the silence.

Soon we'd completed our task and Clementine shone the light on our handiwork: *Votes for Women* carved into the turf in letters two feet long.

'Well, they won't miss it,' I said. 'And it will disrupt their play.' I felt elated. We'd done it without being followed or harassed.

'That it will,' said Clementine. 'But we have one more job to do.' She lifted the bottles she'd been carrying.

We trudged through the darkness to the designated spot. Clementine handed me a bottle – acid. 'Hold your breath,' she whispered. I nodded. We didn't want to breathe in the fumes.

I poured the liquid onto the grass in a thin but steady stream while Clementine did the same nearby. My nerves had dissipated by now and I felt quite emboldened by my work.

'What did you write?' I asked when we were finished.

'"Votes or War",' she said. 'And you?'

'"Justice before Sport". They should get the message,' I said with grim satisfaction.

'I'd love to see their smug faces when they see this.'

A shout rent the darkness and, in the distance, I could see the light from torches moving quickly through the night. Someone had discovered our work. I prayed that nobody had been apprehended.

I grabbed Clementine's arm. 'We've got to go.' We knew what to do and dropped the bottles and trowels on the ground. We didn't want to be caught with evidence. We hitched our skirts up and ran across the golf course, the little torch showing us the way towards the road where the motor car was waiting to pick us up. I grasped Clementine's hand as we skirted the edge of the trees. I wasn't going to lose her again.

'Wait,' I whispered when the motor car came into view. Everything looked quiet and we watched as women made their way back, quickly getting in. 'Let's go.'

We ran as fast as we could to the motor car and climbed in.

I exhaled sharply as we sped away from the golf course, still squeezing Clementine's hand. 'We did it!' I exclaimed.

She laughed with abandon. 'They won't know what's hit them when they come in tomorrow.'

'That'll dampen their mood,' said another woman, laughing heartily.

'Votes for women!' I shouted in jubilation.

26

It feels as though the entire world is breaking apart. The Balkan League is at war against the Ottomans. Serbia, Bulgaria, Montenegro and Greece want to drive the Ottomans out of Europe and the Balkans and assert their independence as nations. What lengths will empires go to, to hang on to power?

'More tea?' asked Richard.

We were still in bed. I'd brought up tea and biscuits earlier before the children were up. We wanted to be discreet in front of them and Esther had thoughtfully taken Annie and William back to the Science Museum to visit a new exhibition, after William's excitement when we'd viewed the machines and scientific instruments a month earlier. I hadn't seen Richard since Christmas and I'd missed him. But now he was in London for a week to help Almroth in the lab at St Mary's and we had the morning together. I cherished every minute I had with him.

I held out my cup. 'I could get used to this,' I said. Richard smiled. 'I have to write back to Sarah soon, she's been pressuring me to move north. She means well but she's very stubborn.' Since losing Mary, I had felt myself softening with Sarah – she would never replace Mama, but I knew she only wanted to watch out for me.

Richard took my hand in his. 'A family trait?' he asked. I huffed a laugh and batted his hand away. 'That's what I love about you,' he continued, 'your fire and passion. And if your sister doesn't understand you by now, understand what you're doing here in London, then you can't worry about that. Maybe she never will.'

Heat rose within me and a glow rested in my chest. 'Thank you, Richard. You always know just what to say.' Until that moment, I hadn't realised that I'd always known what I had to do within myself, all along. Even the impossible decisions. Everything I did came from love.

It was a mild summer day, and Clementine paced the parlour with a cigarette in her hand. I turned back to my letter.

> June 1913
>
> Dear Alice,
>
> We are a very sombre household. One of the suffragettes Clementine was in prison with and deeply admired, Emily Davison, has died. She was knocked over by the King's horse at the Derby and terribly injured. You may have seen it in the newspapers. Clementine is terribly upset as you can imagine. We all are. Not a soul knew she was there or what possessed her to put herself in the path of oncoming horses when she stepped out in front of the King's horse during the race, causing the horse to fall and the jockey to be thrown. But we heard that she had a scarf in the suffragette colours around her waist as she went out onto the field and a couple of WSPU flags in her coat ...

I looked up as Esther shuffled in, her cheeks a mottled red. 'You're not ready yet? We need to leave soon for the funeral,' she said to Clementine, wiping her face. The whole household was attending to support Clementine.

Clementine nodded mutely and departed the room like a wraith. Esther turned to me.

'Do you think Emily sacrificed herself for the cause? The WSPU is calling her a martyr,' she whispered then looked back over her shoulder.

I sighed, rubbing my eyes. 'I don't know. She had a return train ticket in her pocket. Did something go terribly wrong? Why would she put herself in harm's way if not for the cause?'

'But is this kind of sacrifice a step too far? When human life is taken, surely we have to reassess what we're prepared to do to achieve our aims.' Esther began to pace restlessly in Clementine's footsteps and then stopped short, meeting my gaze. 'I'll always support you and Clem in your choice to become WSPU members, but is this death going too far?' she asked quietly.

Emily's death was confronting, not just because a life had been lost, but because of the lengths a suffragette had gone to, to make the government take our cause seriously. What else did a woman have but her own life and her own body to make a statement?

'Is it acceptable if it makes a difference to women getting the vote?' I paused. 'I really don't know.'

The massive funeral procession was an impressive sight, thousands of union members dressed in white, purple or black with our WSPU sashes and many in black armbands. We walked to the beat of the funeral march that our band played, one of eleven groups, each with a captain and band. We were all in white and carried white lilies. Other groups in black carried purple irises and those wearing purple carried laurel wreaths and red peonies.

'She was very loved,' said Clementine, wiping away her tears with a gloved hand. 'She dedicated her life to the movement.'

I nodded. *Even in death.* The streets were lined with onlookers, there to witness the spectacle, and every single one of them could hardly fail to know our cause. And then there was the press attention: journalists and silent filmmakers and cameras clicking away. Part of me wondered if any of them were Special Branch.

'Everybody will know about the suffragette cause, right across the world.'

Clementine, Marjorie and I joined other WSPU members at a speech given by the Chancellor, Mr Lloyd George, a week or so later. Esther had made it clear after Emily Davison's funeral that she disapproved of any further WSPU activity, and had offered to stay home with Annie and William. Mr Lloyd George had just begun his address on a village green outside London when one of the women in the crowd stepped forward.

'When are you going to give the vote to women?' she asked.

With this cue, we all shouted, 'Votes for Women!'

Immediately the crowd surged and dozens of men rushed towards our colleague. The men caught her around the waist, dragging her away from the crowd as she screamed in terror. The men tore the hat from her head and began to beat her with sticks. We all pushed through the crowd to get to her side and I noticed the policemen do the same. Suffragettes had been subjected to violence at our demonstrations before but the idea that it had followed us to a public address by the Chancellor was unthinkable.

'Get away from her,' shouted Clementine. One man turned and punched her in the face and Clementine staggered under the blow, falling to the ground.

I screamed and forced my way to her side, where I covered her with my own body until the police officers were able to lift her.

I heard the Chancellor appeal for mercy from the crowd and begin his speech again. I couldn't believe that he would allow the beating of two unarmed women to continue.

'No!' I shouted. 'Brutalising women is unacceptable. Is there no shame?'

The crowd howled in anger and the men turned on us as one again. I heard Marjorie scream as men tore at her clothing, ripping the fabric to shreds until she was stripped to the waist. I was grabbed by the hair, my screams shrill in my ears, and dragged towards a ditch. I hit the ground hard, winding myself. Before I could recover, I was pelted with rocks and cabbage stumps, and curled into a ball to protect my face. When the crowd turned to a new diversion, I crawled away until I could climb from the ditch. I stumbled towards the cottages where I'd seen Marjorie flee to and knocked on one of the doors. 'Please, help me,' I cried.

But the door remained shut. I saw the crowd closing in on the cottages and rushed to the next one, where I spied Marjorie hiding under the stairs, covering herself in an old blanket, her eyes large with fear. I kept running, hoping the men hadn't seen her take cover, and finally found a cottage door I could open. Men rushed towards me and I went through the door and slammed it behind me, trying to latch it closed with shaky fingers.

'Open the door,' they shouted. 'If we have to break it down, it will be worse for you.'

I stifled the scream that rose to my throat, inching myself into the corner and out of sight. Terror overtook me as the blows against the door vibrated through the walls and I looked around wildly for any means of escape.

Then the noise stopped and I heard the shouts of the policemen and the sounds of them using their truncheons.

A polite knock on the door and then a voice. 'This is the police. You're safe now. Open the door.'

I looked through the window, never more relieved to see a policeman in my life, and opened the door.

'Thank you,' I said with a shaky voice as I was escorted from the building. I noticed Clementine standing nearby with Marjorie, who was wearing someone's coat. Policemen and men must have been plain-clothes officers were standing around the women to keep them safe while others dispersed the crowd. Among them was Sykes, the white-haired policeman.

I stiffened when I saw him and I wondered if our attackers were roughs employed by the police. Had this angry mob been whipped up by Special Branch to teach us a lesson, or were they here genuinely to keep the peace and keep us safe? Perhaps I'd never know, but what was clear was that many men were incensed by the suffragettes and threatened by our cause. They hated us. *How many more women had to die for the cause?*

27

> Forcible feeding is repugnant, though the new *Cat and Mouse Act*, which allows women on hunger strike to be released from prison to recover their health before returning to complete their sentence, is horrifying in its own way. I have no doubt that the escalation between the WSPU and police will continue.

The next month passed quickly with the end of the school year and our household shattered from the chaos following Emily Davison's death. It was a balm to my spirits to receive further correspondence from Mrs Fawcett. I read her letter in the sun-drenched garden, among the cheerful summer stocks, dahlias and foxgloves.

> After months of organising, our pilgrimage has begun. The NUWSS is intending to raise the profile of our cause following Emily's tragic death. You know our frustration after the failure of the various government bills and we have come to realise that a government measure backed by a united cabinet is the only way we will ever achieve women's suffrage. We must push forward by lobbying for support in a constitutional manner across non-party lines. If the government can see thousands of suffrage supporters, women and men, committed to walking from their homes to London, understanding that there is a

great desire across all sections of society for the vote for women, it will give them pause.

Our pilgrimage will end when all eight branches converge on London at our demonstration in Hyde Park on Saturday, 26 July. I hope you will join us there to support the cause close to all our hearts.

It was wonderful to see Alice, Emily and Jenny when they arrived in London after the pilgrimage. Emily and Alice had walked part of the way while Jenny joined them in London.

'I was surprised that although we were camping and walking muddy roads, I really enjoyed the experience,' said Emily. 'You should have been there with us; you would have loved it.'

'We met up with old associates and made new friends,' said Alice. 'We had banners, music and conversation, and when we stopped at villages and towns along the way to speak about our cause and collect funds, inviting others to join us, we had the most wonderful hospitality of locals.'

'Were there problems with any of the men during your travels?' I asked. I had a few fading bruises and my scalp felt tender from where I'd been dragged by the hair. Clementine's face was still discoloured. Thankfully, she hadn't broken any bones. And Marjorie had been rattled by the whole experience, which brought back memories of her abuse by her husband, Edward, more than fifteen years earlier. She told us that she'd been receiving threatening notes since she'd joined the WSPU too, and even though we hadn't received any recently, I wondered that if by association with me, she was now also a target. I admitted my worry to her and explained the trouble with Police Special Branch and the white-haired policeman who she'd seen at the Chancellor's meeting. We were all more cautious stepping out onto the street.

Emily nodded. 'Unfortunately, there were a few instances of women being roughed up by local hooligans and pelted with potatoes, rotten eggs ... even dead rats and cow pats.'

'They thought we were militant suffragettes,' said Alice, grinning wryly. 'But once we explained that we weren't suffragettes nor terrorists intent on damaging their property, they left us alone and some even came around to our cause.'

'Tommy sends his love,' said Jenny. 'He's written to you.'

'How is he?' I'd written to him after Sarah's letter, to tell him that I wanted to see him happy, whether it was to go to Newcastle or stay on the farm.

'He's restless after playing football at such a high level,' said Emily. 'But I think he missed the farm more.'

'The city isn't for him,' agreed Jenny.

'It's not just that. He hasn't settled since coming back to the farm. I think perhaps he needs new challenges and experiences.'

I nodded. Richard had said the same thing. 'Tommy has to work out what makes him happy. He's so stubborn – and nobody can tell him what he should do, least of all me.'

I worried about all of my children but William and Annie seemed settled. William was enjoying London and high school and I had high hopes he'd study at university after. Annie had just finished school and wanted to attend London University in the autumn to study Archaeology and History; the first in our family to go to university. She was living the life I had dreamed of when I was her age. I only wished Roger and my parents were here to see her achieve something that women were only able to dream of not long ago.

The following day we all joined the demonstration at Hyde Park. There were nineteen platforms for the nineteen federations of the NUWSS, with flags, banners and sashes in their colours of red, white and green. And there were tens of thousands present.

'I can't believe there are so many people,' said Annie.

'The newspapers are predicting there could be up to fifty thousand,' said Jenny.

'We gathered over forty thousand new signatures for our petitions along the way to present to the Prime Minister,' said Alice. 'And Mrs Fawcett is taking a deputation to see Mr Asquith and there will be other deputations to Members of Parliament empathetic to women's suffrage.'

I noticed the *Law-Abiding Suffragists* part of the banners and grimaced. I wondered if any of these women had ever been cornered through desperation or lost everything? It was well and good to be law abiding until your very survival was threatened. If breaking the law was the only way you could make yourself heard, then surely you were bound to break it to ensure survival of yourself and those you loved. When peaceful protest failed, when even the police targeted you instead of protected you, I believed in acts of civil disobedience, actions to raise the awareness of our cause, even acts of violence against properties.

The WSPU had lost many members from pushing the boundaries too far. Arson and bombs that risked and endangered people's lives were where many drew the line, especially when the attacks became more public and people were hurt and some even killed. After the death of Emily Davison and the violence that followed, I found that it was a line I could not, in good conscience, cross.

But I knew that Mrs Fawcett would also lobby the Prime Minister in support of the suffragettes who had suffered violence at the government's hand.

*

A note arrived at Notting Hill, addressed to me. I was sure it was from Sykes, our policeman.

> You know what happens to people who are desperate. They make stupid, selfish decisions and pay the consequences. They lose everything dear to them. Now you understand.

Cold fear coalesced in my belly. Maybe he'd seen us at the WSPU meetings or worse still, knew that we'd attacked the golf course.

Since we'd told other suffragettes about him, his harassment had quietened for a time, but he was still always there in the shadows, always watching. And I was sure he was the one who'd begun to send notes to Marjorie since she started attending WSPU meetings. What were the consequences of this latest note? What consequences had we experienced because of him and his threats? I thought for a minute and frowned. I had been beaten by him at the Black Friday demonstration, he had come to our door when Clementine was in prison and he had sent us threatening notes.

I paused, my mind turning over. How could he have been the cause of Clementine's arrest when I wasn't caught? Why would he send notes to Marjorie when she wasn't involved in any militant action?

Something didn't fit. All his threats had been empty.

Something rose in the far recesses of my mind. A condolence card someone wrote about losing everything, years ago. And I remembered a snippet of a conversation from the past, someone talking about how desperate people behaved.

I drew my breath in sharply. What if it was someone else who was trying to scare us?

I climbed the stairs to my room two at a time and pulled the other notes from the bottom drawer. I put each of them on my bed with shaky hands and compared them. The handwriting was the same for them all. I frowned, trying to remember where I'd put the tin filled with the condolence cards I'd received after Roger's death. I stood on the chair to search the back of the wardrobe until my fingers touched the tin.

I sat on the floor, turning each of the cards over, determined not to think back to that time, to stop the memories flooding back and with it, the terrible grief, loss and pain. I found the card I was looking for and held my breath while I read the message again.

> My condolences, Hannah. When you lose everything, you understand the true meaning of loss.

I compared it to the notes on the bed. The language was similar but more importantly, the handwriting was the same – the same looping 'd's and scratchy 's's pressed heavily into the paper.

I exhaled slowly, unable to believe the connection. This person had begun their harassment of me before I came to London. That meant the notes had not come from Sykes or Special Branch.

I dropped to the bed, my mind reeling with the implications. This was a personal vendetta against me and against Clementine, Esther, and now Marjorie, possibly by association. But who would do this to us, and why? I looked at the notes again and the base of my spine tingled as long-forgotten words returned to me like a spectre. I remembered the conversation now and who had spoken those words.

The two pieces of the puzzle fell into place.

It couldn't be.

I paced my room, unable to sit still, my mouth dry. Movement always helped me think and, slowly, I put a plan together.

Then I sat and wrote a letter. I needed evidence.

Later that week, Richard took me dancing at one of the supper clubs that had opened in London. An evening out was the perfect distraction while I waited for the reply to my letter. It was difficult not to tell anyone my hunch, especially Clementine and Esther. I didn't want to worry them until I was sure. So, I pushed my suspicions away for one night of enjoyment and excitement. Tango was the latest craze and after watching professionals dance, we took to the dance floor to try it for ourselves.

'You need a close and comfortable embrace,' said the teacher. 'Contact of the torso is good but the arms must remain relaxed.'

Richard and I mimicked his position. We were so close, I could feel the planes of his body and the heat between us. But I doubted the embrace would be comfortable to anybody but those who were already intimate.

'It would have been scandalous to dance so close not that long ago,' said Richard.

'Yes, but isn't it so liberating?'

Until recently, I would never have imagined dancing with anyone, let alone coming to a fashionable London club. My life had changed so dramatically since coming to London. I loved it here, and I got to be close to Annie and William while they learnt at the local high schools. It was bittersweet, to have lost the pub but to be thriving in a job I was passionate about, at the coalface of women's suffrage and with most of my children under one roof. But if I got the pub back, I would move home to Ebberfield in a heartbeat. I would build the reputation of The Ox and Plough once again, make my pub the community heart and hub it had been before I left. Tommy would be so happy.

Before long I could feel the tension between us, the slow, deliberate movements that Richard danced countering the lively steps that I tried to emulate. This was a dance I could really enjoy once I'd mastered it.

'We'll have to come again,' I said, my arm in his as we walked back to his car.

'I thought you might like it,' he said with a smile.

'Where did you learn to dance like that? You had me swooning from the start.'

He laughed. 'I'm not so good anymore. I haven't danced in years. But I learnt when I was at university. Trying to impress a girl from a good family.'

'What happened?'

Richard was quiet for a moment. 'She died of smallpox. It's what got me interested in vaccinations and prevention of infectious diseases. It was before anyone realised that the protection of the vaccine given to babies didn't last into adulthood.'

I felt chastened, struck by my own self-absorption. I'd had no idea he'd suffered loss as I had. 'My sister Beth died as a baby – that's why I've always been a passionate supporter of vaccination.'

'It brought us together too,' he said softly, putting his arm around me.

'Good things can come out of heartache and difficulty,' I agreed, kissing him.

Finally, the letter I'd been waiting for arrived. I took it up to my bedroom, ripped open the envelope and pulled out the contents.

November 1913

Dear Hannah,

Here's the document you were after. I'm not sure I understand why you want it, but I hope everything is well. I want you to know that Tommy's been looking in the newspaper for another farm job. He's been upset since finding out he wasn't picked for the team in Newcastle. David and John told him to try again next season. He's only seventeen and still so young. But he can't seem to get past it. As much as I'll hate to see him go, I think a new environment will be good for him. I hope he'll talk to you about it when you next see him at Christmas.

Sending love to you, Annie and William.

Emily

My heart ached that Tommy hadn't been chosen – it had meant so much to him. I'd have to talk to him about it, understand what he wanted from a new job. But for now, I had another problem to deal with.

I put the document on the bed and pulled out all the notes I'd received, including the card of condolence. I drew a shuddering breath as I viewed them together.

The document I'd asked Emily to send was the agreement to provide financial support for one of the Ebberfield Suffrage Society's projects twenty years earlier. It was written and signed by Edward Partridge.

The handwriting was all the same – the card, the notes and now this document. I sank to the floor as my head whirled.

The following day, I arranged to meet Amy Sanderson at Alan's Tea Rooms on Oxford Street. We were tucked in a corner, somewhere we wouldn't be disturbed. I told her about the card and the notes we'd received, showing them to her alongside the document.

'The wording of the note reminded me of Edward talking about desperate people and the decisions they made when he was a magistrate on the district session courts. That's when I first thought it might be him.'

'I'd agree with you,' she said. 'I think it's likely the threats are from him.'

I told her about Marjorie's fears of being followed and about our original beliefs that the police, especially Sykes, had been watching us and writing threatening notes in response to our suffragette work – and how Marjorie had recently begun receiving notes too. Perhaps Edward had been seeking a reaction from Clementine, Esther and me but grew bored and moved on to Marjorie. Edward could only live in the shadows for so long. Maybe he wanted me to know he'd sent the notes. He was a smart man, though I was unsure what prison had done to his psyche.

'But why would Edward target you like this?'

'Revenge for testifying against him in court?'

'But I heard from Papa that he's no threat to anyone except himself. Didn't Marjorie's detective, Mr Stevens, see him?'

I nodded. 'I'm sure that's what Edward wants everyone to think. But I believe he's still dangerous. I'll never forget the look on his face when he was taken away after the verdict. He's a man who doesn't forget.' Edward hadn't only gone to prison for manslaughter after testimony from me, Esther and Marjorie, but he'd lost everything he'd inherited from his uncle, Philip Usher, including his estate, Dalleymoor.

Amy shook her head, dubiously. 'It's been a long time since he's been released from prison. Even for a man who doesn't forget. He's been free for over ten years. Why now?'

'I've been wondering the same thing.' I stared into the distance, barely noticing the silverware and small vase of flowers on each table. I'd had enough of Edward's notes. The long shadow of his hatred had weighed upon us for long enough. 'Let's ask Mr Stevens to find him.' The only way to know what he was up to was to confront him.

I waited outside the hostel Edward stayed at in Bethnal Green. I'd told nobody that I'd gone to find him. I searched the end-of-day traffic and pedestrians for his face, or someone who resembled Mr Stevens' description of him. But by the time the street had calmed and sunset had come and gone, I started to worry that I'd missed him.

But then I spotted him, and I shivered. It had been nearly sixteen years since I'd last set eyes on him but I recognised him immediately. He was thinner, more hunched, but still walked with that arrogant swagger I'd never forget. I ran my hands over my face. What had I been thinking? He was dangerous before and there was no telling how much more treacherous he was now. But I couldn't turn back. I took a deep breath before I lost my nerve and strode up to him.

He'd seen me coming and rushed forward, grabbing my arm in a vice-like grip. 'I wouldn't think about screaming, if I were you,' he said in a low voice. 'You've found me, but I know where Marjorie and you and your lovely family live.' He squeezed my arm painfully, and I sucked in a breath. 'I gather you've come to talk, so let's go somewhere you'll be comfortable. The Old George will do.' He hauled me along with him.

'Let go of me,' I hissed. 'I'm perfectly capable of walking under my own steam.'

'Oh, no. I don't want to lose you now that I have you.'

'Let *go* of me,' I said, wrenching my arm out of his grip.

'Fine, fine. Just remember what I said.' He shoved me in front of him and pointed the way to the Old George.

We sat in the back corner of the saloon and ordered our drinks like old friends. A memory jolted through me of the days when we *had* been friends, working together on community projects in the upstairs meeting room of The Ox and Plough. The days before I knew what he truly was, a murderer, an abuser and a liar. But Edward had caused so many people such misery and pain that I would never forget.

'Did you send me a card after Roger died?' I demanded. There was no point beating around the bush.

'What card?' He sipped at his beer and I wondered if he'd found a taste for it after the good whiskey he'd been used to.

'Sending your condolences and threatening that I'd lose everything.'

'Oh, that card.' He nodded. 'It wasn't a threat, Hannah. It was a reminder from one who understands. From an old friend.'

'You can't be friends with a snake.'

He raised a nonchalant eyebrow. 'Such a terrible loss, first, your husband, and then the pub ...'

White-hot anger rushed through me, every part of me tingling with the urge to strike him. 'This is not a game, Edward. People's lives are not a game.'

He looked at me pointedly, his eyes boring into mine. 'No, they're not, are they? Maybe you should have thought of that before you decided to ruin mine.'

'You know what you did, Edward. You had to take responsibility for your actions.'

'Just as you do. You were the one who protected my wife when she left Dalleymoor and persuaded her and Esther to talk to the police about Fred Duggan. Without your interference, I would never have gone to prison.'

I shivered. I couldn't afford to lash out at him now, show him the depths of my fury. I had to remain cool and level-headed, allow him to do what he wanted more than anything in this moment, to gloat, and by breaking me down with his truth, reap the visceral reward of his revenge.

'So you decided to start harassing us with the notes.' All I needed was his confession, the truth of what he'd done.

A slow smile spread across his face. 'A lovely piece of work, I'll admit. How else can I exact retribution for what my life has become? I came out of prison a criminal, a nobody, and with nothing. All due to you and your friends.'

'You deserved to go to prison. You murdered a man, you raped Esther and beat Marjorie.' I gripped the edge of the table to steady myself and swallowed. This was not the time to lose my focus.

'I believe Esther has completely turned away from men … because of me, I suppose. And Marjorie will never be free of me. Looking behind her wherever she goes.' He smirked. 'For a clever woman, I can't believe it took you so long to put two and two together. Your involvement with the suffragettes was the perfect bait to terrorise your household and then Marjorie. And I know what you've been up to. You haven't yet been to prison but perhaps my good friends in the police force could help you with that, they'll do anything for a few dimes. I hear suffragettes are arrested and imprisoned all the time. Didn't your friend Clementine spend some time inside?' Fury swept through my body, burning me up like a raging fire. He was cruel and malicious. I stood and threw my drink in his face. 'It's you who should be worried about going to prison. I sent you there once and I'll send you there again. You won't get away with this.'

Edward's demeanour changed in an instant. Now he was red-faced and his eyes bulged with anger. 'I spent five years in prison thinking about my revenge, and I won't be going back,' he hissed. 'When I got out of prison, I wanted any information on you and your *friends*. I put the word out and I've been a patient man. Imagine my surprise when I found that Esther and Clementine were lesbians. When I heard that the brewery was looking for an underwritten loan—'

I couldn't stay a minute more, listening to his foul words, and rushed from the lounge.

I ran down the streets, looking behind me in fear, but Edward did not follow. I made my way to the high street, numb to anything but getting as far away as possible. I climbed aboard a motor bus and finally felt safe, surrounded by strangers in the pale-yellow light. I began to shake, allowing the tears to bubble up and flow freely down my cheeks.

28

When I heard that the brewery was looking for an underwritten loan ... Could it be? How could it be?

I met with Mr Stevens, Amy, Marjorie, Esther and Clementine. I'd had time for my thoughts to coalesce and galvanise, and I knew what I had to do now that it was all written down in my journal. I told them what I'd found about the notes and where I'd gone, including my conversation with Edward in the pub, and when I'd finished, it was as though everyone released the breath they'd been holding.

'My God, Hannah,' said Marjorie, leaning back in her chair, her face the colour of milk. 'You took such a risk.'

'What were you thinking, seeking Edward out?' asked Esther, incredulous.

I felt myself flush. 'I had to know for sure,' I said, shaking with the shock of retelling it. Until now, I didn't realise how much danger I'd put myself in. 'About the notes and harassment.'

Amy nodded. 'Edward was motivated by revenge and was responsible for the notes but he still has an agenda.'

'I thought he was harmless,' said Clementine. 'I can't believe he sent the notes, not Special Branch nor Sykes.'

I nodded. 'Edward indicated he has corrupt police in his pocket. I don't know if police were involved in all of it; the threats, our treatment and your arrest and imprisonment, Clem, or if Sykes had anything to do with it. Maybe he just had a bone to pick with me ...'

We all stared at each other, thoughts and theories chasing one another.

'Marjorie, have you employed the man I suggested to watch out for your safety?' asked Mr Stevens, eventually breaking the silence.

She shook her head. 'I kept a low profile when Edward was released from prison, living in fear of being found. But when I enlisted you to find him for me all those years ago, and I saw him for myself, I realised he was no threat. He might send me notes but if he was going to do anything more, he would already have been on my doorstep. He's bluffing, and I refuse to be afraid of him any longer.'

'Please consider it. This is clearly not a man to trifle with.' Mr Stevens turned to me. 'What about your children, Mrs Rainforth? Should we take his threats seriously?'

I thought for a moment. 'He's known where we all live since I came to London. Like Marjorie said, he could have done anything at any time. Having notes delivered to us is one thing but I think he's too much of a coward to act on those threats. He's a braggart and an opportunist. He practically claimed to have Clem arrested, but it's hard to say what's true and what's fiction.'

'And Esther?' asked Clementine.

'I wouldn't worry, Clem,' said Esther, softly. 'I don't think he'd dare to come to our home or approach me in public or at work.'

Mr Stevens nodded. 'But don't forget how underhanded he is. I think you should all be on your guard.'

I dropped my head. 'I'm sorry ... I've brought Edward's attention to your doors.'

'Don't apologise,' said Esther, her face a mask of ferocity. 'You didn't. We were his targets all along. Now we need to expose him for what he is. If we have to flush him out to get to the bottom of what he's done, and that means we have to be on our guard, then we will.'

'Mr Partridge knows you went looking for him out of desperation. The longer he believes he has you where he wants you, the better,' said Mr Stevens.

'There's something I've been mulling over,' I said. 'I got under Edward's skin as much as he got under mine. I don't think he meant to tell me but he knew the brewery was looking for an underwritten loan for Roger and me.'

'Maybe he wanted you to know he's had his ear to the ground for years,' said Mr Stevens.

'But what if this all started before the first note?'

Esther frowned. 'What are you saying Hannah?'

'What if Edward had something to do with influencing the loan? He was a financial advisor, after all.'

'You can't be serious,' said Clementine, her eyebrows raised in incredulity.

Amy nodded slowly. 'Perhaps ...'

'How can we find out?' asked Marjorie. 'If he's involved, it could be the thing that sends him back to prison. The evil bastard.'

Amy leant forward, her eyes shining. 'We have to find the evidence.'

Richard took Annie, William and me to Ebberfield for Christmas. I had to get to the bottom of what was going on with Tommy.

'I hear you're looking for a new job,' I said to my eldest son. We were walking to Mrs Scruton's tea rooms. I wanted to spend some time with him away from the chaos of Jenny's place with Sarah and the children.

'Did Emily tell you?' he asked, on the defensive immediately.

'She did, but only because she's worried about you. I know you're upset about not being picked for the team after a wonderful season in the squad at Newcastle but you can try again next season. The timing wasn't right and—'

'It's not that. Football is fun but it's not my life. I want to do something different, make a change.'

'What *do* you want to do?' I shrugged further into my coat. It hadn't snowed yet and the village was bitingly cold in a way that London wasn't.

'You wouldn't understand,' he muttered, pushing his hands into his pockets.

'Try me,' I said.

He shook his head. 'What's the point?'

'When I was your age, I wanted to go to teachers' college in Durham. It was far from home and part of me was afraid. I'd never left Hartlepool before but realised that teaching was my passion. I wanted to help others and I was determined to do something different with my life from everyone else I knew. Maybe you have the same adventurous spirit, that restless nature that makes you want to step into the unknown. When I left teachers' college, I wanted to teach in London, but I had to help my father with the pub because he was unwell. Then I met your father and the rest you know.'

Tommy glanced at me, curious now. 'What if I want to go further than London to follow my dream?' I breathed a sigh of relief, he was going to let me in. He had a dream.

'Well, if your dream is about following your heart and your passion in life, then I say consider it seriously. All I want is for you to be happy.'

'Happy,' he echoed, with such sadness that my heart wanted to break.

'Oh, Tommy. I wish things could have been different for you. I know how much you miss your father. You two were always so close and had a special bond. When he died, I did my best, but I was never going to replace him. I thought I was doing the best for all of you when I went to London after we lost the pub. I couldn't drag you to London kicking and screaming, I thought you'd be happier out of school and on the farm with John.'

He shrugged. 'I was happy on the farm, but I felt like an orphan. Your belief in suffrage took you away from me and tore us all apart. I never understood how you could fight for strangers and not your flesh and blood family, and I never will.'

I gaped; his words stabbed like daggers in my heart. I brushed at the moisture clinging to my lashes. Maybe one day, he'd understand that I did it for them.

'I know you believed you were doing the right thing,' he said gently before I could respond. Could he see the pain I was in? 'You had to do what you had to do. Just as I'm doing now.'

I steeled myself to move on – lecturing my son on suffrage and my own loss of financial autonomy would only drive him further away. Nothing I could say would change how he felt or saw things in this moment. 'Is your dream still farming?'

He nodded.

'But further than London? Have you found a job in Kent or Cornwall? It would be wonderful if you were closer to me, Annie and William. We could see more of you.'

Only then did I see his reluctant expression and stopped walking to face him.

'What is it, Tommy?'

'I'm thinking of going to Australia.'

'No!' I pressed my hand to my mouth, stunned. 'Why would you go so far away?'

'I'll explain, but it's cold out here.' Tommy took my arm.

'I've just seen Mr Sanderson,' I said desperately. 'We're making progress but we have to put together some more evidence for the case. I'm hoping to get the pub back soon. We can be a family again.'

'It makes no difference, Mama. I don't want to be in Ebberfield. I was never going to work in the pub or go to university like you wanted. I love the land and farming. This is my path.'

I couldn't breathe for a moment as all the air rushed out of me.

'Let's talk about it over a cup of tea.' Tommy's look of sympathy was almost more than I could bear.

The room was thankfully empty except for us. I made small talk with Mrs Scruton that I barely remembered but she must have seen I was more than distracted and after serving us tea and cake, quickly withdrew.

'Tell me, Tommy,' I said finally.

'I'm applying for a program for farm workers run by the Australian government. It's called the Dreadnought Scheme and British boys aged between sixteen and nineteen are eligible. I've noticed the advertisements in the newspapers for some time.'

I took a deep breath. I wanted to tell him that he didn't have to go, that he could get a good job here. 'What kind of program?' I asked instead.

'Australia hasn't got enough agricultural workers. It's their biggest industry and the government pays for passage to Australia and for training at one of their farms for three or four months, before being placed on a farm in Victoria or New South Wales.'

'And you want to go?'

He nodded. 'Maybe it's that sense of adventure that you mentioned, but I feel like I'm suffocating here.'

My breath caught. I had felt the same things when I had moved to Ebberfield all those years ago. 'When do you know if you've been chosen?'

'The application process takes a while. I have to provide references and do an interview, then have a physical examination. I think I find out after that.'

'So you've looked into it thoroughly,' I said. This was his path. He had to follow it to discover if it was right for him.

Tommy covered my hand with his own. It was large and broad like Roger's, strong and capable. 'You're the first I've told. But if I'm picked, I'll go. I wanted to let you know, give you time to get used to the idea.'

Tears pricked my eyes. My mother's intuition told me he would be chosen, but I could hold on to a small hope that after his adventure he would come home. In many ways, he was so much like me. I couldn't constrain Tommy. I wasn't in control of my path when I was young, but he could be; he could be free.

'Thank you for telling me,' I said, looking into his hazel eyes and touching his beautiful face framed by the dark, curly hair that was so much like his father's. 'Let me know how you fare.'

As much as it would break my heart, I had to let him go.

Early in the new year, Sylvia and Adela Pankhurst were expelled from the WSPU.

'I can't believe it,' said Clementine. 'All Sylvia did was rename the local branch of the WSPU as the East London Federation of Suffragettes. Her mother and sister wanted her to dissociate the group from the WSPU because it's open to trade unionists and male supporters of women's suffrage.' Mrs Pankhurst was in Paris with Christabel after returning from a speaking tour of the United States but she couldn't come home because she'd be rearrested after absconding from her prison sentence. 'Sylvia wants to concentrate on the bigger picture, using collective workers' action, not individual attacks. You were both right, bombings and arson, and even vandalising property, isn't the way to change. It's not working. Strikes have more power to force change to include workers' rights and the vote for all women.'

Esther nodded. 'Churches have been the latest targets of the bombings and arson attacks. I know it's about applying pressure on the clergy and their complaints to politicians but ordinary people are suffering.'

'Can you believe that Mary Richardson slashed the *Rokeby Venus* at the National Gallery?' said Clementine.

'How did she get in?' asked Annie. 'I thought everyone was checked for weapons at the gallery and suffragettes were banned.'

'I don't think it matters how she got in, an attack on art won't change the government's mind, it will only destroy beautiful art,' said Esther.

'Where do we go from here?' I asked. 'If lobbying Parliament and militant action aren't enough to make the government listen, then what is?' I gazed at them both and their expressions were just as troubled as my own. Not even the deaths of people in the conflict between women and government and police had made a difference: Emily Davison, the women who had never recovered from the Black Friday brutality, the women who perished from poor health after the hunger strikes and forcible feeding, the innocent men and women who were victims of the bombings. 'What will it take for them to grant us the vote?'

March 1914

Dear Mama,

Just a short note. I've finally received the news about my application to the Dreadnought Scheme. I've been chosen and my passage to Australia has been booked on the *Hawkes Bay*. I leave London on 11 June.

I'm very happy and excited but I have a lot to do between now and then. Can I come and stay with you before I leave? I'd like to spend time with you and Annie and William.

I'll write again soon.

I looked up from the page, the faces of Annie, Clementine and Esther blurred through my tears.

'What is it, Mama?' asked Annie, sitting by my side.

'It's Tommy. He's going to Australia.' I couldn't hold it any longer and the sobs burst from my throat.

'It's all right. It's what he wants,' said Clementine softly, reading the letter.

'No, I-I've failed him,' I stammered. 'I haven't been there for him since Roger died. I've lost the pub and any income we might have had from it. I don't have much to give him, just some of what I've saved since I've been here. He thinks I've abandoned him, that I chose to fight for the vote here in London, rather than be with him in Ebberfield. He blames me for not keeping our family together.'

'You can't think like that,' said Esther, wrapping her arms around me. 'There was no way you could know what would happen.'

'I wish I'd taken him to the suffrage marches when he was younger, like I did with Annie. Maybe then he'd understand that I've been doing it as much for him, as for Annie. I hate that he's going to leave, believing that the vote for women is a foolish and unattainable ideal. Roger would be mortified.'

Esther drew away to look into my face. 'He's young and thinks he knows it all. But you brought him up with good values and one day he'll come to understand the importance of equality and why you fought so hard.'

'He's like me at that age,' said Clementine, kissing the top of my head. 'I wanted to get out of the village I grew up in as soon as I could and I've never gone back. And it had nothing to do with my family – I just knew it wasn't the right place for me. I wanted to begin somewhere new, find my people.'

'Tommy wants adventure, freedom to make his own choices and the chance to be seen and known for who he is, not what family he belongs to,' said Annie, squeezing my hand.

'He doesn't want to even be in the same country as me, his mother, the suffragette,' I replied bitterly.

'No, Mama, it's not like that. I understand what he's doing, because I'm doing the same thing. Archaeology isn't seen as a profession for women but it's what I love. I've stepped into the unknown, just like Tommy is about to, because the idea of being an archaeologist lights me up. The only difference is that I'm doing it closer to home while I study. But one day, I hope to be working on archaeological sites all over the world.'

She smiled at my frown of concern. 'Mama, you taught us to follow our hearts, to be true to ourselves, to be passionate and inquiring and to push ourselves past what is easy and comfortable. How can you expect us to be any less?'

I stared at her then. My eighteen-year-old daughter was wise beyond her years. 'You're right,' I said. 'I'm so proud of you all.' I thought back to the early days when Roger and I were first together. These were the qualities he'd loved in me. I was headstrong, passionate and fiercely independent. 'And I know that Dadda would be just as proud of you and Tommy too.'

I joined the deputation to Buckingham Palace to see King George in May. Between tensions in Europe and whispers of war and my own sense of helplessness, the whole world felt like it was careening out of control. Tommy was leaving when the world was on the brink of danger, and we seemed to be getting nowhere with the vote for women. Tensions between the suffragettes and the government were the highest they'd ever been, with women desperate to do anything for our cause. What would it take? Did we have to go to war with the men of our own nation?

I didn't know what else we could do. An appeal to the King about the treatment of the suffragettes by none other than Mrs Pankhurst, who was back in the country and willing to risk rearrest, seemed only reasonable and if the Prime Minister wouldn't listen to why women should have the vote, then maybe the King would. The only silver lining was that, despite our worries about Edward's threats and his police friends, it looked like he was a coward after all, and his threats were all bluffs. Although we were still under surveillance, aware of men photographing us coming and going from tea rooms and walking in the company of WSPU members, we'd had no contact from the police in months.

There were about two hundred of us but crowds of onlookers lined the street as we approached Buckingham Palace.

'Hopefully they're here to make sure we're not assaulted by police,' I said to Marjorie and Clementine.

'That's what the WSPU flyer said,' replied Marjorie.

Ahead of us were the gates of Buckingham Palace, rows of uniformed police on standby. 'That's a lot of police for a group of women,' I said, suddenly nervous.

When the marchers reached the gates, the police moved in and the screaming began. Women were dragged away, hats were knocked off, their hair pulled loose, and those who hung on to the railings were hit with truncheons until they let go.

'They can't do that!' I yelled. 'We've done nothing wrong!' I rushed ahead, with Clementine and Marjorie by my side. There were police everywhere, hitting women, ripping at their clothes. I looked wildly around me and saw that the crowd was cheering the police on, jeering at the women. 'Where's our protection?' I screamed.

A woman went down in front of me and I helped her up. She had mud and blood smeared across her stunned face. Then something hard connected with my jaw and I stumbled.

I heard Mrs Pankhurst shout, 'That's right. Arrested at the gates of the palace. Tell the King.'

I looked up towards the palace and wondered if the King was watching. Somebody surely was but nobody did a thing to intervene.

The woman I had helped was gone and Marjorie and Clementine were holding me up. My face ached and my head swam. 'We have to go,' Clementine said. 'Otherwise, we'll be arrested too.'

Somehow, we made our way to the edges of the crowd.

'I'm finished with the WSPU,' I said, unpinning the WSPU badge from my lapel.

We watched Mrs Pankhurst being marched away by a contingent of police. The march on the palace had been a useless exercise. 'The more violent the measures the WSPU resort to, the more violence they're met with,' I continued. 'All it achieves is even more hatred on both sides. And it does nothing to progress the suffrage cause.'

'I agree. I should have got out when Sylvia Pankhurst was expelled,' said Clementine, as we melted away into the bustle of London. 'I'd hoped things would change but nothing has.'

'Oh, but it has,' said Marjorie grimly. 'The streets are more dangerous for women than they've ever been. I'm done too. This can't continue.'

29

As I watch my children grow, I can't help but marvel at how much things have already changed since I was a girl. In twenty-five years, clothing has become much more practical for women. Annie will usually wear a light cotton blouse, boater hat and her skirt is much shorter, the hem brushing her knee. She wears leggings underneath her skirt so that she can lift it while cycling.

Tommy stayed with us at Notting Hill for a week before he left for Australia. We took him sightseeing, to the cinema and out to the tea rooms, showing him the best of London.

'Come on, Tommy,' said Annie, grinning. 'Keep up.' We were riding bicycles along the Thames to a picnic spot she had found and then we were going boating.

'What are you talking about?' replied Tommy. 'I'm right behind you but I don't know where we're going.'

'Don't worry about that,' she said. 'I'll tell you when we get there.' She looked at Tommy and William. 'Let's race.' She took off.

'That's not fair,' shouted William as Annie sped ahead, her skirt flying behind her, and he was in chase immediately.

Tommy glanced at me.

'Go, Tommy. I'm good.'

That was all he needed – he was gone.

I watched my three children laughing in the sunshine, riding easily and so carefree. My heart squeezed with joy to see them together. They'd learnt to ride when they were small and it was second nature to them, but I remembered the time it had taken me to learn as an adult, especially with a long skirt. They were doing things I had only imagined when I was their age. Annie was off to her first archaeological dig over summer and Tommy was to begin a new life in Australia. William, now sixteen, was fascinated with motor cars and aeroplanes and had taken a course in mechanics. He happily kept Esther's new motor car maintained and she'd even taught him to drive it just a little. I was so proud of them all.

I met them under the willows by the river, the picnic blankets already spread over the grass. I unpacked the luncheon I'd brought while Annie took photographs of us all.

'It's a feast,' said Tommy, inspecting the sandwiches and cake. 'All my favourite things.' It was good to see him smile.

'Yep, even chocolate cake,' said William, rolling his eyes.

'Lucky you're such a good sport,' Tommy replied, punching his brother in the shoulder.

'Where are you going once you get to Australia?' asked Annie, taking a curried egg sandwich.

'Well, I don't have to go to one of the training farms when I get there, since I already have farming experience,' said Tommy. 'I'm docking in Melbourne and I'll have a job waiting for me somewhere in Victoria. But I don't find out what that is until I get there.'

'What then?' asked William.

'I'm going as a farm student, so I'll learn everything I need that's specific to Australian farming from the farmer who takes me on. Agriculture is Australia's biggest industry so I'll be earning decent money. Maybe one day, I can buy my own farm.'

'Is that what you really want?' asked Annie.

Tommy nodded, a faraway look on his face. 'A dream come true. If it's mine, nobody can take it away from me.' I looked away for a moment and swallowed hard. He wanted a life he could control but that was impossible.

'But you'll come home again, won't you?' asked William.

'Of course, little brother,' Tommy said, ruffling William's blond hair.

'Don't touch his *hair*,' said Annie, seeing William's mock anger.

'Or what?' asked Tommy with a grin.

'Argh!' William chased his brother down to the riverbank and before I knew it, both boys were in the water, laughing and splashing each other.

'Looks like fun,' said Annie, smiling wickedly. 'But I'll splash them from one of the boats.'

I watched as she ran down to join them and laughed until tears ran down my face. They were a riot all together. I was so happy we would all have this day to remember and sustain us when we were apart.

Tommy and I took a walk afterwards along the river, the water sparkling in the sunlight. 'I'll be fine, Mama,' he said, answering my unspoken question.

'But you'll be so far away, on the other side of the world. What if something happens and you need me?'

He touched my arm and smiled wistfully. 'I haven't needed you like that since I was a boy … since Dadda died.'

I blinked furiously, determined not to cry.

Tommy took my hand. 'I'm sorry I've been difficult, Mama. You did the best you could.'

I wanted to get down on my knees and beg him to stay but the certainty in his voice and the light in his eyes when he spoke of Australia made me realise it would be a mistake to try to stop him. This was his big adventure, his way to make his mark on the world, as teachers' college and my dream of working in London and making a difference in the world had been for me. I couldn't be the one to pull that dream away from him. I had to let him go in the knowledge that he could always come home to us if he needed to.

So instead, when I got home, I gave him the savings I had put together for him, fifty pounds. 'I'm sorry that's all I have to give you,' I said, wishing I could have given him more.

Tommy flushed with surprise, then kissed me on the cheek. 'It's a king's fortune for me, Mama.'

Time went too quickly and the day of Tommy's departure arrived. He was ready to go, to fly the nest. I was surprisingly calm as I waved off my first-born son, Richard by my side. I had thought it best to tell the children while we were all together about what Richard was to me, and thankfully they had all taken it in their stride. I was so proud of Tommy, he had courage and conviction, and we had found an understanding at last. I only prayed that this would be the adventure he sought and that he'd be safe, fulfilled and happy.

Mr Stevens – Marjorie's private investigator – sent me a note, letting me know he and Amy had been investigating the possibility of Edward's involvement in the loan. Though it pained me to dip into my savings to afford his services, I knew it was necessary to push for a solution.

> We've started with the names of the men he was in prison with and we're looking for connections with anyone who had anything to do with the loan. If we can trace the movements and associations of these men, we hope to uncover any fraudulent activity perpetrated by Mr Partridge.

I gripped the letter tightly. I thought about the network of associates who had kept Edward's secrets: the failed financial dealings, the whispers of fraud and the possibility that he'd even had a hand in his uncle's death. They could be another avenue of inquiry.

Not even two weeks after I received the note, the newspapers were screaming with the news of Archduke Franz Ferdinand's assassination.

'Shot in Sarajevo, in cold blood, along with his wife,' said Esther.

'Austria-Hungary won't like this, especially after Serbia's role in the Balkans war,' said Clementine. There had been news articles speculating that Serbians wanted to be free from the yoke of Austria-Hungary.

'The Balkans is a tinderbox,' I said. 'This could be the spark that causes it to burst into flames.'

The papers continued to report on the diplomatic back and forth in the following weeks, which they called 'the July Crisis'. The demands of each country were like a row of dominoes, with Austria-Hungary's need for retribution, Germany's support of its neighbour, Russia backing Serbia and Britain calling for calm: one wrong move and they'd all fall. And while we waited and worried what would happen, all I could do was count the days that Tommy was at sea, estimating when he'd reach Cape Town, in South Africa, and then reach the port of Fremantle in Australia.

The day Tommy's ship was supposed to arrive in Melbourne, the headlines told the story: Austria-Hungary had declared war on Serbia.

'What if nobody backs down?' asked Annie. She had been working on a research project between university semesters, investigating the period of the artifacts found at the remains of a Roman city in Shropshire, before going to the dig herself in a few weeks.

'They will,' I said optimistically. 'But I'm glad that Tommy has reached Australia and will be out of harm's way if anything does happen.'

In the end, it happened quite suddenly. By 1 August, Germany had declared war on Russia and invaded Luxembourg. Two days later, Germany declared war on France, who was allied with Russia, and invaded Belgium.

'The world is going mad,' said Clementine, as we read the news reports. 'Our government has warned Germany that if it invades Belgium, we will have to get involved in the conflict.'

'Let's pray that Germany has had enough sabre rattling and has the sense to back down,' I said grimly.

Esther shook her head. 'I can't believe how this whole conflict has blown up in a matter of days.'

'It's been escalating for the last ten years or more,' said Annie. 'My professor said it's all linked to imperialism and all the big powers of Europe wanting to exert influence in territories in Africa, China and the Ottoman Empire as it fell.'

The following evening, our government issued an ultimatum to Germany: withdraw by midnight.

'What if we wake up to a different world tomorrow?' asked William.

'Well, you'll know before the rest of us,' said Annie. William had a job as a newspaper boy, delivering newspapers each morning. He had two more years at school before he had to step out into the world and decide what his future would be.

'What will happen to us?' he asked.

'Nothing will happen to us, Will. It's a European conflict that will only last as long as it takes to calm all parties down.'

But none of us slept well that night and I woke with a start when I heard the front door slam and what could only be William's footsteps stomping up the stairs.

'We're at war!' he yelled. 'Britain is at war with Germany!'

30

Our cause is on hold. Mrs Pankhurst has called on WSPU members to defend Britain and the government has released all suffragette prisoners. Many suffrage supporters are pacifists, including Millicent Fawcett, but the NUWSS has decided their involvement in the war effort will raise the profile of our movement and show the government that we are all patriots, ready to do our bit for our nation.

I was in West Hartlepool in December, over four months after the outbreak of war. Jane had been unwell and Sarah and I were visiting.

'It's nothing,' said Jane with a wave of her hand at our concern, but she was pale, drawn and thin. 'How's Tommy?'

'His job in Victoria fell through because of the drought, so he and most of the boys continued the voyage up to Sydney, where he found work straight away. He's on a farm near a town called Yass, working on a wheat and sheep property. He says the farmer is very kind.' I couldn't help but wonder what had gone through Tommy's head when he'd arrived in Sydney to hear that Britain – and therefore Australia – was at war.

Jane squeezed my hand. 'I'm glad he's doing well.'

'You look worn out,' said Sarah, coming back to the point. 'It's time for you to let Bert and Eliza do more to help you. And you can't be looking after the grandchildren all the time.'

'But I love it. The little ones remind me of when mine

were that small and it brings joy and laughter into the house. Besides, there's too much to do with this war. We've been trying to help the poor Belgian refugees, putting together care packages for them and finding them somewhere to live.'

Sarah shook her head. 'It's hard to imagine what they witnessed.' Belgian refugees had fled to Britain with nothing following Germany's invasion and had told stories of horrific atrocities.

'But what about the Germans living here, forced out of their jobs?' I thought of the German pastry shop in London which had suddenly been boarded up. Those who were discovered or who didn't change their names were interned in detention camps. Worse were the riots and the destruction of German businesses and homes.

'The casualties of war,' said Sarah grimly.

I wondered how many more innocent people would become victims before this conflict was over. The newspaper reports were bleak, speaking of a deadlock in France between our allies and the German army.

The following morning, we began my birthday celebrations by having breakfast in Jane's kitchen, the stove keeping us toasty against the chill, when a heavy rumbling sound broke the quiet of the house.

'Is that thunder?' Sarah asked as she brought the last of the pancakes to the table. They were a childhood favourite, something our mother used to make, especially on our birthdays, and Sarah had decided to make them for me.

The rumbling continued. I got up and looked out the kitchen window, only to see the mist coming in from the sea. 'It doesn't look like a storm,' I said, perplexed.

'What could it be?' Sarah asked.

'It'll be gun practice at the batteries or our ships practising at sea,' said Jane, nodding decisively. 'A few fishing trawlers disappeared lately and they're saying there are German U-boats along the coast.'

'You must be used to it,' I said. The noise was a real reminder that we were at war. In London, the conflict was all talk, but here in the north, the British navy was patrolling the coastline and the North Sea.

'It happens sometimes,' Jane said, taking a bite of a pancake. The windows rattled. 'We think local fishing crews are watching and mapping the coast for German activity and sending information to our navy. I worry sometimes about John and his boys on their fishing excursions.' It was hard to believe that Jane's eldest already had sons old enough to go out on the trawler with him.

An ear-splitting boom cut through the air, shaking the house around us and making me jump. Jane's expression changed to one of alarm and she tried to rise from her chair.

I put my hand on her shoulder. 'I'll find out what's happening.'

I rushed out the front door. 'What's going on?' I shouted to men running down the street.

'We don't know,' said one man. 'It could be a battle at sea. We've had naval destroyers nearby.'

'What, a battle with the German navy?'

The man nodded and was gone.

Surely he was mistaken. I ran further down the street to find out the real cause of the noise.

Another boom sounded and I crouched on the ground, my hands over my ears until it ceased. There was smoke in the distance and I ran towards the hill to see more. It was coming from the direction of the gasworks and timber yards on the waterfront and then I saw the flicker of flames. I stared, horrified, then staggered away as another explosion rent the air, my ears ringing. We were under fire.

I ran back to the house, the sky filled with a smoky haze.

'Sarah, Jane!' I yelled. 'We're under attack.'

'What? What do we do?' Sarah looked from me to Jane.

'Bert and the children are in town!' Jane's face was bloodless.

I shook my head. 'It looks like the Germans are targeting the industrial sites on the waterfront. The gasworks has been hit and the timber yards.' It would only be a matter of time before they hit the steelworks, railway and shipyards.

'So, we stay?' Sarah's pinched expression didn't assure me. But Jane wouldn't be able to walk far in her condition.

'Jane!' Bert's voice carried down the hall as the front door crashed open.

'Bert! I'm here.' Jane fell into her husband's arms as he strode into the kitchen. 'You're safe. What's happening?'

'The Germans are shelling the town.' His face was grey with shock. 'We've lost soldiers, they were killed when the Heugh Battery was bombarded. There are three German warships sitting just off shore.' He shook his head. 'We didn't see it coming.'

'How the hell did they get so close?' asked Jane.

'I don't know. We have two light cruisers and a submarine in the harbour but the sub has been hit, blocking the cruisers from leaving the harbour.'

'I saw smoke and flames over at the gasworks,' I said.

Bert nodded. 'The docks and shipyards have been hit and the entire headland has been shelled – houses, shops, everything. People are dead and injured.'

'What? Innocent civilians?' asked Sarah.

Bert nodded again.

The cottage shook as though it was being ripped asunder and the noise that accompanied it was like nothing I had ever heard. I screamed as I dropped to the floor, taking Sarah with me. I was still holding on to her as the explosion subsided, both of us dazed and my ears ringing.

'That was too close for comfort,' said Bert.

I looked around, expecting to see the cottage flattened, but it remained standing. We followed Bert out onto the street. Everywhere there were people running from their houses, women half-dressed, carrying babies and small children. Other children, on their way to school, were crying and screaming, and I thought I saw a man in a suit and bowler hat carrying a frying pan with cooked bacon and sausages in it.

'What just happened?' asked a neighbour.

'It was the tailor's shop on Grosvenor Street,' said a man rushing past.

'Oh, my lord,' breathed Jane. 'He's just a few blocks from here.' Her look of shock turned to horror. 'John, Eliza and the children!'

Bert nodded. 'I'll go and make sure they're safe after I get you out of here.'

Jane shook her head vigorously. 'No! Hannah and Sarah will help me. You see to them.'

Bert hugged her tight. 'Walk through the cemetery and head for Ward Jackson Park. I'll meet you there.'

'Be careful,' Jane shouted, as he ran down the street.

We left the house with our breakfast still on the table and made our way through the cemetery at the end of the street, Sarah and I supporting Jane between us. The road beyond was full of fleeing residents just like us, who had only the clothes on their backs. Some people were crying but most wore shocked and terrified expressions, and were shepherding family members and children ahead of them. What had happened, what was still happening, was incomprehensible. The worry for Jane's family weighed heavily on us. We walked for what seemed like hours before the sound of a motorcycle caused us to stop.

'It's over,' said the man on the bike. 'The German boats have gone.'

We looked at each other in relief and trepidation. What would we find when we returned to the cottage?

The aftermath was just as horrific. All around was the devastation of the bombardment. Houses had gaping holes in them, and we heard stories of people killed on the streets on their way to work and school. All in under an hour. Jane's children and grandchildren were safe, which was the greatest relief of all, and the cottage was still standing.

'The Germans will have to pay for this,' said Bert darkly. 'Nobody can say how many are dead until we finish removing the rubble from the buildings, but from what I've seen, there are hundreds of homes and buildings that have been damaged or destroyed.' Bert was part of the rescue and clean-up crew, removing debris with his horse and cart.

'How did they get away?' asked Sarah. 'Jane told us the navy is patrolling these waters.'

Bert shrugged. 'They disappeared through the fog, like ghosts.'

I left Jane with Sarah and went with Bert to help in any way I could. I was stunned to witness the devastation as we got closer to the Heugh Battery on the headland. Windows were blown out everywhere, whole sides of buildings had collapsed and the front of homes were open to the world, like doll houses. Holes gaped in buildings where shells had gone straight through them, leaving the bottom floor and the rest of the terraces around them intact yet in others, roofs had caved in. Buildings stood precariously, like block towers built by small children. If not for the people wandering aimlessly through the streets, I would almost have thought that I'd stepped into some old, derelict settlement.

Roads were obstructed by bricks, litter and debris, so that Bert had to gently persuade his horse to take us around. Then I saw the carnage. Beds thrown onto roofs or the street, sheets covered in bright blood, people lying motionless on the road, some with mangled limbs, some without parts of their body. And blood, so much blood among the rubble.

I stared at a woman crumpled on the side of the road, covered in shrapnel.

'Bert! She's alive,' I shouted, jumping from the cart. I picked my way through the mass of splintered timbers and furnishings to the woman's side.

'Can you hear me?' I asked, taking her limp and almost bloodless hand in mine.

'My children,' she managed to rasp. Her eyes were wild and clouded in pain.

I glanced at the house behind us. There was very little left. 'Were they with you?'

She shut her eyes and tried to nod, then screamed in pain. Glass shards were embedded in the back of her neck.

'Bert!' I yelled. 'She needs help.' I waited until he reached my side. 'Her children were with her when the shell exploded.'

He shook his head. 'Hannah, it's no good. Her children wouldn't have had a chance.'

'I have to look. Can you stay with her?' I didn't wait for a reply only ran towards the ruined building, ready to check under every piece of debris.

Someone grabbed my arm and stopped me. It was a man in a police uniform. 'Are you mad?'

'There are children in there,' I said.

'You'll get yourself killed if you rush in. We have a rescue team. If you want to help, stretcher that poor woman to the waiting cart and make sure she gets transported to hospital.' He waved in the direction of Bert's cart.

Men gathered around, carefully removing bricks and beams from the inside of the building. I turned to look at the mother. Her eyes were closed and she was quiet.

I went to her side and held her hand once more. 'We're looking for your children.'

Her eyelids fluttered. Bert and others helped lift her from the ground. Her scream rent the air and then she fell into a faint.

'She's not going to make it,' said an older man, leaning over the woman, now laid carefully in the back of Bert's cart. I looked over her body with growing horror. Metal pieces were lodged in her belly and her clothes were sodden with blood.

'Will you go with her to the hospital?' I asked. 'I have to find her children.'

The man nodded and climbed into the back.

'Be careful,' said Bert to me, as he flicked his reins and the cart rolled away.

I looked around. If the mother had been thrown this far from her home, then could her children have been thrown even further? I moved into the front yard of the house next door, my eyes glued to the ground and the surrounding rubble for any movement. And then I saw a child's shod feet poking from under the roof of a lean-to which had been flung onto the ground.

'I've found someone,' I yelled. 'One of the children.' I made my way towards the child as men and women rushed to my aid. Together, we carefully moved the flimsy roof until we could see the child underneath. It was a boy, about six years old, dressed for school, from the looks of it. One of the women touched his face and sought a pulse at his neck. I held my breath. But then she shook her head and sighed.

The muffled sound of a baby's cry came clearly from somewhere near the boy. We scrambled towards the sound, pushing the bricks and splintered wood out of the way. 'I can see something,' I gasped, reaching towards the back of the hole. My fingers touched soft fabric. I carefully reached further into the darkness and felt movement. 'Here, someone help me,' I called, concentrating on grasping the child.

People gathered around to move more of the debris and I crawled through the dirt and rubble until I could get a firm grip on the cloth. I began to pull it gently towards me. There was some resistance but I continued pulling, until I was able to gather the bundle into my hands and finally lift it out of the hole. It was a soft quilt. Then the bundle in my arms wiggled. I tore the bedding away and found a toddler – a little girl. I stared at her, amazed. She didn't have a scratch on her. 'She's alive and well,' I shouted, jubilant. I hugged her against me. She was warm, her face red with her lusty cries.

'That's little Ava,' said one of the women. 'How did she survive when her brother didn't and her mother's fightin' for her life?'

'She must have been cocooned in the bedding,' said one of the other women, in wonder.

The girl's father arrived shortly after, crying with joy and grief as he hugged his tiny daughter to him.

I continued to help move the injured and sent the children without parents to the women who were marshalling those who had survived.

Bert returned to collect me sometime later and he took Jane, Eliza, Sarah and me to Ebberfield, to Jenny's house. With the hit on the gasworks, the town had no lighting or heating.

I held in my sorrow and only began to sob when I was alone in bed. I was forty-four years old, and had been through much in my life, but nothing like this.

31

My former student Jemima Johnson is a qualified doctor but has been prohibited from entering the Royal Army Medical Corps because she's a woman. Instead, she joined the Scottish Women's Hospitals for Foreign Service, run by women and funded by the NUWSS and has gone to France to treat the wounded.

Over the following days, while we were banded together at Jenny's house, the outrage was everywhere but was especially acerbic in the newspapers. How had German warships been able to attack British citizens on British soil?

'They're saying our defences are weak along the coastline,' said Sarah. 'Scarborough is a resort town, for goodness' sake, and has no defences.'

'Not for much longer,' said Jane. 'Heads will roll for this. The papers are saying the soldiers who died at the battery are the first to die on English soil in two hundred years.'

'But not only that,' I continued, 'many innocent people died, civilians who had nothing to do with the war. They were just going about their business.' So many people had been killed immediately, but some took days to die, and I knew for the ones who would survive it would be a struggle to find a way to manage their injuries and pick up the pieces of their lives. Worse, I couldn't get the dying mother out of my mind, taken away in the back of Bert's cart. It could have been me.

The final death toll still wasn't known. Some newspapers

were saying about thirty people had perished and seventy were injured, but by Bert's estimates, it was at least quadruple those numbers. The clean-up would take weeks. Bert had told us that the rescue efforts had been scaled back, because anyone still under rubble would no longer be alive. Then there were the dead and injured in Scarborough and Whitby. I buried my hands in Duke's and Shandy's coats. They were a balm to my frayed nerves. They had settled here with Jenny and her family, since Tommy had left for Australia.

Jane shuddered. 'It's not a fate you'd wish on anyone. It's bad enough for the brave soldiers on the front line in France but for British people, especially children … it's unthinkable.'

Over thirty children died during the bombardment, at home with their families or on their way to school. The feeling of despair when I'd found the woman's small son under the rubble, dead, and the surge of joy when I found his sister wrapped in bedding, alive and well, was indescribable and something I hoped never to experience again. I understood why the pacifists were against this war. Recruitment drives had increased over the last days, exploiting the brutal attack on English soil. Sylvia Pankhurst had come to see the carnage in Scarborough, and was in direct opposition to the recruitment efforts of her mother and sister and the WSPU, and even Millicent Fawcett and the NUWSS.

'That's what the Germans want, maximum fear and panic among ordinary British people,' Sarah said. 'Maybe the Germans are worried about our successes in Belgium.'

I nodded. 'The Germans are hoping we'll keep reinforcements here to protect our citizens rather than send them to fight on the Continent, but they're wrong. The Admiralty won't change their naval policy. The general opinion is that our fleet, although superior to German ships, can't control every part of the North Sea.'

'But what about our defenceless towns?' asked Jane. 'What if this happens again? What if, next time, they invade?'

'I don't know,' I said, shaking my head sadly. Anti-German feeling was high and nobody knew what was to come. The wife of the pork butcher near the colliery had been terrorised after the bombardment, the windows of her shop and home smashed by an angry mob. She and her husband were both German but had been here for years, though her husband was already interned in a detention camp. She only escaped the attack on her shop through the back door, taking her children to the neighbour's place.

Richard and I had planned to meet at his cottage in Ebberfield to celebrate my birthday after my visit to Jane in Hartlepool, and I was pleased and relieved to hear that he had arrived. After such a traumatic time, I wanted nothing more than to be in his arms. Seeing families destroyed, loved ones gone, I needed the security and reassurance of his love and it was a relief to have the solid feel of him as he pulled me into one of his bear hugs.

'You were so brave,' Richard whispered into my hair after I'd told him all of it. 'I was worried about you but you've always had a lion's heart. Now it's going to take you time to get over that day.'

I was crying again, the memories all too fresh. 'All I want now is to be with you and then go home to Annie and William,' I told him.

Suddenly we were all arms and legs, bodies pressed together, mouths searching for one another, until there was nothing else.

'Hannah, I think it's time your family knows about us,' he said afterwards, stretching beside me.

'What are you talking about?' I replied sleepily. 'Annie, Tommy and William know.'

'No, I mean your sisters and Jenny.'

I frowned. 'Why? Aren't you happy the way we are?' I enjoyed the freedom of our relationship, without judgement or pressure. It was enough that the children and Esther and Clementine knew about us. All they wanted was my happiness and allowed me to be and do what I wanted. As a widowed woman, I had a lot more freedom and independence than I'd ever experienced in my life and I wasn't about to give it up.

'Of course, but I don't want us to have to sneak around like a pair of young ones. We're both mature adults and I'd feel more comfortable if your family knew.'

I kissed his chest, the hairs tickling my nose. 'Does it mean that much to you?'

He nodded.

I thought for a moment. We *were* mature adults and could do what we wanted. My reputation hardly mattered any longer, after everything that had happened. And my sisters were entitled to their own opinions, but I no longer felt pressured by whatever they might think. I knew Jenny would be happy for me, if she didn't already know. Anyone else, I didn't care about. 'Well then, why don't you come back to Jenny's with me? You can have a look at Jane and see what you can do to help her and then stay for dinner. We're having a small family celebration for my birthday, since I missed out on the day of the bombardment.'

'Wonderful,' he said, gathering me close.

'And I think I want to get back to London as soon as possible and hold my children in my arms too.'

'I'll drive you back to London and take you to dinner there.'

'You've only just come back,' I said. 'What about your patients?'

'Dr Williams has been filling in for me and he's agreed to

continue.' He took my hands in his and sighed. 'I want to spend as much time with you as I can.'

'What is it?' I asked, suddenly worried.

He shifted. 'I didn't want to tell you like this, but Almroth is moving the entire inoculation unit from St Mary's to France.'

'Why? Is it about getting the typhoid vaccine to our soldiers?'

'The War Office has agreed to take the vaccine and although it's voluntary, troops will only be eligible for overseas service if they have it. But that's not why we're going. We have to take the opportunity to conduct our research on bacteria and pathogens where it makes most sense: in a clinical setting where we will see more cases than ever before.'

My heart began to pound. 'And you're going?'

'I can do more good if I go and continue the work we're doing. When we see injuries and disease first-hand in the field, I know we can find ways to help that we would never discover here at home.'

'You're going to the front?'

'No! God, no. I'm too old for that. Almroth's lab is attached to the general hospital in Boulogne. The rest of the team from St Mary's has been asked to go. The problem is that, because it's a military hospital, I most likely have to join the Royal Army Medical Corps. I'd prefer to go as a civilian doctor and researcher but that may not be possible. I'll know more in a few weeks.' He caressed my face. 'I wanted to tell you about it but after what you've just been through, I didn't want to burden you. I'm sorry it came out like this.'

I nodded, mute from shock. I knew it was an important opportunity. He was as passionate about this type of medicine as I was about achieving the vote for women.

'Let's make the most of the time we have, then,' I whispered, pulling him to me, willing my voice not to shake. I couldn't bear to lose Richard too.

32

The bombardment hasn't just affected the towns that were hit – it has shocked all of Britain. Recruitment posters with the words *REMEMBER SCARBOROUGH! ENLIST NOW,* have been posted in all the visible places across London. The attack has been an affront to our national pride, the British fighting spirit has been roused and we will not take this lying down.

Jane had finally written to me since my return to London. She had gone home to Hartlepool after Richard's ministrations. She had a heart condition, but it would be managed with his help.

I put the letter down and wiped my eyes, my vision blurry. Everything had been going well with Richard. I wasn't in the habit of thinking very much about the future, besides getting the pub back. Since Roger's death, I'd tried to live in the moment, because nobody knew what the future would bring. But my relationship with Richard had changed that habit. With the knowledge that he was leaving, I'd realised the strength of my feelings, and with it, my hopes for a future together.

I picked Jane's letter back up, smiling to myself.

Everywhere we go reminds us of that terrible day in Hartlepool. The clean-up continues. Bert works from dawn to dusk, carting rubble away. But our morale isn't broken, we are not a town defeated, a people cowed. We are a strong community. We are northerners. If the Germans thought they would break us, they were very much mistaken. We have come together, got on with the job of burying our dead, looked after our injured, cleaned up our town and got on with our lives. If anything, local men have joined up in their hundreds, ready to fight the Germans.

Of course, we live in a state of readiness and the police and special constables have distributed information on what to do when we're next under attack. I'd like to say it's unlikely the Germans will ever get so close again, but I can't be so naive. Another attack will surely come.

But our fears have been allayed with more troops stationed here to man and improve our batteries and guns, and to build fortifications against the enemy, should they try to land. Trenches have been dug in the beach and barbed wire roadblocks have been constructed to prevent the Germans from advancing into the town on foot. High barricades have also been built from large sacks of sand and planks, with holes at regular intervals for the guns, mainly to provide cover for our docks.

Clementine and I continued teaching, while Esther's research now focused on converting different engines for use in the war, including aeroplanes and the tractor engines she'd been working on. But with the loss of our suffrage work, a hole had been left in our lives. Clementine turned her attention to Sylvia Pankhurst's East London Federation of Suffragettes, which offered practical assistance to working women through childcare and free medical services, cheap restaurants and employment in a toy factory. I was involved in helping at Crosby Hall, a Belgian refuge in Chelsea for women and children, teaching them English, cooking in the kitchen and bringing relief packages of donated clothing and small gifts that I'd organised. Annie and William joined me when they could and Esther helped both Clementine and me when she wasn't working.

'Can you believe this?' I gestured to the newspaper in disbelief. 'The King has issued a statement that "no wines, spirits or beer will be consumed in any of His Majesty's palaces and houses after today, Tuesday, April sixth, 1915".'

'I know that Mr Lloyd George has been campaigning for a prohibition of alcohol during the war,' said Esther, looking up from her writing.

'He'll never have that passed,' said Clementine, drawing on a cigarette. 'It's against personal liberties and there's nothing the British public – that's men, of course – hate more than a violation of their rights.'

'Well, the Chancellor's push for complete abstinence has got the King on side,' I said. 'And this last budget increased duties on alcohol. I'm not sure I'd want to be a publican in this environment. They've already restricted opening hours for pubs around munitions factories.'

'Strange times,' said Esther, shaking her head. 'And I for one am very glad that you're here with us. You and the children have added much joy to our lives. Haven't they?' she asked, kissing Clementine's cheek.

'They most definitely have,' said Clementine with a smile. 'But you know how much Hannah wants the pub back and hopefully that will happen soon.' Mr Stevens and Amy continued with their search for connections between Edward Partridge and the pub loan. There had been no more threatening notes since I'd confronted him, and the police surveillance had stopped after the war began. Edward himself had disappeared. I wondered if he'd moved on to seek new opportunities to prey on vulnerable people with the chaos of war.

With the temperance movement's new campaign and posters everywhere encouraging readers to 'FOLLOW THE KING'S LEAD' and new changes to the *Defence of the Realm Act* in the following weeks, which banned people from drinking on trains and from buying alcoholic drinks for others in the long tradition of 'treating', I thought long and hard about my future and my desire to move back to the pub. I enjoyed my life in Notting Hill. As much as I missed him, Tommy was happy in Australia and had sent a few letters telling me about the farm and how much he was learning about farming in a different climate. Annie and William had settled into university and school and made new friends. It was a shame that war had suspended football just when William was on the brink of success with Chelsea. Did I want to disrupt their lives all over again by going back to Ebberfield?

Duty on alcohol was increasing and the strength of beer was reduced and watered down. The Central Control Board (Liquor Traffic) had been recently set up and had national control over alcohol production. It also had the ability to take over public houses and breweries in naval, military munitions or transport areas. The life of a publican was only going to get harder, the tougher restrictions became. For the first time, I considered that perhaps I was fortunate, ending up in London, where the children could be properly educated and where I had a stable income.

After a long day at school and working at Crosby House with the refugees, it was a welcome sight to come home to Richard's letter.

May 1915
My dear Hannah,
I feel like I've been at the Number 13 General Hospital in Boulogne for months. Between missing you and the long days and high workload, I have been learning all about military protocol and finding my way around the different specialist departments and units. We've set up in what was a casino just south of the city and have seen our first cases of chlorine gas poisoning. Men returning from Ypres have terrible burns to their throat and lungs from drinking water after being gassed. There are the men suffering from 'shell shock', so traumatised by their experiences on the front. But I am happy to be doing something eminently useful here, for the men and for medical science.

I was so grateful that Richard was nowhere near the front line. That might keep him safe but I could hardly imagine what he'd have to face, dealing with the casualties of such a brutal war. All in a tortuously slow crawl to gain ground.

Did I tell you that Alex Fleming and I have been made captains? We've been working with Almroth on an exciting project that may very well change the way wounds are treated. Only the seriously injured or ill are sent to our hospital and we've seen some terrible injuries to faces and heads especially, from exposure above the trench when men look out. Shrapnel also cuts deep into tissue and is difficult to find and remove, increasing the risk of infection. The antiseptics can't get down to the wounds, and limbs and lives are too often lost. Instead, we're trialling the good cleaning of wounds and leaving them open when the previous policy was to close them after administering the antiseptic. This way, the body's own defence system can take over and promote healing through the development of pus. I'm sorry if this all sounds a bit graphic but I am so elated about this new breakthrough that I wanted to share the process with you.

I will leave you for now. The laboratory and our unit are not well heated and so at night when I have time to write the reports on the day's surgeries, findings, and events, as well as write to you, I must wear my gloves and my coat. So much for enjoying the French coast! The locals tell us that it will heat up soon. I must say, I'm looking forward to some good weather to come.

I keep your photograph with me to remind me of the wonderful times we've had. I miss your smile, the sound of your voice and the touch of your skin against mine. I can't wait to hold you in my arms again.

All my love,
Richard

Richard, a captain! He was doing well, then, despite his reservations about joining the RAMC. I was so happy that his work was making a difference and giving him purpose. I missed him more than I'd realised. Sometimes I wished we hadn't waited so long – we'd had so little time. My only hope was that, like Tommy, he'd stay safe until I could see him again.

It was the end of May and our household was up late when we heard a ruckus outside, the sound of a whistle piercing the quiet of the night and dogs barking all over the neighbourhood. I peered out the window and noticed the neighbours looking to the sky.

'Something's going on outside,' I called to the others. I went out curious to know what was happening, William, Annie, Esther and Clementine following behind.

We looked up too. I was struck dumb by the strange sight that met my eyes. A silver, cigar-shaped object was moving slowly across the sky.

'It's a zeppelin,' Esther whispered in awe. We watched its silent progress, blotting out stars as it passed, transfixed until it disappeared from view.

'Take cover!' shouted a policeman bicycling past us on the street. He blew his whistle again, before continuing down the road.

Then we heard the bang, like the crash of thunder. Annie and William jumped. A flash of light followed in the distance and I shuddered, as the terror of that day in Hartlepool came back to me.

'Is that a bomb?' asked William. His voice was curious, not afraid, but he hadn't seen first-hand what those things could do, and I prayed that he never would.

'Come on, inside,' I said urgently to William and Annie. 'Down to the cellar.'

'But it's not coming this way,' said William.

'You don't know that,' I said, grabbing his dressing gown roughly and pulling him away. Nobody could see what destruction those bombs were doing from here but I knew. The Germans had found another way to get to us, to terrorise the British people.

'Let's do what your mother says,' said Clementine tightly.

The windows rattled with each boom of explosion as we bundled into the small cellar space to wait it out. I had left a few blankets down here in a half-hearted attempt to do something after Jane's latest letter, never really believing an attack on London could happen. She'd suggested preparing a 'safety room' with an exit and to store a pick to dig our way out if necessary. We were to keep water, non-perishable food, warm clothes and matches in the room. But here we were without any of that and, as we huddled under the thin coverings, I vowed the very next day to implement Jane's instructions.

'At least we're safer here,' I said, in an attempt at optimism.

But it was in the light of day that the real damage was seen.

'Houses have been hit,' said a white-faced Annie, on her return from university that afternoon. 'And the London Music Hall. All civilian, not a single military target.'

I nodded. 'The newspaper said a few people died and there are others in hospital from their injuries.' But the photographs of smashed buildings and the rubble surrounding them didn't do justice to the reality I knew ordinary people were suffering.

'Children, Mama. Children have died and innocent people in their beds.' Annie shook her head, her mouth grim. 'This is only the beginning. If the Germans think they can attack us on our own shores with such impunity, they'll do it again.'

'We're not prepared for these attacks, not even remotely,' said Clementine.

'But this – this will inflame the imagination of everyone. An attack on all that is sacred – the capital of the British Empire,' said Esther.

'Perhaps now we'll get serious about protecting our people and our homes,' said Clementine.

Annie's face darkened further. 'I saw some of the damaged buildings from the motor bus. At university, I heard about attacks on anyone with a German accent. Mobs of people shouting abuse at them or beating them for having something to do with what's happened, but of course they haven't. It's not constructive, only makes the chaos worse and divides us more.'

'I'm sorry you had to witness that,' I said, kissing the top of her head. 'There is so much fear out there and people don't know what to do with it.'

A few days later, Annie came into my bedroom. 'Mama, can I talk to you?'

'Of course.' I put down the letter from Tommy I was reading. 'What is it, my sweet girl?'

She sat on the edge of the bed, fidgeting with the bedcover. Nervous about something. Perhaps she'd met a boy, I thought. She was twenty years old and spending a lot of time at university.

'Mama, I've made a decision.'

'What's that?'

I watched as she took a deep breath. Whatever it was, it was difficult for her to say. I steeled myself.

'I've decided to postpone the rest of my university studies. I've finished my exams and I've done enough to complete my second year with flying colours. I've spoken to my professor and he understands my decision.'

I frowned. 'It's wonderful that you've done well but what do you want to do in the meantime?'

'I'm joining the Voluntary Aid Detachment.'

I stared at her as the breath rushed out of me. Since Roger's death and our family scattering, Annie had always been by my side. I had never imagined she would leave me, not until she'd finished university at least. I took a shaky breath.

'Before you say anything, let me explain. After the raid on London, I couldn't shake the feeling that I wanted to do something to stop the Germans and to help the war effort, help our citizens ... I'd felt it after hearing about what you went through in Hartlepool and what you saw there.'

My eyes widened in alarm. 'I'm so sorry if I upset you,' I began, guilt bringing me back to myself.

She shook her head. 'No, I'm glad you told me, but I didn't really understand it until the attacks on London. We're vulnerable here, and ordinary people have been oblivious to what the war is really about. My eyes have been opened. We all have a responsibility to protect our homes and families, our country.'

'But Annie, we've been doing that, helping the Belgian refugees, and anyone else who's been affected by this war.'

'I know, Mama, that's what got me thinking. What if I can do more? I want to train as a nurse, to help in the hospitals. You know how short-staffed they are. I love archaeology but I can't travel to dig sites now and I'll just be stuck at a desk doing paperwork and research papers. I'll come back to it after the war. Until then, I want to feel like I'm making a real difference.'

I felt dazed. Annie's words echoed those I'd spoken to my sisters and parents when I was her age. Clearly I'd passed on my passion for social justice but maybe I'd taught her too well, including the value of independence, I thought wryly.

'What's involved?' I asked, swallowing hard.

'The Red Cross offers training for first aid and home nursing certificates, then a trial placement at one of the hospitals across Britain before they'll accept me full time. It's not as long as the training for a professional nurse, but we can do the less technical parts of their work.'

I breathed a sigh of relief. Nursing was demanding and backbreaking, but the main thing was that Annie would be safe. 'What made you decide on nursing as a way to help?'

'Listening to Dr Jenkins and you talking about medicine and health for all these years,' she said. 'Training to be a nurse would take too long and women aren't accepted to become ambulance drivers or stretcher bearers, but I couldn't see myself as a clerk, sitting at a desk all day long, and we both know my cooking skills aren't up to scratch.' She smiled weakly.

I took her hands in mine. 'Is this really what you want to do? Because there's no shame in continuing the aid work you do with me while you study.'

'Come on, Mama. I'm too much like you. I've seen you give everything you've got to the causes you believe in. This is my way of showing what I believe in.'

A burst of pride flooded me. I couldn't be a hypocrite – I had to let her do this, otherwise I'd lose her as surely as sending her to the battlefront. 'All right,' I said. 'Make sure you have everything organised with the university before you apply.'

She hugged me tight. 'I will, Mama.'

33

The sinking of the *Lusitania* made headlines in May and prompted riots against German businesses and homes. As if Germans here are to blame for the sinking and lives lost! Police made more than eight hundred and fifty arrests and over two hundred and fifty people were injured. Attacks on innocent people continue. The world has surely gone mad.

'Women want to work in the munitions factories,' said Clementine, as we marched along the Embankment in the Women's Great Procession organised by Mrs Pankhurst and the WSPU. Though we had broken with the WSPU, we still would continue marching to the beat of the cause – women's rights and equality. There was a shortage of artillery shells since more men were leaving the factories and enlisting. 'Especially if they're paid the same as men.'

'We need to show the new Munitions Minister that women are ready to step up into men's jobs,' said Esther. Mr Lloyd George had just taken up the new portfolio. 'Those of us already working in men's occupations can inspire women, show them that they can do more than they realise, that we can do what men do.' Esther was always so modest about her accomplishments. She'd recently been involved in redesigning engines to allow aircraft to have more power and fly faster.

'If only all women were as capable as you,' said Clementine grasping her hand.

I nodded, shrugging into my coat even further. It was cold for July, and wet. 'Why shouldn't women be in all the occupations men are in?'

'But this march is also about showing strength and unity,' said Marjorie. 'We're just as patriotic as our men and we want to do more than help our soldiers overseas. We can help Britain at home. Look at the women office workers now, the bus conductors and drivers, the postal workers and the women in banking.'

In the mornings and evenings, women flooded the city streets, many of them clerks and secretaries. And, after being qualified for years, Amy Sanderson was finally working as a solicitor at the War Office.

'That's true,' I said, as we gathered in Trafalgar Square where the minister waited to address us. There were thousands of women, many dressed in costume to support the floats representing our allies: France with the red caps of Liberty on their heads; Belgium; Russia; Poland; and Italy. Others were dressed in our national colours: red, white and blue.

'This is how it should always have been,' I said as Mr Lloyd George welcomed us in his speech.

'We're giving the government what it wants,' said Clementine bitterly.

'But maybe this is a beginning,' I said. 'If we're respected as valuable members of this nation, then the vote must surely follow.'

Annie arrived home after seven weeks of training at Tredegar House in Bow with her double certificate and extra training. 'Because I was doing so well, I was asked if I'd like to do the X-ray course,' she said proudly. 'And I found out that I'm doing my placement at the Fifth London General Hospital. That's St Thomas'.'

'So you're to treat military men with injuries,' said Esther, impressed.

'That's right. I start on a trial basis and if I do well enough, I get a full-time position.' She kissed my cheek. 'I know that you won't be happy, Mama, but I have to stay in the nurses' quarters and can only come home on my days off.'

'I'm proud of you, my girl,' I said, hugging her tight. 'I'll miss you, we all will, but knowing you're just over the Westminster Bridge means you're not far away.'

It was wonderful to receive another letter from Tommy not long after.

June 1915

Dear Mama,

We've finally finished sowing the paddocks. Roy and I are home after weeks of moving between the different farms across the district where we've planted wheat, barley and oats. I've learnt how to cook over a campfire and make billy tea, and I'm now expert in setting up and packing away our camp. I've enjoyed living and eating outdoors and often sleeping under the stars in my swag but now the weather has turned cold, I'm glad to be in my small space in the tack room at night, near the horses in the stables.

Many men have enlisted for the war, often in the Light Horse regiments, and workers are in short supply to keep the farms running. The news about the heroic Australian advances against the Turks and the terrible conditions at Gallipoli are in all the newspapers and inspire pride and patriotism, even though I haven't been here a year. But Roy has more work than he can poke a stick at and I've promised to stay.

I gazed at the framed photo of Tommy beside my bed, happy and smiling at our picnic on the Thames before he left, and breathed a sigh of relief. He might be on the other side of the world but at least he was safe. I sent a silent prayer of thanks to God and to Roy Reid for watching over my boy.

William began his last year of school and we endured another zeppelin raid. I woke to the sound of a policeman's whistle and as I roused William from his bed, I heard a strange whirring outside. I peeked through the closed curtain and gasped.

'What is it, Mama?'

'The zeppelin is right above us.'

The throbbing was loud now.

'That's the engine we can hear,' he said, fascinated.

'Down to the cellar, fast,' I said, grabbing him by the arm.

We met Clementine and Esther on the stairs and were barely in the cellar when the familiar booming began, this time shaking the walls.

'It's closer this time,' said Clementine as we huddled together.

'Annie! Oh God, I hope she's safe.' I could hardly breathe for fear.

'She'll be safe, Mama,' said William, putting his arm around me. 'The hospital will be well prepared.'

All I could do was nod. There was nothing else I could do. The helplessness was almost overwhelming. The wait seemed the longest of my life.

I didn't sleep a wink that night, worried sick about Annie.

The next morning when we emerged from the cellar, we learnt that bombs had fallen on the centre of London, St Paul's Cathedral and Liverpool St Station, causing considerable damage and killing twenty-two civilians and injuring eighty-seven. Six of the dead were children. I was terrified that the hospital just across the river had been hit too, but thankfully it had been spared. But only when I got word from Annie did I relax. She was safe and well.

Another round of attacks on the Germans living in London began and, this time, I saw it first-hand. I was walking near the Electric Cinema, a favourite haunt of ours, when I was confronted with an angry mob trying to get inside the building.

'What's happening here?' I asked an elderly shopkeeper standing at the front of his store.

'The poor fellow is German,' he said, shaking his head. 'Someone believes that he is to blame for the zeppelin attack on us, signalling from the roof of the cinema.'

'How ridiculous,' I said, horrified.

'I agree. I've telephoned the police. I hope they're here soon, before the mob tears the man to shreds.'

'Isn't there anything else we can do?'

He shook his head. 'Unless you want to go in there and break it up yourself.'

I stared, unable to help the lovely man who provided us with the most wonderful movies. He was a kind and gentle soul. I remembered the first time we'd gone to the cinema, not long after it had opened and we'd just arrived in London.

The police arrived not long after, breaking up the crowd and arresting those who refused to move on. I shivered, the sight bringing back memories of the days when me and my friends were the ones who were the focus of police action. I was relieved to learn that the cinema owner was safe, although he was sent to a detention camp not long after, leaving the cinema to be run by his daughter.

Annie returned to us after three months at St Thomas', but I could sense she was on edge.

'Is something wrong, Annie?' I asked one evening, drawing the blackout curtains we'd installed; anything we could do to hide our position from the zeppelins in the air. Massive searchlights and anti-aircraft guns were being installed across London, but still our guns and aircraft had trouble reaching the airships and hitting them.

'I've been offered another placement,' she said slowly.

'Well, that's good,' I said. 'Maybe it's better you're out of London, with these raids.'

She looked at me with an expression of regret and my insides turned to ice.

'I'm going to Egypt, to one of the military hospitals in Alexandria.'

'What are you talking about? You're supposed to stay in the hospitals here.'

'They need us over there. They're desperate for nurses,' she said. We'd heard how the Gallipoli campaign to secure the Dardanelles Strait from the Ottomans wasn't going well.

'But why you?' I asked, distraught. 'And why there?'

'Mama, I can help there. And I've always wanted to go to Egypt. This is my chance to help our soldiers and to see some of the best archaeological sites in the world: the pyramids, the Valley of the Kings and the temples and tombs at Luxor; and the work of our very own Professor Flinders Petrie.' Her eyes were alight.

'So, this is what you want?'

'It is, Mama.' The determination in her eyes told me everything I needed to know. She was breaking my heart but I could not deny her. She had to fly on the wings that beat within her own heart, just as I had wanted to at her age. My dreams weren't fulfilled then because of my duty to my family but these were different times. She would go anyway and I would lose her. Like Tommy, I had to let her go with my blessing. I only prayed that she'd come back to me.

'Then go, my darling. Be safe and remember, we all love you here.'

I hugged her gently but endeavoured to remember the feel of her with a fierce intensity to fuel the long months she'd be away from me. I'd thought my family had scattered when I moved to London but now two of my children would be halfway around the world. For the first time, I realised that perhaps it was too late to gather them all together again. Perhaps I would never reunite my family.

The possibility of that was the hardest to bear.

Clementine and Esther decided it was time to share their love and commitment in a ceremony before Annie's departure.

'None of us knows what's ahead of us in these uncertain times,' said Clementine. 'We want to do this with our loved ones around us.'

'You are our family,' said Esther, squeezing my hand, 'and we want to share it with you.'

We assembled in the garden at Notting Hill, on a clear day in September. Marjorie was there as well as a few of Esther and Clementine's London friends. William had erected a small arch and we'd wrapped it in greenery and small white flowers. The happy couple now stood under it, facing each other. Esther wore a green dress with a calf-length hemline and carried a small bouquet of late-blooming roses, and Clementine was in a navy-blue suit, holding a posy of chrysanthemums and daisies. The flowers were Annie's and my gift to them.

Clementine held a simple wedding band that had been her grandmother's. 'Esther, I love you more than life itself. You are my heart and joy. I want you to have this ring as a symbol of my enduring love and everlasting commitment to you.'

Esther's eyes were filled with tears as she extended her hand and Clementine slipped the ring onto her finger. I clasped Annie's and William's hands.

Esther touched the ring almost reverently before she reached for another ring, which sat on the table beside her, a band encrusted with small diamonds. It had been her grandmother's as well.

Esther smiled at Clementine. 'Clementine, I never expected to find love, but here we are. You are my best friend, my heart and joy and my life partner. I love you more than I knew was possible. Take this ring as a symbol of my eternal love and devotion and my commitment to you.'

Clementine made no attempt to brush away the tears that rolled down her face as she held out her hand. 'We continue to live our beautiful life together,' she said, her voice breaking.

'And I wouldn't have it any other way,' replied Esther, taking Clementine's hands in hers.

'To Clementine and Esther,' I announced. 'May they live a long and happy life together.'

We clapped and cheered as they kissed.

I smiled through my tears. It was the anniversary of the day I married Roger. We would have been married twenty-one years. Clementine and Esther had given me a beautiful gift.

'I wish you all the joy and happiness that Roger and I had,' I whispered, returning that gift to them, before hugging Annie and William to me, the ultimate expression of our love.

34

November 1915

Dear Mama,

Alexandria is a lively and fascinating city with many cafes, bars and restaurants and large marketplaces called souks. I keep pinching myself that I'm here, in the ancient land of the pharaohs. But it certainly is very different, with the Arabic culture, traditions, language and food and, most of all, the heat. The locals dress in more suitable robes for the conditions of this place and I wish our nursing uniforms were made of lighter fabric to allow the skin to breathe.

There is still a shortage of nurses and we VAD nurses have to take on greater responsibility, often learning as we go. Many of our patients are Australian and make me think of Tommy. But it's not just injury that we have to combat, it's dehydration, frostbite – if you can believe – jaundice and sickness from dysentery, trench fever and malaria. Despite how overwhelmed we are, I am happy to be here. There is a real sense of camaraderie, even from the professional nurses, who are pleased they now have help.

I was overjoyed to finally come face to face with the pyramids of Giza and the Sphinx. This is the land of ancient Egypt, the place I studied at university. Thanks to contacts at London University and having studied under Professor Petrie, I was fortunate enough to tour some of the excavations of the royal cemeteries near the pyramids as well as see some of the incredible relics discovered here and in the Valley of the Kings, which are housed in the Cairo Museum. I always hoped that one day I would see such ancient treasures but to be doing this now is an absolute gift.

Give my love to Aunt Esther and Aunt Clem and give Will a big hug from me. I miss you all.

Your loving daughter,

Annie

I was relieved that Annie was stationed at the General Hospital, far from the front line. She'd told me in her previous letter that the journey by hospital ship was three or four days from Gallipoli. Annie's experiences were so far removed from my own. When I was twenty, most young women would never have had the opportunity to visit exotic and ancient lands like this.

The new year saw the passing of the *Military Service Act*, making conscription compulsory for single men between the ages of eighteen and forty-one.

'Not enough men are joining up,' said Esther, looking up from the newspaper she was reading while she ate breakfast.

'You know what that means: too many casualties on the battlefield. The Western Front is a pit of death and injury,' said Clementine in disgust.

'William will be eligible this year,' I said in a strangled voice. I'd prayed that the legislation wouldn't be passed. Millicent Fawcett had told me there was intense debate about conscription and the moral issues and rights around individual choice, much as there had been with the vaccination debate. It was still not mandatory for soldiers to receive the typhoid vaccination; the only consolation was that if they chose not to have it, they could not serve overseas.

'He can apply for a conscientious objection,' said Clementine.

'He'll need to go before a tribunal, but if he's successful, he won't need to fight overseas – he'll do war work here at home.'

I nodded, feeling sick in my stomach. 'I don't think I can bear to have him gone as well.'

Mr Stevens and Amy Sanderson calling on us at Notting Hill was a brief distraction from my worries about my children.

'How's work at the War Office?' I asked Amy as she sat across from me. She looked smart in a tailored suit and with a three-quarter length skirt. Short skirts were much more practical when working and were being seen all over London since so many women now worked in office jobs, on buses and trains, and as police officers.

'The hours are long but the work is rewarding. I'm enjoying being able to practise law as a fully qualified solicitor.' She smiled. 'But Hannah, we came to give you news.'

'We've been able to find Edward Partridge's link with the company that underwrote the loan,' said Mr Stevens.

I breathed out slowly, the words settling heavily in my belly. Then I felt a thrill of elation fizz through me. I had waited for this moment for over two years. 'How?'

'It's the director who was on the board of both Philip Usher's company when Edward was running it and the financial company who underwrote the loan. He was seen with Edward's prison associates and now we know he was bribed to change the wording in the loan contract.'

I nodded slowly. The mere stroke of this man's pen had done so much damage. But while Edward still had his network of corrupt associates from before he left prison, perhaps their loyalty would only stretch so far. This was surely the evidence we needed.

'I've spoken to Papa on the telephone and we're working out how we proceed with the legal case,' said Amy. 'But I must warn you ... We're having trouble finding Edward, and without anything more than hearsay, we may not be able to pin him to the crime.'

I stared at her. All the excitement drained away. 'He can't get away with it,' I said. 'After everything, he just can't.'

Amy squeezed my hand. 'The main thing is we have clear evidence of wrongdoing by the director who's been charged and will go to prison. That should be enough to move ahead with your case.'

A pinpoint of light and hope at the thought I might get the pub back. For years, it had been so uncertain and at times, I wondered if it would ever become a reality. I had to put my crushing disappointment about Edward to one side. This was the first time I felt that we were getting close.

'If we can find the informant who gave Edward the information that the brewery was looking for a loan for you and your husband, you'll be in a much stronger position to get your pub back,' said Mr Stevens.

Amy nodded. 'And find Edward.'

Annie was a prolific letter writer and each one gave me strength, knowing she was safe and happy.

February 1916

Dear Mama,

The Gallipoli campaign has come to an end. The Allied troops have been pulled out, although some will remain here.

I've decided to stay on in my role as a VAD nurse. I'm not sure where I will be posted next but I've been granted a month's leave – or more – to join an American dig of the temple of Pharaoh Merneptah, which was first discovered by Professor Petrie. I've also been asked to join some fieldwork at Deir el-Bahari. This is part of the Theban Necropolis, opposite Luxor, and the site of Hatshepsut's temple, the pharaoh I'm fascinated with. I'm hoping my skill with X-ray machines may be useful in learning more about the mummies.

We've been hearing distressing news about the continued massacres of the Armenian people and of the women and children who survived being forced from their homes by the Ottomans and marched into the Syrian desert to refugee camps, where they have little hope of survival. Others have been forced to convert to the Muslim faith or be sold as slaves. We must speak up about these atrocities in countries as fortunate as our own, when women and children so downtrodden have no voice of their own left to cry for help. It's a travesty that the Ottomans continue to decimate a race of people with such impunity.

I put Annie's letter down on the desk, and opened my treasured album of family photographs and looked through its pages. Images of the children when they were young, laughing, happy in the dene with Roger, at the school play, at birthday celebrations and Christmases. Memories of another time. I could never have imagined Annie's life to be anything like the one she was describing. She was young, independent, doing what she loved, and had the world at her fingertips. I couldn't be any happier for her, despite my worry about her safety.

At the same time, I grieved for the powerless women who were always the victims of violence. My hope was that the world could change if women came together to raise their collective voices. I paused at a photograph of Annie, beaming in her nurse's uniform. I was so proud of her and her social conscience. She was the next generation. She was educated, independent and confident, and knew what needed to be done. With more women like her banding together, the world would undeniably be a better place.

'Will you help me draft a letter to Prime Minister Asquith?' I asked Clementine and Esther one evening as we sat listening to music on Esther's gramophone.

'Whatever for?' asked Clementine with a frown, sipping on her after-dinner tea.

'I've spoken to Millicent Fawcett. Apparently, there's talk about putting together a new register of voters before the next election. There's support for a new franchise bill based on military service. Many men have lost their right to vote since they haven't been at a single residence for a continuous period due to their war service.'

Millicent Fawcett seemed to be the only one who had kept focus on parliamentary reform. Now, with attitudes to women within the government shifting, there was a real chance we could be successful in gaining the vote.

'Ahh,' said Clementine. 'It's about conscription. If all conscripted men are expected to give their lives in protection of their country, then they should also have the right to vote.'

'But we want the bill to be based on national service, not just military service. Women can't enlist but it doesn't mean our service isn't important in helping our country win this war.'

Esther nodded, tapping her fingers in time to the music. 'Women have to be valued for taking on the jobs and roles of men with equal capability and, in some respects, even exceeding their success.'

'And what about the sacrifice of their sons and husbands, fathers and brothers?' asked Clementine. 'Let's face it, the longer this war continues, the population of women is going to far exceed men as the casualties rise.'

'Women have proved their worth as patriotic citizens and with support for women's franchise increasing, now is the time to consider including women in any new franchise bill,' I said.

Clementine's and Esther's faces mirrored the hope that I felt. 'Let's give it a shot,' said Clementine.

We spent much time and energy in perfecting our letter only to receive a short reply, weeks later, that no such legislation was in contemplation. It was another let-down. I remembered why I had turned to the suffragettes and felt like smashing every pane of glass in Parliament and Downing Street. But the government couldn't ignore the problem of the register and Mrs Fawcett had promised to keep me informed on the progress within Parliament.

'It's with Cabinet now,' I told Clementine and Esther. 'But each proposal has been rejected by the House of Commons. Eventually they'll have to deal with the issue of women's contributions to our nation.'

Esther agreed. 'They can't consider soldiers and not women who have worked towards the war effort and sacrificed so much.'

'But there has to be equality to the work men and women do. Until women have equal pay and conditions to men, women's work won't be valued in the same way and nothing will change,' said Clementine.

I sighed. 'I know. Let's do what we can, one step at a time.'

35

I'm so proud that William has already begun some engineering courses at the London Technical College and has assisted on some of Esther's aeronautic projects. He has a good understanding of engines, like his grandfather. Esther is over the moon about his career choice. But my worry about him being conscripted leaves me wound tight. Is all his work for nothing? Will he have the future that he deserves?

There was much public objection to the new conscription laws and with the frustration I was feeling about the new franchise bill, I decided I had to do something, take some action – William's future was in the balance. I joined Clementine in a demonstration organised by Sylvia Pankhurst against conscription at Trafalgar Square.

'This is the first time in British history that we've forced our men into war,' I said as we congregated with thousands of other objectors.

'Conscription is against our basic human rights,' said Clementine. 'It's wrong on moral grounds.'

'So many men already support the war through the work they do here at home,' said Marjorie.

'Too many men have been injured or perished in this terrible war and now we want to send more young men to their slaughter,' replied Clementine.

I could only nod. I was close to tears. In a matter of months,

William would be called up. My only hope was conscientious objection.

A crowd of onlookers was gathering, including soldiers and sailors in uniform, and I began to feel uneasy. Then the men in uniform charged and it was chaos as banners were ripped from the protesters' hands and shouts turned to screams as the men threw red and yellow liquid into our faces.

'What is that?' I shouted as I dodged the liquid. Some splashed on my dress anyway.

'Dye,' replied Marjorie. 'The bastards have thrown dye at us.' She wiped her face in distaste, yellow clinging to her skin. 'Yellow for cowardice and red for sacrifice and the blood spilled in war, I assume.'

'Like women don't understand courage or sacrifice.' I shook my head in disgust. 'Come on,' I said. 'Let's get out of here.'

Police moved in but whether they were there to arrest the soldiers and sailors or us, I didn't want to find out. I'd learnt that if we did what the government wanted, we were welcomed with open arms, but once we disagreed with them, those who attacked us were treated with impunity.

After the protest, I was angry and feeling a little reckless. I persuaded Clementine, Esther and Marjorie to come to one of the growing number of nightclubs in London. Thanks to the wartime blackout, London at night reminded me of Ebberfield when I was young: no street lights and most homes shrouded in darkness. But the fear that danger lurked in the inky blackness was more exaggerated now and women always travelled in groups.

I blinked in the brightness of the club, my senses overwhelmed with the lights, the loud music of a band playing ragtime, the soulful voice of a Black woman singing and the chatter of men and women in evening wear as they drank and danced the foxtrot. The atmosphere made me feel that the war was just a dream.

'Come on, ladies, let's live a little,' I said with a grin. We were four women, older than most, but we could still dance and make conversation, and for many soldiers that would be enough.

'We have to give these poor sods a good time,' said Marjorie, when men in uniform offered to buy us drinks.

'It's fine for you,' whispered Clementine, 'but I haven't danced with a man since I was a girl.'

'Do it for your country,' Marjorie shot back with a wicked smile.

We obliged various gentlemen, accepting lemon squash and whiskey and soda – masquerading as ginger ale with the alcohol restrictions – and danced the waltz. The man I was dancing with was in his late twenties and had somehow been stuck with me rather than some of the younger women in the room. We shared small talk, him telling me he was off to France for the first time after being conscripted. He reminded me of William and when the dance finished, I made sure he had another girl to dance with, someone much younger and prettier. I prayed he'd return home safe and well.

Then it was time to dance the foxtrot once more.

'Time to let our hair down,' said Clementine, taking Esther's hand.

'But there are so many men free to dance with,' said Esther, glancing around the room nervously.

'We've done our duty. Nobody can tell us who we can and can't partner with.' I took Marjorie's hand. 'Let's dance.'

I concentrated on dancing the man's part, the slow, slow, quick, quick steps. I noticed that Clementine and Esther were dancing effortlessly. I knew they sometimes danced at home.

'They're beautiful together,' I said to Marjorie. But then I noticed a few scandalised stares. 'You'd think they've never seen women dance together.'

'Well, they'd better get used to it,' replied Marjorie. 'Because with more and more men away, women have to step into their shoes.' She arched an eyebrow at her double meaning. I'd forgotten how funny she could be. We'd all had a drink or two and it did us good to loosen up and forget our worries for a while. 'But I have a confession to make.'

I frowned. 'What is it?'

'I've been seeing Mr Stevens ... Nicholas. He's been worried about me, ever since you confronted Edward. And when I refused to have someone watch over me, he began visiting me to make sure I was safe. We became friends at first and then it became something more. We've been careful, and Nicholas knows how to be discreet.' She grinned and I laughed. Although Edward had disappeared, it didn't hurt to remember he was still dangerous. A private investigator was the perfect man to be involved with.

'Are you happy?'

'I am. For the first time in too long.'

'You deserve it,' I said, embracing her as the song concluded.

'Time to switch,' said Clementine, as we clapped.

'I haven't had so much fun in years,' said Esther, puffing with the exertion. She was red-faced and happy. 'Dancing like this is so liberating and freeing. I never imagined it possible.'

'The world is changing,' said Clementine, pecking Esther on the cheek. 'One day we'll be able to behave as any other couple does in public.'

Here in this club, with music and dance, the war had brought men and women together in their desperate need and longing, and it felt like anything might be possible.

'Do you think this will become the new dance craze?' I asked, lightly. If the war went on for too much longer, Britain would be a nation of women.

'Why not? Women can do everything a man can,' replied Clementine.

The train ground to a halt as I stood waiting on the platform. Steam swirled around as the doors opened and passengers began to alight. I stood on my toes, peering through the mist. Then I saw them.

'Jenny, Sarah, Jane!' I called across the platform. Jenny looked in my direction and I waved, and then I was running towards them in my excitement. 'You're here, you're finally here!' I cried as we all embraced. It was the first time I'd seen them in over eighteen months.

'You've seen Robert?' I asked Jenny, taking her arm. She'd come to see her husband before he left for France. He'd enlisted a year earlier, leaving his parents and Jenny to run the butchery.

She nodded. 'He's set sail. I'm glad I came. Having those few extra hours with him was wonderful.'

'It's time for me to cheer you up and show you all around London. First stop is Selfridges!'

After we'd finished our shopping, we stopped to relax in my new favourite place, the coffee shop.

'Mrs Scruton would be scandalised,' said Jenny with a smile.

'Don't tell her,' I whispered conspiratorially. 'I've never really enjoyed coffee until recently. It gives me a wonderful boost when I'm tired.' There were days between teaching, working at the refuge and doing what I could for the Red Cross when I needed all the energy I could get.

'That sounds like something for me,' agreed Jane. 'A little pep to get through the rest of the day.'

Once we'd ordered coffee and cake, the conversation turned to family and home.

'Oliver wanted to come with us, but with Robert away, we needed the extra hands in the shop. George has been helping out when he can but he doesn't have much time, now that he's working in the mine as well as his shop,' said Jenny.

She was lucky to have his parents there to help, although they had been retired for some time. Oliver had been apprenticed to his father but now his grandfather was teaching him the finer skills of butchery and all about running the business that he would one day own.

'William misses Oliver, but he's thriving here. He's just finished school and is doing a mechanics course that Esther suggested before he begins engineering at university in autumn.'

Jenny shook her head. 'You must be worried about him being conscripted.'

'I am, but he's agreed to keep doing everything that he'd planned until it actually happens.' I'd talk to William about becoming a conscientious objector when he was called up.

'You have your head in the sand,' said Sarah. 'The war's not about to end, nor is the government about to end conscription.'

I blinked. I didn't want to argue with her about my choices.

'Don't listen to Mama,' said Jenny, squeezing my hand. 'Sometimes focusing on what's in front of us is the only way we can cope. With the recent submarine attack on Seaham, Oliver was convinced he was ready to fight the Germans. It caused such fear that they could shell towns and villages on the coast without us knowing they were there. Many families of his friends had just received news that their husbands and boys had been injured or killed on the Somme. It's hard to tell them that it's not like they think it will be. They're not invincible, but even Oliver's time will come when he's called up and that scares me most of all.'

'What about Tommy? How's he going in Australia?' asked Jane, watching us both with compassion. Her sons had already been called up, so she knew what was ahead of us.

I told her about Tommy's last letters, about the harvest of wheat, his work in the shearing sheds and how good he was on a horse now. 'He's thriving and happy,' I said. Australia had been a blessing in disguise. Perhaps Roger had been watching over him.

'And Annie?'

'She's in Malta now,' I said.

'How's she finding it after Egypt?' asked Sarah.

'She's enjoying the climate much more. It's a beautiful location and it's safe. She calls it the "hospital centre of the Mediterranean" and she's been overwhelmed with casualties from the recent campaign in Salonika.'

'Where's that?' asked Jane.

'It's in Greece, on the Aegean Sea,' I replied, sipping on my coffee. 'But the hospital she's working at has a specialist surgical unit and an excellent X-ray unit where she gets to work with the surgeons and doctors. She told me that they have women doctors now, recently arrived, who are very experienced.'

'I suppose it's because there are so many injured men,' said Sarah, nodding solemnly. 'They need more doctors everywhere and finally the army realises that women are just as qualified and as good as the men.'

I thought of Richard. Since he'd returned to France after Annie's departure for Egypt, he was doing more and more hands-on medicine in Boulogne, with special departments for problems of the eye, ear, nose and throat, especially after the mustard gas attacks. The busier he became, the less regular his letters were. I hoped he'd be home again for Christmas but that was still months away.

'It sounds like a close-knit community,' I said, 'and the Red Cross makes sure they're well supported, with entertainment and comfort for the soldiers with care packages and concerts.'

'She's very lucky to be there,' agreed Jenny. 'Lily has begun work with Eliza at the munitions factory. And as much as I'm worried about how dangerous the work is, I'm grateful she's close and can come home to me each night, especially with Robert away in France.'

'Eliza has been working with explosives, which I'm sure has aged me,' said Jane. 'But she's done well and has been promoted to forewoman so she can keep an eye on Lily.'

'But did you know that both girls are playing football?' Sarah grinned at the look of surprise on my face. 'The munitions factory has a team and they play against other teams in the district.'

'I wanted the girls at school to play when the boys first began all those years ago. Never did I imagine ...' The war had changed so much. Among all the pain, sacrifice and death, there were some good things.

It had been lovely to find that one of the street windows at Selfridges had been again dressed in a suffragette theme with mannequins in green, white and purple, with *Votes for Women* sashes across their chests, WSPU medals around their necks and brooches pinned on their lapels. I had mixed feelings about the WSPU but was glad that women's suffrage was still a popular topic of conversation, with more women working than ever before. The confidence of women was growing. Women were independent, making their own money and their own choices while the menfolk were away. The vote had to come soon.

That feeling of hope only grew when Clementine and I were at a Red Cross working party one afternoon that summer. I'd seen an article in an open newspaper someone had left on a table about a new Special Register Bill that Mr Asquith had presented to the House of Commons.

'Clementine!' I called out, grabbing her arm. 'The Prime Minister has just acknowledged how valuable and effective women's service is during the war!'

'What? Where?'

'In the House of Commons. He went on to say that when the war ends, he won't be able to deny the special claim women have to be heard on questions that affect their interests.' I reread the speech that had been reported in the newspaper and looked up in amazement. 'He's giving his support to women's suffrage after the war.'

But Clementine only glanced coolly at the paper and then at me with some sympathy. 'He's made promises before and broken them. I don't trust a word he says.'

But I had to hope.

36

Annie's letters have me thinking about Hatshepsut, one of the greatest pharaohs and a woman, even though she had to style herself as a man. She was lost in Egyptian history, her great reign erased by the men who came after her. But with the discovery of some of her great temples, monuments and achievements, archaeologists and historians are coming to understand her power and success as a ruler.

'I've been called up,' said William, waving the letter.

I went pale. 'You don't have to go,' I said hotly.

'I'm eighteen and a half, Mama. We knew this day was coming.'

'Yes, I know, but we'll put in a conscientious objection form. You're too young to go to war.' Clementine's idea was my anchor, the only way out of this situation.

'No!' William shook his head vehemently. 'No, I won't be branded a coward.'

'Conscientious objectors aren't cowards. Most of them are pacifists who are opposed to the violence and killing of other humans. They're against the war in principle,' I said, trying to remain calm although my anxiety rolled through me in waves.

'It doesn't matter what pacifists believe, only what others believe of them, and people believe they are cowards. Look at the white feathers that women force onto anyone they believe should be enlisted. The women of the WSPU, who you've rubbed shoulders with. It doesn't matter what reasons men have for remaining at home and in their jobs. What will they think of those who try to flout the law?'

I frowned. I had never agreed with the handing out of white feathers, shaming men into enlisting. It was another reason I was glad to have broken with the WSPU. They were all or nothing, no matter what issue they were campaigning about, continually pushing the boundaries without any thought for the consequences.

'But William,' I pleaded, 'I can't let you go. I need to know you're safe. And you're just about to begin studying what you love.'

'I'm sorry, Mama. How can I shirk my duty when Annie has gone to Egypt and Malta? I have to do my bit too.'

'Annie was twenty when she made her decision – older and wiser. Why don't you wait a year or two? If you want to enlist for active duty then ...'

William stared at me, his jaw set in determination. For the first time I saw resentment in his face. 'If you don't support me in this, Mama, I'll do it without you.'

His fire was a punch to my gut. I couldn't lose him over this. I needed to allow him to make his own decision. I exhaled. 'You have my support, Will.'

'I have to present to the recruitment office in a week.'

I watched as he stalked away, tall, proud and angry. He didn't have the sense to be afraid.

Later that evening, I told Clementine and Esther about William's decision. He was out on the town, celebrating with his friends at one of the new jazz nightclubs. I wasn't sure what he was celebrating – the end of his schooling life or the beginning of his new life as a soldier. I felt adrift in a sea of despair. The feeling reminded me of when I'd lost Roger. If William left, all my family would be gone, scattered across the globe with no way for me to protect any of them. What would be the point of everything I'd been fighting for?

'Why is he so stubborn and pig-headed? Why can't he see sense? He thinks he knows it all, but he knows so little of life,' I moaned. 'Why are all my children so set on causing me grief?'

'You can't force him,' said Clementine gently. 'Conscientious objection is a good solution, but the only other option is to evade call-up.'

'You know he won't do that. He wouldn't want to live with the shame.'

'You have to let him go, then, and find his own path,' said Clementine with real regret in her voice. Annie and William were the closest she and Esther would ever have to children of their own.

I dropped my head, beaten. 'At least he has to serve on British soil until he's nineteen, before he's eligible for service overseas.'

I felt Esther's hand slip into mine and squeeze in sympathy. 'Do you remember when we were young? We thought we were invincible, thought we could change the world, and that, armed with our passion, we could make a difference. We were idealistic and didn't understand the world like we do now, but looking back, I wouldn't change a moment. We were inspired, full of energy, ready to get things done.'

'You can't crush his spirit,' said Clementine. 'After everything you've done to raise him to follow his heart, his conscience and his passion.'

'All we can do is pray for his safety and that the war doesn't spoil his zest for life,' said Esther.

I nodded. 'I know, but it breaks my heart.'

Hot on the heels of William's call-up, I received a letter from Mrs Fawcett.

My dear Hannah,

The time for constitutional reform is now. Although we are in the midst of the greatest war in history, reform is imperative if we are to be involved in the necessary reconstruction after the war. This reconstruction involves legislation and, because of our part in supporting our nation during the war, women must be part of the new franchise bill that is required to be passed with some urgency during the war.

To consider how best to frame the new bill, a new electoral reform conference has been established in secret. The NUWSS has requested they be allowed to give evidence but it has been declined. Instead, we will draw up a memorandum to be sent to the chairman of the conference, containing the points we wish to give evidence on and will send it to every conference member, as well as a number of resolutions from women's societies, town councils, trade unions and political associations supporting women's suffrage.

I trust your instincts and would appreciate your help in gathering and collating this information from different sources. I feel that we are getting ever closer.

Your friend,

Millicent Fawcett

I picked up my pen immediately to reply to her letter and accept her request. It felt wonderful to do something useful, something tangible, that had to get us closer to the vote.

*

It was after school when I took the telephone call that had been booked at the local post office. I knew it was from Sarah and wondered what was wrong. I couldn't help worrying and feeling distracted all day, especially with William having just left for basic training. I picked up the receiver and heard the line click as the transfer was made.

'Hannah?'

'Hello, Sarah,' I said through the mouthpiece.

'Hannah, are you there?' Sarah's voice seemed a long way away but it was her voice. It still seemed incredible that she could be in Trimdon and me in London, yet we could talk.

'I'm here. Is something wrong?'

'Hannah, I'm in Ebberfield.' Her voice sounded hesitant. 'It's Jenny. Her Robert was killed in France during the battle in Passchendaele.'

I gasped, nearly dropping the receiver in shock. Robert had lived across the road from me since he was a boy, working in his father's butcher shop and I was there right through their courtship and the early days of their marriage as they became a family.

'Hannah, did you hear me?'

'I'm so sorry, Sarah. How is she?' But I knew how Jenny was. Shocked, broken, shattered. I thought about her fatherless children. She was a war widow now, with three children to raise on her own. And I knew with Oliver turning eighteen in just over a year, she'd be petrified for him too. 'How's Oliver, Lily, Rose? And Robert's parents?' Poor Amelia and Tom.

I heard her sigh. 'As you'd expect.'

'What can I do?' What could anyone do?

'Nothing. It's going to take time. I'm here, Jane is coming tomorrow. George is working the butcher shop for them. Christopher is here to help too.' Christopher had been ineligible for war service because of the damage to his heart following diphtheria.

'Do you want me to come?'

'There's no need. You have your work. Maybe you can come at Christmas – it will be just you, after all. I think Jenny would like to see you then.'

I felt the sting in her words, even though I knew she didn't mean it. I would have gone to visit for a couple of weeks, or even just a few days, to give Jenny my support as she had given me hers. I felt unneeded, unwanted, but Sarah was Jenny's mother and who Jenny needed right now.

'Of course. Give Jenny and the children my love. Tell her I'll talk to her on the telephone soon, when she's ready.'

I heard the click on the other end and the telephone went dead. Poor Jenny. If the war could reach its deathly finger out and touch her family, what was stopping it from touching mine?

Jenny's loss made me realise that I had no control over the war, who lived and who died. When I read William's next letter, I had to be happy for him and I decided to celebrate his success. I waited until Clementine, Esther and I had finished working on the list of supplies we needed for Queen Mary's Needlework Guild. I was lonely without William around and Annie had encouraged me to become involved with the guild, which supplied a number of items for military hospitals at home and abroad including pyjamas, bed socks, bandages and dressings. I kept as busy as possible, trying to fill the hole his departure had left.

I brought a bottle of cheap champagne into the parlour and put three glasses on the table.

What's this for?' asked Esther.

'I have some news,' I said, popping the cork.

'Well, spit it out,' said Clem, more than a little curious.

'You know how William received his preference, joining the Royal Flying Corps as a third-class mechanic?'

They nodded.

'Well, he's been selected for cadet training at the School of Military Aeronautics in Reading, as an observer.'

'That's wonderful,' said Esther, smiling widely.

'It's thanks to you. All those conversations you had with him, the visits to your engineering projects, the courses you suggested he do. And the private word I'm sure you had with some of your military contacts involved in aeroplanes.'

Esther's raised eyebrows told me I was right but I knew she couldn't say anything.

'It's because of you both taking us in, and your attention to him and his studies, that he's been able to do something he loves.' If we were still in Ebberfield, he'd be an infantryman and soon on his way to the trenches in France, where the chances of him ever coming home would be slim.

'What does an observer do?' asked Clementine. For such a strong woman, she was surprisingly uncomfortable with compliments, praise and thanks.

'It's a reconnaissance role,' said Esther. 'They fly with the pilot and navigate and take photographs.'

I nodded. 'He loves working on aircraft engines but he's excited about artillery observation and the opportunity to fly and use his photography skills, something he enjoyed with Roger.'

'And how do you feel about it?' asked Clementine, her gaze fixed on me.

I poured the champagne carefully. 'He's happy doing what lights him up. And in these times, I'm grateful for that.' It was William's ultimate dream to learn to fly and perhaps this way he would.

'Oh, Hannah, how extraordinary,' said Esther softly. 'All three of your children are following their passions, living lives we never thought possible at their age, and it's because of your dedication.'

'You're incredible,' agreed Clementine. 'We've been so blessed to share in your children's lives.'

Tears sprang to my eyes. Now I was the one having trouble accepting compliments. 'Here's to William living his dream,' I said picking up my glass and clinking it with theirs. 'And seeing him and Annie come home safely.'

37

I am a northerner. We have always been a resilient people. We come from a long line of farmers, industrial workers, miners and fisher folk. We overcome obstacles with little fuss and with great practicality. We are headstrong and stubborn. We are fighters.

It was a fine August morning when I took the phone call from Jenny.

'How are you?' I asked. I'd written to her and we'd spoken briefly on the telephone a few weeks earlier.

'I was managing but now ...'

My heart started pounding. 'What's wrong, Jenny? What's happened?'

'There was an explosion in the mine early this morning.'

'No. How bad is it?'

'It was a change of shift and they're saying about eighty miners are trapped down there. A roof fall blocked the tunnel but even once they got through, rescue teams had to wait because the canaries were overcome. A rescue team got a little way in and found three men dead before they had to turn back. One of them was George.'

I closed my eyes, grief rushing through me. 'And Christopher?'

'No, he wasn't down there. But he's in a bad way. George was all he had left.'

Christopher had lost Nicholas when he was a boy and then Mary, eleven years later. His family was gone.

'I'm coming, Jenny,' I said. 'I'll be there soon.' And it was then that I knew it was time to return home to Ebberfield – for good.

I couldn't deny it any longer. The world as I had known it had changed irrevocably. I no longer needed London to keep my family secure and the fires of my passions lit – my children were grown and spread across the globe, and I had been able to give the fight for suffrage my full attention in London, exactly as I had always dreamed of doing. Clementine and Esther had created a home for us that had pieced my broken heart back together, but the family that needed me most now were in Ebberfield. My relatives and the wider community required more from me as we all reeled from this mining disaster.

I realised that I'd found my peace whether I got the pub back or not. Everything pointed to Edward being behind the loan but while the search for the person who informed him of our application to the brewery continued, there was no hard evidence against him. Despite this, wrongdoing had been determined and the director had been sent to prison for two years. Amy and Robert Sanderson continued the thankless work on the legal case, pushing the financial company for a settlement or to follow it to its conclusion in court.

Christopher needed me, and Jenny too. What I had formed with the Lighthouse community, I knew I could build again, with or without the pub. I needed the people of Ebberfield too.

The actions of the WSPU had been incredibly successful in drawing attention to the cause. Though I had my differences with Mrs Pankhurst's methods, especially now as she spearheaded a campaign to shame men to enlist in this war,

I was proud that I had followed my heart, and my gut, as a suffragist and suffragette. I was glad too, that I kept my friendship with Millicent Fawcett. Her strong, consistent and patient voice in Parliament continued as it always had. She had stayed the course: our guiding star. It was important for me to get behind her efforts once again and push for the vote at a time when women had proved to the nation that they could wield it. I had helped her from Ebberfield in the beginning, I could do it just as effectively from the north again. And with a disaster of this scale, the village needed all the help it could get; the community were as much my family as my flesh and blood. It was time to go home.

Although male teachers were exempt from conscription, many had felt the pressure of remaining at home and had enlisted and the local school was in need of staff. I applied for and was offered the role of headmistress at the elementary school in Ebberfield for the beginning of the school year in September. It was a job I'd dreamed of having when I was a young teacher, but I'd never have imagined everything I'd have to get through to finally be in this position.

'I can't believe you're going,' said Clementine, hugging me in the entry of the Notting Hill terrace. I was packed and ready to go, waiting for the taxi cab to take me to the train. 'All the things we've done together, all the tears we've shed and the laughter we've shared.'

'I know. This has been my home for the last six years and you have been my family.'

'We're going to miss you,' whispered Esther, taking my hands in hers. 'And we'll always be your family.'

I nodded. 'I don't know what I would have done without you both. And the thought of not seeing you every day ...'

'We'll see each other often. And you know you always have a home here,' she said, kissing my cheek.

The tears fell once I was in the taxi cab. The familiar streets blurred as I tried to take in every detail of the city I loved. There was no doubt I'd miss London. But I felt a sudden frisson of excitement ripple through me.

I was going home.

Despite the tragic circumstances, it was heartwarming to arrive at the new train station at Ebberfield. I alighted to the beloved faces of Sarah, Emily, Alice, Jenny and the children, who were waiting for me.

'Welcome home, Aunt Hannah!' yelled Rose, Jenny's youngest, across the platform.

I dropped my bags and ran to them. Hugs, kisses, arms around me, faces pressed together.

'I'm so glad you're back,' whispered Jenny. I held her close, the bones of her back and shoulders more prominent than I remembered. She began to shake with unshed tears.

I kissed her cheek, her hair whipping across her face. 'I'm here.'

Sarah took my hand. 'Hannah, I'm so happy you've come. You should never have left.' I bit my tongue; some things never change.

'Mrs Scruton and Amelia wanted to come to the station too, but they're preparing the food for George's wake,' said Emily, as we walked towards her car.

'We'll have a special celebratory reunion with the suffrage society and all your friends and family when life gets back to some normality,' said Alice, looping her arm with mine.

'Thank you,' I said, overcome with emotion and touched by their welcome.

We gathered for George's wake after the funeral service and burial. There were so many familiar faces, some people I hadn't seen in years, and they greeted me with a friendly smile, a nod of the head. But there were faces I didn't know, customers of George's butchery and miners with sad and thoughtful expressions, some straight from their shift with dirty faces.

George's funeral was difficult for me. Everywhere I looked reminded me of the day we'd buried Roger, but at least I'd had that day, that closure. Jenny's Robert was buried in a mud-sodden field somewhere in France. And many women didn't know the fate of their men, who were missing, presumed dead. Worse still was walking to The Ox and Plough for the wake. I'd done that walk so many times, on my wedding day and after the christenings of my children, those happy days of family members and dear friends, and finally to remember the life of my beloved husband who had left us too soon.

Now those dear friends surrounded me, welcoming me home after so many years away.

'It's about time,' said Mrs Scruton, engulfing me in her embrace. 'It's not been the same without you.'

'Are you back home to stay?' asked Dorothy Duggan.

'I am.'

'And staying with us,' said Amelia, squeezing my hand. Tom and Amelia had been living behind the butcher shop ever since Jenny and Robert started their family, giving them the home above the shop and the space they needed to grow.

'She's headmistress at the elementary school,' said Mrs Scruton. 'The Education Authority got somethin' right. We finally have a woman in the job and the right woman too.'

I smiled, glad to be among friends, people who knew me and accepted me as I was. Gone was the overwhelming sense of shame I'd carried with me when I first left for London. These were my people.

'Will you come back to the suffrage society, dear?' asked Esther's mother, Mrs Burrows. 'We could use your help in setting up relief for families from the mining disaster.'

'If you'll have me. I'd like to help with whatever efforts are planned.'

'Don't be daft,' said Mrs Scruton, waving her hand dismissively. 'You started our society and were our president until you left. It's time for you to put those organisational skills of yours to good use. London's had you for long enough.'

'I'll get started right away,' I said, a pleasant glow enveloping me.

The entire district had been rocked by the mining disaster. The funerals continued for weeks as the recovery continued. More than fifty men had been found dead and a few rescue workers had succumbed to the poisoned air. I wished Richard was here with me, more times than I could count. Poor Dr Williams was overwhelmed with patients suffering grief and anxiety.

The town I had left was different. It was two towns now, the colliery town, which was thriving and bigger than the rural village of Ebberfield, with its own elementary school that catered for over one thousand students, its own churches, pubs, shops, fishmongers, doctors, solicitors, clubs and sporting facilities, and a new branch of Barclays Bank. We now had tailors, hairdressers, a fish frier, a coast guard station, a factory and searchlights and a landing ground used by the Royal Flying Corps 36 squadron, a night-flying unit that was engaged in home defence of North East England and patrolling of the North Sea. We even had defensive trenches built on the coast just north of the colliery.

But the Ebberfield elementary school was much the same as the day I'd begun there, fresh out of teachers' college, nearly twenty-six years ago. It had grown but the feeling was the same, as I walked through the schoolyard that first morning. A place of learning, excitement and joy. My role now was the nurturing of bodies, hearts and, of course, minds. I'd dreamed of this day, to be the headmistress of a school, but it had become an impossibility after I married and couldn't teach any longer. After everything I'd gone through, I was finally here.

'Good morning, Mrs Rainforth,' said Mandy Kellerman, as I took my place in front of the whole school. She had been one of Annie's friends at school, but now she was a teacher. 'Congratulations on becoming Ebberfield's first headmistress,' she said with a grin. 'We're delighted to have you here and the breath of fresh air I know you'll bring to the school.'

I smiled at her enthusiasm. 'I'm looking forward to working with you and all the teachers.' I looked across the school hall, at the sea of faces: boys, girls, some eager, some reluctant. The journey began here to make school somewhere children wanted to be, to foster the love of learning through practical application of their studies, and to support children and their families through these difficult war years. It would be challenging and exciting. 'Good morning, Ebberfield Elementary,' I began.

When I wasn't at school, I threw myself into the work of helping the families of the mining disaster. The Ox and Plough was no longer supporting local community projects, which made me angry and disappointed, after the years I'd spent building the pub as a community hub. Instead, as headmistress, I offered the use of the school hall, with the consent of the vicar, Reverend Proctor, to begin putting together donations and care packages for all the families of the dead. We organised the food for many of the wakes in the school kitchen, often liaising with the close-knit mining community and the Miners' Welfare Institute.

'It gladdens my heart to see Jenny get so involved,' said Sarah, helping me carry platters of sandwiches to the school hall for another fundraising event for the grieving families. 'I was so worried about her.'

'There's more to do every day,' I said, watching Jenny direct suffrage society members to move the chairs and tables across the room. 'It gives them purpose, you know, a way for them to cope with their own loss.'

Sarah nodded. 'I'm glad you're here and it's good that you're staying with Jenny and the children.' I'd been offered the schoolmaster's residence but I couldn't imagine living on my own. Christopher had his own miner's cottage that he'd shared with his father, although he was more often at Jenny's than not. There I cooked for the family each night, so he was well fed, surrounded by love and family and the attentions of Duke and Shandy. The dogs were old now, happy to lie about the house and indulge in scraps of meat from the butchery and soak up affection from the various members of the household. I was happy to be reunited with them, they reminded me of old times and how much I missed the children. I lavished my love on them, as much as on Christopher, Jenny and her family.

'I think Tom and Amelia are happy to have a full house again,' I said. They'd lost both their boys in the war and their daughter lived in Yorkshire with her family and these days spent most of their time upstairs with us, only returning downstairs behind the shop to sleep.

People began to make their way into the hall. They were mainly women and the elderly, mothers, aunts and grandparents of the students. Some men remained in the village but not many: those who were older or not fit for the army and whose skill made them exempt and important for the war effort at home. But I was happy to see members of the mining community too, miners with their families. Sometimes it took a tragedy to bring people together. We might be twin towns but we were becoming one community.

'How's Harry?' I asked Emily when I returned to the school kitchenette. Emily's eldest wasn't much younger than Tommy.

'He's driving ambulances in Boulogne, not far from Richard. He's called on Harry a few times.'

I nodded. 'Richard said he would. And John?' Some men over the conscription age of forty-five, like John Duffield and Roger's brother David, had joined the Durham County Volunteer Corps, doing important work here at home assisting in our coastal defence. Emily ran the farm with her daughter Matilda when John was away but the recent poor harvests made trying to keep the stock alive with barely enough feed difficult.

'He's away at meetings with the civil authorities. If it's not zeppelin air raids, guarding munitions factories and railways, it's to do with communication, transportation and ambulance work.' The volunteer corps was the vital link between the town and the organisation and deployment of civil responses, preparing for any invasion by Germany.

'It's hard having them away,' I said, thinking of Richard. I prayed he'd be home for Christmas.

I attended my first suffrage meeting since I'd been back a few days later. 'It's one thing to help with care packages for them, but for many families to survive in the longer term, women have to become independent,' I said to the gathering. I'd been asked to share my insights on how to help the mining families, after my work in London with the Belgian refugees and the Red Cross.

'So many of us already have,' said Mrs Graham, one of the new members from the colliery village.

I nodded. 'Yes. Women all over Britain and overseas are working as drivers, farmers, clerks, doctors and nurses. Anything a man can do, so can we. We need to make sure the widows of the mining disaster know there's paid work at the nearby auxiliary hospital run by the Red Cross and at the colliery.'

'What about the munitions factory?' asked Jenny. 'It employs mainly women and is one of the most productive in the country,' she said proudly.

I smiled. Lily was doing well there and, at fifteen was already in charge of her small section. She'd wanted to do her part when her beau, like many miners, had been drafted to the Corps of Royal Engineers.

'There too. There's also a register of women for war service. Placing women in jobs is good for them, good for their community and for our country.'

'Now for our final order of business for this evening,' said Emily, stepping forward. 'I'm stepping down as president of the suffrage society and I'd like to nominate Hannah Rainforth as my replacement.'

I shook my head and pulled Emily aside. 'I don't want to take your place, just because I'm back,' I whispered.

'Don't be ridiculous,' said Mrs Scruton, joining our huddle. 'You were here in the beginnin' and with your experience and connections in London, you're most qualified of all of us.'

'Mrs Scruton is right,' said Emily. 'We discussed this last meeting and agreed we wouldn't have it any other way. I've only been keeping your seat warm after all and with John away so much, I'm busier than ever, filling in for committees that John's on.'

'Let the women of Ebberfield decide,' said Mrs Scruton, in response to my dubious expression.

'Only if you're sure,' I said quietly.

'A show of hands for the ayes,' said Emily, when we stood in front of the meeting. I watched with wonder as most of the women raised their hands.

'The ayes have it,' said Emily, with a broad grin.

'Hannah Rainforth is the new president of the Ebberfield Suffrage Society,' announced Mrs Scruton, patting me on the back. 'Congratulations, Hannah!' I could only smile with gratitude as the faces of the women of our community looked at me with acceptance.

The popularity of women's football in the north, especially with the growing competition between the munitions factories, inspired me in my role as headmistress.

'There's no reason girls shouldn't play football at school,' I said at one of our staff meetings a few weeks later. 'The season will begin soon and I'd like to introduce girls to the sport.' I was finally pushing for the changes I had dreamed of when I was a fledgling teacher.

'But what's the point?' asked Miss Sloane, one of the teachers. 'There's no competition for girls.'

'We have to start somewhere. With training each week, the girls will develop their skills. Perhaps they can play with the boys in the school competitions,' I suggested.

'But that's unfair,' said another teacher. 'Boys are better players, they're stronger, faster and have better skills and the girls will only get hurt.'

I smiled. 'There's no difference between the abilities of boys and girls at the elementary level. Sport is good exercise for *everyone*. And it will be good for the boys to teach the girls, and to develop patience and cooperation.'

'Maybe if the colliery school have a team, we could have a local competition,' said Mandy, nodding enthusiastically.

'That's a good idea,' I said. 'Perhaps one day, we'll even have a girls' competition, like the boys.'

With some further debate, I was able to gain the support of the teachers and we began training sessions for girls after school. There wasn't much resistance from parents, mostly because exhausted mothers were happy their daughters were expending energy at school, not pestering them at home. And the girls loved it, many coming to watch the women's games between rival munitions teams when the season began.

Many of my nights in Ebberfield were occupied with reading letters from Annie, Clem, Esther, Marjorie, Richard and less regularly from Tommy, and then replying to them. It was late when I opened my mail three months after my homecoming. I was only just back from a meeting at the Miners' Welfare Institute, where I'd invited the colliery women to join our suffrage society. With the new voter register and the fact that Britain was run almost entirely by women, I felt sure that it wouldn't be long until we had the vote.

I kicked my shoes off and put my legs up on the bed. It was Rose's bedroom, but she slept with her mother now. There were two letters, one from William and the other from Richard. I scanned them quickly.

Then I read the last lines of each letter again and laughed out loud. My prayers had been answered. They were both coming home for Christmas.

As I pressed the letters to my chest, a boom rent the air, shaking the walls and floor around me. The breath caught in my throat. Memories of the attacks on Hartlepool and London returned to me instantly, the visceral fear flooding my body, rooting me to the spot.

'Aunt Hannah, come quick!' called Oliver up the stairwell. His voice broke the spell and I scrambled down the stairs after him, another boom vibrating the building. Dust sprinkled down, catching in my throat and I coughed. How close were the bombs?

I raced outside to where Jenny, the children, and Tom and Amelia stood. I followed their gazes to where flashes lit up the night sky. A boom reached us as the rays of the searchlights appeared in the distance. And then I saw it.

'A zeppelin attack over Hartlepool,' Oliver shouted, his arms around the cowering dogs.

My thoughts went to Jane and her family. And then I saw Jenny's face filled with terror, clutching at Lily's and Rose's hands. All she had left were her children. Nothing else mattered but their survival. Zeppelins could drift from their target and reports of damage to inconsequential coastal villages appeared in the newspaper all the time. We were only a couple of miles from the coast.

'Down to the basement, quickly,' I said with as much calm as could muster, shepherding Jenny and her girls ahead of me. 'We'll be safe there.'

38

Happy news! Mr Lloyd George has become Prime Minister. Mrs Fawcett feels confident that the franchise bill will be passed. He has always expressed his support for women's suffrage but has been stymied politically. Is it too soon to hope that we can achieve what we've been working towards for so many years?

With the dawning of 1917, I was riding on a wave of happiness. Though the war had been taxing for all of us, I was excited for the future of the women's suffrage movement. William had been home in Ebberfield for Christmas, telling us all about his training. The passion in his voice was enough to make me see that this was right for him, despite the dangers ahead. I understood now that life was uncertain for all of us, even those at home. All the same, I was relieved that he'd been assigned to a squadron involved in home defence. He would be nineteen soon and eligible for overseas duty; at home, I hoped he'd be safer.

Richard was home on leave too and my days and nights had passed in bliss and joy.

My contentment was brief and pushed to one side with the news that Germany had begun unrestricted warfare.

'I can't believe German U-boats are sinking merchant ships,' said Lily, reading the newspaper. 'They have nothing to do with the war.'

'Ah, but they do,' said Jenny. 'If they can prevent ships

arriving on our shores with food and produce that we need, that we can't grow or supply ourselves with here, then the Germans put pressure on everyone in Britain: the government, the people, the military.'

'A naval blockade forces us to be more self-sufficient,' I said. 'We can't rely on the British Empire, we have to fend for ourselves.'

'But we're not the small vulnerable island that Germany thinks we are,' said Lily with a frown.

'No, we are not,' I said. 'But you've heard how the last potato crop has failed in many places and prices for many basics have risen and, for some people, have become unaffordable. Things are about to get tougher.'

I put thoughts of the worsening conditions of day-to-day life away, when Mrs Fawcett sent me the key points of the Electoral Reform Report to share with the suffrage society.

'They recommend changes to the vote for men, essentially suggesting manhood suffrage but the support for women's suffrage is less convincing. The backing is there but not for the vote for all women,' I said at the next meeting.

'It's two steps forward and one step back,' said Alice, shaking her head.

'Will we ever get what we're askin' for?' called out Dorothy Duggan.

'Mrs Fawcett writes that the report recommends that if women's suffrage is considered, then it will be limited. Since the number of women is greater than the number of men, the government wants equal representation between men and women.'

'How ridiculous,' scoffed Mrs Graham. 'Anyone can see what a stellar job women have done during the war. Better than men, I say. More women voters than men means a better country.'

'Hear, hear!' cried women from across the room.

I smiled. 'That may very well be, but it's not reality. Men will not loosen their control of power. The report proposes that women aged thirty and over and householders or wives of householders be eligible for the vote.'

'And yet young women and girls are asked to enlist for war work,' said Jenny. 'How many young women work in hospitals caring for our soldiers, at home and abroad? If our men are entrusted to such capable hands of these young women under pressure and war conditions, then why won't the conference trust them with the vote?'

The room burst into applause as the heated debate became a venting session of very frustrated women, mothers, wives and sisters. We'd hurled everything we had at an uncompromising, unyielding government and in the process had our bodies and dignity violated by men who would not see us as equal. It had come to an untenable position before the war. In some respects, it was just like the battlefront our soldiers were fighting on now. Both sides believed in their absolute truth and were fighting to protect that truth. But I had also learnt that there were other ways of fighting for what we believed in, with dogged determination and persistence.

After the room had quietened, I gave them the final message from Mrs Fawcett. 'We've been asked to join the NUWSS in helping organise a deputation of women war workers to be received by the Prime Minister in March. Every form of active war service is to be included and delegations from all the major women's organisations will also be involved. And some of us will join the deputation as well. We have a lot of work to do but I'm confident we can show the Prime Minister that younger women should be included in the suffrage bill.'

*

Soon it was time for Richard to return to France.

'You're thriving here,' he said to me, kissing my eyelids. 'I hope you understand how much you are loved.'

'There's so much to hope for,' I said. 'The vote for women, getting the pub back ... and you and me.' I sighed. 'If only this war would end and you, Annie and William could return to me, safe and sound.'

'That sounds like a bright future,' he said, caressing my face. 'And I'll hold that vision in my heart while I'm away.'

'I'll have my family again,' I whispered.

Emily came to see me not long after Richard's departure. 'The government has set up the Women's Land Army to provide farm workers to help with our agricultural crisis. I've applied for help and the first land girls should arrive soon to help prepare the fields for planting of crops. I pray next harvest is better than the last.'

'I see that the government has also taken over extra land for farming purposes.'

Emily nodded. 'But it will take a while to grow crops and produce and the shortages will only get worse.'

Emily's words were prophetic and the government soon began a campaign for voluntary food rationing. Food shortages had already been felt but a sense of panic began when the government announced suggested allowances per person, based on three staples of the daily diet: bread, meat and sugar.

Jenny and I were discussing ways we could change the way we cooked at school and at home with the new rations and the shortages when Rose piped up. She was part of the local Girl Guide brigade that was peeling potatoes at the auxiliary hospital run by the Red Cross in a nearby village, where injured soldiers were cared for. But recently she had joined a select group that worked in the kitchen.

'The Red Cross has provided a cookery manual at the hospital to suggest different ways to cook potatoes. But it doesn't matter if there aren't enough potatoes to go round.'

'What does the cook think about these new allowances?' asked Jenny.

'She doesn't know if she'll have enough food to feed all the men even on those allowances,' said Rose. 'Four pounds of bread including cakes, twelve ounces of sugar and two and a half pounds of meat, including bacon, which is off the menu now – it's too expensive to buy. And we have to use sugar, golden syrup and jam sparingly. She reckons it won't be long before tea, butter, suet and cheese are also in short supply, and meat and fish are all getting expensive to buy in big quantities.'

'This is something we're all going to have to work our way through. If the Germans blockade our ships with supplies from around the Empire, then we'll have to show them that we'll manage anyway,' I said. But I knew it was going to be difficult to persuade everyone to do the right thing.

Within weeks, there were queues at the local shops, as the owners struggled to keep up with demand. We heard stories of panic buying and hoarding but soon we were face to face with fights and arguments on the streets.

'Stop! You can't take that!' I heard someone shout outside the butcher's one afternoon.

'Help! Help! I'm being attacked!'

I rushed downstairs and out onto the street to the sight of two people tussling on the ground. Christopher was between them in a moment, pulling a man away. I rushed to help a woman still on the ground, her arm bleeding and her bag of meat scraps and bones open and strewn across the dirt. Only when we had them both on their feet did the woman, Mrs Clancy, tell us she'd seen the man buy more than his ration of meat by going to different butchers around town. All she could get were meat scraps.

The main street had become a war zone of its own, tensions running high, locals becoming frustrated with waiting for hours only to be turned away with nothing, learning that neighbours and friends had bought more than their recommended share.

'Mrs Clancy and many like her can't afford the exorbitant prices,' said Jenny afterwards. I nodded. Only the wealthy could buy luxury foods, while the poor couldn't even get the basics. 'She was telling me she can't even get the coal she needs to keep her cottage warm.' It was ironic that even coal was in short supply and we had to abide by the rations when we had coal at our fingertips.

'Soon people will be fighting over coal,' said Christopher, closing the shop. 'It's bad enough that fights are breaking out between the seasoned miners and the fresh ones. When the inexperienced men put the others at risk, nobody will want them to stay.'

As the stalemate stretched on in the trenches of France and Belgium, more of our miners had been enlisted to build tunnels and lay mines to beat the efforts of the Germans and progress in gaining territory. Conscientious objectors were drafted in as substitute miners to improve our supply of coal but as we'd learnt, the mines could be just as dangerous as the trenches.

'Well, they're here to stay,' I said with a sigh. 'At least until the end of the war.' We all had sacrifices to make and if only people understood that we had to come together for the sake of our community, then maybe we'd all survive this war.

I returned to Notting Hill the day before the deputation to the Prime Minister, ecstatic to be back in London to see Clementine and Esther.

'I've missed you both so much,' I said, hugging them both. I'd yearned for the bustle of London, being at the beating heart of all the progressive ideas and conversations, not to mention the convenience of all the amenities at my fingertips. I knew I'd have to return regularly to get my fix of London: time with Clementine and Esther and to keep me in touch with new and modern thinking.

'It's been too quiet without you,' said Esther, her eyes shiny.

'And the children,' agreed Clementine. 'Now we know how you feel without your family.'

'I have so much to tell you,' I said, once we'd settled in the parlour with tea. It was just like old times. I was sitting in my favourite chair and we talked for what seemed like hours about Ebberfield, London, our work – everything. But finally, the conversation turned to the government bill.

'The House of Commons has agreed on a motion to introduce a bill including women's suffrage,' said Esther. 'Members will be able to vote in any way they see fit in both houses and across party lines.'

'That is progress. I can't believe it's finally happening,' I said.

'Let's not get ahead of ourselves,' said Clementine. 'This is the government we're talking about. They can change their mind and break their promises if it suits them.'

'We have to make the Prime Minister understand that the support of the suffrage societies is dependent on women's enfranchisement being an integral part of the bill from the beginning, not an amendment,' I said.

'You see, there's the problem,' said Clementine. 'They won't agree to that. They never have.' The ashtray was full of cigarette stubs.

Esther rested her hand on Clementine's. 'But times have

changed, my love. Without women, this country would fall and the government knows it.'

'It's different this time,' I insisted. 'We're so close now.'

We were disturbed by knocking at the door.

'Who can that be?' asked Clementine, peering out the window. Somehow it had become dark outside, we'd been talking that long.

'Amy!' I heard Esther exclaim in the hallway. 'What a lovely surprise.'

'I'm sorry to disturb you so late,' said Amy, coming into the parlour. She turned to me. 'I knew you were coming today and wanted to tell you the news about the loan in person. We found the informant. He was in the brewery all along. It was the finance officer.'

'Mr Phelps?' I frowned. 'He was the one who refused to give me a loan on my own to buy my sisters out,' I explained.

Amy sat. 'That's right. He used to work for Philip Usher's company in London, when Edward was there. He was a tough nut to crack but, in the end, he told us everything. Edward's prison associates blackmailed him into being the eyes and ears in the brewery and he was coerced into using the financial company where Edward already had contacts. He knew the clauses had been changed and chose to say nothing when Roger signed the contract.'

'We never took to each other, but I never imagined Mr Phelps had an agenda all along …' I stared at her, stunned.

Clementine scowled. 'What a filthy low-life.'

'I'm sorry, Hannah,' said Esther, shaking her head.

Amy grasped my hand. 'You'll be pleased to know that he's been charged. And the police are looking for the ex-cons now, and Edward himself.'

'What happens next?' asked Clementine, clasping my other hand.

'There's no doubt about the evidence of fraud. That in itself is enough to prove that the loan should be declared null and void. The financial company will have no option except to settle or proceed to court. Papa also wants to file for compensation, for the loss of income and your family home. But it will all come down to the negotiations and the court case.'

'Are you saying I'll get the pub back?' I could hardly say the words. It seemed unbelievable after all this time.

'It's likely,' said Amy with a smile.

'What about Edward?' I asked. 'Regardless of what happens with the pub, he needs to be punished for what he's done.'

Amy nodded. 'We know he's behind it all. But without physical proof, we can't do anything. It's out there, we just have to find it, but it will take time. We will keep going until we do.'

Words failed me at that moment and I leant forward and kissed Amy on the cheek. I was so grateful for this woman, her father, Mr Stevens and my friends who had supported me all along.

Amy stood. 'I won't stay. I just wanted to tell you as soon as I could.' She took my hands. 'Stay strong, we're almost there.'

'Thank you, Amy,' I whispered, the words coming now. I hugged her tight, tears in my eyes.

As Clementine and Esther accompanied Amy to the door, I remained in the parlour, staring into space. Running the pub again might be within reach, if the twists and turns of legal argument went my way. But the fight had been exhausting, demeaning and humiliating, bringing me to my knees and stripping me of everything I held dear. But it had also brought me to London, where I'd found a new family, rediscovered my vocation with teaching and renewed the fight for the vote with a fresh sense of urgency, a fight for my very survival. Now I'd returned to Ebberfield, a different person from when I'd left: stronger, more resilient; like the pieces of me that had shattered were glued back together in a way that was stronger and better than before. I was the same, but not the same. I could survive without the pub if I had to. I had rebuilt my life based on purpose and my vocation to make the lives of my friends, family, neighbours and locals of Ebberfield better in a way that mattered to them. That was what gave my life meaning and if getting the pub back aided in that vision, then I'd embrace that victory. But regaining the pub didn't have to define my life anymore.

The burden of fear and doubt I'd been carrying for years slipped from my shoulders and, for the first time, I felt like I could breathe properly. The rush of relief, loss and grief of everything Edward Partridge had been the cause of followed swiftly, and I bent double, gasps turning to sobs that racked my body, and my beautiful friends rushed to my side to comfort me once more.

39

We feel the war at a personal level, with telegrams of loss and despair, the deaths of our soldiers, food and coal shortages and too many families going hungry and cold at night. But governments treat this war like a chess game. It's all about strategy, territorial wins and losses and of course, political gain.

I returned home from London to a visit from William. My initial joy turned to fear when he told me he was being deployed to France. He was only just nineteen.

'It will be all right, Mama,' he said. 'My job will be to see whether Allied artillery fire hits their targets. If they're off, I let them know using wireless telegraphy communication. And I might photograph German positions at the front.' Roger and I had taught William to take photographs with joy but I'd never imagined that he'd one day take them to use as a weapon of war.

'It sounds exciting, my darling. I know how hard you've trained for this. And I know you'll do a good job.' I kissed the top of his head. But Esther had explained that aircraft were now fitted with machine guns and I understood enough to know that he'd be expected to engage with the enemy.

'I want to become a pilot one day soon. Maybe I'll apply after this posting.'

'It's something you've dreamed of for years,' I said with a smile.

He nodded. 'The feeling in the air is like nothing else. I feel free, invincible.'

I frowned. I wanted to tell him that he wasn't invincible but what good would that do? It was a worry I'd have to hold close, as his mother, as I'd done so many times before.

'Have you heard about the Red Baron?'

I shook my head.

'He's German and one of the most accomplished pilots in the air, admired and feared by Allied pilots and observers. He has one of the highest hit counts of any airman. Nobody wants to encounter him but everyone wants to be the one to shoot him down. I'd like to fly like him.'

'Here, let me hug you,' I said, wrapping my arms around my youngest child and squeezing my eyes shut to remember the feel of him. He was muscled after his training but he was still my baby, really just an idealistic boy, and I prayed he could cope with the things he'd have to do in battle and to survive. He would come home different, there was no doubt about that. But I had to let him go, like I had first with Tommy then with Annie, no matter how my heart was breaking.

With William gone, all of my children were scattered to the wind and I had no idea if I'd ever get them together again. It was the most frightening thing to contemplate.

I received a letter from Tommy. He was safe on the farm, working hard to finish sowing the crop. Recruitment drives had come through the district; 'snowball marches', he called them, men travelling to Sydney, where country contingents were being formed. Roy Reid did a lot of farming for one of the biggest farmers in the district, James Black, and they both insisted that Tommy stay behind. Tommy had never liked being told what to do, but for some reason, this time, he'd listened. I wondered if his decision had been influenced by the daughter of James Black. He had written about Madeleine a few times now.

> Maddie wants to one day own her own farm and run a business in her own right. She thought I'd laugh when she told me because her father and brothers don't believe it's something a woman can do. But Maddie understands the land and farming life and has a good head for figures. I told her that you ran the pub for years. I think you'd like her, you have a lot in common. Women have the vote here in Australia and I can see it benefits them in ways I didn't imagine, like an independence and confidence to imagine a life that wasn't possible for their mothers and grandmothers. Women have a say and can influence what happens in our district and the local MPs listen to them. But Maddie believes that women still have a long way to go in achieving equality to men and I think she's right.

I closed my eyes and sent a swift prayer of thanks to Maddie Black, for Tommy's education and his safety.

Annie had written too, to tell me that everyone from her hospital was moving to Salonika, because the surge of submarine attacks on hospital ships made evacuating casualties to Malta unsafe.

I didn't know if my fears were allayed or intensified when I read that America declared war on Germany in early April. Everything felt more perilous with Annie and William in the danger zones.

'America has come to our aid,' said Miss Sloane, one of the teachers at the school. 'They're joining the war because Germany is trying to starve us into submission.'

'Perhaps,' I said diplomatically. I was a bit more cynical. 'But don't forget, Germany has been sinking American merchant ships too.' With US troops in Europe, perhaps the deadlock on the Western Front would end and this war could be brought to a swift conclusion.

I was asked to join the War Savings and Food Economy Committee, where we would discuss the best ways to encourage food saving and how to economise what we had.

'It's only voluntary rationing,' said the chairman, Mr Cavanagh. We were in the new council chambers that had been built in Ebberfield. 'We have a terrible shortage of wheat and flour, and after the failure of the corn harvest last year, other grains will follow. To make matters worse, we don't have enough workers on the farms, and German submarines are blockading any imported food.'

'When the Americans arrive in Europe, now they've finally joined this infernal war,' said Mrs Scruton, 'the Germans ain't got no choice but to end the blockade when they realise they ain't gonna win.'

'That may be,' said the chairman. 'But nobody knows what will happen. If we can't make what we have last as long as possible, we'll all be on the brink of starvation. The county meeting even discussed the last resort of killing our herd animals, to free up more grain for the population.'

'That's ridiculous,' said Emily, who had stepped into John's official roles on council. 'If we have no stock, how will we have milk and meat? And when circumstances improve, how will we ever build a new herd?'

The chairman nodded. 'But with growing desperation out there, decisions are made that aren't necessarily in everyone's best interest.'

'Last night, my shop window was broken, and my stores of tea, sugar and flour stolen,' said Mrs Scruton, shaking her head. 'This behaviour can't keep goin'.'

'The culprit has been caught,' said Constable Williamson.

'His neighbours noticed him coming home with a sack stuffed with food. They confronted him this morning and barged into the cottage and discovered he's been hoarding sugar and flour and poaching game.'

'I hope you make an example of him, pet,' said Mrs Scruton grimly. 'If everyone thinks they can do these things, there'll be nothin' left for the rest of us.'

'Especially the vulnerable, like old Mrs Ainsworth,' I said. 'She forages for berries and edible leaves in the fields and the dene. Her granddaughter brought her what she thought was wild carrot but was in fact hemlock. I'd hate to think what would have happened if either of them had eaten it.'

'So many people don't know which plants and berries are poisonous,' said Emily. 'And when they're desperate to put food on the table … I know it's not right but at least when children pilfer fruit and vegetables from gardens after school, they won't die from eating what they bring home.'

'So, we must find a way to make this voluntary rationing acceptable for the district,' asserted the chairman.

'Then there have to be no privileges for anyone, everyone will get the same,' said Mrs Graham, looking pointedly at Mrs Burrows. Mrs Graham was a known socialist and resented the privileges of the large, landowning families and gentry.

'What about miners?' piped up Mr Gould, a representative of the Ebberfield Colliery. 'Surely they are entitled to more food than someone who sits behind a desk all day?'

'As do pregnant and nursing mothers,' said Mrs Burrows. 'And our soldiers here at home and in our hospitals.'

I nodded. It was going to be difficult to manage the different needs of our community.

'What about a prohibition on alcohol?' asked Reverend Proctor. 'How much grain and sugar would that save?'

'You couldn't do that!' shouted Mr Gould, jumping from his seat. 'What else can a man look forward to at the end of his working day?'

My thoughts precisely. Women too! Besides, pubs across the country wouldn't be able to stay in business. It was enough that beer was watered down, spirits were too expensive to buy, the prices of drinks had been fixed by the government in some areas, and opening hours reduced even further. I was glad to not be tearing my hair out wondering how I was going to make a living and keep the doors of The Ox and Plough open, but it wouldn't be long before I'd have to think about it. Robert Sanderson was making progress with the case and I hoped to find out soon if it was going to be settled. At least I had my job at the school and steady, regular and reliable income.

'Now, Mr Gould,' said the chairman, raising his hands in appeasement. 'If we can make voluntary rationing work, it won't be necessary to consider anything like that.'

'What about promoting ways to minimise food waste and using substitute foods in cooking?' I suggested, wanting to get to the real issues. 'We've begun to put such measures in place at school when we cook for the children at lunchtime.'

'What if parents came in to watch what you're doing at school?' suggested Emily. 'To give them ideas of what they can do in the home?'

'It's a good idea,' said Mrs Burrows, 'but the kitchen at the school is too small and we won't be able to expose enough people to the ideas quickly enough.'

'What about the community hall? We can do two large cookery demonstrations at the village hall as well as the one at the Welly,' said Mrs Graham, nodding enthusiastically. The Miners' Welfare Institute was new and had a large hall with a kitchen attached. Perhaps mining families would come too.

'I think that will work,' said the chairman.

*

I took a telephone call from Esther at the Ebberfield post office. The *Representation of the People Act*, the franchise bill, had passed its second reading in the House of Commons and was now at the committee stage, where a detailed examination of the bill would occur and any amendments and changes voted on.

'I'm calling from Mrs Fawcett's office. She sends her love,' said Esther.

I smiled to myself. 'I wish I could have been there for this important stage of the bill.'

'Well, perhaps it's better you're there. The Americans in France seem to have sparked a new attack by the Germans. Gotha aeroplanes, heavy bombers. They hit London in the daytime a few days ago, killing children at a school in Poplar.'

'It's inconceivable. I was horrified when I read about it in the newspaper.'

'People didn't know what it was and went out onto the street to look.' She sighed. 'Over one hundred killed and five hundred injured. It's the worst raid we've seen in London. Our aeroplanes are old and couldn't fly high enough to reach them. I wish the government would deploy the more powerful aircraft we've designed.'

I huffed. 'When will it end?'

'It's terrible. But enough about that ...' There was a long pause over the telephone.

'Esther, is everything all right?' The convenience of the telephone was wonderful but without looking at someone's body language and facial expressions it was often difficult to decipher the more subtle meanings in conversations.

'The committee have finished their deliberations.'

I waited, hardly able to breathe, the frisson of anticipation coursing through me. Was this the moment we'd been waiting for? Or had it ended like every other time. We'd been fighting for a bill to reach this stage for over twenty years. If now wasn't our moment, I didn't know when we'd next have the opportunity and public and government support for the vote for women. Everything now hung on the committee's decision.

'Hannah, they've accepted the bill! It was passed by a majority. Three hundred and eighty-five to fifty-five.'

I whooped and everyone in the post office turned to stare, the postmaster frowning in displeasure, but I didn't care. 'That's incredible. It passed so easily. We've never got this far before, not with the Bryce Bill, not with the Conciliation Bill, none of them.'

'We might really do it this time.' I could hear the excitement in Esther's voice.

'I wish I was there to celebrate with you,' I said wistfully.

'Tell the others and celebrate with the suffrage society. Clem and I will be with you in spirit. We'll see you soon.'

I took Esther's news back to the special suffrage meeting we'd organised that night.

'The bill has been passed by the committee,' I said. 'Next step is the House of Lords.'

There was cheering and clapping, and we hugged and kissed, and slapped each other's backs.

'After twenty-four years of us fighting for it,' said Amelia, shaking her head.

'The war's what's done it,' said Mrs Scruton. 'Who knows how long we'd be waitin' otherwise.'

'It has been a long fight,' I agreed. 'But we're nearly there. 'Let's order lemonade to celebrate.'

I gazed at the women around me. I hoped we'd now make it all the way through the parliamentary process to the end.

And I hoped that soon, I'd hear about whether the legal fight for the pub had been successful. Everything I'd worked for was so close; I could almost touch it.

A letter from Annie waited for me that night. I was exhausted but elated after the news of the day as I swung my legs up on the bed and turned my lamp up to read the small writing.

Dear Mama,
Salonika is so different from Alexandria and Malta. Here we are close to the front. The hospital has been erected with marquees all arranged in lines but fully equipped with everything we need. We wear white uniforms and have to wear net veils and long sleeves to prevent mosquito bites that cause malaria. We live on rations, like everyone here. Sometimes we can get eggs, goat's milk or fresh vegetables and the edible fruit of the prickly pear, a cactus bush with fruit which must be peeled. The terrain is harsh, rugged and dry and the locals live very rough here. I hear that the winters are very cold and snow falls, with blizzards and rain that causes mud everywhere, making conditions even more difficult.

Men bring wounded soldiers from the front on mules along treacherous paths through the mountains and hills. It's never-ending, but with our surgical team, they have a greater chance of earlier treatment and the best outcome.

When things get too much, I walk a little way from the tents and look out over the beautiful bay to the fabled Mount Olympus in the distance and wonder what marvels I might one day be able to explore in this ancient land.

Your loving daughter,
Annie

I put the letter down and sighed, then picked up the photograph of her and William on the day of Clementine and Esther's wedding which sat on my bedside table next to one of Tommy. They were both smiling and carefree. It was foolish to believe that all Annie's experiences would be happy and exciting, especially in wartime. I could read the weariness between the lines, the jaded perception. The war was changing her, as it was changing all of us.

40

It feels good to get my hands dirty with the suffrage society again. We converted all the small allotments around the village into vegetable gardens. Everyone got involved – women, old men, miners, children – and we gave classes on gardening. We added our newly grown produce to our cookery demonstrations, the meal club at school and the new community kitchen where locals can buy cheap, nutritious meals.

Robert Sanderson came to see me at school.

'Robert! What brings you here?' I asked as he walked into my office.

'Hannah, I think you'd better sit down,' he said gravely.

My heart fell. I'd known Robert's legal case could go either way. Clearly something had happened to the negotiations with the financial institution. They were a big, powerful company and had money to throw at solicitors to tie our case up in knots, even though we were in the right.

I took a deep breath as I sat, steeling myself for the worst. I would manage without the pub. I was happy and secure with my friends and family around me.

'Tell me,' I said, my mouth dry.

Robert took my hands in his, and his eyes shone with unshed tears. He had worked so hard all these years and was just as invested as me in the outcome.

'Hannah, we've done it. We've got the pub back.'

I stared at him. Had I misheard? 'What ... What did you say?'

Robert smiled broadly now, his hands reassuring around mine. 'We've won the case, Hannah. The Ox and Plough is yours.'

I felt dizzy and light-headed. 'The pub ... is mine?'

He nodded. 'The loan is null and void.'

I pressed a hand to my mouth. Thoughts collided and jostled as enormous emotions swelled within me: joy and relief, and then grief for all the years lost.

'Oh Robert, thank you. I ... I'm in shock.' I laughed breathily. 'But what happened?' I asked finally. 'Tell me.'

'The financial company wasn't going to settle but with both men confessing to what they'd done and being convicted, the evidence of fraudulent activity was irrefutable. A scandal of this nature would destroy their reputation and even the hint of suspicion that a convicted criminal had been able to infiltrate their ranks and influence one of their documents was enough to make them settle out of court. They had no choice but to keep it quiet. We're still finalising the details of your compensation, but you should get money from the brewery as well. I'm only disappointed that we weren't able to find Edward. The police can't trace him and for all we know he could be dead. But I think for you, the result is still the same.'

I shook my head in wonder. This was more than I could have hoped for. Maybe it was time to let go of Edward. He'd tried to destroy me but I'd survived.

'Robert, we did it!' I grasped his hands, squeezing them in gratitude. 'Thank you, thank you. You and Amy have worked tirelessly for years, never wavering, always committed. I can never repay you for all you've done for me.'

Robert dipped his head, blushing from the praise. 'It was my pleasure to help you. We've righted a terrible wrong.

I'm only sorry you had to go through any of this in the first place. Now you can carry on you and your father's legacy and make The Ox and Plough the centre of our community again.'

I walked back into The Ox and Plough a week later and gazed at the timber counter of the main bar. It wasn't as neat and tidy as I'd left it seven years earlier, but it was mine. The sign above the door was being restored with my name as owner and publican once more. I was the sole owner of this business, finally stepping into my inheritance with the power to do things my way, the businesswoman I had always been. But now I was recognised legally; as a widow, I was independent.

I was still waiting on the settlement from the financial company but the brewery had been most apologetic for what had happened with the loan and, in lieu of a settlement from them, I was awarded full ownership of the pub and cottage, my liquor licence had been renewed so I could resume trading as publican, and I no longer had any tied arrangement with the brewery. I was free to do whatever I wanted, to buy beer and alcohol from any brewery I liked. I'd wondered how the teachers and parents of the children at school would take their headmistress being a publican but those who remembered the old days were delighted for me and for those who had reservations, I'd just have to prove I could be both and serve the community well in these roles.

With Robert's news, my thoughts had turned once more to the vote for women. If women had had total financial and legal independence, I would never have been in the position where Roger signing a loan contract could cause me to lose everything. We needed the vote so we could change the laws limiting women's financial and legal freedom. I had that independence now and it was something I wanted for all women, the same rights that men had.

My heart was thumping as I ran my hand over the counter. 'We've done it,' I whispered, feeling the strength of Papa, Mama and Roger at my shoulders. 'The Ox and Plough is ours. Nobody can take it from our family now. It's safe. The lighthouse can shine again.' Tears streamed down my face. I was home. I felt it in my bones. All I wanted now was to have my children with me.

I turned at the sound of footsteps on the wooden floor. Jenny, Emily, Alice, Amelia, Dorothy Duggan, Mrs Scruton and Mrs Burrows stood in a row just inside the door.

'We've come to help,' said Mrs Scruton.

Jenny smiled. 'With whatever you need.'

'Well, we have time to give it the once-over, at least,' said Mrs Burrows, glancing around the room, her lips thinned.

'We'll have the floors gleaming in no time,' said Alice.

It was then that I cried with gratitude for my friends who I knew would always be there for me through thick and thin.

'Don't mind me,' I said as the heartfelt embraces of my friends brought me to the present. 'These are happy tears.'

I visited Roger's grave later that day, taking a bunch of wildflowers with me.

'Roger, it's finally mine. Our legacy hasn't been lost. The pub is in a stronger position than ever before, and I have so many plans for the place. It's time to make new memories.' I kissed his headstone and placing the flowers at the foot of the stone, I turned to leave.

Maybe it was my imagination or the wind in the trees, but I felt a sense of strength rush through me, and so much love.

'I love you, Roger. I always will,' I whispered and continued down the hill.

*

The reopening of The Ox and Plough was more than I had ever dreamed it would be. Every inch of the pub was sparkling, and friends, family and neighbours came to congratulate me and help me celebrate. Sarah and Jane were there, as were Mrs Scruton, the Sandersons and Dorothy Duggan. And Esther had driven up in her motor car with Clementine. I pushed the pain in my chest aside every time I thought about Annie, Tommy and William and how they should be here. I kept looking behind the bar, expecting to see Roger, or Reg and Bobby, who were both in France. I had new barmaids, as accomplished as any barman: Jenny, who'd watched Papa and Roger for years; and Susie Duggan, Bobby's sister, who I'd spent hours training. Bella was still here, working the floor and helping in the kitchen. We had certainly come full circle.

The crowd was just as raucous as in the old days, even if the restrictions on our trade meant there was less alcohol. It was more about our joy of being together and remembering those who weren't. Our windows were blacked out but we now had electric lighting. Women and families gathered in the lounge and upstairs rooms, and many played billiards and pub games, while men congregated in the main bar.

Amy, Marjorie and Mr Stevens arrived unexpectedly with a man trailing behind them. I shouted with excitement to see them, overjoyed to have them there in my hour of triumph.

'I didn't think you could get here but I'm so happy you could come,' I said, full of emotion. 'I wouldn't be here if it wasn't for you,' I said to Amy and Mr Stevens.

'We had an offer we couldn't refuse,' said Marjorie. She stepped aside and there, in all his glory, was Richard, grinning from ear to ear.

'You're here!' My smile spread across my face to match his. 'I didn't think you were back from France.'

'I am,' he said simply. He was too far away from me and I rushed into his arms.

Closing time came all too quickly and before long, the pub was empty except for Richard and me. We sat with cups of the precious coffee he had brought back from the Americans in France.

'I've never tasted anything better,' I said, closing my eyes in bliss and savouring every sip. 'We've been using roasted ground acorns. We can't even get chicory.'

'I'm glad you like it,' he said, reaching for my hand.

I wondered if I could be any happier.

'Are you home for a while?' I asked, barely daring to breathe.

'I don't know. The Americans have taken over the hospital in Boulogne and have their own medical staff and researchers. I worked with them for a bit. I have some time off now while I wait to hear about my next posting. I've asked for somewhere here, preferably the military hospital in Newcastle. It's as close as I can get to you.' He brought my hand to his lips. 'I'm not as young as I used to be, after all, and they have plenty of young surgeons and researchers on the Continent.'

I nodded. Richard was already in his early fifties and I would be fifty in three years.

'I can't wait for this war to be over and to have you, Annie, William and everyone we love home with us, safe and sound again. I feel that part of me goes with you and the children every time you leave. And that I won't be whole until you're all here again.'

Richard kissed my cheek gently. 'One thing I've learnt with this war is that time is the most precious gift of all. We have to make the most of every moment we have together, because nobody knows what's ahead of us nor what will happen.'

'Let's enjoy the time we have then.' My lips met his and, with practised hands, we undressed each other in the light of the smouldering fire until we were burning with desire. He lifted me onto the kitchen table, and I arched towards him, wrapping my legs around him and hearing him sigh as we became one.

41

Soviet Russia has signed an armistice with our enemies. The war rages on and I don't know how long it will continue for, even with the American involvement and 'tanks', Esther's armoured cars, taking to the battlefields in France. Clem insists that the revolution in Russia has our government scared, given the rise of socialism at home. She believes that this is the real reason the vote for women has been considered, to prevent a socialist uprising here.

Jenny and the children moved in with me at the cottage next to the pub and there was a bed for Christopher too. The children loved having space because above the butcher's had become cramped, with Amelia and Tom's daughter and grandchildren also living with them. Duke and Shandy finally returned to the place they'd known as puppies, even though they were very old dogs now.

Flashes of memory came to me as I moved through the rooms, the joyful chaos of washing and grooming the dogs, tea and biscuits at the kitchen table, Roger dressing in the morning while I watched him in the pale light of morning. But life was different now and I had to build new memories with Jenny, Christopher and the children bringing life and joy back into our home.

I spent most nights at Richard's residence. I'd walk across after finishing at the pub or he'd come before closing. It was the most time we'd ever spent with each other and I was floating on a cloud of bliss. Each night I'd lie in his arms, happier than I had ever expected to be again. But pressure from Almroth Wright and the Royal Army Medical Corps meant that Richard would return to the laboratory and Boulogne soon.

The business of running a pub at the same time as running a school swiftly hit me. Government restrictions and the tighter controls around licences caused me to rethink many of my strategies. I couldn't return to the way things had been before I left. Government taxes on beer and spirits – so that whiskey was five times the price it had been at the beginning of the war – but not on wine or champagne, affected what I could buy for my very working-class clientele, and there were few ingredients with which to cook enticing food for the lunch and dinner service. I worked long days at school, then at the pub during dinner and late into the night, checking my stock and accounts, and the meetings and events we had booked in, few though they were, were mainly funerals and memorials. When we didn't have enough beer, we'd resort to serving teas brewed from various herbs. And then there was the community work, all based from the pub.

'I'd like to raise a problem I've just encountered,' said Mrs Graham at the last suffrage meeting for the year. 'Me and some other women were told we wouldn't be served in the pubs.'

'What do you mean?' I asked.

'We went in to get a drink after work. Me friends work as pit bank women, haulin' heavy tubs and sortin' coal, and at the end of a long shift, we like to have a beer together at one of the pubs in the colliery town. But we were told we couldn't order alcohol, only lemonade, when we could clearly see that men from the pit were orderin' beer and being served it.'

'Surely it's just one pub,' said Reverend Proctor. 'Maybe it's because he's rationing his beer.' The reverend was at the meeting in his capacity as overseer of the community charity works that the church was continuing with.

'No.' Mrs Graham shook her head violently. 'We went to other pubs and they each said the same thing. Then we came to the village in disgust and went to The Rose and Crown. They wouldn't even let us in!' she exclaimed. 'I was horrified. Women barred from entering a pub.'

The issue of restricting the sale of beer and alcohol due to ongoing difficulties in supply had been debated by the pubs across the two villages but there had been no consensus on what should be done about restricting sales to certain days. There had, however, been mention of restricting sales to women by Charlie Franks, the publican of The Rose and Crown. It looked like he'd inherited the narrow-minded attitudes of his father and had decided to go ahead on his own. The Hare's Foot was still deciding what course of action to take, but would likely follow The Rose and Crown.

'This is the first I've heard of barring women from pubs,' I said. 'I don't agree with not serving women alcohol, either. We have as much right as men to buy and drink what we like. I will never discriminate or deny my customers choice in what they order.'

'That might be so, Mrs Rainforth, and no doubt you will gain new patronage among the working women of the colliery village after this. But what are we going to do about it? Do these publicans have authority to deny women?'

I shook my head. 'Publicans were meant to agree on how to prolong our supply of beer but nothing like this. And I'm not sure they can deny serving sober women alcohol. There is no law saying that they can.'

'Besides, when women drink, they remain more sober than men,' said Alice.

'But surely Mr Franks has done it to protect women, just like a parent protects his child by putting a shield around the fire,' said the reverend.

'Now, Reverend, you're not comparing women to children, are you?' I asked. 'You know what Mr Franks has done is unjust and what the other publicans have done in preventing women from buying alcohol isn't right.'

'Yes, of course,' he mumbled, turning red. The old attitudes were still so ingrained in men, especially the older generations and men of wealth and privilege.

'I agree, Mrs Graham. We have to let them know they can't do something like this,' I said.

'I know just the thing,' said Alice, a wicked smile spreading across her face.

Some of the ladies of the suffrage society met the following evening to take a tour of the public houses between the two villages. At the pubs in the colliery village, we were denied alcohol but not lemonade.

'Would you accept restrictions like this on men?' asked Mrs Graham, addressing the room full of men. They all knew her and her friends, and many had worked side by side with them at the pit. Some men dropped their heads or shook them in shame.

'Not on your life!' said one miner.

'We'd let our Member of Parliament know,' said another foreman. 'He'd make sure our rights were protected.'

'That's exactly right,' I said. 'But there's no reason for women's interests to be protected in the same way as men's when women can't vote. Does that seem right to you?'

'These restrictions do seem unnecessary,' said another man. 'Personally, I think it's insulting to respectable women, especially the hard-working women of this town. If it's about rationing, perhaps a more equitable way could be found.'

Some nodded in agreement while other men became stony-faced. I could see an argument brewing that would turn into a fight and that wasn't what we wanted to achieve.

'We came to let you know our objection and to make you all aware of the situation. Now it's time for us to go,' I said, taking Mrs Graham's arm.

Outside the pub, I pulled out the chalk from my pocket. 'Let's leave them a reminder, so that everyone who walks past will know what's going on here.'

Alice took the chalk and began writing on the pavement in large letters: *Women not served alcohol here. We object to not being treated the same as men. Women matter.*

We left a message on the pavement outside each pub we visited.

'I'm sorry, I can't serve you,' said Charlie Franks when we entered The Rose and Crown.

'Why not?' asked Jenny.

'We're a men-only pub.'

'What?' I spluttered. 'When did you decide this?'

'Recently,' said Charlie, folding his arms. 'You know the supply problem we're all having.'

'But we didn't reach any consensus on restrictions.' I had hoped, perhaps naively, that he'd be reasonable about this.

'We didn't,' he agreed, his lips pulled into a thin line. 'But I am the publican here and it's my choice.'

'It's not even legal,' said Alice, in a loud voice.

Charlie shrugged. 'I've received no complaints from anyone who matters.' He stared at us, his eyes hard. 'I think you should leave.'

'You lily-livered coward!' said Alice in disgust.

While men held the power to write and change legislation, women's opinions were secondary. I prayed that things would soon change with the franchise bill that was finally in the House of Lords.

'Let's go,' I said to the women. 'We've seen what we came here to see.'

Alice stormed out first, scrawling her message on the pavement: *No women allowed at this pub. Publicans must serve all members of the public, including women. Seven men get drunk to one woman.*

When we returned to The Ox and Plough, all the women bought an alcoholic drink.

'This is our new place,' said Mrs Graham to her colliery friends. 'This is a place where women are respected and valued.'

'I feel I must apologise for the bad behaviour of my fellow publicans,' I said. 'They may think they have won a battle over us but their victory *will* be short-lived. With the new franchise bill, women will finally be recognised as valuable citizens for our role in supporting our nation through war. It is my hope that soon women will have a say in the important issues and laws. Once we have the vote, our Members of Parliament won't dare dismiss our voice.'

'Is she always like this?' asked one woman, eyes wide with admiration.

'She is,' said Alice. 'And now she's back, The Ox and Plough will become our lighthouse again.'

'The Lighthouse? What a good name for a pub that supports women and their community,' said Mrs Graham.

I nodded, an idea falling into place like the piece of a jigsaw. The Ox and Plough had been a good name for a pub that served a small agricultural village, but now we were a modern and thriving town – twin towns, in fact.

'I think it's time to rename this pub,' I said. 'The Ox and Plough doesn't fit anymore, but The Lighthouse does.'

Nods of approval, whoops and clapping erupted from the crowd.

'Three cheers for The Lighthouse,' I said, raising my glass.

I received a letter from William in December, arriving on my birthday.

> Dear Mama,
> I'm coming back to England. I've been accepted into pilot training and begin in Oxford next week. I can't tell you how excited I am. You know I've always wanted to learn to fly. Can you imagine? Me, a fighter pilot. Maybe one day I'll be as good as the Red Baron.
>
> When I'm back, I hope to see a little more of you if I can get a few days off at a time.
>
> I hope I've made you proud.
>
> Happy Birthday.

Tears sprang to my eyes. Of course I was proud. He'd worked hard to achieve this wonderful opportunity to fulfil his dream. Not just anyone could become a fighter pilot. But I also knew it was a dangerous job and I worried for him. Some of the most celebrated pilots in Britain had met a fiery death, crashing after some malfunction of their aircraft, some human error or from being shot down by our enemies. There was little chance of survival after crashing an aeroplane.

William was young, not even twenty years old, and he believed he was invincible. I was forty-seven and knew better.

It was Christmas Eve, traditionally the busiest time of the year for the pub, and the perfect time to celebrate its new name. We began the unveiling ceremony in the afternoon, before the light had faded.

I glanced at the gathered crowd, all eagerly anticipating the big reveal. I'd invited Clementine, Esther, Amy and Marjorie and Mr Stevens from London and they'd made the trip north, despite only being here four months ago. Marjorie was glowing, four months pregnant, an unexpected joy to her in her forties. In peacetime, an unmarried woman like Marjorie expecting a baby would have been a scandal, but in these days of war and loss, new life was accepted with warmth and many turned a blind eye. We were so happy for her and Mr Stevens. Family and friends, new and old, members of the suffrage society and customers of the pub all gathered outside, rugged up in coats and hats, where the new sign above the door of the pub was hidden by a sheet. Inside, the fire roared, the Christmas tree groaned under its decorations, hot food and snacks awaited, and performers, musicians and magicians were ready to draw people into the various cosy and welcoming rooms that I'd made my own, to begin the festivities. The first Christmas since I'd got the pub back.

'Are you ready, Mama?' asked William, squeezing my hand. He was by my side and Jenny, Christopher, Sarah and Jane stood nearby too.

I nodded; my mouth suddenly dry as the significance of this moment hit me. This was the culmination of everything I'd been through.

'Dadda, Grandda and Grandma would be proud,' he whispered.

I smiled at him gratefully. I pulled on the rope and the sheet covering the sign above the door fell away.

THE LIGHTHOUSE
PUBLICAN OWNER – MRS HANNAH RAINFORTH

'I present to you, The Lighthouse,' I proclaimed. My heart swelled with pride at the bold new sign. For the first time, my name was above the door as publican and owner. I gathered myself together. 'A place for friendship, support and community. A place for all of you.'

Applause erupted from the crowd, cheers and whistles too.

I beamed. These were my people and this was my new beginning.

42

Gotha attacks still plague London, and Marjorie has told me that the sound of aeroplanes sends terror into her heart. War is still raging, with little gain in territory on the Western Front. I have new cause to be frightened of aeroplanes, given William is determined to become a fighter pilot.

'Today's the day,' I said to Esther, Clementine and Marjorie, as we walked from one of the committee rooms, where we'd been waiting, towards the tiny area allotted to us in the House of Lords.

It was 11 January 1918. I'd returned with them to London, after we'd celebrated a loud and joyful Christmas with all my family in Ebberfield. We were here to witness this momentous event.

Esther nodded. 'If America can pass the federal amendment on women's suffrage, then we have no excuse not to.'

We'd been following the discussion of our franchise bill for three days after members of the house, hereditary and appointed peers, had tried to take the women's suffrage clauses out of the bill and remove the amendment. For much of the time, we'd had absolutely no idea whether the bill would be passed with the women's enfranchisement clauses intact. But with the passing of the American law the day before, hope bloomed among all the suffrage supporters.

'Let's hope they do this soon,' said Clementine as we squeezed into the small area and nodded to women we knew.

Suffragists, suffragettes and anti-suffragists were all jammed together. I squeezed Millicent Fawcett's hand in passing.

Further discussion and final comments were made before the leader of the house, Lord Curzon, stood to speak and close the debate. I felt the muscles in my neck and shoulders tighten and my stomach clench with worry. Curzon was a known anti-suffragist. 'If he denies his support for the bill, it will open the door to others still sitting on the fence,' I whispered.

We fell silent, listening to him talk but my heart began to sink, hearing the standard rhetoric against women's suffrage coming from his mouth. I noticed the look of disappointment on Mrs Fawcett's face and the look of triumph on those who didn't support the vote for women. If we failed now, who knew when we'd ever succeed? It could be years – maybe not even in my lifetime. I'd always imagined Annie's future would be liberated but what if I was wrong? Without the vote, we were denied our basic rights and we'd never achieve equality with men, never gain the legal and financial freedom women so desperately needed.

But then I frowned. 'Did he just say that he won't vote on the amendment at all?' I asked quietly. The women around me nodded.

'He doesn't want to take responsibility for the conflict that will happen in the House either way,' whispered Clementine, her eyes wide with wonder. 'It must be closer than anyone thinks.'

Sure enough, when I looked around the room, the anti-suffragists were red-faced with fury. 'It doesn't mean anything,' spat one of the women nearby. 'The House will never vote for it.' She glared at us scathingly before turning her attention to the action in the room. It was time for the peers to vote and I wondered how many others would abstain, following Lord Curzon's example.

The four of us clasped hands as the votes were ready to be read out.

I glanced at the women around me, their faces rigid with tension. There were women in this room who had given everything for the vote for women: their jobs, their marriages, their families, their respectability, their dignity and their health.

'Let it be what we want,' I intoned like a prayer.

Clementine nodded. 'After everything we've fought for.'

'And everything we've been through,' Esther added.

'For the future of our children,' said Marjorie, resting her free hand on her belly.

The room went quiet and, in the silence, I was sure I could hear my own heart beating. The tension in the room was palpable and the pause between moments seemed to go on forever. It was excruciating.

'One hundred and thirty-four for and seventy-one against,' announced the speaker. All around me, women were looking at each other with expressions of disbelief. But the speaker's words made no sense to me, just a garbled mix of numbers.

Clementine shook me. 'Hannah! We did it!' The breath rushed from my lungs and only then did I realise that I'd been holding it.

'We did it?' There were expressions of jubilation all around me. How could the fight over the last twenty-five years come down to some numbers spoken by a man in a single moment? And yet it was the culmination of everything we'd worked so hard for. The lives that were lost and destroyed. I trembled; the magnitude of the moment crashed though me like a storm. And suddenly I was back in the present, whooping with joy. I hugged Clementine, Esther and Marjorie. 'We did it!'

'All these years,' said Clementine. She was shaking with emotion too. 'Everything we went through was worth it.'

'We'll remember this moment forever,' said Esther through her tears.

'Women all over the country will tell their children and grandchildren about this moment for the rest of their lives,' exclaimed Marjorie.

'And we can say we were here, at the centre of it all,' I said in amazement. 'We're part of history.'

I met with Millicent Fawcett afterwards for a private moment.

'Congratulations, my dear friend,' I said to her, remembering when we first met, decades ago, now. She was getting old, I realised.

She smiled. 'We've waited a long time for this.'

'Only you could have done it. Despite all the disappointments, the protests, the attitudes of the government, you remained patient. You played the long game and because of that, we've succeeded and the bill passed with ease.'

'Thank you, Hannah.'

'Do you know that your determination, perseverance and persistence inspired me to keep going when I was at my lowest point? I refused to give up the fight when I lost the pub, reminded by your example.'

She took my hand in hers. 'Hannah, you've been through so much and I'm so proud that I helped you in some small way. And I hear you're calling the pub The Lighthouse – such an apt and worthy name. But don't forget you played your part too. You've always been dedicated to the cause. But not all women have the vote. This bill is just the start.'

I smiled. 'You can count on me.'

She was whisked away by her committee members and supporters to a nearby tea room, and we were invited to the celebration.

'I won't join you,' said Marjorie. 'I've been advised by my doctor to rest when I'm tired and it's been a long day.' Her pregnancy was high risk, because of her age and the fact she'd never carried a child to term. She'd lost two babies with Edward, both to violence, and believing she could never fall pregnant again, she was doing everything she could to keep this one. She and Nicholas were living as a married couple, but although Edward had disappeared, she could not remarry. 'Come for a light supper afterwards, so we can celebrate.'

We were jubilant, despite the pressures of the new compulsory rationing on our celebratory treats. Tea, sugar and cake were scarce. Mrs Fawcett gave a speech and we toasted our success with herbal tea.

'Cheers to us all,' said Esther, dabbing her eyes with her free hand after Mrs Fawcett sat down. We clinked teacups. 'Our friendships were forged on this single passion and goal,' Esther continued, 'and I couldn't be prouder ...' She put her head in her hands and started weeping in earnest.

'My love,' Clementine whispered, reaching for her. 'We know.'

After the tears and joy at the team room, we went to Marjorie's house to continue celebrating. We were a raucous group walking through the streets of London. We felt invincible.

'She must have fallen asleep,' I said, when Marjorie didn't answer the door. 'And Nicholas isn't home.'

'How can we wake her?' Esther stepped back from the porch to look up to the windows above.

'Which is her bedroom?' I asked, joining her in the small front garden.

'No need,' called Clementine. 'The door is unlocked.' She pushed the door open.

I frowned. 'That's unlike Marjorie. Maybe she was more tired than she realised.'

We went inside.

'Marjorie, we're here,' called Esther.

'And we've brought wine we've saved for the occasion and a few things for supper,' I shouted. We walked through to the kitchen and deposited the food and wine on the small table.

'I'll go up and wake her,' said Esther.

Clementine nodded. 'We'll open the wine and rustle up some supper.'

I went to the pantry to see what I could find to add to our supper. 'There's bread, pickles and tinned bee—'

A scream echoed through the house.

My eyes met Clementine's and we raced up the stairs.

I stopped in the doorway of Marjorie's bedroom. Esther was inside the room, trembling violently and sobbing, eyes wide with horror. Clementine rushed to her, holding her tight. I looked beyond Esther to the sickening scene and I recoiled. Marjorie was lying motionless on her bed, eyes unseeing. There was blood everywhere.

I stood rigid with shock, my brain scrambled. I didn't know which detail to register first. Blood … there was so much blood. The sheets and bedclothes were soaked with it and red was sprayed over the wall. Then I saw the large, jagged gash at her throat. 'Oh God, no!' My eyes travelled down and I fell to my knees. Her belly had been slashed: her baby killed too. I turned my gaze to my friends, arms around each other, their eyes wild.

The police questions seemed to last forever but finally we were back at Notting Hill, hunched around the kitchen table with hot, dark tea and a bottle of brandy, half empty in the middle.

'Who would do something like this?' asked Esther. 'The police say nothing was taken.'

'Someone who knew she was alone,' said Clementine. 'Someone who's been watching her.'

'After all Nicholas's efforts to keep her safe,' said Esther. He'd been called out with the development of a case he was on, only to come home to the chaos of the police and the brutal horror that awaited.

I shook my head. I would never forget what I'd seen, as long as I lived. I rubbed at my face, then my heart stilled. 'Could it have been Edward?'

We all looked at each other, with the question in our eyes.

It was the day of Marjorie's funeral. People gathered around her grave in coats and hats, hunched under umbrellas as the rain fell.

'Oh, poor Marjorie.' Esther sighed, her breath a white trail through the cold morning air. 'She didn't deserve this, and after the hard life she's had ...'

'She was never free of Edward,' I said. Only that morning we'd had word that he'd been arrested, but scant other details. I clenched both my fists. Though the legal system demanded to presume perpetrators as innocent until proven guilty, I had no doubt in my mind. The pits of hell wouldn't be worthy of Edward's crimes.

'How is it that women aren't safe in their own homes?' asked Clementine, her mouth a thin line. We had drunk our way through the rest of the brandy bottle the night we found Marjorie, the night we'd won the vote, and cried, and talked and held each other. But nothing would feel right again. If only we had caught him sooner.

My nostrils flared at the smell of the fresh earth, heaped on Marjorie's grave. Rain-splattered mud stains marked the hems of ladies' skirts and men's trousers. My feeling of desolation grew when I thought of all the abused women we'd supported over the years, including Marjorie, but in the end we couldn't protect her.

'I always feared that one day it would end like this for her,' said Becky desolately. She had travelled down from Ebberfield when we telephoned her about her sister.

'I thought Edward would get away with everything he's done,' I said.

'Maybe if he'd stayed away, stayed hidden, he would have. But he couldn't help himself,' said Clementine scathingly.

'I bet he thought he was untouchable. Getting away with what he'd done to me with the pub was the last in a long line of crimes he escaped justice for,' I said. The director of the financial company, Mr Phelps, and even his prison associates who had threatened them were in prison. But Edward had escaped capture until now. He'd been found, drunk – and defiant to the end – at the Old George. Police had been tipped off by his boasting at a boarding house for itinerants at the docks and, to me, it seemed almost as if he'd wanted to be caught.

'And it emboldened him to murder Marjorie.' Esther pressed her hand against her mouth, tears in her eyes.

'But we got him, didn't we?' I felt the heat rush through me. Finally, now he'd face the consequences of his actions. 'He won't get away with this.'

'Nothing has changed. We're all at the mercy of men,' whispered Becky, twisting a handkerchief in her hands.

I shook my head. 'We can't think like that, Becky.' We had changed some things, but not enough, and not soon enough for Marjorie and countless other women and children subject to male violence. With the vote for women we could change the law and with it, the fundamental attitudes towards women. Mrs Fawcett put it plainly: we needed to keep fighting and this was only the first step. A step that had taken half a lifetime to accomplish. 'We are the arbiters of change. We keep pushing now, for Marjorie. And our children and grandchildren will continue to make the world better than we left it.'

'You're right, Hannah,' Clementine said, smiling grimly. Becky nodded into her handkerchief then dabbed at her tears. 'This is only the beginning.'

'The *Representation of the People Act* has received royal assent and has passed into law today,' I announced to the suffrage society in Ebberfield. It was 6 February 1918.

'To celebrate this momentous occasion,' I continued, 'we'd like each of you to cast your symbolic vote into our ballot box. This is a new beginning for women. We've achieved so much together but we have so much still to do. But we'll do it together,' I said.

'I'll go first,' said Mrs Scruton. 'I am the oldest here, after all.'

'We'd be honoured if you were the first,' I said with a smile. 'You're a founding member of our suffrage society.'

She nodded. 'You're the other one.' She stepped up to the ballot box, an old box sitting on the table of the meeting room at The Lighthouse. We'd draped the box in fabric and decorated it with flowers and a sign, *Votes for Women*. 'I cast my vote for women,' she announced, placing the paper inside.

We all applauded and I hugged her as she came back to the group. 'We did it, Mrs Scruton,' I said, tears in my eyes. Then I thought of Marjorie, who had worked by my side in London, but she would never see the benefit of the power of her own vote.

'Well, at least I've lived long enough to see it,' she said. 'And I'll vote at the next election, but don't you stop until all women have the vote same as men, do you hear?'

I nodded, wiping my eyes.

Soon everyone was lining up to cast their vote, including Lily, Rose and some of the little girls from school.

Finally, Becky stepped forward and Amelia, Mrs Scruton, Jenny, Alice, Emily, Amy and I, all of us who knew and remembered Marjorie, gathered around her. 'This is for Marjorie,' she whispered, as she slipped the final paper into the box.

'For women everywhere,' I said, looking into the faces of friends, family, neighbours. The community I loved.

43

Marjorie was finally empowered with her political freedom, a baby on the way and a family she'd built. Edward killed her for it, of that I am sure. Murder is a capital offence: a life for a life. So much death when too many men and women have lost their lives in war. If he's convicted, Edward won't have to suffer like we did, like Marjorie did. But he won't be able to hurt anyone ever again.

The courtroom fell silent. I clasped Clementine's and Esther's hands as we waited for the verdict to be announced in Edward's murder trial. The trial had taken only a week.

'Guilty!'

Edward's head dropped and I jumped to my feet.

'Finally!' I hugged Clementine and Esther, shaking with emotion.

The words we'd been waiting to hear ever since the Fred Duggan trial, twenty-one years ago. Words we were denied then, but we had them now.

I turned to Becky and embraced her. 'Marjorie finally has justice,' I said.

The judge's gavel fell and a hush descended on the courtroom one more time as we sat. I grasped Esther's and Clementine's hands again. 'I sentence you Edward Partridge to death for the crime of murder.'

The police investigation had been swift. A crime of passion they called it. Edward had lured Nicholas Stevens away with a note, planning to talk to Marjorie. That note was the first piece of evidence that irrefutably pointed to Edward. We'd showed the police that it was the same handwriting as the notes we'd received and the letter to the suffrage society that Edward had penned with his signature.

He'd known about her relationship with Nicholas but when he'd heard that she was pregnant, he'd had to see her, he couldn't help himself. They had been denied the family he'd always wanted when she'd lost her child after that night in the graveyard with Fred Duggan. Marjorie had let Edward in, perhaps thinking it was Nicholas or hoping Edward would agree to a divorce – we would never know. But neighbours had seen Edward arrive, had heard screams. And he had been sloppy, left too many clues and when he was arrested, drunk in The Old George only days later, his fingerprints were a match with those at the scene. With the weight of evidence against him, he was charged with murder.

'Edward will never bother us again,' I said grimly. He had lurked in the shadows for far too long, but now we were vindicated. 'His sentence is justice for all the crimes he committed and was never convicted for.' The murder of Fred Duggan, rather than manslaughter, the abuse of Marjorie, Esther's rape, changing the loan that caused me to lose the pub, terrorising us with threatening notes and possibly even our harassment. Maybe even his uncle's death. We'd never know what really happened to Philip Usher.

'Marjorie's murder was the desperate act of a desperate man, his last grab for power and revenge,' said Esther.

I nodded. Desperate men were dangerous men, and so many had hidden behind layers of laws, rules and words to disadvantage women, to threaten them and disempower them – Edward Partridge, Parliament, men in power. We had tried to protect ourselves, to find a language that men of influence would understand; peaceful protest, using rhetoric and parliamentary procedures and militant action. The war had changed everything and some women finally had the vote, but I was galvanised to keep fighting.

'He's gone,' said Clementine.

'But while we fight for all women, we will always remember Marjorie,' I said. Clementine, Esther, Becky and I joined hands. There was strength and solidarity in the unity of women. It was a power that men underestimated, but a force they would now have to reckon with.

March 1918

My dearest Richard,

The months following Marjorie's death, the court case and Edward's execution have been tumultuous, but I read in the newspaper that Boulogne, Dunkirk and Calais have been attacked by German Gothas. I had to write immediately, I hope you are safe and that the hospital hasn't been damaged.

The children are all as well as you would hope during this war. William is on the North Yorkshire coast at the Royal Flying Corps base and the School of Aerial Gunnery, finishing his pilot's training in tactics and aerial combat. I know that he's safe there, and that he has the skills he needs to fight any attack.

Annie is enjoying working with experienced female surgeons in Salonika, but malaria is indiscriminate and striking down nurses and doctors as well as soldiers.

Tommy sends me letters when he can – while I miss him terribly, I'm so blessed that he has avoided all the violence, bloodshed and uncertainty here and at the Western Front.

My nephew Oliver received his conscription letter while I was in London, at eighteen years and one month. Jenny has been beside herself, especially following Robert's death in France. I can't do much to console her. He's enlisted in the Young Soldier battalion of Durham Light Infantry and has basic training for four months. We all pray that the war is over before he turns nineteen and becomes eligible for overseas service.

In happy news, I've been elected to the parish council to fill the year remaining on the three-year term of Mr Jackson, who died of old age. I remember when Millicent Fawcett asked me to run for local government nearly twenty-four years ago but I wasn't eligible to stand. It's something I've always wanted to do and it feels like a wonderful achievement after all this time.

I miss you every day and wish you were here with me. I pray you remain safe too.

Your Hannah

44

I don't think we've evolved as a species at all when powerful men decide the fate of humankind without understanding the consequences. Survival of the fittest, should be survival of the biggest weapons. I can't imagine this is what Darwin had in mind.

'I've been deployed, Mama,' William said as we sat in the kitchen of The Lighthouse. 'I'm going to France as a pilot.'

My lip quivered and I swallowed the lump in my throat.

'Don't worry about me. I'm flying, doing what I love. And every day I'm in the air, I'm happy and I learn a little more about myself and about my plane. It's under pressure that I know I'll refine my skills and become a better flyer.'

I hugged him tight. 'I'm so proud of you, William. But you stay safe and come home to me in one piece.' I looked into his face, such a sweet mix of Roger and me. 'Do you hear me? You are my heart and I couldn't bear to lose you.'

William cupped my face with his hands. They were big and strong. He wasn't a child anymore but a grown man now, like his brother. 'I'll be careful, Mama.' Then he kissed my forehead.

My baby was charging fearlessly straight into danger and there was nothing I could do to stop him or protect him.

'Watch over him, Roger,' I whispered as he left.

*

A month later, I picked up the mail, holding my breath, hoping there was a letter from William. But I realised it was too soon to hear from him.

It was from Richard. He'd been back in Boulogne for nearly four months and every letter meant he was safe and well.

April 1918

My dear Hannah,

We have a new enemy among us. A terrible gripe, much like the influenza you suffered all those years ago, but also very different. We've heard stories of it spreading across Europe, although there are no public or newspaper reports. But let me tell you, it is cutting through our men. There are the usual symptoms of aches, sore throat, headache, fatigue and some nasal discharge. But I'm worried that with the constant stress on the men at the front, and the injuries and illness those already in hospital suffer, they may be more prone to contracting this influenza and not recovering as quickly as they should. We can't afford to have more men in hospital and in isolation conditions.

Please watch for any flu symptoms at home and tell the parish council to begin the preventative measures before the epidemic has a chance to spread in Ebberfield. Warn Esther and Clementine too. It will be worse in London.

Look after yourself.

All my love,

Richard

I mentioned Richard's letter at the next council meeting but I was outnumbered in my plan to increase our vigilance and state of preparedness when Charlie Franks persuaded some of the other councillors that I was scaremongering. All I could do was warn the suffrage society, keep a watchful eye at school and the pub, and encourage people to take preventative measures when they or others were unwell.

'Have you seen the newspaper?' I asked Jenny one morning in June.

She shook her head as she made us tea from the mint in our garden.

'The new gripe epidemic that Richard was telling me about is here on British soil. They're calling it "Spanish Influenza". Cases are growing every day. I wish he was here. He was always the one to galvanise the community and put the correct measures in place.'

'What are you talking about?' Jenny frowned. 'You've done this with him so many times. You know exactly what to do, what measures to put in place. Now that there's no doubt we have an epidemic in Britain, the parish council will have to take you seriously about keeping our town safe.'

But rationing and the war had worn people out and many refused to take heed of simple measures like staying at home when they were unwell and limiting the size of social gatherings. The epidemic didn't bypass us, and many locals became unwell, but most were better within a few days. By some miracle, more didn't get sick and the threat receded within a few weeks.

I wrote to Richard to tell him we were all well.

> We have ration books now for butter, margarine, lard, meat, sugar and cheese. The new system is more orderly and is working but we continue growing as much food as we can and many people with small allotments are making butter and cream from their own milking cow. Thank goodness we have Emily's cows for the school meals and the restaurant.

Oliver's battalion has been sent to Boulogne to train before he begins his active service. Jenny was shocked when he told her but the rules have changed and he can leave for overseas service now he's eighteen and a half. Of course, she's distraught, but what can she do? What can any of us do? Please visit him if you can, I'm sure a friendly face will help him and allay Jenny's fears.

William has written. He's in France, that much I know, engaged in air patrols, he says. I know he can't tell me what he's doing. But he could be attacking German positions behind enemy lines and doing night-bombing runs or air-to-air combat. It pains me that I don't know and can only imagine the worst. I never imagined my boy being the instrument of such destruction but I've come to understand that, with war, all things become possible. It's kill or be killed. Perhaps he's fortunate being in the sky. I could hardly imagine him in the horror of the trenches, it would break my heart.

Please stay safe and well, my darling.

Your Hannah

After writing the letter, I spoke to Esther on the telephone to check on how she and Clementine were. It was easier than writing and I missed the sound of their voices.

'We're well here,' she said. 'But so many have fallen ill to the Spanish flu. As if the war wasn't enough ...'

'The war has to end soon.' With the worry and everything I had to do, I was exhausted.

'Have you noticed we've had fewer attacks? The Germans are concentrating their forces on the front in France. We're making headway, finally.'

I thought for a moment. 'It's the tanks and aeroplanes and submarines. They've made the difference. It's not just a battle against men anymore, it's a battle against machines and, thanks to you and your colleagues, advances in technology can be used to fight this war.'

'I only hope it helps to end the fighting soon. If we keep going like we are, I think it won't be much longer.'

But Richard's next letter was a warning of things to come. I braced myself as I read his terrible account of the flu epidemic on the front.

> September 1918
>
> Dear Hannah,
>
> The second wave of the Spanish flu has hit us hard. Soldiers are falling like flies, young men, not the old or children, like we'd expect. The symptoms are the same as earlier in the year but something we haven't seen before is a blue colouring of the face, followed by black discolouration of extremities, limbs and then torso. It happens so swiftly and death follows soon after, from pneumonia. Some have speculated that it's cholera, the plague or even typhus, but we've isolated it to a secondary bacterial infection. Many bleed from the mouth, nose and ears and haemorrhage from the intestines and skin too. I've been told that, in the civilian hospitals, women are miscarrying healthy pregnancies. I've never seen anything like it. It is brutal, fast and ferocious, with death occurring within a couple of days of first symptoms.

A shot of anxiety rushed through me. I couldn't do anything for William and Annie, except write to tell them to be careful, but I could keep a close eye on Christopher. Mary had died from the flu because of her damaged heart and Christopher could too.

> Soldiers are sent from the front to hospitals set up for this flu as it is so contagious but it's difficult to isolate patients on their journey from the trench to the hospital. They are often transported by train and I fear the spread will only grow.
>
> I am well, taking all the precautions I can, as we try to find anything to mitigate this pandemic. It is all over the world now and so far our vaccines only deal with one of the bacteria involved in the secondary infection, and not the virus itself. But if we can get enough people inoculated before they are infected then we can minimise symptoms and death.

We didn't need Richard's letter to know that this second strain had come to Britain's shores. Servicemen were returning home from the front and others were travelling from abroad, no doubt bringing it with them.

Parish councillors met with the district council, who agreed to enforce measures limiting numbers at the cinemas and dance halls, theatres, churches and any public gatherings. Any indoor spaces where people other than family met should ensure a good supply of fresh air and ventilation, and people were advised to dress warmly. We closed the schools for a couple of weeks at a time, reviewing the quarantine measures each fortnight. Anyone nursing the sick should wear goggles and a mask made from four layers of gauze. The local doctors suggested those who were only mildly unwell take aspirin for their pain and fever and formamint tablets, a commercial preparation taken for four or five days, to minimise or even prevent infection.

Our communal kitchen was restricted to serving a fewer number of customers so we began serving at tables outside or offering meals to take home in small containers; we thought it important to keep nutritious food available to boost the immunity of vulnerable people. But what Richard had told me about was happening in Ebberfield: young people between the ages of twenty and thirty were falling sick with the terrible bacterial pneumonia. It was heartbreaking to see the pages of newspapers filled with obituaries. Young, fit, healthy miners and girls in the munitions factories who were well in the morning, were dead by evening, among them Mrs Graham's grandson, and friends of Lily and Eliza in the factory. Thank God, Christopher was untouched.

I took the girls' school football team to a game of the Munitionettes' Cup, between the Blythe Spartans, one of the north's most successful women's sides, and a team from a rival munitions factory at the stadium in Hartlepool. The competition went ahead as it was held in the open air and was considered safe from the Spanish flu but I insisted they all wear masks. I wanted them to see what was possible for women's sport and the skill level women could achieve. And with the challenging times we were having, I wanted them to have fun. To have some respite from the hardship around them.

'Why weren't women allowed to play before the war?' asked one of the girls.

'It wasn't considered ladylike,' I replied as we took our seats in the stadium. It was the home to my favourite team, West Hartlepool, before I'd met Roger and David. 'But the factory managers realised that women had to play some kind of sport to keep them fit and healthy for their munitions work.' Annie would have the opportunity to play when she came home and I was looking forward to the pleasure I knew it would bring her.

'We're the same as boys,' said another girl, scornfully. 'Of course we need exercise to keep us healthy.'

The players came out onto the field in their jerseys, shorts and long socks to great applause. The stadium was packed and the roar of the crowd was deafening. I hadn't been to a high-profile game like this in years, since David was playing for Newcastle.

'Look, it's Bella Raey,' shouted one of the girls in excitement. Bella was one of the biggest stars in women's football.

'I want to play like her,' said another girl.

'She kicked six goals in a single match.'

All the girls gazed at Bella in awe. She was their idol and it was wonderful to see that an ordinary girl from a coal-mining family could inspire so many. She was a trailblazer for women doing anything a man could. She was strong, capable and unpretentious. Women like her boded well for our future.

'Then train hard and reach for the stars,' I said with a smile. 'Anything is possible.'

For the first time in a long time, I really felt that it was.

45

War can only lead to humanity's demise. Even nature knows that what we're doing has upset the balance of things. Maybe the Spanish flu has come as a warning to us, before we destroy the world and everything in it.

I received a telegram in early November. The war was nearly over, the Germans all but defeated, and we were waiting for the end of the war to be declared. I had no choice but to take the envelope from the hand of the delivery girl. I forced myself to walk slow, leaden steps to the scullery, the only place I would find privacy at the pub.

I glanced at the fire, the urge to throw the paper into the flames overwhelming, but I took a deep breath and, with the apprehension rising within my chest and my hands shaking, I opened it. All the possible contents flashed through my mind. Was it Annie, William, Tommy somehow, or Richard? Any of these were too horrible to contemplate but there was no other reason to receive a telegram.

I pulled the page from the envelope. It was from the Royal Flying Corps. My stomach dropped. *William*. I forced myself to read its contents, and in a few short seconds, my whole world changed.

Dear Mrs Rainforth,
I regret to inform you that your son William is missing, presumed shot down behind enemy lines in France.

My legs gave way and I collapsed to the floor. I stared at the letter in my hand, no longer able to make sense of the words and struggling to breathe.

'Hannah!'

Jenny was by my side in an instant. She and Susie Duggan helped me from the floor.

'Get her a glass of something strong,' Jenny barked to Susie once I was sitting at the kitchen table.

Time blurred. This was where we'd learnt of my father's death from a telegram. This was where I understood that Roger was dead and never coming back.

Jenny put the glass in my hand and guided it to my mouth. I swallowed in reflex and felt the liquid burn its way down.

I gasped, back in the present, and a keening wail rose from deep within me. I rocked back and forth as the grief filled every part of my being. What I had always feared had come to pass.

I had a vague recollection of the doctor giving me something to dull my senses before I was put to bed, where mercifully I knew no more.

The next day, Sarah and Jane were by my bedside, but I couldn't look at them. I didn't want their sympathy and with it, their inevitable belief that William was gone from me forever. I didn't want it to be real. He was my beautiful boy. I could see him in my mind's eye, running to me as a small child, the fierce love on his face, his little arms around me, holding as tightly as he could to show me how much he loved me, the feel of his blond head as I kissed it fervently. He was my baby. The idea that I would never hug him again, that he was gone, was unbearable.

Richard had heard and sent a telegram, telling me he would do everything he could to learn more about what had happened.

I knew there was little hope. There was little chance of survival for any pilot who was shot down. Perhaps William had emulated the famous Red Baron after all; the infamous German pilot had been shot down and killed some months ago.

'Jenny needs you,' said Sarah about a week later. She had stayed to help at the pub and to support me. 'She hasn't wanted to tell you, but she has received news that Oliver has been injured and she doesn't know where he's been sent. It could be any hospital in France.'

'She didn't tell me.' I stared at Sarah. 'Jenny's been through as much as I have – as much as any of us have.'

My sister nodded. The news was what I needed to pull me up and out of my misery. Not one of us was untouched by this war. We had to stand together and support one another.

'I'll let Richard know. If anyone can find Oliver, it will be him, and he can tell Jenny about his condition.'

Armistice Day followed soon after: 11 November 1918. But it was too late for those who had fallen and maybe William and Oliver too.

Jenny and I walked through the crowds that filled the streets to the village green, where most of the locals waited.

'They were so close,' she whispered, holding my hand tightly.

'What was it all for?' All those boys and men who would never come home. Families destroyed everywhere and a country that would never be the same. The world would bear the scars for years to come.

Mrs Scruton and Amelia stood with us.

'Not long now,' said Mrs Scruton. 'At eleven o'clock it will all be over, just like that. The armistice signed and peace declared. If men can stop war like this, it's a wonder they never stopped it before it began.'

It was a sobering thought. If women had been in power, would we have had the same outcome? I liked to think not. Maybe with women in government and positions of power, we could make sure a world war like this would never happen again.

'No need for such dark thoughts at a time like this,' said Amelia. 'However the war has ended, it's time to celebrate. Loved ones can come home and there will be no more death and destruction.'

I nodded. 'There is much to be grateful for.'

Motor car horns hooted into the silence and bells rang as the clock struck the hour. A loud roar rippled through the crowd.

I squeezed Jenny's hand. 'It's over.' We had survived the war and Ebberfield had survived too.

She hugged me tightly and began to cry and I found I was crying too, relief, grief and loss rushing through me.

'No more,' said Mrs Scruton, wrapping her beefy arms around us and Amelia too. 'Now we start the healin'.'

Cheering and singing began and the military band that had assembled on the village green struck up a lively tune.

'Come on, let's join the procession,' said Amelia, taking Jenny's arm. 'It's important we mark this moment, no matter what we've lost.'

Mrs Scruton and I followed behind them, a sea of British flags waving everywhere we looked, faces filled with relief and joy. Couples kissed, friends and neighbours hugged. I squinted, looking into the crowd.

I grinned. 'Isn't that Christopher and Amy Sanderson?' They were kissing.

'Leave them be, pet,' advised Mrs Scruton with a nod. 'If a day like today ain't ripe for love and comfort, then when is?'

She was right. We had to take love wherever we found it; the war taught us that; and Clementine and Esther.

Life could be fleeting. My thoughts turned to Tommy and Madeleine, he'd mentioned her more with every letter. Then they shifted to Richard. How I missed him and wished him home.

The war was over but in the days after, excitement was tempered by grief, loss and the continuing scourge of the flu. After everything we'd done to get the town through the war, we were still on high alert, trying to protect our own. Many who had survived the dangers of the war fell to the influenza and died. It was unbelievable, heartbreakingly unfair.

We were ecstatic when Richard sent word a week later that he had found Oliver. Jenny's son had finally arrived in Boulogne at the best surgical hospital. They had been trying to save his leg but he had taken ill with influenza and deteriorated too quickly to operate. His life hung by a thread. If he survived, it would likely be too late to save his leg.

It was all too terrible to contemplate. Jenny had already lost her husband and might lose her son. She refused to eat and I knew she didn't sleep.

'Come on, you have to have a little something,' I coaxed. 'Look, it's bone broth with meat in it.'

She shook her head. I didn't know how much more she could take.

'Jenny, you have to keep going for Lily and Rose.'

Sarah arrived from Trimdon to look after Jenny and me. I kept my worries about William to myself. There was no news of him and I didn't want to burden them with my fears. I knew there were boys over there who would never be found. But Sarah knew me too well.

'He's still missing,' I told her after we'd settled Jenny for the evening. 'Richard's done everything he can to trace his movements ...' I shook my head, despair threatening to derail my emotions. 'It's the nightmares ... Whenever I close my eyes, I see William lying dead in a field of mud somewhere in enemy territory.'

'But it's not enemy territory anymore, and there's more of a chance than ever of finding him.'

'I pray for that every day, but what if they never do? What if we never know where he is, never know what his last minutes or hours were? That uncertainty of whether he's really dead, not having his body to bury and properly mourn …' I buried my head in my hands.

'You shouldn't think like that,' said Sarah gently.

'I know, but it's my worst fear and I can't shake it. It terrifies me.' I took a deep breath, trying to centre myself, then sighed. 'I worry for Oliver and Jenny. She's been through so much and I would never dream of sharing these fears with anyone but you. I just wish I knew when Annie was coming home. Maybe if she were here, safe and well, I'd feel less fearful.'

'It's understandable, Hannah, but remember, Jane and I are here for you too.' She enfolded me in a comforting embrace and somehow I felt better. Sometimes a mother needed mothering too.

Jenny was up early the next morning, dressed for travelling. My heart squeezed. She was thin and wraithlike.

'What are you doing, my darling?' asked Sarah, looking up from making porridge.

'I want to go over there,' she said, desperately. 'If he's going to die, I want to see him. If he lives, I want to be there for him and make sure he comes home.'

'You can't go,' said her mother gently. 'It's chaos over there, and you can barely stand.'

'I don't care. I'm leaving for France today.' Her face was set in grim determination.

Sarah stopped stirring the porridge. 'You have to eat first.' Jenny nodded. 'And you're not going alone.'

I frowned for a moment, and then I understood. We were Todd women, strong and just as determined as each other. 'I'll look after Lily and Rose while your mother goes with you.'

Jenny opened her mouth and then shut it again. Sarah shot me a look of gratitude.

'We don't want to have to worry about you too,' I said.

'Well,' said Sarah, untying her apron. 'I should pack.'

I still had a stack of mail to open on my desk; I just didn't have the energy to do it. But Christopher had seen the state of my office, usually so orderly, and insisted on aiding me to get on top of it all. He'd been a wonderful help to Jenny and me in our grief and assisting Tom and Amelia at the butcher's. And a support to Lily and Rose while Jenny was away.

'Let's open this letter,' he said. It was from Millicent Fawcett.

I nodded and he pulled out the pages and gave them to me. Then he turned to organise the essential correspondence I had to attend to. He had a good business head on his shoulders, I realised.

November 1918

My dear Hannah,

I'm writing to you about the upcoming general election. Now that the *Parliament (Qualification of Women) Act* has been passed, the election of women to the House of Commons from the age of twenty-one is a possibility. It seems unbelievable that we did not need to fight so hard to get this Act passed – it was all but unopposed. We have under three weeks until the election – little time or opportunity for women to select constituencies and work up their candidature. I urge you to speak to the women in your suffrage society and within the district about their preferences and if indeed any women are ready to step forward for nomination.

I thought for a moment. We didn't have much time to put our support behind a nominee, much less prepare a woman candidate. I sighed. It was something I'd have to discuss with the suffrage society as soon as possible.

I have been working with other members of the National Peace Council to ensure that issues important to women everywhere are included in the agenda of the Paris Peace Conference, which begins next month. With the end of the war, treaties involving the defeated nations must be moral and humane so that we have an enduring peace. A war of this scale and magnitude must never happen again.

We vigorously support the idea of a League of Nations, a form of multinational governance that maintains world security and peace through diplomacy and negotiation, but is also concerned with important issues like just treatment of all peoples, the protection of minority groups, fair work and conditions of labour, and the prevention of human and drug trafficking.

Once the conference is underway, I hope to turn my attention to the work we still have ahead of us. On reflection, we have achieved so much already. To think how far we've come since our early petitions to the government more than fifty years ago. But we must continue to work for enfranchisement for women on the same terms as men, not just for women over thirty. Now it is also our duty to assist women in understanding and realising their full responsibility as voters. But I feel that to do this, we must obtain all reforms - economic, legislative and social - to ensure equality in all areas between men and women. These must be our objectives and the NUWSS must not rest until we have achieved full enfranchisement for women. I know it will happen. It is only a matter of time. But I must admit to you, my dear Hannah, that I am weary. We will have much to discuss at our meeting in April and I am sure you will bring with you your usual vigour and keen insights, to make our organisation relevant moving into the future.

Your friend,
Millicent Fawcett

We had achieved so very much and we'd come such a long way, but there was much still to do. I couldn't hide from the world with my pain, when so many endured so much more. I had to keep putting one foot in front of the other. William would want that.

Jenny and Sarah returned from France before the general election.

'Oliver pulled through,' said Jenny, rushing to hold Rose in her arms. 'He'll be coming home soon.'

I glanced up at Sarah, who nodded grimly. Rose burst into tears and Jenny sobbed, hugging her daughter tight. Lily would be beside herself too, still grieving the loss of her beau not long after Oliver's conscription.

I followed Sarah into the kitchen. 'How bad is it?' I asked.

'He was so close to death,' whispered Sarah. 'We got to him just in time. Another day and he would have been gone. I am a woman of faith but I have never been one to believe in miracles.' She stared into the distance. 'I might be silly for saying this, but I think Jenny brought him back from the brink. Ollie heard her voice and knew her touch. His face was blue and his skin was black, yet he turned the corner and made a full recovery.'

I shivered, my spine tingling at her words. 'The power of love,' I whispered. If only love could bring William back to me. But I couldn't touch him or talk to him. I took a breath. 'What about his injuries?'

She shook her head. 'He survived the flu, but his life was still in danger. His leg had turned septic and the only option the surgeons had to save his life was to amputate.'

I gasped. 'He was always such an active boy. How will he manage?'

Sarah shook her head. 'I don't know. But he's alive and that's a blessing.' She dashed her tears away with the back of her hand. 'He's being repatriated back to England and will be sent to a convalescent home so he can have special treatment and training for amputees. We have to take each day as it comes. Perhaps, in time, he'll learn to walk again.'

I nodded. The news was bittersweet. But at least Oliver was alive and we knew what challenges were ahead.

'You must be so proud of Richard and Annie,' said Sarah. 'The doctors and nurses are the ones who take our boys, stitch them up and care for them. I can't imagine what they endure each day with the endless casualties coming through the door, some of them in such pitiful condition. I've seen it with my own eyes. But they're the ones who give the rest of us hope.'

Hope. It was what fuelled us. The war was over, but until everyone returned home, it was what we all lived on. We had to hope for a better future, whatever that looked like to each of us.

*

The general election was held on 14 December.

'How many women did you succeed in putting up as candidates?' asked Emily. We were both eligible to vote.

I shook my head. 'None. There just wasn't enough time.'

'What about you?'

'Don't be ridiculous.' I scanned the newspaper before we went to the polling booth. 'There are seventeen women standing as candidates, including Christabel Pankhurst, but nobody in our county.' I didn't tell her that I'd been approached but I hadn't felt ready, not with William missing and Annie and Richard still away. If I was going to stand, I had to be fully focused.

'Let's meet the others,' Emily said, not commenting any further.

We met the members of the suffrage society and a large crowd of women, and we cast our votes to the loud applause of the crowd.

'How did that feel?' asked Jenny.

'Amazing,' I said, grinning. 'For the first time, I chose who I want as our voice in Parliament. All we need now is for that to be a woman who shares our own views and passion.'

'It will be you one day,' said Jenny with absolute sincerity.

'You never know,' I said with a shrug. But her words lit a fire within me. Women's voices had been raised and we were now heard. Whatever I did next, whatever I chose in the future, I knew that it would involve making my voice count, making women's voices everywhere count.

46

The results of the general election have been announced. The coalition has been re-elected and David Lloyd George returns as Prime Minister. It's good news; better the devil you know for the further reforms we want. It's something special to see the very first woman elected to Parliament, a member of the Irish, Sinn Fein. But it's a shame she hasn't accepted her seat, in protest against British rule in Ireland and in support of Irish Independence.

Richard came home after Christmas.

'You're here,' I sobbed, hugging him on the threshold. He was real, alive and well.

'I am. Home for good.' He smiled, a tired smile, but I could see how relieved he was.

'You're frozen,' I whispered, kissing his cold lips. I drew him into the parlour, where I still had the fire going. Everyone was in bed but I had stayed up, working on the plans for a new menu for the community kitchen. 'You look exhausted.'

'I am,' he said, his shoulders dropping as though the burden had become too much. 'But I had to come home tonight. I wanted to get back as soon as I was able.'

The breath froze in my chest. 'Did you find him?'

He shook his head, collapsing into the armchair by the fireplace. 'I'm so sorry, Hannah. I haven't found any trace. I scoured hospital lists, traced every transport he might have been loaded onto and even visited the place they think he crashed. But nobody really knows. It's chaos out there.'

My heart fell as tears welled in my eyes. Up until now, I'd had hope. Hope allowed for possibility, even if it was remote. But I had to ask the question, had to know for sure.

'Is there any chance he might be alive somewhere?' My voice sounded tremulous to my own ears.

Richard took my hands in his. 'There are so many – too many – men missing. It will take months, if not years, to fully understand the degree of our losses on the battlefields. Even the hospitals are overwhelmed. But to survive being shot down and the crash would have been a miracle in itself. And that was weeks ago now.'

I gasped as my glimmer of hope began to fade.

He brought my hand to his lips. 'I think you should prepare yourself for the worst.'

I nodded, my body suddenly wooden. I knew what he was telling me. It had been two months since William was shot down. Most pilots and observers died in the air or on impact, gone in a blaze of glory like a shooting star. And yet, I could not let go of that tiny ember of hope that continued to smoulder. I couldn't let go, not yet.

It was 1919 and the new year was subdued as the third wave of the influenza epidemic rushed through Britain in the coldest part of winter.

Jenny and Rose visited Oliver in the convalescent hospital each week. Lily went whenever she could and Christopher went too.

'He's getting stronger,' said Jenny. 'I think he's finally accepting what's happened to him. So many of his friends didn't make it home. He's coming to understand how lucky he is to be here at all.'

I was delighted for Jenny but I had existed in an agonising limbo, torn between faith and despair for weeks. William's body hadn't been found and as each day passed with no news of him, my grief overtook any last remnant of hope. Perhaps I would be one of the many mothers who would never know what had happened to their sons and daughters. And that would be the greatest heartbreak of all.

I nodded. 'Like William. Richard told me to prepare for the worst.' I hid my face in my hands. It was so much harder to say out loud.

Jenny took my hands in hers. 'No. Look at me. You can't think like that.'

I gazed into her eyes, which were filled with determination and hope.

'He might still be alive. Oliver is here against the odds and William could be out there somewhere, trying to get home to you.' She kissed my cheek. 'Don't give up.'

I nodded, not sure what to think anymore. Jenny's positivity buoyed me, despite the odds. While hope remained, my boy still lived, if only in my heart and mind.

The war was over but life remained hard for everyone. Rations were still in place and it would take months to build reserves of foodstuffs imported from across the globe and to get our agricultural industry back into full gear to provide produce.

Fuel for heating was still hard to come by and the government advice was to dress warmly and to remain in well-ventilated spaces. Richard was busy at the isolation hospital, where too many cases of influenza were admitted each day, and at the workhouse hospital, as the district medical officer, where people were admitted with illnesses accentuated by being under nourished and constantly cold. Dr Williams, well into his eighties, continued to help Richard in the practice.

Dr Williams was a godsend and without him, the village wouldn't have managed throughout the war. The suffrage society endured and helped in any way we could, from sewing masks, making brochures and providing educational lectures and practical tips to the public to reminding them of all the public health measures that would help protect our community.

Meanwhile, the schools opened and closed as the cases rose and fell. We continued to run our community kitchen, as well as the cookery demonstrations.

The elections for the Ebberfield Rural District Council took place in March. I had been nominated to run before I knew about William. Despite my grief – everyone suffered from loss within our community – I campaigned through the early part of the year. In some ways, being so busy pushed my emotions deep within me. Action was a balm.

A few weeks later, Richard came into the pub between patients at the surgery. I had a day off from school and was working behind the bar with one of the barmaids, showing her how to pull a beer.

'The results of the election,' he said, raising the newspaper.

I doubted I'd been successful as I hadn't received a letter, but I watched out of the corner of my eye as he opened the paper on the bar and flipped the pages until he found the announcement.

'Don't keep me in suspense,' I said as he continued to look through the list.

He raised his head, a big grin on his face. 'You've been elected. You're a district councillor!'

'Really?' I would represent Ebberfield and fight for what our town needed. It was the culmination of all my work in the community and schools. Now I could advise Durham County Council on anything to do with the schools in our district. And I was delighted to be working with Robert Sanderson who was still clerk on the district council.

He nodded and turned to the men in the main bar. 'Hannah Rainforth is not only the best publican in Ebberfield and headmistress of our elementary school, she is now also our district councillor,' he announced.

'Congratulations,' said Tom Brown, who had come in with Christopher to have a beer after work. 'Couldn't imagine anyone better for the job.'

'You're the best, Aunt Hannah,' said Christopher, leaning across the bar and giving me a peck on the cheek. He was doing well, surrounded by family, love and support. 'And you won't have to fight anymore with Charlie Franks.'

I couldn't help but smile. Charlie had been elected again for the parish council.

Other customers wished me well too.

'Thank you,' I said, feeling myself blush. I was doing everything I had ever dreamed of but I was doing it without the people who mattered most. My two eldest children were far from me, Annie, just like me, and Tommy who had always been my challenge, and my baby, my William, my heart, was probably dead. I knew I had to accept it, but I feared doing that would destroy me. I remembered William as a baby, his chubby little legs and uncertain steps across the grass, holding up a dandelion flower to show me, with the glow of the afternoon sun behind him. He brought me so much joy and unconditional love. But now he was gone. I was mortified to feel my lip quiver.

'Excuse me,' I said, turning away suddenly and rushing to the quiet and privacy of the kitchen. Only then did I let the silent tears fall.

'It's all right,' whispered Richard, wrapping his arms around me. 'It's natural to be sad. But know how very proud I am, how proud we all are. And we're here for you as much as you're here for us.'

I nodded. Ebberfield was my family too and it was time to accept their love and support in my time of need.

Soon, fathers, sons and brothers began to return home, and daughters, sisters and mothers too. As the reality that William would likely never come home began to set in, I continued to wait, this time for Annie. I yearned to see her but I hadn't heard from her in months, which was so unlike her. I began to fear the worst. Maybe my daughter wasn't coming home.

Finally, I received a letter, the envelope bearing the mark of the Red Cross. It could only be about William. He would have been twenty-one years old and eligible to vote.

I tore open the envelope and wrenched out the paper. I took large, heaving breaths as I unfolded the page.

'It's from Annie,' I whispered to myself. Joy and despair collided.

> March 1919
>
> Dear Mama,
>
> I'm coming home. The 65 General Hospital in Salonika has been officially disbanded. All the Red Cross nurses and VAD nurses are boarding ships bound for London. I will be home in about a month and when I have been debriefed, will send word from Notting Hill.

'Annie's coming home,' I shouted across the pub, to anyone who could hear.

Thankfully, I hadn't contracted the flu during the latest wave. Richard wondered if I had developed some immunity from it after catching it all those years ago. Influenza was still around when I went to London in April, so I wore a mask and stayed away from the most crowded carriages. I was so overjoyed about seeing Annie that I could barely sit still on the train, imagining what it would be like to hold her, hear her voice and see her smile.

'Annie!'

She met me at the door of the house in Notting Hill and I dropped my bags and held her tight. She smelt of lavender and lilac and the curves of her body were leaner than I remembered but still familiar. I drew away to look at her better. She had dark circles under her eyes and the planes of her face were more angular. It had been three and a half years since I'd seen her, three and a half years that she'd been abroad.

'You're well?'

She nodded. 'I'm well, Mama. And glad to be home. I can't believe William is gone.'

'Oh, Annie, come and tell me everything,' I said, overwhelmed. I would cry with her later but she was with me now, alive and well. I'd missed so much time with her and was desperate to catch up on all her news.

'I will.' She smiled, still holding my hand as we walked into the parlour. 'But first I think Aunt Clem and Aunt Esther want to see you.'

Then I was surrounded by my oldest friends and reminded that they had always been with me through the darkest and the most joyful times of my life.

It was just like old times. I shared my frustration, fears and grief with them. Annie shared stories of nursing, the hospitals and her time exploring Egypt, Malta and Salonika, before we spoke about what was ahead of us now that the war was over.

'Women have been holding this country up,' said Clementine. 'But now that their war duty is done, it's time to demand equal pay for equal work. Women in factories, in offices and even professional women, doctors, nurses, solicitors and engineers must have the same rate of pay and conditions as men. We've proven that we can do the same work as men.'

Annie nodded. 'Nurses definitely deserve recognition for the work they do and respect and credibility for their occupation. There's been talk that VAD nurses won't be accepted into the professional nursing body. We may not have the same qualifications as professionally trained nurses, but we've learnt on the job, under war conditions, and some of us are just as skilled if not more so than the professional nurses.'

'Without doctors and nurses, we would have lost so many more ...' I said, thinking of Oliver.

'Female doctors were only accepted into our hospitals when there was a shortage of men. But the female doctors I worked with in Malta and Salonika had more experience and skill than many of the men. The nurses always had the utmost respect for them, but they weren't regarded in the same way by the men, and their rank within the military hospital hierarchy was much lower than men with much less ability, experience and skill. I know that some of them were lobbying for legislation that allows women doctors who served under the War Office to claim for the rank and privileges they were entitled to and to be paid the same as their male counterparts.'

'How is that going?' asked Clementine.

Annie shook her head. 'They were told that it was no longer necessary now that the war is over. The attitude that female doctors can't perform the same duties as male medical officers within the army is ridiculous. I saw women step up all the time and show incredible leadership and discipline. No patient has ever complained about being treated by a woman. They perform the same duties as a man and many times with more compassion.' She shrugged. 'At least the government has agreed to pay them more and award the pay retrospectively. But with the attitudes that are still out there,

I wonder whether female doctors will be taken seriously in male-dominated specialties, fields many women worked in during the war, now it's over.'

Esther nodded. 'It's much the same in engineering. Women worked on some of the most groundbreaking projects, which changed the course of the war and led to victory. But now many of them have lost their jobs, especially women working in munitions and the armament factories. The work is no longer needed. But my concern is that women will be fired from their jobs to be replaced by the men who held those roles before the war.'

'But so much has changed since then,' I said. 'Technology and science have advanced and these women are more qualified than the men to continue in those positions.'

'Katharine Parsons is considering beginning an engineering society for women, to promote women in engineering and give them a voice and share opportunities for employment and training,' said Esther.

'To think that women are expected to step up for the war effort but are excluded from the ongoing work of peace,' I said. 'Rebuilding the world, society, the economy, and the day-to-day lives of ordinary people will take so much work,' I added. 'It will take all of us to do it.'

'Men are blind,' said Clementine bitterly. 'Attitudes haven't changed. They still think of us as their subordinates. Women are expected to return to the social expectations that existed at the beginning of the war. Return to the home.'

'But that will never work,' I said, shaking my head. 'Too much *has* changed.'

We attended the meeting of the NUWSS. Mrs Fawcett had seen the wisdom of changing with the times. The name of the national organisation was changed to the National Union of Societies for Equal Citizenship and much to my sadness but not my surprise, she stepped down as president, naming the very capable Emily Rathbone as her successor.

New principles and aims were set down and even Clementine was impressed.

'I didn't know Millicent had it in her,' she whispered to me. 'Equal pay for equal work! You might even think that she was a socialist at heart!'

But there were real, practical aims that were achievable more immediately to provide equity between women and men, such as overhauling the divorce law and custody of children, and lobbying for pensions for civilian widows.

'I wholeheartedly agree with demanding that women be admitted to legal professions,' said Amy, enthusiastically. 'I could see myself as a barrister or magistrate.' She was still at the War Office, but she knew she was on borrowed time. The last thing she wanted was to return to the job as a legal assistant she'd had before the war.

'The most important thing for me is for women to be allowed to speak for themselves,' I said. 'It's all well and good that women can vote – well, some of us, for now – but women candidates who promote issues important to us must be supported in their campaign to become members of Parliament. We had no time to prepare for the last general election but we will be ready for the next one. Women's voices must count now and make a difference for the future of this country and for the future of our children and grandchildren.'

Too soon, the time came when I had to get back to Ebberfield, as much as I wanted to spend longer with Annie.

'I'm going to stay, Mama,' she said. I had expected as much after her time abroad. 'I'm continuing my studies in archaeology under Professor Petrie and I've been accepted to join the dig around the Lahun pyramid in Egypt later in the year.'

I hugged her tight. Leaving her behind didn't hurt as much as I'd expected. Annie had proven she knew how to look after herself and she was following her passion and her dream. It was time to let her fly. But I couldn't expect Esther and Clementine to look after her.

I glanced anxiously at Esther.

'You know she's welcome to stay for as long as she likes,' she said. 'She's the daughter Clem and I never had.' She kissed Annie's head. 'Don't worry. We'll look after her, especially as that means we'll get to see more of you.'

'Thank you. You know I love London. I'll come as often as I can but there is so much to do in Ebberfield.'

Esther nodded. 'I'll keep you updated with the progress once the bill goes through the House of Commons and on whatever Annie gets up to,' she said with a grin.

I returned home to share the results of the NUSEC meeting with the suffrage society, relieved to find that the scourge of influenza had faded once more and Dr Williams could finally retire, for good this time. It meant Richard was home to stay, committed to his practice, and although he still worked hard, we had more time together and could begin to explore what a life together might be like.

He was so different from Roger. Roger had been my soul mate and I would always love him but I had changed over the years and what I needed when we were young was different from what I needed or even wanted now. Although our ideals and vision had always aligned, Richard and I would never have worked as a couple when we were young. I'd needed Roger's raw energy and passion, which had equalled mine. Now that I was older, I understood Richard and I had a different kind of love. He was kind, considerate, gentle. We were a meeting of minds, true partners in our hopes for the future. I loved him just as much as I did Roger. I was fortunate in finding love a second time.

It was a special day when Oliver arrived home, alighting from the back of Richard's car and balancing on his crutches, one leg of his trousers pinned over his stump. Much of the village had turned out and we held a special lunch at the pub for him. Jenny, Lily and Rose were moving back into the butcher's residence, joining Tom and Amelia upstairs, now that her sister-in-law and her family had returned to their home. Oliver had his room on the ground floor but he'd already been fitted for an artificial leg and had spoken with his mother and grandparents about helping run the butchery.

Having Oliver home finally forced me to accept that William would never return to me. It had been more than seven months since he was reported missing and nobody had been able to trace him, not the Royal Air Force or the Red Cross. I knew that I would never be whole again. That part of my heart would remain with him wherever he was.

For the first time, I was on my own, living alone. Richard and I spoke about living together, but I wasn't ready for marriage again. I enjoyed my independence and standing as a widow, and I knew Richard understood and respected me for it. Instead, we decided to give the village time to accept us together; we were both prominent members of the community. So we each kept our own places and moved between each other's beds as the day suited.

But no sooner had we settled back into our daily routine and I began preparing the children for the end of the school year, than I received a letter from the NUSEC.

Dear Mrs Rainforth,
Mrs Fawcett advised me to write to ask you to join our committee to lobby for legislation against discrimination in public office or the legal profession based on sex. She tells me that you have worked with her for many years and you have great experience and insights that will be valuable in achieving our aims and objectives as we move into the future.

However, I find myself writing to you about another matter too. As much as we have made incredible progress with our work advocating for women to remain in their professional capacities after the war, as you know, there has been much pressure put on the government from employers and trade unions against continuing to employ women in their wartime capacities.

The Restoration of Pre-War Practices Bill has gone to the House of Commons. The substance of the bill allows a return to pre-war practices in various industries, making women ineligible to work in their wartime roles and to return soldiers to their pre-war jobs. We have all lobbied hard against it but the bill has just had its second reading. I worry that it will be passed before Parliament recesses for the summer with few changes. It is a blow against women everywhere and the wartime work we have all done. It shows little respect and takes our cause backwards in many respects to before the war began, especially in the field of munitions and engineering.

We must do all we can to promote women in the professional roles they were clearly capable of during the war. Women must be able to continue their professional careers, training and development, not be relegated back to the domestic sphere women were expected to remain in before the war.

I urge you to speak to your women's society and any women in your area who will suffer from this legislation. It's imperative we remain united and stronger than ever.

Yours sincerely,

Emily Rathbone

I asked Alice, Jenny and Emily to join me at The Lighthouse, to discuss Emily's letter.

'We knew our path forward wasn't going to be easy,' I said with a sigh.

'It doesn't look like we can prevent this bill from being passed,' said Jenny.

'We should have known it would come to this,' said Alice bitterly. 'Men's attitudes haven't really changed. War forced their hand in relation to allowing women into their jobs. Now they are scrambling to hold on to any power they can for as long as possible.'

'There will be many women out of work because of this,' said Emily. 'Perhaps we can employ women on the farms? The girls of the Land Army were good and efficient workers.'

I nodded. 'We have to spread the word to our friends and associates. Anyone who can help support groups of workers in a particular field. I'll reach out to Esther and Katharine Parsons to help women in the munitions and engineering fields.'

'Perhaps we can create opportunities here in the village and district,' said Jenny.

I nodded. 'Let's put our heads together to find solutions.'

I went to London for a few days to meet the NUSEC committee dedicated to the new legislation. It felt like the old days with Esther and Clementine by my side as we fought to change the world, except now we were the elder stateswomen with wisdom and experience behind us. We discussed the various problems women had encountered since the end of the war in relation to recognition of professional standing and qualifications for women and many of us realised this legislation had to go further than just the legal profession. We included Amy and Annie in our discussions and their input was illuminating. They were the next generation of activists, demanding change for the world they lived in.

'Women, married or single, must be allowed to continue working in their chosen professions as they did during the war,' said Esther. 'And also to join their professional bodies and to be awarded degrees for the equal qualifications that a man undergoes.'

'That's a three-year degree for law,' clarified Amy. 'And women must be able to be eligible for any civil service position.'

'And if women can apply to be magistrates, surely it follows that women should be able to become jurors too,' I said. Esther smiled and we shared knowing glances with Clementine, thinking about the Fred Duggan case against Edward Partridge. We knew how cases involving women were disadvantaged when magistrates and jurors were only men. Perhaps if women were involved in that level of legal procedure, more cases involving sexual and domestic violence would make it to court, and more fair and equitable rulings would result. Marjorie would be alive today.

'Now that the government has recognised that women provide a real and valuable contribution to society, we have to ride the momentum before it's lost and push for full equality,' I said.

'Do you really think we can achieve equality?' asked Amy wistfully.

I laughed. 'When we first began fighting for women's rights and the vote, we were young and idealistic and there came a time when we wondered if we would ever achieve our aims. I'll admit it took a long time. Esther, Clem and I have been fighting for thirty years, but with persistence and determination and through trying different tactics and approaches, we've achieved so much and we now have the vote.'

'Not for all women. Not for me,' said Amy.

'Or me,' said Annie.

I nodded. 'We still have much to do. But I'm confident about the future. We have something we didn't have before.'

'What's that?' asked Annie.

'No man can ever question our loyalty to our country, our intelligence or our ability to do men's work or make important decisions. We have gained expertise and insight. A woman's place is not just in the home any longer,' said Esther.

'And not only that, we're stronger than ever,' I said. 'We have been tempered by sacrifice, war service, hard work, deprivations, and the loss of our sons, fathers, brothers, husbands, and our friends and neighbours in bombings and air raids and the flu. We are survivors and we know how to take care of ourselves and our communities. We know we can do whatever we set out to do.'

'We've fought for so much already, given a great deal for our country and survived,' said Clementine. 'The world has changed. Britain has changed and nobody in their right mind can expect things to go back to the way they were before the war. People will continue to demand change; people will no longer be afraid to speak up after what they have endured. The world is a very different place.'

I smiled. 'Who ever imagined a world with aeroplanes, X-ray machines that see inside a body and shorter skirts for women?'

Much had changed. Millions of young men had perished, every person had been touched by loss and tragedy, powerful empires that had existed for hundreds of years had fallen, Bolshevik Russia was engulfed in civil war, and the brutality of war and the dark and light of human nature, the very worst and the very best, were on display for the world to see. We could never think the same way ever again.

47

The stories of women have always been relegated to the mists of time, but times are changing. Annie wants to be involved in resurrecting a great female leader, Hatshepsut – her mummy hasn't yet been found. If the voice of a female pharaoh can reverberate through time, surely it shows us that the voices of all women can no longer be denied.

It was a beautiful summer's day. I opened the upstairs window of The Lighthouse and breathed in the fresh air. The town had grown, but from my window at least, the view was much the same as it had always been, the rooftops and trees that lined the road, now resplendent in verdant green and the rolling countryside beyond the village. I marvelled at how it shifted and changed with every passing season. The light played over the ancient stonework of the church that dominated the hill. It was a sight I would never tire of.

I started downstairs, holding the letter that had arrived from Tommy in my hand. I wanted to read it surrounded by the bustle of the pub and life unfolding around me, rather than alone, in the quiet of my office. And I had to check on the pork pies that had just come out of the oven. I hadn't heard from him since he'd replied to my letter about William. He hadn't written too much, only acknowledged his brother's disappearance and probable death and then told me about the wheat harvest. I could imagine how the news had affected him on the other side of the world, so far from his family.

I sat at the kitchen table, where the pork pies – cooked to golden perfection – were cooling. I slit the top of the envelope with a sharp knife and a photograph dropped out. I gazed at the couple. Tommy and Madeleine. They looked happy and very much in love. Tommy looked different, grown up, a man with purpose.

July 1919

Dear Mama,

I'm writing to let you know that I am getting married! Maddie is a wonderful woman - beautiful, smart, warm and kind. We have plans to buy some Crown land released by the government. It will only be a small block to begin with but enough to begin farming. Maddie loves the land as much as I do and she wants to buy her own block one day and run a farm. She's determined and I know she'll do it. Maddie reminds me a lot of you. You're both women who are independent and push the boundaries of what others say you can do. The Lighthouse is successful because of your determination and hard work. I understand now what you were trying to achieve when you went to London. I'm sorry about what I said to you then. I was wrapped up in my own bitterness and grief and lashed out at you. I deeply regret it.

We're getting married in the local church. All her family will be there to help us celebrate. We wanted to marry sooner but decided to wait until all our friends and family had returned from the war. I wish you and Annie could be here but I understand that you're in no position to come. I miss Will every day but know he and Dadda will be there with me in spirit.

Your loving son,

Tommy

Bittersweet emotion rushed through me. I put my hand over my mouth as the sob escaped my lips. The rift between Tommy and I was healed. And I wanted to meet Maddie, who had changed the way Tommy thought, kiss and hug them both, watch their happiness unfold. I had never imagined any of this for my family. Roger gone, William too. Annie in London to continue her career in archaeology and Tommy in Australia. Grief and sorrow had seeped deep into my bones with every loss. But life went on anyway.

I had to find a way to take joy from doing what made me happy, what I felt passionate about and what was important to me. And I wasn't alone. I had Richard, Sarah and Jane, Jenny, Lily and Rose, and Annie, Clementine and Esther in London. And The Lighthouse.

I'd see Tommy and his wife and family one day. The most important thing was that he was safe and well. There was much to celebrate.

Sounds of the lunchtime service about to begin broke through my reverie. It was hot and stifling in the kitchen and I suddenly needed air. I rushed out the back door, through our beer garden to the field beyond. A cool sea breeze tempered the summer heat and I sighed. I walked past the old trees that formed a boundary with the pub, remembering the days when I walked here all the time, when my parents still ran the pub. The space was soothing then, as it was now.

I stopped by the trees and smiled. This was where Roger and I had shared our first kiss, twenty-five years ago. The branches were bare then, but now, at the height of summer, they were green and lush. Young love was a special time. Anything felt possible and the world was a wonderful place.

'Tommy's happy, Roger. He'll make a good life for himself. That's all we could possibly want for him,' I said, clicking the old farm gate closed behind me and walking back to the street.

Standing outside The Lighthouse, I looked over the village to the colliery town and beyond, to the sparkling sea. Much had altered since the day I'd arrived as a young woman out of teachers' college. I had had a hand in some of the positive change that had followed – both locally and nationally – and now the possibilities for the future were suspended like stars in the night sky, guiding our way. This was my home and these were my people and I'd continue to make it a place where they wanted to live. I was so proud that The Lighthouse was the heart of the community, the beacon that continued to shine.

Ebberfield was where I belonged.

I peered into the distance at a figure walking up the hill towards the pub. Perhaps someone coming for the lunch service. As the figure came closer, I realised it was a man in military uniform.

I squinted, unable to make him out, and felt my heart leap before my mind could comprehend.

Then I was running towards him, shouting his name.

'William!'

AUTHOR'S NOTE

An Undeniable Voice is inspired by the life of Eleanor Blanchard, my husband's great-great-grandmother. I first heard the story about the Blanchards who ran a pub in Durham, Northern England, from my father-in-law, Terry Blanchard. The story was then told to me again by his cousin based in the United Kingdom. The family were all enormously proud of their ancestor, Robert Blanchard, and his achievement as owner and publican of his pub around the turn of the twentieth century. But I was intrigued by his wife, Eleanor, and what her life might have been like.

After I researched the family tree, I discovered that Eleanor's father had originally owned the pub – he purchased it after a long career as an engine fitter in Hartlepool's shipyards. I first found the family at the pub in 1891 and suspect that Eleanor ran the pub with her mother after her father fell ill until she and Robert Blanchard married in 1894. That intrigued me: it was unusual for a woman to be managing a pub on her own at that time. I was fascinated at how this story had changed over the successive generations of its retelling, so that nobody knew much about Eleanor, besides her roles as wife and mother, when the story was passed to me.

Robert Blanchard died in 1907 at the age of thirty-eight, leaving Eleanor with three young children, the youngest only five years old. She ran the pub on her own and looked after her family for the next five years. She did lose the pub sometime between 1913 and 1915 when documents show her no longer living at or running the pub.

Tommy Rainforth follows a similar trajectory to Terry's grandfather, who came to Australia in 1914 at the age of eighteen as part of the Dreadnought Scheme. He left on the *Hawkes Bay* in June 1914, one of the last ships to make the journey before the outbreak of WWI. In fact, after docking in Sydney and the announcement that Australia was now at war, the *Hawkes Bay* collected some of the first New Zealand and Australian troops, taking them to Alexandria in Egypt to begin their training exercises.

In *An Undeniable Voice*, I wanted to continue the exploration of the women's suffrage movement that I began in *A Woman of Courage*, and I took Hannah to London, to the heart of the action in the early 1900s.

Millicent Fawcett led the National Union of Women's Suffrage Societies through successive Private Members' bills through the first years of the twentieth century. But the frustrating failure of each bill that made it to Parliament led to a split in the NUWSS and the formation of the Women's Social and Political Union in 1903, led by Emmeline Pankhurst. The WSPU didn't believe that women would acquire the vote purely through parliamentary process and with their motto, 'Deeds not Words', they became increasingly militant in promoting the cause and increasing its awareness with politicians, media and the public alike. With the failure of the Conciliation Bills, the WSPU began their campaign to pressure the government with vocal demonstrations and window smashing, which then escalated to arson and bombings.

I am fascinated by the role of women at this pivotal time in history. It was the beginning of the modern age and technological advances changed the way people lived, but still women were not regarded as citizens: they had no voice.

Their continued fight for the right to vote was symbolic of their fight to be heard, to be seen as equal to men. And their oppression led to many putting their bodies on the line with hunger strikes and enduring horrific forcible feeding. Emily Davison's death, today considered an accident but at the time seen as martyrdom, was one of the most famous examples of physical protest, but many more women hidden in history were under surveillance, and some were harassed and beaten during peaceful protests. Women ultimately had only one currency they could use, that of their own bodies – and the WSPU understood this currency politically. But even the sacrifice of women's lives, their bodies, incomes, families and reputations was not enough to persuade men in power that women should have the right to vote until towards the end of the Great War.

WWI changed the course of history for women everywhere. As they stepped up on the home front and as volunteers serving overseas, they were seen as the backbone of Britain – patriotic and dependable. Women essentially ran British industry during the war, taking on the jobs men had left. And this changed not just the perception of women by the public, but how women saw themselves and what they were capable of doing. Women had endured loss, conscription of their sons, rationing, air raids and the Spanish flu while gaining and using their valuable skills and expertise in important war work. As the war drew to a close, not only were women fighting for the vote, but equal pay to men, improved conditions in war industries, the recognition of university qualifications and the right to remain in their jobs and continue their work and careers after the war.

Women did finally receive the vote in 1918 with the *People's Representation Act*, giving the vote to women thirty years and over who met the property qualification. With this

Act, all men over twenty-one could also vote. But the fight was not over and only in 1928 was there universal suffrage for men and women.

I wonder where the fight between the WSPU members and the authorities would have ended if WWI hadn't intervened? How long would women have waited until they received the vote if they didn't have the opportunity to prove themselves under the circumstances of such a cataclysmic event? And how many more women would have suffered, putting everything on the line for the cause if attitudes towards them didn't change?

Certainly, we've come a long way since the end of WWI, but we still have a long way to go. Our journey towards equality with men continues and while women band together with a unified voice to fight with passion, determination and persistence, as they did over one hundred years ago, our voices are undeniable. I have no doubt we will make the world a better place for women everywhere.

ACKNOWLEDGEMENTS

My first and biggest thank you goes to Terry Blanchard, my father-in-law and keeper of the Blanchard family stories. I feel blessed that he has shared his family history with me. Thank you, Terry, for your warmth, generosity and support, and for being the best father-in-law I could ever hope for.

I would never have got this story off the ground without the help of Melvyn Blanchard in the UK. He is the keeper of the English Blanchard family history and was able to shed light on the lives of Robert and Eleanor Blanchard and the pub that they owned. Thank you, Melvyn, for trusting me with your memories and stories of your family and supplying me with useful information, documentation and photos.

A big shout out to all the team at HarperCollins Australia for your wonderful efforts in making *An Undeniable Voice* the beautiful finished product it has become. The fabulous sales and marketing team always do an amazing job and have outdone themselves in bringing this book out into the world. My heartfelt thanks to you for showcasing my pride and joy. I also feel incredibly fortunate to have the talented and gifted Louisa Maggio work on the cover. She's nailed it again, embodying everything that the story is about with vibrance, urgency and action. And using the WSPU colours of purple, green and white was the perfect choice! Thank you, Louisa – it's utterly gorgeous. Much of the behind-the-scenes work is done by the editorial team who help me sculpt and refine the novel so that it sparkles and sings. And to them, I am especially grateful. My thanks go especially to Kylie Mason and to Rachel Cramp for their invaluable insights. Rachel, your energy and inspired ideas are a breath of fresh air when I need it most, and your patience and guidance are much appreciated. But most of all, thank you to my publisher, Roberta Ivers, my champion, mentor and friend, who has been with me every step of the way. I feel blessed to have your experience and wisdom behind me.

To my beautiful readers, thank you for your loyalty, support and generous spirit. My books would be nothing without you. It's been wonderful to get to meet and know some of you at my author events and it always touches my heart when you share your thoughts and experiences of my books and your own family stories. I feel that we are a wonderful community that love stories – that sense of connection is very special to me.

To my lovely friends in the writing community, my writing journey is more meaningful because of you. Your friendships bring me joy and sustain me, especially through the process of writing, which can be a solitary pursuit. But most of all, I feel that I belong to this fabulous community of like-minded people. I am nourished, replenished and inspired through the connections I've made with all of you.

My family and friends are my biggest supporters and encouraged me while I wrote *An Undeniable Voice*. The network of love and nurturing has buoyed me through the periods of intense writing. The biggest thanks to my mother, Giselle Brame, and my sister-in-law Trish Casey for their unwavering belief in me and to Jane O'Keefe for her encouragement and interest in the family stories.

Finally, to my wonderful husband, Chris, and my three gorgeous children. I love you with all my heart. You are the ones who inspire me and the ones I write stories for. It has been a delight and honour to tell the Blanchard story for you, and incredibly precious to have you with me every step of the way. It has been a journey: learning about the family history, understanding the world your ancestors lived in and bringing their stories to life. This narrative of strength, resilience, speaking out and fighting for justice – qualities you all share in spades – is for you.

Vaugha[illegible]ms

An Autobiography … and more!

Bet Vaughan Williams 15.7.2006.

Published by Bet Vaughan Williams

I dedicate this book to the memory of my dear husband Arthur and to my grandchildren, Rebecca, Marcus, Faye, Geraint, Morgan, Aled, and Huw.

I hope they will continue to value their roots and history in general.

Contents

Acknowledgement of help and support

I thank everyone who helped me in different ways to produce this book.

The contributions made are not in any order of importance because each is valued by me, but I must acknowledge in particular the many hundreds of hours, after arduous days running her school, during weekends and holidays that Glenys spent editing the script.
I also thank:

Rebecca, Marcus and Morgan for being the catalysts to my starting to write the stories.

Arthur, his parents, my parents and Fergus Armstrong for the details of the past.

Glenys, Bryn and Elsie for accompanying me to the archives at Hereford, Ruthin and Aberystwyth and helping to find and study old documents, and Geraint too at Ruthin.

Myself for believing in the project and investing many hundreds of hours writing long-hand.

Kath, for typing the original script.

Marcus for building me a PC, setting it up in Eglwysbach and providing a helpline.

Kerry, Glenys, Marcus & Morgan for encouraging me to use a computer, and Kerry for teaching me how to use one for this book and being on the other end of the telephone to talk me out of difficulties many times in the early months.

Glenys for editing, planning and implementing the process of publication in its entirety.

Kerry and Bryn for choosing and sorting out the photographs and Kerry for preparing them on the computer to improve quality, size, shading and preparing titles.

Ivor Howatson, Denbigh and Bobi Morris Roberts, Brecon for information.

Glen and Kerry for printing sections of the script regularly and the whole thing many times.

Myself for many hours of frustrating search for details of births, marriages and deaths of people with similar names in different generations and forming the family trees.

Kerry for succeeding in displaying the family trees in easy-to-follow computerised plans, and for working for hours with the printer in the latter stages to get every detail just right.

You for purchasing my book … I thank you all and hope you enjoy reading it.

Foreword

Rydw i'n adnabod Bet Vaughan Williams ers dyddiau plentyndod yn Llanrwst. Mrs Williams Llys Cerdd neu Mrs Arthur Vaughan oedd hi bryd hynny i mi. Fy nhad y diweddar Parch W.E.Thomas oedd Gweinidog y Capel Mawr, Seion, a'r diweddar Arthur Vaughan Williams yr Organydd a Chorfeistr oedd y cerddor proffesiynol cyntaf i mi ei adnabod. 'Rwyf yn cofio llais soprano Mrs Arthur Vaughan yn atsain yn y capel fel unawdydd a phan ymunai gyda'r lleisiau cyfoethog eraill mewn cor gyda Arthur Vaughan wrth yr organ llanwyd y capel gyda sain nodedig.

Roedd fy niweddar chwaer Elin Mair a minnau yn gyfoedion a'u plant Elsie, Glenys a Bryn, Llys Cerdd ac eu cefndryd Emyr (y diweddar Gari Williams), Elinor a'r diweddar Elwyn, Fern Lea. Rhyfedd yw sgrifennu "diweddar" am gynifer o deulu a chyfoedion. Ond daw'r cyfnod yn ol yn fyw yn yr atgofion hyn.

Mae Bet wedi ysgrifennu yn deimladwy a gonest, gyda chynhesrwydd a hiwmor am ei bywyd hir a llawn. Mae'r llyfr yn gyfoethog fel hanes personol a chymdeithasol, yn llawn cymeriadau lliwgar byw o wahanol genedlaethau. Mwynhewch ei ddarllen.

D. Elis-Thomas.

Arglwydd Dafydd Elis-Thomas AC - Llywydd Cynulliad Cenedlaethol Cymru

....

I have known Bet Vaughan Williams since childhood in Llanrwst. She was known to me as Mrs Williams Llys Cerdd or Mrs Arthur Vaughan. At that time my father, the late Rev.W.E.Thomas was Minister of Seion Chapel (Capel Mawr) and the late Arthur Vaughan Williams was the Organist and Choirmaster. He was the first professional musician for me to know. I remember the soprano voice of Mrs Arthur Vaughan resounding in the Chapel as a soloist and when she joined the other rich voices in a choir with Arthur Vaughan at the organ, the big chapel was filled with a magnificent sound.

My late sister, Elin Mair and I were friendly contemporaries of the children Elsie, Glenys and Bryn, Llys Cerdd and their cousins Emyr (the late Gari Williams), Elinor and the late Elwyn, Fern Lea. How strange it is to write "the late" in referring to so many family members and contemporaries.

Bet has written movingly and honestly with warmth and humour about her long and full life. The book is rich as a personal account and social history, full of colourful and lively characters from different generations. Enjoy reading it.

D. Elis-Thomas.

Lord Dafydd Elis-Thomas - Presiding Officer of the National Assembly for Wales

NOW I KNOW WHO I AM

Bet Vaughan Williams

Introduction

How on earth do I start the task that I have been given? Should I even have consented to do it? Well, the truth is that I had no option really because love is a hard taskmaster.

I am a retired grandmother, a widow, living alone for the first time in my life. I have two daughters and a son who are married with children of their own. My bungalow is very comfortable and pleasing, with pretty gardens at the front and back. I am always busy doing something or other including participating in several local clubs, attending Chapel services, and indulging in my love of reading, gardening and singing. I am a Trustee of an ancient Almshouses Trust in Llanrwst, a member of the Village Hall Committee in Eglwysbach, and an elected member of the local Community Council too. Consequently, I have little spare time to achieve this mammoth task despite my habit of retiring to bed late each night. My mother said many times, "Bet, you are an owl, you were born at 10.00 p.m. just as it started to rain." Well, it *was* St. Swithin's Day after all.

But my taskmasters would have none of my excuses about lack of time. They, my grandchildren, insisted that I must write down my stories. They said it would be an easy task for me because I knew the stories so well having told them so many times on request.

I said to my own children, "Why don't *you* tell your children about the past? You heard these things from your grandparents, your father and me during your childhood years, you've grown up enjoying the tales … now *you* share them with your children." "Oh yes we want to," they said, "But we don't remember everything and don't know all the details either, not in the way you do Mam. You also know how our children love to hear *you* talk about our family and the events of the past, and we want them to enjoy their family roots … so please Mam, write it down *for all of us*."

I was influenced by this encouragement especially when it came in addition to my grandchildren's plea of, "Oh, come on *Nain*, you know we want to hear it all again because you tell it so well." They call me *Nain* for it is the Welsh word for Grandmother (pronounced *nine*). They knew that soft soap gets you everywhere with Nain!

They were all so insistent that I finally capitulated and agreed, but immediately doubts surfaced when I started wondering where I should begin, what I should include, and how I could make it interesting. I was required to reflect on the fact that I have one foot still in the distant past and another firmly in the present. Having aired all my deliberations I had to admit that apart from the soft-soaping, there were other reasons for my agreeing to write down my recollections. For instance, I never knew or even saw any of my grandparents because they had all died before my birth. That fact didn't bother me in childhood, but in adulthood however, I came to recognise how greatly deprived I was from not having known them. Also, when I reflect on my life I can hardly believe my own experiences, for the world has changed so much in 80 years. People are much the same fundamentally, the human nature being as it is, but the trappings of our existence are very different indeed.

When I finally began gathering my thoughts I discovered a growing sense of enthusiasm and energy for the task ahead. But before I could begin to write, I had a dilemma to consider. Should I write in Welsh, which seemed the most natural thing to do in view of my background, or in English? I quickly realised that writing my memoirs in Welsh would not serve the main purpose of the task at all because, although my three children, Elsie, Glenys and Bryn are Welsh speakers, my grandchildren are not, having all been born and bred in England. Only one of them, Geraint, understands some of what I say to him in Welsh. My other grandchildren, Rebecca, Marcus, Faye, Morgan, Aled and Huw are English speakers only. That brief deliberation settled the dilemma for me, and that is the reason this book is written in English. I have written it *for them*, and have dedicated it *to them*.

Some years ago, my eldest grandchild Rebecca decided at primary school to write and illustrate a project on 'The Life and Times of My Nain'. She worked hard on it and her teacher recognised its quality because it was put on display in the school library. Remembering this, I fetched out my copy and having read it again decided on the format of my book's rambling story.

"Life is a story in volumes three:
The Past, The Present, and the Yet to Be.
The first is finished and stored away
The second we are reading day by day
The third and the last of the volumes three
Is locked from sight. God keepeth the key."

Anon.

Note to readers: many Welsh people are referred to by their own name followed by the name of their house. An example is 'John Jones Penglogor'. In order to help my English readers to understand i) this Welsh custom and ii) the meanings of the Welsh house names, I have written the house names in italics followed by an English translation in brackets. The house name refers very often to its position or location, so it must be noted that the translation refers to the house and not the person. So, the earlier example will look like this in the book: John Jones *Penglogor* (head of the hill). The bracketed translation refers to the house not to the man.

Chapter 1

WE BEGIN

I was born in 1924 just after the Great War or World War 1 as it is now known. My brother Percy, eldest child of the family, was eleven when I was born, and our sister Elsie, nine. Their birthdays were a day apart, hers being on the 6th of January and his on the 7th. They had a good relationship and were very close. Tragically, Elsie died when she was twelve years old from heart failure, following rheumatic fever. Had she been treated with today's modern drugs, she would almost certainly have survived. She was very pretty with curly, auburn hair, intensely blue eyes and a striking vivacious manner. She was also clever. Both she and our brother passed the entrance examination to the Grammar School. She was buried on the day of the Total Eclipse of the Sun in June 1927. I can remember being lifted onto a table by a kind neighbour to see the crowds that had gathered at the cemetery.

Also during that turbulent year my brother was taken to the Infirmary in Denbigh to have his appendix removed, and three months after Elsie's funeral, our younger sister Isabella was born. It was only then that my mother was finally able to weep and grieve for her lost child. However, there was no respite for her - all the stress and trauma had left their mark on the baby girl, who was born at home, as was the normal practice in those days. The birth had been a difficult experience for both mother and child: the baby's head leaned onto one shoulder, her face was severely marked, and her legs were crossed. Worst of all, she could not take a feed - nothing stayed down. Dr. Leiper, the village doctor who attended was a Scot and friendly with my mother, who was herself half-Scottish. My mother also had cousins who were doctors who had studied medicine in Edinburgh with Dr. Leiper.

The first few weeks after my sister's birth were full of worry, but the difficulties were overcome. The baby was laid always on one side and her legs were straightened and tied together until they became normal and straight. After many tries and failures the first nourishment that stayed down was a very weak mixture of *Benger's Food* mixed with water not milk. Thankfully in the end, she grew up healthy and strong and became a very successful nursing Sister.

At the time I was just three years old and cannot remember very much of my sister's illness, perhaps I was taken care of by kind neighbours, which was customary in the village. But I do recall collecting a handful of flowers and giving them to her as she lay in bed on many occasions. Treatment of rheumatic fever in those days entailed staying in bed for many weeks.

Many years later when I had children of my own my mother told me the details of that terrible morning when Death came without warning. Elsie May, for that was my sister's name was still required to stay in bed although she was getting better every day. My father was working away at this time and my brother was at school leaving only Mam, Elsie May and me at home. It was a beautiful sunny morning in June and my sister had been singing several times with joy because she felt so much better. The song that she kept repeating was the hymn 'There is a green hill far away without a city wall, where our dear Lord was crucified and died to save us all'.

Mam had been sitting with her most of the morning but had gone to the adjoining room to prepare lunch for us. Everything was quiet except for the sounds of my playing outside and then Elsie May called out, “Mam, come here to open the curtains I can't see.” My mother was struck with fear because the bedroom curtains had been fully open for hours and so she hurried to the bedroom and gathered her child to her heart. Gently she soothed her with soft words and caresses but fearful that something was seriously wrong. After a short while, Elsie May became agitated and cried out, “Hold me tight Mam I'm falling and I can't breathe.” At that moment Mam knew that her beautiful daughter was dying. She told me that her heart was being torn apart but she felt a strange strength enveloping them both. She remained motionless until she knew that her little girl's spirit was in the care of Jesus. Calmly but completely devastated she found me and went to fetch help from her kind neighbours.

We lived in *Pengraig*, a cottage that had two rooms, a living room and a bedroom, both on the ground floor. The rooms were fairly spacious. There were three beds in the bedroom, one double and two singles. There was a large wooden post in the middle of the room to ensure that the roof did not cave in. Hung under the slated roof was a large calico sheet. I do not know how it was held in place but I remember when the wind was high, it would flap and billow and I was scared to death of it. Whenever the weather was stormy I would bury my head under the bedclothes so I could neither see nor hear the flapping sheet. In the living room was a fireplace - a cooking range with an oven on one side and a boiler on the other. My mother did all the cooking on the range which she black-leaded every week - a dirty, messy job. All I can remember of the furniture were chairs, a stool, a large long table and a small round one, a homemade bookcase and odds and ends. Our bathroom consisted of an upright orange box with an enamel basin placed upon it and a large tin bath for weekly bathing in the living room. There was a small sash window in both rooms and the only door was very sturdy with a strong lock. I was born in this cottage, but my brother and elder sister had been born in a very different house, a much bigger one, and in those days a very comfortable home that was convenient and well-furnished - a lovely place in which to live. I will explain the story relating to the change later on.

I was very happy in our little home. I did not feel deprived. We were always warm, well fed, much loved and cared for, and there were always books available. There were eight volumes of Harmsworth's Self-Educator, which were large, heavy books with hard, dark red covers. There was also a set of Arthur Mee's Children's Encyclopaedia consisting of ten large books with hard blue covers. We were required to ask permission to look at and read these books and warned not to scribble on the pages or to mistreat any volume. I loved those books and spent many hours reading them. They were full of all kinds of information on every imaginable subject and I owe them a great deal. There was one particular page that held a fascination for me because I hated it. It was a full-page picture of a giant anaconda snake in the Amazon River. It had me spellbound for I hated snakes and I still fear them today.

For years we had to carry every drop of water from a well at the bottom of a slope covered in gorse bushes and brambles where there were many snakes in the summer. We had to be very careful and watchful when walking on the path, but it was quite safe as long as you did not tread on a snake snoozing in the sunshine. The water in that well was clear and had a wonderful taste. We had to make sure to replace the wooden cover on the well every time we used it and never to disturb the sediment at the bottom. Of course there was no electricity in the village, and we relied on oil lamps and candles for light. Today when I read in the newspapers about house fires and people dying, I wonder how it is that I cannot recall any such fires and tragedies when we were young. But I can remember being warned to be very careful in handling naked flames when using matches, oil lamps and the kitchen range.

Outside our home was a large garden, devoted mainly to growing vegetables. It was a rocky place and my father and brother had spent many hours of very hard work carrying soil there to create the garden. My father was a good gardener who won many prizes over the years in the local horticultural shows. Those events created a lot of friendly rivalry and those people who had no garden at home rented a plot at the allotment ground. Thirty years later, long after we had left Pengraig, a man from the village, who had dug over the garden there in order to grow food came to my married home in Llanrwst. He gave my mother, who lived with us at the time, a tiny toy smoothing iron. “I found it in the soil at *Pengraig* and thought it must have belonged to your girls when they were very young. I cannot remember anyone else living there so it must be theirs,” said the man as he handed over the rusty toy iron. “Well thank you, it's very kind of you to take such trouble over a toy,” my mother replied. “It was no trouble at all,” he said as he left. “I just thought after all this time that you'd like to have it back again.”

I cleaned and polished the little iron and felt sure it must have been very old, certainly much older than my sister or me. Since then, it has had pride of place on the dresser in my present home. What a pity it cannot speak to us for I'm sure it would have quite a story to tell.

At *Pengraig* there was also a large shed that housed chickens and items that could not be stored in the house. There was a path from the house to the shed and thence on to the lavatory. This consisted of a very small stone built cubbyhole with a wooden door and a bench seat that had a hole cut out above a bucket that had to be emptied regularly by my father. How primitive it all seems when I look back. I realise now that things must have remained unchanged for generations for ordinary folk. Below the shed was another piece of land called the lower garden that was completely overgrown with nettles and weeds, where I never set foot. Behind the house was an area of grassy mounds and rocks where nothing much grew except brambles. The cottage and grounds were called *Pengraig* and no one knew who owned them. Consequently, I do not believe that rent was paid while we were there. We must have been 'squatters'.

There was a glorious view of the countryside from our home on the hill above the village, hence the name *Pengraig* which means 'head of the rock'. In the late 1920s when my brother caught the bus for school in Abergele, he used to look out for it making its way along the Elwy Valley Road from Llangernyw. As soon as it got to a certain spot en route he would run down the very steep hill to get to the village-square just before the bus arrived there. But during his first couple of years at the County Grammar School he andtwo others had to travel to Abergele on Monday mornings in a car owned by Dafydd Jones the Carrier, because there was no bus to take them. They had to stay in lodgings during the week before returning home again on Fridays.

I recall the years when my younger sister Bella was a toddler and I a mere child when both of us were energetic and noisy, and I marvel at my brother Percy Elfyn, who was then a teenager studying for his Matriculation and Higher Exams. I am still astonished at how well he was able to concentrate on his work in such difficult circumstances. Frequently neighbours and friends called at the house when there would be much talk and conviviality, but my brother was oblivious to it all for he had mastered the art of perfect concentration. He was a clever lad and when he matriculated, the whole school was given a half-day holiday to celebrate the fact that he had come top of the achievement list of the London Matriculation Examination throughout England and Wales

A few yards up the hill from our home was a smallholding called *Pencoed* (head of the woods), where a middle-aged couple lived. They were very kind people and we loved them. We were not related but my sister and I called them Uncle and Auntie and I went to see them every day. They had a big sheepdog called *Pero* and we loved him too. Many Welsh farmers gave their sheepdogs the name Pero, which is the Spanish word for dog. I wonder if it harks back to the ancient period when the Iberians had moved to this land before the Celts, Romans or Anglo Saxons? We can only surmise. Pero's coat was made of long, silky, black and white hairs, and his eyes were so soft. They had one son and two daughters who were grown up, their son and elder daughter had left home and were working elsewhere. The younger daughter was a pretty girl called Dolly who worked away during the week in an office at the Mental Health Hospital in Denbigh, but returned home at weekends. The Hospital was a large, fine building set in beautiful grounds that served North Wales and employed many people. Sadly, it is not in use today. Dolly would give me her empty jars of *Pond's Face Cream* that were made of lovely twisted green glass, and almost-empty circular face-powder boxes that were cream-coloured with a motif of gold and tan on the lids.

I loved going to *Pencoed* because the house appeared to me at the time to be exceptionally smart. It was a bungalow with two bedrooms, a large sitting room and a small kitchen with a scullery cum-larder cum-dairy leading off it. I was allowed to go into the sitting-room only on rare occasions, indeed the room was used only when the family was entertaining visitors. The furnishings were 'posh' and on the sideboard was a huge carved wooden eagle that fascinated me so much that I would ask to go to see it.

There were several small fields at Pencoed where three or four cows and some sheep were grazed. There were chickens and occasionally a couple of pigs too. We bought our milk from *Pencoed* where it was obtained from the large round earthenware basins in which it was kept in the dairy. Periodically, Auntie Williams would skim off the cream from the top of the milk and use it to make butter in the up-and-over churn that we were sometimes allowed to operate by turning the handle. In earlier times and on larger farms, a horse would be used to turn the churn - the horse would plod round and round in circles until the butter was formed. The churn's lid had a small viewing circle made of glass through which we could see the butter forming. The buttermilk that remained in the churn once the butter had been removed was delicious, and was a favourite drink of harvest workers to quench their thirst on hot days.

Living with the family was an old lady called Miss Bartlett and I know nothing about her except that she was a paying guest. She was truly a lady in the best sense of the word and she was almost always working on some exquisite piece of embroidery, knitting or sewing. She was an English lady and from time to time would say pathetically, “I can't drive my senses away, I can't drive my senses away.” I cannot remember ever thinking that this was strange behaviour in any way, but I do recall Uncle Williams throwing a cushion at her if she went on and on, and ordering her to be quiet. However, we liked Miss Bartlett and spent many happy hours in her company. I feel certain that it was she who was instrumental in my being able to speak English at an early age for I do not remember not understanding the language or of learning it either, my first language being Welsh.

From time to time parties were held at *Pencoed* and visitors came to supper. The family owned a gramophone and there would be dancing on the small lawns at the front of the house. There was one occasion when I managed to watch the proceedings for a short time and I can still sense the feeling of music and rhythm and the enjoyment of the dancers. Sadly for me, my presence was missed at home and I was escorted away because it was not nice to spy on people! On such occasions, because of the preparations of food and so on, my visits were curtailed and I would be very disappointed. Miss Bartlett had given me a doll. It was only a cheap little thing with a canvas body stuffed with straw, but it was precious to me. One day however, having been refused entry at *Pencoed* I returned home, fetched the doll and threw it as far as I could into the nettles in the wilderness of the lower garden. Some older children on their way home from school saw this performance and one of them, being my best friend's sister went to retrieve the doll. There she stood on the doorstep handing the doll to my mother. I can see her now, with her back to me and her waist length hair tied at the back. I rushed up to her and grabbed her hair and yanked her flat on her back and threw the doll back into the nettles where it remained, as far as I know. Terrible behaviour I know, but by now I can relate it to the feelings of fury and hurt I experienced at being rejected and refused entry at *Pencoed* that day.

One year the Wesleyan Chapel organised a picnic for its Sunday-School children and although I was Presbyterian I had nevertheless been invited to join the picnic. My sister had to stay at home because she was too young to attend being only about two years old at the time. However, during the picnic a strange figure appeared. My baby sister landed in our midst wearing three hats on her head, one on top of the other and completely nude. There were gasps and gales of laughter and she was allowed some sweets before being carried home.

There was another occasion during the school summer holidays when a nephew of the Williams' came to stay for a week. He must have been in his early teens, was very friendly and kind to us small children, and was called Hugh. He was our hero and we followed him and Pero everywhere. But the lad must have had a surfeit of our company because we never saw him again, and who could blame him for not wanting more of the pestering we must have given him!

There were other incidents that happened during our time at Pengraig that I remember clearly. For instance, my mother had an uncle who farmed three or four miles up the road, and periodically he used to visit the village for an alcoholic spree. On his way home on horseback, he would call at our home and demand supper. We could not afford to feed him regularly, and although he was reasonable enough when sober, he was nevertheless nasty in drink. In the end my mother decided enough was enough, and the next time he came noisily up the hill on his way home, she was waiting for him at the big double gates at the end of the path leading to our cottage. When he demanded that she opened the gates, she refused and told him to go home. I was only about three years old and she was carrying me on her arm. For a second or two he was stunned, then he lunged forward and swung his stick. My mother turned to save me and took the full force of the blow on her face. He swore and raged at us and my brother threw stones after him, but he never called again.

Round about the same time, the firm of McAlpine was building a new road from

Llanfair to Llansannan, a distance of some four miles. There were many 'navvies' working on the road and with them were female 'camp followers'. One of them was a woman called Kate who lived for a while in a tumbled down cottage up the road and had many male visitors. I remember seeing her on one occasion on her way home from the pub when she stopped on a clearing by the roadside and danced within a circle of men. She was laughing and singing, shouting and lifting her skirts high to show more than she should. On seeing this, my mother quickly 'shooed us' into the house with a warning never to go near, “That dreadful woman.”

Another incident took place one night when one of the 'navvies' knocked on our door and shouted that he wanted his supper. He was obviously drunk and unfortunately my father was not at home to deal with him. My mother asked the 'navvy' where he was looking for, and all the while edged slowly and silently towards the door, then quickly turned the key in the lock. After that we felt safe again, and Mam told the man to continue up the road until he came to the workmen's canteen. Finally he left, and later we learned that he had gone into another cottage up the road and had demanded supper there too. But fortunately in that case the man of the house had been at home.

As I mentioned earlier, there were snakes around Pengraig, and Mam told me that when I was very young and playing outside on a hot day, she'd heard my laughing and squealing and had gone out to see what was amusing me so much. “There you were, trying to get baby snakes into an old mustard tin with a spoon,” she said. She knew that the mother snake must have been nearby because a large adder had been spotted in the garden a few weeks earlier. At the time, Mam had heard a hen clucking in the way hens do when there is danger to their chicks, and had gone to investigate. She had come across a hen and a big adder mesmerising each other. Both had been motionless, but totally engaged with the activity. Mam had gone for Uncle Williams to bring his gun, but he'd arrived too late to deal with the snake for it had slithered off by that time and could not be found again. Mam had been rightly frightened for my safety that day, and I can still remember how she pulled me quickly to safety, away from the scene.

I also remember how my mother kept the cinders from the fire in a rusty old bucket outside the house and that one day I had been dancing round the bucket and had been warned that I would get dizzy and fall if I continued. And sure enough I fell onto the bucket cutting my left eyebrow on one of the rusty ears that held the handle. I was lucky enough not to have lost an eye, but I still carry the scar to this day. During a recent eye test I was told that a small area on the outer corner of my left eye shows very old scarring indicating that this part of my eye is useless to me. I have wondered whether the childhood accident I sustained all those years ago in running round the bucket caused the damage described.

I started school when I was three years old. In those days little children just tagged along in the care of older girls and boys who were trusted to look after them. And that's how it was for me.

The village school with an attached Headmaster's house was a grey stone building situated next to the Church Cemetery. The newer Council Cemetery was just further down the road. The well-built and imposing Council School had replaced the older National school or Church school as it was known. On one side of the building was the girls' entrance that opened into the cloakroom, where we hung our coats on designated pegs. The first door leading off the cloakroom was into the *Babies Section* where there were two female teachers, both of whom were very kind. Here, we were taught to read and write, and I can still visualise the blackboard on which was written 'The cat was on the mat'. Also we learned to do *sums* - by adding up and taking away: but dividing and multiplying came later in the next class. We were taught the *multiplication tables* by rote, in parrot fashion, and I still believe that all children should learn the multiplication tables up to the twelve times in this fashion. I know that some younger people will disagree with that opinion because everyone now has calculators - but I still think it's important.

As children, we loved to sing songs together, and once learnt, those songs were firmly fixed in our minds forever. During my time in the *Babies Section* we wrote with squeaky slate pencils onto slate slabs fixed in wooden frames. When the slabs were covered with writing or there were mistakes that required correcting, we simply erased them by rubbing out with the sleeve of our garment, and if necessary by spitting first to make the task easier. The only mishap that I can remember experiencing during this time caused a commotion when the teachers discovered that I had swallowed a staple pin from a book. I still don't know why children put things in their mouths, noses and ears, but on that day I must have put a staple in my mouth for some reason, and in so doing, caused consternation at school!

I can also remember drinking blue ink from a bottle at home because it looked pretty in the light. It tasted tangy at the time in comparison with what seemed like gallons of bland water that I had to drink after the event to attempt to flush it out. I wonder what my intestines looked like at the time? I can also remember being given a severe 'ticking-off' for scribbling on pages of a hymnbook, and I nearly ruined a beautiful rosewood glove box belonging to my mother when I tried to pencil 'Mary May' her name, onto the wooden lid. Unfortunately, children do such things occasionally without thinking of the consequences.

The next room off the cloakroom in school was the big room where two classes were taught - Standard 4 and Standard 5. Between the two was a large table and directly in front of Standard 5 was the exit into the boys' cloakroom and to the left was Standard 3, a large airy room. There were big windows in all the rooms and the school had open fires in the classrooms with high fireguards. On cold days we would envy the teachers when they stood with their backs to the fire to warm their bottoms.

In those days if children were regarded as bright pupils they could sit the scholarship examination when they were eleven years of age and if successful, went to the County Grammar School at Abergele. All the children who passed the scholarship had their names added onto a big black Honours Board in the village school. My brother, elder sister, younger sister and I had our names on the Board, and as far as I know, they're still there. The other children stayed at the village school until they were fourteen years old, at which point they could leave and go to work. The big boys learned some gardening on a small strip of land between the school building and the wall next to the road, and the older girls went once a week to Abergele to learn to cook at the new Secondary Modern School. At the time, there was a strong snobbish attitude in the community that considered the Modern School inferior because it concentrated on practical subjects whilst the County School or Grammar School as it later became known, concentrated on teaching the more valued academic subjects. It was the 1944 Education Act that ensured that only children up to the age of eleven could attend elementary schools, and that all children had to remain at school until the age of fifteen, which later became 16. Eleven year-old children who passed the scholarship examination, or the *11 Plus* as it was later known, were sent to the Grammar School and the ones who failed or did not attempt the exam were sent to the Secondary Modern School. It wasn't until the 1970s when Comprehensive Schools were introduced that the process of segregating children at the age of eleven finally stopped. The old ways might have been suitable at the time, but the world evolves constantly, and education, like many other things must change with the times. Today, there are tremendous changes still taking place in the field of education that are not always welcomed by everyone, but are really necessary if children are to be successful in the modern world.

My village school was built on a slope and its entrances were approached by a series of steps. At the back of the school under the boys' cloakroom were cellars used as storerooms, and under the girls' cloakroom was a large room where children ate their mid-day dinner. The children who lived in the village went home for their mid-day meal, but there were many others who walked three miles or more to and from school who had no choice but to eat their dinner there. They brought packed lunches and tin cans with handles in which they had tea and sugar. There was a big fireplace in the room with a large geyser that provided boiling water. The caretaker, who also cleaned the school, lit the fire daily and filled the geyser with water for us. It had a tap on the front and children of all ages used it to fill their cans with boiling water to make tea. There was no supervision by adults, but I cannot remember even one accident happening as a result of this potentially dangerous practice.

The toilets were in a row between the girls' and the boys' yards (playgrounds), one lot for girls and another for boys. The playground was quite large and on a bit of a slope, and it was surrounded by a metre-high stone wall. We were strictly forbidden to climb the wall because there was a very steep drop down to the road below on one side of it. Many boys climbed over the wall as a dare and survived to tell the tale, and only once to my knowledge did a boy fall and seriously injure himself.

My first Headmaster at the school was a tall, distinguished looking man who taught mostly in English, and we were all afraid of him. If a class was noisy he had only to appear in the room and there would be an immediate hush. Later, another Headmaster came and I remember that my father did not think that he was effective enough. He had previously been an Attendance Officer, a *Children's Policeman* as the children called him, and after undertaking a short crash-course at the end of World War 1, had become an elementary school teacher. I believe his grandfather was a well-known poet. The most senior class teacher was a graduate who had an M.A. in the classics but because of poor health, had been reduced from teaching in a Grammar School to teaching in an Elementary School. I remember one incident concerning him that happened during a lesson when one of the boys, who was always getting into scrapes, had misbehaved and disrupted the lesson and had consequently been called out to the front of the class to be caned as a punishment. The boy reluctantly left his desk, but had no intention of being caned, and as soon as the teacher advanced towards him, started running round and round the centre table with the teacher chasing behind. There was uproar from both classes with all the children laughing and shouting until the boy finally ran out of the building. I don't know what the eventual repercussions were for the boy or teacher, but peace was soon restored that day.

We were taught lessons in: reading, mental and written arithmetic, spelling, English, simple knitting and sewing for girls and penmanship. The slates used in earlier years were finally disposed of and replaced with proper writing books printed with red and blue guidelines - an improvement we valued very much. Thank goodness for the enlightened people of the time. Some children had better handwriting than others, but everyone's writing was legible.

We had a break from lessons to play outside mid-morning, at dinnertime and mid-afternoon, and the school day ended at half past three. The games we played in the school playground during breaks were varied, depending on age groups and the weather. Boys predominantly played football all year round, marbles in the spring and conkers in the autumn, but girls played many different games including rounders. We played hopscotch too, a game that required using a stone to draw a large rectangle on the ground that was divided into a minimum of six squares. Players would individually push a flat stone from one square to the next with one foot whilst hopping continuously from one square to the next until they had hopped on all squares and arrived back at the beginning.

Children who had standard skipping-ropes used them singly and there was also a long rope that enabled many skippers to participate in turn. The long rope was flipped over and over by a child at each end, and each skipper had to develop the skill of timing her jump into the moving rope to avoid touching it and therefore stopping its rhythmical movement in the process. The crowd watching counted the number of times each girl managed to jump successfully over the rope at any one time - the girl with the most jumps was considered the most skilful. We played marbles in the spring by drawing a circle on the ground, setting a larger master marble in the centre and flicking marbles or 'gingers' as we called them from the edge of the ring to try to hit the master out of the ring. If you won, you got to keep the loser's ginger. Some of the marbles were very pretty in having colourful patterns within their glass spheres: some were small and others large. Whatever the activity at playtime, we often played in groups - for one game a child would stand alone facing a wall and at a distance a couple of yards behind, several girls would link hands in a row and walk up to her chanting, "What time is it Mr. Wolf". She would call out such and such a time, and the line would recede and go through the same motions again until suddenly 'Mr. Wolf' would turn and shout, "Time to eat you." If she succeeded in catching one of the girls in the line, they would exchange places.

At other times we would stand in a circle with a small space in between us, and one girl would stand in the middle of the circle. With a handkerchief in her hand, she would then skip in and out of the spaces between the girls. She would be singing, "I wrote a letter to my love and on the way I lost it, one of you has picked it up and put it in your pocket - not you, not you, not you but you!" She would then drop the hanky behind one of the girls in the circle. It was then a race between the two to get into the centre. They were such innocent games, but we had a lot of fun playing them.

There were two bells in the village. One was the Church bell that tolled to call worshippers to attend the morning and evening Sunday services. I don't remember whether there was a joyful ringing for weddings, but I do remember there was a knell tolled at funerals - '*y cnul*' we Welsh speakers called it.

The other was the school bell, to call children to attend the morning and afternoon lessons on Mondays to Fridays. There was a first bell followed in five minutes by a second bell, and woe betide anyone who arrived late for school. Before being allowed into our classrooms we had to line-up on the yard with our right hand resting on the left shoulder of the child next to us. Once we had been called to attention, we were told to lower our arms, turn left and march inside. There was no rushing or pushing - it was good discipline for us.

Visitors sometimes arrived at the school including the nurse who came periodically to inspect our hair for general cleanliness as well as looking for evidence of headlice. My mother would comb our hair regularly with a very fine tooth-comb over a plate to catch and destroy any 'livestock' that had been passed on from other children's hair. The eggs and empty shells called 'nits' had to be destroyed as well. The school doctor came about once a year and we had to strip to the waist so he could listen to our chests with a stethoscope. But the attendance officer would come quite often to chase-up children who did not attend school regularly. Some were absent very often, and on reappearing at school would be questioned quite severely. The answers given by the children were many and varied - some were funny, but others were very sad and tragic.

There was a great deal of deprivation during the Depression in the late 1920s and early 1930s and I can remember some children coming to school with holes in their boots, wearing ragged clothes and with runny noses, but I have to say that they were in the minority. The diseases of the time that often killed adults and children were tuberculosis, scarlet fever, diphtheria and polio. Most of us had suffered from measles and chickenpox at some time or other but all of us had received the vaccination against smallpox. I remember a special occasion once in the village school when a lady, presumably a nurse, came to talk to the whole school about the danger of infectious diseases being spread through spitting and sneezing. We were amused by the fact that she was encouraging us to get an old medicine bottle from home into which we should spit any phlegm whenever we coughed it up. The purpose of her visit was to reduce the growing increase in the number of TB cases at the time. Numerous isolation hospitals and sanitaria were set up to manage the crisis. It was unfortunate however, that these establishments did not impact upon the cause of these diseases, they only dealt with the results of bad housing, poor sanitation and a lack of nutrition - all symptoms of social deprivation, poverty and unemployment.

But the visitor who scared us the most was the Inspector of Schools because he questioned us in English about history, geography, Scripture, mental arithmetic, spelling and other subjects. We held the Inspector in awe for we had been warned that he was an extremely important person. It was the teachers who instilled that fear in us because I think they were themselves scared of the Inspector. We were warned to be quiet, to answer questions properly and not to forget to say 'Sir', for the Inspectors were always men.

I wore a cotton dress in summer and a jumper and skirt in winter with a *'brat'* over the top of the outfit to prevent soiling it. We wore socks up to our knees with garters to hold them up in the winter and ankle socks in summer. We wore black lace-up boots that reached well above our ankles for everyday use, and in winter I can remember wearing gaiters that wrapped over our legs from ankle to knee and were fastened on the side by snap-on buttons. On Sundays however, we wore prettier clothes and were allowed to wear shoes, not boots. We also used muffs on cold days to keep our hands warm.

Once, I can remember the company Dunlop giving every child at school a pair of wellington boots free of charge, but I don't remember why it happened. Maybe it was Dunlop's way of advertising its products, or more likely perhaps a charitable gesture during the Depression. Anyway, I had never worn wellingtons previously but considered them to be great fun. My friends and I turned down their tops to show the lining so we could pretend to be pirates climbing trees just like ships' rigging and yelling at the tops of our voices … “Ships ahoy!”

After school and in the holidays we often played at making 'little houses' - we would build them in any suitable space or corner using whatever materials came to hand. We used old sacks as walls and bits of broken crockery as ornaments. Once, we had a little house under the bank of the river until the floods washed it away. On another occasion we chose a corner of land that had wire fencing in a diamond-mesh pattern and we stuffed all the diamond spaces with bundles of grass and created the other two walls with sacks and sticks - it had no roof. But it was 'our house'.

There were so few cars about that we could play 'tennis' on the main road, moving aside when cyclists or horses and carts came along. The sound of an aeroplane would bring people out of their homes to watch it fly by and I noticed that sometimes the wings would be double on both sides, presumably meaning that it was a biplane - it would be slow moving and a wondrous sight for us to behold.

During the time we lived in Pengraig I did not eat my dinner at the school. Perhaps my mother was scared that I would get hurt with the open fire or the geyser. I don't know, but every day I took my sandwiches to a house in the village where Auntie Lizzie, Denbigh Road, lived. She was a very kind lady who not only allowed me to eat there but the youngest daughter of the Baptist Minister too, whose family lived halfway up the Bodran Mountain. Auntie Lizzie and her family were faithful Baptists who attended her father's chapel every Sunday. At this time my best friend was Hannah, who was six weeks older than me, and her home was a smallholding further up the hill from us. She and I started school together, and were shepherded by her older sister, Dinah. I liked going to their home because Mrs. Morris, their mother would give me a sugar butty - a piece of bread and butter with sugar plastered on it. Their home was also a two-roomed cottage, with a sort of 'lean-to' where the milking utensils were kept as well as the churn for the butter. There was a small inglenook around the fireplace with settles on both sides. These were chests for storage that doubled-up as bench seating with high backs that provided warm places to sit by the fire. Above the fireplace was a high mantelshelf with about twenty or more horse brasses hanging all along the edge. I can remember sitting on a chair by the door on a fine day, with the sun shining on the brasses that had probably just recently been polished, and saying, “Mrs. Morris, I did not know you had so much gold in your house.” This amused her very much and she repeatedly reminded me of it for many years. The name of the smallholding was *Pant y Chware* (Valley of playing). I think it must originally have been *Pant y Chwarel* (Valley of the quarry) but perhaps not. This was where we obtained our buttermilk - the real stuff, because the milk was not mechanically separated before butter making as is done today. I have always preferred buttermilk to milk, the sharp, clean, tangy taste is nicer and lighter than milk.

One day after school, Hannah and I were walking along the road somewhere between our two homes when one of us, goodness knows which one, had a sudden idea. We agreed we would exchange clothes and then she would go to my home and I would go to hers and no one would know the difference, and everyone would be fooled. We were so excited as we sat on a tree trunk on the roadside where we took off and exchanged every item of clothing, including boots and socks before dressing again according to plan. I fared the best I believe. When I got to Hannah's home her mother's face was a picture: she gasped, then smiled broadly and after asking questions and getting to know what was going on, gave me a sugar butty, then sent me home. On the way I met Hannah returning from my home, and realised immediately that my mother's reception had been rather cool to say the least for there had been no smiles or sugar butties for her. So, once again we stripped and exchanged clothes before going home wearing our own garments this time. Hannah and I had a lot of fun together.

The house just below *Pant y Chware* was a nice bungalow and I think it was partly built of timber. The owners did not live there all the time. It must have been a holiday home and there were three or four such houses in the village at that time. When the owners were there I always felt scared of passing the place because they had three large dogs that barked fiercely whenever anyone approached the house. There was a big, wide and strong wooden gate to the garden, but the dogs jumped up against it and I was frightened that they would jump over, but thankfully they never did. Situated lower down the hill was another holiday home where Mrs. Cooper and her daughters went to stay quite often. They lived in Judges Drive in Liverpool, and they too had a large dog, but he was a docile old thing unlike the others, and we liked him.

Just below our cottage was another timber bungalow called Windy Ridge, where Mr. and Mrs. Pickering lived. All I remember about Mr Pickering was that he walked very slowly with a stick, was always well dressed and never spoke to us children. He died very soon after arriving in the house, and Mrs Pickering was then left to live on her own. She was a tiny lady and very quiet. The next place along the road from us was called *Hen Ysgol* (old school) where Miss Davies the dressmaker lived with her mother. Miss Davies made all our new dresses, my sister's and mine. First we took the material there and were measured and told to go back at a certain date for a fitting. This was the tricky bit for us because at that point, the dress would be held together by tacking and pins. We had to stand perfectly still for the fitting, and what a performance it was because sometimes the pins stuck into our flesh but we dared not protest. With her mouth full of pins Miss Davies would order us to, "Stand still, and stop wriggling." Anyway she was a good seamstress and the clothes she made for us were always nice and fitted neatly. I don't know why the place was called *Hen Ysgol*, I can only guess that there must once have been a school of some kind there.

Just above the Wesleyan Chapel was a house called *Bron Llan* (overlooking the village). Another Miss Davies lived there who let part of the house to a tall, thin man called Mr. Sweeney. There might have been a Mrs. Sweeney but I cannot remember one. The entrance to the house from the road on the hill had a wide step that took in the slope. Here, the children from up the hill, including me, would pause and sit to talk or crack nuts or whatever children did in a bunch. There must have been six or seven of us - boys and girls, but never once did Miss Davies scold us for messing about on her step although I am sure we were noisy. She knew however, that we did not get up to mischief or cause any damage. The one thing we did do there was crack hazel nuts on the step with a stone and I am sorry to say that we left all the debris of shells and husks on the step, which poor Miss Davies would have had to clear away - but she never complained.

In school, our lessons were taught sometimes in English and other times in Welsh, but mostly they were in English. Welsh was spoken everywhere else in our community. From time to time a new family of English speakers would move to live in the village, and if they stayed long enough, their children learned to speak Welsh because we continued to speak our mother tongue at all times. They made the best of the situation by learning to join in the Welsh conversations, and under those conditions, picked up the language naturally and quickly. There was no animosity for it was a natural process that the English newcomers recognised and accepted completely.

At the end of the morning session in school the children stood to sing a blessing, which began with, “Be present at our table Lord…” I didn't know anymore of the correct words because most of us sang a garbled version of the rest of the verse. No one had bothered to teach us the proper words, tell us what they meant, or show us the words in writing to help us make sense of them. But, what we sang must have sounded alright to those who heard us because no one ever said anything - perhaps the School Inspector was also taken in by our garbled version … we must have sounded quite convincing!

Chapter 2

LIFE'S TWISTS

In 1931 when I was seven years old, two important things happened: firstly my brother left home and went to work in London, and secondly my family and I moved from Pengraig down to the village. Strangely, I do not remember any details of my brother's departure and things must have been very different after he'd gone and I know that I missed him, but somehow life with its twists and turns went on from day to day. I think that in some providential way the very young and the very old are able to accept death and parting without undue pain. In much the same way, although I loved Elsie my older sister, and enjoyed being with her when she was alive, I did not suffer pain when she died. She just went away to Heaven and that was that. It sounds cruel, but it is a benign situation. Sometimes I think adults can make things more difficult for children by their own extreme reactions to grief.

Later, after I had grown up I learned that my brother was very homesick in the big city at first and also very poor. His earnings were not sufficient to cover his expenses and for some years my mother sent him money to help make ends meet. This was not easy because of the Depression, but at least he had a job. There were millions of people who were unemployed all over the country. Many of the young men in my village had no work, and during the early 1920s my father had to work away in Colwyn Bay where he stayed during the week and came home at weekends. In time he obtained work at the local Mansion, *Garthewin*, where he became head gardener for the Squire who at that time was an elderly, eccentric bachelor, but my father got on well with him. There were many employees on the estate and the Squire owned properties not only in Llanfair but in Betws yn Rhos and the Llanddulas area too.

Old Mr. Wynne used to get his hot lunch delivered every day from Chester, which was many miles away: it came in a hay-box on the train to Abergele and then fetched from there by one of the estate employees driving a horse and carriage. When the Squire died the estate passed to his nephew Robert Oliver Francis Wynne who moved to Garthewin with his mother from the south of England. In the early thirties Mrs. Wynne would sometimes come to the village in a carriage drawn by a pony and Mr. Wynne rode a horse and went fox hunting with the local Hunt. The Wynnes were members of a very ancient Welsh family and there are memorial tablets to various members on the walls of St. Mary's Church in Llanfair Talhaearn.

Within a few years of arriving at Garthewin, Mrs Wynne and later her son, converted to Roman Catholicism, which somehow created a division between them and the villagers, most of whom were Non-Conformists. Mrs. Wynne wrote a book explaining why she had changed and I read her book and found it very honest in revealing that she had pondered long and hard before taking the decision. Mr. Wynne became a member of *Plaid Cymru* (Welsh Nationalist Party) and learned to speak Welsh. He also published a book of poems in English. He married an Anglo-Irish lady and they eventually had three daughters. The elder Mrs. Wynne moved to live in South Wales and called her new home *Garthewin*, after her former home in Llanfair Talhaearn.

The *Garthewin* Mansion in Llanfair is a beautiful place standing on a hill overlooking the Vale of Elwy. The building is decorated in a pale golden yellow and white and has a large drawing room on one side of the main house. This is where the *Nosweithau Llawen* (Happy Evenings of song and poetry) were held, to which the great and the good in Welsh life were invited. I was invited to sing at these gatherings and thoroughly enjoyed them. I met several leading persons in the world of the Arts in Wales at that time and still have the signatures of most of them in my autograph book. After becoming Roman Catholic the Wynnes had a small church built in the grounds for the family that had marble decorations from Italy.

In the grounds at the back of the Mansion was a big stone archway leading to a courtyard, the stables and a large barn. On the archway was a striking clock. There was also a house where the chauffeur, Mr. Falvey lived, whose son, Francis attended the local school for a time and in adulthood became a Priest. The barn was converted to a fine theatre that became the home of a distinguished drama company called *Cwmni Drama Garthewin* (Garthewin's Drama Company). Mr. Wynne gave a lot of money and support to the Arts in Wales.

There were three drives and lodges leading to the house and in the grounds were rose terraces, lawns and a large lake with water lilies and swans. On the main drive was a building called the 'Book Room' used I believe by the villagers at one time. During the Depression, the Wynnes paid for a large building in the village-square to be converted into an Institute for the men, many of whom were unemployed at the time. A library was created on the first floor, and the ground floor was transformed into a billiard room with a large table above which, were electric lights. A private generator produced the power for the lights in the building for there was no general electricity supply in the village at that time - everyone else had to use oil lamps and candles for light. They also encouraged sporting activities by allowing the local football team to play on one of their fields in the valley. I cannot give a judgement on the quality of the Llanfair team, but we children knew where our loyalties lay as we yelled and screeched our support like banshees whenever our team played a match.

The other important event in 1931 was my family's move from *Pengraig* down to the village. A row of attractive semi-detached council houses had been built in Llanfair that became available to local people. They are still there today, but I daresay that most, if not all of them will now probably be privately owned. The houses are arranged in a crescent shape with each one having gardens to the front and back. Originally, ten houses were built with some having two bedrooms and others three, and the two in the centre of the curve had parlours as well as a living room. They were all brick built and had bathrooms and water closets (toilets)! My parents had been offered one of the houses with a parlour but unfortunately, could not afford the rent of 7/6d. per week which was 7 shillings and 6 pence or the equivalent of 0.37 pence today, and so we moved to a two-bedroomed house at a rent of 5/9d, which was 5 shillings and 9 pence or 0.28pence per week.

One of the bedrooms was large with several fitted cupboards and the other was small. On the tiny landing was a cupboard for storing linen. Later on, it housed the hot water cylinder too. Downstairs, the living room was large with a red tiled floor, and leading off it was a small wardrobe for coats, a pantry and a bathroom. The front door opened directly into this room and Dad erected a wooden screen to give some privacy to the family when people called. The fireplace was a black range with an oven but there was no boiler, but after the War a modern range replaced the old grate. There was a large sink in the kitchen and outside the back door was a covered porch that housed the lavatory. All the window casements were large and made of metal and the staircase wound round on itself. On the outside of the house was the door to the coal shed that was situated under the stairs, but it could only be accessed from outside the house. There was a useful brick-built shed for storing tools and other items, a big garden at the back and a smaller one at the front.

I remember very well the day of our departure from *Pengraig*. My memories are not of the packing and preparation, but of the thoughts I had as I stood by the big gate watching an ordinary farm wagon being pulled by a horse that took all our worldly goods in one load to our new house - so few were our possessions. I also remember the excitement of being in a new house, of going upstairs to bed, and of not having a flapping ceiling sheet. The local Baptist Minister, the Rev. John Phillips from South Wales moved to live in one of the parlour-type houses with his family, having previously lived in a house on Bodran Mountain. His daughter Minnie, and I became great friends and we were friendly with Iris, the only child of Mr. & Mrs. Parry who kept the local newsagent and general grocery et al shop in the village. Hannah was also my friend, but mostly at school. Our free time was spent separately because of the distance between our homes. She was six weeks older than I, and an intelligent girl: she and I would vie with one another to be 'top of the class' at school. She should have gone with me to the Grammar School, but instead opted to help her father with the threshing machine that moved from farm to farm to deal with the threshing of corn. It was hard manual work done usually by men and she seemed to enjoy it, but I sometimes wonder if it had a detrimental effect on her health. Later in life she was crippled with rheumatism although it did not dampen her cheery disposition and smiling demeanour. Sadly, she recently passed away.

After we moved from *Pengraig* into the new council house, Uncle Williams and Pero the dog would go at dinner-time each day to the top of a field that we called *Cae Owen Jones* (Owen Jones' field). From there he would shout our names at the top of his voice, *"Bet a Bella Hello,"* so that we would go out and wave to him. He missed us as much as we missed him. Not long afterwards he died and I gathered some flowers from our garden and asked a neighbour if she would arrange them and write a card to go with them to the family. When she asked what she should write on the card I answered, *"Dymuniadau gorau oddiwrth Bet a Bella,"* (best wishes from Bet and Bella). It was a child's wish and could not have been improved upon, although it raised a smile at the time.

Chapter 3

THE VILLAGE

In the thirties just before the start of World War II, Llanfair was a typical Welsh village where practically everyone spoke Welsh. Most people understood English but some found it difficult to express their meaning in the language because they rarely needed to use it. During the summer a number of families came on holiday, usually year after year so we came to know them quite well. Coaches or charabancs as they were known came from Rhyl on evening trips through the 'Switzerland of Wales' along the *Bryn y Pin Pass* to St. Asaph. The coaches were large, wide and rounded like fat ladies, were white in colour and had an emblem of a rose on both sides. The roof covering was made from heavy calico that folded down to the back in fine weather to give passengers a splendid view of the pretty countryside. Occasionally some passengers would throw coins to us children as we gathered to stare in fascination at the strangers in their charabanc. And oh, how I remember the sound and sight of the vehicle's hooter, which was certainly not a standard horn by any stretch of the imagination. The front of it was shaped like a horn that tapered to a narrow middle where it was attached to a large black rubber balloon that had to be squeezed hard by the driver to emit a warning sound. But to us, the hooter was a wonderfully entertaining gadget that made a ridiculously humorous noise: a sort of a rude slap-stick comedy sound that was flat, hard and very loud. The 'boom ... boom' sound made us jump about, laugh aloud and beg to hear it again. I marvel at the simple things that gave us enormous pleasure and talking points before the onset of modern technology.

In the summer months silver and brass bands visited the village, and the ones I remember were the Llanddulas, and Rhyl Silver Bands. I loved to hear their wonderful music and see the instrumentalists dressed in their smart uniforms standing in a semi-circle on the Village Square with their music sheets clipped onto the instruments. They created a wonderful sound and we loved their visits.

Llanfair Talhaearn is a very pretty village and interesting too. It takes its first name from the Church of St. Mary, but the *Talhaearn* is a bit of a mystery. One distinguished poet took it as his bardic name. The bust of Talhaearn is in the Memorial Hall in Llanfair. He was a competent, but not outstanding bard, and was better-known in his day during the last century as an architect. He was involved in the erection of a glass building in France for one of the Rothschild family and on the strength of that took part in the planning of the Crystal Palace in London during the reign of Queen Victoria. It was regarded as one of the sights of London and it must have been very sad when it burnt to the ground. Talhaearn also drew up the plans for Worsley Church (St. Marks) near Manchester, the spire of which can be seen from the M62 motorway. Talhearn lived in a tavern in Llanfair called *Hafod y Gan* at the top of the hill near the village church. The tavern, with its lovely name, which means 'the summer place of song' is now a private house. The Church is at the top end of the village and can be reached by a public pathway as well as the road. It is quite old, and the weather vane is unusual in the fact that it is a fish: the sign of the early Christians.

On the way home from school sometimes the boys would dare us girls to go into the graveyard to look inside some of the old slate chest tombstones in which skulls could be seen! Opposite the church was the Smithy, another interesting place to us especially when Mr. Davies the Smith and his son were making iron bands and placing them on the wheels of carts. A circle of fire would be built on the ground and then a made-to-measure hoop would be placed on the fire until it expanded sufficiently to fit over the wheel. Then it was doused with cold water to cool the metal ensuring a tight fit. Many times we watched the Smith driving nails into a horse's hoof to fit a new shoe and wondered why the horse did not object to the seemingly painful operation.

Further along the road was a stone building within the Church cemetery where the hearse was kept. This was the big, ugly black box that was used to carry coffins at funerals, and was horse-drawn. On the opposite side of the road was a stable used only when stallions were brought to the area to service mares. On those occasions we were naturally intrigued by the proceedings, and more than interested to see what happened to the horses, and discover the role men played in the process. We wanted to know the facts of course, as all children in every generation do but … we were shooed away quickly every time!

At this point in the road there is a 'T' junction and the left hand turn leads up to the *Barrog* area in the hills where there are many farms. The Rectory, a large imposing stone building is up there on the left and not too far from the junction, and I can remember being in its grounds once only, just after the War when a garden party was held to raise funds for the Church. Nearby, but on the other side of the road is a large bungalow with tennis courts, which was owned by *Jones y Moch* (Mr. Jones the Pigs), for there was also a piggery there. Mr. Jones was a successful businessman in Liverpool who manufactured and sold pies, sausages and such like. The family came to stay from time to time, especially in the summer.

By returning now to the main road we immediately notice at the junction the first addition to the Church cemetery which had earlier reached capacity, then further along on the right hand side we see the Council school. Then immediately on the left we see the second additional cemetery that has been provided by the Council and is the one in current use. It is an exceptionally well-maintained cemetery and there is plenty of evidence to indicate that the site is tended by people who take a real pride in their work and care about the place and all that it represents.

If we continued along this road, known as the old road, we would get to the next village of Llangernyw. But by staying in Llanfair, we see that within a hundred yards or so of the new cemetery stands a fine house overlooking marshland and the valley, but as a child I always thought it looked rather forlorn in its isolation. Near the house on the old Llangernyw Road is a sharp hairpin bend that leads back to the centre of Llanfair where the old bridge and the National School stand, behind which is a playing field where sports days and carnivals were held in my day. Many times after torrential rain this field and others in the village were flooded by the swelling river. Usually the *Elwy River* was a pleasant stretch of water rippling along, but flash-floods transformed it into a raging torrent. As children, we played on the river's edge and paddled and bathed in the water during the summer months, but we were warned very seriously about its dangers. We were told that if we stared at the river flowing in flood it could draw us into itself, and I have stood on the old bridge looking upriver during a flood and felt the sensation of literally moving up river as if in a ship! I can also remember being very frightened one fine summer's day as a group of us were playing about on the river's edge when quite suddenly there was a loud noise and a great surge of water bore down on us and we just managed to scramble onto the bank. That was a lesson I never forgot. We knew that if there was any froth on the surface of the water we were to keep away from the river because it was a sign of potentially dangerous turbulence somewhere upstream.

However, the river was not very deep in and around the village most of the time, but its uneven bed varied the depth from about ten inches to four feet or so, and there were dangerous deeper pools in places and a couple of whirlpools too. We thought we knew where they were and tried to avoid them. Such intrinsic knowledge was, and still is part of the folklore of country life.

The river was well known to anglers especially trout and salmon fishermen. An English gentleman who lived in the village was particularly partial to the Elwy eels and we were told that having cut them into steaks to fry, during cooking the steaks would jump about in the pan.

Down river from the village was a weir with salmon jumps, and paths ran along both sides of the river. These were favourite walks, and very interesting too because it was a lovely experience to watch the fish jumping and struggling from one jump pool to the next up-stream, and finally onto the top. In the summer we could walk across the weir when it was completely dry in hot weather, and when there was even a little trickle of water too. On one side of the jumps was a lock gate to section off a waterway that flowed to the nearby Mill where flour was produced. This lock was hand operated by the miller when necessary. A little way down from the weir was the sewage treatment area from where the effluent went into the river. It was fenced off to the public and although in the summer there were always large juicy tomatoes to be seen within this enclosed area, I never saw anyone gathering them! Nearby, were two smallholdings within half a mile of each other, both of which were referred to as mills: *y Felin Falu* (the Grinding Mill) which was the operating flour mill, and *y Felin Crempog* (the Pancake Mill) which was not a working mill when I was a child. This smallholding was also known as *Tyddyn Clefi*, (Clefi Cottage) but I have no idea what Clefi means. Within this second mill's grounds were old disused lead mines, and I can remember seeing two shafts, one was situated close to the house, another a little further away and I knew there were others in a wood nearby. As far as could be seen there were no safety barriers on the entrances, just some old dilapidated brickwork, brambles and weeds. We were warned to keep away from them and were wise enough to understand how dangerous they were. My father had worked in these lead mines for a time when he was a youth and knew their danger.

Llanfair is at the heart of the beautiful Vale of Elwy. The village has two bridges: the old traditional stone one which is highly visible in the village has a large arch and two smaller ones on either side; and the other is less visible being an integral part of the new road to Llansannan, which was opened in 1927.

Up river from the old bridge are the beautiful Seven Sisters - seven large identical trees with seats resting against their trunks and facing the river, a lovely place to rest on a fine day. But the favourite place in Llanfair where young people congregated was the top of the old bridge where we must have stood around for hours talking and having fun. In fact, we sat on the flat stones positioned on top of the arch supports so often they became shiny from being polished by our bottoms!

Facing the bridge is a fine house that used to be the Doctor's residence and surgery, and on the opposite side is the Black Lion Hotel, which is just a few metres away from the centre of the village. The Square itself had: the Swan Inn, two rows of cottages and a bakery, a cobbler's shop, a grocery shop known as 'shop Harrison', and a Newsagent-cum-general store known as 'shop Parry' where the Midland Bank hired a room for a day each week as a local service to its customers.

The other business establishment on the Square that I remember was firstly run as a Post Office by *Miss Davies bach Post* (little Miss Davies the Post). She was indeed small and wore gold pince nez spectacles perched on the tip of her nose. She was very genteel in her manner, but all of us children were afraid of her because we knew she was frightfully strict and would not tolerate any nonsense on our part. Eventually she left, but I can't remember whether she died or went away from Llanfair. The Post Office business was then moved to different premises and Miss Davies' building remained empty for a time before it became a Butcher's shop. It operated successfully for a few years, but eventually collapsed as a business owing to difficulties encountered during the Depression.

The butcher's shop left behind something of great interest to me: a family of black and white cats - six beautiful creatures that had been reared on scraps of meat. I decided that I wanted one of them, and indeed managed to catch one with great difficulty because they were all completely wild. I grabbed my chosen' moggy' and held it tightly, but it was struggling frantically, hissing loudly, and biting and scratching me too. But I was determined, so I started to make my way home along the back path towards the main road when suddenly, the cat sprang free and ran up a tree. I knew that it was useless trying to coax it down so I hurried home and got a sack. As fast as I could, I went back down the road hoping that the cat had not run away, and when I reached the tree I felt elated because I could see it cowering at the very top. Without causing too much disturbance for fear of frightening the cat, I climbed up and quickly put the sack over it and grabbed the content tightly to form a neat bundle before setting off home again. When I arrived I was covered in scratches and blood, but I didn't care because I was happy - I'd got my first cat! My mother knew what was in the sack because she could hear the yowling, but all she said was, “Just look at you, what on earth have you been doing?” She was quite sure the cat would return to its old home, but I insisted that I could tame it. My father supported me for he was very fond of cats, he loved to see them washing themselves especially their faces and ears. In the end I was allowed to keep *Tom Mouse* for that is what I called him. He was a marvellous mouse catcher and was successful in catching rats and rabbits too.

There was a henhouse in the field behind our back garden where Tom went often and he eventually cleaned the place of mice and rats. We knew this because he proudly brought his prey home to show us, but we noticed something else that he brought back with him too: fleas! My father showed me how to smear fat inside the cat's ears and when the fleas had gathered in there it was easy to kill them and then clean the cat completely. Tom sat quite still while I went through this performance and purred happily - he seemed to sense that he was being looked after and made to feel better. Of course there were no patented cat foods available then, at least not to my knowledge, and even if there had been I would not have been able to afford them. Anyway, he didn't need anything special because he ate what he caught himself and devoured any spare bits left from our meals … and he flourished on it all. Occasionally he would disappear for two or three days to hunt in the fields or make love to any willing Miss Pussies around. Lovemaking always involved much screeching and caterwauling. If it took place near a house the family would more than likely throw a dousing of cold water onto them to send them on their way. After his exploits, Tom Mouse then returned home looking scruffy and very much the worse for wear, so I would wash him, comb his fur and make him look his usual magnificent self again, until the next time at least. Yes, I can hear you protest that cats hate getting bathed, but I tell you truly that Tom loved that treatment. He followed me around everywhere, and when I had to go to hospital Mam said that he sat on the stairs and wailed for days. After two or three years he went off on one of his jaunts and never came back. I missed him terribly and hoped that he had not been caught in a trap.

Following the departure of the Butcher, the next occupant of the shop was Miss Gwen Davies, daughter of the village Tailor. She opened a sweet shop and a small café, and without ado, it became known by everyone in the village as *Shop Newydd* (new shop). When Miss Davies married, and a very grand event it was too, the business was taken over by her brother David, and once again, the villagers renamed the shop as *Shop Dei* (Dei's shop). He and his wife expanded the business and were very successful. There were two other shops, both grocers that were known as *Shop Williams* and *Shop Royle*. The former was just round a corner from the Square behind the Men's Club where a path led up to Penllan and the Church past Rosehill and Rose Cottage. At the start of the path was a house named *Penbanc* (top of the bank) because it was situated on a bank and owned by the Williams family from the shop: I remember that it was let out to visitors in the summer.

The shop was a fascinating place where raw ingredients such as flour, sugar and tea were all in large sacks and were packed by the shopkeeper into separate 1 or 2 pound packets made of thick blue paper. I can visualise him now in his spotless white apron weighing the ingredients into the packets on the shop's beautifully graceful brass scales. Heavier packages were weighed by a spring stilage that had a ring at the top to hang onto a peg, and a hook at the bottom on which to hang whatever was being weighed. The middle part was a long and narrow brass plate on which grades of weight, ozs and lbs were marked. Sometimes when we entered the shop we had to wait to be served because Mr Williams would be busy weighing and making up the various packets. We did not mind this because it was a revelation to see how skilfully he used the scoop to fill each bag, weigh it accurately, then close it at the top with a series of specialist folds before banging it on the counter to settle the contents. The circular cheeses were big and covered with a hard rind to keep in the taste and freshness, and a thin wire was needed to cut them into manageable segments. The shop had a lovely aroma of all good food smells from bacon and hams covered in muslin that hung from the rafters to coffee, tea, herbs and spices. Directly opposite the shop was a Tea Garden surrounded by a low white-washed wall on which was an attractive row of plant pots filled with red geraniums. Here, afternoon tea would be on sale to visitors in the summer and homemade ice cream too, and I must say that it was really the nicest ice cream that I have ever tasted.

On returning to the Square we pass three more attached cottages, the last having become the new Post Office. I was always impressed by the way the Postmaster and his wife used the official stamper on the letters and parcels by bringing it down on the inkpad with an almighty thump before marking the items to be posted. Round the corner to the left is the lane where The Crown public house used to be situated, and the licensee was the daughter of my father's cousin. I can remember the Public Room had a stone-flagged floor covered with sawdust and round receptacles called spittoons that resembled dogs' feeding bowls. In those days many men smoked pipes and chewed tobacco and they frequently attempted to spit into the spittoons - and often missed, hence the sawdust! But today, The Crown is an imposing private house.

Behind The Crown was a lane that led to two semi-detached cottages called *The Mount*, aptly named because they were on a slope that overlooked the Square: it was an extremely pleasant spot. By going back to the main lane known as *Y Gerddi* (the gardens) thus named because at one stage it passed between gardens, we walk along the back view of the houses on Water Street below. Because the lane was sloping, the roof of the houses also sloped and came increasingly lower towards the level of the road until finally people could lean on it. By using small stones we would write all kinds of messages on the slates, usually along the lines that So and So loved So and So.

Positioned nearby was a small gate with a path that led to a house with a large garden - the house, for some unknown reason was called Bingo, although it had the proper name of *Bryn Hyfryd* (delightful hill). The lady who lived there was known to everyone as Mrs Jones Bingo who earned her living by wallpapering and painting in people's houses. It was not an easy job in those days because the paper was stuck to the walls with a flour paste and was difficult to manage, and paint was very difficult to use smoothly too. Only a professional painter could get an even surface with few brush marks for there were no silicones in paint then.

On the other side of the lane was *Capel'Rofft* (Rofft Chapel), which was one large room that had been the local Baptist Chapel at one time with an attached cottage. This is where the lane went between the gardens and became very narrow. There were many unpaved paths and lanes in Llanfair, but their surfaces had become hardened by many feet over the years. The lane ended in a small cobbled area between Morris Street and a large house called *Ty'n Llidiart* (Gate House) and then it joined Denbigh Road at the foot of a very steep hill known as *Allt y Powls* (the hill of the Powls), which was the old road to Llansannan.

In Denbigh Road stands the World War 1 Memorial Hall that has served the community well since 1924, and is still being maintained very efficiently for that purpose today. On the opposite side there is a group of three attached houses, a gap, and then another group of three followed by a large house in extensive grounds called *Glasfryn* (grassy hill). There were tennis courts and a Pavilion here, but more about this later. Next, there was a strip of land that was divided into several allotments and let to villagers who tended them very well. Running alongside those, is the new road to Llansannan, and the new council houses called *Glan Elwy* (Elwy shores) where my family and I moved to when I was seven years old. We lived in the house directly opposite *Ffarm Dolhaearn* (iron meadow farm). Further along past my old home, *Llys Alaw* (the residence of tunes) the lane leads up to the lower reaches of *Mynydd Bodran* (Bodran Mountain), where it divides to the left and right. On the left there are five houses and a smallholding after which the lane peters out, but I believe that at one time, it continued to *Pont y Gwyddyl* (Bridge of the Irish). There is an historical explanation, but I cannot follow that up at this juncture.

By retracing our steps to the fork in the lane, we see an attractive house named *Bodran Grange* and the people who I remember living there were Mr and Mrs Hughes. He was a businessman in Abergele and a Deacon at the Presbyterian Chapel in the village and was highly regarded by everyone. Mrs Hughes was a small thin lady, who was always well-dressed, but fancied herself in her furs and gave the impression that she thought she was better than anyone else. I never heard her speak Welsh although I believe she was able to speak the language.

Returning once more to the Square we branch up Water Street, where there are several houses on the left hand side facing the garden of *Hafod y Gan* and the Church at the top of the hill. At the end of the street there is a house called *Minafon* (near the river) which at that time, was a Grocer's shop run by Mrs Royle. Over the road there was a small depot from where Mr Royle managed his business as a Coal merchant. We have now reached the small square known as *Llan bach* (little village) where there was a very nice Butcher's shop known as *Siop y Borth* (the gateway shop). Next to it was the Policeman's house and opposite that, the Presbyterian Chapel and the house of *Dafydd Jones the Carrier*, behind which was another house called *Llan Draw* (beyond the village). To the right is a short steep hill leading to *Pen llan* (a street of houses), the Smithy and the Church. On the opposite side of the small square is another short, steep hill where stands the old Baptist Chapel on the left and a Saw Mill on the right. Halfway up is another house called *New Street* part of which used to be a Butcher's Shop. Further up on the right is the Wesleyan Chapel at the foot of *Allt y Powls* (Powls Hill) and a street of cottages Ffordd Groes (Cross Street).

Well, there you have the village - a complete community of a Church, three Chapels, two Inns, a Hotel, a Cobbler, Butcher, Coalman, five Grocers, a Smithy, Flour Mill, Doctor's Surgery, Post Office and a School. I hope the trek through the village was not too confusing especially when I compared it in my childhood with the way it is today

I can assure you that Llanfair Talhaearn is a very pretty and intriguing place and warrants a visit to enable you to see its enchantments for yourself. Take this book and follow the trail I have described to you - I challenge you to get to know the village and some of its inhabitants … you'll be glad you did!

Chapter 4

MY CHILDHOOD

When we moved to the village from *Pengraig*, life changed for us. It expanded a bit as I made new friends and roamed the lanes and paths of the neighbourhood. It was perfectly safe then although I remember that we were frightened of tramps and gypsies. I cannot remember anyone coming to any harm from these people but they were different, and some of the tramps were very scruffy and smelly. Looking back, I think most of the gypsies were genuine Romany people - we saw the women mainly, for it was they who went from door to door selling lace and pegs and reading the palms of credulous women looking for hope and excitement. Some were loud and a bit 'pushy' with their goods, and would describe good fortune to those who bought from them, and ill fortune to those who refused their wares. Their homes were authentic gypsy caravans and very colourful as far as I understood. There were very few tinkers about, only the odd scissor and knife sharpener, and onion-selling Breton ... *Sioni Winwins*. The tramps were all males who were possibly victims of abuse of some sort, unemployed, perhaps suffering from health problems, alone in the world maybe and going from place to place working short periods on farms and sleeping rough. Some were very dirty and obviously bothered by lice and fleas. Sometimes they would beg for food. It was said that they used secret signs that they marked on the gates of houses and farms where they had been helped. The signs were left for their own future benefit and for other 'gentlemen of the road' who travelled those areas.

One particular occasion comes to mind when I was playing with a group of about eight children on the road near our homes. Suddenly one of the children called out, “Gypsies!” which made us all stop playing. Then Alice, one of the younger ones amongst us shouted, “Come on, we'll go to my house.” So off we all went and barged into her house shouting, “Gypsies are coming, gypsies are coming.” Alice's mother immediately locked the front and back doors, drew the curtains in the living room and back kitchen and warned us to be absolutely quiet. “Rover will frighten them away,” she said. Rover was their dog, a terrier I think. Sure enough we heard knocking on both doors and we held our breath in terror! Rover started to bark so fiercely that eventually the gypsy women gave up and went away. Really and truly there was little to fear if anything, but the experience was a prime example of how ignorance, irrational fear, intolerance and hysteria can ignite a powerful feeling within us all. Once the coast was clear, we returned outside to finish our game, we laughed and chatted non-stop about the incident, and by then viewed it as a marvellous adventure - it had made our day!

Most of us attended Chapel or Church and Sunday School on Sunday and the Band of Hope mid-week. I learned to read Welsh in Sunday School before starting in the village school. We learned the words and tunes of hymns and stories from the Bible. The Sunday School teachers were volunteers and although some were a bit strait-laced, were nevertheless kind and gentle with us. They taught and demonstrated the rules of decent living, and ways of showing respect for other people and kindness to those who were unfortunate in life. I retain an enormous respect for those people who gave their time and patience to help us find our way in the world.

At this time, a religious family, the Bevans lived in the big house called *Glasfryn*. They were Non-conformists for they came to our Presbyterian Chapel, and always sat in the long pew directly behind my family's short pew. I believe they understood Welsh, but I don't recall ever hearing them speak the language. However, at some point they set up a children's club called *'The Snowdrop Band'* and members met in the pavillion in the grounds of their house. All I can remember is that each child was given a plot of land on which to grow vegetables to sell in order to give the proceeds to the Missionary fund. We all began with gusto but somehow the whole experiment petered out very soon and that was that. I can remember three of the four grown-up Bevan children because the three daughters took it in turn to play the organ in Chapel, but I cannot recall the son. Mr. Bevan reared chickens but when one was required for the dinner table he was unable to kill it so he would bring it to my mother to carry out the dastardly deed and dress up the fowl ready for the oven, for which she would charge 6d., 6 pence in old money.

My sister and I went to Sunday School every Sunday afternoon and then I went to evening service with my father. I have no recollection of my sister being with Dad and me at the evening service, neither can I remember Mam being there. Years later when I mentioned this to her, she said that she did not have a decent coat to wear for Chapel - this might have been true, but I have sometimes wondered whether it was because she could not come to terms with the sorrowful events in her life. Certainly she had kept her faith in God in spite of everything.

I remember one winter evening having just returned home from attending a meeting of the Band of Hope in Chapel and walking into the living room to see Mam and Dad sitting by the fire with my sister on a stool between them. It was very cold outside and I was pushing to get to warm my hands and I said, “Bella, move up, I've got cold hands and you are nice and warm,” when my mother said, “That is not Bella,” and I replied, “Yes it is because she knew her name just now.” “Oh no,” said Mam, “That one is gypsy Bella, we exchanged our Bella for this little gypsy.” Well, I didn't know what to think, although I was pretty sure she was my sister. But they kept up the pretence and my Dad joined in to assure me that she was indeed gypsy Bella. I can remember being upset by the incident and actually smelling her because we believed all gypsies smelled differently. It was only when it was time to go to bed that my parents finally confessed that it had all been a big joke and that of course Bella was my real sister. I was very relieved to be told that, but I felt then, and still do today, that it was a very cruel and unwise trick to play on a child. I cannot think what came over them for it was completely different from their usual behaviour.

In those days the Chapel would be full when services were held, and the singing was wonderful. Everyone in the congregation sang the hymns and some had very good voices, but one lady called Mrs Hughes, known as *Llinos Elwy* (the nightingale of the Elwy) was an outstanding singer. She was a farmer's wife who had a wonderful soprano voice, although it had a bit of a wobble by that time, and her daughter Anne, who had a powerful contralto voice. Anne studied Music at the Royal Academy in London where she gained the diploma L.R.A.M., but had to give up her studies and return home because of tragic sickness in the family. They were the mainstays of the singing, but there were many others who had good voices too. My father had a very good bass voice and loved singing. I would sit dutifully listening to the sermons and at that time I could not have understood a lot, but there were powerful preachers and their personalities held our attention. Sometimes I think that they could have become very good actors given the opportunity.

Occasionally, on a fine summer Sunday evening, my father would decide to go for a walk up Bodran Mountain and we enjoyed this very much, although we felt very guilty when the Church bell tolled and we were playing truant! We were not allowed to play ball, shout, gather sticks or do any of our usual everyday things on Sundays. We were told that it was wrong to do so, and that something bad would happen if we did. This was the way of life then and we mostly obeyed, but sometimes it was with bad grace.

The various Chapel denominations were taken very seriously and there was little co-operation between them although I am sure most people did not know or understand the ethics involved in the separation. However, there was one event that served to override any prejudice. The Wesleyans and Methodists baptised their babies by wetting their foreheads as a token of bringing them into the church, and then they were received as full members of their own accord in their teens. The Baptists baptised adults, and then they were received into the Chapel as full members. Their baptism was a total immersion in water and not a token of a splash on the forehead. It was just like the account of baptism in the river Jordan written in the Bible.

So most years, there would be baptisms carried out in the River Elwy during the summer months. The special baptism service was held near the Seven Sisters on Sunday afternoon at about 3.15 p.m, following the Sunday School service. Always on those occasions we finished Sunday School early in the Methodist chapel so we could join in the prayers and hymns on the banks of the river. Often visitors would stop their cars and stand on the opposite bank to watch the proceedings. The Minister, the Rev. John Phillips was short in stature but must have been strong because he would stand in the centre of the river in thigh high waders and immerse 4, 5 or 6 young men and women in turn. The lads would be in their good suits and the girls in dresses with elastic bands round their knees to stop the water lifting their skirts. The minister, holding a Bible aloft in his left hand, and with his right hand grasping the clothing at the nape of the neck, baptised them in the name of the Father, the Son and the Holy Spirit. He lowered each one of them backwards, fully into the water then managed to lift them out again, heavy with water, with his right hand. He was a good man and very diligent. He held services in Llanfair, Llansannan and remote Chapels in the hills every Sunday, and he walked there and back in all weathers, which was a journey of many miles. I doubt whether anyone would do that today. He had four daughters, the youngest being one of my best friends.

Every summer the various Sunday Schools had an outing, a trip to somewhere special by coach or charabanc. Most times we went to Rhyl. I cannot remember ever going to Colwyn Bay or Llandudno, but in later years we went further afield to Southport. There would be a lot of friendly rivalry between the different coaches and we would urge the driver to, "Pass them, pass them." Most times our mothers would make picnic meals and we would eat them on the promenade or on the beach. Sometimes arrangements would have been made for everyone to eat in a lecture room at a Chapel or at long trestle tables in a café. It was very utilitarian but no matter, it was extremely exciting for us. We had some money to spend too. Volunteers at Sunday School organised a club whereby we could save a few pence towards trip day. One year just before the War in the late 1930s, our Sunday School trip went to Southport. I don't think we went on the beach because the tide was out and it was a very long stretch of sand to the water. But there were shops and we had money to spend. The most popular shop for us in those days was Woolworth because nothing cost over 6d. I cannot remember what I bought that day except for one item. I wanted to take home a present and I had sixpence left with which to buy one.

Finally after much thought I bought a toilet roll! When I got home and presented it to my mother, she and my father thought it was a huge joke and laughed and related the story several times to others. I was very hurt by this because I had bought the toilet roll as a luxury item - all we used at home were squares of newspaper hung with string in the toilet.

When you consider that our weekly pocket money was exactly one penny on a Saturday you can appreciate that having four or five shillings to spend in one day made us feel like millionaires. In old money there were twelve pence in one shilling and twenty shillings in one pound. When we got our Saturday penny we had a big decision to make - whether to have 2ozs. of sweets or one ice cream. I remember once, walking along a path that led from the village Square past the Swan Hotel towards the Llansannan Road, and finding a half crown piece, which was two shillings and sixpence - a fortune! I can still recall the feeling of elation - pennies from heaven! I don't know what the margin of profit was for the shopkeepers but they were very kind and welcoming always when we went to spend our pennies and taking time in making our choice.

An annual event was the *Gymanfa Ganu* (the Singing Festival). The Chapels were organised in areas that were controlled by various committees. An annual booklet was produced with hymns chosen from the main Hymn Book alongside new ones composed by various professionals and amateurs. For months, practices and rehearsals were held to teach the tunes in full harmony with the four voices: Tenor, Soprano, Alto and Bass. There would also be a main anthem, a short anthem and a psalm to learn. Generally there would be some difficulty in singing the psalms because Non-Conformist congregations did not use them in their services. But when the big day arrived people from all the Chapels in the area would congregate in one of the bigger chapels to sing their hearts out under the baton of some well known conductor - children in the afternoon and adults in the evening. There was something very thrilling about those Festivals. I think it is such a shame that only the really dedicated singers attend them nowadays. The absentees do not know what they are missing.

Also held annually were Preaching Meetings with prominent and gifted preachers participating - three well-attended meetings were held during the day, and lunch and tea were provided in local homes for the visitors.

I must not forget to mention the Horticultural Show held annually. It must be remembered that most people grew vegetables for their own use and for others too when there were surplus items to requirement. Flowers were also grown, but were of secondary importance. There was intense rivalry between the gardeners, but it was mostly in a good-natured manner. It was known that some minor 'hanky-panky' took place on occasion, but such things would be difficult to prove and no one bothered much. Other classes would be for the ladies: eggs, dressed fowl, butter, jam, pickles, cakes, bread, scones, *bara brith* (currant bread) and so on and some flower arranging. The garden competitions were very important - best vegetable garden and best flower garden. My father was successful many times. He always entered the vegetable competitions, and woe betide us if we were found raiding the radishes or peas in the garden before the big day. The night before the Show all the best specimens of potatoes, beans (French and runner) peas, onions, lettuce and cabbage were gathered and laid out on the kitchen table and put together into groups of five or six, measured and judged for size, similarity, shape and colour. What a performance!

In addition, my mother entered the cookery section - cakes, bread, jams, chutneys, pickles, and dressed fowl and she was always successful, so much so that she finally stopped entering because her wins were stifling competition.

With all this garden produce ready for harvesting simultaneously, there was surplus produce to our family's needs - remember we had no fridges or freezers and it was summertime. Because everyone knew how good the produce was, people in the village were keen to buy it and so, with a large basket, woven by my father, I would set off to deliver the goods. I remember one lady in particular who had been brought up very well and had attended a private school, but through no fault of her own had come down in the world, liked to buy garden produce from Dad, but at one particular time had no money to pay. Instead, we received two large tins of Australian honey from her- they were very large tins approx. 14” x 12” x 8” with a smaller insert lid in the top centre. It was solid honey, beautifully creamy in colour and texture and I have never tasted anything like it since. Apparently several of these tins had arrived from someone in Australia in recompense for something. There were so many they were considering burying them in the ground for storage for a time. I wonder whether there could be any still left?

In the winter, when snow fell we went sledging in *Cae Owen Jones* (Owen Jones' field), a field owned by an Owen Jones who did not live in the village. It was quite big and sloped quite steeply at the lower end and ideal for sledging. We did not have a sledge, just a flat piece of wood that served the purpose, and we had a jolly time, screaming and laughing as we tumbled about.

Once Spring arrived with its 'foxy days' as my mother called them when a couple of bright days with warm sunshine were followed by cold days, we children immediately clamoured to throw off our woolly winter wear in favour of thinner and lighter summer clothes. We desperately wanted to wear our pretty dresses and short white socks, but Mam's word was law, and we had to be patient. She would quote, “Cast not a clout until the May (tree) is out.”

We had a May Queen for two years running when I was 8 and 9 years old and on both occasions it was the same Queen because she, or rather her parents, owned the invalid wheelchair in which the Queen travelled in state. Adults took no part in this event. We sat making long daisy chains and gathered wild primroses and violets and used them to decorate the chair and the occupant. Her crown was made of flowers and she was swathed in a large white patterned net curtain. Then off we went in a crowd along the roads and lanes of the village just to show off and have fun.

Another custom amongst children was to go to every shop on New Year's morning to be given a *'calennig'* - some sweets, an apple or an orange.

Also, on the day before Shrove Tuesday some children would visit farms to be given eggs, flour or milk with which to make pancakes. This was probably a very old custom in the countryside, which may appear odd to us today, but I must remind you that there was no help for poor people in those days except parish relief and charity. Pride is not important if you are hungry.

There was also a custom of *Dydd Gwyl Tomos* (Thomas' Celebration Day), a day when the Rector gave away charity money to poor people. I think it was about one shilling and six pence, which was not a small sum when you realise that you could buy a large loaf for two and a half pence. I can remember my mother sending me once only to receive this money and I quite cheerfully went and felt no shame. Indeed, it never entered my mind. This happened on one occasion only.

There was some Carol singing at Christmas time, but it was rather haphazard. So my father took the matter in hand and sent away for some English and Welsh carol books. Then a group of about twelve or so came to practise at our house. We had no piano or organ and my father used a music pitch-fork to start us off in the correct key. I am sure we were not perfect, but at least we were organised and presentable. We must have been fairly good for we were invited to sing at *Garthewin* for Mr. Wynne and his mother.

About this time I began to be bullied by a small group of girls, slightly older than me. At the time I had no idea why it was happening. The group leader was a girl, named Sally. She and the others would call names, walk behind me, shove me forward, jostle me in the playground, pinch me and be generally very obnoxious. This went on for quite some time and it was very, very upsetting. Then one day, the worm turned. I got really mad! It happened as we were going home from school and the girl who was the ringleader happened to be wearing a new red blazer. She was walking at my side and taunting me when I suddenly turned, lunged at her, hit and shook her, and my hand must have slipped and caught the side of the blazer pocket and I tore it off. Consternation!

She stopped in her tracks. Her mood changed and she was crying. Throughout the bullying I had never cried. I would not give them that satisfaction. She ran home with her entourage following. When I passed her house her mother was at the door shouting abuse and threats at me, but I went on my way. It was many years later that I got to know what was behind all of it. Lies had been told about my brother, but everyone knew that they were lies. His unblemished character was his shield. But the bad feeling flowed over into my life. However, after I turned upon this clique, I was left in peace and there was no more bullying and unpleasantness.

During those years, my father was the head gardener at *Garthewin*, and during the school holidays I would sometimes take his lunch box to him at work. He would eat this in the small brick building where there was an open fire that heated a large greenhouse of fruit, which was in the kitchen garden. And what a garden! It was on a slope with a flat lower section surrounded by a high wall. Growing against the wall, espalier fashion, were apples, pears, and peaches. Soft fruits including strawberries, raspberries, blackcurrants and red currants were grown on the flat area within a large wire cage. There were also vegetables of all kinds grown in their season and pot and cut flowers too. Flowers were taken every morning to the big house on the order of the housekeeper.

Sadly, in the mid-thirties, because of the Depression, heavy Death duties and other taxes perhaps, the number of staff employed at Garthewin was cut drastically and as a consequence, my father had to join many others in the dole queue. Life became more difficult for my mother, but my sister and I, blissfully unaware of such difficulties, were quite happy. We were well fed and were always clean and tidy.

Mam had a first cousin called Mary who lived at the farm over the road from our house in the village. She and her husband were childless, their only son having died in infancy. Mr. Owen liked children and we were allowed to have rides on the hay cart to and from the fields to the farm and to stamp down the hay in the store building. His wife on the other hand always gave the impression of being less welcoming and somehow critical. They were dairy farmers and sold most of their milk to the Milk Marketing Board. Records had to be kept for claiming the payments and of course, for tax purposes. My mother used to do these for them. After a couple of years, Uncle Owen died in a very sad way. Every evening after supper he went with his faithful dog Jim for a short walk along a path that ran along a steep slope above the meadow by the river. It was part of his land and provided a very pleasant walk. He liked to smoke his pipe at that time of day but was not allowed to smoke it in the house. On this particular evening the weather was atrocious, indeed it had been stormy all day with a very high wind and rain was lashing down, but it seems that he had gone out to check that all was well on the farmyard. After a while his wife became worried, knowing that a long time had elapsed since he had gone out and so she went to look for him but could find no sign of him or Jim. In a panic she came to our house and explained the situation and straight away my father organised a search party from among the neighbours who were more than willing to help.

Eventually, they found his body with the ever faithful dog Jim lying alongside. The Post Mortem established that he had died as a result of a massive heart attack. Everyone was sad that such a tragedy had happened to him because he was very well liked even though he was a quiet man. Realising that she could not possibly run the farm on her own Auntie Mary sold the farm and built a new house on a corner of the farmland near the crossroads. It cost approximately £1000.00. She was unwell from time to time and Mam cared for her, taking nourishing soups to her, seeing she was safe in bed at night and locking up. Once, when she went there in the morning she found her lying on the floor after suffering a heart attack. Mam called the Doctor and got Mary into bed. Dr. Leiper told her that if Mam had not found her and tended to her needs she would have died. And so it went on until she finally passed away. In the weeks before she died some people visited, making sympathetic noises and there was much holding of hands. They were not her relatives and some had not been seen for years. However, they benefited, one getting the house, others the money. My mother - nothing! She was hurt and should have claimed against the estate for all the food and services provided. But she would not. She'd helped because she'd been sorry for her being lonely and friendless and because she was 'family'. This world can be very cruel sometimes and was especially so to our mother, but she always held her head high.

Every Sunday I went to the cemetery with flowers, a pair of ordinary kitchen scissors and a trowel, to tend to my sister's grave. There was no head stone, but the grave mound had been raised about ten inches, had grass on all sides, and soil on top on which rested a glass dome covered with wire. Within the dome were china flowers and foliage and a plaque that displayed my sister's name, age and date of death. I placed my flowers in water in a jam jar pushed into the soil - and sometimes my index finger and thumb would get very sore and blisters would form because there was so much grass to cut with the scissors. It was many years later that a gravestone was erected. I still go to tend the area of the grave, and my mother and father are also there by now. I go twice a year, and at Christmas make nice wreaths to lay on the grave, the grave of my late husband's parents, and Neville's grave too.

After my brother Percy went to London, we missed him terribly and every week I wrote a long letter giving him all the news. He kept some of these letters for years. Sometimes the letters went in the parcel of freshly washed and ironed clean clothes that was sent to him every week and he would send home a parcel of soiled clothes and enclosing a letter. My mother was an expert at packing the parcel and never once was there delivered a damaged one. However, on occasion we would just send a letter, and if we missed the afternoon post then we would go down to the village in the evening to meet the nine o'clock bus from Llanrwst to Rhyl. This bus had a mailbox on the back that provided the community with a late post. The village shops too, were open until late - some until 9 o'clock.

There were jobs that had to be done at different times of the year that involved all my family. When the spring frosts occurred without warning the children had to help in the evening in spreading newspapers over the leaves of growing potatoes and other plants and taking them off the next morning. In the autumn we went to gather sticks as kindling for the winter. We tried to get longish ones and then tied them together - we had been shown how to use a strong piece of wood as a lever to insert under the twine and twist it to make a tight and secure bundle that was easy to carry.

After the summer holidays we collected hazelnuts and twice we went up into the hills to a farm to collect walnuts. This was the only walnut tree I knew about in the village. It was a very big one and it shed its large nuts covered in a mushy thick green coating that gave off the rusty-yellow iodine fluid. It stained our fingers for days but came off the nut easily when it was ripe. The taste of those fresh walnuts was wonderful and it was well worth walking the miles in cold weather to get them.

Looking back, I think of the summers, or perhaps the summer holidays as always being sunny, warm and fine days. But sense tells me that it can't have been the case always for it must have rained some days! I think it must be because I enjoyed the warm summer months so much.

I cannot remember exactly which year it was in the mid thirties during a very hot, dry spell, a 'heat wave' in the summer when a fire started on Bodran Mountain. The mountain, being quite high and covered in gorse, bracken, heather and rough grasses, enabled the fire to spread very quickly, and as it neared the farms and houses on the lower reaches caused great concern and worry. All the available men and boys and some women too took it in turns to beat the flames and dampen them down as best they could. There was no water supply available, and it was very hard, hot and dirty work that continued day and night for more than a week. As soon as the fire in one area was believed to be extinguished, the volunteers tackled another area, but the wind could get up and re-kindle the smouldering roots and grasses thus sometimes reigniting the flames. Eventually however, a big thunderstorm with torrential rain put out the fire completely, which was a great relief for everyone in the village. It took five years for the blackened mountain to become green again.

Chapter 5

LIFE'S TRIBULATIONS

Three distressing things happened in the village during these years. A young man shot himself, a young woman drowned herself on the eve of her wedding, and another young woman ran away from home for several days suffering from stress. There was a great deal of talk amongst the grown-ups, but in those days such serious matters were not openly discussed in front of children which meant that we did not know much and indeed, I still do not know the ins and outs of those sad happenings. But nowadays when tragedies happen newspaper reports provide all the related details while television and radio reports embellish them further. Not many people, even children, are in ignorance these days because most things are discussed openly. On balance perhaps, the old way enabled the youngsters to retain their innocence during childhood.

I cannot recall any cases of sexual abuse, but of course such things including incest, could have been going on without anyone ever knowing. No one would talk about such things - anything at all to do with sex was taboo, at least in the open. So much hypocrisy! The punishment for failing to maintain these 'appearances' was severe. Physical punishment of children was much more prevalent. Children were thumped, slapped and caned at school for being late, cheeky, disobedient and lazy. It was no use going home to complain about these punishments because parents mostly took the side of the teacher and some boys would get another whacking. But I can remember two or three families who would watch out for the teacher if their child had been punished, however well deservedly, and a right old shouting harangue would ensue, but I don't recall a teacher ever coming to any harm. It was common practice for parents to slap children at home, but I know of only one case where the slapping became serious physical abuse - the victim was a girl. She would be seen crying almost daily and we knew what was going on at home, but she never ever admitted to being hit, and no one did anything about the situation. Strangely enough, her brothers never seemed to suffer from the abuse.

In our house punishment was mostly the occasional slap that was administered by my mother. She always said that it was wrong for men to smack children because they did not know their own strength. Also, that it was quite wrong to hit a child about the head. My father never raised a hand against us. But, we did have a birch rod, a small branch tied in the middle. It was kept high up out of reach by the mantelpiece. It was rarely used, only for really bad behaviour and even then only on the backs of our legs. But the sight of this weapon of punishment was enough of a threat to bring us to our senses.

In February 1933 I was taken ill with stomach pains. Apart from the occasional common cold or sore throat up until then I had been generally a very healthy child. But I had never been able to tolerate fat in food, somehow I could not digest it. Fat in a meal would form like a candle in my oesophagus and I could bring it up easily. Somehow I have always been able to get rid of similar unwanted matter via a simple reflex action. Coconut was another food that I could not tolerate even in a little sweet because it made me feel sick. For years I wondered why I had a sick headache every Sunday after tea, and eventually I came to recognise the culprit. My mother always made a delicious sponge cake for Sunday tea that was coated with butter-cream and smothered in large flakes of coconut because we all loved it, but I came to realise that my headaches were caused by eating large slices of the cake. When I learned to forgo the cake, the headaches ceased.

However, in early spring 1933 I was actually in bed, ill with a pain that Dr. Leiper diagnosed as a 'chill on the bowel' and I was allowed no food, only drinks. This went on for a week when I experienced fluctuating temperature, pains that appeared and disappeared, moved from side to side and varied in severity. The doctor maintained her diagnosis but my brother wrote home daily from London urging my parents to disregard the doctor. He was adamant that I had appendicitis. He'd had his appendix removed at the age of fourteen, at about the time Elsie, our sister had died. Several of my cousins had needed to have the operation too. However, at the end of the week the doctor visited again, and as the pain had subsided that day, said that I could have something to eat and asked what I would like. Without hesitation I said I would like cooked potatoes in buttermilk. My mother thought this was rather a heavy meal on an empty stomach and suggested a beaten egg in milk. This was agreed, and at 7.00 p.m. I had half a glass of beaten egg in milk with sugar before falling asleep. I must have drunk gallons of this stuff as a child because I loved its taste and it had the added advantage of being very nourishing too.

At approximately 11.00 p.m. I awoke screaming in pain and rolling about in bed. Someone went into the village for the doctor who came straight away. She fell to her knees and pressed my tummy gently and quite suddenly jerked out the words, “Oh my God I've found it, she must be taken immediately to the Infirmary at Denbigh. You must carry her flat and move her as little as possible. Oh my God!”

And so it was at midnight that Charlie Sackett, the owner of the Black Lion Hotel drove his brand new black and royal blue limousine up to our house. I was carried on a plank of wood on to the back seat with my father in attendance, to make the journey of about ten miles on country lanes to Denbigh. During the journey I was violently sick all over this beautiful car and even though I was only aged nine and in pain, I was dreadfully sorry to have made such a mess. However, I can still remember Charlie saying gently, “Never mind lass, you're worth more than the car.”

Looking back now I can appreciate the terrible, heart-rending worry that must have hit my Mam and Dad. They had already lost one little girl aged 12, now here was another daughter aged 9, likely to die as well. For in those days peritonitis was very, very serious - any poison seeping into your system would eventually kill, for there were no drugs with which to fight the infection.

As soon as I had been sick the pain went and I felt better, but the adults knew that this was dangerous, and speedy treatment was vital. They knew that the festering appendix had burst and was leaking poison into my body. When we reached the Hospital the doctor was called and the duty nurse, Sister Joyce whose family had a jewellery shop on Vale Street in Denbigh, painted iodine all over my tummy. She then wrapped me in a blanket and carried me in her arms. “We are now going to the theatre,” she said, and being the little country girl that I was, thought we were going to a place of entertainment - at 1.00 a.m! The surgeon was Dr. Duff, a young Scotsman who had served as a doctor in the First World War. I know personally of several people whose lives were saved by his skill during his service at Denbigh. It was said that he never performed an operation before first praying in a little room adjacent to the theatre. I shall be eternally grateful to him for saving my life that night.

The following morning when I woke up in the ward, I was very, very sick again from the effects of the anaesthetic that had been given to me. I think it was chloroform that was in general use then. Another fact I remember was that I had to lie flat on my back all the time. I tried to turn, but the pain was so excruciating that I was forced to lie flat again. It was no wonder because I had a five-inch slit in the lower right side of my tummy with a long piece of tubing sticking out of its centre. The wound was covered by a thick dressing that was held in place by wide bandages, all of which were changed every day because of the pus draining out. I was in hospital for two or three weeks during which time I read books, wrote letters and chatted to staff and patients.

It is interesting to note here that I was able to go to that Hospital and be treated free of charge because my parents paid a few pence each week into a Hospital Fund. I was not well enough to go to school for many more weeks and could not do anything strenuous for a couple of months. The other nice thing was that our next-door neighbour, a good seamstress with a sewing machine, had made two new night-dresses for me from one of my mother's large night-gowns. She'd used the white cotton material with a lavender stripe to make night-dresses with long sleeves, frills at the wrist and neck, and buttons to fasten at the top. They were very pretty and warm and I loved wearing them. They were the very first garments that actually belonged to me and for that reason, were very special to me. While I was in hospital my pussycat Tom Mouse apparently sat on the stairs at home and meowed and cried for days before disappearing. When I returned home again having regained some of my strength I picked a huge bunch of snowdrops, packed them in moss in a cardboard box and sent them on the bus to Sister Joyce. I received a very nice note of thanks and for several years I sent the snowdrops. I only hope they were still alive when they reached their destination.

Later that spring I was introduced to a new arrival of which I became very fond. It was a pet lamb that a neighbour had been given as a wedding present. It was kept in a field at the back of our house and I fed it with milk from a baby's bottle. As it grew up it could push me around in play, sadly one day it wasn't there. No explanation was forthcoming, but I instinctively knew that I would never see it again, and for some days I felt very sad.

I cannot say that I love dogs but there were some that were special to me. Uncle Williams Pen Coed had Pero, Robert Owen at Dolhaearn Farm had Jim, both were big dogs and very friendly. Minnie, my friend had a small, cream coloured dog with a bushy tail called Gyp. I liked them all but not as much as I liked the cats I've known.

Dr. Leiper lived in a big house in the village and would turn out to calls day and night, summer and winter, in sunshine and in rain. Sometimes she had to walk miles to her destination, but mostly she travelled by car driven by a chauffeur because she was not a driver. Her chauffeur had fought in some of the worst battles of the First World War and had been the victim of mustard gas, the effects of which affected him very badly at times.

In those days, people did not routinely call out the doctor or go to the surgery for medicine or treatment if they could help it because it all cost money. They were the days prior to the establishment of the National Health Service in the U.K. - a time when women had their babies at home attended by other mothers. These women had experienced birth and could cope with straight-forward deliveries, but had to call for a District Nurse or Doctor to deal with complications. There were no antenatal clinics and things like ready-made baby foods. An unsettled crying baby would be given gripe water or filtered boiled water that had been poured on a hot coal, or in some families, watered gin!

Also, there was no Dentist for miles, except for a large beery-looking genial chap wearing a plus-fours suit who visited houses periodically for extractions only. He could not do fillings for there was no electricity in the village. I was never afraid of him or the tooth extractions. My father wore dentures, but quite out of the blue a tooth started to grow through his palate. This was painful and eventually the situation became impossible for him. I remember seeing my father sitting on a chair in the kitchen one day with a friend restraining him and another using ordinary pincers to pull the tooth until it finally came out. My father, having received no anaesthetic made a horrific noise and was bleeding profusely but … the action solved his problem!

Many youngsters had bad teeth and too many lost teeth through extractions at an early age when they could have been repaired. We used old-fashioned remedies for things like toothache that involved putting drops of vinegar and pepper onto brown wrapping paper and holding it against the cheek next to the painful tooth. The heat created by the concoction affected the flesh thus hopefully reducing the pain. My mother said that when she and her sisters had toothache they heated a steel knitting needle against a hot coal and put the point into the hole in the tooth.

With the UK's current shortage of dentists unable or unwilling to take on National Health patients, it looks as if some people will have to go back to the bad old days of having to suffer bad teeth and the related pain

As a family we looked forward to Thursday evenings because certain people would call for a chat and a cup of tea on their way home from visiting the farm across the road from our house, where Mam's cousin lived. They were farmers who sometimes brought their wives and I remember Mrs. Catherine Jones from Glan Conwy who came with her son in a lorry. They used a dry and clean disused stable on the farm as a temporary shop to sell sugar, tea, biscuits, sweets, tinned goods and other items and the farmers brought their eggs, butter and chickens to sell in the shop or be exchanged for goods. She in turn would sell the goods the following day to the hotels and guest-houses in Colwyn Bay and Llandudno. She probably made a living in this way and it certainly helped the farmers during those very hard times between the two World Wars. The prices they received for their produce were probably at rock bottom, but they were able to get household commodities by exchanging in this way. My sister and I looked forward to these evenings partly because we could listen in sometimes to whispered gossip and especially because sweets were brought and handed round. Such were our simple pleasures of childhood.

During this period my father bought 'The Daily News Chronicle' newspaper and he taught me to read it. There were articles by very good journalists including James Cameron, a very distinguished man whose writing I came to appreciate increasingly as I matured. Dad also had the 'Weekly Post' on Saturdays and 'The People' on Sundays. My father had a great regard for the writings of James Cameron and also Hannen Swaffer who wrote for 'The People' and I learned to do crosswords in 'The People'.

The period from my being five to ten years of age is very vivid in my mind because so much happened and I had so many new experiences. Days were never long enough and I cannot ever remember being bored. I wrote an account of a summer holiday for a Welsh newspaper *'Y Cymro'* (Welsh person), and won a book as the first prize, which I still have. I also entered an essay competition in the 'Weekly Post' on the subject of the Union Jack and won a beautiful 'Conway Stewart' gold-nibbed fountain pen that served me well for many years.

Life was so predictable then with one day following another in much the same way as before. Little really changed in our lives, so when a new lady came to live in the village we were very curious about her. We noticed that she had very tanned skin and wore leather sandals without socks. After a while she called a number of us into her house, and although we were not too keen to go at first being a bit suspicious of her, felt later that we were perhaps safe to go in a group! She told us she was Miss Gerbier and was French, and she struggled to teach us a French song that started, *'Frère Jacques, Frère Jacques'*. Knowing the song made us feel frightfully clever, but we can't have been brilliant linguists because that was the extent of our learning in French at that time. After a couple of years she left the village and went to live in the Penmaenmawr area. I don't know why she came to Llanfair in the first place or why she left.

One of my mother's sisters was married to my father's first cousin, and they were farmers. They lived near Denbigh, and every Monday on their way home from market at Abergele they called at our home. Mam would prepare a meal and Auntie Lil always brought cold meats and bread, butter, cakes and Tomato Sauce! There was always enough for everyone to eat and more besides. The talk was always lively, but I was not interested in the subject matter, only in the genial atmosphere and joviality of the occasion. *'Uncle Groes'* as we called him always gave each of us a sixpence coin, which was quite a sum. These visits ended when one of their daughters married and they changed their route home in order to visit her instead. They invited me to go to the farm to stay during the holidays and being an obedient child I allowed myself to be persuaded. I must have been around 8 or 9 years old at the time and can remember the ride in the car being exciting. Once, when I was sitting in the back seat and about half way through the journey I noticed a wheel rolling downhill in front of us and then a lurch. The near-side rear wheel had come loose! I don't remember how we got home because few farmers had telephones in those days and certainly there were no mobile phones.

Everyone was very kind except for my eldest cousin who was 13 or 14 years older than I. She was a fine looking girl but knew it, and was very bossy. Once, when she thought I had nits in my hair, immersed my head in sheep dip! Another time when I had abscesses on two fingers, stuck them into a bottle of nearly boiling water and forcibly held them there. I was screaming and struggling, but she took not the slightest bit of notice. Her treatment may have done some good, I can't remember, but I have never forgotten her cruelty and arrogance. There was something else that I disliked about her too. She came to see my mother once or twice and took a fancy to a beautiful, glazed two-pint jug. It was old - in a royal blue colour with green leaves, pink roses and gold trim. It was one of about half a dozen pieces of crockery that my mother treasured and brought out only when we had visitors. This cousin coveted it and managed to persuade my mother to let her have it. She then added insult to injury by bringing a cheap white pot jug in exchange.

Later, when I requested the jug back she claimed to have sent it to a daughter in Canada who was oblivious of the way her mother had acquired it. My cousin said that my mother did not appreciate such a beautiful object because she used it for every day purposes. Her comment was made in ignorance of the fact that my mother had been raised with beautiful things and had a deep appreciation of the arts, which added to my fury and sense of injustice. Her sisters were much more amenable and I got on really well with them. As far as I am aware, my mother's jug is still in Canada in the hands of a distant unknown relative.

Auntie Lil and Uncle *Groes* raised their daughters and a young lad, a blood relative who lived with them. My Auntie had raised him as her own because his father was her cousin and his mother had died during his birth. In doing so she had emulated her own mother, my grandmother, who also had daughters and had raised a boy whose father was her cousin and whose mother had died at his birth.

I should really have enjoyed myself at the farm during those holidays, but I didn't because I was full of *Hiraeth* - a deep longing that made me want to go home! However, I could not let it show because I would have been teased unmercifully, so I stuck it out. Later, when I was older, I loved going there. I enjoyed every minute from the beginning of the holiday until the end. But, more detail about my holidays at *Groes* comes later in the book.

On Saturdays and during holidays we occupied ourselves with the games we played at school. In addition, my father and brother had made a truck for us from an old wooden box that had once brought butter from New Zealand to Britain, two wheels from an old pram and two pieces of wood as shafts. The rides were exciting, especially if the pusher ran full tilt down a hill! But it was not so good to have to push it uphill again. My father had also made bows and arrows with hazel twigs and string for us, and I got quite proficient at using them although I doubt if anyone would have volunteered to be a living target like the son of William Tell! We also amused ourselves by making lots of mud pies covered with floral decorations and it was such a pity that we could not eat them.

A lady who lived nearby had recently acquired a radio so she gave us her gramophone, which was quite big in lovely grey casing. With the player came a pile of records, most of which were recordings of dance music, but some were of Peter Dawson, a marvellous Australian singer. My father took possession of the Dawson records, but we were allowed to play the others. My mother would not have what she called, "This noise," in the house, so we had to have our musical sessions in the garden shed. This applied to Dad and Peter Dawson too!

One day my sister, friends and I had a brainwave! We decided to hold concerts in the shed and charge a half-penny as an entrance fee. They were very successful, and the highlight of each session was a solo sung by an unknown male singer. The title of his song eludes me, but in the middle of the song, the gramophone needle got stuck in the groove. It went, "Oh I wonder, Yes I wonder, Oh I wonder, Yes I wonder, Will the angels play their harp, harp, harp…" until we moved the needle to finish the phrase, "…For me." Everyone always rolled about with laughter at this point and looked forward to hearing it again the next time - it was without a doubt a good half-penny worth of entertainment!

Once a 'hurdy-gurdy' came to the village, a decorated barrel organ on wheels that had to be wound up by a handle. On it was a monkey that frightened us because it ate nuts and threw the shells at us and the man shouted at it to stop. I don't think he made much money for he never returned to Llanfair.

We played at making little houses out of sacks, broken crockery, old clothes, and pots and pans. We loved mimicking our elders too - mothers, fathers, uncles, aunts, teachers, preachers - we had a go at being anyone and everyone and had such fun! In the evenings at home when not reading, we played shops, school and sometimes Chapel. One of us would be the preacher, another the organist, just thumping the kitchen table with fingers and singing at the tops of our voices. I had quite a good voice and Dad taught me to sing songs and recite poetry. I was successful too and won many prizes at *Eisteddfodau*.

We were members of *Urdd Gobaith Cymru* - the Welsh League of Youth. This was, and continues to be a marvellous Youth Association that has gone from strength to strength and is reputed to be the biggest of its kind in Europe. Ifan ap Owen Edwards, who was later knighted, started it. His father, O. M. Edwards was an outstanding man of academic qualification after an illustrious career at Oxford University, receiving many honours, becoming a Member of Parliament and being knighted by the King. He was appointed the first Chief Inspector of Schools for Wales who abolished the dreadfully cruel 'Welsh Not'.

The 'Welsh Not' signified the deliberate suppression of the Welsh language in schools. Children were not allowed to speak Welsh in the classroom or on the playground. The 'Welsh Not' was a wooden 'necklet' that was placed on a child's shoulders first thing every morning after they had been overheard speaking Welsh at school. During the course of the day if any other child was heard speaking in Welsh, then the necklet was transferred on to his or her shoulders and so on until the end of the school day. The unfortunate child who was then wearing the Welsh Not was severely punished. Is it any wonder that a lot of bitterness and resentment was created in this way? Children were being forced not to speak their mother tongue in their homeland!

If you want to read about a really worthwhile movement that is successful and effective and run by dedicated volunteers, get a book from the Library that tells the story of *URDD GOBAITH CYMRU.* Literally thousands and thousands of Welsh children have come under its influence, which is entirely non-political and non-denominational. The logo represents loyalty to country, fellowman, and God. Recently there was an organised March along the streets of Cardiff, our Capital city, when thousands of members of the Urdd created a sensational impact by their sheer numbers and by wearing the green, white and red colours of our Welsh flag - the Red Dragon. I benefited from my involvement with the URDD and so have my children.

I qualified to compete at the Urdd National Eisteddfod in the recitation section when I was 9 years old and went with a group of competitors from North Wales to Carmarthen in South Wales. Accommodation overnight is freely provided for competitors by kind Welsh people in the localities in which the festival is held annually, alternating between north and south Wales. A distant cousin, who was five years older than I, stayed with me in a beautiful house with a lovely couple who had just returned from a holiday in Paris. I can remember sleeping in the guest bedroom in a lovely bed covered with a thick eiderdown. My cousin kept pulling the bed-clothes off me so I pulled them back again! I had never slept in such luxury before and was enjoying myself, but I had difficulty understanding the speech of our hosts. Although we all spoke Welsh I was lost, for I could not follow what they said, and they had some difficulty with us too!

Credit must be given to our Welsh Television and Radio stations for bringing more understanding of the north and south dialects to each of us. They call *North-Walians - 'Gogs'* and we call *South-Walians 'Hwntws'*, meaning north and south residents - they are friendly and endearing labels.

Sometimes, the life we led was humdrum with little real excitement, but we were never bored because we always found something to do. In the spring and summer we were out paddling in the river, playing ball, collecting nuts or gathering mushrooms. There was a kind of anticipation in the process of gathering mushrooms. We had to get up early, well before anyone else got there first, especially on hot, sunny days that followed a downpour in the night. Most people knew the fields where they grew being the ones that had not been ploughed for sometime. There was a thrill in arriving early enough to see those white clusters dotted about the field, and then lifting them carefully into a dish to take home, discarding those spoiled by animals and insects. We never collected mushrooms in fields where freshly dipped sheep grazed because of the effects of the poisonous dip fluid. The taste of wild mushrooms is wonderful and I love it. My mother used to say that the 'manna' referred to in the Bible was blackberries and mushrooms! Farmers were very tolerant as long as we did no harm and we shut gates.

At that time there was a fair amount of poaching going on for trout and salmon in particular. Although we were not involved, we knew very well who was skilled in the art of poaching fish and not being caught in the act. Many times I was sent to Mrs Sarah Jane Jones' house to buy a rabbit, but that was in the days before the outbreak of myxomatosis, a disease affecting rabbits deliberately imported to counteract the fact that rabbits had become too numerous in the countryside. Some children would whisper that she skinned cats too, but I don't think there was ever any truth in those allegations. My mother could roast a rabbit to make it taste like chicken, but I liked it best boiled with vegetables and served in a thick parsley sauce. Mrs. Jones' house was situated on the road, along which we used to walk to school, and there were times when we had to be very careful as we passed the house. We were cautious because she would sometimes open an upstairs window and empty the contents of a chamber pot into a sink below, and she was not particular about trying to avoid splashing passers-by! She used to look peculiar sometimes because she powdered her face with flour, but my father could remember when she first came as a parlour maid to Garthewin and was a very pretty young woman. Poverty trapped most people then and made life very hard for them.

There were rituals at our home with which we had to abide whether we liked them or not. We had to have a dessertspoonful of sulphur mixed with treacle every week to clear our blood and if we became anaemic we had some 'Parish's Chemical Food' that contained iron. Another remedy was an infusion of wormwood. My mother would steep the wormwood leaves in a jug of water, cover it, then leave it on a cupboard with a large eggcup nearby for us to use when we felt inclined. If we children ever felt sick, we had only to drink an eggcup full of this potion, and we would soon feel fine again. We did not think the taste was so awful really, but it could never be described as pleasant. Perhaps it is an acquired taste, after all, is wormwood not used in the making of Vermouth?

We did odd jobs and ran errands for people for which we were rewarded with a few pence. My sister delivered milk from the farm to a few customers after tea and she also weeded between crazy paving slabs for a certain family on our road. The lady of the house was obese and with her lived a middle-aged husband and wife and their unmarried daughter. They were kind people and every 'Guy Fawkes Night' would treat us to a show of fireworks that we thought were spectacular - Catherine wheels, sparklers, jack-jumpers, rockets and fountains. By today's standards they were probably nothing much, but we had great pleasure in watching them followed by the setting alight of the bonfire. For weeks we had been collecting a huge pile of flammable material for the bonfire, and it can be said that much unwanted rubbish was burnt on it.

At night, there would be no lighting outside except from the moon and the lights that came from shop windows. There were no street-lights because there was no supply of gas or electricity to the village. On walking past others on the road in the dark, people would say '*Nos dawch*' meaning 'good night to you' and a similar response would be made in return. Thus we always knew who was about because we recognised voices and manner of speech.

There was enormous trust in the village, doors were left wide open on hot summer days and keys were stored under doormats and plant pots as well as hanging on string just behind letterboxes. Probably it was possible to maintain the trust on the strength of the community's Christian moral standards, but it could also be said that most ordinary people had little of worth to steal anyway.

Sometimes on dark winter evenings, we would make rag rugs having begged for hessian bags and old garments. We cut the clothing into strips and fixed them into the hessian with a special hook. The rugs were not luxurious, but were colourful and warm underfoot and we liked making them. The few who could afford to buy proper canvas and balls of wool made much prettier rugs, but we had a special satisfaction with our rag rugs that perhaps eluded them.

Country life was enjoyable in the main, but I never liked bats or '*ystlum*' as they are called in Welsh. I found their behaviour frightening in the way they seemed to appear from nowhere in the dark and brush past my face scaring me to death. Owls on the other hand did not worry me, indeed I liked them with their big eyes and funny cries, especially the white ones. I have no fear of mice or spiders either, nor do I fear ants, although they can sometimes be a great nuisance. But I do really loathe snakes. I cannot abide them in any shape or form and can remember one frightening occasion when I had gone with a group of friends for a picnic on Bodran Mountain. The day was hot and sunny and we'd gone off with our sandwiches, crisps, and Corona lemonade, and while we were still on the road leading to the mountain paths I saw an adder climbing up the side of the hedge, and that was enough for me. I simply refused to go any further, and we all trooped back and ate the picnic on our front lawn. For years I had a recurring nightmare that involved my standing on a mountain and snakes would appear from holes in the ground all around me and I couldn't move to get away and neither could I scream. It was horrible and it frightened me very much.

On another occasion I was gathering violets and primroses in the hedgerows and ensuring that the flowers had stalks long enough to go into a vase, I was sliding my finger down the stalk of a violet when I touched a curled up snake snoozing in the warm sunshine. This was in the days before farmers used insecticides. It was like having an electric shock. I shot away as quickly as my legs would carry me. Ever since I have had a horror of snakes and will not even look at them, never mind touch them. My daughter tells me this is a psychological problem for me and that I should not try to influence my grandchildren into being afraid of snakes. I disagree. I think all children should be warned that the adder is dangerous and should not be meddled with and that there are very dangerous snakes abroad. My mother warned us not to sit on stone walls when the weather was hot and not to walk in undergrowth in sandals.

However, the best time of year was around Christmas. I cannot recall any great excitement when we lived at Pengraig, we must have had a special meal, but we were very young and there was no money for toys and gifts. But after we moved house and my brother went to work in London, things changed. We had a Christmas tree with lights - little candles in holders with hinges that gripped the branches, fragile, delicate ornaments to hang on the tree and silvery lengths of tinsel and a huge star on the top. Dad got the tree and Percy our brother, brought the decorations from London. No one was allowed to leave work early in those days, which meant that Percy would arrive home very late on

Christmas Eve having had to make a frantic dash by the underground Tube from Trafalgar Square where he worked at County Hall to Euston Station to catch the Holyhead train. He would arrive at Pensarn Station at 11.30p.m. then walk five miles to Llanfair with two heavy cases. One would hold his personal things and the other would be full of wonderful Christmas things for his little sisters, Bella and me. My father would walk to meet him and help carry the cases. We were fast asleep in bed before he arrived - otherwise Santa Claus would not come.

We hung up two pillowcases - one each. A stocking would be far too small! My brother loved being our Santa and it gave him great pleasure to see our happy faces in the early morning when we woke up and groped in the dark to see if the pillowcase had been filled. We would be shivering with cold but that was of no importance, the candle was lit and we could see our new treasures. Wonderful! We had fruit, sweets, chocolates, games, books, coloured pencils, drawing books, puzzles and so on. There were no bikes or radios, televisions, computers or clothes, and we would never have expected to receive such things because only rich people could afford luxuries and there were very few of those around anyway. Indeed, televisions and computers were not then available and radios were very primitive sets by today's standards. My sister and I loved what we received and we took great care of everything for they had to amuse us for a whole year until the following Christmas. Two seasonal episodes stand out in my memory.

One Christmas morning as we rummaged in our pillowcases finding all the presents, my sister held up a pretty rubber rabbit that had to be blown up. At once my hands plunged into my pillowcase, fully expecting the same. But, the dreadful disappointment of finding not a pretty rabbit, but a grinning monkey was too much to bear! Well, I could have wept. It sounds so silly does it not, and so trivial too, but at the time it was horrible. I never did play with that monkey.

On another occasion, my brother's landlady, Mrs. Butt had very kindly sent us each a doll. They had china faces with a mass of curly brown hair and their china-blue eyes opened and closed. Mrs. Butt had made some lovely clothes for them and had attached them with elastic bands onto the boxes. Later that morning we saw my friend Minnie in her back garden and we shouted to ask what she had received from Santa Claus and she shouted back and lifted up a doll to show us. My sister, who was only about 5 or 6 years old at the time, held up her doll still in its box to show Minnie and horror of horrors it fell out and smashed on the ground. Bella was inconsolable and would not stop crying. I must admit that it was with bad grace that I agreed to share my doll with her.

During Christmas morning Bella and I would play with our presents while my mother would prepare and cook our Christmas dinner. We always had a goose with all the trimmings and vegetables followed by plum pudding and white brandy sauce. After eating and enjoying our dinner we would go for a walk, weather permitting, leaving poor Mam to clear and wash up. We would arrive back home in time for tea and more of Mam's wonderful cooking including the special Christmas cake and mince pies. This meal was also delicious in being totally home made and perfect. My mother was a wonderful cook. As soon as it was dark enough we lit the candles on the tree and the little lights would twinkle and reflect the shining trimmings on it and the coloured festoons stretching from the four corners of the ceiling to the huge paper ball in the centre. Magic! Just like fairyland. In fact all the festivities of Christmas were magical.

Christmas Day was the culmination of a very busy but enjoyable time. The anticipation in the preceding weeks involved writing our letters to Santa Claus, practising singing Christmas Carols, and making and delivering Christmas cards to our friends. All the activity served to enhance the enjoyment of the Festival. Mam would start buying the fruit, nuts, sugars and other ingredients necessary for the Christmas fare at the end of the summer because there was no money to buy them all at once. Round about October she made the cake and puddings. We loved these proceedings especially after permission had been given for us to scrape and lick the basins at the end of the mixing process. The preparation was meticulous. My sister and I watched with interest while Mam greased the cake tin and wrapped brown paper around the edges and finally spooned the delicious mixture into the tin. But that was not the end of the story of course because the heat of the oven had to be maintained constantly to enable the cake to cook slowly for hours, without burning. The puddings were in white basins covered with grease-proof paper and clean white cotton cloths tied in a knot on the top and they would boil merrily in the wash boiler for a few hours. These major operations were all safely dealt with at least two months before Christmas.

From the beginning of December, Mam would be extremely busy preparing fowl. She was an expert in feathering and dressing hens, turkeys, geese, ducks and other fowl. There was never a tear in the skin and no quills or feathers left in the flesh. There were 'shows' held in the markets, and farmers brought their fowl to Mam to be prepared expertly for the shows. There were always tens of these corpses waiting for attention and my job was to label them according to their owners. During these days Mam would take up residence in the shed outside and would appear only to eat. She would emerge from the shed covered from head to toe in down and feathers like some outsize fowl herself and looking very funny. We laughed at her but she did not mind that at all, she had a good sense of humour. However, it was very hard work for the hands, and her fingers would get sore with plucking the feathers, but she never complained.

Once, a farmer brought a huge turkey to be feathered, cleaned and dressed for a show. Mam looked it over and said, “Good gracious me, this bird is as old as the hills.” “Old? No, no, it's just been fed very well,” said the farmer, and Mam replied, “Well-fed it may be, but it has been well-fed for a long time. You cannot sell this as a young bird, it will be as tough as old boots, just look at its spine with its high ridge.” The farmer was well aware that he was beaten, but he still wanted Mam to deal with it. He who pays the piper, calls the tune! It feathered well and its appearance looked alright, skin nice and pink, but the peaked back was there for all to see and so she folded a towel, put it on the bone and whacked hard with a wooden rolling pin. And the result was a nice rounded bone! That bird, dressed by Mam went into the Christmas poultry show and won a prize! I pity those who bought it, and tried to chew it.

On another occasion, when an elderly fowl was brought to her, she pulled all the tendons from the legs otherwise no one would have been able to sink their teeth into the flesh. However, she had trouble with the last tendon, her middle finger was pulling it away, slowly easing it out of the leg flesh when suddenly it came away and wrapped itself round her finger, cutting through the flesh and into the bone. She could not get it off with her left hand so she called over the hedge to her younger neighbour, “Jenny, can you unwind this off my finger please?” Jenny was a wonderful friend and would help in any way she could but she took one look at the finger and promptly fell down in a faint! Mam did what she could, but a piece of tendon was still trapped in the bone. For weeks she had to have a kaolin poultice on it resulting in the piece of tendon being drawn to the surface. The pain eventually went and the finger healed. This poultry work paid for our Christmas treats. We always managed to get every fowl away to our customers before Christmas Eve.

I remember once when I was quite young, going with my mother and sister to the farm where one of my mother's sisters lived about 10 miles away. We had to get up that morning while it was still dark and cold and someone came to fetch us in a car. The purpose of the visit was for my mother to help with feathering a great number of fowls. I do not remember anything about the day and we fell fast asleep in the car on the way home, but I remember the early start.

Early on Christmas Eve we went to sing carols round the village and once or twice to the Hall at Garthewin too. My father took a group of about ten of us in hand and after sending away for music copies we learned new carols. We had three or four practices in our living room before going out, and 70 years later, I can still remember the tunes and all the words to those carols. Can you just imagine the state of the living-room floor tiles after all the muddy shoes and boots had been there for rehearsals? There was no carpet or linoleum on the floors in our house in those days, but the tiles could be washed fairly easily. There was no piano or organ either, just the pitch fork that my father used to pitch the key of the music. Later on Christmas Eve a group of men would walk round the village singing Welsh and English carols, in full harmony. It was a wonderful sound they created that seemed magical on a clear, still and frosty night, and in my mind I can still hear and appreciate them even now. It was particularly poignant because many of those men were unemployed at the time and struggling to make ends meet. Anne, the young farmer's daughter who had trained and qualified at The London Royal Academy of Music taught those men to sing at such a high standard. There were no fees involved, just goodwill and a love of music. She was home at the time to look after her very sick brother who died young, and she managed to enrich the lives of those local singers at the same time.

Tea-time on Christmas Day would be a little later than usual to ensure that the delights of the meal could be enjoyed fully after the equally wonderful Christmas dinner consumed earlier in the day. We had such a delightful spread of white bread and butter, *bara brith* (slightly spiced fruited bread), warm mince pies, rich trifle and the Christmas cake in all its glory. The cake, cooked weeks earlier was by then covered in marzipan and smooth white icing that had been decorated with piped icing and ornaments. Christmas night supper consisted of cold meat and a wide range of pickles. Mam always had a store of wonderful tasting home-made beetroot, piccalilli, onions and chutney. How we coped with so much food in one day I will never know, perhaps we had only small portions of the many different things. But what I do know is that eating beautifully prepared food in good company is an important part of the Festival don't you agree?

One Christmas, three young male friends of my brother came to tea. They had been school friends who had done well for themselves. Two were brothers, a teacher and a chemist who, like my brother had moved to England to work. The other one remained in Wales and is now sadly the sole survivor of the quartet. That day I well remember much lively discussion at the table and friendly argument in putting the world to rights. They were young unmarried men at the time with most of their lives still ahead of them - they were happy times for all of us.

Boxing Day was an easygoing day for everyone. The remains of the Christmas

Day feasting tasted just as good, if not better. We played a lot of games including cards, Ludo, Lotto, and Snakes and Ladders. There was much squealing and shouting and laughing and rivalry but all was done in good spirit. Except once! We had visitors that year who were included in the general melee of games. One lady was losing in a particular game and of course no quarter was given or taken, but everyone was having fun. Then quite suddenly the lady swept the board with her hand declaring that she was not going to play such stupid games. We were all aghast, but good manners prevailed and all play was ended. However I remember the remark that was made to me privately later, "Anyone who can do a thing like that is not a pleasant person." People very often reveal facets of their character in such trivial ways.

I think I am correct in saying that it was on Boxing Day evening that the so-called 'Coffee Evening' that was such great fun was held in the village. I don't know who organised it or why coffee was never served, at least not at the evenings that I attended. The event was held in Capel Rofft, the old Baptist Chapel being used as a Community Meeting room. The Coffee Evening was not meant for any specific age group for in those days everyone, young, old and middle aged, went to all meetings and concerts and I maintain that it was good for the community because we all got to know each other well. In fact, I believe that we could do with a bit more of that spirit today in our communities. The Coffee Evening was made up of simple competitions, for instance, reading a passage without punctuation. This is not easy to do of course, but the audience would be in stitches when completely wrong interpretations produced gales of laughter as most of the sentences referred to local people. Another was whistling the tune of the Welsh National Anthem with everyone trying to make the whistler laugh. Try it - it's difficult, a bit painful too, but absolutely hilarious! Another competition would be making up sentences from a given word, playing the mouth organ or producing music by blowing through tissue paper on a comb. Such simple things gave us lovely times.

During the winter we sometimes had 'magic lantern' shows that resembled showing picture slides. The pictures on the screen would be of poor quality usually, rather jerky and hazy, but oh, the wonder and amazement we felt at the time of watching them. How we marvelled at that simple entertainment.

Just before Christmas when I was ten years old I suddenly realised that we did not have a Christmas tree and there was no prospect of having one either. It upset me to think we wouldn't have one on Christmas day, but I suddenly remembered a fir tree in the wild garden at *Pengraig* where we used to live. It had remained unoccupied since we left so I decided to go there to have a look around and, after tea, before it became dark, I fetched the medium sized saw from the shed, just in case I might need it. I did not tell anyone where I was going and hid as much of the saw as I could under my coat. I hurried up the road and scrambled to the top of *Cae Owen Jones,* over the stile and a spurt up the hill and into the wilderness at *Pengraig*. Even though I knew there would be no snakes around in winter I still felt very uneasy as I made my way down to the hedge at the bottom of the garden. There, in all its glory was the fir tree.

I knew that people were supposed to cut only the branches and leave the top to continue growing but all the branches on this tree were thin and spindly with no shape. But the top was lovely! It was also very high. I stood there on my own and thought a great deal, but in the end I decided we were going to have a Christmas tree. Slowly, carefully and painfully I climbed up that scrawny tree getting scratched by the rough hard branches.

It was not easy because I had to manoeuvre my feet and hands upwards holding on to the saw. When I reached a point where I thought I could cut off the top, I suddenly became aware of my surroundings. No one could see me from behind but directly in front, over the valley was the Rectory! I froze and then became hot all over and felt sure that the Rector was at that moment watching me through binoculars and would know I was stealing the top of the tree. Everyone would get to know including Mr Griffiths the local Policeman. Such is the power of guilt, but then I calmed down and realised that it was almost dark and anyway, the deed was done.

I came down that tree in double quick time and grabbed the top part and the saw and raced home. After putting away the saw and the tree in the shed I went into the house. As soon as Mam saw me she stared in disbelief and said, “Look at you covered in scratches, twigs and blood, what on earth have you been doing and where have you been, what have you been up to this time?” I told her, but all she did was tell me to get washed and tidied up. For days afterwards I was so worried there might be repercussions but … at least we had a Christmas tree.

About the same time there was a man in Llansannan, the next village, who became known as the 'One-Man Band' because he used his feet, arms, hands and mouth to play several instruments simultaneously. I still remember how we all marvelled at his ability because it all sounded so good. He also possessed an outstanding baritone voice, but unfortunately, had never had singing tuition to develop the necessary skills and techniques to perform professionally. What a pity it was that his voice was not heard further afield!

During the school holiday if the weather was wet or very cold, we played in the house, or in the shed if all the feathers were gone. It was a good time to do jigsaws and we all enjoyed this challenging activity and I still do the larger ones today with the help of the new generation.

When I now look back into my childhood and consider my reactions to it, I find that my overall impression is one of happiness despite being poor. I can see that we took what the days had to offer and enjoyed the blessing of general good health despite having lost a sister to rheumatic fever. Other families in the village grieved for children who had died from other major diseases of the time - diphtheria, scarlet fever, poliomyelitis or tuberculosis. There were no miracle drugs available because they had yet to be discovered. Treatment consisted of nourishing food, good nursing, hygiene, fresh air and warmth. Doctors' services were expensive, not because their fees were exorbitant but because their patients had little money. Minor, run of the mill complaints were dealt with at home using simple remedies passed from one generation to the next. There were some families who knew a lot about herbs, lotions and creams made from plants and I can remember an ointment being made from small, round green leaves for cuts and small wounds. The leaves are easy to find in the countryside where they grow on rocks in damp places, but I don't remember the recipe for the ointment.

The following are home remedies that were used by most people:

A mixture of soap and sugar kneaded into a soft ball, applied to a festering wound to draw out the pus and any foreign body

An infusion of wormwood used to treat nausea and acidity in the stomach

A mixture of sulphur and treacle to be given once a week to children to clean the blood and the system of any impurities

Iodine dabbed on cuts and small wounds as a disinfectant

A piece of greaseproof paper with butter was applied to stop bleeding from small cuts

Asafoetida swallowed for worms

Onions, raw or cooked for constipation

Blackberries were used for constipation in children

A piece of brown paper with a dash of vinegar and scattered with pepper was held to a cheek to alleviate toothache

Goose grease, melted and softened during the cooking process then solidifying after cooling, was used to cure a sore throat, it was applied to the neck and covered with a strip of woollen material - an old sock or blanket, the strip being reduced bit by bit as treatment became successful

Tincture of rhubarb and spirit nitre for bad colds and feverishness or hot milk and lemon with a teaspoonful of whisky or brandy

Gargling with salty water for sore throat

Aspirin, of course, for aches and pains

Buttermilk for sunburn

Soft green soap for shampooing hair and a dash of vinegar or lemon juice in the rinsing

water for shine.

Nowadays, despite the existence of modern medicine there still seems to be a great interest in homeopathy. Have the simple remedies of the past made a comeback I wonder, packaged today as sophisticated products in marketable containers with high price tags?

Chapter 6

GROWING UP

The decade before World War II was very eventful because in the U.K. the Depression had caused very high unemployment and dreadful poverty. Due to these unacceptable conditions many people were starving, and the great human suffering resulted in strikes being called in the coalfields, quarries and heavy industries. Desperation drove men to participate in protest marches to London to plead for improvement in work conditions and pay. But nothing much seemed to happen until re-armament began in the late thirties.

Elsewhere in the world there were unrests, and although only children at the time, we knew about the wars even though we did not fully understand the reasons why they happened.

The Headmaster of our village School had served in the First World War and had told us about the dreadful conditions he had experienced in the trenches. He described the lice, rats, filth, extreme danger, and dead bodies that had surrounded the soldiers day and night, and my vivid imagination had been ignited by his words, which had made a deep impression on my mind.

China and Japan were at war, the Japanese having invaded China and driven out the main Chinese opposition. Those countries seemed very distant to us, different too, and the stories we heard about them were surrounded by an air of mystery and mythology. We found it impossible to relate closely to them. Then Mussolini, the dictator in Italy attacked Abyssinia, now known as Ethiopia in Africa, and Emperor Haile Selassie was overthrown. News of this seemed more real to us than hearing about China and Japan, but we still did not really believe it had anything to do with us personally.

Following on, General Franco a fascist Dictator in Spain started a civil war assisted by the Italian Mussolini and the German Adolf Hitler, and cities were bombed. There were many casualties. Some men from Britain and other countries joined the International Brigade to fight Franco, but to no avail. Franco took control. There was persistent talk that these Dictators were practising for something bigger. This talk made an impression on me and the other children, and it scared us. I remember when it was announced on the radio that the Government forces in Spain had capitulated because I cried noisily and ran home as fast as my legs would carry me because I was afraid for my brother in London. I knew there were diplomatic comings and goings and that Prime Minister Neville Chamberlain had returned from Germany with a scrap of paper announcing, “Peace in our Time,” despite German Panzer divisions having already occupied Czechoslovakia.

In the meantime, here in Britain life went on normally, and at school I passed the Scholarship examination. It was a selection examination where only a few children chosen by the Headmaster were allowed to sit the exam. I was not old enough to qualify to sit the exam in the spring of 1935 because I would not be 11 years old until July. My father however was adamant and told the Headmaster that if he did not allow me to sit it that year then he would teach me himself. So, winter and spring of 1934/5 were taken up with swotting for the examination. There was a choice of Welsh or English and it was decided that I would sit the Welsh exam. I remember learning a long poem by I. D.

Hooson called *Y Fantell Fraith*, based on the story of The Pied Piper of Hamlyn and being able to recite it from memory having learned two lines every day. Anyway, I passed and therefore would attend the County School in Abergele after the summer holidays.

In 1935 the whole country celebrated the Silver Jubilee of the reign of King George V and Queen Mary. All we knew of them was that they lived in Buckingham Palace in London and wore rich, fancy clothes. The pictures in the newspapers showed them as two stern looking people and that was our impression of them. However, the importance of the Silver Jubilee to us was the fact that there were celebrations to be enjoyed. Flags and coloured bunting, tea parties and Gala days were everywhere. There was a Grand Sports Day held with decorated wagons and fancy dress competitions. We loved it all! Most girls wanted to be pretty and dress up as a fairy, flower girl, or a milk maid, but I wanted to be different, so I dressed up as an old lady using a crutch. I think I won a prize, but I cannot remember what it was.

Then the King died and there was mourning. A new King was declared immediately and as tradition dictated, it was the eldest son, Edward, named after his grandfather, King Edward VII. He was Prince of Wales and was popular in the country as he was thought to be more concerned for ordinary people than his predecessor. Whilst visiting a very poor area in South Wales he was very touched by the suffering and declared, "Something must be done." This did not go down very well amongst senior politicians in Government who thought it was none of the Prince's business. However, after he was declared King, but before he was crowned, news leaked out in the newspapers that he loved a certain American lady called Mrs. Wallis Simpson who had previously been divorced and was a married woman. There are some very strict rules that apply to the Monarchy because the Monarch is Head of the Church of England. Edward VIII had obviously transgressed and there was a great furore. He was advised by the Prime Minister to give up Mrs. Simpson if he wanted to be King. He refused and finally abdicated and left Britain for France where he and Mrs. Simpson were married after her second divorce.

Therefore, another King was declared, a younger son called George who became George VI. He was married to a beautiful Scots girl and they had two little girls Elizabeth and Margaret. In 1937 George VI was crowned in Westminster Abbey with his Queen Elizabeth. So hurrah! hurrah! We could look forward to yet more celebrations and flags and tea parties and Galas. Life was fun. Queen Elizabeth, later to be known as the Queen Mother died in the year 2002.

When the annual village Sports Day was held we had all the usual races for young and older children, *a tug of war* for the young men that brought much heaving and grunting and supportive shouting, and a fancy dress competition. Once, there was a *stilt* race when competitors walked round on long sticks, as clowns do in a Circus. I was never amongst the winners for running, but I loved competing in the egg and spoon race, sack race and the three-legged race.

Chapter Seven

THIS ABOVE ALL - TO THINE OWN SELF BE TRUE

After the summer holidays in 1935 my life changed completely when I became a pupil at the County Grammar School at Abergele. County schools were like Grammar schools in as much as they emphasised academic subjects.

I recall the first morning and getting up early to catch the bus for the five mile journey to Abergele. There I was decked out in my new outfit, the regulation uniform of the school - black shoes, long black woollen stockings, green serge gymslip with three pleats at the back and front with a narrow sash around the waist. The green blazer had the school badge on the breast-pocket, outlined in white and the blouse was white with long-sleeves. The girls' cap was a peculiar shape, green in colour with the white school badge set centre front. It was similar to a soldier's forage cap set from side to side instead of front to back. In addition, there were two covered buttons either side holding a band over the edges. It looked like a round cap with an ear sticking out on both sides. I never liked it but we were obliged to wear it outside whilst wearing the school uniform. The boys' cap was ordinary with stripes and a badge. The school Motto was *"Oni Heuir ni Fedir"* (If you don't sow you will not reap).

Most children had leather school satchels, but I had a large case probably because it cost less: it was much too big for me because I was small in size and only just turned 11 years of age. I followed the older pupils to school but cannot remember many details of that first day. It was all so different and confusing and I believe that the move from the small village school to the big secondary school in town was the biggest step I ever experienced. It probably sounds a bit exaggerated now, but it was another world to me. Bear in mind that I had been to Abergele only three times in my whole life before that day.

The reception classes were 2A and 2B. All the scholarship winners were in the A form where we studied Latin while the others were in the B form where they were taught commercial subjects - book-keeping and shorthand. I would much rather have done the latter and not the Latin!

We were introduced to our Form teacher, a pretty lady called Miss Frankel, who was the Geography and Games mistress. She was a very good teacher and we all liked her very much. Unfortunately, we had her for one year only before she left to become Headmistress of a Girls' school in England. Her replacement was her exact opposite. We did not dislike her, but she had no discipline in her classes. Most of the other teachers were good at their work, but there were two or three who were never cut-out to be teachers because they were ineffective. The Headmaster, Mr. D.B. Jones, was always referred to as, "D.B.," behind his back of course. He was a good leader who said everything three times for emphasis. We had nicknames for most of the teachers - passed down from year to year: 'Daddy' Holden, 'Uncle' Ivor, Mr. Walters was 'Willie Wet', 'Daddy' Easom. Miss Dwynwen Owen was *Dwy-wningen* (two rabbits), Mr. Hughes was 'Hugs', and so on. The headmistress was Miss Wynne who was a bit of a dragon, very precise, unbending and a stickler for rules. She taught French. There was a set list of homework subjects every night. Miss Wynne however gave us homework not just on the set-list days but on other days as well. Whenever we protested she would insist, "Never mind anything else, do your French homework" - and we had to comply or suffer the consequences!

Once we were installed at our desks on that first day we were introduced to our form teacher and given timetables. It was a big surprise to find a different teacher for every subject. Two things stand out in my memory from that day. Firstly, the children who had come from the country schools were a bit apprehensive but the girl who sat in front of me must have been very scared indeed. She was a quiet, timid looking girl who wet herself and the drips fell onto my shoes and I felt a little disgusted, but I did not say anything.

Secondly, during the afternoon, our English teacher took the class and we were each given a book and asked to read a paragraph out loud in turn. I cannot remember the book's title or its contents but I remember full-well when my turn came and I stood up and started to read. I knew I could read English very well but I came upon a word I had never seen before - metropolis. I pronounced it with the accent on the third vowel and there were immediate sniggers and guffaws, especially from the boys. The teacher corrected me and reprimanded the class for rudeness. I felt awful. I wished for the earth to swallow me up, but I vowed there and then that I would show them that they could never do that to me again. When the end of term exam results came at Christmas I was pleased to come 5th out of a class of 35 and I was the youngest. The girl who was top of the class was aged 14. I believe she was a paying pupil, for there was that facility within the system. Abergele County School at that time had a very good reputation - buses brought pupils from Rhyl, St. Asaph and Colwyn Bay, even though there were County schools in those towns.

I didn't really enjoy the first years at Abergele because it took me a long time to settle in. The town children seemed so different. They were used to going to the cinema and talking about film stars and swimming and going out to various events, things of which I knew nothing. I had been to *the pictures*, 'cinema' once only when Mrs Roberts, my neighbour in Llanfair wanted to see a film called 'Sanders of the River' because Paul Robeson was the star in it. Mrs. Roberts had a good contralto voice and came from a very musical family with a long line of outstanding singers. She was a fan of Paul Robeson and asked if I would accompany her to the Abergele Cinema to see the film. She treated me to the outing and I loved the film. I can still picture scenes in my mind and hear Robeson singing that wonderful song 'Old Man River'. That however, was the sum total of my cinema experience at that time.

Having already said that I did not enjoy school in my early teens, I must admit that I did not hate it because I enjoyed some things about it such as having good friends. In winter when ice and snow stopped buses from travelling to Abergele we would struggle to walk the ten mile round trip to and from school. On the way to school when we'd got to the top of the Sanatorium Hill, being young and with a group of friends we sat on our bags and cases and slid to the bottom. We would arrive in school somewhere between 11.00 a.m. and 12noon and would be hailed as heroes. At about 2.30 p.m. we were allowed to leave early to return home before dark. I remember one year we had learned a short play to perform on St. David's Day and, being the star performers, were looking forward to our moment of glory. But it was not to be - all the learning and practising had been in vain because as the first day of March dawned, everywhere was a wonderland of snow and it was still falling heavily. We could not possibly get to school that day and so my chance of becoming an actress had been cruelly snatched away at the last minute. Alas, Alack, Woe is me!

I concentrated on my studies and retained my position in the exams. I would have achieved a higher overall mark had I not had to study Art. I was hopeless at the subject and was awarded very low marks. But you cannot excel at everything, or so I told myself until I saw what one of the 6th form boys had achieved. He was a fine looking lad of mixed race who was outstanding in cricket and football and won the Victor Laudorum Cup each Sports Day. He also won a State Scholarship to either Oxford or Cambridge, but I can only remember his nickname which was 'Hockey Ball'. I never knew the reason for his nickname but I admired him and his achievements.

I participated in organised games without much enthusiasm in the early years but as I grew to like playing hockey I joined the 1st XI team and played for the school. I made new friends who were mostly from a similar country background to my own, but at the same time I remained true to my village friends. There was a trio of us who went around together, Minnie, the Baptist minister's youngest daughter, Iris, the only child of Mr. and Mrs. Parry who had a general store and newsagent shop in the village and myself. Iris was a privileged child. She had many things we could only dream of - a brand new bike, a new piano and music lessons and so on but I was never really envious because in other ways we were on equal terms.

During the time before our teens we had a kind of club going in one of the empty rooms at the back of Mr and Mrs Parry's shop. Not everyone was allowed to enter. I don't remember that we did anything very special except gather to talk. However, there was another group of girls who asked to join and they were allowed to come one day but that was the one and only time because they transgressed. Firstly, they introduced cigarettes and proudly showed off their mastery of smoking with nonchalance. We were urged to have a go and with some reluctance started taking puffs. We felt very daring, but then the coughing and spluttering began and most of us gave up. I know I never again smoked anything because I did not see the point of suffering discomfort and besides, I had no money for such things.

Secondly, the leader of this group of girls suddenly asked if we knew where babies came from. No one did of course. I don't believe I had ever really thought about the matter previously. The girl then proceeded to explain in great detail not only where babies came from but also how they were made! Consternation!! We were speechless and then all started protesting at once and arguing that she was talking nonsense because OUR fathers and mothers would never act in such a manner. Well, my friends and I were really upset by all this. We could not believe, and did not want to believe what the girl said, and yet she seemed to know the facts and was quite adamant about them. Not surprisingly, the girls were never allowed into the group after this episode and the clubhouse closed its doors not long after!

How wrong and unfair parents are who do not explain the facts of life to their children in a loving way. Children accept things in a very natural way and it is adults who bring embarrassment into situations and it should not be so.

This reminds me of something else in the same vein because one morning I went to the toilet before leaving to catch the bus for school and had the fright of my life. I really thought there was something dreadfully wrong with me because I was bleeding. I called to my mother and told her about the blood and she just said that I wasn't to worry, I was growing up and it happened to all girls. She had never even hinted to me, never mind explained about menstruation or anything else. She just acted in the way she had been brought up and of course the climate of opinion was very different then from today. We now believe in children being given information about the changes that will happen to them as they grow up and opportunities to think and discuss matters openly.

During the summer holidays, a gentleman called Mr. Page brought some boys to camp in tents in a field not far from the village. They belonged to the 'Old Swan Club' in Liverpool and as far as I can remember, there were about six of them. Mr. Page was a customer at the Newsagents so Iris knew all about them and of course she told Minnie and me and we became friendly with these lads in an off-hand fashion.

One particular group came twice and I remember the names of two of them - John Page was one and the oldest of the boys was Reggie Brown. Iris targeted John … he was the son of Mr. Page after all. One afternoon when we had been 'messing about' at the riverside near the Seven Sisters, Reggie called my name and then opened his arms wide. I can still remember the wave of emotion, a mixture of feelings that swept through me - pleasure, excitement and apprehension too. Reggie was all of fifteen years old and I was thirteen. He held me close and I began to feel a bit foolish because of the onlookers so he let me go but he fiercely whispered to me to remember that I was his girl. Later, Mr. Page took us all to Pensarn to the beach and the boys had a go in the Amusement Arcade. Reggie won a 'Three Wise Monkeys' figure and promptly presented it to me! I was sincerely happy to accept and kept it until it finally disintegrated. I have often wondered what happened to those lads, did they survive the War? In recent years there have been items of news in the business section of the 'Daily Post' about a Mr. John Page and his business matters and I wondered whether he was the same John that we knew all those years ago.

One year we had a Junior School Choir made up of girls and one boy, Glyn, who had a good singing voice and was from a very musical family. Iris and I competed in most of the local Eisteddfodau singing solos and also duets when she sang soprano and I sang alto, although I too had a high voice. We were quite successful too. But Glyn's father thought that it would be a good idea for Glyn and me to sing duet too with me singing soprano and Glyn, alto. We too were successful, in fact we beat the duet I sang with Iris! Well, that was O.K. with me.

With all these activities and our growing up, an attachment flourished between Glyn and me. We wrote little notes to each other leaving them in secret places. We met here and there on Saturdays, he accompanied by his mates and I by one of mine! Once or twice we were alone and we experienced a few self-conscious kisses. Oh! - I still remember the wonderful sweetness and innocence of those days. It was a marvellous way to slowly savour the interaction between girl and boy. Glyn's voice broke so the duets ended and our 'affair' ended too … it just petered out.

As an adult he married a girl who had also sung in the choir. We remained friends. But sadly, a few years ago Glyn became ill and lost his voice due to cancer, and has since died.

How different things are today. Youngsters are pressurised by television and magazines to experiment with sex long before they are grown up and able to cope with the intense feelings and urges that beset the teenage years. They have no experience to help them to take control because adult practices are urged upon them much too soon. I really do feel sorry for youngsters who get into difficulties because in some cases it is because older people have not helped by explaining things to them long before they reach puberty.

Whenever we visited villages where *Eisteddfodau* or Concerts were held, a group of about eight of us would simply pack into a car just like sardines in a tin and travel there laughing and joking all the way. Being cramped together was fun of course and much better than sitting sedately on a seat. We were young teenagers with mixed up feelings, sometimes feeling gauche and ungainly and then at other times feeling full of energy and anticipation. The world was our oyster - we were not children any more nor were we adults. We were safe in our village environment at that time but we eagerly looked out onto the wider world and dreamed our dreams too.

I progressed through the County School with satisfying success. At this time I was bothered with spots on my face from time to time and was very self-conscious about them. My physical appearance meant that my self-esteem was low, but I always reminded myself that I had a good brain and was intelligent and bright. As I grew up of course, things improved, the spots disappeared and I learned to recognise what was truly important and what was not. Teenage years are very hard to live through.

I enjoyed the challenge of learning and the examinations at the end of each term before the holiday breaks. We had no money to go away for real holidays as such, but from the beginning of the holiday period until the very last day I would be away staying at my Auntie Lil's farm. It was always a working holiday that I experienced there, and I liked that very much. We were always busy and I learned to milk cows and develop many other country skills too.

During term time my mother would give me money to buy fruit to eat after lunch. I saved some of it until I had enough to buy compacted powder and lipstick. I don't know whether Mam ever guessed what was going on but I certainly felt guilty because it was a real sacrifice on her part. My father was unemployed, like thousands of other people, and there was no money to spare at all.

However, the make up boosted my self-esteem and I learned to use cosmetics with some skill but make-up was certainly not for use in school. Oh no! In summer we were allowed to wear cotton gingham dresses, but even then we were still made to wear the long black stockings. It was so stupid! During the summer term of 1938 when I was in Form IV, all the girls decided to attend school the following day wearing white ankle socks. Wow! We were rebels and were all sent home in the afternoon and warned to wear the long black stockings the following day. End of revolution!

The Headmistress was an elderly spinster, who lived in a time warp and refused to move with the times. However, World War11 broke out and we were finally allowed to wear white ankle socks. Clothing was rationed by the use of coupons.

In our part of the world the only escapade we got up to was sneaking behind the bicycle shed or the sports pavilion to smoke and of course that was for boys only. The girls had to make do with magazines and in those days they were very innocent in content and there were not many of them and certainly they could not be compared at all with the avalanche of magazines we have today. There must be hundreds of different ones today specialising in various things such as sports, home, fashion, hobbies, fiction
and of course, sex - and from being THE taboo subject of our day, it has now become THE most popular subject ever!

The early teenage years, I think, are the most difficult for girls and boys. The world of our childhood is so secure in that things mostly remain the same and the world and its people are accepted as they are. During childhood we grow slowly and steadily, almost without being aware of any changes happening, but then there comes a time when Nature seems to take over and everything appears to change dramatically. Life becomes full of contradictions and one day we feel on top of the world then suddenly without any reason life feels flat, drab, and disappointing. There appears to be no moderation in anything, things are either high or low, good or bad, and at other times happy or sad. The world beckons and one moment we are confident that we are cut out to be a hero and a success, and then quite suddenly the world becomes a frightening place and we long to hide away and be safe. Our body seems incapable of doing what we want it to do. Parts of it grow at different rates and we look in the mirror and see someone else looking back at us. Everyone seems to be against us and we lash out and behave in a way that we do not approve of normally. We are excited by all the change and yet there are times when we almost hate ourselves. This period is the most difficult on the road to becoming an adult. If we are fortunate to live in a loving, caring and understanding family, then things are not too bad and we are helped along the way. But I pity the unfortunate youngsters who have to struggle through the changes unsupported or on their own in ignorance.

Well, that's enough philosophy for a while I think, but I have to say that I have always 'thought' about matters and wondered why and how certain things happen, when and where they happen, and who they happen to. Thinking about things makes life a lot more interesting, but you have to be careful not to carry things too far and risk becoming intrusive or plain 'nosey'.

At that time it seemed to me that the pupils in Forms V and VI at school were very grown up. They looked so tall and grown up, perhaps it was because I was small and very slim, a mere 5ft.1in.without shoes. Two or three of the senior pupils stayed on at school that year because they could not find jobs and I remember one lad acted as a clerk to the Headmaster and was called 'Sharpie'.

I mentioned earlier that my family had no money at all to spare and that is what made me feel so guilty about spending money on makeup instead of fruit. I remember the occasions when Mr. Davies, the rent man called and Mam asked him to leave it until the following week. He never made a fuss because he knew very well that the rent would be paid. At that time, there was a shop in Abergele that had a system of order and deliver. On a certain day of the week a man called to take an order and the following week came in a van to deliver the goods, receive payment and take another order. That was the pattern. There were times when Mam had to ask for payment to be delayed and again there was no quibbling because she always did pay.

During the war, the local Guesthouse was full of people who had come to the country to avoid the air raids on the large towns. The owner was very busy and somehow, I don't know who approached whom, but it was arranged for my mother to do all the washing - bed linen, dining room linen, bathroom and kitchen towels too, and eventually some of the guests also brought their personal clothing to be laundered. I remember one lady very well because she was young and beautiful and very well dressed. She was Jewish and had one little boy and everyone called her Mrs. Rab. She was very orthodox in her religion and kept to the religious rules on the days of fasting and other rituals.

The laundry work was very laborious for there was no washing machine, only a tub, a dolly, the boiler, sink and one pair of hands. There was no dryer either or an electric iron, just two flat irons in the red coals of the fire. When hot enough, one iron was fastened into a 'fender' or 'slipper' that covered the sole plate. You needed to be experienced about achieving the right heat - too hot and clothes would be scorched, too cool and the creases could not be ironed out. In winter and on rainy days the task of drying the clothes was a huge challenge, and in summer the heat of the fire and the irons was a constant problem too. But, by doing the work, Mam managed to keep us going - we never wanted for necessities.

Mam baked her own bread and we used to go to Mrs. Jones in the village to buy yeast, which is the raising agent that we called 'barm'. Mam even mended our boots when we were younger, but when we went to Grammar School our shoes were repaired by the village cobbler. However, when her own shoes or my father's needed repairing she did those as well. There was an iron stand with four separate shoe shapes on it, varying in size called the 'Foot'. A piece of sole leather was bought from the cobbler, nails too, then the shoe was placed on the correct 'foot' on the stand, the leather placed on the sole and the nails hammered in to secure it firmly. Then a sharp knife was used to neatly cut the surplus leather all round.

My mother had a 'thing' about shoes. She always insisted that our footwear should be of good quality, always polished well and kept in a good state of repair. “If your coat is old and ragged but your shoes are good, you will always look neat and tidy,” she used to say.

Even though we were aware of how long and hard she worked, we did not really appreciate exactly what it entailed. She must have been exhausted sometimes, but she never complained. On Sundays, after clearing up the dinner dishes she would sit down to read ‘The People’ newspaper … and then go to sleep in the rocking chair with the newspaper over her face and head!

I worked diligently at the various subjects at school and all the homework too although I was not so keen on some. I knew that to achieve a better and easier life, the only way was to learn, qualify and get a good job. When moved up from Form 3 to Form 4, I had to make one or two choices. I wanted to continue with Chemistry, but because I would have been the only girl amongst boys, the teachers talked me out of it - not exactly by prevention but by pressure, and so I started Spanish lessons with the girls and a couple of boys. Who knows what loss it was to the world being deprived of my scientific skill, but I quite liked Spanish and progressed very well. Perhaps the 'old boys' might have been right after all.

I liked Arithmetic and found it easy. I understood Geometry and could do Algebra at first, but somewhere along the line I lost track of Algebra and it became unsatisfying and a burden to me. An added problem was that my brother, who had preceded me at school, had been a 'whiz-kid' at Maths and the teacher expected me to be the same.

Then in Form VB I studied for the Central Welsh Board School Certificate - the equivalent of yesterday's G.C.Es and today's G.C.S.Es. By this time I felt a lot happier at school. I had friends, had proved my ability to the teachers and my co-students, and was always in the top three in the examinations. We were given a homework rota and were expected to do half an hour for each subject i.e. two hours every night.

In each classroom we sat at individual wooden desks comprising of a bench seat attached to a compartment in front with an opening lid that sloped towards the user for comfort when writing. We were allowed to fit a padlock to the desk because it was the only place we could safely leave our books, money and other small belongings. There were instances of thieving, but only very few. We could store all our reading and exercise books, rulers, pencils, pens, and protractors too knowing that no one could copy our work without our consent. There were inkwells on the desks and at first I used a pen with a 'relief' nib, which ensured neat writing. However, it was not long before I received my 'Conway Stewart' fountain pen from the 'Liverpool Weekly Post' for winning an essay writing competition. A fountain pen had an inner rubber tube and a small lever on the outer casing of the pen. The nib part was inserted into a bottle of ink, the lever lifted to flatten the tube and then slowly lowered again to allow the ink to flow into the rubber tube and fill it. You could write an awful lot before having to re-fill. Ink came in three colours, black, blue and red. These fountain pens replaced the ordinary steel pens that had to be dipped in the inkwell on the desk many, many times and wasted time during exams.

I treasured that pen and used it all the way through Grammar School. I think I gave it to my elder daughter when she passed her 11 plus exam. But we were not allowed to use fountain pens at the Inland Revenue where I later worked as a young woman. We had to use a scratchy pen so that the ink went into the paper and would last a long time - for record purposes. There were no biros in those days of course.

It seems to me now that I had succeeded in winning a fair number of books in Welsh and English for writing essays in competitions. Also I received a book Prize every year I was at school in Abergele and two in the last year at Primary school, one for attendance and one for being top of the class. At Abergele we were allowed to choose the prize books: some of mine were Spurrell's Welsh/English Dictionary, a complete Works of Shakespeare, a Collection of Essays based on Shakespeare's plays by Charles and Mary Lamb, The Splendour of Wales and some other Welsh books.

My year in FormVB was momentous - the storm clouds were gathering in Europe and Hitler and Mussolini were throwing their weight about and getting away with it. We teenagers were aware of these things but in an unreal way.

Somehow, international upheavals did not impinge on our lives. That summer term was very busy for me as I worked towards the School Certificate, and we had really beautiful weather as I recall. Came the end of term, and away I went to my Auntie Lil's farm. The end-of-year exams were always held mid-July, which meant that I had my birthday in the middle of them. The year was 1939 and I was 15 years old.

The 'National Eisteddfod in Wales' is a Festival of the Arts and is an old institution going back over the centuries. It is always held during the first complete week in August, and in recent years has been extended by a few days. Welsh men and women from all over the world come home to Wales especially at this time for a grand ceremony of welcome at this great Festival.

In 1939 it was held at Denbigh, an old town situated 3 or 4 miles from *Groes Farm* where I went for my holidays. Every year, on the Thursday during Eisteddfod week, David Lloyd George was President and he always made a grand speech. Lloyd George was a remarkable man. He was born in Manchester of Welsh parents. His father was a teacher who died when comparatively young, leaving two sons and a widow who returned to Llanystumdwy, a small village near Criccieth to live with her brother who was a cobbler. He must have been a very intelligent and far-seeing man for Lloyd George thought the world of him and consulted him on many occasions during the older man's life.

Lloyd George became a lawyer and a Member of Parliament. He opposed the Boer War in 1901 and was very outspoken about it. After making a speech in Birmingham he was lucky to get away with his life. Indeed, he had to don a policeman's uniform and leave from the back of the building. He was a marvellous orator and needed no notes as prompts.

He very rarely lost any debates held in the House of Commons. Winston Churchill admired him greatly and copied his style in many ways. When Lloyd George died Winston Churchill paid him a wonderful tribute. Both became Prime Ministers and led Britain in wartime. At Llanystumdwy there is a Museum that celebrates the life of the great man, including a small cinema showing old contemporaneous films of events during his lifetime. The old cobbler's workroom and home have also been preserved. Complying with his known request, Lloyd George was buried on the bank of the river in the village. He could have been buried with the Great in Westminster Abbey, but he lies in Wales with only a large boulder to mark his grave.

He became Prime Minister during the Great War of 1914-1918 and his energetic leadership played a vital role in winning the War. Before that, during 1909/10, when he was Chancellor of the Exchequer, he defeated the House of Lords and forced through Parliament the Act that entitled old people to receive a pension, thus starting off the Plan for a Welfare State in this country.

However, on that Thursday in August 1939, his manner was very grim and he warned of dark storm clouds over Europe. It was then that we felt fear and trepidation in our hearts. We remembered the newspaper pictures of bombings in Abyssinia or Ethiopia as it is now known, and Spain and we remembered the Headmaster at our village school telling us of his experiences in the trenches in France. He had described to us how terrible, how inhuman it had been, just sheer hell. Rats and dead bodies, lice, wounded, unwashed and unshaven soldiers who were hungry and cold, wet and afraid. Only the camaraderie had kept the men sane. All these horrible accounts came flooding back and we were afraid.

Very few people had a radio (or wireless as it was then known) and there were no televisions. However, Auntie Lil had a small radio but it was not used very often.

The results of the C.W.B. School Exams were published in the Liverpool Daily Post on the 1st September 1939 and I went to Denbigh that morning on the bus. I bought the newspaper and was almost afraid to look for the results. However, I was delighted to see that I had done very well in the exams and had passed in all subjects except Latin, which I had not revised or tried very hard to learn. I could hardly wait to go back to tell everyone, but I had to wait around for the next bus. I wandered about the town in an aimless fashion for I had no money to spend. I went into Woolworth and heard the girls at the counters talking about the latest news that Hitler had invaded Poland. I knew that Britain had signed a pact with Poland guaranteeing that country's sovereignty and so it was highly likely that this country would be embroiled somehow. This news cast a dark shadow over my day of good news. There were news bulletins all day Saturday after Mr. Chamberlain, the Prime Minister had sent an ultimatum to Hitler telling him to withdraw his forces from Poland or face the consequences. Months before, Mr. Chamberlain had flown to Munich to see Hitler and had come back with a signed declaration guaranteeing 'Peace in our time'. I don't know whether the Tory government was playing for time to re-arm or whether they really thought that Hitler would not attack Britain.

The Anglo-German Fellowship was in existence then, and many high-ranking persons supported it and were members of it. Indeed, Hitler had feted the Duke of Windsor and his wife when they visited him. For a short period, even the canny Lloyd George had been taken-in by Hitler.

On Sunday the 3rd of September 1939, at 11.00 a.m. when the ultimatum expired, the Prime Minister broadcast on the radio. He said that no answer had been received from Hitler and therefore we were at War with Germany.

There is no need for me to go further into national matters - it is all history now, and everyone knows about the events. I shall comment only on the way the War affected our lives in the six long years that elapsed before peace in 1945.

Everyone in my Auntie's house that morning listened to the Prime Minister in total silence and no one knew quite what to say afterwards. We all understood the seriousness of the situation and knew about the bombing, and the 'crack' S.S. Stormtroopers and the 'blitzkrieg' that had made Hitler's march into the countries of Europe so easy. It was frightening, but we really had no idea how totally ruthless they were. But we were soon to learn.

Before long, gas masks were issued to everyone and we were required to carry them everywhere in their boxes. Arthur, my husband to be, refused to have one because he said they were useless, otherwise why should the ones issued to the troops be so very different. He said that the issue of civilian gas masks was to stop panic developing amongst the population if poison gas were ever to be used by the enemy.

Arrangements were soon put in hand for children from the great cities to be evacuated to the country. It so happened that two little girls from Liverpool came to stay with us. They came amongst a group of evacuee children who were brought to our area with their teachers and taken to the Village Hall. There, the villagers who were prepared to give a home to evacuees had gathered to take their pick of the children in turn. It must have been awful for those little children for they were crying, frightened, homesick and lost amongst strangers who spoke differently. My father came home with two sisters, Peggy and Josie. I cannot remember their surname. The Government paid a small sum for their keep. The sisters came from Back Strickland Street, an area of deprivation near the docks.

We were poor, my father had only just started work after more than three years on the dole, like most of the men in the village, but we came to learn that there were many people in Great Britain who were much worse off than us. The first thing I noticed was that both of the girls had squints in their eyes. My mother gave them supper, then put them in a warm bath and washed them thoroughly. They had no fleas or lice, but each had a plug of dirt and grease in their navels and there was a certain smell about them, even after many baths. That night we put them to bed and they settled without any trouble, but later, when we went to check on them there was no sign of the two little girls. They could not have run away we thought, and when we called their names they appeared from *under* the bed. They told us that was where they slept at home. Those poor little girls! They were very affectionate, cheerful and happy, and well-behaved too. We learned of the culture that was familiar to them simply by observing the manner in which they played in the evenings. They would be under the kitchen table acting out the various characters and happenings of their home life. The gossiping, the borrowing of money from the moneylenders, the Priest of their Church, and so on, it was fascinating and amusing too!

On Sundays when my sister and I went to Sunday School they pleaded to go with us. We had to refuse because the Priest and their teachers would disapprove for they were Roman Catholics and we were Protestants. Once however, they followed us and sure enough as soon as the Priest got to know he came to see my mother and told her that the girls were required to go to Garthewin, the big house where there was a Catholic Church, for services. My mother had no objection provided there was an adult to accompany them on dark nights on the one and a half-mile journey on foot. Soon they were removed to Garthewin where they lived in a big barn, very much against their will. Later on we had a little girl called Rosemary from London who was also very loveable. Rosemary was a bonny girl, but she could not run having never been used to it when playing. I have often wondered what happened to those girls as they grew up. Did they survive the War?

Our troops went off to France and were lucky to escape back to Britain from Dunkirk. There were some very brave withdrawal actions and some very cruel ambushes by S.S. German troops. Hundreds of large and small boats and all available ships made their way to the French coast to rescue our soldiers even though there was strafing and bombing by German planes. There was outstanding bravery by those soldiers who fought the rearguard action to enable the evacuation to take place. Many lives were lost but many, many more were saved. There was widespread dissatisfaction with the leadership of Chamberlain in the Coalition Government and finally, Lloyd George made an outstanding speech in the Commons and told Chamberlain to go. He resigned, and Winston Churchill became Prime Minister. Like his friend Lloyd George, Churchill was a powerful orator and he rallied the country. He said that the lights were going out all over Europe, but Britain still stood alone and free. There was a frenzied effort to dig trenches everywhere, build obstacles to stop an invasion, and lookouts to sea. Those refugees who had escaped from Europe formed army divisions of their own and our troops re-formed. There was a lull for many months. We were expecting an invasion by Hitler, but it never came. However, preparations for such an eventuality went on apace, but we were not affected to any great degree at first in our quiet part of the country. However, there was a real possibility of an invasion of Britain, and the stark reality was that only twenty miles of sea separated us from a mighty military force such as the world had never seen before, and we faced it alone. Observation posts were set up all round our coasts including the western areas because only a narrow stretch of sea exists between Wales and Eire, which was a neutral country.

But soon, there was to be a change. Immediately, all buildings had to have blackout curtains, not a chink of light could appear from any window, and there could be no street lights anywhere even in the cities. Air Raid Precaution Wardens went round checking there was total darkness. The vehicles that were absolutely essential had to be driven with their lamps covered to leave only a small slit, just enough to see where they were going. Pre-war, there had been few vehicles on the roads, but during the war, petrol rationing restricted all movement, and most journeys were for business purposes only. Food was also rationed, and any that had hitherto been imported to Britain either disappeared completely from the shops or was strictly rationed. No bananas were seen throughout the War and oranges appeared only now and again. We grew our own apples, so they were plentiful. Children had bottles of concentrated orange juice to keep them healthy. The rationing was very necessary because our ships were being sunk by German U-boats - submarines regularly. Although the convoy system was in operation, at one stage our ships were being sunk at a terrifying rate.

There were volunteers for the Home Guard to man the observation posts even in the country areas. Farmers and anyone who had a garden were encouraged to 'Dig for Victory'. The food ration was small - 2oz. of butter per person for one week, small joints of meat for families and so on and yet strangely, we were healthier then as a nation than we are now. Everyone had to carry an 'identity card' and use 'clothing coupons' to buy clothes. We had 'dockets' to buy new furniture - rationed of course. Second-hand furniture was very expensive to buy.

When Hitler finally launched his offensive on Britain there were many planes in the sky and dogfights took place, especially in the southern part of the country. Our big cities were bombed systematically, night after night. In our village we could hear the deep heavy hum of the loaded bomber planes and their accompanying fighter planes long before they passed overhead on their way to Liverpool or Manchester. We were not afraid when they were on their inward flight, but we certainly were when they were being chased by our fighters for it was then that they dropped their bombs anywhere in order to get away quickly. We caught glimpses of them when the searchlights picked them out. The heavy guns situated around vulnerable areas brought some down, but it was the fighter pilots who were the heroes. Churchill said, “Never was so much owed by so many to so few.” Many, many young pilots lost their lives, but the Battle of Britain in the skies was won. Goering boasted about his German Airforce that had wreaked so much havoc everywhere, but our young pilots in those tiny 'Spitfire' planes proved more than a match for the German planes, and their Air Force never was supreme again. Some of those lads in the R.A.F. and the other armed services, had been my fellow pupils at school, and it was very upsetting to hear of their death, or of their suffering terrible wounds and injuries.

After signing a Treaty with Russia, Hitler reneged and attacked the country. The German tanks and guns quickly pushed forward and the fighting that resulted was terrible. Japan attacked the American Navy in Pearl Harbour, succeeding in sinking and damaging a large number of ships and killing hundreds of men. This brought America into the War. The Japanese pushed into Malaysia, and Singapore fell. Many troops from New Zealand, Australia and Britain were captured and all civilian colonials were herded together then marched into terrible war camps where many thousands died from starvation and disease. There was so much cruelty it is a wonder anyone survived. Civilians, including women and children were also rounded up and forcibly marched into captivity in camps where they suffered terrible deprivation.

Those were very dark days for Britain and the British. We had stood alone for over two years and suffered greatly. However, the great victory of the British and Commonwealth troops under the command of General Montgomery in North Africa when they defeated General Rommel's crack troops was a great boost and was the turning point of the War. Churchill gave an order that all Church bells were to be rung throughout the land in celebration. As from the outbreak of war the peals of the bells had been used only as warnings. Although the dark clouds and fears were always there, people were cheerful and helped each other. There was a good feeling around - the silly divisions of class were forgotten in the struggle to survive. Women, who pre-war worked only until they were married, now worked in ammunition factories and on the land, or joined the armed forces. Young men and women had to register at a certain age, I think it was 18, and were then conscripted into the forces or some other vital work.

In towns people registered on rota lists for fire fighting duties. When the air raids started in earnest they began with incendiary bombs that destroyed and flattened large areas of the towns and cities. As soon as word came that enemy bombers were on their way the siren wailed - a horrible sound, and people went into air raid shelters underground, and in London into the Underground Tube Stations. When the raid was over the siren sounded the 'all clear', which was a much less frightening sound. My brother, who was in London during the War, said he admired tremendously the bus and ambulance drivers and the fire fighters. In the chaos and confusion after a raid with burst gas and water mains, fallen masonry from destroyed buildings and the danger from live electricity cables, they toiled hour after hour, day after day, night after night, during and after raids, to keep the city moving and working. They were wonderful taking it all in their stride without any fuss. The devastation affected most of our other great towns and cities too.

Gradually, hope reappeared. After the defeat of General Rommel's armies in North Africa there was heavy fighting when the Allies pushed the Germans out of Italy, especially on Monte Cassino. The Italians had already capitulated, but Russia was crying out for a 'second front' which was an invasion of Europe proper. The Russians were holding out in devastated cities with no food, in winter weather. British ships were delivering tanks, guns, and other equipment to them from ships sailing in the Baltic Sea. This was very risky because of the presence of U-boats and the severe weather conditions. Eventually, the Russians succeeded in driving back the Germans who promptly used the 'scorched earth' system, that is, they burned everything behind them as they withdrew.

In Britain, a huge stockpile of vehicles, tanks, and guns was being built and hidden on the south coast. There were thousands of servicemen and women, from Britain, America, Canada, Australia, New Zealand and all parts of the Commonwealth including those who had fled from Europe, all waiting all over the country for a signal to act. There was great secrecy and people were told on the radio and in the newspapers that, "Careless Talk Costs Lives." Finally, the invasion of Europe began with an assault on the French coast. There were a number of coded landings on Normandy coasts and inevitably there was heavy loss of life. That was the beginning of the end for Hitler who eventually committed suicide. He knew what would happen to him if the Russians got to him first because of the cruelties the German forces had inflicted upon them, and it was they who in fact got to Berlin first, followed quickly by the other Allied troops. As the Allies made their way through Europe freeing the countries, they came upon terrible death camps where Jews and others had been humiliated and made to suffer and had died in their millions. How could supposedly civilised people possibly have inflicted those dreadful atrocities on fellow human beings … it is beyond understanding.

But then came 'Victory in Europe' - V.E. day, when Germany finally capitulated. Fighting still went on in the Far East until Japan surrendered after the bombing with atomic bombs of Hiroshima and Nagasaki. This new type of bomb was horrifying and although people were glad to have the War finished, many wanted atom bombs banned. This argument still goes on with weapons today, weapons becoming bigger and much more frightening. Countries spend millions of pounds on these weapons, which cannot be used unless we want the whole world destroyed.

Hitler had used different types of bombs before the end of the war, including the unmanned 'doodle-bugs' and 'buzz bombs' that were remote controlled. It was fortunate that he was defeated just in time, for the Germans were on the point of being able to produce atomic bombs. The 'doodle-bugs' and 'buzz-bombs' were directed at the Greater London area and could be seen and heard as they approached. As soon as the sound of their motor stopped, people on the ground knew that the bomb would land and explode within minutes, and it was very scary to watch and listen to them knowing more or less where the devastation would happen. The trail of destruction after the explosion affected a wide area.

There was great jubilation and street parties were held when the War finally ended. Everyone was tired of the war effort, but there was then a lot of re-building work to be done in Britain and Europe and therefore more had to be achieved. Although the Americans had sent troops to fight and had supplied us with goods, Britain still had to pay for them. We were a rich nation before the War but at the end of it, we were nearly bankrupt, all our gold reserves had gone to pay for the War effort and the gold ingots held in the Bank of England were by that time sitting in Fort Knox in the U.S.A. I read in a newspaper article recently that we finally cleared the debt in 2003!

During those War years I was growing and changing from a gauche schoolgirl, plagued by periodic spots to an attractive young woman, well that is what I was led to believe at least!

At school, pupil numbers doubled as a result of evacuees coming to the district from many areas, but mostly from large cities in England. School routine went on as usual. Obviously, the many deprivations caused by the War affected our lives in many ways. We were encouraged to knit for the troops, and women went to meetings arranged by the Women's Institute (W.I.) and the Women's Royal Voluntary Service (W.RV.S,) to learn how to eke out our meagre food rations. It must have been easier in the country areas because we could grow vegetables and fruit, keep hens and catch rabbits. We could also get the occasional pot of salted butter that consisted of alternative layers of salt and butter, which was made on farms and pressed firmly into pots. The butter had to be thoroughly rinsed before use because of its extreme saltiness. A 'black market' most certainly existed although it was very 'hush-hush', and the penalties for breaking the law were heavy, but some very prominent people were involved in it. Overall however, the system of rationing was fair and it ensured that everyone had a reasonable share of vital food. The system of fair shares in clothing, controlled by the issue of coupons was also acceptable. In addition, we made do with sacking, bleached flour bags and bits of parachute material for curtaining and items of clothing.

There were various campaigns to raise money for aeroplanes and arms, but I cannot remember whether contributions were made by unofficial voluntary donations or official savings. Metal railings around buildings were taken to be melted down and used to make armaments. There were posters warning everyone to be careful who they spoketo and why, and how they spoke of their work and family members serving in the forces, as there might be spies about. Members of the forces writing home, were not allowed to say where they were, what they were doing or where they were going next, and understandably so.

As the years went by, camps were set up in the UK for German and Italian prisoners of war captured in the North African campaign and later in Italy and France. The prisoners were screened, and those thought to be safe were put to work on the land, helping to grow food for us in Britain.

Dances, whist drives and other events were held in the Llanfair Village Hall and the soldiers who were guards at the camps or stationed at the big training camp at Kinmel, would come to join in. When I was around seventeen years old, I organised a concert in the Village Hall, in aid of the Red Cross. I emulated my father in this respect because he had done this during the 1914/18 World War. I wrote to the Commander at Kinmel Camp explaining my intention and asked if there were any entertainers at the Camp who could support the effort. He was extremely helpful and sent along a comedian and others to help with the event. Together with local talent, we had a jolly good show. We made a profit of £17.10s.0d, which in those days was a tidy sum.

After the summer holidays I returned to school and my form master and Headmaster decided between them that I had done well enough in the School Certificate Exam to warrant going straight to the VIB Form, thus by-passing the VA Form. This meant that I would begin the two-year study course for the Higher School Certificate, today's 'A' level, and that I had to make my final choice of subjects: three main plus one other. I decided on English, Welsh and Spanish. Very few of my old classmates went up with me, most of them either left school or went into Form VA. Some older pupils came up from Form VA of course. Further education in those days was an option for the few and so numerically, VIA and VIB, together was only a small form which was just as well because the room that housed us was also small. There were no desks, instead there was a large table and chairs, it was more of a study room really.

To complicate matters the Education Authority had at last agreed to build long-awaited and long-needed extensions to the school, and building-work had commenced even though it was wartime. Our study was to become a library and the main hall was to be divided into two sections. A new hall was to be built. What I remember is the sound of clanking, banging and knocking and general disturbance every day. For a while, I can remember some of us being huddled round an oil heater at the end of the old hall, wearing our coats. Later, that area was partly finished and the beautiful long table from the old classroom was moved there with some of the chairs and we were again able to have lessons. I was the only pupil taking Spanish and I remember an occasion when my teacher, who was a local Welsh-speaking man sat at one end of the table and I at the other studying Don Quijote, the classic novel by Cervantes. During the lesson he leant back in his chair and because the parquet floor was new and very highly polished, his chair slid forwards and he landed under the table almost at my feet! I was nearly bursting with suppressed laughter, but his pride had suffered from his downfall and I deemed it wiser to appear nonchalant as though teachers sliding under tables was the norm. I never did see the end product of alterations for two reasons, I had left school and the project ran out of money: it was quite a considerable time before the new buildings were finished.

During the last year at school there were only three of us taking English, and lessons were held in the staffroom of women teachers. There was always a nice warm fire in the room. Welsh lessons were taken by the Headmaster in the library. I was fortunate in having three very good teachers, especially in English. Miss Davies was an exceptional teacher and I found it easy to study with her. She showed me how to appreciate good poetry and prose. Unfortunately, because of the War, visits to theatres and the production of plays at school had to be discontinued and I had always looked forward to taking part and enjoying such activities. So, there was disappointment in that respect, but we dare not, could not, and did not complain, it was a time of war after all.

At this time there were many soldiers and other servicemen in the area, and also 'land girls'. The girls were from all walks of life, not all from farming backgrounds by any means. They looked very smart in their uniforms and it was surprising how soon they adapted to their new life in the countryside.

On one occasion, the Headmaster asked me as a prefect to keep an eye on one of the schoolgirls from my village to make sure she went straight home from the bus on arrival at Llanfair. Apparently she was missing one night, having spent time on the beach with a soldier. I did not care to be a spy, I did not think it was fair of him to ask me to do such a thing and so I did what was asked of me, in a very casual way. This girl was attractive and all the boys were around her like bees around a honey pot. Today, she is very successfully running her own business and very well off.

In 1939 when War broke out I was just fifteen years old, therefore my remaining teenage years were spent with the clouds of War hanging over everybody and everything in my life. However, there were lighter moments of course because my brother came home on holidays and we were still very close in those days. We went walking many miles in the countryside together. One day we decided to go to Llandudno, but there was no bus due for hours, so we tried hitching a lift. A lorry stopped and we were told by the driver that if we wanted a lift we could get into the back of the lorry, which we did thankfully. But lo and behold! What was hidden under the tarpaulin? Well whatever it was, the smell was atrocious. The lorry was driven by a business man whose work involved collecting the bodies of dead animals from farms, in order to acquire hides and skins for tanning. We were only co-travellers with the corpse of a dead cow - ugh! We went to stand right behind the cab so that the wind and fresh air blew the smell downwind. In such a way we completed part of our journey because for the next part, we sat comfortably in a bus.

When we reached Llandudno we decided to walk to the Happy Valley and Haulfre Gardens situated on the side of the headland known as the Great Orme. This was, and is, a lovely spot. I am very pleased that now at last, money has been received to clean up, re-plant and generally make more beautiful this lovely area.

As in all seaside towns, seagulls sometimes become a nuisance. On the day of our trip our mother had given us a packet of chicken sandwiches. We sat on a grassy slope to enjoy both the sandwiches and the view when suddenly, a big greedy seagull swooped down and snatched the last sandwich from my hand. I was flabbergasted and so cross! Unfortunately, it happens quite frequently, these large birds are so cheeky and can be quite fearsome. Looking back, I think Percy tried to bring happiness and joy into the lives of my sister and me, and it is very clear that we admired him for his cleverness and loved him very much for his generosity of spirit and care of us as younger siblings.

For the last two years at school, life was quite humdrum. The War did not affect us in any serious way. We concentrated on our schoolwork and of course at sixth form level there was a lot to do. I sat the Higher Schools Certificate Exams in 1941 celebrating my seventeenth birthday in the middle of them in July. I remember that the oral test in Spanish was on the first Monday of the summer holidays. It was a strange experience going to an empty school with just my teacher, for there were no other entrants. I was told that the Examiner had come from South Wales specially to test me, and my teacher knew I was a little nervous. However he said, "Answer his questions, take your time but don't dry up. Talk about anything and everything as long as it is in Spanish." Well, I know that I didn't stop talking, but I could not remember what on earth I had said. When my teacher was ushering me out of school before taking the Examiner to the railway station, he said to me, "Well of course Bet, I don't know how you fared but I think you frightened him more than you were scared of him." The Examiner was a Mr. Phillips. Afterwards, it was just a case of waiting for the result that finally came at the end of the summer holiday. We had been told that unless we had a job to go to, it would be advisable to go back to school, and this is what I did.

My exam results were good. I had passed in English and Welsh with Distinction and had achieved a Credit in Spanish which included Oral Proficiency. It was good enough to go to University, but there were difficulties. Although my father was now working away from home in the Wrexham area, we were still poor and my mother still had to struggle. My younger sister was now fourteen years old and at the same school as I attended. Also, in those days there were no grants or financial help at all for fees. On top of that I could not attend any college before I was eighteen and that would not be for another twelve months. My Spanish teacher was leaving the school and going into the Royal Air Force as an Intelligence Officer and I can remember his pleading with me to stay at school for the next year and try for a Scholarship, which he was confident I could win. It was a big decision and I found it hard to focus on the situation. For years it had been taken for granted in my family that I would go into some branch of the Civil Service, maybe the Post Office or something similar.

In the event, within a few weeks, certainly before half-term, the Headmaster brought to our notice a letter he had received from the Inland Revenue inviting applications for jobs in the Estate Duty Office that dealt with death duties - nowadays they are known as Inheritance Taxes. The minimum requirement was a good Higher School Certificate. Due to the War, most of the large government offices had been evacuated from London to various parts of the country and the Revenue Offices had gone to Llandudno. I applied for a position and was called for interview. The Controller was the head of the Estate Duty Office and it was he who interviewed me at the St. George's Hotel in a large room on the first floor, facing the sea. He said that although the work did not call into use the subjects of my Higher School Certificate except for English, it was the quality of intelligence that he was looking for. He offered me a post and I was happy to accept.

Chapter Eight

EARNING MY LIVING

And so it was that my working life began, but first I had to buy some suitable clothes. All I had was my school uniform, some good Sunday clothes and a few odds and ends for every day use. My mother was very annoyed with my bossy cousin, she, of the sheep dip shampoo fiasco, who took me to Denbigh to buy a navy blue dress. It was quite a nice one actually but very expensive, and mother had to pay for it. At that time, although this cousin was married with a baby, her husband was away in the Royal Navy. They lived in Holyhead, but she returned to her parents' farm in his absence because she feared bombs, although none had fallen in Holyhead at that time.

It was a long bus journey from Llanfair to get to work in Llandudno. I caught the 7.10a.m bus to Abergele, waited there for 15 minutes to catch the Llandudno bus that got in at 8.50am in time for work at 9.00a.m. There were three other people from Llanfair who travelled on that early bus, but only as far as Colwyn Bay to work at the Ministry of Food offices. Returning from work I caught the 6.00p.m bus to Abergele and then the 6.50p.m bus destined for Llanrwst that got to Llanfair at 7.10p.m., which was exactly 12 hours since starting the journey in the morning.

Sometimes during the summer months I could not get onto the usual bus home from Llandudno because it was full of visitors to the area, which meant having to wait another hour for the next one to Abergele. The delay made it impossible for me to catch my connection to Llanfair leaving me with no alternative but to walk the last five miles home. This did not happen very often but it was tiring and annoying when it did. Even during the war there were holiday-makers in the coastal resorts. On reflection I marvel at the fact that I could walk home alone during wartime, with servicemen everywhere, and prisoner of war camps around, and never did I feel afraid, nor was I ever in any danger of interference or attack from anyone. The incidence of crime such as stealing and personal attacks was minimal in our part of the world anyway. How different from today when I will not venture very far on my own, even during the daytime in some districts.

After a few weeks of travelling 4 hours a day to and from work it was arranged that I should lodge during the week at a small Guesthouse owned by my father's unmarried elderly cousins in Colwyn Bay and return home for weekends. I shared the front sitting room with a girl who worked at the Ministry of Food and we kept our weekly rations of food in a cupboard - we had no fridge of course! Each of us had a small bedroom, but also living there was a much older woman, a maid who we considered to be a pest because she was always after us telling us not to do certain things, but to do this, that and the other. For instance, she made us push our slippers under the frill of chair covers so they were hidden … and then we couldn't find them! Well, after six months I could stand it no longer! I decided I much preferred the tedious daily journey to and from work to living in that place, and that is how it was for the rest of my time at the Estate Duty Office.

But during my time in the Guesthouse, I still travelled the short distance to Llandudno on the bus that I had always used, and every morning a young man would sit with me whenever he had the chance. He seemed decent enough and when he asked me to go to the pictures with him, I agreed. After the film he saw me home and wanted a good night kiss, and for some reason, I knew that I did not want this to happen. Something in his manner had gone against the grain and I had concluded that I did not like him. For nearly two weeks I had to take another bus in the morning so I would not see him again. Perhaps I misjudged him - perhaps not, but I followed my intuition because I have great faith in it - it has only once let me down.

Now, I will say a little about my job which was temporarily situated in the St. George's Hotel in Llandudno during the war years. Mary, a girl from Westmoorland started with me in a section called 'Review' that also employed an older lady and the Section boss. We were known as Assistant Examiners and were given five Law Books each pertaining to the work. For the first few days we were shown the content of some of the files that we had later to requisition every morning to be brought up to our desks from the cellars. Each file held an affidavit sworn by administrators or trustees of a deceased person's estate, and then details of the Will with legacies or details of the successions of persons entitled were set out in abbreviated form on one side and particulars of what duties were payable on the other. Sometimes, in larger estates there would be a further section outlining Deeds that the deceased person had assigned, and the duties payable on such transactions. That is a simplistic explanation of the complex work, but we are not concerned about that now.

On a daily basis, we were required to requisition a number of affidavit files for perusal thereby enabling us to control our workload, but we had to keep a log of the number of files we dealt with and the amount of work involved in each. Some of the files consisted of just a few sheets of paper but others could be up to a foot deep, bound in hard covers with straps and metal clasps that were brought to us on trolleys - these would represent old estates with many Deeds and long-term reversionary entitlements and were dealt with in the main by senior staff. At first the work was confusing because of the abbreviations used and the range of titles given to various processes that were peculiar to each office. For example, there was a *W/Wash* on some files and this *white wash* meant that the work on the file was completed, all dues paid and a letter sent confirming this. Mary and I had little trouble in getting the work done once we understood all the idiosyncrasies and were quite happy to deal with Solicitors in Wales and England, and their equivalent Writers to the Signet in Scotland. Our work consisted of checking and reviewing processes to ensure that all the procedures were dealt with in a satisfactory way and within reasonable timescales. Mary and I made good friends with Nan, a girl from Motherwell who started with us in the Review Office, but worked in a different room. We chatted in our break times and got to know her well, but she eventually went to work in the Control Commission in Germany at the end of the War.

Mr. Lea, our boss, was a Senior Examiner. He had lost most of his right arm in the First World War and used what remained to hold down papers on the desk while he wrote with his left hand - a skill he'd had to develop. I remember him as being a very kind man. He once told me that I had a tidy mind and on another occasion he said that I thought like a man, a statement that puzzled me at the time, and even now I wonder what he really meant.

We had a one-hour break for dinner, but mid-session tea-breaks were spent still working at our desks. We drank tea without sugar - something I eventually got used to! We took it in turns to go to the basement to fill a large enamel teapot with boiling water from an enormous geyser that frightened me to death because of the gurgling, belching and hissing sounds it made when I turned on the tap. How primitive were those basement kitchens compared with the modern facilities of today's hotels. At first I ate my dinner in a small café in town where I could read my newspaper by a warm coal fire. The waitress was a nice Irish girl who invited me to attend her wedding to a Canadian soldier at the local Roman Catholic Church. It was a full Mass Service in Latin that took many hours to unfold and it was a new experience for me - the smell of the incense was too.

Once I'd made friends, I went with them to the Revenue canteen where we could get hot meals or salads. The food was cooked well and presented nicely, and the staff deserved medals for their efforts considering the food shortages of the time. I can still visualise individual salads beautifully laid out on plates ready to be eaten.

We were paid in cash, and collected our monthly pay packets from the Administration Office. In today's terms, our earnings were paltry, but fifty years ago they were good salaries. I gave my mother £1.00 a week and saved most of the rest.

After six months or so I was entitled to some leave of absence and I went to stay with my brother in his digs in London. The great firestorm of incendiary bombs that rained on London just after Christmas had caused great devastation especially in the City area. Thankfully, there was a lull in air raids during the week I was there, and one way or other I managed to visit most of London's famous landmarks. My brother had warned me to wear a comfortable pair of walking shoes because the stone in London pavements is harder on the feet than elsewhere he explained - I believed him too! Admittedly, we walked for miles and used the Underground tube trains and buses too but still my feet complained. Two particular outings still remain very vividly in my mind.

The first was the day we went to the world-famous Kew Gardens where we enjoyed ourselves very much. Having spent the day appreciating the beauty of the plants it came time to return to Percy's lodgings which required queuing for a bus. As we waited we chatted about the day's activities in Welsh but suddenly realised that others in the queue had stopped speaking which caused an unnatural hush. Then the same thought occurred to us simultaneously, "They think we're Germans!" Percy said to me in Welsh. "Just continue normally and take no notice - that's best," and sure enough everything then settled down again. If we had stopped speaking they would have become even more suspicious of us, our language, and motives - after all it was war time.

The second outing that has remained clear in my mind involved the day we walked in the City when I fully appreciated the devastating results of mass bombing. As we walked along the scarred and pitted streets I saw the remains of walls, twisted metal and charred remains of people's homes. I learnt that the destruction had been caused by firebombs, incendiaries that had been dropped by a first wave of aeroplanes followed closely by exploding bombs dropped by a second wave of planes. However, the most dramatic, poignant and surreal feature of the area was St. Paul's Cathedral that still stood intact amidst the ruins all around. My brother said that its survival was symbolic to Londoners and served to give them courage to carry on through those terrible years. As we stood there looking at acres of devastation, a scene I could never have imagined had I not seen it, I could almost sense the fright and terror of people caught in the hell of the attacks, even if most of them had been physically protected in shelters. When they emerged following an attack, many would find their homes and chattels, offices and places of work flattened to a pile of rubble. It is only the people who experienced the awful events who really understood the impact of war.

In the past, men went to fight in battles and many were killed and maimed but in modern times, civilians too, are in the line of battle especially in strategic areas. Perhaps we will learn someday that, nobody wins wars because we are all losers in them. At the end of any conflict people must thrash things out and come to some sensible agreement so … we should do our utmost to take such action *before* guns are fired. We must be alert to the fact that armaments are mass produced and sold for profit often to amass fortunes for unscrupulous people and governments. It can be argued that their production can have the effect of providing employment for some, but conversely their production can also wreak havoc on others. Surely there must be other ways of creating employment opportunities and building a nation's infrastructure without having to resort to mass killing and the destruction of communities? Most people in the world just want to get on with their lives, but there will always be the few who lust for money and power, and care nothing about the misery and suffering they cause to others in their pursuit.

There were a number of Welsh Chapels in London during the war and my brother was a member of the Jewin Presbyterian one in the City area. This Chapel was bombed like most other buildings causing the congregation to have to find another meeting place. They were fortunate enough to be allowed to use an Anglican Church nearby until that too was bombed. They then moved to premises in Grays Inn Road where the Welsh Forces Club met and that is where they remained until a new Jewin Chapel was built at the end of the war. My brother by then had been elected a Deacon who worked terrifically hard in getting the new Church built and free of debt. Several years passed before I was able to visit London again.

There was a very special visit I made after the War to another devastated city that impressed me greatly: Coventry. A new church had been built there that had been paid for by residents of a German city as a token of goodwill and repentance because they too had suffered mass bombing: I believe it was Cologne. I visited the Church when I was on business in the area, and was totally unprepared for the experience. It was so completely different from any other church I had visited because it was so beautiful and I was overwhelmed by the feeling of peace and tranquillity that permeated the place. I would have stayed there longer but for the lack of time. I really felt a deep and wonderful calming of my spirit there - a sensation that I have never forgotten.

The war years rolled by affecting our lives in many ways, but we were fortunate not to have suffered in the way many did. But it is true to say that regrettably I did not experience, freedom and the carefree time that is usually associated with early youth, but happily I did not experience bitter losses and grief either. At that time when young people reached the age of eighteen they were required to register to become eligible for call-up to the armed forces or to do other essential work such as coal mining, factory work or working on the land. After registering I was informed that I must stay at my job of working for the Inland Revenue in place of the young men who had been called to war. The Revenue Offices, temporarily set up in Llandudno during the war included the Income Tax Office, which was probably the largest section, but there were other smaller sections too. Many of the staff eventually settled in reasonably well and availed themselves of whatever leisure activities were available in the Welsh coastal resort at the time, and they came to appreciate the beautiful countryside surrounding the area, such as Snowdonia, or *Eryri* to give it its proper name. However, to Londoners and other city dwellers, Llandudno was a delightful but small seaside town, quite unlike home, and most longed to return to their families and where they had come from. They moaned and groaned and finally the Estate Duty Office left Llandudno, but it was to Worthing in Sussex that it was relocated not London.

Our offices were installed in the larger hotels of the town where all the rooms including the bedrooms were used. The office structure included the Clerical, Administrative and Executive sections. The storage area was in the basement, the clerical section used the largest rooms on the ground floor whilst the rest of us were upstairs in various sized bedrooms. Nothing much had changed in the hotels in the years between the Wars, for example, there were still coalfire grates in the bedrooms. After we left work in the evening, cleaners carried out their cleaning duties and prepared fires for us to light on our arrival the following morning. Fires were only provided in winter, none was available in the summer, whatever the weather.

I have often thought how hard it must have been for the people who worked in those hotels in the dark kitchens and having to go up and down all the stairs. I remember one morning in the late autumn of 1946 when young men were returning to work after demobilisation from the armed forces, and on this particular morning I was on my knees trying to light the fire and having some difficulty in getting it going. I was blowing into the feeble flames, my hands were black, and my face red with my exertions, when the door opened and someone entered. I automatically said, “Good morning” and the greeting was returned. Straight away I knew this was a stranger and quickly got to my feet. We stared at each other and the expressions on our faces were identical - surprise and puzzlement. He thought I was a charwoman and I thought he was some kind of Inspector. There he stood, a very nice looking young man in all his glory - dressed smartly in a suit, carrying an umbrella and an attaché case and a newspaper tucked under his arm. He was returning to work at the end of the war dressed in the style he had been used to when he left to go to war in 1939. I cannot remember whether we had been told of his arrival, but obviously no one had informed him of the much more relaxed dress style imposed on office workers by the restrictions of war. In the end we both burst out laughing and after introductions settled to work. It must have been difficult for those young men to return to civilian life after demobilisation. His name eludes me but he was a member of the religious movement called 'The Plymouth Brethren'. He was married and very interested in antiques. He arrived at work one Monday morning and informed us animatedly that he and his wife had been lucky enough to buy a four-poster bed!

Our treats were little ones: periodically, but not often, oranges arrived in the shops. Word spread like wildfire when they appeared and within minutes long queues would form outside the shops in the hope of obtaining the fruit. At other times we had to make do with bottles of rose-hip syrup for our vitamin C to cure spots and keep us healthy. There were very few overweight people around in those days - maybe it was something to do with the fact that sweets and chocolate were rationed, or that the concept of fast-food was unknown.

By returning to Llanfair every evening after work I could spend my leisure hours in the usual recreations of village life. I was a member of the *Aelwyd Club*, which was the senior section of *Urdd Gobaith Cymru*, Welsh League of Youth. We held social evenings and had picnics in the summer. Big functions such as the *Eisteddfod Genedlaethol yr URDD*, National Eisteddfod had been discontinued for the duration of the War except one Urdd Rally that was held in Aberystwyth, but I cannot remember in which year. However, I do recall that it must have been during the winter months because it became dark early while we were there. Three or four of us went walking along the Promenade in Aberystwyth and of course there were no lights. We were laughing and talking as we went along when quite suddenly we heard a male voice shouting, “Stop, who goes there?” We giggled and went on, thinking it was some boy trying to be funny. Again the command came, and still we took no notice, and then - WOW! A soldier with his rifle pointed at us stood and barred our way. We froze! We were speechless, but the soldier wasn't. He gave us a complete dressing down, and left us in no doubt that we should consider ourselves lucky that no serious consequences would come from our foolishness. We had learned our lesson, and much chastened, hurried away to board the train for home in a much more responsible mood.

The train journey home took hours and we felt tired and bored. When we got to Bangor some soldiers boarded making the train overcrowded and even darker than before. Somehow we got into a conversation with some Scottish soldiers who were stationed at Kinmel Camp, which was within a few miles of our neighbourhood. We chatted about this and that in the way you do with complete strangers and then they said they wanted to date us and finally my friend and I arranged to meet them in Abergele the following Saturday. We did not tell them who we were or where we lived but we went to Abergele the following Saturday to the agreed place but cautiously viewed the chaps from a safe distance before approaching them. One look was enough in daylight to know that we didn't like them, and we calmly walked by, ignoring them - they were clearly very worldly and far too old for us. So much for romantic train rides!

I had a number of boy friends over a period of time but I have never gone out with lads just for the sake of having a date. First of all, a boy had to be attractive and intelligent and had to know how to behave in a decent manner, with respect for me, just as I would behave towards him. Nothing was to be taken for granted. In this way I made many good friends even after I stopped seeing them regularly. There were one or two who thought that because I was petite and friendly, that they could go further in their advances than I wished but they soon got their marching orders. Once, when I was stood up, I felt anger and resentment, and humiliation too, although no one else was aware of my being stood up. Very soon afterwards I heard that the lad had been called up to war and that he was in the habit of drinking heavily. That was one time when my judgement of a person had been faulty, but it was one of those mistakes from which you learn about life.

During this time Minnie, one of my close friends joined the Royal Navy and eventually landed up in Ceylon (Sri Lanka today) in a place called Trincomalee. We kept in touch for a while, but she later married and settled in the south of England and since then I have seen her only twice.

I also had a pen friend called Eileen Corrigan, an American girl whose father was in the U.S Navy and stationed at Manila in the Philippines. We corresponded for a number of years and when I married she sent me nylon stockings and a set of beautiful, large white cotton sheets that I still use today. Eventually she stopped writing and I wondered whether her father had returned to the U.S.A. or perhaps she herself had got married - something had changed, but I know not what.

I think that my mother, like all mothers, was concerned during the War years when we were growing up that we did not get into bad company, get too intimate with boys, or worse still, get pregnant which was a frightful disgrace at the time. Youngsters were ignorant about sex and only a little information was available about precautionary aids such as condoms, known as French letters. They were available but not openly on sale and were very unattractive and awkward to use. I suppose it must have been a slight relief for my mother when I was appointed as a Precentor in Chapel and my friend Iris was appointed as an Organist. This involvement in Chapel work labelled us as 'good girls' and we were then committed to the monthly Rota system that meant we were expected to attend the morning and evening services in addition to our long-standing faithful membership of Sunday School.

Since childhood we had been fortunate enough to have attended good quality Sunday School classes run by effective teachers and are indebted to those people for opening our minds and for sharing their knowledge and wisdom with us: their very skilful insight into the developing minds of young people was remarkable. I think especially about one elderly gentleman who had seen hard days and experienced a lot of heartache, but had still kept his faith in God. A friend of my brother was our teacher in our late teens until he was called up for national service. He made a lasting impression on us because he taught us to think for ourselves.

I do not believe my being made a Precentor went down very well with the other two much older gentlemen in the Rota system, especially one who was downright awkward. Nevertheless, I enjoyed doing it and was quite capable I think. Many years later when the Chapel members were celebrating a Centenary and a half of the Chapel they asked me to conduct the *Gymanfa Ganu* (Singing Festival). I was very proud to do so. We had some marvellous singing that day: sopranos, altos, tenors and basses singing together in full harmony to create an absolutely thrilling sound.

In our youth Iris and I sang duets together and also competed against each other in solos in Eisteddfodau. After Iris left the village I continued to lead the singing in Chapel and had a Sunday School class as well, until I married and I too moved away from the village. She worked in a bank on the Wirral and eventually married a colleague. After her husband died, she continued to live there and we kept in touch each Christmas until she passed away two years ago.

When I was eighteen years of age and my sister Bella fifteen, we became closer and developed a more mature relationship. The age difference then seemed less important somehow and we spent more time together in the period before she left school to go to London to become a nurse. One Saturday evening in early summer, we had been for a walk and were returning home via a narrow public footpath above a meadow. The path led behind our aunt's farm and out into the road, close to our home. As we approached the gate leading to the farmyard, we saw a small tent against the wall and two lads crouching near a Primus stove. In those days I was very self-conscious and shy - and those who know me today find that statement unbelievable, but it is true. I have had to school myself along the years to change. Now I am self-confident and quite extrovert, but it was a struggle at one time and a hard one too. My sister on the other hand was not at all bothered about such things. When we saw the campers she called out, "Hello, who are you and what are you doing here?" They must have been surprised but replied in an equally friendly manner. Off she marched, with me following to see what was going on.

They were obviously cooking a meal in a frying pan and you never saw such a messy fry-up - everything in a heap frying away. The eggs had been cracked open and just dropped on top of the contents of the pan. Bella said, “That's no way to treat good food,” and one replied, “Why not - that's what it is like when it gets into your stomach.” A profound remark indeed that required no response! However, they were Welsh, had arrived on a motor bike and decided that it was a nice place to stop for the night. One was called Robin and the other, Wil Sam. They were very funny, especially Wil Sam, who asked, "And who are you?" When we told them our names he said, "Bet and Bella - I like that." It's strange how we can be so relaxed in the company of some people and feel as though we have known them all our lives. That is how it was with those two. We talked and laughed, then Bella and I went home, having promised to return the following day, which we did.

The weather was fine and we sat on the grass and the chatting and frivolity went backwards and forwards in such a natural fashion. I can remember that Robin lay on his back with his head on my lap, twiddling a piece of grass in his mouth. It was natural and lovely. They came from a village near Criccieth in the vicinity of Lloyd George's childhood home and were fervent Welsh patriots. Wil Sam was a mechanic and Robin worked in a milk factory before starting at University. Then they were gone.

However, some time later when he was at Bangor University I received a long, passionate letter from Robin. It was the first 'love' letter I had ever received and was surely the longest and most poetic too. My feelings were mixed - I was extremely flattered, very impressed and glad, and yet the whole thing was surreal. I showed the letter to no-one not even Bella nor did I divulge the contents to anyone, but I kept it safe for a long time. I eventually replied. I cannot remember exactly what I said, but I know it was a very stilted letter that conveyed friendly but not loving sentiments, it lacked the warmth that I would have preferred it to have had. A reply came in the same vein, which served me right, but I was disappointed all the same. While Robin was at college he became quite famous in Wales as part of a singing trio called *Triawd y Coleg* that broadcast a lot on the radio. He later became a Minister of Religion and Wil Sam, who owned a garage wrote very funny and successful plays. I feel privileged to have known them both.

During the War a lady from London and her young son stayed in the village as refugees from the bombing. The boy was to sit an entrance exam to a famous public school and she wanted someone to help him to prepare for the exam. My name was mentioned to her and she asked me to pay her a visit, which I did. She was pleasant enough in a supercilious and rather patronising way, which frankly 'grated' on me but she was offering to pay me quite well and I agreed to coach the boy. He responded well and apparently passed the exam and became a boarder and his mother eventually returned to London I suppose. However, during the weeks when I was coaching the young lad, his older brother arrived for a holiday from his placement at Sandhurst Military College. He was very nice and his manners were those of a perfect gentleman: later on when I was older, I am quite sure that I would have appreciated his demeanour much more than I did then. At that time however, his 'far-back' voice and perfect enunciation seemed affected and artificial, which of course was nonsense. That was his natural culture. He asked me once to go walking with him, and my sister and his young brother decided to go as well. We decided to climb Bodran Mountain by going up the side facing the village and along a fairly easy, zigzag pathway. When we reached the top the air was clear and the weather fine and we could see for miles. I regretted not having taken a picnic with us, but we sat a while to rest and enjoy the lovely views. Then I purposefully decided that we should descend on the other side of the mountain, which was covered in bracken and had the River Elwy flowing at the bottom. With wicked intent I sped down and shouted out,

"Come on, come on." Bella and I were used to the hills and steep slopes of the mountains and knew how to use our feet sideways thus braking the speed but they were novices obviously. Anyhow, the older lad, not to be outdone and willing to join in the fun started to run down and went faster and faster until he fell and then rolled down through the bracken and over the loose stone scree. Luckily, he managed to stop before reaching the river. He was shaken, scratched and probably bruised, and his suit was covered in grass and bits of undergrowth. He was courteous even then and I was ashamed. I think he knew that I had played a mean game, but he bore me no ill will and I learned a useful lesson. Never again did I presume to judge anyone before getting to know the person properly.

I found the travelling to and from work every day tiring on top of the busy day itself. But by this time I was judged to be competent enough to be moved to another part of the office where it was hectic and we no longer called for our work in measured amounts because it was brought to us daily according to the mail that had been received. Clerks opened the mail and attached letters and documents received to related files: they placed a pile of them on each desk. We just plodded along balancing the task of dealing with easy cases and more complex and time consuming ones too. All mental calculations were checked for accuracy on machines operated by the clerks. Perhaps the machines in use at that time were not capable of working out complicated calculations in the way calculators do today, but they were useful nonetheless. We have to remember the tremendous advance in technology that has taken place in the last 50 years! There was a need also for me to learn quickly the skill of dictating letters accurately to a typist who came round every morning for this purpose. The letters were sent to Solicitors, so they had to be done with care.

We all managed quite well on the whole, except when we'd been on holiday and had to return to a huge pile of work that had accumulated in our absence. It was not conducive to enjoying a holiday I have to say! If anyone was sick however, then everyone else was obliged to take on some of the work involved in the absence. In the five and a half years I worked there, I was on sick leave for only ten days. In fact, for the whole of my working life of twenty-seven and a half years, I was absent on sick-leave for a total of only two and a half weeks. I have been lucky enough to enjoy good health, although I have struggled to work many times having a bad cold, or suffering aches and pains when I would dearly have liked to stay at home. Many people behaved in the same way, such was the ethos of the time. We actually felt guilty when we were absent on sick leave, especially when we were at the stage of 'getting better'. I suppose we felt proud and appreciative of having a job per se and of being able and fit enough to do it. We believed that it was right and proper to do a good day's work for a good day's pay. I believe there is also a certain satisfaction and blessedness to be derived from the discipline involved in work when it is done well, its accomplishment is good for our soul and self-esteem. It is a cure for many ailments too. The reason why youth unemployment in particular should be avoided at all costs is because of its soul-destroying nature. Everyone should have opportunities to achieve worthwhile things and experience work satisfaction because they are so important to our wellbeing.

The Chief of my new Section was a much nicer man than the Chief of Review, who was short and overweight, rather supercilious and bossy. I don't think he was generally well liked, but my new boss was the complete opposite in being younger, slimmer and kinder, which is not to say that he was easy-going because he was a stickler for competence. I remember one day when I had arranged to go out after work for a meal and to a concert, I needed to leave work fifteen minutes early. Well, we all knew that no one could just go off early because we had to obtain permission to do so. So off I went to Mr. Reay's office. I was wearing a smart brown suit and a green Tyrolean hat with a brown feather stuck through the side. The style of the hat was such that it had to be worn at an angle, and it really was very attractive. I loved it. I also wore some green earrings. I knocked on the door and was told to enter. I explained my request and he said, "Well, what about your work. When will you be able to make up the time?" I replied that I had worked the time during the lunch hour and I had a clear desk. "Oh well, it seems you have it all planned so off you go." I thanked him and turned to leave. "By the way you should wear that hat more often. I like your earrings too," he said. I thanked him again and left feeling as if I'd won a million pounds.

From time to time difficulties arose with travelling home after work. It was fine in the morning but in the evening, things were apt to go wrong. For one thing, the bus company was expected to save on petrol consumption because many ships were being sunk and sailors killed attempting to bring goods including petrol into the country. So, all sorts of ways to save fuel were being trialled. Some buses had big containers on the back that were full of gas made from coal, which was plentiful of course. When travelling on level ground this worked well, but when going uphill it was such a slow process that the passengers could have walked faster. Consequently, if the bus was loaded it became so slow on the hills that it ran late and we would miss our connection.

On one such occasion, two of my friends and I were standing at the bus stop in Abergele waiting impatiently for the next bus home to Llanfair. Now you must remember that few people owned a car at that time and as there was petrol rationing only essential travel was possible, so there was very little hope of getting a lift. We were chatting and laughing and trying to kill time when, out of boredom more than anything, I declared that I would thumb a lift from the next vehicle that came round the corner. The girls laughed and joked about it knowing there was very little chance of anything coming along except the bus. Then along came a motorbike. The rider was a man in a scruffy cap and long coat and wearing gauntlet gloves. At once the girls shouted with glee … "Go on, go on, you said you would. You can't go back on your promise." They were enjoying my predicament and never thought I would dare to do it. Well I did … partly because I had recognised the rider. The bike came to a standstill and I was told to get on the pillion and hold on to him tightly, which I did. When we arrived near my home he stopped for me to get off and I thanked him and then out of politeness asked, "How much do I owe you?" as I was truly grateful to get home. He laughed saying he did not want any money from me. He was on his way home from work anyway but I could do something else if I liked. I glanced at him and he was looking quite serious, so I replied, "Well yes, of course I can," and he said "You can come to the pictures with me next Saturday - I shall be on the five o'clock bus to Rhyl." For a moment I was nonplussed, but I knew him to be a gifted musician and of a respected family, so I gathered my wits together and said, "Thank you: that would be nice." In such a fashion I started going out with Arthur, who was to become my husband.

Chapter Nine

ROMANCE IN THE AIR

The day I hitched a lift with Arthur was not the first time I had enjoyed a ride seated on the pillion of a motor bike, but never had I been on one quite so big and powerful. His bike was called 'The Panther' and there was a picture of one on it as I recall. In an attempt to use less petrol Arthur sold the powerful bike and replaced it with a smaller one.

I can understand why present day youngsters are attracted to glamorous, powerful bikes. There is something very alluring about the power of such machines and the ride is exhilarating. Now that I am older and I hope wiser, I can see how very dangerous they are too and how they need to be handled with great respect and skill.

Going to Rhyl to the cinema and coming home on the last bus at 9.30p.m at the end of the week was a treat for most young people and we had a good time travelling with our crowd. A few went dancing at The Queen's Pavilion but most went to one of the 3 cinemas - the Plaza, the Odeon or the Regal - we had a choice. Afterwards we went to the Chip Shop for fish and chips wrapped in greaseproof paper and old newspaper. We then had to rush to the bus station to queue in our usual orderly fashion for the bus, so the pleasure of eating our supper had to be postponed until we were seated on the bus.

Sometimes in the summer months, holidaymakers visiting caravan sites in the area would shove and push us in the queue. This caused some resentment because we knew they had only a short journey to make and had a choice of buses to use whilst we had a much longer way to go and had only the one bus available to us at that time of night. Once, I remember a large English lady trying her best to edge herself forward in the queue when one of the Welsh lads in front of her turned round, smiled broadly and said to her, "Stop huffing Mrs." And when she swore badly at him, he jovially said to her in Welsh, "*Cer yn ol i dy wlad dy hun yr hen chwaer*" (go back to your own country you old fool), and the whole crowd burst out laughing and she calmed down. That put a stop to her that night.

Sometimes, there would be one or two chaps who had imbibed too well and would be a bit of a nuisance especially for the poor bus conductor, but there was very little real drunkenness on the bus. Before I started going out with Arthur I would get off the bus in the village and make my way home with the other girls or a boy friend. There had been a few of these lads, but the relationships rarely lasted more than a few weeks. My sister recalled their names better than I did. There was Joel, an engineer who worked locally as a contractor - he was very tall and even when I wore my highest heels the top of my head still tucked nicely under his chin, which did not make kissing an easy option. Matters were resolved when his contract was completed and away he went.

Soon a new family came to live in the neighbourhood and I started going out with their son, Douglas. All that I remember about him is that he had nice manners and auburn hair and I liked him well enough, but before long he was called up to train in the Royal Air Force. And that was that! Later, towards the end of the summer I met a very good-looking lad called Meirion. He was tall and fair and very amusing and we had lots of fun together. He was a farmer who lived quite a distance away near Chester. He came to meet me on a motor bike and that was the fly in the ointment. The time came when he could neither beg nor borrow any more petrol coupons and so we were stuck. I hoped something would turn up because I liked him, but it was not to be and that was the end of a very promising romance.

My relationship with Arthur became steady after a few dates. He used to travel from his home on a bicycle round the Bodran Mountain and we would then go together on the bus to Rhyl. On our return to Llanfair we would have supper with my family before he walked or rode his bike back to his home in Llansannan again.

At first, I was a bit aloof but polite with him because he'd given me the impression that he rather fancied himself from the way he walked, but I was wrong. He was seven years older than me and was already a very successful pianist having gained a Silver Medal with Honours and had been elected a Licentiate of the London Guildhall School of Music and Drama. He also had an impish sense of humour. but could also discuss various matters very seriously and with great skill. He was a committed Christian who held very deep convictions and during the war worked on the land because he was a conscientious objector to killing, on account of the Christian teachings. It took tremendous courage to openly hold such views during wartime and many chapel people were very hostile indeed but strangely, the people who showed understanding and empathy were the veterans of World War I. Arthur told me he would gladly have done medical work in the war except that he was forced by the Tribunal he faced to do heavy agricultural work instead. The work he and other conscientious objectors ended up doing during the war was hard and often dangerous.

On leaving Denbigh Grammar School at sixteen having done well in his School Certificate Exam Arthur wanted to join a Solicitors Office in Denbigh as an articled clerk, but his father said he could not afford to pay the £75.00 deposit required, and so Arthur, like many other young men left school without having secured a job with prospects for the future. He found temporary jobs such as being a clerk for the Royal Welsh Show, and carrying out a survey for the local Council on overcrowding in houses. But finally, he worked for a local farmer as a general factotum - in the office, as a representative for his seed business and generally helping on the farm at busy times such as haymaking and harvesting - all for £1.00 per week! During the war, farmers were expected to turn over rough and overgrown land, often found in hard-to-access places on steep hillsides in an attempt to produce more food for families and fodder for animals. Risks were taken, accidents happened, and life was tough.

As a boy his father had taught him to play the piano and then in his late teens he advanced his studies and skills with a distinguished organist, Mr. John Williams F.R.C.O. in Bangor. Arthur rode his bicycle to Abergele then travelled by train to Bangor to his weekly lesson. He also studied Harmony with Dr. E.L.M. Pritchard by going to Trefnant on his bike after work. During the period of study before his Guildhall Examination in pianoforte playing he used to rise at 6.00 a.m. every day to practise scales, arpeggios and musical test pieces for two hours and a further three hours every evening after work. This was when he was nineteen years of age and was on the point of completing his studies for the L.R.A.M. Diploma when War put a stop to all exams. However, he was able to continue his harmony studies for composing music with Dr. Pritchard who was a Doctor of Music and Organist of Rhyl Parish Church unlike his father who had been a medical Doctor. Dr Pritchard had studied Music at Oxford with Dr. C. H. Kitson who was recognised by all as an authority in his field. Dr. Pritchard himself was a great teacher, but was a good example of the 'absent-minded professor'. He was a bachelor and lived in the village of Bodfari and on Saturdays he travelled by train to Denbigh to give lessons. He was around sixty years of age at the time.

On one occasion, after the teaching session in Denbigh, he made his way to the railway station to catch the train home. He had about ten minutes to wait so he started pacing up and down the platform becoming mentally engrossed in a harmony problem in music. Eventually, he returned to the reality of his situation and looked at his watch. "Well, well, this train is very late today, I'll speak to the station master" he said to himself. So he marched off to the office and very politely asked the man why the train was late.

"What train are you talking about?" asked the stationmaster. "Do you mean the train for Bodfari?" "Yes," he replied. "Well, goodness me, it's been and gone, some twenty minutes ago!" Poor Dr. Pritchard hadn't noticed, and there was nothing he could do except wait another hour and a half for the next train.

Fortunately, he had a very good housekeeper to look after him, and he really appreciated her, for he was forever singing her praises. On another occasion, he had invited the organist of St. Asaph Cathedral, his wife and daughter to tea at the house. The housekeeper had prepared a feast of goodies and laid everything out on the main table and additional side tables ready for serving. She was not available to serve the meal, but her presence was really not essential because she had attended to every detail before leaving the house. Everyone came to the table and Dr. Pritchard proceeded to serve the trifle, the cakes, and all the sweets, and then the organist's wife asked, "Dr. Pritchard, are we supposed to eat this cold meat and salad as well?" The old teacher was embarrassed and did not know what to say or do. Later on, relating the story to Arthur, he said, "I wished the floor would have swallowed me up." He was not a pompous man otherwise no one would have known of these mishaps.

Arthur was good looking and attractive to girls. His hair was a golden colour with a hint of a curl, he had blue eyes, nice teeth and a lovely smile.

We got engaged after a year or so of dating. I remember that we bought the ring in a shop on the High Street in Rhyl - a diamond solitaire in a setting of 18 carat gold. It was difficult to find a ring to fit, as my finger was so small. However, my ring was a second-hand one and cost just over £10.00. Don't forget, that was not a small sum then and all new rings during the war were made of only 9 carat gold. My wedding ring was one of those, and in time wore away the softer 18ct. gold band of my engagement ring, so I had to have it built up again. Luckily, I had my great-grandmother's wedding ring that had also suffered wear, and the jeweller was able to use it to repair my engagement ring. I still wear my ring at all times and never take it off. At that time, the jeweller valued my ring at £250.

After we became engaged I was invited to spend a weekend at Arthur's home. Although I knew his parents by sight I had never really spoken to them properly. I had a very warm reception and they had clearly gone to some trouble to make nice meals. The house had two bedrooms and a very small one under the eaves. Downstairs was a parlour, a kitchen/living room, a pantry and a scullery. There was no bathroom and the toilet was outside. Arthur's father slept with Arthur so his mother could share the double bed with me. The bed linen was fresh and shining white, but I was so embarrassed and uncomfortable and feeling guilty knowing how much work and bother my visit had caused. I was truly glad when it was time to leave. Probably his mother experienced similar feelings, I don't know. In all the time we spent together I had a certain feeling that although my pedigree was acceptable there was a little reluctance to be wholly pleased for

Arthur and me because I was 'modern', wore makeup and had a mind of my own. Nothing was ever said, well nothing directly, but it hung in the air from time to time. Well, it was the old 'no win' situation I suppose. No mother is ever 100% satisfied with her son's wife!

My father's cousin, Uncle Edward *Groes*, Aunty Lil's husband, was a successful farmer and District Councillor and was fond of buying things at sales. He'd bought a small organ and I was able to buy it from him. Arthur played it when he came to visit Llanfair and we had good old-fashioned singalongs with friends who visited from time to time and joined in the singing with us.

Finally, Peace was announced and The War came to an end. But during the latter years many political tracts and books were on sale, by the publisher, Victor Gollanz. The ideas outlined in these books started up public debate. 'Why not trust the Tories' was one book that outlined the case against the Tories who had been in power for many years, except for the Coalition during the War. Many men and women who had served in the armed forces wanted to return to a better lifestyle than the one that had met soldiers returning from the First World War 25 years earlier. In response to this, Labour was explaining its plans to provide work for all, a Welfare State, and a National Health Service. But despite the plans, many people believed that Winston Churchill and his Tory party would win the forthcoming General Election because he was held by many in high esteem as a heroic War leader. The lead-up to the election was all very exciting with big public meetings, speeches, heckling and posters everywhere. Arthur was a supporter of the Labour Party and I helped him by going round the constituency distributing leaflets and posters.

The day of the General Election finally dawned, and there was a very heavy poll. As the results came through, there was mounting tension and excitement on all sides, mostly because final results from all the constituencies were not as quickly available as they are nowadays. There was no Television to keep people informed, only the Radio and Newspapers. The result was a landslide for Labour and a shock for Mr. Churchill because it was his deputy, Mr. Clement Attlee who became Prime Minister. He was a very able man who had done a remarkable job during the War in organising the tasks of government. But it was Mr. Churchill who had inspired the people and whose spirit kept this country going when things looked very bleak after Dunkirk, and it was quiet Mr. Attlee who had kept the home fires burning.

Gradually things improved. We had lighting once again at night and no longer had to have blackout. Restrictions were eased in many ways but we still had rationing for some time after the war ended. Germany was a devastated land and the great Powers divided it into four zones, Russian, American, French and British. The British Zone was the industrialised area that had been heavily bombed and was completely ruined.

When the Russians became awkward at the start of the Cold War, Britain had to airlift food and supplies into the British Zone and that meant we in Britain had to share our food, therefore rationing remained. There was so much to do in the country: soldiers, sailors, airmen and women were returning to civilian life; factories that had all been converted to wartime production, had to be changed back again to produce the many things that were needed for replacement or renewal. Our country had spent all its financial resources on the War effort. Our bombed cities had to be rebuilt, houses for people, offices, shops and other essential items like schools and hospitals. At first everyone was so glad that the War was over that they tolerated the inevitable discomforts of its aftermath. However, just as we felt things improving, there was a war in Korea against the Communists that upset everything again and in the early 1950s the Tories were able to stir up resentment against the continuing rationing and shortages in the UK. It was not then surprising that the Tories won the next General Election and formed the Government in 1951 despite the fact that the Labour Government had done so much to improve life in Britain in such a short time in the face of so many difficulties. It is only people of my generation who can fully understand and appreciate the tremendous improvements that were brought about by the vision and determination of the post war Labour Government.

I can remember waiting for my bus home from work in Llandudno the evening when Peace was announced; I saw a crowd of office cleaning women emerging from a public house in town - presumably having been thrown out. They were celebrating the Peace by having a right old fight amongst themselves and were screaming, swearing, punching and shoving each other and pulling hair. I was not quite sure whether I ought to feel disgusted by the scene or not, but the bus came before I had reached a conclusion on the matter. I think on reflection however, that my opinion was that they were demeaning themselves at the time, but I suppose it could have been their way of finally throwing off the worries of a long War that had affected us all in some way or other.

My father was now home again and working for the Council. Also, due to ill health, one of the local butchers employed my father part-time as his stand-in. Dad was a fully qualified time-served Master Butcher and the shop opened in the evening only, so it suited him. Eventually, my father was able to purchase the business and take on the work full-time with my mother's help, and they ran a good business for themselves. There were no fridges then, only netting cupboards, but the tables and chopping stands were scraped and scrubbed every night. The cleaver, knives and cutters were scalded and everything was cleaned scrupulously. There were never any Salmonella or E-coli outbreaks in those days. Shops treated food with respect and care. The meat ration for every person was not very big and naturally everyone wanted the best joints for their share. At the end of the week there would be small bits left over and Mam boiled them on the bone in a large pan that produced stock for soup and enough meat for our supper on Saturday evenings that was piled on a platter, from which we happily helped ourselves. It sounds like poor fare, but believe you me, we thoroughly enjoyed it, and were grateful for it too. My father and mother also made sausages from their own special recipe, which were very popular with everyone.

I had a new friend at work called Sal Thomas from Carmarthenshire. She had a B.A. degree and was a Welsh speaking girl. We got on very well together and had some great times. We still keep in touch at Christmas, and last year, were able to meet at the National Eisteddfod in Denbigh. We had not seen each other for nearly fifty years and yet, our meeting felt so natural and pleasant and we knew each other straight away in spite of grey hairs!

My sister, who had always wanted to be a Nurse, was accepted to train at St. Mary's Hospital in Paddington and although it was one of the finest hospitals in London, Bella was not happy there. Going from a small village in Wales to a large bustling hospital in a noisy city area was too much of a cultural shock and she moved to Hampstead General Hospital near the Heath, where she was very happy.

On one occasion, Arthur and I had arranged to go to Rhyl to see a special film. I had been looking forward to seeing the film for days, but when Saturday afternoon came, there was no sign of Arthur, nor any message. I was terribly disappointed and I am very sorry to say that I was extremely petulant. My parents tried to reason with me saying there must be some very good reason and anyway, there would be other good films to see. Well, none of us is perfect and my behaviour on that occasion was immature and unfair. Later that evening, Arthur turned up and got a very cool reception until he explained that he had been bargaining for a second hand car - a little Austin Seven.

The film was soon forgotten in the exciting news and the following weekend saw us both busy cleaning and polishing that little car. I was doing the inside and I took out and cleaned everything that would come out, because it had been used previously by a farmer for farm work and was in need of a really good clean. When we finished the job, the little Austin was shining and gleaming and we were very proud of it. We had a lot of pleasure driving round the neighbourhood in the car and it was also a cosy little area of privacy for a courting couple. It was a useful vehicle for Arthur to use to travel to various villages to give piano lessons that brought in useful money for our savings account.

Before the advent of our car we travelled everywhere by bus, and once, when Arthur had an afternoon off he came to Llandudno to meet me. He wanted to buy me a present for Christmas and I fancied an umbrella. We went round the shops and finally decided on a nice blue one from Arnolds, a very elegant shop, regrettably not there any more. We caught the 6.00 p.m bus for home and of course it was dark at that time at the end of November. I remember that it was very foggy and I believed there was a sea mist too that we sometimes saw inland in Llandudno. By the time we got to Colwyn Bay the double-decker bus was full with many people having to stand, and the fog had become so dense that the conductor had to walk up the hill in front of the bus with a torch in his hand to guide the driver. When we reached Penmaen Head the driver could not, or would not go any further so we had to use Shanks' pony. We had to walk quite far through Llanddulas and had reached the Lodge to Gwrych Castle when a passing single-decker bus stopped and let us on despite also being packed. We were pleased that it got us to Abergele, but then we had to start the 5 mile walk home to Llanfair.

The fog was absolutely thick - you could not see your hand in front of your face. Still, we knew the road well and there was no traffic, but there was an eerie muffled silence all around. We were whispering as we spoke to each other: I don't know why we didn't speak normally, it seems very odd now. When we started going uphill we knew we were near the 'Sanatorium' but after about five hundred yards we realised we were on the wrong road, the ground was much too soft underfoot. So we had to move right across to the hedge to retrace our steps down to the main road. We started climbing again and believed that the fog at the top of the hill would not be quite as problematic, but it was only marginally better. We could now however just about make out the outline of the white line at the centre of the road. This was progress, so we peered at the line and followed it all the way home. How glad we were to get into the house! We were frozen and damp and both of us had a headache from staring at the road. When I got to bed I could not sleep and I could not get rid of that white line from my mind. Arthur still had to get his bike and walk home - another three miles. Luckily, the next day was a Saturday, and we did not have to go to work. I have never forgotten that night and although I was not frightened because I was with Arthur, I was nevertheless mindful of the eerie and strange effects of the fog.

Arthur was still working for the Agriculture Board and was chafing to get free because he had decided to start his own business in music teaching. However, his old employers wanted him back and Arthur did not want that because of the poor wages. So the situation was at an impasse. The Board Committee would not release him unless he went back to his old job. The Chair of the Committee was an old aristocratic woman, who really was a tyrant - a typical 'throw-back' to a previous century. But the war had changed many things and Arthur was advised to go and consult with a man who was in the Employment Office. When that man heard how matters stood, he immediately reacted by saying it was unjustified and smacked of bullying. “They can't do this. They have no right. Leave it to me. I'll sort them out,” he said. A meeting was arranged and true to his word that man stood up and demolished the spurious arguments, and Arthur was free to get on with his life.

At this time during 1946, Arthur lost a very dear friend. Both were the same age and had known each other for a long time. The Rev. Herber Evans was from Llanrhaeadr in the Vale of Clwyd and had not received the benefit of secondary schooling. But, in his late teens he entered *Coleg Clwyd* in Rhyl, which was a preparatory establishment for students entering the Ministry, before going to College. It was part of the Presbyterian Church in Wales. After passing exams he entered the University of Wales at Aberystwyth, had to overcome many hardships and work extremely hard before finally succeeding in gaining his degrees BA, and BD. He also had an outstanding and unforgettable baritone singing voice. He lived meagrely in order to pay for singing lessons from a well-known and distinguished professional singer. Herber became well known by winning prizes singing at Eisteddfodau and concerts all over Wales. He was an impressive preacher too, not least because of his sincerity and warmth. He was a very special personality.

Soon after his induction he was appointed as Minister of a Chapel in mid Wales and was overjoyed to be able to carry out the work of God that he was so eager to do. He was a handsome man with twinkling eyes, and was always cheerful and helpful. He was engaged to a lovely girl who was a French teacher in Macclesfield. Everything he had striven for in all those years had come right for him, but soon however, he was plagued by health problems, and before long was admitted to hospital. Within the year he was dead. Arthur and I found it very hard to come to terms with his loss, it was inexplicable. Herber's friends were devastated, his family and fiancée must have suffered beyond words. To the end his faith in Jesus was as strong as ever and he passed away serenely. He was only twenty-eight years old.

Herber was a wonderful person, and there are two special things that stand out in my memory about him. One is that he preached a sermon about God being in charge of the world and his Creation, and to illustrate his message he spoke of a ship on the high seas being tossed around in a terrible storm. Many of those on board were in fear of their lives, but the small daughter of the Captain was full of confidence and was shouting to everyone, “Daddy is by the wheel.” I can still hear him repeating those words, singing them out loudly in his wonderful voice. In fact my sister subsequently used to call him, “Daddy is by the wheel.”

Once, when Herber was at my home in Llanfair with Arthur, we all enjoyed a wonderful sing-along and then Herber sang a solo to Arthur's accompaniment on the organ. He sang, 'There is No Death' and I can truly say that his rendering of it seemed to enter into the depths of my very soul. I cannot express it any other way. His death was a tragic loss, not only for his nearest and dearest, but also for society at large. Sometimes I am unable to understand or explain how or why such an outstandingly gifted and dedicated person should be struck down at such an early age when he had so much to give of benefit to others.

Before the War our Chapel had organised an annual Eisteddfod that was held in a small marquee and refreshments were prepared in the adjacent Memorial Hall. It was a very popular event and competitors came from far and near. One who used to come on his motor bike was a young joiner with a wonderful tenor voice. He was David Lloyd who became a celebrity after winning a scholarship to the London Guildhall School of Music. Indeed most of the competitors had wonderful voices. On the morning of the Eisteddfod the children and young people competed. I took part myself in the singing and elocution classes and won prizes on many occasions. The Eisteddfod was always held on a Saturday and as a special treat, we children were allowed to stay up late so we could enjoy the evening meeting until the end, which was around midnight. The only stipulation was that we had to sit in the front row and behave! Sometimes this was difficult, for some of the singers and elocutionists showed some very funny expressions on their faces during their performances and we had to stifle our giggles and stuff our hankies into our mouths so that no sound emerged. We listened to solos from the oratorios and operas and unconsciously absorbed much culture.

When I was very young there was one occasion when I sang a solo in a competition and felt a little nervous at first until I started to sing, and then immediately settled down. Everything was then going well until suddenly - calamity! I felt a ping … and I knew that the elastic band in my knickers had snapped. For a second I felt panic, then quickly decided to carry on clutching desperately at the clothes around my waist. Perhaps it added a degree of *oomph* to my performance, for I won first prize! On an earlier occasion when only four years old and competing for the first time on stage, I was very nervous, and when 'Uncle Pencoed' asked me how I had fared I replied, “Oh fine, but I would have done better if the stage had kept still.”

During the year after the end of the War, I suggested to the Deacons of the Chapel that we should restart the Eisteddfod and they agreed provided that I became the Secretary. I agreed and a Committee was set up. It all went very well and the following year's event was also a success. By the time the third year's preparations were starting I had left Llanfair and other people had taken over and succeeded likewise. I am glad to say that the *Llanfair Eisteddfod* is still being held annually and is very popular with competitors.

Chapter Ten

SUDDEN CHANGE

The Labour Government did a tremendous amount of work during those years after the War. There was such devastation and the difficulties were colossal. There was a determination that all the returning service men and women should have jobs to go to and so there was very little unemployment. Public utilities were nationalised, indeed, there was no other way to rationalise and organise services. Gas, electricity, coal, water, the railways had struggled during the War years and during the Depression in the 1930s. Only what was strictly necessary had been spent on the country's infrastructure during those bleak years. These essential industries were spread over parts of the country in small disparate units but most of the rural areas had no gas or electricity supplies at all. The numerous companies that existed within the industries were finally brought under one command by the Labour Government and a slow process of integration and investment was introduced. A supply of electricity was offered to every habitation in the land for a subsidised price and most people were glad to accept. It took a number of years to complete the project and a few more to break even financially. But as soon as profits started to flow, the Tory government, in power at the time, decided to split up the industries again and privatise the lot. Madness! The Treasury could have benefited so much and our taxes reduced as a result.

The biggest improvement however was the birth of the Welfare State and the National Health Service. The original plans had been put forward by Lord Beveridge, a Liberal, but they were adopted and implemented with some amendments by the Labour government.

Aneurin Bevan, a Member of Parliament from Tredegar, South Wales, was the Minister entrusted with the National Health Service (NHS) Act and to steer it through Parliament. He was able, skilful and passionately determined, and succeeded in the face of fierce opposition from the Tory members. To a man, they fought against it and voted accordingly. Arthur and I were in London for a few days at the time and we spent a day in the Public Gallery at the House of Commons listening to the Debate. Aneurin Bevan was in total command of the proceedings and had memorised and internalised every related detail of the Act and could answer all the questions without having to consult any notes or documentation - he was very impressive. Our M.P. at the time was Sir Henry Morris Jones, a medical Doctor practising from Harley Street in London. He belonged to the Liberal-National Party upholding Tory policies. He rose to speak and put forward all sorts of objections but Mr. Bevan rose to answer all the points made. He then added words to the effect that the Bill would ensure that all doctors including those from exclusive practices in wealthy areas would in future have to exercise their skills for the benefit of all people wherever there was a need.

After we became engaged, Arthur and I started to save money in earnest and it was not too difficult really because there were still shortages and some rationing, which meant that there was not a lot available to entice us to spend our money. However, we did manage to have a short holiday in Holyhead. A friend of mine knew of a lady who owned a Guesthouse there, which was recommended. I had been working for a number of years and my salary had increased accordingly. We decided to make a reservation for a week there, and when the time came we set off in the little Austin.

It was summertime so it was warm. The Guesthouse needed redecoration but it was clean and the food was plain but wholesome. We had a bedroom each but spent some time together in each other's rooms, for there was no separate lounge. We did not sleep together however - you just did not do things like that in those days. Besides, it would have seemed to be tempting Fate!

The weather was gorgeous and we sunbathed - we were quite tanned on our return home. We also explored Anglesey and got lost many times - there were so many class B roads and lanes and no signposts. When War started all the signposts and names of places everywhere were taken away in case of infiltrators and spies.

If this story has been a little higgledy-piggledy in relating how things were during the time just before the end of the War and afterwards, then dear Reader, you have to bear with me because that was precisely the situation with much upheaval and change. Fifty years have elapsed and memories don't always come in the right order. Recollections are buried under a mountain of events and thoughts, and influences occur without any probing or prodding.

Our brains are surely and truly wonderful, but I believe that we are merely on the fringes of understanding the capability of the human brain. It will eventually become as good as, if not better than the most powerful computer. This, to me, is one of the most compelling of reasons for believing that there is a God or some Supreme Being. We have come a long way since humans first appeared on Earth, but all along we have developed because we DISCOVER the rules and theories of the Universe: Man did not INVENT the formulae, they were already there and in place since the Beginning. And who knows what else lies undiscovered.

I must not get carried away with these wondrous things because I have a lot more of the story to relate.

The year of 1946 drew to a close and Christmas was much the same as every other year except that my sister was not at home with us. She was on duty at the hospital in London. I asked her once how they could have celebrations in a hospital with very ill people being treated there. She said that they did not have really noisy celebrations and that seriously ill patients were protected at all times. Carol singers toured the wards, children's wards were decorated, Santa Claus arrived and presents were given and received, and games were played. Off duty nurses enjoyed the usual Christmas festivities. She said that unless Doctors and Nurses let their hair down sometimes they would be unable to cope, working as they did every day amidst suffering. It was the restoration to health and well being of the patients that made it all worth their while.

My brother came home as usual. His friends were married by now so their little social gatherings at our house were no more. My mother was not isolated in the shed in the middle of feathers any more either, but she and Dad were busy until the last hours before Christmas serving their customers with fowls, meat and their popular sausages and stuffing. We had a nice family Christmas Day: Arthur came in the evening and on Boxing Day too. Then everyone went back to work and normality returned - until mid January 1947 when Mam became seriously ill and had to remain in bed to rest. This meant that I had to stay home from work to look after her and also help my father in the shop.

It was a strange feeling. I had gone to work and completed a busy day, tidied my desk and saw everything right for the following morning then left the office and the building. Never to return! My life as a Civil Servant working in an office came abruptly to an end after five and a half years. I had learned a lot from various people who were very much like the rest of us in Wales in many ways, but different too - they were Londoners. I made a number of new friends and became used to being an independent young woman. Looking back I can honestly say that there was only one obnoxious person with whom I had to work and fortunately, it was only for a relatively short time. He was disabled and in his sixties - he walked with two sticks. He must have been crippled with rheumatism for he was very bandy-legged. I felt very sorry for him, but he had a sarcastic manner and was literally a chain smoker. He always had a cigarette between his lips, with little piles of ash all over his suit and a full ashtray and he refused point blank to let us open a window. We sat, worked, and breathed in this smoke laden air with goodness knows what damage to our eyes and lungs. It was horrible.

Thank goodness there were others who were friendly, jovial and good-humoured. One young man who returned after the War was just such a one. He would stand behind my chair and EAT my hair, well not exactly! He would gather strands of my hair and pass them through his lips. He said he liked the smell of my hair! But that was all, he liked me, but he never made a pass at me or took any advantage. He was married, I was engaged and that was that. It must be hard for today's young people to understand that this was how things were in those days. There was much more restraint and self-discipline I believe.

When I reached home from work to learn that Mam was ill and ordered to rest for some weeks, I had to tender my resignation. Normally, it was necessary to work a period of notice but in the circumstances this was impossible. I cannot recall what happened about my pay. In any case, all the staff knew that the offices were leaving Llandudno before long, not to return to London, but to the Home Counties. My office was going to Worthing and of course, I could not go because I was engaged to be married, and would continue to live in North Wales. There followed a new phase in my life.

It was necessary for me to get up very early to get breakfast and make a packed lunch for my father who was now working for the local Council as a road-maintenance man. It was January, dark and freezing cold. There was no electricity or gas, just coal fires, lamps and candles. Brrr! At the time, although far from enjoyable, it was not so bad because it was what we were used to and had to make the best of things. Getting up early was nothing new for me because to get to work I had always got up just after 6.30a.m in time to eat some breakfast and catch the 7.10a.m bus. Anyhow in this new phase of my life, the days were very full. Mam was getting better, but of course she needed attendance. I soon got into a routine and January came and went and February came along with sunny weather and frosts. Towards the end of the month, snow started to fall and it was the fine powdery snow that packed hard and was slow to thaw. Then we had a hard frost overnight and the sun on the following day melted the surface until it was like glass and very hard to walk upon. More snow fell and the wind got up and there were snowdrifts … deep ones. This pattern was repeated many times with the result that it was impossible for cars or buses to travel. For over six weeks, no bus came to the village. The roads were blocked and people walked on top of hedges. Indeed, that was the only way to get to Abergele town to buy bread and other necessities. Gangs of men were hard at work trying to clear the roads but as soon as they were partially opened, down came more snow and more frost. At some exposed high areas, the walls of frozen snow were even higher than the tallest of the workmen who were attempting to cut a way through them. I cannot remember anything like it, before or after 1947.

I can remember a couple buying a smallholding near the village - they were very cultured people, especially the wife and he was a clever man with a B.Sc. degree but sadly, he was also an alcoholic. During this time, spirits were in short supply, especially whisky and whenever it was reported on the grapevine that there were supplies at such and such a pub, the couple would drive there at once. His wife would accompany him to drive the car if necessary. One night he heard that a pub in a nearby village had whisky, so off he went driving at speed on the treacherous roads. He finally landed in the middle of a snowdrift and the more he revved to get the car out, the more embedded it became. He was stuck there until a farmer on a tractor helped him when he happened to go by the next day, but even that experience did not cure him.

From time to time, when government rules allowed, he would kill a pig, or rather ask my father to slaughter the animal and cut the carcass into appropriate parts. Some pieces were salted and processed as normal, but Dad was given special recipes for curing and was required to treat the meat in unusual ways. It meant using sugars, salt, honey, spirits and spices, and all with wonderful results! The couple left the village eventually but the man died quite young. I believe his wife remarried.

I got my second cat from that smallholding, another black and white one that I named Whiskers. This one was also wild, having lived with a group of feral cats on the farm and I had to spend time taming him, but he was lovely and worth all the bother.

During the snowbound weeks my sister had her appendix removed in the London hospital and came home to recuperate. She arrived by train at Pensarn Station in Abergele and Arthur went to fetch her in the Austin. This was not at all easy. By now the snowplough had managed to cut a track in the snow to Abergele but the space between the wheels of the Austin Seven was much narrower and the car kept sliding about on the icy surface. However, the journey was completed successfully and it was very nice to have my sister's company again. While she was home she took Arthur and me to task, and wanted to know what our plans were about getting married. Quite honestly, we did not have any. “Well it's about time you started thinking seriously about it” she declared, “You *are* going to get married aren't you?”

“Well, yes of course, but what with the war and now the weather, things have not been normal or easy have they?” I replied. “Good heavens, you have been engaged for nearly four years, how long do you need? All through the war years, when the future was very uncertain, couples continued to get married. Come on, fix a date and we can all start planning” said bossy sister. Well, she had a point I had to admit, so we finally came up with the date of the wedding - Saturday 2nd August 1947.

My sister recovered and returned to London, my mother was getting better and Arthur and I began to discuss plans - where were we going to settle, where and how would we find a house? Very few new houses had been built since the war and most were small pre-fabricated houses with priority given to the bombed town areas. As it happened, events caught up with us. Arthur's mother saw an advertisement in a religious paper, a vacancy for an Organist and Choir Master at Seion Chapel, Llanrwst. It carried a monthly salary of £8.00, a tidy sum in 1947 and Arthur was interested in the job, and his parents were very keen on the idea. Some people from the Llanrwst area visited their home and urged Arthur to put in for the post, which he finally did. He was interviewed and the requirements of the job explained. He would need to attend morning and evening services and afternoon Sunday School every Sunday and prayer meetings every evening during the first full week in the New Year - plus any special events that could take place from time to time. He would play at all funerals and weddings at the Chapel but he could charge for his services at such events. There was no regular choir as in a Church, but one would be formed from the congregation as and when required. The demands were quite onerous but at that time the post carried a high status and his services as a Teacher of Music would be in demand. Arthur already had quite a number of pupils scattered in the villages, some who would continue to have lessons when we moved to Llanrwst. He was appointed to the job and would start on the first Sunday in May. It was a testing time because on this particular Sunday every year there were special services and the day was known as *Sul y Blodau* (The Sunday of the Flowers).

I was getting really interested by now and quite excited by what was in store. Arthur was naturally a bit apprehensive but confident in his ability. His favourite instrument was the piano and although he had played organs at chapel services for years, the pipe organ at Seion was something else! It had been built in 1914 at a cost of £1000.00, to a specification of the distinguished resident Organist of the time. It is still there at Seion and has three manuals with a full range of wooden foot pedals and many stops on both sides of the manuals that help create different effects including a thrillingly powerful bass sound. Arthur consulted another church organist friend who advised him and explained the finer points of playing such a wonderful instrument. Arthur began practising on local pipe organs for many hours. Most of these were old and required someone to pump air into the bellows and of course, most of the time, that someone would be yours truly - well, I was young and strong and glad to be of use. The organ in Seion however did not require air provided manually I am glad to say, and Arthur soon started to enjoy playing it. He had the skills needed to fill the chapel with soul-stirring music that was conducive to high quality singing too.

However, there had been another happening in 1947 of which I knew nothing at the time. Before accepting the Llanrwst job, Arthur had been approached by an old school friend who had offered him a job in Llansannan. Readers will perhaps remember that before the war Arthur had worked at a local farm as a general factotum doing office and farm work, but mostly selling seeds and other materials used by farmers. This school friend was the elder son of the owner of another local firm. The mother was dead, the father was middle-aged, a Councillor and a busy man. The family also had a general store and Post Office in the village. The friend was a very successful Barrister in London who believed that his younger brother needed some assistance from a trusted person to promote and develop the seed business and he offered the job to Arthur. He in turn discussed the offer with his parents who thought that the Chapel Organist job would be more suitable as it carried more prestige. I was not informed or consulted until after he had refused the local job and had accepted the Chapel position. I was furious, mostly because I had not even been told anything, and I told Arthur that he had made a mistake, but of course the deed was done. I wanted him to change the decision, but he did not think that it would be honourable to do so.

Many years later Arthur confessed that he had regretted his decision, and that I had been right. Life would have been much easier and so much more beneficial for him.

With the decision having been made, I accepted the situation with good grace and started to think of the practicalities. We knew we had to look for a house in Llanrwst, but it was easier said than done. We hunted, we enquired and we walked. There were no houses to let. Arthur and I had both saved and I remember that I had just over £500.00 and he had a little less. We would make a down payment on a house, but of course lots of other things were needed too, furniture, curtains, crockery and so on let alone the expenses of a wedding. Finally we heard of a nice semi-detached house built and owned by a local builder, occupied by the wife and children of an insurance agent who had been moved to another agency in South Wales. He also had the problem of not being able to find a house but the owner promised to give us the first option to buy this house when it was vacated. It was an attractive modern house, built in the 1930s in a pleasant area. I was very happy about everything then and looking forward to setting up home there. While we were still in the process of hunting for a house, we had seen and passed by, several times, a big tall house in Llanrwst that we were told was vacant and for sale. We never even considered acquiring the house, because it was far too big and not at all suitable.

Happy that we had the promise of a house, Arthur was getting organised for the first Sunday in May, when he would begin his work. For two weeks beforehand, he had to attend rehearsals. Every year the format was the same and programmes were printed giving particulars of all the service items, and the names and titles of those taking part. In the morning it was the turn of the young children, starting with the toddlers singing as groups. Some were shy, others knew exactly what they had to do and a few could not have cared less and just looked round the building staring at people in the congregation. It was all so lovely and wonderful. Sometimes it would not be particularly harmonious because even at that tender age there were singers who sang 'bass' in their boots and little sopranos singing 'descants' but everyone was giving of his or her best. Of course, there would be individual singers, readers and speakers who had been practising and aiming for near perfection. There was also hymn singing by the congregation and around half way through the programme a guest speaker addressed the children. Depending on how interesting the subject was, and how able the speaker, there would be concentration and reaction from the children or lots of shuffling feet, whispering and teachers hush-hushing. In the afternoon it was the turn of young teenagers taking part and another speaker. In the evening the service included some items by individuals, solos, duets, readings, sometimes sketches and a short address by the Minister. Everyone wore a posy of fresh flowers and children showed off their new clothes … and some grown-ups as well! Everyone looked happy and very pleased with themselves. This was a special day and it was always uplifting and enjoyable.

However, on this first occasion it was full of care for Arthur. There was no master of ceremonies and the programme was followed with each person going forward to take part quietly and without announcement. The organ was very powerful and those little children had to have the musical accompaniment without drowning their little voices. On the other hand adults would require appropriate background music to suit their voices and their songs. Arthur did this superbly, without a hitch. He had come through his first test with flying colours.

In the same month of May, the District *Gymanfa Ganu* (Singing Festival) was held at Seion. All the Chapels in the surrounding areas, 10 or 12 of them, gathered to sing hymns from a specially printed Schedule. Rehearsals had been held for weeks and all singers would know the hymn tunes, the chant and the anthem. There was a guest Conductor and with that great organ and a good Organist, it really was a thrilling event.

Seion Chapel has a large gallery and in all, can accommodate over one thousand people. In those early years, late 1940s/50s, you had to be in Chapel at least 30 minutes before the start, otherwise you would have to sit on an inner windowsill, steps or extra benches.

Seion is a beautiful Chapel. Even though I had come from a small village Chapel, I always felt at ease in that great Chapel. The building consisted of the Deacons' Room and the Caretaker's house and up the stone stairs leading from the back door was the Lecture Room where weekday services were held, concerts, the children's Eisteddfod in February and the Sunday School for the older children. The younger children used a separate small building in the Chapel grounds, and had it all to themselves. It was part of an older Chapel and by now has been demolished, and not before time either, for it was very damp and musty and not at all suitable for children of any age.

The Organ at Seion is magnificent. I believe that it was built by 'Norman and Beard' - a renowned firm. There was only one other like it in Wales and that was in Aberystwyth. Recently the chapel in Aberystwyth was demolished and the organ given to a Church in Sri Lanka where it was rebuilt. The frontage of the organ is imposing with all the pipes that are for show only, but it's the large area behind the facade where the action takes place. There is one stop in the bass section that has housing nearly as large as a small room. It is to the credit of the Chapel that the Organ has been looked after so well for all the years since 1914. Qualified tuners from the firm that built the organ came regularly and once, I remember a major overhaul being done that involved two men working for six weeks. It all cost a lot of money.

Now I return to that first Gymanfa Ganu for Arthur as Organist. The conductor that year was a lady, a gifted vocalist of great vigour who had decided that the congregation should be woken up and encouraged to put some spirit into their singing. This was all very well for some of the hymns but others needed more sensitive treatment. However, all were conducted with pace, indeed with speed! The singers scarcely had time to take a breath. It was a lively meeting but not one of her better ones. I knew the lady well, one of the best. But for Arthur with all the stops, three keyboards and foot pedals it needed nerves of steel and total concentration to follow the Conductor's movements. Again he successfully got through his second test with honours. Having been thrown in at the deep end in his first month, he was away in the job! He mastered that Organ and used it to great effectiveness. During services there was no need of a Precentor, Arthur played the music with his right hand and both feet and conducted with a raised left hand. People said that he made the Organ speak!

I remember a cortege leaving the Chapel after a funeral service when he played the 'Dead March' with such profound effect that most people were openly weeping. There was something in the music with that deep note, the 32ft stop recurring again and again that touched a raw nerve and seemed to stir one's very soul.

Eventually, he ceased to use that particular music unless it was specifically asked for because he felt it was too distressing for the bereaved.

Weddings were quite different of course, but equally effective. None was like any other. Each couple wanted their day to be special and most were specific in their choices. Sometimes Arthur would help couples in choosing the music because he had an extensive repertoire to offer.

One of the 'different' weddings that took place in Seion was when the late Leila Megane, the famous opera singer and diva, married her second husband. This lady was born in the Lleyn Peninsula, near Pwllheli. She had a remarkable Mezzo Soprano voice and had trained with Jean de Reske in Paris. She had sung opera in all the great cities including London, New York, and Milan. Her first husband was a well-known musician and composer, Osborne Roberts, and they led a very successful life together. Eventually, they returned to Pentrefoelas where he had been born, and they helped many aspiring singers for some years. After the death of Osborne Roberts, Leila Megane was eventually sought out by a widower from Lleyn who had been a great friend of hers in their youth and finally they decided to marry. Now Leila was a Diva and acted accordingly. Everything had to be different and special and perfect! If she visited our house once, she visited a dozen times. Of course, no one dreamt of gainsaying her at all, for she was Leila Megane. Well, thank goodness for some characters like that with a bit of colour about them. They may drive you up the wall sometimes but they get away with it because they make it all worthwhile. Many of the great and the good had been invited to the wedding ceremony but only a few were invited to the wedding reception!

After the May start, Arthur travelled to Llanrwst every Sunday for the day. He was excused the weekday meetings until we had actually taken up residence in Llanrwst. People were very good to him and he was invited to several homes for lunch and tea, but there was one family that was exceptionally good to him - Mr. and Mrs. Solomon Jones in Watling Street. Mrs. Jones had a small café open on weekdays and had a band of loyal customers because of the good food she cooked and served. She fed Arthur so many times, free of charge, until it became embarrassing, but she would not take payment. The house we wanted was still occupied and June, July, August, September and October, had come and gone and still no house.

Chapter 11

MARRIED LIFE

We arranged our wedding day to take place on the 2nd of August and happily prepared for it. Shortages and restrictions were still with us after the war and there was very little in wedding finery available and even that was very expensive. My sister and I went to a fine shop in Colwyn Bay called Woods in Station Road, and bought two lots of similar material, a fine crepe, orchid pink for me and a lovely pale lime colour for Bella with her auburn hair. Miss Davies, the skilled dressmaker who had made all our best clothes since childhood made the wedding dresses too. The style of the dresses was classically simple, but there were dozens of small round buttons covered in the dress material that ran down from the nape of the neck to a low waist at the back and from the elbows to the wrists on the long sleeves. Miss Davies said to me, "The guests will see more of your back than your front, so it must be interesting." We carried enormous bouquets of sweet peas and maidenhair fern. We had two or three fittings and I hated them because of the need to stand still for long periods, getting pins stuck in all kinds of delicate places and having to hang around in a petticoat, waiting for permission to move. But, the dresses did look nice. We each had a plaited band of the dress material in our hair. There were no veils or anything like that and I cannot remember the shoes I wore, but I do recall my 'going-away' ones because they were so very special. I had bought them in Llandudno. They had very high heels, were a size two and a half and made of beautiful royal blue leather with peep toes. The dressmaker had also made a suit for me to wear when going away on honeymoon - a lovely skirt and blouse-type top in a cerise colour with an off-white wool coat, navy hat, gloves and handbag. I had all this to wear on a scorching hot day in August! Well, we had to conform to conventional style - and it was our special day for showing off after all!

The wedding took place at Soar Chapel in Llanfair, and the service was led by the Rev. Cadnant Griffith. Our wedding breakfast was held in the Memorial Hall in Llanfair and a couple from Llansannan did the catering. It was a very nice meal - salads, cold meats, pickles, bread and butter, trifles, and cakes, but Mam had made and decorated the wedding cake in her own inimitable way. We had quite a number of guests, mostly relatives and my brother had brought a lady friend with him from London. He said she was a friend of many years standing and that the relationship was platonic because it was only a short time since the war years during which her husband had died in tragic circumstances. However, in the month of March following our wedding, they were married.

At that time, my father was still in business as a butcher and my mother had recovered from her illness and was once more about her work as before. On the evening before our wedding everyone was busy, the last deliveries of meat were made, and my sister and I were finishing getting things organised at home. Clothes had been washed and ironed and were being aired in the living room on a maiden by the fire. Then there was a knock at the door and my sister went to open it and in stepped the gentleman from the smallholding mentioned earlier who got stuck in the snow chasing whiskey. He had been drinking, but seemed quite affable. He greeted us all and looked round the room and then suddenly declared, "Well, I'll be damned Isaac, you've got an awful lot of knickers around!" He then turned on his heel and went. We all burst out laughing and no one knew why he had called!

The following day dawned fine and clear and we all dressed in our finery and drove to the Chapel. The marriage service was suitably solemn but happy, and then came the wedding feast with all the usual speeches, jokes and good wishes. Everything had gone very successfully to my mother's relief. After all the photographs had been taken, Arthur and I returned to my home in order to change our clothes. Celebrations over, we set off on our honeymoon in the Austin Seven car, which had been suitably decorated by 'well-wishers' using jolly balloons and ribbons and not forgetting the rattling old tin cans and the advice for newly-married couples chalked up on the body of the car.

We had made no arrangements beforehand for accommodation, but that evening we landed at Harlech and found a room in a guesthouse.

The first night of a honeymoon is always supposed to be the wonderful culmination of great longing and emotion, romance and excitement, and in a way it was so for us. We were now married and could give way to our feelings and sexual desires without restraint, but we were also tired and exhausted. We cuddled and loved and then fell into a deep sleep but not in each other's arms for the weather was much too hot. Things improved over the next few days and nights! We went exploring the beautiful countryside of the Lleyn peninsula. One day we went to Barmouth where Arthur's parents had spent their honeymoon - I have no idea where my parents went for theirs. Barmouth is a nice seaside place and apart from the seashore there are some beautiful walks there, one of which is the renowned Panorama Walk. We decided to walk up the mountain path to the top and the view from there is absolutely glorious all around, especially over the Mawddach estuary. Strangely for August, we had the place to ourselves and the romance and the beauty, the sunshine and happiness led to our making love on the grass. It was pleasantly satisfying but the earth did not move and I saw no stars. Well, I have always liked comfort, I will put up with any amount of hardship and discomfort when I am working but when I am at ease or resting, then I like to be comfortable and that grassy hilltop was so hard!

After a couple more days we got bored. Bored? Bored on our honeymoon? Yes! Not with each other but with doing nothing and we knew that the National Eisteddfod was being held in Colwyn Bay that very week. So we decided to go back home to Llanfair and spend time at the Eisteddfod, which we both enjoyed. But there were raised eyebrows … coming home early from a honeymoon? Unheard of!

For the next ten weeks we lived at my home and sometimes at Arthur's home. We were starting to despair of getting a house in Llanrwst and Arthur had decided to give up the job at the end of the year if things remained unchanged.

Then one night, quite late, about 10.30 p.m, there was a knock on the door and when Dad went to open up, there was a man and a woman on the step asking for Arthur. They were invited to come in to sit down. Finally they explained that they knew we were looking for a house and had come to offer us a house that they had for sale. They were mother and son - the father was dead. She owned quite a lot of property in Llanrwst - a newsagent, a printing works and various houses. The house in question was the big one that we had ignored in Watling Street. My first reaction was that I did not want to live there. She told some tale about the Council threatening to issue an order to requisition the house unless it was occupied before the end of the week, but I did not believe a word of it! However, they said they wanted £2,500 for it and we said we would think about it and let them know our decision as soon as possible. Then they left. Well, there was no time to arrange a mortgage and after a long discussion we decided that we had no alternative other than to buy the house. We decided to go to see Uncle Edward and Auntie Lil, in *Groes Farm*, Denbigh. They were by then retired and he had bought several properties in the Denbigh area as investments. We thought he could put up the money to buy this house and we could repay him as soon as we could arrange a loan from the Bank.

The following morning we went to Denbigh to explain the situation to them. Uncle was immediately interested and decided that we should all go to see it the following day, which we did.

It was an imposing house with three storeys built in 1901 with red and cream coloured bricks. There was a narrow flower border at the front of the house and a low wall with railings. The front door opened into a small vestibule and had a fine brass letterbox. We were told that the whole house had just been decorated internally, but on inspection we saw that the lower half of most walls had been covered in dark brown gloss paint and the upper part distempered in a pale orange colour. The word *'awful'* does not adequately convey the depressing effect of such a colour scheme but we were in no position to air our views on such matters. I silently reminded myself that beggars cannot be choosers and should be thankful for small mercies. The whole group of us, having marched through the house following Uncle Edward, who was a well set-up figure of a man, heard him pronounce that he was satisfied with the soundness of the building before even organising a survey. He immediately proceeded to discuss the price, to bargain as he would say and that was finally settled at £2,500. And so, that is how we ended up with a house that was far too big for our needs and we knew that our few chattels would have fitted easily into one of the 11 rooms. However, we were so glad to have solved our biggest problem, and I felt quite confident that we could manage the rest somehow.

But the first surprise for us came when we learned that my Uncle had no intention of relinquishing ownership of the house. He had bought it as an investment and we would pay him £8.00 per month in rent. And as it happened, that was precisely the salary being paid to Arthur by the Chapel for his work as Organist and Choirmaster. We were disappointed with the fact that we were not buying the property, but readily agreed to my Uncle's terms: he then ensured that the legal side of the purchase was completed quite speedily.

As soon as we received the keys to the house I set out to start getting the house ready for occupation. I arranged for a young woman from Llanfair, a friend called Alice to come along with me and Arthur and his brother Harry, who was a carpenter, to Llanrwst to give the house a really good clean. We couldn't do much in a week about the state of the décor but we could ensure that everywhere was spotlessly clean and tidy. There were also a number of small jobs that needed attention. Curtain rails had to be fixed on the windows for instance and we decided to board up the fireplaces in the bedrooms on the first floor. We had no plans at that time to use the top floor, and it might as well have been non-existent. We had no need of it and certainly no money to spend on it. Later on, I found the 'L' shaped bedroom useful for drying clothes on wet days and also for storage purposes. Later still, it became a play area for our children.

The house still stands in Llanrwst with its two large bay windows on either side of the front door with two more directly above on the first floor and a smaller landing window in between them, and two bedroom windows on the second floor. It has 3 living rooms downstairs, a kitchen, 7 bedrooms, a bathroom, and outhouses. The rooms have high ceilings with lovely picture rails and heavy solid doors and the floor in the lobby is beautifully covered in smooth good quality square and triangular tiles in beige, white, light and dark blue in the Roman style. When we lived there, the square sitting room had an old-fashioned Victorian fireplace with a high mantle-piece with rounded columns on both sides and a grate made of iron decorated with scrolls and tiles with coloured flowers. The grate would be worth a small fortune today but unfortunately I gave it away in 1960 when we modernised the room. In fact, there were ornate fireplaces in all the other rooms too including the first floor bedrooms, but the ones at the top of the house were small, plain and black - obviously thought to be good enough for the servants of the house at the turn of the century.

Above the door in the rear living room was a glass-fronted box with room numbers on the front panel and inside the box separate bells for each main room that indicated when service was required somewhere in the house. Needless to say we immediately disconnected them from the beautiful bell pushes situated in the front reception rooms and bedrooms. My only servants were my own two feet and two hands and I would order them around as *I* saw fit and no one else!

One afternoon shortly after obtaining the house keys the house was empty because Arthur had gone to the funeral of a Chapel member and I had gone to a shop to buy curtain material. When I returned I went upstairs to the toilet and heard a movement on the upper stairs. It startled me but I immediately went to investigate and there, sitting on the stairs as cool as a cucumber was the ex-owner. She explained that she had come to view the funeral cortege leaving the house down the road. I was appalled and disgusted with such cheek and bad taste. It was also illegal of course. However, she made no move to leave until the cortege had gone and I went downstairs. When she eventually came down I demanded and finally received the key, which she had deliberately not handed over, and I then let her know how I felt about her actions. I could never respect her ever again. Someone told me afterwards that she had acquired the house because a mortgagee had defaulted.

Another rather unnerving event followed a few days later when I was alone in the house preparing a snack for myself at midday when there was a knock on the back door. There stood a strange looking woman with very straight white hair wearing a cape. She startled me and before I could speak, she said in a 'pushy' and menacing way, “I've been watching you … can I come in?” and promptly pushed past me. I suddenly felt decidedly uneasy and my mind raced but I told myself that on no account should I panic. So I calmly asked where had she been watching us from, and why. “I live over there,” she said pointing to the second house of Mona Villas which were behind our house, “And I have been watching you a lot ... I can see everything from my bedroom window.” I didn't like her message nor her manner so I told her there hadn't been much for her to see and … anyhow, why had she come? She then rambled on saying she was alone and had no money and could she stay and have a meal with me. Well, I am not an uncharitable person, but I could not risk entering into further dialogue with her - she made me feel uneasy and decidedly unsafe. I did not know anything about the woman and I needed to establish our privacy from the start. So I told her I could not give her any food for I had only a snack for myself, which was true. She was so reluctant to leave that I practically had to propel her out of the house and the back yard and then I firmly bolted the yard door.

Later on I went to see Mrs. Solomon Jones, our dear friend to tell her what had occurred and she warned me not to encourage the woman in any way because she was a nuisance to the neighbours, always begging for food when she was not destitute. That yard door remained bolted at all times thereafter.

I later learned that Mrs. Griffiths, for that was her name, had come to Llanrwst from the Isle of Man and was known for her strange ways. She sometimes appeared with a small, plump and rather timid woman whom she apparently often abused physically. I was glad when eventually, both of them left Llanrwst - I believe that Mrs. Griffiths went back to her native Isle of Man.

With our coupons and tokens we were allowed to buy one three-piece suite, one dining table, four chairs and one bed. They were stamped with the utility kite mark and were quite sturdy and I still have the table. The suite, upholstered in green woollen moquette, gave good service for many years.

I had enough coupons to buy some very nice peachy cream material for the two big bay windows upstairs and Irish linen with a floral pattern in pinks, blues and greens for the other two downstairs. For the back windows, all I could get was dyed sacking - deep brown with some sort of pattern on them. The condition of the linoleum on the floor in the Music Room was good enough for it to be left in place, especially after the good scrub and polish we gave it. We stained the sitting room floor a dark oak colour, and the large rug we placed on the hearth made the room look a little cosier. The living room had red and black tiles and those polished up quite nicely too and helped make the homemade rag rug on the hearth very acceptable.

The next step was more difficult because we had to buy the rest of our furniture second hand and although it was available, was nevertheless expensive. We also had to be very careful to find the good stuff for there was a lot of junk about and many otherwise good pieces had woodworm hidden in parts.

The priority was to buy a piano. We certainly could not afford a new one, but Arthur was very pleased to find an excellent *'Ibach'* piano that had been reconditioned by Wagstaff's Music shop in Llandudno. It was iron framed and over-strung, in a lovely mahogany case. A refugee from war-torn Europe had done the excellent reconditioning work on the piano. He was a middle-aged Polish man who spoke no English, but was obviously a master craftsman with pianos. The tone of that piano was beautiful and wonderful, and it was played by hundreds of hands, large and small for 38 years. Even when we had to part with it, the working parts inside were perfect, but the outer wood frame had been attacked by woodworm.

Having ordered the three-piece suite, table, chairs and bed and handed over our official furniture *tokens*, and cash of course, we set forth to scour second hand furniture shops. When you take part in such a hunting expedition with an objective in mind, a short timescale and limited money, then the searching can become a frustrating chore. On the other hand, if you are setting out in a leisurely fashion to look around with no particular objective in mind except bargain hunting and there is loose cash in your purse, then the operation can be enjoyable, and even exciting. We started off in the latter category, but ultimately ended up in the former!

We found a small, solid oak bedroom suite from the Edwardian period, which I still have and is probably classed as an antique by now. Also a dressing table and chest of drawers in dark oak, some odd chairs, a chiffonier, a couple of occasional tables for the sitting room, some small tables for bedsides, a Lloyd loom chair, linen basket, and other small accessories. Then something special caught my eye in a furniture shop in Denbigh, it was not new but it took my fancy: it was a lady's escritoire, a beautiful compact French piece in rosewood with inlays and fine narrow legs. The top opened out on two sides to form a table with a leather centre. When the leaves were opened a section rose up at the back that comprised of compartments to hold papers. I paid £5.00 for it and Arthur used it in his study for 5 or 6 years before acquiring a larger desk. He sold the little desk to his brother for the same price but it was disposed of fairly soon afterwards and then I lost sight of it. I have often wished I could have had the chance to buy it back for two reasons: firstly because it was a beautiful piece of furniture, and secondly because it was an antique. Several years later, I was browsing in an antiques shop when I came across a very similar desk and was told that the asking price was £400.00. I felt quite faint when I heard that, and mentally thumped myself for letting Arthur sell our desk. Well, it's easy to be wise after the event, but it taught me an expensive and useful lesson. We live and learn.

Auntie Lil had given us a big iron bed with brass knobs with an old-fashioned wire mesh base set in a solid wooden frame and we had bought a new mattress for it. We had to practically climb into that bed it was so high off the ground. I painted the iron white and polished the brass knobs until they shone and it looked quite presentable. Arthur and I slept in that bed and we put the new one in the spare bedroom. Aunty Lil also gave us a wall clock that we used for many years in the living room. The new table and chairs and suite went into the front sitting room with a nice Victorian round occasional table and the chiffonier that later went into the study. We had a second hand dining table and 4 chairs in the living room, two new fireside chairs, a desk with two cupboards below, and a glass fronted top cupboard that Arthur had made years before. My mother had bought a lovely solid oak cupboard cum bookcase for me at a sale in a country house for £17.00 that I still have. The top part has wooden shelves and glass doors and the bottom part has two drawers and ornately carved doors on two cupboards. We put that bookcase, the little desk and chair, piano, and a fireside chair in the study and they completed the room. I had also found a perfect 'high chair' for use at the piano. It was one of those chairs that shops especially drapers' shops provided for their customers that are rarely seen nowadays - long tapering legs, small circular seat, and a high open oval-shaped back. Arthur always preferred to have his hands above the keys of a piano, not flat, but in a sort of grasping position. He said that it ensured better control ... so the chair was ideal for him and his pupils' needs too.

The other big purchase was a Jackson electric cooker - a pale green vitreous enamel one with four splayed legs. It had an oven, a large and small cooking ring, a rectangular solid cooking plate, and a grill. How modern and how convenient - I loved it! I also bought some heavy aluminium saucepans and frying pan. I had no washing machine or fridge at that time but stored food perfectly well in what we called a *food safe*, a ventilated large shelved wooden cupboard on legs. The safe served us as a family for fifteen years and no one ever had Salmonella or anything else, but I must emphasise that it was situated in an extremely cold walk-in pantry that was built outside the house and accessed from the inside. In addition to that, perishable food was never stored for more than two, possibly three days depending on weather temperatures.

We had received numerous wedding presents in the form of cash, and some useful and not so useful goods too. We received an electric clock, bed linen, cushions, cutlery, four butter dishes, ornaments and such like, and I particularly remember a gift given to us by a Londoner married to a Welshman who had managed to learn some Welsh. I was very fond of this old lady for she truly was a lady. She gave me three old plates and said, "I have no money to buy you a present my dear, but I'd like you to have these plates because they were given to me by a very old lady when I got married and she told me they were old." I was very pleased to have them for they are pretty and decorated in pink, white and gold. There are only two now because the third was accidentally broken. They must be very old by now and possibly valuable too. Another wedding gift with sentimental value was a butter dish made of patterned glass that was given to me by the widowed lady at whose house my friend and I ate our dinners during our school days in Llanfair. On reaching into her *'cwpwrdd gwydr'* (display cupboard) to take out the dish she said, "I can't give you a costly present but I would like you to have this to wish you luck." It meant a great deal to me because she had taken it from amongst her treasured possessions - to part with something you value gives it that added worth.

The last place to visit was the hardware shop to buy kitchen utensils, shoe cleaning brushes and polish, a poker, an electric kettle and crockery. Even after extensive shopping sprees we still identified essential items to purchase - it seemed never ending, but we were discovering the many things that we needed to set up home. They were happy days however, and we enjoyed building our own nest and making a cosy home.

The day came when Mr. William Jones, a lorry driver, went on his journey with Arthur to pick up all the different items from Denbigh and Llanfair. His lorry had none of the fittings and fixtures of present day furniture removing vans, it was just an open lorry. However, the care was there and absolutely nothing was broken or even scratched. Mr. Jones was a careful worker and very kind too. And so it was that we were installed in our own home on the threshold of a new life in time for Christmas 1947. There was another wonderful 'extra' benefit in our new home that made a terrific and spectacular difference - we had ELECTRICITY!

I believe that this is a good place to pause in my story to enable me to give details about the background of our two families: Arthur's and my own.

Chapter Twelve

MY FATHER AND MOTHER

My father's name was Isaac Owen, pronounced *'Eesac'* in Welsh - very similar to the Jewish way of saying the name. There was no Jewish connection as far as I know, but there are numerous Hebrew names given to people, Chapels, and even villages in Wales, the influence being the Bible of course. My Headmaster at the County School in Abergele used to say that the Welsh and Jewish people were alike in many ways. They belong to small nations, are very religious, remarkably musical, and fond of dramatics. It is true that there are many Welsh-speaking people with Jewish names such as Elias, Isaac and Samuel, but these are mostly in South Wales because they are mainly descendants of the Jews who settled in Wales during the boom time of the industrial revolution.

Having gone off at a tangent again I now return to my father who was born on the 1st of June 1883 in the parish of Llannefydd on a smallholding called *Garreg Lithrig* (slippery stone). It was a small house but my father was one of nine children born and raised there: Edward who died aged 6 months, Mary who died aged 13 years, John, Owen, Robert, Isaac, Dinah, Jane and Ann, who died when she was a young adult. Their father was Robert Owen, a butcher who ran the family's smallholding and managed a shop in a hut near the 'Hawk and Buckle Inn' in the village of Llannefydd near Denbigh. He went about the countryside in a horse and trap selling meat. It is said that he was a very strong man who could handle large carcasses of meat. He was the conductor of a local choir and a Precentor in the chapel at Ffynhonnau and had been born in Llansannan, but nothing more was known of him until recently when I was able to compile a Family Tree, which is shown in this book.

His wife, mother of his 9 children was Catherine who came from a well-known family in Llannefydd. She was the youngest daughter of John and Mary Jones, *Ty Gwyn* (white house) Pont y Gwyddel, and one of twelve children. Her twin did not survive as can be seen on the Family Tree for this family, which is also shown in the book. Members of the family were renowned for their love of singing and it was said of them that, “Twelve children have John and Mary - no one weeping - everyone singing.”

I am delighted to possess a torn out section of an old Welsh newspaper with the heading 'Old memories' written by Mr. Robert Roberts, *Bont Bach* (small bridge) Llannefydd that fascinatingly refers to outstanding men and women members of Ffynhonnau Chapel during the years 1859 to 1922 amongst whom were members of the *Ty Gwyn* family. I often heard my father speak about the family that he referred to as, “*hen deulu Ty Gwyn*” who consisted of his mother Catherine, his aunts and uncles, and grandparents John and Mary Jones. My father's grandfather, John Jones, a Deacon and Precentor in the Chapel had to use a pitchfork to gauge the right key for hymns because there were no organs in Chapels in those times. The newspaper writer, Mr. Roberts, says that, “Mary Jones was every inch a lady who was always calm and dignified whilst John was inclined to be rather impatient. As a family they were clever, kind and always happy. They never tired of singing. Friends and neighbours who visited would find themselves singing with their hosts late into the night.” It is known that Catherine, my grandmother had a powerful soprano voice and tradition says that she was offered a scholarship to the Royal College in London that she was unable to take up. She died in her late sixties.

When my father was a little boy there was a lot of unrest, almost rioting in the North Wales countryside because of Church tithes, a form of tax. People who had left the Anglican Church in Wales to become members of Nonconformist Chapels objected to having to pay the tithes and many refused to do so. This meant that officials would go along to take animals in lieu, and by force. In some cases, soldiers were involved and the reading of the Riot Act happened. Lookouts would take turns in watching out for such officials and if any were seen approaching, people ran from one place to another to warn small-holders (big landowners were not involved) so they could gather their livestock and lock them up in the outbuildings. When Lloyd George got an Act through Parliament to Disestablish the Church in Wales, the tithes were abolished and peace was established once more.

One of the most active and effective of the protestors was a lady called 'The Queen of Llannefydd'. The eldest brother of Catherine, my paternal grandmother, was married to this lady. He was not a big man but she was enormous. When they went to Chapel services, visiting friends, or to market, they had to travel in separate pony traps because of her size. When she died at the age of sixty-six years the bearers were not able to get the coffin out of the house and so a window had to be removed. Although she fiercely protested against the tithes and marched to face the Collectors, waving a black banner, she never broke the law and she paid the tithes. But her actions were published in newspapers and brought publicity to the cause.

My mother told me years after the event that she was amazed to see and hear my father and all his brothers and sisters singing their hearts out on the day of their mother's funeral, my grandmother Catherine. “How can they sing in their grief?” she asked after the funeral. She was told that it would have been their mother's dearest wish for them to sing from the heart, at her final resting-place.

Her husband outlived her and was nursed faithfully through a long illness by Robert his son whom we used to call Uncle Butch. We know that Robert never married, but John the eldest child was married with a son, but his wife died very soon after the birth. Owen, a carpenter was married with three children and the family lived in Rockferry. Dinah was married with a daughter and they lived in Pwllheli, and Jane was married with two sons and two daughters and the family lived near Abergele.

For a short while before helping his father in the butchery business my father had worked in the lead mines at Llanfair T.H. That qualified him to say to my sister and me that he had been underground, on the ground and above the ground. He justified the claim to having been above the ground because he had once been on an aeroplane trip from Rhyl. When he was old enough, he was apprenticed as a butcher to 'Cutlers Butchers' at Colwyn Bay and 'John Jones Butchers' at Conwy, and finally he became a Master butcher himself. He told a story of how, one night in going to his lodgings in Conwy he saw a man beating his wife and dragging her by the hair along the street. Feeling chivalrous, he tackled the man and freed the woman, only to be set upon by her for attacking her husband! That was enough to disillusion the chivalrous would-be knight!

During the time when he was an apprentice, there were two other young men who were also training with the firm, and being keen, vied with each other for work that carried status. In those days there was an annual animal fair at Llanbedr, a village further up the Conwy Valley and the local *Y Bedol Inn* (The Horseshoe) always placed an order for a whole side of beef from the butcher to feed the many farmers who came from far and wide.

The beef was purchased on condition that a butcher came along with the meat to organise the spit roasting and more importantly, the carving afterwards. My father's chance came along, and he was all geared up to do the job and show what he could do, and have a day out into the bargain. However, it didn't turn out quite as he thought. After about three hours of non-stop carving and slicing, his forearms were ready to drop off. Far from being a holiday it was hot, non-stop toil. Needless to say, he did not ask to go again, but of course he had to take his turn with the rest. I think he went home every weekend, but the shop was open fairly late on Saturdays so I suppose it was early evening when he got on a train to Abergele then walked home to *Garreg Lithrig*, or perhaps someone came to meet him along the way with a pony and trap.

On Sundays he went with the family to Chapel and took part in all the singing in the services, and the singing at home too. His Uncle John had learned to read old notation, but my father relied on the *Sol-fa* system at which he was an expert. He had a very resonant bass/baritone voice. He truly loved Music.

He thoroughly enjoyed listening to music played by bands, especially brass bands and was highly appreciative of the sounds they created. When he was about 17 years of age he taught and conducted a Choir of children. One of the prizes they won in a competition was a pair of Chinese vases that I still have today.

He told me stories about the old times and the small, local *Eisteddfodau*, (competitive events with adjudicators) that were held in most villages in Chapels, vestries or schools. Each village had a choir and there was fierce rivalry between the villages. There were no cars, buses or trains in the country, and few people had bikes so it was Shanks' pony (walking) and no one minded walking miles there and back. If the meeting ran late, who cared? “It is night until morning,” they said.

My father told me about an incident that happened on one occasion at an evening concert held in a small hamlet where the only lighting available in the room came from two candelabras, one positioned above the platform and the other above the centre of the room. He said there were no seats available so everyone stood in the way that people stand at football matches. The room was crowded with local and neighbouring villagers and whenever one person moved, the whole crowd moved, and as the evening wore on it became very hot causing the wax of the candles to melt even faster. No one wanted candle wax in their hair, but then someone spotted a bald man in the crowd from a rival village, so they slowly eased the poor man under the candelabra! Ouch! They thought it best for only one person to suffer the dripping wax and somehow reasoned that it would be easier for him to remove it from his smooth scalp than to pull it from their own hair. Such were the lengths that some went to in rivalry, but I wonder what the bald man thought!

On another occasion, at an Eisteddfod held in a Memorial Hall conditions were much better with lamplight, seats and a policeman to keep order. As was customary, the chief recitation competition was highly popular with audiences because competitors chose to recite very dramatic, emotive poetry that was written to stir emotions. One elocution competitor named Richard recited the story of a happy sea voyage that turned to a disaster when a raging storm blew up. He had arranged with a friend named Roger to stand by the door to start singing a very well-known hymn about a storm when the climax of the piece was reached. Richard was getting along very well with his recitation, and describing in ever-mounting excitement how the wind was howling and the mountainous waves were crashing onto the ship. The crew and passengers were in fear of their lives and panic was rising. The audience was enthralled, and then suddenly, a voice at the back of the hall started singing the hymn as arranged. Immediately the policeman grabbed hold of Roger. "Oh, how dare you interrupt such a performance," he said, and pushed him out. Richard was shouting from the stage, "No, no, leave him alone. He is with me. Let him go." The audience was in stitches. Everyone understood that the keen policeman had believed poor old Roger to be drunk and disorderly! Calm was finally restored and a new start given to Richard, but it wasn't the same, couldn't be the same when everyone in the audience then knew what was coming at the climax. Without a doubt, Richard had been disadvantaged in the competition because it was difficult for him to generate spontaneity the second time round. Such was the strength of the competitive element of Eisteddfodau!

At an *Eisteddfod* in Llansannan, the musical piece set for the chief choral competition was a religious anthem, and two choirs were competing, one from Llansannan and the other from Llanfair T.H. - villages five miles apart. Both choirs had performed well and the adjudication was awaited with eagerness. As soon as they had sung in the competition and heard their rivals sing, some of the choristers wended their way to the Cross Keys Inn (later called The Saracen's Head) I know not whether from thirst or nervous exhaustion, but what I do know is that one of them was the conductor of one of the choirs. As soon as the adjudicator announced the result of the competition, the conductor of the victorious choir was called on stage to receive the prize and the plaudits, but to no avail. He was not in the audience and had therefore not heard the result, and a choir member who was there had become so excited about the outcome that he decided to race down to the pub to announce it to the conductor and take him back on stage to receive the glory. But the conductor spotted him running towards the Inn, immediately read his hugely obvious body language and started waving his arms, shouting excitedly, "Hurrah, Hurrah." Then just as dramatically, and to the great amusement of others, stopped suddenly, and became deadly serious as if he was having enormous doubts about his interpretation of the body language, then he grabbed the chorister, looked him straight in the eye and asked nervously, "Who won lad?" I'm sure that as soon as he had obtained absolute confirmation of the result he would have shot onto that stage as fast as greased lightning!

Dad, who was a year older than my mother courted, then married her in 1909 and moved to Llanfair to set up a Butchery business in Water Street. They owned land and other buildings in Llanfair including a slaughter-house in *Pen Llan*, and had sheep and cattle livestock, and a milk round in the village. I believe they also owned some cottages. Both were good at their jobs and not afraid of hard work and their business flourished.

They moved to better premises in the village, a nice roomy house with a bigger shop - a building called 'New Street'. The house was on a slope and the shop was under the lower end of the building. Their house was one of the best furnished in the village with all the 'mod.cons' of the time. They had a lad helping with the outside work and a maid for the housework. The young woman was very good in the house and kept everything spick and span, but my mother told me that there was one drawback, the maid hated seeing my mother use the pots and pans for cooking after she had earlier worked hard polishing them!

At the beginning of January 1913 my brother Percy Elfyn was born, which brought further happiness, but more work for my mother. She was very active in the business - well, she had to be. My father was involved with the milk round, buying animals, slaughtering, butchering and carving. I remember my mother telling me how one day, a couple of gypsy women came into the shop when she was alone, asking for free handouts. When my mother offered some scrag-end of neck of lamb for making stew, they were not satisfied and demanded 'proper' meat. This angered my mother and she said, “Take it or leave it.” They left, but no sooner had they gone out of the door than two scruffy men entered with a big dog and, seeing my mother on her own, started making demands. She remained quite calm, lifted a cleaver and said, “If you are not out of that door in five seconds this cleaver will show you the way,” and she advanced towards them. They fled down the street, cursing and swearing. She was strong and courageous, but was also known for her kindness to poor people and sick children.

There were many poor people in those days with no permanent home. They worked here and there on the farms, as and when needed. When they had money in their pockets they would have a 'spree', a long alcoholic session of drinking themselves silly, then going to sleep in someone's barn or hay-shed. One such person was *Ned Bach* (little Ned) from another village. One night when my mother had gone up to the farm buildings to put the cows into the shed for the night, she noticed that the cows would not go in at all. She was puzzled, but finally went inside and found Ned asleep in the hay. She called to him and told him to get out so that she could feed the cattle and settle them for the night. He took no notice, so she got a bucket of cold water and threw it over him. That sobered *Ned Bach* a bit and he got up swearing and cursing, then left. The cows went in, and Ned went over the road to the Church cemetery and lay down on one of the gravestones and fell asleep for the night.

When war came, Ned joined up and saw action at Ypres and the Somme, but the worst experience for him had been the hand to hand fighting in Mametz Woods, “And for what?” said Ned, “We gained nothing, but thousands of young men died that day.” He was battle-hardened like many of the others, but amongst the soldiers were very young boys having just been called up or volunteered for the armed services who were petrified and calling out for their mothers during the fighting in Mametz Woods - such was the terror and horror of the experience. Ned said it upset the older soldiers, as they thought it was wrong and senseless to have youngsters who were hardly out of childhood in such a situation. He said that many a time in the trenches, when he was thirsty and there was no clean water to drink he would remember with affection the bucket of good Welsh water that Mam had thrown over him in the cowshed.

Mam also told us of a man from the village, who had suffered mustard gas poisoning in the First War. The Germans tried it out one day but unfortunately for them the wind changed and most of the gas blew back into their own trenches. But sadly, those British soldiers, including the man from the village who did breathe in the deadly gas suffered all their lives. Their lungs were scarred with the burns and once, when this man had been for a drink, called at my parents' house and suffered an awful attack of coughing and was literally choking. They loosened his tie and lay him sideways on the floor and the beer and the froth flowed out of his mouth.

The Great War started in 1914 but it did not really affect the general life of the village although there were some major changes that occurred for some families. Men left for the Army and prisoners of war arrived to work on some farms. Kinmel Camp in Bodelwydden was extended and some officers came to the village to drink in the Black Lion Hotel and the Swan Inn. The Crown Inn had spittoons and sawdust on the floor and was a little more old fashioned but many of the locals were happy to use it.

One German soldier prisoner of war who came to work for my parents was from Wilhelmshaven and his father owned the big Hotel near the railway station in that city. He had been in the Kaiser's special Life-Guards and was a fine looking man who spoke English. He was appalled when he saw my mother carrying a quarter of beef on her shoulder from the slaughterhouse to the shop, a distance of some 500 yards. "You should not have to do this, it is too heavy for a woman," he said. "Needs must," was my mother's reply.

My father was rejected medically from serving in the First World War because of problems he'd experienced with a hernia and he wore a truss all his life.

In 1915, again in the month of January, my sister, Elsie May was born on the 7th of the month. Her brother had already enjoyed his own birthday on the previous day, on the 6th. They were now a lovely family of four!

In 1917 my father bought a new Ford T car that travelled at 30 miles an hour! It was round about this time that my father began to spend too much time in the Black Lion Hotel. He was such good company - a natural and amusing raconteur, a wonderful mimic and always entertaining. He was also kind hearted. Because of his nature he was popular and had many good friends. He also had false friends and some relatives who were scroungers.

The officers from Kinmel would ply him with drinks and he would drive them back to camp. I do not know whether they paid him or not. The scroungers would sweet-talk him and ask for so called 'loans' just to tide them over - giving him I.O.Us that proved absolutely worthless in the fullness of time.

The situation became serious and could not continue for much longer because he had a tin full of IOUs and the family business was suffering. His real friends tried to warn him to revert to his usual efficient ways, but it appears to have been to no avail. I had not been born at that time, so I do not know the exact details, but I do know that the successful family business that my parents had worked so hard to establish 'crashed' round about 1922/23.

This was an instant disaster for the family, and life would never again be the same. The repercussions were immediate starting with a public sale of all assets to clear creditors. Everything was sold including property, furniture, personal belongings, and equipment. Not surprisingly, my father was missing all day. My mother was determined come what may, that all had to be paid in full in order to do right by everyone and avoid the stigma of bankruptcy. But it made them homeless with two little children. My father's sister Jane took them into her house out of compassion. But she too was married and had a family of her own, so it must have been very difficult for everyone concerned. I think Auntie Jane and her husband showed wonderful kindness and loyalty in helping in this way, and I know that during that difficult time my brother and sister attended the local school at St. George near Abergele. Not surprisingly, my mother became ill and was confined to bed, and I think she must have suffered stress and a nervous breakdown perhaps after such a traumatic time. After all that hard work and effort to achieve success in their business and then to have it all taken away was nothing short of tragic. It must have been hell for both my parents. My father was a very intelligent man, well brought up, never violent or abusive in any way and yet he had brought them all to such an awful plight.

My mother never talked about this time or said anything derogatory about my father whilst we were children - it was only when we were grown up and curious that we got some answers to our questions.

I remember my mother telling me once about the time she was ill in bed being low in spirit, desperately unhappy, feeling beholden and knowing that they were a burden on her sister-in-law's family. Then one morning she suddenly sat up in bed and in a loud voice she declared, "I have to get up and go. I have a family to bring up." She got up and despatched my father back to Llanfair to find somewhere for them to live, "Anywhere and anything as long as we have a roof over our heads." And so it was that they moved back to Llanfair to a small two-roomed cottage with a few sticks of furniture but with their health and strength and pride regained. That cottage was to be their home for nine years - *Pengraig*, the place where my sister and I were born, and the house that I described at the start of this book.

One factor helped the family to survive. My mother had received a legacy of £300.00 from her Aunt Margaret, her Scottish grandmother's sister who was a spinster lady. The Bank manager had kept the money in my mother's name so she was able to draw on it as and when things got desperate.

I was born in July 1924, but have no real recollection of my early years. I have a vague memory of my sister Elsie lying in bed and at the age of three giving her flowers when she was ill. I remember the awful day of her funeral in 1927, the day of the Total Eclipse of the sun when the world became dark at 3 o'clock in the afternoon. The terrible darkness of grief remained with my parents and my brother for a very long time. Three months later on the 12th September 1927 my younger sister was born and the floodgates of my mother's grief burst open. She was finally able to weep for her lost child.

Elsie May was, I was told, a very pretty child with very blue eyes and golden ringlets, she was quite tough, but very popular. She fought her brother's battles and they were inseparable. Her death was especially traumatic for him because he was in hospital with appendicitis round about the same time.

On the day of the funeral several teachers and children from the County School at Abergele where she was a successful pupil, came to join the very long funeral procession.

After returning to the village to live, my father obtained a job in Colwyn Bay working for a butcher. He stayed there during the week and returned home at weekends. And it was on his way home at the end of the week as he queued up for a connecting bus at Abergele that an acquaintance from Llanfair went to my father to sympathise with him in his great loss. This must have been a terrible gut-wrenching shock for Dad for he did not know that his Elsie May was dead!

Very soon afterwards he got a job as Head Gardener at *Garthewin* Hall and was living at home again. He and my brother set about making a garden at Pen Graig and my brother spoke of carrying tons of top-soil in a wheelbarrow to cover the rocky area. It flourished and we had plenty of vegetables and fruit each year thereafter. My mother kept hens, so we had eggs too, but we enjoyed chicken only occasionally when it was regarded as a treat.

My mother was born on the 9th of May in 1884 at a farm called *Gerdden Isa*, Bryn Rhyd yr Arian barely a mile away from where my father was born one year earlier. Her father was Joseph Jones a Welsh farmer who came from a good lineage from both his parents. They were literate and were descendants of ancient families. Her mother was Betsy Barton Howatson a Scots girl, but more of that later.

Now I will tell you more about my mother's background: she was the eldest of five surviving girls out of a total of twelve children born to the family. None of the boys survived, but one named Thomas lived until he was 8 months old. My grandmother died in childbirth when she was 40 years old after the still-birth of her twelfth child. She had been warned that she would not survive another pregnancy, and for some reason did not heed the warning and died of a haemorrhage in 1901. Before she finally passed away she managed to arrange her own funeral with instructions about suitable clothes for her girls to wear. My mother was seventeen years old and devastated when her mother died as was her father who never really got over the loss of his wife and who himself died 8 years later in 1909. This was the year that my mother and father were about to marry, and here was my mother aged 24 with both parents dead.

Her paternal grandparents had already died: her grandmother in 1886 when she was 2 years old & her grandfather in 1899 when she was 15 years old, but the Howatsons, her maternal grandparents were still alive. They were still living at *Plas Newydd*, the home farm of the *Dyffryn Aled* estate, the mansion where the Wynne-Yorke's lived. Her grandfather, Thomas Howatson was the Estate Manager. It appears that the girls lived at home at *Gerddan Isa* but spent a lot of time at *Plas Newydd* especially my mother. She had been at *Plas Newydd* with her grand parents on and off for lengthy periods of time and when she had finished at the local Church School at 14 years of age, it was arranged for her to become a pupil at a Private Girls' School in Denbigh run by a Miss Foulkes. This was a finishing school, typical of the time that aimed to turn out obedient young women with a good background of religious studies who would be ideal wives and mothers.

My mother was a fine looking girl with long blonde hair reaching down to her waist. Every Monday, the man who was known as the 'Carter' at the farm accompanied my mother to Denbigh: she rode a donkey for the best part of the way. During the week, the girls were taught the '3Rs' and Religious Instruction and ways of becoming nice young ladies. They attended a class run by Mrs.Gee the wife of Thomas Gee, the renowned Editor of the newspaper *Y Faner*, in Denbigh. The girls sat exams based on the Scriptures and my mother was very successful. She must have been interested because for quite some time she wanted to be a missionary. The Carter accompanied her home again every Friday afternoon. When this finishing school period was over it seems that she was at *Plas Newydd* permanently more or less, and one or other of her sisters also, from time to time.

They had to work very hard, getting up at 5.30 a.m every day and going straight to the cowshed to do the milking. On very cold mornings they used to hide a jug of very hot *Camp Coffee* in a pail hidden by clean cloths that they used to wipe the cows' teats. They would then add fresh milk from the cows to the coffee and enjoy a deliciously warming drink. As soon as the milking session was completed, the milk was poured into large earthenware pots and creaming dishes in the dairy. After the pails had been washed first in cold water, scoured in hot water, then scalded with boiling water, they would be left to dry upside down on the slate slabs. There was no respite for the girls for there was work waiting in the kitchen where they had to prepare breakfast for the men - porridge of course with salt, the Scottish way, not with the customary sugar. Some had '*brwas*' - broken crusts covered in good dripping and scalded with boiling water, sometimes with coarse oatmeal mixed in. A little later in the morning came cooked breakfast of egg and bacon.

Finally, the women themselves were able to eat breakfast before tackling the rest of the day's chores. Dinner had to be on the table at 12 noon prompt. The estate bell called everyone in. Tea was at 3.30p.m and by that time the women had to be clean and tidy in fresh pinafores. Supper was at 6.30p.m. Tea was also taken out periodically to the men in the fields or on the farmyard.

On Wednesdays, Mr & Mrs Howatson, my mother's grandparents went to Market at Denbigh, which gave the youngsters some freedom back at the farm. I remember my mother telling us how she started to cook cakes one Wednesday afternoon having hurried through her chores earlier in the day. Will, her cousin had asked Mam to make some scones but she had no idea how to go about it, or what quantities of ingredients to use. Anyhow, when the scones came out of the oven no one could even bite them - rock cakes in the true sense of the word!

Will, by the way, was the son of my mother's uncle. His mother had died when he was born and his aunt, my grandmother, having no boys of her own, had raised him.

After the scone fiasco they had to get rid of the incriminating evidence and so they decided to crush the scones with heavy stones and drop some crumbs every morning from their bedroom window onto the yard below. Their grandmother said in her Scottish accent, "I dinna ken the fussing of these hens - they are always picking and poking about the house these mornings." No one else knew either!

On another occasion, Will went to gather eggs, one from each nest, and persuaded Mam to make a sponge cake this time. Again no one knew what was needed for the perfect recipe but having collected six eggs they were stirred into goodness knows how much sugar and flour until the mixture looked right. Then the cake was cooked until it looked wonderfully golden and risen. They allowed it to cool slightly before Will eagerly took a bite, and within a second or two had decided to walk to the far end of the kitchen, cake in hand, from where he threw the 'sponge' cake at the opposite wall and found that it bounced right back again at him! His action brought about gales of laughter, and I'm sure that it was repeated more than once too for the effect. Who would have thought then that my mother was to become a prize cook and much sought after to make 'special cakes'. She also had the reputation of being able to produce a tasty meal from practically nothing. Experience really is a powerful teacher.

During the time my mother was at *Plas Newydd*, her mother's younger brother, a very handsome young man called Robert, or Bob, was growing up there as well, but he died when only 23 years old. All I know about the circumstances surrounding his death was that he was bed-ridden for quite some time, and towards the end of his life was in terrible pain, and the old nurse who attended to him had to lie in the bed holding him tightly whenever he had spasms until they were over. I have no idea what was wrong with him and never thought to ask. He died two years after his sister, my grandmother.

During the years that the Howatsons were at *Plas Newydd*, the *Dyffryn Aled* mansion was sold. The widowed Mrs. Wynne-Yorke went to live at Plas Cornel (corner mansion) and Dyffryn Aled became an expensive Private Mental Asylum.

My mother spoke about a patient there, a nice but eccentric old gentleman who was a Lord of the Realm and attended at all times by his butler. She said that he kept asking her to marry him. Just fancy … had she done so I might have been a Lady! All day and every day when the weather permitted he would roam the fields gathering stones into small piles - he who had been a captain of industry. At other times he pestered my mother to show him, "The cow that gave the cream." And being the impish teenager that she was, finally took him to see the bull! She was severely scolded by her grandmother, who was scandalised by such behaviour.

When my mother, her sisters and Will were children they wore clogs, and in the summer very often ran about with bare feet. Once, when they were chasing each other in the farmyard my mother climbed onto a haystack and in the excitement of the moment went too near the edge and fell down onto a hay-cutting machine. She fell onto the blade and cut a three-inch wound in her cheek. It started bleeding profusely and she was scared of going into the house in such a mess. She sat by the door of the cowshed crying until someone came looking for her and saw her dreadful wound. The Doctor's surgery was four miles away, but fortunately down at the bottom of the hill lived a lady who was skilful with herbs. She attended to the gaping wound by washing it and placing on it a thin layer of some ointment she had made herself. She then tied a bandage round my mother's head to cover the wound and told her to leave it untouched for a week. It healed beautifully and left only a very thin pale scarline that could barely be seen. Later on, the Doctor told her that he would have had to use stitches had he been called to attend, which would have scarred her face forever. Today, although we have forgotten many of these old country ways and rely on artificial cures, there is a growing trend to re-discover the natural remedies because in some instances they have proved superior.

My mother and her sisters had to retire to bed at 9.30p.m. at *Plas Newydd* and that meant 'lights out'. Whenever they managed to get hold of a book or other reading material, they had to push squashed newspaper between the bedroom door and its frame to avoid the light from a smuggled candle being seen through the cracks thus giving the game away. Their grandfather was strict about such things!

When my mother was sixteen years old, her grandfather's brother came to visit *Plas Newydd.* He was William Howatson who was eight years older than his brother Thomas, and coincidentally, both of them died at the age of 83. William was a kindly man and my mother liked him much better than her grandfather, who was very strict, terse and very forbidding. When the girls were laughing and having fun, their grandfather would tell them to be quiet, but his brother said, "Leave them be Tom, it is good to hear the lassies laughing." The Howatsons were Scots from Middlebie in Dumfriesshire where they had been sheep farmers. The family had arrived there from the Highlands at some time in the past.

William Howatson was a shepherd working for a Laird who had a pretty daughter. She fell in love with William and became pregnant, and as was the general custom in those days among the upper classes, the shepherd was packed off with £50.00 and ordered to disappear. He went to South Africa. When the Boer War broke out he fought on the side of the British and was taken prisoner and feared for his life. He was a lad brought up in the Scottish Presbyterian Kirk who knew his Bible, and realised that the Boers also laid great store by the Holy Book. And by quoting chunks of the Scriptures to his captors and reminding them of the wrath of Almighty God, they let him go!

Eventually he married a Boer lady named Martha Hanger, and at the time of his visit to Wales had a large ranch at Tbaba 'Nebu on the outskirts of Johannesburg. It took two days for him to ride a horse along the perimeter of his ranch.

He had come over to London at that time when he was 70 years of age to find the child that he had fathered years earlier. I don't know why or for what purpose but it seems that he had managed to find his Scottish son. He wanted my mother to go back with him for a holiday and she was eager to go. However, my grandmother, who was expecting her twelfth child did not want her to go - perhaps she had a premonition of her own imminent death, for she had been warned by the Doctor not to become pregnant again. Sadly, his warning had not been heeded, and the pregnancy resulted in a stillbirth that caused her to haemorrhage to death.

My mother was only seventeen years old when her mother died: she was the eldest of the children and felt the loss very badly. Her father survived for eight more years. During the next few years things continued to change: Auntie Lil, one of my mother's sisters was married to a first cousin of my father and they moved to *Groes farm* near Denbigh; another sister Auntie Janet went into service at a farm in the Vale of Clwyd; another sister Auntie Mag married at the age of l6, and she and her husband stayed on at the family farm at *Garddan Isa* and raised a family there.

When the girls' father, Joseph Jones became ill with what is now known as 'farmers' lung' and became confined to bed, Mam being the eldest was the one who had to nurse him. No one was allowed to enter the room except her and the doctor. No dusting was allowed and the least disturbance had to be achieved. It was not pleasant because of all the discharge that he struggled to cough up in order to breathe. During this time he asked my mother to go into a drawer and bring him a pile of papers, which she did. He studied them for a time and then asked her to put them away again explaining that the papers were I.O.Us from people who owed him money.

Finally, he passed away and the doctor was sent for, and someone went to inform his brothers who lived some distance away in the same neighbourhood. Two brothers arrived first and went upstairs and asked my mother to leave the room so they could be alone with their relative. She was surprised they wanted her out of the room now that her father was dead, but complied and left the room. Her uncles closed the bedroom door. Several minutes later they solemnly emerged and one uncle said to my mother, “He said my name.” Mam knew this was nonsense for her father had passed away hours before. She replied, “He did not say your name any more than he called my name.” Without another word they left. Mam went in again and began to tidy up before the doctor came. She looked into the chest of drawers and saw that many of the I.O.Us had gone. So much for brotherly love, never mind sympathy and fair play for young girls left orphaned.

Joseph Jones died on the 9th April 1909 just before Easter when my mother and father had planned to marry. In those days it would have been regarded as unseemly, and lacking in respect to enjoy any celebrations in a time of bereavement. However, after consulting with members of the family, taking note of all considerations, they decided to go ahead with the wedding, but it was a quiet affair at a Chapel in Denbigh. I have no idea where they went for their honeymoon - I find it strange that I do not know this detail and yet I know where my in-laws spent theirs. Looking back I realise that there is so much that I don't know and I wonder why this is so. Was it a lack of interest on my part, an inherent sense of being loath to pry, or was it an exaggerated sense of propriety or personal privacy on my parents' part for some reason? Perhaps today it might be suggested that they just did not want to talk about those things for some reason. I cannot remember having intimate chats or conversations with them. My sister Bella was closer to my mother, I think because she was the baby of the family or perhaps because there had been such a struggle for her survival. But I believe that my lack of intimacy with my mother especially arose because of the big age gap, there were forty years between my parents and me. The interaction between us was influenced by the exaggerated respect that was expected of children towards their parents at that time, but strangely enough, it was not apparent with my younger sister.

I have never known how much my mother inherited on her father's death, if anything, but it could not have been a lot because the farm was rented and there were five girls and he had been ill for a long time. I feel sure though that her grandparents Howatson would have given her a sum of money when she got married, but I cannot be certain. However, I am fairly confident that my parents must have had some capital to set up in business when they got married.

My mother was a good-looking woman with fair hair and grey eyes. She had a good figure, was strong, well educated, confident and very competent. She knew everything about farming and dairy work, was an excellent cook, and could knit, sew and crochet. She did not care very much for housework, for she took no delight in it. It was just a chore that had to be done, but I can remember that people came to her for advice because she was well respected and trusted: they knew that she had been through a lot in life and was wise. It seems that her grandparents were against her marrying my father and must have made their views known on many occasions. She once said to me, "If they had not gone on and on so much about it I might not have married your father, but the more they harped on the matter the more determined I became." My belief is that my mother's Scottish grandparents deliberately groomed her from childhood to marry a rich farmer from the Vale of Clwyd, or a man of similar means. I do not believe they were against my dad as a person because he was of good character and came from a decent, cultured and religious Welsh family, but his family were not wealthy by any means. The Howatsons had their sights set on enabling their lovely granddaughter Mary May Jones to do very well for herself in life.

My father was extremely intelligent, was a great reader and seeker of knowledge. When he was very young he saved to buy a set of books called 'The Harmsworth Self-Educator' and when we were children he bought a set of Arthur Mee's Children's Encyclopaedia. We were never without books. He was also very interested in politics - not as an avid party man, but as a man hungry for ideas, progress, humanity, oratory and ingenuity. He was popular because he could debate politics and other important world matters in an enlightened and intelligent way with anyone. He was well mannered, good humoured, well behaved, very much liked, highly amusing, respected, and considered to be highly entertaining. I am very fortunate to have been born to such wonderful parents.

There are two interesting facts that emerge from studying the maternal family tree of my mother's father. My mother's great, great grandfather Morris Davies (or Maurice) of *Llys Aled* was the Contractor who built the new Church at Llansannan, the present building that replaced the old building that was demolished in 1787. As such, he was entitled to the timber from the old church that he sold to Col. Biddulph of Chirk Castle who was the landlord of *Llys Aled*. Some of this timber was used for the principals of the barn that was built on the site of the old house at *Llys Aled*. His wife Mary, (nee Lloyd) was one of the first members of the Calvinistic Methodists who established 'the Cause' at *Tan y Fron*. The son of Mary and Morris Davies was Joseph who married a lady called Elizabeth. Morris Davies was a hard-working tenant farmer who was born in 1790. He was a poet and a man of learning who was also a good musician. He was a Precentor at his M.C. Chapel at Llansannan and many thought him to be way ahead of his time. He was a cultured man with a consuming interest in his country's history, a man of principle who was well respected. As well as being a farmer, he was a part-time drover. Towards the end of each year he would buy fatted pigs and take them to be sold at markets in Shrewsbury and Wolverhampton. On one of these trips he received a letter at Shrewsbury on a Saturday morning informing him that his wife was seriously ill, and if he wished to see her alive, had better make his way home as quickly as possible. He travelled the better part of the journey by train and reached Cerrig y Drudion by nightfall. It would have been highly dangerous to attempt to cross Hiraethog Mountain in the dark with not even a footpath to follow, quite apart from the fact that he was carrying a lot of money on his person and there were areas where notorious robbers had hideouts. So he stayed overnight at Cerrig y Drudion, then made his way home on foot the following morning, which was a Sunday. When he arrived home he was relieved to see his wife still alive and feeling much better. But in the afternoon he walked to Llansannan to attend Sunday School where he told his friends about the difficulties of his journey and his trek over the mountain that Sunday morning. The result was that he suffered a disciplining by the Elders of the Chapel for journeying on a Sunday, and was deprived of his Chapel membership. He and some others then left the Methodists to worship on their own. Some of the people who left with him were:

1) Edward Llwyd of *Llwyn Derw* son of Joseph Llwyd a Chapel deacon. Edward was a writer and two of his Manuscripts have survived - one is at Aberystwyth in the National Library that gives the history of the Independent cause in Llansannan.

2) Hugh Roberts (Sawyer)
   and

3) William Rees (Gwilym Hiraethog) a famous preacher and writer of international repute.

   This walkout was the first step in establishing the Independent cause in Llansannan.

   The Calvinistic Chapel in Llansannan is known as *Henry Rees' Chapel* after

William's brother. It begs the question of what brotherly relations were like after the religious split, but it must be remembered that these people were educated men in an age when many were unable to read or write. They were also philosophers and as such would not have been afflicted by personal animosities, not to any great extent anyway.

It is interesting to note also that the grandfather of the Rees brothers was Henry Rice who first came to Llansannan from Llandeilo Fawr in Carmarthenshire as an Exciseman around 1765 and married Gwen Llwyd the heiress of *Chwibren*. The name *Llwyd*, is now known as Lloyd and the name Rice or Rees was originally *Rhys*. The Welsh form is of course the original. A *Llwyd* family from mid-Wales formed Lloyds Bank so that drovers could deposit their money after sales and not risk carrying it on their person. Highwaymen, who were robbers were very much part of the scene in those days, and drovers were known to carry a lot of money.

There were many small landed-gentry in Wales after the big landowners left to follow the Tudors to London after Henry Tudor (Harri Tudur) became Henry VII following the Battle of Bosworth. One of the most influential families in England, the Cecils, is a prime example. They were a Welsh family called *Seisyllt*, a name that became anglicised to Cecil. On the other hand there are distinguished Welsh families today who are descendants of the Normans who came over from France with William the Conqueror. The Salisbury or Salesbury families are examples to be found in the Denbigh area, William Salesbury, translator of the New Testament into Welsh, and *Myddleton* is Sir Hugh Myddleton who brought the first public water supply to London. The Myddleton family seat was Chirk Castle. The connection was with Denbigh Castle, which was a Norman stronghold until Cromwell and his Roundheads blasted it during the Civil War.

Chapter Thirteen

THE HOWATSONS

Mam's mother was a Howatson. They were Scots from Middlebie near Ecclefechan in the border country. Earlier in the 1700s they were at Eskdalemuir, which was a wild remote area where they were shepherds. According to the books and maps of Scotland over which I have pored, the Howatsons were part of the great MacDonald clan but they lived in Douglas Clan country. I read that the Douglas family was very powerful and married into the Scottish Royal family eleven times. During the years of border raids they were known as the Black Douglas.

The Howatson family-tree goes back to William Howatson who was born in 1721 and who died in 1798. He married a Marty Anderson and they had four children. Their son Robert was born in 1754 and died in 1838. He married Isabella Laidlaw who lived until she was 92 having had nine children. Their son William moved to Middlebie and is described as a shepherd who married Isabella Armstrong who lived until she was 87 years of age after having had ten children. The youngest of the brood, Thomas, described as a farmer married Elizabeth Richardson who lived until she was 79 years of age having had nine children. Elizabeth Richardson also came of farming stock but they were dairy farmers and looked upon as being one step higher than sheep farmers on the pecking order. I was told by one of my mother's cousins that the Richardson family lived at East Scotsbrig or West Scotsbrig on the northern edge of Westmoreland. I shall have to go looking for this soon. Elizabeth Richardson had a sister called Isabella Richardson who married Charles Armstrong: they also had another unmarried sister called Margaret. Their mother's maiden name was Barton.

Thomas and Elizabeth Howatson with three children and one servant moved from Scotland to Wales around 1865//66. They came to a village called Llangernyw to work at an estate farm called *Maesol*. A daughter Agnes was born and died in 1869 and was buried at Llangernyw churchyard. Shortly afterwards, Thomas was appointed as Estate Manager for the Wynne-Yorke Family, at their Mansion *Dyffryn Aled*, in the village of Llansannan, and he moved to live at the Home Farm at *Plas Newydd.*

The family at this time consisted of Betsy Barton Howatson the eldest, who was my grandmother, also Isabella Richardson Howatson and John Howatson, who were born in Scotland, and William Howatson who was born in Llangernyw. Later were born George who died aged 12 years, and Charles who was born in 1875 who became a Veterinary Surgeon in St. Asaph and married Mary Elizabeth and had two daughters. He was a clever fellow who became an alcoholic and died aged 62 - the tale was that his wife favoured the life of a lady and never had meals ready and so Charles went to the local hotel for his lunch! One of the daughters became a pharmacist and worked for Boots in London. Another child was Margaret, born in 1876 and died 1877.

Robert, the youngest was born in 1880 and died aged 23. He was the very handsome young man whose death I have described earlier, and I very much regret not questioning my parents more vigorously about him.

The Howatson family has now become very large in North Wales and is gradually spilling over into other countries. Most of them are resourceful people, not afraid of hard work and successful in business. Some are farmers, engineers, technicians, builders, funeral directors and a lady beautician. All of the females of course, have lost the paternal surname by getting married but most of us still like to link up with the old family.

Some people wonder how a Scotsman came to be employed here in Wales. Well the truth is that at that time, education in Scotland was way ahead of England and Wales. Thomas Howatson was an able and intelligent man, very strict, kept his books neatly and in meticulous style. I believe he became the first Returning Officer for his Area after the introduction of Local Government elections. He was also fond of growing flowers and had a fine collection of geraniums growing in the porch at *Plas Newydd.*

The surviving four children grew up and got married. They produced large families and many members became the backbone of various communities.

Betsy, my grandmother, married Joseph Jones, an attractive farmer. As I have mentioned earlier, she had twelve children of which only five girls survived, my mother being the eldest. Her sisters were Elizabeth (Lil), Isabella, Margaret and Janet. Auntie Lil had four girls and was the one who emulated her mother by rearing as her own, a baby boy, whose mother had died at his birth, the son of a cousin.

Isabella was working as a mother's help with an English family. After a time, the family announced that they were going to visit the U.S.A. and Isabella spoke of her wish to travel to the United States. Much to her mother's dismay, her grandfather promised to pay her fare as long as she would be travelling with her employers. She was only 18 years old when she arrived in New York, and found a job at one of the best hotels as the Housekeeper's Assistant. Eventually she married an Italian and became Mrs. Sparacco. Five children were born, the eldest was named Joseph after his grandfather and one of the girls was named Isabella after her mother. While the children were still very young Mr. Sparacco departed, never to be seen again. When I was a teenager I somehow came across her address and began writing to her. For some years she responded and then - silence! During the war, unbeknown to us, her son Joseph was lying in a London hospital having been badly wounded. If only we had known, my brother could have visited him and brought him some comfort. After the war my sister and husband Stanley who lived in New York State found her again and got to know the family. They were all decent people bringing up their children, and of course they were our cousins. My sister kept in contact with Aunt Isabella and met her on several occasions in the USA, but she and Stan were never invited to visit her home: they always met in a public place and parted the same way. How sad!

Aunt Isabella went safely to the States on the Lusitania on her maiden voyage before World War 1 - but during the war the ship was torpedoed and sunk by the German Navy - the event is believed to be the reason the U.S.A. belatedly became involved in the War. Apparently Joseph had tried to persuade his mother to return to Wales for a visit to the family - he promised to pay her fare, but she would not move from the USA. She had suffered horribly from sea-sickness on the voyage to America, and was unwilling to repeat the experience ever again.

After a time, there was silence once more, no one answered my sister's telephone calls and that was the end. We have no more knowledge of the family. Aunt Isabella herself would not now be alive anyway. I regret the ending of our contact with this branch of the family. Perhaps in future, with a lot of effort and good fortune, contact may be re-established once more.

Margaret (Mag) married at 16 years of age and had one girl, Kit, and three boys -

Owen Emlyn; Tecwyn (his mam called him Tecs); and Aled. For a while they lived at her home at *Garddan Isa* but later moved to a Chapel House at Rhuallt near St. Asaph. Kit married and had one son. Owen Emlyn married and had four sons. Tecwyn married but I don't know about his family, and Aled was in the Army in the Far East and picked up some jungle bug. He was not well for a time and died quite young. Auntie Mag's husband Owen was a heavy man who died suddenly, leaving her a widow. Then Kit died, followed by her husband and their son also. Owen Emlyn also died early. And in addition, Auntie Mag suffered for years with ulcers on her legs, but nothing stopped her energetic way of life. She was always cheerful - but then she too passed away.

When I was about 10 years old, Owen Emlyn was self-employed as a timber-feller. He bought an area of trees and systematically felled them, turned them into planks and then sold them. He also sold logs from the branches. At that time he was newly married and lived in a caravan. It wasn't a modern caravan, but a gypsy type van and between the two of them Owen Emlyn and his wife fashioned a lovely home. For a few months he was working in our village area and I loved going to that caravan. I decided that I too would live in such a caravan when I grew up. The nearest I ever came to that ideal was spending a holiday with my younger daughter and her family in a modern caravan, which was pleasant and enjoyable but not a patch on that old gypsy caravan with its magic and romance.

When Janet left school she went into service at a farm in the Vale of Clwyd. When she was a child she had suffered an acute attack of measles that had affected her eyes. For many weeks she could go outside, only after dark. Gradually however, things improved, and she lived normally again. She was a tall lady, not particularly pretty, but with a special elegance. In her late teens she became pregnant by a farmer's son and therefore lost her job. She had no home to call upon and her parents were dead so, she went to my mother for help. She lived at my parents` house for several weeks and just before Christmas gave birth to a beautiful baby boy. She suckled the baby for a few weeks. No one knew she was there because the baby was so quiet. My mother wanted to adopt the baby, but she was expecting her own first-born child within a month and was still working in their butchers' business - especially busy at Christmastime. It became obvious that Janet could not keep the child, so my father, with the help of a solicitor friend, arranged the adoption of the little boy by a well-to-do couple from Cheshire. The handing over was at Rhyl railway station.

Janet went to see the little lad once, when he was about two years old. She saw him coming down a staircase at his home looking like a little angel. She could not take any more and fled. She became a housekeeper to a farmer whose wife was an invalid. She worked hard, looking after the lady of the house, bringing up the little daughter of the house and coping with the farm work. This went on for years. The daughter grew up and went to a Private School, and after some years, married and had a little girl of her own, Janet idolised her. The invalid wife finally died. They left the farm and moved to a smallholding where they farmed on a small scale, and Janet did 'Bed and Breakfast' for visitors. With pressure from her family, the farmer married Janet. A few years later he died and she moved to a house in the village and finally to a nursing home where she died. I used to visit her at her house and then later at the nursing home because I felt sorry for her. She was intensely proud with a high regard for certain people whom she called, 'county families' the aristocracy and wealthy people. My sister Bella was a legatee in her

Will - £50.00. I was not mentioned, but there again I never thought I would be. Bella used to spend some holiday time with them at the smallholding. I went once, but felt uncomfortable there. I don't know exactly why, but I much preferred going to Auntie Lil's farm.

There was a sequel to Janet's story, a few years after her death I was told that a man had been to Llansannan looking for a Janet Jones and giving a few details of her life. He had been advised to contact me. A little later, I received a letter from a gentleman in London who worked free-lance tracing people and making up family trees. He explained his current mission and asked if a certain person could visit me. After consulting my husband and re-reading the letter many times, I could think of no valid reason why I should refuse. The person wrote to us and we agreed that he, his wife and son should visit one Sunday afternoon.

The situation was that this person was known to be a son of Janet Jones and the accompanying details gave reason to believe that she was my Aunt Janet. This made me realise that my Auntie Jen must have given birth to two boys and had given them both up for adoption.

Even though I had agreed to the meeting with this man I still felt pangs of trepidation wondering what he was like, would I be happy for him to be my cousin? Feelings and thoughts rushed through my brain, almost overwhelming me. After all I knew nothing about him. However, the deed was done and that was that. Came the hour and the doorbell pealed and I walked to the door, hesitated slightly, then with composure opened the door. I looked at the man on the doorstep and instantly knew he was indeed, who it was said he was. He had Auntie Jen's features - the same shaped face and mouth and I knew who his father was too - the same unusual complexion and hair colour was evident. I invited him into the house with his wife and their eleven year old son. We went through the usual social graces and then he told me the whole story.

There was never really any question about his mother, for his birth certificate gave her proper name and address. He had been born in a small town about 10 miles from the farm where she lived and worked. He had subsequently been taken by the family of a farm labourer who went from farm to farm as work became available. It was a poor family, and the sum of money paid over when the child was given to the family was very welcome. The family lived in a poor area of St. Asaph and the baby took the surname of Roberts, which was the family name. He could remember a woman coming to see him when he was a small boy and bringing him a sailor suit to wear. He hated wearing the suit because it stood out like a sore thumb amongst the clothes worn by the poor children in the area. During the early part of his childhood he was not treated too badly. The father was always kindly towards him but the wife grew increasingly abusive. She went to work at the military camp nearby and started to drink. He showed me the large scar on the back of his neck where a knife had struck him having been thrown by this woman in a temper. As a teenager he got a job in a shop at Denbigh and my husband remembered seeing him making deliveries in the town. When he was sixteen, he ran away from home and joined the Army.

There was one daughter in the Roberts family who was some years older than the lad, and was always good to him. Once, when he came home on leave he pestered this girl about his parentage until finally she told him about the farm where his mother lived and described the farmer who was his father, but she mentioned no names. One day, he walked to the farm and as he approached it along the lane he could see a woman standing at the doorway. He was tempted to rush up to her and announce who he was, but the thought came to his mind - "She didn't want me when I was born. I don't want her now," so he hurriedly left. As he was on his way from the farm, a car sped by driven by a man whom he recognised from his sister's description. He never had any further contact with them. Indeed he was averse even to thinking about them.

War broke out and he was sent to France where he was captured by the Germans and sent to work in the coal mines in Germany. His co-workers were very much against him and treated him badly, but one elderly man was very good to him. He shared his lunch and taught him to speak German. When the War was over and he was set free, he was appointed to work with the Control Commission in Germany because of his ability to speak the language. He went on courses for ex-servicemen and finally landed a good job with the Electricity Board. He continued to study and became Head of Department. Well, we had one thing in common: we both worked for the same firm! He had been married before and had a lovely daughter. He showed me some photos and was obviously very proud of her and also of his young son and second wife who also worked for the Board.

The whole business of tracing his parents had come about by accident. He was a guest at a wedding in Denbigh and got into conversation with a man from London who was also a guest. In the course of chatting about work and so on the London man explained that he traced the whereabouts of families and people, and having heard Mr. Roberts' story volunteered to find his mother. His offer was not accepted because Mr. Roberts did not want to open old wounds after so many years. However, his wife, who had a very gentle manner, persuaded him to accept, "If your mother is still alive she might be lonely and would really like to know you," she said. And so it came about that I met another cousin. He was a gentleman in the true sense of the word, he had suffered many tribulations and come through with dignity. I was proud to know him as my cousin. He wanted nothing from his mother or father or anyone else. He was self-sufficient.

I asked if he would like to see a photograph of his mother and he said he would. I gave him a photograph of Auntie Jen taken when she was a young woman. He held it faced downwards in his hand for a long time until his wife said, "Why don't you look at it?" He said, "I am afraid of what I shall see." Finally however he turned over the photograph and gazed at it for some time. I offered it to him and he gladly accepted in the knowledge that his mother was by this time deceased.

The Roberts family lived in Wrexham and they warmly invited us to visit their home. Unfortunately that period was a very busy time for me working full time and running a Guesthouse with my husband. I never really had time to go anywhere, not even on holiday, so we never got to Wrexham. However, I am glad that my cousin finally got to know who he was and yes, I am glad that he knows he has Howatson blood in his veins.

I mentioned earlier that Auntie Lil was my favourite aunt. When I went on holiday to the farm, every week on a Wednesday we went to the market at Denbigh. People would say to my Auntie, "Oh, is this your youngest daughter then?" Our first call was to the grocers to give her order, to be called for later on, and then to whatever various other shops she wanted to visit. Our progress from one place to another was very slow on account of the frequent stops we made to chat to people. She was very well liked because she was kind and interested in people. Some conversations were more interesting than others. I can hear her now saying in Welsh "*Cer oma*" - literally,"Go away" (slang geraway) when some surprising bit of gossip was passed on or she would exclaim, "Fancy, well fancy that!" Such funny little things, quite unimportant, that stayed in my memory.

Although I worked quite hard on my visits to the farm, doing whatever jobs Auntie Lil asked me to do, I really enjoyed myself. There was no time to get bored. Every summer on a fine day, Auntie Lil, one or two of my older cousins and I would go to *Bryn Trillyn* on the Denbigh Moors to gather bilberries. We would eat our fill and then gather lots of berries to take home. My face was always puce from the juice of the berries and so were my fingers and clothes. The berries were cooked into jam or jelly and some just for tarts. I would love to have one of those teas at *Groes Farm* again. Tea with creamy milk, fresh from the cows, wholemeal bread baked by Auntie Lil in the brick oven in the kitchen wall, butter made by Auntie Lil and that fantastic bilberry jam. With all the fancy food that is available today in freezers, tins or bakeries, there is nothing to compare with that farmhouse tea.

My grandmother's sister was Isabella who married David Vaughan and had ten children. Two sons emigrated to Australia. I came to know one of the brothers named Tom, who had a hill farm near Llanrwst and his sons and daughters. One of the sons, John, became President of the Welsh Black Cattle Society and won many, many trophies for his cattle. His sister Glenys was the owner of the Abbey Grange Hotel at the foot of the Horseshoe Pass at Llangollen, a girl who thrived on hard work all her life. She was a very kind lady, and most welcoming. Whenever we called to visit her she was never too busy to serve tea and sit to chat about old times with us. I also knew Mary, one of the daughters of Isabella, who was married to a stage actor, and lived at Ecclefechan in Scotland. One of her daughters married the famous Scott of the Manchester Guardian. Mim lived at Llan Ffestiniog and was a widow when I knew her. Blodwen married a Llanrwst man and I knew her in her later years. Her son Chris, one of twins, came for holidays to Groes once or twice.

Isabella or Bella as she was known lived with her mother. When I was a small child they kept the Saracen's Head Hotel in Llansannan. Bella had a daughter called Olive who was about my age. She was spoilt and was given everything she asked for, including a rocking horse. When my mother and I visited once, Olive would not let me have a go on the rocking horse and so I stuck a finger in her bottom and she jumped off crying and squealing, mostly in surprise I think. What a dreadful thing to do but I got my ride! They also had a gramophone, a HMV with a picture of a listening dog. The record I remember was called "*Robin Goch*" - Robin Redbreast.

Isabella's daughter Bella, was a very attractive woman who later lived with a married man. There was apparently a very good reason for his leaving his wife, but of course in those days divorce was out of the question. However, after the wife died, Bella and the man did get married. Isabella, the mother reminded me of Queen Victoria because she had a similar figure and was always enveloped in long black clothes, in the same way I suppose.

William Howatson, the youngest of the four brothers married a Jane Owens and had seven children. The eldest son was John Howatson, my grandmother's brother. He was a farmer, and his first wife was Mary Beattie a Scots girl whose family had came to Wales after the Howatsons. She had four sons, but died when the fourth one was born, William, the Will who was brought up by my grandmother. Later, John was married again, to Jane Hughes.

Three children were born to them, a boy Charles, and a girl Alice. Another girl, Barbara died when she was aged 16. Johnny was devastated when Mary Beattie died. He was inconsolable and it is said that it was her death that made him hit the bottle. I only know that Charles, his son, had to suffer a lot of unhappiness when he was the only one left at home with his father until the old man died aged 84 years of age. Johnny was the uncle, who hit my mother across her face when I was a toddler held on her arm at *Pengraig*, as I related earlier.

Chapter Fourteen

RETURN TO SCOTLAND

When the Wynne-Yorke family sold the Dyffryn Aled Estate, the Mansion itself was converted into a Mental Asylum for wealthy people for a few years and when that closed down, Tom and Elizabeth Howatson retired. They went to *Llety'r Eos* nearby for a while until they finalised the purchase of 'Castle View' in Abergele, which was a nice home. My mother used to visit them every week taking eggs, butter, chicken, and other foods like cakes. She took with her my brother, a cute little boy dressed in a kilt.

After a while Tom and Elizabeth grew restless. They had retired from a very active life and now were amongst relative strangers in a town. For whatever reason, they decided to return to Scotland. They bought a fine stone-built house called 'Mayfield' in Ecclefechan. It appears that some repairs were necessary and a new kitchen range was fitted, at a cost of £5.00. The house in Abergele had also to be sold.

It must have been around the end of World War1 in 1918 when they moved back to Scotland. In view of the fact that they both died in 1921, they did not live in Mayfield for long. It is probable that they eventually realised that they had left all their family in Wales. There is a saying, 'A native never returns'.

I remember my mother telling me something her grandfather had told her after her grandmother's death, after she'd travelled up to Scotland for the funeral. My mother said many times that she had never heard a cross word spoken between her grandparents in all the years she had lived with them, but the old man told her of an incident that happened one evening when they were sitting quietly, not speaking on either side of the fireplace. Suddenly the old lady got up and picked up the poker and made to hit him with it. He was heart-broken. I wonder if it was he, who wanted to return to Scotland and she was pining for her children and grandchildren far away in Wales and in her heart blamed him for depriving her of their family?

Who knows? Tom lived for only six months after Elizabeth died. Almost immediately, he went into decline. Now the eldest daughter, my grandmother Betsy was dead, but her sister Bella was alive and it was she who went to Scotland to tend to her father. At the time Mary, the daughter of Bella, was living in the village of Ecclefechan so it was very convenient for Bella to be able to stay in Scotland. When Tom died, his brother-in-law Charles Armstrong, who was the Executor of the Will and Estate wrote to my mother, "Dear Mary. Do not trouble to come to Scotland for the funeral of your grandfather. It was with shock and grief and dismay that I learned that he had changed his Will recently and has left you nothing. If I'd had any idea of what he had done, I would certainly have tried to reason with him. It is so unfair and unjust."

The letter was a terrific shock for my mother for it was she who was the favourite. It was not just the financial side that impacted on her but the thought that she had become out of favour for no reason at all. I do not know what the details of the Will were, but Bella certainly benefited well from it.

Who can guess what had gone on in those last few weeks? My mother knew. There was not much luck attached to that legacy. About ten years later, when Bella and her daughter and granddaughter were living in a big old house at Pensarn in Abergele, they arrived one day at our house as early as 9 o'clock in the morning and stayed until late in the evening. Mam gave them a welcome and fed them, but was very puzzled about the visit. Later she found out why they had come. That day there was a big sale at their home. The money had run out. I cannot remember any more about them except that many years later I met Olive again, at a funeral, and she was a very nice lady. I liked her.

Chapter Fifteen

THE ARMSTRONGS

After the Howatsons' arrival in Wales, a fair number of other Scots families followed - the Bells, McGills, Beatties and the Armstrongs. Mrs. Howatson's sister, Isabella, had married Charles Armstrong and they too migrated from Scotland to Wales where they took over a hill farm of 500 acres, *Bryn Kenrick* in Llanfair T.H. They had eleven children. Charles also had a seed business that he later sold to a local businessman in Llansannan, and it expanded very successfully. Three boys and one girl became Doctors of Medicine, another son became a bank manager, a daughter Elizabeth became housekeeper to her brother, Dr John. Another daughter, Kate trained as a Dairy expert and travelled about teaching and lecturing. Amongst other things she taught farmers' wives how to make cheese. At the time, a number of cheese schools were set up in North and Mid Wales. The garage at Auntie Lil's farm was called 'The Cheese School'. I always thought it was a funny name for a garage!

On one occasion, King Edward VII and his Queen Alexandra came to visit Kinmel Hall, and at a banquet in their honour the centrepiece on the dining table was an impressive model of the Hall made of butter, created and beautifully decorated by Kate. It stood on a thick base of industrial ice - not edible but marvellous to look at. Kate married Yak Atkinson and they had a dairy farm in Derbyshire. At one point the motor firm of Rolls Royce bought some of their land for a very good price and so they became tax exiles on the Isle of Man. I corresponded with Kate for some years. A daughter, Mrs. Barr, lived in a large house on a hill in Penrith where her son was a successful Veterinary Surgeon.

The bank manager died young. His wife was French and they had one son, John. When his father died and his mother was ill, John went to his Uncle Fergus and was raised by him. Although Dr. Fergus was a bachelor, he nevertheless had a very good home run by a kind and efficient housekeeper named Rosie.

John had everything he could possibly want. He was educated at an exclusive private school for boys at Cowbridge, but never settled down or made anything of himself. He drifted along, returning home periodically. Each time he was rigged out with several sets of clothes and money. In the end he just disappeared. How sad, because he might have become a great man and inherited a small fortune too.

George became a Doctor and went into General Practice at Pontllanfraith in the county of Monmouth. Janet qualified as a Doctor and became a Schools' Medical Officer. She married an estate agent in Cardiff and became Mrs. Herdman. They had a son and daughter, both of whom became doctors, the lad in Canada and Biddy as a Medical Officer of Health in Buckinghamshire.

John Richardson Armstrong was educated at the Grammar School in St. Asaph, and at 16 years of age, passed the examination admitting him to Edinburgh University Medical School. Four years later, he graduated with the degrees of M.B. and C.M. but had to wait until he was 21 to be admitted to the Medical Register. He held posts as a locum doctor, and made a round voyage to Japan as a ship's surgeon. When he was 24 he took the M.D. degree. Finally he answered an advertisement for a colliery doctor at Cwmparc in the Rhondda valley. There were 144 applicants and the choice was made as a result of a ballot of the miners and their choice was the 'young North Walian'. He was a success and before very long he had built a large house for himself which he called 'Gilnockie' after the ancestral home of the Armstrong clan. Life for a colliery doctor was hard - three surgeries a day, and patients to visit on his rounds totalling up to seventy a day. Night calls were never refused. At its peak, Dr. John's practice had four surgeries and employed two doctors, two dispensers and a trained nurse. As there was no dentist in the area, he also extracted teeth without anaesthetic. Emergency operations were carried out on the kitchen table until a Cottage Hospital was built.

His sister Elizabeth was his housekeeper. After 35 years in practice he died in 1931 and was buried locally. The miners voted unanimously that his brother Dr. Fergus Armstrong should take over the practice. At the time Fergus was in practice at nearby Tonpentre.

He was the youngest of the family and had received his education at the Abergele County School where his father was a Governor. He achieved a first class pass in the London Matriculation Examination when he was 16 years old. After five years as a medical student at Edinburgh University he gained the degree of M.B.Ch.B. at the age of 21. He joined his brother at Treorchy then applied for, and became a house physician at Cardiff Royal Infirmary. He submitted a thesis for the M.D Edinburgh Degree and succeeded with Honours. Still not satisfied he went to Edinburgh to work for the Fellowship. To keep himself, he became a supervisor of medical students in the Anaesthetics Department. He had been the first to introduce the 'open ether' method at the Royal Infirmary Cardiff and at the Gynaecological Wards of the Edinburgh Royal Infirmary. Fergus estimated that he gave some five thousand general anaesthetics without a death. In 1913 he passed the examination for the F.R.C.S. at the minimum age of 25. He passed all his exams in the shortest possible time and at the youngest possible age. He could have obtained a very senior post anywhere, or gone into private practice, but he decided to become a partner in a colliery practice at Tonpentre at a salary of £250.p.a.

When War broke out in 1914 he immediately decided to enlist, and was given a temporary commission as first lieutenant in the R.A.M.C. Then he became a Captain at the Welsh Hospital at Natley. He became bored and frustrated with the routine work and longed for the operating theatre. On Good Friday 1915 he was on board ship bound for Salonika to be Chief Surgeon at the First British Hospital in Serbia. With Professor Strong of Harvard University, U.S.A. he travelled through Albania and Macedonia to inoculate some 30,000 troops and on the way they found soldiers dying of malaria through lack of quinine.

When his contract with the First British Hospital ran out he joined the Serbian Relief Fund's Hospital. There were 1250 beds and here he gained a wide and varied experience of war surgery. In October 1915 the Serbian Army was defeated and crushed by the Austrian and Bulgarian armies and everyone in the Hospital including staff were taken prisoner. In the middle of the bombardment Fergus was attending to casualties in the operating theatre when a Bulgarian officer entered and spoke to him in perfect English announcing, “You are my prisoner”. Fergus worked non-stop for seventy two hours during the battle. After six months of captivity he was released by the Red Cross organisation, and in October 1916 was repatriated.

During his time in Roumania Fergus met Queen Marie and worked as a surgeon in her hospital. He lived an interesting life, and as a King's Messenger he delivered thirty two dispatch cases to the British Foreign Office.

On his way home to Treorchy, he fell and fractured his ankle at Euston Station, London. Before being fully recovered from this injury he received a telegram from Queen Marie that said, "Come out at once to Palace Bucharest." In October 1916 he set out for Roumania with a team that included an American surgeon, Dr. Breckinridge Bayne, Sister O'Neill his theatre sister in Serbia, and an actor whom Fergus had trained as an anaesthetist using the 'open ether' method. Queen Marie had great faith in Fergus, and a high regard for him too, and in her Autobiography there is a full-page photograph of him. When the Germans finally invaded Roumania, Fergus and Sister O'Neill were advised to leave the country. Before leaving, Fergus developed a pustule on his hand, which was diagnosed as the deadly Anthrax. He was treated successfully but it left scars. The party left, and eventually reached Stockholm where they lunched with the Crown Prince and Princess of Sweden, but on the way Fergus had experienced some difficulty at St. Petersburg because the Russian Revolution had broken out. Fergus had a trunk full of surgical instruments and the officials would not let him take the trunk with him on his journey. He was sent to see Trotsky who also refused. However, he decided to take a chance and went to the station and took the trunk with him. He found an official who spoke English and told him the trunk contained, "the tools of my trade." The official was immediately satisfied and put a chalk mark on the trunk, which was promptly passed through the barrier.

He returned from the War with decorations conferred on him by the Kings of Serbia and Roumania, 'The Royal Red Cross of Serbia' and 'The Order of Officer of the Star of Roumania' the country's highest decoration.

After his capture by the Bulgarians, the enemy wanted to give him a medal for bravery and were very disappointed that the British government could not allow such recognition to be bestowed in wartime.

Ironically, although he was recommended to receive a British decoration for his work and bravery, he was nevertheless deemed to be ineligible because he was under the command of the Serbian army at the time!

While at St. Petersburg he bought a magnificent sable fur coat, and when he wore it on his return home, was considered to be "every inch the Baron" which was how he was addressed by his fellow residents at Cardiff Royal Infirmary - "the Baron."

On his return to Wales he took up the Medical Practice he had left in 1914. His first post war emergency operation was performed on an elderly lady on her bed in her own home, and during the operation the electric light failed, but Fergus concluded the process successfully in the light of candles. Between 1946 and 1951 he carried out five hundred appendectomies without a death.

For a long time he had himself suffered with a duodenal ulcer and in 1938 had an operation to attend to the problem. He was 51 years old. To recuperate he joined the R.M.S. Franconia as ship's surgeon for a voyage lasting over five months. During his time on the high seas he performed one appendectomy on a young lad of 14 who recovered well.

Although he had worked under shell-fire and bombs during the War the nearest he came to being killed was locally in 1941 during an air raid when twenty-three people died and many more were injured.

Fergus told me these stories and gave me related newspaper cuttings when I used to visit him in Treorchy. He loved to play host to celebrities at his home at 'Gilnockie' that included singers, musicians, adjudicators and actors. My husband, who was a professional musician and a Silver Medalist of the London Guildhall School of Music, had many conversations with him especially about his friends during his youth in North Wales. Fergus would say, "I knew him, of course I knew him, I knew them all."

He had signed portraits of Queen Marie and her daughter who was connected to the Greek royal family. The 'long' room upstairs in Gilnockie held these portraits and countless marvellous souvenirs from his travels.

It seemed strange that he was unable to drive, but then of course he did not need the skill because he was always driven around by a chauffer. At one time, he had been engaged to be married to a lady from North Wales but it did not result in marriage. How could a Scottish Presbyterian marry a Roman Catholic in those days? He asked me once if I thought he had made a mistake in not getting married. What a question! "How could anyone know" I said, "You might have been very happy or on the other hand you might have been miserable." That is how things work out in a marriage, you can never really know the outcome in advance.

When the would-be doctors were students at Edinburgh, their father wisely took precautions to ensure that Fergus and his brothers and sister worked hard, but suffered no hardship. He installed his wife's sister Margaret in a cottage that he had purchased in Edinburgh, and it was she who saw to their needs and kept a strict but motherly eye on them.

There was a generation gap between my mother and her cousin Fergus but because he was the youngest of his family and my mother was the oldest of hers they were about the same age and were fond of each other. She told me that he chased the nurses, and he told me that she once ate a whole cucumber, which made her extremely sick. While on holiday from University he used to go to *Plas Newydd* where my mother lived and they always had fun.

I liked Fergus, and I shall always be grateful to him for lending us the capital to buy our Llanrwst home when the owner was selling it, and the loan was interest free! He also let us repay the loan as and when we could. This generosity helped us immensely.

When Dr. Fergus Armstrong retired he was over 70 years old and a great Presentation send-off was arranged for him in the Parc & Dare Hall, Treorchy. Arthur and I were invited to attend the celebrations and were happy to be there. People said it was, "the end of a dynasty" and there was a palpable sadness as well as a rejoicing in the air. The Treorchy Male Voice Choir was in full voice; the local M.P. spoke; and colleagues reminisced about his life. He was presented with a beautiful solitaire diamond ring, a miner's lamp and other gifts of appreciation including a special plaque bearing the Borough Coat of Arms. The local people idolised him. He could quite easily have worked in the highest places in the land but he had opted to stay in the Rhondda, through the sufferings of the Depression and the World Wars. I saw photographs of him playing golf with King Edward VIII, Lord Davies of Llandinam and other high ranking people but he was never snooty or supercilious. He was always 'down to earth' and proud of his achievements but never boastful. The newspaper report that followed his special presentation stated that, "There are few people in Britain, let alone the Rhondda Valley who could rightly claim to be a living legend, and a benefactor to thousands. Dr. Fergus Armstrong certainly could, though he would not be so immodest as to do so." The Plaque signified the love and respect held for him by the people of the Rhondda. "He was larger than life, a powerful personality, a compassionate nature hidden under a smoothly rough exterior and his tireless efforts to aid the sick were the qualities which made him a dominant figure, a legend in his own lifetime throughout his years in the Rhondda."

He suffered quite a lot at the end because of cancer but he bore it all with fortitude and grace. He died aged 89 years.

I have written at length about him because I admired him immensely and was very fond of him. He was a true Scot who spoke English magnificently well with a Welsh accent.

When he retired he had made provision for all his staff, and Rosie, his devoted housekeeper retired with him to a terraced house which was roomy enough, but small in comparison with Gilnockie. His sister Janet did not approve of Fergus living in such an insignificant house but Fergus was glad at the end to be taken care of by Rosie in her 'small house'. He continued to receive the loving care to which he was accustomed.

Chapter Sixteen

MY MOTHER-IN-LAW

I had a mother-in-law for nearly forty years, who actually shared our home with us for eight of those years. Later, I too became a mother in law to two sons and one daughter. I do not like the title because it has an unappealing connotation, promoted by jokes and innuendo that portrays the role holder as an unfriendly person. It shouldn't be too difficult for society to create a much more user-friendly and attractive title for those in such roles … and what about the mothers of unmarried couples, should they not also be given a similar title? Will someone suddenly have a brainwave and create a lovely new title for mothers-in-law that has the feel-good factor? But I hope not one akin to the irritatingly awkward title 'Ms' that has been created of late. I have great difficulty pronouncing Ms because it has a sibilance that resembles being accosted surreptitiously with a loud "pssstt"!

Well, I suppose like everyone else, mothers-in-law come in all shapes and sizes, character, mannerisms, peculiarities, talents and abilities because they are persons in their own right and members of the human race.

I remember Arthur's mother as a kindly and generally helpful person who was a good conversationalist with a remarkable memory for names and places. She was very religious and read the Welsh Bible every day. She was a trained and talented dressmaker who could make wonderful things with her hands and the sewing machine. She could sometimes be critical in a subtle and annoying way, and occasionally be in a sulk that no one could explain or understand. At first I tried to understand her moods and help her out of them, but life was hectic and I was busy. We never had arguments or rows and my father-in law said that she always snapped-out of a mood very brightly, and told me not to worry.

To differentiate between the two grandmothers, we called her *Nain Gaerwen*, literally Grandma and her house name *Gaerwen*, and this is how I shall now refer to her. She was born with four sisters and two brothers, one of whom died in infancy. Her mother, Margaret was born in Trefor, which is between Llangollen and Wrexham and that is all I know about her. I cannot recall anyone speaking of her family or relatives. Nain's father was from a village called Betws Garmon, a country area near Caernarfon. He had been adopted by an uncle and aunt when he was very young, but I am unsure of the reason for the adoption. This childless couple raised the boy on more than one farm, having moved once or twice because of the wife's health difficulties.

Before the couple were married, a carpenter from Anglesey had been brought to the bride's home, to make a full set of furniture from seasoned oak grown on the farm. This was a normal custom - trees, mostly oak on the farmland would be cut down, the branches used for firewood and the timber put aside to season for quite some time, sometimes years, to be used when the need arose. This particular suite of oak furniture would have been made around 1820 and used by the couple throughout their married life. Following the couple's death, the individual items of furniture in the suite were disposed of in different ways and ended up in various places. For instance, I can remember a *'tridarn'* cupboard (three piece cupboard), a 'press' cupboard, a grandfather clock, some chairs and a small table at the home of *Nain Gaerwen's* youngest sister, Aunty Gusta. But towards the end of her long life when she was still living on her own, these lovely old pieces of furniture disappeared gradually, and very valuable tea sets and silverware that she had inherited from a friend went too. In addition, other items of more modern furniture also disappeared from her house without explanation. Later, it came to light that an antique dealer, so called, had visited her house many times, and items of worth had then disappeared, but worryingly, her finances did not reflect any substantial increases as a result.

However, to come back to where we were, after *Nain Gaerwen's* father died, her mother and three sisters moved from the farm to a house in Bangor, and not long afterwards, around five years after their mother's death, three of her girls bought a new house in Deganwy. These were my husband's aunts. It was at this time that a 'dresser' and 'cheese cupboard', from the original set of hand-made oak furniture, were handed over to their sister Katie (Catherine Ellen) viz *Nain Gaerwen*. She had been working in a large store in Caernarfon called 'The Nelson' as a dressmaker and subsequently moved to a similar post in a country store at Llansannan, near Denbigh. In 1915 she married Thomas Vaughan Williams, *Taid Gaerwen* (Grandfather Gaerwen), my husband's father, and went to live at his home at *Bryn Rodyn*, or as it was known 'The Factory' at *Bryn Rhyd yr Arian* near Llansannan. She took the dresser and cheese cupboard with her. And so it was when Catherine Ellen and Thomas Vaughan Williams (*Nain & Taid Gaerwen*) retired to a house in Llansannan, which they called Gaerwen after her old home in Anglesey, the dresser and the cheese cupboard went with them there too.

Later when they were in their seventies, and owing to ill health they had to give up their home to live alternately with their two sons, Arthur and Harry and their families. The dresser and cheese cupboard came into our home in Llanrwst at that time and a smaller dresser and other items went to Harry's home. When Arthur and I retired in 1985 and moved to live in Eglwysbach, the dresser and cheese cupboard were moved there too, and that is where they are today.

The cupboard was in a sorry state when it first arrived in Llanrwst. Slabs of salt had been stored on the top of it and a mouse had nibbled a hole at the front, but after a lot of rubbing and polishing the wood came up well and it became a useful piece of furniture, needless to say not for storing food. The dresser too, had suffered a little in use - there were stains on the surface of the lower half, and the back panel of the open shelves had been wallpapered with paste. I had to painstakingly scratch it off bit by bit to restore it to its former glory. Taid's chair happened to be at the side of the dresser and I think the sound of the scratching irritated him because one afternoon he blurted out, “How long are you going on with that scratching, you sound like a rat!” Poor Taid! But the dresser looked much better afterwards. Nain was very pleased to see it being restored to its former glory and looked after so well and fortunately, the different sized Amaranth blue plates that are as old as the dresser, were intact. The dresser, with plates displayed, took pride of place in our living room in Llys Cerdd for many years, as it does today in my dining room in Eglwysbach.

Interestingly, I have a sepia coloured photograph of the couple, for whom the furniture was made, and my husband listed all the homes that had the dresser and cheese cupboard since 1820 as follows:

1) The farm at Betws Garmon;
2) Gorsedd Grucyn Farm, Nebo, Llanrwst 1850;
3) Garnedd Ucha Farm. Peniel, Nr.Denbigh;
4) Llanfair P.G. Village House, Ynys Mon (Anglesey);
5) Gaerwen Isa Farm, Gaerwen, Ynys Mon;
6) Dyffryn, Bangor;
7) The Ffactory, Bryn Rhyd Yr Arian, Denbighshire;
8) Y Gaerwen, Llansannan;
9) Llys Cerdd, Llanrwst;
10) Rhyd Yr Arian, Eglwysbach. (Present home)

Nain Gaerwen was born in the village of Llanfair P.G, - yes, *the* very place with that long, long name. *LLANFAIR PWLL GWYN GYLL GO GER Y CHWYRN DRO BWLL LLANTYSILIO OGO GOCH*. Can you pronounce it? Later they moved to a farm called *Gaerwen Isa*, Anglesey, or *Ynys Mon*, to give it its proper name. Anglesey has many villages and hamlets, and towns too such as Holyhead at the far end where there is a busy port with boats going to and from Eire. Ynys Mon is an island, and Holyhead is situated on a smaller island just off the mainland, but linked of course. The South Stack lighthouse is on a still smaller island linked by a bridge over the rocks and pounding seas. The new major road that cuts through the island from the Menai Bridges to Holyhead is an extension of the A55 that runs along the North Wales coast. The A5, built by the famous Scottish engineer Thomas Telford is still in use passing through many small villages and towns in the hinterland of North Wales.

Nain Gaerwen and her siblings grew up in a typical Victorian family - decent, hardworking, deeply religious and happy. Their father, Pierce Williams, was a highly-respected Deacon in the Presbyterian Chapel and although very strict, was kindly and loved by his children. Two of the girls, Martha Grace and Margaret, trained as nurses and were S.R.Ns. They trained in London and Margaret won a Gold Medal. They tended the servicemen wounded during World War 1 and later did private nursing based in Manchester, until they retired.

Mary was a milliner who opened a drapery and millinery shop in Deganwy that was very successful for over 15 years until the Depression years between the Wars, when she was forced to close her shop. She did not live long after the closure.

Myfanwy (Myfi) decided to emigrate to Chicago in the U.S.A. and for some years worked for the well known store in Chicago called 'Marshall Field'. However, after some years she became ill with tuberculosis and Margaret went out to the States to nurse her sister for just over a year until she died. During this time, Martha was working in this country and sending money to her sisters in the U.S.A. as they had no other means of sustenance.

The youngest, Augusta (Elizabeth) stayed at home to look after her parents. After her father died she and her mother left *Gaerwen Isa* and moved to Bangor and later after her mother's death, Aunty Gusta moved to Warren Drive, Deganwy, where she remained and where her two nursing sisters joined her when they retired, and lived there until they died.

Although she had not trained as a nurse Aunty Gusta worked periodically, nursing people in their homes and was in great demand. As a young woman, she had been engaged to a young man who was killed in action serving as a soldier in World War I. She was ill for a time and suffered from alopecia and thereafter had to wear a wig for the rest of her life. During all the time I knew her she was always cheerful and friendly and loved going on outings in the car. She lived for 97 years. Her last years were spent in a residential home, and although her sight and hearing were not good and she yearned for, "God to take her" as she often said in Welsh, she still retained her lively interest in everything and everyone.

I have pictures of the three girls when they were young women and they were pretty. Why, I wonder, did they remain unmarried? Of the four sisters, Arthur's mother was the only one to marry and have a family.

My favourite was Aunty Martha for she had a tranquil personality, was unassuming and had the loveliest and most unusual eyes.

These maiden aunts were very generous to their nephews, Arthur and his brother Harry. Every birthday they received cards and gifts. Every Christmas when they were children, the postman had to make a special delivery for them - there was always a sackful of presents. When you think that the round journey for the postman on foot, was in the region of ten miles and in all weather conditions it would not have been surprising for him to have been non-too-pleased. But no, the joy for the little boys, their excitement, and the welcome cup of tea and cake were enough to mellow the postman, who like other country postmen became a family friend.

When the boys grew up and married there grew a new ritual at Christmas. At first it involved each couple, and later, when children were born, each family was invited to visit the aunts in Deganwy for an evening meal during the week before Christmas. They always prepared a feast. Cold meats and salads, pickles and condiments of all kinds, and bread and butter followed by big dishes of lovely trifle followed by Christmas cake and hot mince pies. The food was always beautifully prepared, presented and served, but I always had mixed feelings about the visits because we were expected to eat everything in sight, and pressed upon us too were second and third helpings that appeared by magic from somewhere. "Come on, eat up, everything must go," said the aunties in their welcome to us. To make matters worse still, every time the ladies left the dining room for the kitchen, all three of our children would pile things onto my plate from theirs. "I'm full," "Don't like it," or, "I've had enough," or more pleadingly they would say, "*Please* will you eat it Mam." I would never have hurt the aunts' feelings because they were so kind and consequently, I was absolutely full up and could hardly move at the end of the evening. A visit to the toilet became an absolute necessity. Luckily I have always been able to regurgitate without any fuss when 'full to busting'. I think the Good Lord must have planned this very necessary facility for me, otherwise there would have been dire consequences.

The sisters had a brother, Arthur, who died in infancy. The other son, David was a joiner who decided to go to the United States of America. From what I remember being told, he lived in a hostel for a while, until he had settled in permanent work. He married a Welsh girl from Anglesey who followed him to the States. They had three children, Peggy, David and Arthur. When the children were quite young their mother died. Later, their father had an awful accident when a nail ricocheted into one eye with the result that he lost his sight in it, but worse was the constant pain that followed. Eventually, he committed suicide leaving the children without a mother or father. However, his wife's sister from

Anglesey went to America and brought up the children. They were extremely fond of their Aunty Parry and did not forget how good she had been to them. She returned to Wales when they had all flown the nest.

Peggy married, had no children of her own, but with her husband adopted a young boy. Her husband died quite soon after the adoption. The elder boy, David, who was in the U.S.Navy, married an Australian girl but they parted. He died young, shortly after the separation, but I have no knowledge of the circumstances of his death. The younger boy, Arthur, was a U.S.A. Government Contracts Attorney with the Department of Defense. He set up bases and completed all the legal formalities. He was married to a lovely American/Hungarian woman and they had a son and a daughter. They once came to visit their Welsh relatives including us, en route to Italy. Their children were highly spirited and full of fun. I seem to remember that the parents eventually separated. The girl became a teacher in Japan: the family had lived there for a time when Arthur was working for the U.S. Air Force. After Arthur died, another son was mentioned, who had a different surname from Williams, a David Koch of Los Angeles.

Apparently, Arthur loved to talk, tell jokes and laugh a lot, very much like his cousin Arthur - my husband.

While he was an Attorney for the Air Force assigned in Japan Arthur filed 'Williams vs. NEC', one of the first major 'Federal False Claims Act' cases, as a *qui tam relator*, charging a conglomerate of Japanese Telecommunications companies with 'bid rigging' that had been going on for 25 years. It resulted in a major Department of Justice settlement. Nobody else could find it, but Arthur. He was a true patriot.

He served with the Navy Submarine Service in the Pacific Theatre of World War II. He graduated from the University of Miami Law School in 1951 and was admitted to practice before the U.S. Allied High Commission Court in Nuremberg, Germany, and the United States Supreme Court. He is buried in 'Arlington National Cemetery' where President J.F. Kennedy also lies at rest.

Peggy and I kept in touch every Christmas - she lived in Michigan and came over to visit once and seemed a very nice person. I did not hear from her last Christmas. I know she was ill, but no one has written to me with any news.

Then there was Catherine Ellen, *Nain Gaerwen*, my husband's mother. She moved to Llansannan near Denbigh to be in charge of the dressmaking department in a village store. There were a number of shops in the village, amongst which were two that employed dressmakers. She lived as one of the family because she was much too far from home to go there very often. Today of course, the journey by car, train or bus is quite easy.

She met Thomas Vaughan Williams when he came to the village on a Sunday to play the organ in the Henry Rees Chapel. They courted for many years and married when Thomas' mother died. She had suffered a stroke, and for seven years her son had carried her up and down the stairs every day. I wonder what went through Catherine Ellen's mind as she waited during those long years. She must have been frustrated as she watched the years pass by and herself getting older. She was 39 years old when they finally married and she moved into 'The Factory' with Thomas and his father.

Chapter Seventeen

HENRY VAUGHAN WILLIAMS

He was Arthur's paternal grandfather. I never knew him because he died in 1932, but I have heard so many interesting things about him that I must record them. He was the only child of his father's first marriage, but he had several half brothers and sisters from the second marriage. It appears that his mother was a Miss Vaughan, originally from Scotland and this was a little puzzling as it is well known that 'Vaughan' is the modern form of an old Welsh name, Vychan meaning small of stature. My husband asked Bob Owen of Croesor, a renowned expert on the old families of Wales, if he could explain how a Scots lady could be a 'Vaughan' and was told most emphatically that there was a clear explanation. The 'Vaughans' were a renowned and prominent South Wales clan in the Middle Ages but some members were headstrong and had murdered a member of a rival clan. Because of this, the guilty members of the 'Vaughan' family fled to Scotland. Problem solved!

That was how the name of 'Vaughan' became a family name. The lady had come down to Wales from Scotland to work at the St. George's Hotel, Llandudno, as a chambermaid. Presumably she must have moved later on to Llansannan, to work in one of the large houses or manors in that area, probably the estate of *Dyffryn Aled.* There was an Elizabeth Vaughan aged 32 years and described as a servant who lived at The Lodge, Llansannan, listed in the Census records of 1841. We also know that she was the daughter of a Thomas Vaughan of *Bryn*, who is described as a Book-binder. She died in 1853.

Henry's father was called John who was a weaver. But as a youth he had been apprenticed as a Stonemason. One day when he and the other stonemasons were working at the *Dyffryn Aled Mansion*, the weather became so bad that they had to take shelter in the stables. John, a fourteen year old lad, was bored with standing around and went to join some other workers who were cutting hay for the horses. A horse operated the machine that they were using for this purpose by plodding around in a circle outside the building. The man in charge of the machine was called away for a time and during his absence, John gathered an armful of hay and pushed it into the machine. Sadly in his ignorance he pushed his hand too far and the machine chopped off the fingers of his right hand. What remained were his thumb, half an inch of an index finger and stumps on the other three. The pain must have been excruciating but the seriousness of the situation was worse. How was he to earn his living without fingers? He could no longer continue as a stonemason.

It was decided that he would train to be a weaver. The most difficult problem he had was tying the threads, but with practice he became very proficient and quick with the whole procedure. Amazingly he had very clear and tidy handwriting too and he became well known locally as a proxy letter writer. During this period there were many people who were illiterate and they went to John for help. He would agree to do this and then asked, “Well what do you want to say?” The reply more often than not was, “Tell them I am well and send my regards.” John, of his own accord would then make up the rest, giving details of local events and so on. Having finished writing the letter, John read it through to the sender, who would be delighted. This of course begs the question of who actually read the letter at the end of its journey - was it the recipient or a proxy? Elizabeth Vaughan, John's wife, was born in 1809 and died in 1853 aged 44 years.

Henry was born in 1845 so he was a little boy aged 8 when his mum died. After a suitable interval, John remarried and there were seven children of the second marriage. Working at his loom he managed to bring up his large family in a decent God-fearing way. Henry played a large part in helping to bring up his half brothers and sisters. His father worked at one loom and Henry at another.

There were a fair number of independent weavers operating in their homes in country districts in those times before the advent of woollen factories. Henry developed some infection in the thigh of one leg when he was still a boy. He spent many weeks in the Infirmary at Denbigh, but the medical people there could not diagnose the trouble, and he was sent home. He lay in bed in the cottage getting weaker and his father despaired. The rooms were all at ground level so, when a customer from the Gwytherin area called one morning with wool to be woven, she noticed the little boy lying in bed and asked his father, "What is the matter with him?" "No one is able to find out or say what is wrong," said his father. "Would you mind if I look at him?" she asked. "No, of course not, go in, he will be glad to talk to someone other than me." The lady went into the boy's room and talked with him, asking questions and examining his leg. She finally emerged and said to his father, "Tomorrow morning I will return. Please have lots of boiled water ready for me." The father didn't know what to think but was prepared to agree to anything if there was a glimmer of hope of curing his little lad.

True to her word the lady arrived at the house the following morning carrying an armful of different foliage and a package of small plants. All these were washed and then scalded with boiling water and left to soften. Then she asked for a clean white cloth and proceeded to scald it with boiling water before washing the boy's leg thoroughly. She wrapped the softened leaves in the cloth and laid the package on the sore spot on Henry's leg. Then she wrapped strips of the cloth round the leg and over the leaf package quite firmly. "Now," she said to the father, "Leave that on his leg without touching it for the next week, at which time I shall return."

She did return as promised, and proceeded to untie the wrappings on the boy's leg. The cloth was saturated with pus and blood and the mess smelled terribly, but she was pleased with the outcome. She washed the wound then wrapped another clean cloth over it. "There you are" she said, "It's clean, and now it will heal." And heal it did. The boy got better and regained his strength.

What a loss it is for us these days that the knowledge and skill that ordinary woman had with plants has probably been lost. Unfortunately, no one recorded the precise leaves she used, or their quantity. It is possible that she could neither read nor write, but what is certain is that she could definitely heal!

In such a fashion, Henry's life was saved, but he grew up with one leg approximately eight inches shorter than the other. But this handicap did not inhibit him in any way whatsoever. He was as agile and nimble as anyone else, and needed a walking stick only when he became old.

All the family members were faithful worshipers at the Church at Llansannan and many had lovely singing voices. Henry had a good tenor voice and was a member of the Church choir. The organist, Mrs. Pugh, wife of the Rector, noticed that Henry as a young lad enjoyed the singing and was keen to learn. She was growing older and thought that maybe young Henry was bright enough to learn to read music and play the Church organ when she herself was not able to do so. Whether she approached him by cajoling, pressurising or using some other means I cannot say, I only know that he agreed, and then started having music lessons. Obviously he had no instrument of his own on which to practise, so he had to go into the Church to use the organ there. He found it all rather hard at first especially in the winter when it was cold and dark in the Church where he felt a bit scared by himself.

It is important to remember that these were times of Puritan influence and there were no musical instruments of any kind in Chapels nor were there in every Church. Harps, fiddles and such like would be played only in taverns, not in places of worship. Mrs. Pugh was an educated lady and able to read old notation and play an organ. She was also a lady of means and it was she who arranged for an organ to be installed in the church at Llansannan. She also had a harmonium in the Vicarage.

Henry attended the Church School in the village and the Headmaster was a kind man who knew about the music lessons. He sent away to a London firm that sold musical instruments for a list of prices of harmoniums. The cheapest in the catalogue was £12.12s.0d., a large sum in those days. Henry had been saving every penny he could spare but still had not enough. The London firm gave a special discount of around 25% to Churches, Chapels and schools, so the kindly schoolmaster purchased the harmonium in his own name as a schoolmaster, and Henry was allowed to pay the remainder to him as and when he could.

Eventually the organ arrived and was installed in the little cottage. And so began the musical dynasty of three generations of one family who taught, performed and generally brought music into the lives of hundreds of people living in a very large area.

Word spread like wildfire in the neighbourhood that Henry had got a thing that made music and had paid dearly for it. He was thought to be a fool by some, one farmer remarking that he would have been wiser buying a cow, at least he would have some benefit from a cow. This is always the way of the world is it not: when someone dares to do something different, and to venture into setting up something new. Most times this kind of reaction is due either to ignorance, fear or jealousy.

Henry could not have cared less. He was delighted and practised hard until the day came when he was allowed to play at Church services, eventually taking over completely. He could play all the hymn tunes in every key and could also play anthems and psalms. He was Church organist for twenty-five years without a break. Not many people could read music, and they learned the hymns, psalms and anthems by memory. There were a number of Non-Conformist Chapels opening up in the area, but no musical instrument was allowed in them. This was because music, other than singing, was thought to be of the Devil, just like dancing and drinking, and so the Precentor would sing out one line of the hymn and the congregation would repeat it and so on to the end.

At Christmas time, carols were very popular and Henry knew many of them, some very old and handed down from one generation to the next. There was one carol service called the '*Plygain*' which was held in the early hours of Christmas Day. According to things I heard from old people, there was something very special about this service, that it had a certain peaceful and mystical aura about it. What is certain is that many people attended and probably missed their sleep completely on Christmas Eve.

In 1913 Lady Lewis went to Henry's home with her phonograph, a very early type of recorder that she used to record him singing several of the old carols. The late Mr. W.S. Gwyn Williams of Llangollen later published at least one in his carol booklet. It was a joyful surprise for Arthur, my husband and me to see and hear a choir of nurses and doctors, working at a famous hospital in London, singing one of Henry's old tunes with English words on a Christmas television programme some years ago.

Henry was learning the craft and skills of weaving from his father and eventually moved from the village of Llansannan to a nearby hamlet called *Bryn Rhyd Yr Arian* (hill by the silver stream), a lovely name with a beautiful sound. He had married a lady called Elizabeth Davies who had come to the Rectory at Llansannan as a maid. She had a child called Sarah from a previous marriage.

There were many second and even third marriages because many women died in childbirth and husbands were left with small children. Some of these children were sometimes given to members of the same family to be reared, some were adopted and others acquired step-parents. Also, there was a lot of poverty and only Church charity was available. I wonder whether we, who complain so much about our Welfare State have any idea what it was like to suffer real hardship as our ancestors did. They just had to accept their fate and get on with life. 'We do not know that we are born' as they say, and never let us forget those brave and compassionate pioneers, who had to struggle so long to change things for the better.

Henry was also in demand in the surrounding villages as a ballad singer because of his remarkable voice and large repertoire. No printed solos were available and Henry depended mostly on local bards for lyrics. He was very friendly with a renowned bard called Iorwerth Glan Aled who was many years older than Henry. When this bard was on his death-bed, he gave Henry his silver half-hunter watch and naturally Henry valued and appreciated the gift. It was greatly valued by his family too. Indeed, I had this watch in my display cabinet together with my father's watch and my father-in-law's watch, until they were stolen in a burglary some years ago, much to my dismay and disappointment.

Once, when Henry was to sing at Llangernyw, a village some eight miles away, there was a calamity. His friend, Hughes the tailor, was going with him for company because they were walking to the concert. Some way along when they had descended a steep hill and were climbing up another, they passed by a farm called *Hafod y Gog* (summer home of the cuckoo). What a pretty name that is! They noticed a gap in the hedge into the field where there was a pump that drew water from a pond. They were young lads, full of life and fun, and they decided to have a go at pulling up a full bucket of water. Henry, having filled the bucket, let it down by its own weight and then let go of the handle, which then turned hard and fast with the result that the handle caught the bottom of his trousers and tore them from the bottom to the top! Henry was devastated and wanted to go home. Hughes was doubled up with laughter and said, “Come on Henry, I'll fix you up when we get to Llangernyw.” True to his word he managed to make Henry look respectable but the singer was concentrating more on his trousers than his singing. However, the following morning after getting home, the trousers were despatched to his friend Hughes the tailor who made them look as new again. It's good to have useful friends is it not?

There must have been something rather special about living in villages and town neighbourhoods in those days. Everyone knew everyone else and there were tailors, cobblers, weavers, butchers, bakers, smiths and millers, et al. They were completely self-sufficient and life was colourful if nothing else. We may be financially richer now but do we enjoy our everyday lives as much?

Henry married Elizabeth Davies who was a maid at the Rectory, Llansannan. She had a child, Sarah, from a previous marriage. Henry and his wife Elizabeth moved to *Bryn Rodyn*, a small holding with a building in a corner of a meadow where there had been an early woollen factory. The river Aled flowed alongside the meadow. The property was part of the *Dyffryn Aled* Estate, the Squire being one of the sons of the prominent Wynne-Yorke family.

During the time Henry and his wife had worked the small holding and operated the machine in the Factory, they must have saved some money. Henry had seen how small woollen factories had been set up and organised in other areas such as Trefriw and Penmachno, and had decided that he could do better if he had more modern machines installed in his Factory too. So Henry and his wife set about saving even harder until there was enough money in the kitty to purchase what was necessary.

Eventually he and his wife went by train to Huddersfield in Yorkshire, to buy new machinery. They stayed in lodgings there overnight but Henry did not sleep a wink. Indeed he did not even go to bed, because he was fearful of being robbed as he was carrying so much cash on his person.

Just before dawn there was a commotion in the street as the factory workers made their way to work. At the same time, a street vendor wheeled his trolley onto the pavement. He sold hot drinks and some kind of buns or muffins to the workers. For some time he was very busy and then it became quiet again and he started to pack up. He still had some buns left in a pile on the trolley and then quite suddenly a small crowd of children - street urchins in rags and no shoes, rushed up to the trolley and several buns fell onto the road. Immediately the children pounced upon the buns and pushing and shoving ate them ravenously. Henry thought the kindly stall-holder had deliberately upset the pile of buns!

During the day the two of them found what they wanted and having completed the purchase, returned to North Wales. The machinery arrived in a couple of weeks and was set up and operations began at the Factory.

Henry and his wife had two children, a boy called Thomas Vaughan (Arthur's father) and Elizabeth. There was also Sarah, their half sister of course, but she was older. Eventually, she married a Mr. Edward Douglas. They lived not far away, near the village of Llannefydd.

Henry still had his little organ and he taught his son Thomas Vaughan how to read and play music. He was not a very good pupil at first but his father persevered for he was determined that Vaughan should learn to make music. His sister Elizabeth was a pretty girl who had a good soprano voice. The parents paid for lessons for her with a Mr. Dafydd Parry in Llanrwst and for a short time Vaughan also had piano tuition from this man.

Vaughan learned how to operate the machinery in the factory and how to work out patterns in cloth. Henry's half brother Richard was also part of the team but he was the salesman. He went off in his horse and cart to the seaside towns of Abergele, Colwyn Bay, and Rhos on Sea to sell the products of the Factory. Eventually he married and went to live at Dyserth. The seaside towns were expanding very rapidly, as it became fashionable for families who were rich enough, to spend holidays at the seaside. Some of the pretty villages in the countryside also became popular and large Hotels were built to accommodate the visitors.

For some years, there was a man called Dafydd Owen from Dinas Mawddwy who was hired to work in the Factory, and he lived with the family. He was an experienced weaver having worked previously at a woollen factory in mid Wales.

Elizabeth married and set up home on one of the *Dyffryn Aled* estate farms called *Pen Coed*. A little girl was born and she too was named Elizabeth although she was known as Lizzie. While she was still small her father died, which left her mother alone to run a sizeable farm for which she had no training or experience.

At the time Tom Howatson, my mother's grandfather was the Estate Manager at Dyffryn Aled and he did not think that the young widow was capable of running one of the best farms on the estate. However, Mrs. Howatson intervened and pleaded on the young woman's behalf, “Give her a chance Tom, give her a chance.” I know this is true because my mother was there at the time.

Elizabeth Roberts was given a chance, and proved herself able to meet the challenge. She worked so hard and diligently, and so did Lizzie as she grew up, that the farm became one of the best in the district. Lizzie married a local man, Johnny Roberts, and they had one son, Bobi Morris Roberts. His grandma doted on him. Lizzie was related to my mother through her father. If you find it hard to follow these inter-linking relationships, take a look at one or other of the family trees.

You can read more details about Thomas Vaughan Williams, known as Vaughan later in the book, but first read more about Henry Vaughan Williams, his father, who was an interesting character.

Chapter Eighteen

TRY, TRY AND TRY AGAIN

There was a vegetable garden and orchard between the house at the Factory and the river, and Henry was a keen gardener - he grew many different vegetables and worked the soil and planted until he was an old man.

He was also a good fisherman and not only with a rod, he liked to lie flat on his stomach on the river bank and feel for the trout with his hand, under the stones. Apparently the method of catching the fish was to tickle their bellies!

The fishing rights on the river belonged to the estate and I don't know whether Henry had permission to fish or whether he was poaching. He fished in the river at the bottom of his garden to feed himself and his family. It would be a very hard and greedy river rights owner who would gainsay that natural custom.

The thought of the river brings to mind a very turbulent day for Henry. His wife was known as a kind and generous woman. Incidentally, she was also known for her herbal remedies and creams. Well, on this particular day it was sunny and the weather was fine, around August/September, and Henry had gone fishing. Everything went well until he missed his footing and slid into the river. Soaked to the skin he went into the house and changed into his second best suit. Not much harm had been done. Later, a customer called at the factory and during a friendly chat while her purchase was being packed, remarked on the gorgeous Denbigh plums on a tree in the garden similar to, but to my mind better than Victoria plums. Mrs. Henry asked, “Would you like some?” and in the same breath, “Henry, go and get some nice ones.” The customer must have been a good one, for Henry dutifully went with a bag and his stick to gather some plums. He used his stick to pull down branches but suddenly one branch sprang back and Henry found himself in the river again, soaked through. Once again he went into the house for a change of clothing - his best Sunday suit, but the customer still had no plums and Henry insisted that he could get some for her if he climbed into the tree on the land-side. Although his wife and the other lady were loud in their protestations that he should not bother further, Henry went up the tree, not far up but he clung to a branch that overhung the water. This time he was successful and handed down a large bag of plums but, just as he was manoeuvring himself backwards, there was an ominous crack and the branch gave way and he was once more in the river. Wet through again!

There were no more clothes, so poor Henry had to go to bed until the following day, when hopefully, some of his clothes would be dry! It seems very funny in the telling now and would probably make for a very entertaining scene on television but it must have been quite traumatic for Henry especially when we recall that he had the disability of having one leg much shorter than the other and no fingers on his right hand. It appears however, that he himself was the least bothered about it all.

Elizabeth, Henry's wife, suffered a damaging stroke in 1907 but lived for another seven years during which time, her son Vaughan had to carry her downstairs every morning and back upstairs to bed every night. I think that during this time, her older daughter Sarah was there to manage the household.

When Henry's wife died it became possible for Vaughan to marry his fiancée, after a suitable period of mourning of course. So, Catherine Ellen (Katie) went to live at the

Factory and became mistress of the family. Henry, who sported a bushy beard, remained at the Factory and worked until he grew too old. He got on very well with his daughter-in-law and was always very appreciative of her, saying she treated him like a king. The two must have been tolerant people. Henry used to go to Llansannan from time to time to have a couple of pints with his old pals - he was never drunk, tipsy or rowdy, just happy and mellow. But Katie, his daughter-in-law, had been brought up in a very strict teetotal family where alcoholic drink was totally absent - her father was Senior Deacon at the Chapel.

Henry was still there when Arthur and his brother Harry were born and throughout their childhood. They loved him very much and together they had a wonderful time. "Taid" was much easier to coerce than Dad! He told them tales of bygone days amongst which was the true story of his family background. I shall treat that subject separately as there is quite a lot to tell.

These story-telling sessions took place on Mondays and Wednesdays usually because Vaughan and his wife went to the markets at Abergele and Denbigh on those days. Henry told tales of the old days when he was a youth in the village of Llansannan. In the springtime when the weather was warmer and everyone became livelier after Lent and Easter, a group of dancers would arrive on their village green. This group was a merry one and dressed outlandishly and some painted their faces. One would carry a maypole and another would carry the *Cadi Ha* - a piece of wood with an image of a horse's head on top. They never seemed to tire of singing and dancing and making merry. There being an inn and a tavern nearby possibly added to the general hoo-ha.

Another big annual event in the village, probably held on a Saturday, was the occasion of the 'Club Band Day'. I do not know a lot about it, but I have a photograph taken in 1897 when Vaughan was 21 years old. It appears that members of the Club, wearing their sashes, marched behind a brass band that possibly visited from elsewhere. I think the Club was the 'Buffalos' but I cannot be sure. In those days, this kind of Club was quite common everywhere - possibly they declined in popularity after World War I. There was also an annual trip to Rhyl to the seaside when everyone dressed in their Sunday best clothes. Even the children wore grand hats. They travelled in horse-drawn farm wagons and it was always a great day out, or so I have been assured.

Another occasion to look forward to, was the Singing Festival when everyone who could sing at all came together to glorify God and enjoy making music. It was after all, a great social occasion too. At first, people sang in unison but after the advent of the Solffa system of reading music, the singing was in harmony: Tenor, Bass, Soprano and Alto. It really must have been a splendid sound and very moving. We in Wales had such a wonderful tradition of singing in harmony and now sadly, generally it is in decline, it is a great loss and a deep sadness for me. Some choirs are finding it difficult to recruit young singers to their ranks, especially men. I wonder if the fact that the Solffa system is no longer taught in schools or Sunday schools has any bearing on the situation. I believe that the Solffa system should be reintroduced in schools so that future generations can also experience the deeply satisfying and uplifting delights of massed singing in 4 part harmony. It is assumed, that because Old Notation is taught nowadays in schools, that there is no longer a need for Solffa, but I think they should be in tandem, learning the octave from the modulator is similar to learning the times tables in maths!

Another 'tall' story that Henry told the boys involved a stonemason friend who had worked on the wonderful Marble Church at Bodelwyddan, between Abergele and St. Asaph. It really is a wonderful church and the building is illuminated from time to time. It was built for a lady in memory of her husband. The Church spire is quite high and tapers to the end as spires do.

"Well," said Henry, "Let me tell you that my friend was the man who laid the last stone on that spire, and he also stood on his head on that stone." The boys were duly astonished and wondered at the man's daring. "He must have been very brave because he could have fallen and got himself … killed in the process." "Well" said Henry chuckling, "You see … he certainly stood on his head on that stone, there is no question about that, but he did it on the ground before taking it to the top of the spire!"

Another subject was the Plas (mansion) of *Dyffryn Aled*. The family of Dyffryn Aled could trace their origins very far back in history. The family name was Wynne or Wynn and the last heir was Pyrs Wynne. The original Plas was on the ridge on the other side of the river. Pyrs Wynne's daughter Diana married twice. During the period of her widowhood she built the new *Dyffryn Aled* mansion on the opposite side of the river. No expense was spared. Later, she married Philip Yorke from the Erddig Estate in Wrexham.

It is said, that the last member of the Wynne-Yorke family to live at Dyffryn Aled used to visit Inns in Llanfair TH and was seen to light up his pipe with a £1.note! He also offered to give £1.00 to any man who would allow him to hit him in the face! It is sad to think that he died in a workhouse with nothing to leave but his walking stick.

Henry said that his father remembered Dyffryn Aled as a very beautiful building, large, with many rooms. It was necessary for bridges to be built because it was situated on a high bank above the river Aled, The main drive to the house from the village was planted on both sides of its entire length with flowering trees - lilac alternating with laburnum. It must have been a magnificent sight. Although they were protected at first from the animals in the fields, over the years unfortunately they disappeared, and what a pity it was! However, there were other drives that provided pleasant walks and one in particular that was cared for was boxed in with privet hedges that provided walkers with cooling shade on hot days. It was also a kind of "lovers' lane." In late autumn, when the hedges had shed their leaves, the path was swept and cleared by workmen who looked forward to the job because of the possibility of finding lost coins. On one occasion a poor man from the village swept the path and as he did, found a gold necklace and locket. The discovery of the necklace would have set off an enquiry at the house that might have been embarrassing to someone. However, the man was honest and handed it in at the House - and was rewarded with only a "Thank you." He must have wondered if honesty really was the best policy, but then, what could a poor man have done with such a valuable piece of jewellery in Llansannan at that time?

For years there were many people employed at *Dyffryn Aled* itself and on the Estate's land, but around the turn of the century parcels of the land were sold, leaving the big House and Home Farm to become a residential Hospital for wealthy people who had nervous or mental problems. After some years, during the early months of World War 1, the House was taken over to provide accommodation for high ranking German Naval Officers who were prisoners during the 1914/18 War.

During this time a group of the naval officers plotted to escape from Dyffryn Aled. A meticulous plan had been drawn up by them and agreed with the German High Command, which meant that there must have been German spies about in Llansannan for this to have been achieved. Or had there been a letter (in German of course) sent to the senior ranking Officer and handed over to him without any security check being made? The plan involved a German U-Boat being present just off Great Orme's Head in Llandudno bay for a specified number of hours and would signal her presence discreetly to them. In Llansannan, the naval officers succeeded in giving their guards the slip and made their getaway. Having escaped from the village, the journey to Llandudno could have been made fairly easily in those days because the terrain was rural and dotted with farmsteads and isolated cottages. They reached their destination safely and remained hidden until nightfall. Eagerly they watched and waited for the signal all night. They saw nothing, and when morning dawned they were all recaptured. How confused and disappointed they must have felt when they learned that the U-Boat had been in the sea off Llandudno all the time they'd been waiting, and had indeed signalled to them as planned. Unknown to them at the time, the U-Boat had positioned itself on the wrong side of the Great Orme!

I remember my father-in-law telling us about an adventure he'd had during this time. He explained that tenants of the estate had been allowed to use the *Dyffryn Aled* private road as a short cut from the village to their homes at *Bryn Rhyd yr Arian.* One night, he'd been to the village on his bicycle, possibly to meet his fiancée, and on the way home along this route, the light on his bike went out. As he neared the prisoner camp he was challenged orally by a guard shouting, "Halt! Who goes there?" This had never happened before and naively he ignored the command and rode off into the darkness at full speed. He was caught of course and treated as a suspicious character. By now, Vaughan had become frightened of the armed guards and their military manner and a senior officer then appeared and Vaughan explained where he had been, and that he was using the short cut in order to get home quickly to carry his invalid mother upstairs to bed. It was obvious that they disbelieved his story. However, in the end he was escorted home under armed guard, and only then did the soldiers see that he was indeed telling the truth. From then on they were friendly and helpful but issued a warning to be more careful in future!

At the end of the War there was no further need of the camp and accommodation for prisoners and so *Dyffryn Aled* became vacant and gradually, derelict.

After World War II the estate was sold to the Bibby family, who are well known in the business world, especially in the Liverpool area, and they built a fine new house on the site.

Chapter Nineteen

FAVOURITE BABYSITTER

Sometimes when Henry had been left in charge of the two little boys while their parents were out on business, being an old gentleman, he would fall asleep and then the two boys had a chance to get into mischief, but there was little harm done, except on a couple of occasions. Once, the fire must have burned low in the grate and Arthur who was a very small boy at the time started to find things to throw onto the embers, anything, including his smart cap with a tassel. As the fire became brighter and the flames burned higher, the arsonist became more excited. Luckily the crackling of the flames and the jubilant cries of the stoker woke Henry who soon put a stop to the jubilation. Luckily too, that was the end of Arthur's career as a stoker, but not to his curiosity.

Again it was on a Market day and Henry was in charge. At the end of the afternoon it was time to prepare the table for tea in readiness for the return of Mam and Dad. To ensure the safety of the boys, Henry sat both of them on the window seat and pushed the table up against them. He then proceeded to bring all the necessary crockery and cutlery and set the table. He then sat down in his favourite chair to smoke his pipe, and have a little rest after his labours. At first, the boys were quiet, but they soon got restless in their enforced confinement and it was then that Arthur noticed and took a fancy to a blue sugar bowl and matching milk jug. He became fascinated by the beautiful patterns created by the effect of the flames from the fire reflecting on the shape of the glass bowl. Quite suddenly he reached over and grabbed the bowl sending its contents all over the place. Henry jumped up and went to retrieve the bowl. Sensing that there was trouble brewing, Arthur flung the bowl onto the hard floor, on which it smashed into pieces. Poor Henry was very upset, because he knew that Katie loved the blue dishes - they had been given as wedding presents. He scolded Arthur and in return, saw the wrecker grab the milk jug and send that crashing too. Well, what a terrible mess! I don't know any details of the sequel - Arthur did not remember. Probably he had deliberately decided not to retain that memory, and fortunately he turned his thoughts to more normal and less damaging excitements!

Another time, Henry asked the boys if they knew that ducks could talk. They laughed and said, "No Taid, don't be silly." "Oh yes they can," said Henry, " Listen," and proceeded to imitate duck sounds - the boys were so surprised they stopped laughing and went off immediately to find the ducks and imitate their Taid. Unfortunately I cannot explain these sounds to you dear English reader, because those ducks spoke only in Welsh!

There was certainly a great bond of affection between old Henry and his two grandsons, as indeed there was with Lizzie his granddaughter, who was older and lived elsewhere but no great distance away and came to visit her grandparents quite often.

Henry died of old age in 1932 at a grand age of 87 having made a significant mark on the lives of his descendants and also on the life of his neighbourhood

Chapter Twenty

THOMAS VAUGHAN WILLIAMS

This gentleman was Arthur's father - I use the term gentleman deliberately. He never had wealth, but had a certain air about him, some culture and bearing that was quite apparent. He walked with a certain grace and panache.

When my parents and Arthur's father were children they lived fairly close, and knew each other well. Arthur's father recalled my father as a young man, full of fun, who was witty and good company. In fact, Vaughan and my mother went on holiday together when she was a little girl and he was a grown lad. They went to stay at a large farm *Llewesog* in the Vale of Clwyd because both were related to the hosts on different sides of the family. Of course I remember Vaughan only as an older man.

Between the wars during the Depression of the 1920s & 30s, business was diminishing and the actual Factory closed down. Times were changing and people's way of life changed too. Suits and woollen goods were in abundance in shops at reasonable prices. So Vaughan reverted to the single loom to satisfy the needs of older people who clung to the old ways. Together with the smallholding they made a reasonable living. In addition he made a little more money by teaching pupils to play the piano. Some years before, he had bought a new piano.

Fortunately, while Vaughan was still a schoolboy, the Llansannan Church School headmaster was a Mr. Emanuel Davies who recognised Vaughan's ability. Mr. Davies knew all about the way Henry had become a church organist and deduced that Vaughan needed further tuition in music. He acquired a Hamilton's Tutor book for him. It was a difficult project for a young Welsh lad but Mr. Davies encouraged Vaughan and indeed gave of his time every Monday evening to teach him. This went on throughout the time that Mr Davies lived in Llansannan. He taught his pupil to play the Hallelujah Chorus whilst he was still only twelve years old. Vaughan became a very good pianist and an accomplished accompanist. He was in great demand and many came to him to be taught to sing solos so they could compete in the many *Eisteddfodau* that were held in the towns and villages. Some paid for the tuition, others did not because they could not, and a few just took advantage. Those pupils, mostly children and youngsters who came to learn to play the piano were charged, but the fees were minimal. Vaughan was in much demand as the official accompanist at concerts and *Eisteddfodau*. Many of the singers he accompanied on the piano had very good voices and some had musical intelligence as well. The best went on to greater things, becoming professional musicians.

Vaughan played the pipe organ at the Presbyterian Chapel in Llansannan and having taught Arthur his eldest son to play the piano Arthur was able to play the harmonium at Horeb Chapel, which was their local Chapel. So, for some years, Henry was organist at the Church in Llansannan, Vaughan, his son was organist at the Henry Rees Chapel, and Arthur, Vaughan's son was organist at Horeb Chapel. Three generations of the same family - father, son and grandson played organs in Church services in 3 places of worship in the same local area during the same period: what an achievement!

When Vaughan bought his piano and his father Henry had died, Henry's original little organ went to *Pen Coed* (head of the trees) to Elizabeth his daughter, and later it went to *'Rallt Ddu* (black hill) the home of Lizzie, her daughter. Now, I think it is at the home of Lizzie's son, Bobi Morris, in Brecon.

It is an interesting fact that Vaughan began accompanying in public when Robert Owen, *Garreg Lithrig*, my grandfather asked him to be the official accompanist at a Christmas competitive event in Llannefydd. The usual practice in those days was for every competitor to go on stage and sing his or her song, unaccompanied. However, Robert Owen managed to get a harmonium from somewhere, possibly Denbigh, and Vaughan had promised to undertake the work, the importance of which, he had no idea, having never done it before. There was a printed programme giving details of the competitions and also the names of the officials, i.e. Adjudicators, Secretary and Treasurer of the Committee, and the Accompanist, who in this instance was Vaughan. Once this was published, the would-be competitors started beating a path to the Factory to ask for a practice run with Vaughan. Fortunately, this cut both ways because he also was able to gain valuable practice of the songs that he would have to play at the event. At the end of the competitive meeting the music Adjudicator congratulated members of the Committee for their initiative in breaking new ground. He said that at the meetings he normally attended, he rarely saw a musical instrument. He also gave Vaughan great praise for his skill, which encouraged him enormously.

Later, following this debut, there was talk in the neighbourhood of the possibility of getting a harmonium for Chapels. There were strong feelings on both sides. The Puritan effect was still strong among Dissenters and music and dancing were frowned upon. Eventually a farmer, Mr. Evan Roberts of *Plas Isa Farm* (lower mansion), approached the deacons at Horeb Chapel with a suggestion that a harmonium should be bought for the Chapel. Repeatedly the request was refused. In the end he asked if Henry Williams would accompany him to Liverpool to buy a harmonium for Horeb. He was fed up with the refusals and decided that an organ would be in the Chapel the following Sunday. Vaughan was invited to go with them since he was the one who would be the organist. And so it came to pass. Surprise, delight, consternation, anger, and fury were some of the emotions reflected on the faces of members of the congregation. The Precentor was John Jones, *Penglogor* (top of the hill) my grandmother's brother, who Vaughan described as being highly effective in the role and always in the correct key. Like all Precentors of the time he used a pitchfork, but it was always hidden in the palm of his hand.

On that Sunday morning when the organ was first used, Vaughan as the organist took the brunt of the fury of the antagonists. He was pushed, shoved, and kicked on the shins and all kinds of difficulties were set against him. He said that after that morning he very nearly decided to resign and return to Llansannan Church with his father Henry, but on account of the help he received from other members, such as the organ donor and the Precentor and his family, he decided to soldier on. John Jones made sure that Vaughan always knew the hymn to be sung by calling the number out loudly. The resentment continued for some time, but eventually the quality of the singing at Horeb Chapel was so improved that word got round and others wanted a harmonium in their place of worship. The snag however, was the dearth of people able to read music and play the instrument. The immediate result was a sudden surge in the number of pupils coming to Vaughan for tuition.

Later, a Liverpool businessman, Mr E Morris, who had a house locally at *Llety'r Eos* (home of the nightingale) gave a fine pipe organ to the Henry Rees Chapel at Llansannan. At the same time, Vaughan was invited to become organist of the new instrument with the added attraction of a regular remuneration. Finally he agreed, and started the job on 1st August 1901. He was to continue for over 25 years. Before leaving Horeb Chapel however, he had taught someone else to take his place. His pupils came from all the surrounding villages, Llanfair TH, Llansannan, Gwytherin and Llannefydd and as they became proficient, so were harmoniums brought into places of worship and congregational singing improved everywhere. Vaughan was happy to have made a contribution to this success and he thanked God for blessing him with the skill to do so.

As a result of such an improvement, annual Singing Festivals were held in districts and a booklet of hymns and tunes was published every year. Regular rehearsals were held leading up to the event and finally, when the Festival was held, it was invariably a feast of harmonious song. These are the kinds of meetings that I remember as a child and in my youth, and I can categorically state that they were thrilling. I wish today's young people could experience such body and soul of ecstasy and I use that word intentionally.

When work in the Woollen Factory building was in full swing, Henry and Vaughan and other workers were skilled in putting the wool through the various stages until it became the thread that was used in weaving cloth. They dyed the wool in different colours. Vaughan was clever at working out patterns of different tweeds for suits for men and women. He had samples to show when people came to buy cloth, and having measured clients, knew how much material they would need.

The owners of the small holding and Factory at that time in the 1920s were the Dundonalds of Gwrych Castle in Abergele and two brothers used to come to the Factory to choose and buy tweed to make 'plus fours' suits. These were very popular at that time. The brothers were tall and broad and very straight, and were treated very respectfully in accordance with their station in life.

One day while Vaughan was showing the brothers some of his woollen patterns, the two small boys, Arthur and Harry, were standing with their father, quite still and silent. They were monoglot Welsh at that time, and did not understand any of the English that was being spoken - except that is, for two words that they heard being repeated several times. Suddenly, they both scampered off to find their mother. They were giggling and laughing as they told their Mam that the two men were being very rude. “Dad kept saying 'for shame, for shame' to them.” Now I have to explain here that these were the words that the boys' mother used when she reproved them for letting out disagreeable smelly bursts of wind from their bottoms, and now they thought that the two visitors were doing just that! Only later was the mystery solved when Vaughan explained that what he had actually said was, “The same, the same” meaning, “Yes, yes of course,” in agreement!

Arthur Vaughan was the elder son born in 1917, two years before his brother Harry Pierce, and life must have been very happy for the little family at the Factory.

Arthur started going to school at Llansannan when he was five years old and had to walk the three miles both ways every day, probably in the company of older children. One of the teachers was a Mrs. Dick, who was apparently exceptionally good at her job and popular with the children. The following year when Arthur was six years old he became unwell, had pains in his tummy, could not eat and became wan and listless. The usual practice was to try to ease the pain by applying heat to it, therefore hot plates were suitably wrapped and placed on his tummy. We must remember that the doctor lived miles away and his services were expensive, so home remedies were always tried first. In this instance, the hot plates did indeed ease the pain but at what price. Arthur became worse and the doctor was called. Without delay, Dr. Leiper from Llanfair T.H. arrived and after examining the little boy advised the parents to take him to the Infirmary in Denbigh where he was attended to immediately as an emergency. The pain had gone because the infected ulcer on the duodenum had burst when the heat of the plates had been applied to it and the poison began circulating all through the little boy's body. Today an injection of penicillin would have dealt with the problem, but no one then knew about penicillin or any of the wonderful drugs that we have at our disposal today. Only people who have gone through such a traumatic experience are able to appreciate fully what we take for granted today.

The Chief Surgeon at the Infirmary was a young man called Dr. Duff. I have already written about this Doctor because he was the one who also operated on me in the same hospital. However, in this instance, repetition will not come amiss. He was a Scot and had seen service as a surgeon at the front during World War I. He was a wonderful doctor. I was told that before he operated on a patient, he would go alone into his office and pray for guidance.

A local doctor from Ruthin Dr Trefor Jones, who assisted at the hospital, was there when Arthur was examined. Dr. Duff was disheartened and said that he thought there was no purpose in operating because it was too late, the poison had circulated too far. Dr Jones pleaded with him to operate, "What have we got to lose?" said Dr Jones, "If you do not operate he will die anyway. At least he will have some chance of living, if you operate." Finally, Dr. Duff took the advice of his older colleague and indeed, Arthur pulled through. He was terribly emaciated and weak and was in hospital for many weeks. When he finally went home his little brother did not recognise him. Gradually, Arthur became stronger, and I can remember his mother telling me that a lady restaurant owner in Denbigh gave her a large pot of meat juice jelly every week in order to help the boy regain his strength.

It must have been a very distressful time for Arthur's parents. When a crisis occurs and children become ill parents become frantic, feeling so helpless and unable to help their little ones in their pain and distress.

It was an extremely difficult situation in the hospital for Arthur for as well as being extremely ill he could not speak English nor could he understand the language. The nurses and staff were all English speaking and so he felt very isolated and unsure, and was unable to make his needs known. He was merely six years old! But his life had been saved and he was certainly getting better.

The Infirmary at Denbigh is still there and giving sterling service. There were no large hospitals in North Wales at the time, but those district hospitals gave of their best. I wonder how many lives were saved by the dedication of those nurses and doctors - Arthur's and mine for a start.

Another skill that Vaughan had developed was the cutting of letters and figures on gravestones. It was painstaking work and needed concentration and once the chiselling work was completed, the names and figures were then painted in white, black or gold. He used gold leaf for the latter option. A similar skill that he used less often involved inscribing presentation books or pictures. This work was very special and that ruled out even the slightest error because the work was done on the actual gift. I remember once, when he had undertaken to do rather a long inscription on a gift from a Society to an important person, he shut himself in the parlour and no one was allowed to speak to him or approach him in any way until he had finished: the work took hours and hours. He had wonderful handwriting, but these inscriptions needed decoration and flourish and indeed, his skill was such that he always succeeded in producing an artistic presentation, perfect and beautiful. He was truly an artist in many ways.

In addition to all his other work, Vaughan wrote short stories for children and articles for periodicals, mostly religious ones. He enjoyed doing them but the work was voluntary and there was no payment involved, like so many other things he did in his life. He was never a rich man as far as having money was concerned, indeed there were times when life was a struggle, but he never thought of himself as being poor.

For most of his adult life he suffered from a stomach ulcer and from time to time he would need to keep to his bed, eating bread and milk only. This was the recognised treatment. Eventually, the pain subsided and he would return to work even harder, to make up for lost time. This was the set pattern of his life until just after World War 2, when a distinguished London surgeon, Mr. Ivor Lewis, decided to return to his homeland, Wales. When Vaughan was referred by his G.P. to see the Consultant he was told that he was to enter hospital immediately. This of course was after the Labour Government had set up the National Health Service. For seventeen weeks the Hospital persevered in building up Vaughan's strength because he had become very thin, and trying to heal the ulcer. This was successful except for its inner core, which had become impossible to heal. In November 1951, at the age of 75, he was operated upon and half his stomach was taken away. Everything healed so well that when Christmas came he was able to eat Christmas dinner for the first time for years, and thoroughly enjoy it too. He was told that it was essential for him to eat small meals often at first, but in time, as his stomach grew back to normal size he would be able to manage larger meals. Vaughan was delighted to be able to enjoy eating again and as a result started to gain weight and look much healthier. He developed diabetes in his 80s then had to be careful with sugar intake, but he lived until he was 86. He was tall and lean, had a white moustache and a head of beautiful thick white hair. Vaughan was always courteous and mannerly and had a very amiable presence.

All of us have our personal foibles and Vaughan was no exception. He was very fastidious, liked to be well groomed and was particular about his food. After his operation every meal time was an occasion to be savoured, and he always used a large white napkin. He enjoyed a bowlful of stewed apples as a pudding every dinnertime and although it had become a standard daily item, he still asked the same question each day, “Are there apples today?” If someone coughed or sneezed near him he would purse his lips and, using his hand as a fan blow away the air around his face in ever such a genteel manner. Although we were amused by this, we smothered any smiles because it was his way and was very natural, and we loved him for it. He was highly respected by everyone. His grandchildren loved him and he had a way with children and never tired of telling them stories that they still remember.

Chapter Twenty-one

ANOTHER DIMENSION

The twentieth century has drawn to a close and a new Millennium has dawned on the world. On looking back, my life appears to me as having been a series of ever widening horizons. It began with a carefree childhood in a safe environment that moved from the village school to the Grammar School in Abergele, followed by starting work to earn my own living amongst strangers with totally different backgrounds. Each step was a completely new experience, uncomfortable and unnerving at the time, but useful in having added to my self-assurance and confidence. My experiences enabled me to realise that I could cope quite well and operate satisfactorily too. However, all such steps had been taken within the warmth and safety of the home that my parents had provided, and later within the warmth of my own home too. My roots were still in the earth from which they sprang. At this point, when I married Arthur and we moved to Llanrwst, my roots were transplanted to another spot. I was leaving my parents' home in order to set up my own with my husband. In common with most young people, I was looking forward to this new phase in my life, but I was not longing to leave my erstwhile home. I had been quite content there. However, I was not moving that far away, only a dozen or so miles, and it was comforting to know that we could always nip home to Llanfair in the little Austin car now and again.

During those first months in my new home I had plenty of things to do and organise. Slowly but surely, the number of Arthur's pupils increased and people got to know of his skills. He really was a first class teacher. He had patience and knew exactly how to deal with children and adults. In other words, he had charisma. In addition, he was a professional musician to his finger tips, an appropriate euphemism for a pianist! At first, he had free time in the mornings when he did his own practising on the piano or organ. At midday, a couple of pupils who lived in country areas who attended school in Llanrwst came for lessons and then, as soon as 3.30 p.m came, the stream of pupils began and carried on until 8 or 9 o'clock. Saturdays were free but Sundays were not.

Arthur was in the senior men's class in Sunday School. He had always been a member of Sunday School and enjoyed the cut and thrust of argument and discussion. The leader of this particular class in Seion, Mr. Solomon Jones was a unique character. He knew his Bible and was very able at getting discussions going. It was a very lively class and not particularly quiet at all times. Mr. Solomon Jones was not what is generally thought of as being pious, indeed at times he was almost irreverent but he was an honest man and had no façade. His qualities were real and there was no veneer. Once he asked Arthur, “Have you seen the Chamber of Horrors in Seion yet?” Arthur said, “No, what is it?” He replied, “The Deacons' room!” This was a fine room, furnished with a marvellously long and polished table, surrounded by comfortable leather chairs. All the walls were hung with large pictures of mostly long-gone deacons and ministers, who all looked serious, dour and stern, which was the right look for God-fearing men to show in those days - not even a hint of a smile - and all male. Solomon Jones' sense of humour came in many guises and I think that his honesty and humour were the qualities that appealed to the men in his class.

There were about half a dozen adult classes, all held in the Chapel itself and there was much talk going on, everyone intent on their own class, seemingly unaware of all the others! It was much as it was in the old schools where you had two or even three classes, within the same room.

Even now, in our day, when scores of people have stopped going to services in Churches and Chapels, Sunday Schools for children are thriving in some communities, which is very pleasing. This is due largely to the dedicated people, who give freely of their spare time every Sunday to teach our children about good and bad and the basics of our civilisation. I remember reading an article written by a highly respected Judge, who stated that in all the years that he had been involved in court cases, he could count on one hand the number of people who had stood before him who had attended Sunday School as children or young people.

With Arthur now fully involved with the different duties of his work, what was I doing? Well, I had the usual chores of any housewife - cooking, washing and ironing, cleaning, sewing and darning. Cooking was easier because I had a brand new electric stove with an oven and a full set of heavy gauge aluminium saucepans. But washing was still done by hand in the old stone sink using blocks of soap, Lux soap flakes for delicates, and Rinso or Persil powder for general washing. The job of ironing was also made easier now that I had an electric iron.

The task of cleaning remained relatively unchanged. It still entailed dusters and Mansion Polish and a lot of effort. I used Brasso liquid and Silvo, although I had no real silverware except six special teaspoons! But I had no need to 'black lead' grates any more thank goodness, for there was a beige vitreous enamel grate in the living room. There were no polishes with silicon, and the necessary ingredient to all cleaning was still 'elbow grease' - you youngsters can deduce for yourselves what that was.

One needed to sew all the time, it went on forever - there was always a need for a needle and thread. We had to look after our clothes, firstly because of rationing during the war and secondly because we had to take care of the pennies. I darned rips and rents, re-fixed buttons, turned collars on shirts, cuffs on sleeves, and of course darned all socks. For this task I had a wooden mushroom that was pushed into the sock, held by the stalk with the material placed on the rounded top. There was an art to the mending and darning, you could not bunch up the material otherwise many complaints from the wearer about blisters and pain would soon be made! I had to learn how to darn the proper way, the hard way, oh dear me, yes I did!

In addition, I was also the music business' receptionist and unpaid of course! We had an electric bell fitted near the front door to sound over the piano when it was in use, and when it rang, I dropped whatever I was doing to greet whichever pupil was there. If he or she was early, or Arthur was running late, then I would invite the pupil to take a seat in the living room where I ensured that everything was always ship-shape, clean and tidy. Some were young adults, others teenagers, but most were children. Like people in general, some were shy, others were talkative, and a few were nervous, but all of them were well behaved. Only once did I ever have to admonish a child, a little boy who had been left alone in the living room whilst I dealt with a phone call in the next room. When I returned to him, he was rummaging through a drawer in the dresser. I am sure he was not intent on stealing anything but he was too curious for his own good.

Soon after we had settled into our new home a young teacher at a school in the area called to enquire whether she could lodge with us during the week. This came as a total surprise and we had to think about the implications. We decided that we could do with the money and we knew that we had a big enough, decent bedroom that she could use as a bed-sit. We bought a fireside chair and an electric fire for her room that was conveniently positioned next to the bathroom. We were happy for her to eat her breakfast and evening meal with us downstairs. We outlined this arrangement to her and she accepted. We found her to be a nice, quiet and decent girl and things worked out quite well in view of the fact that we had lost our privacy for six days out of seven. We were resigned to the fact that you can't have everything, and it was probably a good introduction to what was to come later. As things transpired, the arrangement lasted for a few months only because Arthur and I decided that we valued our privacy and wanted the house to ourselves.

I must now tell you about a boy called Marcus, one of Arthur's pupils. He was such a cheerful and happy child who had many interests including music - he practised his piano exercises well. One day he was sitting at the piano concentrating on his lesson and Arthur was sitting nearby watching and listening when suddenly he said, "Marcus, what have you got in your pocket?" Marcus completely unruffled turned to Arthur, put his hand in his pocket and took out a snake! Not a big one I hasten to add, but a snake nevertheless that was all mixed up with string and sweets and other bits and bobs in Marcus' pocket. "Marcus … don't you ever bring a snake in here again, do you hear?" said Arthur, "Mrs. Williams would have a fit if she saw a snake, so put it back in your pocket and finish your piece and I will see you next week … without the snake!"

From thereon things went well, and Marcus made good progress with his piano studies, and was as always very well behaved. However, one afternoon during a lesson, Arthur became aware of some movement in Marcus' jacket pocket again. "Marcus, have you brought that snake here again?" "No, Mr. Williams, you told me not to do so." "Well, what have you got in your pocket this time?" And calmly, Marcus put his hand in his pocket and brought out a little frog, which he stroked gently. Arthur warmed to Marcus straight away and just smiled and said, "Frogs don't like music, so you had better leave him at home next time." "Oh, alright, I never knew that frogs didn't like music Mr Williams!" Marcus Bailey and his family moved from the district before long, but after nearly fifty years have elapsed I remember him and his name and the fact that he was a remarkable little boy. I wonder what became of him.

I went to Sunday School every Sunday afternoon and to the evening service too which was what I had always done in Llanfair, but I have to admit that as a wife, I stayed at home in the morning to cook the Sunday dinner.

Almost immediately after becoming the organist's wife, I was asked to teach a class of young girls in Sunday School. They turned out to be six very pleasant and intelligent young ladies. I had been a Sunday School teacher in Llanfair, but the class there was made up of young children whom I had known from babyhood. I had found it easy to deal with them. When I was asked to take this class of teenage girls, I was flattered but felt a little uncertain about the task that was asked of me because I knew so little about them, except their names. I felt uncomfortable because I did not feel old enough to talk to them wisely, but not young enough to be on their level either, but gradually, we came to a point where we understood each other and I have pleasant memories of them.

During those early months of settling in at *Llys Cerdd* (Music Abode) Llanrwst, I remember a very pleasant and friendly postman who was middle-aged I suppose. Every time there was any mail for our house he did not just push it through the letter-box the normal way, he rang the doorbell and of course I had to answer the call. The postman would then compose a little verse for me by way of a reward. Sometimes the verses were written down, and how I wish I had kept them. They were whimsical and funny. He was Mr. Idwal Glynne Davies, father of the crowned bard at the National Eisteddfod (at Llanrwst in 1951) novelist and journalist Mr. Tom Glynne Davies.

Early one morning in March, Arthur was getting ready to set off to an Eisteddfod somewhere and I was cooking breakfast in the kitchen when I heard a knocking on the inner front door and someone calling out, "Oes yma bobl?" - "Anyone at home?" Then I heard footsteps, and I turned away from the cooker and saw a tall man, hat on his head, mac on his arm and a wide grin all over his face standing there looking at me. He took a very good look at me standing there with surprise all over my face and shouted, "*Wel myn diawcs,...lefren*!" And when Arthur came into the room, *"Wel, Arthur, fachgen, dyma lefren dda sginti"* (Well by Jove a leveret - Arthur lad, you've got a leveret, that's good). By this time I too was grinning, because his enthusiasm and easy friendly manner were contagious. I knew who he was, although I had never met him before, I knew that he could only be the one and only *Llwyd o'r Bryn* (non-de plume). Everyone connected with the Eisteddfod, poetry and music in Wales knew of *Llwyd o'r Bryn*. He travelled extensively throughout Wales but had no car. He hitched lifts! That particular morning he had left his home on a farm near Bala very early and travelled in a milk collection lorry as far as Betws y Coed and from there he had started to walk to Llanrwst. He thumbed a lift from someone who was driving to work, and landed in good time to travel with Arthur to the Eisteddfod. His journey had been pre-planned with precision as always. I offered him some breakfast and he quickly accepted, false modesty was not in his line. He was one of three of the outstanding Welsh characters of the time - the three Bobs - *Bob Lloyd* (Llwyd o'r Bryn), *Bob Owen Croesor*, and *Bob Roberts,* the ballad singer.

When Bob Roberts was quite elderly it was arranged for him to go to Alexandra Palace in London, from where television programmes were broadcast in the early days of television, to sing before an invited audience and he was presented at the end of the programme to the Queen Mother. He had been told to address her as 'Ma'am' but when the Queen Mother asked him a question, Bob answered, "Yes, my mother!" (Mam in Welsh means mother). Fortunately, the Queen had a sense of humour, but on the other hand, old Bob might have made the remark with his tongue firmly set in his cheek! On the same occasion Bob sang a Welsh ballad that told the story of the love of a young lad for a girl. At the end of his song the female compère of the show approached Bob and asked him if the girl in the song was the young man's sweetheart, "Oh yes," replied Bob with enthusiasm and gazing in admiration at the famous and beautiful lady. "And was she very pretty Bob?" asked the compere, "Yes, yes indeed," said the incorrigible Bob grabbing the lady's arm and adding even more enthusiastically, "But not as pretty as you!"

Bob Owen Croesor was a *walking encyclopaedia* because his knowledge of the old families of Wales was tremendous. He knew all the history of Wales and had hundreds, if not thousands of books about the subject. It is said that there were books all over the place in his home. The story also goes that when he got married he and his new wife went on honeymoon to Aberystwyth. For her part, she spent her time sitting on a seat on the promenade whilst Bob researched something or other in the National Library. We might say, "Oh, how unfair, and poor lady," but she knew his ways before they were married and was therefore happy to go along with them. They were a content and happy couple as far as I knew.

Christmas time came. We formed a choir to sing carols in the Christmas services and there were practices. There were many good singers of all ages in Seion in those days. They are too numerous to mention and most have sadly passed away by now. They sang because they loved to sing and everyone who heard them loved to listen. As well as the choir we had duets, trios, quartets and solos, there was no shortage of talent. The congregational singing was wonderful for there was full harmony: tenor, bass, soprano and alto and Arthur leading with that great organ. Oh, to have those wonderful services again! I can still hear the marvellous music that those people brought forth from their very souls, and in that, they live on for ever for me. We were all friends.

Seion Chapel is a fine building inside and out and was known in the town as *Capel Mawr* (the Big Chapel). Apparently, in the distant past, there was a certain amount of snobbery associated with the chapel. Don't misunderstand me, I am speaking from second hand knowledge concerning a few people only, who appeared to go to Seion Chapel not to worship God but to be seen showing-off new clothes, airing their grand manners, and looking down their noses at poorer people. I cannot recall any real snobbery when we were there, but there were certainly one or two men who thought they were more important than they really were… and I well remember them!

The war had changed things. Men and women had been in the services, had met different people, had seen many places and experienced good and bad things. The great spirit of camaraderie that grew between people going through the hardships of war still flourished in the late 1940s and early 50s and helped to even-out the nonsense of 'class'.

There is always something special about the Christmas service in Church or Chapel. It may be the lovely decoration, the spiritual sound of the Carols old and new, or the warmth and light inside contrasting against the dark and cold outside. But whatever it is, I believe that all men and women have the divine spark of the spiritual within them, whether they are Christian or believers of another faith, or indeed, have as yet no belief. They may not acknowledge it, but the human race is continually seeking something that has no name, but the need is there for all to see. Fortunate are they who have found the 'Divine Power' that is the source of their spirituality. I will now put away my 'soap box' and continue the tale.

Arthur and I went to my parents' home at Llanfair for Christmas Day in 1947 and to Arthur's parents at the Factory for Boxing Day. We also visited Arthur's aunties at Deganwy for high tea that meant cold meats and pickles, salads, cakes, trifles, mince pies Christmas cake and everything else imaginable during the week before the New Year. They were extraordinarily kind, and wanted to please us so much.

My brother was home for Christmas and his friend Eluned was visiting relatives in the area. We were assured that she was only a good friend, a daughter of the Minister of the London Church at Jewin Chapel, where my brother was a Deacon. We enjoyed the Christmas break and then happily returned to our home in Llanrwst where by now we had established a satisfying routine to our lives.

During the following February we received an invitation to my brother's wedding. It was to take place at a Chapel in Colwyn Bay, and Arthur was asked to play the organ. We were very pleased for them. We knew that Eluned had suffered severely a few years previously. She had been married to a Welshman from South Wales, who had a delicatessen shop in the West End of London. They had a beautiful home and voluntarily helped to 'settle in' the young men and women who came to London from the rural areas of Wales. I remember going there on a Sunday evening after Chapel service, for supper. This was when I visited London during the war. I cannot remember what we had to eat but I do recall that the long table was set with fine glassware and a full set of silver cutlery. After grace was said everyone set to, and I had no idea which of the knives and forks I was supposed to use. Willy, the host, immediately noticed my discomfort and came up behind my chair and asked me which vegetables I would like and served my choice onto my plate. Quietly he whispered in my ear, "Work in from the outside." I was so relieved that my embarrassing ignorance of table skills had not been shown up to all the others at table. That kind act I have never forgotten. It proved to me, that he had a kind heart.

A few years later Eluned was in hospital having her appendix removed and during this time her husband died in tragic circumstances. She was devastated and suffered for a long time. My brother helped her a great deal during her convalescence, walking for hours with her along the streets of north London and trying to help her to come to terms with the tragic circumstances. Slowly she re-arranged her life but I feel sure that the events had left deep scars. Now she and my brother were getting married.

Sadly her mother was very ill with cancer but bravely came to her daughter's wedding service, smiled for the cameras and attended the reception. Within a few weeks she was dead. She was a lovely lady with smiling eyes and a kind nature. That is how I remember her.

Everything went well in the service except for one funny thing that happened in the chapel. Arthur had been given the signal that the bride was about to begin her entrance down the aisle and so he started to play the Bridal March. However, one of the bride's aunts arrived late and insisted on going into the church ahead of the Bride, and so it was she who appeared to the first strains of the Bridal March.

Later, at the wedding breakfast, I initially felt shocked and angry and then later disgusted when I saw the seating arrangements that had been organised. Traditionally, the 'u' shaped table arrangement so familiar in weddings at the time would have had the bride, groom and both sets of parents as centre stage on the top table, with the bridesmaids, best man and ushers on either side of them and then came other close family members. Friends and more distanced family members would be seated down the side tables. That was the customary way of doing things, and that was what everyone always expected at weddings. It was therefore humiliating and degrading for us on entering the room to discover that arrangements had been made for the groom's closest family members to sit as far away from the wedding group as was possible.

The bride, groom, bride's parents, bridesmaids and best man were all seated at the top table as expected, but the groom's parents, two sisters and brother-in-law, who had also been the organist at the service, had all been put to sit at the bottom end of one of the side tables. How unwelcoming and ungracious of them to have arranged the seating places in such a way.

Many times over the years I have thought about the message that was conveyed to both families via the seating arrangements that day. The powerful message was in evidence not only to the groom's close family members, but to everyone else present too. I could not have cared less on my own account and neither could Arthur nor my sister, but we felt to the quick regarding the blatant disrespect and lack of value shown to my mother and father. Despite the shameful arrangement, my parents said not a word - they were educated, intelligent, dignified and honourable people, and everyone present knew that. The message conveyed more about the mentality of the people arranging the breakfast than those attending!

Chapter Twenty-two

THE START OF A FAMILY

The name of our house was 'Gwydir View' when we first moved in, we think it was because Gwydir Castle could just about be seen over the river at the far end of the park and fields. But we wanted a Welsh name for the house conveying if possible the nature of Arthur's work, which of course was carried out at our home. In the end we called it *Llys Cerdd* (music court). In centuries gone by, *Llys* meant a Court, a kind of manor, but over the years it had assumed a less grand meaning - an abode or residence. *Cerdd* is Welsh for music. The house is still known as Llys Cerdd, possibly because it became known far and wide as the house of music.

During March, I became concerned because I had not menstruated for two months. Neither Arthur nor I had any cause to visit a doctor since coming to Llanrwst, so I decided to go quietly by bus to Llanfair to consult Dr.Leiper who had brought me into the world. She questioned and examined me and announced that I was pregnant and should arrange to see a local doctor at Llanrwst. I went to see my parents and told my mother the news. She took it all in her stride, made no fuss or bother, and was very matter of fact about the whole thing.

I returned home to Llanrwst and told Arthur. His reaction was also quiet and matter of fact, but he was pleased. He was concerned that I was feeling quite well and kept saying that I should take extra care of myself. I was glad there was no fuss. I could not have coped with fuss. It all seemed so unreal. There I was, looking and feeling normal, but with this tremendous knowledge that there was a child growing within me. I needed time to get accustomed to the new situation and therefore we told no one, except my sister and Arthur's parents.

Mrs. Solomon Jones who had been so kind to Arthur before we moved to Llanrwst, had been very helpful and friendly to me as well, and so I asked her for advice regarding which doctor we should register with. She immediately said Dr. Bowden in Betws y Coed. He was her family's doctor and was marvellous, the best. So he became our doctor too until he retired. He was a small, thin man but an excellent doctor. He drove a car with a 'dickey', that is, his car had room for the driver and a passenger at the front and a seat for two at the back which was outside, under a hinged cover. When not in use the seat closed into the car like a lid. He wore long gauntlet gloves and you could call for him any time, day or night, and he would come, without delay.

I consulted Dr. Bowden and told him about my being pregnant and he then advised me to go to the Clinic half way up Watling Street. The year was 1948, and the start of the new National Health Act that had been enacted by the Labour Government, as part of the new Welfare State and so we had a free Clinic. There was a full time Nurse and a caretaker on the premises, each of whom had a flat in the building. Various clinics were held there at different times. A visiting lady doctor was in charge, Dr. Peggy Roberts. I presented myself and I was thoroughly checked and found to be okay. I was given vitamin tablets and other things and many instructions. They were very good to me and really looked after my welfare, just as they did with all their patients. I needed some dental treatment and a visiting dentist at the Clinic provided this free of charge. That was that - I was then in another new routine.

I had a trouble-free pregnancy and as I grew in size of course, more people could see my condition. We had a heat wave during June and that was the only time I felt uncomfortable. I lived my life as before, doing my chores and I went to Sunday service, but gave up the Sunday School class because I felt the girls were becoming a little embarrassed by my 'bump'. Well, the climate of openness that we practise today did not exist in those days. Anything to do with sex, even within marriage, was strictly taboo and young girls were expected to be ignorant of the important facts of life.

I had also got to know one of the women who lived in Mona Villas at the back of our house, a Mrs. Downey who was clean, tidy and decent. Her husband had gone off and she was single-handedly bringing up a son and a daughter and caring for her aged mother. I arranged for her to come to give me a hand with some chores during the last few weeks before the birth. We got on very well and she continued to help me for some months afterwards too.

As the months of the pregnancy passed I became restless and wanted to do things. I was tired of the brown and cream décor and decided to paper the upper half of the walls in the living room. I bought some rolls of patterned paper, pink flowers and foliage on a cream background and Mrs. Downey volunteered to do the job. In those days flour paste was used to fasten the paper to the walls and as those walls in our house were far from being level it was no easy task. However, when the job was finished it looked good enough, not perfect, but a great improvement and it cheered me up no end.

I have to report too, that in the summer of 1948, the Australian Cricket team was over in Britain for the Test Matches for the Ashes. Both teams, England and Australia, were outstanding and well matched. The players were superb and the matches exciting. I knew the names of all the players and listened to the radio for every minute of every match! The weather that summer was wonderful. I have always liked cricket. There is something satisfying in sitting around watching the bowlers and batsmen and the movements without fuss. That is not to say that it is uneventful or quiet. There is an undercurrent of excitement in the knowledge that suddenly there will be drama and change. In those days of 1948 very few people had television and we relied on the radio commentators to convey the atmosphere and changing patterns in the action during a match. Most of them were very good and one or two were outstanding, they could convey the picture with their words. From time to time, the onlookers would clap or cheer and that would be heard, but there was no shouting, uproar or continuous noise, which unfortunately accompanies many of today's matches.

I was advised by the Clinic Nurse to pack a case well in advance to contain all that was necessary for my admittance to a maternity home at Colwyn Bay for the birth of the baby, During the last few days I grew impatient and wanted to get on with things. I thoroughly cleaned all the rooms that we used at that time and washed and ironed all I could lay hands on. I had no Hoover, so I dry mopped and swept the bedrooms upstairs. Arthur was very concerned about all this activity, especially when I got stuck under the bed! My mother laughed and told him that this behaviour was perfectly natural and can be seen in nature. She told him that animals too prepare a birthing place, and added that it was a sign that things would begin to happen very soon.

On Tuesday, 14th September 1948, I woke at 5.00a.m with vague pains in my tummy. I did not wake Arthur straight away but waited for further developments. The pains went and I settled back to sleep, but not for long. The pains came back. They were different from other tummy pains that I had experienced and I knew that my time had come. I woke Arthur who immediately jumped out of bed and thought I had to go to Colwyn Bay straight away. I calmed him down and sent him downstairs to make me a cup of tea that I enjoyed enormously. Fully awake, I could not settle to sleep any more. The knowledge that I had a tremendous job of work ahead of me, the culmination of months of preparation and imagination fully occupied my mind. I had no feelings of apprehension, more of excitement and certainly no thoughts of panic or failure. I got up and went downstairs about 9.00a.m and ate a light breakfast. Then I had a bath and checked my bag. The pains were a bit stronger but I knew that things were only just beginning. Arthur went to see Nurse Evans at the Clinic to say my labour pains had started and having ascertained their nature, advised me to wait until 3.00 p.m before going to the maternity home. Arthur went to the shops and told Mrs. Solomon Jones who immediately volunteered to accompany me to Colwyn Bay with Arthur driving the car. He was profoundly thankful for he was like a cat on hot bricks. The day dragged for us both, but at last it was 3.00 p.m. and then the three of us set forth.

I cannot remember any detail of our arrival except that my bag was emptied and taken home again by Arthur. The next thing I recall was being led to a large room, shown a bed with a bedside chair and that is all. There was no one else there but I did not mind. I had brought the daily newspaper and a magazine with me. The pains were strong now but not unbearable. I read the paper and the magazine from beginning to end and during that time saw nobody. Night came and I remember wandering down the hall to the toilet and looking at the clock several times and wishing that the action would begin. At daybreak I was feeling very frustrated with nothing to take my interest and no one to talk to, but I noticed there were three large bay windows in the room and the lower panes had been painted white so no one could see inside. I remember climbing onto the low sills and looking out of the top panes just to make sure I was still on earth. The pains were very strong now and I recall talking to myself saying, "These pains will end soon, think of that against the pain some people suffer that go on till they die." I remember gripping the rail at the bottom of the bed and willing myself not to shout or scream. During that day, the Wednesday, I was still alone but a nurse popped in once or twice asking, "Are you alright?" Well, I didn't know whether I was alright, or not. All I knew was that I was wracked with intense pain coming more and more often. I remember drinking but not eating, going to the toilet and hearing terrible screams. I asked a nurse coming from somewhere what was happening and she said, "Oh, it's a nurse having her baby." I had made up my mind that if humanly possible, I would not scream or shriek, and as far as I know, I did not.

I don't remember the rest of the day. I was in a haze and not at all aware of what was going on. At some point someone spoke in my ear asking who my G.P. was and I told them Dr. Bowden of Betws y Coed and then I was asked if I minded having a doctor from Colwyn Bay to attend to me as it was the middle of the night. I could not have cared less in my maze of pain.

When I came to, it was daylight, and I was in a bed in a two-bed ward. Gradually my mind cleared and then a nurse came to say I had a perfect little girl, and that was when I saw my baby for the first time. She had been born at 1.20a.m on Thursday 16th September. She had taken all that time from 5.00 a.m Tuesday to 1.20 a.m Thursday to make an appearance. Did she delay deliberately do you think, for the 16th was her Dad's birthday!

After I had washed my face and hands, still in bed, a Sister came to see me to ask how I felt. I said I was tired but happy and content. She said that she had attended to me at the birth, but was sorry she could not look after me any longer because she was leaving that morning. Apparently she and the Matron had a tremendous row, but I don't know the reason why. She said, “Your little girl slept all night without a break. That is very unusual in a new baby. Let's hope she keeps it up.” Then she went. When I sat up in bed to eat I noticed there was a lady in the other bed who was also from Llanrwst. She was Maltese and married to a local painter and decorator. She had given birth to twin girls. She spoke English very well.

The babies were not with us. They were in the nursery and were brought in when it was feeding time. When I helped my baby and coaxed her little mouth onto my breast, the wonder of it all made me feel as if I was watching a film. Was this because I could remember nothing of the birth and then finally handed my baby all clean and beautiful when I was in my bed, several hours later? All I could remember was the pain. However, all was well. It was over and I had a perfect little girl who was hungry.

Later on in the afternoon, Arthur came with all kinds of goodies from my mother, all special treats to build up my strength. He was laughing when he entered the ward. He explained that as he entered the building after parking the car, he was met in the hallway by a cleaning lady, an Irish girl. He told her who he was and that he had come to see his wife who had given birth to a little girl that day. “Where are you from?” she asked, and Arthur replied he was from Llanrwst. “Oh” she said, “Congratulations, you've got twins!” He nearly fainted. “No” he said “One little girl only.” “Well, I tell you, you've got two little girls.” She showed him the way to my ward and he couldn't get there fast enough. He was most relieved when he realised that it was the other Llanrwst lady who'd had twins.

The night came and I slept well. My baby slept well too, after her feeds. The following day I was puzzled as to why I was bleeding so little - much less than an ordinary menstruation. The pads supplied were large which was to be expected but I lost hardly any blood at all. I was not worried, but on the Saturday I felt a movement in my tummy and it was not a bowel movement. I told the staff nurse about it and she laughed and said, “Oh come on, you have had your baby, it must be wind.”

During that morning, the Maltese lady was not feeling well at all and rang her bell for attention. No one came. She started to shiver until the bed was shaking, so I rang my bell and kept my finger on it. A nurse appeared and asked me what I wanted and I explained about the other lady. The nurse was very terse with me for interfering until she saw for herself what was happening, then curtains were drawn round the bed and there was much to-ing and fro-ing. I cannot remember what was wrong, but it was serious. However, she got over it.

After tea, I felt the tummy movement again and I knew something was wrong. I rang the bell and the staff nurse appeared. I told her there was something moving down inside me. She got quite cross and not very nice but I was not going to be bullied and told her that I was not playing games and that there was something there and she must look. I was quite firm and she finally took a look. Immediately she said, “Oh my God you're right” and rushed off before returning with another nurse. They rid me of half of the placenta - the after-birth.

Well, I knew what it was because my sister, a nurse had told me that after a baby was born, two people were required to check that all the 'after-birth' had come away as it was dangerous for any of it to be left inside the body.

I don't know how long I had to stay in that place, but I knew that I would never go there again and that I would have any further confinements at home, with my own doctor and the local nurse in attendance.

I do hope that all the previous details have not been too much for you. After all, birth is a very normal function that happens every minute somewhere in the world, but to the mother it is a very intense and personal experience, especially the first time. It was necessary for me to give a true and detailed description of how things were, because the situation was far from satisfactory. Perhaps the place functioned well usually, or perhaps they were short-staffed that night. The National Health Service had only just started to take effect. Perhaps it was a case of my being there at an unfortunate time. I doubt whether it could happen now. Sometimes I think that the sudden departure of the Sister had something to do with the situation.

I was glad to return home and happy to see that my mother had come to stay for a few days. The baby weighed 7lb.loz. at birth, but felt so small with a floppy head that had to be supported when held. I was so afraid at first of dropping her. Mam explained that I had to hold her firmly because any nervousness or fear that I felt would be sensed by the baby and transferred to her. When I bathed her for the first time in a small bath on the table in the living room, I must have appeared clumsy in handling her for Mam said, “Here, give her to me, I'll wash her and you can watch and learn.” But I would not let her, and my words of reply were, “No, I'll do it myself, she's mine, I brought her into the world and I shall look after her.” How ungracious and unappreciative was my behaviour. But that was how I felt. We decided to call her Elsie Vaughan after my dead sister Elsie and Arthur's family name Vaughan. Mam seemed at ease with the idea.

Elsie continued to sleep all night, waking up for the 6.00 a.m feed and thereafter she would be awake most of the day and demanding attention - not crying or wailing, but just making persistent noises that meant I had to turn my daily routine upside down. I bathed her in the evening in front of the fire and quite often, some pupil or other, usually teenagers, sat and watched the proceedings. They were so fascinated and there was never any embarrassment. I breast fed her for a couple of months before changing to bottle feeds - *'Cow and Gate'* powdered milk, and she thrived on both. Every week we went to the Clinic where she was weighed and checked. My mother showed me how to wrap up a baby before laying her down in her cot to sleep. Newly born babies have no control over their arms and hands and they wave them about which seems to prevent them from settling down. The way Mam wrapped Elsie in a small shawl made of Merino wool, which is soft and warm, ensured that her little arms were within the wraps - not tight, but confined, which gave a sense of safety to the baby.

We were now a little family. We were the classical doting parents, thrilled when the first tooth appeared and enjoying the little baby antics. I became an efficient mother, losing all nervousness as practice made perfect.

When Elsie was a few weeks old my sister Bella came home for a holiday to see her. She had knitted so many things for her including a beautiful shawl. Bella knew that I could not go out anywhere in the evenings at all because there was no one else to look after the baby, so she announced to Arthur one morning that she and I were going to the cinema that evening. There was a very nice, small cinema in Llanrwst at that time. “Fine, that's good. You go and enjoy yourselves. I'll be fine. You can bathe and feed the little one and put her down. She sleeps well so there will be no problem", he said. I really looked forward to this outing and we both enjoyed ourselves. We called at the chip shop on our way home and bought a take-away supper of fish, chips and mushy peas for the three of us. We arrived back to a hullabaloo - Elsie had woken up and had cried all evening. "She must have known you were out," said Arthur very shaken up and glad to see our return.

Although we spent Christmas with my parents, we still put up a little tree at home, covering it with decorations. Arthur picked up Elsie and took her to see the tree, circling it and pointing things out to her. I don't know what response he expected - she was only three months old!

During our stay with Nain and Taid (grandparents) Elsie slept in the open drawer of a tallboy! She did not care and it did away with having to bring the cot: there were no soft carry cots around then.

Arrangements had been made for Elsie to be christened at Seion Chapel and Arthur went to fetch the four grandparents to stay with us overnight to attend the ceremony that was held the following Sunday morning. My mother had brought her best outfit and was looking forward to the event. Everyone was up early, had breakfast and prepared to leave for Chapel. Then, consternation! Mam could not find her shoes, "I've looked everywhere for them. I must have brought them surely?" I looked round the bedroom and there were slippers and everyday shoes, but not the best navy ones. "They are not here Mam. Are you sure you brought them?" "Oh, I don't know. I must have forgotten to put them in my bag. I will have to stay here and you had better get a move on or you will all be late. Go on. I'll be alright."

It was too late to think of any way to solve the problem and so, poor Mam could not come to the service. What a disappointment and it took a long time for her to live down that episode! It really was not fair to tease her. It was her ingrained care and thought for others first and then thinking of her own affairs that was the root cause of her mishap. She was most upset at missing the Christening of her first grandchild.

Obviously my work-load had increased with the arrival of a young baby. There were soiled nappies to deal with. I had no washing machine. I did all my washing in the stone sink in the kitchen. I used terry cloth nappies with muslin ones next to the skin. Soiled nappies were rinsed in cold water and then soaked for some hours in cold water, rinsed again and then boiled, using soap flakes, for ten or fifteen minutes on top of the stove. Soon it became a matter of routine.

Another time-consuming job was preparing the bottles of milk food for the day. Feeding time and burping time, you cannot rush these things or you suffer with a fractious baby! After use, it was necessary to rinse the bottle and teat in cold water, washed properly, then scalded with boiling water and then left to dry under a muslin cloth. I never had any trouble with sickness or stomach upsets. I am a firm believer in strict hygiene when it comes to food and cleanliness. I washed my hands, dozens of times every day, and I still do and no, I am not obsessive, but I will not risk my family's health and wellbeing.

Arthur was getting on well in his music business. He no longer went out to the villages to give lessons because all pupils came to our house for their lessons, which was much better all round.

The weekly visits to the Clinic showed Elsie to be gaining weight and growing. As the months passed, she started crawling, but had a peculiar way of her own, with one leg tucked under her bottom. As we did not have carpets, I had to make her some pantaloons using heavy cotton, but in every pair she wore out the one leg in no time at all. She could move like greased lightning. She was bright, but spoke no words except one, "*Doh-doh*". This was her word to convey several things using different nuances, expressions and pointing. Somehow, we knew exactly what she was saying. This went on until she was nearly three years old and then suddenly she started speaking normally. She never used baby talk. Her musical sense was extraordinary for her age. She could sing tunes, la, la, la, in perfect pitch before she was two years old, even negotiating an octave.

In August 1949 we were invited to go to London to stay with my brother Percy, his wife and their baby son Alun. We were all very pleased when Alun was born: he had been named after Percy's great friend who had died when still young. Now my parents had two grandchildren, a girl and a boy and they were very happy.

However, on reading *The Visitor*, the local newspaper, my father noticed an announcement of Alun's birth that referred to him as being the grandson of his maternal grandfather only - there was no mention of his paternal grandparents, no mention at all. My parents were hurt by this deliberate and cruel omission, but once again said nothing about the fact that they had been ignored and de-valued, and somehow once more thought it best not to make a fuss. They were cultured and courteous people and too refined to share their disappointment and dismay outside the immediate family.

Arthur and I shared their hurt and disappointment, but despite this we were also excited about going to London to visit the new baby. We were going in the little Austin that was piled high with all the stuff we needed, mostly baby things. Come the day, which was fine, we set out on our journey. We had everything we needed, a large flask of coffee, plenty of sandwiches, Elsie's bottles and food, and a tankful of petrol in the car.

When we reached Chirk and the English border we stopped to stretch our legs and have a bite to eat. You may think it was too soon on the long journey to stop for a break, but bear in mind that we had eaten breakfast very early that day and the little Austin was capable of only 35 miles an hour!

Refreshed, we then continued on our way. We left the A5 road somewhere around Whitchurch and travelled along a road that ran parallel to it most of the time. It was not as busy as the A5 and had the added advantage of being more scenic. We passed places called Wem and Wig Wig would you believe, Ludlow, Kidderminster, Aynho, where, if my memory serves me correctly, there are lovely cottages with espalier peach trees on the walls. We travelled through Banbury Cross where the 'lady rode her white horse', and all the way I had Elsie on my lap. There were no baby seats in cars in those days and no room for her on the back seat anyway. She was quite a handful at eleven months old and extremely lively. She was not tired at all for most of the journey until the last stage when she finally slept. We used a map to the North Circular Road then followed directions to Highgate Hill. Considering we had never driven to London before, we did very well indeed, but my left arm was absolutely numb from holding Elsie for so long in a confined place.

We were warmly welcomed by Percy and Eluned. They had nearly given up on us - well, the journey had taken all day!

I can remember very little of our stay except that we enjoyed ourselves. I remember we spent one pleasant sunny afternoon on Hampstead Heath with my sister Bella, who was a nurse at the Hampstead General Hospital at the time.

Oh yes! I remember one moment of panic. It happened on the first evening there after Arthur had put up the cot and I had washed and fed Elsie and put her into it with the sides pulled up. Having made sure everything was safe and sound I closed the bedroom door and went to join the others. Later, I went to check that she was alright. I opened the door, tip-toed to the cot and had the fright of my life. "Oh no, she's gone. Someone has stolen her!" After all, this was London, a big place with bad people about!

I looked round the room and there was no sign of her. "What do I do now?" I turned to leave the room and there she was, behind the door! Quiet as a mouse and very pleased with herself. She must have climbed out of the cot and crawled to the door. She had never climbed out of the cot before! The open door had hidden her from view. But I was so happy and relieved to see her safe and happy. I learned a lesson that night, never to underestimate what children can do, even very young ones!

Chapter Twenty-three

CHOIRS AND BABIES

When we returned home our busy routine recommenced. Several young men had approached Arthur to ask him to become the conductor and trainer of a male voice choir that had been convened. In the past there had been a very good choir in Llanrwst and district, but the war had put an end to it. Arthur was happy to oblige and soon there were 120 members in the Llanrwst Male Voice Choir. Some of them had very good voices and were extremely keen to sing well.

Each year since 1924 I believe, an Eisteddfod had been held in a marquee on the school playing field behind Watling Street. It was a very well known Festival in North Wales, a *Cyngerdd* (concert) on Friday night, the Eisteddfod on Saturday and a *Gymanfa Ganu* (singing festival) on Sunday evening with an invited guest soloist each year.

During those high days of male voice choirs, The Llanrwst Choir had competed once at a smaller eisteddfod against other good competitors, and had performed well, but not won the prize. However, when Arthur became the conductor he trained the choir to sing the test piece for the Llanrwst Eisteddfod. It was called 'The Village Blacksmith' and in one section the music split into eight different voice parts. The choir members worked very hard and Arthur loved coaching and conducting them: he was passionate about conducting and often referred to the fact that it was his favourite music activity, it even surpassed his love of playing the piano and organ! Conducting gave him the biggest thrill: he oozed confidence, expertise, passion, power and strength in all his music work, but it was inspirational and pure magic when he conducted, and the larger the audience, the better! His inner joy seeped through his enormous smile, twinkly eyes, and engaging manner ... and audiences were captivated and responded by giving him exactly what he wanted.

The Llanrwst Male Voice Choir was no exception. The chief adjudicator at the Llanrwst Eisteddfod that year was Dr. Frederick Wood from London who wrote a glowing adjudication for the choir. The Llanrwst Choir, under Arthur's leadership had won first prize by beating twelve other choirs! All the singers were overjoyed, and the success motivated them to continue to work hard and attend all practices faithfully. Arthur told me once that when he was in his early 20s in the pre-war period, years before we met, he had made a special effort to attend most of the concerts held in North Wales that featured a celebrated conductor and orchestra. He had used the opportunity to enjoy the music created, but more importantly to study the craft of conducting, and to emulate the skill and technique that he witnessed at the concerts, and in time to develop his own unique style. His favourite conductor was Sir Malcolm Sargent.

At this time there was talk in the town of inviting the National Eisteddfod of Wales to come to Llanrwst. A local committee was formed with representatives from the town and villages in the surrounding area. A formal invitation was sent to the National Eisteddfod Council that eventually decided to hold the National Eisteddfod in Llanrwst in 1951, a year that also happened to be the 'Festival of Britain Year', a national celebration of the regeneration of Britain after the war years. News of the Eisteddfod stirred up some excitement, and people gathered in earnest to plan the work that had to be done in order to host the prestigious event. Suffice it to say, most local people were involved in some way. One very important task involved forming and training the official 'Eisteddfod Choir' that consisted of mixed voices. The Choir would perform several times during the 'Eisteddfod Week' not in competitions, but in concerts and ceremonies. Sections of it were formed in surrounding villages as well as in Llanrwst itself. Local musicians held section rehearsals, and once a month they all gathered in Seion Chapel for a full rehearsal with the appointed conductor. Arthur was the trainer in Llanrwst town and was the accompanist for the main rehearsals. These arrangements continued for several months. They sang Dvorak's 'Stabat Mater' and choruses from Brahms's 'Requiem' and other compositions- it was a choir of more than five hundred voices!

Arthur wanted the Llanrwst Male Voice Choir to become part of the Eisteddfod Choir for the following eighteen months and he explained to the choristers that they would all learn and benefit from the experience. Also, it would have been impossible for him to work with two choirs because he just did not have the time.

All this raised a problem for some members of the successful and 'raring to go' Llanrwst Male Voice Choir, so the choir committee met to discuss the situation. Approximately a third of the members were keen for the choir to compete in the Eisteddfod. Eventually, after discussing the matter, more than half the choir opted to join the big Choir, and the others stayed away. But it affected that wonderful Llanrwst Male Voice Choir and sadly, membership never reached over one hundred ever again although the choir won prizes from time to time in the ensuing years.

That big Eisteddfod Choir was a tremendous success. It was one of the best, dare I say arguably the best of any choirs that have been formed and performed for the National Eisteddfod in Wales. I am not alone in holding this view, but probably all singers believe the same about their particular choir. There was also a Children's Choir of six hundred voices.

Despite wanting to contribute to the Eisteddfod, I had no chance of getting involved at all because Arthur was wholly occupied with his work and the Eisteddfod committees and rehearsals. I knew the situation had to be like this because it was his field of expertise, but I nevertheless felt deprived. I longed to join the Choir, my voice had developed well and I had always sung in choirs. But of course it was impossible and I accepted the situation with good grace. More to the point, I was pregnant again with another baby due in May 1950. I had no problems with carrying this baby either, except for the normal increase in size and so on. Of course, towards the end of the pregnancy I became tired periodically, but that was to be expected, especially as Elsie was such a lively child.

We stayed at home that Christmas and my parents came to stay with us. My mother had made a Christmas cake, pudding, and mince pies and had bought a goose. She took care of all the cooking over the period, which helped me enormously. *Nain and Taid* (Grandma and Grandpa) thoroughly enjoyed their new role and fussed over Elsie and of course she thrived on all the attention.

Glenys Vaughan was born on Whit Sunday May 28th 1950 at 5.55 pm just before her father left to go to Chapel for the evening service. He left the house with a smile on his face with relief and delight after the anxious wait for the birth - he had held on until the last minute before having to go to the Chapel to play the organ. I had no difficulties at all with Glen's birth, everything was straightforward, and she weighed 8 lbs 8oz.

I visited the Clinic regularly, obeyed all the instructions, ate good nourishing food, and relaxed when I breast fed her, but she cried a lot and I could not get her to burp. I did not think I could produce enough milk to feed her because I was on my feet for most of the day getting on with things in the home. Finally, I changed over to bottle-feeding. But still she cried, even screamed. I felt dreadful when I went shopping with a baby wailing endlessly in the pram, it was so embarrassing. I was getting very little sleep - it was so awful at night, sitting up in bed feeding Glenys, then trying to get her to sleep, when soon after she would start crying again. This went on for six weeks and I was at the end of my tether. We had tried all sorts of things, but nothing made any difference to the situation. I began to understand a little about how some mothers can get to a point where they end up harming their babies because of sleep deprivation. Not for the world would I ever have harmed my little girls, but I understood the feelings of helplessness that are experienced by some mothers who have fractious babies. Then one day I was out shopping with Glenys who was crying in the pram, when a lady came to me and asked, “What's wrong with the baby?” I replied, “I don't know - she's a bonny girl, and perfect in every way, except for the fact that she hardly ever stops crying.”

“Well,” said the lady, “Go to 'Boots the Chemist' and buy a bottle of *Dinnefords Clear Magnesia* - not the thick white stuff, but the clear liquid that resembles water. Put a teaspoonful in every bottle of feed she has … good luck.” And away she went.

I don't know who she was, but I did as she suggested with the next feed. Glenys was hungry and soon finished off the bottle of baby milk containing the Clear Magnesia. I lifted her against my shoulder and got her to burp immediately! But she was already fast asleep so I put her down in the pram as usual. I hurriedly had something to eat, fully expecting the crying to start any minute. Miracle of miracles she did not cry. Glen slept on and on and I finally had to wake her for the next feed. This became the normal pattern. There was no more crying and I could hardly believe the reality of the situation. I still have difficulty in adequately expressing the joy and relief of that miraculous change.

All summer long Glenys was out in the fresh air asleep in the pram, and even when the cold of winter arrived she was still out in all weathers, fast asleep. In my mind's eye I can still see the pram outside with Glenys well wrapped up and cosy inside it with snow covering the hood and the apron. Both girls were bonny and healthy, and never had a cold. Immediately life became easier for me and I could then cope. I am eternally grateful to that lady for her advice. I wish I could have known who she was in order to have thanked her personally.

A gentleman named Harry who lived up the road had recently retired from his job as a foreman at the Dolgarrog Aluminium Plant. He was very fond of music and thoroughly enjoyed participating in every minute of each rehearsal of the Eisteddfod Choir. One of his daughters came to Arthur for piano lessons. Each morning Harry went for a short walk before calling at our house on his way home. He was fond of our girls and many times took them to the park, baby in the pram and Elsie helping to push it. This helped me to get some chores done quickly and I was very grateful to him.

When Arthur was adjudicating at an Eisteddfod or conducting a singing Festival that did not entail an overnight stay, *Harry Fron* (he lived at *Fron View*) would accompany him to enjoy the journey in the car and the events of the day. He was a good friend and we were very sorry when he passed away. I remember his telling of a story from the Works that involved a worker who was forever complaining about something or other. One day when Harry was discussing the latest of these complaints with his boss he said, "I think he's got a bee in his bonnet again," to which the boss replied, "A bee in his bonnet, eh, Harry? It's more likely he's got a bloody hive in there!"

Christmas arrived again and it was so nice with having two little girls to enjoy the happiness, although Glenys was still only a baby. They didn't understand much about it, but they loved the decorations - the Christmas tree with the lights and baubles and the lovely aura of Christmas with the carol singing. I have always loved Christmas and I think they could sense the happiness in the air. My parents came to stay over the holiday and Arthur's parents were with Harry and Nance and their children in Llansannan.

During the time that Arthur was visiting villages to give lessons he had a call centre at a house in the village of Gwytherin. The son of the household was one of Arthur's pupils who had his lesson during the visit along with other pupils who called at the house at designated times for their lessons too. Mrs. Jones, the lady of the house was a very kind person. There were also two daughters in the family, one of whom was married and the other was Win, (Winifred) named after the Saint of Holywell and Gwytherin of course. Mrs. Jones came from a well-known family, some of whom were outstanding singers. Win had a marvellously deep and rich contralto voice - and still has today. During the war she served on the base camp of General Eisenhower. When she was de-mobbed and having returned home, she lost her sight for six months. It gradually returned with the aid of treatment and glasses, but has been a problem to her ever since. However, she accepted the situation and never let it get her down. She always has a joke and a laugh with everyone she meets.

Win and I first met when competing in Eisteddfodau, but round about 1950 her family moved to live in Llanrwst and she and I became friends. I am pleased to say that the friendship has lasted to this day. It is not a 'bosom pals and the baring of souls' kind of friendship, but is always there and we understand and trust each other. During the time when the children were very small she kept me up to date with what was going on in the community. I was confined to barracks as it were because Arthur was either giving lessons or at some meeting or other.

At this time, rehearsals for the National Eisteddfod Choir were in full swing and every member was keen in his or her own way. Most could read music and had good voices, but there were one or two of the singers, who were perhaps … well … not as musical as they might have been. Once, when the sections of the Choir from the surrounding villages had gathered for a combined rehearsal under the baton of Mr John Hughes the chief Conductor, he remarked to Arthur during the half-time break, "I wish they would look up at me from their copies to watch my conducting more than they do, and be more like the chap amongst the baritones in the gallery who is a fine role model to them all, he watches my every move. I wish they were all like that." "Oh" said Arthur, "I wonder who he is, I'll have to look out for him."

And during the second half Arthur watched in the organ's rear view mirror and sure enough, there he was singing away as enthusiastically as ever. Arthur was amused because he knew the man to be a keen member of the Male Voice Choir who had a passable voice, but lacked the ability to read music and therefore sometimes unknowingly held his old notation copy upside-down. It says a lot for the other members of the choir that no one ever said anything detrimental or teased him in any way.

One member of the sopranos had been nicknamed 'Top Lah' - a high note.

Apparently she would stop singing just before the end of a piece especially if it ended on a high note, then take an obvious deep breath before launching into the last few notes holding on to the last one well beyond the point at which everyone else had obeyed the conductor and stopped singing. But alas, far from being praised for her extraordinary efforts she discovered that her vocal efforts did not find favour when she was roundly reprimanded by the Conductor!

In addition to providing private piano and vocal lessons to individual pupils; carrying out his duties as organist in Seion; and leading choir rehearsals for the Eisteddfod, Arthur was also in regular demand as an adjudicator, conductor and accompanist at eisteddfodau and singing festivals, near and far. He was always busy, which meant that at certain periods, the only outings I experienced involved going shopping with the children, but I did not find it wearisome. It was my life and I got on with it. The girls were cute, incredibly funny and so loving. I would not have missed this stage of their upbringing for anything. I took great interest and care in preparing their food and making up their clothes. My sister was marvellous with handwork and knitted many garments for them. I too could knit, but not as well as Bella. I once bought nice natural coloured wool from Lerwick in Scotland and knitted plain jumpers for Elsie and Glenys that lasted through many washes before being passed on to someone else.

Chapter Twenty-four

A CARING DAUGHTER

In the latter part of spring my mother became ill and Dr. Ball said she had to go into hospital in Chester. She had suffered for some years with a prolapse and needed to have an operation. I could not go to Llanfair with two children, one being just a baby, so Percy phoned our sister at Hampstead Hospital and said she had to go home to nurse our mother. Bella was a night Sister at the time and had to have the Matron's permission to leave her post to go home. The Matron was very nice although she was loath to lose a good nurse and become short-staffed.

Mam had the operation, but was sent home much too soon because she became very ill with a high temperature. She had an internal abscess that finally ruptured and Dr. Ball ordered an ambulance and sent her back to the hospital. My sister could get no information from the Ward Sister, although she herself was a qualified nursing Sister. We never did get the full facts about Mam's treatment. My brother managed to get hold of the hospital doctor who wrote back a letter of apology for sending mam home too soon. What would have happened if my sister had not been home to realise just how ill mam was? She could have died because it had been touch-and-go. When Mam was better, Bella took a job nursing at the old C. and A. Hospital in Bangor for six months and went home for weekends, always calling at our house on the way, which the girls loved. Before her arrival they repeated over and over to anyone in sight, "*Mae Anti Bella'n dod i ty ni. Mae Anti Bella'n dod i ty ni fory,*" (Aunty Bella's coming to our house).

Meanwhile my father was just about coping with the butcher's business on his own except for a little help from Bella when she was there. It was very difficult for him, but there was nothing anyone could do.

After six months, Bella went to a hospital in Surrey to do her midwifery training and became a licensed qualified midwife. She was Isabella Owen S.R.N., S.C.M. She then moved on to Cuckfield Hospital as a theatre sister. She was an extremely capable and caring nurse.

I asked her once what had been her worst experience in nursing and she told me about a little girl, three years of age, whose whole body had been terribly burned although her face was unmarked. The surgeons, doctors and nurses had laboured all night to try to save her, but finally had to accept defeat. They were all devastated and weeping openly. My sister took it upon herself to layout the poor little body and she went to great pains to ensure that her little head with its curls, looked pretty, and her tiny hands were crossed tidily upon her chest. She also put a posy at her side. She herself spoke to the parents and helped them to bear their terrible tragedy.

Chapter Twenty-five

EXCITEMENT AND UPHEAVAL

Throughout the summer, preparations of all kinds were going on for the National Eisteddfod to be held in a large pavillion during the first week in August 1951. Thousands of people attend the event each year from all over Wales and England and from countries abroad too. The Festival is held annually in different towns alternating between North and South Wales.

Llanrwst is a small town and accommodation was required for the visitors in as many private homes as possible. A survey was made in 1951 and bookings taken and I promised to take two married couples and a single lady for full board for the week. Also, the Eisteddfod Committee supplied camp beds for three female students to use in our empty rooms on the second floor! They required breakfast only, but the other five required breakfast, lunch, and dinner at 6.00p.m. to give them plenty of time to attend the evening concerts, *Noson Lawen* (merry night) and drama productions. Arthur and I and our girls therefore had to make do by sleeping in rooms on the top floor during the Eisteddfod. I planned the whole week with precision including the menus. My sister Bella came home on holiday for the week to help! I cannot remember what I was paid for the students, but it was adequate in view of the conditions. Each of the family of five paid one guinea a day £1.1s.0d, which was one pound and one shilling, and my mother kindly supplied the meat and vegetables free of charge. I must admit to having been a little apprehensive about the whole thing because I had never done anything like it before and wanted the visit to be a success. With hindsight, I realised that my charge of a guinea per person per day was totally inadequate considering all the work involved in catering for the guests 3 times each day. But we live and learn do we not!

The week before the Festival Elsie and Glenys went down with whooping cough. I had heard of it previously, but had no personal experience of it. I concluded that they must have become infected during their regular visits to the Clinic in view of the fact that it was highly contagious. Elsie was three years old and coped fairly well with it, but Glenys, who was only fifteen months old, had a harder time. She had never even had a cold before, but both of them were whooping in a dramatic way. It was very distressing to see them struggling to bring up the slimy matter from their lungs. When my sister saw the girls having a whooping spasm, she placed newspaper on the floor, grabbed their legs and held them upside down over it. And sure enough the horrible stuff that looked like a small jellyfish slipped out of their mouths onto the paper, with immediate relief for everyone. During the day, coping was fairly easy because the whoops did not disturb anyone really, but during the night, with all the guests in bed it was a different matter. We decided to put the cots and a bed downstairs in the music study and take it in turns to sleep with the girls in order to deal with night attacks before they disturbed the household. Another one of us slept upstairs on a camp bed in a bedroom on the second floor and the third slept on a large chair in the living room. Thus we managed to get sufficient sleep to enable us to attend to the following day's activities.

Another snag existed in the fact that on the opposite side of the road was the Church House, the venue of the nightly *Noson Lawen*, and sometime between midnight and 1.00 a.m. a crowd of around two hundred or so happy people would pour onto the street laughing and joking and banging doors as they got into cars, and who could really complain because they were enjoying the Festival. But the noise was loud enough to wake the girls, then it was difficult to get them settled once more.

However, we coped successfully every day and everything went like clockwork including us! At the end of the week we felt like robots on automatic pilot. One thing is certain, I could never have managed without Bella: she shared the burden of nursing the sick children with Arthur and me, despite having come with the purpose of enjoying the Eisteddfod! Arthur had to attend the evening concerts and I believe my sister finally managed to enjoy some of the later events too. On the last Saturday afternoon, which was warm and sunny, I took the girls onto the Eisteddfod field just to look around.

Before leaving on the Sunday evening, all the guests thanked us for the welcome and the service they had received. The lady from the group of five was particularly effusive in her thanks and asked me if I was sure that my fees were enough to cover the costs. I was young, inexperienced in catering and not wishing to appear greedy, replied that I had stated my price and would stick to it - I felt that I could hardly change it at that stage! But her eloquence in praise did not stretch to any tips being forthcoming, which they could easily have afforded especially knowing they had been very fortunate in staying with us.

It was a valuable experience for me, although I did not realise it at the time. We had not made a loss on the venture, but had earned very little if anything for our hard work. We were very grateful to have survived and coped so well in a difficult situation. We then had until the end of August to relax and recover before the start of the next term.

After the involvement of so many people over a period of two years in planning, anticipating and preparing for the Festival followed by the enormous enjoyment, excitement and thrill of the week's activities, sadly the final moment of the last session arrives and reluctantly, everyone has to pack up and go home. The site of the main Pavillion and small marquees is cleared immediately and quickly leaving behind litter on the ground and a 'flat' feeling all around. There is quietness in the place that hours earlier, had been so vibrant and enchanting. There is also a sense of anti climax about the scene, strengthened by the visual impact of the desolate, dull and dejected site. From high to low! But gradually however, the normality of routine takes over again and life gets back onto an even keel.

At the end of September 1951 Arthur and I went to London for 2 nights having left the girls with my parents. I had been invited to sing at a concert being held in the Welsh Club at Gray's Inn Road and Arthur had been asked to accompany me on the piano. I remember very little about the occasion except for the fact that I felt nervous, and rather overawed. I cannot even recall whether we drove to London or travelled by train. Maybe I was still not quite back to being on top form having giving birth to 2 children in 3 years, or perhaps I felt emotionally drained after such a hectic summer. But whatever the reason … I know that the London concert, although well-received, was not one of my better ones.

Christmas 1951 came and went. The girls were healthy and growing well and brought great joy into our lives. Elsie was slow in talking but she could sing all kinds of tunes. She would sit on the stairs near the music room and sing la-la-la to all the different melodies that the pupils played. Once, when a young boy was learning to play a well-known Welsh tune, and Elsie was la-la-ing on the stairs and having to stop time after time again while the lad struggled through the piece, she barged through the door and announced, much to her father's amusement, … “Dad … you play!” I'm not sure what effect this three year old's request had on the boy's musical confidence however!

I mentioned earlier, that for a long time when she was little Elsie called practically everything, “Doh doh” and strangely we knew exactly what she meant by her nuances and gestures. However, when she finally decided to speak, she did so properly more or less immediately having somehow missed the gradual 'baby talk' stage.

Glenys on the other hand advanced in the expected way, learning an increasing range of words with each passing week. Of course children learn from one another and it is easier for siblings to pick up from the eldest. We always spoke properly to the children and corrected their mispronunciations. It is amusing when children say certain words in funny little ways, but it becomes embarrassing for them when they go to school unless they have been helped to eliminate the peculiarities.

In winter, I bathed the babies in the living room in front of the coal fire. As Arthur's pupils waited to be called into the music room for their lessons, they loved to watch the performance of the babies frolicking, splashing and squealing. Many have told me in later years how pleasant and homely it was at *Llys Cerdd*. The living room was by far the warmest place in the house for we did not have central heating, very few people did in those days. We had a coal fire in all the downstairs rooms until they were replaced later with electric ones.

Chapter Twenty-six

THE LAST ARRIVAL

In 1952 Arthur's parents moved from the Factory into a council house in the village of Llansannan. Arthur's father had suffered for years with an ulcer that had finally been operated upon successfully in 1951, but despite the improvement to his health they could no longer continue to live alone in the isolated countryside without electricity or mains water supply.

In preparation for the move Arthur and his brother Harry undertook the job of clearing and sorting the Factory, and they decided to be ruthless - too ruthless maybe, for they had a big fire burning in the garden for a couple of days as they worked through their parents' belongings! In the meantime, Nance and I, the two daughters-in-law went about cleaning and getting the new home in the village ready for *Taid and Nain*. With the best of their old furniture and the acquisition of selected new furnishings including pretty curtains and a few rugs, we managed to prepare a cosy home for them. My parents looked after Elsie and Glenys during the period of this work and did not regard it as a chore, but saw it as labour of love.

A few weeks before Christmas 1952 I realised that I was pregnant again. Somehow it seemed pre-ordained, I don't know why, but it felt right. I was very well indeed and never suffered morning sickness with any of my children.

We decided to go to Liverpool to do some shopping before Christmas and Mam came with us in the little Austin 7. The weather had been very stormy over the past few days and there was still dampness in the air, but the wind had calmed by the morning of our trip. About halfway to Liverpool we filled the fuel tank at a petrol station in the knowledge that it would be enough to get us to Liverpool and back home again. We therefore continued merrily on our way, but not for long because half a mile down the road the engine started to splutter and finally stopped. Arthur opened the bonnet and found the carburettor full of water. He emptied it and got the engine going again. A couple of minutes later the same thing happened again … and again … and again. This was serious - a major disaster we thought in view of the fact that the Mersey Tunnel lay ahead and we knew that a penalty of £15.00 would be levied if we broke down inside it. Having to pay a fine would substantially deplete the Christmas spending money that we'd scraped together over the previous weeks. We were not a happy group of travellers at all!

Finally, an AA man on a motor cycle stopped, investigated then immediately reached the conclusion that we had received a tankful of watery petrol at the station, the result of the recent stormy weather we speculated. He advised Arthur to empty the tank of its contents and replace it with proper petrol at another local station. What a waste of money, time and energy! We reasoned that we had no choice but to follow the advice, but couldn't help but wonder how many other motorists had been affected in the same way. Having obtained more petrol we continued with the journey, crossed our fingers as we entered the tunnel, and shouted "hurrah!" as we drove out of it without a hitch! Our spirits rose again especially after finding a parking place, enjoying a meal, and starting on the shopping.

Elsie was old enough at 4 to really appreciate the Christmas lights and decorations - and Glenys being only 2 was wide-eyed and pointing in awe and wonder. Having completed the shopping for Father Christmas we then went to buy a carpet square for the lounge. We went to Lewis' Department Store and having gone in the lift to the carpet section found it difficult to make an instant choice from the wide range available. It took a long time … and in the meanwhile Glen had had enough. Although she'd been carried around quite a lot, her little legs were tired, so she climbed on top of a pile of carpets and sat there and would not budge! This meant that my mother had to stand guard while Arthur had Elsie in tow and I finally managed to choose a very big square rug with cream, pink and rose garlands on a green background. I was very pleased with my purchase and we all went home quite satisfied. The girls were exhausted but happy after the adventures of the day and slept all the way back to Llanrwst.

The lounge looked so much cosier and more colourful with the arrival of the new rug and it covered most of the polished wooden floor. Made of good quality cotton it served me well for years. Later, Elsie and Neville used it in their first flat and later still Bryn and Kath used it for a while - it had become a little faded by then, but was still unworn.

1953 is prominent in my memory for a number of reasons including the death of King George V1 that resulted in his daughter becoming Queen Elizabeth II. The King had not enjoyed good health for some time, but it must still have been a terrific shock to the Princess to be told of her father's death while she and Prince Philip were away on safari in Africa.

In June, the annual Sunday-School trip was to Rhyl and we were fortunate that the day was warm and sunny. Rhyl in those days was lovely, just as nice as it was when I was a child. Golden sands, lovely promenade with flowers everywhere, a paddling pool, designated bicycle area, the domed Pavillion, lots of ice cream kiosks and candy floss stalls, a fishing pool, donkey rides and of course the Marine Lake with all its wonderfully thrilling rides. I remember the ghost train, bumping cars, the little train puffing round the lake and a host of other exciting adventures. Oh! it was such a wonderful place for children and adults too. There were all sorts of shops to suit everyone and a range of shows available in the theatres too. Somehow the place is not the same today, but then everywhere else is different too - very little remains unchanged in the space of half a century. Mam had come on the bus from Llanfair to meet us wearing her best clothes and hat and she enjoyed watching the girls making sand castles with their father. I was heavily pregnant with our third child at the time and due to give birth mid-August, but I still enjoyed the day.

Within a couple of weeks we had a phone call to say that Mam at the age of 69 had suffered a stroke, was paralysed down one side, and her speech had been affected. We went to Llanfair straight away and learnt that the previous evening she had left my father to clear up and wash down the butcher's shop whilst she'd gone home to prepare supper. She had taken a delivery basket with her and about half-way home had begun to feel unwell. She vomited, so she sensibly turned into the drive of the police house where she collapsed. I don't know how long she lay there or whether she lost consciousness but an old man passing by, although hard of hearing, heard her moaning and making noises and went to investigate. That is how she was found and then received care.

The event shocked everyone, especially her family - she was such a healthy and strong woman, but of course had suffered shocks, disappointments and struggles all her life. The reason for her stroke was given as stress. The doctor was very good with her and she obeyed him absolutely even to the point of giving up salt in her food. Within a few weeks she was herself again, but naturally she and dad had to give up the butcher's business.

August came and my sister had arranged to return home for two weeks to be with me for the birth of the baby due on the 16th August. She and my mother, who was feeling well again, duly arrived at our house, and the girls were extremely pleased and excited because their Nain *and* their favourite Aunty Bella were there. They were also on tenterhooks looking forward to seeing the new, *"Ba bach"* (little one). Every morning our bedroom door opened and two little heads appeared round it asking in unison, "Has the little baby arrived yet?" And every morning they were disappointed because the baby was late!

I was very uncomfortable with pain in my upper back just under my shoulder blades caused by the size of the baby in relation to my own. In the evenings my sister walked me along the river paths and all over the town in order to bring on my labour but to no avail. We were both getting anxious in the knowledge that she would have to return to London at the end of the fortnight, and each precious day spent waiting for the birth, at worst meant greater risk of running out of time, and at best meant less time to look after the baby.

Wednesday the 25th August dawned bright and sunny and I woke up and knew straight away that this was to be the day. Arthur got up and the household was quickly astir. The midwife, Nurse Llywelyn and Dr. Bowden were alerted, and I was very happy that my sister was with me and that the whole process would not take too long.

I had reached the stage in labour where Nature was insisting that I push to help the baby make its way into the world, but my sister was anxious for the Doctor and Nurse to appear before labour proceeded any further. She asked me to refrain from pushing, which is, as every mother knows, like trying to close the flood gates once partially opened! Fortunately, within minutes they both arrived and I was given gas and air to help me with the pain. Our third baby arrived at 11.20a.m and was laid at the foot of the bed. The medics attended to me because I was torn again and was probably in a bit of a mess. As they attended to my needs, my sister held up and gently smacked the baby which resulted in a little cry. I then remember her coming to me and saying, "You have a beautiful little boy." I was so happy and content with everything that I just lay there, half asleep. The baby weighed a massive 10lbs - less 1oz. It was no wonder I had suffered so much from discomfort at the end of the pregnancy.

When order had been restored and the little boy lay nice, clean and warm in his cot, the girls were allowed to come in to see him. They could not contain their excitement, wanting to hold him, watch him, and stroke his face. It was wonderful!

We could not decide on a name for him until my mother suggested we called him *Bryn*. We agreed that it was a nice short name that was easy to pronounce correctly and was linked to the village of *Bryn Rhyd yr Arian* where his father, one Nain and two Taids had been born and bred. The baby was finally baptised Bryn Vaughan whose birth had made us a family of five - Arthur Vaughan Williams, Bet Vaughan Williams and our children Elsie Vaughan Williams, Glenys Vaughan Williams and Bryn Vaughan Williams.

Bryn was a good baby especially when he was very young, and his sisters doted on him. They helped by pushing his pram to and fro to get him to sleep and later entertained him when he was awake during the day and demanding attention. Elsie was now at school in the infant class and loving it. Glenys was only three years old and still at home. She had a passion for jigsaws, and still has - she spent many hours sitting or lying on her tummy on the hearth rug working out how to join the pieces to make a picture and all the time would be humming some tune or other.

My sister claimed Bryn as her own although she was back nursing in Sussex. She was a very good knitter and made many jumpers, cardigans and pullovers for the children. She knitted a cute Pluto-type cuddly dog for Bryn named Sammy that had a slim body and very long, floppy limbs. Bryn thought the world of it and carried it about everywhere during his early years of childhood. When Bryn was around 3-4 years old he would go upstairs after lunch dragging Sammy along into bed and go to sleep - all of his own accord! Sammy had great facial features that gave him a character of his own. All the children who knew the family also knew Sammy - he was highly popular, very well-known and some would even say famous too! One day, on his travels up the street with Sammy in tow Bryn became interested in some wonderful puddles that were great fun to splash in and explore with friends. When the two of them returned home we found that Sammy was no longer the yellow dog that we all knew and loved but a soggy mustard coloured character. “What happened to Sammy?” we all enquired. But Bryn was oblivious to the change of appearance - Sammy was Sammy whatever the colour of his coat!

Each day, after I had washed him, Glen would dress Bryn and attend to his every whim. The girls shared a double bed at that time and, after Bryn had got too big for the little cot, we moved him to the larger one in the girls' bedroom. All three thought this was wonderful and Bryn exploited his popularity to the full. After I had tucked them in, kissed them goodnight and put out the light, he would get out of his cot and call out softly, *“Dwi'n ramblo”* (I am rambling), and the girls would answer, “Oh, alright, come on, get in here with us,” and there he would be in the middle of the bed, between them. Sometimes the girls would encourage him to go onto their side of the bed instead of in the middle, and at other times when he was in the middle there would be an argument and one would say, "He's mine,” and then the other would say, "No, he's mine,” each one pulling his arms in different directions. It's a wonder he was able to stay in one piece - but Bryn loved it all - every bit of the attention and popularity!

My workload had increased even more and I was very busy every hour of the day. We were a happy family, so the work did not present as a chore. On Sunday mornings, Arthur would take Elsie with him to Chapel and she would sit quietly all by herself in the gallery by the great organ, while her father played it. We never gave her pencils or paper or anything else and she never misbehaved or created a fuss, she just watched the people and copied whatever they did. Eventually, when Glen was old enough she too went with Elsie to Chapel and Sunday School.

When my friend Win and her family moved to Llanrwst she looked after them, brought them home after Sunday School and her kind mother always gave them little treats whenever they visited her home. They liked going to 'River View'.

I remember my father-in-law telling me that he'd discovered that, “if you explain to children why you want them to do, or not do something then they are more likely to obey. Children are naturally reasonable as long as grown ups leave them alone and trust them.” I found what he said to be absolutely true. We had very little trouble with the behaviour of our children. We tried to ensure they understood what was required and gave them lots of praise and encouragement to help them to achieve.

These days I see some children of six or seven years of age walking about with dummies in their mouths and I must say that I think it looks awful. My three children used dummies as very small babies and I am prepared to say that they were a help at that time, but I wanted to get rid of them as soon as possible thereafter. They were free of dummies before the age of three months. Dummies are unhygienic because they fall onto the floor, get sticky and grubby, have a tendency to distort the child's gums and lips and worst of all, impede the development of speech. I have witnessed big children trying desperately to explain something with great difficulty because of having a dummy in their mouth!

My children were potty trained regularly but playfully, with the result that they were clean at 18 months and dry before the age of two years. This all sounds very smug and pompous I'm sure, but it is perfectly true and I believe it was due mainly to listening to them and carrying out my father-in-law's advice. Explain to children and then trust them!

Oh yes, I nearly forgot to tell you the story of what happened one afternoon about two or three days after Bryn was born. Two spinster ladies who lived just down the road from us, one of whom was a retired, qualified and experienced nurse, and her sister came to our front door and rang the bell. I was still in bed, my sister was in the bathroom, and my mother was in the living room with Elsie and Glenys. As soon as they heard the doorbell the girls rushed to open the door to greet the callers. The kind ladies had brought a beautiful bunch of flowers for me and were no doubt hoping to be asked inside, but meanwhile they were engaging the girls in conversation, in Welsh of course. I could hear all that was said. "Hello, what are your names?" "Elsie and Glenys and we have a new ba-bach." "Have you now, and what do you think of your little brother?" "He's lovely and we love him very much." "What is his name?" "Bryn." "Well, that is a nice name and where did he come from?" In unison they answered proudly, … "From Mam's tummy!"

The incredulous gasps were audible even to me upstairs and obviously the ladies were scandalised! In general, children at that time were not told about the real details of birth and reproduction in the way they are taught today. There was a conspiracy of silence to keep them in the dark and when Elsie and Glenys came out with an obvious truth … the spinster ladies were stunned at first, then shocked and horrified … and basically, just couldn't take it! "Oh dear, oh dear, is that so?" they said hurriedly. "Well here you are, give these to your mother." "Thank you very much" the girls said together, and came tearing upstairs quite unabashed.

My sister who had been sitting on the landing throughout the conversation could not speak for laughing. She thought it was absolutely hilarious. But my mother was ranting downstairs. "This is dreadful, quite disgraceful. How can you teach children in such a manner? Quite unseemly! What on earth will those ladies think? They will think we are all mad. What is the world coming to?"

My sister thought it was best to go downstairs to my mother and try to console and quieten her. She tried to explain that people were being more open and honest with their children in many ways and it was a much more sensible way to go about things. It was unfortunate that no adult had been able to greet the ladies, my sister being in the toilet, my mother still unsteady after her stroke and Arthur out somewhere. Later my sister called at the ladies' house, not to apologise for the girls but to thank them for their kindness and generosity and explain why there was no adult to greet them when they called.

Summer melted into autumn, and I was a very busy mum when Elsie contracted mumps, not very seriously, but badly enough for us to keep her home from school. Glen got off very lightly and Bryn was fine. It was poor old me who suffered most. I did not have mumps as a child, and I am told that when adults are attacked by illnesses that are regarded as childhood ailments they are much more severely affected. My neck swelled up on one side and I could barely open my mouth to sip a drink. Eating and chewing were out of the question because the pain was acute. I looked grotesque, especially with a scarf tied round my face and my loving family thought it very funny and even tried to make me laugh, which was unfair because of the pain. Like Bryn, Arthur was not affected, and this was a good thing because mumps can cause serious complications for males.

The one good thing about the attack is that it did not last long and when Christmas came we had a jolly time with a tree and decorations that I had brought from Llanfair, and by then 'Santa Claus' had become very important. For weeks the girls had been looking forward to Christmas and telling everyone what they wanted from the nice old man. Arthur and I found this period very useful to get easy obedience to rules of the house, such as bedtime and sleep time. Santa Claus had a helper called Johnny who came to visit homes without warning to find out how well the children were behaving and what time they went to bed. Periodically of an evening, oddly enough, round about bedtime, Arthur would go out to ring the doorbell and followed it up with a conversation with Johnny! The topic of conversation depended on how the listeners had behaved during the day!

With the arrival of Christmas morning they would be up before dawn rummaging in their pillowcases to see what marvels lay within. How wonderful it was to watch their pleasure and excitement! We made sure they received as many toys, games, fruit and sweets as Bella and I had received when our brother was Santa Claus, and Arthur and Harry had received from their aunts in Deganwy. But there was more to come! There were many wrapped presents stacked under the Christmas tree too, so enticing in shining coloured paper, and not to be opened until after the Christmas dinner had been eaten and cleared away. The wait was long and many were the pleadings to be allowed to open, "Just one." When they were a little older, Glen would surreptitiously finger, feel, shake and smell all the packages, then excitedly announce the contents. Not always wrong! This led to a period when the Vaughan Williams presents to each other were being very, very heavily disguised to avoid Glen's detection! Tiny presents would end up wrapped in huge boxes and circular items would end up square. Even this treatment sometimes failed!

During the latter part of 1953, Harry, Arthur's brother had decided to go into business on his own account. He was a carpenter who took on the tenancy of a yard in Llanrwst where he set up the business. He travelled from Llansannan every day and came to our house to eat his lunch. The children had great fun with him and he enjoyed chatting and joking with them. He had three children of his own; Emyr born March 1946, Elinor his sister, born on the same date in March 1949 and a brother Elwyn, born in February 1952. Harry loved making Glen laugh and he found a way of doing this by asking her in Welsh, "Glen, what will Father Christmas bring for you in his sack?" To his great amusement Glen would answer by saying, *"Joni dro drons a cises i mi,"* which was a toddler's way of saying, *"Mae Johnny Santa Clause yn dod a cylleth i mi"* (Santa will bring me a knife). Glen's sister had received a knife, fork and spoon set, and now she wanted one too.

During the early months of Harry's setting up in business in Llanrwst, Arthur helped him a great deal. He would spend full mornings working with him either at the yard, or out on a job. Arthur enjoyed the work and his brother's company and really wanted to help Harry make a success of his new business. So much so that he sometimes risked the success of his own business in the process. Arthur would sometimes cram in as much work as possible for Harry and delay coming home at lunchtime until the very last moment, which sometimes made him a little late for his own work with pupils. In the end I had to call a halt to this practice because he had no time to get changed into clean clothes suitable for a professional teacher, or to eat his lunch until it was very late in the afternoon.

Chapter Twenty-seven

CHALLENGES FOR THE FAMILY

In the spring, Arthur was always busy as an adjudicator at *Eisteddfodau*, the competitive meetings that were very entertaining for the audience but rather nerve-wracking for the competitors, some more than others of course. The quality of the competitors, adjudicators, accompanists and performers, varied from mediocre to excellent. At the larger events there were preliminary tests before any stage appearance that usually weeded out the poorest attempts.

The smaller events too had their uses; they provided children and adults with an opportunity to appear before an audience, to stand on a stage alone and try to please a crowd of people by singing, reciting poetry or some other form of art. Many famous Welsh people respected for their skills, started in this way. Long may the *Eisteddfod* flourish! Incidentally, many emigrants from Wales took their culture and traditions with them to their new land, and in the U.S.A. during the 19th and most of the 20th centuries many *Eisteddfodau* and other cultural festivals flourished. My own children came out of this mould and all three have flourished in the world.

Apart from the competitions that involve stage appearances at the *Eisteddfod* are many others that involve creating an item skilfully beforehand e.g. a composition of prose, poetry or music, art and crafts, items of cookery, handwriting, flower arranging, anything and everything really. At the *National Eisteddfod* a chair and a crown are prizes awarded for poetry, a gold medal for prose and these awards are highly regarded, and much sought-after by the competitors. They have real value and prestige because the prizes are not easily won at all, and they confer great honour on the recipients.

Snow came at the end of February after frost, so that St. David's Day on the 1st of March dawned to a white wonderland, at least that's what our children thought. They loved it, and wrapped up well against the cold the snow represented fun and great enjoyment in sliding about and making snowmen. However, adults were not quite as enthusiastic. Arthur needed to go to an *Eisteddfod* in a village on the outskirts of Denbigh that meant driving up and down steep hills and negotiating narrow country lanes. When you are country born and bred you learn to take these weather problems in your stride, and Arthur set off in the Austin with a spade, some sacking, rags, an old blanket and a good dollop of faith! He got as far as the village of Llansannan but had to leave the car at his parents' house and continue the journey on foot because of the depth of snow. The main roads had not been too bad but the country lanes were untouched by snowploughs. When he finally arrived it was as he had expected, the little hall was packed with people not wanting to be deprived by the weather of their annual event and eagerly looking forward to the competitions. He was so pleased he had made the effort to get there to do the work … and they were equally delighted that he had managed it because they had been worried about his safety knowing the state of the roads.

During the daylight hours more snow came and as darkness fell, Jack Frost went on his rounds again. When proceedings were concluded and tea and sandwiches had been consumed, Arthur then set out on his four-mile walk back to his car in Llansannan. En route there is a very steep hill and he slipped on the ice and fell heavily. He felt a sharp stab in his back, but got up and continued painfully on his way. Although his parents had waited up for him and wanted him to stay overnight, he continued on his way home to Llanrwst because he knew that I would be worried and would be waiting up for him. It was very late when he reached home, but after a cup of tea, with no milk or sugar which was the way he liked it, and a couple of aspirin tablets, he fell into bed and was asleep at once. Arthur was fortunate in the fact that he could sleep anywhere at any time, whereas I can sleep only at night providing I am not disturbed.

In the morning he was no worse for his fall except that he was very stiff! The weather changed during the week and the snow and ice disappeared, which was just as well for Arthur had many engagements booked for March, April, May and June. However, he started to suffer pain in his lower back and leg and by June was having to take pain killers regularly and was finding it very difficult to walk properly: he could not bend over which was very worrying. We discussed the situation and Arthur decided that he would soldier on until the end of July when the schools would start the summer holidays and he would have the whole of August free from organ duties in Chapel too. His last engagement was in mid July, which meant he could have seven weeks of rest to recuperate. This also meant of course that we had no money coming in during that period! From the beginning of our marriage we had dealt with the summer holiday situation by ensuring that outstanding bills had been paid and we had enough money saved to cover household expenses. That year was no exception, we enjoyed little trips to Llandudno and were visited by my parents and Arthur's mum and dad, and as always we had fun with the children - Elsie was six, Glenys, four and Bryn was one year old.

Then it was time to start the new term in September 1954. Arthur was still in great pain, indeed the pain was getting worse and he walked by bringing one foot up to the other and inclining his body to the side. His right leg had almost no flesh on it, just skin and bone, but he would not go to the doctor. Well, it's not easy to be sick and go off work when you are self-employed and have a business to conduct.

September was nearly over, and one evening Arthur had dragged himself to a Workers Educational Association (WEA) meeting at the school next door. He was a member of a class studying Welsh History and always enjoyed the sessions. The tutor was Frank Price Jones from Bangor, a distinguished historian and a friend from school days.

I had finished putting the children to bed and was just about to sit down with a cup of tea when the doorbell rang and rang continuously … on and on it went non stop, so I hurriedly went to open the door and there was Arthur slumped against the bell push and looking as white as a sheet. I helped him in and sat him down, but he could not stay seated because he was in so much pain, he did not know what to do to relieve it. I got him a cup of tea and a couple of aspirins and advised him to lie down in bed.

Frank Price Jones, the tutor called at Llys Cerdd on his way from the class to enquire about Arthur, having noticed his condition on leaving his class that evening. He willingly agreed to telephone Dr. Bowden on our behalf from the telephone box on the square, and I knew that the Doctor would come to see Arthur, despite the late hour. And come he did. I took him upstairs and Arthur was back in bed after pacing the floor. The Doctor sat on the side of the bed and Arthur and I described how things had been getting worse during the summer. Then there was a long silence … many minutes went by. The doctor had his head lowered, resting on his hand and I really thought he had gone to sleep, exhausted by his long day. But no, suddenly he lifted his head and said quietly, “I think you have a slipped disc Arthur.” Now, I had already read about this complaint, a condition that had been recognised as such during the war. Previously all who suffered in this way had been bundled into the large group of people who suffered from 'rheumatics'. People became crippled and bent and were treated with only pain killers, but then it became known that because of various accidents, discs between the bones in the spine protruded and chafed against the sciatic nerve, causing intense pain. Therefore, when the doctor proclaimed his diagnosis I blurted out, "He can't have" forgetting that a little knowledge is a dangerous thing. "He has not done anything to cause that," I said in all innocence. "Well," said the good doctor, "I am afraid that is what is wrong and we must arrange for him to have it seen to at once. I will arrange things as soon as I can in the morning, but meanwhile Arthur, I've given you a prescription for very strong pain-killing tablets to help ease your pain."

Next morning Dr. Bowden came to see Arthur as soon as he had finished his morning surgery work. He was as good as his word, having arranged for Arthur to be treated at the Colwyn Bay Hospital, but he would have to wait for three or four days for the consultant and doctors to deal with previous appointments. I obtained the prescribed tablets from the chemist. One, and only one was to be taken every four hours, and the doctor had warned me not to allow Arthur to exceed the dose. As soon as Arthur had taken a tablet the pain eased, but after three hours the effect wore off and he pleaded for another one.

Remembering the doctor's warning I had to refuse, and found it so very hard to do so. Later, I told Dr. Bowden about it and explained with a wry smile that Arthur, "Would have murdered me for one of those tablets had he been able," to which the Doctor replied with an extremely serious tone in his voice and look on his face that required me to consider the severity of pain normally associated with toothache. He asked me whether I had experienced it and I must have smiled, at which point he said, "Oh my dear, don't smile … if you have ever had toothache you will know how much it hurts?" I replied that yes indeed, I had suffered with toothache at times. "Well then, just remember that the sciatic nerve is the biggest nerve in your body and the pain your husband is experiencing is a hundred times worse than any toothache," he said. I realised how facetious my remarks had seemed to the doctor and I then remained silent and downcast. I could not possibly experience the intensity of the pain that was prolonged for Arthur, but Dr Bowden helped me to understand it better and be able to empathise with Arthur. I knew well the temporary pains of childbirth, and the fact that Nature has arranged for us to eventually forget them, but I learnt from Arthur's problem that it is a different matter to suffer pain week after week without relief or rest.

Thankfully, Arthur was taken to the Colwyn Bay Hospital within a week where treatment began immediately. He was taken to a room where a strap was fitted under his chin and his whole body raised up by a pulley so that his feet were clear of the floor. This enabled his spine to be fully stretched to enable the offending disc to be returned to its proper place between the vertebrae. Arthur told me several times that the moment of suspension was the most perfect sensation ever - he was completely free of pain! However, the two doctors continued the operation by slapping 'Plaster of Paris' all over his torso, from his armpits to his legs. When this was sufficiently hard he was released from the pulley and returned home. Of course, the pain was still there because of the inflammation of the nerve so he still had to have tablets. For about ten days Arthur was despondent believing the operation had not been successful. The Clinic Nurse was very kind and took the trouble to visit and explain that he would find a gradual improvement, and that was exactly how it worked out. He had to wear that plaster for over four months!

At the clinic he was warned not to do anything except relax and do gentle exercises. Well he could not bend and that meant that I had to hold him by the arms when he sat down or got up or went to bed. One of the other patients at thc clinic advised Arthur to follow the doctor's instructions implicitly. "I disobeyed and as I got better and the pain was fading I started working, with the result that I am back again to square one," he said. Arthur decided to follow the doctor's orders even though the plaster became loose on his body. Eventually it was taken off and he enjoyed the luxury of a bath once more. He was then measured and fitted with a leather and steel waistcoat to sustain and protect the spine. This, he wore every day for two years. He could have discarded it earlier, but he was so afraid of the terrible pain returning that he kept to the recommendation.

Looking back and wondering what had caused all the trouble he remembered helping on the farm where he worked as a general factotum during potato harvesting when he was eighteen years old. There were many sacksful of potatoes that he had been lifting up onto a cart. Arthur was strong and had a rhythm going - bending, lifting and so on. But there was one sack heavier than the rest, and as he lifted it, felt a terrific pain in the small of his back as if someone had stabbed him. It stopped him momentarily on the day, but he felt alright again in a few days. Months later, he had a similar experience, but again the pain disappeared in a couple of days. He was young, strong and healthy at the time and everything adjusted naturally. However, during his fall on the ice in March, he was nearly 20 years older and the disc must then have slipped out and stayed out. He was thirty-seven years old and that was the difference. Perhaps if he had rested for a couple of weeks in March, the disc might have adjusted naturally again. Who knows, but you have to keep going when you have a family to feed, clothe and shelter.

We were all very glad when Arthur began to feel better, but our worries were just starting especially for me. How were we going to pay our way - Arthur was self-employed? But somehow, my faith never faltered. We knew that Arthur would not be working for some weeks, but I do not think we realised quite how long it would be. Maybe it was just as well, especially at first!

Fortunately, we had no immediate debts and had a small 'rainy day' fund in the bank. There were also a few delayed payments due from pupils that were then paid to us. The Sickness Allowance that we received to provide for our family, all five of us, was under £4.00 per week and out of the blue, we had a visitor one day! A man called without warning to check that Arthur was not working! The Authorities were more vigilant in those days methinks.

Arthur had sold the car. I cannot remember why, unless he envisaged that we would need the money. But he would need a car as soon as he was well because he had a number of engagements booked. One fact stands out for me from this period: I found out who our true friends were. People stood in for him at the organ on Sundays, and one man especially officiated at weddings on Saturdays and gave us the fees. This kindness meant that we were able to pay the rent. My parents supplied us with vegetables, my sister and one of Arthur's aunts sent us money, some of our farmer friends brought eggs, carrots and potatoes. What wonderful, wonderful friends those people were. There was one other donation - a mystery. One evening, just before Christmas, our Minister called as usual, and handed over an envelope, addressed to me. I opened it and took out a £5.00 note - a large sum in 1954. There was no note attached, and the Rev.W.E.Thomas was held by a promise not to reveal the donor's name. I could only ask him to convey my heartfelt thanks to the donor. It was specifically to buy things for the children for Christmas Day. I kept that envelope because the spelling of Vaughan had an 'a' missing - Vaughn.

Some years later, my dentist gave me a prescription for a mouthwash and I noticed that my surname was written as Vaughn. A few days later our Minister Rev. W. E. Thomas visited and I decided to ask him a question. “Do you remember the Christmas when Arthur was ill and you gave me an envelope with £5.00 in it?” “Yes I do” the Rev. Thomas said. “Well, if I deduce the name correctly, will you tell me please if I am correct?” I asked. He pondered for a while then said, “It's a long time ago so I think it will be alright, but please let it remain confidential.” I agreed then explained about the prescription and asked, “Am I correct in saying that the donor of that money was Mr. Emrys Jones, the Dentist?” “Yes” said the Rev. Thomas. Wonderful again - God works in wondrous ways.

By Christmas time in the year of 1954, Arthur was feeling much better and was able to enjoy short walks outside. On Christmas Eve he walked to the end of the street and came across two friends who were very pleased to see him, and they chatted for some time. When they went their separate ways, each wished the others a, "Happy Christmas and a good New Year," in Welsh of course. As he walked home Arthur, who had been feeling despondent, thought how lucky the others were, going home to a fine holiday with no money or health worries. But by the time he had reached our gate, he stopped suddenly. He could hear our children laughing and playing in the house and he thought, “No, *I* am the lucky one, at the centre of my little family.” The other two men had no children to love and enjoy. Christmas is different and magnificent if you have children.

When the new term started after Christmas, Arthur was able to start working again and things looked more hopeful.

Chapter Twenty-eight

HELLO HARRY ... GOODBYE BELLA

In August 1954 I hurt my right hand seriously. One morning as I unlatched the top part of the bay window in one of the bedrooms, the cord holding the weights snapped and the window fell onto the upper part of my right hand between the middle knuckles and nails. I could not move it so I shouted to Arthur to come and release me. As soon as he heard my screams he came, but had to go looking for an iron bar to push the two frames apart. He finally managed to separate them and I got my hand free. I could feel no pain but I sat on the bed and looked at the mess on my fingers - the skin was broken and I could see some bone through the bits of paint and crushed skin. I went to the bathroom to wash the wounds and held my hand under the warm water to gently clean away the debris. Then the feeling returned and the pain I experienced was horrific. My head started to go round and I thought I was going to pass out. I had never fainted in my life so I grabbed the washbasin and took control of myself. Slowly, I managed to sit on the chair and finally succeeded in dressing the wounds myself. I did not go to the doctor or hospital and eventually everything healed up nicely, but I still have the indentation on three fingers. Thank goodness no bones were broken.

Another thing I remember about that eventful year was the atrocious weather during the autumn season. It was quite normal for there to be one or two river floods during August because of torrential rainfall: these were times when the river Conwy was affected by the tides in the lower reaches. 1954 was no exception to that - but between August and the middle of November there were five serious floods. In November the water reached the top of the platform at the railway station, and the river had become a lake five miles long and two miles wide between Llanrwst and Dolgarrog. Traffic was at a halt and many animals were lost.

Nowadays, orange or red alerts are issued as warnings and a cob has been built to reduce the widespread flooding. But prior to this, despite using sandbags in doorways, Llanrwst people were used to having river water regularly in their houses, and having to call out the electricity board because of the danger of the water coming into contact with meters and electricity supplies.

However, 1955 had arrived and we looked forward to better times. During this period the General Secretary of the Dyffryn Conwy Chair Eisteddfod, Llanrwst, retired and Arthur was offered the job, which he accepted. He had been a secretary of the local Eisteddfod in his old home area and knew the ropes as it were, but of course, the Llanrwst Eisteddfod was a much bigger proposition. It was known far and wide and people flocked to it to compete and to listen. I too, had been secretary to our local Eisteddfod at Llanfair, which meant that I could help Arthur with some of the work. There was some remuneration, not much, but we needed the money! Most of the various committees had completed their items of competition and Arthur needed to draw up the syllabus - the Main Programme, then send copies to various shops, schools and individuals in order to get as many prospective competitors interested as possible. All the Adjudicators and Accompanists had to be booked too. There was a lot more to be done, but not until the beginning of May and onwards. In addition to working with his pupils and Chapel work, Arthur had many engagements as music adjudicator, conductor of singing festivals, accompanist in concerts, working in television and radio, and making music recordings on disc (records).

Although he had reluctantly relinquished his role as Conductor of the Male Voice Choir because of pressure of work, he still continued to conduct training sessions from time to time with the Choir - good training and regular practices are vital to any good choir.

I can see from his Diary that March, April, May and June that year were very busy for him and involved an awful lot of driving. He had bought a second hand Austin Big 7 car, which was a bit better than the Baby Austin.

He went to Porthmadog, Caernarfon, Talybont in Cardiganshire and Corwen, and he drove to London for a festival on the 4th and 5th of May. On the 6th, he was back in Corwen, and on the 7th in Ruthin. He recorded that he was dead beat with working and driving so much, especially considering it was barely six months since he had been seriously ill with his back.

On June 1st, 2nd, 3rd and 4th he was adjudicating in the URDD National Eisteddfod at Abertridwr in South Wales. On the 11th, he was at Llandyssul in Cardiganshire where proceedings ended at 2.30a.m. and after a cup of tea Arthur started his long drive back on the Sunday morning, arriving home at 8.30a.m. After a good wash and breakfast it was then onto playing the organ in Chapel for morning service at 10.00am, afternoon Sunday School and evening service at 6.00pm. During the sermon in the evening session he fell asleep and woke to hear the congregation singing a hymn without the organ! His good friend, Mr. Hywel Thomas, had started them off. There was some good-natured leg-pulling afterwards of course, but you can push the human body only so far - sleep is vital to us all. You can function mechanically but you are never 100% efficient if lacking sleep.

After Easter, *Taid and Nain Gaerwen* (my in-laws) came to stay for a holiday again. It was a change for them and they were company for me while Arthur was on his travels.

One morning I had seen the girls off to school next door, and had sat Bryn in front of the fireplace on a little chair that his Uncle Harry had made for Elsie for her second Christmas. I had tied a scarf around him and the chair and given Bryn a comic to look at so I could get breakfast for the rest of us. Taid and Nain were sitting on either side of the fireplace and because they were complaining of being cold, I had removed the big fireguard that I always used for the safety of the children and asked them to keep a special eye on Bryn. Having laid the table in the living room I returned to the kitchen to brew tea. The kettle was almost boiling when I heard the most awful scream and I flew through to the living room. My heart turned over when I saw Bryn had overturned the chair, probably reaching for the comic that he had dropped, and was lying face down against the all-night fire grate which was very, very hot. I grabbed him and the chair, undid the scarf and held my little boy tightly. He was still screaming and gasping and I was fearful of shock to his system so I murmured soft words to him and nursed him for a long, long time until he grew calmer and I could look at his poor face.

His right cheek just under his eye was burned, the skin all frazzled and raw flesh. I could have cried, I cannot tell you how I felt but I kept calm. Still holding him I reached into my First Aid box for the tube of 'Valderma' and ever so gently covered the wound with the cream using cotton wool. Initially it had a slight stinging effect that led to sobs again, but they soon stopped as the cream soothed his face. I had used this cream for years and had faith in its healing capacity, therefore I did not consult anybody, I just carried on applying the cream twice a day and explaining to Bryn why he should not touch his face. In ten days he had new skin, the scab had dropped off and there was no scarring. In a month he was as good as new. I thanked God many times over for giving me the strength to cope. I failed to understand how Taid and Nain could not have seen Bryn drop the comic, try to reach it, and fall forward onto the fireplace. How could they not have anticipated the danger, but I did not reproach them. I decided there was no point in upsetting them further because they were already close to tears. Furthermore, they were getting old and their reactions were not as quick as they had been when they were younger.

During 1955 a house became vacant in Watling Street just a few doors up from us and Harry and his family decided to move there. It would be much more convenient for Harry not having to make the journey to and from Llansannan every day. His business was doing very well in Llanrwst and he was expanding it all the time. The news of the impending move by Harry and his family to Llanrwst was heard by our three children with glee - Harry's three children were more or less in the same age groups. Elsie and Glenys were especially excited with Eleanor coming. Elwyn was about eighteen months older than Bryn and as they grew up they became firm friends, almost like brothers. When summer came with warm weather, everyone felt better and more cheerful, although I must say we were always a happy crew. There were childhood bickerings but never big rows or fights.

My sister Bella announced that she and Kay, the Irish friend who had trained with her had decided to go to Canada for two years. They were going as nurses to a Catholic hospital at St. Catherine in Toronto. Bella was then 28 years old. She was a fully qualified nurse who had been a theatre Sister and a night Sister, and had been offered the job of Sister Tutor. She told the Matron at her hospital that she had reached a point where she needed to reach out to new horizons, or it would be too late, so she and Kay made their plans. They would set sail in August 1955.

In July Elsie and Glenys went down with measles, the infection was doing the rounds. I knew that care had to be taken with this ailment because it could have complications. I remember my mother telling me about the experience of her sister, Janet when she fell ill with measles when it affected her eyes very badly. For many months she could not tolerate any light and could go out of the house only when it was dark. She got better of course, but always had weak eyes. Therefore I took great care with my girls, but they were as healthy as could be generally, suffered no ill effects and were soon well again. Then Bryn went down with measles in August, when he was still of the nappy-wearing age during a heat wave, and the spots all came out on his skin under the nappy - he suffered badly. My sister stayed with us for a couple of weeks before sailing to Canada, but could go nowhere near him because measles are contagious. She loved all three kids, but Bryn was 'her baby'. She had looked after him when he was born and kept him with her through the first night. She was very upset that she could not go to comfort him when he was ill.

Came the day of departure, she said her farewells then Arthur and I took her in the car to Liverpool where she met up with her friend and boarded a beautiful new ship called the 'Saxonia'. As we stood waving on the landing stage I had a strong feeling that she would not return to live here again.

My mother was very upset at her going. Bella was the youngest of her children and had arrived just after Mam had lost Elsie May. It was a miracle that she had survived. She and Mam were very close. They were very alike in many ways, not in appearance for Bella took after my father's family with auburn hair and very blue eyes. Also of course, history was repeating itself, my mother's younger sister also called Isabella had gone off to America when she was 18 years old and had never returned. So, although Mam wished her 'bon voyage' she was inwardly very sad.

I missed my sister! The difference in our ages was a major factor in our early teens, but later we had a good relationship, and had kept in touch even when she moved to London.

We received news to say that the two nurses had landed safely in Canada and were settling down well to working in a different country.

Later, Bella wrote home to inform my parents of her engagement to Stan and their marriage plans. My parents were pleased for Bella, but also upset for a number of reasons - my mother was particularly upset. She had kept her hopes alive that my sister would return at the end of the planned two years, but the news brought an end to her dreams. “We haven't even seen him,” she wailed as I tried to console her, and I said, “She's not silly Mam, she is 29 years old, an experienced nurse, and a sensible person. She would not marry just anybody.”

Stan and his friends were from Liverpool and were in Canada to find work. Stan had a sister who was a nurse at the same hospital as Bella in the UK. She had written to Stan suggesting that he and the lads welcomed Bella and Kay off the ship on their arrival in the USA, which they did. The rest is history!

Chapter Twenty-nine

SUMMER HOLIDAYS

My brother and his wife had a son and two little girls. During the summer they came on holiday to stay at the Hydro Hotel in Llandudno. Alun, their son sometimes stayed at our cousin's farm because he was very fond of animals. The family came to visit us once in a while and the children got on very well together which pleased my brother, but I am afraid their mother did not exactly encourage any close connections. She was always in a hurry to leave. I remember once when Elsie and Glenys had gone to a lot of trouble to set up a wonderful tea for all of us on the day of their visit to Llys Cerdd. We always ate well and healthily as a family, and the girls had followed our usual meal time pattern. There were thin sandwiches, a home-made trifle, an assortment of dainty home made cakes, tea and fruit juice. When we sat down at the beautifully set out dining table, Percy and Eluned's children were allowed to drink only a sip or two of the juices and eat nothing because … it would spoil their supper, four hours later! I thought it was rude to my girls who had made the tea, and a shame too for Alun, Nerys and Hefina who were longing to eat the goodies.

Once, when they visited my parents, one of Percy's little girls, I will not say which one for I don't blame her because she was merely repeating what she had heard, went up to my father in all innocence. He was sitting in his favourite chair at the time and he put his arm round her shoulders. She said, "Taid" and he said, "Yes?" She continued, "You are not like us are you Taid, you are ordinary people." My father was shocked, but he sympathised with the little girl and said nothing, just patted her on the back. He remembered another occasion, when we were all having tea during one of their visits and the talk was about how well all the children were doing at school. We all agreed that we were blessed with bright and intelligent children, thank goodness. Then my father said that Percy, my brother was clever and how proud he was when Percy gained his B.Sc. Degree in 1946 - extramural London University in 2 years instead of 5, which was the norm. His wife immediately retorted, and I use the word intentionally, "Percy is not clever, lots of people are cleverer than he is." She said this of her own husband, and in his presence! I could not believe my ears and said, "Of course he is clever. He has always been clever, his record proves that." We let the matter drop, but the atmosphere was no longer conducive to any further friendly association at that time, so we took our leave and went home.

During August, after Bella's departure, we prepared to enjoy our break from duties and that year was a good one. Things were looking up. That year's Eisteddfod, the first time experience for Arthur as Secretary, had been a great success although he had identified certain things that could be improved. He himself was stronger and had coped very well with the heavy workload. We were solvent again and although money was not plentiful, the children were healthy and happy. The weather was sunny and warm and we went somewhere every day: the seaside at Llandudno, the dunes at Conwy, further afield to Black Rocks at Porthmadog, Abersoch and Criccieth on the Lleyn Peninsula, and onto several beaches in Anglesey. We also went for trips in the car to see the beautiful lakes and mountains of our own land of *Cymru* (Wales).

My children, now middle-aged with their own families still have fond memories of those days. One of the best compliments I have ever received was when Bryn said to me, "You know Mam, I had a wonderful childhood. I really enjoyed it all."

That particular year was better than usual especially for the children because Harry and Nance and their three children had joined us on some of the seaside trips, and the experience was very enjoyable also for us adults. The kids were busy all day carving out a big boat in the sand with seats and legroom. I have many photographs that record all this and it is a joy to look at them and remember those special moments. We used an old 1937 Kodak box camera: I think Arthur said he had bought it including a cloth case with a shoulder strap in Woolworths for about one shilling and sixpence!

The fine weather came to an abrupt end with a terrific thunderstorm. We had been for a trip to Bala Lake and were on our way home over the mountains above Penmachno when it really started. Most of the day had been fine, then it became very close, and felt as though a storm was brewing as we prepared to set off for home after eating our picnic tea (we always took a picnic lunch and enough for a snack at teatime too). We never let it get too late before setting off because children get tired and fractious and everything is then spoiled. Anyway, dark clouds were gathering, and when we got to the top of the mountain it became very dark indeed, thunder cracks were extremely near and lightning flashes were continuous. Arthur stopped the car so we could watch the flashes dancing on the peaks of Snowdonia. It was truly wonderful and awesome. The children were not afraid for we had explained that the rubber tyres on the car wheels acted as insulators so that the electric flashes could not earth, so we were safe closed up in the car. I had experienced many thunderstorms like everyone else, but I had never before seen such a spectacular sight. In later years I was to see another in the U.S.A., but much nearer - watching through the window of a Yacht Club as the lightning danced among the masts of the yachts in the Marina. So beautiful, but so dangerous too in certain circumstances.

We finally reached home tired but happy, and after a wash and a light supper, the children were soon fast asleep in bed. The doorbell rang and Arthur opened the door to find a policeman standing on the threshold with a group of people huddled behind him. It was pouring with rain as it had been for hours. The constable explained that the storm with its rushing wind and rain had washed away the tents of many campers who had set up in the valley. Every hotel and guest-house was full and still they had people without a roof over their heads. The couple with the constable had two small children with them and their clothes were soaking wet. "Could you please put them up for the night Mrs Williams? They are willing to sleep on the floor or anything. They are desperate," said the policeman in Welsh. It took some time for me to think straight, it had all happened so suddenly and we had not had strangers sleeping in our house since the family of 5 at the National Eisteddfod.

I turned to Arthur who said, "Well, it's up to you, but we do have a spare bed." Then it dawned on me just how awful it must have been for them having come to enjoy a simple holiday in the country and ending up suffering through no fault of their own. How would I like being in such a situation if my family and I were ever in a similar position? If we called ourselves Christians, there was only one option. "Come in, come in. We will sort something out for you," I said. They came in shivering and very thankful. We hung their wet clothes to dry on banister rails, gave them plenty of warming blankets then prepared a meal of hot soup and sandwiches for them. The double bed was already made up so the parents and the smaller child slept in that, while the older one used a camp bed. After a good night's sleep I got up early and cooked breakfast for 9 people. It was just as well I had good stocks of food in the house ready for our trips. Our children were bewildered: who were these people; where had they come from; and why were they staying with us? The questions were never ending. But as soon as our unexpected guests were washed, dressed and fed, they left. They were so grateful and thanked us profusely. They wanted to pay, but we did not think we should take anything. After all they would have a lot of extra expense sorting things out at the camp. The storm had passed, the sun was shining and everywhere was steaming. We cleared up, stripped and washed the bed linen and hung it out to dry. Soon everything was ship-shape again, then we had lunch and went to visit our parents - the children bursting to tell the tales of our adventures.

During the following years the Police would contact us again if they had enquiries for accommodation from tourists. At that time most people took holidays in this country. Europe was still bearing the scars of the War and air travel was expensive. There were some chartered plane journeys but no cheap holiday packages like today and of course, there was no Channel tunnel.

By taking in the tent family on that stormy night, unwittingly we began a little enterprise that gave us much pleasure and helped us to settle our bills too.

At the end of August with the long summer holiday over, it was back to routine and now Glen was starting school. Elsie was very proud taking care of her little sister and she really was a very good carer, you could depend on that. If I was harbouring hopes of having an easier time, well, I soon knew differently because Bryn was now two years old and missing his adoring sisters, especially Glen, who was now also at school. Early in the day he would amuse himself with his toys or if the weather was fine, he played outside with his little tricycle.

Our neighbour had a large shed that backed onto our back yard. I knew that part of it was used to store coal and I also knew rats were there because I could hear them squealing and fighting as I pegged out the washing during late evening. When I noticed holes appearing at ground level in the wooden shed, I became very uneasy and eventually told the teacher who lodged next door about the noises and the holes and she told her landlady, who was a little old lady who rarely appeared outside. However, one morning as Bryn was playing in the yard, he suddenly ran in, grabbed my hand and said in Welsh, “Mam, mam, pussy over there” and indicated he had stroked the 'pussy'. I was horrified to see in my flower border an enormous rat. I grabbed Bryn, took him in and washed his hands thoroughly and called Arthur to come to sort things out. He investigated, then said, “Don't worry. I've shooed it back through a hole that I have now blocked so no more can come into our garden. It looks as though the Council has already put down poison because the rat was very slow to move. It was dying, and others in there will be too.” Well, it was a relief. It was even better a couple of weeks later when workmen demolished the shed and built a 6ft.stone wall between our yards.

In missing his sisters, Bryn was bored and therefore into everything: every cupboard was emptied in turn and anything that made a clatter was banged. He even managed to work out how to unlock and open the middle door, and it was fortunate that the iron railings and heavy gate were there to stop him getting into the street. Bryn copied Glen in many respects, but there was one incident that happened that he most certainly didn't copy. It involved an occasion when I had left Glen in the pushchair inside the front gate so that she could see something of the world going by. Later when I came to check that she was alright, I found her happily crunching a large snail and shell, with another in hand, ready for the next course!

Nain and Taid Gaerwen, Arthur's parents, came to stay for a week periodically. I could attend the Sunday evening service when they did and I sat in a pew with friends. On one such occasion, Mr. Norman Rogers Jones, a Deacon, called me aside and said that he would be very pleased if I sat in his family's pew. His only son was married to an English lady so only he came to Chapel - Mr. Jones' wife was an invalid. I thought it was a very thoughtful gesture because Arthur had no choice but to sit up in the gallery, next to the organ. I thanked Mr. Jones for his kindness. He really was a gentleman. The seating was very comfortable for it had a thick plush cushion fitted along the whole length of the pew. The pew was also very well positioned by being right in the centre of the chapel - it was excellent for seeing and hearing everything. Incidentally, it was also a great place to sit where we could see Arthur, and by leaning forward slightly, he could see us too. That is where we sat as a family in services throughout our years of being members at Seion Chapel. Elsie and Glenys can still visualise their father proudly looking over the balcony periodically at them whenever he had an opportunity in a service, grinning and winking at them in the process and showing just how much he loved them.

One Sunday evening in October 1955, there was a drizzle as we left Chapel at the end of the service. I had my umbrella up as I hurried onto the main road to go home. Quite suddenly through the mist I saw a little figure looking so forlorn standing on the pavement - it was Bryn wearing only slippers and a vest! I couldn't believe my eyes. I quickly scooped him up on to my left arm and under the umbrella. He was soaking wet. The only thing I could get out of him was that he was looking for me, but I had no idea how he could have found his way, or how long he had been standing there. I hurried home and Nain tried to explain that she had attempted to get Bryn to undress and put on his pyjamas before we returned from Chapel. She said that he did not want to do it, perhaps because he had always had a wash in the bathroom first before donning his pyjamas, but whatever the reason, she had managed to partly undress him when he suddenly sprang out of her grasp and ran out of the house. She went after him, but could see that he was half way up the street and she was unable to run after him. Els and Glen were in their bedroom on the second floor and were quite unaware of the consternation going on downstairs. Although there was a comic side to the incident I was very aware of the seriousness of it too. I decided new rules would have to be implemented regarding the locking of doors.

Chapter Thirty

CONCERTS FOR CHARITY

During the autumn and spring months the Llanrwst Male Voice Choir was being invited to hold concerts in various places and I was invited to go along to sing with the choir and perform solos too. I was pleased to be asked but knew that I had not sung solo in public for some years - well, I'd had other things to do in the meantime, had I not? I mentioned this to the Secretary of the Choir and asked if my friend Win could also attend because she too could sing solos for them, and could also sing duets with me. Other combinations were arranged too - she sang duets with male singers from the choir and so did I. The choir members were pleased with the idea and so we started to practise regularly and Arthur gave us a lot of tuition, which we needed. Win had a very rich contralto voice and I had a strong, clear soprano voice. We learned many songs and duets and were appreciated everywhere we went. We sang in Welsh and English: we chose some of the classics, songs from the shows, serious religious songs, and some comical ones too that involved great drama with exaggerated, flamboyant gestures that were always well received by audiences! Win and I wore attractive evening wear for our appearances with the choir. This arrangement went on until the Male Voice Choir disbanded and a mixed choir was formed.

Win and I were being invited increasingly to sing at charity concerts held in Chapels, Churches and halls and we had a lot of fun together. Arthur and Mr D. J Williams (Choir Accompanist) accompanied us on the piano and sometimes others would come along to vary the programme. We sang solos and duets, and occasionally we'd have a poetry recitation, a story telling, or a short sketch. I have lost count of how many concerts we did over the years, and in all that time, we never charged anything for our services.

A lady once said to me, “When you are asked your fee, name a sum then if you wish, give it back as a donation. That way you will put a value on your contribution, and you will be more respected for it.” She was right of course! But a lifelong habit is difficult to break.

Once, Win and I were asked to sing in the vestry of a chapel high up in the foothills of Snowdonia. It was not a big audience, about fifty farming folk, but they were so friendly and enthusiastic. Anyway, mid-way through the programme Win and I were required to sing a duet that had quite a few parts requiring 'forte' volume and much gusto - we always sang it well and audiences enjoyed it. As in all Chapel vestries, on the wall there was a large round clock, of which no one took any notice. I don't think Win and I were even aware of it. Anyway, we launched into the duet: first I sang a section on my own, then Win sang her part and then we sang together to the climax. Everything started well and I ended my solo and the accompanist played the music in between and then Win began her part, but she had sung only a couple of bars when the clock began to strike … loudly! What a nuisance! But then, that's what clocks do. The time was 9.00 p.m. and so, knowing Win's powerful voice, we believed that she could drown nine chimes of the clock, but then the clock continued to chime ten and eleven, surely it would stop at twelve, but no, on it went to thirteen, fourteen, and fifteen. By now Win had given up her valiant attempt to beat the clock! Everyone, including me was bursting with surpressed laughter but trying to look concerned and then Win, the good old trouper that she is, burst out laughing and said, "Well, that is the first time that a clock has managed to shut me up." Everyone was in stitches and glad to let go. A man put a stop to the chimes and said to Win, "Well thank you very much. You have done something that many have attempted. That old clock has not functioned for years!" Maybe it was making up for lost time!

We sang with different groups, and as neither of us could drive a car in those days we had to have lifts. There was always laughter and a great deal of banter and we were all good friends. Once, when Win and I were returning home in the car of a man who was one of the group, Win was first to be dropped off because her house came first en route. Then we had only a couple of blocks to get to my home. To my surprise, the man whizzed by my house, and I said, "Hey, hold on. You've gone past my house." He laughed and said, "Okay, don't get het up. I want to talk to you." Then quite suddenly he turned the car into the local cemetery! I did not know whether to laugh or thump him. Wisely, I did neither. "Well, come on it's late. What do you want to say?" He turned round in the seat and looked at me seriously and said, "From the first time I saw you when you came with that group to sing at our Chapel I have known that you were the one I wanted." I told him to stop talking nonsense and for us to get going. "No, no, I mean it. You have always been top of the list." Now this man did not drink so he was stone cold sober and I decided enough was enough or things would get out of hand. I said, "I don't believe a word, and in any case it makes no difference. I am married, have three children and a good husband. Now, are you going to be sensible or do I have to scream my head off and have everyone in the district think the dead are being raised in the cemetery?" He laughed, but knew me well enough to know that I would do what I threatened. He switched on the engine and away we went and I was home in a couple of minutes, none the worse. I told no one, and we remained on friendly terms. It was the first and last time that I was 'kidnapped' and taken to a cemetery!

One other event comes to mind. The choir was going on a coach to compete at an Eisteddfod in Dolgellau and in order to achieve best value, every seat on the coach needed to be occupied. Choir members had priority but a number of other people went along too to fill the otherwise empty seats - Bella and I occupied 2 of them. She and I used that opportunity to spend quality time together before she sailed to Canada. It was a lovely summer's evening and the journey was a pleasure to experience. As the coach weaved its way along the beautiful *Lledr* Valley my sister said, "When I settle in Canada and have a moment to think of home, I shall remember this breathtakingly stunning scenery … it is so typical of Wales and so wonderful." As we marvelled at the beauty of the area, praising it to high heavens and basking in its delights, Bella quite suddenly let out a squeal and pointed at something she had spotted outside the coach. This was much to the delight and amusement of our fellow passengers because she had managed to draw their attention to a group of nudists splashing, bathing, laughing and generally having fun in a stream. Immediately, all the passangers rushed to the appropriate side of the coach to enjoy the best view, which caused the vehicle to tilt somewhat. The driver did not stop, but slowed down to savour the view, much to the approval of the passengers. The bathers were oblivious to the effects of their nudity on the Eisteddfod seekers, but would have smiled no doubt had they known the mild consternation it caused. We both thoroughly enjoyed the breathtaking Welsh views and were glad we'd made the effort to fill those empty seats.

Our experience at the eisteddfod was also dramatic, but in a very different way. The event was being held in a long, narrow tent with poor lighting as I recall. Bella and I sat a little behind the centre block and had enjoyed a number of items of music and elocution during the evening including two choirs that sang very well. But then when the Llanrwst Choir was on stage singing and giving of its best, a strange thing happened that led me to believe that my eyes were deceiving me. The choir appeared to be sinking backwards and then the accompanist and conductor disappeared followed swiftly by the piano. There was consternation amongst the audience by then because it became obvious that the stage had collapsed! We made our way forward to find out what was happening and see if we could help - were there any casualties? … my sister was a nurse after all. There was a right old mess at the front of the tent and with time, all the choir members were accounted for and found to be very shaken but unhurt except for scratches and bumps.

Finally, we returned home on the coach. Dear reader, there are no prizes for guessing the two main topics of conversation in Llanrwst over the following week or so!

Chapter Thirty-one

OPPORTUNITIES AND TRAUMAS

Another Christmas arrived with all its Christian customs and other non-religious rituals. I know that some people do not involve themselves at all with the religious part of the celebration, but as a family we always have done. Recordings of Christmas Carols are played in the big shops with the intention of getting people to spend money on gifts. The concept of giving to one another is certainly a Christian value and many people have this goodness and generosity in their hearts. Others get carried away to excess, or fall into the trap of 'keeping up with the Joneses'. Not many people go to a place of worship any more and I am afraid that the Christmas Religious Festival is fast losing out to pagan Yuletide practices.

I love Christmas and my family does too. Long may it survive as a Christian Festival I say! The New Year of 1956 came with all good wishes for a better year. Arthur was adjudicating at the village of Gwytherin on New Year's Day, and there is a note in his *Diary of Events* that states that 22 years previously he had started his career as an Accompanist at that same Eisteddfod and his father had been the Music Adjudicator.

The weather was extremely cold and wintry with much frost day and night. It was difficult and expensive to keep the house warm - very few people had any sort of central heating. We had to keep an eye on water in pipes and storage tanks all the time too in case it froze and caused bursts. But life went on normally. Monday was the week's main washday. It took most of the day to wash, rinse and mangle the bed linen and personal clothing for all of us. One Monday, due to the weather being so cold and wet, I was late making 'tea', our late afternoon meal, therefore Elsie and Glenys were late going to the 'Band of Hope' in the Chapel vestry. Before they left however, I checked to make sure they were both wrapped up well against the cold and I said to them, "Now if Mrs. Williams comments on the fact that you are late, you must tell her that it is my fault because I have been so busy today." Then, quick as a flash, Glen said in a very matter of fact way, "No Mam ...if Mrs. Williams says we are late, I'll tell her that I know we are late." Out of the mouths of babes! No nonsense logic, from a six year old! Glen was always the realist and the one with all the questions. My brother used to say that she was the philosopher of the family.

I used a room at the top of the house to hang out the wet clothes on washday when it was too wet outside. We allowed this room to be used as a playroom by our children, their cousins and some close friends. The walls became covered with children's drawings over a period of time, all created during playtimes up there. The children also had access to a superb play-shop that had been built-up over the years with packaging saved by many people. They had all my friends opening food cans and cereal boxes bottom-up and all packets were filled with newspaper and sellotaped to seal them in order to make them seem full and realistic. It looked to the world like a real shop because they had a counter with shelves to display the goods and a till to hold the money they had made for themselves. They had toiletries and foodstuff and even a life-sized cardboard figure that Boots the Chemist in Llanrwst had used to advertise Kodak films. The children played up there for hours and I knew they were safe, not getting into mischief, or catching colds in the wet, cold weather. The only specified rules were that they had to wear slippers, and there were to be no more than 6 children up there at a time. The shop grew larger and larger until the time came that we dismantled it completely because all seven upstairs rooms were needed as bedrooms.

With the world still sorting itself out after the war, there were all sorts of different schemes whereby young people went on exchange visits. We were asked if we would accommodate someone from Europe for two weeks. We decided that we should do so and that is how Katarina came to stay with us. She was a young woman of around 20 years of age from Yugoslavia. The children took to her immediately because she was interesting, pleasant and spoke English very well. She also had a good knowledge of German and some Russian and spoke the three languages of the regions in Yugoslavia. I asked her if she knew Latin and she replied she did, so I handed her a Welsh newspaper and suggested she read it. She looked at it and thought she could not possibly do so. I briefly explained the 'll' and 'ch' pronunciations in Welsh, then suggested she read the words in the way she would read Latin, because Welsh too is phonetic. It was fascinating to hear her read Welsh effectively knowing she did not comprehend the text. She was quiet, polite and unassuming and yet she had a proud dignity. We had many discussions with her about the communism practised in her country. Tito, the national hero of the Resistance, was alive and in power. She explained that the system was more liberal than in Russia. For instance, anyone could start a business and run it privately as long as the number of employees did not exceed five. I distinctly remember one comment she made which was, "I may not be a communist for ever, who knows … but one thing I am certain of … I shall never again be a Catholic." I asked her why she felt like that, and she explained that some good Catholics who had been active in the Resistance during the war had told their priests about their actions during Confession, and had in turn been betrayed by them. The Priests had revealed the information to the Germans who had then taken action against them, their families and in some cases whole communities too.

Katarina's diet was quite different from ours and she would not eat raw cucumber, but she never complained about the food we gave her. She always wanted cucumber sliced thickly and fried. We missed her when she returned to Yugoslavia and I have often wondered what happened to her since, especially during the recent troubles there.

There is a small cottage on the far side of the old bridge in Llanrwst called *Tu Hwnt i'r Bont* (beyond the bridge). It is very old, dating back to the fourteenth century if not earlier. It had at one time been in use as a house, and a courthouse, but is now a café and owned by the National Trust. It is known all over the world. In the 1950/60s the tenant was Olwen Caradog Evans and it was she who made the place famous. She worked very hard and before very long was awarded a major Diploma, one of only six, for an interesting Tourist Attraction, awarded by the British Travel Association. Olwen was always ready with new ideas. She was charming but determined. During the mid 1950s she had the bright idea of holding a *Noson Lawen* (merry evening) periodically at *Tu Hwnt I'r Bont*. First there was a dinner served that comprised of Welsh food - soup, beef, lamb or fish from the river Conwy, puddings from old Welsh recipes and Welsh cheeses with oatcakes. Following the meal there was excellent entertainment in the Welsh fashion. Taking part were a harpist, a soloist, poetry-singers and a group of very young girl singers. One of the poetry singers was a bit of a wag, who told funny stories, mostly against himself. These evenings were a tremendous success and many famous people came, more than once. The cost per person was £1.ls.0d. - one guinea!

One of the young girls in the group was our eldest daughter, Elsie. Olwen had arranged for Welsh costumes to be made specially to fit the girls. In 1956, British Travel Association (BTA), which was similar to the present Tourist Board except that it operated for Britain as a whole, decided to make a film in the Llanrwst area, in Technicolor. The girls, Olwen, Tu Hwnt i'r Bont, George Jones a local farmer and his horse and cart and others, were the cast. We were invited to a preview at the Savoy Cinema in Llandudno and it really was very colourful and interesting. It was seen in all the countries of the British Commonwealth, as we were to find out later.

During the summer Elsie and Glenys were asked to pose in their Welsh national costumes on the bank of the river Conwy, for a group of professional photographers. The picture was used with a long caption in German by the B.T.A. Later, wearing our Welsh costumes, Elsie, Glenys and I were taken by taxi one Sunday afternoon to Conwy town to be photographed with the famous castle and bridge in the background. It was all very exciting and we felt like film stars with all the cameras and tourists watching the proceedings. The photographs were used to publicise Wales.

I think that it was in September that Olwen asked me if she could take Elsie with Margaret, the eldest of the group of girls to her home in London for a long weekend in order to entertain special travellers returning to Canada from a holiday in the UK. The large group of Canadians, who were either Welsh speaking or had Welsh roots had chartered a plane to visit Wales and were being made to feel special before departing for Canada on their return journey. Several of them had been to a *Noson Lawen* and Olwen wanted to give them a fond farewell by having the girls sing to them.

Olwen had been a nurse in London and was the wife of a Doctor of Medicine at the St. George's Hospital. She travelled between London and Llanrwst in a sports car and *she* didn't dilly dally on the way! I pondered over the request, after all Elsie was only eight years old and London was a long way away. I did not know what to do. I knew Olwen had a nice home and she was very fond of Elsie, 'with her funny little walk', and I knew that both girls would be looked after very well. I also knew that Elsie wanted to go and would enjoy the whole adventure. I did not think it was fair to stand in her way just because I would be on tenterhooks until she was home again. Eventually, Arthur and I agreed to let her go … and she enjoyed every minute of it!

Chapter Thirty-Two

HOME-MAKERS

Each Easter holiday, I would spring clean the whole house from top to bottom. That however does not quite convey the reality of the performance at Llys Cerdd. People vary in their conception of the term *spring clean*. Some housewives say, "I don't need to spring clean because I keep the place clean all the time." I am sure they do, and so do I like many others, but inevitably there are jobs that no one does weekly or monthly. Curtains and covers for instance need washing, windows and paintwork need cleaning, furniture needs to be cleaned on top, behind and underneath, carpets need cleaning and ornaments and other items need washing. Cupboards and drawers also get 'higgledy piggledy' during the year and need sorting out. Everyone has a couple of drawers where all 'homeless' articles get shoved out of sight. Check how the following list of bits and pieces compares with yours: nails, screws, pencils, pieces of ribbon and string, an assortment of keys, incomplete packs of playing cards, a collection of live and dud batteries, out-of-date raffle tickets, used birthday cards, catalogues, letters awaiting attention, and so the list goes on! And that is only the start of course because spring cleaning at Llys Cerdd also meant a programme of re-decoration too. Dark winter months hide a lot of things we don't want to see, but come a glorious spring morning with the sunshine acting as a searchlight in all the dark corners and those previously unseen or ignored cobwebs suddenly loom very large indeed! There must be spiders too lurking in strange places, so ... the ceiling brush was an essential spring cleaning tool for me that often became lost amongst the hockey sticks, tennis rackets, sports items, caps, scarves and gloves et al in the cloakroom during the rest of the year. But at spring cleaning time it really had to be found. Well, the spring sunshine brings such a revealing moment to all households … and insists that people spring clean .... whatever their usual cleaning style!

Some go mad - stripping everything including bed linen and curtains from all over the house with resulting bedlam. We live and learn! But I concentrate on one room at a time, and start at the top of the house and finish at the bottom. It is interesting to do the variety of jobs required in one room and get the satisfaction of completing all the work in it over a short period. With the exception of the kitchen you can also close the door on the upheaval if someone calls, or you get tired and take a break, or the job takes longer than you planned. It is in my genes to be particular, inherited from my father's side of the family by all accounts! I have had to train myself not to be obsessive about details but even so, Arthur used to say that I licked every square inch of those rooms! Having done the cleaning we could concentrate on whatever decorating that was needed and enjoy doing the work. In this way we managed room by room as we could afford to change the appearance of our home, getting rid of the dull, boring colours and using fresh light colours and patterns reflecting cheerfulness. I think the old house loved it and we certainly did.

Arthur was the chief decorator and I was the chief problem finder and sorter. In later years we were a family unit of cleaners, decorators and problem solvers. This was an ideal way of getting things done and in passing on skills and knowledge to our children. Glenys has always said that she learnt the skills of painting and decorating rooms from having had opportunities to do so with her father when she was younger in Llys Cerdd.

I do not enjoy the task of painting anything, although I have to do it sometimes. I attribute this dislike to the experience of painting the walls of the bathroom in Llanfair in the mid 1940s using the standard paint of the day that did not incorporate silicone! Arthur was particularly good at papering round 'awkward' corners, and Llys Cerdd had many awkward corners to paper! The house was 100 years old in 2001. I always prepared the walls meticulously with Polyfilla and glasspaper before painting and wall-papering commenced, and we always took time to get the job done just right!

Each day I paid great attention to the cleanliness of the black-leaded step and brass fittings at the main entrance to the house. For standards to be maintained, the step had to be black and really shiny, and the brass letterbox, keyhole and step-strip had to be exceptionally glossy and bright. In addition, the beautifully coloured floor-tiles outside the house, yellow, maroon and navy-blue were scrubbed daily to bring out their aesthetic beauty. To achieve the best results I did this job down on my hands and knees. This became a task for the girls when I went to work. I was also very keen on having clean windows in and out of the house and I took my life into my hands whenever I hung out of the top windows to clean them on the outside!

Chapter Thirty-Three

EISTEDDFOD GADEIRIOL DYFFRYN CONWY, LLANRWST

1957 was an extremely busy year for Arthur because he was fully involved as secretary of the Llanrwst Eisteddfod as well as being away most Saturdays in his own right as adjudicator of other eisteddfodau, conductor of singing festivals and accompanist at concerts. These events were held all over Wales, which meant constant travelling for him from north to south, and east to west. In addition to these commitments he still had his standard daily work of providing music lessons to his private pupils in Llanrwst, and being the resident Organist in Seion Chapel.

Preparation for the Llanrwst Eisteddfod, held in June, always commenced with vigour the previous September. There were many different committees associated with the Eisteddfod, and each had its own terms of reference. After a series of meetings of the various committees, each one submitted recommendations to the Main Eisteddfod Committee that dealt with the most important details and this usually took place before Christmas. These included matters such as: lists of competitions, names of suitable judges and accompanists, artistes performing in the Friday evening concert, a Conductor and artiste at the Cymanfa Ganu on the Sunday evening, and a group of Compères and Stewards to ensure the smooth running of the Festival. The Syllabus was published as soon as possible in the New Year to ensure that the bards and authors who wanted to compete in the Eisteddfod had sufficient time to compose their poetry and prose on the set themes. The Syllabus was sent or taken to various individuals and centres in North Wales early in the spring. The Programmes for the 3 separate events of the Festival were compiled and sold nearer the time of the Festival.

In late spring, by which time most of the entries would have been received, the Day Programme was drawn up, together with details of Preliminary tests in the competitions.

Each committee was important in its own right, but I remember the work of the Field Committee in particular because of its importance on the actual days of the Festival. This was because so many people were involved in fulfilling particular roles and responsibilities that had to be done accurately and according to agreed policy. There were very many stewards to do the different roles on a rota basis and the Eisteddfod always benefited from having conscientious stewards for its smooth running.

The Ladies Committee planned and organised the catering arrangements. Members were also involved in arranging competitions in the Arts and Crafts Competitions. They organised and ran a special fund-raising concert earlier in the year to provide funds for the running of the Festival. There was quite an expense to the Eisteddfod, and this is the reason why so many roles were done voluntarily.

I think that here I should say more about the background and story of the Llanrwst Eisteddfod because as a family, we were involved with it for so long in working for it, and competing in it. Its full history however, stretches much further back than the time of our involvement.

Llanrwst has been noted for its Eisteddfodau for many years and it is known that the *Gwyneddigion* held an Eisteddfod in the now demolished Town Hall in 1791 and amongst the notables present were William Jones, Llangadfan, Owain Myfyr who was William Owen Pugh, Twm o'r Nant, and Gwallter Meichion. One remarkable happening at that Eisteddfod was the start of the movement to send a Welshman to America to look for the Welsh Red Indians. They were supposed to be descended from the sailors under the command of Prince Madog who is said to have sailed from Wales and reached America before Columbus: there is a commemorative Plaque placed on a rock on the eastern sea board of the U.S.A. These people were Mandan Indians who had blue eyes. It was generally believed that there was some truth in these legends and so it was decided to send someone to the area to find these unique Indians.

Here are some of the subjects at the *Eisteddfod* in 1791 and you will note that they were for *bards* only:

- *Pont Llanrwst* (The Bridge)
- *Ty Marchnad Llanrwst* (The Market Place)
- *Yr Iaith Gymraeg* (The Welsh language)
- *Y Beibl* (The Bible)
- *Dyffryn Llanrwst* (The Vale of Llanrwst).

The subject of the *Englyn* (stanza) was *Rhyddid* (liberty), this being the time of the French Revolution.

I feel sure that there would have been other *Eisteddfodau* held in the following years but I have seen no records. There were certainly some held in the surrounding villages like Trefriw and some were held at Pentrefoelas that offered very generous prizes.

However, from the available records that we saw, the current series of the Llanrwst Eisteddfod started in 1924. Five men met in the Cobbler's shop at Compton House, Station Road, Llanrwst, and called a meeting for a fortnight later that set up the Eisteddfod. They were Humphrey Roberts, William Hughes, R.O. Edwards, David Jones and W.O. Jones a retired veterinary surgeon and chemist. Every year during the ceremony of 'Chairing the successful bard', a sword is used, half unsheathed from its scabbard at first and then symbolically sheathed when all persons present shout, “Peace” to denote that agreement prevails in the awarding of the Chair. The sword used in Llanrwst was an Army Officer's dress sword lent annually by the late Mrs. W.J. Roberts, *Manorafon*. It belonged to her husband the late Mr. W.J. Roberts, a local auctioneer and a one-time Officer in the old Denbighshire Hussars. He wore it during the military ceremonials at a Royal visit to Caernarfon in the 1890s, probably that of the Duke and Duchess of York, later to become King George V and Queen Mary. There was one year of exception when the late *Cynan*, the chief architect of the National Eisteddfod ceremonials, was the poetry adjudicator and lent a ceremonial sword.

The Llanrwst Eisteddfod was, and is still held in high esteem by competitors and adjudicators alike. The town has been very fortunate in the quality and dedication of the hard working volunteers who have striven to make the event a success every year.

I can speak only of the years when Arthur was General Secretary. Our children grew up during those years and when they were old enough, played their part in tackling the work schedule. There was a lot of what I call 'donkey work', repetitive and somewhat boring but absolutely essential, and then there were exciting and rewarding times that made it all worthwhile.

Arthur was an outstanding manager and leader. Entries for competitions were very numerous and there had to be enough time allocated to the preliminary tests. There were judges and accompanists to cover the preliminary tests, and the actual stage competitions, both of which were on-going throughout the day. This had to be worked out so there was never a hold up. But this was easier said than done when we had big numbers with which to contend.

There would be an average of 15-25 competitors for each competition, but once, I remember 59 hopeful youngsters entering the solo for children under 12 years of age! All were given equal opportunity to perform well with an accompanist, who played the same piece of music 59 times, and were listened to carefully by the adjudicator who chose the best 3 or 4 to perform the same song later on the main Eisteddfod stage. It was just the same in the adult classes. The various items of elocution and especially solo singing would have 20 or more contestants. Arthur was an expert at arranging this and I cannot remember any gaps in the day's stage proceedings, a situation for which the Compères and Stage Managers were profoundly grateful. There is nothing worse for a Compère than having to fill in time trying to keep an audience happy. Such an occurrence shows up the difference between the clever and the ordinary. Some could hold an audience in the palm of their hand, literally be in command, whilst others would have an audience restless and noisy. I suppose it is true of anyone in a public role, you either 'have it' or you 'don't'.

Arthur embraced change and innovation. He made several minor changes straight away in the job but of course you have to tread carefully at first in a new job - you must not frighten the horses or risk throwing out the baby with the bath water!

Smaller eisteddfodau were held in halls or vestries whilst the bigger ones took place in tents and marquees. The tents were long and relatively narrow meaning that the people at the back could neither hear nor see properly what was happening on the stage especially during evening sessions. The loudspeakers shrilled, squeaked and whooshed, and any possible mischief makers or drunks always congregated at the back of the tent. I was firmly of the opinion that if conditions were improved then people would be more likely to behave better. We had discussions at *Llys Cerdd* about these things and 'on our rounds' of other eisteddfodau Arthur and I came across Clwyd,a technician who had a perfect loudspeaker system with a clear output. Arthur approached him with a view to hiring him for the Llanrwst event, and there and then, a deal was made. That was the first major improvement he made to the event.

Subsequently I visited a theatre somewhere, I cannot remember where, but the stage where all the action took place was almost in the centre of the room. I was very impressed and wondered whether the idea could be incorporated into a marquee. When I got home and told Arthur about the seating plan, he was immediately interested. He was a good draughtsman and drew several tentative plans, working out the pros and cons and ironing out snags. Eventually he contacted Mr. Davies, the owner of the Chester firm who supplied the tent every year. He was sufficiently interested to come all the way to Llanrwst to discuss this new idea with Arthur. After a few hours he went home taking the plans with him and promising to draw up a viable plan for consideration. Meanwhile Arthur had a word with this one and that one on the Committee about the 'nuisance problem' at the back of the tent. All agreed that something needed to be done. Finally Mr. Davies turned up with his master plan and a General Committee was called to view the drawing and discuss the situation. The majority was very impressed with the plan that had the stage positioned much further forward with three semi-circular seating sections coming right up to it.

As always, there were some people who questioned the need for such a plan because it would entail more expense. In any Committee there are always people who quibble, and let's face it, they are needed to counterbalance those who would throw all caution to the winds and rush forward.

Mr. Davies would not construct this new marquee unless the Eisteddfod Committee signed a contract to hire it for three years - it would be costly for his Firm to construct a brand new Marquee that might only be hired once! It was felt that this was reasonable.

Arthur was a firm believer in the 'Lloyd George system': whenever the great Prime Minister had a measure to put before Parliament that might be controversial, he worked out a case 'for' and an argument 'against' so that he was always prepared with answers to any objections.

Arthur envisaged that there would be opposition in the Finance Committee because the aim of the Eisteddfod, apart from the cultural aspect, was to raise funds to build a Community Hall and so some members were duty-bound to argue with Mr. Davies against a three-year contract. Arthur pointed out there was no great risk for the Company because it was almost certain that other big events would want to use the new Marquee. This did happen due to the fact that the Marquee was so adaptable: extra 'wings' could be added so the Powys and Ynys Mon Eisteddfodau hired it, as indeed did the Urdd National Eisteddfod, and a number of other events that were held in Wales and England.,

However, Mr. Davies was adamant about the contract, and so Arthur had his work cut out to persuade the Committee that it would be advantageous in the long term to have this new-style marquee. Sooner or later people would become disenchanted with inadequate conditions and audience numbers would suffer, perhaps even competitors too. Furthermore, it would be Llanrwst Eisteddfod that would be the first to introduce the new concept. In the end and to their credit the Committee agreed to go ahead. It was an immediate success. When measurements were provided, I suggested that it would be an improvement to have a wall to separate the main body of the marquee from the areas at the sides and back of the stage. Within days, Arthur's brother Harry had built a panel with a door for each side of the stage and the panels had the advantage of being collapsible for storage each year. Ivy-patterned wallpaper was pasted onto the panels that looked very attractive and in harmony with the huge fresh flower arrangements prepared beautifully by a group of ladies each year that adorned the front of the stage. All in all, the whole scene was delightful, and it was complemented magnificently by the display of a big 'Red Dragon Flag' hung as a backdrop.

The next objective was to ensure that sufficient numbers of people came to the festival in order to generate more income. It was also agreed that there had to be a modest increase in entrance fees too. The importance of publicity could not be over-emphasised because it was crucial to success, just as it always will be. Announcements were made about the Llanrwst Eisteddfod at all large gatherings in North Wales in the months leading up to it. Large and small posters were taken to every corner of North Wales where people in shops, Chapels and halls were kind enough to display them for us. Programmes too were left at these places. Arthur had very few refusals. He and I also attended other eisteddfodau held on dates prior to Llanrwst where we 'sweet-talked' and touted for competitors, and gained publicity at the same time.

One year we heard that a group of dancers from abroad en route to the Llangollen International Eisteddfod were sight-seeing in the Conwy Valley area. On making enquiries about their availability, were told they would appreciate an opportunity to practise their dance to a live audience at Llanrwst before going to Llangollen. We were delighted with the prospect, and duly arranged for them to dance at the evening session where they walked down the centre aisle onto the stage wearing beautiful costumes. They danced and sang magnificently well and the audience was stunned and enthralled by our visitors - they loved it all. Some of us wanted to make an annual event of such an international arts display, but sadly, a small but significant group of traditionalists were very much opposed to such radical change.

The Llanrwst Eisteddfod was really a three-day event - on Friday evening a *Cyngerdd* (Concert) was held where well-known artistes and choirs participated. On Saturday, the actual *Eisteddfod* took place that consisted of a full programme of events organised into 3 sessions starting with: the children's competitions in the morning, followed by the young people's competitions, Chairing Ceremony and the mixed choirs in the afternoon. In the evening adult elecution, solo singing competitions and the male voice choir competition took place. The format may well have changed over subsequent years. Choirs came from far and wide including Manchester, Birkenhead, Nelson and Colne, Northwich, Runcorn, Wrexham, Mid Wales and Anglesey. To round off the week-end there was a *Cymanfa Ganu* (Hymn Singing Festival) on Sunday evening with a guest Conductor, with songs sung by well-known artistes such as Richard Rees, Richie Thomas, Stuart Burrows and Tom Davies (Bryniog). Gwenllian Dwyryd and Nansi Richards accompanied on the harp and Maelor Richards, Eluned Douglas Williams, and David Jones accompanied on the piano. These wonderful musicians and many others contributed extremely effectively and professionally to the success of the *Eisteddfod*.

Bus companies provided lots of extra transport that spread throughout North Wales collecting passengers from Corwen, Capel Curig, Gwytherin, Rhyl, Glan Conwy and Conwy, and about 20 other towns and villages en route.

People really enjoyed the Eisteddfod and its peripherals and looked forward to it each year, and when reserved tickets were released for sale on a specific *Fair Day* beforehand, there would always be a long queue waiting to purchase them.

Arthur was General Secretary of the Eisteddfod for 20 years. He enjoyed the role and was successful in it. Each year we would prepare well in the lead up to the Eisteddfod in June, and 1961 was not an exceptional year in that respect, but I can nevertheless recall every detail of it vividly. The weather was always a major factor in ensuring the Eisteddfod's financial success, and people often speculated about it prior to the event. As the Conwy Valley and its surroundings are mainly agricultural areas, fine weather is crucial to farmers in their hay-making at that time of year, and the activity can take priority over enjoying themselves, even at the Eisteddfod. On the other hand, if the weather was cold, wet and miserable, few people would brave the elements. Fortunately however, there were very few years when inclement weather resulted in dramatically poor attendance that caused major financial concern. The new style marquee had proved to be very successful because it was much more comfortable and effective for competitors and audiences alike.

The weather in June 1961 had not been too bad leading up to the Eisteddfod, it had been dry, but there had been a prevailing high wind for some days. The Friday night Concert went off well and everything looked set for the morrow. The security guard was in his caravan close by and the acoustics engineer was in his van too. After the concert had finished it was customary to clear the marquee and field of all persons then lock the gates for the night. The field stewards were always very particular about security. Saturday dawned with the usual bustle of activity, all the stewards were in position, the marquee had been cleared of litter from the previous evening and chairs had been re-positioned tidily. The rooms at the nearby junior school being used for the preliminary tests were checked to ensure readiness for the elocutionists, singers and dancers. The Chief Steward was the person charged with organising the stewards in these various places and efficiency in this job contributed to the smooth running of the day. Arthur was fairly free of chores on the actual days of the festival and people wondered how he was able to have time to walk around chatting to competitors, officials and visitors. His answer was that most of his work had been done in the weeks and months before the event, unless an emergency arose unexpectedly. And sure enough, 1961 was the year when such an emergency did arise, and Arthur had to manage it as effectively and efficiently as possible.

On that fateful day, the morning session had been very successful and had come to an end precisely at the specified time. The marquee made of thick, strong white canvas, held solidly in place by very long sturdy thick poles stood majestically on the field in Llanrwst patiently awaiting the crowd to return from lunch to enjoy the second session of the day. Practically everyone had left the field to go for lunch at the end of the morning session but three people chose to remain in their seats to eat a picnic lunch. It was not a sunny day, but was dry and rather cold for June and many people wore overcoats to keep out the draughts. During the morning the wind had strengthened, and by lunchtime, was gusting with some force. Those who were present spoke later about a flapping sound they'd heard that was followed quickly by a terrible tearing sound that was very loud and almost like a snarl.

Those few people, who were milling around outside the marquee that lunchtime and the 3 eating their picnic on the inside looked up towards the sloping roof and saw a split in the canvas into which the wind immediately rushed and ripped the split further and wider causing the structure to lift up the poles out of their sockets then fall back down again to the ground with an enormous crash. It all happened so quickly that for a few moments the few people present stood still and dumbstruck from shock, a few screamed and then there was much shouting, but almost by magic the stewards appeared and ushered everyone off the field. Arthur was soon on the scene too and together with the stewards and some local volunteers, managed to pull and drag some of the heavy canvas to one side to get into the only area of the marquee left standing. Five out of the seven main supporting poles were broken and lying on the ground amongst the chairs, flowers, ropes and signs that were strewn about the place. The scene literally resembled a war zone - it was surreal. The electricity supply was immediately switched off. Thankfully only three people were slightly hurt and received prompt treatment from a Doctor. Shock and disappointment were felt by everyone, but there was also an immense sense of relief that a much worse disaster had not happened that day involving fatality. People who were queuing for tickets for the afternoon session were informed that the rest of the day's events and the Singing Festival on the Sunday evening would have to be postponed to a later date. Meanwhile, Arthur had started a long session of telephone calls to try to contact competitors due to participate later in the day to inform them of the situation, especially the choirs. However, it was impossible to stop some who were coming from afar and amongst these were members of the Birkenhead Choral Society and the Northwich Festival Choir. Without exception everyone was sympathetic in spite of the inconvenience and disappointment, not one person complained.

Immediately, arrangements went ahead to resume the Eisteddfod, which took place on Saturday July 8th in a similar Marquee. The most marvellous thing was that all competitors, including Choirs, Adjudicators, Presidents, Compères, Accompanists and guest Soloists came for the second time, and a most successful Festival took place. Bearing in mind that some of these people were professionals, they insisted on returning and waived their usual fee. It was really remarkable and demonstrated their high regard for the Llanrwst Eisteddfod. The Eisteddfod Committee and all who worked to create the Festival were very appreciative of the outstanding goodwill of those people. The fact that Arthur knew them all on a professional basis and regarded many of them as friends also helped in such a situation.

The Eisteddfod is still held annually, but like other similar festivals in England and Wales, times have changed and people's interests have changed too alongside the introduction of modern technology. Operation costs have increased, many people now work shifts, television offers instant entertainment at home, and everyone has so many extra irons in fires. Some young people would rather have pop music and gigs these days and of course they have every right to indulge in whatever appeals to them. I enjoy fine singing of any kind, but am less eager to listen to the shouters and screamers who sometimes jiggle and prance about to the continuous thump, thumping of the beat while constantly repeating the same words and phrases!

The modern music culture embraces many different genres and encourages today's musicians to experiment with sounds and effects that help to generate massive income in the music industry. I realise, understand, and accept that the way I was taught to sing is but one genre of music making. I approve of young people's involvement with the arts - its positive effect can help to reach the soul, refine values and strengthen character.

I like the dances of pre-war days: the graceful movements of the waltz and the vigour and energy of the foxtrot, the quickstep - they had real tunes such as the Blue Danube. Oh, dear. I've got to stop or my grandchildren will never speak to me again. "Oh go on Nain, you know our rock and pop music is fun really, don't you! What shall we do with you … we'll just have to take you to a rock concert to convince you once and for all!"

Well, the world has changed and I have had to change with it. Now I journey through a different world. But there are still young people who sing in choirs, recite poetry, and keep on with our old traditions and there are young people who venture into new terrain to discover new themes evolving from modern technology, and others still who do both or none at all. God bless them all.

Chapter Thirty-Four

A NEW BUSINESS VENTURE

A surprise came to us in the summer of 1957. A policeman came to our door with a middle-aged couple, who looked pleasant. They were looking for accommodation and we decided to let them have one of the front bedrooms. After all, we had some experience of catering by then. They were a Mr. and Mrs. Hughes, who made themselves quite at home. I thought they spoke slightly differently from English people, but I could not quite place their accent at first. However, on the third morning when they were having breakfast Mrs. Hughes said to me, “Do you know I've been racking my brains for the last couple of days because I thought I knew your little girl - the one with the auburn hair in plaits and yet how could I, for we are from Australia. But now, I've solved the problem! When we landed in London we called at Australia House and were given lots of leaflets, one of which featured 3 young girls in Welsh national costume, and that is how I saw a coloured picture of your little girl.” It had been a photo of the three girls singing in the *Noson Lawen* at *Tu Hwnt i'r Bont*! Always creative, entrepreneurial, and 'on the ball' was clever Olwen Caradog … always ahead of the game with publicity and ideas.

Mrs. Hughes told us that her husband had made a fortune selling wood for stoves because there is no coal in Australia - then he spent it all, then made another fortune in the same way. Now she was making sure they could enjoy a fine holiday. Their young daughter was touring in Europe while they were seeing what the old country looked like. They stayed with us for a week before moving on elsewhere.

It was the summer holiday for school children. This meant that there were no music lessons being taught for 7 weeks and no money coming in. So we decided to try our luck at taking visitors as paying guests. We put up a 'Bed & Breakfast' sign in the front garden and hoped for the best. A week later a young couple from Stockholm in Sweden stayed overnight. The following week a young couple and their little daughter, Colleen, from Pretoria, South Africa stayed with us for 3 nights. The man worked in South Africa House, Trafalgar Square in London. He had English roots and his wife was half Irish and half French. We learned a lot about South Africa and the system of apartheid. At home in South Africa the little girl was looked after by a nanny, a black nurse whom she adored. The parents explained that they had every trust in her because black people never harmed children. Anyhow, little Colleen could speak English, French and Zulu.

During the rest of August, we had visitors from the Wirral, Essex, Nottingham, Hampshire, Pontypool and Yorkshire. Also, a couple from Barking in Essex came and stayed for a week. They asked if I would make an evening meal for them and I did. They enjoyed their stay so much that they kept coming back for several years … they were Mr & Mrs Keay.

Another visitor was a maiden lady who announced that she was a musician who had a LRAM Diploma from the London Royal Academy of Music. We did not ask her to demonstrate her prowess because she was very high-handed and demanding, but we made sure she was well looked after like everyone else. She stayed for four days. On her first full day with us she had breakfast and then disappeared into her bedroom. We had other people staying too, keen crown green bowlers who were out all day and did not return until the evening. On that particular day we finished our chores of washing up, making beds, cleaning the toilet and bathroom, and generally tidying up and then had lunch. We heard the musician lady leaving the house for the day so we quickly sorted out her room, locked up and went to my parents' house in Llanfair where Elsie, Glenys and Bryn were staying. My father was very good with the children, making bows and arrows for them, taking them for walks, and so on. We got long letters written in pencil on blue paper by Glen at the suggestion of my mother, to keep them quiet for a while I suppose. Elsie added a short bit and Bryn printed his name and lots of xxxxs. They were very funny and comical letters. I have kept them and they still make me laugh every time I read them.

We came away from Llanfair that day with lots of vegetables and fruit, and on arriving home entered through the front door as usual. As I put away the vegetables in the larder, I thought I heard a noise in the back yard. I unlocked the back door and noticed that the door of the outside toilet was wide open. I wondered what had happened and went to shut the door. And there, sitting on the toilet seat, was our Musician! I asked her if she was alright and she snapped, "Of course I'm alright!" "Are you not well?" I asked and, "How did you get into our yard?"

"I am very annoyed" she said, "I came back this afternoon and found myself locked out. This is a disgraceful way to treat me. I found the yard door unlocked and so there was nothing to do but sit here and waiting for you." This was unusual for we always kept the back door locked.

"Well. I am very sorry you feel like that. I thought you understood the B. & B. system. You have a bed for the night and a good breakfast and that is it, this is not a hotel. If you want hotel service then you must go to a hotel and pay hotel prices!" Although I was annoyed with her for treating us like servants I stayed calm and dealt with her in a civil manner. I can only say that I was very glad when she left.

During all the time we had guests there was only one other incident that was unpleasant. It was in September, and we had no one else staying at the time. During the afternoon two young couples called and booked two rooms for one night. It was a lovely day, sunny and warm. After unpacking and having a wash they went out, after I had explained to them, as I did to everyone, that we locked the front door at midnight. When they returned around 11.30 p.m I could tell that they had been drinking, one of the men was very unsteady on his feet. He stumbled up the stairs. Arthur and I never went to bed before the house was silent, so we waited for them to settle down. The table was already laid for breakfast and we were ready to go to bed. However, there were strange sounds coming from upstairs that resembled furniture being moved. I could not make out what was going on and I was uneasy. Eventually things quietened and we decided to go to bed. On my way to the bedroom I went to the toilet and found it reeked of a horrible sour smell. I switched on the light and was horrified. Someone had been sick all over the place, the walls, door and floor were covered in bits of chips and other stomach contents. I lifted the pedestal mat and threw it out of the window and there, underneath was a heap more of the same. I was heaving and went for the stairs just as one of the men came out of a bedroom and when he saw the state of the toilet, gasped and said, "It wasn't me, honest, it wasn't me." I knew he was telling the truth, but I raced downstairs for a bucket of hot water, cloths, a scrubbing brush, disinfectant and a pair of rubber gloves.

It took a long time to clean the mess and throughout the exercise I had the windows open. I decided to wash it all down again and so I went to get some clean water from the bathroom only to be confronted by a similar scene. I was shaking with anger. There I was at one o'clock in the morning cleaning up pig swill! I opened the bathroom window, threw out another pedestal mat into the back yard and scooped up another lot of vomit into the toilet pan and flushed it three times. I then continued with the washing down and sponging the carpet. I did not try to be quiet and it was all of three o'clock in the morning before I was satisfied with the state of my house. We went to bed and got up early the following morning. We cooked a nice breakfast for four but only three appeared. One of the girls said, "Our friend is not feeling too good this morning." I merely said, "You had better share his food between you because you will have to pay for it." I left it at that for the moment.

When they had finished, I told them what they owed plus an extra £5.00 for the mats that I wanted them to take away with them.I should have charged them for cleaning during the night too, but I didn't. However, I gave them a right rollicking. I told them I was ashamed that the only people who had messed up my home were my compatriots. The four of them were Welsh from South Wales. They were not ruffians, they were just silly and stupid and rather immature.

To finish 1957 in a more cheerful fashion, we were delighted to learn that my sister and her husband were coming over for Christmas. They would be visiting Stan's family in Liverpool first, then coming to us for Christmas. The children were so excited and looking forward to seeing their Aunty Bella again and meeting Uncle Stan for the first time and … well to top it all, their *Taid and Nain Llanfair* were coming as well. Even Santa Claus and Johnny Santa Claus had to take second place.

My parents were in two minds about the visit, well my mother at least! She wanted to see Bella so very much, but she could not bring herself to think about meeting her new husband.

School was closed, the holidays had arrived, the Christmas tree was decorated, and paper chains and coloured balls created a lovely effect in the house. Lots of green holly with bright red berries completed the festive look and … everyone was happy, well … nearly!

My father was more philosophical than Mam. "What's done is done. Let's be friendly and welcoming," he said. And that's how it was. We liked Stan straight away and the kids were very happy - they received lovely gifts from America. I remember that Glenys was given a pale blue and beige checked jacket that fitted and suited her very well and she loved it. She wanted to wear it all the time. Stan was very charming to Mam and he eventually won her over completely, he was helped along by Arthur who could always get Mam into a good mood. He knew exactly how to make her laugh until the tears rolled, and then everything was hunky dory. The visit was too short because Stan had to get back to work. Bella did not work then. I will re-word that statement more accurately ... Bella was not nursing then and in fact, did not return to paid employment ever again. But of course she worked hard at home. For one thing, even though she was a fully trained and experienced Sister, S.R.N. and S.C.M. in the UK, was not allowed to practise in the USA without completing basic training again, unlike Canada where she could, and did. Interestingly, when she herself went into hospital to have her babies she concluded that her nursing training in London had been of a higher calibre than that on offer in the USA at the time.

At the end of January 1958, a Tutor from the Normal College Bangor came to see me to ask if we would accommodate four student teachers who would be doing their teaching practice at Llanrwst Primary School, the school next door to us from February to March. They would require breakfast and tea and an evening meal, and a suitable room in which to do their written studies and lesson preparation every evening. We decided that we could provide all that was required for the student teachers, and knew that we could do with the extra money too. The girls were growing quickly and Bryn was no longer a baby, and that is how and when we began another brand new experience for the family.

The four male students were well-mannered and no trouble at all. Elsie, Glenys and Bryn were very pleased with their presence in the house because they were fun to have around. I cooked good meals and varied them quite a lot during their time with us. There was always enough to go round for all of us. The children had their cooked meal at lunch time, but when the students were with us they had some fish, chips and mushy peas or sausage, mash, carrots, apple sauce and gravy for supper as well, instead of their usual sandwiches. When the students departed at Easter time and I wanted to do my cleaning, Glenys and Bryn went off to stay with my parents in Llanfair T.H., but Elsie, who was now 9 years old, stayed at home to run errands and help about the house while I cleaned. Arthur was busy adjudicating and conducting at different venues all over Wales.

One morning I sent Elsie to a nearby shop to get something or other and when she came back said, "There was a lady in the shop who said she had seen me in a film in Winnipeg in Canada." Olwen's film had travelled in yet another direction!

On returning to school after the holidays the girls caught chickenpox, then Bryn caught it too. But fortunately, all had a mild dose and were left with no visible scars.

We knew that other student teachers would be coming the following March and most probably more visitors too, therefore we had to decorate and furnish a bedroom for the girls on the second floor. It was a nice airy room with plenty of space and a lovely view of the river and beyond. We bought two new divans for the front bedrooms on the first floor and took the replaced beds upstairs. At the start of the holiday season I emptied all the wardrobes and chests in the bedrooms on the first floor to make room for our paying guests' belongings. The clothes and personal items were taken upstairs to the empty rooms until the end of the holidays. We had a shower fitted in the bathroom, just an ordinary mixer shower above the bath that accessed water directly from the bath taps. Later on, we replaced it with a very good electric shower. Then we decided to install wash-basins in the three first floor bedrooms. Nowadays of course, visitors expect 'en suite' facilities. We had to work hard to complete the improvements in the short time available before visitors started to arrive and we succeeded too.

During that summer we had many visitors, all were British, with no foreign tourists at all. Some came for the second time having pre-booked, a useful practice and much appreciated by us. Elsie and Glenys were old enough to help with the visitors, and were also entertaining at the *Noson Lawen* evenings held at *Tu Hwnt i'r Bont*.

Bryn needed no cajoling to go to Llanfair T.H., he went quite happily and was spoilt because Mam used to store up treats for him. Bryn loved mandarin oranges and Mam had dozens of tins of them in the pantry. He also liked to mooch about in the garden whilst his Taid was digging the vegetable section. On one such afternoon Bryn was getting fretful. Taid had promised to go to the village with him to buy sweets, but Taid would not stop digging. "When are we going Taid?" Bryn asked in Welsh. "Oh, I won't be very long. I must finish this patch today because I want to sow seeds tomorrow. If you are a good boy you can sow some seeds yourself, then you can watch them grow," he said. After that, there was silence for a while, but within five minutes, the little boy of four said, “Taid, come on, or it will be dark soon.” “Dark! … of course not Bryn! Look, the sun is shining and it will be light for a long while yet.” Silence again, until suddenly there came a reply. “You wait Taid, until Jesus Christ switches off the light, … then it will be dark!” What could poor old Taid say to that response? He couldn't stop laughing lightly and tenderly because little Bryn was right! Summer gave way to autumn, and then Bryn too started going to school.

Using some of the money we had made from the B & B work, we purchased a twin-tub washing machine that made life a lot easier for me. Of course, there was still the ironing to do, but at least I could amuse myself by listening to the little radio. *Taid Gaerwen* had recently been invited to participate in a radio broadcast, and we had bought a very special radio so we could listen to the programme. After all, not everyone was asked to broadcast on air.

One Sunday evening the children had been bathed and fed and were in bed by 7.30 p.m. I had prepared our supper of cold meat, pickles and bread and butter and was sitting quietly reading by the fire enjoying the peace and contentment at the end of the day when an incident happened that had Arthur dancing up and down.

Arthur had not yet arrived home from Chapel when I decided to switch the kettle on in time for his arrival and … lo and behold … sitting on the kettle lead was a tiny little mouse very busily trimming its whiskers. It took one look at me, then nonchalantly carried on grooming regardless of my presence. I have never been afraid of mice, but I did not fancy the idea of having a rodent in my kitchen from a health point of view. I had no idea where it had come from, so I closed the kitchen door and tried to get hold of it, but the mouse had other ideas. Quick as a flash it jumped down and scampered into the pantry where it hid behind the bottles and boxes on the floor. So I closed the door on it and waited for Arthur to come home! I explained the situation when he arrived, then he grabbed a walking stick and set forth to battle with the mouse … for that is what it sounded like when he got into the pantry shutting the door behind him. There was no light fitting in there, and so the only light available to him came through the door panels from the kitchen.

From the banging and thumping going on in the pantry it would have been easy to believe that an enormous wild animal was on the loose in there with Arthur, not a little mouse. After all, this was my easy-going husband, the calm man who always took things in his stride even when delivering controversial adjudications in highly competitive male voice choir competitions. Here was the man who performed complex pieces on piano and organ becoming increasingly frustrated in the pantry with a tiny mouse! The noise and commotion continued for some time … then there was silence! “Have you found it yet Arthur, have you got it?” I asked anxiously. But before I had a chance to make any more enquiries, Arthur let out an almighty yell and came darting out of the pantry as if being chased by a ravenous lion. “You got it?” I asked enthusiastically. Arthur yelped and jumped about as he desperately rummaged around in his trousers, “The little blighter's only gone up my trouser leg” he said.

He finally tracked it down, and trapped the offending little mouse by clutching it through his trouser leg then pushing it down onto the kitchen floor and hitting it dead with a saucepan. I wouldn't have dared giggle at that time of the hunt, but that is exactly what I was inclined to do! When I related the story to the children next morning, in unison they declared, “Oh Dad. Why did you have to kill it? Poor little mouse.” But by then even Arthur had recovered enough to see the funny side of it.

Arthur went to collect his parents to come to us for a holiday: on arrival Nain came straight into the living room to see me and Taid made a bee-line for the Music Room where he gave Arthur a piece of paper. On it was a new and wonderful hymn tune that he had composed, and he asked Arthur to play it. He enquired tentatively, “What do you think of it Arthur?” Taid had composed many wonderful tunes over the years for which he had won many prizes. Arthur played it eagerly a couple of times, praising his father's composition each time, then he stopped, turned to face his father and said, *“'Nhad, mae hi'n don dda iawn - ardderchog wir - llongyfarchiadau”*, (Father, this is a very good tune, truly excellent - congratulations). His father then said in Welsh, “That's good … that's it then”, and went to the living room, sat in the fireside chair where he had always sat, and was then completely silent. Thereafter he never spoke in conversation, he simply answered questions and asked for whatever he needed. This was completely out of character, but even stranger behaviour was to follow. He kept sliding out of his chair and looking about him in a fearful way. In the end we decided to put him to bed with Arthur helping him to undress. Then he would not let Arthur leave the bedroom. He had to stand by the window without moving because Taid was complaining of strangers in the room. Clearly there was something seriously wrong.

First thing the following morning we telephoned his doctor in Llanfair T.H. who came later that morning. Dr Jones examined his patient thoroughly but was rather unsure about the reason for the odd behaviour. Remembering my faux pas with our own Doctor when Arthur had the slipped disk and the accepted protocol in dealing with doctors, I was not inclined to remark about something I had observed. However, I decided that because our lives had been turned upside down on account of Taid's strange behaviour we needed to do something about the situation. I ventured to say, “Excuse me Dr. Jones, I think I should tell you that when Taid has used the toilet, his urine smells strongly of 'pear drop sweets' and I have read that it is a sign of diabetes.” “Well thank you for that information, I will do a test straight away,” said the Doctor. The result of the test was positive. Taid was diagnosed diabetic, which meant that he had to take tablets daily and follow a strict diet from thereon. The strange behaviour ceased and everyone was happier, but Taid was never quite the same again.

Since Harry and family had moved to Llanrwst from Llansannan, the families had made special efforts to visit Taid and Nain at least once a week and a lady from the village called every day to see to their needs. However, we had to look anew at the situation. Both Taid and Nain were getting old and illness had caught up with them. All of us decided that we would have to take care of them. They would stay with us for six months at a time and go to the other household for the next 6 months. Both family households were quite near each other in Llanrwst, which meant very little upheaval for Nain and Taid in making the moves every 6 months, and it also meant that both families would be sure of a break from time to time. It was not an ideal situation, but it was the best we could do. I felt a little guilty because my own parents were in a similar situation. My mother had been operated upon and had been very seriously ill. She had suffered a stroke and Dad suffered badly from rheumatoid arthritis and both were managing as best as they could, my mother using a trolley to get around the house.

Anyway, Taid and Nain Gaerwen arrived, and the Welsh dresser arrived as well.

The cheese cupboard came later when Harry had inserted a new piece of wood where a mouse had gnawed away at a rear leg.

It was a difficult situation for all of us because our little family of 5 had suddenly been extended to 7 people, and it felt a bit strange to say the least. Taid sat on one side of the hearth and Nain on the other so it meant that those chairs were more or less always fully occupied by our extended family. However, we found other places to sit in the house, but the trouble was that our new, modern radio was situated right next to Taid's chair, which meant that Elsie and Glenys, now approaching their teens could no longer listen to Radio Luxembourg because it upset him. It did not go down too well with the girls, but they were enormously understanding and tolerant of their Taid's feelings and willingly made huge sacrifices to accommodate his needs.

Nain and Taid's income consisted only of their old age pension and they gave me a share towards their food. There was extra work for me with cooking and cleaning, but we soon got into a routine. Nain helped as much as she could but her eyesight was not very good. Every day she cooked apples for Taid's pudding. I started sending the bed linen to the laundry, but up until that time I had washed everything by hand because I had no washing machine. That was the moment when I finally decided to buy a twin tub washing machine.

During the late 1950s I became involved with the local section of *Urdd Gobaith Cymru* (Welsh League of Youth), which was and still is, doing a tremendous job for Wales and its language. A weekly meeting was held in the school next door and the Headmaster was the leader. There were about four of us helping in various ways with singing, elocution, drama, sports, and all sorts of other things. The age range was 5-15 years and there would be around 20-25 youngsters at every meeting. When the Urdd National Eisteddfod and its related local and district eisteddfodau were looming, we would be extra busy practising for the events. However, it did not matter how busy we were because we would always make time at the end of the meetings for the older children to display their acting skills. At that time there were 5 or 6 boys of around 12 years of age who would make their way down to the stage then get into a huddle. Within 5 minutes they had discussed and agreed a sketch, and would be ready to perform their impromptu drama. Their efforts would be completely spontaneous and unrehearsed, and the dialogue would be made up as they went along - all they had was the skeleton of a story they had cooked-up in the huddle. It worked every time! There were benefits all round: we all looked forward to their sketches and enjoyed every one, it was good experience for the boys themselves, and the children in the audience learnt a great deal from them too. I have to say that those boys were clever and talented - they could think on their feet! They grew up and developed into very successful persons in their own metier. Emyr Pierce Williams, our nephew, otherwise known as *Gari Williams* in his professional life was one of them and Lord Dafydd Elis-Thomas is another!

The Urdd Eisteddfod also had sections for folk dancing and action songs, and several parties competed in these highly entertaining and enjoyable competitions. In 1961 two groups of young people competed in the Drama Section, coached by the late Rev.& Mrs.W.E.Thomas. Both made it to County level and took 1st and 2nd positions. Elin Mair Thomas, Nesta Jones and Glenys were three of the members of one group, and Elsie and others made up the second group. Incidentally, no money prizes are given at Urdd Eisteddfodau, only marks that contribute towards winning the highly valued plaques, cups and shields presented at the end to the winning groups. This lack of pecuniary awards does not dim the passion and total commitment of the competitors in anyway.

The Urdd has a separate club for young people from the age of 15 to 25 called *Yr Aelwyd*, (the Hearth) that offers a range of activities to its members. The Urdd has a summer holiday camp in Llangrannog for children, that provides a dry ski slope, swimming pool, and all sorts of outdoor and indoor activities and there is an outstanding Youth Camp for the older groups on the shores of Bala Lake, *Llyn Tegid*. They are wonderful places. Elsie and Glenys went to Llangrannog many times as children and thoroughly enjoyed the experience.

We were a family of nine for Christmas 1958, Arthur's parents and mine, Arthur and I and Elsie, Glenys and Bryn. But on Christmas Day itself Arthur was away adjudicating at Rhostryfan in the old Caernarfonshire County, which seemed an unusual day to have a competitive event, but he was happy to attend. Despite this, we still celebrated Christmas on the day for the children's sake, but agreed to save the Christmas dinner until Boxing Day when Arthur would be home. When we were all gathered together as a family, I thought how nice it was for the children to experience the company of their grandparents - all four of them. I never saw any of mine and I have felt a loss in not having known them.

When Taid and Nain Gaerwen moved in with us Arthur and I decided we needed another bedroom on the top floor for ourselves to avoid having to shift our clothes and personal belongings before the summer visitors arrived. These bedrooms at the top of the house were quite spacious although ours was not as big as the one the girls had next door. First of all I had to buy stair carpet for the second flight and for the top landing. We had already papered the stairway walls with a very pretty pattern that had a white background with ivy trailers and deep pink rosebuds. It lasted well over 20 years, and still looked good even when we left *Llys Cerdd*!

All the alterations we carried out cost money, and we would not have been able to do them without the revenue earned from our B & B work each summer holiday. We bought a new bed because the hand-me-down one that Auntie Lil had given us when we married had finally collapsed, and I tackled the job of restoring the Welsh dresser that Nain and Taid had brought with them from Llansannan. It took many days to complete the work, but it was worth the effort.

Spring arrived and Taid and Nain went to stay with Harry and Nance at 'Fern Lea', their home. Then shortly after, the next group of student teachers arrived at *Llys Cerdd*, three of them this time. I shall always remember each of them fondly, I believe we all will, because all three became part of our family straight away. Two came from slate quarry areas in Wales, and both had fathers suffering from silicosis. They told us that their fathers could hardly breathe, and were forever panting and having to be near an open door for air. The fine dust had formed a wall inside their lungs that was absolutely tragic of course. Their sons were so concerned about their dads.

The three lads were very keen, and took their studies seriously, for this was their way out from having to follow their fathers into the quarry. They were very nice-looking lads and word soon got round amongst the local girls that there were some lovely new faces at *Llys Cerdd*. Very soon we could see a group of girls taking evening walks round the block where our house stood, ever so casually of course, just taking the air, and Elsie and Glenys suddenly became very popular with the older girls! Naturally, it didn't take long for the lads and lassies to get together!

The college students were a jovial lot and we had a lot of fun with them. Vincent (Hughes) asked me to make a 'French bed' for Arfon (Roberts); readers will perhaps know of the prank. You fold and loosely sew the lower half of the top sheet so that the person's legs can go no further than half way down the bed. Another time the cardboard Kodak lady was brought down from the 'shop' upstairs, laid in the bed with her head on the pillow and a bolster pillow strategically placed to pad her out, then covered normally with the bed-clothes. From the doorway, in the relative darkness of the curtain-drawn room, she looked quite real and Arfon, on entering his room thought that a visitor had taken over his bed. He backed away onto the landing shutting the bedroom door quietly behind him and went looking for Vincent who was trying to keep a straight face. "There's a woman in my bed," he said. "Who is she?" "Good Lord, are you sure?" asked Vincent. "I don't think Mrs. Williams would have left you without a bed Arfon, go and ask her." He came downstairs to see me, very puzzled and said, "I don't quite understand Mrs Williams, but I seem to have a woman in my bed." "What? … we can't have that Arfon, can we, you'll have to get rid of her right away, but how did she get there?" "I don't know Mrs Williams, I've asked Vincent, but he says he knows nothing about her." Their pals were laughing themselves silly upstairs listening to all this, and were having to hold their heads in pillows to muffle the sounds. In the end we trooped upstairs with me in front and Arfon and Arthur following. I marched up to the bed trying to look stern, but then just burst out laughing. "I don't think you need worry about this one," I said in Welsh, "She's dead to the world."

I'm not sure whether Arfon was relieved, disappointed, amused, or annoyed by the prank … but he laughed about it as much as everyone else afterwards because he knew that it had just been a bit of fun! The students were up to all sorts of tricks, Arfon included, but all of them were very harmless. Our three children loved being with them, were very much involved with, what seemed to them to be their exciting and daring pranks, and squealed with delight when they were being planned, executed, and discussed fully afterwards.

On his way to bed one night, Bryn, being about five years old decided he needed to visit the toilet and he sat there quietly in the dark for a while with only the landing light showing round the partly closed door. At about the same time, not knowing about Bryn's visitation, Vincent left his lesson planning to go upstairs to use the toilet. He dropped his pants and was about to sit on the seat when out of the darkness a squeaky little voice said, "I'm here." Vincent literally jumped up and ran out of the room like greased lightening, then fell about laughing on the landing and just couldn't stop for ever such a long time. The commotion was to be heard all over the house and then we all laughed and laughed until the tears rolled when we realised what had happened. It was hilarious!

Then Elsie was of the age to sit the dreaded 'eleven-plus' examination! She was clever enough to pass it, which meant that henceforth she would attend the senior school known as Llanrwst Grammar School.

The following summer, the visitors who came to us for B&B were mostly British with one or two American exceptions. Some came for a second or third time, which pleased us! The returners booked in advance for bed, breakfast and an evening meal. I made no money out of making the evening meal, but provided it as an option for people who stayed three nights or more at our home. People who stayed longer than one night enabled me to save on the daily grind of washing and ironing that was associated with visitors who left every day. During August, we had a party of eight Catholic teachers from Eire who stayed with us and spoke the Gaelic language, which of course comes from the same root as Welsh. Some of them spoke Welsh as well. We had most interesting talks especially with the accompanying Fathers, the priests. That is what was so satisfying about B & B work - it provided opportunities to meet so many different people from all over the world that consequently added interest to our lives and helped widen our horizons.

As the school holidays came to an end we had to go shopping for Elsie's new school uniform. Some of her friends from primary school were also headed for the Grammar School and in time, they settled quite happily. Llanrwst Grammar School was the second oldest Grammar School in North Wales going back to the year 1610, and was part of a Trust set up by Sir John Wynne of Gwydir Castle. It was a Free School that educated poor boys only at first. It was mandatory that the Headteacher had to be a Master of the Classics (M.A.). Of course, along the ages the school changed and was incorporated into the Local Education Authority system (LEA). Glenys and Bryn also passed the 11-plus examination and subsequently attended the Grammar School. I shall relate the story of the Trust later.

Chapter Thirty-five

A MERRY HEART GOES ALL THE WAY

Taid and Nain *Gaerwen* returned again to our house from 'Fern Lea' at the end of the six month period, and we all settled down for the winter months ahead. Arthur had been very busy during the first half of the year adjudicating in various festivals, especially during May and June. A week before the Llanrwst Eisteddfod was due to be held, he was up at 4.45 a.m. bathed, shaved and dressed, and after eating a good breakfast travelled to Ffestiniog. There he picked up the elocution adjudicator before continuing to Brecon to arrive at 9.30a.m. for an Eisteddfod that started at 10.00 a.m. Everyone was pleased to see them and the event went very well, but the proceedings went on until 1.00 a.m. the following day. After some tea and sandwiches Arthur drove home again and arrived in Llanrwst at 6.15 a.m. having driven and worked for 25 hours non-stop. He went to bed for a few hours, then got up again to go to Seion Chapel for the evening service. He was very tired after the demanding schedule. At times like that I waited up for his return home more often than not, but that night I went to bed because there was so much to do the next day. Arthur always insisted that I went to bed and not wait up for him at such times, but I didn't always follow the well-meaning instruction.

The Christmas holidays fell during the six month period when Arthur's parents were with us, and I must admit that things were a bit tense sometimes because my parents were also with us. My parents and Arthur's father were very well acquainted despite Arthur's father being a bit older than my parents: they'd all been born and bred in homes situated within a mile of each other. Nain *Gaerwen* however, was from Anglesey and was sometimes a bit miffed when the conversation turned into reminiscences. She and my mother were sometimes like chalk and cheese, both of them good people of course, but completely different in temperament. My father however, was the diplomat who steered them all into calmer waters. Nowadays a lot is written in magazines and newspapers about the friction that can occur in households when families gather together at Christmas time and how upsetting it is when there is backbiting and falling out. The Christmas Festival should be a happy one when we should celebrate the arrival of the Christ Child into our world in order to save our souls. If we forget ourselves and concentrate on trying to please others we find that we ourselves feel much happier. This is so strange, but true.

Nain and Taid returned to 'Fern Lea' from our house in March, just before the next group of student teachers arrived, who were with us for three weeks. They were a happy lot: two were from the same town but one was a mature student about 10 years older than the rest, who teased one of the younger ones about his liking for the girls. He gently reprimanded him for not attending to his preparatory work as much as he ought. "Yes, yes I know. I really, really will settle down to it tonight, honestly," said the younger, good-looking student. "How many times have I heard that promise this week eh? But it's still one whiff of '*Evening in Paris perfume*' and you're out like a flash again following it home!" But he was a lovely person who did get on with his work in the end … and still somehow managed to pull the girls!

However, he was not alone in having a keen eye for the girls: another of the students was also very nice-looking and much admired by the local girls. But very soon after arriving he became quite attached to a girl in the town. He settled down straight after tea to do his work, then after supper, went out on his own. Well, as the days went by, he started coming in later and later and sometimes it would be midnight when he returned. It meant that he needed to ring the doorbell to be let in and of course in so doing, managed to wake everyone in the house. The other students got fed up with this in the end and one night, they opened the landing window, which was directly above the front doorway, and as soon as he rang the bell, one of them threw a bucket of water over him! "That will cool you down," they said. Luckily he managed to dodge most of the water, but he was still rather wet going to bed: things improved after that. Those lads had their own code of behaviour, and dealt with problems in the accepted way - amongst themselves. Too soon it came time for them to return to College, which meant less work for me, but I always missed them long after they'd gone ... we all did.

We also made improvements in the back yard at *Llys Cerdd*. When we first moved into the house in 1947, a flower border ran the length of the back yard, but there were no plants in it. I went to Mr. Holmes' Nursery in Llanrwst and bought plants, some little bushes and colourful annuals. Arthur planted a stone from a peach: it grew and was fixed to the wall espalier fashion. It flowered, but only three peaches appeared that were unfortunately completely inedible, but the plant looked very pleasant against the white wall. I also planted a cherry tree in the far corner by the wall that was very pretty in the springtime. We removed the heavy iron railings at the front of the house and made the wall double the width so it had a centre cavity and a square pot either side of the path where we put two dwarf bushes. We planted annuals in the walls that looked glorious in the summer and filled the narrow borders just under the house wall with hydrangeas, potentilla and hypericum. It was very attractive and drew many compliments during the flowering months.

Arthur was very busy with all his work throughout this time. The number of pupils he had for piano teaching was as much as he could manage, but he also had the adjudicating and conducting work, including his weekend engagements. We had a fair number of summer holiday visitors as well, and more student teachers each September and March. Then a wonderful thing happened. The Council demolished the old tall houses called 'Mona Villas' situated behind our house. The difference was startling! The increase in light, open outlook, and freedom from the glowering windows were all a delight to the eyes, and I could have shouted with glee. When Elsie came home from school that day, the first thing she said was, "Have you washed the plates on the dresser Mam, they look very shiny?" She had not noticed that the houses had gone until I said, "No, but look outside." As soon as the last of the rubble had been taken away we swept up and hosed down our back yard. Then I settled down to the annual spring cleaning just after Easter. Glenys sat her eleven-plus examination and passed. We were so pleased that she had succeeded like Elsie. 1961 was the year when we first obtained a telephone at Llys Cerdd, when Glenys rang her grandfather at the Post Office in Llanfair to tell him the outcome of the 11-plus exam.

During a short lull between the Llanrwst Eisteddfod and the August Bank Holiday a young couple from London came to stay at Llys Cerdd, who decided to go to visit Lake Elsi high above Betws y Coed, and invited Elsie, Glenys and Bryn to go with them. The children were of course delighted to accept the invitation, but I had some reservations - not many, but some. Arthur was away at a festival at the time and was not part of the decision, but I decided that the girls should go, but Bryn was too young to cope with the climb. He was not pleased at all about the decision, but I said that he and I would go up to the lakes above the village of Trefriw instead.

I prepared a picnic tea for all of us and away we went on our different ways. Bryn and I took a bus ride to Trefriw then walked up the road leading to the first lake, *Geirionnydd*, and then on to the others, *Crafnant* and *Eigiau*.

Bryn and I reached the open heath at the top of the mountain passing a ruined house and a roofless chapel where sheep were happily resting. We saw the old railway track used in the building of the dam and the huge pipelines that carry the water down to the turbines below. The pipelines showed the direction to get down to the valley again, so we followed them. Unfortunately, there was no path to go down and we therefore gingerly came down the precipitous slope covered in fallen leaves, and were half leaning against the high pipeline for support most of the way. A fall from that height would have meant serious injuries or worse. We were therefore relieved to reach the main road at the bottom of the incline then hastened towards the bus stop timetable that unfortunately showed that no bus was due for Llanrwst for another hour. We decided to walk the three miles or so to Trefriw then two more miles over Gower's Bridge to Llanrwst Railway Station and into the town and home. I was shattered when we arrived at *Llys Cerdd*, and fell into a chair, but Bryn was alright. Finally, hunger compelled me to get up to prepare some tea. The two of us enjoyed it thoroughly, and I then felt a bit livelier especially with slippers on my feet. But Bryn immediately went out to play! We'd walked at least 10 miles earlier that day before he scampered off again to play with his friends, but then he was only eight years old, very healthy and full of vitality. I was astonished at his resilience! The other walkers eventually reached home tired and happy, having had a wonderful time by Lake Elsi.

A couple of years later the children and I went to Llyn Elsi again on Easter Bank Holiday Monday. We made the mistake of walking on the main road instead of the minor road on the other side of the river, and I was constantly on tenterhooks leading them single-file with a non-stop stream of cars and buses passing by, close to us. We would have been much safer on the old road. Having reached Betws we then had a steep hill to climb to get to the lake. We enjoyed the outing, but I vowed I would never again walk on the busy road on a Bank Holiday.

We had student teachers in the following February and September and visitors during the summer holidays. The visitors were mainly British, but we had a Swedish couple and some Hungarians too. Taid and Nain *Gaerwen* came back for the winter months and we noticed a deterioration in Taid. He was lost in his own world and spoke only to answer questions, and that was mostly in monosyllables. It was sad, very sad, because he had always been lively and ready to entertain the children, making up stories about birds and animals. We tried to reach him, without success, and in the end we thought it was kinder to let him be, although we always included him in conversations saying, “Isn't it Taid?” or, “We will, won't we Taid?” without making a fuss about a reply. Nain also was slower, although she did her best with Taid. They had been fond of going to sit on a bench by the riverside in Llanrwst to chat or watch the world go by, but that too had lost its appeal. I had to cajole them to take even a short walk. There was also some tension growing, now that the girls were teenagers. When they came home from school they would immediately switch on the radio in the living room and within a few minutes Taid would switch it off. They would also ask, “Why does Nain always want to know where we're going, when we're coming back, where we went last night and what happened, all the time?" "Well try and be patient," I said, "They're old, and their world is very small now. Besides, she is your grandmother and is interested in all you do," and to be fair, Elsie and Glenys did indeed give both Taids and Nains due respect and helped them a great deal. But I knew how they felt because I came in for the same treatment at my age, and Arthur too sometimes. I must admit that I felt the questions had an edge of criticism, but then I would hold my tongue because it was so unimportant and not worth creating bother and fuss about.

I could look forward to Christmas again with all the preparations, special food, presents, decorations, and cards. Taid and Nain *Llanfair* came to stay with us again and everyone was convivial. No sooner was the holiday over than we were preparing for the arrival of students once more, and Taid and Nain *Gaerwen* returned to 'Fern Lea'. Although the extra cooking, cleaning and washing meant more work for me, there was relief as well. It was a change to have young people around the house and a lot of laughter too. It lifted my spirits, and as soon as they departed I started the usual spring cleaning and decorating in earnest because we were busy with the 'Urdd' youth movement that year. Elsie and Glenys were in two separate drama competitions and both groups were very successful and won prizes. I was teaching a group of young girls to sing Elizabethan madrigals and they had lovely voices, all six of them. Indeed some had won prizes as soloists. Today, I have no doubt they would be in the limelight, but in those days, in the early sixties, the opportunities that youngsters have in radio and television today were not available then. However, the girls came to practise regularly and reached a very high standard. They won at district level, then county level and qualified for the National Eisteddfod to be held that year in South Wales. The adjudicators had all been so emphatic that the girls should go to South Wales to compete at National level that I broached the matter with the other leaders. They however were very lukewarm and said that it was a long way to go for such youngsters, they were all of 14/15 years old for goodness sake!

I had been that far when I was 9 years old! It was a shame, for after the National Festival was over, several people phoned me to ask, "Where was the party of girls you had, and why were they not at the National, there was no one to touch them?" I felt so awful because of the missed opportunity for the girls. Why are some people such wet blankets? The girls themselves were disappointed, but did not look upon the episode as a waste of time, but rather, a valuable experience to help them to achieve more in the future. What a positive and mature attitude! I was really proud of them.

Llanrwst Eisteddfod was a big success too, and there were no calamities, unlike the previous year!

Bet's Sister, Elsie

Arthur in his lovely Austin 7

Bryn Rodyn - Smallholding & Woollen Mill (The Factory)

Henry Vaughan

Thomas Vaughan

Bet and Arthur in 1945

Bryn and Elwyn- ushers at Elsie's wedding

The entrance to Dyffryn Aled - the manor house of the Wynne-Yorke estate in Llansannon. The lady in the carriage is the Lady of the Manor.

Bet, Morgan, Glenys and Kerry in New York

Llanrwst Bridge in Winter with Ty Hwnt i'r Bont in the background.

Arthur Vaughan Williams

Christmas at Ty Hwnt i'r Bont in 1956 when Elsie was 8 years old

Glenys & Elsie at the Urdd Eisteddford in Carmarthen

Elinor, Elwyn & Emyr (Gari Williams)

Toodles & Pwji Pwj Cats at Llys Cerdd

Glenys aged 6 in 1956

Bet & Arthur near the Britannia Hotel on the Horseshoe Pass, Llangollen

Glenys, Bryn, Nain Llanfair & Elsie

Alun, Hefina & Nerys

Elsie May, Bet andPercy in 1925

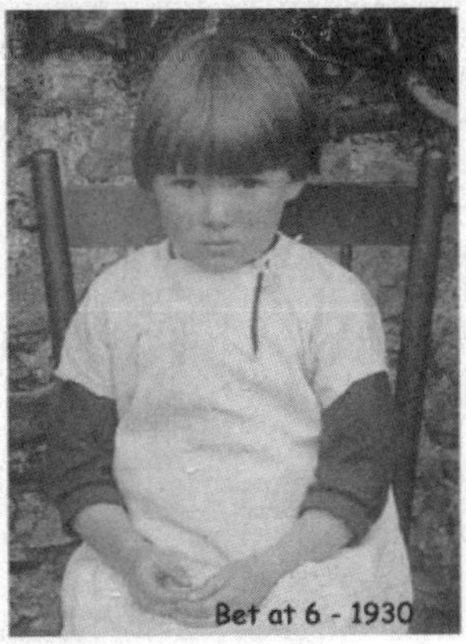
Bet at 6 - 1930

Bet aged 9 years after a major operation at that time for peritonitis

Bet (circled) in the 1st eleven Hockey team at Abergele County School in 1940

Bet aged 20

MANWEB Llandudno Office

1927 Sister Esie's grave with the school in the background

The "At Home" Tea Rooms in Llanfairtalhaiarn - 1937

Bet & Bryn in Horwich

Wedding of Elsie and Neville 1969

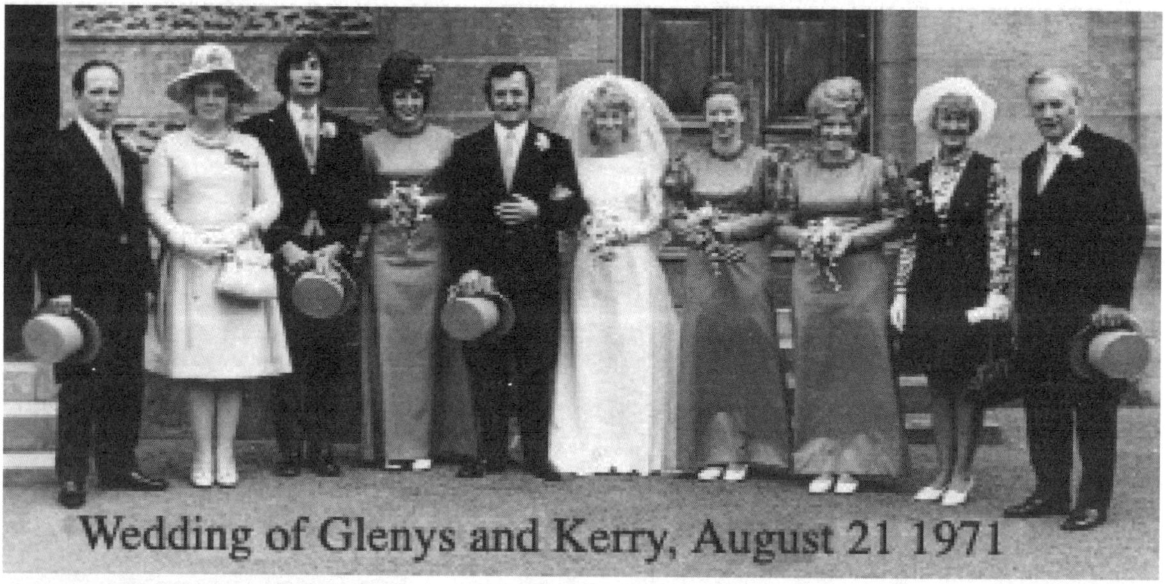

Wedding of Glenys and Kerry, August 21 1971

Sunday School
Seion Chapel 1954-5

Putting the final touches to the Electrolux "Top of th Bill" winning window exhibition at the MANWEB shop in Llanrwst. 1970s

DR. FERGUS ARMSTRONG M.D. F.R.C.S

Aunty Gusta

Percy E. Owen B. Sc.

Ellen and her son

Older Ellen and son in L.A. 1954

Philip Owen's family in Chicago. Mary, sister of Catherine, Bet's grandmother. Younger lady is Ellen, cousin of Bet's father Isaac.

Bet, Elsie, Arthur & Glenys

Llanfair T.H. School in 1932

BET

Arthur arriving to play the organ for the wedding of Glenys and Kerry

Bet at the wedding of Glenys and Kerry in 1971

Bet and Arthur's Wedding Day in 1947

Wedding Day 1947

Family and friends at the
Wedding of Bet and Arthur in 1947

Henry Vaughan Williams with family. Thomas Vaughan, his son, is on the right. Lizzie 'Rallt Ddu'is the child at the front.

Bet's Father

Garreg Lithrig Family

Mary May & Isaac Owen

1909 Wedding Day

Betsy Barton & Joseph Jones (Bet's Grandparents)

Bet's Uncle Edward & Aunty Lil

A view from the church over the village of Llanfairtalhaearn

Children's tea party in Seion Chapel in 1955

Aunty Martha

My friend, Betty Algieri, whilst we were on holiday in Switzerland 2002

Grandparents with Hefina, Bryn, Elsie, Alun, Nerys & Glenys

Arthur working on his model threshing machine at the rear of 'Llys Cerdd'

Family in 'Llys Cerdd'

Morgan is fascinated with Taid's 'disappearing coin'

Elsie, Bryn & Glenys at Black Rock Sands, 1957

A Summer Evening at Rhyd yr Arian

Ken, Mary, Andrea & Kevin at home in Washington D.C.

Petrine and Brian in Horwich at Christmas time

Bet in Niagara looking over the American Falls

Ray, Kathy, Morgan & Bet in Horwich

All the Grandchildren in Horwich

Harry(circled) & Arthur(rectangled) During the 1961 Llanrwst Eisteddford when the marquee collapsed

Bet on holiday in South Carolina with Marcus Newton in 2003

Bet in South Carolina in 2003

The Caring Nain

Cottage where John Williams brought up his family of 9 children (2nd marriage). Also home of Henry Williams (Arthur's Taid's first marriage)

The Caring Taid

Llys Alaw, Llanfair TH Bet's home from 1931

Family in Trafalgar Square, London

'Llys Cerdd'

Bet & Percy in the ruins of 'Pengraig'

The old bridge at Llanfair T.H. from a card posted in 1946

Bet in the ruins of her first home - 'Pengraig'

Llansannan Old School with lodge & gates of drive to Dyffryn Aled. Statue now in centre of village

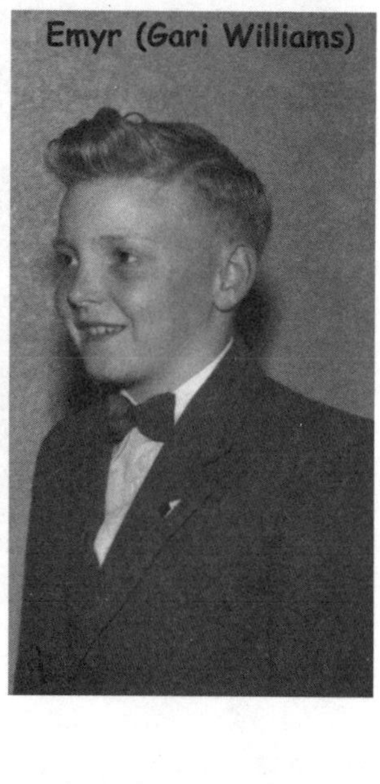
Emyr (Gari Williams)

80th Birthday Celebrations

Elsie

Arthur in Horwich

Photo of Glenys for TEACHER magazine

Bet's 80th Birthday

Bryn

Kerry

Neville

Kath

Rebecca

Marcus

Faye

Geraint

Morgan

Aled

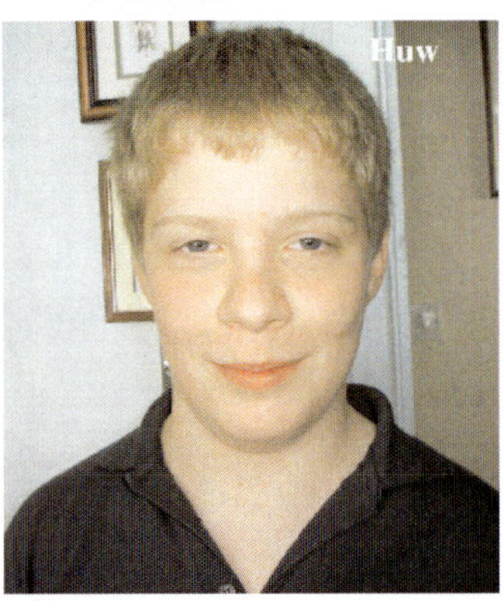
Huw

Alexander

Ethan

'Rhyd yr Arian', Bet's present home

Irene & Bet

A view from the house to the sunhouse

Back Garden of 'Rhyd yr Arian'

Bet tending her beloved garden

Seating area of the garden

The small back garden at Llys Cerdd

Arthur loved his tomatoes

Family assembled, following the funeral of Arthur

Arthur at the organ in Seion Chapel

Newspaper cutting showing Bet holding up the cup she won 12 consecutive times for best-kept garden at Eglwysbach Show

Bet ready to present a trophy at the Urdd Eisteddford in memory of Arthur

Bet ready for the Eglwysbach Show

Glenys & family at her Masters Award ceremony at Manchester University in 1990

Bet & Kerry at the wedding of Elsie & Neville

The whole family in Horwich at Christmas time in 1988

Bet & Glenys at a wedding in 1970

Chapter Thirty-Six

SPREADING OUR WINGS

Our house was never a quiet place. It was an orderly home, but there was always something going on and you never knew who was around - children, pupils, friends, relatives, student teachers, visitors, always on the go and never a dull moment. The busiest time of year for our household was the week-end of the *Llanrwst Eisteddfod.* It felt as though a stream of people ran through the house for days, which was very stimulating and exciting in many ways, but afterwards, there was an immediate slowing down and a quietening of the household that provided an essential calming lull, and oddly enough, a deflation to the spirit too for a while.

Our B&B visitors that summer had again been predominantly British, but some had been continental European, mostly German. One couple from Barking in Essex returned five times, the husband worked in the marine section of Ford Motors. It just so happened that on their second visit to us, another couple called looking for accommodation, and it transpired that they too were from Barking and worked for Ford. I told them about the coincidence and the man playfully groaned, "Oh no! I have just left all that to come on holiday, and here we are banging into Ford people again." "Well" I said, "They are a lovely couple who are on their second visit to us and I need to hurry now to finish preparing an evening meal for them, so you need to decide quickly whether you want to stay or not because I really must go. Are you staying or going? It's up to you, but please be quick." "Oh, so you're making a meal are you … any chance of a meal for us then?" they asked. "If you like," I said. "I can easily include two more." And so it was that Mr. & Mrs. Keay and Mr. & Mrs. Tully became very friendly with us and each other. They came on their holidays to *Llys Cerdd* on the same fortnight for three successive summers when Ford shut down for the workers' annual break, and we spent many happy evenings in their company.

On some occasions after evening dinner, Mr.Tully would ask, nay command me to tell stories from the turbulent times in Welsh history, or explain about the Welsh way of life and culture and I would do so willingly. Although I had tables to clear after their evening meal, dishes and pans to wash and put away and tables to set for breakfast I nevertheless felt that the interest shown by them deserved a proper response, and anyway it was all good fun too. Three hours later, after the meal had been eaten, stories had been told and an enjoyable time had been had by all, our guests were relaxed and satisfied. But then, late at night after everyone else had gone to bed, Arthur and I still needed to tackle the jobs awaiting us in such a way that didn't disturb the rest of the household. Although challenging at the time, and self-inflicted too some would argue, we nevertheless saw it as being part and parcel of providing a good holiday for our guests, and we also knew that our all-round efforts were appreciated.

I remember once telling them about an ancient Church in the hills near the lakes where Llywelyn the Great, a powerful and brave Welsh Prince and his wife Joan, who was the daughter of the English King John (of Magna Charta fame) used to go to worship. At once Mr. Tully said, "We must go there. We will go to that Church now." He would suffer no excuses and so off we went in his car with Arthur leading the way in our car. It was a lovely evening and the old Church was aglow with the rays of the setting sun. There was a certain aura of stillness, peace and tranquillity at the scene that we all felt and benefited from that evening. But finally, having enjoyed the visit, we agreed to go home on a different route along another narrow country lane that Mr Tully wanted to explore. At one point Arthur slowed down to edge past 2 cars parked alongside a small-holding, followed by Mr. Tully who drove passed them with a wider sweep and nearer the hedge than Arthur. In Wales, many hedges in the country are grown on top of stone walls that are not always visible. Being in the back of the car with Mrs Tully and nearest to the hedge I heard a slight grinding noise and knew instinctively that he had scratched his car. My heart fell into my stomach because it was brand new. “I have watched this car being made from start to finish,” he had explained with pride. “It has been made especially for our daughter Angela's wedding in two weeks' time.” I whispered to Mrs. Tully and alerted her to my suspicion and she gasped and whispered back, “Oh my God! … he will be furious.” Then she added hopefully … “Maybe it's only superficial.”

By the time we parked the car it was twilight, and although Mrs Tully and I could not see the damage, we could nevertheless feel the scratch with our fingers. Mr. Tully was happily chatting to Arthur and both were blissfully unaware of the disaster. “I'll have to tell him,” Mrs Tully said, “But I really don't know how to do it because he'll be so cross.” So I said that there was no easy way, and then added … “Just tell him straight.” And she did!

Fury was an inadequate word for the explosion that followed! He was so upset because he wanted Angela's wedding to be perfect. He ranted and raved and we let him get it off his chest. I said how extremely sorry we were about the damage to his car, but we also became concerned because he was upsetting Mrs. Tully by making it seem her fault. “You have to accept Mr. Tully, that it was your fault for being so impetuous. I should never have agreed to take you up there in the first instance. I regret very much being persuaded by that Irish charm.” His mood changed, and he said, “Don't worry my dear. I shall soon have it put right when I get back home - it will look as new again.” He did too! I received a letter from Mrs. Tully telling me about the success of the wedding … and the car! After all … he *was* the night Manager at the plant.

With the summer holidays over, we welcomed a new, but last batch of students at the start of another term. We'd been planning a family holiday at half term in October and London had been suggested as a venue by Elsie and Glenys because they had both visted the city and wanted to return again. Elsie had been on a short visit with Olwen Caradog Evans when she was eight years old and Glenys had been on holiday for a week staying with my brother's family. Her cousin Nerys, who was used to jumping on buses and tubes and generally finding her way around London had escorted Glenys to places such as Madame Tussaud's, the Planetarium, and the Victoria and Albert Museum. Such freedom and carefree behaviour in 1961 was fine, but would be considered risky today for two unsupervised eleven year old girls. Glenys had enjoyed herself very much during the week and the highlight had been the family's visit to the theatre one evening to enjoy the 'Sound of Music' musical. The children had spent the week preparing for the show by learning all the songs, and throughout the production had enjoyed singing them in their heads and giving each other smiles and knowing looks.The success of the trip followed a rather shaky start for Glenys because she had travelled to London alone on a 'Midland Red Coach' with a plan to leave the coach at a certain bus stop in North Islington where she would be met by my brother.

The journey went well and a kindly elderly couple took Glenys under their wing. She asked the driver to drop her at the designated stop, but when he did he told Glen he wasn't sure of the place, nor were the elderly couple or anyone else on the coach, which left Glen feeling vulnerable to say the least. When she finally decided to alight from the coach that evening having considered all the facts Glenys lacked confidence in her own decision because there was no sign of my brother. It was a scary experience for her because she questioned, as she sat on the bench, whether she was in the right or the wrong place. Had Uncle Percy forgotten to come, or had he gone somewhere else - the correct place perhaps. Her mind went into overdrive and ideas of what to do flooded in: she could walk along the pavement until she found someone to ask; she could find a 'phone box to ring home; ring Uncle Percy's home; or even ring the Police. What should she do? She looked at her watch and saw that the expected time of arrival had gone, the coach had been on time, give or take a few minutes, so she decided to wait right there for 15 minutes or so before taking any further action. She waited and waited … and waited and waited, and every minute seemed like an hour to her. Then suddenly a car came round a corner at great speed, leaning over to one side, and travelled in Glenys' direction before coming to a halt at the bus stop. All the doors of the car opened immediately and simultaneously and out poured the whole family waving their arms, welcoming her and shouting apologies and greeting her in the same breath. The relief was without bounds, and Glenys was extremely pleased to see them. There was a perfectly good reason why they had been held up of course, but it had been an unnerving experience for Glenys.

We had not enjoyed a proper family holiday for quite a while because there had not been an opportunity for one in the year and there had not been money for one either. I felt restless and unsettled whenever I looked into the future because our children were no longer little, they were bright and intelligent and deserved opportunities to access further education and obtain good jobs. From getting married in 1947 I had not gone out to work preferring to stay at home to look after my family, but in 1961 I considered the possibility of going to college as an adult student to train to become a teacher by accessing grant funding that had recently become available. I had the necessary qualifications and was capable of the academic study involved, but after much deliberation about the potential upheaval arising from the daily travelling to Bangor to college for 3 years I concluded that, although I deserved the opportunity, the children came first. That time was theirs - not mine. I also tried to persuade Arthur to do his final year of teacher training to enable him to teach Music in the Grammar School. He already was a Licentiate of the Guildhall School of Music and Drama in London. But he would have none of it. He said that it was out of the question. "How are you and the children going to manage for a whole year without my earnings? How will we pay our way?" They were fair questions, but as it was for one year only with holidays that could still be used for B&B work, I was confident we could manage. I tried every pursuasive argument I could muster including the fact that at the end of the year he would have a regular income, access to a good pension, better holidays and so on, but to no avail. There was no changing his decision and I eventually let the matter rest.

Then Fate seemed to take a hand during October, when I happened to see a job advertisement in the newspaper that interested me - a Clerk was required at Llanrwst's Manweb Office - the Electricity Board. I was unsure about pursuing the job, but my mind kept returning to the advert until I decided to request and complete an application form.

But then, I delayed posting it until one evening I realised I was dithering because I was apprehensive of taking on a job after an absence of fifteen years from the workforce. But the idea of returning to work was strong in my mind despite being busy preparing for our London trip.

We travelled by car to the hotel we'd booked in Russell Square and I took the application form with me in my handbag, but kept putting off posting it. Then the closing date was just two days away and I had to make a decision there and then to apply or not … to post the envelope or not … to go back to work or not. I argued with myself that if I were meant to have the job, I would be offered it, and if I were not, then I would accept that also as Divine guidance. But I also knew that if I didn't post the envelope I would never know the outcome. I finally dropped the letter into a Royal Mail post box in London on the Wednesday and waited for something, or nothing to happen. Que sera, sera!

We enjoyed our hectic stay in London and the children were insatiable. We took them to see the Houses of Parliament, the Embankment, St. Paul's Cathedral, Trafalgar Square, Hyde Park, Oxford Street, Bond Street, and so on, but that wasn't enough! They wanted more, and still more, they wanted to go on the river, but we took them up the Mall to see Buckingham Palace instead. Unfortunately, the Queen was not at home, so we were not invited to tea. What a shame! Some of the pigeons in Trafalgar Square took a huge interest in us by deciding to perch on our heads, a very painful experience as I recall, they perched on our shoulders and arms too which was decidedly a less objectionable practice, but they also squawked loudly in our ears. The whole experience was quite unnerving really for they would not let go of us until they realised that we would not feed them. Somehow, the scene was captured on film showing the horrors and slight pleasures of the moment. But safely back at the hotel, we had a good laugh about those pigeons. Fortunately, steps have been taken in the interim to outlaw the pigions that became a nuisance for tourists visiting Trafalgar Square

We decided to return home via South Wales calling on the way to see my mother's cousin Dr. Fergus Armstrong in Treorchy. En route we stopped in Oxford for a meal but there was no time for proper sightseeing on that occasion.

We arrived in Treorchy in the late afternoon and I went to ring the doorbell at a large house called 'Gilnockie'. I had never seen Fergus nor had any contact with him at all. I had been writing to his sister Kate for some time, and my mother had told me a lot about her Armstrong cousins. Partly it was on her behalf that I was making this call and partly out of curiosity. I was not apprehensive, but I had no idea what kind of reception awaited us. I did not hesitate, but pressed the bell button confidently. I could hear the ringing within, and then the door opened and a middle-aged woman stood there. "Good evening" I said, "Is this where Dr. Fergus Armstrong lives?" "Yes it is, who are you, please?" she asked in a kindly way. "We're from North Wales but are calling on our way home from a holiday in London. Dr. Armstrong is my mother's cousin, and …" Then I heard a man's voice calling out, "Who is it Rosie. Who is it?" "It's relatives from North Wales Doctor." Instantly he said, "Well bring them in, bring them in." I beckoned to Arthur and the children in the car and we all trooped in to be met by a tall man with a quizzical look on his face who said enthusiastically, "Come in, come in." I hurriedly explained who we were and why we had called on him. "I'm sorry we could not get here earlier, we don't want to inconvenience you, and will continue our journey soon, but I really wanted to meet you having heard my mother speak so often about you." To be honest, I was beginning to regret having called as I stood there thinking how presumptuous the visit must have appeared to him. But no, how wrong were my thoughts. "No, no," he insisted, "You have only just come … you *cannot* go home tonight … you *must* stay with me and talk. Rosie, prepare beds for them please." He was not a man to be gainsaid!

With the introductions over with, and after a lovely meal served formally in the splendid dining room, a session of questions and answers took place. I had never before heard a Scotsman speaking English with a Welsh accent in a booming voice … and I liked it … very much! He was so welcoming and interested in everything and was forever asking after people he had known in his early years in North Wales, some who had been at school with him. "Know him? … of course I knew him … I knew them all." And he did!

A larger than life man was Dr. Fergus Armstrong. My children sat looking on in awe and fascination. "You must be very bored listening to all this." he said to them. "Do you want to go and watch television?" "Oh yes please" they chorused with enormous joy because it was a new and exciting experience for them - not having one of their own at home. "Right then!" he said. "Rosie, show them where the television is situated. I have three sets, one in my bedroom, one in the sitting room and a small one somewhere else in the house. Have you got one at home?" Like a shot the three in perfect unison bewailed "No-o-o-o. Mam won't let us have one." This was fact at the time because I believed that a television would interfere with their studies. "Oh, you *have* to have a television set. You can have one of mine to take home," he said. The chorus came on again, "Oh, thank you, thank you so much," they said looking at me in triumph and with glee. What could I say but, "That is very kind of you Fergus, thank you." With the children happily settled with 'square eyes' in the study, talk of old times and family history went on for two hours or more and Fergus was in his element. I learned a lot of family history that night. He laughed when I told him what my mother had said about him as a young man in as much as, "Fergus was always chasing the nurses as a student you know." "She did, did she? … Well I remember your mother eating a whole cucumber and being very sick." It went on and on … one story after another, but we finally got to bed and enjoyed a restful sleep in a lovely room.

In the morning after a good breakfast cooked by Rosie, Dr Armstrong showed us his home, which had been built by his brother. It was large with a very long gallery room upstairs full to the brim of wonderful artefacts that Fergus had collected on his travels all over the world. The house was called 'Gilnockie' after the Armstrong historical stronghold in Scotland. When we were finally allowed to leave, it seemed as though we had known each other for years. Arthur got on famously with Fergus, and as we were leaving the house he said, "Children, have you got your television?" "Yes, thank you," they said very excitedly. Of course they had, for they would not have forgotten that! They also spoke for a long time about the luxurious beds they had slept in at 'Gilnockie' and the wonderful time they'd had there.

We had quite a journey ahead of us, but it was one that Arthur had done many times over the years on his travels to and from festivals. The children slept for part of the way home feeling happy with their television, but as soon as we reached Llanrwst they wanted to get it to work straight away. Arthur and I had quite a job convincing them that we needed an aerial and cables to make it work and we couldn't organise them until at least the next day. However, after a wash and a drink they were soon fast asleep, this time in their own beds. Arthur and I then sifted through the mail that had built up over the week we'd been away from home. As usual, most of it was for him. "Look, there's one for you," Arthur said. My heart was in my mouth when I opened the envelope and read that I was being invited to attend an interview on Monday in the Llandudno branch of Manweb. That was the next day - it wasn't panic as much as shock that I experienced at that point. What had I let myself in for I wondered, but gradually I calmed down and started to think sensibly.

What was I going to wear; what time did I need to be there; where was my copy of my application; and where were my certificates and references from my job with the Inland Revenue? There were so many things to think about, but once I'd got myself organised, felt more composed, and got on with getting the household geared up for Monday morning as usual. Sleep was a little hard to come by that night, but when morning dawned I was ready for the day. Arthur and I set off mid-morning for Llandudno. He dropped me off on the Broadway and I went to the Manweb offices shortly before the appointed time for the interview. There were hundreds of butterflies whizzing about in my stomach during the few minutes that I had to wait, but strangely they all flew away as soon as I was called in and asked to sit down. There was a semi-circle of men sitting in front of me, their manner was very pleasant, but they asked some very searching questions. I was quite calm and confident. I think this was attributable to the fact that I was well-accustomed to standing on stage in front of audiences to perform. Then it was all over, and I rejoined Arthur to do a spot of shopping to replenish the larder, then went home. Did I think I would get the job? Well, there were five applicants, but who was to know - que sera, sera. The children came home for lunch, then in the afternoon I attacked a pile of washing. I had no sooner finished that and was about to get tea ready when the phone rang. It was the secretary of Manweb in Llandudno informing me that I had got the job, and could I start on Wednesday?

I agreed immediately without a second thought, and that was that. I remember the date being the 5th of November - 'Guy Fawkes' night, and of course there was the excitement of a bonfire with fireworks in the field by the river, but it was nothing in comparison with my excitement at being offered the job and the thought of starting work all over again.

The following morning, Tuesday the 6th of November, Taid *Gaerwen* died peacefully at 'Fern Lea', aged 86 years. With our having been away in London, and the busy activities of the Monday, we had not known that Taid had not been feeling well, and so it came as a shock to learn of his death. The start of my new job therefore came at a very sad time with Taid's passing away. I went to work on the Wednesday and Thursday and had a day off on the Friday to attend the funeral. It had been a period of very mixed emotions.

Chapter Thirty-Seven

BACK TO WORK

On my first day back working in an office after an absence of fifteen years I felt very strange. No two offices are alike because the jargon is different and it takes time to become accustomed to routine, methods and procedure. Everyone was kind and helpful, but there was no way of overcoming that feeling of inadequacy from having to ask lots of questions of busy people, and believe me, it was a busy office, and one that was about to get even busier. Hectic would be a better word to describe it. I went from saying to myself, "I can't leave after two days," to, "I can't leave after just a week." And so it went on. In our room all the records were on draw-out plates and files in cabinets, and there were just two of us - a very good shorthand typist and me. The bulk of the clerical work fell onto me as well as coping with a three-line switchboard. However, there were times when we had to really co-operate, co-ordinate and collaborate to stay in business!

Electricity bills were sent out quarterly, the outcomes of which had no impact on us. Our work involved counting all the coins that were collected in a heap from prepayment meters, emptied by the meter reading team. They had special cards for meters that were used to calculate the money due to Manweb for electricity used. Surplus money was repaid to the householder, but if the meter had insufficient money in it, the meter reader would re-calibrate it so more money would have to be inserted in future for the usual supply in order to make up the deficiency. We issued the cards, and at the end of each day the meter readers brought the cards and the money for us to check the balances against the receipts issued. We then put the money in the safe until the following day's banking. We dealt with meter readers for 7 or 8 weeks during a period of 13 weeks.

Another regular job was the recertification of meters on a quarterly cycle. By law, meters have to be taken off circuit after a certain number of years and new ones installed. For us, this meant drawing up paperwork to cover the change, which was easy as far as credit meters went, but less so for pre-paid meters. Electricians had to bring back the unopened slot meters, and we had to empty them, work out any amounts due and enter all details onto the P.P. card. This was very time consuming, and there were occasions when many meters were still on the office floor awaiting our attention when we left work in the evening. There were many more electricians than clerks!

During the first few weeks in Llanrwst, I almost despaired that I would ever become competent enough to get on top of the workload. Our office was sub-district to the main one in Llandudno, and one day the boss came to visit. He asked how I was coping and I told him how I felt and he said, "Don't worry about it my dear, we are all the same, a new job seems so hard at first, but gradually everything falls into place, then the day comes when you know you've cracked it. However, the day you leave, you will still be learning." And that is exactly how it happened.

Suddenly, I knew I was operating at 100% proficiency, and it was just as well because the work on the development project was about to begin in earnest. The engineers had been visiting the far removed farms, dwellings and outlying villages in the countryside working on plans to take a supply of electricity to every house, farm, school, shop and all establishments to be connected to the mains electricity supply. The offer of supply was mandatory, and the connection fees were heavily subsidised especially when it meant fixing pylons and high power cables for miles across the countryside. Our job involved opening files and recording all the jobs done, and when metering started, there was a team of eleven electricians, a foreman and an installation inspector at work. Electricians were also working on contracting jobs such as wiring buildings for sockets and ceiling lights. In the shop, two people were busy selling cookers, washing machines, and refrigerators that needed to be delivered and connected to the power supply in the dwellings for the first time. All this activity was in addition to the normal routine, so there was a lot of additional pressure for us to manage. Most of the time all was well and work went smoothly, but occasionally, there would be an outburst of frustration or tension about something, but then calm would soon be restored.

This happened once and once only in our office. My colleague came to work one morning and I knew there was an 'atmosphere' present. I had no clue as to why this should be and so I carried on calmly as normal, then quite suddenly, she lashed out saying she worked harder than I did, implying that I was not pulling my weight. Had she said something in previous months when I was new there might have been some substance to her complaint, but that was no longer the case. I was totally competent, I knew it, and she knew it too. It takes a long time for me to blow up, but from previous experience I recognised that a matter of this nature had to be settled once and for all and as soon as possible too. So I turned round to face her and told her emphatically without shouting that she was talking nonsense, that she was unfair and knew it, and that I would not stand for it. I then turned back to my work and got on with it.

You could have cut the atmosphere with a knife and I hated it. Soon she was called to the boss for dictation and stormed out of the room crashing the door behind her. What went on in the boss' office I will never know, but she returned to her desk, and I took no notice, and we did not speak all day. The following morning she came in and said, “Good morning” to me, and I returned the greeting and from then on we got on famously with never a cross word again. We were both good workers, and in time grew to respect each other. Much later, there was Local Authority reorganisation and she left Manweb to take up a better job with a Local Authority.

While the Llanrwst Manweb office existed, four women came to work with me. They were all competent shorthand typists, but the rest of the work was mine on the whole. Things eased up a little when work on development areas gradually came to an end. All the employees in the Llanrwst depot were friendly and courteous and we interacted very well as a group, and were willing to help each other. There was not much status seeking, although in the office we were never called by our Christian names - it was always Miss, Mrs or Mr. It did not seem strange to me at the time to be called Mrs Williams because that is how it was in Manweb when I was there, and before that, when I worked in the Inland Revenue, I had been known as Miss Owen.

Chapter Thirty-Eight

A TRAGIC TURN OF EVENTS

Many things happened during that time at home within the family. After *Taid Gaerwen* had been buried, *Nain Gaerwen* came back to live with us at *Llys Cerdd*, and was very sad of course. She missed Taid terribly, but did not have the responsibility of meeting his every whim anymore. It must be said that a great burden had been lifted from her shoulders and she was once more able to do a little of what gave her pleasure. Her memory was astounding and she could recite accurately who was related to whom and the size and make up of families in North Wales especially the families of Ministers of Religion. She was sad that she could no longer sew as she'd been used to because of her failing eyesight, although she could read large print quite well with the aid of a magnifying glass. Nain read the Bible every day and was proud of being able to quote accurately from the Scriptures - she certainly knew the Bible.

Because I was working full time, Elsie and Glenys were very good at doing the shopping and making the tea, and sometimes if I was late home, they would cook supper as well.

We could not take students any more because of my job at Manweb. We had also acquired another member of the family - a cat! Bryn was nine years old at the time and really wanted a pony! "Where do you think a pony is going to live?" we asked, "In our yard," he said. "Well there isn't enough space there for a pony and anyway, it would eat the flowers." There were no more talks of ponies, but not long after, Bryn watched a nature programme on television and decided he wanted a monkey and this time … *he was serious!* He went on and on about this, and the rest of us were getting nowhere in dissuading him. *HE WANTED A MONKEY!*

Then one afternoon our Minister Rev.W.E.Thomas called and during the conversation was told about the 'monkey problem'. Mr. Thomas was a diplomat by nature and he said to Bryn, "When I was the Minister at another chapel before I came to Llanrwst, I was very friendly with an old sailor. He had sailed all over the world and when he retired decided to have a pet monkey as a companion. He trained the monkey to do all kinds of tricks and he often sat on the old man's shoulders. Everything went well at first, but the monkey began to disobey his master. One day when playing games, the monkey attacked the old man, biting and scratching him and began to climb and tear the curtains. It jumped about smashing pots and making an awful mess and the man was very frightened and had to get rid of it. The monkey was not in its natural habitat - and that was not good for it. So you see Bryn, you will have to be prepared for surprises and not all pleasant ones either. Monkeys are fun in zoos but not at home. You think about it Bryn."

We heard no more about monkeys. Then one day Bryn came home from school and brought another boy with him. "Deio has two cats and he says I can have one. *Please* may I have a kitten?" I had been allowed as a child to have cats and I felt sorry for Bryn after the pony and monkey refusals, so I said, "Perhaps, but I would like to see it first." No sooner said than done.

They were off like greased lightning and returned with a beautiful young cat - pure white fur with one black patch in the shape of a heart on the side. She appeared healthy, eyes clear and beautiful. Two sets of eyes were staring at me, one human and one feline, but both were impatient to know the verdict. “All right, you can keep her, but don't forget you have to look after her. Feed her and train her to our way of life.” “I will, I will,” said a delighted Bryn. They played with the cat for a while and I said that the cat needed a name. It was decided to wait until the girls were there too. Meanwhile I sent them off to play and had a chance to examine it further in case of fleas, but she was clean. Later I set the table for tea with a cloth and crockery in time for everyone arriving home. Suddenly the outer door burst open and Bryn ran in and was crying his heart out, tears all over his face. “What's the matter … tell me?” Then it came tumbling out that Deio's father had decided to keep the white cat and Bryn would have to take her brother, a black and white Tom cat. I tried to soothe him by saying that all my cats had been black, white and beautiful.” “No I want the white one,” said Bryn, and with that he grabbed the ends of the tablecloth and plucked it clean off the table, but would you believe it - the crockery and everything else stayed in place on the table! I had heard of this being done, but would not have believed it had I not seen it at first hand. The shock made Bryn stop crying and he stood still, holding the cloth. Then I saw the funny side of it and smiled. The boys too laughed, in relief I dare say, and the whole situation was resolved.

The white cat went to Deio's home and we welcomed the black and white cat, which was a fine looking Tom. He was named then and there - Toodles! He grew to be a fine specimen and we all loved him very much. It is hard to describe how he was always trying to please us - his eyes 'said' it all. He loved to stretch full length on top of the television, and in those days, the last television programme ended at midnight when the National Anthem would be played. As soon as he heard the strains of the anthem, Toodles stood up as if displaying fervent patriotism. The reality of the situation was that Toodles had realised that the television lost its heat at that time of night when switched off after the anthem had sounded!

In *Llys Cerdd* there was a little ledge on the side of the sink unit in the kitchen near the larder door, and if Toodles felt hungry he would try to gain our attention by sitting on the ledge and lifting his paw to 'shake hands' with whoever went into the larder. While we had Toodles there were no rats or mice or anything else near the house. He went hunting, and came home bearing his prey and laying it on the doormat as a present for us. Once, he brought a young rabbit home. Toodles was a magestic and beautiful cat and we loved him very much.

Just before the Christmas holiday I bought my first fridge. It was not large, but had a small and useful extra-cold compartment. Working full-time meant I could no longer shop frequently and needed adequate cold space to store food safely for a few days. The fridge pleased me enormously and gave good service for twenty years until I replaced it with a fridge/freezer just before retiring.

Some years prior to acquiring the original fridge I had baked a lovely jam and cream sponge birthday cake for Glenys and covered it with fondant icing. After eating the best part of the cake at her birthday party we were still left with a large enough piece to save, so I placed it in a tin container with a tight fitting lid and stored it in the usual way.

Later, I noticed what I thought was a long piece of thread on the hall floor that turned out to be a column of ants marching along the side of the wall each carrying a pupa. I was horrified, yet fascinated at the scene, so I followed it to the front of the queue that led into the 'food safe' and into the cake box. There were dozens of ants, hundreds of them enjoying a fine meal!

Half the icing had already been eaten by the time I discovered the activity, and we had no stomach to eat any of the cake afterwards. The whole lot went straight into the bin: I managed to kill most of the ants and felt awful doing so. As creepy crawlies go, the ant is a very clean insect that leads a very ordered life in an orderly community, and I admire the structure and discipline that ants accept. My admiration however, does not inhibit my ability to spray a substance to kill them and make known to the rest they are not welcome in our house.

Seeing ants reminds me of Friday afternoons in Form VA in Abergele Grammar School when our form master Mr. William Waters, or 'Willy Wet' as he was lovingly known would give out Bibles during the very last lesson of the week and tell us to turn to page 149. He would then read out some verses that began, "Go to the ant thou sluggard, consider her ways and…" This happened every Friday, and I think he was trying to get us to change our idle ways by comparing us to the industrious ant.

We had Taid and Nain *Llanfair* and Nain *Gaerwen* with us for Christmas, and as usual had our customary goose for Christmas day, not turkey. Some people do not care for goose meat, but I find that a shame because there is no other bird to touch it for flavour. The secret is to drain away the fat in good time. We always clarified the fat. Some of the oil was kept for cooking for it was the best for making crisp, tasty chips. But the thick and creamy white fat was kept to rub on the outside of throats when there was soreness inside. On Christmas day Taid *Llanfair* kept things on an even keel ensuring everyone had a nice time. My father was a wonderful raconteur who could entertain for hours: he was always highly involved with all the current national political affairs. He also liked to play card and board games that made him very popular with the children. He loved to eat chocolate and nuts too.

The 1963 New Year brought very bad weather that persisted for weeks. We had a lot of snow, but not as much as we had experienced in 1947. Frost and ice played havoc with everything and resulted in temperatures plummeting. When I recall the worst frosty weather within my experience, I remember the 1963 winter. At work in the office it was nice and warm because we had electric storage heaters, but at home, as in most other homes of the time there was no central heating at all. In *Llys Cerdd* we had a nice coal fire in the living room, plenty of hot water, and electric fires in all the downstairs rooms, but there was no heating at all in the ice-cold bedrooms, and there was only a wall heater in the bathroom. When we wanted a bath or shower the bathroom had to be pre-heated for over an hour, then the heater had to be removed because it was too steamy to leave exposed elements switched on, for safety reasons.

There was one rare and wonderful spectacle that I saw that winter. It was a haystack in a field that had the sun shining onto it making it appear to have a glass dome placed over it. I also saw a beautiful photograph that my friend had taken in Rhos-on-Sea that showed the *sea* actually frozen for up to two yards and more from the shore. Although the weather and its effect were most uncomfortable, we were nevertheless able to cope. However, things were much more serious for people such as farmers who were obliged to check their flocks constantly. Builders too could not continue with their contracts and therefore had a hard time in the snow. Building materials cannot be used successfully when there is a frost. Others suffered tremendously too.

My brother-in-law Harry had succeeded in building up a good business at his yard in Llanrwst. He worked very hard and was always prepared to study books, magazines and trade brochures to modernise his methods of building. Farmers were anxious to have large sheds to shelter their flocks over the winter months and Harry was an expert in building them. His order books were bulging, he had five men working for him, and his yard was fully stocked with timber, nails and other essentials for the job. His machines were new: everything and everyone was raring to go. Then the frosty weather came very suddenly, and without realising it a week went by without managing to work, then another without any change in the weather. Yet another week passed, but surely it would end soon! But it didn't, and another week went by, and yet another after that, and no work could be done. Harry was desperate to keep his workers because they were skilled men with families to feed, and he would need them as soon as they could start work again after the thaw. This went on for five weeks and Harry continued to pay his men full wages without any work being done - without any income being generated. Soon the bills started building up, but the orders kept piling up too, and although Harry had shown his order books to the Manager of his Bank, he would simply not grant a further loan. Other creditors were willing to wait for payment knowing that was all that was needed, but the manager would not agree and the Bank foreclosed. This was a shattering blow for Harry because it meant that he and his family were given short notice to vacate their house, workyard and buildings. There was a sale of all the equipment, when almost new machinery went for a song. Harry could not even cash any cheques made out to him personally - he was totally stuck for cash.

Harry came to see Arthur on that awful day and showed that he had only a few shillings in his pocket. He could not even buy food for his family. Arthur gave him some cash to keep him going and they were both so very upset about the situation. Arthur and Harry were very close and had been since childhood. When I heard the news I was lost for words and felt disgusted with the Bank, and thought the manager was acting in a very short-sighted manner. Harry did not know where to turn because he and his family had only a few days to find a roof over their heads. We could, and would have put them up in the short term.

In all the sorrow, sadness and worry however, there came a stroke of luck. The following Saturday Arthur and I had been to Colwyn Bay on business and were on our way home through Mochdre, a suburb of Colwyn Bay, when purely by chance I noticed a sign outside a house. I quickly told Arthur to slow down as we went past. The sign said 'To Let'. We noted the particulars and went racing back to Llanrwst as fast as we could. Arthur found Harry and told him to go immediately to phone the Agency. He used our phone and was informed that the owners lived elsewhere and that they wanted to interview all would-be tenants. After another phone call, Harry and Nance were on their way to be interviewed. The owners were a very nice elderly couple. The two sides liked each other straight away. Harry was perfectly open and honest with them about their situation and they in turn were most sympathetic. Thus began many years of friendly co-operation between them. Harry and Nance lived in that house for nearly twenty years.

Within a week Harry had found a good job and was able to start a new life. He must have felt so bitter in being forced to lose everything that he had worked so hard to achieve. But he was strong enough to put it all behind him and not let it sour his spirit. I have always felt that there were certain people within the family who could easily have helped him financially before and during his hour of need, but chose not to. Anyway, I thank God that He made me turn my head that day to see that blessed sign - 'To Let' in

Mochdre.

The move was perhaps a blessing in disguise. Emyr, the elder boy, had been a boy soprano and had won many prizes over the years. He was also a showman and a stand-up comedian. Elwyn, his brother, was more academic and did well at school, but he also had a good voice and played the guitar. Within a few years they were in demand locally as a duo and then in the wider sphere too. Their first record was issued in 1969, then in 1970 'Romani' became a big success by going to Number 1 in the Welsh Charts They were on their way!

At the time Emyr was working for a frozen food firm travelling round North Wales establishing lots of contacts. He had also adopted a different forename that meant from then on he was known as *Gari Williams* not his birth name of 'Emyr Williams'. Elwyn had done well in his school exams and had landed a clerical job in Manweb. I was consulted when he applied for the job and was glad to be able to provide him with a good reference. Incidentally, the same thing happened when Edwina, who became his wife, was taken on as a typist. During this period Elwyn completed a study course with the Open University in his spare time that earned him a Bachelor of Arts (B.A.) degree. It had cost a great deal in time and effort, but he was well pleased and we were very happy for him.

In 1981 Emyr and Elwyn established a company called *'Cwmni'r Castell'* and by that time they were both married, Emyr to Hafwen and Elwyn to Edwina, and they worked solely for their own company producing programmes for television. They combined their different talents to ensure the company's success. *Gari* (Emyr), took on many different comic characters for his appearances and his humour speckled with gently wicked asides was very popular. Their parents were very proud of them and their sister Eleanor too, who had also married and set up home with her husband Elwyn. Everything had finally worked out very well for them as a family. Nance had a part-time job at the local school and Harry had his hobbies. They were members of the local Chapel and Harry became quite an expert in growing fuchsias, and had many different plants. He also followed in Arthur's footsteps by becoming the Conductor of the local mixed Choir.

Chapter Thirty-Nine

A WELL-DESERVED HONOUR FOR ARTHUR

I now return to 1963 to my own family when we were very sad at Harry's misfortune and missed having the family as neighbours in Llanrwst. But, there was work to be done and life had to go on: I was very busy with my job and also had the annual spring cleaning to do at home. I took a few days off work to add to the Easter Bank Holiday week-end in order to clean the whole house from top to bottom. That was as much as I could do in my holiday: therefore no decorating was done that year.

In June, the *Llanrwst Eisteddfod* was held as usual and Elsie won first prize in a competition for accompanists. She was a very good musician and could easily have achieved a degree in the subject, but her father advised her to treat it as a hobby to enjoy in the hope that she would avoid the financial worries that he had experienced in life. Elsie also excelled in other subjects, so it seemed the right thing to do. I have thought many times since that perhaps he was wrong in his advice to her, but it was well intentioned advice nevertheless. By nature and temperament I believe it would have suited her better to have been a performer than to have gone into business. It is so easy for parents to make mistakes. Despite this, Elsie made a success of her career at ICI.as a manager.

In August 1963 the *National Eisteddfod* was held in Llandudno, but unfortunately I had little chance of going to the meetings because we were busy with B&B visitors. Luckily Elsie and Glenys were able to help with the work, which they did willingly to give them their due. During the week Arthur was received into the ranks of the Gorsedd of Bards in the order of green robes. He was the organist at all the *Gorsedd* Ceremonies that week.

It was later in 1986 at the *Eisteddfod in Dyffryn Lliw* in South Wales that he was received into the ranks of the *Gorsedd* of Bards in the order of white robes, signifying the highest of the Orders, except of course for those who were distinguished poets who had won the Chair or Crown competitions. The honour was given to Arthur in recognition of his services to music in Wales and the Eisteddfod per se. I was greatly pleased because he deserved to be honoured and the *Gorsedd* are to be praised for their gesture.

The same could not be said for the Music section where his talents and experience were ignored and neglected. I have found the record book he kept of all his engagements during his working years and they numbered well over a thousand ranging from small local festivals to the greatest. He co-adjudicated with the most distinguished in England and Wales and even had letters from some of them thanking him for his support and assistance. He was engaged as adjudicator at the annual Miners' Eisteddfod in Porthcawl for thirteen consecutive years. He was the one chosen to present and deliver the judgement on the Chief Male Voice Choir competition. This was not done lightly because all the great Male Choirs competed against each other, and it was no use just announcing the names of the winners. The judge had to explain in detail and prove the judgement was correct. The President of the National Union of Miners (N.U.M.) always attended the Eisteddfod and on one occasion Joe Gormley, President of the NUM spoke to Arthur just as he was about to go onto the stage to deliver the adjudication and final verdict. He said, “I would not be in your shoes for all the tea in China Arthur,” and Arthur said, “What? That's strange coming from you Joe.” Mr. Gormley replied, “Don't I know them.” He knew them for their passion, singing and fair play.

Arthur had been told on several occasions by different people that he had been nominated many times at local committees of the Welsh National Eisteddfod to be invited to adjudicate at the Eisteddfod, but nothing had ever developed from this stage. Then one year when the Eisteddfod was being held in South Wales he knew without any shadow of a doubt that his name had headed the list, but he heard nothing from the Eisteddfod Office. It was getting near the time for the publication of the Programme, and it just so happened that a very distinguished musician from the area in South Wales was at the Llanrwst Eisteddfod and staying overnight at our house. As we were chatting that night I mentioned to him about our puzzlement about such events and he promised to look into the matter.

Within the week he wrote to Arthur and said that he would be hearing from the Eisteddfod Office very soon. It seemed that some papers had been mislaid and that was the reason for the delay! Sure enough, the letter came and Arthur accepted and was a great success there. But that was the one and only time that he adjudicated at the National Eisteddfod. He always had a strong feeling there was a degree of antipathy against him and other worthy musicians too for whatever reason - he suspected it was one created by one or two self-seeking individuals who were influential in the committees that mattered most. Those committees seemed to have been dominated by them at that time. Perhaps things are different now - I do hope so.

Arthur won first prize for composing a tenor solo at the Eisteddfod with high praise from the adjudicator who was one of the most distinguished of Welsh composers. It was never used as a set piece for a tenor competition at the Eisteddfod, although it has been sung by several esteemed Tenors in concerts and enjoyed throughout Wales. It seems a waste of a very good composition because it would be an excellent Test piece for any Tenor competition.

During the summer of 1962 we had been quite busy with visitors: a fair number of them came from abroad. We also had a young lady who called to see if we would have her as a lodger because she was starting a teaching job in Llanrwst and we had been recommended to her. I was a little wary because of our previous experience many years previously, but this young lady was quite different. She was lively and pleasant, had a good sense of humour, was very open and had an easy manner about her. It felt as though we'd known her for a long time, so we decided she could come and live with us: we never regretted having her. She soon became part of the family and the girls regarded her as an older sister, especially Elsie. She was happy and carefree, and loved life. After some years, she met a young man from one of the villages in the Valley and became enchanted by him and they married. They lived in a flat at first then moved into a house in Llanrwst. They were very happy together for some years before drifting apart when she became extremely unhappy. She found it difficult to believe that their love had gone. Finally, she left Llanrwst for good: I have not seen her since, but understand she is her old happy self again, and I am very pleased for her.

Elsie, Glenys and Bryn passed the 11 plus examination that enabled them to go from the Llanrwst Primary School to the Llanrwst Grammar School. This selection process meant that some of their primary school friends went with them to the Grammar School on School Bank Terrace on their first day while others had to go to the Secondary Modern School on Nebo Road.

In 1963 Glen went to Paris on a trip organised by the Grammar School and loved the Parisian lifestyle, the coffee and croissants at breakfast and the leisurely evening dinner under the stars on the city streets. Elsie went on a cruise trip to the Mediterranean calling at various ports such as Gibraltar and Malta. The pupils had lessons for part of the day, then went sight-seeing. There were fees to pay but we thought it was a splendid idea. In 1964 there was a cruise to other destinations and Elsie and Glenys went on that one too and thoroughly enjoyed the experience. Glenys suffered sea sickness for a couple of days until she got her sea legs, but as soon as she disembarked to go sight-seeing and then returned on board, she was very sick again. It rather spoiled things for her although for most of the time, she was well. In 1966 it was Bryn's turn to go on a cruise with the school to a destination he had always wanted to visit - Egypt. The cruise suited him down to the ground because it started with a luxury air-conditioned coach journey from Llanrwst to London, then a flight to the Italian Riviera where they spent two days sight-seeing by coach. Later, they joined the ship to cruise to the Holy Land where they saw all the Holy places that we read about in the Bible that form part of the history of Christianity. Bryn loved the experience but felt somewhat disillusioned at seeing so much commercial activity in all the holy places such as the Via Dolorosa. The group sailed on the Sea of Galilee the day before war broke out in that area and there was heavy gunfire. Having rejoined the ship they went to Egypt and up the Valley of the Nile River, saw the Pyramids, the Sphinx and Tutankhamun's tomb. On the return journey they called at Malta. It was a dream trip for Bryn. He wrote 20 postcards to his friends and family and delivered them as soon as he arrived back home again!

Chapter Forty

WORRIES AND LOSSES

One of the young ladies who came to work as a typist in the Manweb Office in Llanrwst was Lyn who lived with her husband in a very isolated area, beyond Dolwyddelan. Lyn was a farmer's daughter who was vivacious and very pretty with big brown eyes, and I had known her since she was very young. I liked her and enjoyed working with a younger woman who taught me a lot of make-up tips and encouraged me to use eye shadow. I did not care for mascara and eye liner because I thought they made me look as though I had black eyes. But her other recommendations were taken seriously and the trifling experience had a very rejuvenating effect on me and I felt much lighter, happier and more confident.

I even ventured to Chapel without wearing a hat! You may laugh, but I tell you it was no small thing in those days. Everyone wore a hat for special occasions and most certainly for going to Church or Chapel. Men were obliged to take off their hats on entering Chapel or Church. The first time I went to evening service without a hat on my head I knew that every eye was overtly or covertly beamed onto my head. Whatever thoughts were going on in people's minds were not necessarily religious I know that much, more on the lines of, "Good gracious, what next, it's all that going out to work I'm sure." However, before long the young ones and many older women too were going hatless … and why not! God is concerned about our souls, not our hats! Besides, I was more concerned about paying off the loan on our house than buying hats.

I was never afraid of being different or of not conforming, but I would never risk appearing silly or ridiculous. I have always accepted that society must have rules in order to avoid chaos and uncivilised behaviour. But sometimes the rules become more important than the need for their existence and that is not acceptable to me. I like to read 'The Observer' - the first Sunday newspaper to be published on the 4th of December 1791. I have read it for over 50 years because it has good writers and thought provoking articles. In the 1960s period I read an article in the paper about a new birth control system that appealed to me - the Intra Uterine Device (I.U.D.). I asked my Doctor about it who arranged for me to see a Consultant at the St. David's Hospital in Bangor. He was very pleasant and explained that it was new and did not suit everyone. But I was happy with what I heard and agreed to have the device implanted and everything turned out well. Thereafter, I returned for a brief annual check until I reached the age when it was no longer needed. I had a brief stay in hospital to have the device removed when it was thought to have been lost at first, only to be discovered having embedded itself. It was removed after giving me years of not worrying about pregnancy. I believe that I was one of the first women to have the device fitted in Bangor.

I went through the menopause without any bother. I had H.R.T. tablets for three months and then the doctor took me off them. I think I was too busy to have time to dwell on any symptoms.

Lyn and her husband had a small menagerie of animals at their home in the countryside, and when her husband changed his job and they moved to live in Colwyn Bay they had to find homes for the animals too. Did I want a kitten? Well no, not really, because I already had a cat. "Oh, but this one is lovely. He is so playful and you'd love him Bet." When I mentioned this conversation at home someone suggested it would be a good idea to have the kitten and give it to Nain and Taid *Llanfair*. We knew Taid liked cats. So the cat arrived in the office one morning and created mayhem. He thought that piles of papers were there for his entertainment and he jumped into the middle of them sending them flying in all directions. While I hurriedly went to rescue the papers, Lyn tried to grab the kitten, but it had other ideas thinking no doubt that the chairs and desk tops were there for his physical exercises. He jumped up and down like greased lightning daring Lyn to catch him. She however was well acquainted with his antics and in less than two minutes had him safely back in his basket. Panic over, but not before a small group from the adjacent office had assembled to see the show! I went home early for lunch and the kitten went too. We had to put it in a large cardboard box with the grill grid from the cooker tied on top.

When the children came home from school they released him and he purred so loudly they immediately christened him Figaro after Pinoccio's cat. Next day was Saturday and Bryn was despatched on the bus to Llanfair with Figaro in the box with the grid on top tied down tightly. He could not get out but he surely put up a tremendous effort to get free, and the bus conductor had to help Bryn to push his head back into the box. Once he was safely at Nain and Taid's home, Bryn heaved a great sigh of relief. They were not expecting him, but that did not matter. They were always glad to see Bryn. "Oh you've brought your cat with you," said Nain. "No Nain, this is not Toodles, this is Figaro and he is only a kitten." When we went to see them later we heard a tale of woe, they'd had lots of trouble with the cat. However, when we said we would take him home Mam said, "No, leave him here. I think he is slowly settling in." What we had overlooked was the fact that my parents were getting old and could not be doing with a lively, playful kitten.

Bryn sat the 11 plus exam and passed. It had been suggested to me by the school that perhaps he should wait for another year before sitting it because his birthday fell on the 25th August - just 6 days too early to be included naturally in the following year's cohort. Anyway, he'd passed to go to the Grammar School, so that is where he went. At the end of the first year at the Grammar School they advised me to allow Bryn another year before moving on so he would be on a par with his age group. I agreed to the suggestion, rationale and plan. It all turned out to be a very big mistake and I have regretted it ever since. For a start it separated him from the peer group he had been with ever since starting school together, and that dealt a hefty blow to Bryn's self-esteem. During the following year a study of pupils' I.Q. was made by a group of undergraduates from the University and Bryn was amongst the highest in the School.

I accepted advice from professional teachers and thought I was doing the best for Bryn, but they were wrong and it was unwise of me to have listened to them. Bryn himself was inadequately consulted about the matter because that too was not accepted practice at the time. Training of teachers today is very different.

The following year Mam had another slight stroke, but would not give in to her ill-health. She struggled through her difficulties until she was able to move around the house using a tea-trolley to balance herself. Later, after making progress she could manage with a stick. She really was an indomitable woman.

During the Whitsun Bank Holiday Arthur and I went to another eisteddfod in Anglesey to publicise the Llanrwst Eisteddfod and tout for competitors. Nain and Taid Llanfair were in Llys Cerdd with Glenys, and Bryn and his friend Ithel had gone to the forest on the hills because it was a nice day. They did this quite often because it was not too far and they were mindful of snakes and old mine shafts. It was nice for Arthur and me to be able to participate in the event without having to do anything other than enjoy the singing and chatting to the many people with whom Arthur was friendly or acquainted, and by this time I also knew the competitors who frequented the eisteddfodau. There was great rivalry between them, but no ill-feeling. Many times at these competitive meetings I have listened to wonderful singers with voices that touched the very soul, some of whom became successful professional entertainers, others failed to control their nerves other than by partaking of alcohol that led to nothing at all except disappointment.

The evening session had already started when Arthur suddenly remembered that one of his pupils was due to be at our house that evening for a final practice before an important concert. Hurriedly we left and made for home as quickly as we could. Fortunately we managed to return on time and Arthur went straight ahead with the lesson. It was a lovely evening but Glenys was rather worried for no one had seen Bryn since he left that morning with Ithel. I prepared a light meal but no one had much of an appetite and when Arthur was free, we told him of Bryn's non-appearance and then he too was very worried. Immediately he went to Ithel's home in case Bryn was there but no, neither of them had been seen. Ithel's father suggested that he and Arthur should go looking for the boys. It seemed the right thing to do, and Arthur came back to tell us what the plan was and to change his shoes. Ithel's father arrived in his car with ropes and goodness knows what else and off they went up the hills and along to the lakes, scouring the usual walking areas.

They saw some soldiers camping and enquired if they had seen the boys. "Yes, we saw them this morning. The little lads were in fine fettle, but we have not seen them since." Another group of campers further on had also seen them early in the day but not since. They called at the café by the lakeside and were told that the boys had eaten a snack there at lunchtime. Apparently they had three shillings and threepence (old money) between them and had eaten egg on toast and a drink. The men could go no further with the car and so they decided to return home. This entailed coming down the steep, narrow and winding lane. Mr. Jones was at that time only a learner driver and Arthur was terrified because of the speed of the car and told him to slow down. "You are going much too fast, you will lose control and not be able to stop," said Arthur. "Oh no, I am a very good driver and besides I am not afraid at all."

Never in his life was Arthur so relieved as when he got out of the car and landed on his own two feet. The relief was short lived when he learned that the boys were still missing. It was getting late, half past eight. They had been gone for ten hours. Everyone was on tenterhooks. Should we phone the police or what? We decided to wait until 9 o'clock. No one had anything to say and so we were all quiet, and that fact in itself was extraordinary and exposed the tension and worry. After a while Glenys got up and went to the front door, then quite suddenly shouted, "There they are, look at them." And look at them we did! They were walking up the street, laughing and chatting without a care in the world. We didn't know whether to laugh or cry. Bryn said, "Ta-ra. See you in the morning," to Ithel, then ambled in saying, "Is there anything to eat, I'm starving." I could have shaken him for the anxiety, stress and fear that we had suffered, but I was so very, very glad to see him unhurt and safe once more that I just went to prepare food for us all. He told us they had walked miles and miles round the lakes, Crafnant and Geirionydd, had eaten two pieces of toast and an egg and had found some berries on the mountain. They had enjoyed their outing very much.

Afterwards he was warned never again to go off anywhere without telling us where he was going and when he would be back. Of course he promised to do just that and was very sorry and contrite about the bother they had caused. There were other times, when the boys lost all sense of time when they were enjoying themselves, but never for as long as that day. Really, looking back he was always full of curiosity about everything. Even when he was only six or seven years old and should have come home for his lunch at midday from school like his sisters, Bryn would be missing. If he heard the fire engine going off somewhere he would run after it. More than once Arthur went in the car to fetch him home. Boys will be boys I suppose. He never came to any serious harm and although some of his friends were somewhat older than him, he managed to organise things with them very well. Bryn really enjoyed going fishing and became very proficient during his time in Llanrwst. He had his own fishing tackle and learnt skills from others who were experienced and successful fishermen. He still enjoys the sport, but does not participate as often now that he has a family of his own with whom to spend time.

I saved enough money to buy a bicycle for Bryn on his thirteenth birthday because his pals had bikes and he wanted one too. He was very pleased and used it well, but within months had pulled it apart because, "I wanted to see if I could put it together again," he explained!

The girls were no longer little children. They were growing quickly, and were naturally a little gauche for a few months perhaps, but learning all the time and were a great help to me because they were capable of shopping, cleaning the house and making our tea. I let them experiment. I believe it is important for parents to show their children how to do things then let them try things out so they learn how to cope in the world. In their late teens Elsie and Glenys gleefully admitted to me that when they were little girls on Sunday evenings after I had gone to Chapel they would raid my wardrobe and parade about upstairs in my finery - shoes, handbags, jewellery, evening stoles and all! I did not have an extensive range of clothes but I had a variety of attractive tops, skirts and shoes that I wore for concerts whenever I sang solo. There was a lovely black taffeta skirt I remember that had panels cut on the bias that swirled out with movement and made a magnificent 'swishy' sound that they loved. When it caught the light it shone and came alive with different hues. That was a favourite apparently! They also had favourite high heeled shoes that they wore with delight. But I had no inkling of this fashion parade because everything was put away neatly before I arrived home. I already knew they paraded about in the flamboyant and beautiful ball gowns that my sister had left behind in a wardrobe at Llys Cerdd when she left to go to Canada. There must have been over half a dozen dresses there and each having its own delightful features such as a covering of netting, low-cut neckline, strapless top, tight waisted, swooshy skirt, clingyskirt with a slit at the back, bows and sashes and glorious belts, and each made in a magical colour. How they loved wearing those dresses and shoes and all the time yearning to be old enough to fit them properly!

My father died suddenly in March 1965 aged 81. A Policeman rang our door-bell continuously at 6.30am that morning to give us the sad news. Dad must have got out of bed to go to the toilet during the night and had fallen down by the side of the bed. Mam could only move very slowly after her second stroke, so it took some time for her to walk round the bed to get to him, but once there, couldn't do anything to help him. She struggled to get to the wall they shared with their neighbours and knocked as hard as she could with her walking stick. Jenny and Jack came immediately as they held a key, then went for the Doctor, but by then Dad had left us without creating much bother. We learnt later that he had suffered a fatal heart attack. He had suffered from rheumatoid arthritis for years and had deliberately kept himself going, "Otherwise I'll seize up," he'd said. He was also a believer in the power of Aspirin - he had taken at least one tablet daily for many years and was convinced they helped his pains. He dug his garden and planted it until the last couple of years of his life. When we were clearing up the outside shed prior to vacating the premises we found dozens of empty Aspirin bottles. Possibly Aspirin did help to keep him going, it certainly helped him cope with the athritic pain especially when it was at its worst in the wet and cold winter months. He had a very healthy stomach and was never really ill apart from the arthritis. He had suffered rheumatic fever as a young man. We were deeply saddened on receiving the news.

What I recall most clearly from the day of the funeral was the service at the graveside and the Rev. Cadnant Griffith, his Minister, saying that the quality that epitomised Dad was his friendliness to everyone. "When I pass over to the other side I know that Mr. Owen will be there and he will approach me with an outstretched hand in friendship and welcome," he said. I felt a real glow of pride in that. Following the internment when we were at my parents' home, Percy, my brother and I talked about making arrangements for clearing and vacating the house. There was no question of Mam being able to stay there. She could never manage on her own. My sister Bella could not be present because she was in America with her own very young family.

Both Taids were now dead but both Nains were thankfully very much alive. Arthur's mother still came to stay with us as usual and of course I was working full time. I asked Percy if he was willing to adopt the same pattern of sharing responsibility for our mother as had proved so practical with Arthur's parents, staying alternately at our house and Harry's house. "Of course," he replied. I was very relieved to have this shared commitment.

After the funeral Nain *Llanfair* immediately moved in with us in Llanrwst bringing only her personal things, toiletries, clothes and a couple of boxes of odds and ends. Later, I was not able to be at Llanfair to help clear up because I could not get leave of absence at that time on account of pressure of work. I was told that my parents' large items of furniture were sold, but wasn't informed about Dad's tools and garden implements, therefore I naturally supposed they were just given away to whoever wanted them. But of all my parents' belongings, the items that I requested then, and still really desire in 2005 are photographs they had in a box … the one that my brother took away with him for safe keeping all those years ago. I am sure that at that time he had no desire to keep them all to himself, thus depriving his two sisters of their fair share … none at all … but that is exactly how things have transpired over the years. Some of the photographs are still with his daughter Nerys. Her father would have wanted her to share them equally between the Owen, Sherlock and Williams families as is right and proper. This is what my parents too would have desired, without a shadow of a doubt.

I do not believe that Nerys has any concept of the hurt and frustration she caused when she failed to respond to our requests for photographs needed for this book. She kept promising that I could borrow a few in order to make copies, but they didn't materialise.

Instead, she provided a dozen copies of some of the photographs that I had requested, but unfortunately the copies were of poor quality and could not be used. I knew that Nerys had difficulty dealing with this, and other matters during her grief following her parents' death, but time has long ago healed her sadness: she should now deal with the matter urgently, for my sister and I are pensioners and no longer getting any younger.

I felt that it was very important for me to include the original photographs of my own parents and their ancestors in the book that I have written about our family, and that is why I pursued the matter. Finally, in time for printing, Nerys sent two original group pictures and one of my parents' wedding and I thank her for that: if there are more in her possession then some of them should be given to my sister Bella and me.

For a few months we had the two Nains with us and there were happy moments, and a few awkward ones too. Arthur was the one who always managed to calm troubled waters because he could at all times make my mother laugh and that was a salvation.

At the end of June our summer B&B visitors started arriving and Arthur's mother moved to Mochdre to Harry's house. Then she was invited to go and stay for a while with her sisters at their house in Deganwy. But suddenly, she was taken ill and sadly died there in her sisters' home on the 1st August aged 86. We were deeply saddened to receive the news about Nain's death.

The grave of Taid and Nain *Gaerwen* is at Llanrwst Cemetery and I go there with Bryn to tidy up and place a wreath every Christmas. It was their wish to be buried at Llanrwst thinking that the family was established there, but I think it was the wrong thing to do for there is no relative at Llanrwst now. Llansannan had been the family area for over three centuries and it seems sad to me that the family connection has been broken. Of course the world is a different place now and people move about the world just as they moved about between parishes in the old days.

My sister Bella had been upset when Dad died because she was so far away and couldn't return home for the funeral because she had a young baby and two little boys and there was no one to look after them. But she and Stan decided to come over with their three children to visit the family as soon as they could afterwards. There was great excitement about the impending visit because Elsie, Glenys and Bryn remembered their Aunty Bella and Uncle Stan visiting some years prior to having children. Now they had Raymond, Kenneth and baby, Brian. It must have been a tremendous feat of planning for them, but one made easier I like to think because they were coming to stay with us at *Llys Cerdd* and not at a formal hotel. They also visited Stan's relatives on the Wirral. They knew they could feel free and easy at both homes.

My mother was very much looking forward to meeting her American grandchildren for the first time. What a lovely moment it promised to be for the children too - meeting their Welsh Nain for the first time! I realised the significance of the visit and therefore concentrated upon paying attention to details such as planning the meals, beds, entertainment and so on. Getting time off work was a challenge. But … it all worked out beautifully, thank goodness!

They came, they saw, they conquered! My lot thought the little boys were lovely and cute, and they were too! We had good weather during the family's stay and were able to visit different places of interest in the area. One day we went to the Lleyn peninsula and stopped at Criccieth where my sister stayed in the car to feed the baby and Stan took the older boys up to the Castle. The castle is in a marvellous position on a high promontory above the bay. There are steps cut in the rock to form a path to the top. Raymond, the eldest was a strong little lad who took the lead, Ken followed behind and all the way up he yelled at the top of his voice, “I'm King of the castle, you're a dirty rascal,” over and over again to the delight of several other tourists round about.

A couple of years before the Sherlock family visited Wales, Arthur's American first cousin, wife and two small children, a girl and a boy visited us. There was a little confusion at the time because he too was called Arthur! I have outlined a little of their history elsewhere, but what I remember mostly is the children's exuberance. They were never still except when asleep. They too loved whooping and yelling and having a good time. They loved running up the stairs then sliding down the banister. We were concerned for their safety at times, but they never came to any harm I'm glad to say!

As I walked home from work one day while Bella and family were with us, I noticed black smoke billowing out of *Llys Cerdd's* chimney pot - our three storied house. Immediately I became alarmed because there should only have been a token fire in the living room grate for my mother's benefit only, there was no real need for it because the weather was fine and warm! *'Haf bach codi tatws'* as we say in Welsh (a little bit of summer to lift the potatoes). I ran home expecting the worst and was relieved when I opened the front door to hear much laughter and merriment, but as I walked into the living room I was aghast. There was a really huge fire in the grate, literally roaring up the chimney, the heat was intense and there were two small stokers working as hard as they could, carrying coal from the outhouse and piling it on the fire. Their faces, hands and clothes were streaked black and there were bits of coal scattered on the floor. My mother was in the middle of it all enjoying the whole performance, there she was, sitting in her chair at the fireside laughing and chatting with the boys and being thoroughly enchanted by it all. Slowly, gently, but firmly, I had to collar the stokers and stop the supplies! Next I had to throw masses of salt on the fire and luckily, we had an old sack that I soaked in water and placed across the grate to stifle the fire from receiving a strong flow of oxygen, and we shut the doors and windows to help the process along. It was suffocatingly hot in the house, but I had to reduce the amount of air circulating because the chimney was on fire. Sparks and spurts of flame were issuing out of the chimney pot, which surprisingly was still intact.

It just so happened that everyone was out of the house and my mother had been deemed able to keep an eye on the youngsters. Of course, they had never seen a proper 'live fire' before and wanted to experiment a little! It was all very understandable, children sometimes do such things, but I thanked God that I had arrived home in time to save things. Children and fires don't mix well!

However, with that escapade out of the way, I can say that all of us enjoyed their visit even though they'd missed seeing Dad. They also had the immense sadness of saying goodbye to Mam when they departed from Wales. The parting was particularly poignant in view of the fact that Mam and Bella never did see each other again, and both knew at the time that it was likely to be the case. Life can be so cruel. Sadly, sometimes it can be of our own making, but for the best reasons usually.

After our visitors had departed and routine reigned once more I was badgered by my children into learning to drive the car, badgered sounds better than bullied I think!

But I did not see why I should bother because I was quite content to be driven to different places by someone else. Arthur was neutral in the debate … he thought it better to own a reasonable looking vehicle than a battered one, but also thought it would be useful to have a second driver in the family. The children's view was different from their dad's of course because they knew their father was often working during social hours, and they were of an age to go gadding-about visiting shops in Colwyn Bay and Llandudno during the day, and dancing and doing other things that young people did at that time in the evenings. They believed that having their mum able to drive would be a huge advantage to everyone all round! They were very determined and sent away for the necessary forms for me, and I stood by while they posted them. In due course, Arthur went off to the local garage for L plates and without further ado, fixed them onto the car.

Mindful that they could not order their father about, the three cajoled and sweet-talked him into giving me the necessary tuition. He had no doubts regarding his ability to teach me, but had many doubts regarding my ability to learn to drive. Truth to tell I knew little about the inside or outside of cars, beyond the obvious! I had previously never had to think about making a car move and had no idea what to do with the pedals or gear stick. When I actually got into the driver's seat for the first time, I felt really scared.

Anyhow, Arthur explained the mechanics and movements before we went for a trip round the car park. Slowly I learned, but I had to do my driving practice after work when it was dark and usually on a quiet road up in the hills. Once, when I drove in Llandudno Arthur emphasised something really important to me in such a way that made me stop the car and get out! I know he was only trying to help me, but he was only succeeding in making me feel 'tizzy'. I suppose it is not ideal for a husband to teach his own wife to drive, but beggars cannot be choosers, money was still tight. Eventually, I went for the Driving Test and failed and failed the next time too. Arthur kept telling me to drive as I would usually, but I was so busy trying to be perfect that I failed the next time too. On the fourth attempt I finally passed because I decided that I would ignore the Test Examiner and just drive normally as Arthur had been telling me - I just did things naturally - and I got through. The previous examiner had said that I was too slow, so Bryn told me in a very convincing and funny way, “Mam, just pretend you're Stirling Moss.” Youngsters these days pass first time without any bother because they are young and so full of confidence, but the truth is that anyone can do it really … at any age!

That morning, I went through my paces for the driving examiner at the exact time of the Aberfan tragedy. I could never have imagined the awfulness of the main news item on the television that night! My jubilation in driving round Llandudno on my own and then meeting Arthur to tell him the good news was simply drained away in horror and disbelief when he told me about the horrendous burial of little children under mud, water and coal slack in Aberfan. There was a strange silence everywhere as people tried to imagine and believe what had happened in that South Wales village that morning. I suddenly remembered the time when I was a child and hearing of another tragic accident that happened in a coal mine at Gresford when hundreds of men were entombed in the mine when it collapsed, and then the awful horrors of the second world war when hundreds of thousands of men, women and children perished, but this was different and worse because it happened in peacetime and predominantly involved children. It was impossible to imagine the anguish, grief and torment of the parents and grandparents of those little ones who had left home that morning so full of life to go to the safety and enjoyment of their school in Aberfan. My heart, and countless others too went out to them.

Chapter Forty-One

MORE CHANGES

In a little over a month we were told at work that the office part of Manweb in Llanrwst would be closing down shortly and staff would be transferred to the District Office at Llandudno. I had been aware that the work relating to the rural development was more or less finished and there were just a few loose ends to tie up. The chief clerk at District Office came to inform us of the changes. He said that the nature of our work would change and would no longer be concerned with all the different aspects of Manweb work that had been the case to date. Everyone would have their own work and would belong to a larger related group. He asked me what I would like to do and I replied that I did not really have any preference as long as it was interesting work. I was landed with disconnections for debt! It was certainly interesting work without a doubt!

I had enjoyed working on the provision of electrical power to the outlying villages and rural areas. I knew what a wonderful change it had brought to all those homes. I had experienced life without electricity as a child and teenager - lamps, candles and coal fires. Even now it amazes me when I recall doing my homework and reading with only an oil lamp on the table beside me for light.

It became time for Nain (my mother) to go for her annual visit to Percy and Eluned and their family home in Berriew near Newtown in mid Wales. My brother had finally moved from London because he had grown very tired of being stuck in traffic for hours. He had been engaged as Bursar at *Gregynog Hall*, the Estate that is owned by Aberystwyth University of Wales. The two ladies of Gregynog, daughters of the famous Davies family of Llandinam had made a gift of it to the University. Percy had made a lot of necessary improvements and was enjoying the work. It was a completely different life from London and at first had seemed very strange to the children who had been born and bred in the Capital.

When the invitation had arrived, Mam was not very keen to go because she said, "They leave me on my own most of the time in the front room." We thought that she should go - it would provide a change of scenery for her and a short respite for us. Arthur took her in the car. Within a few days there came a telephone call in the morning saying that Nain was not well and wanted to come home. Without any hesitation Arthur told them to bring her back home to us as soon as it was convenient for them.

In the afternoon they arrived: Eluned my sister-in-law was driving and had a companion in the front with her whilst Mam sat on her own in the back seat. Arthur said that they half carried Mam into the house and put her to sit in an armchair. They declined a cup of tea and left immediately. Nain was clearly upset and unwell so Arthur phoned me and I managed to get home. I could not get any sense from Mam as she was so upset, but she said something about falling on the landing at my brother's house, so I decided to call her Doctor from Llanfair. He came as soon as he could and very gently asked her some questions and got a little more information, but not a great deal. However she complained of a bad pain in her arm and shoulder, so the Doctor examined her. He opened her blouse, then stopped. "Mrs. Owen," he said, "When did you hurt yourself, did you have a fall?" Arthur did not hear her reply properly except for the fact that she kept saying, "They wouldn't stop, I was thirsty and was being banged from side to side in the car." The doctor told me to have a look.

Half of Mam's chest, one shoulder and her arm were black and blue. Dr. Jones exploded, “Criminal negligence,” he said. “She's got a dislocated shoulder and should never have had to travel without some support.” He repeated, “Criminal negligence.” He explained that she would have to go to hospital and arranged for an ambulance to take her immediately to Rhyl to the Alexandra Hospital. I followed later in the car after packing a case for her. When I got to the hospital she was in bed and a doctor had attended to her and prescribed the medication required. Apparently the shock had made her unable to pass urine and she had to be given something to help her in that respect. Consequently and immediately she became incontinent.

When I arrived home from the hospital that night it was very late because I stayed with Mam as long as I could for she was very upset indeed, which in turn made my insides feel very churned up. As soon as I came into the house and told Arthur how things had turned out in the hospital I decided to phone my brother there and then. Arthur demurred, but I would have to go to work in the morning and there wouldn't be time to phone. Besides I was really furious. When my brother finally answered the phone, having had to get up from bed probably, he sounded irritated and said I could have waited till morning. This made me even angrier and I lashed out at him and I am not easily moved to anger, far from it. Mam used to say, “Neither fire nor water will move that girl,” meaning me, but when I finally let go, then look out!

Everything came tumbling out, the slings and the arrows, the discourtesy, the disdain, which my parents, especially my mother, had endured. I know that Mam could be difficult on rare occasions, but she was old and ill and had suffered a great deal of worry and hardship in her life. I doubt whether anything or anyone could have stopped me and I am surprised that Percy did not hang up on me, but I felt a lot better having unloaded a weight off my back. It was a relief. After that there was no contact between us for some years. I did not want a feud or split for I did not feel bitter, but if they felt alienated well, so be it. Everything I had said had been the truth. Looking back, perhaps it would have been better had I spoken to them as things happened, instead of bottling it all up, but I thought it was for the best since I don't like squabbling in families especially when there are children involved.

When Elsie got married she would not send an invitation to Percy and Eluned, but she did invite their children who did not attend, but sent a nice present of good bed linen. However, when Hefina, their younger cousin got married, Arthur and I were invited. We pondered some time over it, but decided it would be churlish to refuse since the children obviously wanted to heal the rift. We accepted, and on the day of the wedding although at first we felt distinctly uncomfortable, everything went smoothly, everyone was natural and the girls Nerys and Hefina were most pleasant. Arthur and I were both glad that reconciliation had taken place. Nothing was said, but it felt right for the family to be whole again. We were all older and wiser and my brother and I had been very close in our younger days.

Elsie and Glenys were chosen in the VI Form to be in separate teams for a Public Speaking competition held at Bangor University. They did not win but one team was the runner up. I think I am right in saying that Lord Dafydd Elis Thomas who is Presiding Officer of the Welsh National Assembly in Cardiff was a member of the winning group.

Elsie sat her final exams (A levels) and was expected to do very well having gained 12 excellent passes in her ‘O levels’ two years previously. I had emphasised the need for a lot of study and revising and was assured that everything was going well. She was at home regularly, but it was impossible for me to monitor her efforts all the time. When the results arrived in the summer holidays she was working as a waitress at a top class hotel in Llandudno and I took the envelope to her that morning. When she opened it and read the contents I could tell from her face that it was bad news. She went pale and just handed the paper to me then burst into tears. I felt the pain and disappointment as much as she did, but I kept calm and told her to get her coat and request the morning off. We walked the streets and I tried to help her to come to terms with the results. It was not a poor result by any means, but was not good enough for her plan to go to the University of her choice. She was so disappointed. I suggested she could return to school to re-sit a couple of subjects and with extra study could still attain the required results. She would have none of it so I suggested that she could go to one of the new Colleges of Advanced Technology instead. I truly ached for her and decided to let the matter rest for the moment.

Later she applied to several colleges and had interviews at three or four. Arthur took her in the car to all the places and Glen went along too. I cannot honestly recall exactly where they went but Arthur made those long journeys gladly despite Elsie being rather ungracious at times. In the end she decided to accept the furthest away - Hitchin, near London.

Glenys sat her O level exams and passed with a good result enabling her go to the VI Form in the autumn term. She too was working at a hotel in Llandudno during the summer holidays. Both girls were getting work experience and earning money that they used to buy clothes and save a little. It was hard work but they enjoyed it. Arthur and I worried now and again, but we knew they were sensible girls and we had done our best to give them a good start with the right values. They had been allowed to go out dancing and to cinemas and so on, but Arthur was always available and willing to collect them from venues should they not have a lift home - they only had to 'phone. The time was known as the 'swinging sixties', but despite that, I believe they were far safer times than the present.

Arrangements had been made for Elsie to live with an elderly widow who wanted a lodger. Elsie would have her own bed sitting room and would be quite independent. I bought a Baby Belling cooker, an electric iron and kettle and everything else that she needed. We also had a shopping spree for clothes and that was a nightmare! She had good taste, but I was so embarrassed sometimes when she would have the assistants bring this and that and half the shop sometimes and then would leave without a purchase. This is perhaps what we should all do unless we are totally happy about purchasing clothes. In a similar situation I would not buy either if it was not what I wanted, but I would feel a bit guilty and be rather apologetic in my thanks knowing the trouble and time they'd taken over my demanding requests. She didn't feel like this at all and saw it as a right to make demands on shop staff, who were being paid to please customers.

I remember the day we took Elsie to Letchworth and found the house where she would stay. It was a lovely house with a nice garden, and the lady was pleasant although a little patronising in her manner, but was obviously glad to have company. We settled Elsie into her room and saw that everything was in place and then it became time to go. I can still see her leaning out of the window and waving farewell, and even though she was quite composed there was a forlorn look about her. The exam disappointment knocked her for six and there was a subtle change in her. She grew a hard exterior to protect her vulnerability. She has a high intelligence and learns very quickly, but does not like protracted study. In the event it proved to be an advantage for her to study at a C.A.T. College in view of the fact that she would later go to work with I.C.I. and get promotion to a senior post within the company.

Arthur and I went home feeling glad that Elsie had found good digs, but within six weeks we received a letter saying that she had to leave because the landlady needed the room for a lady from Europe, a refugee who had been a close friend. This was worrying news because we were so far away. However, Elsie had met a girl at college whose family had fled from Kenya at the time of terror under Idi Amin, the cruel Dictator. They had very kindly offered to have Elsie to stay at their home until she could find somewhere else to stay and that was a relief.

Meanwhile the Llanrwst Manweb office had closed and I had started to work in Llandudno. I felt so glad that I had passed my driving test and could travel to work by car. There was a train available and buses too but they were not as convenient as the car and the time spent travelling on them would have been lengthy and tiring.

There were two open plan offices either side of a long corridor behind the shop, a typing-pool room and smaller offices for the bosses. All staff members in our office were female except for one male who was our superior. I sat opposite him. We were a happy crowd and I liked every one of them. They were all different, but each one was pleasant and friendly. I settled in very quickly and soon knew the routine. As I said earlier I dealt with the disconnection of electricity supply for non-payment of bills, but there was a strict system of procedure before any supply was cut off. First the bill was sent, then a reminder, then a letter threatening disconnection on a certain date. If there still was no payment then we had to obtain a Magistrate's warrant and then send a recorded letter giving the date and time of the proposed disconnection. Then an electrician would go to the premises accompanied by a policeman and if necessary, break in to disconnect the supply. If this meant that a window had to be broken, it was then made secure with a temporary cover until such time as it was repaired. Any reconnection would be charged for. In some instances, outside engineers would have to disconnect the supply from an electricity pole outside the premises, and that would be even more costly to reconnect. It was nonsense when people complained that they had not been warned of a disconnection. In one case, in addition to the Police we had to arrange for a man from the R.S.P.C.A. to accompany the electrician to carry out a disconnection because the customer had a fierce dog that he encouraged to attack the men. The man took great delight in doing this but he was finally thwarted when the R.S.P.C.A. man used a long pole at the end of which was a snap-on cover that fitted over the dog's head. Households with children present were always viewed sympathetically.

Disconnection letters had to be sent by recorded delivery, but if the postman failed to get anyone to receive and sign for the letter then Jim our Supervisor and I had to go together to stick the letter securely onto the door of the house. Many times I had to listen to verbal abuse, but it did not bother me at all. Once, a woman shouted at me so loudly over the phone, that I had to hold the telephone receiver at arm's length and everyone in the office could hear her. It would appear that a supply engineer had cut off the supply to her ice-cream kiosk on the beach and all the ice-cream had melted away. She had been warned many times that she must pay her mounting electricity bills, but to no avail - she had failed to take heed of the advice given and suffered the consequences. Others phoned to complain about food in fridges and freezers going to waste. Most were chronic bad payers and guilty of blaming others for their own irresponsibility.

On many occasions I helped customers, especially young mums who had fallen behind with payments. We had a small booth available where customers could talk confidentially to staff about their financial difficulties and I found that if we were sympathetic and they were prepared to co-operate we could always work out a payment plan to suit them. I warned them that if they failed to comply or did not inform us of any snags then I would have to arrange disconnection. The majority did co-operate and managed to clear their debt. It was obvious to me that many of those young women had not the foggiest idea about budgeting and living within their means. No one had ever taught them at home or school how to manage their income and expenditure. Once they'd been shown, then many coped quite well in avoiding further debt.

The weight of work at the Llandudno office was much lighter than in Llanrwst. That is not to say that we did not work steadily all day and every day, but the pressure of too much work was gone and it meant that I could finally concentrate on the specific job genre for which I was responsible. Travelling every day gave me plenty of practice in driving and I really enjoyed it. Practice really does make perfect, yes indeed!

We were all home for Christmas and my mother was quite well considering everything. She had made good steady progress and was managing to get about reasonably well with the aid of a stick. She was eating properly and enjoying life in her own way. We arranged for her to have her hair permed and she was quite chuffed: her hair was thick and strong and looked well. By this time she was the only grandparent left and Elsie, Glenys and Bryn thought the world of her. They had a good relationship and were on easy-going-terms with her and with my father too when he was alive: they used the familiar *"ti"* (thou) in conversation. They loved their other Taid and Nain too, but their manner towards them was more deferential and they used the more formal *"chi"* (you), which is how Taid and Nain *Gaerwen* spoke to each other too.

When the children were still in primary school and went to stay with my parents in Llanfair, which they frequently did, my mother prepared well for their visit by stacking favourite things in the pantry. Bryn's favourite tinned Mandarin oranges were stacked next to other treats such as biscuits, chocolates and sweets, many of which had been carefully hidden away to be doled out on suitable occasions. Elsie in particular learned a lot from her Nain - how to clean out a fowl, how to cook it and make a meal. Taid made bows and arrows for them and took them for walks. All four grandparents will continue to live on while my children are alive.

We enjoyed Christmas and it was so good to have the family together again but we all missed Taid and his cheerfulness, especially first thing in the morning when he would come downstairs to the living room and announced himself with a deep, booming, "Morning."

All good things come to an end and everyone had to return to work after the festivities. I drove Elsie back to Hitchin, to her friend's home where I had been invited to stay overnight. They were very pleasant people and very welcoming. During dinner they described the terror they had experienced before being forced to leave Kenya and finding safety in the UK.

It froze hard overnight but the morning was clear and bright with sunshine, and before I could start my journey home I had to call at a garage to have a nail taken out of a tyre and have the damage repaired. I left about 11.00a.m. and made good progress until I approached the Midlands where traffic was heavier and I noticed what seemed like the odd white feather floating down at first except they were not feathers, but snow flakes. I felt an awful foreboding and hoped against hope that the flakes did not augur a snowfall. The sunshine had gone but it was still bright, so onward I sped, and by then was confident enough in my driving to travel at speed. Then I noticed the sky become grey and heavy with snow, and then darker still and very soon vehicles were displaying low lights. It was no use switching on headlights because they blurred everything - by then the snowflakes were falling heavily and sticking fast. The wind rose and was blowing from the north. Pretty soon 4 inches of snow lay on the ground and I was attempting to drive my offside wheels in the track of a lorry in front. The back of the car was swinging and swaying but I managed to put all fears out of my mind by concentrating on steering the car in the track on the road and ignoring the falling snow being swished across the windscreen by the wipers. I was approaching a very big roundabout at Whitchurch and wondered if the brakes would stop the car without its sliding on the snow into the path of other vehicles. By this time there were fewer cars about, but still plenty of trucks and lorries. As luck would have it, I did not have to stop at the roundabout and was able to slowly make my way round it. Although the snow was thick on the ground the road ahead was level with no hills to worry about and I steadily made my way to Llangollen. Then the climbing started and it was very scary with the car sliding about. Traffic was light so I had the road to myself most of the time. I passed through the stillness of the villages and Corwen but I was very aware that I had very little petrol left in the tank. I decided that I would have to try to get some at Cerrig y Drudion and Providence was with me.

There was a car at the pump and I eased up towards it as the other car drove off. The attendant was still there which meant that I could stay in the car. I switched off the engine and felt better knowing that I had fuel anyway. I paid the man and switched on again starting off in second gear as Arthur had taught me to do in snow. I could not see a thing as I drove along the straight sections of the A5 because the wind was blowing a blizzard of snow across from right to left and there were no hedges to follow. The lights of a car came out of the gloom so I stopped, but after it had passed I knew where the road was and was able to move straight ahead slowly, keeping the steering wheel steady all the way through Pentrefoelas and down towards Betws y Coed. A mile or so from Betws the snow was falling as sleet and when I reached the turning for Llanrwst there was no snow at all on the road. I could not believe my eyes, but nevertheless I was extremely pleased to see those conditions and know that I was then safe. At home everyone was glad to see me but they were quite unaware of the bad weather elsewhere. Within twenty minutes of my arrival Glenys called out that it had just been announced on the television that the A5 was blocked by snow and closed to traffic. I thanked God for my safe return.

Chapter Forty-Two

GOOD JOB I LEARNED TO DRIVE

My cousin Doris inherited our house on her father's death and we paid rent to her for a few years until she decided to sell the property. She gave us the chance of first refusal. We chose to buy it despite having paid rent for almost twenty years. Arthur and I paid a visit to her farm with a view to making a deal: Arthur and Doris would negotiate and agree a price. He was much better than I in matters of business within close family. They haggled - Arthur made a bid, but it was not enough, so he withdrew. Doris was in the kitchen preparing a meal at the time of speaking with Arthur. Her husband and I were in the living room and after a while Arthur joined us. "How is it going?" asked Albert her husband. "Not well. She is as immovable as a rock," said Arthur. To our amazement he said, "Keep going Arthur, don't give in easily. She is bound to give way in the end." And so she did, bless her heart. We bought the house at a very reasonable price. We still had to raise the money, so I wrote to Fergus Armstrong and explained the situation to him. I asked if he would be kind enough to lend us the capital and we would repay him by instalments over a short period. Within two days the cheque had arrived by post and subject to the usual procedures we were then the owners of our home. We felt quite proud, but had to work out how to repay the money. Fergus was so good, he did not charge a penny in interest and it took us just over two years to repay him in full.

I shall always be grateful to Uncle Edward, Fergus, and Doris for helping us along the way to owning our own home. They knew we were honest, trustworthy and appreciative but even so, it was very generous of them. I saved sums of £250.00, then travelled by car to Treorchy on days off periodically to pay Fergus. In winter I stayed at the Bear Hotel in Newtown overnight on my way down and travelled over the Brecon Beacons and down the valleys in the morning. Fergus and I got to know each other very well in that time. Once, he invited me to join him in Llandudno at the Grand Hotel for lunch. A liner with Americans on board used to anchor off Llandudno each year and passengers would be ferried into town. That particular time, Fergus was expecting a guest from the liner to join him at the Grand, the widow of an American Doctor who had been a prisoner of war with him working in a hospital in Rumania with Queen Marie. Fergus knew Llandudno quite well because he had spent many holidays there staying at the Craigside Hotel. I accepted the invitation despite feeling nervous of playing hostess for a man who had dined with Edward, Prince of Wales, Lord Davies of Llandinam and other distinguished and important high ranking people. Although a stickler for manners, Fergus was always at ease without any airs and graces, so his guests were also at ease. We had a lovely lunch, but unfortunately the lady guest did not arrive. As the sea was rather choppy that day we concluded that perhaps she was not feeling comfortable and safe enough to travel ashore in the ferry - she was elderly after all. We learned later that she had not been able to board the liner at all because she had become ill before it set sail. I enjoyed the occasion at the Grand with Fergus and notched up another interesting experience.

As Easter approached and I took time off to do my spring cleaning again, we had to plan things a little differently because Mam was with us. She took it all in her stride and far from complaining about the disruption, took a keen interest and even helped to do small jobs. This gave me a chance to get on with things as we were having a new floor laid in the kitchen and some cupboards and cabinets fitted too. We were doing away with the spence which was the broom cupboard under the stairs in order to make a doorway from the kitchen through to the lobby. Once the workmen had completed their tasks there was much cleaning and decorating to do: Arthur made a professional job of the paper hanging and the rest of us got stuck into the painting, clearing up and clcaning jobs. Somehow, by working all hours of the day and most of the night we completed the planned jobs. Arthur was also away every Saturday adjudicating at Eisteddfodau in various places.

In May it was Glenys' seventeenth birthday and she wanted to learn to drive. Everything was arranged and she started with Arthur, who said she was a natural driver. We took her out in the car as often as we could to help her improve her skills. One sultry Sunday afternoon after tea, Glenys asked if one of us would accompany her for a practice drive along the Conwy Valley road. Having other things to do at the end of the weekend I was rather reluctant at first, but finally agreed to go as far as the Talycafn Hotel. Off we went and Glen was driving very well indeed, and on reaching a suitable turning point just beyond the destination, turned the car round to return home. It was very quiet on the road that Sunday afternoon with only a couple of cars coming towards us. We passed the Maenan Abbey Hotel and negotiated a series of bends for about half a mile at a speed of around 35m.p.h then came up to *Tyn Ddol farm* where there was a sharp bend in the road. Suddenly, a car driver travelling towards us came fast out of the bend, spinning his car round as he did, then hitting our car on the driver's side and ending up with his vehicle pointing in the wrong direction. The driver must have approached the bend in the road much too fast.

We could not get out of the car because there was just an inch between the passenger door and the roadside wall, and the driver's door was jammed. Glenys was hopping mad and that was her salvation I think. She was not crying or shaking or feeling frightened, just totally furious with the other driver who had by then approached us to see if we were alright. He was extremely shaken, ashen white and very apologetic. Passing motorists stopped at the scene and forced Glen's door open, enabling us to get out of the car. Finally the Police arrived who told Glenys there was no fault on her part because she had clearly steered as much to the left as possible away from the oncoming vehicle. Insurance particulars were obtained then the Police took Glen and me home.

From then on Arthur took care of everything. Our Hillman Minx was a well-built, robust car which is why we were both unhurt. It also helped that we had not been travelling fast. Both front tyres were flat, the doors were buckled, so too the engine, but amazingly, the windows were all intact. However the car was a write-off. The young chap who caused the accident was a representative for a drinks firm who had driven all the way from Oxford that day. He could possibly have been feeling sleepy at that stage in his journey on that sultry afternoon. It was also a time before motorists involved in accidents were breathalysed. It is believed that having managed to travel fast along the few miles leading up to the sharp bend at *Ty'n Ddol farm* he came upon it unexpectedly, went into it too fast, failed to reduce the speed sufficiently and lost control of the car.

A court case was held in the old courthouse at Betws y Coed where the Police charged the driver with 'Dangerous Driving' initially, then reduced it to 'Driving without due care and attention'. On the day of the hearing however, there was deep snow everywhere and local people struggled to get to the courthouse, but the chap being prosecuted failed to attend. The case was postponed for several weeks and when it finally took place the chap got away scot free. He claimed his car had skidded on the road because it was wet causing him to lose control, whereas the truth of the matter was that at the time of the accident the road was dry. It was only afterwards when we were standing around waiting for the Police to arrive that it started raining and Glen and I got back into the car for shelter, but the prosecution could not prove him wrong! The Police Inspector said in court that there was not a vestige of fault on the part of Glenys and that she had acted very responsibly. Shortly after, Glenys passed her Driving Test first time.

In late spring Elsie managed to find new digs. She had joined three other girls in an arrangement to rent a groud floor flat in Letchworth. Two of the girls were Irish waitresses, the other was a clerk in an office. Elsie had warned us that the flat was not as nice as they would have liked, and that it could never be mistaken for *The Ritz*! When I took her back for the new term, I helped her to clean the place, but I was very concerned because there was a problem with condensation there and the flat was damp.

For some time Bryn had been complaining of a pain in his knee. He was a very good footballer and sometimes played in goal. He loved to jump, dive and do all the acrobatic things that goalkeepers do. After a game he would come home in agony and sit with his leg straight out in front until it clicked and he could move again. Our concerns were such that we took him to see Dr. Chown, our G.P. who said that Bryn had damaged cartilage and would have to have an operation. This took place in the Abergele Cottage Hospital - the old Manchester Sanatorium. An older man who'd had the operation explained to us that it was an extremely painful operation and would take some weeks before he could walk properly. He advised Bryn to do exactly as he was told. He himself had been foolish and disregarded the advice and paid the price by having to return for more surgery. Bryn was very sensible and did exactly as he was told, but he still missed several weeks of schooling. No professional person provided hospital or home tuition for Bryn during that time and no one from the school offered to help him with the work he'd missed: he inevitably fell behind with his studies at an extremely important stage in his educational development - when he was 14 years of age. It was a crying shame it happened as it did. Bryn's knee eventually settled down and he was then as right as rain, able to attend school again and play football eventually. We were all extremely worried about Bryn at this stage because he had so many things stacked against him, and none of them of his own making. Everyone knew how intelligent he was and recognised openly that his potential was not being realised. His school was failing him - it just did not seem to have any provision available for children who missed school through long-term ill health. We all agonised over Bryn's misfortune - Glen tried her best to help him because she cared deeply for her younger brother and wanted him to achieve his potential, but at the time did not have the necessary skills to support him as successfully as she would do today.

Glenys had taken her 'A level' exams and succeeded in doing well enough to go to College. She and I visited many shops in Llandudno and Chester to buy new clothes in preparation for the start of her 3 year teacher training course at the Normal College in Bangor. Arthur and I had been very successful that summer with B&B visitors, many of whom were from the European Continent: we could afford to kit Glenys out well. As a family we also obtained tickets for a whole week of opera performed by the Welsh National Opera at the Winter Gardens in Llandudno. We really looked forward to that week each summer in the knowledge that we would experienced high standards of music and drama and thoroughly enjoy each performance.

There were rumours at work that the Manweb district office in Llandudno would close and amalgamate with the office in Rhyl, but nothing had been said officially. In addition, the office clerk who shared a flat with Elsie and two Irish girls got married and moved to live in Scotland where her husband had a good job in the field of computers. It meant that the Irish girls could no longer afford to stay on and would have to leave in a few weeks. Once again Elsie did not know where to turn. All the addresses on the official college register had been taken up and there were no vacancies advertised. Earlier on in late spring, Glenys and I had gone to Letchworth to help clean up the house and make it a bit more comfortable for Elsie and the other girls. During our stay Elsie, Glenys and I went to Cambridge for the day in our car. We spent a pleasant time walking round the town seeing its attractions, looking for, and finding an excellent restaurant for our evening meal, which incidentally I failed to locate on another visit to Cambridge some years later when I attended a Manweb Summer School.

We also went by train to London to see the play 'The Mousetrap' at the Drury Lane Theatre. We enjoyed it very much, so much that we decided to stay until the very end thereby cutting it fine and risking not catching the last train to Letchworth that night: a decision made worse by not having checked the location of the nearest Tube Station beforehand! We hurried out of the theatre as soon as the play had finished and looked round frantically for a policeman who could give directions. Then we spotted one and Elsie rushed up to him and asked, "Do you know where the Tube station for Letchworth is please?" In her hurry she had not chosen her words well! Quite unaware that we were at the mercy of the clock, he replied jokingly, "Yes … do you?" She could have thumped him except that he represented the Law. When Glenys and I rushed up breathlessly the policeman got the drift of what was going on and told us exactly what we wanted to know. Off we went full pelt to reach the platform just as the train was leaving the station - the last one that night! A helpful porter suggested taking the next train to Hitchin, which was nearer to Letchworth than London. We took his advice and arrived at Hitchin very late, much too late to think of walking, so we had to hire a taxi. However we returned safe and sound which was good. Later on we had a good laugh about Elsie and the policeman!

In the long term Elsie was getting worried. In spite of her extensive efforts she could not find anywhere to live. However, one morning on my way to work in Llandudno, I called at the Llandudno Junction Manweb shop as usual to collect the mail for the District office. I passed the time of day with the Manager of the shop, the late Mr. Bill Wakelin, and purely by chance somehow, reference was made to Elsie's predicament and he said, "Wait a minute. I've got a sister living in Letchworth and her husband has just died. Her house is quite large. I think perhaps she might like to have a lodger. I'll phone her tonight and find out what she thinks of the idea." And that is how Elsie was lucky enough to move into Mrs. Charteris' house where she was most comfortable and lived there until she finished at college.

Elsie brought a cat home when she arrived for the Christmas holiday after leaving the flat. It had belonged to the girl who got married, and Elsie had phoned to ask if we would allow her to bring it home because she could not abandon it to its fate. We had to consider the matter carefully as we already had two cats. There was Toodles, Bryn's cat - a big, fine-looking black and white Tom, a real gentleman with wonderful manners. Then there was Pwji Pwj (Figaro), the cat we had given to Taid *Llanfair* that came with Nain to live with us when Taid died. He was a Tomcat too, small, fierce and streetwise who sometimes got into scraps with other cats. He would tease Toodles until the bigger cat got fed up with Pwj and would give him a sharp clip over the ears, which meant an end to the teasing and fighting, resulting in peace again. After some weeks of being together they came to an understanding and lived quite happily together. Toodles, was gentle, but was without a doubt the boss, and Pwj knew that: he learned to be subordinate, but only to Toodles. All other felines were aliens to be chased away.

Having been assured that the 'saved' cat was house-trained we decided that Elsie could bring her home to live with us. On arrival she was not happy at all with two Toms in residence and must have decided that she was the boss because they did not hiss or snarl but she did! In the end the two Toms decided to ignore her completely. Her name was Sherry because of her colouring and I have never before or since seen such a beautiful cat. She was fluffy, her underside was cream coloured, gradually deepening upwards through tan to dark ginger. There were dark stripes all the way from the top of her head to the tip of her tail, which was long and bushy. Her face was a deep cream colour with long whiskers and deep green eyes. She looked and walked like a Queen and eventually established her superiority, at which time the household settled down.

At Easter time the weather was superbly sunny and warm and I was busy spring cleaning. I am sorry about this recurring theme and must admit that it is my one and only obsession. On the Saturday afternoon somehow we were all out except Mam who was in bed as usual. She was never the same after her last stay in hospital because she had lost confidence and her spirit was more subdued, but she still retained her sense of humour. When we returned home, no one had a key to get into the house, we were locked out, but fortunately the lower part of Mam's bedroom window was open so Kerry, who was Glenys's boyfriend went to fetch a ladder from the school next door and climbed in through the open window fully expecting to have to calm Mam and stop her screams because she had never seen him before. Well the truth is that as soon as he stood up at the open window and looked towards Mam inside sitting up in bed she said, “Who are you then and what do you want?” as cool as a cucumber!

Anyhow, in the evening at suppertime, Toodles and Pwj turned up as usual for their feed and we thought it was strange that Sherry was not there too. We never saw her again! Everyone was upset and Bryn went looking everywhere for her, but there was no sign of her, dead or alive. She was quite happy with us and was treated very well and would not have run away or gone with anyone of her own free will. She would have scratched, bitten and snarled at anyone who tried to pick her up. I think I know what happened. There was a large car park behind our house before the swimming pool was built, where lorries parked and drivers rested. On that warm sunny day I believe Sherry might have jumped into one of those lorries and fallen asleep. When the lorry drove off she might not have been able to jump out. I have wondered many times what befell that beautiful cat. We missed her terribly, including the Toms who were wailing.

Every morning I helped Mam to wash herself, get dressed and into her easy chair - she could not get downstairs any longer. Even though the toilet was next door on the landing we put a commode in the bedroom because we were afraid she might fall downstairs en route. We went through this routine every day, but since starting work in Llandudno I found it difficult to get Mam to accomplish the tasks with me before having to set off for work. Arthur therefore ended up bearing the brunt of her care during the day, taking her breakfast and lunch on a tray: I took over when I came home around 5.30p.m.

In late spring however, Mam deteriorated quickly because she could not stand without help and had to start wearing large sanitary towels for her bladder weakness. During the day, Arthur would change and fit these for her and it is to his eternal credit that he did it without complaint. She was a proud and independent woman and must have suffered great mental stress as her condition worsened. Arthur had great respect and liking for her and that I think is why he did not baulk at looking after her in such a personal way. Slowly, things got more difficult. Mam had a walking stick with which she banged the floor if she needed something. This became a constant recurrence and interfered with Arthur's work when he gave piano lessons to his pupils. In the end it was a case of no sooner had he been upstairs to attend to whatever was required and returned downstairs again to re-start his work, than there was further banging on the floor of the bedroom. It was as if she was frightened of being alone. It was obvious however, that he and his work were suffering. I did not know what to do for the best. We were all suffering.

We had looked after grandparents for over twenty years - eight of those in our own home during which time our children were growing into adults and I had acted as a buffer between the generations. They were old and vulnerable and we had never thought other than we should look after them. Only my father had passed away without seeking help and succour even though he also was not well. Now however, the situation had changed. In the end I felt drained and decided to visit my G.P. to request a tonic to act as a pick-me-up. Dr. Chown knew our family well, he was a keen musician, and was very observant and caring. He questioned me and I was glad to receive his advice. I told him that I hated the thought of my mother going into a nursing home, but what else was there to do? The Doctor said, "Look at the facts. You have come to me for medicine, which means that there is something wrong, and there is. You are under a great deal of stress and unless you give way you will really fall very ill and what will happen then? Besides, your mother needs full time nursing care now. You have done your best all these years. You have nothing to blame yourself for … you must let her go now for everyone's sake."

I knew in my heart that the Doctor was right, but the awful sorrow that I felt for my mother weighed heavily on me. Arthur agreed with Doctor Chown and I contacted my mother's Doctor in Llanfair. He came and saw for himself how things were at that time. He spoke so kindly to my mother and explained that she needed special care in hospital and promised to arrange things. Because she was still registered with Dr. Jones in Llanfair she had to have attention in the region covering that village which was Clwyd, whilst we were in Gwynedd. The upshot was that she became a patient at a hospital in Holywell, a town that was quite a distance away. I went to see her once a fortnight after work, sometimes more often in the summer. She was in very good hands. The nurses were wonderful, so kind and thoughtful, nothing was too much trouble, and best of all, Mam was content.

I must confess that the relief was enormous, a great weight lifted off my shoulders, but still a sense of guilt haunted me from time to time because of my being able to have a little time to do the things I enjoyed: reading, singing, gardening and improving our home. This I will say: unless you have actually experienced this type of situation you cannot possibly know what it is like and you should never tell anyone else how to cope with it. In all, we had our parents who were also our children's grandparents, living with us in our home during eight years and certainly their presence impinged on our life as a family. At times it was difficult and hard to bear, but it was also rewarding and instructive. We all learned tolerance and appreciation.

Chapter Forty-Three

UPS AND DOWNS

Over the years we had worked very hard to improve our home by decorating it to our taste, and from time to time buying new furniture, curtains and carpets. We had removed old fire grates and installed modern ones, and had workmen put in a new floor in the kitchen then fit new kitchen units. We'd had heavy iron railings at the front of the house removed and Arthur had built a low brick wall with a cavity to hold soil in which we had put lovely plants. He and Bryn had built the curved wall round the back yard because it bulged and we feared its collapse and potential to cause damage to man and beast. We had also improved the yard at the back of the house.

We already had a small lawn with a long double step onto it with lots of flowers. It really was a very pretty space, especially in the summer. There was a peach tree growing espalier fashion on our next door neighbour's wall that looked delightful. That small external patio area was a real sun trap, and after the old houses had been demolished behind Watling Street, the high surrounding wall gave us a very private relaxing area. The only snag then being insufficient time for relaxing, except for very short periods here and there during the day. Nevertheless, just looking at it was soothing and pleasing.

Now that Mam was in hospital, the bedroom she had occupied and Arthur's parents before her, was in need of a complete refurbishment. We had a washbasin installed, decorated it from top to bottom, with new curtains, carpet and furniture. This operation and the annual spring clean took the usual two weeks over Easter plus many extra hours at weekends.

Then we received a letter from a young man called Neville who was asking for permission to get engaged to Elsie. We knew she had a boyfriend because we had met Neville, but had not realised that the relationship had progressed that far. He had completed his studies and was a graduate Chemical Engineer working for I.C.I. on Teeside. Elsie was to leave college at the end of the summer term and they were hoping to get married in August. Arthur and I discussed the request and talked about things with Elsie and decided that they were both sensible and understood what they were about to do, so we agreed to their plans, which meant some very busy months ahead. It was a happy occasion, my spirits were lifted and I could stretch my wings a little again. There was more fun around, or perhaps I was feeling more aware of outside interests and reacting accordingly. Arthur was busier than ever and was away every Saturday at Festivals, which meant long hours and loss of sleep for him because of having to be back home for the Sunday morning services in Chapel. He really enjoyed these engagements and the adrenalin flowed. Periodically however, there followed a time of coming down to earth with fatigue, and once at such a period I unwisely badgered him to paper the walls of one of the main bedrooms because he was so good at doing the job with support with the pasting and cleaning. He somehow finished the job despite his fatigue and Elsie, Glenys and I complimented him on the results. But what happened next!

At the time Arthur was displaying similar symptoms to his father by complaining of stomach pains and indigestion. I suggested once again that he should give up smoking because there was increasing evidence in the media that smoking caused serious health problems. At the time he was smoking even more than ever, but he heeded not the advice.

In June, Glenys' boyfriend Kerry completed his teacher training course at the Normal College and secured a teaching job at St Mark's CE School in Worsley, near Manchester which was to start in September. In order to pay his way through the summer months he'd also found a holiday job collecting rents in the Wrexham area where he lived with his parents. He had an Austin A30 car that he used round about college and to travel to Llanrwst and Wrexham.

On the Saturday morning after finishing in Bangor Kerry phoned us to say that he and Glenys had been in a car accident the previous night that he had sustained a broken arm and Glenys was quite badly hurt. He said they had both received treatment in hospital and needed to be collected because his car was a wreck. The news came as a shock, but I set out straight away and Kerry told me to go to the Outpatients Department at the C. & A. Hospital at Bangor.

Later, Kerry told me of his apprehension about phoning me, fearing I would blame him for the accident and injury to Glenys: he said he could hardly believe it when he heard my voice sounding so calm and normal. Well, I suppose it was because my mind was racing ahead to get to the hospital as quickly as possible, but also I knew that Kerry never drank alcohol.

The weather that June morning was lovely, and after parking the car I went to look for Glenys and found rows of chairs outside the Outpatients Department with patients sitting in the sunshine. I too sat and waited and was shocked when she finally came towards me because she was hardly recognisable. Her face was badly swollen especially round the mouth, her hair was matted with blood and she looked unkempt. Glenys was limping and her leg was swollen, painful and heavily bandaged. She was still in shock from the accident and crying. She was also very thirsty so I found a nurse and asked if it was possible for my daughter to have a cup of tea. I was told that it was Saturday and no refreshments were available despite my being able to see a kettle, mugs and condiments in a kitchen. I suppose the nurses were so busy they could not spare the time, but several minutes later a nurse brought her a glass of water which was greatfully accepted. We then waited for Glenys to be seen by a doctor again that morning.

Kerry had sustained a compound fracture to his arm and had already had a plastercast fitted and a sling to hold it in place. He'd managed by then to get hold of most of the facts, and was able to tell us what happened because Glenys could not remember a thing from the previous evening. The accident happened in a part of Bangor called 'The Lookout' as they were driving home from attending an end-of-year student dinner at an Indian restaurant. As they approached the top of the hill Kerry suddenly saw a car come tearing round the bend at the top towards them, it flipped over mid-air and finally landed on top of their car. Glenys went head-first through the windscreen and back again and Kerry's arm was broken with a compound fracture. Those were the days before the seat-belt legislation had been introduced. The whole car was buckled and damaged, but he managed to get out and got Glenys out too. She was unconscious and therefore difficult to move, and although several cars passed by, no one stopped. Luckily, Mike, one of Kerry's housemate came along and was shocked to see what had happened. He helped to lay Glenys on the pavement, where she was in and out of consciousness and crying in pain. Kerry explained to her what had happened, but it did not seem to sink in and she kept asking what had happened over and over again. Mike took them to hospital in his car.

The two men in the offending car were drunk and had somehow managed to sustain only minor scratches, or so Kerry was told. The hospital dealt with them first for some reason, maybe because they realised just how angry Kerry was with them. Fortunately, Kerry still had his wits about him even during the aftermath of the accident and had managed to get all the particulars that the police required. Kerry was next to receive treatment, and then lastly, Glenys, who was the most badly hurt of all.

The nursing staff dealt with her leg that night, they also put fifteen stitches in the zig-zag wounds under her chin and six in her upper lip on the inside and out. Kerry said she had moaned about the back of her head too that night but no one appeared to have listened and therefore no attention was paid to it. She had still not been fully conscious and totally aware at three o'clock in the morning when they were discharged and told to leave. Mike stayed with them throughout and took them to the house until the morning. He truly was a good Samaritan to them that night, and they were enormously grateful to him for his kindness and generosity of spirit.

They returned to the hospital the following morning, Saturday, as instructed. Glenys had to wait a long time and was attended to briefly and told to return to the Clinic on Monday morning. She was still complaining about the back of her head, but it was difficult to see anything because of her blood-matted hair. I told the staff that I intended taking Glenys to Llandudno Hospital on Monday and requested a medical note to take with me. The journey there was shorter from Llanrwst, but Glenys had also lost a front tooth and I really was not at all happy about the way she had been treated in Bangor, in a way that seemed to have been rather offhand.

Later in the day, having returned to Llanrwst and rested a while, Glenys still as white as a sheet and complaining about her head, agreed for me to clean her hair sufficiently to have a better view of her scalp. And there, under the matted hair and blood, was a wound about seven inches long. I bathed and cleaned it gently with diluted Dettol and covered it lightly. On Monday at Llandudno the nurses were very concerned when they realised it had not been discovered and attended to on Friday night, but of course professional conduct would not have allowed them to be too critical.

Eventually, we came to learn that the two men in the offending car had been drinking, had no licence or insurance, and had equipment in the boot of their car used in burglaries. In addition to this, the tyres on their car were bald. They were arrested, tried in court and given a two month suspended sentence. During the period of the suspended sentence they were arrested for another crime, then tried for it and finally served six months in prison.

Kerry had not only lost his car, but his summer holiday rent-collecting job too because of his injuries. Glenys had not only sustained the obvious injuries, but had lost a front tooth and felt battered, bruised and very sore and was still in shock for some time after the accident. Kerry's car was a write-off and neither he nor Glenys could work that summer, so things were pretty grim for them. To make matters worse, because the offenders had no insurance, Kerry had to contact the Motor Insurance Board, a body set up to help the victims of accidents where insurance was unavailable. What a palaver it was for them in having to go to Gobowen to have their injuries assessed, going to Liverpool periodically to the offices of the Motor Insurance Board, going to their Solicitor regularly in Wrexham, having to wait long periods in between appointments and worst of all having to personally push the matter along every step of the way! It took four years to obtain £400.00 compensation ... the inadequate amount hardly seemed worthy of all the effort they had put into the process let alone make up for the loss of a car and earnings, the inconvenience of it all, and the personal injuries suffered by them. Glenys was a good patient and we looked after her until she became well again. She was young, strong and healthy thank goodness, and Kerry's arm healed too. Eventually he bought another car.

Elsie came home from college after her course ended in Letchworth, and for 6 weeks prior to her wedding to Neville, worked in the Manweb office at Llandudno with me to earn some money. It was standard practice at Manweb to employ students during the summer holidays in order to give them practical experience of working in a busy office, and help existing staff to clear backlog of filing and cross referencing work.

Neville had managed to rent a large flat above a bakery in Redcar, where they would live after their wedding, but it greatly needed cleaning and decorating. One Friday evening in July Elsie and I left work in Llandudno just after 5.00p.m, and began our journey to Redcar in Yorkshire. It was my first visit to the area and I knew it would be dark when we arrived. It was a long journey at a time before the M56 and M62 had been built and there were always long delays round Helsby and Frodsham. Elsie was not a driver then and could not share the task. The traffic was heavy and at first Elsie navigated well but gradually, having done a day's work became sleepy and stopped giving me directions. She just did not want to wake up and I had to shout to wake her at crucial points in the journey: between us we somehow reached our destination. I will never forget my first sight of the I.C.I. works at Wilton - as we came down towards the sea at Redcar in the dark we saw a sight that resembled fairyland - there were thousands of lights in yellow, white, green and red. During daylight of course it looked quite different when we could see only steel structures, gantries and chimneys, so very drab and utilitarian and in complete contrast to the attractive night view.

We were exhausted on arrival at Redcar so we ate a light meal and went to bed only to rise again at 6 o'clock to start decorating. Neville and I did most of the painting whilst Elsie saw to the meals and the task of unpacking all the bits and pieces we had taken with us. It was very hot weather and I was standing on top of a table painting the ceiling clad only in my underwear. The flat was up the stairs above the shop, and when we heard footsteps on the stairs, Elsie called to me to get dressed properly because someone had arrived. Well, I had not come all that way to waste time so I called back saying, “I am not coming down from this table so if anyone is nervous of seeing me in my slip then they had better not come in.” We worked very hard indeed all day and the following day too. The living room, which was long, large and airy, was transformed with a bit of colour and elbow grease. We scrubbed the wooden floor, then stained it. The large green carpet square that Arthur and I had bought in Liverpool all those years ago was laid in front of the electric fire and suddenly there was a hearth and a home! We had supper, then Elsie and I set off home at 8.00p.m. Neville had been urging us to leave earlier, but I wanted to finish what we had set out to do. We left with tired muscles, but with great satisfaction in our hearts too.

It was the early hours of Monday morning when we reached Llanrwst, but despite that fact, we were still on time for work again in Llandudno later that morning. Of course there was also all the excitement of planning the big day: the invitations and the service and reception, without forgetting the trip to Liverpool to buy *the* dress. There were so many beautiful ones to choose from, but there was one special very close-fitting one with lace that was a perfect fit for Elsie and suited her as if it had been made for her. Glenys was the chief bridesmaid of course, and Neville's niece Ann, and Ruth, Elsie's best friend were the other two bridesmaids who all wore beautiful sugar pink dresses. I was so pleased when a beautiful day dawned for Elsie and Neville's wedding. Everything was set: Arthur was to be the organist at the service because he felt his best contribution to the ceremony would be at the organ, and Bryn would give away the bride. He was only 16 years old, but I felt proud of him because he bore himself well and was very dignified. All the men were in morning suits and looked very distinguished. Our Chapel Minister, the Rev. W. E. Thomas, who had christened my three children in infancy and later received them into the fellowship of the Christian Church, was not with us on that day because sadly he had died recently.

Fortunately we were able to arrange for another Minister to officiate at Elsie's wedding, a man who had known Arthur from being a child, and although retired at the time, was nevertheless still very pleased to marry them.

There was a lovely crowd of family members and friends at the wedding and the singing in Chapel was great. There was the usual traditional celebration at the reception, which was held in a very old hostelry, *'The Tal-y-Cafn Hotel'*, situated a little out of town. The oldest person there was Aunty 'Gusta who was the sister of Nain *Gaerwen* (Arthur's mother). There were no grandparents because they were all gone except Mam, poor mam, who was in hospital at the time. Aunty Gusta had written some poetry and was so pleased when called upon to read the verses, at the time she was well into her eighties. On their way to Manchester airport for their honeymoon in Portugal, Elsie and Neville dropped into the hospital to give Mam the bridal bouquet of flowers. That pleased her very much. It had been a really lovely day and everything had gone very well. Of course the whole thing was expensive, but nothing remotely equalling the money paid for weddings today with discos and evening banquets totalling anything between £10,000 and £15,000. Surely this money would be far better spent on helping the young couple to set up their new home.

Together with the feelings of happiness and satisfaction at the end of the day I also felt a trifle sad because the first of the little ones had flown the nest!

Neville, Elsie's husband was a local lad who was Welsh speaking. He worked for I.C.I. as a qualified Chemical Engineer and had lived in Redcar for five or six years. He was already well established with a circle of English and Welsh friends and very soon Elsie too became part of the same coterie. Wherever in the world Welsh people find themselves, they tend to gather together into clubs, and this is how it was in the North East of Yorkshire at the time. The group met regularly and enjoyed the interests they had shared during their time in Wales.

At half term Arthur and Harry set out in Harry's little pick-up to deliver some larger items to Elsie and Neville in their new flat. On the way to north Yorkshire the weather was stormy and wet and suddenly the windscreen wipers stopped working. The brothers decided to tie a piece of string to each blade and for Arthur to hold the string to one blade and pull it steadily alternating with Harry doing the same with the other. It was very tiring especially for Harry who was driving with one hand and doing the windscreen bit with the other. Both had a good sense of humour however, and found it hilarious despite the potential hazards of the incident.

The makeshift wipers got them to Redcar safely. It was still very early in the morning when they parked the pickup and were getting out of it when a group of young lads passed and stared at the sign on the pick-up with the address '*Mochdre,* Colwyn Bay' and one said to the others in a loud voice, "Colwyn Bay, where the hell is that?" Harry, with his usual 'cool' reaction and response said in an even louder voice, "We have just landed from Mars and have come to get you lot," and marched towards them in a very aggressive manner. The youngsters took to their heels and fled leaving Harry and Arthur laughing themselves silly!

Elsie and Neville lived in the flat for a comparatively short period of time before moving to a semi-detached house with gardens at the back and front. The house they chose was directly opposite the starting gate of the Redcar Racecourse. When there was a meeting Elsie and Neville would be in the front garden watching and when the race was televised we'd ring to say we could see them. This went on until the novelty wore off. I liked Redcar as a town, but like some other seaside towns of the time, had its 'grotty' areas too.

In spite of the hectic time before and after Elsie's wedding we still had visitors to cater for - we had only a week kept free to do all that needed doing. In September, my sister Bella and Stan invited me over to the U.S. to 'recuperate'. I have to say that by that time I was feeling rather drained, but when there is work to be done you just have to keep going and do it, but afterwards, when the tiredness arrives and the flat feeling with it, there is only one thing to do … that is to RELAX!.

So, off I went to the U.S.A. for two weeks. I flew alone from Manchester to Toronto airport and there to greet me was the family: Bella, Stan, Raymond, Kenneth and Brian. It was lovely to see them again and I noticed immediately how much the boys had grown since I had last seen them. Ray and Ken were now well established at school and Brian was nearly five years old. Stan drove the car carefully for 150 miles home to Hamburg despite all the chattering and great excitement in the front and back seats. I had to show my Visa as we passed through Customs on the Peace Bridge going over the Niagara River from Canada to the U.S.A. but all was well. We then rode along the Queen Elizabeth Highway passing the big town of Buffalo, and later that week I had the pleasure of watching a game of American Football played by the family's heroes at the world famous Buffalo Bills Stadium.

We relaxed a lot in the garden in the sunshine - the kids had a large inflatable pool and were in and out of it happily splashing water on themselves - and us! But poor Stan had no choice but to be at work some days: he had a very responsible management job at Ford Motors working as a tool and die engineer, but he did manage to have some days off in order to take us out on trips. We roamed around locally and also went sightseeing in specific places of interest further afield - we had a wonderful time together. Stan and Bella were extremely good to me during my visit to them - they went out of their way to give me a first class welcome. Their neighbours and friends were also friendly and welcoming and many invited Bella and me to meals or for drinks in the evening. I have never been one for drinking much, just the odd ones at celebrations and so on, but there was no gainsaying those people - they plied me with unusual cocktails, which tasted very nice, but were also quite potent. One evening we went to the home of an Irish couple, Iris and Norval, who were so pleasant and would not let us go home until it was late. When Norval drove my sister and me home we were singing - she says I was the loudest, but it was the other way about I'd say! As the days went by I grew a bit wiser to the cocktails - I still enjoyed them, but in moderation!

One Sunday I was to sing a solo at Stan and Bella's Church where Stan was a

Sunday School teacher and a leader in special services and ceremonies too. I had received the invitation before leaving Llanrwst and had taken music with me. I went for a practice run on Saturday with the organist and everything was fine, and during the rehearsal they asked me to sing in the choir too. They gave me a copy of the music and I was able to follow and join in quite well. The first Service was at 8.00a.m. All members received a printed programme of each Sunday service and on that particular day the programme had my name on it and an English translation of the song that I would sing in Welsh as requested. The acoustics of the Church were wonderful and I found it easy to sing there. I enjoyed the service and was then taken on a tour of the building. Apart from the Church itself there were many other rooms including an office, a large stainless steel kitchen that could cater for 500 people, and a large carpeted lounge with easy chairs and a grand piano. There were several rooms for individual Sunday School Classes that were used during the week by kindergarten classes and crèches. There were two Pastors who shared the pastoral and preaching work. It was a very impressive Church in many ways including its family-friendly services.

When the early morning Service ended most of us went straight to a Sunday School Class for about 45 minutes and then for coffee or soft drinks in the lounge followed by the last Service that ended at 1.00p.m. Then we were free to do as we pleased. Of course, we did not have to stay on after the first Service and not everyone did, but most people attended all the services.

In the afternoon we went to the Welland Canal and on to the Observation Platform at Lock 3 at St. Catherine's in Canada. This lock is one of seven lift locks on the Welland Canal, a part of the St. Lawrence Seaway system. Ships from all over the world sail through the locks, in and out of the Great Lakes. At the time I was there in September I saw each one in turn pass out to sea, but in colder months some can be locked in all winter. It was fascinating to see the operation - I had never seen anything like it before.

Another time we went to Letchworth State Park in New York State in the beautiful valley of the Genesee River. The Genesee River Gorge is known as the 'Grand Canyon of the East U.S', and there are cliffs several hundreds of feet high. The Mount Morris Dam at the north end of the Park is 246 feet high. There are three major waterfalls with forests covering the slopes down to the river that winds its way into the gorge below. There are several trails and evidence of Indian and pioneering life in the region that can be seen in a Museum there. I saw the mighty glaciers that blocked the original riverbed and created 17 miles of deep winding canyons and valleys, thus forming the gorge. Within the park there are restaurants, an Inn, a Lodge, camping cabins and a swimming pool. The former home of William Pryor Letchworth is preserved in its original setting and is now the Glen Iris Inn. It is a lovely area at any time, but in the autumn, the fiery reds and golden tints of the foliage are absolutely wonderful.

Then early one morning when the sun was shining brightly we travelled along the lovely Canadian road to get to Niagara Falls. Within half a mile of the Falls, I could hear the roar of the water and glimpse the spume rising above the ridge and see the rapids as they appear immediately before the plunge. As we approached, I also noticed the old wreck of a boat stuck on the rocks at the centre of the river that has been there for some time apparently, but unfortunately no one knows its history or significance.

But the scene reminded me of a popular vocal solo composed by the late Dr. Joseph Parry, a musician from Wales who spent many years working in the U.S.A. The words tell the story of three young men who sailed down river on the Niagara on a beautiful day. They were laughing and singing merrily on their way and then suddenly, the people standing on the river bank started calling to them to warn them, "Ahoy, ahoy, the rapids are near." The three took no notice and happily continued on their way. Again there were shouts, and then the music becomes turbulent suggesting the Rapids are very near … and suddenly. Nothing! They had disappeared. It was all very dramatic and the song was a favourite of singers in my young days.

We too reached the famous Falls, but safely on dry land I'm pleased to say. The 'Vantage point' at the roadside on the Canadian side of the river gave us a marvellous view of the water as it plunged over the sheer edge of the rock. I could see the distinctive horseshoe shape of the Falls and noticed that the water as it came over the edge looked like very thick blue-green glass. It was awesome! Then we drove to Niagara on the Lake, a very pretty village preserved as it was in colonial days. The region had many battles in the pioneering days between the English and French, English and Americans, and there are a number of old forts and stone memorials telling the story of the bloody battles that took place there. It had been such an interesting and enjoyable outing.

On another occasion we went to Niagara Falls on the American side and walked through a park on Goat Island. The island is in the middle of the Niagara River where it becomes two channels, the larger heading towards the Canadian Horseshoe Falls and the other towards the American Falls and the smaller Bridal Veil. On the day we visited, there were American Army engineers busily boring holes in the ground right on the edge of the Falls. We stopped nearby to watch and they called across to us to, "Come, come on, come over, you will never again be able to walk over the edge of these Falls on dry land." And so we did! It just so happened that the water had been diverted to the other channel while the engineers carried out their task of discovering why there was so much rockfall especially on the American side of the river. Soon afterwards we discovered that the river was allowed once more to run in its own bed and we realised how fortunate we had been that day.

Geologists estimate that the Falls are between 10,000 to 30,000 years old. About 12,000 years ago the Falls were located seven miles further down the river but in the meantime, the Falls have eroded as much as six feet per year. The American Falls are 1100 ft. wide along the brink, and have a drop from the brink down to the river below of 180 ft. The Canadian Falls are 2500 ft. wide along the brink, and have a drop from the brink down to the river below of 170 ft. The water that flows over the Niagara Falls comes from four of the five Great Lakes and continues on its way down the Niagara River into Lake Ontario, then down the St. Lawrence River to the Atlantic Ocean. The volume of water flowing in the Niagara River is calculated to be 1400 gallons per second. Five and a half billion gallons of water flowed over the Falls before a decision was taken by the Governments of the U.S.A and Canada to divert three-quarters of this water to generate electrical power for both countries.

The Niagara Falls have been producing power since colonial days and are now one of the largest producer of electric power in the free world. I plucked up courage and went to the Power Station itself and asked if I could possibly just take a quick look inside. The gentleman to whom I spoke, stared at me in amazement, no doubt wondering why on earth this little lady tourist would want to look inside a power station. Finally he agreed, after all, what damage could I possibly do to the plant? I explained that back in Wales I worked for the British Electricity Board and that I was overawed by the tremendous power of the Niagara water. He then understood my interest and showed me some of the controls and explained in layman terms how the plant worked. Having satisfied my curiosity I thanked the power worker and joined the others. They couldn't believe that I had the nerve to even ask for admission, never mind actually go inside. We did not have enough time to visit all the museums, but we saw the huge statue of an immigrant who had pioneered the use of water for generating electrical power, but I am ashamed to say that I cannot remember his name. In the depths of winter, much of the Falls is frozen, but I was told that it never happens entirely. Now let me tell you about the really exciting part!

On the American side we stepped from the Park into the top of a giant tower and descended in a lift to the edge of the river below. We were going on a boat trip in the 'Maid of the Mist' on a gloriously hot day and everyone wore cool summer clothes. As we stepped onto the boat we were given plastic macs with hoods and I said to my sister, "What on earth do we want these for?" With a wry smile she replied, "You will see - put it on." I obeyed, and soon we were moving slowly and gently on the great river. The scene was fantastic … we were very low down on the surface of the water and could see that the buildings we'd been in earlier were very high above us. The people on the viewing landings looked like ants, but I could still see the beautiful Bridal Veil Falls at that point. I then became aware of a feeling of dampness around and then a cold mist: the sun had suddenly become paler too and there was drizzle and then rain. Very soon the rain became very heavy and I heard the sound of thunder - the thunderous sound of water. The river water became rough and the boat rocked and rolled in spite of the weight of all the people on board as it navigated into the basin at the foot of the Horseshoe Falls. The wind was blowing fiercely as in a gale and I must be honest and say that I was scared, even though my sister Bella and Stan kept reassuring me that we would survive! But it was also very exciting and thrilling as we struggled to keep our balance in the boat alongside all the other tourists on board.

Then the boat started its journey back and we had the incredible reverse experience of returning gradually to warmer and drier conditions until we were back in the full heat of the day. The trip had been a truly invigorating experience for me and from start to finish the whole episode had been surreal and wonderful.

Since then I have been on the 'Maid of the Mist' twice more and would go again if given an opportunity. I have never however found the courage to venture on the Spanish Aerocar over the fearsome Whirlpool in the river below. Steel cables have suspended the steel car since 1918 as it carries visitors safely to and fro above the Whirlpool. Yes I know, but what if it were to break down whilst I was riding in it! No thank you!

As I gazed over the Horseshoe that links America and Canada geographically I marvelled at the historic exploits of Blondini who walked a tight wire over the ridge, and another brave person who agreed to be hurled over the Falls in a sealed barrel. I tried to imagine how they managed those highly dangerous feats, and concluded that they must have had tremendous vision, highly developed skill and expertise, nerves of steel, great courage and enormous determination. I also knew that I could never in a month of Sundays have done anything remotely like that. In the area there are some lovely sounding Indian names such as Chippewa, Lakawanda and Tonawanda.

Interspersed with these thrilling visits I enjoyed lovely, peaceful days with Bella's family relaxing in the sunshine, chatting and reminiscing about our earlier life together in

Wales. On the eve of my departure Stan took Bella and me to dine at a special restaurant, and I distinctly remember the great secrecy that surrounded the venue. It was getting dark when we set out on the 45 minute journey by car, but on arrival, all I could see was what looked like a large barn with a flaming torch above the entrance. I was not disconcerted at all, but my curiosity was roused and I quickly realised on entering the building that Stan had taken us to a really unusual and expensive restaurant. There was a raised dais all round the room where people sat eating, and I noticed decorative rails, beautiful iron works, colourful light shades and floral decorations all around. It had a Spanish look that appealed to me. In the centre was a very large circular platform piled high with every kind of hot and cold meat, fish, vegetables, salads, fruit, sauces, spices, gravies - everything! There were four chefs in tall white hats to slice and serve with a smile and Stan explained to me that I could have anything and everything, and as much as I liked! I was stunned by it all and everything I chose was perfect. It was 1969 and this was my first experience of Smorgaasbord, and I have never seen or had quite the same selection or taste anywhere since. I delighted in going to choose all the bits and pieces and the chef was amused by my delight and actively encouraged me to, "have some more," which I did until I could eat no more.

The exterior of the restaurant had been extremely deceptive and it reminded me of an old hut in Hamburg that turned out to be a lovely café where we enjoyed delicious coffee. It was the place where I had first seen a policeman enter a café, drink coffee with other customers whilst wearing a gun! When he first entered I immediately remembered films like *The Fugitive* and scary little thoughts buzzed in my head. Oh, silly me! All he was chasing that morning was a cup of lovely coffee.

Our return journey to Toronto Airport was an artificially jolly experience. We knew that soon we would be saying farewell and that thousands of miles of land and sea would separate us again. The air was heavy with emotion as we kissed and waved before I boarded the plane and the boys seemed inconsolable. Children soon forget such disappointments when something new appeals to them, but it was pleasing for me to realise their affection for me, and I had so enjoyed their company too.

I was home again and had so much to tell, but found that it came out in spurts over a period of time. I had to return to work and catch up on matters awaiting attention on my desk, and settle again to routines at home.

Elsie was married and working in her new job at I.C.I., Glen was back at College missing Kerry who was working in his first teaching job, and Bryn was back at school. Arthur was as busy as ever teaching his pupils, adjudicating at festivals, conducting at *Cymanfaoedd Canu*, being the organist at Seion Chapel, and reporting news to the local newspaper.

At half-term Glen came home for the break and had recovered from the car accident except for the continuing dental treatment she was receiving on her front teeth. The scars from her injuries were still visible, but were less noticeable than before. Really, it was quite remarkable how well she had looked as Elsie's bridesmaid. Indeed, they both looked very pretty and Bryn looked every inch an attractive young lad, and Arthur and I were very proud of them.

During the half-term holiday Bryn complained of not feeling well, he had no appetite and was very lethargic. For Bryn to complain that he was unwell was unheard of for he was always healthy and on the go. One evening he went to the Youth Club to play table tennis where he drank a bottle of pop, but soon after started feeling very queasy. He decided to return home, which was only a quarter of a mile away, down two streets. He'd had to stop many times on the way and had experienced great difficulty in reaching home. He rang the doorbell and as soon as the door was opened, stumbled upstairs on all fours. He had stomach pains and went to the toilet where he experienced a great gush from his body, then he went to bed. He had a pain at the top of his head like a crushing weight as he described, and I told him to stay in bed to rest and supplied him with plenty to drink but gave him no food. I thought he had a stomach upset or had picked up some kind of bug. He was compliant and that too was different somehow, coming from Bryn.

However, on the Friday evening Arthur and I were due to take part in a concert somewhere with the Llanrwst Choir. As I went upstairs to get ready, I saw Bryn walking from the toilet along the landing in front of me. He moved so slowly with his arms hanging by his side, then I noticed his hands. They were absolutely white, there was no colour in them at all. I was shocked and knew immediately that he was suffering from something more serious than a tummy upset. I went downstairs and asked Glen to phone Dr. Chown as soon as his patients' surgery was over. Arthur and I had to leave, but I was very worried and could not settle down at all during the evening.

When we arrived back home that night, Glen told us that Dr. Chown had been and said that Bryn was very ill and had to go into hospital early the next morning. The haemoglobin count in his blood was extremely low and would have to be rectified immediately. Tests were also necessary to discover the cause of the imbalance. I was very, very worried and could not sleep that night. Bryn said he still had the pain at the top of his head, but I did not know what medicine was safe to give him for relief.

At 8 o'clock the next morning Arthur took Bryn to Colwyn Bay and Bryn insisted on walking into the Hospital, whistling! Years later he told me that he was scared, but would not show it. I asked why and he replied, “I didn't want them to think that I was a softie.” Would you believe it! Tests began straight away and confirmed what Dr. Chown had said regarding the blood count and it was also discovered that he was bleeding internally. In the ensuing days he had to suffer barium meals from up and down his stomach and intestines, in an attempt to find out why he was bleeding. He was also given blood transfusions. This treatment went on for several days and it was extremely unpleasant, but he began to feel better. He was in a Male Ward with five elderly men who had bad chests and kept waking up at night and making noises. Of course the poor men could not help this, after all that is why they were in hospital, but it was hard to bear for a sixteen-year-old lad who was also ill himself. Two of the old gentlemen died while Bryn was there which covered a period of several weeks. We understood from the doctors that nothing had been found to indicate what had caused the damage, but the bleeding eventually stopped and with the transfusions, medication and good food he slowly regained his health and strength and was discharged from hospital. Although the doctors and nurses had been extremely kind to him, Bryn was glad to come home and we were delighted to have him back again. Now it was up to us to continue to build up his strength. Arthur undertook this responsibility and ensured that he had prepared a proper meal of meat, four vegetables and gravy for Bryn every day. He took a pride in doing it knowing that Bryn loved a gravy dinner and would eat it with relish.

During this time of stress, there was another family in town going through the worry of having a son of Bryn's age unwell with a blood illness. Sadly, their worry turned to sorrow and grief for their beloved son died. We understood the worry, but thankfully not the loss. This resulted in a rumour spreading in Llanrwst that Bryn too had gone down with the same illness. For weeks we were required to contradict the rumours - naturally we were happy to do so, and understood I suppose that it was a reflection of the concern that people had for Bryn in our small town.

Bryn regained his health but suffered again in the loss of time from school. He was miles behind in his studies by this time. No help had been forthcoming from Llanrwst Grammar School or Denbighshire County Council, and he struggled as best he could to try to catch up, but three long periods of absence at critical periods had created 'a bridge too far'. We tried as a family to motivate him but he knew and we knew that we all lacked the skills required at such a critical stage in a young person's life to get him going again to fill in the gaps. This was a real travesty for Bryn, he knew it, and we knew it ... but the school did nothing about it ... nothing at all. There was no communication between the school and us, the staff did not seem able to show concern or have ideas about helping Bryn to become a sucessful learner again. No compassionate interest whatsoever was shown in his medical progress or in his educational progress either. I am so glad that today's schools have much better practice in place to accommodate pupils' long-term illnesses. Bryn's entire life has been affected by the unfortunate turn of events in his teenage years, and I bitterly regret that period and those involved in it. Bryn on the other hand has remained the giving and forgiving person that he is, strong and brave, resilient and determined to make his life a success. I am so proud of his achievements, for he has raised two wonderfully confident daughters with his wife Kath and has earned sufficient to raise his family and purchase a house by having always been in paid employment.

Some years after Bryn's illness, I read in a newspaper about a school dinner lady who had died. No one knew what had been wrong with her until a post-mortem was done and it was discovered that she had bled to death. A sliver of aluminium foil had torn something inside her. We learned that after serving all the children their meals she would scrape the dishes and eat the remainder herself and it was thought that in such a way she must have swallowed the metal sliver.

Thinking back to Bryn, I knew that when he arrived home from school he was in the habit of going into the fridge and helping himself to a bottle of milk. He would drink the whole pint straight out of the bottle. I had warned him not to do this because at the time I was complaining to the Milk Company in Llanrwst that the tops of their glass milk bottles were often chipped and cracked and therefore dangerous. I told them they could cause cuts and bleeding and should not be in circulation in that state - they would also spread disease. In my opinion the damage was caused to the bottles when the metal foil tops were clamped on, or when the bottles were washed and sterilised, or maybe through rough handling in some other way. Eventually, the danger was rectified, but I am pretty certain that it was a piece of glass from a damaged milk bottle that ripped Bryn's intestines causing his problems, and was probably passed out in the thick barium meals that were part of his treatment. We were so relieved when Bryn started to make great progress with his health again.

1969 was certainly a remarkable year for us in many ways as a family, but for the world, I believe it was unique because in July, man walked on the Moon for the first time.

Chapter Forty-Four

FROM OFFICE TO SHOP

We were all home for Christmas in 1969 including the newcomer into the family, Neville. Glen and Kerry were now engaged, with the wedding planned for 1971 when Glen finished in College … well they'd given us plenty of warning at least. Meanwhile, we were into the New Year of 1970 and the Manager of the Manweb Shop in Llanrwst had taken another job elsewhere, thus creating a vacancy. By then we knew that our office in Llandudno would be amalgamated with the Manweb Office in Rhyl within a few months and all the girls in my office thought I should apply for the post at the Llanrwst shop. "It's on your doorstep and no travelling Bet. You can virtually jump out of bed and be at work in five minutes," they said. But I was not sure. I knew everything about Manweb Offices but nothing about the Manweb Shops or the work therein. I was not so keen at the thought of a great deal more learning. I had really enjoyed the last four years at the Llandudno Office with a group of people who were pleasant and friendly. But in the end I trusted to Fate or Providence again and, *"Que sera, sera"* as they say in Spain … I applied for the shop job and was called for interview. There were five applicants. The panel consisted of people who knew me and the quality of my work, but they still questioned closely, explained the job description, and told me what would be required of me. I got the job.

I was told by one of the men on the panel that I would drop one step in my salary, "Because you don't know the work and will regain the loss within a short period." I should have insisted on that in writing, or rather I should have refused it point blank. It was a mean thing to do, but then he was a mean old man and I had to fight to get that drop re-instated.

I was sad to leave the crowd in Llandudno and there are a couple of events that I remember distinctly from my period there. During my second Christmas after moving to the Llandudno office those of us who used the un-manned canteen every day to prepare and eat our lunch, decided that we would have a slap-up Christmas dinner. Everyone had a task to do, mine was to obtain a nice big turkey and cook it. Others got the vegetables, the pudding, decorations and so on, and we even had some Asti Spumante sparkling wine that I had never tasted before, but liked, and still do today. On the day of the dinner I had brought the turkey ready stuffed and prepared for the big oven pan in the canteen cooker. It went in early and cooked all morning. We had not spread the news too much because the dinner was for the regulars only. However, the gorgeous aroma of the cooking turkey wafted down the corridor and into the offices with the result that the Boss, the Manager, came to investigate. He was not liked by some, and feared by others, but I found him to be alright. Provided you were honest with him he would always stand up for you, but *woe betide* anyone who lied or tried to cover up. When he landed in the Canteen there were only two of us there and we explained that we were merely checking that all was well. He was very nice about it and hoped we would enjoy a very good lunch, which indeed we did.

Another time, during the summer the girl who helped Jim, our supervisor, to prepare the wage packets for the electricians was away on holiday and I stepped in to cover her duties. It was a lovely sunny day as Jim and I drove to the Bank for the money. As soon as the cash was in the black bag, locked and strapped to Jim's arm, we drove back to the Office which was situated on the Mostyn Broadway between Craig y Don and

Llandudno town centre. The Broadway, in being a wide road similar to most of the main roads in the town, could accommodate the cars of six or seven of us who used to park them each day outside the Manweb building. On that particular morning as we came down the road I saw a crowd of people standing near Manweb with Tom and Ena, the sales people from the shop amongst them. Jim slowed down and we saw they were all Manweb people plus Police. We parked the car and Jim took the Cashbag into the safe. We were told that a little old lady had driven up from *Craig y Don* and for some unknown reason had gone crashing into the back of the last car on the line. The brand new car that was the pride and joy of its owner had in turn pushed the front of my Hillman Minx under the expensive car in front. The old lady's car had bounced off into the road then crashed again into the cars in front of the line. The lady was in a very confused and upset state, as well she might be, having damaged five cars in one go. They all had to be repaired and courtesy cars provided for the convenience of the owners. It must have cost the old lady's insurance company a packet of money. The only good thing to come from the occurrence was that no one was hurt.

When I first came to the District Office I was given a stand-up file with a whole pile of dockets on it representing unpaid bills that the company was chasing. I was pleased that when I left, there were only two dockets on that file.

Before I could start at the Llanrwst shop, for two weeks I went to observe, then practise the work and learn the job at the Manweb shop in the 'Round House' in Llandudno Junction. I was shown the basic routine of cash collection and balancing, the different models of appliances, ordering, booking in and out of stores as well as many other things I'd need to know about. It was all so very new, but I memorised most of it. Fortunately my part-time assistant in Llanrwst was someone I knew very well. We had been at Grammar School together in Abergele all those years before. She had been working in the shop for some time and knew the ropes. This was very helpful of course. People who know her will tell you that there is only one Norah - a real character! You would never guess that she was a Reverend Minister's wife and a very good one at that. She would never have made it in the Diplomatic Service, but you always knew where you were with her. She had a ready laugh and yet kept her dignity. She has unfortunately suffered ill health in recent years, but has battled through it all. We got on well together and still do.

Within a few weeks of settling in, I was told to attend the Training School at Wallasey. Each course lasted a week and we were billeted in a nice hotel and attended the School every day. I had been warned by other shop personnel that the Chief Instructor was a bit of a tartar and very strict, and there would be an examination at the end. Some of the women were scared to death of all of this, but when I discussed it with Norah she said, “No, it's not that bad, don't worry about it, you'll be alright, after all … he's only a man!” Still, it was with some trepidation that I set out for the Training School not knowing quite what to expect. Well Norah was right, the trainer was indeed just a man, and not an ogre! He was very pleasant but strict, and insisted that we took the tuition seriously. I could tell that he tolerated no nonsense, but he also had a sense of humour. I could accept his strictness without difficulty because I wanted the information in order to become a successful manager - I needed to learn, so I set about acquiring it willingly.

The following months represented a period of concentration and learning mostly. I was getting into the routine of the shopwork quite easily and everyone I dealt with was very helpful. Whenever I attended training courses at Wallasey, cover was supplied during my absence and whoever came, did what they could, but left the problems and difficulties for me to deal with on my return to work. They were not dodging work but simply leaving some matters that only a manager could deal with. Finally I completed the training courses and passed the tests successfully. I was glad to receive the tuition because I needed the knowledge about different appliances in order to make the required sales. I believe that Manweb staff members were the best trained in all electrical retail outlets at that time anyway. There were many other outlets selling appliances at marginally cheaper prices, but customers did not get the necessary details and advice in making their preferred choice, or so my customers informed me. There were some people who had the nerve to visit the shop to pick my brains before going elsewhere to make their purchases. It was not long before I got wise to their game and I knew exactly how to deal with them. It is a kind of intuitive awareness that is acquired by experience, I relied on an extra sense when deciding whether or not to receive bed and breakfast guests into my home as well.

At this time, my mother was in Hospital in Holywell, and I visited her as often as I could, usually on my afternoon off on Thursday. She was comfortable and safe and very well cared for, but I could see that she was getting weaker. Although my reason told me that there was no other way open to us I still felt sorrow and regret at having to leave her there every time I visited.

In the weeks leading up to Christmas there was increased activity in my shopwork. More small appliances were bought as gifts and special offers and decorations were brought into stock for display. Finally the Christmas window had to be in place and we had general instructions from head office of course, but the actual placings depended on the size and shape of the shop window. Although nowhere near the size of the large shop windows, ours was a good one for showing an attractive and striking display to the public, and I always made good use of the really lovely decorations provided for us by Head Office. Although it was extra work and fiddly, I always enjoyed doing the Christmas window simply because it was Christmas I suppose. With the exception of one year, I arranged the Christmas window for all the fourteen years that I managed the Llanrwst shop, with some help of course when my part time assistant was not dealing with customers or doing other duties.

The one exception that I referred to was the time when we were having a new floor put in place. The Manweb building was one of the oldest buildings in Llanrwst, probably built of stone in the fifteenth century. In the cubbyhole office we had at the back of the shop near the backdoor, there was an enormous lump of solid rock that had been incorporated into the back wall but jutted out. Anyhow, I had been complaining to the senior bosses about the state of the floor in the shop because the surface was uneven and slippery when many wet feet had trodden on it. The powers that be decided in the end that it was necessary to lay a new floor and arranged for the work to be done with just one month to go before Christmas.

The work started at 9.00a.m. on a Thursday morning when a large Manweb wagon arrived and all the large appliances were taken from the shop and put in it. The counter and till were moved down towards the window area where we dealt with customers all morning. Meanwhile, three men moved in with all sorts of tools and started on the work. The shop was closed as usual in the afternoon and work began in earnest. My boss arrived with a colleague who was in charge of another shop. There was not a lot we could do while the men were at it and they worked hard, stopping only for lunch and tea breaks. Somehow, providing the continual supply of drinks of tea became my job. When the workmen finished and departed, the rest of us then had to buckle down to clearing up and cleaning the place. There was vacuuming, dusting, washing and polishing to be done. While my boss, Bob, colleague John, and the wagon driver brought back the appliances and replaced them in their correct positions, I was busy cooking bacon, eggs and beans in tomato sauce on a Baby Belling cooker at the back of the shop. They then sat down on boxes using a storage heater as a table and really enjoyed the repast.

But the Christmas Window still needed attention even after all the upheaval of the day. My instructions from head office indicated that it needed to be in place for the next day! And it was! With appreciation, gratitude and lots of well deserved pride, we all stood outside on the pavement and looked at a most wonderful display all ready for Christmas, at exactly midnight. What an achievement … and what dedication to our work!

Chapter Forty-Five

MAM DIES

Glen was now in her final year at College and in March 1971 was doing School Practice at the Welsh School in Rhyl where Glyndwr Richards, a long-standing friend of Arthur was Headteacher. Early one morning while I was at work, Arthur received a phone call from the Holywell Hospital saying that Mam had been taken ill and was slowly dying. Arthur immediately phoned me in the Shop and fortunately, my assistant Nora was working that morning which meant I was able to get away. We managed to contact Glen who said she wanted to go with me to see Nain. I left Llanrwst immediately in the Hillman Minx and called for Glenys at her digs in Rhyl then, we departed together for Holywell as fast as we could. We did not talk much on the way, but as soon as we parked the car we rushed into the foyer and announced ourselves. A senior nurse came and ushered us into an office where we were told that Mam had passed away peacefully shortly before we arrived. We were both shocked and disappointed, but Glen was devastated. The children had always been close to their Nain. Glen wept uncontrollably and could not be consoled. She told me later that she'd had a premonition of Nain's death. A kind nurse served us tea and biscuits, but I have to admit that I found it very hard to swallow them.

We were too late to see Mam alive, and there was nothing more we could do at the Hospital so we decided to return to Llanrwst to set things in motion for the funeral. Glen asked if she could drive the car and I asked if she felt calm enough, she said she was and appeared to be composed by that time. I thought that concentrating on the driving would be good for her because she was an excellent driver. We spoke quite a lot on the way back about Mam and previous times when Glen, Elsie and Bryn had spent so much time in Llanfair and being cared for by Nain and Taid. As we came to a long stretch of straight road we saw a blue light flashing in the distance on the opposite side of the road, Glen reduced her speed and we could see two or three cars moving slowly ahead of us. As we got nearer to the car in front, Glen decreased her speed even more, but quite suddenly it stopped abruptly. Glen braked hard and turned the wheel sharply so that the car veered to the left down a lane and just clipped the corner of the car in front causing only a little damage to a side lamp. There were no seat belts in those days and I hit my forehead on the sun visor and was stunned for about twenty seconds. Glen seemed alright but instinctively jumped into my arms crying, “What have I done, what have I done?” We both got out and went to see what damage had been done. There was only minimal grazing on the right side of the bonnet of our car and a smashed lamp on the near side at the back of the other car. However, the male driver was making a big fuss because the Police were on site seeing to another matter. We went through the official procedures, insurance addresses and so on, but the Police would not let me drive our car. They gave us a lift to their headquarters in Colwyn Bay and then abandoned us. There was no point in phoning Arthur because he could not get to us, so I phoned by trusted friend Win, and her husband David who very kindly came to fetch us. Glen and I were profoundly thankful to them for their Christian good deed. When we arrived home Arthur took over and sorted things out and no case was brought against Glen ... and quite rightly so.

My brother arranged Mam's funeral and we shared the expenses. I had managed to keep calm up until the funeral, but after the service in the Chapel, I burst out sobbing and shaking in distress. I suppose a lot of it was pent up stress, but the main cause was the feeling of profound pity. I was thinking how cruel life had been to Mam, the unfairness she had suffered, one thing after another. She had looked after us incredibly well; raised us to value the right things; ensured we were well educated; and struggled to make ends meet until we were making our way in the world. She had lost both parents as a very young woman; lost a dearly beloved little girl to death; survived a major operation and two strokes without complaint; seen the successful family business go down the drain; and lost her lovely home. Then at the end, she had died in hospital away from home, with none of her family there to comfort her. I was shattered, and although I had done my best, still felt I had let her down. Arthur helped by reminding me that Mam was a grand person who had a wonderful sense of humour, a person who could laugh at life and enjoy herself most of the time. She loved her grandchildren, and was proud that her own children had done well in the world. In spite of all her tribulations, she had lived until she was nearly 87 years of age. She could be awkward, obstinate and determined at times, but these were the very traits that had helped her to overcome so many of her troubles in life. Even after suffering her first stroke, she resumed a favourite pastime as soon as possible by going once more for car rides to interesting places, the highlight of which was calling at nice tea places to savour the fare. Sometimes we would take her to Llandudno or Colwyn Bay for a treat, and as soon as she was out of the car, would say, “Now, where can we start spending - money is meant to be spent,” but not on herself you understand! She would have been saving for weeks until she had a tidy sum of money, then she had the pleasure of being able to give the children and the rest of the family a treat or something they needed.

Life goes on even after a parent's death, and I had to settle back to work at the shop and at home. There was spring-cleaning as usual in preparation for visitors, without forgetting another big occasion, which was Glen's wedding in the summer.

The date of the ceremony was the 21st of August 1971, they had the reception at the *Tal y Cafn Hotel* where Elsie and Neville had theirs. The bridal dress was the same too, Glenys couldn't afford a new one and Elsie was generous enough to allow her to use hers. They were both the same size: a wonderful size 8. It really was a most beautiful gown and fitted them perfectly. Kerry's sister, Kay, kindly let Glen borrow her lace veil, and Glenys looked really, really lovely. The bridesmaids' dresses were a pretty shade of lavender. Elsie was the chief bridesmaid assisted by Kay, Kerry's sister and Rhiannon, Glen's friend from College. The best man was Gareth Hughes Jones another friend from College. It was a warm sunny day and everything went well. Bryn did the honours again by giving away the bride, as he had done at Elsie's wedding, but this time he was two years older and knew the ropes. The reception was very pleasant indeed with everyone chatting, smiling and happy. Afterwards the newly-weds left for their honeymoon, Glenys wearing a beige dress under a lovely petrol-blue coat with matching accessories. We later took the girls' bouquets and laid them on the graves of their Grandparents.

After the busy preparations and excitement leading up to the great day we had to step off cloud nine and come down to earth, which we did with a bump. It was strange to think that the second of our brood had fled the nest. The house seemed quiet and empty. Welcoming and entertaining paying guests helped us overcome melancholy and sadness.

Chapter Forty-Six

HELPING EACH OTHER

Now that Glen had qualified as a teacher, she had been appointed to a post in a school not far from where Kerry was employed. She had trained for teaching through the medium of Welsh that meant in reality being able to teach in English and Welsh. However this ability gave her an extra insight into the means of teaching English as a second language to ethnic minority groups. For six years, in addition to teaching at school, Glenys had an evening class of 16 adults learning to speak Welsh at the Bolton Community College on Manchester Road! A hard-core of eight of them stayed with her all that time and made exceptional progress.

After some searching, Kerry and Glen bought a semi-detached house in Bradshaw, a pleasant little community with a village atmosphere. Elsie, Neville and I went to help with the decorating and moving-in jobs. The house was in good condition, but needed some decorating inside. There was a job for everyone, and having a cooker already there meant we were all fed and watered as required. Elsie was the cook and Kerry saw to the lighting, power points and general modifications. Neville and Glen tackled the painting and paperhanging and I was the cleaning woman. Everything was going like clockwork until a most unfortunate calamity happened.

The downstairs main room was an 'L' shape with a dividing sliding door to separate the dining area from the sitting room. The whole area was carpeted in a lovely black carpet with a pattern of pink roses and foliage and was of a very good quality. Glen had set up her pasting table and was preparing to start cutting lengths of paper, when she shook the tin of white paint that Neville was about to use causing the entire contents of the big tin to explode all over the black carpet. Oh no, what a catastrophe! Neville, Glen and I screamed and dashed for cloths, but to no avail. Five litres of white paint had gone all over the carpet! So Neville and I, each with a tablespoon started to scrape the paint into an old box. Moving with the pile of the carpet we worked until we had taken away all the loose paint, but what a matted mess was left. Glen was convinced they would need to replace the carpet. None of us really had any hope of success, but we persevered. Neville's Chemical Engineering background helped enormously and he advised that we should saturate the patch with white spirit pressing the cloths hard onto it to absorb the liquid then repeat the procedure with water and detergent. It took time and determination, and for a few days the house smelled like a paint factory, but it didn't matter because the carpet looked immaculate, and after a general shampooing of the whole carpet, looked newly laid and perfect. The secret was a combination of the quality of the carpet, expert knowledge, and the persistence and determination demonstrated by Neville and me.

The only other memory I have of that house is of the back garden, which was badly neglected when Glen and Kerry moved in. It was not a small garden either, but I soon got to work on it because I enjoy gardening as an activity, and viewed it as a challenge. It needed a massive overhaul, more than just pruning I can say, more like de-branching, which resulted in a small mountain of garden debris being created in the middle of the lawn, where it stayed for a time. We finally found the outlines of the flower borders, which made it possible to weed and fork the soil. Suddenly, after a lot of very hard work, the area looked like a garden again. The only blip on the horizon was the pile of debris on the lawn, no one could think of what to do with it, after all we couldn't have a bonfire because it would have ruined the lawn. Then I had an idea: just behind the garage at the bottom of the garden was a rough area of around 6ft. x 3ft. with lots of stones and rubbish thrown in a heap. My idea involved taking out the big stones, cutting up the larger branches in the pile on the lawn and throwing them onto the rubbish heap behind the garage, then transporting the rest of the debris in a wheelbarrow onto the mounting pile. Once the lawn was cleared of the debris Kerry was able to cut the grass and put the cuttings on it too. We obtained soil from somewhere to top it all then finished it by placing the stones haphazardly on top. And hey presto! before too long, we had a rockery with plants that flourished throughout the three years that Glen and Kerry lived there.

We sold the Hillman Minx and bought a nearly new Hillman Imp that had its engine at the back. It was a great little car, very easy and enjoyable to drive and within weeks Bryn had passed his driving test too. He also became a student at an engineering College in Wrexham. He came home at weekends, usually by hitching lifts, but we always drove him back on Sunday nights.

In the spring, his knee started to trouble him again, he was in a great deal of pain at times, but in remembering his earlier experiences, would not go to the see the Doctor. Finally however, he had no choice because stiffness was setting in. The Doctor said that another operation was inevitable and it was a case of waiting to have it done and suffering in the meantime. Fortunately, he did not have to wait too long and was fortunate in having the same Surgeon as before, who performed a more extensive operation this time by opening up the knee all the way round. It was to prove a complete success and Bryn has never had any more trouble with it. The convalescence time however was just as long as before and he had to give up the course at the College although he had already concluded that it was not suitable for him. When he was able, he got a job in an engineering factory at Colwyn Bay. His overalls got so oily and dirty that I had to clean the washing machine after washing his clothes! But he was not happy there. Eventually, I spotted an advert in a newspaper calling for people to train guide dogs for the blind at the GDfTB headquarters in Bolton. I showed Bryn the advert and he was very interested in it. He applied, was interviewed and appointed. Glen and Kerry very kindly let him lodge with them. They had by this time moved from Bradshaw and were living in Bolton.

He settled down to learning about the work of training dogs starting off at the bottom - cleaning out the kennels and such work. He did this willingly realising that it was part of the early training. However, as months passed, and no real opportunities to work with the dogs materialised, he became disillusioned and believed that he was being used as cheap labour. He stuck it out for a year then one day noticed an R.A.F. recruitment van in Bolton town centre and went in for information. He told Arthur and me about this and gave us to understand that he was keen to enlist. His Dad was less than enthusiastic, but after giving the matter serious thought I came to the conclusion that it might provide the stability and training that he needed. Soon after, he made the decision to enlist, was kitted up and sent away to the preliminary training centre.

Everyone came home to *Llys Cerdd* for Christmas in 1975: Elsie and Neville, Glen and Kerry, and Bryn. It was wonderful to have them home once more because it was all so enjoyable. We played games, laughed a lot, and enjoyed scrumptious meals. Arthur recorded the Christmas dinner table talk without anyone's knowledge and I still have the tape. It is hilarious. You should try it at your table for a laugh.

Arthur gave up being Secretary of the Llanrwst Eisteddfod after 20 years in the job. It had been interesting and rewarding, but had also meant a lot of hard work and sometimes very long hours. It did not mean relinquishing all interest in the Eisteddfod, not at all, but the responsibilities had been transferred to someone else. In the same year, Elsie was invited to be the President of the morning session at the Eisteddfod when she made a speech to the audience.

Arthur was the guest of honour at the St. David's Day dinner of the Teesside Welsh Society and I had been invited to sing. We had a very warm welcome. Welsh people who are away from Wales are always keen to celebrate anything Welsh, the *hiraeth* is assuaged I suppose. I think the Celtic people - Scots, Irish, Cornish and Bretons have the same response to the stirrings of the spirit.

Chapter Forty-Seven

WORK AND PLAY

My workload at the Manweb Shop started increasing rapidly because we were forever widening the range of appliances in stock and thereby gaining more customers. Our sales figures were increasing too. I attended the annual Sales Conferences held at the Head Office in Chester where Senior Managers outlined their plans by quoting figures and urging increases in sales in all the shops. Some of the things I heard were new and of interest to me, other things I'd heard before, but a few presentations were just boring. Each year shop managers were given sales targets to meet with the understanding that the main criterion for keeping a Manweb Shop open was for it to make a good profit. The trouble was that the goal posts were moved annually! We'd work hard to achieve our target for the year, only to be rewarded with a tougher target to achieve the following year. This went on year after year!

Despite this, we were a happy staff team in the Llanrwst shop, which consisted of a part time sales assistant, cleaning lady, various electricians who called in to make necessary phone calls and me. The company representatives who visited the shop were also regarded as colleagues and friends because they were always very helpful. I can honestly say that we were very willing to help one another within reason, and that was true of other Shop Managers in our group too.

In 1973 the UK Government changed our currency to decimalisation. There had been many discussions on Radio and Television and countless articles written in newspapers about the change in preparation for the big moment. All Manweb staff had received training beforehand, but there was still some apprehension about the change, after all, we had dealt in pounds, shillings, and pence all our lives from the early days of infant school. Being expected to deal with pounds and pence only was going to be quite a challenge for the whole country!

Well, the new Cash Till arrived ahead of the big day, and my assistant and I looked at it more than once in the knowledge that we were required to use it efficiently from the transitional day onwards. I well remember the high level of intensive care that surrounded the way we issued our first receipts that day. I will never forget the very first time my assistant, Norah pressed the figured tabs - very dramatically she held out her index finger at arm's length as if setting off 'Big Bertha' the cannon, fully expecting the till to blow up the shop and the whole world in the process!

Sooner than expected decimalisation became routine, and money calculations became so easy to manage in comparison with the previous cumbersome system. Perhaps too much had been made of the change, I'm not sure, but the nation was certainly aware of it. However, it must be said that some older people found it very difficult to accept the change and adapt to it. They were vulnerable in shops in being short-changed by uncaring traders when they held out a handful of cash saying, "Take what is required, I don't understand this new money. Unscrupulous traders also increased prices under the guise of decimals, but it was short lived.

In 1974 we started to sell audio equipment in the Manweb shops: radios, radio/recorders, record players, and music centres which meant all staff had to be trained in their use. Everyone knew what they were and what they did, but we needed to learn about their finer points in order to capitalise upon sales. To save time and money we were required to attend training sessions at places that were geographically central to a number of shops. I attended training in Bala, and after the session, joined colleagues for an evening meal at a Hotel on the outskirts of the town. During the meal we experienced a terrific noise and vibration resembling a long and very loud rumble of thunder: wall pictures went askew and cutlery and china did a little dance on the table. And then there was silence, followed by dramatic speculations from the group about the cause of the bizzare experience. There was no further disturbance that evening and normality returned. Later we wondered further about the incident - there was no evidence of a storm, nothing appeared in the press, and no reference was made to it on news bulletins. Years later I read an article on the subject of U.F.Os in which reference was made to the Bala incident, but it discounted speculation that the incident had been a U.F.O.landing. Apparently some local people had seen strange lights and soldiers, but there was no explanation from Authorities or anyone else. This year I read again about the occurrence, but with still no further enlightenment I'm sorry to say. It remains a mystery! We all like a mystery, but we all like to know the explanation and solution too.

Round about this time our pay structure was changed. A bar was placed at a certain point on the scale and in order to progress beyond it we were required to obtain an Electricity Board Salesmanship Certificate. I decided to enrol for training, as did two young men from other Shops. We attended sessions at the Training School again for some weeks, then sat the examination, which was not a doddle I have to say. There was written work to complete and practical role tests too. Happily, all three of us passed well and celebrated together at a dinner in a hotel with our immediate Boss and our Trainer. This success meant we were awarded a rise in salary, but no sooner had that happened when loud protests were made by other staff about the bar, and the Union successfully negotiated automatic rises on behalf of some of the grades. I had no objection to anyone gaining extra pay because we worked hard enough for it. However, it did not seem fair that three of us had given our time and energy to study and improve our skills for the benefit of the Board only to find we were no better off than others who had done nothing extra. I had to battle on my own for months before being given some financial recognition for my extra effort and additional skills. I was disappointed too that the Union did nothing to help.

By this time Elsie and Neville had both passed the driving test and bought a Hillman Imp like ours before replacing it quite quickly with a new and much bigger Fiat. Elsie's job with I.C.I. involved travelling on the Continent. Over five years she visited many of the western European countries when she enjoyed the food and culture. This is very different from today when many places look the same, and all business people see are hotels and airports. She went to several different countries, and although sightseeing was not part of the programme, she nevertheless enjoyed a range of different experience. It was during one of her trips to Italy that she noticed a car that impressed her so much that she bought one on her return to the UK - it was the Fiat that replaced the Imp.

During the summer, Arthur and I went to stay with Elsie and Neville for a couple of days before going further north to Scotland with Elsie. She wanted to drive most of the way having recently become a fully fledged driver. We went through the old counties of Northumberland and Durham and were amazed at the wonderful scenery. As a child I had been told that those areas were covered with coalfields, woollen factories and heavy industry, as I'm sure children elsewhere were told that Wales was covered with coalfields, steel and slate quarries, and Lancashire with cotton factories. I marvel at the way children today have a much more accurate knowledge of geographical locations due to computers and the Internet, and modern interactive whiteboards and video-conferencing facilities being available in schools.

We had written to Bryn to tell him we were hoping to stay overnight at Alnwick, where he was stationed with the RAF. When we arrived we met him at a hotel and were introduced to his girlfriend. Together we went for a walk along the seashore and took some photographs of the occasion.

The following day we went to the local Tourist Board Office to arrange accommodation for the night. The Edinburgh Festival was on, so we knew it would be pointless even trying to obtain accommodation locally. After many phone calls we finally secured rooms at a large country hotel with a golf course. We spent the rest of the day enjoying the views, then drove to the Hotel in our little Hillman Imp. The long drive led to the car park where we parked our little car next to impressive-looking vehicles such as Rolls Royce, Daimler, and Mercedes. We checked-in at reception and Arthur and I were taken down the drive to a lodge where we were the sole occupants. An electric heater was switched on and hot water bottles put in the most enormous bed that I have ever seen … it was huge! Arthur and I were searching for each other in it! Meanwhile Elsie had been escorted to a tower in the Hotel building where her room was located. She and I dined at the hotel that evening, but Arthur went for a walk in the grounds instead because his stomach trouble had flared up again, so he took *'Complan'* instead of the meal.

In the morning Arthur and I made our way up the drive to the Hotel for breakfast, but there was no sign of Elsie, and after waiting some time, we became worried. She finally appeared and was not in a very happy mood. We learnt that she'd been kept awake during the night by noisy pigeons in a loft at the top of the tower, and this had made her late for breakfast. Even so, she took her time over it and ate well, determined to get her 'pound of flesh'!

We could very easily have disappeared without paying that morning because we looked and looked for someone to pay, or somewhere to settle our account - but without success. In the end, Elsie and Arthur gave up the ghost and went out to the car leaving me to deal with the situation. I looked round every door and corner and called out, but to no avail. Finally I lost patience and banged hard on what appeared to be a small cupboard and called out, "Hello," loudly many times. And lo and behold, all of a sudden one part of the little cupboard opened to reveal a man's head. "Yes?" said the head abruptly. "I would like our bill please," I said in a reasonable manner considering the annoyance of the situation. "What name?" he asked curtly. "Vaughan Williams," I replied immediately. "Just a minute," he said and disappeared closing the cupboard doors behind him. I then waited, and waited, and waited for a very long time and was really tempted to leave, but then thought better of it. My hand was preparing to bang on the cupboard door again when it opened and an arm appeared with a bill attached. I took it and was shocked at its outrageousness.

My pride was up however, so I moved over to a small table and made a great display of putting on my glasses, finding my special fountain pen and using it in a flamboyant manner on my open chequebook. I made that man wait as long as I could, then handed the bill and cheque to him and thrust out my arm to stop him being able to close the cupboard door. He then handed back the bill without a word. "I would like a receipt please," I said coldly. "No receipt is needed with a cheque," he said equally coldly. "Nevertheless, I want a receipt, after all, one cannot be too careful these days can one?" I insisted, looking him straight in the eyes. He reluctantly stamped the bill and thrust it at me without a smile, a word of thanks, or a please, and he certainly did not enquire whether we had enjoyed our stay. I found myself comparing this experience with the considerate way in which we treated our guests at *Llys Cerdd* and the enormous difference also in the cost of the accommodation - I was of the opinion that we gave value for money at our guest house, whereas that particular hotel didn't achieve the status and neither did it care.

Anyway, we were glad to get away from such a place, but disappointed at the rude and disgruntled treatment we had experienced on our first visit to the land of my mother's forebears in Scotland.

We headed for Ecclefechan, booked in at a clean, bright and cheerful Guesthouse and immediately felt better. We spent the day visiting the churchyard on the way to Annan where some of my mother's people are buried. The Church building was no longer there, having somehow been burned to the ground. Fergus, my mother's cousin had told me to look in the cemetery for a Memorial stone to one of the cousins who had been in Van Diemen's Land, (Tasmania) in the mid 1880s, where he had been acclaimed a Chief by the local people because he was so tall and could jump so high! I scraped the moss off the base of the Celtic cross gravestone that bore the names and death dates of my maternal great-grandparents and photographed it. We also visited their retirement home, 'Mayfield' and photographed it too. I remember our Guesthouse landlady being a good cook, and we ate very well that evening and at breakfast the following morning too.

Before leaving Scotland we went to see 'Gilnockie', the ancestral home of the Armstrongs who were cousins of the Howatsons. It was a traditional stronghold, ground level for the animals, middle region for the defence and the upper region for the household. We also saw and walked a little by Hadrian's Wall - the Romans' 'keep out' to the Picts and Scots.

Arthur, Glenys and I had travelled to Scotland a few years earlier, and had gone from Bolton via Penrith where Kate (nee Armstrong) had lived. Her daughter, Mrs. Barr, still lived in the big house (I cannot remember the name of it), and I met her son who was a partner in a Veterinary business in the town. He was a tall, good-looking and pleasant man who wanted me to go to see his mother, but we did not have the time unfortunately. We liked Penrith, such a clean and bright town and it was where I saw a young man nestling a very young fox cub against his chest. It was so lovely and cuddly and had obviously been tamed and adopted as a pet.

Penrith was also the place where Arthur had an unfortunate experience. We had visited a tourist shop that sold all kinds of souvenirs and had bought a plant holder made of heavy granite that Arthur carried on his arm. As we left the shop Arthur swung round suddenly to call to me and in so doing swung the granite piece into the vastly protruding stomach of a man standing nearby who yelped … naturally! Arthur apologised profusely and asked if he was alright. However, the victim was in no mood that day to accept apologies from clumsy tourists and he cursed Arthur and his companions very loudly! We all three again said how sorry we were and left without further ado, which seemed the most sensible thing to do in the circumstances.

On that day we managed to speak to a member of the Howatson clan who was still farming at Middlebie. He said, "There are now more of us down there in Wales than there are up here in Scotland," and indeed, I think he was right. However, he told me also of a retired bank manager who lived in Annan so we went to visit the town. Arthur and Glenys refused point blank to accompany me to visit the man, so I had to go on my own. He was extremely surprised to see me, but received me into his home very courteously. He explained that his wife, a teacher, was still at school, and was not there to act as hostess. But he managed very well because we drank coffee and ate shortcake, which seemed very appropriate to me. We chatted about the Clans and it was he who told me about the Church where I would find the family graves.

We returned to Bolton safe and sound having taken Elsie back to her new home in Redcar on the way. All our extended family members were busily going about their lives, but managing to keep in touch from time to time. The contact was sometimes intermittent, but was often enough to know how everyone was faring, including my sister and her family in the States. But we had no such news of my brother and his family.

Before joining the Royal Air Force Bryn had met Kath while working at the Guide Dogs for the Blind Training Centre in Bolton. After Bryn left the Centre and joined the Air Force, Kath phoned Glenys for Bryn's address, and started writing to him. Kath then got a job near to Bryn's posting in Northumberland as a Receptionist at first, then as Assistant Manager at a hotel in Alnmouth, just outside Alnwick.

In 1976 they decided to get married very quietly, telling no-one other than a friend of Bryn's who stood as best-man and a friend of Kath's who was to stand for her and take photographs with a good camera. Sadly, on the day, Kath's friend phoned the Registry Office to say that she could not attend the wedding because her children had developed measles. So not only did Kath have to ask the girl who was typing in the Registry Office to sign for her, but ended up with no photographs either!

It was quite some time before Arthur and I received a letter from Bryn telling us that he was married. To say that we were shocked, hurt and disappointed is putting it mildly. Even though Bryn was 23 years old he had not had an opportunity to really think about his aims in life or settle into a proper job on account of the months he had spent in hospitals and recuperating at home - and this worried us greatly. Also, we did not know anything about Kath, and therefore felt concerned about Bryn's future happiness. Elsie and Glenys were stunned with the news - Bryn, their much loved younger brother, who had played his part so well at their own weddings by giving them away, had got married without involving them or his parents - in fact without telling any of us of the event! The whole thing sounded so unlike Bryn somehow. Glenys and Kerry were especially taken aback because Bryn had lived with them for several months when he worked in Bolton before joining the RAF, and they had established a good relationship .... they were friends! It stands to reason they were disappointed at not being invited to Bryn's wedding - that none of the family had been invited or told about it.

It took several weeks of reflection for us to come to terms with the marriage, but we finally accepted the situation with as much good grace as we could muster because it was not in our nature to create ill feeling. Above all, we wanted our children to be happy and for our family to remain close.

I am able to thank God that our wishes were realised. All of us let bygones be bygones and relegated this experience to the past. I believe everyone learned from it in time and became stronger and wiser as a result. My family is a delight and a support to me and I feel blessed by their affection and respect.

Chapter Forty-Eight

NEW AND BRIGHT

During the following year I applied for an opportunity to achieve the Electricity Council Salesmanship Diploma. A minimum period of two years had to elapse after gaining the Salesmanship Certificate before the Diploma could be sought. Usually candidates were required to go to Head Office in Chester to be interviewed and tested, but the powers that be decided to come to Llanrwst to my workplace to conduct the proceedings. There was no real office in which to do this, so the two interrogators and I had to sit on boxes in the storeroom - it could easily have become farcical if the proper demeanour and procedures had not been maintained. As it was, the two Examiners were very keen, questioning very closely and, as I later learned, going beyond what was required, by asking questions on shop management too. However I had no fears on that score either because there was nothing in big shop management that did not also crop up constantly in smaller shops too. Anyhow I must have satisfied them because I obtained the Diploma. It did not bring any increase to my salary, but it boosted my self-esteem and gave me extra confidence.

The Llanrwst Manweb shop was a busy place, not only for sales of appliances, but for payment of electricity bills too. We turned over many thousands of pounds per day during billing time. There were also many queries regarding all kinds of things to do with supply of power. During storms or heavy snows and floods when lines were brought down and various areas had no power supply, the phone would be 'red hot' with anxious customers experiencing problems. I must say that during all the years at the shop, I never had unreasonable people to deal with at such times. Once a proper explanation had been given, people managed with very little grumbling. Very often customers would come to see me at the shop with problems of one kind or another. They were aware that I had worked in Manweb offices before working in the shop and they found it easier and more effective to talk to me in the shop than phone or write to the District Office. And at the risk of sounding pompous - they were right, because I knew the ropes. I helped them and the office staff too, but at the expense of my own precious time. Frequently I was late going home at the end of a busy day, but it gave me a great feeling of satisfaction having solved a problem somewhere, helped someone who was struggling, or avoided a problem arising by being pro-active in some way.

When Norah left and went to work for an Optician in town a new assistant, Ethel, was appointed and we worked together very well for a few years. Eventually, Ethel decided to leave and I was sorry to see her go, but was lucky to have Betty come to work with me. In January 1977 there was a newspaper report and I quote from it:

" ... BRIGHT IDEA SHINES THROUGH THE SNOW"

A bright idea proposed by Mrs. Bet Vaughan Williams, Supervisor of Llanrwst Manweb shop was the victim of atrocious weather last week.

Mrs. Williams had planned a big demonstration of electrical appliances in the local Community Centre, and had received responses from 600 people who wanted to attend it over two evenings Then came the blizzard - and cut Wednesday's expected attendance of 300 to 200, and Thursday's attendance to only 60. Even so, the event was a big success. Mrs. Williams got the idea when she realised that village groups often could not book a Manweb Cookery demonstration for a meeting, because economies meant that only ten demonstrations would be given during 1977 throughout the whole of the Board's Clwyd district. So Mrs. Williams suggested a mass demonstration for 100s of women at a time, coming from a lot of Organisations in an area. The result was that 28 organisations, W.I., Young Wives, Inner Wheel, Y.F.C.s, Parent/Teachers Associations, Mothers' Union and other groups from the Conwy Valley and hinterland accepted invitations to the show at the Community Centre, Llanrwst. The attendances were encouraging enough, considering the atrocious weather, for three more big-scale meetings to be planned by Manweb in towns in Clwyd later this year.

One of the chief talking points for the audiences at Llanrwst was a Microwave Oven recently brought on the market, at a price within the range of ordinary homes. The high speed of cooking by the microwave method makes it one of the biggest timesavers ever introduced into the kitchen. Some dishes can be cooked 30 times faster than by conventional means. Pre-cooked meals can be re-heated in almost, unbelievably, 15/20 seconds. The Cookery demonstrations were by Mrs. Lynette Gibson, Clwyd District demonstrator and her counterpart from Gwynedd, Mrs. Eirlys Hughes.

Mr. Eric Richardson, Senior Instructor from Manweb's Training School, Wallasey, gave a talk about a scheme for planning complete New Kitchens. The programme on both evenings also described a range of other appliances, safety measures and costs. Mrs. Bet Vaughan Williams gave the introductory talks."

We had organised dozens of different electrical appliances to be on display in the Hall to help generate interest. The event had entailed a lot of planning and hard work for a number of people including me, and my disappointment when the snow storm arrived to disrupt our plans was beyond words. Still, it was not a disaster and the results were good for our shops.

Writing this account now brings back many thoughts. It was a different world then, and we were introducing the concept of a new and different way of living especially in the kitchen. When I first joined Manweb, I was involved in the work of introducing Electric Power for the first time into rural areas. When I moved to work in the Llanrwst Manweb shop, it was exciting to be able to sell modern electrical appliances that required the power that had so recently been taken to those remote areas. Such appliances included: cookers with double ovens or fan ovens and ceramic tops, microwave cookers, automatic washing machines, dishwashers, suction cleaners, radios, recorders and television and all the other necessities and luxuries of modern life, even planned fitted kitchens. But sadly, Manweb does not exist separately today because it has been incorporated into a Scottish Company, albeit a very good one. The familiar Manweb shops have gone from our town centres, and I find it strange to think that all the work that we did and the activity that took place in the Manweb shops in the past, happens no longer.

Many years earlier, in late January 1977 a memo was sent to all sections from our Head Office in Chester inviting applications from staff to attend the Electricity Council Spring & Summer Schools. The invitation was open to all employees in every sector. I applied, was successful, and found myself setting out at the crack of dawn on 30th March to arrive at Cambridge Railway Station, at 3.00p.m, where a coach took the assembled group to Corpus Christi College. There were 100 persons attending the School of whom only 10 were women. Every section of the Industry was represented - fitters, electricians, store-keepers, typists, work-study clerks, meter readers, engineers, labourers, shop staff, private secretaries, health personnel, linesmen and managers. All the women were housed in one block and each had a separate, comfortable room.

Every morning we attended lectures by leading members of the Industry, then attended discussion groups for an hour before re-assembling to put forward questions to the speaker. After lunch we visited places of interest such as Ely Cathedral.

All in all, it was a very interesting and informative experience and I was extremely glad to have been given the opportunity to participate. I was required to write a report on my return to work, which was very favourably received.

Although Cambridge itself and the surrounding area are full of items and matters of interest, I nevertheless decided quite quickly that I would not want to live there long-term. For having come from North Wales with its naturally beautiful landscape of rugged rocks and rolling hills and valleys, I found the Cambridge countryside far too flat for my liking, too bare, cold and wind-blown, and with too few trees!

Despite having enjoyed the wonderful training opportunity at Cambridge, I was pleased to return to the beauty of Snowdonia and home. Spring came and went, and summer brought news of a baby's birth. Kath had given birth to a little girl whose name was Rebecca Jo Vaughan Williams - she was carrying on the 'Vaughan Williams' surname. She was our first grandchild!

As soon as we could arrange things we journeyed to Alnwick to meet the new arrival! It is obviously a great emotional feeling for parents to hold their newborn child for the first time, but it is equally thrilling for grandparents to hold their newborn grandchild. Rebecca was lovely! I know that all doting grandmothers say that, but she really was a pretty baby. Arthur and I were very happy - Rebecca was the first of the new generation in our immediate family.

For me, things were going well at work. Sales were up and statistics were showing that we were more than holding our own by way of percentages in the commercial area. I have kept the Memos informing us of these successes and the congratulations from our immediate superiors.

Betty, my part-time assistant eventually left to work full time in a Solicitor's office and Marian, an adult teenager, was appointed to replace her. She needed training and development, but was intelligent and eager to learn. Interestingly, Marian still worked at the shop when I retired and wisely attended evening classes to learn about computers and new technology in order to keep up-to-date with developments and safeguard her career. When the Manweb shops were finally closed Marian found it easy to transfer her skills to office work. I had the privilege of mentoring and coaching her development commercially, and nurturing her personally in many ways to become the mature, capable and lovely lady she is today. She herself acknowledges she learnt a lot by working with me, and how happy she was playing her role in our little group.

There were sales promotions arranged quite often by the various companies and manufacturers with whom we traded. I won many small items over the years such as a vacuum cleaner, an iron, a copper saucepan, stepladder, and so on, but the best prize was for a 'shop window display competition' organised by Electrolux called the 'Top of the Bill' display. We were thrilled to win first prize in the knowledge that we were competing against much larger shops with better window space and more staff to help.

Our competition entry showed a display of Electrolux appliances in the background of the window with two lady models in the foreground. One was sitting down exhausted, dressed drably in mobcap and apron, holding dusters, a dust pan and sweeping brush, and the other looking very glamorous was standing dressed very smartly using a new model Electrolux cleaner. A large sign hung above the scene that posed a question 'Which is your life?'

My prize was to travel to London with Marian as my guest, where we enjoyed the best reserved seats at the London Palladium to see 'The Two Ronnies Show'. Following the show we went by special coach to the Beefeater Restaurant near the Tower of London where we enjoyed a Mediaeval Banquet. It was certainly a different experience, and one that we would not have had at home! A twin room had been reserved for us at the Marble Arch Holiday Inn for an overnight stay where we were comfortable and looked after well. We both had a wonderful time and thoroughly enjoyed the prize.

I was known to enjoy and appreciate training and development opportunities, and was therefore given a chance to attend a special course at the 'Horsley Towers Training Establishment'. This was the Headquarters of the Electricity Council in Surrey. It was a course designed for Supervisors and Managers with the purpose of developing their higher order skills in - 'Effective Reading and Writing'. Although I valued the opportunity and went willingly on the course, I did wonder initially however, what I could possibly gain from it that would be new and useful to me. After all, I had always been an excellent reader and writer, a fact verified by the 'A' grades attained at A Levels in the VIth Form all those years ago. But, I was soon to be enlightened!

I discovered that Horsley Towers was a large mansion in the country with a long drive to the main entrance. It had originally been owned by a rich man who obviously wanted to lead a grand lifestyle. He did not want any contact with the lower classes however because he had an underground passageway built for the servants and tradesmen leading to another entrance! When I was there however, everyone seemed to use the driveway, the course participants certainly did, but I was intrigued to know whether or not the underground passageways were still in use: and by whom?

It was a very useful training course because it taught me to *read* letters and memos quickly, grasping the essentials in a short time, it also taught me to *write* letters and memos succinctly in a short time too. It proved to be invaluable for I received a daily bag of mail from District Office as well as letters delivered by the Postman every morning that I dealt with whenever opportunity presented between customers. I did not have the luxury of a large staff to deal with the public while I dealt with management duties, so I often had to wait until closing time to attend to such matters.

For several years Arthur had suffered periodically with stomach upsets just as his father had done in previous years. For over two years he more or less lived on *'Complan'*, a fortified milk drink. This was the only way he could avoid stomach pain. He did not seek medical advice from our G.P. because he believed nothing could be done without major surgery. Some years earlier, he had undergone minor surgery on a salivary gland in his mouth. He'd been puzzled by symptoms that appeared as soon as he started eating when his face and neck would swell up and become flushed. It was very strange indeed. The Doctor sent him to hospital where stones were discovered in a salivary gland. The Surgeon decided to operate from inside the mouth and in so doing accidentally damaged a nerve on Arthur's tongue with the result that thereafter he had no feeling in half his tongue. It took him a very long time to become accustomed to the lack of sensation in half his tongue - a feeling I would imagine to be similar to having been permanently injected for numbness at the dentist before treatment. When the trouble recurred at a later date, the same Surgeon operated on Arthur, but did so through an incision in the neck the second time, he removed the offending gland completely. He was told not to worry about the loss of the gland because there were many such glands in the mouth. Arthur was given one of the stones, which he kept as a souvenir. Ugh! He wasn't keen on having another operation, if he could help it.

However, the pain from the stomach trouble became worse and eventually on August Bank Holiday, Arthur was really ill all night and finally vomited blood several times. The previous day, despite his suffering, he had conducted a successful singing Festival. We also had a houseful of B. & B. guests, all wanting to be fed. But before doing anything else the following morning, Arthur finally went to see our Doctor at his surgery in Betws y Coed, who immediately arranged for an emergency entry into hospital at Llandudno. Fortunately, I did not have to go to work that day and Glenys and Kerry also happened to be home for a few days, so together, we were able to cope. Glen went with her father to the hospital that day and stayed with him until he was settled and comfortable. I remained at home to sort out the guests, do the washing and ironing, then clean bedrooms, toilets and the bathroom. It was a very worrying time for all of us. Glen and Kerry returned home to Bolton after a few days when things had calmed down at *Llys Cerdd.* Arthur, at this time was doing most of the B&B work while I was at work, but he had been admitted to hospital and I knew I could not cope with guests alone. Either I had to have a replacement for Arthur or close the B&B until he was recovered again. I rang Glen and asked if she would come back home to do the work because we relied on the income in the summer. She agreed immediately to help out for a week as requested, which was so very good of her for she had plenty of other things to do during the school holidays.

Following tests and X-rays it was found that Arthur had a duodenal ulcer, and it was decided to operate upon it immediately. As luck would have it, the usual Senior Surgeon was absent, and a young Swedish Surgeon was the locum tenens. He explained that he had used a piece of the stomach to create a new opening into the duodenum thereby by-passing the ulcerated section which would then either wither or heal. He had also cut a vagus nerve, which meant that Arthur would never again have trouble with over-acidity. My niece, Nerys, who was a professional nursing Sister, explained to us that it was the very latest operation of its kind. This all proved to be 'spot on,' but after the operation Arthur was still very poorly. He was allowed drinks, but there was very little urine being produced. His stomach was distended and he could feel the liquid sloshing about inside. This lasted for 24 hours until the problem was observed and immediately thereafter a notice appeared above his bed that said 'Nil By Mouth' and all sorts of tubes and drips were attached to his body. He was allowed only enough liquid to wash out his mouth. The reason was that the flesh of the internal wound had become swollen and was blocking the outlet from the stomach.

While he was still lying in bed at the hospital, feeling very poorly and groggy, a local dignitary from Llanrwst visited him, stood at the end of the bed looking very serious, and announced in a loud voice, “Well Arthur old chap, you do look pretty awful!” Another man present, one of Arthur's friends was aghast and told him not to talk nonsense. Somehow you do not expect a professional man to be so lacking in common sense, never mind tact, especially when a person is very weak, ill and in pain. However, after three weeks in hospital Arthur was considered well enough to return home.

Glenys worked hard making breakfast for the guests, cleaning the house, making beds, washing, ironing, shopping and also simply being at home to answer the door-bell to new visitors who called on-speck. A week became a fortnight, and before we knew it, the fortnight became three weeks by the time Arthur returned home: Glen stayed all that time. She went for him from hospital that morning in the car, while I was at work. He had been told he could then eat anything he fancied in moderation. Glen asked, “What would you like for your lunch Dad?” “Bacon, eggs and mashed potatoes,” was the reply. That was what she cooked, and he ate it with relish! He could hardly believe how his life had changed - no more feeling ill, no more having to exist on *'Complan'* and especially, no more pain!

He was so pleased to be home, but felt very weak and totally drained after the operation and repercussions, but insisted on Glen telling him what she wanted as a 'thank-you' gift. She protested that she didn't want anything, but he was determined, so they ended up walking along Watling Street as far as 'Lloyd Jones and Bebb' - the store that sold everything for the discerning householder, to buy a set of kitchen knives, an item that Glenys, as a newly-wed had not yet managed to purchase. Glenys said that her father had taken a very long time to walk the short distance that day because he was so weak, but she was immensely moved by his expression of gratitude to her - she still remembers it with great fondness.

By mid October Arthur felt well enough to drive down to Porthcawl in South Wales to adjudicate at the Miners' Eisteddfod for a whole day, and then drive back home again after a full day's work. On this occasion I accompanied him, just in case he started to feel unwell, but he was fine and we both thoroughly enjoyed the occasion.

Chapter Forty-Nine

TRY - AND YOU MIGHT, DON'T - AND YOU CERTAINLY WON'T

Early in the New Year a television company in Cardiff advertised for entrants to appear in a televised Quiz Competition. Someone put forward my name, and a group of us were interviewed to see if we were suitable. Four were chosen: two men and two women. We travelled by car, starting out after lunch, travelling on the eastern side of Wales through Ludlow where we stopped for refreshments. During the journey the weather deteriorated for it started snowing. Sarah, the other lady and I wanted to get going, but the driver was fortifying himself for the rest of the journey and we were dependent on his goodwill.

It was getting dark when we set forth once more and the snow was being driven by a biting wind. However, we were warm enough in the car and our chauffeur was competent, but things were not quite as rosy for the fourth member of our party sitting in the front passenger seat. We relied on minor roads, small road signs and finger posts to get to Cardiff, but that night, snow covered the directions they provided. Whenever a decision had to be made at crossroads or a fork in the road, out came the command, "Well, go on Ifor, get out and see what it says … and close the car door behind you!" Several times poor Ifor had to scrape snow from signs and return to the car with the required information. He became very wet and frozen in the process. During the last part of the journey we could feel the car sliding and slipping increasingly on the road, and we heaved a huge sigh of relief on eventually reaching our hotel in Cardiff. Credit was given to Harry for driving us safely to our destination despite all the hazards en route and to Ifor too, for his willingness to navigate in uncomfortable circumstances.

Next day we went to the Studio to start rehearsing the programme. Well, the state of the studio can only be described as seriously breathtaking! Where were the luxurious settings seen on our television sets each evening? It was baffling, not only was there no luxury, colour and splendour, but absolute chaos reigned everywhere. The place seemed full of big thick cables stretching for miles, enormous lamps, cameras, spotlights and lots of people walking about with clipboards. Perhaps modern technology has changed all that because more recently I was in the audience of another televised Quiz Show and noticed that its programme setting was similar to a floor show in a theatre. Incidentally, we had great fun on that occasion … and I won a small dishwasher for answering a general knowledge question correctly! However, on the Quiz Programme in Cardiff, we did not do very well as a team and did not win. However, that did not matter. It was a completely new experience: we had learned how things worked in Television Studios, and enjoyed a lot of fun working together on a joint project.

Back to work again, humdrum chores and all that! Work at home meant spring cleaning the house from top to bottom again by working round the Easter holiday as usual. We could never take visitors during that time because the holiday was the only chance I had to buckle down to the annual deep cleaning of the house. I had a lot to do at home, and things were extremely busy at the shop too: the days flew by; I achieved my goals; and lived to tell the tale!

The Manweb building was owned by a firm that sold menswear nationally. After closing its Llanrwst branch, the firm leased the building to Manweb, and sent a representative each year to ensure it was being maintained properly. One afternoon, having recently carried out the annual check, the representative appeared again and requested the keys to go upstairs. I fetched the keys, and decided to walk with him on his rounds. "You've already done your annual check," I said. "Why have you come again so soon?" He told me that his clients were selling the shop as an investment property, and the sale would take place in London imminently.

As soon as the man departed, I phoned Manweb Head Office at Chester and requested the 'Buildings Section'. I knew the chap who was in charge of the Maintenance Division and eventually got to speak to him to ask if he knew about the sale of our building, and it was obvious that he didn't. He said he would get in touch with Head Office straight away.

Soon, I had Manweb Management on the phone wanting to know all about the visit and my conversation with the Agent. I told them they had to move quickly if they wanted to acquire the premises because the sale was to be held within a week. Well, they were obviously interested because Manweb ended up purchasing the property at the sale in London!

Before long, Manweb had decided to increase the area of the shop floor in Llanrwst by incorporating the space occupied by the rear storeroom. A new storeroom would be created by purchasing a couple of derelict cottages behind the shop and converting them appropriately. The floors upstairs would become flats to be rented out. All the plans were drawn up, but then a snag appeared! The grocery shop next door objected to the Manweb plans on the grounds of 'loss of light'. So the whole plan was scuppered! It was very unfair, but that was the law I suppose. I was disappointed because our hard work had led to an increase in business, and more space and better facilities would have made things better still. But it was not to be, and that was that.

A firm of builders later purchased the derelict cottages behind the stores, repaired and converted them into pretty little homes. The passageway between our shop and the big adjacent Store led from the Square past the cottages and a house, directly to the river. It was called 'Steam Packet Alley' and I am certain there is a fascinating history to the Alley. Much to my annoyance at the time, someone with a vested interest suddenly built a brick wall that blocked off that ancient passageway. It was a thoroughfare no longer, but no one objected officially to it as far as I am aware. Shame on whoever did such a thing because they had no respect for the rights of Llanrwst people and no appreciation of Llanrwst's ancient history. I wish someone would take up the gauntlet and challenge the perpetrator even now in 2005!

Manweb ran many promotions in collaboration with manufacturers, some were very successful, others less so, but they all represented good value. I would not have promoted anything that did not represent genuinely good value for money. 'Hoover' then manufactured many different appliances of good quality and I had no hesitation in presenting their qualities to my customers.

On one occasion 'Hoover' ran a competition for sales people, and I was one of the winners. The prize was a weekend in France. I travelled to Chester by train, then flew to France with the other winners, but I cannot recall from which airport we went - I presume it was Manchester. It was a small plane and its frame creaked and bumped a bit in the air streams giving the impression that it was about to fall apart any minute. But the experience was very exciting, and the company I was in, extremely jolly and joyous. We spent some time sightseeing in Paris and had lunch at a lovely restaurant in the city centre. There were many French families lunching together and we were told it was customary for families to dine out on Sundays. Afterwards, we boarded a coach and drove south to Burgundy country. We arrived at Dijon, famous for its mustard and I was very impressed by a Church in the town. It had the most beautiful roof, different coloured tiles in amazing patterns, and inside were curtained alcoves on both sides where the sick used to be tended. We were told that the sick were no longer treated there, but the last patient had only just recently left. That Church had been a Hospice, and this had been the case in certain Churches in Britain in times gone by too. I can think now of some villages in Wales that are named after their old Church Hospices such as *Ysbyty Ifan* and *Ysbyty Ystwyth*, (*Ysbyty* - means 'Hospital' in today's speech).

We were then taken to a Chateau and its vineyard to do some 'wine tasting'. We saw where the vines grew, then went down into the caves underground. There, we saw the huge wooden corkscrew winepresses that were used in the past. Leading out of the main gangway were smaller caves where bottles were stored, some had strong iron gates with big padlocks on them. Inside, absolutely covered in dust, were hundreds of bottles of vintage wines that were so valuable as to be priceless. I wonder whether the contents would ever be fit to drink!

I am an absolute ignoramus as far as wines are concerned but, I do know the ones I like to drink occasionally, and they are the lovely ones. I am not bothered in the least with any others. We were given small, shallow, round tasting dishes at the vineyard and expected to queue to receive our 'splash' of different wines. The queues were quite long because there were many people there and some were very merry indeed. We were not far from the Swiss border and some French and Swiss people made a habit apparently of visiting all the free wine-tasting vineyards within travelling distance! The notion seemed a bit far-fetched to me, but who knows? What did it say about the people involved I wonder? Anyhow, we enjoyed our visit and soon the weekend in France was over, and we returned home. What a prize we received! I hasten to add here that Manweb shop staff members were never paid commission on sales.

Chapter Fifty

SOCIAL INVOLVEMENTS

In 1980, Soar, the Presbyterian Chapel in Llanfair Talhaearn, where I had been a member for years was celebrating its 150th birthday. I had been baptised there; attended Sunday School and learned to read Welsh there; attended the Band of Hope; been received into full membership of the Chapel there; been a Sunday School teacher and a Precentor; and been married there too. The place was, and still is very special to me!

Out of the blue arrived an ivitation for me to conduct a Singing Festival at the Chapel, the occasion was to be one of several meetings planned for a week of celebration. I was very proud and pleased to accept the invitation and glad too that Arthur had been invited to play the organ. Of course the organ was not a huge pipe organ such as the one at Seion Llanrwst, nor was the Chapel itself as large as Seion, but there was a full house in Llanfair that evening of about 300 people, all singing four part harmony. They had *wonderful* voices: tenors, bass, alto and soprano. It was a thrilling experience and I was so very proud and privileged to be their Conductor.

I had chosen the hymns and their tunes personally to represent a special event or someone extraordinary who had touched my life in some way. As members of the congregation stood and sang from their hearts and souls, I could see in my mind's eye the various people being represented by the hymns, and I wondered if my father could hear us singing his favourite tune 'Builth,' a tremendous tune with the different voices rising and falling and interweaving to create wonderful waves of harmony. I was reminded of my paternal grandmother's ancestors with their reputation of 'never quarrelling because they were always singing'. This is far-fetched maybe, but how inspirational and memorable it was!

A tape-recording was made of the event, but unfortunately the recorder was positioned too near the organ causing the sound to drown the voices at times. Despite its imperfection, I treasure that recording and thoroughly enjoy listening to it periodically. The day itself was magnificent in every way, and the only regret I had was not having access to the old American organ that was played at the Chapel in my youth - for it had a soul! How unlike the modern electronic one currently in use at the Chapel that has many automatic features, but none of the beauty of tone and soul of its predecessor. I would have been overjoyed had I been given the chance to purchase the old organ when it was being pensioned off.

At another meeting during the week of celebration, different people who no longer lived in Llanfair spoke of their growing-up years there, when the goodness and dedication of older members guided them to the Christian way of life. My brother was one who spoke extremely well and very movingly about his childhood and teenage years in Llanfair. The entire event made a deep impression on me, and I shall always remember it as a blessing.

The group of singers I had sung with in concerts for many years still got together occasionally for special charity events. One year we received an invitation to perform at the St. David's Day Celebration at the Welsh Club on Teesside. There were five of us in the group - Arthur accompanist, Richie Thomas tenor, Meirion Jones baritone, Win Owen contralto and me, soprano. All the singers had excellent voices and sang solos, duets and as a group too, and Arthur was an exceptional accompanist. We provided a rousing Welsh

Concert that evening that was thoroughly enjoyed by many people who were either Welsh or had connections with Wales and living in the Teesside area and further afield. They even held an annual Eisteddfod there at one time, such was their love of all things Welsh!

We stayed overnight with Elsie and Neville who had by then moved from Redcar to live in a village called Loftus. There were some fine old buildings there, many smaller dwellings, and few shops. Many local people worked in either potash or coal mines in the hinterland. Els and Nev's property consisted of a very fine detached house with large grounds near the old Hall.

We had travelled to Teesside in two cars and enjoyed a splendid journey there: the men in Meirion's car and Win and me in the Hillman Imp. But the following morning, the weather was very cold as we departed for home, and snow had fallen overnight. However, the main roads had been cleared so we set out in good heart, having earlier eaten an excellent breakfast. The men led the way and we followed and all was well until we reached the turning from the A19 into the A1 when the heater in the Imp stopped working. I hooted the horn and flashed the lights to get the men's attention, but of course they were talking and joking as usual and totally oblivious to us in our hour of need. I had to stop at a layby to fetch a rug from the boot and insisted that Win wrapped herself in it because it was so cold in the car. I then drew up my coat collar, put on a scarf and a pair of warm boots, but unfortunately failed to find gloves to wear. We then set off again knowing that the others by then would probably be miles away, unless they'd stopped somewhere to enable us to catch up with them. As we travelled along, half expecting to see them waiting for us in one of the many laybys, it soon became apparent that they were not concerned about us even when crossing the Pennines in the snow. We learnt later that they hadn't given us a thought until their arrival in Llanrwst reminded them of our existence! We could have been stranded for all they knew…and we were not best pleased I can tell you! It is a long journey at the best of times, but it seemed twice as long in the cold without a heater!

When we finally reached home I was so cold I could not get my legs to move and my hands were almost frozen to the wheel. What a journey, but at least we had arrived back safely. At Christmas time I often admired the attractiveness of cards showing people travelling on stage coaches pulled by horses in the snow in 'ye olden days' without considering just how terribly cold such travellers must have been in those days with no heating, or any form of basic comfort. Brrrrrrr.

We were looking forward to Christmas time and Bryn had hinted that he and Kath would like to visit *Llys Cerdd* for the festivity, and of course Rebecca would come too. How exciting it would be to have a child in our home at Christmas time once more. Arthur set out to make a matching little table and chair for Rebecca and painted them in bright colours. I had no problem getting a box big enough to hold them because there were plenty in the stores at work, but covering such a big parcel with Christmas paper was another matter! Elsie and Neville were also home and entered into the spirit of the occasion with gusto - the more the merrier as we say! But Glenys and Kerry were on holiday abroad in Tenerife, and on Christmas morning telephoned to say they were in shorts by the poolside enjoying blue skies and brilliant sunshine. This was in direct contrast to the equally beautiful Christmas snow-scene that met our gaze in Llanrwst that morning.

I have to say that I love going to hot countries to enjoy the sunshine and warmth, but definitely not during the festive season! At that time of year, I enjoy the luxury of looking out onto a winter scene whilst being warm and cosy inside surrounded by lots of lights and decorations, a Christmas tree and holly, food and drink, and lots of games and laughter. Last but not least, I also enjoy the Carol Services in Church and Chapel that remind us of the real meaning of Christmas.

Well, we had a very happy Christmas, and it was a joy to see little Rebecca's face when she finally tore her way into the big box to see what her Taid had made for her. Wonderful!

Each summer the Royal Welsh Show is held at the showground in Builth Wells, in mid Wales. It is mainly an agricultural event, sponsored in turn by individual Counties. However, the Show encompasses much more than agriculture alone: it is a huge event that lasts a whole week. It has a large central ring where all the competitions are held, and large marquees that focus on horticulture, cookery, arts and crafts, and all sorts of things that touch on country life in some way. In addition there are hundreds of trade stands and exhibitions, restaurants, coffee bars, beer tents, T.V. studios, Banks, a Post Office, all sorts of entertainment, various reception tents serving drinks and biscuits by different clubs and societies, Police, First Aid - you name it ... it is bound to be there! The Show is very highly regarded and extremely well attended. Some people say it is the best of all the shows held in the U.K.

The Electricity Board had a permanent building on site and its exhibition was organised by the South Wales Electricity Board assisted by members of the Merseyside and North Wales Electricity Board. I was invited by the Marketing Section at Chester to be part of the team. It was flattering to be asked to do this and no doubt it was due to our Shop's excellent sales figures, but I suspect it was also very useful to have a bilingual experienced sales staff member on the stands. Other members of the team represented 'Energy Sales Marketing', and 'District Sales Marketing'. I was happy to accept and looked forward to the event.

All the Manweb staff stayed at the same hotel in Llandrindod Wells where we were well looked after, and entertained in the evenings. But by Jove, it was hard work! It was not so bad for colleagues who were expected to roam the Show Ground promoting goods because they had freedom of movement and fresh air, and could sit down periodically, but for those of us who were working within the confines of the building where all the different appliances were exhibited, conditions were very different. The floor, in being concrete made obvious demands on our feet, a fact made worse by having little scope to move about because of the need always to be available at the stands, and worse still by having nowhere to sit for even a minute or two! Our feet ached having been on duty from 9.00a.m. until well after 6.00p.m. Even so, I would not have missed it for the world, the experience was highly challenging, very stimulating and extremely rewarding in many ways. It was also a change from my usual routine and an interesting opportunity to meet all sorts of different people - it was a window on the world one might say! I enjoyed it and returned for some years. I received a nice letter from the Chief Commercial Officer in Chester relaying the thanks of his counterpart in South Wales, "for the valuable assistance provided by yourself as Manweb Staff in the successful presentation at the Show," and also adding his own appreciation of my contribution. Nice to be appreciated - 'Thank you' goes a long way.

Later that year I was invited to become a member of the Conwy Valley branch of Soroptimists International, an association of clubs for professional and business-women believing in friendship, striving for the ultimate triumph of goodness over evil in the world, and working for charity. It was a great honour to be invited to become a member of the club and I enjoyed the good fellowship of its members for many years. During that period I learned a great deal from listening to various guest speakers and visiting interesting venues. On one occasion, my friend Tilly Goodwin and I attended a gathering at Chester and we met the Duchess of Westminster and enjoyed a speech given by her. She was a very gracious lady.

My next venture came very unexpectedly and was in connection with historical Llanrwst. I had known for some time that the old Almshouses on the street leading to the Church had finally become empty. I could remember a time when three or four people lived there, one was a cultured elderly gentleman who deputised for Arthur as organist at Seion Chapel during the August holiday break. I had always found it difficult somehow to associate a musician capable of playing that great organ with someone living in an almshouse, but it was so. I believe that being alone in the world was the main reason for his being there, and all he wanted in life at that stage was contained in his spartan one room bed-sit. He had no luxuries, but managed to look after himself reasonably well, staying clean and keeping his dignity. However, as the years went by he became more and more frail and finally died, which left only one woman in the Almshouses. Years earlier there had been a number of people living there including an old gypsy lady who arrived after becoming a widow. It is said that she and her husband used to entertain visitors on the promenade in Rhyl in the '20s and '30s, when he played harp music and she danced to the tunes.

Sometime after the last person had left the Almshouses it was discovered that the fabric of the building had deteriorated seriously within a relatively short period of time. The Almshouses were in desperate need of urgent attention: their demolition would have been totally inexcusable and a complete travesty, not least because of their history. Surely someone in the community would see a need to undertake responsibility for the situation and take swift action to 'save' the Almshouses from oblivion!

Their history started in 1610 when Sir John Wynne of Gwydir erected on a site adjoining the Parish Church of St.Grwst, the almshouses to which he gave the name 'Jesus Hospital' - for the reception of twelve poor men of the town. He endowed this Charity very well with the rectorial tithes of Eglwys Bach, the village where I now live, tithes that in 1770 were worth £200 per annum - a princely sum in those days. The Almshouses continued for nearly 200 years as Sir John Wynne had left them, but were then improved a little so they could continue to give shelter for another 160 years right up to recent times.

By 1981 a number of local people had become increasingly concerned about the state of the historic building, and finally a Steering Committee for the 'Almshouses Museum Project' was set up. The Committee met five times and considered all the relevant matters concerning the importance of the Almshouses building. At the final meeting of the Committee on 29.06.82, it was unanimously agreed to form a 'Charitable Trust' with the objective of acquiring the property and then urgently pursuing its renovation and conversion. Representatives from different Oranisations and Societies in Llanrwst were called to meet on 06.09.82. to arrange the setting up of a 'CharitableTrust', which was eventually founded on 07.12.83 after two years of discussion between the Llanrwst Community Council and many other interested local parties. The Trustees who had been elected from voluntary local organisations and individuals were all unpaid, and had a

dedication to the objectives of the Trust, as follows:
1.To purchase and completely restore the Llanrwst Almshouses, so saving them from a probable fate of dereliction and by so doing conserving an important part of our Welsh architectural heritage.
2.To adapt the interior of the Almshouses to provide a museum of local history. This educational facility was to serve the people of Llanrwst and the Conwy Valley, presenting its history in both permanent and changing temporary exhibitions. The title was: The Llanrwst Almshouses and Museum Trust.

I am proud to say that I was one of the ten original trustees, and served as Treasurer for some years too. We set up an appeal fund and held different functions to raise money, but it was a very challenging effort because there were no significant grants available at the time, unlike today.

Eventually, when 'Heritage' became more fashionable nationally, grants became available, but in order to claim them we had to abide by strict rules and conditions, and in order to comply with the Charity Commissioners rules, the Almshouses had to be operated by the Trustees of the original Sir John Wynne Charity. At that time only two were left, and when they both died the new Trust had to nominate fresh trustees for the old original Trust. I will not delve into any further detail, suffice it to say that those new Trustees worked long and hard and succeeded in rescuing and renovating the Almshouses with support from various grant providers.

We, in the *Llanrwst Almshouses and Museum Trust* have by now succeeded also in setting up a Museum in the Almshouses, with the aid of grants. It has been such a long haul, but I am so glad to be associated still with such a dedicated group of people who have held faith for over 22 years. During that time other people with similar aspirations also became involved in the work and have contributed effectively to the cause. The building is now beautifully kitted out with furniture, modern displays and artefacts.

We had a Grand Official Opening Event on 26th April 2002 with Lord Dafydd Elis-Thomas A.M., Presiding Officer of the National Assembly for Wales, doing the honours. He was born and bred in Llanrwst of course, and knew the Almshouses well. He acknowledged that for 22 years a small group of people in Llanrwst had worked diligently to save the historic building, and in achieving success had needed to overcome many frustrations and disappointments by maintaining their hope and being persistant. He welcomed the restoration of the Almshouses and delighted at the fact that they were being opened to the general public as a historic venue of interest.

The Museum is open to the public, and to date, many thousands of visitors have been to the Almshouses in Llanrwst. Entrance is free, but there is a donation box and a small souvenir shop.

Throughout life we gradually learn about, and come to know the many facets of human nature, good and bad. But it was during my time in the Manweb shop, as I dealt with people face to face that I learned to evaluate human behaviour and identify personal qualities. Training was part of it, instinct yes, and intuition too, but it was also in the course of my ordinary chit-chat with customers that I really learned to understand human nature. We show our real selves during life's lighter moments do we not!

Chapter Fifty-One

ESPAÑA - HERE WE COME!

During the summer holidays, Glenys, Kerry and I went to Spain for two weeks. Friends of mine, Ken and Norah owned a beautiful villa in Javea and allowed us to use it for holidays, which was very generous of them. Javea was a small fishing village until it was 'discovered', so the old part still had fishing boats and little cottages and the new part modern hotels, shops, arcades and golf clubs. A couple of miles away from the village on a hill covered in Spanish pine trees in the shape of an umbrella a consortium of firms from abroad had developed beautiful properties in pleasant communities. Scores of villas, differing in size and shape had been built on individual plots, all with swimming pools and extensive, beautiful gardens. About half a mile away and convenient for the villa was a supermarket that sold everything we needed. On the hilltop stood a lighthouse and another could be seen further down the enormously craggy coastline. Javea village has a large stretch of sandy beach, and a wide tree-lined promenade with pleasant cafes and bars. Local artists sold their work there and I bought a picture from a pretty young girl and asked the artist to sign it so, "I'll be rich when you become famous," and she actually put her name on the back of it much to the amusement of her artist friends. It was also very pleasant to walk in the evenings to the nearest lighthouse and a nearby café. It was such a glorious experiemce to sit there enjoying the panoramic view in the cooler air of the evening after spending the day revelling in blue skies and spendid sunshine. Yes, sunshine, all day and every day - heaven!

Our villa was lovely, and had the Welsh name *Haulfryn* meaning (sunny hill) displayed in wrought iron at the main entrance. The external walls were painted white and a large Spanish style garden surrounded the villa. Pink and white oleanders grew along the perimeter walls and splashes of vivid colour were provided by geraniums and bougainvillaea. Ken and Nora had once planted a fig tree that bore fruit for the first time while we were there, but we had to rise early to gather the sweet green figs before the bees got to them first. When I say 'we' I mean Neville and me, when I holidayed there with Elsie and her family on another occasion.

The sun lounge opened onto a large sun terrace where a lovely pool was situated. We often had barbeques on the patio overlooking the pool side. The villa was refreshingly cool and spacious inside, it had a large sitting room with a fireside for warmth on cool evenings in winter, two bedrooms, a bathroom with shower, kitchen and a sun lounge. It was furnished in the traditional Spanish style which added to the charm of our relaxing holiday. Everything had to be kept clean to avoid infestations developing in the heat: a man cleaned out the pool regularly, and all our rubbish was deposited in a large communal bin at a designated site that was cleared daily.

There were several lovely restaurants in the vicinity. One that we frequented was run by an English woman and her Spanish husband who had met when he'd been working in an hotel in England. Another, owned by a Swiss man stood out because its garden had very green grass and borders of beautiful multi-coloured flowers. Masses of bougainvillaea grew rampantly everywhere and the stately yucca plants with their huge spires of white flowers contrasted dramatically with them. I was told that the yucca is native to the Caribbean and I wondered if the Spanish conquistadores had taken them to

Spain centuries earlier. The restaurant owner was very keen to ensure that his guests received good service and enjoyed themselves, he was always present, but never intrusive. The food was never anything less that wonderful … absolutely wonderful! The menu was printed in French, but had an English translation - we were told it had been translated by a group of Spanish High School girls. Their literal translation was very comical, but the meaning was clearly conveyed and we were appreciative of the girls' efforts.

A gardener came to tend the Villa's garden, but I watered it in the evenings and dead-headed plants after the sun had gradually disappeared below the horizon having created wonderful shades of gold and crimson. While watering, we could see hundreds of tiny lights in the garden: the eyes of small creatures that displayed fluorescent light in the darkness. Fairyland!

We visited several seaside towns and villages during those lovely sunny days and ventured to a couple in the mountains too. We had been told about an idyllic small hamlet in a bay at the foot of the cliff, where the water was warm and very clean. So we decided to visit, and Kerry initially drove past small-holdings with poultry, goats and donkeys in small fields and I saw the cockerel that woke me up every morning at the crack of dawn much to my annoyance!

Then the journey took us off the main road onto a much narrower and steeply descending road above a gorge. On both sides of the road were houses that looked as though they were hanging precariously in mid-air. The road became a zig-zag route on the steep hill and the car was gathering speed. Kerry decided enough was enough and decided to turn back - but the question was how was he going to do it? We came to a passing place that measured about 3 square metres. After a short while, Glen got out of the car having decided it was not possible to do a three point turn there, as the nose of the car was right up to the ledge and there were no railings or anything else between us and a long drop. I too was very frightened but decided that if I also left the car, Kerry might well lose his nerve. After a few minutes of calmer thought, Kerry decided it was safer to proceed down and Glen got into the car again.

Slowly but surely with our hearts in our mouths we reached the bottom which was an extremely pretty fishing bay that looked like the setting of the proverbial 'smugglers' hide-out'. But there was little else there, just one inn serving drinks and snacks, a few houses and local people staring openly at us - there were no other tourists there! We felt a little uncomfortable and bare in our holiday gear at first, but soon relaxed because we were treated with respect. We did not stay there long because of the thought of the drive back up to the top again, which incidentally turned out to be a little less scary than the drive down.

Then we explored the road behind the Church that led to a pretty village of whitewashed cottages, outside of which were lots of brilliantly coloured geraniums displayed in the sunshine. We enjoyed strolling, discovering this and that including an interesting little shop that sold refreshments and all sorts of souvenirs, some of them hand-made. Behind the counter two women chatted in Spanish. We chose some postcards and a few small pieces of pottery and Kerry found a small chrome figureine of a man riding a horse. When pushed gently, the figure rocked backwards and forwards for a very long timc and we decided to buy it as a gift for Arthur.

During our time in the shop Glenys and I must have spoken to each other in Welsh at some point because as we were being served, I ventured to use my rusty Spanish to ask,

"Cuanto es por favor?" and the younger lady smiled and said in perfect Welsh, *"Gwell imi ei roi yn rhatach i chi ynte,"* which means 'I had better charge you less I think.' Glen and I nearly fell over with shock, pleasure and excitement! The last thing we would have expected was to hear anyone speaking Welsh in that little village. She was originally from South Wales and had married a handsome Spaniard who had visited her home town on a three month job placement some years earlier. She was very happy in her new life, but had time on her hands and had decided to open her small shop during the tourist season in the village of Moraira.

She was as delighted to meet us as we were to talk to her, and I think she would have talked all day to delay our departure because she was suffering a touch of the Welsh 'hiraeth' on meeting us that day. Eventually we paid for our purchases and went on our way talking about our unusual experiences that day. Incidentally, the horseman ornamant that Kerry gave to Arthur still rocks on my Welsh dresser whenever I give it a gentle push after dusting it, and I am reminded of the Welsh lady in Spain and wonder how she fares.

The Spanish days flew by in pure bliss and soon we were returning home feeling relaxed and refreshed and looking well and truly tanned, for those were the 1970s, the days of serious sunbathing. Today we know better!

Chapter Fifty-Two

DIFFERENT EXPERIENCES

During the time Kerry and Glen lived in Radcliffe Road in Bolton they had the unfortunate experience of a robbery at their beautiful home. During one of the school half-term holiday breaks, Kerry had taken a group of pupils to a camp in the Isle of Man leaving Glen at home. She planned to collect Kerry from Blackpool airport on the Saturday when the group was due to fly back. Glenys set off for Blackpool at 2 o'clock and Kerry and his charges arrived on time at the airport, where they all met up and chatted about the holiday. Kerry and Glenys arrived back home in Bolton at about 5 o'clock. They unlocked the front door and immediately sensed something was wrong: they felt a draught and quickly realised the back door was ajar - it had been forced open. Glenys felt a sudden fear as she wondered whether intruders might still be in the house. Fortunately the house was empty.

They phoned the Police who arrived shortly thereafter to carry out their enquiries. They went round the house and saw that every cupboard and drawer had been ransacked and their contents strewn all over the place. It was difficult to identify what was missing straight away, beyond the obvious items. A brand new set of red suitcases had gone - full of the pickings no doubt. Certain items of jewellery had been taken, a beautiful carriage-clock and a new radio/recorder too. The instruction booklet for the radio/recorder showing a picture and serial number was given to the Police to aid their investigations.

After the Police had gone Kerry said, “Well, it could have been a lot worse, but we can say goodbye to what's gone. Thank goodness they did not see or could not get at the expensive Leak music equipment in the lounge.” Glen was upset by the thought of their hands going through her clothes. “Just think” she said, “They have seen our photographs, they know our faces, we could pass them in the street without knowing, but they would recognise us. Horrible! Horrible!” Both were upset, but calm, and set about putting the place to rights and getting a new lock fitted on the back door.

At approximately 11.00 p.m, the Police returned with the news that the thieves had been caught. Glen and Kerry could not believe what they were hearing. The two detectives explained that just as they were driving on the last lap of their tour of duty a call came from base instructing them to go to Bolton town centre to attend to a disturbance outside a nightclub. Two men had been refused entry because they were not properly dressed. The younger of the two was wearing Kerry's velvet evening jacket with a frilled shirt, and ragged jeans (not the done thing in those days)! He was also carrying a radio/recorder, which was thought by the detectives to look very much like the one on the instruction booklet in their possession. They questioned the men and the replies were highly suspicious so they detained them. The older man asked if he could use the toilet at the Club and was allowed to do so. Later the owner of the club found Kerry's gold rings in the waste bin and was honest enough to hand them to the Police.

After investigations it became clear that the robbers had operated on a large scale in different parts of the country. They were from Glasgow, lived in a mobile caravan moving from place to place. The mode of operation was to carry out robberies and stash the loot in a rented room wherever they happened to be. The Police found the red suitcases and many stolen items in the caravan in Radcliffe. They returned all the items that belonged to Glenys and Kerry amongst which was a pair of absolutely putrid socks that the Police had kindly sealed in a plastic bag. With a wry smile the Policeman said they had brought them along with the other things … just incase …they belonged to Kerry! Their humour was appreciated and all had a good laugh about the socks. Thus ended one criminal set up - at least, for a while. The two were imprisoned for two and a half years.

Glen and Kerry worked hard on the house - they converted the garage into a dining room, transformed the original dining room and kitchen into a large, splendid modern dining kitchen, installed fitted wardrobes in all the bedrooms, extended the drive and erected a double garage. I had helped to improve the large gardens that were difficult to manage on account of a pernicious weed known as Mare's Tail and Couch Grass - a devilish combination. But the robbery had unsettled them and they were determined to find another house.

During their time there, every Sunday morning the late ubiquitous Fred Dibnah would drive his wonderful steamroller slowly up and down Radcliffe Road, past their house, operating the whistle as he went. I enjoyed the spectacle, but apparently some local people were not amused. Arthur absolutely loved it however because of his passion for giant steam machines. He often went to visit Fred's yard and stayed there for hours at a time, he even had tea with the family once. Those were the days before Fred became famous.

However, the most important event to happen at that house was Marcus Vaughan's birth on the 17th May 1982. He was a fine healthy baby and a joy to his Mum and Dad and we all loved him straight away. He cried a lot at first and, remembering his mother's own first weeks of life, I hastily went in search of the wonderful *Dinnefords Clear Magnesia* that had wrought a miracle with her as a baby. I tramped from chemist to chemist but with no success. However, Glenys and Marcus bonded well from the start and she breast-fed him for 10 weeks, but was unhappy that a nurse had given him a bottle of powdered milk the night after his birth, against her specific spoken and written instructions, and she linked this to his crying. It had been done apparently with the explanation that the nurse had wanted to give Glen a peaceful night's sleep! What a short-term solution it was!

Glenys is as determined today as she was then that maternity nurses should respect the wishes of new mothers. She feels that maternity nurses should be held accountable for their actions when they contravene mothers' expressed written wishes regarding feeding. So, for the first 6 weeks of his life we did what we could to make Marcus as comfortable as possible by rubbing and patting his back after feeds until the 'burp' came, and soothing him by carrying him in a certain way over the shoulder at other times. After the first few weeks, things improved and Marcus established a regular sleep pattern. Weeks passed into months and he made good progress with all the baby/toddler milestones, and his parents revelled in it all. He was such fun to be around and we all enjoyed his company. Glen went back at work as Deputy Head at Cherry Tree Primary School after taking maternity leave, and Marcus was in the care of Ann Ford, a childminder who had once worked as a nursery nurse at Glen's school and was keen to look after him. Glen had confidence in her, and Marcus seemed happy with Ann and her teenage children. Some people do not approve of mothers going out to work leaving their children in the care of others, but if great care is taken in their choice and in monitoring the provision, it can be a good experience for the child, leading to self-assurance and independence. It was certainly a success with Marcus and later with his brother Morgan too.

In 1982, I was co-opted to serve on the Llanrwst Town Council. This pleased me very much, not only because it was an honour and an implied trust in my competence and suitability, but it gave me an opportunity to play a part in looking after the town and its residents. I found the work very interesting because there were many important issues to be dealt with at the time, including the controversy surrounding the ownership of *Llyn Crafnant* (Lake) set in the magnificent hills above the Conwy Valley. It had been, "given to the people of Llanrwst," i.e. the Town Council, by a local gentleman in his Will and had always provided the town with its water supply. When Local government was changed in the 70s, the 'Water Board' was formed and later 'Water' was privatised, and so, quite rightly, the question of *Llyn Crafnant's* ownership arose. There is also a property on the shores of the lake that is currently used by the tenant as a café, and rent is paid to the owner of the lake. There was a possibility of High Court action. Ultimately, after long negotiations an agreement was reached that pronounced Llanrwst town the owner of the lake having been the beneficiary under a legal Will, with the Water Authority, the District Council and the Town Council as joint Trustees.

In the spring, Arthur and I decided to improve our backyard. We had already introduced a flower border and small lawn that looked pretty, but knew we could make it better still. So we introduced an area of crazy paving, and the slate we used had beautiful colours and hues of greys, blues, pinks and greens shot through here and there with a touch of russet red and black too. Delighted with our purchase we were fortunate enough to have a very careful and artistic man to set out and fix the patterns for us. Our yard was then a wonderfully restful area, full of subtle and tasteful colour and was easy to care for. Flower pots and hanging baskets were everywhere and I loved tending them. The little shed cum greenhouse that Arthur and Bryn had built still looked good, and I remember it as the particular spot where I had disposed of an old piece of carpet that mysteriously continued to be ignored by the bin men. I would place the wet dirty piece of carpet in the bin and then later find it on the ground again, and even in dry weather the horrible thing was always wet.

In the end, I came across Bryn poking about behind the bin and discovered the 'factory' he was running. He was about ten years old at the time and loved messing about by the river. He was very interested in watching fishermen who waited patiently for a fish to bite in the Conwy River - Bryn watched their every move and chatted with them about fishing - he learnt a great deal this way. He saw some of them using worms and sometimes was asked to look for some. He decided to mass-produce worms in his nursery under the old carpet behind the bin … and sell them! It was no wonder I was not allowed to throw away such a valued source of wealth.

Mid-summer I was reminded, in the nicest possible way of course, of how time marches on: Manweb Head Office wrote to me to say that I would soon complete 20 years service with the company, and they wanted to present me with a long-service award. There was a good choice of gifts to choose from and I decided upon a Music Centre. That was the name given at that time to a unit consisting of a record turntable, VHF radio, tape recorder/player, and I chose the top of the range by adding my own cash contribution tothe Award. It was a marvellous choice and I have enjoyed hours and hours of beautiful music from it. Prior to this we had a radiogram at *Llys Cerdd* that consisted of a radio and a record player encased in a long, low wooden item of furniture. The sound was rich and mellow, and when that radiogram was in its heyday it was used regularly by all the family, especially Elsie and Glenys who played classical and pop records on it each day and danced to the music on their arrival home from school. Bryn too used it to savour the sounds of Shirley Bassey and a range of orchestral music too.

1982 turned out to be an eventful year in many ways that included a birth and a death in the family. We had all been looking forward to Christmas when out of the blue came news of the death of Arthur's brother Harry in November, aged 63. We found it difficult to believe the news because Harry was a strong and healthy man who was never ill and had a passion for his garden and singing. In retrospect I remember his telling me that he was looking forward to retirement - he was tired and his arms ached, but it seemed such an ordinary complaint at the time, and one that bothered most of us periodically.

However, he had become unwell on Friday and his condition worsened on Saturday, but he would not let Nance call the doctor. She eventually became so worried that she called Emyr, their elder son who, on arrival, immediately telephoned the doctor who arranged an ambulance to take Harry to hospital. As he was being carried out of the house on a stretcher he said to Emyr, “Look after your mother.” Shortly afterwards he died in hospital of an aneurism - a burst artery. It was a tremendous shock for everyone and it took a long time to become used to Harry's absence.

Arthur felt the loss keenly because he and Harry had been close from being little boys, and had always helped each other in different ways. They took a pride in not ever having rows or falling out with each other. The loss affected all the family greatly especially his wife Nance and children Emyr, Elinor and Elwyn because it happened so unexpectedly. Emyr was really shaken by his father's death as he confessed to Arthur, he said he would make sure that he had time to enjoy his own retirement. Nance then moved from *Bronllys* in Mochdre to a small bungalow just around the corner where she made a cosy home for herself.

A month later we had news that cheered us - a happy event on the 8th December when our third grandchild was born, a sister for Rebecca. The proud parents called her Faye Elizabeth, a lovely name, especially for me. Well, it's a step towards immortality is it not!

Arthur and I travelled to Driffield in Yorkshire for Christmas especially as we wanted to see the newest arrival into the family. She was a lovely baby girl, who was a joy to her Mum and Dad. Her sister Rebecca was so proud of Faye and was continually telling us to look at her. During our visit Elsie and Neville arrived and announced, they too were going to welcome a little one the following year - after fourteen years of marriage! I believe the delay was planned, but we wondered what had been the catalyst for ending the freedom years. I think it was seeing how happy the others were with their little ones. Granted, having children meant new ties, hard work and planning, but the joy and love made up for it all ... and more!

Life had become much more enriching for Elsie and Neville and so, on the 4th July 1983, Geraint Vaughan Lloyd was born - a fine healthy boy whose doting parents were so happy. Neville was over the moon and could not do enough to care for the baby. He gladly undertook so much of the 'nappy cleaning' jobs involved in baby care and delighted in the bathtime routine too.

Years before Geraint's birth Elsie and Neville adopted a kitten from a litter born to a stray cat in Llanrwst. They called him *Llew* (lion) and he grew into a magnificent specimen of the feline family, and they doted on him. Elsie had wanted a cat for sometime and on hearing about the unwanted kittens I visited them with Glen. We had enormous difficulty choosing just one kitten out of those five lovable balls of fur that were so funny and friendly. However, after watching them playing for a while, we chose the ginger one that seemed to be the leader of the gang, being strong, very active and playful. It eventually turned out to be a very good choice although we had doubts at one point when, en route to Yorkshire with the kitten, Glen and I stopped in Bolton for a respite. There we made the mistake of letting it out of its basket temporarily because within a second of freedom it had disappeared in the lounge. Having moved all the furniture and carried out a full-scale search for this tiny ball of lively fluff we eventually heard a miaowing sound coming from the chimney of all places! The kitten had managed to squeeze through a small gap between the fitted gas fire and the chimney breast. Kerry removed the cover of the gas fire and Glen got a saucer of milk, and finally we managed to entice *Llew* the kitten to re-enter the lounge … much to our relief.

Llew was pampered in his new home but not mollycoddled, and he followed Neville everywhere, but only when it fitted in with his own pursuits! At that time they lived in Loftus where they had a huge garden and orchard that stretched down to a stream - it suited Llew very well because it was a wonderful place for him to roam safely and at will.

Their attractive house had been built in the 1920/30 period and had solid block parquet flooring, solid oak internal doors, and stained glass windows. There was even an air-raid shelter in the orchard. The gardens were nicely laid out with a large lawn, side gardens and steps leading down to the dell with its stream. It was a demanding garden, but Neville enjoyed the outdoor work involved, and so did I when I went on periodic visits. They extended the lounge into the garage that resulted in a spacious leisure room cum-dining area. During this renovation, the floor in the lounge had to be lifted for various service jobs to be done and one evening, Llew could not be found. He was a confident cat, was not frightened of the workmen, and knew his territory well, and no one was unduly worried about him. After all, evening time was hunting time and Llew was an expert, having proudly brought home many specimens of mice, rats, birds and rabbits in his time. However, very late that night Nev heard him miaowing and went to the backdoor to let in the wanderer, but he wasn't there, nor was he at the front door, and the cries grew ever more desperate in tone.

Finally, it dawned upon Nev that the wailings were coming from under the floor in the lounge! Well there was nothing for it but to lift a section of flooring in order to rescue Llew. He was ecstatic at being free once more and although covered in cobwebs, had suffered no harm. His experience as a kitten in Bolton all those years earlier had not curbed his instincts for exploring! Who was it that said, "Curiosity killed the cat".

Then along came Geraint, and everyone believed Llew would feel neglected having been relegated from the comfort of the house to the utility room: he might run away or become jealous of the baby. But no, the new situation was quite the reverse. Llew became very attached to Geraint, and all was well.

My two black and white tomcats, Toodles and Figaro (Pwji Pwj) lived with us in *Llys Cerdd* for many years and we all loved them greatly. One morning as usual, I unlocked the back door for Toodles to come in for his breakfast, but was surprised that day that he wasn't at the door although I could hear his crying. I called his name several times, but to no avail. I asked Arthur to look for Toodles as I had to get to work, but I worried that he had got himself trapped somewhere and was unable to get free. As I crossed the town Square a young lady approached and asked if my black and white cats were alright. I replied that I hadn't seen one of them that morning. She said that she and her children had found a cat that very morning on their way to school and as it appeared to be hurt, had taken it to the Vet. I gave my thanks and hurried along as quickly as possible.

As soon as I had opened the shop I left my assistant in charge and crossed the Square to the Vet's surgery where I could hear Toodles crying and I just knew immediately that it was my cat. As soon as the Vet heard what I had to say he went to fetch Toodles from the cage where he was lying and laid him on the table. When Toodles saw me he stopped crying and started purring so loudly that he sounded like a moving train. The Vet explained that Toodles had been injured somehow: something had fallen onto him, he'd been hit by a car, or someone had been cruel to him. I found it hard to understand how he could have had an accident because he was such a healthy and strong streetwise cat, used to living next to a busy road. There was only a faint smear of blood on his fur, but he was paralysed from halfway down his body. Also the Vet could feel a swelling inside his body, which could mean internal bleeding. I asked the Vet if there was anything he could do and he shook his head.

I was absolutely devastated and sick at heart, but I could not even think of Toodles as a cripple. I knew I had to face a dreadful decision so I asked the Vet to put him to sleep. I put my arm under Toodles' head as he looked intensely into my face, happy and trusting because I was there. He purred loudly while the Vet injected as gently as possible. Slowly and peacefully Toodles closed his eyes and purred his way out of my life. I cannot tell you how heart broken I was because I loved that cat like a good friend and he loved me too. He knew everything about my movements and sentiments because I confided in him. For weeks I kept waiting for him to appear from somewhere and being always so disappointed when he didn't. Sadly I was not the only one to feel lost without Toodles because within weeks Figaro, (Pwji Pwj) just lay down and pined, then died shortly afterwards. He just did not want to live without his pal Toodles. Incidentally, the Vet was also moved to tears when he had to put an end to the life of such a magnificent cat as Toodles. He really was a wonderful, intelligent, loyal, dignified, good-natured and friendly cat. Loosing Pwji Pwj so soon after Toodles made it a double blow because he too had been an important member of our family. His characteristics were different from Toodles but special nevertheless. I treasure my memories of them both.

Christmas with its chores and delights came and went and we entered 1984. I knew it would be an exceptional year because I would celebrate my sixtieth birthday and would need to plan for the changes that would ensue in my life.

I carried out my annual spring clean of the house, and we decided to decorate rather more than usual, until we got our home to look very attractive from top to bottom. Arthur and I had decided that when I retired, we would put the house up for sale and look for a smaller home, preferably a bungalow. After we'd finished our decorating, the house looked so attractive that I had a sudden feeling of not wanting to leave it and I nearly changed my mind but later, common sense prevailed and I knew that it was time for a new phase in our lives.

Chapter Fifty-Three

LIFE WILL BE KINDER IF, HEAD HELD HIGH, YOU KEEP A TWINKLE IN YOUR EYE.

Summer arrived and with it St. Swithin's in July 1984 and my 60th birthday. Things had been going on behind the scenes, and Marian my assistant had been making arrangements with the staff in other Manweb shops, resulting in a most enjoyable 'sending off' party at a hotel in Rhos on Sea. I received numerous bouquets and lovely presents. At the party were current and past colleagues and friends including electricians with whom I had worked during my office days and some 'reps' from supplier firms. The District Manager also came and presented me with gifts. He made a wonderful speech that made me feel happy and sad! A beautiful basket of lilac and mauve flowers arrived from my daughter Glenys and her family and it was so marvellous that so many had attended and said such nice things in the usual bantering way of close friends. And we really were such good friends, no-nonsense pals who were honest and open with each other.

On the very last day at work my staff and I and our immediate friends enjoyed lunch at a local restaurant. Then later in the day, after I'd closed the shop for the last time, I was presented with a special cake and a bottle of bubbly that were shared and enjoyed before I finally handed over the keys and left the premises for the last time as Manageress. It was a peculiar feeling made up of mixed emotions including sadness arising from nostalgia, and happiness arising from looking forward to a happy retirement and having wonderful memories of my time at Manweb. I had worked for the Electricity Board for twenty two years, fourteen of which had been as Shop Manageress in Llanrwst. I can honestly say that I always gave of my best, very often going the extra mile. On the whole, Manweb was a good company to work for, and I always tried to ensure that my customers were satisfied with the service we provided in the shop. I knew most of my efforts were really appreciated by local people, but one or two people were never satisfied no matter how much time and trouble I'd invested in sorting out their plights. But I continued to do it anyway!

Even today, many people still know me as Mrs. Williams, Manweb! I received a very appreciative letter from the District Manager and have kept it, and in one paragraph it reads, "It is my pleasure on behalf of the Board to thank you for almost 22 years of loyal and good service. In particular I would like you to know that during the 14 years we have worked together I very much appreciated your dedication and enthusiasm not only in your service to your employer but also on behalf of our customers. Whenever you thought something was wrong - perhaps you could see that we were not being as efficient as you knew that I would want us to be, you always took the trouble to let me or my colleagues know, and quite frankly we need more people like you." Reading it again now, I can say, "Thank you Mr Mellor."

My time with Manweb spanned the period from when the electricity industry with all the various power companies, large and small, had been nationalised and welded together under the wing of the Electricity Council, and into the period when the successful Council was disbanded and privatised under the Thatcher Government of the 80s.

For many years the industry had been heavily subsidised by Government, necessarily so in order to achieve a safe, efficient supply of energy for the nation. I dread to think what life would be like today without a guaranteed supply of electricity. At first there were many problems to deal with within the industry including a lack of cohesion, but gradually with a plan of action, things improved enormously. For instance, there was comprehensive training available for all staff, and in Manweb most workers were willing and industrious. We were like a family and everyone helped where it was required. We all grumbled of course at times, but most of the staff were pleasant, cracked jokes and generally got on with it. A quick cup of tea was always a wonderful reviver! A qualified Manweb electrician, having been trained through apprenticeship and training school was implicitly trusted by the public because people knew he could be relied upon to do a safe and efficient job. Staff members at the Manweb Shops were equally well prepared at the Training School where we were taught not only to gain a thorough knowledge of the many appliances available on the shop floor, but to achieve customer satisfaction too. We had good products to sell and their many benefits made it easier for us to apply our sales skills to win customers.

Eventually the industry became very successful, the network grid was in place and everyone in the country areas had been offered connection to the main power supply at a subsidised price. Then there was a new Conservative Government elected that decided to privatise the industry and there was certainly no shortage of people wanting to cash in on the successful industry, which was by then booming after surviving the pains of birth and subsequent growth. The work force was pacified with offers of shares and most accepted. I believed that the industry should have been left intact to continue generating profits for the government to repay some of the subsidies that had earlier come out of general taxation.

I did not take up the offer of shares on principle, much to the amazement of some people and probably I was foolish, but I knew it was a carrot and stick offer. Many people benefited financially, but many people lost their jobs too. However it is a free country and everyone has a right to act as they see fit. It all happened round about the time of my leaving Manweb.

The manner in which I left the job - retiring after years of working happily with friends, was very different from the way I had to resign suddenly from my first job with the Inland Revenue when my mother became seriously ill all those years earlier. I had been happy working for Manweb, had worked very hard and gained satisfaction, but I had known all along that I would have to leave on my 60th birthday and I was prepared, or so I thought! The leisure time was welcome, but I missed my colleagues terribly with the camaraderie and socialising. I even missed my customers because they knew me and I knew them too. My assistants and I had worked hard to make the shop successful so that the people in the town and surrounding areas could enjoy the facilities it offered. However, within a few years, many of the Manweb shops including the one in Llanrwst had closed, much to people's regret. However, change is inevitable, the world does not stand still, and we have to learn to adapt in order to survive.

I had plenty of things to do at home to occupy my time. We continued to have visitors from all over the world and had kept a record of them and their comments in a Visitors' Book. I had never really had time to look at the book properly, but a couple of years ago I came across it in a drawer and read it from start to finish! The book was full except for the last page. Over the years, we had paying guests from New Zealand, South America, Canada, Switzerland, Germany, U.S.A., Australia, Spain, Holland, Belgium,

Luxembourg, South Africa, Poland, Bahrain, Malta, Argentina, Isle of Man, Sweden, Sudan, Singapore, France, Denmark, Mauritius and of course many from Scotland, Ireland, England and Wales. Their remarks were so wonderful that I felt like patting myself on the back as well as Arthur, Elsie, Glenys and Bryn and some very willing and friendly young girls who in the later years came to help as waitresses and chambermaids.

Doing B&B was hard work, it never left any of us with much spare time, and the upheaval for us as a family in the early years was considerable. However, it was part of the way we earned our living each year and I have to admit that on the whole I loved it! Meeting new people was exciting and invigorating, and giving them a pleasant stay was important to us. Tourism is essential to the economy of North Wales and I felt a need not only to provide good food and attractive rooms for our guests, but an explanation about our culture too. Our visitors wanted to know things about the Welsh language, our traditions and history, the Welsh people and our way of life. People from all over the world stayed at our house over the years, and I must have responded to thousands of questions and invested hundreds of hours in telling them about Wales. They learned from us and ... we learned from them too. I have lifted the following short list of quotes from the Visitors' Book that represent the thrust of them all:

Hans Hoffer, Germany wrote, “A very good breakfast.”
Laquita Stard, Washington D.C., “Food - wow!”
Mr. Morgan, Kent and Mr. Hatton, Hampstead, “First class in every way”.
Mr. Criedland & Steven, Bloemfontein, S. Africa, “Lovely place and sweet people to look after you.”
Mr. & Mrs. Raymond, Connecticut, “A Glorious gift you have given us. Thank you. A delightful interlude.”
Mr. & Mrs. Webster, Vancouver, “Extremely comfortable. Enjoyed everything. Just delightful.”
Stefan Keller, Dusseldortf, “Our very best B. & B.”
Misses Turcan, Paris, “Very nice holidays. We come back before long time.”
Mr. & Mrs. Abraham, Durban, “Outstanding. We hope to be back again before long.”
Group from Belgium, “Fine Welsh hospitality.”
Mr. & Mrs. Braambeck, Holland, “Nice, and full of music.”
Mr. & Mrs.Simpson & family, Calgary, “Excellent, lovely rooms.”
Mr. & Mrs. Yendel, Pennsylvania, “A very lovely meal and garden.” And on and on...

I feel so proud of what the book and its comments represent. I remember some of the people who stayed with us, but certainly not all: I genuinely miss the B. & B. work. We did not make a fortune, but it provided a useful income during what would otherwise have been lean summer months every year.

In 1984 Bryn received an invitation from the Office of the Lord Chancellor inviting him and his wife Kathryn to attend a Garden Party at Buckingham Palace on the 12th of July. This prestigious invitation was in recognition of his special efforts in the Falkland Islands during his tour of duty there. Bryn and Kath thoroughly enjoyed the occasion and looked the part in their very smart outfits.

After retiring, my life was given a boost again when I went on holiday to my friends' villa in Spain again with Glen, Kerry and Marcus. Arthur had an aversion to flying and would never go with us. I had looked forward to the holiday, and it was even better than the first time because we had 2 year old Marcus with us who was such fun. The journey from the airport at Alicante to the Villa at Javea was around 80 kilometres and of course the weather was very hot. As soon as we were clear of the busy city we travelled on a modern road for quite a distance before stopping for a break and a bite to eat at a small, authentic country café. We were given one huge platter of green salad covered in olives. And that was all - no plates, cutlery, condiments, bread or drinks. It was a novel experience!

The holiday was wonderful and we enjoyed doing the same things as before, dips in the pool, sunbathing, shopping, visiting the seaside and the markets, playing with Marcus and reading his books with him. Marcus made friends with different people such as the man who came to clean the pool, and a little girl of his age playing on the square in the village. Neither understood the other's speech but they were enjoying each other's company and totally accepting of each other as only young children can do.

During this holiday we made fewer visits and relaxed more by the pool when Marcus had his little snooze during the day. Glen was three months pregnant with Morgan and was feeling very well. Marcus often wandered about the villa naked except for a large hat and layers of sun cream, sometimes he pretended to play a toy Spanish guitar we'd bought for him in the local market. He also loved the pool and we had to be careful he didn't deliberately jump into the water unsupervised or accidentally fall in, for he was only a little fellow being two years old and unable to swim properly. But he was a grand little boy and well behaved too. He loved watching the small lizards that scuttled about and disappeared into holes in the garden walls, and spent hours playing with his little toy digger, lifting and moving soil from place to place. Too soon it was time to leave our Spanish haven in the glorious sunshine, to go home again.

Glenys and Kerry returned to their schools and Marcus to the daily care of Ann, his child minder. I felt under-employed on my return home and found it difficult to get used to the idea of not having a strict routine to live within that included going to work each day. And until I took myself in hand, I was really quite miserable. Arthur and I had already decided to sell the house, but chose to wait until after Christmas before putting it on the market.

In the meantime, we received an invitation to the wedding of my brother's younger daughter, Hefina. It came as a bolt out of the blue for we had not heard from them or seen them for several years, except for a chance meeting with Percy one day on the street in Llanrwst. On that occasion he was in town on business and I was on my way to the bank with money from the Manweb shop. Both of us were taken by surprise and felt unsure of what to do, but we stopped and greeted each other civilly, made polite conversation, then went our separate ways. And that was that until the wedding invitation arrived.

Arthur and I discussed the invitation in the wider context of things and finally decided to accept it because Hefina was our niece and had always been pleasant with us. We did not wish to mar her happy day in any way, nor did we wish to appear churlish. We anticipated a little stiffness from Eluned and Percy, but had no idea really how we would be received, but were prepared to play it by ear. The day of the wedding dawned bright and sunny: I put on a pretty dress and Arthur looked smart in a grey suit, and off we went to the Chapel in Conwy. Percy and Eluned had moved to live in Conwy after he retired from *Gregynog*. The wedding service was lovely and everything went very well. After the reception at a hotel we went to Percy and Eluned's house to wait for the bride and groom to get changed before setting off on their honeymoon. When we arrived, there was a small commotion going on for they had no key to get inside … they were locked out! Luckily a small window in the toilet was open and Percy was hoisted up and climbed through it - how he managed to squeeze through I will never know. As future proof, I took a photograph of the clean pair of heels he displayed as he disappeared inside. Everyone was very affable, Percy and Arthur got on well as they always had done and Arthur had found a soulmate in David's father - both were animated by steam power. Mr. Turner had been involved with steam machines commercially and Arthur was fascinated by their power and had a scaled replica of one to power his models of farm machinery. Nerys, our other niece who had been a very attractive bridesmaid escorted me to view all the wedding gifts on display in a bedroom upstairs. Eluned was busy being hostess to the guests who were at the house and was pleasant in her manner to us. All in all the occasion passed off amicably and pleasantly and Arthur and I were glad we had attended the wedding. It certainly broke the ice. Hefina had married a nice-looking, clever lad, and Arthur and I took to him and his family immediately. We were very pleased for them both.

Glenys telephoned in October to say they had sold their house on Radcliffe Road and would need to find another to move into quickly. She was expecting her second child in January and needed to get things sorted before the birth. After searching in the Bolton area for weeks, Glenys and Kerry finally bought a lovely new show house on The Beeches off Belmont Road.

A busy road ran alongside the garden, but the area was pleasantly close to open moorland and there was an *olde-worlde* little shop nearby known as the 'Top Shop'. The first time I walked Marcus to the shop, he noticed the dead body of a little black and white cat on the path by the entrance to the estate. He was most concerned because he thought it was my cat Mickey Mouse who was also black and white and loved very much by Marcus. After much reassurance that the poor dead cat was not Mickey Mouse, he was still talking about it and I had to lift the corpse onto the bank running alongside the path! After Toodles and Pwji Pwj had died in Llanrwst I'd been for a while without a cat and felt a little bereft. So when I heard about kittens on a farm in Glan Conwy needing a home Arthur and I visited and came away with a playful black and white Tomcat whose face reminded us of Mickey Mouse, the Disney cartoon character: hence the name we gave the cat!

A few days before Kerry and Glenys moved into their new home, I went to stay with them to help in any way I could. Moving house always means a great deal of work with packing and cleaning and so on, and because the school term was still ongoing Kerry and Glen had little time to get on with such things, and in addition, Glenys was nearly eight months pregnant. There were also a couple of alterations to be done to the lounge that involved builders and brickwork.

The garden at the back of the house had very wet grassland under established tall trees, and there were young leylandii planted close to the house on one side that were a nuisance and served no purpose where they were positioned. One day at my request, Glen took me to The Beeches and left me there with some tools where I spent the day digging eight big holes by the perimeter fence, uprooting the eight leylandii saplings and replanting them in the holes where they looked much better. At the end of that mid-December afternoon, darkness came early and I was hungry and wanted to use a toilet, but could not get into the house. Glen had promised to collect me as soon as possible after school once she'd collected Marcus, so I waited, and waited, and waited. But there was no sign of her and I got increasingly anxious wondering what had happened. Had she gone into labour? No, it was too early for that. I was desperate to use a toilet so I adopted a country custom and used the newly planted hedge and the darkness to satisfy one body function. I could not contact anyone, so I just went on waiting. Eventually Glen arrived full of apologies - she had completely forgotten I was there. Well, she had a lot on her mind at the time, so I suppose it was no wonder! I was so glad to get inside, have a shower and some food that nothing else mattered then.

They moved shortly before Christmas and I recall joining Glen and some of the staff from Cherry Tree School going to sing Carols one evening in aid of charity, and Marcus went too. After a while his little legs became tired and he wanted his Mum to carry him, which she did despite being heavily pregnant and only a month away from giving birth.

I returned to The Beeches mid January in readiness for the new arrival and he was late, really late, and his Mum was getting increasingly restless because of the weight she was carrying. Christmas had been and gone with all its excitement and activities. The old year of 1984 had gone, and the new year of 1985 had arrived, and on the 30th of January, Morgan Ashley was born, a bonny, healthy boy who was adored by his mum and dad and all of us who knew him.

Chapter Fifty-four

FAREWELL TO 'LLYS CERDD'

Arthur and I returned home from Bolton and arranged for an Estate Agent to value our house for the purpose of selling it. It can be an unsettling feeling when you are in the process of selling your home, it can give rise to a bit of anxiety - and that is how I felt at the time. During the first few weeks after putting it on the market, three or four local people came to inspect the house. I use that word deliberately because that is why they came, 'for a spec' for they had no intention of purchasing and I knew that, but it would have been unwise and churlish to refuse, and anyway I was proud of my home and was pleased to show it. After that, things became very quiet for weeks, but in April the agent told us he had a prospective buyer and the news jolted us into thinking seriously about where we were going to live after selling.

We looked round Llanrwst, but there was only a half-built bungalow available at the time that looked nice and was in a good location, but was priced far too high for its real worth. Then we spread out to nearby villages and the coastal belt and inspected so many places. We studied brochures, made calculations, dashed hither and thither when Arthur was free and generally worked really hard at finding a suitable new home for ourselves. We saw nice houses in unsuitable places and unsuitable houses in desirable locations. We saw some very peculiar houses and marvelled at the unusual décor and colour schemes chosen by some vendors. Well, there is no accounting for personal taste! We reminded ourselves that everyone is different, and how boring it would be if we all had similar ideas. At the same time we knew that a young couple had said that they wanted to buy Llys Cerdd, but had made no serious offer for it to date. They wanted to buy the house to do B. & B. all year round, but they did not have enough money to furnish the whole house. We were quite willing to leave a lot of the furniture, carpets, curtains and fittings because they would be surplus to our requirements and I drew up a list and leant over backwards to be more than fair in pricing them.

At this stage we were getting a little desperate to find a place for ourselves, but quite suddenly our luck changed. My brother put us in touch with an agency for which he had done some valuing of properties that were coming up for sale. The agency arranged for us to view a couple of properties on the coast on a Saturday morning, and as I left their office I just happened to glance at a rotating stand that displayed pictures of various other houses on sale. I saw a flash of white that made me stop in my tracks. I took one look at the photograph and details and immediately asked if we could inspect the white-painted bungalow. We were told it was vacant because the young couple selling it had just moved back to South Wales, and … would we like to view it the following day on our way from the other places arranged earlier? We agreed, but made it our first call - not last!

We met the agent at the bungalow, and after struggling with the key in the lock, he finally opened the door enabling us to enter the hall. Arthur followed him in and I traipsed behind. We had only just taken a couple of steps inside when Arthur declared, "This is it, this is the one." Well, I knew what Arthur meant, but I made suitable sounds only because I wanted to see it all properly first before committing to its purchase. I knew that the whole business was getting on Arthur's nerves and his judgement could be impaired, but after spending some time seriously assessing the pros and cons we decided that we were very interested, subject to my brother making his observations known to us. The agents were very helpful, we made an offer, and it was accepted. We were then in a position to go ahead with our own sale. The fact that our estate agent was acting for us as well as our purchasers was not ideal because he knew that we had found what we wanted in Eglwysbach and were keen to complete the sale of *Llys Cerdd*. As a result we found it difficult to withstand some erosion of our asking price, which we knew was fair. Arthur was keen to complete the sale, so we agreed the new price subject to contract, and the matter was left to our solicitors. We had sold a house in Llanrwst and bought one in Eglwysbach!

Ironically, during the following week two gentlemen rang our doorbell. They stood on the doorstep and declared they had come to view our house with the intention of purchasing it. I told them it was already sold. “That can't be so,” said one of the men holding out a copy of the '*Chester Chronicle*'. In it was a picture of the house and a full description saying it was for sale. They said they had travelled a distance and that I had to let them view the house and make an offer to buy. Well, I did not really know what the legal position was in such matters, nothing had been signed, but we had agreed to sell. Arthur was not at home to consult and I opted not to let them in, and that was that. I believe they were genuine, but I will never know for certain.

Then an even stranger thing happened the following day. A very pretty, nicely dressed young woman rang the doorbell and spoke to me animatedly in a cultured way saying, “I've come to buy this house.” At first I wondered whether I had heard her properly, so I asked her to repeat herself. She said she had come to buy the house and I told her that I was very sorry but it was already sold. She stared at me appalled, and then burst out, “Oh no, that is not true is it? It can't be. Tell me it's not true. I want this house and I have the money with me to pay for it.” She opened her handbag to show me the cash. “Please let me have it, I will pay you more than anyone else,” she said. Well I was flabbergasted! I didn't know what to do for I felt sorry for her and for us too, but having been brought up to behave in an honourable way, it is very difficult to deviate from it. The poor girl cried, and I felt awful as she finally left. I have thought of her many times and wondered what became of her. People have told me I was foolish not to have let her buy the house, and maybe I was. Anyway, it is history by now, and *Llys Cerdd*, our old home in Llanrwst is now over 100 years old.

The bungalow we purchased is modern, being only a few years old, and is part of a small estate of mostly true-bungalows, some having had dormers fitted. The detached true-bungalows have a large lounge, large kitchen, two bedrooms, a bathroom and toilet. They have very generous sized gardens at the back and front and an attached garage. The previous owners had enlarged our bungalow by adding two large bedrooms with dormer windows in the loft space. An open staircase leads to them from the kitchen. The house was in good condition when we purchased it, but needed redecorating throughout. While waiting for completion, I planned an operation that involved five workmen completing jobs to strict timing. First, there were things to be removed from the house including false rafters from the lounge ceiling and a truly monstrous floor to ceiling rough stone fireplace. Another big problem requiring attention was the Artex finish that covered the walls and ceilings of the lounge, hall and a downstairs bedroom. An amateur had done the Artex work, it consisted of smudges with needle-like points that seemed dangerous to me. I managed painstakingly to chip and scrape the ceiling and walls of the bedroom, but the rest had to be re-plastered before any painting or papering could be done.

The front garden was staked out, but very neglected and the back was an absolute wilderness. I tidied up the front and Neville, my son in law dug out borders in the back and mowed the grass. He found a large mound full of ants and a snake that he promptly killed. Then he broke into a wasps' nest and suffered a severe stinging above his eye. In no time at all it had swollen up obliterating the eye socket, and was giving him great pain. A local chemist provided medication that eventually provided some relief for Nev until he returned home to his own garden where he was stung on his arm this time, causing enormous swelling and making him feel very ill indeed. His doctor gave him medication and told him to carry it with him at all times because he had an allergy that made the stings very poisonous to him. He was warned that were he to be attacked by a swarm or even just one, their stings could prove fatal!

The incident brings to mind a tale that Arthur told me about his father's stepsister who many years earlier had been helping at a summer fete in aid of the local Church. It was a fine day and the activities were held in the grounds of the Vicarage. Aunty Sarah, the stepsister had the job of slicing and buttering the bread. In addition to the plain bread there were many loaves of bara brith, the Welsh form of speckled bread. Nowadays *bara brith* looks more like fruit cake than the original homely loaf that was made from ordinary bread mix with spices and raisins thrown in. Anyway, sheltered from the sun Aunty Sarah stood under a tree busily cutting and buttering bread on a table, and from time to time would grab a handful of bread-crumbs and raisins to eat to avoid any waste. There was no harm in that of course until she gathered a particular handful and popped it into her mouth not realising other creatures also enjoyed eating the fruit! Almost immediately she let out a terrifying scream stunning the guests to silence! Aunty Sarah was dancing about, like a dervish, spitting and crying. Someone went to calm her down and within seconds, the poor lady could not speak because her tongue had swollen to double its size. Another lady realised what had happened and obtained from somewhere an onion that she cut and placed on Aunty Sarah's tongue as an antidote to the wasps' sting. What a commotion! Soon after, everything and everyone recommenced proceedings and enjoyed the rest of the day.

The second thing on my action plan at Eglwysbach involved redesigning the bathroom area. We separated the toilet from the bathroom and fitted a small washbasin in there. We erected a wall to create a very handy open-ended cloakroom in the hitherto wasted corner, and Percy and Eluned kindly came to lend a hand with fitting new cupboard units in the kitchen.

Thirdly, a new modern grate was fitted in the lounge and Bert the plasterer, being a fine craftsman, did a great job dealing with the Artex disaster. Then fourthly, with all that work completed the painter came to do his job: everywhere needed to be decorated except the two bedrooms upstairs where we simply replaced the carpets. Everything was finished before removal day, except for some painting, thanks to the wonderful workmen who carried out my action plan.

Removal day was the fifth thing to happen! It had been arranged for a Saturday in June and it turned out to be a fine day as well as being the day of the annual Vale of Conwy

Eisteddfod in Llanrwst. Arthur was no longer the Secretary, but as it happened, the bard who won the Chair was from South Wales and was not well enough to make the journey to receive it. He wrote to Arthur asking him to deputise for him at the Chairing ceremony, which he did of course, and Percy accompanied him.

Fortunately, we had already had one load of small boxes delivered the previous afternoon, which left the rest of the furniture to be taken that day. I had made sure that we left *Llys Cerdd* spotless with everything gleaming. There were many things we left for the new occupants - one bedroom was ready to use, and all they required was seating in the lounge. I had just finished dusting and hoovering when the new owners arrived with several helpers, members of the family I think. I was grieved to see paint being chipped on the stairs as they carried things in, and had to remind myself sternly that *Llys Cerdd* was no longer my home and none of my business any more. Even so, I still felt I was abandoning it to its fate. How silly can you get? I took a last nostalgic look around, handed over the keys and left for our new home in Eglwysbach.

Arthur and Percy returned to Eglwysbach at the end of a successful afternoon at the Eisteddfod. Both were laughing as they told how they had walked from the Eisteddfod field through the car park and down the lane at the side of *Llys Cerdd* and into the porch as usual before realising they shouldn't have been there! Force of habit is so strong - Arthur had walked in and out of that house for 37 years after all!

I had a love/hate relationship with *Llys Cerdd.* It was a hard task-master demanding continual attention, sulking sometimes and punishing us with work to be done urgently. I learned to look carefully at the old house and listen to it too, and in return it rewarded us by glowing brightly and being welcoming. I knew every nook and cranny and loved them all! I still gaze at the house whenever I drive past and am reminded that it represented a long period in my life, so I will now bid it farewell.

Chapter Fifty-Five

ONLY THOSE WHO WEATHER THE STORMS EVER SEE THE RAINBOW

We were both looking forward to our new life of retirement. We had a bungalow that pleased us, a large garden to coax into new life, and time to read, bake and do so many pleasurable things. (I am inwardly smiling ironically as I write these words). Arthur had halved the number of pupils who came for piano lessons and had bought a beautiful brand new piano.

The old piano had been fine except for the woodworm in its casing. Arthur had not wanted to part with it really, but I had insisted that no worms would be moving to our new home, and he had reluctantly agreed! Whilst shopping in Llandudno one day and passing the music shop where we had bought the old piano, my attention was drawn to a new piano in the shop window that proudly bore a German name that was very familiar to me: it was the name of the company that had manufactured the old piano. In my excitement I yelled after Arthur, who was further down the street, to come to see it, and in so doing succeeded in gaining not only his attention, but everyone else's too, but I didn't care. “Look, look it's an Ibach,” I said as I pulled Arthur into the shop where he promptly sat on a stool and ran his hands all over the keys bringing forth wonderful music that pervaded the entire shop. Customers stopped to listen and some drew nearer as Arthur got carried away with this wonderful instrument … it also brought forth a lady shop assistant, who listened with great admiration. This went on for a full ten minutes at least, then Arthur stopped mid-stream and said with enthusiasm, “It's a marvellous instrument, but I cannot possibly afford to buy it.”

Well I knew full well that he longed for the piano, so I asked the assistant to leave us for a few minutes, which she did. I reminded Arthur that he had some insurance money due shortly and he said, “Yes I know, but we shall need that to invest for income.” “Never mind that, you have never owned a brand new piano before. Go on treat yourself, you've worked hard enough to deserve it,” I said. There and then we completed the purchase and arranged delivery. And Arthur was thrilled with the purchase! He was also looking forward immensely to having sufficient leisure time to play it to his heart's content. He had the skill and ability to make that piano speak poetry, do cartwheels, somersaults and even fly as high as the moon and the stars. He was an intelligent, powerful and sensitive musician who could stir deep emotions to the hilt in even the most hardened people. Music is such a wonderfully emotive force, and everyone should be blessed by the experience of being moved by it!

Arthur was also looking forward to using the space in the garage to work on his hobby of making working models of old agricultural machinery. Hitherto, he'd had to make do with the cramped shed at *Llys Cerdd* or the kitchen table that meant having to clear away at meal times. We had so much to look forward to in our new home.

And so it was that after all the comings and goings, the viewings and planning, packing and unpacking and everything else that challenged us, we were finally safely installed in our new home and were gradually getting used to the new routine and doing things in a little more leisurely way. The last of the workmen was still with us finishing off the painting jobs in the house and he sang happily as he worked. He was a member of a local Male Voice Choir and had a lot of respect for Arthur as a successful musician. He told us that he was putting an 'extra effort' into getting the decorating absolutely 'spot on' in Arthur's music study in particular … and he did too!

During the second week we were enjoying a mini heat wave and all the doors and windows were open. Arthur and I had just finished our lunch; the decorator was working in the hallway, and I was clearing up when I heard him say anxiously, "Arc you alright Mr.Williams? Is there anything wrong?" I did not hear any response so I walked into the hallway and saw Arthur walking unsteadily towards the front door. I hurried to him as I saw him leaning towards the right and holding on to the doorpost. He said, "I seem to have lost my balance." At that moment I did not think there was anything seriously wrong. He had eaten a light lunch as normal and had taken his diabetes tablet. A couple of years earlier he had been diagnosed as suffering a mild form of diabetes that was controlled by daily doses of insulin in tablet form.

After his major operation in 1978 Arthur's appetite had improved and he was able to enjoy his meals again. He visited a clinic in Llandudno Hospital regularly where staff did blood tests and checked the balance of the sugar levels in his body. We came to realise that the first sign of diabetes had been in his feet. Once, when we'd stayed with Elsie and Neville, and had visited the local folk museum at Hutton le Hole, Arthur had complained that his feet hurt terribly. On returning home, our Doctor diagnosed diabetes and prescribed the medication.

So, on this day in Eglwysbach, when he said his balance was not right and he didn't feel well, we both thought it was related to the diabetes, so I led him to a chair in the lounge where he sat quietly sipping cold water. After a while he said he felt a little better, but added, "I think I've had a stroke." That shook me as I remembered how it had been with my mother. When I phoned the Doctor's surgery at Betws y Coed, neither of the two doctors who dealt with our family were available, they were both on holiday. However, there was a young Irish locum doctor on call. When I told him what was wrong he told me to take Arthur to the surgery that evening. I was most surprised there would not be a visit made to our home, but I somehow managed to get Arthur into the car. It was very hot in the late afternoon when we arrived in Betws and I had great difficulty in getting Arthur out of the car. I don't know whether the young doctor saw our struggles, but he came out to help me to get Arthur up some steps into the surgery. Arthur took off his jacket and lay down on the table. The doctor examined him carefully and asked Arthur questions including whether he smoked. Arthur and I replied simultaneously that he did. "Well then, you must stop as of now. You have had a stroke, fortunately not a severe one, and you will get better if you do as I suggest. Take this as a warning and remember that the cause of this attack is your smoking. Stop now!" He did. Arthur never smoked another cigarette.

For years he had smoked, consoling himself by saying that he did not inhale deeply at all. I told him regularly to give up the harmful habit and I was forever opening windows and doors to let out the harmful smoke. I would show him the colour of the net curtains from the music study and tell him that his lungs had the same stain. I knew he had sufficient will-power to stop and indeed he had previously given up for over two years before re-starting again. It was a visit to adjudicate at a week-long Eisteddfod that had been his downfall. There were panels of adjudicators staying together at hotels. Arthur was not a drinker, enjoying just half a lager or so, but that was kids' stuff to such a group. Also Arthur was in his element when socialising, he was famous for his stories and jokes, so on being offered a cigarette one evening felt very tempted, and a refusal would have been regarded as being the odd man out. He decided one would do no harm, accepted it and lit up. But that was it! Next morning, he was in a shop buying a packet of cigarettes again, and from then on he smoked until the Doctor's ultimatum. Having stopped once more, he grew to hate the smell of cigarettes and was more anti-smoking than anyone I knew. Elsie, Neville and Glen had given up at least a decade earlier, and Bryn too gave up his pipe.

At 8.30a.m the following morning I had a phone call from the Irish Doctor to say he was sorry he could no longer continue to treat us and we needed to find another practice. I was stunned and on asking why, was told that our new home in Eglwysbach was considered to be outside the *Betws y Coed* catchment area. I just could not believe what I was hearing and was at a loss as to how to proceed, so I phoned my brother and his wife who then lived in a flat in Colwyn Bay. Percy said I should ring Dr. Grout in Conwy who had been their Doctor when they lived there and had treated Alun, their son, when he had fallen ill and no one knew what was wrong with him. Dr. Grout had diagnosed an unusual syndrome that was gradually killing Alun. From being a big lad with an Honours degree in Electronics, Alun had become so thin and frail that his father, a smaller man, had been carrying him to and from bed. They had great faith in Dr. Grout.

Straight away I phoned the Surgery and explained the situation and was told to take Arthur into the surgery that night where Dr. Grout would see him. I was very relieved and drove to Conwy to a friendly and encouraging meeting with Dr. Grout who examined Arthur and finally said, “Well I suppose I had better put you on my list otherwise your niece will never forgive me.” When he had been training as a doctor at Bart's in London, Nerys my niece had been training to be a nurse at the same hospital and they had known each other. Dr. Grout has recently retired and has been replaced by a lovely lady doctor in whom I have equal faith: Arthur and I always felt safe in Dr Grout's care and never lacked proper attention.

The priority then was to get Arthur going again. He had lost strength in his right arm and both hands. He received a soft-ball from Irene our neighbour, and had been squeezing it all the time. At first he felt he was achieving nothing, but slowly things improved. He was prescribed Warfarin tablets to thin his blood and I drove him to attend a monthly clinic to have his blood tested. After some months he was able to play the piano again to a fashion, but the speed of his hands and the fast agility of his mind had suffered and he was very frustrated at his lack of skill for a while. All piano lessons had been terminated, but he was able to return to play the organ at Seion Chapel and everyone was happy about that. He was even able to adjudicate and conduct singing festivals, but not with his usual fervour and gusto. I advised him not to accept any more because of the long hours and stress and he eventually agreed.

He could however re-commence going to the meetings of the club which dealt with old farm machinery and to demonstrate the use of his models at shows. Gone however, were the days when he could make the models. The fingers that had been so sensitive to touch, could no longer contend with the miniature tools and model parts. His interest however was just as acute and alive as ever. What a disappointment it was for him not to be able to activate his retirement plans. I felt to the quick for him.

It was a difficult situation for an artiste to accept the end of his gifted and talented performances. After a life of struggle and commitment it was unfair to be dealt a blow on the very eve of retirement, but I never allowed him to go down that path of depression. I saw it as my task to cheer him on, remark on his visible physical improvement, and encourage him to do the things he was still able to do such as drive, dig a bit in the garden, mow the lawns, and water the plants.

On a cold and windy day Arthur and I needed to visit a government office in Colwyn Bay. Arthur wore a thickly padded long jacket that Glenys had given to him for a Christmas present. We parked the car, and as I had one call to make nearby, Arthur went on ahead leaning into the wind with his hands in his pockets. Suddenly there was an almighty gust of wind and I saw Arthur being partially lifted off his feet, losing his balance and then falling onto his face in the roadway. I rushed to him and found he had suffered several small cuts on his face having been unable to break his fall from having had his hands in his pockets. There was some bleeding, but I managed to clean him up at a supermarket. There was no real damage as far as I could tell, but from then on, he always used a walking stick.

Eventually we settled into another routine consisting of housework requiring attention: cooking, cleaning, washing, and ironing and some people would say it was household drudgery. But, I cannot honestly say that I disliked the work. There is a certain satisfaction in bringing order after disorder, to have a gleam and a shine around you, having the pile of washed clothes neatly ironed all smooth and crisp, sitting down at a beautifully laid table to enjoy the results of an afternoon of cooking. You will say that I am old fashioned and women don't do things like that anymore, and that women now have more freedom to enjoy themselves in other ways. I do not disagree, but there are times and seasons in everyone's life, and the secret is to face up to whatever confronts you and decide to cope with it in a cheerful way because doing so is better for you and everyone else. 'Laugh and the world laughs with you, cry and you cry alone' I would add 'in the long term'. Anyway we are all different, and a good thing too. How awful it would be if we were all the same! Now I will put my soapbox away and recall more family history.

In 1986 Bryn decided to leave the R.A.F. after twelve years' service and the family settled in Manchester where there was work for him. He kept up his interest in gardening and worked in his own garden, and two allotments growing his own vegetables.

I asked my friends Ken and Norah if it would be possible to spend another holiday at *'Haulfryn'*, their lovely villa in Javea, and they kindly agreed. After the upheavals of the previous year I felt I needed a rest and a change. Arthur was deemed well enough to cope alone at home, in fact the Doctor thought it would do him good to be independent for a while, it would give him a boost to his confidence. Our friendly neighbours, David and Irene, living just over the road promised to keep a daily eye on him and I trusted them to keep to their word.

I invited Elsie and Neville and of course Geraint who was then 3 years old to go too, and they were delighted to accept. The weather was perfect, the villa just as lovely as before and the pool as inviting as ever. Neville relaxed visibly and we all pottered about, reading, cooking, messing about in the pool and shopping in the *'supermercado'*, as well as going to different places in the hired car and so on. By wearing armbands Geraint could swim quite well and he jumped into the pool without any fear whatsoever. He loved being in the water, clambering out and then jumping in again. One day however, somehow he missed his footing and slipped, hitting his forehead on the stone edge of the pool. He cut open the skin and was bleeding quite freely so we rushed him into the villa, washed the wound with diluted Dettol, fixed a thick pad over it and took him to the Clinic in Javea where he was treated immediately by a lady doctor. She knew some English words and I remembered an adequate number from my days of school Spanish, so we managed quite well. The little boy had been very upset when he hurt his head and had cried, but between us we managed to soothe him. The doctor was marvellous with him and Pero, the toy dog too who also got a bandage round his head! When she produced a mirror and he could see the swathe of bandage round his head Geraint was quite chuffed. However the pool was barred for a time and he had to be careful not to hurt his head any further. During the next few days he decided to become a gardener and was very busy digging the soil in the borders and playing with his little cars. We, the grown ups were very worried, but the child took it all in his stride and behaved very well. In spite of the mishap we all enjoyed the holiday very much indeed.

Arthur was keen to have a car with a boot big enough to take his models and display material when he went to demonstrate at agricultural shows.A Ford Orion would be just the job, so we bought one from Alan, Nev's friend who owned a garage in Bala. It was a wonderful car and very roomy. Arthur really enjoyed going to the shows and the monthly club meetings with his friends. He was very interested in all steam engines and knew a lot about the power of steam.

Winter arrived and we battened down the hatches and were very cosy in our new home. We had a coal fire in the sitting room and although it meant chopping wood into sticks for kindling, carrying buckets of coal and stacking logs, we could do it all outside the house and it did not impact upon the cosiness and cleanliness indoors. We could empty the ash pan from outside too thereby doing away with the dust indoors.

On Sundays, Arthur drove to Seion Chapel for morning service, returned home for lunch, then both of us went in the afternoon to play our roles as Sunday School teachers. Afterwards we drove to the riverside car park in Llanrwst for a relaxing view, and to eat our picnic of sandwiches, cake and a flask of tea and listen to interesting programmes on the radio. We really enjoyed those quiet interludes and once in a while, when invited to take tea with a kind, cultured widow, went rather reluctantly I must admit. We felt obliged because she was so welcoming and very lonely in missing her husband. After evening service I drove home where we enjoyed supper and read the 'Observer' newspaper until it was time for bed, unless there was something special on the television. Listening to music was another pleasure we shared often.

Chapter Fifty-Six

NO MORE DEADLINES

When Spring burst forth in 1987 we had lived in our new home for nearly two years and Arthur's health was much improved, so we decided to tackle the back garden. In the front we had already planted many bulbs of daffodil, narcissus, hyacinth, and crocus, and they looked delightful. When past their best with the flowers faded, I tidied the borders then cleared the foliage away and scattered fertilizer before planting summer annuals that would suffice for the time being. I had ideas forming and developing daily in my head for the 'back garden restoration plan', but nothing was set in stone yet.

We set forth to see what was on offer in the many Garden Centres and Nurseries in the area, and enjoyed perusing the various catalogues that arrived by post. I loved the visits to the Nurseries and felt almost addicted to them: it was therefore always necessary to be very strict with myself in what I bought for the garden. Even today I have to decide on my 'plant budget' beforehand because of the delightful temptations available - a myriad of plants of all sizes and shapes in wonderful colours and scents. There are eight Nurseries cum Garden Centres within a radius of five miles of Eglwysbach and visits to them are far more enjoyable than visits to clothes shops for instance. I don't want to give the wrong impression here because I love buying new clothes, but I do not enjoy shopping for them because I find it a chore, unlike shopping for plants on the other hand which I find a real pleasure!

However, visiting the Nurseries that year was a necessary and essential part of my garden restoration plan because there were trees and bushes to be bought and many perennials too. But what a pleasure it gave me despite the fact that the overall cost made me feel rather faint … but needs must!

My garden plan also involved planting the purchases and giving them the best start in life. Writing about the methods I used to nurture them will only be of interest to the most serious gardeners, so I will avoid that detail suffice it to say that knowledgeable gardeners usually get excellent results. Gardening programmes on the television can provide excellent tips for all gardeners of course.

The trees and bushes I bought were not fully grown, just a couple of feet high in fact, but planting them still entailed time-consuming and hard physical work. Elsie and Neville had presented us with a greenhouse for Christmas and to his credit, Neville had gone out in freezing conditions to level it for us. It was a wonderful gift, and I made full use of it by growing plants from seeds and cuttings. We had two sizeable plots at the far end of the garden where we grew potatoes, carrots, beans, peas, sprouts, leeks and once, sweetcorn too, and we also grew salad plants, lettuce, tomatoes, cucumber and radish. It was hard work, but so very satisfying when we harvested and enjoyed the wonderful taste of our own home grown vegetables. At the end of that year we had a proper garden, although it was to change and evolve many times more along the years.

Els and Nev had enjoyed our visit to Spain so much the previous year, they decided to return, but this time with an addition to the family. Another little chap had been born on the 5th July, the day following his brother's birthday. He was Aled Vaughan Lloyd, a lovely baby who was much loved by his mum and dad. When we set out for Spain Aled was all of seven weeks old! I was amazed! Never in a month of Sundays would I have ventured abroad with such a young baby, but his Mam and Dad took it all in their stride. They had bought a wonderful carrier - almost like a lined basket, so easy to carry and Aled loved it. I quite often rocked him to sleep in that little Moses basket. This was very new at the time and everyone remarked on it and wanted one. Some of the Spaniards even asked to buy it! The Villa holiday was ideal for the family. Els and Nev had made a fair number of trips abroad connected with their work as well as personal holidays and were mindful of the potential effects of extreme heat on their new baby so we kept him cool in the shade. I was able to baby-sit Geraint and Aled a couple of times during the holiday to enable their Mam and Dad to enjoy evenings out together. We had a lovely holiday, and all too soon it was time to return home. But on arrival at Alicante Airport an unfortunate incident happened that caused injury and much pain to me.

Geraint held my right hand and with my left I carried a bag and small basket, Els followed carrying some bags and Nev came next carrying Aled in his basket and pulling small items of luggage. We made for the escalator, which was very long and extremely steep with high steps. Geraint and I got on quite easily, but I soon realised that he had his little hand underneath the handrail so I tried to get him to place it on top of it, which meant giving him oral instructions and physically helping him to do it. At the same time I was retaining my grip and simultaneously re-positioning myself behind Geraint to protect him from falling down the escalator. In so doing my feet were separated onto 2 steps, and fortunately someone down below noticed my predicament and switched off the escalator giving me a chance to become upright again.

Soon, the escalator was switched on again and we got to the top where the little boy was able to step safely off the elevator. In the process of protecting my little grandson from injury I knew that my movements had resulted in deep grazing to my leg on the steel stairs. It had been a very painful experience, but my injury was not my first priority at the time because I was concerned about my grandson's safety. Elsie and Neville were naturally perturbed and anxious about Geraint's wellbeing and very relieved that he was fine, but were unconcerned for my injured leg and intense pain. My leg was bleeding quite considerably, but I somehow managed to ease the flow and wipe most of the blood away with tissues and my own saliva. I was really shocked and shaken by the painful and terrifying experience, but somehow Els and Nev didn't appear to understand the extent of my suffering because they continued to push on as much as ever to get to the plane without calling for assistance. I somehow managed to push myself to the hilt to keep up with the group by mustering every bit of energy, effort and determination within myself until I boarded the plane, where I gratefully sank into my seat to recover. I also thanked God for his protection during the incident because it had the potential of being much worse - we both might have sustained serious injuries. Elsie and Neville seemed unconcerned about my distress, and even on the plane did not think to enquire about my wellbeing. This may have been because of the way I dealt with the situation, but my extreme pain and injury seemed not to have been noticed by them really, and I was hurt by their lack of concern.

The following three years were extremely hectic as Arthur and I improved things in and out of the house. We bought a large shed to store all our tools and garden things because the garage was bulging with other items - they were all nicely organised because I cannot be doing with disarray, muddle and jumble. The front and back gardens had improved tremendously due to our hard work and the benefits derived from all the natural fertilizers that I had carried in sacksful to mix in with the soil. They included leaves, seaweed, riverside sand and mud thrown up by floods, and my homemade compost made from household waste, newspaper and dead vegetation. I saved all the used tea bags for the garden's benefit and I must have thrown the contents of hundreds and thousands of them onto the compost heap in my time in Eglwysbach.

Perhaps all this feeding of the soil was the reason for my success at the Annual Eglwysbach Agricultural and Horticultural Show - I was urged to compete in the local garden competitions and in competitions for the best specimens of flowers and plants. It was all very exciting, but very hard work and I am glad that I managed to get my grandchildren interested in making things for the children's section - even cooking! One year Bryn, my son, won first prize for the best chocolate Swiss roll. My grandchildren won many first prizes over the years including: best animal modelled from a vegetable, best miniture garden, and so on.

We received an invitation from my sister Bella and husband Stanley to attend the marriage of their second son Ken to Mary and I was very pleased to accept. But, as always, Arthur would not fly. Raymond their eldest son was already married, but I had not been able to attend his wedding because I was required at work and was not able to take time-off. My niece, Nerys, was also a guest at Ken's wedding but we did not travel together to the USA. She went earlier to spend a few days in New York with some friends. I flew into Toronto and was met by Stan and Bella. I had not visited America since 1969 when their sons had been little children, so it was quite a wonderful shock on my arrival to be greeted by three strapping young men. Raymond, the eldest son had worked in the UK for some time, then moved to other countries including Australia.

On a very hot day just before the wedding, Stan drove the three of us hundreds of miles to Ken's house. We stopped once for a picnic and Stan warned me not to wander from the tarmac parking area because of the danger of snakes. One word of warning was enough for me because of my terror and hatred of snakes and thankfully none made an appearance that day. We also stopped at a roadside resting station that had spotlessly clean toilets and babies' changing rooms as well as a nice café. My abiding memory of that place was the sheer cleanliness of the facilities and the fact that they were free.

The house was large with plenty of ground surrounding it, and there was the ubiquitous deck where it was pleasant to sit in the evening for drinks and conversation. Stan took us out for lunch one day and I ordered a 'salad roll' fully expecting a normal one that I could bite into with ease. But that turned out to be the day I was introduced to the concept of eating American 'subs'- sandwich submarines that took real skill to eat and ages to consume because of their enormous size. It looked wonderful and I had to pull it to pieces before I could manage to eat it, but it was delicious nevertheless.

On the eve of the wedding a dinner party had been arranged at the Sailing Club hosted by Stan and Bella. We enjoyed a lovely meal and marvelled at the spectacular electric storm that developed during our time there. Our table was by a window overlooking the Marina and the play of the lightning flashes and streaks amongst the masts of the yachts and boats was awesome. The forked blue flashes seemed to dance and it was wonderful to watch. The experience reminded us that this natural phenomenon is extremely beautiful but also very powerful and highly dangerous.

The day dawned warm and lovely for the wedding and the Church service was very moving. I had been invited to sing a solo during the service and had chosen 'The Holy

City' being a song I had sung many, many times before. The bride and groom looked wonderful but the best man was on crutches having suffered a broken leg playing football - American style of course!

Mary and her sisters are all qualified Engineers as is their father, but the girls looked more like models on that day. Once the photographs had been taken at the Church we moved on to the Reception, which was held in the ballroom of a hotel. By this time Nerys had arrived and we joined everyone else in enjoying the huge piles of fruit, mounds of salads, petits fours, cold meats, cheeses and drinks. The speeches came next followed surprisingly by a hot four course meal! There was so much delicious food, then there was dancing and drinking for hours until everyone was exhausted and went to bed. It had been a very memorable day!

I cannot recall how long I stayed in the USA, but I will never forget the journey home. Nerys had planned to travel with me but her plans had changed and I flew out of Toronto alone. Stan and Bella saw me off on a very hot evening that had a temperature of 99° even with a stiff breeze, I boarded the plane at 8.00 p.m. and the flight took off on time. Procedures were carried out and drinks served prior to dinner. Then the intercom burst into life and a voice said, "This is your Captain speaking. We are having a spot of trouble with one of the engines and have to return to Toronto. Please remain in your seats and move around as little as possible. I will keep you posted."

We were all stunned and rather fearful, but everyone seemed to accept that it would be helpful to remain calm. We did not know what was ahead of us, so we just had to wait. Que sera, sera! Our speed was reduced so it took longer to return, but when we finally landed we were asked to remain seated until instructed to change to another plane or re-start the journey in the same one.

An hour later we were informed that an oil leak had been given attention and the failing engine repaired, and within a few minutes we were taking off again. It was a strange flight in the fact that all the passengers were very quiet thereafter. Perhaps they were sleeping, it was night time after all, but they were probably like me, a bit apprehensive after the blip mid-air. I wondered whether we'd be alright crossing the cold Atlantic Ocean in the dark or would we have to land in the water and need to be rescued, or even worse perhaps! Then I decided to put all such thoughts from my mind and think of other things, which I did, but I was still intensely relieved to get my feet onto terra firma at Manchester Airport.

Bryn had arranged to meet me at the scheduled time of 7.30a.m. British time but it was after 1.00p.m. when the plane finally landed. Instead of taking me to Piccadilly railway station to catch a train for home, he decided to take me to his home to rest and put my feet up before catching a later train. Having been still for hours in a restricted space my feet and legs had swollen up alarmingly and felt very strange indeed. Nowadays we know a lot more than I did then about the risk and danger of blood clots developing due to remaining motionless on long flights.

For some years Glenys had been a Deputy Headteacher at Cherry Tree, a very large primary school in Farnworth, Bolton and had been very successful in introducing new innovative ways of teaching. For instance all the school's pupils had been involved in a mini-enterprise project, which was thought to be among the first of its kind in the country. The school had featured in a B.B.C. television programme where children were shown running and discussing the businesses they had established including a hot-dog stall, a greetings card firm and a school magazine. Profits went to charity. As a result of the publicity, the school was invited to make a presentation of its work at a prestigious event held at the RSA House just off the Strand in London (the Headquarters of the Royal Society for the Encouragement of the Arts, Manufacturing and Commerce). Glenys and a colleague, Pat Hughes who had been implementing one of the projects with her Year 4 class, chose 6 'whiz kids' to participate in the presentation, and took them to London for the weekend. They all had a wonderful time and were given an outstanding welcome by everyone at the event. Glenys was also invited to appear in the BBC 'Education Programme' that was recorded live in London. She was interviewed by Sarah Kennedy, the presenter about the enterprise project.

During the summer term Bolton Local Education Authority (LEA) invited teachers to apply for a secondment for one year to carry out in-depth research into assessment, records of achievement and new teaching methods on behalf of the LEA. Headteacher, Eric Brindle urged Glen, his deputy to apply, and he supported her application: the opportunity appealed to her very much. She was chosen out of over forty applicants and was allowed to choose Manchester University at which to undertake the study. Glenys was fortunate to be allocated Dr. Alex. Robertson as her Personal Tutor. Having got to know Glenys, he advised her to apply to the University to be allowed to study for a bespoke Masters Degree in Education (MEd) incorporating the L.E.A. research work. In order to be able do this, she had to submit a long treatise to be examined, to decide whether she was suitable and capable of the work. The focus she chose for the paper was her work on 'enterprise education in the primary school'. Her work was deemed good enough, and she left Cherry Tree School for a year to begin her studies in Manchester University in September 1988. As events transpired, she never did return to Cherry Tree because a year later, in September 1989 she started as Headteacher at Claypool Primary School.

During the summer holiday of 1988, Glenys, Kerry and the boys were moving house again. There was more than one reason for this including the fact that they were disillusioned with the garden, half of which was waterlogged all year round, and was mostly out of the sun too under the big mature trees - the children could not play out at the back because they always came in covered in mud. Although the house was beautiful, with a lounge, dining room, 4 bedrooms, kitchen with a breakfast bar, utility room, 2 bathrooms with a jacuzzi, downstairs toilet and a double garage, it nevertheless did not have some of the basic requirements that a young family needed. For instance, it did not have a cloakroom for coats and wellingtons, or basic storage for family things, and the kitchen was not designed for a family to congregate on chairs round a table.

But the catalyst for moving house was the fact that Marcus and Morgan were getting too involved with the children of two families on the estate who had very different values from their own family. In particular a little boy from one of the families, who was a little older than Marcus, was extremely spoilt and still used a dummy at the age of 6 when it suited him. He was defiant, disobedient and generally very badly behaved, but was also very daring, risqué and exciting in his play and therefore totally captivating to Marcus at the age of 5. They gravitated towards each other like magnets and the influence was enormously strong. Kerry and Glen thought it best to move to an area where the local families shared their own values and raised their children in a similar way. They bought a true-bungalow in Horwich where Kerry taught at Horwich Parish School and Marcus attended as a pupil. The problem never arose again.

At the time of moving Marcus was six but Morgan was only three years old so I went to help for a couple of weeks. Removal day arrived and everything went well, but it was early evening when we finally landed at the bungalow that they were to make their new home. It was an unusual house in the fact that the back and front doors were next to each other. Once everything was out of the lorry Glen and I stood by the back door talking about our tiredness and hunger when we overheard part of the conversation Kerry was having at the front door with the removal men when one of them asked him, “Why on earth have you moved from that lovely house to this one? Kerry said, “This house has terrific potential, just give us a couple of years to work on it and it will be a very different place”, to which they replied, “Well maybe so but … we still think you're mad!” Later Glen sat on one of the many boxes littering the horrible lounge and said she didn't know whether to laugh or cry. The detached bungalow was in great need of modernising and developing, and it compared very badly with the aesthetically pleasing executive detached show-house they had just left but … it had enormous potential for property development and was located in a good area where they knew families similar to their own.

After the removal men had departed and the doors closed we set about making the place as comfortable as possible for the night. We set up and made the beds, found towels and some personal things that we needed and then prepared some food. The boys were in their element roaming round from room to room and finding their toy boxes. After my initial inspection I decided that as a first job I would throw out the three layers of floor covering in the toilet and then undertake an almighty scrubbing down with cleanser and disinfectant. Following that, I scrubbed out the wall cabinets in the kitchen so things could be put away. It was rather awful at the time, but the potential was there, and both Glen and Kerry knew exactly what they wanted to do to the place.

Eventually they re-designed the internal layout of the bungalow by demolishing walls and erecting others, and moving the front door to the other end of the house. They installed a new bathroom, kitchen and downstairs toilet immediately and completely stripped all other rooms and hallway to re-carpet and decorate from top to bottom. Once the ground floor had been done to their specification they developed the possibilities that lay in the cavernous loft. They installed stairs and created a huge master bedroom with an en-suite bathroom and a further big bedroom with an en-suite shower room. They also had a lovely big driveway installed across the front of the house that runs on as a path all the way round to the back where it becomes a superb patio. It took hours of hard work over 3 or 4 years to get their bungalow as it is today, a lovely, spacious modern home that is functional and easy to run. They made a good move, and their children have grown up happily surrounded by similar families.

Glen settled down well to her studies and enjoyed the course work and the researching too. During the summer term of 1989 she applied for a Headship at Claypool Primary School in Horwich and was appointed. She began her headship in September 1989 and was thrilled to have been appointed because it was what she had aspired to for a couple of years.

During the summer holiday Kerry, Glen, Marcus, Morgan and I went on holiday to France. They had booked a *gite* (holiday cottage) in the Loire area. The weather was lovely and there was plenty to do. Glen had taken her University work with her because she was still working on her dissertation. The secondment had come to an end and her assignments throughout the year had been completed satisfactorily and the report for the

L.E.A. had been accepted. At that point she had still to complete the final part of her Degree course in her spare time, when she was also about to take up her Headship. However, she and Kerry needed a break so we went to France by car and ferry - the Channel Tunnel had not been built at that time. From Caen we travelled past the War Graves Cemeteries, an area where Kerry's father had passed through when he was in the Army during the 2nd World War.

We were all very tired when we finally arrived on an exceptionally hot Sunday afternoon at our destination in a small village in France. Our gite was one part of several farm outbuildings that had been converted for holidaymakers. There was a large, gloomy old fashioned kitchen, a living room with a table and dining chairs and two bedrooms upstairs that were very sparsely furnished. There were no easy chairs or comfortable settees to relax on to read or just chat, no rugs underfoot, just quarry tiles downstairs and cold linoleum upstairs. The two double beds in the bedroom that the boys and I used were dreadful because both made us roll into a hollow in the middle. After one night of rolling, I put the bolster pillow down the centre of the bed to help the boys from ending up on top of each other in the middle, and despite clinging to one side of my bed I still found myself in the hollow each morning. The *gite* was not remotely welcoming, homely or comfortable …just the opposite really. Our hostess, Madame Gijon, was a typical farmer's wife, spoke no English, but was most welcoming and smiley, and very kind to us.

As we were 'self-catering' we had taken lots of basic groceries to tide us over until we could get to a shop. So, our first major task the following morning was to explore the village. It seemed to be a lovely hamlet having developed under the wing of a large *Chateau* (manor house). The main house was situated behind big gates and railings, and the Post Office and other Community Offices were within the compound. The *boulangerie* (bakery) and the general grocery shop were just outside the gates and we were able to obtain lovely fresh *baguettes* and pastries every morning. The Chateau gates opened up to a long straight road with an impressive wide avenue of trees on both sides, and it was easy to visualise grand processions making their way in stately grandeur down such a road.

On that first day, we wandered all over the village in the sunshine and enjoyed the quaint little back streets and the quietness and stillness of the environment. Marcus was chatting and skipping along happily with his Mum, and four year old Morgan and I followed them hand-in-hand, contentedly chatting about this and that and looking with interest at everything. Just before we arrived at the *boulangerie* we came to a stone statue of a soldier sited on a plinth with steps up to it. The armed figure was leaning forward with a flower in one hand and a rifle in the other. Morgan stopped, went up the steps, touched it, and gave it a good inspection. Then he asked me what it was and I explained that it was a memorial to many young Frenchmen who had been killed in two world wars.

"What is a war Nain?" he asked. Well what a question, and how do you explain to a four year old boy what war means? So I said, "Our homes are in a country called Britain and to get to this country called France for our holidays we have had to travel over the sea. Next to France there are other countries too that we can go to without going over the sea because they are part of the same piece of land. You need to have special papers to say who you are before you can go to other countries because different people live there. One of those countries is called Germany, and twice the Germans have marched into France to fight the French and try to steal their land without having those special papers. So Britain went to help the French to stop them. That is war."

Morgan showed a big interest in the explanation so I went on to say, "If you fall out with other boys and you start fighting, hitting and knocking one another about, it is called fighting. But in wars, real guns and bombs are used to fight people, and many are killed. But there is no need for you to worry Morgan because it has all stopped, and we have peace now and are friends again."

He really listened to all I said and I had no idea what was going on in his little head, but I noticed he was silent as we made our way up the road. We passed an icon by the roadside, an image of the Holy Mother. "Who is that?" asked Morgan. "That is Mary, mother of Jesus Christ. You remember the story of baby Jesus?" "Yes, but where is baby Jesus and where is his father?" "I don't really know but probably there will be similar statues to them somewhere else." That seemed to satisfy him until we arrived at the other end of the village, where there was just one shop selling items of pottery and rosaries and other religious artefacts, not far from the Parish Church. Marcus had already reached the end of the road and Glen was calling, urging us to catch up but no, the little fellow was standing very still gazing up at a large statue of Jesus on a plinth. "Who is this and why is he not wearing proper clothes?" "That is Jesus after he grew up, and in the country where he lived they wore robes like that. See, he's holding out his hand because he loves little children and wants to care for them. Now come on or your mum will get annoyed with us."

No matter, Morgan stood absolutely still, gazing up at the face of Jesus. Then he suddenly turned to me and said, "Where was Jesus during the war?" I was stunned. Lord in Heaven, what was the answer to that one? The philosophical aspects would tax the minds of the most learned of theologians so what hope did I have? So I opted for the simple way by saying, "The spirit of Jesus was everywhere during the war helping the Nurses and Doctors to heal the wounds of the soldiers and caring for the people who had lost sons and daughters, fathers, brothers and sisters and sweethearts in the fighting. Jesus does not like fighting, but He loves everyone who comes to him for help." Again Morgan was silent as we returned along the same road. I told him that his grandad had been a British soldier in France. "Oh!" was the only word he said. Minutes later we passed the statue of the soldier and suddenly he burst out, "My Dad is the best fighter in the world." Well there you are you see, that is what is called filial loyalty! I can remember thinking similar thoughts when I was a small child, *my* parents were the best Mam and Dad, capable of coping with anything, and I was safe with them. Sometimes I wish that feeling could be emblazoned in letters of fire in the sky to enable all children to enjoy that feeling of security and safety.

In the field next to the farmhouse were some horses including a big one called Fifi, and as the boys stood by the fence yelling the name, the horse would amble along and they would feed it clumps of grass. Fifi - what a name to call a stallion!

Glen prepared our main meal during the early evening to enable us to go sightseeing during the day, but even then it was extremely hot in the kitchen. Unfortunately, uninvited and unwelcome visitors came in too - they were huge, horrible bluebottles buzzing round like miniature aeroplanes. There were so many that I was practically on permanent duty in the evening with the big swatter. Morgan would shout, "Come on Nain, the Charlies are coming." I had to chase and swat them whilst he gleefully counted each casualty. They were such a nuisance!

The large expanse of flat land in the vicinity was mostly devoted to growing sunflowers, but there were vineyards too. At first it puzzled me that when we drove along the road in the sunshine in the morning, all the beautiful yellow faces of the sunflowers with their green bonnets would be looking at us, and yet there they were again looking at us from a different direction on our return in the evening. But their name explained it all - the sunflowers simply turned their heads to follow the sun!

Some of the time Glen stayed behind in the gite writing her dissertation and Kerry and the boys sailed forth with me in tow most times. One day we visited a large park with a big lake where we paddled and because the lads were wearing only trunks, the sun was burning their skin. I decided to rub some of my sun cream on them and because of its scent we had lots of noisy protestations. "We're not girls, Nain. We don't like it." It was only the promise of large ice cream cornets that finally persuaded them to give in. Funny isn't it how these little lads change their minds when they become big teenagers and they then buy as many creams, lotions and body sprays as girls do, if not more!

Kerry took the boys to *'Futuroscope'* near Poitiers one day and I stayed with Glen in the sunshine, she working on her dissertation as usual. When the chaps returned they were all bursting to tell us about the marvellous place they had visited and all the hands-on activities they had experienced including making music by jumping on giant keys on the ground. Kerry said it had been a wonderful visit and they'd all enjoyed it very much.

On another day we all visited a castle high up on a rock above the Loire River. From the outside it looked like a Fairly Castle but it had big deep and dark dungeons. The boys heard the French way of pronouncing the word and Morgan said they were 'donjohns'. We had some lovely picnics here and there and wandered in the countryside and along the river bank in the glorious sunshine. A visit to one place on the main square where they sold *crepes* was a great success!

The most fascinating place that we visited was a *Troglodyte Village*. We stumbled on it one day as we travelled in the car along the flatlands when we saw the strange sight of chimneys sticking out of the ground. Having driven towards them we found ourselves in the tourist car park of a village of dwellings that had been carved inside the soft rock. The village was at that time a tourist attraction but had once had many families living in it. The houses looked normal from the front, and on entering them we saw that they were quite roomy inside, and apparently when families increased in size, they simply carved out another room from the rock. They were said to be cool in summer and warm in winter. There was even a farm there, and several trees growing up to the surface where they looked like bushes. We tried to imagine living in such a house - there was something tragic and desperate about the place somehow, but perhaps we were associating the place with poverty and helplessness. We were told that the families who lived there were perfectly happy with their lot - and perhaps they were.

I always look forward to going away on holiday, to make the most of it in order to enjoy something different, but I always find it lovely to return home too, to the familiar surroundings, and my own comfortable bed!

In the spring, Arthur and I decided to change our car. The Orion was really too big for just the two of us and we were lucky enough to find a Ford Fiesta that had very low mileage, a wonderful small car, my faithful chariot that I used until 2003 when I bought a Vauxhall Corsa with power steering.

The last months of 1989 and early 1990 were extremely busy for Glenys, and she regularly worked long hours far into the night. She was settling in well at her new school, getting to know the staff and children, never easy of course even at the best of times. The researching part of her dissertation had been done and most of the writing too, but there was some longhand copying to be done before she could get it all on the computer. Nowadays she works everything directly onto the computer, but at that time I was able to help with the fair copy writing from her work with all her very numerous additional notes and alterations added on. I was glad to help in this way and I believe it was also helpful company late at night and also to make gallons of tea. As the deadline date for handing in the dissertation drew near things were getting a little frantic, but she managed it well.

Then there was the waiting for the result. Was the dissertation good enough, could she have done it differently she wondered? At last the report came through indicating that she had been successful. She had been awarded the higher degree of Master of Education (MEd) at the highest category of Distinction. What a relief, and after all the long hours of unrelenting study and writing, there was an emptiness, but not for long.

The invitation arrived for Glen to present herself and her guests at the 1989 presentation ceremony at Manchester University and Glen's personal tutor said to me at the buffet after the event, "I am sure you feel very proud of your daughter today." I said, "Yes I am proud of her," and then he said, "but I don't think you know how well she succeeded." I replied, "Well no, I don't know any details", then he explained, "You know she was required to do 8 assignments with each one carrying a maximum of 4 marks and a dissertation carrying a maximum of 16 marks making a possible total of 48 marks. Well, Glenys scored 44 marks, the highest score ever recorded in the Education Department of the University." Well I was lost for words, but thanked him for telling me and also for his support in guiding her along the way to achieving her success. Afterwards, photographs were taken of Glenys in her cap and gown holding the Scroll of Honour and of course, the boys posed in the Cap and thought it was great fun. Dr Robertson was keen then for Glenys to consider doing a PhD, and told her he would be pleased to continue being her personal tutor. They explored the option once, but by then Glenys was heavily involved in her work at Claypool School and simply never found the time to pursue the matter any further … but I am certain that the quality and quantity of her work at Claypool over the last 16 years would be the equivalent of at least one PhD with all the Honours going!

I am very glad that Arthur was still with us then and well enough to enjoy the great sense of pride in the achievement of our daughter Glenys. After the excitement of the 9th July 1990 at Manchester University we returned home to Eglwysbach where we enjoyed a small celebration of my 66th birthday on the 15th July.

But within days of all this happiness we heard very tragic news about the death of Emyr Pierce, our nephew, on the 18th of July. He was the elder son of Nance and the late Harry Pierce, Arthur's brother. Harry's sudden death at the age of 63 had itself come as a shock to us, but his son Emyr's death at the tender age of 44 surpassed even that in its tragic and untimely circumstance.

Emyr was very well-known throughout Wales as *Gari Williams*, the all-round entertainer who appeared regularly on television. He had started out as a talented boy soprano, and as an adult had been joined by Elwyn Vaughan who sang duets with him and played guitar. They became well-known on the club and theatre circuits and released a number of very successful records. Eventually they formed a company called *Cwmni'r Castell* (the castle company) that produced films for television. Gari's wicked humour and cheeky smile together with non-stop fast chatter won everyone over. The company became successful in making different types of programmes including ones that featured Gari.

It was a beautiful summer's day when the funeral took place at the little Chapel at Mochdre. Many hundreds of people had gathered to pay their last respects. During the service a shaft of sunshine fell onto the coffin, then a cat walked into the Chapel. It jumped onto a Deacon's seat then quietly and serenely walked along until it finally came to rest on Gari's coffin. Everyone present witnessing the scene knew that Gari would have enjoyed the incident enormously, and seen it as a big and wonderful joke. There was a genuine sense of loss amongst the public, not least because of his natural talent and charity work. But the loss to his immediate family was devastating. Never again would we see his impish grin and share his perpetual cheerfulness. He is still remembered fondly.

Four years earlier, in the mid '80s there was considerable activity in the Lloyd Jones family too. Elsie no longer travelled abroad as extensively as before on business for ICI, but she still held an important executive job at ICI in Wilton. Neville had been promoted to Transport Manager for ICI Western Europe, and in February 1986 while Geraint was still a toddler they decided to sell their house in Loftus to buy another, more conveniently situated for work. Elsie especially was sorry to leave the house because it was distinctive and very comfortable, but the garden, although most attractive in layout and colour, was a time consumer - it demanded a great deal of energy and commitment. Initially they had decided on a house in East Harlsey, but at the last minute just before contracts were to be signed, the owner withdrew the house from the market. Not only was this a disappointment, but a waste of money and time for them too.

Immediately, there was a serious problem of finding a roof over their heads because the Loftus house was already sold and occupation was required within days. Fortunately they had friends who owned holiday flats and one happened to be vacant as it was late in the season. Elsie and Neville accepted the offer of the flat, but soon realised that the standard of cleanliness was not to their liking. Because I was retired and deemed to be a lady of leisure with time on my hands, I was invited to visit Teesside again, or maybe I invited myself. Who cares! ... I was pleased to be able to help not only with the packing and unpacking, but the cleaning of both properties too. The move went well, essentials were taken to the flat, but other items were put into storage until they'd found another house to buy. Els and Nev were working during the day and I was looking after Geraint in the flat because Helen, the nanny was on holiday. I cleaned everything in the flat including the paintwork, shelves, cupboards, floors, bath, toilet, and cooker ... absolutely everything! Between us, we got the flat into a decent place in which to live and that was just as well because their stay there became protracted due to their difficulty in finding another property. They finally bought a house in Hutton Rudby, and perhaps Providence had taken a hand in matters because I much preferred the house, and they too soon came to think the same way.

Hutton Rudby village is delightful with the old and new areas blending together nicely round the village green. The villagers have the use of a Church, Chapel, school, and village hall, in addition to three pubs, a Post Office, hairdresser, butcher, greengrocer and a General Store.

Els and Nev gave their new home a Welsh name - *Hafod* meaning (summer place). It was a spacious house consisting of a lounge, kitchen, downstairs toilet, dining room, study, three bedrooms and a bathroom. Then they extended it to include a family room downstairs, and two further bedrooms and shower rooms in the loft space above the first floor. The gardens are extensive with trees, bushes, an orchard and extensive lawns, and there is a big patio and barbecue area too. *Hafod* is an excellent family home with plenty of space inside and out. That's enough, or I shall start to sound like an Estate Agent!

I remember the occasion of Aled's Christening when the Minister walked up and down the aisle in the Chapel with him on his arm. Although still a very young baby, he was quite happily looking round at the assembled people with obvious interest. I have never seen anything like it before or since - he was a remarkable baby! In time, he lost his dark hair and became fair-haired, and was lovely, or should I use the word attractive, now that he is a young man of 17 years of age!

Four years later another little boy arrived in the family, namely Huw Vaughan Lloyd. He was born in February during very cold and wintry weather unlike his brothers who had been born in the summer. When Neville brought Huw and his Mum home from the hospital I had to take a shovel to cut a path through the snow for them to get safely from the car to the front door. Huw was a good and quiet baby, but he has more than made up for the silence since then, because he has a very powerful voice and he likes to exercise it frequently!

At the end of April 1991 Arthur retired from the post of being the Organist at Seion Chapel, Llanrwst having completed 44 years of dedicated service. He was then 74 years of age and not in the best of health, so we decided it was time for him to make the final break. No one can go on forever in any job - not even Arthur. Sooner or later he would have had to retire from the role and we judged that that time had arrived. Naturally, it was a wrench and the Chapel members and Deacons were very sad at his departure, especially the ones who attended his Sunday School Class. He was presented with a generous cheque from the Chapel and a lovely garden seat from his Sunday School Class in appreciation of his services. We proudly placed the seat on the verandah in Eglwysbach and Arthur enjoyed many hours sitting there, watching people come and go and often passers-by came to sit with him for a chat.

I too, was very sorry to leave my Sunday School Class of young women at Seion Chapel. We'd had some excellent discussions over the years based on Biblical teachings, and they were eager to participate and speak honestly about their views and experiences of life. It is such a pity that people who reject all forms of religion have mistaken ideas about those who do attend Church, Chapel or other places of worship. I suppose it is a throwback to a time long ago when Christians and other religious followers were looked upon as being narrow-minded, strait-laced and spoilsports. Apart from some exceptions, to my knowledge, most Christians and other faith followers today are kind, pleasant and welcoming people who can relate to today's world. I also acknowledge that a minority take their faith to extremes, which sadly and alarmingly has the result of creating fear and disenchantment for others.

Tragically, I am also highly conscious of so many people today who appear lost and stuck on the surface of life, individuals who do not realise that they too are vainly searching for the things that all human beings search for in life: love, peace, trust, happiness, intimacy, contentment, fulfilment and spirituality. They look everywhere for them except the one place where they can find routes to all of them in abundance.

We don't all see things in the same way but the basic truth is the same - God is Love. God is the Holy Spirit. Just as there have always been contrasts in the world such as light and dark, heat and cold, sweet and sour, there has also been the contrast and challenge between God the Holy Spirit, and the Devil, which is the spirit of evil. There is a constant struggle going on in the world and also in the hearts and minds of all human beings between the spirit of the God of Love and the evil spirit of Satan. We see evidence of this contrast every evening on television news bulletins and in newspaper reports. I believe that Jesus Christ came into the World to tell us these truths, as did other faith leaders in their time, to show us Love and Compassion and help all people to overcome evil. That basically, is what the message of all religions is about. It is a pity that the word 'Love' has been narrowly interpreted in today's world to mean *only* sexual pleasure. Its true meaning involves sexual pleasure and so very much more ... so much more! This *Credo* is what I believe, it has influenced me over the years to become the person I am today. Like everyone else, I am a member of the human race that has its frailties and failings, but fortunately also the potential to rise above them with the power of the Holy Spirit.

After saying goodbye to the large Seion Chapel in Llanrwst, Arthur and I became members of the small Presbyterian Chapel in Eglwysbach. Arthur attended one Service only. I don't think he could adapt to the huge change after so many years as Organist at Seion. How could he, it was all too different after 44 years of service elsewhere, to become a 'standard' member of the congregation. In all that time he had been an outstanding and accomplished Organist with one of the finest instruments available nationally, he found it hard to settle passively in a pew. But I have remained a member of the Chapel at Eglwysbach, and have attended as regularly as I can.

In the early '90s Glen was really concentrating on her school, trying hard to achieve her vision for education, to implement the ideas she had put forward so effectively in her Dissertation for the M.Ed. She was enthusiastic about new ideas and methods of teaching children more effectively, but too often she encountered resistance and difficulties with teachers entrenched in set patterns and like many, happy in their own little ruts. It was an extremely difficult time for her, but she has the gift of endurance and perseverance and therefore trained herself to lead and coax rather than push and shove. Gradually and sometimes painfully things improved at the school, and in 1991 new extensions were built resulting in many improvements in accommodation for staff and pupils, but there was much more work for Glen to do to get the school to where she wanted it to be.

Kerry and Glen had bought a caravan in 1989 and had spent their first holiday in it for three weeks in France. The caravan was very popular with Marcus and Morgan because they were able to take their bikes along, television and computer too! One year, plans were made to go touring on the Isle of Wight and I was invited to go with them. I was so pleased and excited because ever since I was a little girl I had wanted to live in a gypsy caravan. Blissfully unaware of the deprivations and difficulties involved I was sure that such a way of life was wonderful and satisfying and even later on, when I was grown up the romantic attraction was still there. It did not matter that Glen and Kerry's caravan was nothing like a Romany home, it was still a caravan for goodness sake with all the 'mod. cons.'!

The Evans family and I went to the Isle of Wight at the end of July. The weather was pleasant as we drove south to catch the ferry and on board it was breezy, but we enjoyed the crossing. The island has a great deal to offer. We spent a day at the delightful 'Black Gang Chine Theme Park' where the boys had a wonderful time with ships and pirates and many other play activities based on different themes. An area of the cliffs above the shore in the Theme Park had been fenced off because of a landslide of crumbling rocks. A few days after returning home, we read in a newspaper that yet another massive landslide had happened there and a large area had fallen into the sea leaving a house clinging onto the very edge of the cliff. No one had lived in it for a while because of its predicament. We felt very sorry for the owners of the theme-park because we noticed evidence of continual erosion of land, in fact at the time it was one meter per annum and increasing each year. Despite this, we saw much evidence of their continuing investment of money in the Park, and most importantly their care in maintaining high standards for their customers - we were very impressed!

We visited the tourist sights of the island, had fun and enjoyed the good weather. On the one rainy afternoon the boys and I did some cooking in the caravan when we baked little fairy cakes for tea. Really scrumptious they were too! We'd spent ages talking about how we would decorate the cakes, and then even more time fulfilling the detailed plans. Each little cake was unique and very special, and we'd used enormous creativity in making the most of the limited cake decoration material available to us in the caravan. We managed to make fondant icing for the surface of the cakes, butter icing for the inside and then used Smarties, Jelly Babies, Chocolate Buttons, and Chocolate Flake to achieve variety and individuality on top!

As usual, we phoned Arthur every day to make sure he was alright - Irene and David, my kind neighbours were keeping an eye on him and the cat, Mickey Mouse too. Living in a caravan imposes its own rules and everyone has to abide by them to ensure a smooth routine. I loved it, and the days sped by and much too soon it was time to return home. I always think it's nice to go away for a break, but it's also nice to go home again too. I really missed the kids, my conversations with them, and their little ways, once back in Eglwysbach.

I believe I'm very lucky to have children who are generous enough to extend an open invitation to stay with them at their homes whenever I care to visit and also join them on holidays at times. I greatly appreciate this and try not to take advantage of their goodwill. Even more, I delight in the wonderful rapport that I have with my grandchildren.

I love them all and they love me. I am their Nain.

Nain is a Welsh word full of affection, and there is only the one word for the roleholder unlike in English where there is a preponderance of different titles - grandmother, grandmamma, granny, gran, nanna, nanny and so on, but in Welsh there is only *'Nain'*. I am proud that all my 7 grandchildren call me Nain - a title and role that I love.

As always, there was a warm welcome on my return home from holidays. I cannot tell you who was the more enthusiastic - Arthur or the cat! There was plenty to do on my return including, catching up on the washing, ironing, gardening, shopping, and cooking! Attending Chapel, the W.I. and meetings of the *Merched y Wawr* (Welsh Women's Society) were a huge interest and goal for me. There were never dull moments, including appointments that Arthur had to keep in relation to his health situation. His blood pressure was still being monitored regularly and he visited a wonderful chiropodist at the clinic. Arthur nearly lost his toes on both feet through the diabetes, but Mr. Jones the chiropodist rescued them. I cannot praise his efforts enough for it wasn't easy for him … Arthur was extremely ticklish and had very tickly feet! He found it difficult to keep them still while Mr. Jones used very sharp instruments, so Arthur placed his hands on his knees and I placed mine over his in order to control the involuntary movements and Arthur's,"whooo whooo whoooing," when he felt the tickling sensations during treatment. Arthur was so ticklish, he even laughed out loud *before* the tickling even happened.

Glen and Kerry started on the loft space of their bungalow and there followed a period of chaos. It never ceased to amaze me how cool they always were at such times. I was involved from time to time helping as much as I could in some way or other, but they somehow sailed through the upheavals alongside their full time jobs, and always achieved their goals.

We spent the following Christmas at their home - well most of the holiday at least before we received a disturbing phone call from Irene, our neighbour to tell us that someone had broken into our home and suggesting that we should return right away. We were absolutely shocked, such awful things didn't happen in Eglwysbach! We hurriedly packed clothes, presents and everything else and off we went, but when we arrived home, everything looked quite normal. There was no mess or disturbance to be seen and we were puzzled. Then Irene and David came over and pointed out that the casement window in the kitchen had been forced open. I had three potted plants on the window sill but it was only when we went outside that we discovered that all three had been set unharmed in the border on the opposite side of the path - that was strange behaviour for burglars, but there was more. I knew that Irene looked round our house every day to check on things in our absence, and on that day she noticed that the curtains of our bedroom had been drawn. She told David she thought it was odd that we had returned home and not phoned to tell them of our return. So David decided to go over just in case something was wrong, and it took him some time to realise exactly what was amiss because everything looked normal. After careful scrutiny he noticed that the kitchen window had been forced open but carefully pushed closed as the intruders had left. He immediately called the police and phoned us too.

The police had already visited by the time of our return and had taken finger and footprints. They returned when we arrived home and asked if anything had been stolen. It was difficult to say offhand so I had a tour of the house to inspect for lost items. I knew they had been rifling through drawers, but I could see no signs of damage. I was beginning to think that nothing was missing until I searched the lounge, which also appeared at first to be untouched. The decorations were still up and all the Christmas cards in place too. The large cabinet in the lounge that has a central drinks compartment, glass fronted display cupboards on both sides and drawers and cupboards below looked exactly as we'd left it. Then I glanced through the panes of glass for closer inspection and saw immediately that three antique breast-pocket watches were missing. One was my father's, another belonged to my father-in-law, while the third was silver and very old - it had been given to Arthur's grandfather by a very old poet on his deathbed. It was a 'half hunter' watch, that is, the outer case had an inner circle cut out of the front so that part of the face was always exposed. This one was very valuable. To get to the watches the burglars had to remove three or four Christmas cards to open the cabinet door, but curiously, they had all been replaced neatly. The police said that prints showed there had been two intruders, and they had their suspicions as to their identity. They believed the intruders were local, but had yet to discover sufficient proof to make arrests. If their suppositions were correct then I too had an idea of who they were!

Another house, two doors away had also been burgled that night. The owners were also away for the Christmas holiday and from the cemetery at the back of the properties it would have been obvious that there were no lights in either of the two houses. For those young thieves, getting over the fence would not have been a problem. But that is no longer the case, because on the advice of the Police, security measures have been set in place.

Watches stored on top of a cabinet had been stolen from the other house, and later we were told that watches had changed hands at a pub in a nearby village the following evening. Although little damage occurred to my house, I nevertheless hated the idea that strangers had been in my home looking round and fingering personal items. It brought feelings of disgust and soiling, an intrusion of my privacy, quite apart from the loss of valued family heirlooms. Most of all, we lost piece of mind - for a long time we were on tenterhooks wondering if they would come back. The Police were very helpful and advised us about steps to take to make our home safer. We had special windows and locks fitted, security lights and other measures too. If anyone came over fences now they surely would have the marks to show for it!

Chapter Fifty-Seven

GARDEN HERITAGE

Plants are living things sharing our world and environment - indeed we are more dependent on them than they are on us. In many ways they react like humans in the way they respond to care and respect. If we love them they will repay us in beauty, form, scent and colours of many hues and shades. I remember as a child being upset at seeing bunches of wild flowers collected by children only to be thoughtlessly disposed of later to lie broken, crushed and dying underfoot. I was once asked which flowers were my favourites and I found it a very difficult question to answer because flowers excel in different ways from the point of view of scent, form and colour. Some are easy to tend, but others are fussy. Examples of scented flowers are Daphne bushes, Roses, Jasmine, Honeysuckle and Phlox, and flowers representing interesting form and colour are large Begonias and the smaller non-stop varieties, especially when they are placed in baskets and tubs. Jolly-looking flowers include Pansies, Daisies, and Sunflowers, and examples of elegant flowers are Columbines, Lilies, and Peonies. Easy, non-fussy plants are the many summer bedding plants that include, Lobelia, Alyssum, Ageratums, Geraniums, Zinnias, and Marigolds, and not forgetting the pretty Forget-me-nots that conveniently re-seed twice every year. Eagerly awaited spring flowers include Daffodils, Narcissi, Snowdrops, Tulips, and Crocuses. I love them all … every single one!

My mother had her own plants to look after and her pride and joy were her Fuchsias. They bore the ordinary purple and scarlet flowers, but they were huge. She grew them in two large, low earthenware pots that had formerly been used to skim milk. We lived on a road that led to a flour mill, and I think the secret of the success with the Fuchsias was due to the horses' deposits on the road that I had to collect as manure for the garden. My mother fed the plants with the liquid from the dung. This was also used on two rows of Sweet William and Columbines (Aquilegia) that grew under a low hedge at the bottom of the back garden. They looked wonderful in flower.

I love Busy Lizzies, or Impatience, to give them their 'posh' name, I first saw them in gardens in the USA and then later in great profusion in the parks and municipal areas in France. I have used them in abundance in my garden ever since discovering them. The many colours are lovely and they are long-suffering in droughts. In recent years I have gradually added more and more camellias to my garden too because they look so lovely in the Spring, and the story in the opera La Bohème gives them an even stronger appeal for me.

I remember the outstanding horticultural gardens in Niagara Falls in Canada where I was bewitched by a large tree with what looked like beautiful white bows all over it. I took a photograph of it and made a note of the genre. For a long time I looked for one to buy in this country, but they were all huge specimens. But I achieved success eventually, I managed to buy one that did not grow as much as the others. It was so slow to flower that I gave it to my son Bryn, who planted it in his arboretum. This year it produced 4 or 5 white bracts that pleased me so much.

Today, as I gaze at my garden I experience a certain feeling of pride and satisfaction in my achievement. I planted every single plant, tree and bush, and designed the different layouts too. Bryn did all the heavy work in laying out the paths, patio and the base for my lovely summerhouse that I named *Hafan* (summer place), and my friend Gary, a past colleague from Manweb put in the electric power supply for it and the 'Adam and Eve' water feature, and rock fountain. All the features make a wonderful sight to see - I have been told many times over that the effect of what I have created is wonderful!

The lawns have interesting curves, and there are two areas covered in pea gravel with lovely dwarf bushes of different shades of green and cream, there are bird baths, small boulders, mounds and large black pieces of drift-wood from the river that look like weird creatures. There are benches in interesting positions where the garden can be viewed from different angles, and an arch over the path covered in Jasmine that gives off an overwhelmingly delightful scent. Also growing on the arch is white double Clematis. There are other Clematis plants here and there, and in the Spring I look forward to the one that smothers the branches of a dead tree with lavender blue bells hanging so delicately in profusion.

As I write, I note that my garden is just as lovely now at the end of September as it was when the Eglwysbach Show judges came to visit at the beginning of August, when I won the Challenge Cup for the 12th time for 'the best kept and most attractive garden' in the village. I work in the garden because I enjoy it, but I must admit that winning such a prestigious competition in an area where there are so many other lovely gardens, is the gilt on the gingerbread.

The masses of white flowers on the twin weeping Cotoneasters at the drive entrance have now become mantles of red berries. Sadly, before the end of November there will be only bare branches, but there are two pairs of Blackbirds who love the berries, and they have to eat something tasty occasionally, as we all do. Besides, they deserve them all as thanks for their glorious songs in the evenings when, perched high on a branch they pour out melodies in a never-ending stream, so sweet and soothing to the ear.

My advice to any would-be gardener is to treat your plants as children, care for them, feed them, protect and love them. Life would not be the same without my garden or my children.

Chapter Fifty-Eight

MY NAIN KNOWS EVERYTHING

Once, during a spring weekend not long after the Evans family had moved to live in the bungalow in Bottom o'th' Moor, Marcus and Morgan, or the M & Ms as I call them, went for an afternoon walk with me. It was a lovely sunny day and we ambled along to the lower end of the village where there are some very old and interesting cottages. Eventually we reached the main road and decided to wend our way back through 'Daffodil Hill', a lovely name and a lovely place, especially in the Spring. As I led the way past the lodge, Marcus suddenly came up close and under his breath and looking very concerned said, “Nain, Nain, you can't go that way.” “Why ever not?” I asked. “No, no you mustn't go that way”, he replied. “Of course we can, come on.” Marcus still looking very serious and concerned said, “But that is a graveyard.” So that was the reason … and probably schoolyard talk amongst the youngsters had conjured up spooky tales of ghosts and such like especially in the knowledge that children in his school needed to walk through another graveyard to get to their dinners each day at that time. I knew that young children loved that sort of thing. “Come on, it's only a short path through the cemetery and the flowers will be lovely,” I said, grabbing his hand. And as soon as we reached the open field he was away bouncing his football again, but Morgan was still clutching my hand.

Then the questions started. “Nain, what is a graveyard?” He was naturally curious, but I also suspected that Marcus' air of mystery and concern had made an impression too. I considered how best to explain without making a big thing of it. I have always answered children's questions truthfully, but only as far as they are capable of understanding at that stage. “A graveyard is called a cemetery and it is where people who die are buried.” There was a silence, but then he said, “Why do they bury people when they are dead and why do people die?” So I said, “Well some people have accidents, when they fall and hurt themselves very badly, some people become very ill, and others die because they are very, very old and tired.” There was silence again, “But Nain, how do people become dead?” Morgan's questions always challenged me so I said, “When people die, the spirit that represents the real person when they are alive leaves the body and goes to Jesus in Heaven. But at that time their body can no longer walk or run, see or feel, eat or sleep, it is useless … but the person's spirit remains alive and active within us.” It is a joy to me to know that Arthur's spirit is still actively alive in my grandchildren today, many years after his death. I explained to Morgan that because it is not possible to keep bodies for too long after death they are put into a coffin and buried in the ground, or cremated when the casket containing the ashes is buried in ground that has been blessed or the ashes are scattered there.

Morgan remembered the time we saw the poor cat that had been run over near 'The Beeches' when the family lived there. I explained to him that the way the cat appeared is how people appear too when they die. Then there was silence, followed by, “But why do people get old and have to die?” I sent up a silent prayer for guidance, so I said, “Morgan, you have seen lots of beautiful new cars that have lovely shiny colours and when you ride in them their engines work well climbing hills and speeding along the roads so easily. After many years, the cars begin to look shabby and the paint fails to shine any more.

Bumps and scratches appear on the bodies and the engines get tired, and they have to be taken to garages where mechanics alter things and fit new parts. There comes a time when the cars won't go any more and they have to be taken to a scrap yard. Well, our bodies are something like that, because they also wear out." Immediately Marcus, who had rejoined us said, "Like Aunty Gusta?" and I said, "Yes, just like Aunty Gusta", and that was that. The old lady was Arthur's last surviving aunt who had lived until she was 98 years old and to the end, she still had an interest in life despite being wrinkled and doddery. Glen and Kerry used to visit the old lady at her Nursing Home in Llanrwst, and Marcus went too. She loved children and always made a fuss of Marcus, and in a funny way, despite a huge age gap of 97 years, she and Marcus were somehow able to connect with each other.

When I visited the M&Ms as little boys they would want me to read a story aloud to them every night, but mostly they wanted me to tell them stories, some of which were true while others were pure fiction. But every night, following the stories, came the demand, "Sing for us Nain." In response I would sing the usual repertoire of nursery jingles such as: *Jack and Jill*; *Mary, Mary quite contrary*; *Polly put the kettle on*, then gradually more and more were added including: *Where are you going to my pretty maid*; Daisy, *Daisy; Kkkk...Katie, beautiful Katie*, and Welsh songs too. The favourites were: *At six o'clock on a shining morn, we start our busy day; Migildi Magildi; Hen fran fawr ddu* (Big old back raven), and finally the *Skye boat song* - and before I'd sung the last few notes they were fast asleep! This was a ritual of the biggest and most powerful kind. I would be on my knees by their bunk beds and the songs had to be sung in strict order and woe betide me if I made a mistake. I would be corrected forthwith and there were no short-cuts in the programme either. I was so tired sometimes my knees would be aching, or I was almost asleep myself, but it was a privilege for me because I was allowed into their world and was the richer for it, and hopefully, they were too.

The boys soon made a new friend in Horwich called Adam, who had a very deep voice for a little boy. One day, as he played with Morgan Adam asked me, "Nain, can I call you Nain?" to which I responded, "Well yes of course Adam if you want to." What a compliment it was!

I remember an occasion when Glen had driven Morgan, Adam and me into Manchester when, during the afternoon the boys announced they were hungry, small boys are always hungry, and we ended up at Pizzaland, and had to sit at separate tables although near to each other. The boys sat together at one table and Glen and I sat at another. We had finished eating but still had our drinks to consume and conversations to finish when suddenly and with pleasure Glen said to me, "Listen to them jabbering away." What we heard was very funny, but we had to appear to be unaware of it. Morgan said to Adam, "My Nain knows everything, and she's got anything you want in her handbag." Of course the latter part was not far from the truth! My bag gets so heavy that periodically I have to empty its contents onto the table and trawl through it. The contents usually include: a load of tissues, plasters, tablets for headaches and sore throats, nail scissors and files, biros and writing pads, spectacles for all weathers, headscarf, an empty wallet, purse, keys, hankies, safety pins, compact, comb and lipstick and sometimes even more. I have to admit that all the items have proved useful at some time or other, but they are undoubtedly surplus to requirement most of the time … they are simply there to be handy … and you never know when!

The following poem was composed and written by my grandson Morgan … and I am so proud of the piece because it is well written, and is the masterpiece of Morgan Evans, aged eight years, who wrote it as a dedication to his Nain in Llanrwst.

NAIN'S GARDEN

1

Nain loves her garden at all times of the year,
And doesn't stop when Winter's here,
She weeds and waters 'til her hands turn brown,
She's the garden queen and wears the crown!

2

Nain uses a fork to dig up the veg.,
At the top of the garden near the hedge,
She hoes away when weeding the border,
She's off to the nursery to collect her order!

3

Nain works in her garden every day,
And doesn't stop 'till it's all okay,
She grows plants, tomatoes and also fruit,
She grows cauliflower, potatoes and beetroot!

4

Nain enters her garden in a competition,
And ends up in the first position,
She always makes me feel so fine,
She's the best in the land - she's MY NAIN!

By: Morgan Evans aged 10

I also read to Geraint, Aled and Huw when they were little boys, but somehow the singing didn't appear on the list. I don't know why because they too are musical. I suppose that's how different things happen to appeal to different people. I read Welsh books to Geraint because he understood a lot of Welsh and could speak a little. Although his Mam and Dad were Welsh-speaking, they nevertheless lived in England and the children went to English schools and listened to English radio and television and that makes it very difficult to speak Welsh fluently unless the language of the hearth is Welsh. Also their live-in Nanny was English.

When I visited Bryn's home, Faye always wanted me to set sums for her, she just wanted more and more arithmetic and I really thought she would excel in this subject, which in fact she did. Now that she is grown up she has a very good job in the Finance office of a large Company. She recently completed a two-year course to gain a Diploma relevant to her work.

Rebecca compiled a dossier of my life when she was at Primary School that was regarded as excellent by her primary school teacher. Rebecca, on leaving secondary school went to work in an office related to customer care. She completed work-related studies that enabled her to move to better jobs. Now she is married to Ross, who is currently serving in Iraq, and they have two little boys called Alexander and Ethan who are absolutely adorable.

I am very proud of all my grandchildren for they are all bright and intelligent. But also, they are kind, thoughtful and sensible, although they do have their moments like all other children.

Whenever Arthur and I spent a week or more with our children and families we had to take Mickey Mouse with us because the little ones loved him so much. He was a great favourite and had excellent house manners! He had settled in very well when we moved to Eglwysbach because there was a better hunting area there and few cats in the neighbourhood. When a small estate of houses was built just off our road, a few more cats appeared as families moved in, but Mickey did not approve. Not one of them was allowed to roam about on his territory.

One day I heard snarling and terrible yells coming from our back garden and I rushed out to see a terrible fight in progress, Mickey was fighting with a much bigger cat, they clung on to each other, biting and scratching, they looked like one big ball of fur. The enemy was younger, and poor Mickey was elderly. It was impossible for me to separate them with my bare hands, so I had to get a brush handle to force them apart, shooing the stranger away and Mickey chasing him off as fiercely as ever. Eventually peace was restored and Mickey went off to have a snooze. He did not look any the worse for wear other than the loss of tufts of fur. However, as the afternoon wore on, Mickey remained at rest, ignoring his food and wanting only to lie in peace. At this point I wasn't really worried, his exertions had taken their toll and his body needed to relax. But later in the evening after Arthur had to gone to bed, Mickey got up and stretched and then proceeded towards his food basin. He ate a little and then went back towards his bed but his gait was very unsteady. He lay down again to rest, but before long I heard strange sounds, squeaky, laboured sounds of breathing and I knew something was wrong. I went over to lift and comfort him, but he objected strongly to being disturbed, so I let him be, but kept a watch over him.

Soon, he was fighting for breath and throwing his body about, thrashing and crashing against the wall. I was torn at the sight of him suffering, I wanted to hold him and calm him, but he was beyond anything I could do for him. I prayed that God would end his torture quickly … and then suddenly, he just lay still and his brave spirit gave up. Poor Mickey… poor Mickey … poor Mickey Mouse. Mercifully, he passed away eventually, much to my relief. I cannot describe properly how I felt, my heart was hurting from seeing his pain and anguish and I thanked God for releasing Mickey from it. I don't know how long I was there, but I just sat remembering the affection that little cat had given so freely. Eventually, I formed his little body into a sleeping shape and wrapped it in cloth. In the morning I buried him in the garden where he used to lie in the sun. For weeks I kept hoping to see him loping down the path, but of course he never came.

When Marcus and Morgan heard of Mickey's death they were terribly concerned and upset and during their next visit, their first action was to find a suitable piece of stone on which to paint Mickey's name and date of death. Then they solemnly and sadly placed it on the spot where he was buried. It showed their love for Mickey and his pure, enduring goodness.

Several months passed before I could even think of getting another cat, and even then it was only because I'd seen an appeal in the local newspaper from the 'Cat Protection Society' for homes for the cats that the Society had in its care. Arthur and I went to the home of the lady volunteer who was caring for a number of cats brought to her for various reasons. One mother cat was ill and had given birth to five kittens. She was obviously a street cat that must once have been a pet because of the way she reacted to affection. The kittens were not all the same colour, but three of them were ginger with white markings, lovely little balls of fluff. One had been chosen by someone else, so I watched the other four frolicking and playing and decided to have the one with white paws and shoulders and an interesting and lively face with unusual markings. The carer was happy for us tohave our choice, but no one was allowed to have the kittens until they were over 8 weeks old and had received all the recommended injections, had been spayed, and our homes had been inspected for suitability. Before we left that afternoon I stressed that my chosen kitten should be reserved for us and we were reassured that it would be.

But having arranged on the phone on Friday to collect our kitten on the Sunday, we were taken aback on our arrival to be told that the lady carer had gone out for the day and left her husband in charge of the smallholding and the kittens.There was no sign of our chosen kitten because the lady who had earlier chosen a ginger kitten had decided to have two we were told, and the husband had mistakenly handed over my kitten to her. He was very sorry and extremely apologetic, but I was very disappointed nonetheless and had to accept the situation. I decided to take the other ginger kitten that needed a home.

Training started immediately. I had a tray of litter with a handful of fine soil added to it. Cats are fastidious animals, and always clean up after their toilet activities, and their natural instinct is to use clean soil. I have found that when kittens are taken out to a soil patch at regular times, and holding their front paws and making them do scratching movements in the soil whilst repeating any phrase over and over again they quickly pick up the procedure. In this way my cats quickly learned to use outside soil for their toilet. Unless I am travelling abroad, my current cat, known as Shonna, always goes travelling with me. She is a perfect house-guest and is given a right royal welcome and uses her little tray although she does not use one at home. All seven of my grandchildren love animals, especially Shonna, indeed I am firmly of the opinion that my welcome at their homes hinges on Shonna's presence! They feed her, buy presents for her, stroke her, in short they love her to bits and her ladyship of course believes that she deserves all of this idolatry. On one occasion, when I went on holiday to the U.S.A. Shonna pined and lost weight at a local Cattery despite being well looked after. Now when I go away from home I am happy to leave Shonna in the tender care of Glen, Kerry and the boys, where she is thoroughly spoiled and is perfectly happy and free to come and go as she pleases.

Before we were allowed to take Shonna home, a person from the Society came to inspect our premises to make sure we had a good home for her. She was tiny, just eight weeks old, and so trusting and playful. She was especially fond of Arthur because he would play with her and very soon she became a part of our lives. She's just a cat, some people said laughingly, but I have seen her make slaves of such people, given the chance. Some time ago, someone sent me a birthday card entitled *Cat Truths*. I don't know who wrote the text but it was definitely someone who knew cats.

10 CAT TRUTHS

1. Cats do what they want, when they want.
2. They rarely listen to you.
3. They're totally unpredictable.
4. They whine when they're not happy.
5. When you want to play, they want to be alone.
6. When you want to be alone, they want to play.
7. They expect you to cater to their every whim.
8. They leave hair everywhere.
9. They're moody.
10. They drive you nuts.

I quite like dogs too, well, some dogs. I don't like big, fierce dogs and am very fond of Sheepdogs, Scotties, St. Bernards and Labradors, they are ideal pets for other people, but not for me because I am a *cat person*.

Bryn and Kath have three Shi Tzu's puppies, they are Temple dogs from the Far East and are very lovable. They have big liquid eyes that look straight into people's eyes, captivatingly. When I visit them and open the car door the three - mother, son and daughter jump onto the back seat and show they are ready to go somewhere although we never have done. They give such a warm welcome, everytime!

During the summer holidays in 1992, Kerry, Glen and the boys very kindly asked me if I would like to go with them again in the caravan. They planned to go touring in the South Wales area and I jumped at the chance. I needed a change, and Arthur was well enough to look after himself for a week or so. Of course, I had to prepare stacks of food and so on for Arthur, but that was no problem because we had a little freezer by then.

The weather was very changeable, but we managed to spend some days at a big pleasure park where the boys enjoyed the usual things like the bumping cars, water chutes, and so on. But the highlight of that holiday came by chance. Kerry had taken a berth at a Touring Caravan park and learned that we were near the summer camp of *Urdd Gobaith Cymru* at Llangrannog where Glen and Elsie had spent some happy times at the camp when they were younger. Since those days of course facilities at the camp had been improved, and there were wonderful opportunities available to non-camp residents after 5.00 p.m.to use some of the facilities for a reasonable charge. The magnet for our boys was the dry Ski Slope, where there were professional skiers to train the youngsters. One trainer in particular took to Marcus and Morgan and gave them hours of marvellous tuition, well beyond what was required of him. He also had conversations with us in Welsh about this, that and the other. He was excellent at his job and the boys soon mastered the art of using skis, first on the nursery slope and then on the high run. After the first evening of non-stop skiing, that was all they wanted to do every evening throughout the holiday even when the weather was wet and miserable. They had the place to themselves during those wet times and spent 4 hours every evening of that holiday going up and down the slope following the high quality tutoring of that professional skier. He was a skiing tutor at one of the best resorts in the Alps. Marcus and Morgan still love skiing and have been to Italy and France to enjoy real ski slopes in high mountains and have loved it, and maintain that skiing on real snow is much easier that skiing on artificial slopes.

As the year wore on Arthur became more frail and slower in his movements. He seemed to be increasingly affected by the diabetes and medication, but he still enjoyed his food and chatting at every opportunity. He could not do any heavy work of course, but liked pottering about in the house and garden. We went to spend Christmas with Glen, Kerry and the boys and they arranged a get together for the family - Elsie and Neville and the boys came and Bryn, Kath and the girls too. In addition there was Brian, my sister's youngest son from America and his fiancé Petrine. At the time, Brian was living in Britain, working for two years at Harrogate and Petrine had come over to visit him. We had a lovely time and Brian took a photograph of us all together, the only one I have of all our immediate family in a group.

Chapter Fifty-Nine

FAREWELL TO ARTHUR

As soon as the winter months gave way to signs of spring Arthur and I decided to prepare things for the spring and summer garden. For some years we had grown vegetables at the far end of the back garden and always had favourites - lettuce, radish, beetroot, peas and runner beans outside, and tomatoes and cucumber in the greenhouse. We tried leeks and sweetcorn a couple of times with minimal success. The difficulty lay in the fact that we had so many plants at different points in their development stored in the greenhouse, and it was therefore difficult to tend to them all. We protected lots of big, established plants like fuschias in there until the weather became warm enough to put them outside again, but we also had countless trays of seedlings and small potted plants in there too and, as every gardener knows, the spring months mean non-stop work.

Arthur enjoyed it all very much, but for some time he had not been able to do as much as he'd been used to. For instance, he could no longer plant potatoes because he had lost his balance and would fall over, but he still enjoyed choosing and setting early potatoes in boxes to sprout growths, and he liked watching me tend the plants. There was always a tradition of friendly rivalry in the village to be the first to lift early potatoes, and he enjoyed that. He also loved admiring the garden, and always praised my efforts to visitors who called.

During the cold months after Christmas I delight in looking through the many colourful catalogues that are sent to me, enjoying the colours, shapes and descriptions and making long lists of the plants and seeds that I would like to order. Inevitably, common sense ensures that drastic reductions are made to the lists and related cost. I plan my activities so that the seed-growing period is in full swing in the greenhouse before I become embroiled in the task of spring cleaning the house. Even though there were only the two of us at that time, there was still a need for an extra clean, or so I told myself. The rays of the spring sun always show up dust, smears and dirty windows and the most colourful fabrics can look dull and in need of a refreshing wash. Ornaments lack lustre, items of brass and copper benefit from a good, vigorous polishing, paintwork requires cleaning and sometimes walls need papering or painting too.

The spring months of 1993 were no exception, and my time was taken up with spring cleaning the house, tending the plants in the greenhouse, mowing the lawns and preparing the borders. I was very pleased with the progress of the plants, Arthur was very keen to water and feed the tomatoes and cucumbers, the weather was fine and sunny, and all danger of frost was gone. All the plants that were sufficiently hardened were firmly placed in the garden. Life was good!

After a few weeks we wondered whether some potatoes might be ready, so we lifted a couple of plants and lo and behold found lovely clusters of new potatoes ready to eat. Tradition involved eating the first 'earlies' on their own with no other item of food on the plate to mar their wonderful taste, peas and beans had the same treatment in turn. And so it was, that on that particular Tuesday, we had new potatoes for lunch with melted Welsh butter, pepper, salt and bread and butter. It was all in moderation of course, on account of Arthur having to take care with his diet. But I have to say that both of us thoroughly enjoyed that special meal!

After lunch, later in the afternoon Arthur did not feel well. He said he felt dizzy, weak, tired and disorientated, and that his chest felt tight. I sat him down - he always liked to sit in a chair with a straight back - and I prepared a fizzy antacid drink for him. I said, "You've probably eaten too many new potatoes … that's what! I told you to go easy on them didn't I," and I thought that was the reason, although I knew he hadn't overindulged really. But before long I knew for certain that it was not the case.

Arthur became very pale, almost ashen and his lips and ears had a bluish tinge. Without hesitation I phoned the Doctor's surgery in Conwy and within twenty minutes a lady Doctor had come all the way from Penmaenmawr to our house. She must have responded immediately and driven very fast, I was very relieved to see her, and she was so nice. She was calm, quiet and friendly and I could see Arthur relaxing even as she examined him. She explained that he had suffered a touch of angina and she sprayed something under his tongue and gave him the spray to carry around with him in his jacket pocket. He would also get a supply on prescription in the morning. Almost immediately, Arthur felt a lot better and managed to have a good night's sleep, but I did not sleep much that night.

The following morning Dr. Grout phoned to say that he wanted Arthur to have a series of tests, ones that he could conduct in the surgery over a number of visits or Arthur could go to Llandudno Hospital and have them done there altogether. It was his choice and we were to phone back at 11.00a.m. with the decision. I explained all this to Arthur while we ate breakfast, but he wasn't sure what to do. I said that he had plenty of time to think about it and Dr. Grout wanted him to decide for himself, he should do whatever he was happy to do.

Eventually Arthur said that he would go into Hospital to get the tests all done at once and I asked if he was happy doing that and he replied that he was. He had been there so many times as an outpatient and inpatient, and everyone had always been very good to him. He didn't mind going there at all. So I phoned the Surgery and they said that an ambulance would be arranged to fetch Arthur and take his records to the Hospital. I told them there was no need for an ambulance because I would gladly take him in the car. They told me which ward to take him to, and after getting everything ready for his stay, we set off in the car. I parked as near to the side entrance as I could and managed to get a wheelchair for Arthur for there was a fair distance to walk to the ward. Fortunately, a gentleman came along who took control of the wheelchair. When we got upstairs to the ward we were told there had been a change in plans and Arthur was to go to another ward.

Quite recently there had been unusually heavy flooding in Llandudno and the ground floor of the Hospital had been badly affected. Some areas needed new surfaces and some re-arrangements were to be expected. Anyway, Arthur was to be in a small ward and it just so happened that the man in the opposite bed was a Welsh-speaking farmer and very soon he and Arthur were having an animated conversation. I was very pleased that he was settled and would be getting early tests.

I returned home and continued with my late spring cleaning - most of it was already done but, I have always found that if I have worries about anything, I find it easier to cope if I have physical work to do. After tea, when I thought the children would be home from work, I phoned to tell them all what had happened. I explained that their father was settled into a nice ward, had made a friend, and that I was going to visit him the following afternoon. Glen immediately said she would meet me at the hospital, and I told her there was no need for that and it would be better if she came at the weekend, but she was adamant. It was impossible for Bryn to come at such short notice and Elsie would find it extremely difficult being so far away and there being no perceived immediate danger.

The next day I gathered some periodicals, fruit drinks and some clean clothes and went to the Hospital to find Glen already there with Arthur's favourite nibbles from Marks and Spencer and a couple of interesting things to read, and everyone was in good spirits. Arthur was eager to tell us that he had undergone some tests, including X-rays that had detected an infection in one lung. He had been a little worried because he had mislaid his walking stick, but someone had later found it for him. We chatted about different things, and Arthur was more like himself. He said that the Consultant was due to see him the following afternoon and wanted me to be present too. He warned me to arrive early as it was well known, he said, that Doctors liked going home early on Friday afternoons! I promised that I would get there early the following day. When visiting time was over Glen and I left and were both pleased to see Arthur putting on his spectacles and having a look at a newspaper. Glen returned home to Bolton and I went back to Eglwysbach.

I arose early on Friday to finish cleaning and polishing the lounge in order to complete the spring cleaning. The weather was sunny and hot and I was feeling very warm indeed. After having lunch and then a shower I went to the hospital and arrived there at 1.40 p.m. in good time for the 2.00 p.m. Consultant visit.

When I entered the ward I was shocked to see Arthur sitting up in bed with an oxygen mask on his face, arms outstretched and rocking from side to side and repeating over and over in Welsh, "I'm dying, I'm dying." I tried to calm him, but to no avail. The gentleman opposite said to me in Welsh, "Don't worry, he'll be alright. I think he's upset because he's had a little mishap in the bed." I could see a group of Nurses by the desk in the corridor so I hurried over to them and said, "My husband needs attention and he also needs a Doctor - call one immediately." I returned to Arthur and tried to soothe him and in seconds a Doctor came with another following on his heels. One of the Nurses came and took me aside then led me to the dayroom - I was told to stay there until they had sorted things out. I did not want to go to the dayroom because I wanted to stay with Arthur. Even if I could not do anything, I knew that my being there would have consoled him and given him strength and confidence, but they insisted! It must have been Hospital Policy at the time, and was user-friendly to the staff perhaps, but certainly not to the patient or relatives.

I don't know how long I sat in that dayroom, but Nurses popped in from time to time to ask if I was alright. Well of course I was not alright, and I kept asking for information and was told that Doctors were still with Arthur. I was really worried and then one of the Doctors came and said they were getting him ready to go down to Intensive Care and someone would come to fetch me as soon as everything was in place. This talk of intensive care scared me. What was going on?

I waited and waited and eventually a young Nurse appeared and said they were not quite ready yet for me to see him. Then I got up and told her to go back and ask the doctors for detailed information because I had to telephone our children and I wanted full facts and wanted them straight away. Poor girl, it was not her problem, but it was certainly mine. I decided to phone Glen immediately and told her that Dad was seriously ill and I thought she should come as soon as possible and would she please phone Elsie and Bryn. Glen was shocked and upset, but wasted no more time in talking - she said she would ring Elsie and Bryn at work and arrange things with Kerry and the boys, then leave right away.

I can't remember how long it was before anyone came back to that room, but eventually a Nurse took me downstairs and asked me to sit just outside one of the operating theatres. I sat there for a long time and Nurses passed by going in and out and I was told nothing. Then a Doctor came out and asked me some questions, which made me wonder why they were being asked because all the answers were to be found in Arthur's records, wherever they were. He explained about the infection and that Arthur was having difficulty with his breathing. The Doctor wanted to use a ventilator to help him until the infection had been dealt with, but there was no ventilator available at Llandudno, and Arthur would have to be taken to the larger hospital at Bangor. Another difficulty was the heavy traffic delay en route resulting from major roadworks. What did I think and what action should be taken? I replied, "I don't know. You are the Doctor and you should know. All I am asking is that you do not make him suffer any more than he has to. He does not deserve that." The Doctor said nothing, just grasped my shoulder and patted my back. I sat down again and suddenly felt so lonely and lost. No one seemed to be around and everything looked so bleak and bare including the water-damaged floors.

And then out of the blue, Win and David were there. Win and I had sung duets with the Llanrwst Male Voice Choir when younger. David explained that they had been visiting another patient and had heard someone say that Arthur was in the Hospital too. They enquired and were told that he was in Intensive Care and that I was present too, but they would not be allowed to join me. That comment had an immediate reaction from Win because she insisted that she must see me - she told the staff that she had been my friend for years and she was going to see me. The Nurse must have realised that Win was sincere, trustworthy and totally determined! Win and David were eventually allowed to come downstairs to sit with me. Sometime afterwards the Sister came along and asked if we would like to wait in her office, where it was more comfortable than the corridor, although there had been flood damage in that room too. We waited and drank several cups of tea.

Hours had passed and then the door opened and a very young Nurse quietly said, "The Doctor says your husband is sinking fast, and would you like to go to him now?" I got up and followed her. She led me into the theatre and I saw Arthur lying there all in white up to his chin. His eyes were closed but his mouth was wide open and that upset me. I took hold of his hand, which was quite warm and spoke to him. Immediately I thought how foolish that was, but the Nurse encouraged me to continue talking to him, as the hearing was the last faculty to go. There was no one there except Arthur and me, and the nurse quietly withdrew. I continued to touch him and say comforting things - just like a robot - I had no feeling in me, it had all drained away during the awful afternoon and evening - I was in shock. After a while, the Nurse returned and we left the room. I asked if they could close Arthur's mouth. I took one more look, but somehow it all seemed unreal, as if I was a bystander watching a scene unfolding before me. It all felt so strange - it was surreal. There was tea and sympathy again when we sat in Sister's office and I was glad Win was there - she represented reality. They must all have thought that I was either very hard-hearted, extremely brave, or simply in shock because I was not crying or weeping. I wasn't feeling anything and my mind was just completely numb. Nerys, my niece arrived and helped as much as she could.

Glen arrived late afternoon, then later, Elsie and Neville and Bryn and Kath. They were all extremely supportive and so very upset, and I envied their ability to weep. Win, David and Nerys left and we thanked them and said goodbye.

After that my mind is blank. I have no recall of any details. The girls took charge and arranged things. I know that I was involved and was consulted about everything, but I was detached as if watching myself doing things, but feeling nothing.

We decided that the Funeral Service should be at Seion Chapel, Llanrwst, where Arthur had been Organist for so long, followed by a short service at the Crematorium in Colwyn Bay. A few weeks later Arthur's ashes were scattered on Bodran Mountain, at Llanfair T.H., just as he had requested in his will. He always liked Llanfair because it was a happy place for him, he said.

The days after Arthur's death were sunny and very hot. Scores of people phoned and there were visitors to the house all day and every day. Glen, Kerry, Marcus and Morgan stayed with me for a few days, I can remember that because I sometimes became tearful when speaking to friends, and then Marcus would come and put his arm round my shoulders and Morgan fetched the box of tissues for me. They were 11 and 8 years old at the time and were quite understanding of the situation that involved their Nain's sadness over Taid's death. Glen and Elsie stayed on for the week to provide support for me, help with the funeral arrangements, and host visitors and callers.

The service at Seion Chapel was very moving and many people had come to bid farewell to Arthur including relatives, many, many friends, former pupils and associates from the music world. I was very glad that the singing was uplifting just as Arthur would have wanted. Most of the family members sang with fervour - there was always a tradition in my father's family that if you decided to sing at a funeral then you should do so as well as you could. My own mother could never understand this, believing that grief could not give vent to song, Glenys and Bryn are the same.

But I understood the desire to create the uplifting music, and I sang to please Arthur. But, as we sang one particular hymn, I glanced at the coffin on the bier in front of us and experienced an overpowering feeling that engulfed me with the belief that the scenario was all wrong. “Arthur should not be lying motionless in that box, he should be up there at the organ creating wonderful music just as he had done at the Chapel for 44 years, and conducting the singing with his left hand as was his usual custom.” That thought was the catalyst - my throat constricted and I could no longer sing, and the tears washed down my face. It was like a dam bursting and my feelings came alive again and with that, the pain of reality set in. During the rest of the Service I tried hard to compose myself again, people were so kind and my children and their families were a wonderful consolation.

Tea had been arranged in the Village Hall in Eglwysbach by the girls and some ladies from the village who very kindly prepared and served it. Afterwards, our nearest relatives went home with me to *Rhyd yr Arian* and a photograph of the group was taken in the back garden on that very sunny afternoon. Although the girls wanted me to return home with them for a few days, I thought it would be better for me in the long run to get used to my new circumstances, and so I decided to stay at home. True to fashion, I threw myself into work in the garden and spent many hours outside. There is a saying, “One is nearer to God's heart in a garden than anywhere else on earth”, and it's true.

Gradually I became used to my different life, but on many occasions I found myself returning home from a concert, a meeting or even a simple conversation with someone and saying to myself, "I must remember to tell Arthur about that", and realising that he was not there any more. And then one day I stopped in my tracks with the realisation that now, for the first time in my life, I was living alone. As a little girl I had lived within a family of father, mother, brother and sister, and then I was married with a husband, and quickly became a mother of three children, again within a family. In the course of time our children had left home, but I was not alone. Now however, I was completely on my own. I had been a daughter, a wife, a mother and a grandmother. Now, it was just me and it was frightening, but also challenging. I had total responsibility for myself and all decisions surrounding my life. It was fortunate that I'd had to cope with many decisions for some months before Arthur died because the experience had prepared me in some ways for what was to come. But even then I had still been able to discuss some matters with Arthur, unlike the period after his death when he wasn't there at all.

We had already had a number of double-glazed windows fitted in the house, and the effect had been so significant that we had decided to have the rest done before the winter set in, so I arranged for the job to be done. The house was so much warmer and I really dislike cold weather. However, I had to be careful with the pennies because when a partner dies the only saving is in the cost of food and clothes for one. All other expenses remain the same, heating, lighting, household expenses, car expenses and having only one income coming in instead of two also makes a difference.

During all the years after Arthur had suffered his stroke in 1985 I had coped on my own, helping him to do whatever he was unable to deal with and always alert to his movements at night, in case he fell when not quite awake. I ferried him in the car to and from visits to the Doctor's surgery and for regular tests at the hospital. I did not, and do not begrudge doing what I did. I was thankful that I had the health and strength to do so. Still, I must admit that it was with mixed feelings that I became aware in 1993 of the availability of financial assistance in such circumstances. I obtained and completed an application form on Arthur's behalf for an Attendance Allowance. I had only to obtain the Doctor's signature on the form, but all to no avail. Arthur died before I could post it.

Well, life had to go on. The world was not standing still and I had to get moving likewise. I joined the Women's Institute. I was already a member of *Merched y Wawr*, the Welsh Women's Club. It felt strange at first, but the members were so friendly and welcoming and I tried to take part in the many activities until everything became familiar. I had unfortunately not been able to keep up my membership of Soroptomist International when Arthur became ill, and had missed the comradeship.

I talked to Shonna, the cat. She is now fourteen years old, completely bi-lingual and wise in many ways! I talked to the people who appeared on the television, disagreeing and shouting at them or clapping my hands when they made me laugh. Eccentric behaviour you think? No, no of course not! Letting it all out and remaining stable, was much the best thing to do. And none of the television characters could shout back at me!

Chapter Sixty

STRESS

Neville came to fetch me to stay with them for Christmas and I was very grateful and really enjoyed myself. The antics of the three lads, three distinctly different personalities, were amusing to say the least. Geraint was 10 years old, Aled, 6 and Huw, not yet 3. At those ages boys can be just like puppies rolling about, jostling each other, shouting, running around, laughing and enjoying being alive.

On Christmas Eve, Elsie and I went to midnight Mass in the local Church. It was a dry and extremely frosty night and paths were slippery underfoot. Being well wrapped-up, we walked the half-mile down to the Church by the river with Elsie leading the way. I wore knee high boots and we walked briskly because of the cold weather. Half way there, as we descended a short but steep path I felt my left heel slip on a patch of ice just as I lifted my right foot to take another step. I fell awkwardly onto my bent left leg. I could not grasp anything to lever myself into any position to get up, but Elsie heard my exclamation as I fell and came back towards me. Just then a group of young lads going home after their revels came up the hill and very kindly offered their help. I thanked them, but said I could manage. Elsie offered to go back home to bring Neville with the car, but I did not want to be left on my own after midnight in such a situation, so with her help I struggled upright and limped the rest of the way to the Church. It was full as usual and Elsie and I had to sit separately. I was able to get up to sing the Carols, but wasn't sure how I would manage to go down to the altar for the Holy Sacrament of bread and wine. I was determined to do so and although my leg hurt intensely, made my way down without limping too much by gritting my teeth. At the end of the service Elsie again offered to fetch Neville and the car, but I decided to walk. With her help and going slowly I made it to the house and thankfully sat down. There was nothing much to see, but I certainly had enormous pain. After hot tea and a couple of tablets I went to bed and slept soundly.

Christmas morning dawned very early in the house - the three boys were up and about in the dark, groping for light switches and presents. Strange noises emanated from their rooms before they descended on their parents and then me in turn, to show what Santa Claus had given them. Sure enough, Santa had been good to them and had also eaten the mince pie left for him and taken the carrot for Rudolf. Elsie and Neville were tired but delighted and satisfied.

Then the great bustle began, preparing the Christmas dinner. Elsie had already prepared the turkey and stuffing the previous evening and it was already cooking nicely, filling the kitchen with a beautiful aroma when we came downstairs for breakfast. We were invited next door to Dr. and Mrs. Bryson's home for preprandial drinks and although my lower leg was very painful I had not bargained for the swollen state of my foot. I could not get my shoe on and had to make do with a slipper. When Dr. Bryson saw me limping he asked what was wrong and I told him. He had a good look at my foot and I suggested that I had sprained my ankle in the fall. He said he didn't think so and considered that I should go along to the Hospital for an X-ray to determine whether there was a fracture or not. Neville was all for going to Northallerton Hospital immediately, but I said no, it was Christmas Day and the foot could wait another day. I would sit down and rest my foot.

So we all enjoyed our Christmas dinner and followed it with the family's long tradition of opening presents together from under the tree. That produced sounds of paper being torn and whoops of joy and jubilation, growing piles of individual gifts, and an enormous pile of waste wrapping paper. Then there was peace and quiet for a while until teatime when mince pies, Yule log and Christmas cake appeared with a very welcome cup of tea. We all played games even though I didn't feel up to it, but I made a special effort for the sake of the boys. This was the stuff of bonding and family tradition and unity after all. The joy remains within children for ever and helps them when they reach their teens and the adult world.

After a light supper I went to bed, and sleep came easily even with my gammy leg. On Boxing Day, Neville would stand no more procrastination, so he took me to the hospital at Northallerton. An X-ray showed I had broken a bone in my left leg, so they set it straight and encased it in plaster. However, they then decided after much measuring that it was not straight enough, so off came the plaster and the process was repeated. The Nurses were so nice and waved away my apologies for being a nuisance during the festivities. They gave me crutches and a warning not to let my foot touch the ground and to return after a period of time for a check up, which I did and everything was O.K.

Glen came to fetch me to spend New Year with them and this was enjoyable too, although I missed Arthur from the festivities. At this time of the year one tends to look back with memories and look forward to the future with a degree of apprehension. Although Glen wanted me to stay longer I felt I should be going home. There was no real reason why I could not cope even with a wonky leg.

On the day that I was to return home I had two strange feelings of 'waking up' as though I had been asleep. Glen called a Doctor who examined me and said all was well for me to travel home. In the car on the way home I felt again as though I was 'going off' but managed not to do so. When we reached home I was very cold and could not get warm. Of course the house was not too warm even though I always left some heating on during my absences, but it was January and the weather was really cold. Glen sat me in front of a two bar electric fire with a thick rug round my shoulders and made some hot tea, but I was still shivering. I'd had a chest cold before Christmas, but nothing to worry about. Anyway, Glen phoned Dr. Grout and on being told about my broken leg, the funny turns, the shivering and the fact that there would be no one with me at home, he sent me to the Hospital at Llandudno. There, they put me through a series of tests including an E.C.G., but could not find anything radically wrong. After a few days I returned home.

In the meantime, Glen had got in touch with Betty Whelan, who was by now living in Anglesey and she came to stay with me. She stayed with me for six weeks and we got on very well together. Betty was born and bred in a village Post Office in Anglesey. When the War broke out, soldiers were stationed in the village because of its proximity to Ireland, and the Post Office was an important communication point. One of the soldiers was John Whelan and he and Betty fell in love and eventually married. After the War they moved to Bolton where they settled and raised a son and daughter. For some years Betty worked as a telephonist at the Bolton Telephone Exchange. John always wanted to return to live in Anglesey so when he retired they bought a bungalow in Betty's home village Llanerchymedd, and set up home there. They were very happy and John loved it, working on home improvements and creating a nice garden.

One day however, tragedy struck unexpectedly. Both had been clearing up the dead vegetation and grass cuttings, and as Betty held a plastic bag for John to fill from the pile of rubbish, he collapsed at her feet and within minutes was dead. He had suffered a fatal heart attack and Betty was distraught. She could not believe what had happened. For a long time she blamed herself for not having learned some First Aid, but there was nothing she could have done to save John. The attack was too severe.

Betty is one of the nicest and kindest people I know, and I am proud to call her my friend. She is so good hearted, so willing to help with so little thought of her own welfare. For a long time she found it hard to become accustomed to John's death, which was quite natural, they were a very close and loving couple. Fortunately, she had family living nearby: her brother and family ran the business at their old home and her sister was not too far away. Slowly the twinkle came back into her eyes and her familiar smile returned. She bought a new automatic car and loved driving around.

Betty had experience of becoming a widow suddenly, and that is why she came to help me. We are both talkers so there were never any strange silences or discomfort. Every day she liked to watch Countdown on the television and I was amazed at her ability especially with the figures part. I counted myself good at arithmetic but she left me standing!

The day came when I could dispose of the crutches and manage with a walking stick and by then, was fully capable of looking after myself. I was loath to lose Betty's company because I'd enjoyed it so much, but her own home needed her and she departed. I was so very grateful to her for all that she had done to help me in my hour of need. I really felt lost for quite a while, but there were things that needed doing and I had to get down to brass tacks.

I was able to drive the car once more and it felt a little strange at first, but after a couple of outings everything was fine again. I went to Abergele to take the car for its annual full-service and M.O.T. and visited my brother Percy and his wife Eluned who had a nice bungalow there. Percy had worked hard to get the gardens just as he wanted them and I was eager to see the end product.

During the short visit I detected a subtle change in his demeanour. He had not long since had two operations for a hernia and was possibly not fully recovered yet. I thought no more about it until they decided to sell the bungalow in Abergele in order to move to a very nice flat in a modern complex in Rhos on Sea because Eluned was not too well. But Percy's health gradually deteriorated too and the change became more noticeable because he had previously been so full of energy, so healthy and fit. His balance and memory were being affected and finally, when Eluned's failing health made it impossible for her to cope, Percy became a resident of a Nursing Home in the vicinity of the flat. She was able to visit him regularly and Nerys, their daughter too, who had secured a senior nursing job in North Wales and had made her home nearby in Deganwy. I went to visit my brother fairly regularly although it upset me every time to see his condition.

In late spring I was not feeling too good myself: I had lost my appetite and had no energy. I went shopping and filled my fridge/freezer with a range of foods, but whenever I prepared a meal for myself I just could not work up any interest in it or appetite for it. I bought a tonic at the Pharmacy, but there was no improvement. Then I found difficulty in sleeping, and after struggling for a few weeks and telling myself to get a grip on things, again to no avail, I finally went to see Dr. Grout.

I felt so foolish because I wasn't ill in the normal sense of the word, but I just wasn't myself. Dr. Grout had been so good with Arthur, and I had great faith in his judgement. He listened and then pronounced that I had been sensible to consult him instead of floundering in self-medication: events had taken their toll and I was suffering from clinical depression. “But I'm not feeling depressed,” I said. The Doctor explained that clinical depression was a medical term and he prescribed tablets to relax my muscles. I don't like taking pills, but I trusted my doctor so I swallowed two tablets at bedtime and lay on my back in bed. Soon, I could feel the relaxation taking effect and a lovely feeling akin to sinking into cotton wool, and miraculously, I slept for hours. The next night I took another two tablets and again slept the whole night through. The following night I took one tablet only with the same result, and then for a week after that I took half a tablet each night, then no tablets at all, but I slept every night. My sleep rhythm had returned and I felt so much better. My appetite returned too, and I was well again! Hurrah for Dr. Grout.

Chapter Sixty-One

AMERICAN WELCOME

Glenys and family had made arrangements to visit the U.S.A. during the summer holiday and had been invited to spend time with our family over there. Bella and Stan insisted that I too should join them and I was very pleased to accept the invitation. David and Irene my friends across the road very kindly said they would keep an eye on my house and water the plants during my absence, and Bryn helped them to look after Shonna. I was also a little apprehensive about my health so I consulted Dr Grout who urged me to go and enjoy myself. He provided me with a dozen tablets that would benefit me should I need them, explaining that medication was very expensive in the U.S.A. As luck would have it, I didn't require them at all.

Our flight from Manchester took us south to Atlanta Airport first, before another plane took us north again to our destination at Dulles Airport in Washington DC. There was a delay in disembarking at Dulles because airline stewards were obliged by strict rules to arrange for Police to remove a young man who was drunk and disorderly on board. He was still protesting and shouting as they took him away, but was not physically violent. It was nearly midnight by the time we had collected our baggage and gone through Customs, and were very pleased to be greeted by Raymond, my nephew, a Financial Consultant, and his wife Cathy who had come to take us home. We collected a Buick hire car, and some of us travelled in that and the others went in their car. We had quite a distance to travel, but when we arrived at their lovely home they made us a cup of tea and we chatted for a while before tumbling gratefully into bed.

During breakfast the following morning we were introduced to Oggie, their very friendly and intelligent Dachshund dog. He was long and low and Marcus and Morgan loved him immediately, and he gloried in their attention. Their house was large with a garden at the front and a large expanse of grass at the back that ended at the edge of wild woodland. We were warned not to go into the woods, as there were snakes there and deer too. The weather was sunny and very hot. Ray and Cathy took us to very interesting places including Hershey's Chocolate World, a huge factory and retail outlet where we hopped on to moving platforms to get from one active display to another. A very 'sweet' place, with temptation all around! On the way there we drove through a town where stalls were being set up by Fire Brigades under the shade of trees on the riverside. It was a very pleasant location and the exhibition was interesting to view alongside a fascinating collection of new and old fire fighting machines. We also watched a dozen fire vehicles spouting water in arcs into the river creating a fascinating display. The arresting sight had an artistic aura about it too. We would have stayed longer, but there was a lot more in store for us.

We also visited Pennsylvania Dutch country where the Amish people live their lives according to their unique beliefs. Initially they arrived to settle in the USA from Europe, and brought with them their own distinctive way of life. They are sometimes referred to as the *plain people* because they have not changed their lifestyle or plain dress codes for centuries. They farm in the old traditional ways paying great heed to the demands of the seasons, they travel about in horse and buggy, and are very religious. The Bible is their handbook, and they believe that photographs in which they can be recognised violate the commandment in the Bible: “Thou shalt not make unto thyself a graven image." They have no mirrors, items of clothing are fastened with straight pins not buttons, they have no televisions or computers, wear no jewellery, always cover their heads to go outside, and cherish their children. They look and behave differently from everyone else but in accordance with their beliefs. They are ordinary people who have chosen to live according to the traditions that have been passed down to them from generation to generation. They are thrifty, hard-working, happy and content with their humble life-style, they value the simple and most important things in life such as kindness, honesty, generosity, sacrifice and endeavour. They have shops where beautiful hand-made articles are sold: magnificent large patchwork quilts, carved wooden crafts, delicious fudge, dolls, pottery and much more. The meal that I enjoyed the most in America was served in the Amish Barn Restaurant, which consisted of wonderful wholesome food. The Amish people are fascinating because they have managed to hold on to important fundamental things that most other people have cast aside as unimportant, and are the poorer for it. We all thoroughly enjoyed the visit and were reluctant to leave the special community.

On the way home we visited a very unusual and fascinating antique shop located in the middle of nowhere. The building resembled an old barn with two floors, and the items for sale were displayed higgledy-piggledy all over the place. There were thousands of small, interesting articles as well as big old furniture and other household things. Some items in this Aladdin's cave were beautiful and splendid and others were rickety and cheap. It was incredibly hot and humid in the shop especially on the first floor, but we were not in a hurry to leave. There were many things that I would have loved to purchase to take home with me, and it was just as well that it was closing time otherwise we would have been there all night. It was a surprise I suppose to see the shop because I don't usually associate Americans with selling antiques, only with buying them.

We visited Philadelphia, which has the reputation of being the cradle of American history, but it so happens that it is also a very lovely modern city. The Independence National Historical Park contains the actual buildings where the Nation was founded. The City has exciting shops and restaurants, successful and popular sports teams, and the world famous Philadelphia Orchestra. Obviously we could not savour them all, but visited the Independence Hall that witnessed the appointment of George Washington as Commander-in-Chief of the Union Army. Here, the Declaration of Independence was adopted, the Articles of Confederation prepared, and the Constitution written: a veritable shrine of daring and commitment. It was all the more impressive for our knowing that many Welshmen had been involved who signed the historical documents. Thomas Jefferson stated that members of his family hailed from the foothills of Snowdon, Yr Wyddfa as we know it in Wales. Of the persons who had signed the American Constitution eighteen were descendants of Welshmen/women - the largest ethnic influence at the time.

Three of the first six Presidents of the USA were of Welsh descent.

It was extremely hot and humid on the day of our visit, and although I enjoy very hot weather, the extremity of heat and humidity made even me long for shade. I was more than grateful to stand in the shade of some trees while we waited for a bus, and queuing to see the Liberty Bell mid-afternoon had us all wilting and exhausted. We literally dragged ourselves into the air-conditioned building and uttered a huge sigh of relief on escaping the oppressive conditions outside. Seeing and touching the famous cracked old bell made all the effort totally worthwhile.

On the way home we were treated to a cinema visit to see the animation film, 'The Lion King'. Before entering the cinema on this extremely hot day, Cathy gave each of us a jacket. We were already wearing the lightest summer clothes in our possession and certainly were in no need of another layer of clothing, so I wondered about the purpose of the jackets. We politely thanked Cathy and went to our seats where we quickly realised the usefulness of the jackets! The really cold air that blasted from the air-conditioning system made us shiver and shudder and we were grateful to Cathy for her thoughtfulness and care. At first I was not at all enthusiastic about the film because I believed it to be a film intended for children only. But how wrong I was! It was clever, wonderful, and marvellous in every way and I loved it. The human voices linked to the animal characters were so remarkably suitable that it all seemed so real and natural and the beautiful songs added yet more special wonder and quality to the film. The overall impression was of pure delight. Everyone, young and old enjoyed the film tremendously and spoke excitedly about it as we walked outside. The contrasting experience of walking out of that extremely cold cinema into the tremendous heat of the day felt as though we were walking out of a refrigerator straight into a very hot oven!

We also visited New York City, which meant staying overnight at a large motel that provided accommodation only. We ate breakfast the following morning in real style - out of the car's trunk! Ray stopped at a Plaza to buy cheese, salami and ham, fresh bread, fruit, orange juice and other tasty food and we had such a laugh preparing and eating it on the car park! But Ray told us not to let his Mother know about it or she would be so cross with him! He said she would think it an inappropriate way to treat guests. Nothing could have been further from the truth because we actually enjoyed the experience! Having satisfied our hunger, we made our way to a car park on the outskirts of the city and travelled to the World Trade Centre by train.

I had seen many images of the high-rise buildings in New York, but seeing them in reality was awesome and wonderful. As we had only one day, our programme was obviously limited, but we achieved so much. First, we went by boat to Ellis Island where all the immigrants to the U.S.A. had undergone all sorts of checks and interrogations in order to be allowed into the country. We viewed excellent displays of enlarged authentic old photographs of immigrants seen walking up the wide and impressive stairway that we stood on that day, and we thought about the thousands who had walked up the stone stairway and passed through the building on the island. It must have been a fearful experience for those people after a long and hazardous journey by ship from Europe. Most were poor, some were unwell or had disabilities, few could speak English and some were rejected outright and sent straight back home without ever leaving the island or seeing anything of the city in which they had hoped to work and live. We felt a strange sadness for a process that had been seen to have been essential for many years in the USA.

Then we went to the nearby Statue of Liberty and I find it difficult to convey its hugeness. Most people will be familiar with the image of the flaming torch held aloft by the female figure. We were told that because of some defect that made it potentially unsafe, the original torch had been replaced by an exact replica. However, we were able to view the massive original torch in a very large room on the ground floor ... it filled the room! It gave a perspective to the overall size of the whole monument. We walked up the stairs inside the monument but only as far as the general viewing balcony where we had a wonderful view of the New York shore and skyline. We dearly wanted to continue walking up as far as the statue's hand and torch, but the heat and humidity of the New York summer made it a strenuous task for those of us who were unused to such conditions. Instead, we rested and relaxed with ice creams and cold drinks in the café and gardens at the base of the statue. It goes without saying that the place was heaving with tourists. As we journeyd on the ferry from Ellis Island to the Statue of Liberty amongst visitors from all over the world who spoke various languages, it was reminiscent I thought of the Biblical story of the Tower of Babel.

We intended to view more of the City, but Kerry had developed a migraine, and added to that an almighty downpour of rain made us call it a day. We were very grateful to Ray and Cathy for planning such interesting trips and escorting us so knowledgeably and efficiently everywhere.

We also stayed with Ken and Mary, my sister's second son and his wife. Both are qualified engineers who work on defence projects for the Government. I had attended their wedding and had sung during the marriage service. We had a warm welcome from three people in this home because they had a little daughter, Andrea. She was a lively little girl and the boys had a great time entertaining her. Bella and Stan were also there for a shared birthday party because Stan and I enjoyed the same birth date on the 15th of July, and he always said that he had to defer to me because he was a year younger! Andrea's birthday was also due the following week, so we had a triple celebration. Ken and Mary had gone to a great deal of trouble to lay on a grand feast with a special cake. Ken and Brian, his younger brother, had arranged for Glen, Kerry and the boys to stay with Ken and Mary, while Bella, Stan and I stayed with Brian and Petrine.

One day we all went to Washington D.C. to see the sights, and we certainly saw some fantastic ones! I had been there before, but like all great cities there are so many fascinating places to visit and interesting things to see. Marcus and Morgan wanted to go to the National Air and Space Museum and it was full of exciting things. The "Milestones of Flight" exhibit told the story of flight from Kittyhawk to the Apollo moon landing, and there was a space capsule that was the first command module to land on the moon and recalls the famous John Armstrong quotation, "One small step for man, one giant leap for mankind." Since that first historic landing on the moon, space travel has become a fairly regular feature in the news and we have tended to become quite blasé about it. Quite recently an American businessman paid millions of dollars to be allowed to go as a tourist to a space station - stayed for some days and then returned to earth declaring that he was very satisfied with his trip, but very pleased to return to earth.

We visited the Capitol, an imposing and stately building, and the embodiment of American Government. We looked at the White House, but could not view it inside because of a long queue of visitors waiting with the same intention. We went inside the Washington Monument, which is 555ft. high with an observation platform at level 500ft from where we had a spectacular panoramic view of the city as well as parts of Maryland and Virginia.

We simply had to visit the National Archives Building, where the Declaration of Independence, the Constitution, the Bill of Rights, and other historical government records are displayed. The lighting is deliberately rather dim inside the building and there is a very thick cover of plate glass over the documents in order to preserve them. No cameras are allowed and guards ensure that the queue is constantly moving slowly, visitors are allowed a short time only to view any one document. Near the exit, a copy of the British Magna Carta is also on display in a glass case.

We had our picnic lunch in a park near the Potomac River and it was very satisfying to sit happily with our relatives, chatting and eating on a warm, sunny day. And then suddenly it went dark, and a heavy downpour of rain hit us, literally. We managed to grab our belongings and rush up the steps of the Lincoln Memorial and there we stayed a while under the benign gaze of the great man himself - Abraham Lincoln. The seated statue is 19ft tall and the inscription above it reads, "In this Temple as in the hearts of the people for whom he saved the Union, the memory of Abraham Lincoln is enshrined forever."

I was particularly interested in this statue because Lincoln was descended from British stock. His father's family was from an area on the east coast of England, but his mother's ancestors (Nancy Hanks) on the maternal side were descended from Welsh parents who had both emigrated to America before meeting each other. The lady was from the rural village of *Ysbyty Ifan*, in North Wales, an ancient place on the Pilgrim Trail to *Enlli*, the burial place of the Saints, which is an island situated just off the west coast of North Wales. The house where she was born and reared is still there, but is now used to store farm machinery. After leaving Wales and settling in the U.S.A. she married a young fellow countryman who had emigrated from the beautiful *Lleyn* peninsula in North Wales.

The Welsh race has made a great contribution to the American nation over the centuries. Examples of those contibutions come to light every so often but unfortunately, instead of being credited as Welsh, they are often bundled together under the title British, or even English! But I believe that an increasing number of today's enlightened Americans are interested in *Cymru* (Wales) as a country in its own right, and know that the Welsh people are proud descendants of the Celts and have an ancient Celtic language that is still spoken naturally every day by thousands of us. Our history and culture are illustrious, and I am very proud to be a member of the Welsh race, as are the other members of my family.

My mother's family tree shows clearly that I have also Scottish blood in me, being a quarter Scottish and three quarters Welsh. Of course the Scots also have Celtic origins. I have only to hear the skirl of the bagpipes and I become sentimental - my Scottish pride I suppose. Some people dislike the sound of the pipes but it creates in me a feeling of something special. It is a sound of 'far away', melancholy but also very stirring. The sound conjours visions of a time before modern trimmings existed, when loyalty and honour meant something and people knew who they were. But then again, I have only to hear the strains of the 'Men of Harlech' march, or the Welsh National Anthem, and I become full of Welsh pride and fervour too.

We walked along the famous black marble Commemorative Vietnam Wall. As we approached it we became aware of the 'hush' around us. The place was quiet and tranquil, similar to being in a Church. Various personal items had been laid against the wall by family and friends in memory of the young men who had lost their lives in that awful war. I have rarely been moved to tears on such an occasion but there, I felt to the bottom of my heart such sorrow and depth of sympathy for those young men sacrificed in a war that lasted far too long. It affected me deeply.

During the day we passed Ford's Theatre, which has been restored to look as it did on the 14th of April 1865. We all know it was on that day, in that theatre that President Abraham Lincoln was shot dead by John Wilkes Booth. We were worn out with all the walking by that time, and were glad to return and put our feet up. But what a wonderful day we had experienced.

On another day, Brian took us to the American Mint where all the dollar bills are produced. We stood on a gallery behind a thick glass partition watching a number of black female employees examining sheets of the new dollar bills and packing them. We looked at huge blocks of the dollar sheets worth millions standing on the floor ready to be despatched. So near yet so far away! What a fascinating sight it was, and what an experience overall! The smell of paint in that building was overpowering and we soon discovered that the smell was not of paint, but printing ink … how strong must that smell have been to the employees in the actual processing room!

The weather remained very hot, and Kerry was suffering from it, but he gamely kept up with the rest of us. It was decided that the kids, younger and older, should have some fun and so Glen, Kerry, the boys and Ken, went to an amusement centre for the day and had a rip-roaring time. We, the staid members of the family were taken by Brian on a motoring tour to see some very posh, large and expensive houses, some of which were in small groups enclosed within walls, fences and guarded entrances. We called at Annapolis, the training base for sailors of the U.S. Navy, where we saw them in their uniforms looking very smart. The town has kept its original features and resembles an old English town. We visited a park on the banks of the Potomac River where there was a lovely breeze during the hot mid-day hours, and then we enjoyed tea in another *olde English town* before returning to Brian's house. Bella and Stan's three sons and families had done us more than proud during our visit to the U.S.A! What a country it is … what enormous potential it possesses, and what wonderful individuals abide amongst its people!

We also stayed at Bella and Stan's home, where we had a very warm welcome. Stan took us round to see the sights, but sometimes I stayed home with my sister while the young ones went gallivanting. One day they went aboard an old sailing ship with sails and very tall masts, a wonderful sight indeed. Another day, Stan took the group to a submarine stationed in a dock for upgrading purposes and they had a full viewing tour of the vessel. It was such a hot day and Stan was obviously suffering fatigue, but was determined to give us his best effort … we are eternally grateful to him for that valiant effort - Stan was a generous, kind, and sincere man.

Once again we went to visit Niagara Falls and there continued to be tremendous power and beauty in the waters of the Niagara River as it flowed along. It moved so smoothly until it reached the rapids where the water frothed and agitated as though a giant monster was whipping it up, and then it glided over the lip of the rock and fell into the turbulence way down below. It really was fantastic. Glen and her family were there for the first time and they too were amazed and thrilled with it all, especially the trip on the *Maid of the Mist* boat. It was our last trip of that holiday and it was with mixed feelings that we said goodbye to our American family who had cared for, and entertained us so wonderfully well. Our flight back to Manchester was comfortable.

Once home, there was a great deal of work to be done in the garden, but first, I had to fetch Shonna from the Cattery and I hoped she'd not been pining like dear old Mickey Mouse. The owner said that Shonna had been reasonably settled and had enjoyed her grated cheese every day, but as we chatted I heard Shonna's insistent miawing, she must have recognised my voice. As soon as she was free she jumped onto my shoulder and was purring and rubbing and generally expressing her delight to be with me again. For days she kept following me around as though she was afraid that I might disappear once more. I vowed then that I would not put my cat in a Cattery again, if I could at all help it.

Glen had supplied me with bread, milk and other basic food to tide me over once home, but after a few days I had to go shopping to fill up the gaps in the fridge/freezer once more, but I had to ensure that I left Shonna in the house because she wanted to follow me everywhere.

Chapter Sixty-Two

SADNESS

Late autumn arrived with all the work of clearing the garden in time for the winter. Also, all the different societies started up again and that meant I was kept busy most of the time. Then Christmas came again and I spent it with Glen, Kerry and the boys in Horwich. After their schools had broken up for the holidays everyone became intent on shopping, wrapping presents, and putting up the tree and decorations - and there was much secrecy, hiding things, mysterious murmurings and shifty moves. Christmas time was here once more with all its excitement!

During the morning of Christmas Eve, Glen and I and the *M & Ms*, (Marcus and Morgan), went to do the last minute shopping. It was a very cold day, but we were well wrapped-up against the biting wind. We needed to visit a few places, and finally we went to the supermarket for some last minute groceries. The place was heaving with people queuing in the aisles with baskets piled high with goodies. It was hot, far too hot for people wrapped up against the cold weather. Glen was continually being greeted by someone or other and was chatting for a moment or two with each one, but we met a lady who related a lengthier piece of news than the rest, and the boys and I were hanging around wishing she would go away. After a while, the heat in the store started to affect me, which was unusual for me, and I moved around a bit looking at this and that, but with no real interest or outcome. The boys told me later that I stared at a bottle of sauce for ages, and they moved to see what was so interesting about it. Suddenly I keeled over and was unconscious for about 2/3 minutes apparently. Pandemonium ensued and I regained consciousness wondering why I was lying on the floor. I did not feel ill or shaky, just bruised and so we went to the store's café where I drank a cup of tea and that was that. Everyone was most concerned and kind but all I could feel was surprise. Why did I faint? It was most unusual for me. However, nothing further happened and we all enjoyed the marvellous post-Christmas activities. But Glenys and Kerry continued to keep a watchful eye on me to ensure that I was alright.

When I returned to my own home, I went to visit my brother again to wish him a belated happy birthday and New Year. I found him in a much worse condition than the last time I visited him. He was much more confused and I came to realise that Nerys, his daughter was also having a hard time attending to her mother and being called many times, day and night to calm her father down. It upset me terribly to see my brother, the efficient, capable, affable man, in such a condition. Although it upset me, I continued to visit him because he would listen to me with obvious pleasure talking about the old days when my sister and I were children and he was our big brother. At that stage however, he found it difficult to concentrate for more than a couple of minutes at a time. My heart bled for him, it was all so cruel, but the staff were wonderfully kind to him. I can never understand why good people like Percy, who have served God and man very well, can end up suffering long and cruelly at the end of their life. Thankfully, before the end of January 1995 and just after his 80th birthday, Percy died: I was glad and happy for him to be released from his torment. Even so, there was great sadness in realising that I would see him no longer, but also happiness in recalling the good days of our lives together - I had very mixed feelings. He had always had a strong influence on me, especially when we were young, possibly because of the age gap between us. He was the 'big brother' who was there to advise my sister and me on most things.

Percy was a long-standing member of the *Council for the Preservation Of Rural Wales (CPRW)* having first served as Treasurer and Membership Secretary of the Caernarfonshire Branch, then as a member of the Council for Wales and Vice President of the CPRW.

Elizabeth Colwyn Foulkes wrote the following obituary to Percy in the 1995 summer edition of the *Campaign Magazine for the Protection of Rural Wales*. "He had the gift of being able to work well with other people, and this ability was exercised to its full extent in the collaboration and support he devoted to the great battle to save Conwy Castle and Town from the vandalism of Welsh Office road proposals, during a year-long inquiry into the A55 Conwy crossing." She added, "Percy Owen had made a magnificent presentation at the inquiry into the Welsh Office road proposals for the A497 through the Lledr Valley both in the quality of written material and in person. He had done so much to ensure that proper consideration was given to this exceptionally beautiful and highly sensitive landscape." I believe that my brother was highly deserving of this tribute.

After Percy's death, Eluned's health grew even more fragile. She battled bravely, but became more and more breathless. That winter was very cold and windy and although the flat was nice and cosy she could not face going out of the house. Poor Nerys had a very hard time of it, her sister and brother lived very far away so she was left to bear the brunt of helping her mother. Because of ill health, age and loneliness, and probably being frightened too, her mother made great demands on Nerys and she literally had not a minute to herself. Within a few short months Eluned died. It was a happy release for her too, as there was no joy left in her life after Percy died and her health failed. It was also a relief for Nerys, although losing her mother was traumatic. But the long months of coping and caring for her suffering parents who were very much loved, had taken a heavy toll on Nerys' life. She had done more than her best for them both. Nerys then needed time to recover fully herself.

Spring arrived and everything woke up. The birds were singing, there was warm sunshine, leafy trees, flowering bushes and flowers in their new clothes, and I loved the spring once again! However, all this regeneration meant work as well as pleasure, but I have to admit that work is not a chore or toil if you enjoy doing it.

Then summer arrived and, much too soon for my liking, it slipped into autumn again. My sister wrote to say that Stan was not very well and was having medication, and although I was concerned, the news did not alarm me at the time. Then came the additional news that Stan was very seriously ill in hospital and Bella told me that he had cancer. I was so very sorry for Stan, Bella and the boys. She also admitted that Stan had not been well for several months and that made me wonder how on earth he had managed to accompany us on our outings during our holiday in the USA. He was always smiling and joking and leading the way and had shown only a few signs of fatigue.

Before the year was out Stan had passed away peacefully. I shall always remember him as a good friend who was always ready to help willingly and had a twinkle in his eye. He was very proud of his family. It was good to think that he had lived long enough to see his first grandchild, Ken and Mary's daughter, Andrea, but he did not see her brother Kevin, or Raymond and Kathy's son Colwyn James (CJ), or Brian and Petrine's daughters Bridget and Natasha. But he would have loved them all.

After Christmas, my sister asked if she could come to stay with me and bring a friend with her who was also recently widowed. I replied that I would be very pleased to welcome them both and so, in August 1996 Bella and her friend Jean arrived. Fortunately the weather was fair, not cold and not hot, and we had some nice outings. One nice, warm day we took the train up the slopes of Snowdon Mountain in the village of Llanberis, which is situated at the foot of the mountain. After reaching the top, Bella and I scrambled up the cairn at the summit alongside many other visitors, but Jean declined. Perhaps she did not feel the surge of Celtic passion in the blood or perhaps she just didn't feel like scrambling about in the mist and cold at the top of Snowdon.

We spent days in Llandudno, Queen of the Welsh resorts! I was seventeen before setting foot in the town in wartime, but I fell for its charms straight away and the magic has held throughout the years. Lots of visitors arrive in coaches for day trips, but to really savour the joy of the place, like a good wine you cannot gulp it, it has to be sipped slowly and fully to appreciate its many qualities.

My sister and I had heart to heart chats and that was good for both of us. There is a need to deal with grief and sadness when we lose a loved one, it is necessary to talk and share sad feelings with someone close and trusted. My sister said she felt the loss when Arthur died even though she was far away on the other side of the Atlantic Ocean. "I liked Arthur. I felt that he was my friend, and Stan was always going on about Arthur and what good company he was. Always cheerful and making people laugh with his stories and jokes," she said.

I felt a certain tension between Bella and Jean at times, but I think that it was because of raw emotion in learning to accept the reality of life as it had become for them. It was very difficult for them - for all of us really.

Our American guests were invited to stay at their homes by Elsie and Glenys and were taken on trips on Teesside and in the Bolton area. I felt rather strange when Bella and Jean departed for home because I missed their company, and I don't like saying goodbyes.

However, there were many things awaiting my attention, especially in the garden - including a lot of hard slog in springtime. As I have grown older I have added more bushes and trees to my garden so it has colour all year round that makes the overall effect in summer much more interesting.

The other extremely busy time in the garden is late autumn when self-discipline has to be exercised. Most of the flowers, especially those in tubs and baskets are past their best and look rather tatty and forlorn, yet some are still in bloom. Reluctantly, I set about the task of clearing the straggly plants and generally tidying everywhere, but at that time of year there is little to motivate me in terms of lovely flowers to follow, a thought that always spurs me on. Nevertheless, I still get the job done and derive some satisfaction in the knowledge that the garden then looks tidy for the winter months. I like seeing the clean areas of raw soil between the bushes after the fallen leaves have been taken away from their various hiding places. A gardener has to retrieve the leaves from all the nooks and crannies in the garden, and sometimes, as soon as I have collected a tidy pile of dead leaves ready to be dealt with, the wind pounces and blows them all over the place again as if playing a joke on me!

But there is no point moaning about it, far better to see the funny side and have a good laugh! It can be exhilarating to battle with the wind, but not if it's coming from its icy home up North. I cannot enjoy gardening in very cold winds, and very rarely venture out at such times because I cannot stand being cold and feeling shrivelled up inside. But I quite enjoy listening to the rain being blown against the windows when I am warm and cosy indoors, except when it's a strong gale because that makes me fearful about the prospect of damage to my home and costly repair bills!

Winter departed, then spring arrived, and by the first week of June in 1996 I had finished planting out and was looking forward to enjoying my garden throughout the summer months. But suddenly, one fine afternoon the phone rang, and as I picked up the receiver I heard Elsie say, "Mam, you had better sit down," and my immediate thought was 'bad news'. Then she said, "I'm sorry, but there is only one way for me to say this ... Neville is dead!" I gasped incredulously. "What? What did you say?" Elsie then repeated that Neville was dead. "He died at 4.00p.m during a meeting held in his office when he suddenly stood up then fell down dead. The ICI paramedics were there within 3-4 minutes, but he was already dead and there was nothing they could do to save him." I was shocked and stunned, but I marvelled at my daughter's calmness, but of course the impact had not yet made its mark on her. She was reacting in her usual efficient way. She said she would inform Glenys at school, but asked me to convey the news to the rest of the family, insisting on telling their sons herself, and insisting that she would definitely be strong for that - they were aged 12, 8 and 5 at the time. It was the first time for them to have to cope with tragedy. She said, "We came to work this morning together as usual and separated to our different jobs. Nev was fine. They contacted me at teatime and said Nev was not well, they asked me to go to his office, but I was not allowed to go in. I knew he was dead. I just knew."

Neville was 53 years old, a fine figure of a man, never ill, played hockey and badminton, and was also a strong swimmer. He was a very conscientious worker at ICI and at home where he helped with the preparation of meals, did the ironing, bathed the boys and put them to bed. He was a good handyman and although not a natural gardener, he kept the large garden tidy and helped Elsie with the planting. Although he was a qualified Chemical Engineer he had moved within the ICI Company and was at that time Transport Manager for Western Europe and travelled extensively to different areas of Europe. There was certainly a considerable degree of stress involved in the work that probably contributed to the massive heart failure.

Although Nev loved to get me going on my high horse, especially in politics when he would deliberately provoke me sometimes with outrageous remarks, he was also kind to me and we got along well. In the course of his work he made regular visits to ICI installations in Cheshire and on many occasions at the end of the working day he would drive to North Wales to pick me up with the cat, to go home with him. It was a very long drive at the end of a busy day and he must have been tired, but we talked a lot at such times about different things, especially matters relating to the children. He loved his boys and was very proud of them. He was not without faults and had one or two 'hang-ups,' but then haven't we all?

Shock was immediate and profound for everyone who knew Nev and the regard in which he was held by members of the large congregation at the funeral was very obvious. I found it difficult to accept the reality of the situation because of his apparent health and strength and the startling suddenness of his death. Later I was to recall the previous Easter when the family came to visit me as usual. We had been out for an enjoyable day with the kids kicking up a rumpus in the back of the car on the way home. When supper was over and cleared away, the boys were in bed and Nev was doing some ironing I said, "Come and sit down Nev you must be very tired." He replied, "No. I find it very relaxing to iron and listen to the television." Later we enjoyed a cuppa before bed and Nev had fallen asleep in a chair still holding onto his tea mug. He looked absolutely worn out and his face was a shade of grey, but I attributed it to natural exhaustion at the end of a very busy day.

On the day of the funeral, Kerry and Bryn and a number of Neville's close friends, in their roles as bearers carried Nev's coffin to the final resting place in the cemetery near the Church at Hutton Rudby. Geraint, the eldest of the children was only 12 years of age but he conducted himself with dignity, walking alone behind his father's coffin. Quietly, without any fuss and of his own accord, Marcus, who was 14 years old joined his cousin Geraint and they walked along together. I was touched by their demeanour. Everyone was very supportive, and Elsie was fortunate in having good friends locally because inevitably normal life had to resume.

The boys went back to school, but Elsie did not resume her work at I.C.I. until September after the summer holiday. The shock and the loss were still there and it took a great deal of courage to cope. Apart from all the extra work, she had lost the love and support of her husband in the fullness of their adult life together.

I spent some time with them during that autumn when things had quietened down and I was also there over Christmas. For the sake of the children the Festival was celebrated in the usual way. We went to the Services in the Chapel and Church, sang carols and celebrated the time-honoured rituals of the family at home. This was good for everyone and helped to strengthen the Eternal hope of Christian belief. However, the strain on Elsie must have been immense, but she struggled through.

We use so many clichés in our normal speaking and writing and lots of them are banal, but many also are truisms. One is that time is a great healer, and I thank God for that healing power, for it happens to be very true. I have also noticed that work can be a healer too, especially the kind that requires concentration - perhaps because it uses up the time that is required for healing. Time must be given to the grieving process in order to work the hurt out of our minds and hearts, but we also have to learn to let go of pain and all that is associated with death. This is Nature's way, and no one should feel guilty of acquiescing in any way.

Elsie coped, but the stress of full-time working, running a home and being mother and father to three boys, as well as dealing with her grief and helping her sons' with theirs, was taking its toll. There followed a rough patch when relations were strained between us all, but thanks be to God and some plain, common sense on all sides, we returned to an even keel once more.

Chapter Sixty-Three

BACK TO WALES

I am writing again! Resolutely I have put pen to paper. Months passed when I wrote nothing and made all kinds of excuses for the lapse. Some were conveniently genuine, but served only as a camouflage. I came to realise why I was so reluctant to get on with my recollections. The truth was that I just did not want to re-live such an awful period when the complexities of family life were raw. The traumas and searing grief of losing so many dear ones within a short period of time were scarring to the mind. Of one thing I am sure, the experiences have chastened and strengthened us as a family and yes, made us more tolerant and wiser too.

I kept myself very busy through it all and there were never enough hours in the day. I sometimes managed to enjoy myself in my own little way too. I tried very hard to help my children and their families to be as happy as possible, and also made my own life as happy as I could by being active in the community. Casual visitors to Eglwysbach village often comment on its beauty, tranquillity and peace, and totally fail to see beyond that view into the busy community life of the area. "It's so lovely, but what on earth do you do here? Does it not become rather boring?" they say.

There are so many community activities available in Eglwysbach that if people participated in them all, they would never be at home.There is an indoor Bowling Club, a Historical Society, the very successful Annual Agricultural and Horticultural Show Committees, the Darby and Joan Club, the Women's Insitutute, the Welsh Club '*Merched y Wawr'* and other cultural clubs attached to the Church and Chapels in Eglwysbach. I enjoy being a member of some of these societies. For several years I have also been a member of the Eglwysbach Community Council and for a term, enjoyed the privilege and honour of being the Chairperson.

For quite some time Bryn had become tired of life in a large city: he had always been a country lad at heart and loved country activities. He worked long hours, was Branch Chairman of the T.G.W.U. and was involved in local politics. He had laid out a lovely garden at his home and cultivated two allotments when, out of the blue, an opportunity came along that he seized with enthusiasm. He was appointed Senior Gardener at *Maenan Hall* near Llanrwst. He returned to Wales and the Conwy Valley to develop a career for himself in landscape gardening.

Maenan Hall is the country estate of the Honourable Christopher. M. McLaren. As a young man he had lived at Bodnant, home of the world famous *'Bodnant Gardens'*. When his father Lord Aberconway died, he moved with his mother, the Dowager Lady Aberconway to *Maenan Hall*. At the time, the old house had been used as a farmhouse and there was a great deal of work that needed to be done before they could actually move in. A house was built in the grounds for the Dowager Lady as a temporary abode, which later became the gardener's house. Lady Cristabel together with her son Mr. McLaren started planning and forming gardens within the areas around the drive and the Hall. Over the years a wonderland of beauty has been created and Mr. McLaren and his wife and children are able to enjoy the beauty of the lovely gardens whenever they visit. The hard work of the gardeners goes on and Bryn enjoys being an important part of the endeavour.

Twice a year in May and August the *Maenan Hall Gardens* are open to the public under the National Gardens' Scheme and the proceeds are given to various charities. Considerable sums of money have been raised in this way, but of course, much depends on the weather. A fine sunny day will bring the crowds, but even on the wettest and most miserable day some people arrive, such is the attraction of the place. Many come year after year. Some come for the refreshments alone others for the obvious attractions of the gardens. Bryn's wife Kath, arranges the refreshments and over the years several friends and family have helped out in various ways. All the gateaux, pies and cakes are homemade, which means that for several days before each Open Day Kath, my friend Betty Algieri and I are very busy for hours on end cooking, baking and decorating our creations. Other ladies make savoury sandwiches that are also always in great demand. On the day of the event, the long table groans under the spread of scrumptious scones, cream cakes, fruit cakes, ginger cakes, apple pies, coffee and walnut gateaux, triple chocolate delight, chocolate and ginger gateaux, strawberries with fresh cream, orange cake, lemon cake, cream meringues and so on, and I must include the cheesecakes and trifles too. Most people gasp when they survey the delights and feel spoilt for choice. Visitors also purchase whole cakes to take home with them. There is really no need to tempt the regular visitors to the events because they know what to expect, but I encourage those who have never visited to do so on 'Open Day'. They will certainly enjoy the lovely walks in the grounds with the Tower on the hill, the Dell and the Glade and the refreshing repast afterwards, sitting outside on fine days or inside knowing they have helped a charitable cause.

I have to admit that I was very happy to have my son and his family living within a few miles of my home. Hitherto, my three children lived considerable distances away, which meant that I was not able to enjoy their company regularly. Then at last, one of them was close by and it was a comforting thought. Bryn is very good to me and comes to help out with heavy jobs whenever possible although I do try not to impose too much because he works so hard all day. I especially enjoy the times he comes either alone or with Kath to have a good old natter and put the world in order. It reminds me of the bygone days when, as a family in *Llys Cerdd* we sat round the dining table at meal times, having discussions and debates on all manner of things and arguing about all kinds of worldly affairs. This was almost routine behaviour within the family.

At the end of the school summer holidays and before Bryn moved to Maenan, my grand-daughter Faye came to live with me for six weeks so she could start at her new secondary school *Ysgol Dyffryn Conwy* in Llanrwst at the beginning of term. It must have felt rather strange for her at first in the fact that she was not only moving to a new house and school, but moving to a bilingual school and community. Faye of course was used to hearing Welsh spoken by her father and paternal family, so it wasn't completely new to her, but she still needed to make new friends and settle at the school. To her credit, she did this very well and took the whole experience in her stride. I was also very glad of the chance to get to know Faye well during those few weeks when she stayed with me and I enjoyed having her company. Rebecca, her older sister was already working in Manchester, and remained living in the family home.

Bryn, Glenys and I worked really hard cleaning, decorating and preparing the house in Maenan ready for the family to move in. One day, as I struggled in an awkward position to clean the kitchen window just above the sink, I stretched too far and persevered too long on an empty stomach, but continued to push myself because I was anxious to finish the job. I have no recollection of what happened next, but I found myself on the floor without realising that I had fallen. I seemed unhurt, but was worried about the fact that I had fainted once more.

Dr. Grout sent me for different tests at the hospital in Bangor including an E.C.G. and a Head-Scan. The results of all the tests were negative, a fact that gave me comfort in the knowledge that I was pretty healthy overall. Since that 'funny turn' in 1996 I have been fine. I know that I have low blood pressure and therefore must not let my blood sugar run too low. I also know that when I am busy I have a tendency to keep going with work until it is finished without taking a break occasionally for a drink and a bite to eat. Now that I am wiser, I stop to eat properly periodically and still get the work done without putting my health at risk. We live and learn in this life do we not!

In an earlier Chapter, I wrote about our connection with the Symonds family and explained how I started to get involved with the story. I mentioned articles that had been published in a Denbigh Newspaper that were based on quotations from the Diaries of a Richard Symonds, who was an officer in the army of King Charles I. At that time, Arthur and I had wondered whether this person might be the same Richard Symonds who had lived at 'Mynde Hall' in Herefordshire, but as I read more old papers and records in library archives I realised that the soldier Richard Symonds could not possibly have been the same person as Richard Symonds, the merchant of London because the facts failed to fit accurately. But I find it intriguing that the same name is also recorded in connection with the very same *Maenan Hall* where Bryn is employed. It is such a coincidence that a summary of Richard Symonds comments and descriptions from his Diaries as a Soldier is given great display and prominence at *Maenan Hall* by the owner, the Rt. Hon. C. M. McLaren. I have included my notes based on the Diaries because I found the account very interesting, especially the part that related to *Maenan Abbey* and *Maenan Hall* and Llanrwst.

The Symonds name has popped up for attention at some juncture or other for over four hundred years; is it a restless ghost determined to keep poking our curiosity and wanting to become part of the 21st century. Perhaps it will!

Chapter Sixty-Four

EXTRACTS FROM A CIVIL WAR DIARY

The Extracts are from the Diary of the Marches of the Royal Army during the Great Civil War that was kept by Richard Symonds. (Original MS in the British Museum). Printed for the Camden Society and edited by Charles Edward Long MA.

At the outbreak of the Civil War the author joined the Royal Standard and was in the troop of horse commanded by Lord Bernard Stuart a younger son of the Duke of Lennox. He had a ruling passion - the love of topography, genealogy and heraldry. He jotted down whatever took his fancy at mansions and churches on his travels during the war. At that time he was then a very young man.

Copious extracts of the Diary will be found in Parry's Royal Visit to Wales. The Diary mentions Chirk Castle and its owner Sir Thomas Middleton and many other persons of note and places. There follows details of monuments in Ruthin Church and effigies in Llanrhaeadr Church of Sir Thomas Salusbury of Lleweny, Knight Banneret son of Thomas Salusbury Esq.

Some readers will also have visited this church that has the beautiful Jesse Window, which depicts the family tree of Jesus Christ in glorious stained glass. It is known that this window was removed during the Civil War and buried in the woods above the Church until peace was restored to the land. It is said that the Church building was used, by Cromwell's army, to stable the horses during the time of the Battle of the Green.

The Diary then goes on to say that many monuments of the family of Salusbury are in *Eglwys Wen* (Whitchurch) near Denbigh.

There follows an account of the skirmishes and battles around Denbigh, one of which was The Battle of the Green.

"Foot (soldiers) in Castle at Denbigh. Horse got to Llanrwst that night (12 miles). Foot then joined the rest at Llanrwst. Sir Richard Wynn lives at Gwydur, a faire seate in the parish of Llanrwst yet in Caernarfonshire.

Vert, three eagles displayed in fess or "Wynn". This coate is twice, old, in his window and contrary, one gardant, the other passant. Diverse mottoes about this house one is "Non mihi glis servus nee hospes hirudo".

Manan (Maenan), an old house in the parish of Eglwysfach, co. C'arfon neare Llanrwst. This coate is often carved on the old wainescott, for Kyffin and one Mr Kyffin now lives there, they call him Cuffyn.

Argent, a chevron gules between 3 pheons argent each pointing to the centre of the shield. Roofe of parlour adorned with the second coate. (Here is sketched a buck's head) The roofe of the chamber over the parlour was the old roofe of the chapel of Conway abbey. Family Cuffyn came from Flintshire.

The ruin of the Abbeys was the raysing of them. One of the family fled for Killing a man, formerly, at last returned and changed his name to Vaughan for he was little of stature, for so Vaughan signifies.(Fychan)

The Abbey of Conway stands near this house called Manan; twas antiently built at Aberconway but one of the Princes there (as is reported) likt his seate and gave (the Abbot) him leave to build in any part of Carnarvonshire els. The Abbot liked none better than this seate but twas out of Carnarvonshire over the river in Denbighshire. So this

Abbey was made part of Carnarvonshire. This is the countre story. Now the family of Wynn lives in this Abbey; their coate is Gules, three boar heads erased polewise, argent. This coate also is painted in the Abbey howse: Gules, a "man's head erased" argent "or proper".

Having read and checked many facts and dates I have to conclude that the soldier Richard Symonds is not part of the Mynde Park Symonds family. What a disappointment in not being able to claim kinship with such a dashing and mysterious young man - this conclusion was not popular with my grandchildren, who time and again wanted to hear the story of the soldier and had already decided that they were related to him! It is possible I suppose that the soldier was from another branch of the Symonds family. Buckinghamshire is not far from Herefordshire and Gloucestershire after all!

However, I have included it in my story because of the historical connections with the Llanrwst area. And this is a good opportunity for me to give an account of Llanrwst and surrounding district. This interesting market town at the heart of the beautiful Conwy Valley is the hub of its agricultural hinterland. It has peculiar traditions such as holding an outdoor Market every Tuesday except the first Tuesday of each month when the next day (Wednesday) is used to hold a Fair. In the old days, farm animals were sold in various streets in Llanrwst, cattle in one, sheep in another, and pigs somewhere else. Eventually, an animal Mart was built that still flourishes today despite the Foot and Mouth epidemic that developed a few years ago threatening many agricultural businesses.

When Arthur and I arrived in Llanrwst in 1947, Market day was busy with many stalls set up all over the square selling a whole range of goods, but Fair day was even busier. Many people came to do their weekly shopping, and the place was buzzing with people buying and selling and catching up on news and views. Farmers and their wives arrived in town mid-morning and went about their business of selling their wares - eggs, butter, potatoes, poultry, and of course live animals. At that time the old Town Hall was still standing on the Square, but it has since been demolished to enable traffic to flow more easily in the town centre, more's the pity. Local produce was sold on the ground floor of the old Town Hall on tables set up here and there by farmers' wives, and under canopies in the Square itself.

Stone steps led to the main entrance to the Town Hall. On the first floor was the main hall that had a proper stage with curtains. At the time of demolition, the fine old town clock positioned above the main door was taken to *'San Ffagan'*, the national Folk Museum in South Wales. The old clock was eventually returned to the town, and its face incorporated into a new stone tower built recently near the site of the old Town Hall. The clock's weights and mechanism are on display in the Almshouses Museum in Church Street just off the Square.

Having finished selling their produce, the farmers' wives joined their husbands and made their way to their favourite eating-places for dinner mid-day. Most of these were renowned for the quality of the food they served. Afterwards, the weekly shopping was done and some of the men went to the Inns for a pint or two. On Fair day some went further than 2 pints, it was a bit of a 'spree' day for a few! Most of course simply went for afternoon tea and never ventured into the pubs and inns. Their day out ended when they had to return home in time to attend to the twice daily task of milking and feeding the animals. Most came in carts with horses, others came by bus, but only a few had their own cars or vans - the late 40s being just a couple of years after the end of the war. During those days there was an air of hustle and bustle in the town and local people too enjoyed what was on offer. Things have changed with the passing of the years and the improvements made in agriculture and farmers' acquisition of cars and Land Rovers, but there are still stalls on the Llanrwst Square each week with traders from far and wide still setting up stalls.

Llanrwst is situated at the easiest point for fording *Afon Conwy* (Conwy River), and we know that there has been a settlement there since very early times. There should be many very old buildings still in existence in Llanrwst, but its strategic position left the town vulnerable to attacks from warring opponents. The town was razed to the ground three times, especially the Square, known as *Bryn y Boten* where grass and other vegetation grew as a result. A thousand years ago the Southern Princes of Wales invaded the North and laid-waste the land. Later, the town was ravaged during the revolt of *Owain Glyndwr* who set up a Parliament in Machynlleth and very nearly became ruler of all Wales. Later still, there was fire and destruction during the Wars of the Roses too. One thing is certain however, no one and nothing can take away its long and fascinating history. The river was a bastion of defence for the Welsh in their long struggle against the Saxons and Normans, and many battles were fought there. Llanrwst is on the eastern side of *Afon Conwy*, and on the western side are the foothills of Snowdonia.

Despite its history of destruction, there still remain some very old and interesting buildings in the town. The Church of *St Crwst* is extremely old and has a beautiful 'Rood Screen', which is made of very dark oak with rich carving of foliage, and the fine tracery is so lovely. The top part of the Rood Screen is accessed by steps leading to a balcony where there is bench seating. Initials have been cut into the wood, which must have taken some doing because the wood is so hard. I have often wondered who would have had the time, opportunity, strength, determination and will to carve their own and perhaps others' initials in that way - were they fiddlers in the days before organs had been introduced into churches, were they singers in a choir, or did they perform some other duty perhaps. Obviously they wanted some participation in posterity whoever they were. The Screen came from *Maenan Abbey*, at a time when all such Roman Catholic places of worship were destroyed by order of King Henry V111. It was brought to Llanrwst by boat up the river and a section of the church wall had to be taken down then rebuilt to enable sufficient access. The Screen was also a little too wide for the Church, so a part of it had to be cut away. You can still see today where the cut was made, but no matter, it was preserved for all to enjoy its beauty and that is what matters.

On the lane that leads into the churchyard from the Square, stand the Almshouses, founded as a Charity in Trust, by Sir John Wynne of Gwydir Castle in 1610. The interesting and quaint Museum created by the Llanrwst Almshouses and Museum Trust is now open to visitors and flourishing well.

Part of the Sir John Wynne Trust also involved setting up and maintaining a Free School, and until recently the original building was part of *Ysgol Dyffryn Conwy Llanrwst* (The Conwy Valley Llanrwst School) in School Bank Terrace which was called Llanrwst Grammar School when my children attended as teenagers. The Grammar School, a listed building, was transferred to the care of the Education Authority as a result of the 1944 Education Act. Today, *Ysgol Dyffryn Conwy* exists on one site on Nebo Road and the old Grammar School building on School Bank Terrace remains empty. I can only hope that a purposeful new role will be found for the old building so it can continue to be respected and valued. Its legal ownership is currently in question.

Sir Richard Wynn had a Chapel built next to the Church, which is known as the 'Gwydir Chapel'. Herein, there is an effigy of one of the Wynn ancestors, as well as the lower section of the stone coffin, sarcophagus of *Llywelyn Fawr* (Welsh Prince Llywelyn). Many other interesting items can be viewed there too.

The Eagles Hotel, which is next to the Church, is an old hostelry, and there are one or two other 16th Century buildings on the town Square. Listed buildings there include the *Pen y Bont Inn* (head of the bridge) and the Boot Inn, which is now known as Mr Pickwicks. Once, when lead mining was flourishing in the area men came from other parts of the country to work in the mines, and in those days there were over 50 pubs in the town! They met local girls, married them, and settled to raise Welsh-speaking children who had English surnames.

In the old days, the town was well-known for its production of long-case grandfather clocks, and today, if you are fortunate enough to own one, you posses an item of antique furniture worth a small fortune of several thousands of pounds.

Llanrwst was also a centre for making harps and other stringed instruments: it had leather, metal, and printing works, and for a time, a candle making factory too, near the Square. Ropes for ships and boats were manufactured at Llanrwst, and art, poetry, literature and music were prolific. The output rivalled any other part of Wales.

Approximately half a mile from Llanrwst on the other side of *Afon Conwy* is *Gwydir Castle*. It is not a traditional ancient castle but an attractive large Medieval House that benefited from the dissolution of the old Abbey at Maenan, like many other such properties in the Conwy Valley. There was an earlier building on the site, which was the main residence of the Wynn ancestors who could claim descent from the Welsh Princes. In Tudor times the Wynne family held important Government posts in London, and they were influential and well regarded there, but they might not have been quite as popular locally. One of the sons of Gwydir fathered 11 sons and 2 daughters. Maurice Wynne married the famous *Catrin of Berain*, Llannefydd, a beauty of her day. Several dwellings were built along the valley, and in the villages and the Llanrwst surroundings to accommodate the offsprings. Indeed, there were so many that there were more than 3 times as many listed properties included in the Royal Commissioner's Report for the Upper Conwy Valley than those listed in the same Report for the more well-known historical area around Conwy.

On the hillside just above *Gwydir Castle* is the private *Chapel of Gwydir*, which also dates back to the same period. This is open to visitors and is worthy of a visit if only to see the magnificent decoration on the ceiling. The key is available to visitors in the Forestry Offices nearby. Gwydir Castle, famous for its grounds and peacocks is also open to the public.

For as long as can be recounted there has long been a saying *'Cymru, Lloegr a Llanrwst'*, which means (Wales, England and Llanrwst). There have been many explanations put forward about its origins, but no one knows for certain. It may be that it was to do with the fact that many battles took place in Llanrwst that involved the winning and losing of territory. However, the dominant feature of Llanrwst is the old bridge built in 1636, *Y Bont Fawr,* (The Big Bridge). For over three and a half centuries the Bridge has been an inseparable part of the history and character of Llanrwst.

In 1626 there was a large wooden bridge over the river but it had become unsafe and was finally swept away in a huge flood. As Llanrwst was such an important crossing point, the calamity caused much trouble and inconvenience. In 1634 Sir Richard Wynne of Gwydir presented an application, from merchants, to King Charles for a new bridge to be built. Permission was granted for a new bridge and the architect was the famous Inigo Jones. A sum of £1000 was required and the Counties of Denbigh and Caernarfon each contributed £500. Work was started in 1635 and the opening celebrations day arrived, but as soon as the bridge bore weight the locking stone on the bridge became loose, dropped out of its key position and chaos ensued. Apparently the locking stone had been positoned upsidedown, and it was suggested that Mead Houses nearby were the cause of the mistake! Be that as it may, the builder ordered that there should be no more mead consumed, only buttermilk, and that was one name given to the Bridge - the 'Buttermilk Bridge'.

During the work of cutting into the rocks for the foundations of the Bridge a large pearl was found and taken to Sir Richard Wynne at Gwydir who presented it to the Queen, wife of King Charles 1. After this episode the name given to the bridge was *Pont Y Perl,* (Bridge of the Pearl). Incidentally, during Roman Times *Afon Conwy* was famous for the fine pearls found in its waters. During the Civil War part of the Bridge was destroyed to prevent the passage of heavy cannon, but was restored thereafter.

Today it is still in use. It is said that the bridge has a slight movement when bearing heavy loads and that this is the secret of its strength, something that was unique in all Inigo Jones' bridges at the time. It is interesting to note that there was a notice at the side of the bridge restricting the loads to 12 tons. With the passage of time, rust has completely eaten away the message on the iron notice, but the Bridge is still there and what is more, the loads it carries these days weigh much more that 12 tons.

Sometimes motorists must make many attempts before they finally get over the narrow bridge because of a central hump that makes it impossible for a driver to see traffic on the other side except from the top of the bridge. Locals know that whoever gets to the top first will have priority down the other side. It means that traffic part-way up the other side of the bridge must capitulate by reversing off the bridge to allow the victorious traffic to have right of way. Sometimes it is difficult to determine who should capitulate because of the bumper to bumper positioning at the hump but someone always gives way with good grace. Most times however, the scene is highly amusing to onlookers who sit on benches at the foot of the bridge when they witness motorists in peak times having to go through the process up to a dozen times before successfully getting across. Road-rage has still not arrived in Llanrwst, thank goodness! We have to pay tribute however, to the skills of the architect and those long-gone stonemasons for the beauty and strength of the bridge. For it to have lasted this long I'm sure it will continue to serve the town well for many more centuries to come - in one way or other!

Immediately over the bridge from Llanrwst lies *Tu Hwnt I'r Bont*, (Beyond the Bridge), a very old house, which is now owned by the National Trust and run as a café and shop. Delicious meals are served there, and special cream teas with homemade scones, jam and *bara brith* (fruit bread) can be obtained in authentic oak beamed, low ceiling rooms full of antique furniture and fascinating knick-knacks. *Tu Hwnt I'r Bont* is over 600 years old and was once a Court House and another time 2 cottages. The valley is prone to flooding and when the river overflows its banks, usually at least once a year, the ground floor of the house is flooded and the furniture has to be taken upstairs, nevertheless the old house comes to no harm. I believe that the Virginia Creeper that covers the house is much more harmful to the fabric of such an old building because of its invasive tendrils, although it must be admitted that it looks lovely in the autumn. However, it is the old stone structure that has withstood time and tide that should be admired and protected the most.

For a time Llanrwst had 2 railway stations, the original one built at the northern end of the town was positioned to serve the people of Llanrwst and Trefriw. The walk from Trefriw village over the swinging 'Gower's Bridge' to the station is less than 2 miles, but nowadays very few people walk that way to travel by train. It was decided in recent years to have a station in Llanrwst town itself that is far more central and convenient for everyone. The entrance to the new station is just off Denbigh Street and many people use it to travel into town to savour the delights of Llanrwst's restaurants, hotels and cafes that are well-known for the quality of the food served.

Downriver is the village of Trefriw where *Llywelyn Fawr* had a dwelling and a base for his army. The ancient Church at Llanrhychwyn, where they worshipped is high up in the hills above the village, which meant a hard climb every Sunday for Llewelyn's wife Joan. She was the illegitimate daughter of King John of England of Magna Carta fame, so Llewelyn built a Church specially for her in the village to avoid the hard journey each week.

In Trefriw, there is a long-established woollen factory and shop that is family-owned and managed, called the Trefriw Woollen Mill - it is extremely popular with tourists. A mile or so further on is the 'Trefriw Spa' where healing waters ooze out of the rocks. The Romans had baths there and the Spa became very popular in Victorian and Edwardian times. The medicinal water is now sold in many parts of Europe and several high quality outlets in the UK too. The Spa is now open to visitors and it is possible to tour this interesting place and enjoy refreshments at the delightful café and shop. A little further down the road is the site of a Roman Camp at Caerhun. Here can be seen the remains of the central heating system that enabled the Roman soldiers to enjoy their beloved baths.

High up in the hills above Trefriw is the ancient Church at *Llanrhychwyn* established in the 7th Century. The present church is probably 10th Century and is an old Celtic Church that has fortunately been well looked after. The peace and tranquillity of the place gives rise to a rare ambience.

In the hills above Trefriw are a number of beautiful and peaceful lakes that nestle in the mountains. *Llyn Crafnant* (Lake Crafnant) the lake given to the people of Llanrwst by a Mr James, of Dyffryn Aur Farm as a bequest in his will is one, and next to it is *Llyn Geirionydd* (Lake Geirionydd), a lake just as lovely, which is also enjoyed by many visitors, and *Llyn Cowlyd* (Cowlyd Lake), an extremely deep lake that will never dry up as there are underground springs in addition to the surface rain catchment area. Cowlyd is now the main water supply to the Conwy Valley and coastal area, and lastly there is *Llyn Eigiau* (Eigiau Lake) which is the one that burst its faulty dam, and created such a disaster in Dolgarrog in the 1920s.

There are roads from Llanrwst to Betws-y-Coed on both sides of the river. The one that passes *Gwydir Castle* is the older and there are tree-covered cliffs above the road and one of the outcrops is called *Carreg y Gwalch,* (Rascal's Rock). In the latter part of the 15th Century an outlaw called *Dafydd ap Siencyn* lived in a cave in this area with his henchmen. As this was the only road at that time, all traffic passed below Dafydd's lair. He and his men would pounce on rich travellers and steal whatever they carried of value. The proceeds were then given to the poor and needy. When I first heard the story I thought it was another 'Robin Hood' type of romantic fiction, but it seems there is truth to the tale.

One of many compatriots who had suffered injustice at the hands of the notorious 'Red Judge' was the nobleman *Rhys ap Ieuan* from the Denbigh area of the Vale of Clwyd. He decided to travel all the way to Wigmore Castle in South Wales to outline his case to the Duke of York who was a cousin to King Henry V1 because of the many injustices he had suffered at the hands of the Red Judge. His journey was to no avail, and he returned home thoroughly disillusioned and disappointed. He then decided that, as there was no further recourse to justice, he would take matters into his own hands. At the next Assizes at Denbigh he and his *'kinsman from Nant Conwy'*, together with a dozen followers entered the Court and stabbed to death the Red Judge on the Bench and then escaped. No one made any effort to capture them, which was silent proof from the populace of their approval of their deed. It is said that Dafydd ap Siencyn, and presumably his kinsman also, escaped in disguise. This is proof of the existence of *Dafydd ap Siencyn* and also gives credence to the local story in *Nant Conwy* that Dafydd ap Siencyn had gone to Denbigh and had assassinated the Red Judge, and had escaped capture.

On the other side of the old bridge is the newer road to Betws y Coed, the well-known tourist village that achieved its popularity in the Victorian era when artists congregated there to paint the beauty of the place. Today, rock climbers also congregate there as well as families on country outings, and there are many hotels, restaurants, interesting shops and a tourist information centre for their use. The main road from Betws y Coed to Blaenau Ffestiniog passes through the stunningly beautiful Lledr Valley. At the bottom of the hill from Betws is the entrance to the Fairy Glen where *Afon Conwy* falls and is joined by *Afon Llugwy* (River Llugwy). The road that passes through the village of Betws-y-Coed leads to *Capel Curig* and *Eryri* (Eagles) and *Yr Wyddfa* (Snowdon) - climbers' paradise. At *Penygwryd Hotel* a road leads down to Beddgelert, an award-winning village of great beauty. *Penygwryd Hotel* was the centre for the climbing team that successfully conquered Everest in 1953. This area is becoming very popular with film-makers because of the many lakes, rivers, mountains and natural beauty of landscape.

On retracing our steps to Llanrwst it is possible to travel through the pretty village of *Capel Garmon* where there is an ancient monument called a *Cromlech* and an interesting and very old hostelry called the White Horse Inn.

Chapter Sixty-Five

TRIP TO SCOTLAND

There was great political excitement in 1997 before the General Election because the Labour Party had been changing some of its policies and style of presentation in order to appeal to the electorate. The Conservative Party had been in power for eighteen years and had become stale, and cases of sleaze were constantly being reported in the newspapers. People obviously wanted change because Labour romped home with a landslide majority. There was apparently a great deal of work to be done because of cut-backs that had taken place in the Public Services such as the N.H.S. and the Railways after privatisation had become chaotic. It would take time and money to restore and improve standards, and the new Government, under the leadership of Prime Minister Tony Blair, set to work immediately. There were lots of good things in the Government's manifesto that would benefit everyone.

Purely by chance, I spotted a 'Highland Heritage' advertisment in the holiday section of Glenys' local newspaper in Bolton The advert was very specific and appealed to me greatly so I sent for the relevant brochures. Betty Algieri and I studied them, quickly decided we liked what was being offered then booked a holiday with the company. We were collected by coach at Bolton and driven very comfortably to our hotel at Tyndrum. We were not disappointed because the area is an outstanding tourist attraction in every way. The beauty of the landscape, the five beautiful hotels owned by the family set in grounds with masses of colourful flowers, the comfort of the rooms and coaches, terrific service, lovely entertainment and wonderful food just made the whole experience superb. The daily trips on which we were taken to interesting places by the courier/drivers were also wonderful. The drivers showed care and respect, were always with good humour and knowledge, and gave attention to detail. There was nothing that we could fault because it was all truly superb! This wonderful place came to be because a true Scot, proud of his heritage wanted to share it with all his guests. God willing, Betty and I shall go there again because we enjoyed it so much.

I do not believe there is a holiday company organised along those lines in Wales, but there ought to be, for it would be a very successful business, and a great way of presenting the best of Wales' heritage to tourists. How I sometimes wish that I were thirty years younger!

Betty and I get along very well being two of a kind and at ease in each other's company. We had a lovely time and plenty of fun on that holiday, and have enjoyed others since then too.

The only fly in the ointment at that time was the pain I was suffering in my right knee. I have had arthritic pains in various joints for years, but they come and go and are not debilitating. However, as time went by the pain in my knee worsened, it grated and was swollen, and finally became unreliable as it would quite suddenly give way causing me to stumble or fall. Clearly it was dangerous, and I was sent by Dr. Grout to see a Consultant who decided I needed a new knee.

After a wait of some months I was called to Bangor Hospital for the operation. The surgeon, a big cheerful man explained to me what he would do and showed me the artificial joint that he would use to replace the diseased one. It was made of steel and plastic and I felt confident because I have faith in the fact that the overwhelming majority of the Doctors and Nurses who work in the N.H.S. are conscientious and hard-working and carry out wonderful work. Unfortunately the small minority of medics who fail or transgress are given such prominence and publicity by the media with the result that their importance and effect is completely exaggerated. Over and over again I thank God for the N.H.S., I know it is not perfect, but I dread to think where we would be as a nation without it. Could the majority of us afford the bills if we fell ill and needed medical treatment, especially complicated surgery or ongoing treatment and medication?

Finally, having been prepared for theatre I was wheeled by cheerful, friendly men in gowns and caps down long corridors to a designated area to await my turn to enter one of a number of theatres. There were three or four others on trolleys, then very shortly mine was wheeled into theatre and I was transferred onto the operating table which was surrounded by a cluster of people in gowns and masks. I lay there and wondered why I had not received the jab in the hand that relaxes you before the anaesthetic, but not for long, for I was asked to sit up and swing my legs over one side of the table. From behind the anaesthetist explained I was to have two big injections in the lower back; the first one would feel very cold followed by the second one shortly after that would feel very warm. Without any further delay this was done and I lay back and presumably went to sleep. From time to time I would float to semi consciousness, but could feel no pain. I remember seeing my left foot and decided to lift it. What a hope! I had no power to move anything from my head downwards but I was aware of the various people working on my right leg. I could hear them speaking, but then I would drift off again. Finally I heard the surgeon say that it was a good job well done.

When I woke up afterwards I was in the Recovery Ward on my own and in terrible pain. Glenys arrived and saw my agony and immediately called for a nurse. She asked for something to be given to me to ease my pain and the nurse said that my notes indicated that a tablet should have been given to me on leaving theatre. I told her that I had not had a tablet, so she checked and returned with one that I gladly swallowed. Glen finally left satisfied that I was alright, and I eventually fell asleep once more and the next time I awoke was in the general ward with five other patients. I was told that I had been given an epidural injection before the operation which meant I could eat normally straight away and would suffer no after effects.

After a couple of days in hospital patients tend to fall into a routine of daily care - personal hygiene, food, tablets, exercises, Doctors' visits, and so on, and undoubtedly, this happened to me. One of the assistant doctors, a small, quiet man from the Far East who had wonderful hands told me that a knee operation is always very complicated because of the many tendons, ligaments, tissues, nerves and blood vessels within it that have to join up again properly after severance. My operation had lasted three and a half hours to complete and at first my leg was outstretched in a splint. Within a couple of days I had to get up to stand and walk with crutches around the bed. From then on I underwent physiotherapy and exercise to enable the gradual bending of the knee - an extremely painful procedure, but absolutely necessary. I took tablets to minimise the pain and used a special machine to help with the movement of bending the knee. Every day the extent of the bend was measured. Eventually I walked along the corridor with a stick and exercised by going

up and down steps and so on. Some patients found it very hard and complained of the enormous pain involved, and although I too had enormous pain, I nevertheless decided to co-operate with the physiotherapists and really push through the pain barrier, and it finally worked for me. I was in hospital for just two weeks, returning home before Christmas, which I spent happily with Glenys, Kerry and the boys.

One day, during the time I was with Glen's family and doing exercises to improve movement in my knee and strengthen leg muscles, my son-in-law Kerry, returned from the shops with a toy lawn mower, the top of which he promptly sliced off. He gave it to me and I found it much easier to exercise by placing my right foot on top of the mower and rolling it backwards and forwards along the floor. It was so simple, yet very effective, well done Kerry for being so innovative - it helped my recovery enormously.

When I returned to Eglwysbach I went for three sessions of physiotherapy at Llandudno Hospital that were very beneficial. Everything went very well and the operation was a complete success. I have been for four annual checkups since and each time the surgeon is very satisfied with the new knee.

I have spoken to people who have told of failures and disappointments with knee operations. All I can say is that I obeyed instructions and did my very best with painful exercises and it worked for me. I never think about my knee now other than when I get a bout of pain in all my bones for a period when I take Paracetamol and eventually the pains go away. Today, I have pain in my left knee that will also require attention shortly. I am likely to require surgery again, but that remains to be seen. Whatever the outcome … I am prepared for it!

There was only one major hiccup along the way: on leaving hospital I was prescribed pain-relieving tablets that were different from the much stronger type I'd been taking in hospital. Straight away I experienced a strange feeling of inner trembling, nausea and unreality. It was horrible, so Glenys contacted the Doctor on call at the time and he said that the change had been too drastic and gave me different ones. I was to take four tablets a day initially until things calmed down, but the unpleasant, weird feelings were still present during the gaps between the tablets. The strange and alien experience upset me and I decided to control the gradual reduction of tablets myself by increasing the time between each tablet. This was very difficult to do and I honestly think that the effect on my body was similar to the withdrawal symptoms that habitual drug users suffer when they attempt to come off hard drugs like cocaine, to a much smaller scale of course. It took me a fortnight to wean myself clear of those tablets and it was very hard because it tested my resolve to the limit. I would never ever have thought it possible for my body to demand more of something that was intended to help it deal with pain. It was only the help and encouragement of Glen and my own determination that finally overcame the horrible experience.

However, it was time to celebrate another New Year and look forward to spring again when I would be able to attend to my garden once more. I was warned not to twist my knee and I found that I could kneel on a soft cushion, but only for about 5-10 minutes. I could however bend down from the waist and that was O.K.

During the summer vacation of 1998 Glenys, Kerry and the boys flew to the U.S.A. again. They loved touring New England in a lovely Chevrolet for a week visiting all the sights and then journeying down the east coast to Boston, where they had a wonderful time especially on the quay visiting Quincy's Market and a delightful Magic Shop. They drove through the heavy traffic of New York to Washington D.C. where they met up with Glenys' American cousins and their families. They could not be in America without also meeting up with their Aunty Bella. They received a wonderful welcome from them all and I have to admit there is a warmth and generosity in the welcome that Americans give to visitors in their homes. This has certainly been my experience whenever and wherever I have been in the USA. Marcus and Morgan especially loved the American experience again.

Before the end of 1998 we had lost another member of the family. On a lovely sunny Sunday morning Nance, my sister-in-law had been to Chapel and was making her way home when she must have felt unwell and went to sit on a low wall. Within minutes her daughter-in-law, Hafwen had caught up with her, but sadly Nance passed away quietly. She had never really got over the sudden death of her husband Harry, and then not long afterwards the death of her eldest child Emyr, Hafwen's husband (or Gari as he was known to everyone in Wales) after a very short illness. Nance missed them and felt lonely even though her family visited her regularly and she went to stay at their homes. She loved her grandchildren and was very proud of them all. I visited her from time to time when we would have a cup of tea, some cake and a good old natter, mostly about the good times when Arthur and Harry were alive.

Sadly for the family, Elwyn Vaughan's sudden and untimely death occurred less than 5 years later on the 28th of June 2003. This came as a huge shock for everyone especially for his immediate family, Edwina his wife, Aled and Catrin their children and his sister Elinor. Elwyn had been taking his little grandchild for a ride in the pram at Eirias Park in Colwyn Bay when he collapsed and died.

Chapter Sixty-Six

TOUR OF ANDALUCIA

Age is a quality of mind...
If you have left your dreams behind,
And your ambitions are all dead,
Then you are old...

But if in your life you still have zest,
If love you hold,
No matter how the years go by,
No matter how the birthdays fly,
You are not old.

In the spring of 1999 I felt an urge to go on holiday somewhere warm and interesting. Having pored over holiday brochures and consulted with Betty, we decided on a coach tour of Andalucia in Spain towards the end of summer when the high heat had subsided. We flew from Manchester to Malaga where a coach was waiting to take us to our hotel. It was a lovely Sunday afternoon and we took a walk along the front near the beach. It was busy with Spanish families enjoying themselves as well as the tourists. We had a meal at a small café and successfully found our way back to the hotel.

The next day we travelled to Granada and went sightseeing to view the wonderful Alhambra Palace, a splendid Moorish fortress on a hilltop with the snow capped Sierra Nevada overlooking the city. There are beautiful gardens at the Alhambra with many water features. It was built for members of a Moorish dynasty who ruled the kingdom of Granada for a time. Here I bought a beautiful brooch in the shape of the flower of the pomegranate plant, which is the symbol of Granada. Then we travelled through the vineyards of Andalucia to Cordoba and on the way we visited a wine bodega where we saw various processes of producing fine wines and were treated to small samples, which were not enjoyed by everyone.

A thousand years ago Cordoba was the Capital of the Islamic Empire and was once called the Athens of the West because it was the centre of learning for the Arab world. The wonderful heritage is to be seen everywhere in historic landmarks including the 8th century Mezquita, a huge mosque, which is now a Christian Cathedral. We saw a huge, magnificent altar and a small Chapel and were told that the rich decoration was of solid gold probably brought from the Americas. This area was locked. In the city also is the Roman bridge across the river Guadalquivir and I remembered the name of the river from the days of the Civil War in Spain - it was an important line of defence and continually mentioned in the newspapers of those days.

When we emerged from inside the Cathedral in Cordoba we walked down the many wide steps to the square below - to be besieged by begging gypsies, all women. They were offering white heather for luck but I was not going to oblige, and I warned Betty not to open her purse. However Betty being Betty and kind hearted, said in Welsh to me, "I don't know what to give them, how much is this coin?" and I said, "It's enough, just give it and let's go quickly," for I could see more of them gathering round her. She handed over the coin and waved away the sprig of heather. Well you should have heard them, "Not enough, pah! more…more." It was rather menacing really, but that was the only occasion that it happened during our trip.

It was in Cordoba too that we witnessed a protest march of some kind when there was a small band playing music and a group of men following and chanting. They stopped in front of shops, but the Police stood behind them until the chanting stopped then disbanded the men and ushered them away.

Next day after breakfast Betty and I had to visit a Bureau de Change to buy more pesetas, and had to hurry back before our coach departed. As we rushed down the street we could see a crocodile of people walking in the opposite direction towards the Cathedral and every one dressed in warm clothing including hats and coats. We were suitably dressed in summer dresses and cardigans, but we quickly realised they were calling to us saying it was very, very cold. Well, there was a little breeze I suppose that certainly didn't feel cold to us, but being used to very hot weather conditions in the summer months, they probably did feel cold and thought us outrageous in our summer wear!

With pesetas in our purses off we went to join the group on the coach. As it turned out we were not the last ones of the group to arrive, so we were not in anyone's bad books!

The group members were quiet at first, we thought some were a bit standoffish but, we were wrong. They were a bit shy and I think a wee bit wary of these two Welsh women jabbering away. Well, Betty and I are gregarious and like meeting people and gradually we got things going so that everyone spoke to someone on the coach. They came from all parts of England, and we were from Wales. Then we discovered this Londoner who was so witty and funny and then even the shy ones came out of their shells. On this day we were going to Seville, which was further south in the very heart of Andalucia and I was looking forward very much to Seville. I knew it was the birthplace of Flamenco dancing and that bitter oranges used in making marmalade came from the area. Otherwise I knew little else about the place and had certainly no idea of what was in store!

We arrived at our hotel and then had the rest of the day to explore the city. First things first - both Betty and I were dying for a proper cup of tea. We had brought sweeteners and tea from home but had no utensil to boil water, so off we went and quickly found the main shops where I bought a small jug kettle and some gorgeous fruit. Bliss!

Later we joined a guided tour to see one of the world's largest Gothic cathedrals and the 12th century Royal Palace - the Alcazar. Seville is the proud Capital of Andalucia and to me it was *the* Spanish city with a wonderful vivacious atmosphere. Lively pavement cafes, broad boulevards and huge squares lined with beautiful fine buildings, not forgetting the glorious water fountains.

We returned to the hotel for our evening meal then we and a few others opted for a Flamenco dancing excursion. It was already dark when we set off in the coach and the town was alive with bright lights and sounds. Then we had a lovely surprise, the driver and courier were going to take us on a tour of the town before the dancing started. There were so few of us on the coach that we had a chance of sitting in the front seat with its wide window. Betty was averse to joining me because she was not able to cope with the sensation of being high up and in front. The coach was the Continental type with the passengers high up and the driver and courier downstairs - very comfortable and wonderful for seeing the sights, but I could understand how Betty was affected. However

I was in my element, I gloried in the fairyland spreading ahead, especially the lights playing on the fountains and in the trees on the avenues.

Finally we arrived at the theatre for the dancing. Actually there was no public performance that night, but the young Spanish lady courier had somehow persuaded the troupe to dance for us. We were ushered to the front row where low tables had been provided for us and were asked if we would like sherry, champagne or another drink. One person had sherry, others had soft drinks, but I opted for the champagne, and because I was the only one to request it, was given the whole bottle and encouraged to take it with me to our hotel. Now I am sure it was not the best champagne in the world, but it was pleasant enough and I enjoyed a couple of glasses, which went well with the performance.

You can correctly assume that I thoroughly enjoyed that performance. I have always loved to watch it on television, but to see a live performance … that was something else! All members of the troupe were real Seville gypsies, Romanies if you like, and it is they who are the true exponents of this type of dancing. The men were lean and strong, dressed in the usual black waistcoats and narrow trousers, sometimes wearing flat hats. The girls, all strikingly lovely and wearing their colourful long dresses with the customary flounces and train, which they swished with ease and grace. The men and women wore the special shoes with the clicking heels. With them were two men who provided the music and another who stood and clapped his hands to the beat. He must have had very strong hands for he clapped without stop. There is a story to every one of these dances and the twists, turns and stand offs change patterns accordingly. I loved it all and was almost mesmerised by the movements of the men's feet. I really don't know how they do it, but of course they have been reared in the tradition.

We thanked them for such a display and I think they could see our appreciation. I would not have missed it for the world. Tired but happy we fell into bed and morning came too soon. We had to be up early for a quick tour of the town again, the second for us of course, but it was different again in daylight. We alighted at one of the plazas, I think it was the Plaza de España, a fine piece of architecture, but we could not stay very long. We also saw the 98 metre high Giralda minaret and the lovely Roman style House of Pilate. It struck me as odd that the orange trees everywhere with ripe fruit on the branches had masses of oranges on the ground and no one seemed to want them. But of course the strange thing is that the oranges are nearly all exported to other countries especially the United Kingdom where we all love marmalade of one sort or another. In Spain, marmalade is not used very much and they unbelievably import any that is needed for tourists! The trees are there because they are attractive and a feature of the country - a bit like apple trees here. Seville fascinated me and I would love to go there again preferably during one of the Fiestas. One day I hope I shall.

Our next destination was the busy port of Algeciras on the Costa de la Luz. Then we travelled for a while on a motorway so we had a little snooze until we reached the border at Gibraltar. This small British colony surrounds a 400m rock of Jurassic limestone. Like any other national border we had to alight from the coach and pass through Customs, but we had no difficulty.

We decided to take a trip to the top of the Rock in a taxi. Our driver was a Spaniard who lived in Gibraltar. On the way up we stopped to visit St. Michael's Cave an impressive natural grotto and the Gibraltar Museum that has displays covering the Stone Age to the present day. Within the mountain there is a large theatre and we were told that during

World War II the British were holed up safely in that place for some time.

The most famous residents at the top of the Rock are the Barbary apes that have no tails and are descended from pets brought by sailors from North Africa. They vary in size with none being very big, they are very friendly and some would say cheeky with it. Motorists have to keep car windows and doors closed otherwise they have additional uninvited company. They jump onto car bonnets and peer at occupants with great interest! If you let them, they will paw you or jump on your shoulder. We decided to keep our distance! On the way down we stopped at a viewing point where we could clearly see the coast of North Africa, and at this point the Atlantic Ocean to the right merges with the Mediterranean on the left.

After the taxi trip we could have gone on a guided walk, but we'd had enough. Instead we sat at a table of a street café where we enjoyed the sun and two cups of delicious coffee. Then we ventured into the town and toured the shops - we could easily have believed we were at home because everyone spoke English, and although they accepted pesetas, they much preferred sterling. Later we had a light meal at one of the numerous cafes and finished the day with a drive along the coast road back to Malaga for our overnight stay.

After breakfast we went to Malaga airport for the flight to Manchester where Glen and Morgan met us and took us home for a meal before driving us back to Wales. Tired but satisfied!

No sooner was I back to my normal routine than the Christmas invitations appeared and I had to decide where I should stay for Christmas and New Year, and so on. Some say that journeys are more enjoyable than arrivals. Well, I don't think that is always true, but there is an excitement and delicious anticipation before Christmas. This is a kind of wonderful mixture of love, generosity and a wish to please and give to our loved ones, friends, acquaintances and even strangers, and this lovely feeling mounts as the Festival draws ever nearer. Many people buy enormous amounts of food as though supplies would not be available for months, and then spend more than they can afford on presents thus sending their blood pressure shooting up by worrying about trivialities. Over indulgence in eating too many large meals, chocolates, sweets and nuts, and drinking too much alcohol leaves many people exhausted and bloated. Sitting around all day watching the box is not good for anyone either and before long, we feel deflated and want to get things going again.

The reason we do this is because people through the ages have done something similar in our part of the world, and we tend to continue the trend. At that time of year winter is dark, long and cold in the UK and our ancestors decided to cheer themselves and everyone by having a good old knees-up, and a party. They decorated their homes using evergreens like holly with the bright red berries, and of course the sacred mistletoe. They feasted on roast meat, cheese, bread and copious drinks of mead. In Welsh the word for mead is *medd* (pronounced *mathe* as in *bathe*) and the word for being drunk is *meddwi* as in (mathe-wee)! Later on when Christianity converted the pagan ancient Britons, they had no difficulty in adapting, they simply introduced religious services and customs into their old celebrations.

Now to come back to the ending of 1999 - this period of time was very special - not only was it the end of a century but also the end of a Millennium. We were made very aware of this outstanding event by the media. Another time like this would not happen again for a thousand years, we were living at a time of significant importance.

Plans for the celebration of the dawn of the new Millennium were many and varied and most people took part in some event or other, somewhere. There was much talk by persons of repute on television and much was written in newspapers of some terrible things that would or might happen to televisions and other technological equipment with dire consequences for industrial and commercial institutions. We were told that all the computers in the world would revert to the date 0000 at midnight causing catastrophe everywhere. A lot of money was spent in preparation to avert a disaster … but nothing happened thankfully. The vast majority of ordinary people took it all in their stride, 'que sera, sera'. As far as anyone knows nothing untoward happened, but there were some people who were really afraid and tried desperately to set up precautions.

We celebrated Christmas first of course, believing that it was the birth of Jesus Christ that gave us the beginning. Well, the 25th December is close enough to the 1st January isn't it? But the matter of these few days gave rise to a hotly debated issue by so called experts in the Media but very few of us, the hoi polloi, cared two hoots about a difference of a few days.

I spent the last Christmas of 1999 with Elsie and the boys in Hutton Rudby then spent the first year of the New Millennium with Glenys, Kerry and the boys in Bolton. When New Year's Eve arrived we all dressed up in our loveliest evening clothes, had a special meal together and opened all the silver-wrapped presents that Glen had arranged for us to enjoy at the table. She had bought many things and had made sure there was at least one very special Millennium present for everyone. Everything at the table that evening was silver, including the many candles, presents, and beautiful decorations. She had created a wonderful scene for us to enjoy and remember. At the stroke of Big Ben we counted out 1999 - one, two, three…… and twelve! Hurrah! We toasted the arrival of 2000 with good champagne and went outside into the road. It was remarkably warm for mid-winter and lots of the neighbours were out as well greeting us and each other very warmly and wishing a happy new millennium.

Horwich village is high up near Winter Hill where the big television mast is situated, and we looked down onto the towns on the plains below where thousands of coloured fireworks were going skywards like shooting stars exploding into a myriad of shapes and colours for over an hour - it truly was spectacular. The bangs were effective too. We had to be vigilant as well because fireworks were exploding all around us, just as spectacular as the ones below. Everyone was jolly, chattering and we were all wishing everyone else a, "Very Happy New Year." When finally we started to shiver in the cool air and departed indoors, we proceeded in the time honoured way by putting the kettle on and having a good cup of tea, and wondering what was in store for us in the New Year. Oh well, we would soon find out because tomorrow was already with us, and tomorrow was designated a holiday!

The start of the Millennium Year was celebrated everywhere in some form or other. Here in Eglwysbach, the Community Council arranged a Tea Party in Aberconwy Hall for youngsters and Senior Citizens that everyone enjoyed. The Council also donated a slate paperweight with an exclusive design incorporating a view of St. Martin's Church to every child up to 16 years of age - a change from the ubiquitous mug!

In London, a huge Dome had been built to house innumerable companies taking part with artistic presentations, especially one that involved dancers, trapeze artists and music. Everyone was thrilled with the show and much was written about it all in the press. However there had been serious problems during the official opening and that was enough to dampen the spirits of some faint hearts. Glenys and her hardworking and inspired team of teachers however, arranged to take all the children at Claypool Primary School to see the Dome and its contents, and I was invited to go with them. We travelled by train from Bolton and it was great. We were all excited and the children were very well behaved but, there was so much to see and not a long time to fit everything in. I really and truly enjoyed my visit to the Dome and acquired a good deal of new information, but more importantly made friends with my daughter's wonderful pupils and staff. It was a long journey there and back, and it was gratifying to see how well behaved the children were even on the homeward journey when they were tired.

I found it hard to understand why so many commentators in newspapers and magazines were so ready to condemn and denigrate the Dome for it deserved much better overall evaluation. Everyone to whom we spoke during our visit was so full of praise for all the wonderful exhibitions, and each of us loved the whole experience.

Elsie returned to work on the 31st of March 2000. Six weeks later, all her plans for the future were in tatters.

Out of the blue Elsie phoned to say she had breast cancer. I just thought, “No, that's not fair.” Neville died at 53 years of age and now this with three young sons dependent on her. She had been in hospital for lumpectomy and lymphectomy and the results of the histology at the end of ten days showed there was cancer at the margin. She was back in hospital in September for a full masectomy but prior to that in July, she took the boys on a Mediterranean Cruise and in August as usual to the Hydro Hotel in Crieff, Scotland.

Thankfully tests showed that the cancer had not spread. She had the operation and is now on a daily cocktail of drugs, a routine to be followed for a considerable time yet. She is also monitored on a regular basis, her attitude is positive and she leads a normal life as far as possible. Of course she has her dark days, but is brave and forward-looking. Her friends and neighbours have been wonderful - the ladies from her Chapel took it in turn to help practically by doing her ironing and taking the boys to and from school and so on for a long time to aid her recovery.

Sometimes after reading the newspapers or listening to the News on the television, it is so easy to lapse into despair after hearing about all the ghastly wickedness in the world and the cruelty of people, but then we hear about and see how the majority of ordinary people live their lives with kindness, compassion, and bravery in abundance, thank God.

In May 2000, Glenys was 50 years old and Kerry decided to organise a party for her without her knowledge. He managed to keep the whole arrangement a complete secret. He invited everybody, family, friends and colleagues and we all gathered in the hall of her school in the evening. Glen had been told that we were all going out for a meal in a hotel. Before starting the car Kerry insisted that Glen had to be blind-folded until she reached her destination, then he proceeded on a long and winding detour before finally coming to a stop at the school. Advance messengers had arrived to ensure perfect silence and all doors opened wide. It all worked beautifully and when Glen removed her blindfold she stood before a crowd of about 80 people. She was absolutely flabbergasted! She soon regained her composure and the music played and everyone was singing 'Happy Birthday' and chattering away. Kerry had even organised a “This Is Your Life” book and video. It was truly a marvellous occasion. Everyone had a good time.

Glenys's school, Claypool Primary in Horwich where she has been the Headteacher since 1989 continues to be a leading school in England. It has been a Beacon School for the last 3 years, holds the Ofsted Outstanding School status and a host of prestigious awards such as the Charter Mark for Excellence in Public Service.

Kerry retired in 2005 after 37 years in the teaching profession, 27 of them as Deputy Head at Horwich Parish C.E.School. He is now enjoying lots of leisure time playing golf and generally pleasing himself - and good luck to him.

Chapter Sixty-Seven

TOUR OF ITALY

In 2002 my sister Bella had been thinking of making another visit to Wales and we all urged her to come. I too had been having holiday thoughts and had decided upon Italy. So we had an exchange of ideas by telephone and had decided that she should have a holiday here as well as accompanying me on a holiday to Italy at the end of the summer. We would go to Italy on a coach tour with a Welsh company, so I completed all the arrangements. It was a very satisfying feeling of anticipation for me all through the ensuing months.

Bella duly arrived at Manchester Airport and was met by Glen, Morgan and me. Glen drove us home to Eglwysbach. My sister's birthday falls on the 12th of September. Glenys and Kerry thought it would be nice to have a party for her so we arranged to have it at a Welsh restaurant in Llanrwst, the *Amser Da* (Good Time). First of all we had a little celebration at home in Eglwysbach before going to the *Amser Da* (Restaurant), where we had a wonderful time with speeches and everything, then Glen brought in a special cake with candles that Isabelle managed to blow out with a little help from the boys. Then we all went to the restaurant in Llanrwst, Kerry, Glen, Marcus and Morgan, Isabelle, Bryn and Kath, and me. The atmosphere was lovely despite our sadness about Elsie, and we managed to have fun.

Within days Bella and I we were joining our coach tour to Italy with *Cae Lloi Motors* from Pwllheli. The company celebrated 150 years in the coach business in 2001 and it is the oldest operator in the U.K. Bryn took us to Betws y Coed very early one morning to be picked up by the coach, it was still dark when we started our journey and everyone was quiet on the coach.

The coach had facilities for making coffee and tea, and travelling with us were two friendly ladies, Leah and Mattie who set up a service of providing hot drinks as required and bringing them to us thus avoiding everyone going backwards and forwards. The cost was a mere 50p for a lovely cup of tea or coffee served by the lovely, smiling ladies. They must be well known to many in North Wales because they travel extensively with *Cae Lloi* coaches, and I thank them profusely for their service.

We reached the port in good time and the trip on the Ferry was very pleasant. The English Channel was calm and my sister and I had a meal in the restaurant where we had impeccable waiter service. We arrived at Calais, disembarked and settled into our seats on the coach again to travel through the flat lands of northern France where we saw in the distance some of the Cemeteries established after the two Great Wars of the last century. The fields looked ordinary as we sped passed them, but they had once been the scenes of destruction, fear and barbarity where millions of people had been slaughtered. We were mindful of the fact that those fields also represented heroism, bravery, sacrifice, and compassion too, and we thanked God that humanity is capable of those fine qualities even in the face of cruelty and savagery.

We stayed overnight at Lille and by the time we had checked into our rooms and eaten dinner, were glad to fall into bed for a good sleep at the end of a very long day.

Next morning we were up again bright and bushy-tailed ready for whatever was in store. Our journey took us south passed Rheims and other interesting places until we reached Macon, which was our last overnight stay in France before reaching Italy. We were then in the Alps region and needed to travel through a tunnel that had been closed to traffic due to damage caused by a serious fire. We therefore had to make a long detour through the foothills of the Alps, much to the delight of the passengers but not of Derek our driver who had to take us safely through unfamiliar country. Despite the detour, our driver was absolutely great and nothing dampened his wit or humour at any time. He never intruded, but his experience and skills gave us confidence and he was always helpful too.

I seem to remember that it was at Macon that we had a dreadful evening meal that no one could eat, followed the next morning by a splendid breakfast that compensated somewhat. We had been obliged to leave our designated hotel to move to another in Macon because the police were dealing with a matter that was not divulged to us. Our vivid imaginations led us to conclude that the evening meal problem was connected to this in some way - perhaps the Police had cooked it!

Anyway, no one was grumbling, we were enjoying ourselves and gradually getting to know our fellow travellers. There were no youngsters on board, not in age at least, but we were all young at heart. People should not set out to enjoy a long coach journey unless they have a sense of humour and an essential bonhomie.

We were all Welsh-speaking except for one lady from Rhyl who told us she was an experienced traveller and she joined in very well.

When we left Macon fortified by the good breakfast, the driver explained about the detour and how it would mean a longer day, but that he would make extra stops. Well as far as my sister and I were concerned, we really enjoyed it. Although we were brought up in Wales among the hills and rugged mountains, we were totally amazed by the Mountains in view. I have used a capital 'M' deliberately because they were so beautiful, absolutely gloriously beautiful: the villages, meadows, and everything was so different from Wales. It is hard to find words to adequately express my delight at the place.

Eventually we crossed the border into Italy and arrived at La Spezia where we stayed overnight at a lovely hotel, one of a group of Jolly Hotels. Everything was perfect. We enjoyed a good evening meal then explored the immediate area of the hotel which was close to a palm fringed promenade. We met up with a couple from our party and walked into a Square where local people were laughing and clapping and enjoying an entertainment show. We then joined the rest of our group at the hotel for a leisurely drink and chat before falling into bed. It had been another long but absolutely wonderful day. We all agreed that La Spezia was a lovely town and the driver said he would endeavour to arrive earlier on our return journey to enable us to see it properly!

In the morning excitement was mounting, now that we really were in Italy. Amazing scenery! We travelled along the Italian Riviera passing above Genoa the famous port and the childhood home of Christopher Columbus, I was told that the house is still there. It is a City of picturesque piazzas and fine buildings, but we travelled along one of the big motorways that run along the side of a mountain overlooking the Mediterranean. As we headed further south the weather became sunnier and much hotter, but we had air conditioning in the coach for our comfort. Considering he had not done the journey before, our driver was a mine of information with which he regaled us, on our way. He must have done his homework!

We just glimpsed the domes of Rome in the far distance on one side and themountain peaks on the other. We passed the towering peak of Monte Cassino, famous for its Benedictine Abbey, which brought back memories of the terrible battle that took place in the area during WW2 as the Allies tried to dislodge the Germans who had taken over the Abbey. The Allied armies were battling their way through Italy and the Germans were attempting to stop the advance. They had heavy machine guns placed on top of the mountain and the Allies were suffering heavy casualties. In the end however, after several attempts it was the Polish contingent that succeeded. With dreadful loss of life but indomitable bravery the Allies were able to take Monte Cassino and from then on the Germans were in retreat.

Thoughts and memories like that were not conducive to happy holidays perhaps, but we should remember the sacrifices that were made because they are the reason why we can now indulge in our carefree ways.

We were in the outskirts of the interesting city of Naples where some of the most famous archaeological museums in Europe are situated, but that day we were not visiting them. We could see mighty Mount Vesuvius like a slumbering giant appearing quiet and majestic, looking down over the rolling vineyards on the foothills. Such lush growth in vines, fruit and vegetables growing in the fertile soil created by the ashes spewed out during the Volcano's last eruption. Vesuvius is the only live volcano on the European mainland.

Our destination was Sorrento, which many people associate with the song 'Come back to Sorrento'. But before we could start enjoying the many pleasures of cosmopolitan Sorrento we had to negotiate the road climbing up the mountain high above the Bay of Naples. It is a narrow and very winding road with ever-changing spectacular views. On that day it was my turn to sit by the window and I tell you, it was no use being squeamish. We looked straight down the craggy rocks to see the buildings below like toy houses with the blue waters of the sea lapping at their feet. There are deep gorges, ravines and fishing villages with whitewashed houses and terraces covered in bougainvillea. Absolutely beautiful but scary too if you don't like heights!

Then the narrow, winding and tortuous road descends into the outskirts of the town and I will always remember the skill of Derek our driver on the awesome drive. The passengers were oblivious to the severity of the height and sheer drop along the road but Derek was paying no attention to all that because he was concentrating on driving that big coach round those hairpin bends and avoiding the oncoming traffic. When we reached the bottom and were on level ground in the town, the road continued to be narrow and the pavements too and of course there were dozens of scooters and mopeds weaving in and out of the traffic. There were lots of people standing and chatting, and our coach was very slowly moving forward and then weopped. In the rear view mirror Derek had seen one of the scooters travelling far too close to the back of the coach. Riding pillion on the scooter was a woman carrying a small child with its leg stuck out very close to the wheel of the coach.

He got out of the coach to tell the man to move aside for the sake of the child, but he could not understand and became truculent and abusive, he was also drunk. As soon as Derek turned to get back into his cab the man started kicking and banging the coach and shouting. A coach driver is responsible for his coach and passengers so Derek went back to stop the man who immediately attacked him. Some of the men from the coach went to help Derek who had managed to overcome his assailant with the help of bystanders. And all the while there was a policeman standing nearby, calmly watching the proceedings with nonchalance. Derek managed to get us to our hotel without further disturbance and

I really admired him - he had driven all those miles and negotiated the mountain road with skill and nerve and then suffered the upset in the town. It must have been nerve-wracking. And yet he was calm and debonair in looking after his charges when we reached our hotel.

It was called the Hotel Majestic Palace and it certainly lived up to its name having wide, shallow steps leading up to an impressive entrance hall and foyer. It was still warm outside and the tall French window in our bedroom opened onto a lovely terrace serving four rooms. There were six large tubs joined by an iron trellis on which a jasmine creeper had been trained and its tiny white flowers gave off a lovely scent. At the end of the terrace was an ornate wall behind which were trees covered in bulbous crimson flowers. It was a perfect setting. Our bedroom was large with a high ceiling and modern en-suite facilities. The dining room downstairs was very large and there were numerous waiters led by a major domo who spoke English very well. The service was excellent.

I have described these things to show that this Hotel and many others in Sorrento had been built in the Victorian/Edwardian era to cater for the British visitors who flocked there at the time. After stretching our legs we had a short cat nap followed by a shower. Dressing for dinner I was pleased that I had taken some 'glad rags' with me to wear in such grand surroundings.

The waiters in the dining room wore black suits, white shirts and bow ties and their manner was formal but friendly. There was a choice of food and the quality was good. When the wine waiter arrived, I asked if there was a good house wine and he told us a few different ones. I asked my sister in Welsh if she wanted wine and she said, “Yes, but it has to be sweet.” I would have preferred a demi-sec, but I went along with her. “Shall we have a half-bottle?” I enquired, to which she replied, “No, a glass will be enough.” By now, the waiter was wearing a quizzical half-smile on his face and no wonder! He knew that my sister was from the USA and I was from the UK, and yet there we were, speaking a strange language. I explained to the waiter that Welsh was our mother-tongue and with a smile he then suggested we had a bottle of sweet white wine that afterwards could be stored in a fridge for the following evening.

After an excellent meal the group congregated in a comfortable area near one of the bars. We were a mixed bunch of farmers, retired professional couples, widowed ladies and younger middle aged people who were still working. One of the men, a member of a male voice choir had a good voice, and he and I kept saying, “We will sing a duet as soon as we find a piano.” Well, Leah and Mattie found one in a corridor that had been painted red at some point, but it seemed to be in good working order. One of the ladies could play several Welsh tunes, so we had a good old sing song. We stayed at the hotel for five nights.

Next day my sister and I shopped for a while, sat in the sun writing postcards and generally relaxed before finding a pavement café where we enjoyed a light meal. To our delight we were offered P.G. Tips tea courtesy of a regular English visitor to the café who took her own tea to ensure she did not miss her 'cuppa'!

The following day we visited Pompeii where we were free to do whatever took our fancy. Pompeii is world renowned of course and hundreds of tourists visit the ruins every day all year round, but I have to say that the toilet facilities there were awful. They consisted of only three cramped cubicles, no toilet paper, no soap or hot running water - the toilets were memorable for their serious lack of basic requirements!

We took our time in climbing the slope then rested a while when we reached the actual site at the top: we considered ourselves fortunate in having our own very knowledgable guide who explained everything so well.

I knew from history books that Pompeii had been a thriving, busy town in ancient times but had been destroyed by an eruption of the volcano Mount Vesuvius in A.D.79 and had remained covered by ashes from the volcano for centuries. And there I was standing, looking at the actual remains of houses, a long street, the Forum and the oldest amphitheatre ever discovered - it was surreal. I saw the high graceful columns of the Temple of Apollo, the Arch of Caligula, flourmills and bakeries, the remains of grand houses with beautiful decorations and pools and baths. It was all so marvellous to see these things personally and have time to wonder about bygone times.

On a sharp bend in a street we could see the indentation of chariot wheels as they had swung round the bend all that time ago. We also saw bodies in the streets, some lying face down, and others facing upwards with contorted facial expressions of terror and disbelief - all cast in stone. We looked towards Vesuvius outlined against the skyline and tried to imagine what it might have been like for those people when it erupted and the burning lava spread down the mountain on the other side whilst the red hot rocks and ashes rained down onto Pompeii. But it was not the rocks and ashes that killed the people but the deadly gases that preceded them. The volcano has been quiet for nearly 2000 years but general opinion is that one day it will erupt again, but the circumstances are different now. With special equipment vulcanologists can predict fairly accurately when the mountain will spew out its deadly products. Volcanoes are the safety valves of our world and they have to be treated with respect. It has taken many, many years of patient work to uncover the remains of Pompeii and there is more to do, but what we see today provides the best evidence of the way of life of the ancient Romans. It is a truly fascinating venue, and one that I thoroughly enjoyed visiting. I have watched various archaeological programmes on television and visited Roman sites in Britain and have now visited Pompeii and I am still amazed at the skill, craft, knowledge and organisation of the Romans. In Wales there are Roman roads, bridges, forts, villas and baths and I marvel at them all. What a truly remarkable people were the Romans. I remembered they were in Celtic Britain for four hundred years and had returned to Rome before the Angles and Saxons were able to land. It was very hot at Pompeii but I would not have missed the visit for anything.

We returned to Sorrento and the hotel feeling a little dusty and sticky, but refreshed after a shower, we dressed for dinner. Modern hotels are comfortable and efficient but the ones built a century or more ago have a certain splendour and eminence about them, an ambience that demands that we treat them with the respect that they deserve by conforming to their grand way of life. We imagined ourselves dressed in ball-gowns with fine laces and making our way grandly into dinner on the arms of fine gentlemen.

Wake up, wake up girl and back to reality, ball-gowns and suitcases don't mix well, unless you are super rich with dozens of trunks and servants to carry them, and anyway we have no fine gents of our own. But we do our best in living out of suitcases, we certainly do, for we have learned to roll-pack clothes and make shoes earn their place by filling them with imitation jewellery and other essential knickknacks including our make-up of course. On arrival we unpack our dresses, tops and skirts, press them with the travel iron then hang them ready to be worn. Our undergarments are left in cases and get all jumbled up within a couple of days. Well, that can't be helped, no one will see the creases in them, but then again, you never know! So we do make the effort and we do look quite good in the end although I have to say it myself.

We clip-clopped on the marble floors in our high heels and sat down gracefully at our table and a waiter immediately brought the menu. We began to get used to the grand way of living and after a satisfying meal and a couple of glasses of wine we got even more used to it and enjoyed it very much. "What a pity it is only for ten days" we said. Oh forget about the time factor, simply enjoy! And so we did - very much so!

After our meal, six of us walked down towards the seashore and passed a number of large hotels where there were youngsters laughing and having a good time but strangely, no loud music only the soft strains of melody - ah romance! It seemed appropriate when the word has connotations with 'Roman'. Our companions on the walk enthused about the lights and life down by the seashore having been there before. But disappointment awaited us to discover spooky darkness and only a few mundane street lights. We later learnt that the locals had all gone to Naples to an annual Fiesta - they want a good time too.

We settled comfortably to enjoy a couple of drinks and a chat with the rest of the group: we are Welsh after all! Welsh people love chatting to anyone if they are pleasant. We stayed up late that night because we knew we'd be free to please ourselves the following day.

Next morning we walked the mile and a half to the town centre, risking life and limb from the many moped riders who disregarded pedestrians! We visited the shops in the Square and bought some souveniers. We also wandered down the numerous narrow streets that lead out of the Square where I bought a useful black bag, with "Capri" worked on it in gold, and my sister bought one too. She also bought a pretty dress for her granddaughter, Andrea, and I bought 2 bottles of Limonoro, a lemon liqueur, one for my son and the other for my cakes. I purchased silk scarves, and Capo di Monte ceramic flowers in a picture frame. Most of the articles for sale were well made, attractive and reasonably priced.

We ate lunch *'al fresco'* on the Square under a canopy of course and washed it down with a large glass of Asti Spumante, which I had barely sipped when our table tipped and my wine was spilt. I called the waiter, showed him the table's 'wobbly leg' and my spilt wine. He quickly adjusted the table and rapidly refilled my glass.

Earlier that day we had been chatting to two ladies on the hotel terrace who told us about a delightful ride they had enjoyed the previous day, in a horse-drawn carriage. The owner charged 10,000 lira for a ride round the old town Sorrento, but they had asked him to take them back to the Hotel Majestic too and the total cost was 15,000 lira. Yes, I know the cost sounds horrendous but the value of the lira was very low. Having finished our meal and paid the waiter, what should we see but three ponies and carriages parked at the top of the Square under some trees, so we decided to approach them in a leisurely manner looking at this and that, as tourists do. Three men sat on a low wall close to the ponies, then a couple came along and hired the first carriage and off they went. Casually we walked up and genuinely admired the ponies, which were piebald and very well-groomed. Immediately, one of the men came up to greet us in good English. I said, "You have very fine ponies," and with pride he patted the one at the front. "Yes lady we love our horses. Would you like to go for a ride?" I said, "Perhaps, how much does it cost?" "Only 12,000 lira and we will take you round the old town too." I said to my sister in Welsh that he was an old rogue and that he didn't know we had prior knowledge. This bit of dialogue had the man stumped because he didn't understand a word of it. I told him it was an awful lot of money and that we could not afford it. What a pity, and we turned away.

He shouted after us that as it was a nice day he would give us a special price of 10,000 lira. We turned round and I opened my purse to pay and asked how much more it would be to take us back to the hotel Majestic because we would have to get a taxi back after he'd dropped us. “No, no I will take you to the hotel for 10,000 lira,” for which we thanked him. Then he started to help us into the carriage and I said we could not travel in the one with torn covers so I hoisted myself into the second one. By now the poor man had quite given up and gallantly helped my sister and then took up the reins and we trotted away.

He took us round the old town and down to the waterfront, then along the bottom road where all the large grand houses were situated. The driver was very nice to us and explained all sorts of things that were of interest. We passed a large house with a crest above the entrance gate - it was the coat of arms of the Russian royal family. They were not there any more of course because history had taken care of that. Those great houses had large gardens that stretched down to the sea.

Apparently it was the British who first started visiting the area, and its flourishing tourist industry had grown from their love of the place.

We saw our friends Leah and Mattie taking a walk and they waved and asked the driver to stop in order to take a photograph of us. We insisted that the driver should be included and he said that he hoped he did not spoil the photograph and we all laughed. One of them aimed the camera, we smiled and then realised she couldn't take it because the film had finished in her camera. We were all disappointed, but soon regained our good spirits and saw the funny side of the matter. Our driver was really upset and insisted it was his fault. It would have been nice to have had an actual print because that man had become our friend. We stopped right in front of the Majestic and paid our fare plus a tip, but he would not accept it and wished us well for the rest of the holiday. As we approached the reception desk for our key the receptionist said he'd noticed that we'd been for a tour. We said how much we'd enjoyed it and he said that we'd had the best team of the lot, to which we agreed wholeheartedly. After dinner, as we discussed the events of the day with the others, they told of the amazingly beautiful Amalfi Drive along the cliffs of Sorrento. But Bella and I could not visit it because the following day we were due to take a boat trip to the Isle of Capri.

The morning dawned lovely and sunny for our visit to the Isle of Capri, and the sea and sky were a brilliant blue. We walked along the Terrace with stalls selling all the usual tourist things. The flowers were very pretty. We enjoyed a meal at one of the cafes, but it wasn't the one previously owned by Gracie Fields. Our guide also said that it was the British visitors who gave rise to tourism in Capri and the Neapolitan area which became special when Gracie Fields went to live there. In the days before television, Gracie, the mill girl from Rochdale became famous for her wonderfully strong and vibrant voice. She could sing classical songs with ease, but also loved fooling about with songs like, 'The Biggest Aspidistra in the world' and of course 'Sally in our alley' and the beautiful 'Now is the hour'. Gracie was 'of the people', but had star quality in abundance that flowed naturally from her personality too.

After lunch we had a chance to see a few more sights before going on a boat trip round the island. I cannot describe adequately how marvellous that was, but it was certainly the best way to see the rugged coastline and lofty cliffs, gorgeous grottos and the clean, blue translucent waters of the sea. The beautiful colours of the coral in green, blue, pink and cerise were so stunning. Our guide pointed out the fine houses of the rich and famous as the boat sailed round the rocky pillars and through the arches of nature. There was a general air of calm and relaxation on that boat ride.

When we went ashore we made our way to the busy piazzetta in the centre of the town where there were very smart shops and restaurants. My sister was feeling the effects of the hot mid-afternoon sun so we found a table under the awning of a street café and ordered a coffee and some biscuits. The coffee was wonderful, as only Italians can make it so we had a second cup too. We felt so relaxed and easy that we could have stayed there for hours watching the world go by, but that would have been unfair for the owner and others waiting for a table. Later we bought a cornet of ice cream that also had the quality and special taste that only Italians can produce. We copied other people by going to sit on the wide steps of the Church above the Square and that was pleasant too until everyone was shooed away by a cleric. Jesus would have shooed him away and let us stay I'm sure.

We made our way back to the port area to await our boat. Like all seaside places there were curio shops, ice cream sellers, snack bars and fruit sellers. We noticed one old woman selling particularly nice cherries from her fruit stall: they were big, black and glossy, so we decided to buy some. We waited while she served the people in front of us and my sister noticed that when the old lady was showing the customers the weight of the fruit hanging from the stilage she had her thumb placed strategically to tilt the container. Crafty old so and so, but we made sure her thumbs were in the right place when she served us, although I don't think I would have minded her little tricks too much because those cherries were truly gorgeous. I also bought some fresh walnuts because I had not savoured any since childhood when we would gather them freshly fallen from the tree still covered in thick flesh, mushy with iodine

That evening was the last one in Sorrento and we had been told by Orsino, the waiter, earlier in the day that dinner would be special. Forewarned, it was decided that we too would rise to the occasion. Everyone had gone to extra lengths to dress up as it were. I wore a long black skirt that draped nicely, a loose black silk top with low cut cowl neckline, pearl necklace and drop pearl earrings, silver sandals, usual makeup and perfume. My sister had already gone ahead also looking very swish. I followed as quickly as I could for it would not do to be late. On the other hand you cannot be seen scurrying along in all your finery and anyway it is impossible to scurry anywhere in high heels. In those far away days of youth, I used to be called 'petite' by nice people and 'titch' by not so nice individuals. Now of course the word used is 'small'. But, if you wear high heels you gain not only some inches in height but also in 'amour proper' - self-assurance. However, just then there was no time for such thoughts as I went on my way.

There was quite a long stretch from the foyer to the far end of the dining room and I was thankful that my heels had rubber tips to ensure a quiet entrance. I saw two or three waiters at the end of the room indicating that serving had not begun. I said, “Good Evening” with my best smile and they greeted me in the same way. And then the head waiter, whom we knew as Orsino, stepped forward, held me at arms length and said, “Oh madame, bellisima, bellisima”, and the other two smiled and clapped their hands silently.

Wow! I felt like a queen. I know that the gesture was spontaneous and genuine, but even if it had not been so, I could not have cared less. The effect on me was special. I was on cloud nine as I made my way to the table.

My sister asked where I had been as she thought I was going to be late. I decided I would say nothing about my lovely experience on the way into the dining room because it would sound trivial in the telling and I did not want any silly remarks or teasing about it. Besides it was my special cameo, mine alone. The meal was delicious and the serving of the final course was preceded by a procession of all the waiters, each holding aloft a platter with the pudding flambé. It was a ritual carried out with due aplomb and we all applauded with gusto and then proceeded to enjoy the delicious offering. Some people might scoff at the ceremonial parade but in doing so they would reveal a stuffiness and dismal state of mind. It was altogether lovely and I appreciated it from beginning to end.

There was no time for socialising later that evening because we had to come down to earth and solve the problems of repacking our bags in some semblance of order. Finally we managed it, but I had to sit on my sister's suitcase to make it close. Items required on the journey the following day like fruit, biscuits and drinks went into a separate bag and any new purchases into yet another. We failed to understand how we had accumulated so many things having set out with a firm decision to travel light!

Having solved all the packing problems, enjoyed a good breakfast on yet another gloriously sunny day we were ready to set off again in the coach. In appreciation of very good and pleasant service we offered a worthy tip to the dining room Waiters and it was accepted with grace. And so, with a last look around I went on my way, but just as I was passing the potted palm on the top table, Orsino appeared and held my upper arms and offered me good luck and then kissed me on both cheeks. I smiled and looked him straight in the eyes and saw genuine empathy and sincerity. That made my day. I said, "Thank You" and turned and went on my way.

We had a long journey ahead of us and again Derek would be negotiating the drive over the cliff road above the bay. This time we would be on the inner side of the road, not quite as scary perhaps but I can appreciate why it is such a popular area for there is an aura of relaxation and ease of mind, sunshine and friendliness in abundance there. It is a soothing place and yet exciting too. I would very much like to return to Sorrento at some time in the future. We then started our return journey and ahead of us was our overnight stop at La Spezia, where we had so enjoyed visiting on the outward journey.

We were not disappointed in our second visit to La Spezia and its Jolly Hotel. We couldn't stay too long because of the need to return home through Switzerland and I was really looking forward to seeing some more Alpine country. We passed by Milan, a great industrial city, ancient and modern grand architecture and salons of Italian style haute couture. It was fortunate perhaps for the sake of our bank balances that we were not stopping there - prices in lire would surely have been in the millions! The scenery was truly lovely, the high peaks of the mountains, some wearing their snowcaps reflected in the blue waters of the lakes below. Lake Como and Lake Lucerne and the surrounding pretty villages with their chalets overhung with flowers of all colours. We stopped at various places, especially one centre where there were many interesting items for sale such as plates and mugs, steins, cuckoo clocks and Swiss dolls in national dress. We had no reason to hoard our Swiss francs, so we didn't. We had the pleasure of clearing out our purses with glee, and acquired some very well designed souvenirs in the process.

We had our overnight stop at Lugano and unfortunately the weather was unfavourable. But we had a good rest and excellent food, and it was Saturday night already and the time seemed to be passing with increasing speed as it always seems to do towards the end of good holidays. We continued to enjoy Alpine countryside interspersed by tunnels, not long ones, but no tunnel can be regarded as appealing. However, they serve their purpose so let us be thankful. At the end of the afternoon we bid farewell to Switzerland and said Hello again to France.

We stopped overnight at Letz, in the Bleu Marine Royal Hotel, which was very comfortable. This was an interesting town, but we had no time to wander far because we had to be up early to start a very long journey on Monday morning.

After breakfast Derek was itching to get going, so we obliged because we had to be in Calais at a certain time to catch the Ferry. I did not enjoy the ferry journey on the inward journey home as much as the outward one because there was more of a sea-swell. Before long we were back on British soil and speeding through southern England. Derek knew of a detour to avoid heavy traffic and we passed through several typical English villages instead of busy motorways. As the shadows of evening fell and we could no longer see outside, weariness set in and we dozed, although Leah and Mattie, bless their hearts, helped enormously as they continued to serve their welcomed drinks.

We stopped at a motorway service station in the Midlands somewhere around Birmingham. Here we had to bid farewell to Derek our driver because of a legal requirement concerning the number of hours at the wheel. We were very sorry to see him go and we all trooped out to thank him and give him a good tip. He thoroughly deserved it. We had a snack and a drink, which cost an arm and a leg, then were away again with our new driver who was either a brother or friend of Derek. They swapped vehicles, bus for a car.

We had woken up a little with the stop, but were soon dozing again with a snore to be heard now and again. Then we were back in Wales!

When we reached the Wrexham/Llangollen area we made a short detour to drop off one of the ladies. We all wished her well and hoped to see her again. We next dropped off the singer and his wife who were a nice couple and good company. In Corwen a number of people were leaving our coach for another smaller bus, which would travel towards Bala.

Finally we reached Betws y Coed where Bella and I left the coach and the remaining travellers. Our legs felt a big groggy, but thankfully Bryn was there to take care of absolutely everything including both of us, all our luggage, and our great need to get home to bed. We were absolutely shattered, but it took a long time to get to sleep for we were still in motion!

We rested for a couple of days and talked about Italy and the rest of the trip. It had really been an amazing experience and we had seen so much. My sister and I were very happy and satisfied. However, there was more to come.

Chapter Sixty-Eight

LONDON TRIP

Every year Welsh Male Voice Choirs travel to London to sing *'en masse'* at the Royal Albert Hall under the baton of a distinguished Conductor. There are also solo singers of renown who perform at the events. I had made arrangements with my friend Betty Algieri to book seats for Bella and me to travel with her and the Betws yn Rhos Male Voice Choir. Bus fares and entrance fees had been paid and Betty's brother Ernest and his wife Maureen would give us a lift to meet the coach. They too, were going to London. It was a nice social group. There were many coaches travelling from North Wales full of choristers and partners and enthusiasts like us. Our group was staying at the Kensington Palace Hotel near Hyde Park where we were comfortable and in a nice area of London. Our first priority, having organised ourselves in our hotel rooms was finding a restaurant where we could have supper, so we went exploring. We found a restaurant serving good home cooked food that looked clean and attractive. It was a family-run business, members of which welcomed us warmly. We returned to our rooms and Betty made a pot of tea for us. She really is a champion tea maker amongst her many other capabilities.

We intended going shopping and sightseeing the next day, but such ideas had to be abandoned because the weather was so atrocious. Not to be thwarted, we made the best of things and went on a city tour in a double-decker Red London Bus. That was no pleasure because the rain was being blown into the lower deck and the top deck was open to the elements with the rain being washed downstairs. There were other brave souls like us, but everyone was soaked and fed up. When we returned to the comfort of the hotel, Betty spoke to her brother on the house phone and we arranged to return to the same place for supper before attending the Concert. Again we were very well pleased with our delicious meal. Thankfully the rain stopped towards the evening and we did not have to worry about getting wet, nor did we have to call a taxi because the Albert Hall was within walking distance of the hotel.

If you have ever been to the Royal Albert Hall you will know that it is a round building with several entrances. It was just as well that we were there in good time in order to find our block entrance and then stand to wait for an orderly entry. Everyone was in good humour and there was no pushing or shoving. I edged forward slowly, Bella and Betty followed and we found our seats and they were good ones. Two men sat next to Betty and soon she was in animated conversation with them. They were from South Wales and were not acquainted with the North Wales singers, so Betty was explaining things and filling in the details. They were very grateful to her and one offered to share his ice cream cornet with her! With grace, she declined.

The massed choirs were singing under the baton of a respected Conductor who succeeded in getting the best out of them. From time to time the great Organ accompanied the singing - played brilliantly by a Welsh lady who sadly died recently. The soloists also sang well and the full house expressed their appreciation in fine style. We enjoyed ourselves and the concert was well worth the effort of travelling to London. Back at the hotel after the performance everyone was relaxed and letting their hair down. The atmosphere was convivial and happy, then it became a little too loud at which point we three departed upstairs: Ernest and Maureen also.

In the morning we had a nice surprise - we were woken gently by Betty with a delicious cup of tea. The best way to start the day, and it was a sunny day too. We enjoyed a very good breakfast although the service was a little chaotic at first.

Our journey home included a visit to Stratford upon Avon for a couple of hours, which was a pleasant break, but there were too many people about for comfortable shopping which was good for business in the town of course. We could not complain for we formed part of the crowd. We bought a few small things then went back to our coach. My sister was starting to feel cold and sneezed once or twice. She huddled in the corner of the back seat of the coach and was feeling pretty miserable. Perhaps all the travelling was taking its toll or it may have been the result of the cold and wet weather of the previous day.

Home again and Isabelle went to bed with a hot toddy. The cold remained with her for the last few days with us and until she returned to the U.S. when it became more serious, but after medication and good care, she eventually felt better.

They had been good trips, but we were tired after all the travelling we'd done during the past month. We had tended to overlook the fact that we are no longer the young chicks we used to be. But just give us a few days of respite, and we will once more be ready for anything again!

We were invited to dinner by our niece Nerys, Percy's daughter, and were very happy to join her at a top class Llandudno Hotel. I had often seen newspaper reports of the many awards and accolades that had been given to this particular hotel and it was a treat to enjoy a meal there.

Isabelle's holiday came to an end when she returned home to the U.S.A. It seemed rather strange for me after she'd gone because we'd been so busy and there had been very little time for just talking. But no matter, we do that every week on the phone anyway!

Bryn drove us to Manchester Airport and Bella treated us to a good breakfast before we said our goodbyes. I did not think I would see my sister again for some time. But I was wrong!

Summer's end brought good news. Faye had been successful in securing a job with a large firm in Manchester that offered additional training leading to a Diploma, which she has since succeeded in obtaining. To date, she has been promoted three times within the firm.

Marcus achieved good results in his 'A' level exams then studied for 4 years at the University of Huddersfield. By now, he has his BSc Honours degree and has secured a job at Gresham Office Furniture Ltd, a major manufacturing company in Lostock specialising in office furniture. He too is receiving opportunites to access further training, and is attending evening classes at the new Bolton University to study specific courses of interest and use to him. He is motivated enough to also do a great deal of self-teaching by using manuals, magazines and the internet. Marcus' expertise is in the ever-evolving field of ICT.

I am always so pleased and proud to see my grandchildren doing well in the world.

I had decided that I would write about my life as far as the end of the Millennium year, and then call it a day. After all, there has to be a stopping point sometime and thedate 2000 seemed to be very appropriate. But I have decided to stretch it to 2005 because of some important events that happened during those years.

In the spring, Rebecca, the eldest of my grandchildren announced her engagement to Ross Gowans, a Marine in the Scots Guards. They celebrated by having a party at the Maenan Abbey Hotel, Llanrwst. Their friends, most members of Ross' large family from Scotland, and some of our family attended the celebration and had a good time. Bryn had suffered a fall and had broken his arm a few days beforehand, but was still able to enjoy himself even with one arm in a sling.

The wedding would be held in a Church in Scotland on the 8th June 2002 and we would all be attending. It was a good excuse to buy new clothes! Within a few weeks of the party, Ross had an accident whilst on manoeuvres and was very seriously hurt. However, with hospital treatment he has recovered and is back to his usual smiling self once more, although he had to have further treatment to his shattered leg. Now he is fully recovered and serving in Iraq with the Marines.

For some time I had been planning to reduce my workload in the garden. In winter, I do little in the garden except enjoy looking after the birds that come there: every morning I prepare a whole pile of food for them, then shout and yell like a banshee to scare away the ravens with their long beaks. The small ones repay me when I watch their antics.

Then the catalogues from the various plant growers started piling through my letterbox and I enjoyed perusing them and planning the designs I might work on in the coming months of 2001. Reluctantly however, I decided that I would buy in young plants from various firms that year, and for the first time, not grow my own. It meant letting go of the greenhouse to avoid the temptation of using it. I advertised its sale in the local newspaper and the greenhouse, where I had enjoyed so many happy hours, went to a new home. I was glad that a young woman, who had a keen interest in gardening, was the buyer. Bryn had started to dismantle it, but the lady had a most useful trailer - flat and wide and low and so the main framework was transferred whole.

The next step was to look around for a gazebo, and Bryn and I saw some nice ones, but finally it was a summerhouse that proved most attractive and spacious. I bought one with a guarantee of 20 years. Bryn extended the concrete base, the supplying firm assembled and fitted the structure and I painted the inside walls in a pleasant pale shade of green and covered the floor in grey vinyl. I bought two comfortable wicker chairs with cushions and a matching coffee table. It looks lovely.

At this time Morgan was having his bedroom changed to a bed-sit and during the Christmas holidays his Mum and Dad worked hard to re-decorate according to Morgan's choice - mainly royal blue and silver. It looks really nice with his new furniture and he is very pleased. The replaced furniture was in good condition but not suitable for a modern-minded lad in his new study. I saw that I could make use of a couple of items in the summerhouse and Morgan was willing for me to have them and his Mum and Dad agreed. I already had a bamboo whatnot, shelves one upon the other in a triangular shape to fit into a corner. I was therefore comfortably furnished in my summerhouse. Electric power was also connected for work, rest and play.

This winter the summerhouse has also provided shelter for the plants that needed protection against the cold winds and winter frosts. I could not have financed the whole operation as well as go away on holiday, but I was happy in the thought that I can enjoy my summerhouse for many years to come, I hope. I think that *Hafan* (summer place) is a good name for it.

In the last few years I have said more than once that I would no longer enter *'The best kept and most attractive garden'* competition in the Eglwysbach Agricultural and Horticultural Show, but each time friends have persuaded me to change my mind. But this year, I definitely decided not to enter in view of 12 successive wins, and now, I can really enjoy my garden in a relaxed fashion. I shall of course enter individual items to support the good work of the Show's Committee members who give their time freely to this successful annual event.

Gardening as a pastime is booming at present, you have only to visit the many Garden Centres in the area to see how interested people are in this hobby, and that is very good. If only we could instil this urge to create beauty into the minds of our youngsters. We need their enthusiasm to turn our villages and towns into glorious areas. There would be associated benefits in the way that graffiti, litter and mess would decline and eventually disappear.

Geraint was informed that he had been successful in his 'A'level examinations and had been accepted at Oxford University. He studied at Worcester College and settled into a new way of life very successfully. Everyone was pleased for him especially his mother Elsie and his brothers and I am only sorry that his father was not alive to have relished the moment - he would have been very happy indeed. So would Arthur, his grandfather.

He has since gained a BA Hons. Oxon degree, and a MA degree too. Well done Geraint!

Chapter Sixty-Nine

THE ALPS AND ALL THAT CLIMBING

I have written a great deal about the past, but it is over and done with. It cannot be changed. But it is still with us, it trickles into every day and affects our present lives. The past is done with, but the experience of the past remains with us and affects us all according to its severity and our personalities. Some carry it lightly and gradually shrug it away. To others it is a heavy burden they carry, sometimes forever. If the past was kind to us, then we are glad of its company and remembering it as a delight. The majority of us carry a mixed bag of good and bad.

How do I feel today? How has the past affected me? I have enjoyed my life, which is not to say that life has been a bed of roses all the way, but on balance there has been more joy than sadness. I carry no bitterness and few regrets. Experience is a great teacher if you are willing to learn. Would I change anything, would I have acted differently? In some cases, yes - with the benefit of hindsight I can see things more clearly and I would decide differently, but mostly, I would do things exactly the same.

I had to work hard all my life and now look back and wonder how I coped. Well, the work was there and had to be done, so I just got on with it. It also has to be said that I enjoyed working. I relished the results of my efforts and this was possible to a large degree because of the good health I have enjoyed. I have been in hospital for treatment seven times including surgery for my face and a new knee and I have nothing but the highest praise for doctors and nurses and all staff. There are complaints from some people about the quality of food and cleanliness in some hospitals, and maybe there is a case for bringing back the role of 'Matron'. I marvel at how well the N.H.S. has performed in the last decade. The extra burdens that the service has had to deal with include more people living longer, general chaos in society with some people abusing alcohol, cigarettes, hard drugs, obesity and lack of exercise, and higher expectations increasing the number of patients receiving treatment. Now that extra funding is invested, people in general should cease moaning and whinging about trifles so that the serious problems can be investigated properly. I am very glad however that relevant people have seen fit to demand extreme cleanliness and hygiene in our hospitals. Well done N.H.S. I say.

I believe exactly the same about the teachers, headteachers and schools too. The hard work that goes on is incredible and good heads and teachers work very long hours managing the myriad of initiatives that have come flooding relentlessly from central government since 1997. Head teachers have very little free time and use their holidays to catch up on school work that cannot be done during term-time. This is partly due to the fact that social problems within households spill over into schools with the children. Good teachers know that these problems have to be tackled in order for children to settle down to learning. But mostly, the demands involve complex, important changes that require implementation in order to refine the education service.

I have worked for the Civil Service and also for a nationalised industry. Most people I worked with were hard-working and conscientious, but I think the structures of those offices needed changing. Privatisation appears to have made some necessary changes, but not to the real basics. The chaos and upheaval today on the Railways is indicative of the failure of privatisation in some industries. Services that are vital for national success should be allowed to function without having to put profits first.

Sometimes, after reading newspapers or listening to the news I feel sad and depressed by the reports of so much crime and cruelty and the low self-esteem of people who need drink or drugs or crude sexual practices in the pursuit of fun or happiness. Happiness is not achievable by targeting: it is spontaneous. Real happiness is elusive and can only be enjoyed when it is not being pursued. Happiness is a by-product; it comes of its own accord in the form of feelings that bubble up within us when we are absorbed in non-self thinking or activity. Real happiness is related to generosity of spirit and an inner contentment. Parameters are out of fashion and 'freedom to do your own thing' is the slogan. Freedom is great and it is the right of every human being. But unbridled freedom in a society is very dangerous. Some time ago I read a quotation written by Dr Sydney Cave in the 1950s. I wrote it down and here it is: "A society cannot live forever by a Faith it has abandoned. A time comes when the capital of the past is used up and an abandoned Christian faith ceases to provide the impulse to Christian character." Have we reached this time and are now seeing the results I wonder?

Having said that, I am also heartened when I read reports about truly wonderful people who go beyond the call of duty in their attempt to help their fellow humans, without giving any thought to themselves. There are more of them than we think. They don't make a fuss because they usually work quietly. The things they do are not always outstanding, but are practical and useful. Thank God for such people. Without them humanity would be lost.

How do I compare now with the person I was in my younger days? Goodness knows what answers there would be if the question were asked publicly! I would hope that I have learned to be more composed, more compassionate, more tolerant and more patient. I think I was a good mother: Arthur used to tell our children that they had the best mother in the world. Well, I don't know about that, but I always did my very best for them and always put their welfare first. Some people would argue that my going out to work while the children were still at home was not good. This was in 1961, a time when very few wives and mothers went out to work. I would beg to differ. We needed the money to do well by the children and anyway Elsie was 14, Glenys was 12 and Bryn was 9 and their father was home-based when I returned to work. They also experienced a degree of independence that has stood them in good stead.

I had to face many problems along the way and there were times when I was sorely troubled. There were times when I had to cope with problems on my own and I would seek help and guidance in prayer.

I have never knowingly or deliberately hurt anyone, but possibly I have made decisions that seemed right at the time, but were unwise in the long run. This happens to everybody, we are all human and fallible. There are times when we can seek advice or talk things over or even argue, but there are also other times when we cannot avail ourselves of the advice and guidance of others, when we stand alone and have no option other than to decide within our own judgement. It is not easy and there is an abundance of evidence of people being overwhelmed by the loneliness of their situation with tragic results.

On the whole I coped pretty well and we were a very happy family. Most difficulties were to do with money when we always had to tread carefully and budget wisely. We managed with a tight rein to enjoy trips away in the car and regular treats and new clothes. Very few people went abroad on holiday at that time, but none of us felt deprived. There was enjoyment in planning any trips that we made. After I returned to work, we went for long weekends in London; went out sometimes for an evening meal or spent an afternoon shopping in Llandudno or Chester. When it came to buying clothes we believed in quality and were willing to save in order to afford the best on offer. However, Arthur and I were never able to buy a new car. We had a horror of debt and Arthur was too kind-hearted for his own good. But we counted our blessings and realised that we were rich in all the important things. I was happily married, had three wonderful children, many friends, and led a busy and interesting life.

There are three wonderful love stories in my life. Arthur, my beloved husband was obviously one of them. The other two men shall remain anonymous but not forgotten.

In the spring of 2001 I was elected Chair of our local Community Council. We are a conscientious group and it is amazing how much work we have to deal with at our monthly meetings. We give freely of our time. It just so happened that a long-term plan from the County Council was making an appearance and a proposed plan for housing was being put forward. One way or other a misunderstanding had upset some villagers and a public meeting was called by the Community Council that I was required to Chair. It was a very lively meeting with many speakers giving vent to their feelings, but there was no trouble. As the days passed, everyone calmed down and things were sorted out at further smaller meetings. It was a case of being thrown in at the deep end from the beginning, but fortunately the rest of the year passed by relatively peacefully.

The Eglwysbach Agricultural and Horticultural Show was a victim of the horrendous 'Foot and Mouth' epidemic that hit the nation a few years ago. The 'agricultural programme' of the show had to be cancelled immediately and many other similar events suffered the same fate. Our part of the country did not have infected areas, but nevertheless had no choice but to abide by all the strict regulations. However, the hard-working Committee of the 'horticultural programme' of the show, which was not affected by the epidemic, decided to go ahead and have their 'mini show' in the Aberconwy Hall and St. Martin's Church. It was very successful indeed, much to the relief of everyone concerned. This was to be the pattern for the following couple of years too. Thankfully, the full Eglwysbach Agricultural and Horticultural Show returned to its former glory this year, and was welcomed warmly by everyone in the community.

In June, my granddaughter Rebecca and Ross were married in Scotland. It was a long way to go but most of the family made the journey to enjoy the Church service and Hotel reception and to wish the young couple every blessing in the future. It was a lovely wedding: Rebecca looking very pretty in a beautiful embroidered traditional white dress, Faye her sister, and two other bridesmaids wearing very attractive dresses in a deep rose colour with two little girls, relatives of Ross', as flower girls. The two mothers looked very smart and the two fathers also. My part of the family had also turned out in style and I was very proud of them all.

Bryn, as father of the bride made a very thoughtful speech in his usual relaxed manner and proposed toasts to the happy couple and also to absent friends and members of the family, sadly no longer with us. I was very proud of his naturally dignified manner throughout the day.

Towards the end of June 2003, my friend Betty and I went on holiday. We had decided on a coach tour of the lakes and mountains of Switzerland. We had studied brochures and pictures and held in our minds the kind of land it would be. We were looking forward to something different in the scenery and the special Swiss way of life. Well, we got that and much, much more.

Our first week was hectic in that we moved from place to place and each night was spent in a different hotel. Every shower was different, ranging from the earliest type to the latest and I have never seen such a range of toilet pans and flushing arrangements either. It was not just Betty and I who were perplexed, other tourists were equally puzzled, but every single one was clean and some were automatically cleaned and sterilised after each use. One such type caused consternation and then merriment - as soon as the seat was clear of a bottom, a square box shot out from the back and the seat and cover were tilted and turned and a wash sprayed on them. Then they returned to normal. The first time I experienced this system, I really thought I was seeing things!

We saw very few overweight people there, except amongst the tourists! Another feature we noticed everywhere was the use of bicycles. Hundreds of them of every shape, size and colour were parked neatly in bunches on special parking areas. Babies and children were pulled along behind bikes in all sorts of baskets, cots, back-to-front prams, and so on.

Breakfast was fairly easy: cereal, juice, cold meats, bread and jams, no marmalade as such, and a choice of coffee or tea made with warm water. Ugh! At mid-day we were served sandwiches, plain soups, fish and meat. The food in the evening was wholesome, but the meat and vegetables were cooked differently somehow. Lots of ice-cream and sorbet were used as dessert. Having said that, Betty and I had some delightful meals, especially salads and filo parcels. On three occasions we were also successful in being served a proper English tea with a teapot and boiling water, thin sandwiches and cakes: once was at the top of a mountain and the other times at lovely hotels by the lakesides.

The buildings are all distinctive with their sloping roofs, absolutely necessary in their winters. We saw no litter on the streets and the rivers and lakes look clean with lovely clear green water. The trains buzz along the streets or climb the mountains in a zigzag fashion. I don't know how the people on the plateaux on different levels on the mountains can possibly survive in the winters except with the use of the cable cars and the funiculars. My admiration of Swiss engineers is total. They have achieved mastery of their terrain through their skills.

We went into castles and grounds and admired their many classical statues. We visited pretty little cottages and enjoyed going round admiring the abundance of fruit and vegetables, bread and cakes on sale in their open-air markets. Best of all we had two weeks of glorious sunshine and warm weather. Local people said that a summer like it had not been experienced there for over a hundred years: we felt so fortunate. Rivers and lakes and beautiful cities are all dominated by the great glaciers and peaks.

I had read about St. Moritz as the winter playground of the rich and famous. We stayed overnight in a hotel above the lake and the following day went on the Bernina Express across the Alps to Tirano in Italy - the only railway to cross the Alps without a tunnel and the track drops over the unique spiral viaduct at Brusio. Then our coach took us along the shores of Lake Como to Lugano, a very lovely town where we stayed overnight. Back to Italy and Lake Maggiore, clear water, towering peaks and lush meadows, where there were cattle with their tinkling bells strung around their necks.

In the middle of the lake there are islands amongst which is Isola Bella with a castle. We needed two boats to take our group to the island and we spent an hour or so taking photographs of the castle, its glorious gardens and many sculptured figures. Suddenly there was a very heavy downpour and we hurried down towards the lake. Betty and I had no coats and took shelter for about ten minutes. Then we made a dash for the jetty just in time before the boat left; the other one had already returned. On the way back to the mainland the motor of our boat stopped so we had to transfer from the nose of the boat onto the nose of a rescue boat. We successfully negotiated the move even though a thunderstorm had broken out and the rain was coming down like stair rods, and there was a high wind. We felt like heroes when we returned unscathed and marvelled at the dexterity of the sailor in charge of the rescue boat in easing the nose of his craft alongside our boat to enable us to jump across without fear of falling into the water!

On Wednesday morning we travelled by train to Zermatt at the foot of the mighty Matterhorn (4478m.). The town is a noble place where traffic is not allowed on its streets. We stayed at Lausanne overnight.

Next day we went to Gruyere, the famous cheese making town where the streets are cobbled. The buildings are quaint and are adorned with beautiful flowers in gardens and window boxes. We enjoyed looking round the town and somehow managed to drink a very expensive cup of coffee! The group had the option of visiting a cheese factory, but chose instead to go straight to Berne, the capital of Switzerland where the monumental Federal Place is to be found. We visited the Bear Pits, the bear being the emblem of the City of Berne, where everyone was disgusted with the state of the bears and the conditions in which they lived. The coach then took us to Interlaken where a number of us stayed for the following week at the end of which we rejoined the tour.

At Interlaken we decided to do the unforgettable one-day excursion to the Jungfrau Joch, which is the highest railway station in Europe (11,333ft.). The train passes through beautiful meadows covered in wild flowers of all colours, and then on to forested areas until they too give way to the barren crags of snow covered alpine mountains. The train zigzags its way up until it reaches the ice area.

Interlaken is situated between two beautiful lakes, Brienzersee and Thunersee. We went on a boat trip on Thun, which took over five hours, the boat criss-crossing from one pretty village to another. The day was lovely and we became sunburnt. There were boat trips on Brienz too, but we decided we'd rather walk along the lake to enjoy the views on that very fine day. We took tea, English style, at a grand hotel on the lakeside, which was delightful and memorable. It was also useful to have the facility of trains and buses running frequently across the town.

We went up a steep mountainside on the funicular that rises and falls very steeply, and were so pleased we did because the views from the top are absolutely spectacular and breathtaking! Here too we enjoyed a very satisfying meal … and tea in a teapot!

We walked to the city centre and found an interesting jumble of shops. Some were very modest while others were grand jewellers with frightening prices, and haute couture shops with grand clothes. Nearby, was the 'Big Field' as it was named, a wide, open space on the edge of which was a fine restaurant where we had delicious salads, naughty cakes and English tea in a teapot! We enjoyed Interlaken very much.

On Thursday afternoon another tour coach arrived for us, with different people on board of course, and we travelled to Lucerne. That evening we went to a spccial restaurant where we had a drink and a Swiss cheese fondue. There were many more guests there beyond our group and we were entertained to a Swiss Folk Evening by members of a

Swiss family. They were marvellous and really talented. The elder lady had a fine singing voice and yodelled quite a bit, but not quite as I had heard in the past I have to say. As I did not know the original form of yodelling, I could not form an informed opinion about the performance except to say that it was interesting and entertaining. Someone mentioned that the tradition in Switzerland is for women to yodel. The group consisted also of a man who played the piano, another, an accordion, a third man played a fiddle, and a girl played a xylophone and a set of bottles. A tall, smart man played four long horns and made music using a saw. Just before the end of the performance, a large black and white cow, pantomime style suddenly appeared in the restaurant and moved about amongst members of the audience. It was hilarious and the visitors certainly enjoyed the innocent fun.

On Friday we had a sightseeing tour of the lovely medieval city of Lucerne. We went to the summit of Mount Titlis (approx 9750ft.) in a series of cable cars starting with gondolas, carousel fashion, holding six people. At first the countryside around was gentle, cows grazing, haymaking and so on. Then we transferred to a bigger square car holding forty people and then later the Rotair, the world's first revolving cable car - the floor rotates once around on its axis. At the top we were in the snow and ice where there is a Snow Park with slopes for those who find their entertainment in skiing. There is a restaurant and the view from the windows is stunning. We loved it. Strange to come down from the wintry scenes to the valley below into hot sunshine and ice-cream!

We also enjoyed a boat cruise on the lake before leaving for the Zurich area in the late afternoon and staying overnight at the hotel where we had started our journeys. Then it was early to bed ready for a very early start for the airport in the morning.

What a holiday! Strenuous - yes: walking, riding, climbing, talking, laughing, eating, and always on the move. Both of us had to contend with a tickly cough for some days until a kindly chemist sold us some 'magic' pills, but it did not dampen our spirits. We enjoyed it all! We met some very nice people on this trip, some of whom have kept in touch.

Chapter Seventy

EXCITING EXPERIENCES WITH JUST A HINT OF DANGER!

My sister Bella kept asking when I would visit her and the family in the USA again. She had been to the UK twice recently and now it was my turn to visit her. I sat down and did my sums and finally decided that I would go in 2003. Kerry was kind enough to book the flight *on line* and Elsie arranged insurance cover.

But what was I to do with Shonna for a whole month? I could not take her with me as I do when I visit family here and I did not want to put her in a cattery because she was old, nearly thirteen years of age, and would have missed me terribly and her freedom too of course. Glenys and her family came to the rescue when they kindly offered to have Shonna in their home. They knew her to be a perfect house-guest and she was familiar with the family, their house and locality having been to stay there many times in the past. The M & Ms were quite keen as well because they had known and loved her since they were small boys and she doted on them too. It all worked out extremely well and Shonna was in her element with all the attention lavished upon her in Horwich.

During our coach tour in Switzerland, Betty and I had become friendly with a family from South Carolina and had kept in touch with them. On hearing of my visit to my family in the USA, they invited me to stay with them as well and I was very pleased to accept. Ken, my nephew was kind enough to arrange the internal flights involved from Washington D.C. to South Carolina. So I visited the USA once more! Well, all travellers know that you can't just up and go, because there are so many details to attend to, money, clothes, presents and arrangements for housewatching during the absence. Irene and David, my neighbours have always kept an eye on my house whenever I've been away, but it is not as easy now with both of them being incapacitated. Despite this, they are still sharp-eyed and extremely good neighbours and I am grateful to them for their care.

Very early in the morning on 28th August, Bryn drove me to Manchester Airport and I duly departed on an 8-hour journey through the skies. Since the terrorist attack in New York, security in all airports including Manchester has been tightened, which means that you have to allow plenty of time for all necessary clearance, it is no use getting there late because you could miss your flight.

I had read all about the danger of embolism on long distance flights and had obtained the stretchy knee socks for support. During the flight I obeyed the rules by making sure that I had twitchy feet and restless legs! Like everyone else I read a magazine, snoozed, did crosswords and ate food. Towards the end it became a little tedious, but we reached Dulles Airport safe and sound and I was thankful. After waiting in a long queue for a security check then reclaiming my luggage I pushed my trolley to the reception area, and wondered why I always seemed to pick the trolley that always wants to move sideways! I was very glad to see my sister and her son Ken and his children Andrea and Kevin looking out for me. I could now relax because I had arrived in the USA and was united with my family.

Dulles Airport is quite far from Ken's home and the late afternoon sun was still hot. I was longing for a cup of tea or anything liquid and the others were really hungry. Someone had a brainwave: all of us must go to the wonderful place called the Rainforest Café. Ken soon found it and a parking place for the car too. When we entered the café I thought for a minute that we were in a real rainforest. Everywhere, high and low was covered in foliage and exotic flowers, not the real stuff of course, but in the semi-gloom it looked believable. All around, near and above tables there were animated monkeys and apes, large and small. I could not decide whether the noise came from children or monkeys!

We ordered the food, which was duly served and turned out to be a good meal, but Andrea and Kevin were so excited they ate very little being too busy darting hither and thither, curious to see all the wonders of the place. When it was time to leave, they just didn't want to know because they were completely absorbed in the atmosphere!

Finally, when we were in the car making our way home they should have been tired out, but were instead singing away happily. My sister was busy asking questions in the car, catching up with the news from my side of the 'big pond'. I was by then feeling rather dozy and was glad when we arrived to be greeted by Mary.

I was relieved to fall into bed that night and the following day was spent quietly unpacking and walking round the Zoll Lane neighbourhood of Waldorf, which is part of Metropolitan Washington DC where Ken and his family live. The undulating land was once part of a farm until it was developed into an exclusive rural community of large houses with drives and surrounding grassy areas with trees and bushes.

The weekend was free for Mary and Ken and there was no school for the children so it was all planned already. No need for me to think - a luxury for me.

On Saturday we all went to watch Kevin playing soccer in a match at his school. It was a hot day, but nothing daunted the players. There were two girls in the team who were very good players. Kevin was playing very well too and it was obvious that he was very popular. We were all egging him on and shouting, "Come on Kev." Later, he and I played hockey on the driveway - and achieved wonderful shots!

We visited the Kenilworth Aquatic Gardens and the National Arboretum established in 1927. Later on we escaped the rain by ducking into the newly renovated Conservatory that offers a beautiful and fascinating living plant Museum (nearly 4000 specimens) on the Nation's Mall at the foot of the U.S. Capitol. In the early evening we enjoyed an excellent seafood dinner at the Cedar Knoll on the Potomac, overlooking the river and south Maryland shoreline. I enjoyed it all very much. Delightful!

On Sunday we spent the afternoon and evening with Brian, Bella's youngest son and Petrine his wife who came to visit with their little girls Bridget and Natasha. The girls are so petite and pretty and their parents dote on them as indeed we all do. We spent Monday touring in historic southern Maryland absorbing the sights, smells and sounds of the Port Tobacco River, the Potomac River, the Patuscent River, the St. Mary's River, and Chesapeake Bay. We also visited St. Ignatious Church in Port Tobacco that overlooks the Rivers. The St. Thomas Cemetery and St. Thomas Manor date back to 1860. The present Church was built in 1798. I was interested to see several gravestones bearing Welsh names and wondered which part of Wales they had left before going to America.

From there we went to the original site of St. Mary's City the original Capital of Maryland. It was abandoned for the present Maryland capital of Annapolis in 1695. We walked to the waterfront of the St. Mary's River to view a replica of a ship similar to the Ark and the Dove that brought the original settlers to this site. We then drove to Point Lookout State Park, Scotland, Maryland. This Park's peaceful surroundings belie its history as the location of a prison camp that held as many as 52,264 Confederate Soldiers during the Civil War. There is a Museum on the site that recounts this vivid history. Finally we enjoyed a waterfront dinner (Crab Cakes) at the Stoney's Kingfisher Restaurant on Solomon's Island, Maryland. This is a quiet fishing village where the Patuscent River meets Chesapeake Bay. We took a stroll on the Riverwalk; it is a place of charm and unspoiled beauty. We'd enjoyed such an inspiring day and the weather had been lovely too. We slept well that night.

On Tuesday Mary dropped off Bella and me at the Mall and we went round the shops, "Just looking" we said. It was a good thing we were inside because there came a sudden heavy rainstorm, but because of it I fell into temptation by buying a pair of blue leather sandals and a pair of black court shoes with leaf patterns and transparent tops. Very swish! On Wednesday and Thursday we idled, walked and talked in the sunshine and I did a little gardening to keep my hand in so to speak, and got ready for Friday's trip.

Ken drove me to the International Airport in Washington D.C. It was a very hot day. My sister also came along to see me off safely onto the plane to Greenville Airport, South Carolina. If you have been through an American airport recently you will know that it is no longer straightforward! My family were allowed to accompany me only as far as Customs and Security. Then I was on my own and I reminded myself to keep my wits about me. The queue was like an enormous eight loop snake. Whenever I passed through the 'arch' I 'pinged' because of the metal in my 'new' knee. Like everyone else I had already divested myself of my handluggage, shoes and jewellery, except my watch and ring, by placing them in a basket that also passed through the check point. A woman official called me to an area where I was required to sit on a chair and show the soles of my feet, then stand up and move one foot forward onto a specific 'foot patch' on the ground, then repeat with the other foot. I had to lift my arms shoulder high and straight sideways and all the while she was using the checking rod around my body with resulting 'pinging' from time to time. I had already informed her of my 'new' knee. Then I was released to recover my belongings. Well what a palaver! All the security is as a result of the atrocity of 11th September in New York City and Americans have become a lot more nervous and careful since then. Suitcases and other heavy luggage are also checked even if they are locked, but a card is left to say what has been done. It is a nuisance, but very necessary - we live in violent times. The journey took just under two hours and was relatively pleasant. It was not a big plane and did not fly above the clouds so I could see the shapes and patterns of the land and sea below.

As we approached Greenville I began to feel a little apprehensive. I had already spoken to Mark Newton from Ken's home before departing. He is generally known as Mark, but I prefer his real name, which is Marcus, like my grandson. I told him that I would wear a black and yellow shirt to help him to spot me at the airport. I began to wonder if I could pick him out in a crowd, Greenville is not big and sprawling like large airports, but neither is it small, the reception areas are quite spacious in fact. I found my way, collected my case and made for the exit and realised there were two…so I wondered which one to use. I could see no parked cars so I decided to pace between the two exits keeping an eye open overall. However, it became necessary for me to visit the toilet and a lady directed me to the public conveniences. It was a bit of a struggle to get in with my entire luggage, but it was worth the effort because I felt a lot better afterwards!

The crowd of people had diminished, but I still could not see Marcus Newton. I was not in a panic, but I did begin to wonder what my next move should be, and I decided to keep moving and looking around for a few more minutes. Almost immediately the lady to whom I had spoken previously asked if I needed any help, and I explained the situation to her. "Do you have a telephone number?" she asked. "Yes, I have their home number," I replied. She used her mobile phone and I was so pleased to be able to speak with Vicki Newton who gave me her husband's mobile phone number. The lady said to go ahead and I dialled, then with a sigh of relief I heard his voice answering. He'd had difficulties in finding a parking space, he told me to stand outside the entrance where he would pick me up in a few minutes. I thanked the lady who had been so helpful: she had certainly done her good deed for the day.

I stood outside with my bags for a few minutes then noticed him hurrying towards me. There was no difficulty, we both recognised each other straight away and smilingly greeted like long lost friends. It was a relief for us both that I was not 'lost'. He picked up my luggage, stowed everything in the boot of the car and away we went, Marcus wondered if I would like to go and watch his daughters playing a ball game. I said that would be fine, but I was rather hungry and would appreciate something to eat first. We went looking for a restaurant and a parking place, Marcus had to drive round and round for ages until finally a man, who must have noticed the car passing time and again, motioned with his hand that a space was available outside a restaurant. Without delay Marcus took up the space and thanked the man, then we enjoyed a meal interspersed with points of view about religious Faith. We did not agree on all aspects, but had a long discussion as friends. Marcus has a very strong and deep religious Faith and lives and works accordingly. Suddenly we realized it was getting late and Marcus drove to his home where I was warmly greeted by Vicki and their teenage daughters, Lana and Chrystal. After a welcome cup of tea I sank gratefully into bed and fell asleep immediately.

Next morning had fine weather so I went exploring the territory. The estate, or ranch, was extensive with several acres of grassland, woods and a large paddock where there were seven or eight horses. The house was brick-built and of an unusual design: there was a large outdoor swimming pool with the usual furniture set around it. Vicki likes flowers and has planted bushes and trees in the grounds and filled baskets and tubs and they looked very attractive. They had a dog, Sandy, a retriever who was eleven years old and devoted to Marcus. His brother had died the previous week and Sandy was missing him. When a large bird hove into view, Sandy rushed around barking furiously, but they told me he ignored all other birds and animals unless they were big ones. As soon as Marcus went to attend to the horses, the dog followed and jumped into the back of the pick-up in the paddock, ready to go!

The day passed quietly and we drove into 'Taylors', the nearest small town and the surrounding countryside. On Sunday Marcus thought I would like to join in worship at a Baptist Church in 'Taylors'. It was a very large white building full of adults of all ages, and many children too. There were 150 members in the Choir alone and they sang really well, accompanied by a lovely Organ. There was also a small orchestra. During the service two people were baptised, but all we could see were two heads being immersed in a font at the back of the pulpit. We were given a leaflet with the order of services for the day and the rest of the week - it was an extremely busy Church. The order of service was much the same as in the U.K. with a sermon, congregation singing, children's interlude and blessings.

We returned home, but on the way Marcus stopped at a small shop to buy some fresh doughnuts. He offered me some, but I could not face one before lunch, but he ate three of the smallish ones. Apparently it is customary for people to gather there early on Sunday mornings to chat and eat doughnuts. After lunch all of us went in Vicki's car to a place called Flat Rock in North Carolina. The countryside on the way looked nice and green like North Wales. We reached our destination, a small theatre where there was a stage production of a comedy based on 1920/30 era in London. There was a good audience and I was pleased that the family had managed to find a play they believed I would relate to and enjoy. The play was quite amusing and the acting was good.

We returned home and in the evening Marcus took me on a driving and walking tour of Greenville. I saw where some of his brothers lived, the fine office suite of his Practice from where he used to carry out his professional duties as a lawyer. We stopped for coffee and there was live music nearby where people were dancing, it was a celebration of some kind. It was so lively and melodious I felt like joining them.

Then back to the ranch to do some packing before retiring early to bed because we had an early start the following day. We were going to see Marcus' old home in the area where he had spent his childhood and early teenage years. The family had land and grew cotton, tobacco and vegetables. Their father was disabled and in a wheelchair. His disability had started when he was young: first his legs were affected and in time his arms too. It meant that the whole family, mother, sons and daughter worked very many hours in the fields and their mother took the produce into the shops in town very early in the morning. This was the Depression time in the USA and farmers suffered, there was very little money. Marcus took me to see his home, his school, the Church and the cemetery where all the family members are buried. He also showed me the depot where the cotton and tobacco leaves were packed, weighed and stored. We also went round the campus of the preparatory college that he attended for 4 years in readiness to go into college to study for the Ministry. He had walked nearly 200 miles from home to the college and scrimped and saved on his own during this period.

Then there was the Vietnam War and Marcus was sent for training as a helicopter pilot. When he had served his time, he returned home to the USA, and after a period of indecision, went to study at Law School and qualified as a lawyer. He eventually had his own practice where he worked for 23 years. The practice became very successful and financially rewarding.

All his life, since being a little boy, he had wanted to be a Minister, and all along felt God was pushing him in that direction, and one day he shut everything off in his office and changed his life. You have to respect someone who's determined and brave enough to do that.

After a busy day, evening approached and we set off for Charleston because it was quite a distance away. We stayed at one of those soul-less travellers' hotels that are dotted around the world, but I slept very well. After an early call I was ready to meet up with Marcus for breakfast, but service was so slow that we were able to eat only half our breakfast because we had to skidaddle to catch a Tour Bus to see the town. The day was warm and sunny: the driver was very chatty and explained the interesting details of the town that had been established by British people moving to the Carolinas from Barbados. It had suffered during the Civil War and we saw the gun placements where the first salvos had been fired at the start of the war. There were some very fine buildings from the very early period. There was a Slave Market with a museum attached, but it was unfortunately closed on that day. After stops for toilets and stretching of legs we set off for a tour of the Magnolia Plantation in the afternoon, which was about 12 miles from Charleston. On reaching the plantation we travelled through a beautiful wooded area that had tall, majestic trees, many of which were Magnolias that would have looked magnificent in the spring.

We left the coach and there was time for a very quick snack, which we ate at a stone toadstool and all the while, we were surrounded by geese, hens, pheasants, peacocks and all sorts of unfamiliar birds that were very insistent in wanting to share the food. Then we had a walking tour of the speciality gardens, 'Bible Garden', 'Box Garden', and 'Herb Garden'. We visited one of the huts where the slave women who cleaned the 'big house' lived, and bought cards and souvenirs. Afterwards we walked back to the Tour Bus to ride into the areas of the swamps where we saw alligators sunning themselves everywhere and were told that many poisonous snakes lived in the copses. Lastly we went into the house where we saw typical examples of antique American furniture and valuable paintings. The furniture reflected the fact that the settlers were still very British in their lifestyles, but were having to acclimatize to their living conditions in their new homeland.

I really enjoyed that day because it was so very different for me, but also familiar too! But we had to be thinking about starting the journey back to Taylors. We picked up a few snacks on the way because we hadn't really had a proper meal that day. The journey was not tedious because we talked all the way and really put the world to rights. With the right companion, talking is easy.

When we arrived back it was getting late and Vicki and the girls were already in bed. I had to have my cup of tea of course, and Marcus went to check the horses. He returned and looked very happy although he must have been very tired after driving so far. He asked me, "Do you want to come and see the birth of a foal?" and I replied, "Oh yes please." He said, "Go and put on some sturdy shoes." I followed him to the paddock and found a foal already born and lying on the ground next to its mother. Marcus said he had to get the foal on its feet and suckling. It was a clear night with a full moon, but it was chilly. Marcus was very pleased when I found the placenta. He struggled to get the foal on its feet because it was very heavy, but its mother kept moving around. He asked me to stand within a round metal structure and gave me the halter of the horse while he went to get some hay and food in a bucket. He went to the house to tell the rest of the family, once he saw that I could handle the horse. I did not feel nervous even though there was another horse nearby moving around and new mothers can be very excitable. However, I managed very well by talking soothingly and keeping my movements slow and steady. Even so, I was glad when the others arrived and after Marcus had struggled for longer, the foal stood up: it had very long legs. Then it managed to suckle, but I wondered how the foal would fare overnight with the air being so chilly, but in the morning it was very perky and strong.

I took some very good photographs of the family and foal, but then had to get going so I could catch my plane to Buffalo to visit Bella in Hamburg.

When we arrived at Greenville Airport my name was being called and I had to hurry down to the plane, but even so I still had to go through the security checks with all the checking and 'pinging' going on, and then I was helped to the plane by one of the airport's staff. On the way to Buffalo airport we were calling at Pittsburgh Airport Pennsylvania, where I had to change planes. It was very fortunate that I had asked the staff at Greenville Airport to arrange for me to have a buggy ride at Pittsburgh because it would have been a very long way to carry heavy luggage. As a matter of fact I enjoyed the pleasant ride in the small buggy driven by a lady who whizzed along with no bother. The plane journey was just over an hour and when I arrived at Buffalo my sister Bella and friends were there to collect me and my luggage.

I spent a very enjoyable and restful week with Bella. We pottered about in the garden, which is large at the back of the house with grass and several flower beds under the trees. There is a lawn and flowerbeds and ornamental trees in the front too. We went shopping and dined out a couple times and visited May, the widow of one of Stan's friends. One evening all three of us went out with Iris in her car to a very nice restaurant for dinner. Iris did not remember me, but I remembered going to her home for a meal years earlier when her husband Norval was alive. I have a photograph taken there at that time. Iris is Irish and homesick for Ireland, even after many years of living in the USA. She fully intends to return there permanently. It was Bella's birthday on the 12th September so we went out for supper at a special restaurant where we enjoyed a wonderful meal of fish and chips! Just like the real McCoy at home! Katie and Jim were with us too and Jenny their daughter. Afterwards, we were invited to go to their home for tea and a birthday cake, a nice end to a special day.

Next day Betty came to give Bella a 'shampoo and set' and I was very pleased she could do the same for me. We talked for hours with one thing leading to another, just talking about mundane things of long ago that had been forgotten for many years. We also watched some videos made in Wales and bought in the U.S.A.

Then it was time to return to Washington to Ken and Mary's home. It was a short trip and we were met at the airport by Colwyn James (CJ) and his mother, Cathy who had made a special visit so I could meet C.J. whom I had not seen before. He is the son of Raymond, my sister's eldest son. C.J. is a very lively and happy six-year old and very tall for his age. He and his cousins, Kevin and Andrea, Bridget and Natasha are great friends. Cathy and C.J. took my sister and me to dine at the Red Lobster. After enjoying a very pleasant meal together, we went to collect Andrea and Kevin from school. When we reached Ken's home, C.J. and I went on a walkabout that ended when C.J. saw the playhouse at the bottom of the grassy area. He was in his element on the chute and falling out of the trapdoor. He also had a try on the swing. “Higher, Nain, higher,” he yelled. We then returned to the house to watch Andrea and her friend, Krystal's documentary, 'Ripley's believe it or not!' It really was fascinating to watch those two eleven-year-olds conducting the programme with such panache and ability. I would not have believed it except for the fact that I had actually witnessed their filming and commentary. C.J. and his mum then departed because Cathy had to return to work the next day. But I was so pleased Cathy and C.J. had made the effort to visit me.

During the previous days, we had seen reports on the television relating to 'Hurricane Isabel', which was blowing its way over the sea, and frantic calculations were being made of speed and ferocity, so there could be a good estimation as to where it would touch land.

I was supposed to fly home on Thursday, 18th September, but the flight was cancelled like many others. Everyone in the hurricane's path was battening down the hatches and taking all reasonable precautions, and the news was the favourite programme on television! Electric power was lost from 1p.m. to 3p.m., but was then restored. It went off again at 9.30p.m., and that was that. We all went to bed, the children were frightened and no one slept well at all. We heard the howling wind gusts and the battering rain all night long. I heard one of the shutters come away from the wall and some shingles slithering down the roof. If you have experienced being battered by a hurricane, you will not want to live through it again.

Next morning, the storm had abated, but was still with us. It was a depressing sight for Ken and Mary. All around were the effects of the power of Nature - the damage done to the County neighbourhoods, the flooding and fallen trees on the roadways, and debris everywhere. Electrical power was still not available. Ken and Mary immediately undertook the task of repairing their property to the limit of their skills. Ken replaced two shingles that had been blown off the roof and refitted the shutter. I went with them onto the grass, at the rear of the house to view some saplings that had suffered severe damage - a Bradford pear tree had been split, and hose clamps and glue were used to force it together again, well you have to try, don't you! They pulled the big Willow tree up and held it with a tough cord to another pear tree. They also pruned to shape another tree whose top had been sliced off. To everyone's delight, electric power was restored at 5.00 p.m. and all electric appliances were working once more, and everything seemed to be in order.

However, on Saturday, the sewage grinder pump stopped working. Now, this was serious trouble and caused a great deal of worry, but help was at hand and it was repaired on Sunday afternoon in good time before my departure to Dulles Airport to fly home to Manchester. It was a lovely day and we had time to spare, so Ken thought we could visit a picturesque area to view the Potomac River in its full glory. It is a popular spot, so it was very busy. Disappointment awaited visitors because the area had been closed due to the damage and resulting danger caused by the storm. Nevertheless, we all enjoyed the drive.

I boarded the plane and had a long, uneventful flight to Manchester, arriving early. I passed through customs and security, retrieved my luggage and sat down in the Arrivals Lounge to wait for Bryn. I was not concerned because I knew he would eventually arrive. As it transpired, he too had experienced difficulty in parking. Manchester Airport is always a busy place. We called at Glenys and Kerry's house in Horwich to collect Shonna who was pleased to see me, but not overly so because she was obviously content where she was, flighty pussy cat!

Bryn and I finally arrived in Eglwysbach and I opened my front door and immediately proceeded to open all the windows in the house to let in some fresh air. Shonna decided to make a tour of her territory, miaowing loudly to proclaim her return as she went. When she arrived back she lay down as if to announce that all was well.

Bryn went home and then I felt rather lonely really. There had been so much moving around, momentous and never-to-be-forgotten events in the recent past, new people and new scenes. I had been on five different flights and made my way on my own and even surprised myself. I think it must have been because of the MAGIC HAT that Mary gave me that I wore with some aplomb, to the delight and amusement of others. It was just a wide-brimmed straw hat with a flashy bow, but it certainly was MAGIC!

In October, Elsie collected me and we travelled to Oxford to see Geraint, my grandson at Worcester College. Elsie had booked a room for us as visitors for two nights at the college. The weather was cold, but bright. We made the journey successfully with my navigating and managing to get us through various roads and junctions and Elsie driving. We eventually arrived, complete with a table and four chairs for Geraint's house. Parking is a chronic problem in the city because it was built long before the advent of the motorcar. Once everything was unloaded, the car was parked in a parking area and left untouched until we left for home. There was some concern that the table would not go past the front door, but a screwdriver and some muscle power won the day. Now the boys could sit at a table in comfort.

We ate breakfast in the refectory with students and dons and met one of Geraint's tutors. He was expecting great things from Geraint in his finals. On the first morning, we met Geraint and all three of us went on an open-top bus to view the city. This is by far the best way to view everything, helped along by an excellent commentary from the driver of the vehicle. However, we had to wipe away the frost from the seats before we could sit down. It was very cold and although we were well wrapped-up, it was still freezing throughout the tour. But it was worth it, especially at the end when we went to a small café and had a hot drink - hot chocolate for me, and coffee for Geraint and his Mum.

We went to a smart, but friendly Italian restaurant for dinner and I had just plain fish and mashed potatoes because I had woken up to a 'funny' stomach that morning.

The next day, we visited a fabulous Museum but only managed to see about one third of the contents. Perhaps one day in the future I can return to complete the viewing.

Just before Christmas Betty and I went on a week-end trip to London specifically to yet another concert at the Royal Albert Hall to hear Jose Carreras, the famous Spanish tenor and a supporting cast. He is one of my favourite singers on account of the passion in his singing and also the quality and beauty of voice. He took seven curtain calls at the end of the concert.

The following day we had a whole morning to do as we pleased before returning home. We decided to go to an Exhibition of photographs in the Natural Science Museum. Betty was very keen to go because previously some of the work of her son, Pierino had been exhibited there. I was happy to accompany her to the Museum.

Before we reached the photographs we were obliged to pass in a queue through a very large show of dinosaurs. These prehistoric reptiles had once occupied the earth, and we saw some huge replica animations. Their roars and movements were so lifelike they appeared dangerous and threatening. Thank goodness there are none around today!

Finally we reached the more peaceful setting of the photographs - not just any pictures, but examples of fine art. Each one was absolutely wonderful and I wondered how long the person with the camera had been forced to wait for the perfect picture of an animal or plant, or the perfect colours and hues of sunset, sunrise or storm. It was an exhibition of perfection and I was very glad that I had gone with Betty.

Chapter Seventy-One

THE SYMONDS SAGA

(*Readers may find it useful to refer to the related family trees at the end of this book when reading about the Symonds family.*)

You will remember when I told you the story of Henry Vaughan Williams that I mentioned there was a very interesting background story to his life that goes back a very long way, as far back as 1620!

But I'm putting the cart before the horse as it were - deliberately so - to make sure you stay with me. This is not my story, nor does it relate to my family as such, but I have been intrigued from the moment I was told about it, many years ago.

When my husband's parents were giving up their home they decided that Arthur should have the dresser as the elder son, and as we were packing the various items on it I came across a cup and saucer, or rather a 'dish' and half a saucer. The cup had no handle and so I knew it was old, but there was half a saucer missing! I called out to Arthur and asked if there was any specific reason why this one damaged item was displayed on the dresser and were we going to keep it. He hurried over and told me that of course we must keep it and for goodness sake to take care that no more harm came to it because it was a family relic on his father's side. I asked him to tell me all about it and he told me to wait until we got home so his father could explain. After supper that evening in the late 1950s Vaughan, Arthur's father and son of Henry told me the story, and now I will relate it to you.

Henry's grandmother, Ann, had told her grandson about her father's family. Sometime in the 1770s her father William Symonds had come to North Wales as a Customs and Excise officer. He had come from Mynde Hall in Herefordshire. In May 1780 he married Jane Foulkes from *Llechryd* in Llannefydd near Denbigh

This lady was from a distinguished Welsh family from Llannefydd. Their residence lasted from the middle ages until around 1875. They traced their lineage to *Ithel Goch* (Ithel the Red), father of *Iolo Goch*, who was the family bard of *Owain Glyndwr*. In 1646 was born Peter Foulkes who was educated at Westminster School and Christ's College, Oxford where he graduated thrice as Bachelor and Master of Arts before gaining his Doctorate in Theology.

The Foulkes family had financial means obviously and could be described as 'gentlemen' because they owned their own farm, but they were not wealthy enough to be classed as aristocracy or 'county gentry'. They were however influential in their area.

Jane was born in 1762 and was therefore a daughter of Richard Foulkes and his wife Margaret. She was one of five children. It is not easy to say how well educated she was because it was not customary at the time to educate girls in the same way as boys, but she would certainly have known how to run a large farmhouse with servants, how to entertain, and so on.

Incidentally, the dates of the marriage of Jane and William and the birth of their first child, Ann, seem to indicate that the wedding was none too soon - no birth control of value in those days!

They were married in the Church at Llannefydd and their first home was in the village. Their first-born child was the aforesaid Ann in October 1780. When she was christened, a distinguished gentleman came to the service and celebration in a carriage

driven by four horses and he brought a present for the baby girl - a Japanese tea set of twelve pieces, the damaged cup and saucer on the dresser being part of this set. He stayed overnight in one of the manor houses in the Vale of Clwyd.
Nine children were born:

Ann born October 1780
John died as a baby in 1782
Jane born 1786
William born 1789 died 1816
Mary born 1791
Richard born 1793
Thomas born 1795
Sarah born 1799
Margaret born 1802

Ann, the first born, John, Jane and William were born at Henllan and then the family moved to live in a small manor house, *Dalar Bach* in the village of Llansannan, where the other children were born.

William Symonds the father, continued to work as an Excise Officer, which entailed a fair amount of travelling. Whilst he was at Holyhead he became ill and died of pneumonia in December 1818, aged 68. The children were all grown up and most were married: the youngest was 16 years of age.

However in earlier years one of the girls, either Ann or Jane, was a maidservant at the house of an Attorney at Law in Denbigh who knew the history of the family. He knew that the Mynde Hall Estate was entailed and that at some period it had been in Chancery. The family of William Symonds believed that this was because the heir of the Mynde Park estate at that time was rather reckless and extravagant; he loved the high life and travel. Although the property itself was entailed and therefore safe, there was no money and so the estate was in Chancery. Or could it have been when Sir Richard (Peers) Symonds died in 1796 without issue?

One day the lawyer read in 'The Times' newspaper that the estate was out of Chancery. He called the maidservant, gave her a day off and instructed her to go home and tell her father to travel down to Mynde Park and cut down an oak tree. He would be prosecuted but he, the Attorney, would fight his case in Court and claim his rights. She went home and gave the message. Nothing happened; William Symonds did not do what the Attorney had said. Why? Was it because William knew the Symonds family were well used to Courts and were far too wily for him to make a challenge? Or was it because he knew he had no case? But the Denbigh solicitor believed otherwise and solicitors are rarely gullible. No one seemed to know. Also according to the family, when William the father died, strangers came to their home and took away 'all the papers'. Were these strangers, officials from the Customs and Ex435cise office, or were they perhaps relatives looking for compromising letters or documents? No one seemed to know that either. And that was that! In the ensuing years the family grew and made their way in the world. Some of the more prosperous decided to look further into the matter but without success.

That was the story. I was very interested in it, but at that time far too busy to dwell on it or explore it further.

Some years later Arthur was adjudicating at the Miners' Eisteddfod in Porthcawl and suggested that I should go with him because he was sure I would enjoy it. Well, I went and I did enjoy it. We decided to go home via the Wye valley, which is very beautiful. After setting out and consulting a map I noted that Hereford was in the vicinity and asked Arthur if we could go there to find Mynde Hall. It was a nice day and we had some spare time, so off we went.

We parked the car and walked into town and came upon the Cathedral. In the Cloisters we observed the tablets on the walls bearing the Symonds family names. When we left the Cathedral we noticed the Museum and Library over the road. I said to Arthur that we should call in and ask about the Symonds family. As soon as we asked one of the ladies in the Library for information she dashed off and very courteously brought two large volumes and set them on a podium. I cannot now remember the titles of the books as 40 years or more have elapsed, but in one we found that a Richard Symonds had left the Mynde Estate to his surviving daughter. Our interest was growing by the minute and we frantically tried to find something on which to write down the information. Too diffident to ask the ladies for paper we made do with the back of a cigarette pack, which I still have.

We tried to locate the Mynde Hall itself and were told that it was not occupied any more and that the last event there had involved filming parts of the Pink Panther film. We failed to locate the house and so we returned home. There was no time for further chasing of elusive ancestors.

Some years later we read an article in a local weekly newspaper in Denbigh written by Arthur's retired Headmaster of the local Grammar School. He was a very learned and distinguished man who was very interested in history. He had read some of the Diaries kept by a young soldier, a Cornet of Horse, who had ridden with the regiment accompanying King Charles I during his meanderings in the Civil War. His name was Richard Symonds! Well, we were agog - could this be the same Richard Symonds who had lived at Mynde Park? Again, there was no chance of following this up, but we kept the newspaper cuttings. Well there you are - the story and ensuing tantalising bits of information and there the situation remained for several more years.

After Arthur died and I was alone and looking through masses of papers and books I came across the cigarette pack notes and the newspaper cuttings. I read them again and pondered a long time. Could the story be a figment of imagination with no foundation? I decided that there must be an element of truth - how could a Welsh family in Llansannan in the 18th century have known about Mynde Hall and the Mynde estate in Herefordshire? The fact is that this part of the family history was passed down each generation from Ann, the eldest child of William Symmonds to Henry, her grandson, then on to Thomas Vaughan, and later on to Arthur Vaughan, my husband. Also there was the dish and saucer which had been loyally guarded over many years. This has always been one of the family stories most requested by my grandchildren.

In 1995, I decided to write down all the facts I could find. The next section reports my conclusions. I never dreamt at the start how many hours would be spent poring over old documents, microfilm in archives, gravestones and so on. Glenys accompanied me on a two-day visit to Herefordshire and the National Library at Aberystwyth, and later to the archives in Ruthin; Bryn took me to the National Library and on an overnight visit to Hereford; and on another occasion Elsie took me to the Library in Aberystwyth. They all gave valuable time to help me with the research. I visited Hereford Library four times, Gloucester Archives twice, Ruthin Archives four times and found staff very helpful at those places. I also visited the National Library of Wales three times.

The papers of the Symonds family at Mynde Hall or Mynde Park have been deposited at Aberystwyth because part of the estate was situated in Wales and the family having sold the Mynde estate no longer had an interest therein. It is wonderful how the information is being stored for posterity. We met several people on our trips, some from as far away as Australia, on the track of their roots.

MYNDE PARK ESTATE

The Mynde Hall and estate, anglicised it is believed from the Welsh word *'mynydd'* meaning 'mountain' has roots right back in the 13th century or even earlier. Welsh villeins populated this part of the world during Norman times. The mansion was called *Tregroes* and later Browne's Place in ancient times. Later it was part of the larger estate including the manors and lands of Orcop and Kilpec. It was the home and property of the Pye family for yearly 300 years. Pye is from the Welsh *ap Huw* (son of Hugh). In 1635 Sir Walter Pye senior died and was buried in January. In 1637 it was found by Inquisition that the said Sir Walter Pye Senior, late of the 'Meende' held it of the King in chief by Knight service. He was Attorney General of the Court of Wards of Henry VII for the purpose of regulating inquiries upon the death of the King's tenants and ascertaining heirship and the rights of the King to marriage wardship. Sir Water Pye Junior inherited a large estate from his father; his composition was fixed at £2649. During the Civil War 1642/6 he was taken prisoner at the siege of Hereford and narrowly escaped death.

Elizabeth Pye the eventual heiress to the Mynde married Henry Gorges, whose son sold the Mynde to the Duke of Chandos Marquis and Earl of Caernarfon in April 1723. Grant and consideration of £33,200 of the Manors and Lordships of Kilpec and Orcop and the Mynde Estate.

In 1726 the Duke of Chandos sold the property to *John Symonds* who settled it in a Trust for Richard Symonds his brother who was his heir, to bestow on one of his sons, his elder son John who was his father's heir.

There are several Deeds, etc., of mortgage monies charged on the estate to the Pye family by the Duke of Chandos and some such money also to the Duke by Richard Symonds and others. The records seem to signify that the three Symonds brothers, Thomas, John and Richard (please see family tree) were ready to seize their chance of owning the large Mynde estate in order to establish a Symons dynasty. Richard Symons in his Will entailed the estate in strict settlement directing that each person who inherited should adopt the SYMONS name and arms of Symons.

According to one historical record the family of Symons, one of great antiquity in Cornwall, is stated to have come over with William the Conqueror.

Certainly, the elder son of Richard Symons the London Merchant, named John was accorded a well-to-do rearing; he was termed a 'gentleman'. The records show that John received monies from his father to cover the expenses of his maintenance at Oxford University and his travels abroad in Holland 1727/32. John gave a Covenant to his father Richard, to allow a deduction of £1600, the amount advanced by his father out of his expected inheritance from the estate of Uncle John Symons deceased, brother of Richard.

In his Will, Richard Symons states that it was, "My greatest care and concern for many years to have my now only son John Symons educated so as to render him fit for the enjoyment and management of the provision made by the last Will and Testament of my brother John Symons deceased whereby a very large provision in lands and Real Estate is made for my son John and his issue male and which I hope and trust he is well qualified for the enjoyment of and which he will best continue to be by adhering strictly to the advice given by his said Uncle's Will..."

As soon as the Mynde estate had been acquired Richard Symons and his family moved into the mansion in 1727. 'Grant and Release of the whole estate of the Mynde in Trust for Richard Symons of London on 17th August 1726'.

There followed several Court cases within the family mainly, claiming legacies left by Thomas and John Symons, brothers of Richard who was the sole surviving executor of John who was the executor of their sister Eleanor and Thomas. Perhaps the money was tied up in property and cash was hard to come by, but the matter seems to have dragged on for years. Mostly they concerned the three daughters of Ann, who was the sister of Thomas, John and Richard.

John Symons Junior married Ann Colebrook in 1735, and a Marriage settlement was drawn up. Curiously there is a Declaration of Trust regarding this Marriage Settlement drawn up by Richard Peers in 1763. This was to declare lawfully that shares in the South Sea Bubble had been sold, these formed part of the investments of the settlement on the advice of the Trustees who wisely foresaw the collapse of the Company. Proceeds were then invested in Real Estate.

In 1764 John Symons of Mynde Park died, without issue according to records. His wife Ann survived him by several years. John Junior was born in 1702 according to records and was aged 62 when he died in 1764. William Symmonds was then aged 15 years.

When John Symons Junior, son of *Richard* died in 1764 (legally childless) the estate passed to Richard Peers the son of Anna-Sophia (daughter of *Richard* Symons) and therefore the grandson of *Richard* Symons Senior. In accordance with the terms of his grandfather's Will he had to change his surname to Symons before he could inherit the Mynde Estate and of course he did adopt the Symons name. He was born in 1743 and was therefore 21 years old when he took over the Mynde Estate, which incorporated lands at the Orcop and Kilpek also. In May 1774 he was created a Baronet and became Sir Richard Symons. He died unmarried on 4th July 1797 and the title lapsed because he had no issue (children).

At this time William Symons, Excise man, was 48 years old.

The estate then devolved on Thomas Raymond, son of Mary Raymond who was the daughter of Ann Hampton (nee Symons) sister of John, Thomas, Richard and Eleanor. In the 1800s the estate was heavily mortgaged and many parts of the estate were sold. Eventually the whole estate was sold and the new owners took over.

In the latter years of the 19th century the house was described as a mansion, which was large and handsome, with a noble entrance hall 60ft. wide by 30ft. high. The grounds were rich and well wooded where there was a deer park and a lake.

When we visited the area in 1999 the house was covered in scaffolding and tarpaulins. The drive was in good order and the surrounding park newly planted with young trees. Obviously tremendous improvements were taking place. Good to see life taking over again.

We have looked at many documents pertaining to the family and estate at Mynde Park and we never saw any mention of William Symons. We checked the details of his birth at the Hereford Archives. He was born on 23rd March 1749 in Kingsland, Co. Hereford and his parents were William and Margaret Simonds (nee Meyrick).

The spelling of the surname differs a lot in the records, some are Symmonds, others Simmonds or Simmons, and even Symons. In old records the spelling appears to change according to whom the writer was and how good he was at spelling!
William and Margaret Simmons married February 1741.

1742 - Daughter Mary born February
1744 - Daughter Margaret born September
1745 - Daughter Elizabeth born November - then a gap of nearly 4 years.
1749 - Son William born March - then a gap of 4 years.
1753 - Daughter Mary born September died same year.
The first Mary must have died as well.
1754 - Daughter Ann born May
1755 - Daughter Martha born June and died 1766.

The Symons family we have traced from Clowerwell, or Clearwell as it is now known, on the border of Gloucestershire/Herefordshire Mynde Park is in the Parish of Newland.

There must be a link somewhere between William Symonds the Excise man Llannefydd at Henllan in May 1780.

The story, as handed down in the family, is too detailed to be disregarded. It is what the father told his children - how could they otherwise have known of Mynde Hall in Herefordshire, hundreds of miles from the little Welsh village in the countryside in North Wales? Why should the father name his children - Ann, John, Richard, Thomas and Mary - family names over centuries in the Symons clan?

And then there is the 'dish and saucer' that I have in my possession. Why should this be so treasured in the family, even though the saucer is damaged?

All in all, I feel there is a connection - perhaps William was illegitimate and was brought up by another Symons family, which was common practice in bygone days.

The Symons family had worked long and hard to rise in the world and bring up the younger ones to marry well and become gentry. John Symons, brother of Richard, who was unmarried, had amassed a considerable fortune to pass on to his younger brother, Richard, in Trust for his son, John Junior, laid great importance on 'appearances and good behaviour' (as shown in his Will) and heirs had to be 'lawfully begotten'.

Looking at the dates of births and deaths of the characters I have concluded that if William really was an illegitimate child of the Symons of Mynde Park, then the person who could have been his father was John Symons Junior, son of Richard Symons. He fits in and although John Jnr. had no legitimate children, that could have been because his wife was unable to bear children. John Symons Junior was 47 when William was born. John was living at Mynde Park from the late 1730s to 1764 when he died. The rest of his close family were either dead or lived in London.

The grand gentleman who came up to the christening at Henllan when Ann was born could only have been Sir Richard Symons who inherited after John's death. Sir Richard was only six years older than William and was 37 years old when Ann was christened.

William was still alive when Sir Richard died in 1797 unmarried, and Thomas Raymond succeeded to the estate as was stipulated in Richard Symons' Will. Was it at this juncture that the Denbigh solicitor thought he could have won a Court Case or was it earlier when John Junior died?

Who knows?

One thing is certain. Not one of them ever thought that their history and characters would be scrutinised so closely in the 21st century in North Wales, knowing from the onset that there could never be a financial gain. But this tracing of families is fascinating, you get hooked - going ever backwards looking for clues.

I resent the use of my time, but I have to admit to enjoying the rooting about - I only wish I could have found the irrefutable solution to the mystery!

Chapter Seventy-Two

AFTERTHOUGHT
Life is for Living

When we are born, we are given the gift of Life and a slot in Time. We can control our life; it is ours to do with as we please. Time is different. Time is always on the move and we cannot control it. We talk about it all the time: time to go; time moving slowly; time going so fast; time to start; time to stop; managing time; time wasted; short time and many more; but these are not indicative of control; they are statements of our measuring Time and using Time. We have other Time measures too; eras, ages, millennia, years, months, weeks, days, hours, minutes and seconds. We have fine-tuned Time but we have not altered it one little bit, because Time has no beginning and no end.

Our life and our slot in Time are so precious. But how many of us fully value and appreciate Time, and our slot in it? How many of us are aware of the wonderful make-up of our bodies with all the structures and automatic movements, including the non-stop pumping station of the heart? Think also of the brain and the electrical impulses of the nervous system. Each of us has a body and it is ours, given to us to use, do we look after it enough and appreciate how hard it works quietly, non-stop on our behalf throughout our lives? We should value our bodies and all the miraculous workings within it far more than we do. Life is not for ever, it comes to an end. Time on the other hand is the only thing that goes on for ever.

We are all human beings, but we are all different, because each of us has a special D.N.A. chain that tells of the genes that we have inherited from our ancestors. They make us who we are and they are the tools with which we work to form and control our lives.

I think it is absolutely fascinating and this is why I became so interested in finding out about the people who went before me and who made a contribution to my life. Who were they, what did they do and how did they live?

The best way to start is to ask parents, grandparents, relatives and friends what they know. After that, it is a case of looking in old records of births, marriages and deaths. This is very time consuming, but now it is far easier because of the information stored on microfilm in Local Authority Record Offices and in Archives in some Libraries More recently, the Internet can also be a useful source I am told. I have to warn you that it is very addictive! Life is for living.
I know who I am!

Bet Vaughan William

JOHN SYMONS OF CLEARWELL, IN THE COUNTY OF GLOUCESTER

1620 Yeoman (a person qualified, by holding and possessing free land of an annual value of 40 shillings or more, to serve on juries etc.)
1623/4 Purchased a house called 'Waddams'.
1630 Daughter, ELEANOR married KEDGWIN HOSKINS.
1633 He owned a coalmine in the Forest of Dean. There were several smallish coalmines in this area at that time, also charcoal burning and the very earliest experimentation of iron smelting.
1640 Mention of THOMAS SYMONS and JOHN SYMONS – SONS
1653 Grant and counterpart (copy of a legal document) for life from JOHN SYMONS of Clearwell to THOMAS SYMONS, SON AND HEIR.

John Symons

Elinor - Married 1630 To Kedgwin Hoskins.

John - His will is dated 1707

Thomas - In 1653, given a house and land by his father. In 1659, he is mentioned as a yeoman. He was the eldest and was his father's heir. His wife was called Margaret in 1694.

Thomas Symons
m. Florence Hooper in 1659 – 5 children
Lived Clearwell area. Collected rents and tithes with brother, John. Later lived in London. Died 1718. Eldest of siblings. Left legacies to 3 daughters of his sister Ann in his will. Sponsored, brother, Richard through his apprenticeship in London. This debt was repaid 1716. His brother, John was executor of his will.

John Symons
No record that we have seen of marriage. Lived in Clearwell all his life. Collected rents and tithes with his brother, Thomas. Some clients were: Duke of Gloucester, Duke of Beaufort, Sir Walter Pye of Mynde Park and Sir Thomas Throckmorton. Thomas and John were both described as Attorneys at Law and in practice together - John, at Clearwell and Thomas, later in London. The Practice probably started in 1660. They were industrious, ambitious and very successful. John died 6.4.1734 and his will was dated 1721. He had amassed a considerable fortune and his heir was Richard, his brother, in trust for Richard's sons. From the evidence available, it has been deduced that Thomas and John were considerably older than their other siblings, and that 'family' was important to them, especially John, who was unmarried. Because of the nature of their work, they knew a great deal about the financial affairs of their powerful, wealthy and influential clients (who was solvent and who was not so)! They knew how to use this knowledge for their own advantage.

Eleanor Symons
She was a spinster and lived mostly in London. Returned to Clearwell in 1691. She died before 1732.

Ann Symons
m. Phillip Hampton in 1701/2 and had 3 children – Margaret, Ann and Mary. Mary married William Raymond. Their son, Thomas Raymond changed his name to Symons in order to inherit the Mynde Park Estate on the death of Sir Richard Symons (formerly Peers), who was the son of Anna-Sophia Peers (nee Symons), the surviving daughter of Richard Symons.

Richard Symons
He is referred to in various documents as a Merchant in London, (oilman and fishmonger) and also as an Attorney in Law.
Letters were addressed to him at 'The Rose', near Fishmonger Hall in Thames Street. Bought property in Croydon in 1716. Bought 'Red Lion Inn' at Coalford for £80 in 1732. Married in 1702 and had 5 children.

There was also another sister, but the only reference that could be found was in Richard's Will, where a legacy of £50 each was given to 'my sister, Mrs. Chitty and her son, Abraham".

John was the elder son of Richard Symons and he lived at Mynde Park from 1726 when his Uncle John purchased the whole estate and put it in trust for Richard, his brother, to pass on to his son and heir. John Junior married Ann Colebrook in 1735. He was his father's heir but died without issue in 1764, when Richard Peers, son of Anna-Sophia came into the inheritance.

Thomas was the younger son of Richard. He was still living in 1734 but predeceased his father.

Elizabeth was the eldest daughter of Richard and was born in 1708. She was married to Mr. JUSTICE CLIVE. She had no children. She died in 1762, aged 54 and is buried at Wormbridge in Herefordshire.

Eleanor was the second daughter of Richard and married Mr. Henry Banks of Lincoln's Inn in 1738. She predeceased her father and had no children.

Anna-Sophia was married to Richard Peers of London. She had a daughter, Elizabeth, who was born in 1743 and died in 1772. Elizabeth also had a son, called Richard Peers. Anna-Sophia was buried in Croydon.

Richard Peers later assumed the surname of Symons in order to inherit the Mynde Park Estate. He was created a BARONET on the 23rd May 1774, but died unmarried in 1796, when the title became extinct. The estate devolved to THOMAS RAYMOND SYMONS (the grandson of Ann, the younger sister of Richard Symons) and, on his death in 1818, his son and heir, THOMAS HAMPTON RAYMOND (then Symons) inherited. It is thought that the estate was later sold. Certainly, the Symons family is not at Mynde Park today.

Symmonds/Williams Family Tree (1749-2005)

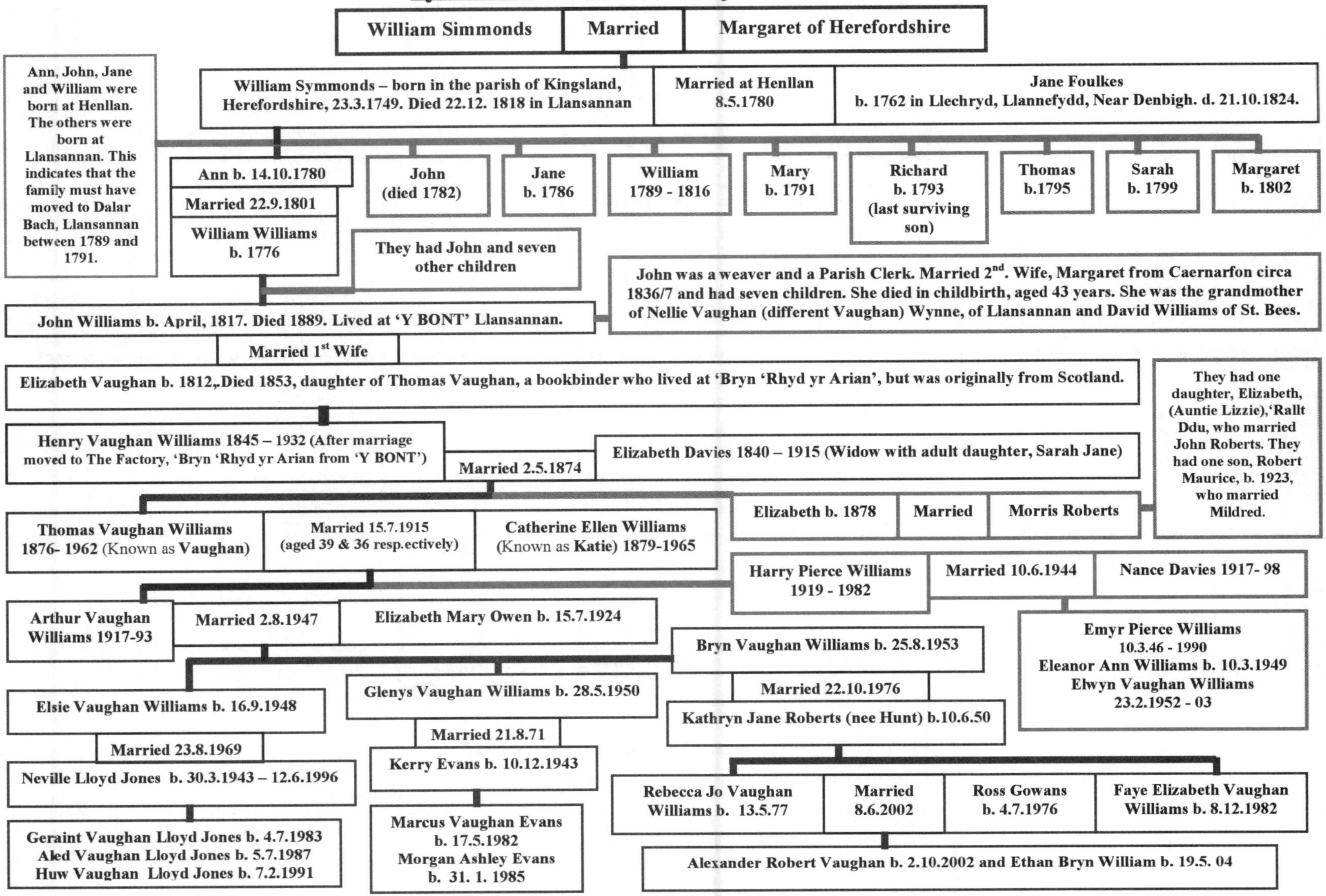

THE HOWATSON FAMILY OF NORTH WALES

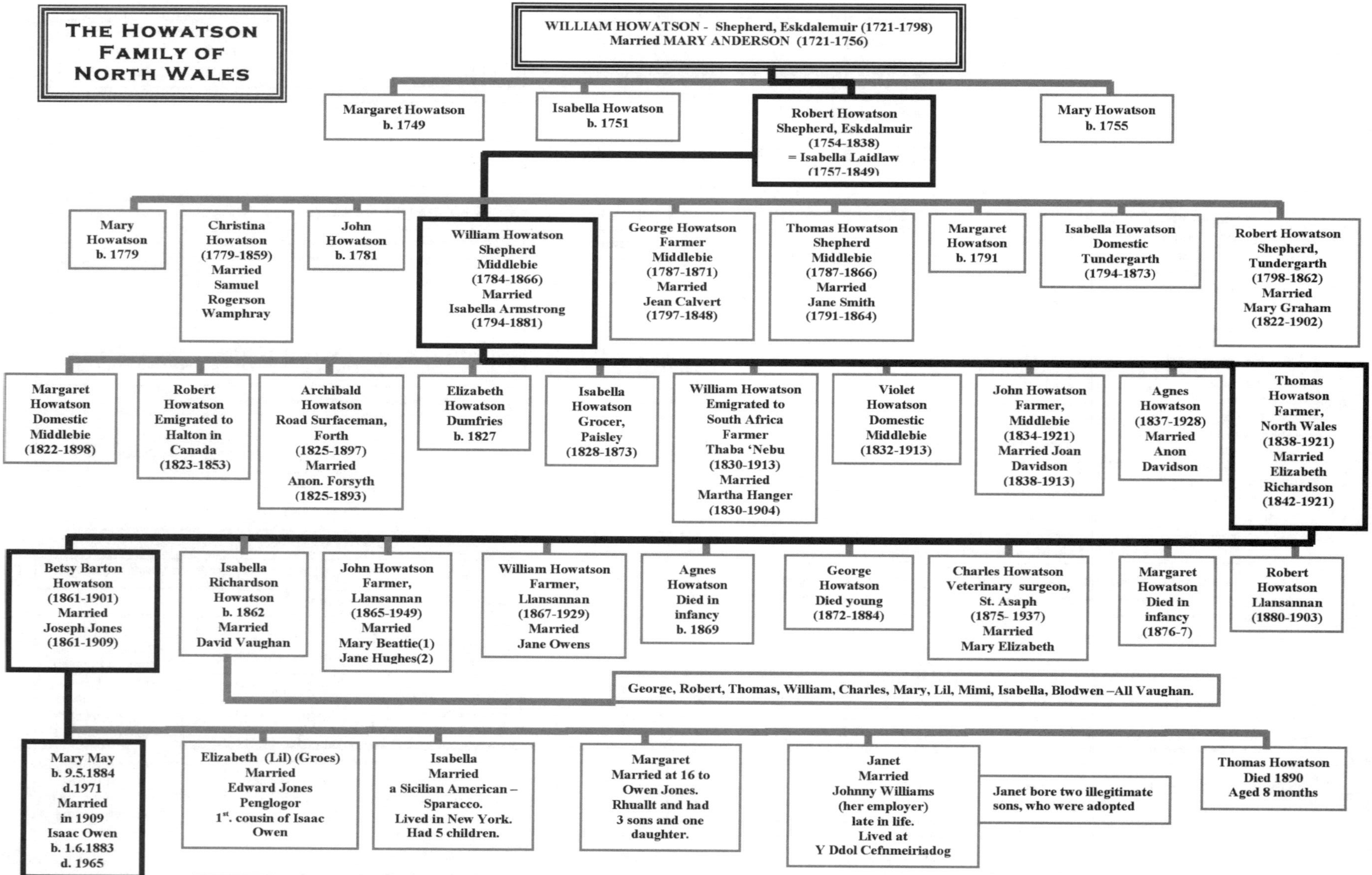

See the other list for ancestors of Joseph Jones. He and his wife had 12 children, with six of them being still-born. The other list also shows the ancestors of Isaac Owen.

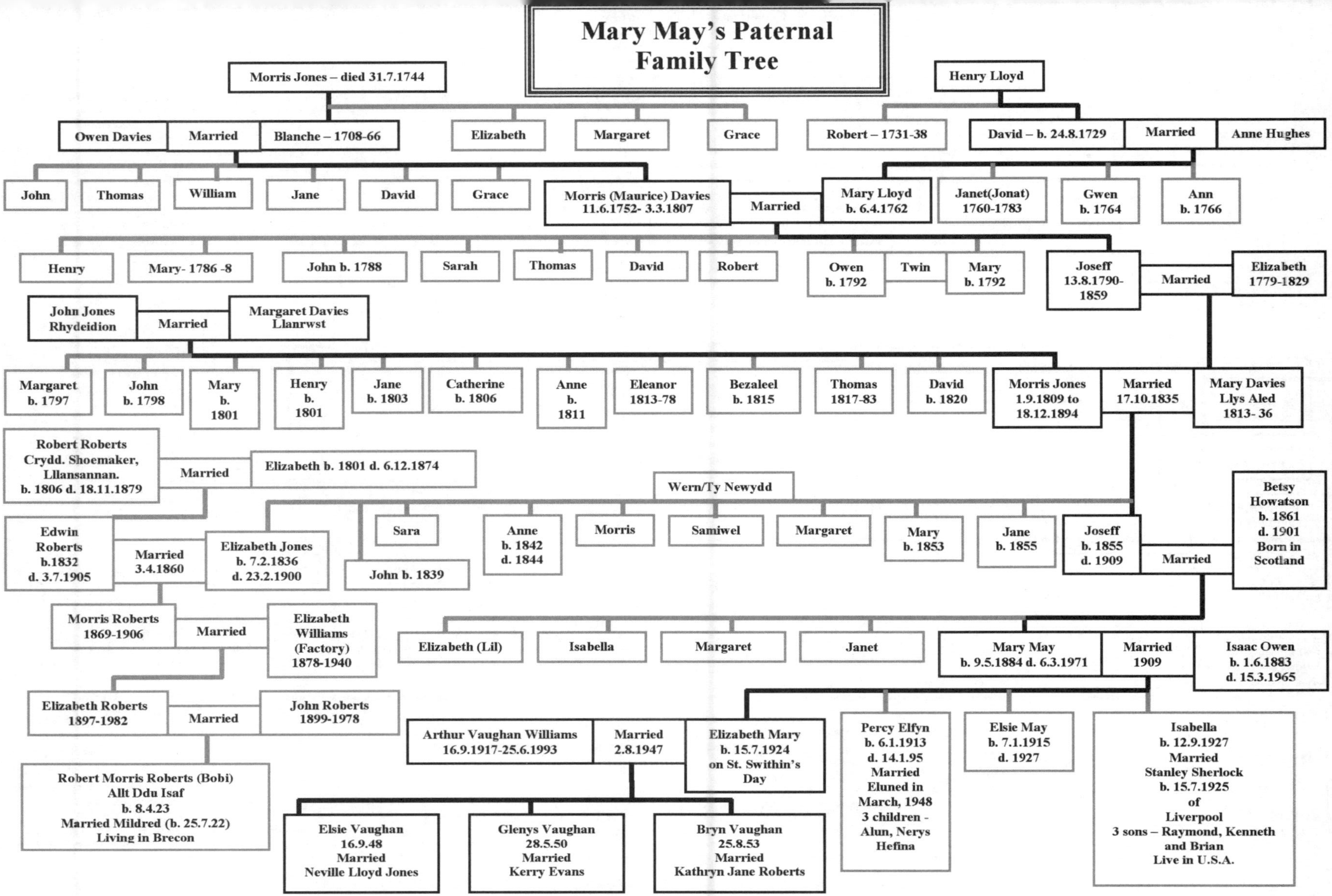
Mary May's Paternal Family Tree
Morris Jones – died 31.7.1744
Henry Lloyd
Owen Davies
Married
Blanche – 1708-66
Elizabeth
Margaret
Grace
Robert – 1731-38
David – b. 24.8.1729
Married
Anne Hughes
John
Thomas
William
Jane
David
Grace
Morris (Maurice) Davies 11.6.1752- 3.3.1807
Married
Mary Lloyd b. 6.4.1762
Janet(Jonat) 1760-1783
Gwen b. 1764
Ann b. 1766
Henry
Mary- 1786 -8
John b. 1788
Sarah
Thomas
David
Robert
Owen b. 1792
Twin
Mary b. 1792
Joseff 13.8.1790- 1859
Married
Elizabeth 1779-1829
John Jones Rhydeidion
Married
Margaret Davies Llanrwst
Margaret b. 1797
John b. 1798
Mary b. 1801
Henry b. 1801
Jane b. 1803
Catherine b. 1806
Anne b. 1811
Eleanor 1813-78
Bezaleel b. 1815
Thomas 1817-83
David b. 1820
Morris Jones 1.9.1809 to 18.12.1894
Married 17.10.1835
Mary Davies Llys Aled 1813- 36
Robert Roberts Crydd. Shoemaker, Lllansannan. b. 1806 d. 18.11.1879
Married
Elizabeth b. 1801 d. 6.12.1874
Wern/Ty Newydd
Edwin Roberts b.1832 d. 3.7.1905
Married 3.4.1860
Elizabeth Jones b. 7.2.1836 d. 23.2.1900
Sara
John b. 1839
Anne b. 1842 d. 1844
Morris
Samiwel
Margaret
Mary b. 1853
Jane b. 1855
Joseff b. 1855 d. 1909
Married
Betsy Howatson b. 1861 d. 1901 Born in Scotland
Morris Roberts 1869-1906
Married
Elizabeth Williams (Factory) 1878-1940
Elizabeth (Lil)
Isabella
Margaret
Janet
Mary May b. 9.5.1884 d. 6.3.1971
Married 1909
Isaac Owen b. 1.6.1883 d. 15.3.1965
Elizabeth Roberts 1897-1982
Married
John Roberts 1899-1978
Arthur Vaughan Williams 16.9.1917-25.6.1993
Married 2.8.1947
Elizabeth Mary b. 15.7.1924 on St. Swithin's Day
Percy Elfyn b. 6.1.1913 d. 14.1.95 Married Eluned in March, 1948 3 children - Alun, Nerys Hefina
Elsie May b. 7.1.1915 d. 1927
Isabella b. 12.9.1927 Married Stanley Sherlock b. 15.7.1925 of Liverpool 3 sons – Raymond, Kenneth and Brian Live in U.S.A.
Robert Morris Roberts (Bobi) Allt Ddu Isaf b. 8.4.23 Married Mildred (b. 25.7.22) Living in Brecon
Elsie Vaughan 16.9.48 Married Neville Lloyd Jones
Glenys Vaughan 28.5.50 Married Kerry Evans
Bryn Vaughan 25.8.53 Married Kathryn Jane Roberts

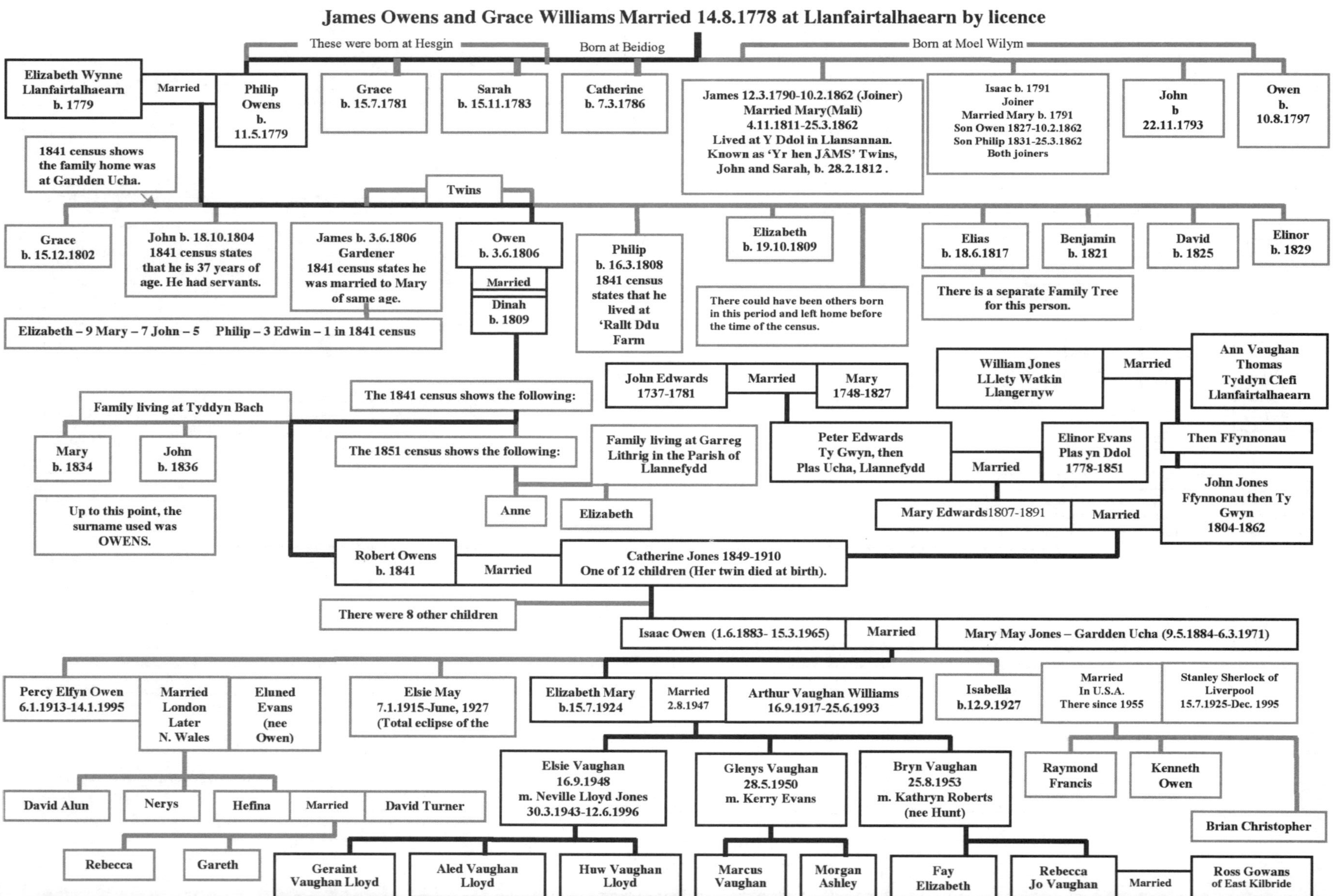

James Owens and Grace Williams Married 14.8.1778 at Llanfairtalhaearn by licence
These were born at Hesgin
Born at Beidiog
Born at Moel Wilym
Elizabeth Wynne Llanfairtalhaearn b. 1779
Married
Philip Owens b. 11.5.1779
Grace b. 15.7.1781
Sarah b. 15.11.1783
Catherine b. 7.3.1786
James 12.3.1790-10.2.1862 (Joiner) Married Mary(Mali) 4.11.1811-25.3.1862 Lived at Y Ddol in Llansannan. Known as 'Yr hen JÂMS' Twins, John and Sarah, b. 28.2.1812 .
Isaac b. 1791 Joiner Married Mary b. 1791 Son Owen 1827-10.2.1862 Son Philip 1831-25.3.1862 Both joiners
John b 22.11.1793
Owen b. 10.8.1797
1841 census shows the family home was at Gardden Ucha.
Twins
Grace b. 15.12.1802
John b. 18.10.1804 1841 census states that he is 37 years of age. He had servants.
James b. 3.6.1806 Gardener 1841 census states he was married to Mary of same age.
Owen b. 3.6.1806
Married
Dinah b. 1809
Philip b. 16.3.1808 1841 census states that he lived at 'Rallt Ddu Farm
Elizabeth b. 19.10.1809
There could have been others born in this period and left home before the time of the census.
Elias b. 18.6.1817
Benjamin b. 1821
David b. 1825
Elinor b. 1829
There is a separate Family Tree for this person.
Elizabeth – 9 Mary – 7 John – 5 Philip – 3 Edwin – 1 in 1841 census
The 1841 census shows the following:
Family living at Tyddyn Bach
Mary b. 1834
John b. 1836
Up to this point, the surname used was OWENS.
The 1851 census shows the following:
Family living at Garreg Lithrig in the Parish of Llannefydd
Anne
Elizabeth
John Edwards 1737-1781
Married
Mary 1748-1827
William Jones LLlety Watkin Llangernyw
Married
Ann Vaughan Thomas Tyddyn Clefi Llanfairtalhaearn
Peter Edwards Ty Gwyn, then Plas Ucha, Llannefydd
Married
Elinor Evans Plas yn Ddol 1778-1851
Then FFynnonau
John Jones Ffynnonau then Ty Gwyn 1804-1862
Mary Edwards1807-1891
Married
Robert Owens b. 1841
Married
Catherine Jones 1849-1910 One of 12 children (Her twin died at birth).
There were 8 other children
Isaac Owen (1.6.1883- 15.3.1965)
Married
Mary May Jones – Gardden Ucha (9.5.1884-6.3.1971)
Percy Elfyn Owen 6.1.1913-14.1.1995
Married London Later N. Wales
Eluned Evans (nee Owen)
Elsie May 7.1.1915-June, 1927 (Total eclipse of the
Elizabeth Mary b.15.7.1924
Married 2.8.1947
Arthur Vaughan Williams 16.9.1917-25.6.1993
Isabella b.12.9.1927
Married In U.S.A. There since 1955
Stanley Sherlock of Liverpool 15.7.1925-Dec. 1995
David Alun
Nerys
Hefina
Married
David Turner
Rebecca
Gareth
Elsie Vaughan 16.9.1948 m. Neville Lloyd Jones 30.3.1943-12.6.1996
Glenys Vaughan 28.5.1950 m. Kerry Evans
Bryn Vaughan 25.8.1953 m. Kathryn Roberts (nee Hunt)
Raymond Francis
Kenneth Owen
Brian Christopher
Geraint Vaughan Lloyd
Aled Vaughan Lloyd
Huw Vaughan Lloyd
Marcus Vaughan
Morgan Ashley
Fay Elizabeth
Rebecca Jo Vaughan
Married
Ross Gowans of East Kilbride

Bibliography

Dyffryn Conwy a'r Creuddyn (E.D. Rowlands) 1947.

Dwyn mae Cof a Ysgrifau Eraill (Pernant Bob Owen Llanrwst) 1982.

Plwyf Llansannan Ei Chwedloniaeth, ei Gymeiriadau hynod (Mr R. Wynne Jones) 1911.

Trem yn ol Y Parch.T. Brynmor Davies Llawlyfrau Llansannan.

Two Colliery Doctors: The Brothers Armstrong of Treorchy (A.D.Morris) Reprinted from Wales and Medicine March 1974.

Inscriptions in Llansannan Churchyard W.C.Wynne - Woodhouse 1974.

Diary of the Marches of the Royal Army during the Great Civil War by Richard Symonds (original in the British Museum). Printed for the Camden Society and edited by Charles Edward Long MA.

Handwritten notes by Thomas Vaughan Williams.

Archives at Ruthin.

Archives at the Public Library in Hereford.

Archives at the National Library of Wales, Aberystwyth.